THE UNAUTHORIZED GUIDE TO
DOCTOR WHO

2005-2006
SERIES 1 & 2

TAT WOOD
with additional material by DOROTHY AIL

Also available from Mad Norwegian Press...

Space Helmet for a Cow: An Unlikely 50-Year History of Doctor Who
by Paul Kirkley (forthcoming)

AHistory: An Unauthorized History of the Doctor Who Universe
(3rd Edition print and ebook now available)
by Lance Parkin and Lars Pearson

Queers Dig Time Lords: A Celebration of Doctor Who by the LGBTQ Fans Who Love It,
edited by Sigrid Ellis and Michael Damian Thomas

Chicks Dig Time Lords: A Celebration of Doctor Who by the Women Who Love It,
edited by Lynne M Thomas and Tara O'Shea
2011 Hugo Award Winner, Best Related Work

*Chicks Unravel Time: Women Journey Through Every Season
of Doctor Who,* edited by Deborah Stanish and LM Myles
2013 Hugo Award Nominee, Best Related Work

Chicks Dig Comics: A Celebration of Comic Books by the Women Who Love Them,
edited by Lynne M Thomas and Sigrid Ellis
2013 Hugo Award Nominee, Best Related Work

*Whedonistas: A Celebration of the Worlds of Joss Whedon by the Women
Who Love Them,* edited by Lynne M. Thomas and Deborah Stanish

*Running Through Corridors: Rob and Toby's Marathon Watch
of Doctor Who* (Vol. 1: The 60s) by Robert Shearman and Toby Hadoke

Dusted: The Unauthorized Guide to Buffy the Vampire Slayer
by Lawrence Miles, Lars Pearson and Christa Dickson

<u>The About Time Series</u>
by Tat Wood and Lawrence Miles
About Time 1: The Unauthorized Guide to Doctor Who (Seasons 1 to 3)
About Time 2: The Unauthorized Guide to Doctor Who (Seasons 4 to 6)
About Time 3: The Unauthorized Guide to Doctor Who
(Seasons 7 to 11) [2nd Edition now available]
About Time 4: The Unauthorized Guide to Doctor Who (Seasons 12 to 17)
About Time 5: The Unauthorized Guide to Doctor Who (Seasons 18 to 21)
About Time 6: The Unauthorized Guide to Doctor Who
(Seasons 22 to 26, the TV Movie)

All rights reserved. No part of this book may be reproduced or transmitted in any form or by any means, electronic or mechanical, including photography, recording or any information storage and retrieval system, without express written permission from the publisher.

Published by Mad Norwegian Press (www.madnorwegian.com).
Copyright © 2013 Tat Wood and Dorothy Ail.
Content Editor: Lars Pearson.
Cover art: Jim Calafiore. Cover colors: Richard Martinez.
Jacket & interior design: Christa Dickson and Matt Dirkx.
ISBN: 978-1935234159. Printed in Illinois. First Edition: August 2013

table of contents

Introduction.................... 5

Series 1

X1.1 Rose 8
X1.2 The End of the World......... 34
X1.3 The Unquiet Dead 51
X1.4 Aliens of London............. 69
X1.5 World War Three 80
X1.6 Dalek 95
X1.7 The Long Game..............113
X1.8 Father's Day.................128
X1.9 The Empty Child 140
X1.10 The Doctor Dances 153
X1.11 Boom Town................170
X1.12 Bad Wolf...................184
X1.13 The Parting of the Ways....195
X1.13a Pudsey Cutaway..........209

Series 2

X2.0 The Christmas Invasion......218
X2.1 New Earth 238
X2.2 Tooth and Claw 255
X2.3 School Reunion..............273
X2.4 The Girl in the Fireplace 295
X2.5 Rise of the Cybermen 312
X2.6 The Age of Steel 322
X2.7 The Idiot's Lantern 340
X2.8 The Impossible Planet.......364
X2.9 The Satan Pit................376
X2.10 Love & Monsters...........389
X2.11 Fear Her 406
X2.12 Army of Ghosts............420
X2.13 Doomsday.................429

table of contents

Essays

Why Now? Why Wales? 9
RT Phone Home? 35
Is the New Series
    More Xenophobic? 53
Why is Trinity Wells
    on Jackie's Telly? 71
He Remembers This *How*? 83
What's Happened to the Daleks? . . 97
Why Doesn't Anyone Read
    Any More? 115
Reapers - Err, *What*? 129
What's So Great
    About the 51st Century? 141
Gay Agenda? What Gay Agenda?
   155
Does Being Made
    in Wales Matter? 171
Did He Fall or Was He Pushed? 185
Bad Wolf - What, How and Why? . .197
What's a "Story" Now? 211

How Long is Harriet in No. 10? 219
Has All the Puff
    "Totally" Changed Things? 239
Stunt Casting:
    What Are the Dos and Don'ts? . . .257
Why the Great Powell Estate
    Date Debate? 275
Is Arthur the Horse
    a Companion? 297
Are Credited Authors
    Just Hired Hands? 313
How Many Cyber-Races
    Are There? 323
Are We Touring
    Theme-Park History? 343
Can He Read Smells? 367
Why's the Doctor So Freaked Out
    by a Big Orange Bloke? 377
Is *Doctor Who* Fandom
    Off-Topic? 391
Was Series Two
    Supposed to be Like This? 407
What Are the Most
    Over-Familiar Locations? 421
Was 2006 the *Annus Mirabilis*? 431

End Notes 452

how does this book work ?

About Time prides itself on being the most comprehensive, wide-ranging and at times almost *unnervingly* detailed handbook to *Doctor Who* that you might ever conceivably need, so great pains have been taken to make sure there's a place for everything and everything's in its place. Here are the "rules"...

Every *Doctor Who* story (or, since 2005's relaunch, episode) gets its own entry, and every entry is divided up into four major sections. The first, which includes the headings **Which One is This?**, **Firsts and Lasts** and **Watch Out For...**, is designed to provide an overview of the story for newcomers to the series (and with BBC America's hefty promotion of Matt Smith's Doctor, this may mean a lot more people even than joined us in 2005/6) or relatively "lightweight" fans who aren't too clued-up on a particular era of the programme's history. We might like to *pretend* that all *Doctor Who* viewers know all parts of the series equally well, but there are an awful lot of people who - for example - know the 70s episodes by heart and don't have a clue about the 80s or 60s. This section also acts as an overall Spotters' Guide to the series, pointing out most of the memorable bits.

After that comes the **Continuity** section, which is where you'll find all the pedantic detail. Here there are notes on the Doctor (personality, props and cryptic mentions of his past), the supporting cast, the TARDIS and any major characters who might happen to wander into the story. Following these are **The Non-Humans**, which can best be described as "high geekery"... we're old enough to remember the *Doctor Who Monster Book*, but not too old to want a more grown-up version of our own, so expect full-length monster profiles.

Next is **History**, for stories set on Earth, and **Planet Notes** otherwise - or sometimes vice versa if it's a messed-up Earth or a planet we've seen before. Within these, *Dating* is our best-guess on available data for when a story happens. Also, given its prominence in the new series, we've added a section on *The Time War*.

To help us with the *Dating*, we may have recourse to **Additional Sources**: facts and factoids not in broadcast *Doctor Who* but nonetheless reliable, such as the DVD commentaries, *The Sarah Jane Adventures, Torchwood* or cut scenes.

Slightly more frivolously, we have included a **Catchphrase Counter** for recurrent turns of phrase and a **Deus ex Machina** list for suspiciously-convenient ways that the story has been made to fit into 42 minutes of screen-time and not end with everyone dead. These form a significant part of the flavour of the twenty-first century episodes, just as cliffhangers were for the earlier iteration.

Of crucial importance: note that throughout the **Continuity** section, *everything* you read is "true" - i.e. based on what's said or seen on-screen - except for sentences in square brackets [like this], where we cross-reference the data to other stories and make some suggestions as to how all of this is supposed to fit together. You can trust us absolutely on the non-bracketed material, but the bracketed sentences are often just speculation. (Another thing to notice here: anything written in single inverted commas - 'like this' - is a word-for-word quote from the script or something printed on screen, whereas anything in double-quote marks "like this" isn't.)

The third main section is **Analysis**, which comprises anything you might need to know to watch the episode the same way that anyone on the first night, sat in front of BBC1 on a Saturday teatime (or whenever), would have; the assumed background knowledge. Some of this is current issues or concerns - part of the "plucked from today's headlines" appeal of *Doctor Who* right from the power-politics over new technology in the very first story (1.1, "An Unearthly Child") - some of it is more nuanced. Overseas or younger viewers might not be aware of the significance of details that don't get flagged up overtly as worth knowing, such as the track-record of a particular performer and what that brings to the episode, or what a mention of a specific district of London would mean to UK viewers. These are your cribnotes. **The Big Picture** handles the politics, social issues and suchlike occupying the minds of the authors. Many *Doctor Who* fans know that 15.4, "The Sun Makers" was supposed to be satirical, but even an apparently throwaway piece of fluff such as 17.1, "Destiny of the Daleks" has a weight of real-world concerns behind it. New for this volume, **English Lessons** (and sometimes **Welsh**

5

how does this book work?

Lessons) tackles the allusions and vocabulary that BBC1 viewers all have at their fingertips and all the nuances underlying apparently innocent remarks. More than ever before, the **Oh, Isn't That...?** listing will tell you why what might seem an innocuous piece of casting means more to us first-nighters than to anyone else.

Up next is **Things That Don't Make Sense**, which in this volume continues to cover plot-logic, anachronisms, science-idiocy, characters' apparent amnesia about earlier stories or incidents and other stupid lapses, but rarely the production flaws or the naff effects and sets for which the series was hitherto notorious. Finally, for this section, **Critique** is as fair-minded a review as we can muster; sometimes, this has required a bipartisan approach with *Prosecution* and *Defence*, but not in Volume 7.

The final section, **The Facts**, covers cast, transmission dates and ratings, overseas translations, edits and what we've now taken to calling **Production**: the behind-the-scenes details that are often so well-known by hardened fans as to have the status of family history. We try to include at least one detail never before made public, although these days finding anything nobody's said to any of the dozens of interviewers hanging around Cardiff is increasingly hard, unless you get into outright gossip or somehow manage to crack BBC Wales' occasionally impenetrable news-management arrangements.

A lot of "issues" relating to the series are so big that they need forums all to themselves, which is why most story entries are followed by mini-essays. Here we've tried to answer all the questions that seem to demand answers, although the logic of these essays changes from case to case. Some of them are actually trying to find *definitive* answers, unravelling what's said in the TV stories and making sense of what the programme-makers had in mind. Some have more to do with the real world than the *Doctor Who* universe, and aim to explain why certain things about the series were so important at the time. Some are purely speculative, some delve into scientific theory and some are just whims, but they're *good* whims and they all seem to have a place here. Occasionally we've included endnotes on the names and events we've cited, for those who aren't old enough or British enough to follow all the references.

We should also mention the idea of "canon" here. Anybody who knows *Doctor Who* well, who's been exposed to the TV series, the novels, the comic-strips, the audio adventures and the trading-cards you used to get with Sky Ray ice-lollies will know that there's always been some doubt about how much of *Doctor Who* counts as "real", as if the TV stories are in some way less made-up than the books or the short stories. We devoted a thumping great chunk of Volume 6 to this topic, but for now it's enough to say that *About Time* has its own specific rules about what's canonical and what isn't. In this book, we accept everything that's shown in the TV series to be the "truth" about the *Doctor Who* universe (although obviously we have to gloss over the parts where the actors fluff their lines). Those non-TV stories which have made a serious attempt to become part of the canon, from Virgin Publishing's New Adventures to the audio adventures from Big Finish, aren't considered to be 100 percent "true", but do count as supporting evidence. Here they're treated as what historians call "secondary sources", not definitive enough to make us change our whole view of the way the *Doctor Who* universe works, but helpful pointers if we're trying to solve any particularly fiddly continuity problems.

It's worth remembering that unlike (say) the stories written for the old *Dalek* annuals, the early Virgin novels were an honest attempt to carry on the *Doctor Who* tradition in the absence of the TV series, so it seems fair to use them to fill the gaps in the programme's folklore even if they're not exactly - so to speak - "fact".

You'll also notice that we've divided up *About Time* according to "era", not according to Doctor. Since we're trying to tell the *story* of the series, both on- and off-screen, this makes sense. The actor playing the Main Man might be the only thing we care about when we're too young to know better, but anyone who's watched the episodes with hindsight will know that there's a vastly bigger stylistic leap between "The Horns of Nimon" and "The Leisure Hive" than there is between "Logopolis" and "Castrovalva". Volume 4 covers the producerships of Philip Hinchcliffe and

---

This product is not authorized by the BBC. Doctor Who and TARDIS are trademarks of the BBC.

how does this book work

Graham Williams, two very distinct stories in themselves, and everything changes again - when Williams leaves the series, not when Tom Baker does - at the start of the 1980s. With Volume 7, the amount of material has necessitated that the remainder of the Russell T Davies era will be covered in Volume 8, with Steven Moffat's tenure discussed in Volume 9 and beyond.

There's a kind of logic here, just as there's a kind of logic to everything in this book. There's so much to *Doctor Who*, so much material to cover and so many ways to approach it, that there's a risk of our methods irritating our audience even if all the information's in the right places. So we need to be consistent, and we have been. As a result, we're confident that this is as solid a reference guide / critical study / monster book as you'll ever find. In the end, we hope you'll agree that the only realistic criticism is: "Haven't you told us *too* much here?"

series 1

X1.1: "Rose"

(26th March, 2005)

Which One is This? For a whole new audience, this is the one where Rose Tyler meets a mysterious stranger called "the Doctor" and an amazing adventure begins. For a lot of other people, it's "Spearhead from Space" (7.1) on 78rpm and with that kid who was married to Chris Evans.[1]

Firsts and Lasts Deep breath, and... the first *Doctor Who* of the twenty-first century is the first episode of the series made in the BBC Wales facilities. (For future reference, BBC Wales is a subdivision of the British Broadcasting Corporation but, being primarily for the population of Wales, makes a lot of local-interest programming that nobody in the rest of the UK ever sees. Some of this is bilingual in Welsh and English, but most Welsh-language broadcasting has, since 1982, been made by S4C: a network partly funded by the BBC but which shows commercials - some of these also in Welsh. See **What Difference Does Being Made in Wales Make?** under X1.11, "Boom Town".) This makes the new *Doctor Who* the first BBC Wales production to have been explicitly made for export, not just to the rest of Britain (they'd done a few dramas like that before), but potentially globally.

It is the first *Doctor Who* story to be made on Field-Removed video, the "film-look" digital technique preferred by most TV drama companies. (See **What Difference Did Field-Removed Video Make?** under X4.15, "Planet of the Dead".) The episodes were shot as if on film - with a single camera, a cinematographer and multiple takes from various angles - rather than the three-camera gallery-directed format that had worked (sometimes, only just) until 1989. "Rose" is also the first orthodox episode since 1966 to have an individual episode-title (see **What's a "Story" Now?** under X1.13a "Pudsey Cutaway"), and, barring the freakish experiment of Season Twenty-Two, the first time a series of thirteen 45-minute episodes has been shown - the BBC doesn't do commercial breaks, so that's the length most imported US dramas come out at when shown by them (and anyone who thinks that *Buffy the Vampire*

Series 1 Cast/Crew

- Christopher Eccleston (the Doctor)
- Billie Piper (Rose Tyler)
- John Barrowman (Captain Jack Harkness, X1.9 to X1.13)

- Russell T Davies (Executive Producer)

Slayer is a bad model for a British-made family-orientated fantasy series will really hate the next few years). As such, this is the first episode to have trailers for the following episode (technically, they are called "throw-forwards") woven into the end-credits as anything other than a provocative title over the closing shot (as per the black and white episodes). It's the first of three episodes this year to be directed by Keith Boak, who, mysteriously, wasn't ever asked back.

This is the first time a series of *Doctor Who* has been "authored", with a designated head writer (who is also one of the three executive producers) not only providing the bulk of the scripts but the ideas for the remainder, and a close supervision of both form and content. Russell T Davies, the *soi-disant* "show-runner", instigated a lot of other American-style procedural changes, running this new, vast operation on more than the memos-and-chats-at-the-bar arrangement that had been common at Television Centre until the 1980s. It's the start of the culture of Tone Meetings and the commissioning of effects from various outside contractors (a practice that had more or less ended with 4.8, "The Faceless Ones", and even then it had generally been one contractor per story for everything - generally in-house, but see 10.4, "Planet of the Daleks") under the aegis of one overall series designer and a number of specialists within his department. (This is perhaps the most fundamental change of all: hitherto, the only people who worked full-time on *Doctor Who* were the producer, the script editor and the production secretary, with various BBC staff assigned to each story and freelancers hired in *ad hoc*; see the accompanying essay for more.) We have the first use of an in-house choreographer to direct alien movements across the series (c.f. 2.5, "The Web Planet"). The full-time composer Murray Gold begins his marathon stint (105 episodes and

Why Now? Why Wales?

A currently "hot" big-name writer is given a sweetheart deal by the BBC to develop whatever pet project they feel like. In the process of negotiations, it turns out that the rights to a hit fantasy show of the 60s are up for re-use, and that the Big Name Writer can do whatever he pleases, cast anyone he feels like and generally indulge himself (so long as the effects budget doesn't go over what's permissible for a Saturday Night drama/adventure show). The result is announced to great excitement to fans of the original, fans of the Big Name Writer and TV pundits generally; the casting for the two main roles causes huge publicity and raised eyebrows; and the list of guest-cast keeps the buzz going. Then, on a Saturday night, the expensive titles roll over the evocative and slightly retro theme and...

... nobody's that impressed. Because Charlie Higson's revamp of *Randall & Hopkirk (Deceased)* doesn't really work as fantasy-drama, isn't funny enough for fans of Vic Reeves and Bob Mortimer, and just looks like Higson's playing with the effects technology simply because he can. Not even Tom Baker playing, essentially, himself in a recurring role can redeem the show in the public's eyes.

This is just one of the many projects to have come and gone from Saturday's schedules over the previous decade. Many of them were vaguely SF/Fantasy-themed, shown in the 8.30 slot hitherto the preserve of cop-shows and made in 45-minute filmed (or film-*look*, see the essay with X4.15, "Planet of the Dead" for the technicalities) episodes. Forty-five minutes, when advert breaks are added on non-BBC transmission, is an hour. These things are made to be sold, although a good size of audience on first transmission is always helpful.

After *Randall & Hopkirk (Deceased)* came *Strange*, a supernatural chiller, and *Sea of Souls*, equally spooky but with a more police-like investigation team. Before had come *Moon and Son*, the notoriously inept *Crime Traveller* and the only one to really catch on: *Jonathan Creek*. This was produced by Verity Lambert (who, if you somehow skipped Volume 1, produced the first two years of *Doctor Who* in the 60s and did loads else besides.) The premise of *Creek* was, however, to look spooky and turn out to be simple tricks that the guy who designs the equipment for a stage magician sees through, theoretically, long before we do. David Renwick, the show's writer, was obviously sick of it when he scripted the Christmas special that ended the first phase - it was all done with mirrors and the butler did it. However, his name and track record were what originally sold the series, and a change of author would have weakened the "brand" even more than when the female lead was replaced. When he wanted a rest, they rested the series, bringing it back with one-off specials and diminishing audiences.

Randall & Hopkirk (Deceased) took the original show's premise (private eyes, one of whom dies on a case and is doomed to stick with his partner - his widow being, like everyone except Jeff Randall, unable to see him) and used as a pretext for green-screen malarkey and *Avengers*-style shenanigans, with the occasional pastiche of well-known ghost stories and interludes where Hopkirk's mentor, Mr Wyvern (Tom Baker, in a role not in the original and invented simply to have Tom Baker in it) teaches the late Marty a new trick that will come in handy at the end of the episode, and then never be mentioned again. Reruns of the original had been moderately successful in the kitsch slot of Fridays at 6.00pm on BBC2, but more for the late 60s London vibe and glimpses of actors who later became more famous than the plots or premise. Higson's use of it for slapstick versions of *The Matrix* and inept spy faff wasn't the best use of Dennis Spooner's original format. The second (and final) series altered the sales-pitch by bringing in other writers, notably Mark Gatiss and Gareth Roberts (of whom we will hear more in this book and the next two). However, the point to make here is that there is nobody watching who isn't thinking that this series is really marking time until the BBC decides to start making *Doctor Who* again.

Why weren't they?

The television landscape in Britain changed a lot after *Doctor Who* ended in 1989. As you'll recall from Volume 6, there were three reasons for the delay in following up the goodwill and ratings from the otherwise disappointing experiment with Paul McGann in 1996. One is that, simply, a lot of people in high-up posts within BBC Television had a grudge against a series that wasn't what

continued on Page 11...

X1.1 Rose

two Proms concerts, four arrangements of the theme-tune and those for *Torchwood* and *The Sarah Jane Adventures*), and we get the first use of a few of his most distinctive motifs, including one - a wordless vocal by Melanie Pappenheim - that has gained a certain notoriety for flagging-up outrageous plot contrivances...

After decades of London standing in for Tombstone, Arizona; the Isop galaxy; the Court of Kublai Khan; and anywhere else the TARDIS lands, we have another city (Cardiff) standing in for London, with shots of the real London recorded as if on a foreign location shoot (in a sense, they were). We get to see a new TARDIS prop, with a metallic plaque instead of the plywood one and the correct proportions for a police box (until now it was slightly smaller, originally made to be conveyed in lifts to and from studios according to fan lore). The interior is new, with a brass/coral look and a permanently fixed chair for the first time ever. We see the first use of a new design of Gallifreyan script, the first of several alien languages devised by senior graphics designer Jenny Bowers (who also designed the logo for Henrik's, the department store where Rose works, and which will be back in later episodes).

This is the first time that episodes have premiered on Saturdays at 7.00pm, rather later than before, and been repeated on digital channel BBC3 twice over the weekend. BBC3 also showed a 30-minute (expanded to 45 minutes with Series Two) behind-the-scenes "puff" show, *Doctor Who Confidential*, immediately after each first-run episode. This and others were allowed access to the making of the series as part of its promotional strategy. (See **Has All the Puff "Totally" Changed Things?** under X2.1, "New Earth".)

In case you hadn't noticed, this story marks the debuts of Christopher Eccleston as the Doctor, Billie Piper as Rose Tyler, Camille Coduri as Jackie Tyler, Noel Clarke as Mickey Smith, monster-actor Paul Kasey (the Pat Gorman *de nos jours*), voice actor Nicholas Briggs and - possibly more important than any of these (certainly for merchandising revenue and plot-convenience) - the new-look sonic screwdriver. That's probably the biggest change since the 1960s: this story sees the start of *Doctor Who* as a huge business venture from the outset, rather than this being an accidental, if welcome and occasionally hilarious, side-effect. (See **Why Was There So Much Merchandising?** under 11.4, "The Monster of Peladon"; **Did They Think We'd Buy Just Any Old Crap?** under 22.5, "Timelash"; and **Great 21st Century Merchandising Disasters** under - where else? - X5.3, "Victory of the Daleks".)

Eccleston is the first Doctor to be younger than *Doctor Who* - he was born during "Marco Polo" (1.4).

Oh, and this was the last episode to be shown without a pre-credits sequence until "Smith and Jones" (X3.1), and the last one broadcast before the star's impending departure was announced (see **Did He Fall or Was He Pushed?** under X1.12, "Bad Wolf").

Watch Out For...

• As we said, this is "Spearhead from Space" on steroids. The opening shots of both stories are views of Earth from space with modishmusic. The original had a NASA photo spun on a rostrum camera and Dudley Simpson's small combo doing 60s spy-movie jazz; this time, we get a computer-generated Earth with oceans glistening in sunlight, and a pseudo-symphonic sweep suitable for a Hollywood movie about aliens invading. There had been speculation about who'd get to score the new series, and the press were keen on rave/electronica outfit Orbital - whose leader, Phil Hartnoll, had struck up a close friendship with original *Doctor Who* theme-maker Delia Derbyshire. Instead, new head honcho Russell T Davies stuck with his chum Murray Gold, and we got a soundtrack exactly like anything else on television.

• Hooray! The Autons are back. Except... they aren't called that any more. *Doctor Who* writer Robert Holmes gets a credit at the end for having created the Nestenes, but they skip the name of the iconic killer shop-dummies. Another change since last time they did this story is that the BBC can afford to have fake glass, so that the remake of the scene from "Spearhead from Space" of the dummies coming to life and shooting down pedestrians in the street ought to look more impressive. (Whether it does is down to personal taste, as is whether the remount of this version in X2.10, "Love & Monsters" is more effective despite being shot over three hours rather than three nights.) But in the carnage and confusion, nobody's sure which city we're in - a prominent Cardiff landmark is clearly visible over Jackie's shoulders as she takes a call from Rose, and then a London bus is overturned right in front of her.

• Another schizoid scene is the one where the

Why Now? Why Wales?

continued from Page 9...

they believed a certain amount of Licence-Fee-Payers' money ought to be spent on. The ringleader of the tormenters, Michael Grade, had left his post as Head of BBC1, the mainstream TV channel, shortly after becoming a household name for mismanaging *Doctor Who*'s suspension in the mid-80s (see 22.4, "The Two Doctors"; 23.1, "Mysterious Planet" and all points thereafter). He had left television altogether after quitting as head of Channel 4, the hitherto highbrow network he had made more commercial but not entirely deracinated, and being on the board of the disastrous Millennium Experience at what is now the O2 Arena.

BBC2, the other terrestrial TV network run by the BBC, had tried showing re-runs of *Doctor Who* in early 2000, putting them on in the slot usually reserved for *Star Trek: Deep Space Nine* and wondering why that audience weren't lapping up the likes of "Doctor Who and the Silurians" (7.2). This followed on from an entire night of *Who*-themed programming, all of which was popular until they put on some actual vintage *Doctor Who*, namely a bodged omnibus of the last three episodes of "The Daleks" (1.2) followed by the McGann TV Movie. However much goodwill the series had when treated as a source of nostalgic clips on Saturday night, it didn't extend to actually watching serialised stories on Tuesdays at 6.00pm when you're expecting a space-soap with effects by Industrial Light and Magic. Nostalgia for a 70s childhood failed to grab the younger audience, just as treating an Earth-based, cerebral, moody serial from 1970 as suitable for space-opera geeks wasn't going to work in however many million years the Silurians had been dormant.

However, the simple fact that has to be acknowledged here is that transmissions of old episodes was largely a shop-window for the sales of videos and DVDs, which had been healthy, and the tie-in books, which were selling to a hard-core of habitual buyers, but were sporadically available in most shops and were largely unknown to the mass of potential viewers. DVD sales were picking up as more people bought the players, just in time for the near exhaustion of the available unreleased stories on video. "Spearhead from Space" (7.1) had been the launch of the BBC2 reruns and was rushed out on DVD with barely any extras (the BBC2 trailers being one of the highlights). Commercially, then, *Doctor Who* was doing good business for a defunct show; because of the unique way the BBC is funded, all revenue from these sales went into making more BBC drama. (This is why the later episodes, despite making more money than they cost, had such scant budgets compared to any similar series - the earning power of *Doctor Who* went into a collective pot for shows such as *Rhodes* and *Holby City*, *Pride and Prejudice* and *Sea of Souls*.)

The BBC, after the governmental witch-hunt of 2003, needed a high-profile popular hit. There is currently a split between the terrestrial channels, available to anyone who pays the TV Licence Fee (for which BBC broadcasts and a percentage of other channels pays) and the subscription-only cable/satellite channels. Although the Licence Fee is set at a level decided by the government of the day, the Corporation is not run by the government, however much each government wished it were otherwise.

In 2005, the BBC was under fire from two fronts: Tony Blair's government had decided not to raise the allotted money, denying strenuously as they did so that this was in any way connected with the uncomplimentary coverage of Blair's statement to the House of Commons about the mythical Weapons of Mass Destruction that could be aimed at Britain from Iraq in 45 minutes (see X1.5, "World War Three"). Meanwhile, the majority of the press, especially those owned by proprietors of digital TV channels, were looking for any excuse to kick against the Corporation. At around the time *Doctor Who* vanished from BBC1, Rupert Murdoch launched the satellite service Sky, while a rival, BSB, sought to undercut the tycoon's bid for Bond-Villain status. Sky had parabolic dishes, and BSB had "Squarials", either mounted on exterior walls. BSB was the exile home of *Doctor Who* reruns in the early 90s, but lacked an owner who also ran the biggest-selling tabloid newspaper and the formerly authoritative paper of record (*The Sun* and *The Times*), and so was subsumed into BSkyB, a compromise foisted on both companies by a government in thrall to Murdoch's News Corporation.

continued on Page 13...

X1.1 Rose

Doctor deflects Rose's questions about who he is by taking her hand and giving a spiel about how he can feel the Earth's motion. The scene begins and ends in London, but the middle was shot in Cardiff as part of the coverage when the episode was found to be under-running. It's one of the best moments on display here, and effectively establishes the Doctor as not-a-local-boy. Still, one has to wonder whether Davies, writing this in a hurry to fill a shorter scene, had been listening to "The Galaxy Song" from *Monty Python's The Meaning of Life*.

- One small detail that might have eluded you: in the first episode of *Queer as Folk*, the Davies-surrogate character Vince Tyler and the impossibly self-assured sex-god Stuart Jones re-enact the "King of the World" scene from *Titanic*. Vince asks "Why am I always Kate Winslett?" During this book, we will see several references to this nautical tragedy, and indeed a couple called "Rose" and "Jack". It's also worth noting that Series Three ends with the TARDIS colliding with what appears to be the *Titanic*, and a whole Christmas episode follows. One of Davies' first television projects was a children's fantasy drama called *Dark Season* (see X2.3, "School Reunion"; X4.14, "The Next Doctor"), which had a protagonist who was like the Doctor if he'd been a chubby 12-year-old girl at a comprehensive school and her two friends, a conventional-looking couple. The girl in the couple was a photogenic youngster called Kate Winslett. Just sayin'...

- And after decades where the public have used "Doctor Who" as the character's name (and not just them, see **Is His Name Really "Who"?** under 3.10, "The War Machines"), we finally get on-screen use of the name, as the title for Clive's website. The website was set up for real by the BBC, but the search-engine Rose uses isn't genuine.

- The episode was *still* under-running, so the "Next Time" sequence was grafted into the end-credits as a slightly desperate ploy - but it allows a glimpse of a story that's still very *Doctor Who*, and yet completely unlike what we've just seen. For anyone worrying that it was going to be week after week of council estates and comic-relief boyfriend and mum, this was a huge relief. For anyone unfamiliar with the basic concept of the series, it was a bit of a shock.

The Continuity

The Doctor As Rose [not one to miss the obvious] spots fairly quickly, he's an alien who talks as if he comes from the North of England. [Specifically, Salford, near Manchester but not so near as to have the same accent - these minutiae matter, as we saw in **What Are the Dodgiest Accents in the Series?** under 4.1, "The Smugglers".] Accordingly, he dresses rather less whimsically than some earlier incarnations. The body he's got now is tall and lean, with cropped hair and striking features. He has a beaky nose and protruding ears, and is dressed as many men his apparent outward age (mid-40s) would in early twenty-first century London, with a dark leather jacket [more formal than a bomber-jacket, but somewhat *hors de combat*], black jeans, Doctor Marten boots [worn by generations of Mods and Soul-Boys, see **What Are the Most Mod Stories?** under 4.6, "The Moonbase"] and a V-neck sweater, with a zip. [The overall effect is if someone had sought to combine Angel from *Buffy the Vampire Slayer* with Wallace from *A Grand Day Out* and *The Wrong Trousers*. Also notice how the sweater is dark red in this and most stories set in the present or future, with dark green for adventures in History and blue for others. Similar colour-coding applies to David Tennant's suits, Matt Smith's bow-ties and the Time Vortex in stories made before 2010.]

He refers to humanity as 'stupid apes' [see also X1.8, "Father's Day"] and 'stupid little people who have only just learnt how to walk', but he also expresses confidence that they're 'capable of so much more'. He's not above a bad pun ('armless'), and is impressed by the rapidity with which Rose adapts to a peculiar situation and asks the right questions. His main techniques for protecting Earth from alien incursion are blowing things up and running away. He drinks his coffee with milk and no sugar.

- *Ethics*. The anti-plastic vial used to destroy the Nestene Consciousness seems to be on hand as insurance - a means of the Doctor negotiating with the Nestene and offering a peaceful way out. To this end, he tells Rose, 'I'm not here to kill [the Consciousness]. I've got to give it a chance.' Mickey's possible fate after the Nestenes abduct and copy him seems too insignificant for the Doctor to think about while he's trying to save the world.

Why Now? Why Wales?

continued from Page 11...

This set-up, even today, accounts for under a fifth of the nation's viewers. Well, domestic viewers at least: Murdoch and his ilk snapped up a lot of the rights for live sport, and pubs invested in big screens and dishes (hence Mickey's assumed interest in going out for a drink in "Rose" and in the TARDIS scanning system in X1.4, "Aliens of London"). Sky One, the front-line of Murdoch's entertainment service, grabbed first UK rights for most US hits (especially, obviously, those from Fox, which he also owns). Thus passionate admirers of "cult" series got the jump on the rest of us - if they could pay for it - and the terrestrial networks (five of them after 1997) got to cherry-pick foreign imports on the back of feedback from a self-selecting test audience (hence a widespread belief, among people who've not been to the States, that US television is uniformly better than ours).

We will be picking up on what this meant for the content of individual episode of *Doctor Who* later (notably in **Why is Trinity Wells on Jackie's Telly?** under "World War Three"), so for now let's just dwell on that last point. The idea that there were certain programmes that only appealed to "anoraks" had been useful when the BBC apparatchiks wanted rid of *Who* (see **What's All This Stuff About Anoraks?** under 22.1, "Attack of the Cybermen", and indeed most of Volume 6). The idea that there was a "cult" demographic of single men in their 20s and 30s, with education and disposable income, had been welcome when Murdoch et al set up their channels. These two stereotypes coalesced into characters such as Vince Tyler in *Queer as Folk* and Clive Finch in "Rose" (X1.1) - precisely the audience most off-putting to the BBC1 schedulers. BBC1 does not do minorities, however well-off they may be. The BBC doesn't need advertisers. What it *needs* is broad audience-appeal.

However, by 2003, it was obvious that *Buffy the Vampire Slayer* had united the audience for re-runs and imports (bracketed together as "cult") with that of teen-dramas such as *Hollyoaks* and the Australian soap operas beloved of students and home-workers. Teenage girls and well-off single male graduates could be united. *Doctor Who* - still widely perceived as a children's series - seemed like a way to grab a slice of that dual audience without having to import it. (A very big dual audience: the minority channel, BBC2, usually considers itself lucky to get audiences about two million. *Buffy* rarely got above five million in the US on first run. On BBC2, *Buffy* got nearly four million, in an era before BBC's online catch-up system, iPlayer, allowed time-shifted viewers to be counted. Both by BBC2 standards and as a ratio of American viewing figures, the twice-weekly run in Britain was a phenomenal success, achieved partly by showing the episodes at 6.30pm on weekdays, edited for violence, and then again after midnight on Fridays, uncut. Even if the calculation was that the "cult" demographic and the teenage girl market were crossing over, the figures for BBC2's run of the series exceeds saturation-level. A far higher proportion of the viewing public here knew of, or watched, this series than in America - even if middle-aged parents of teenage girls sometimes got the programme's name wrong. The word "Slayer" is rather crucial to understanding the whole point of that show.)

However, the rights to the series were tied up. This is the third reason not to have struck while the iron was hot. A potential gold mine like *Doctor Who* was desirable for independent producers even when the ratings were in the toilet. This is where it gets tricky to tell the story in brief, as different parties held different rights. Fox, one of BBC's partners in the McGann movie, made a mess of the rights negotiations and had - largely through inexperience rather than any chicanery - put in a lot more money into the production costs without securing a share of overseas revenue. The 90-minute movie cost the BBC about £1 million, to Fox's £5 million stake, but the BBC got the bulk of £25 million (estimated) from the sales to Australia, Russia, France and elsewhere. Even though the movie was only shown twice in either of the home countries, the project more than broke even. Films based on the series were still being discussed. We saw in Volume 6 that there had been various bids in various stages of production, notably the Johnny Byrne-scripted *The Last Time Lord* starring (depending on who you asked) Rutger Hauer, Donald Sutherland or Dudley Moore.

Even when the rights reverted to the BBC in

continued on Page 15...

X1.1 Rose

- *Background.* From the way he treats his own reflection in Rose's mirror, the Doctor is unfamiliar with his appearance and surprised [if not dismayed] at his ears. [This is generally taken to mean that he has regenerated very recently. His inability to do card-tricks would seem to support this - it seems from earlier stories (for example, 19.3, "Kinda") that a fresh body has to re-learn motor-skills that were hitherto well-practiced. The other explanation offered by some commentators is that he's recently had a haircut ('Could have been worse'), and is moved to independently comment 'Look at those ears!' while checking it out in a mirror. Or, both theories could be true - he could have recently had his first haircut in this incarnation. However, if he selected his clothes to suit his new look, it's unlikely he had a shaggy mop or afro.]

At some point, the Doctor posed for a photo in Edwardian clobber (frock coat, top hat) shortly before rescuing the Daniels family, who were due to sail on the *Titanic*. This is one of a number of photos of this incarnation at historical moments. [He seems to have been badly photoshopped into a still of Kennedy's assassination, but this is a photo from the 'Washington public archive', Clive says. The Doctor was also sketched on the island of Krakatoa the day before the 1883 eruption (see 7.4, "Inferno"; 13.5, "The Brain of Morbius"). If the Doctor has only just regenerated, the most logical (and conceptually neat) explanation is that Rose - knowing that these photos will have been taken and that the Doctor is a time-traveller - later took the snaps herself to make her own past work out correctly, a sort of trial run for sending herself the Bad Wolf messages. This could be why the Kennedy photo has the Doctor staring right at the camera. (A possible caveat is that the Doctor, within hours of Rose opting to travel with him and on their first trip, mentions in X1.2, "The End of the World" that he survived the *Titanic*, suggesting he was there without her. Then again, the Doctor could be at the event more than once - one of the *New Adventures* books, *The Left-Handed Hummingbird*, also has the seventh Doctor sailing on the *Titanic*.)

The Doctor knows, or can tell from photos somehow, about the couple being discussed in *Heat* [then the biggest-selling celebrity gossip magazine]: 'He's gay, she's an alien.' [As we mentioned in Volume 6, the timing of this episode's debut for the very week "Brangelina" came into being was a bonus, but there are several dozen such confected couplings of which it could be true.] Apparently, he'd not read bestselling novel *The Lovely Bones* before, nor seen the subsequent film [mind you, hardly anyone bothered with the film].

Genghis Khan and his Horde tried and failed to batter down the door of the TARDIS once.

- *Inventory: Sonic Screwdriver.* It's back! After being destroyed [for supposedly making the stories too easy to resolve - see 19.4, "The Visitation", for many viewers a rather more traumatic "death" than Adric's later that year], and used by the seventh Doctor [27.0, "The TV Movie"], the Doctor now has a sturdy-looking new model with a powerful blue light on one end, and what could either be bone or coral for a handle [not entirely unlike the new TARDIS, a connection that later stories would reinforce]. The main cylindrical form ends in a black cone, and the metallic end with the light is telescopic, making different sounds for different settings and lengths. In this story, it opens and locks doors, and shorts out lift controls. It also jams the Nestene's psychic link to the animated mannequin arm that has followed Rose home. [This is just the start of a whole slew of improbable new uses for a device originally capable of undoing screws by sound (5.6, "Fury from the Deep" and **How Does the Sonic Screwdriver Work?** under 15.6, "The Invasion of Time").]

- *Inventory: Other.* The Doctor is also packing a small vial of a blue liquid he terms 'anti-plastic'. [It makes the Nestene Consciousness burst into flames and blow up the complex, so it obviously isn't just nail-varnish remover. Fannishly, we might propose that it's the same mix Polly devised for Cybermen in "The Moonbase".]

There's a Yale lock on the TARDIS. [As you will recall from Volumes 3b and 4, this hasn't always been the case (see also *The Sarah Jane Adventures*: "The Death of the Doctor").] The Doctor first meets Rose when planting explosives at Henrik's, and has a chunky remote-control detonator.

The TARDIS Said by the Doctor to stand for 'Time and Relative Dimension in Space'. [Note the singular use of 'Dimension', and compare with 1.1, "An Unearthly Child", et al.]

The exterior now looks almost exactly like a police box from the 1950s instead of approximating for height, layout and the panel over the phone hatch. It still *seems*, outwardly, to be made

Why Now? Why Wales?

continued from Page 13...

2001, a new series was the less-likely option. Despite reopening the closed door of *Doctor Who* as the main Saturday Night family drama, the BBC continued looking into the film option for another two years, causing the BBC's online Cult site to hedge its bets when constantly being asked why there was no new series in the offing. The maker of *Event Horizon*, Paul WS Anderson, was sufficiently interested for the BBC to shelve plans for a low-budget TV version. This version was to have been written by someone with a track-record of spooky children's drama for BBC, Russell T Davies, with an elderly man (or woman) living in an ordinary street and claiming to have been a time-traveller once (so, basically, *The Sarah Jane Adventures*). Laura Mackie, the incoming Head of Drama and Serials in 2001, had ambitions to make US-style smart, popular dramas and a lot of her commissions will be mentioned later in this book. However, the decision to finally commit to *Doctor Who* came later, from people whose jobs she would later take over.

Meanwhile, in Canada (where the "American" McGann movie had been made), Nelvana was adding to its roster of animated cash-ins of old, well-known child-friendly franchises by preparing a cartoon series based on *Doctor Who*, which looks from the production sketches to be like the rejected first script for the TV movie. (You will be pleased to hear that Winston the bulldog wasn't involved, but K9, in the form of a Gladstone Bag on legs, was. Look, it *might* have worked...) Online, the BBC, in association with Cosgrove Hall Studios (makers of *Dangermouse* and others) had produced an animated podcast: *The Scream of the Shalka*, with Richard E Grant as the Doctor, Sophie Okenado (X5.2, "The Beast Below") as the companion and Sir Derek Jacobi as the Master (X3.11, "Utopia"). It was written by Paul Cornell, of whom we will also be hearing later in this book, and featured David Tennant in the cast. (See also **Is Animation the Way Forward?** in Volume 8.)

There had also been a peculiar project called "Death Comes to Time", in which Sylvester McCoy was the Doctor one last time, getting killed all over again four years *after* regenerating into Paul McGann in front of ten million viewers. This had been online. Various theories persist about what this was supposed to achieve; one plausible account is that the drama department of Radio 4 had to use up an amount of its annual expenditure by the end of the fiscal year to avoid being docked for the next allocation, so they made an expensive pilot for a series that would never be commissioned... only to find the departmental head called their bluff by saying "now make the next three episodes and release it as a podcast". It ended with the Time Lords all gone, Ace taking over from them with the help of an enigmatic Doctor-esque figure called the Minister of Chance, played by Stephen Fry as if he were doing a crossword at the same time. (Twitter hadn't been invented, so it can't be that.) However, the publicity for projects of this kind always seemed to be that if it came off, the BBC would finally make a proper television version of *Doctor Who*...

...just as soon as they'd got their co-production spin-off from *Buffy the Vampire Slayer* off the ground. That's right - for most of 2001, it looked as though a series, probably to be called *Ripper*, would follow Rupert Giles as he moved back to England and dealt with his mis-spent youth in a manner not entirely unlike John Constantine in the comic *Hellblazer*. They removed Giles from Sunnydale (and set him up near Glastonbury, so he could help Willow recover from going a bit bonkers and trying to kill everyone on Earth) in part to allow the BBC to develop its very own *Buffy* and grab the all-important teenage-girl/goth/cult crossover market. As you may have noticed, this never quite materialised. However, bear this in mind for later.

When the BBC had "rested" *Doctor Who* in 1989, the official reasons included the number of companies interested in taking over production, in line with the government's strictures on what percentage of the BBC's output should be made by the BBC. However, what a close reading of Volume 6 would indicate is that, logistically, the custom-made Television Centre in West London was no longer up to the task, even for fourteen 25-minute episodes a year. Anyone seeking to revive the series in a way that could hold its head up alongside *Buffy* or even *Stargate SG-1* would have to have a purpose-built studio and staff who were doing little else all year. It is worth remembering that between 1963 and 1989, there were only two

continued on Page 17...

X1.1 Rose

of wood, rather than wooden doors set in a concrete box. The outer door leads straight into the Console Room, with no intervening "atrium" of black [as had been the case on and off since the Patrick Troughton years, and all the time after 14.1, "The Masque of Mandragora"]. Inside the door is white enamelling, and a cage for the phone, as per a real police box [and the second Peter Cushing movie, see "Dalek Invasion Earth 2150 AD" in Volume 6's appendix].

From the door there is a ramp with a bannister, leading up to the first of two disc-shaped gantries. These levels are made of steel mesh and show the lighting and wiring below [a variation on the design for the 1996 TV Movie]. At the centre, the Console is still a mushroom-shaped construction with six panels, although this is now a torus of green glass, lit from within, with assorted domestic objects pressed into service as controls (a chess-piece, a rubber mallet, a bicycle pump, what seems to be a glass paperweight, various sprockets, a nautical compass [see 10.2, "Carnival of Monsters"], a 70s Trimphone...).

The glass is segmented by six coral/bone amber-coloured struts, with a similar band around the rim. The same ambiguous material provides the basic support for the cupola-like roof. The vast room seems to be made of brass and makes a hemisphere of about five metres radius. There are six vast "timbers" of the coral-like substance, separated by four segmented panels that meet at the apex, which is also the top of the central glass column housing the Time Rotor. This rises and falls in flight, as usual, and comprises various glowing glass rods of different heights. The brass segments are studded with hexagonal bosses containing circular lights - a gesture back to the old-style roundels - which get smaller the higher up the walls they go. [There are 320 of these.] There is a perimeter gantry about halfway up, which has lights and a ladder to reach it left of the door. [We never see what's to the right of the door, because the camera is situated there - except for brief shots in the set-up for X4.0, "Voyage of the Damned".] Next to the door ramp is a wooden hatstand, as before. Around the "neck" of the Time Rotor are two brass bands supporting a contemporary flat-screen monitor, on which cryptic swirling glyphs and other handy graphics can appear. There are also Post-It notes in the same hitherto-unseen Gallifreyan language. This screen can be moved around to any panel.

Taking the front door to be six o'clock, the panel at four o'clock seems to be used for tracking the Nestene signal. There is a chair apparently requisitioned from a fighter-plane at two o'clock, and it's bolted to the floor [the Doctor has finally noticed that landings aren't always smooth]. Around this main platform is an intermittent steel bannister, as if from a sports ground, hastily wrapped in foam rubber. Thick electrical cables snake down to the Console from the roof, one of which has what seems to be a section of a disc-brake from a lorry at a strategic point [for radio reception?]. A second ramp seems to lead off from one o'clock to whatever else is inside this vessel.

There is a cavernous echoing sound in the Console Room instead of the old hums or chimes [imagine Talos from the 1963 *Jason and the Argonauts* snoring].

The Supporting Cast

• *Rose*. When the Doctor meets her, she's a 19-year-old Londoner with no idea of where she's going. She's had something of a chequered past - something mentioned briefly in the little pre-rescue speech she gives when announcing that she has the bronze for Gymnastics (Under-Sevens). Since the useless first boyfriend, Jimmy Stone, who caused her to quit school with no real qualifications, she's gone back to living with her mum and working in a major department store - albeit at a menial level - although the loss of her job makes her think about going back to school. There appears to be just one novel in Rose's living room [and we have reason to believe that the copy of *Lovely Bones* is Rose's rather than Jackie's; see X2.12, "Army of Ghosts" for why].

Rose's most noticeable trait is, in the best companion tradition, sheer curiosity. [In something of a hangover from the old show, her persistence in finding out more about this mysterious stranger is seemingly rather against the Doctor's inclinations.] Her gymnastic skills save the day at the last minute against the Nestene, and she's the one to point out the obvious location for the Nestene transmitter [for the rest of the season, she'll show a definite talent for mentioning the key fact we need]. She here takes the TARDIS almost in her stride. She does, on the other hand, fail rather miserably at noticing Mickey's implausible replacement, or for that matter the Doctor showing up again for the third time running.

Rose hesitates when the Doctor first asks her on

Why Now? Why Wales?

continued from Page 15...

people who were full-time of *Doctor Who*; the producer and the script editor/story editor. Everyone else, even the regular cast, were assigned to individual stories or a six-month production run from either the BBC's pool of staff or as freelancers. Therefore, anyone wanting to make *Doctor Who* had to have a big studio, a lot of effects staff, make-up, props (mostly custom-made, even for historical yarns) and ancillary workers. The BBC could do that effortlessly once, when they made it almost as a side-project for directors and writers they'd hired for prestige or routine dramas, and had a lot of sets and props in store with which to realise any combination of period and genre at short notice and with no extra cost. Michael Grade and John Birt had ended that, and sold off the stock on the grounds that "nobody watched" costume dramas or science-fiction shows. No other broadcaster or production company in Britain had this kind of back-up resource either. Any new *Doctor Who* would be starting from scratch and would either be cheap guerrilla-style location filming (as per the singularly odd-looking *Neverwhere* and the hapless ITV cash-in *Demons*) or be co-production with an overseas company and thus compromised (as per *Primeval*). Unless, of course, the BBC had a big drama studio that they could use for *Doctor Who* and nothing else.

You know that part of it: Cardiff became the home of the relaunched series. However, this was less of a *fait accompli* than it looks like today. The long and complex story of broadcasting in Wales need not detain us: for legal reasons, there had been a need for collaboration between the BBC and commercial stations over Welsh-language transmissions and then, from 1997, local news coverage expanded greatly after the decision to grant Wales more independence than it had enjoyed since the twelfth century. (Just to reiterate for anyone who skipped the revised Volume 3 and has no clue about Britain, Wales is one of the three-and-a-half countries that make up Great Britain - the "Great" being the fact of being more than the usual England-Scotland-Wales combo, not any other kind of Greatness per se - and they talk Welsh, a language with 23 letters, few of which work the same way they do in any other language. So anyone who wonders what part of London *Torchwood* is set in, and why they talk funny, can just start again.)

The BBC's facilities included a lot of local-only drama and more than a few nationally shown series. However, due to the institutional changes with the rival ITV network, several BBC programmes were now being made in studios built for other companies that had now been absorbed into the rapidly amalgamating commercial channel. In brief: the set-up of ITV was that 14 local franchises, including two for London on different days of the week, plus a unified news company and later on a Breakfast franchise, were unified and regulated into a loose confederation. Then, with a change in the regulations on ownership, the more profitable ones bought up the remainder. Eventually, this led to the Breakfast company, ITN news and two monoliths: Granada and Carlton. Other local stations which had been making programmes for their own territory as well as occasional national outlet found that they now had studios left idle for much of the time, as they were mainly making local bulletins to follow ITN national news. However, they were now allowed to lease these to other productions, including feature films and BBC series (*The League of Gentlemen* was made at Yorkshire Television's studios in Leeds, for example). Eventually, Granada and Carlton amalgamated, with only the Scottish company STV rebelling, and the whole network was relaunched as "ITV1". Cardiff, the capital of Wales, had been redeveloped extensively and was moving from an industrialised port to being a commercial hub and cultural centre. Local ITV company HTV had had to adjust both to collaboration with the BBC to form S4C, the Welsh-language station, in 1982 and to a shift towards centralised UK-wide organisation as the regional franchises agglomerated into ITV1. There were studios going begging in Cardiff and a lot of experienced staff used to making drama without help from London. It was a bit of a leap from identifying over-capacity in studios to deciding "Let's make *Doctor Who*", though, and the missing steps are still a little obscure. Lots of other BBC studios, and those of ITV companies across Britain, could also have been used. Wales had one deciding factor, namely a separate Drama department with an ambitious head: Julie Gardner.

continued on Page 19...

X1.1 Rose

a trip into space, but immediately believes him when he says that the TARDIS travels in time. She then gives Mickey a quick peck and rushes aboard.

• *Jackie*. Rose's mother [for the next season and a half, she's defined pretty much entirely in terms of this relationship]. Jackie's genuine concern about Rose's welfare after her job is blown to bits quickly bleeds over into (from Rose's perspective) helpful-if-irritatingly-enthusiastic suggestions for how to get some extra cash by exploiting the current compensation-litigation culture. She thinks that the shop has given Rose airs and graces. As Jackie's would-be flirtatious scene with the Doctor indicates, she's on the lookout for romance now that she is no longer fending for her daughter. [This will be something of a running gag (and a plot-point next season; see "Love & Monsters"). What exactly became of Rose's dad is a matter dealt with later in the season.]

• *Mickey*. Like Jackie, he's almost entirely defined in terms of how Rose thinks of him. [He'll gain a semblance of autonomy in later instalments, and more chances to do something useful (although it's more than understandable that Noel Clarke's most enthusiastic acting in this episode comes when he's playing a restaurant-destroying Auton). Still, before being kidnapped by an importunate dustbin, Mickey does come off rather well; he and Rose seem to be having a genuinely good time during their lunch in Trafalgar Square, and he's chivalrous if rather over the top about defending his girlfriend from evil Internet predators if necessary. Naturally, he's not at his best by the time Rose and the Doctor rescue him from the exploding warehouse (this is Mickey's first ride in the TARDIS, although a lot of people seem to overlook this), and by the end of the episode is more or less left blubbering on the ground while his girlfriend runs off with another bloke. During the final confrontation with the Nestene, Mickey clings to Rose shouting 'Leave [the Doctor], there's nothing you can do' - which, for anyone steeped in the programme's lore, is as good as ordering Rose to stage an improbable rescue. Things look up for Mickey later, and eventually he becomes something of an action-hero.]

Mickey is fond of footie [as per the stereotypical English male], and drives a yellow VW Beetle. Like the Doctor, he finds the temptation to mess about with a detached window dummy arm simply irresistible. He has a stud in his left ear.

[There is a school of thought that the odd behaviour of the Nestene facsimile of Mickey results from the real one resisting alien mind-control - which makes him better at this than Martha when the Sontarans clone her in X4.4, "The Sontaran Stratagem".]

The Non-Humans

• *The Nestenes* [last seen on TV in 8.1, "Terror of the Autons"] are a collective mind housed in a lumpen, undulating mass of semi-molten plastic about the size of a tennis-court. They can use the psychic energy with which they came to Earth to animate plastic, including replicas of specific people, shop-dummies and wheelie-bins. The moving plastic people [never identified in this story, but virtually identical to the Autons from the two Nestene invasion attempts in the 1970s, so we'll call them that for now] can kill either by physically beating a human to death or by the use of the energy-weapons built into their right hands - the hand hinges just before the wrist, directly opposite the thumb-joint, as before. Each Auton is independently animated, and the components can also move when separated from the rest. The arm that Rose pulled off one manages to "walk" [like Thing in *The Addams Family*, we presume] and get in through Jackie's cat-flap to hunt down Rose. As with the daffodil-like Auto-Jets ["Terror of the Autons"], the arm attacks the face to smother the victim. A dismembered Auton sends and receives signals, making it easy to immobilise with a jamming pulse from the sonic screwdriver, but on detecting any attempt to home in on the source the body-part melts, possibly automatically. Apparently, despite the entire thing being operated by remote, an Auton's head is more complex than its arm.

The Nestenes have lost all of their 'protein planets' and have selected Earth for conquest because of the various noxious substances humans have introduced to the atmosphere, including dioxins and hydrocarbons. The loss of their worlds was a consequence of a war in which the Doctor was a participant [see **The Time War** entry under **History**], and the Consciousness blames him. They identify the TARDIS as superior technology and a potential threat. [Although most of what the Consciousness says is unintelligible, sharp-eared viewers might discern its dying words as 'Time Lord'; the closed captioning on the Series One DVDs confirms this. Some claim to have heard

Why Now? Why Wales?

continued from Page 17...

One part that is obvious is the luring of one of ITV's key writers to the BBC fold. Although he began with BBC children's dramas, Russell T Davies had become a name through his work with Red Productions (the name being a reference to Manchester United's strip, not politics or gingerness), which had had the *cause celebre* hit of 1999, *Queer as Folk*, on Channel 4 but had thereafter produced several Davies-penned series for ITV1 (but see also X2.8, "The Impossible Planet"). Red came to BBC Wales to make Davies' first project under Gardner's aegis, *Casanova*. Gardner, a key figure in BBC Wales' development as the BBC's main centre of drama production, was quite overtly empire-building at this stage. Her department had a Welsh-language soap (*Pobol Y Cwm*, see 10.5, "The Green Death"), a few hit drama series and the occasional feature-length project, but not regular returning series. She had been head of BBC Wales' Drama department since July 2003, while the negotiations with Davies over *Doctor Who* had been conducted, but had also been in talks with him over *Casanova*. Davies had been persuaded over to the BBC by the overall Controller of Drama, Jane Tranter, and - like Charlie Higson before him - given the chance to make a pet project. His price for joining the BBC's fold was, as you might already have guessed, being given *Doctor Who* to play with. Properly, this time.

Tranter, however, didn't need all that much persuasion. For the reasons hinted at above, the logic of making it, especially once the old stories had all been released on video, was inescapable. As a money-spinner, a home-grown *Buffy*-surrogate and an iconic "brand" with a great deal of residual goodwill after more than a decade since its tailing-off, the only element missing was a big enough name attached to it who was prepared for the potential damage if it failed. In early negotiations, the low-cost option had been discussed. But, as with Davies' previous projects, the scale and complexity grew. (In *The Second Coming*, the special effects had snowballed; in *Bob & Rose*, the crowd-scenes became more complex. *Casanova* had cast Peter O'Toole, just as his stock had risen all over again.) However, the Controller of BBC1, Lorraine Heggessey, was prepared for this.

The key difference between this relaunch of *Doctor Who* and the previous Saturday night fantasies was the timing: this time, the 8.30pm slot was not what anyone had in mind, but instead a return to the early evening family audience that the "experts" said no longer existed. *Doctor Who* was returning to its original function of providing a drama which would appeal to the same audience as the variety shows, game shows and light entertainment that had been slowly returning to the BBC1 Saturday schedule. The current model of such shows was that there should be some form of talent competition where viewers could phone in the votes. This caused a lot of trouble for the BBC later, and ITV's attempts went way off-beam (see X1.12, "Bad Wolf"), but the point is that, as with *Juke Box Jury* back in the early 60s, it was something about which all members of the family could hold different opinions. Arguing the merits of each of the hopefuls was something a family could do collectively in front of the telly, which the conventional wisdom said was no longer how people used television.

Heggessey was gambling on this being wrong. She wanted something on Saturday evenings that had the same broad appeal as the phone-in talent shows that were the dominant life-form, but with a scripted narrative (perhaps we should say an *overtly* scripted one). The cornerstone of this project had to be a high-profile series with a distinct look. The low-cost, safe version of *Doctor Who* entirely set in a street was not going to cut it, so the full range of the programme's potential, aliens, spaceships, costume-drama production values and a different genre every week would have to be shown off. Apart from showing off the potential of the series, they were showing off the abilities and potential of Cardiff. In the course of making this series, the city's facilities and locations would be brought into the spotlight. But that's another story. (See **Does Being Made in Wales Matter?** under X1.11, "Boom Town".)

Gardner, meanwhile, had become Davies' bellwether: he tried ideas out on her and found that she had almost his tastes, but less experience with the so-called "cult" shows pre-*Buffy*. According to legend, Davies lent her "City of Death" (17.2) and said, "This is what *Doctor Who* can be like." He is on record as saying he would never risk an episode

continued on Page 21...

1.1 Rose

"Bad Wolf" there as well, but this is disputed.] The Consciousness is versed in its 'Constitutional rights' and the details of 'Convention 15' of the Shadow Proclamation [something we'll be hearing more of - see X4.12, "The Stolen Earth"]. The Doctor says that the Consciousness makes use of 'warp-shunt technology'.

History
- *Dating*. The missing-persons poster for Rose in "Aliens of London" says that she disappeared on 6th March, 2005. The tax-disc in Mickey's car-window confirms the month and year [although he ought to have sent it off for renewals, as it expires in under a month - he's a motor-mechanic, so he should have known that].
- *The Time War*. Whatever happened in the interim since "Survival" (26.4), it involved a great conflict across time, including many of the most advanced species in the cosmos. The Nestenes lost their homeworld and all their protein-planets, and the Doctor, who says he 'fought' in the war, was powerless to help. There has been some restitution of law and a universally-recognised code of conduct - the Shadow Proclamation maintains relations between the "higher" beings. Convention 15 of the Proclamation governs safe conduct during negotiations.

Additional Sources Panini's *Doctor Who Annual 2006* has a background piece by Russell T Davies that fills in the gaps about Rose, Mickey and Jackie. Rose and Mickey have been on-and-off since she was 14, and Jimmy Stone was the wannabe rock-star who came between them and stole her money. Jackie pays the bills by running a hairdressing service from the flat, which is 48, Bucknall House, SE15 7GO. Rose has been on a school trip to Parc Asterix, Paris (see X1.7, "The Long Game"), but other than that, a week at a Welsh seaside resort every summer is as far afield as she's been.

Catchphrase Counter We get the first of several occasions where the Doctor declares something to be 'fantastic', in this case Rose pointing out the London Eye's suitability as a Nestene transmitter.

Deus Ex Machina [Although the "Flavia" theme - that female vocal we will be hearing whenever the plot needs a helping hand from Fate - is used for Rose's first sight of the TARDIS, the really flagrant scripted cheat is the anti-plastic, which is never explained but does an awful lot of damage for something looking like the complementary shampoo from a cheap hotel.]

The Analysis

The Big Picture Whilst the BBC is predominantly concerned with making radio and television for the public - who pay a Licence fee to get the content without commercial interference - there had been a move since the 1980s to maximise the spread of the Corporation's activities into other, directly remunerative areas such as publishing, CD, video and DVD releases of old programmes and online services.

This was nothing new: it was the BBC Enterprises division that had made sure there were filmed copies of the black and white episodes of *Doctor Who* to be sold to Nigeria, Cyprus, New Zealand and elsewhere. Enterprises, which became BBC Worldwide in the late 1990s, published the tie-in books about Paul McGann's Doctor and supervised the successful exploitation of *Doctor Who* when there were no new episodes being made. It's worth reiterating that *Doctor Who*, even in the last few years when the outlay per episode was higher than whole year's-worth of 1960s episodes, made more money from overseas sales and merchandising than it cost to make. This money, however, went into the BBC's general kitty for television drama, funding *EastEnders*, *Silent Witness* and various things with Michelle Collins in (X3.7, "42"). In the essay with this story, we will look in detail at the logic of bringing back *Doctor Who* in 2005, but the precise nature of the series they made isn't as obvious a choice as it might look now.

To make a twenty-first century version of *Doctor Who*, they had to remove any taint of cheapness. Less-gifted comedians were still making the same three jokes about the wobbly sets, the low budget and Daleks being defeated by stairs. There were economies of scale that follow from making a big-budget series: the quality (or, at least, fame) of actors, the overall look of the series and the use of dedicated staff and facilities - as opposed to just cobbling things together from whatever other productions have just been made at the same complex. Making individual episodes in blocks out of transmission order means utilising resources (including specific actors) efficiently.

Why Now? Why Wales?

continued from Page 19...

she wouldn't have liked. Gardner and Davies became the first two executive producers on the new series (a post only ever held by Barry Letts in Season Eighteen under very different circumstances). The BBC's then Head of Continuing Drama, Mal Young, was, for the first year, the third. He abruptly left the BBC at the end of 2004 after seven years restoring the "bread-and-butter" of regular dramas apart from the prestige projects (he gets a credit right up until X2.0, "The Christmas Invasion").

All these new names to remember might seem a little daunting, but there is one fact to be borne in mind about them. These executives were all roughly the same age, old enough to have spent their childhoods enthralled by Tom Baker or Jon Pertwee. The generation of BBC management who had axed the series were old men from Light Entertainment backgrounds who had never been young enough for *Doctor Who*, and resented any drama taking money away from song-and-dance shows. They had all died, retired or gone on to other jobs with other television companies. (In the case of Michael Grade, virtually all television companies in Britain had at some point hired him, then regretted it.) The old guard had been replaced by people who simply didn't get why *Doctor Who* wasn't being shown. Some had been dyed-in-the-wool fans, some casual viewers in days gone by and some only had a vague idea about the details of the old series - but everyone knew, bone deep, that it belonged on BBC1, on Saturdays and in the twenty-first century.

The gamble would only have been assessed to have paid off if the ratings were favourable. Although the BBC is still not primarily concerned with crude viewing figures, audience-share for BBC1 output is used as a measure of success amongst the Corporation's critics. These were very active at the time, both other media consortia (especially those owned by Rupert Murdoch's News Corporation) and politicians who were increasingly resentful of the BBC's independence from their control. Spending a vast sum of public money on a series watched by a few thousand obsessives would give these critics ammunition at a time when the government was looking for ways to clip the Corporation's wings.

They therefore needed to make a product that would re-ignite interest in a well-established and lucrative brand, and have it be watched by as broad a spread of different categories of viewer as possible. It had to be child-friendly, action-packed, soap-like and clever. The soap aspect is one that US broadcasters never quite "got", given that they work on the assumption that these are two different audiences. This is partly a function of the nature of American soaps (which are occasionally shown in the UK for ironic viewing tinged with outright gobsmacked disbelief). It's also to do with the progressive ghettoisation of any fantasy-themed series onto specialist channels and the image-problem this gave them amongst main-stream viewers in many countries. The BBC had learned the hard way that this didn't work in Britain: the mistaken belief that nobody would be equally interested in *Doctor Who* and *Coronation Street* had caused no end of trouble in the period when Sylvester McCoy was the Doctor.

Many of the writers Davies recruited were veterans of Britain's soaps. As it happened, the whole trend in fantasy television was towards character-led, "novelistic" stories with small details becoming significant much later, and long-term storylines feeding into individual episodes - a radical change since the days when each individual episode of a series was made to be broadcastable in any order, and one that eventually proved the undoing of the anthology series *The X-Files* when it brought in too many conspiracies and recurrent mysteries for any resolution to seem possible. Paradoxically, the best way to make something that spoke to the whole of Britain was to make something that seemed American in form, and the best way to be able to justify that scale of outlay was to sell the result overseas and hope that this secondary audience were smart enough, or patient enough, to follow a series making relatively few concessions to them.

An argument can be made that the BBC deliberately sabotaged the overseas sales of *Doctor Who* in 1985, when they allotted fourteen 25-minute episodes per year. With a slightly larger budget for sets, cast and costumes, the production team could have made two-part stories (or occasionally

X1.1 Rose

traditional-style four-parters) and sold these in batches every two years making, in effect, 28 hour-long episodes - a standard US-style season (sort of). For financial and logistical reasons, however, the minimum length of stories was now three episodes. For a relatively small capital outlay, it could have been possible to make a late-80s *Doctor Who* that looked like it deserved to be on the world's screens. Using post-production techniques similar to the ones used on US shows could have made them look as though they had been originated on film, and thus keeping the savings of video-tape whilst not having the compatibility problems that made British VT-made series look odd on French, US or Indian transmission systems. (And, it must be said, vice-versa: the initial BBC2 run of *Star Trek: The Next Generation* looked like fourth-generation bootlegs of home-movies.)

We're going to talk a lot more about this in Volume 8, but the production of the series from "Rose" onwards is altered to look as much like an American series as possible. Although fewer than half the domestic television sets were configured for it, the episodes were made in the 16:9 aspect ratio preferred by foreign networks (and set manufacturers). There is now a regular Director of Photography (other names for this complex job are "cinematographer" or "lighting cameraman") who arranges the lighting and lenses and works with the post-production colour-grading team to make each individual frame of the episode look a particular way. In the days of film, this was a matter of the right film-stock, lenses and lighting-rigs, but the switch to digital has made it, if anything, more complicated. The Betacam system also meant one camera used for multiple takes from different angles, rather than the conventional TV drama set-up of three to five cameras recording a scene from the different angles in a continuous take.

There is a drawback to this approach. Whereas the kind of American series they are aping in form have a regular base and a large stock company, *Doctor Who* rarely stays in one place or time for two stories in a row. If individual episodes are now self-contained stories (itself a drastic change from the format that had worked for 26 years - see **What's a "Story" Now?** under "Pudsey Cutaway"), this could mean costly set-building and costuming problems for 13 different planets or historical locales. Compared to something like *Star Trek: Deep Space Nine*, where they can do entire episodes with just the usual sets, Federation uniforms and actors - or *Buffy the Vampire Slayer*, where they can go ten episodes without any location shooting - it might have seemed daunting to even consider doing *Doctor Who*. Look at Series One and you can see how they did it: Mickey's flat, Jackie's flat, the TARDIS and Satellite Five and lots and lots of locations, mainly in Cardiff. Other than these, there were a few tiny sets dotted about, most of them in the two-part World War II story.

So the content was British, but the form was American. It was a definite choice and rather cynically made: this time around, *Doctor Who* had a definite "season finale", and something premeditatedly designed as a potential relaunch or "sweeps" episode (X1.6, "Dalek") if the first launch faltered. It is unfortunate that many observers assume that the BBC's overseas sales mean just the US networks. As we will see in Volume 8, the redubbed and re-edited versions of the Welsh-made series are a global phenomenon, albeit one that some territories find baffling.

Something non-British viewers will probably not quite realise is the extent to which this episode's version of London is explicitly tourist-friendly. All the bits where actual Londoners go are removed in favour of a run-through of clichés straight out of *Austin Powers* and Richard Curtis romcoms. (Ironically, the same grotesque parody of London that Noel Clarke has devoted his main career to trashing.) In this and the other two-part story made in the first production-block, director Keith Boak is consciously evoking the trite "Cool Britannia" sales-pitch of the late 90s, one which Tony Blair endorsed (to widespread ridicule). In particular, there are many scenes and shots that seem almost fingerprint-identical to *Spiceworld: The Movie*. (If you think that's a coincidence, look at who got the first line of spoken dialogue on day one of shooting... Naoko Mori, who was the fictitious sixth Spice Girl in that benighted flick.) Just as every American film set in Paris takes place in hotels which magically *all* have views of the Eiffel Tower, so this kind of production is a sort of visual shorthand for the fairy-tale version of England with bad food and Pearly-Kings. (To quote Elton from "Love & Monsters", real London is madder, and darker and a whole lot better.) It's only just a step up from *Murder, She Wrote*'s use of 50s stock-footage of fogbound Piccadilly Circus and

Remington Steele's idea that we had steam-trains in the 80s.

Boak isn't solely responsible, as the script has the London Eye used as the Nestene transmitter. The entire colour-palette of these three episodes is jarringly vibrant and mainly red, white, blue and pink. Lots of pink. The Tyler household, supposedly our benchmark of "real", is one of a kind that only exists in mid-90s TV dramas and sitcoms, to the extent that when they attempt a different sort of TV-drama-"natural" touch, the contradictions and anachronisms trip each other up. (See **Why is Trinity Wells on Jackie's Telly?** under X1.4, "Aliens of London", and **Must They All be Old-Fashioned Cats?** under X3.3, "Gridlock".)

With such a high-profile series taking so much Licence-Fee money, the first episode had to be as low-risk as possible and demonstrate as many aspects of the format as possible in three-quarters of an hour. Subsequent episodes had to capitalise on this and avoid alienating the broad audience expected for the series by looking too much like the nerdy, self-obsessed US space-operas with which the BBC had attempted to bracket the re-runs of 70s episodes during the interregnum. This is the reason so few episodes in the first two years take place any further away than Earth orbit, and why every alien world is being explored by humans from Earth - Davies' faith in the casual viewers was never high (see **Is Kylie from Planet Zog?** under X4.0, "Voyage of the Damned"). As a shop-window for the series' potential, "Rose" is as risk-averse as is conceivable, and allows for as much painless introduction of characters and situations as possible whilst still having things happen rather than just being talked about.

English Lessons *Lottery Money* (n.) The National Lottery, later renamed the Lotto, launched in 1994 and was originally on Saturdays. A second draw on Wednesdays followed, and various other new permutations have come along (including a Europe-wide draw on Tuesdays and Fridays). Many workplaces have syndicates, each donating a pound (the cost of one standard entry) and making multiple entries on an even split of whatever winnings they make. Rose being given custody of the entry-money indicates that she is A) trusted and B) fairly junior. (And yet Jackie seems to be able to join, if the phone call next episode is any guide.) The Saturday Draw should have followed that episode, but there was a bulletin about the death of Lord Callaghan of Cardiff.

• *Coffee* (n.) Although American-style chains have come and almost replaced our indigenous cafés, most people in Britain stick to the simple mug of instant coffee from granules or powder as a work-place alternative to tea, according to taste and time of day. So many people are particular about how they have their tea that making it for strangers is almost as bewildering as ordering coffee in one of the US franchises, whereas "a cup of coffee" is more-or-less uniform with only yes/no milk and sugar choices.

• *Swan Off* (v. trans.) To leave with an affectation of nonchalance, as with a swan (which appears to glide gracefully but, beneath the surface, is paddling away like billy-oh).

• *Beans on Toast* (n.) As hinted at in Volume 6, our baked beans aren't quite like the ones on sale in the US, and the fact that this quick, easy and nutritious meal needed to be explained at all perplexed us.

• *Chips* (n.) Not the same as French Fries. These days, those aren't even potatoes but processed maize (the stuff Americans call "corn"; that being what everyone else uses to denote various grains such as wheat and barley). Chips come in two basic varieties, the ones deep-fried in chip-fat and served with battered fish, doner kebabs etc., or game chips, which are larger chunks of potato roasted in the fat of whichever meat they are served with (as in the "steak and chips" the Doctor orders in X1.11, "Boom Town", although less salubrious establishments fudge the difference or use pre-prepared frozen "oven chips", as do busy housewives). Our basic chips are cut into long cuboids with a 1/2 inch cross-section (thus absorbing less fat than US-style fries) and marinaded in milk or secret-recipe preparations. They are fried twice (so they're fluffier on the inside than they are on the outside), the second time on the premises in front of the customers. Traditionally, this would be done once every two days, as some people prefer the more frangified day-old chips (hence the sign "frying tonight" on chip-shop doors until the 80s). As with all the best British food, it's adapted and altered from overseas, mainly Belgium, and came to the East End with Jewish emigrés in the late 1850s. What we did with the basic format made it all ours (using different varieties of potato and applying salt and vinegar instead of mayonnaise).

• *A Levels* (n.) Originally the intermediate step between school and university, these are now the basic qualification for anyone planning to go

1.1 Rose

beyond menial work. They are sat after the GCSE exams (which generally come when a student is 16) and now have two phases: AS and A2. Without three A Levels, any hope of University has to be at best postponed. However, since their introduction in the early 1950s, they have become the benchmark qualification for employers.

Oh, Isn't That...?

• *Christopher Eccleston* (credited as 'Doctor Who'). He seemed to come out of nowhere in 1993 and just be in every British-made film or major TV drama. First he was the 1991 historical drama *Let Him Have It* (more talked-about than seen until the DVD release), then the by-the-book cop in *Cracker*, against the almost-stereotypical maverick psychological profiler Fitz, played by Robbie Coltrane. His character, DCI Bilborough, was killed slowly by Robert Carlyle's character in an episode that was Jimmy McGovern's first script about the anguish following the Hillsborough Football Stadium disaster (he did another, called *Hillsborough*, starring Eccleston).

And then came *Our Friends in the North*, which told of friends responding to 30 years of British social history and pitched his idealistic character against a more cynical survivor played by Daniel Craig. At the same time, Eccleston was in the first of Danny Boyle's films, *Shallow Grave*, opposite Ewan McGregor. By this time there was a definite type of role he played, and a set of directors whose projects he tended to be in, so later films (*Elizabeth*, where he was the least bewildering piece of casting, *eXistenZ* (sic) and *Gone in 60 Seconds*) saw him moving out of that clique, and his cameo in *The League of Gentlemen* had him play comedy for almost the first time.

We could go on: a couple of films with Michael Winterbottom (*24Hour Party People* for an unannounced cameo as Boethius, and *Jude*, a Thomas Hardy adaptation with Kate Winslett) and (drumroll please) *28 Days Later*, as you probably knew (see "Aliens of London" for the full significance of this), and *The Second Coming*, a two-part TV drama by Russell T Davies. So, in essence, announcing that he'd been cast as the Doctor was a bold statement that the new production-team meant business. The BBC were silent about exactly how much he was getting for his stint as the Doctor, but he could afford to give a reported £10,000 to an appeal to try to stop the Glazer brothers buying Manchester United FC.

• *Billie Piper* (Rose Tyler). Anyone not around in late-90s Britain might need to be told that Billie (no surname needed then) was actually more famous than Eccleston, albeit not for acting. Whilst at stage-school, she had appeared in an advert for sardonic pop mag *Smash Hits* and, on the back of this, had been groomed for a recording career. Her debut single, *Because We Want To*, was a smash hit, appropriately, and several more followed. She was a household name at 15. (NB she's actually four years older than Rose.)

Then the hits dried up (see next story for a sidelong comment on this) and phase two of her extraordinary career began. As a 19-year-old hasbeen, her marriage to disgraced former Radio 1 Breakfast Show DJ Chris Evans (literally twice her age) was tabloid gold, but when the couple embarked on an unrepentant drunken spending-spree for a year, the story wrote itself. Then, after a brief interlude, Piper resumed the acting that had been her first love. A couple of undistinguished roles followed (*The Calcium Kid* for heaven's sake!) and then *The Canterbury Tales*, modern-day retellings of Chaucer, had her as a nightclub singer in *The Miller's Tale*. The marriage was disintegrating during the filming of Series One, which caused headaches for the BBC Wales publicity department. Until she was two days old, she was called "Leanne" and her middle name is still "Paul". And she's not really from London, she was raised in Swindon (we will note a few little slips into a West Country accent here and there).

• *Mark Benson* (amateur conspiracy analyst Clive Finch). From the early 90s hit *Soldier Soldier* onwards, he had cornered the market in fat geordie blokes. At the time of "Rose", he had been the star of a number of ads, notably a series of really annoying bank commercials but, more to the point, had been the anti-Christ to Eccleston's Son of God in *The Second Coming* (a character named, with typical RTD originality, "Johnny Tyler"). This makes "Rose" his second Eccleston/ Davies project where he never actually meets the star on screen. At the time of broadcast, he was sporting a terrifying mullet wig in *Catterick* (a baffling "dark" sitcom of the kind BBC3 made a lot of back then). At time of writing, he is currently in three long-running series.

• *Noel Clarke* (Mickey Smith). Writer, director and actor, Clarke was juggling his *Doctor Who* commitments with work on his feature debut, *Kidulthood*. He was also in the 20-years-on sequel series to comedy-drama *Auf Weidersehen, Pet*, which affected his availability for *Doctor Who*. He had already won awards for his stage acting.

• *Camille Coduri* (Jackie Tyler). Basically, if *Doctor Who* had been made in 1990, she would have been a likely casting as the companion. There was a cultural stereotype of "Essex Girls" (vacuous, promiscuous, gaudy and unambitious) that meant she would always have a bit-part somewhere, often as a murder-victim, but the thing everyone forgets now is that she was the hero's love interest in the feature films *Nuns on the Run* and *King Ralph*.

• *David Sant*. Although Sant was unrecognisable inside an Auton head, it has been brought to our attention that he is noteworthy as both the hitman Cartoon Head in fan-friendly stoner sitcom *Ideal*[2] and as the voice of *Pingu*. (Yes, we know it was German-made originally, but it was bought by a Welsh animation studio who make the new series of the Plasticene penguin's geographically-confused adventures.) He's moved into directing kid's shows.

Things That Don't Make Sense It seems petty to point out that they goof in the first five seconds of the series but... if the sun has reached New York (as the first shot of Earth shows), then it can't be 7.30am in London. (And they keep making this kind of mistake - see X3.1, "Smith and Jones" and X4.17, "The End of Time Part One" for the most glaring ones.)

Rose is chased around a cellar by dummies that can A) kill with an energy-pulse, and B) stay perfectly still and not attract attention. That being the case, either letting her leave or just killing her and evaporating the body would be a sensible course of action, but waking up (slowly), chasing her around (slowly) and being ooh-scary achieves nothing, even if they catch her and beat her to death. The Chief Electrician's office has a hazard warning for electrocution on the door, as if this were the main fuse-box rather than an office - not really such a sensible arrangement. The explosion that devastates Henrik's doesn't shatter any of the shop-windows across the road.

The obvious quibbles concern the extent to which this happens in London or the theme-park version of the city inhabited by Dick Van Dyke and visited by Perry Como at Christmas. In the real 2005 London, the 22 bus route had used the abhorred bendy-buses (instead of double-deckers) for over a year. Even after midnight, when it becomes the N22 and goes a lot further, it never reaches Queen's Parade, Cardiff. Moreover, the Doctor and Rose are standing directly across the Thames from the London Eye, but go all the way to Westminster Bridge, run across that and then go back along the South Bank to the Nestene base, rather than use the Jubilee foot-bridge like anyone else (this would have knocked 15 minutes off their journey - helpful, if you're running). Their journey must take ages, as one second the big famous clock behind them says 10.30pm, then the next the N159 to Streatham is running, as it only does after midnight. (Jackie's late-night shopping is *really* late...)

With this comes the bigger problem that traffic in London is still running a day after what appears to be a major terrorist outrage in the heart of the city. (We can speak from experience from later in that year.) Wherever Henrik's is supposed to be (and we can gloss it as a thinly-disguised "Fenwicks", so possibly Bond Street), Rose can duck out for a packed lunch in Trafalgar Square. This makes it seem likely that she works within walking distance (rather than spend ten minutes of her lunch hour commuting by tube - if she had that kind of money, she could buy a lunch). The most likely location of Henrik's is therefore Regent's Street or maybe Piccadilly. (Oxford Street, where the shops like that are also concentrated, is possible, but they'd meet in Leicester Square instead.) If a major store in Regent's Street blew up, the whole of Central London would be cordoned off for days, nothing else would be on telly all week as the news media go into overdrive (see "Aliens of London"), and nobody, but nobody, would do a bit of late shopping the following evening.

The Nestenes want Earth because of the things we've put into the air. All right, but why not go to Jupiter if they want juicy toxic hydrocarbons? Why not pop over to Titan (see 15.2, "The Invisible Enemy"), a much better candidate for a 'protein planet' and one with a lower gravity-well to overcome for export purposes? Why, indeed, try a ploy with walking shop-dummies that they must know isn't really practical? Even if we go with the theory (fashionable among a minority of fans for a time, but discredited once "School Reunion" proved the new series wasn't a continuity reboot) that the Time War changed everything so "Spearhead from Space" never happened, the logic of taking over Earth by making a few shop-mannequins go on a rampage in London after the

X1.1 Rose

majority of shops have closed is hard to fathom. Indeed, pretending that the two earlier Auton adventures have ceased to exist simply raises the question of how the big blob of Marmite in the cellar made and distributed these dummies, or even installed itself near the Eye without any hands or human servants. The thing that the Doctor talks to in the unexpectedly large, obviously old warehouse under the Thames (did they not run into this when laying the foundations for the Eye?) is a plastic body for a disembodied consciousness. So either a big dollop of plastic fell to Earth and slipped past the radar that detected much smaller hollow plastic spheres in the early 70s (because in "Spearhead", we saw UNIT using radar that can detect plastic spheres the size of watermelons, so they're obviously not the usual kind of plastic that lets radio signals through) or someone on Earth made it, as was the plan in the last two attempts.

This is more alarming when the situation here is compared to that in "Spearhead from Space" and "Terror of the Autons", both of which were about UNIT and the Doctor desperately trying to prevent the embodiment of the Nestene Consciousness in a plastic body. That's already happened here, so again we must ask - what is all the pratting about with shop-dummies attacking late-night customers supposed to achieve? They've won, and all they have to do is avoid drawing attention to themselves until they can do something really evil, such as increasing the supply of tasty dioxins in the air by fiendishly replacing world leaders with replicas who give tax-breaks to major polluters. (As with the Zygons - 13.1, "Terror of the Zygons" - the alien plan would be better served by *not* interfering and letting us turn the planet into something they can use.) But instead of doing all the nasty things the Doctor says they could have done with phone-wires and domestic plastic, they send shop-dummies out on a not-very-efficient rampage.

Whatever 'anti-plastic' is, it causes a big fire just under several major tourist destinations (and the nation's legislature) on a week night. Again, with London on a full security alert after a department store blew up, it's unlikely that the Doctor and Rose got that close to Parliament and into a hitherto undetected alien base without the government agencies knowing all about it, and yet Mickey is questioned about Rose's disappearance ("Aliens of London") and evidently doesn't mention the Doctor at all. (If he had, the accusation that he'd murdered Rose would have been dismissed and either UNIT or Torchwood would have stepped in, alerted by the Code Nine flag-up system.) At the very least, the CCTV would have shown Rose and the mystery man going into a building which is then destroyed, and never coming out. (If you've been to this bit of London, you'll know that the proximity of two railway stations, a vast arts complex - see 10.3, "Frontier in Space" - and Parliament means that this section of the South Bank is monitored very closely.) So if the authorities don't realise that the guy in the leather coat is the Doctor, they'll assume she died - and if they *do* recognise him, they'll surely assume he took her on what the *Radio Times* used to call An Adventure In Space and Time. (And isn't it lucky that the Doctor and Rose stumbled across the entrance at low tide, when that hatchway isn't under six feet of water?)

Clive, the world's leading authority on the Doctor and how everything he touches leads to death, seems amazingly ill-informed on how to get your wife and kids out of life-threatening situations of the kind where the Doctor is usually involved. There's no hint of "I just knew this would happen, as soon as someone started believing me." (Incidentally, Clive's surname being the same as the butcher's shop that might hire Rose would be annoying, if it had been used on-screen.)

Although most of the episode shows Rose doing companion-like things, she ought to cultivate a sense of occasion - Kids, if *you* ever have to stage a last-minute rescue involving an axe and swinging over a vat of molten plastic to free the hero, don't waste time telling anyone who might be watching your entire school record. Still, at least her accent holds: earlier, she described the TARDIS as 'that baax'. (Did we mention that Piper's from Wiltshire? Non-British readers will have to accept that in the West of England, every day is Talk Like a Pirate Day.)

The one that everybody seems to notice: When the Doctor shakes a bottle of champagne enough to propel its cork at Auton-Mickey, there's not a drop of champagne spurting anywhere. Also, while it's fair enough that the Nestene keep Mickey alive to keep refreshing his duplicate's body-print, why does Rose find Mickey just sitting around in the Nestene base, not at all tied up and presumably able to escape?

And... *seriously*, Rose didn't notice that Mickey had been turned into a plastic Max Headroom?

Critique It might sound like damning with faint praise, but... this was designed to do a job, and it does it efficiently.

Seven years or so later, it's easier to see what's there rather than what we *hoped* would be there. It's not as convoluted as the episodes were going to get, not as effects-heavy as the rest of this series - let alone later years - and takes time to establish everything the viewer needs for the story to make sense first go. There's one big set-piece effect of an explosion in the first half-hour, but it almost looks like a routine comedy-drama about a shop-girl until the Nestenes take Mickey, at which point it looks like children's television.

There's nothing wrong with that: the whole object of the exercise is to reassure the British Public, en masse, that this isn't going to be impenetrably nerdy, and set out the stall for what this programme can offer them that others can't. The taint of this relaunch being regarded as "Cult TV" had to be removed (which partly explains the toe-curling interlude with Clive and his wife), but at the same time, all the options open to the series and the basic ground-rules had to be explained succinctly. Four recurring characters needed to be introduced and a major plot-development sketched in for more experienced viewers. And it had to *entertain* casual viewers (which, at that stage, was everyone under 30) along the way. And now, that's all that's left.

And it *is* entertaining, as a piece of television. There's so much energy, such exuberance and such an air of *fun* that it is impossible not to get swept along. (In the interests of full disclosure, it's worth noting that popping the DVD on to check one small fact inevitably led to watching the whole thing all over again.) It tells jokes, sets a mood, makes a decent fist of showing dummies attacking late-night shoppers as a counterpoint to the real story of a girl who thought she was useless saving the World. Cleverly, it withholds things until the right time: there's virtually no dialogue until Rose is in a lift with a stranger who's just saved her from killer shop-dummies, almost no effects until the crisis that causes her to run into the TARDIS, and it keeps explanations until they are absolutely necessary and in character. Everything here is intended to reassure the general public that there is nothing here to scare off normal people or turn them into the anorak-wearing spods they think would usually watch that kind of series.

Paradoxically, in almost every other regard, it's barely distinguishable from the last "proper" story, "Survival". That began in a suburban London setting and had comic-relief "ordinary" housewives. It had, for the time, state-of-the-art effects and a leading-lady faking a London accent and pretending to be a teenager with varying degrees of success. That was in three 25-minute episodes and was paced accordingly. If they'd been told to do it in one 45-minute dollop, it would have been sequenced in much the same way as "Rose". This isn't to say that "Rose" is *therefore* better. Forty five-minute episodes sacrifice a lot to get it all in, and the real achievement of "Rose" as a script is that it retains almost every element one would expect in a *Doctor Who* story from the late 80s rather than looking as if it's edited highlights. Anyone watching this with a basic idea of what's going on was kept in suspense by the mystery of what this new Doctor would be like, what's changed and whether this is really the same series or a completely fresh start. Suspense kept the setting-up process watchable. Suspense, in the more traditional sense of the word, is something that this abbreviated storytelling risked losing, but this time they achieved that too. It's hard to maintain this and keep moving with such zest, but somehow they managed it.

But now we know, and we're all familiar with the series, so coming back to this episode the flaws are more obvious. Mickey is excruciatingly badly handled, and Noel Clarke doesn't do much to offset this. We now know he can do better, but he's going to be playing catch-up for the next two years. The Wheelie-Bin scene is criticised for the comedy burp, but the problem begins earlier, with the set-up seeming like someone had read one of the Peter Haining cash-in books from the 80s and seen the theory about the Yeti in the Loo being more scary, but had failed to watch any of the examples of when it did work and when it didn't. Before all that, the establishing scenes of Rose, whilst neatly done (especially the cutting between the incidental music being in-shop muzak and actual soundtrack) was so modish for 2005 that it's now painfully dated. The sped-up aerial shots of London traffic in particular look like someone trying to pastiche early twenty-first-century sit-com manners from an ironic present-day standpoint. At the moment this isn't much of a problem, but this episode will date as badly as

X1.1 Rose

"Spearhead from Space" has and for the same reason - it was bang up-to-date when it was made.

The simple fact is that everyone has a long list of all the things this new version of the longest-running science-fiction series in the world is going to avoid, but no clear idea of what it *is* going to do and - for obvious reasons - who else is likely to be watching. They planned it to catch the *Buffy* audience of teenage girls and a few goths and die-hards (contrary to what the press thought, *Star Trek* wasn't the main series adopted by *Doctor Who* fans in the 16-year interregnum, *Buffy* and *Press Gang* were), but the whole object of the exercise was to make decent family-friendly action-drama to retain the audience watching BBC1 on Saturdays for *Strictly Come Dancing* and the like. So the tone is uneven. They try to make that a virtue, and back when this was the only episode of the BBC Wales series anyone had seen, they could get away with that. As soon as there were any others with which to compare it, these tensions became obvious.

The scene at Cleopatra's Needle is a good example: it begins as a dramatic scene about a girl whose boyfriend has died and a man who seems not to have noticed, then goes into a comedy-of-manners about aliens trying to pass for human before ending up as a piece of child-friendly panto where something really obvious has passed him by, and the nation's five-year-olds are shouting *it's be-HI-I-I-IND you!*. Then it elides into a rom-com run through the tourist version of London, hand-in-hand before they find the Bond Villain's lair. It never settles down. And, as we suggested, that's both its great strength when watched in isolation, and its biggest problem as a *Doctor Who* episode when judged against the ones that came after it.

At the heart of it is the central dilemma for anyone reviewing this year's episodes: is Eccleston doing a superb job of playing a character who is awkward, uncomfortable in his own skin and wanting the ground to swallow him... or is he really regretting signing the contact? It was hard to tell even before the news broke about his resignation, and his manifest lack of any real rapport with Piper weakens the efforts of the script and directing to move us. Piper almost sells it, and she is holding this episode together. The difference between this and the next is that when Rose is the one thing out-of-place, the Doctor becomes the focus and Eccleston has to pull everything towards him by sheer momentum. That being the case, the *real* heroic performance here is Mark Benton in the thankless role of Clive. Without having seen any episodes of this new version of the series, he could have played it for laughs or mugged the way the guest-cast tended to in the 80s - or Camille Coduri does here. This is a huge vote of confidence that this series is going to be worth doing. It's Benton's restraint and commitment to a potentially ridiculous situation that is the clearest sign of what is to come.

From every other point of view, the rewards here are those of any adequately made piece of television. It's a slightly insubstantial episode, with a perfunctory alien threat that's there just to establish the new team's dynamic. A typical RTD season-opener, you might say. Yet it's even more of a throwaway than most, as if they were unsure of the appeal of the format. Looked at from a point after Steven Moffat's indulgently complex opening episodes, it now seems a lot crisper. And the lack of any convolutions means that this is a 45-minute episode that feels like half an hour. This episode was the ideal jumping-on point for the British public in 2005, but it's really not much more than that.

The Facts

Written by Russell T Davies. Directed by Keith Boak. Overnight figures for the first broadcast were 10.81 million viewers, making it the seventh most-watched programme that week. With the BBC3 repeat adding another 0.6 million, this seems like vindication. The system of data-collection was still geared towards people watching things as they were transmitted, and was thus only able to cite the two broadcasts on different channels as separate figures. From "Voyage of the Damned" (X4.0) onwards, it gets a bit more complicated, but for now we will follow the convention of only citing the two transmissions on BBC in the same week (some weeks they did it three times, but we'll come to that).

Alternate Versions [For the remainder of this season, we will be listing the German, French and Polish titles of episodes, but - as Gertrude Stein once pointed out - a "Rose" est un "Rose" ist ein "Rose".]

Apart from the accidental redubbing on first transmission, with Graham Norton and his audience butting in, the majority of transmissions are as per the original. The French redubbed version substitutes *Boeuf Bourgignon* for "beans on toast".

Production

The announcement of a new series of *Doctor Who* came just before the fortieth anniversary of the first episode. It had been a topic that popped up on slow news days every so often, and the casting of the new Doctor was announced on 20th March, 2004. It was the closing item on most bulletins that day, and ended the parade of "sources close to the BBC" claiming that it would "definitely" be Richard E Grant/Bill Nighy/Alan Davies. Eccleston was a surprising choice until about four seconds after the announcement, at which point everyone remembered that he had worked with Russell T Davies on *The Second Coming* and Mark Gatiss on *The League of Gentlemen*. (In the latter case, as Dougal Seipps, owner of the Cat Cinema - don't ask - he had been visibly relieved at not getting yet another "intense" character and had been dressed as most of the public, Gatiss included, thought the Doctor should look. We'll pick up on this in two episodes' time.)

Many of those same bulletins had comments from Alex Saul, owner of the most famous specialist *Doctor Who* merchandising outlet (The Who Shop), in which she was restraining herself from drooling. This aspect of the new Doctor's potential appeal was one the press picked up on, and almost immediately, Davies was busily teasing the press with the idea that the Doctor-companion relationship could get romantic if there was a good enough story reason for it. Two months later, the casting of Rose was announced (or rather, confirmed). Oddly, the press had decided that Billie Piper was to be the companion long before she or the BBC had even spoken about it. Such was her profile at the time that, after her standout performance in a series of re-worked stories from *The Canterbury Tales*, she was widely seen as a slam-dunk for any significant young female role. *Anything* Piper did was newsworthy. Indeed, this was one reason Davies was hesitant: Piper was known to be living large with her husband, wayward millionaire DJ and TV personality Chris Evans, and their whirlwind romance, year-long bender and his abrupt sacking from BBC Radio 1's flagship breakfast show was the stuff of legends. (See X2.0, "The Christmas Invasion" for what's widely thought to be a dig at Evans - his TV production company was called "Ginger Television",

if that's any help.) Expecting her to come to Cardiff for nine months, and risk the reputation as a serious actress she'd been establishing once enough time had elapsed since her pop career sputtered out, was vaguely absurd. Nevertheless, she was available and enthusiastic and easily passed the audition. Two months after that, in July 2004, they shot the first scenes (for the fourth episode).

Now let's rewind a bit and fill in a few gaps...

• As you may already have gathered, Russell T Davies (actually Stephen Russell Davies CBE[3]) was one of the most lauded and bankable TV writers of his generation. He had made his mark in other people's series before launching a string of successful short series with a Manchester-based production company called Red. He was co-producer on many of these. His breakthrough was the controversial *Queer as Folk*, an eight-part series about gay men in Manchester, which lost its original sponsor as its ratings grew. This was on Channel 4, still in those days rather adventurous if occasionally rather worthy. On the strength of this, he pitched a low-budget revival of *Doctor Who* to the BBC... who declined it. He was grabbed by the main commercial network, ITV, and had several other hits with high-concept, big-scale dramas. *The Second Coming* told the story of, well, the Second Coming. In Manchester. With real-life newscaster Krishnan Guru-Murthy telling us how this was affecting the outside world and lots of set-piece riots and crowds. Steve Baxter (Eccleston) was betrayed by his girlfriend (Lesley Sharp - X4.10, "Midnight"). Sharp returned in the next project, *Bob and Rose*, about a gay man who falls in love with a woman and how this leads to riots, crowd-scenes and so on. (Penelope Wilton was in it, as was Alan Davies, which may be why he was the press front-runner to play the new Doctor after his stint in *Jonathan Creek*.) *Mine All Mine* was about a man who finds he owns Swansea and was laced with *Doctor Who* references, up to and including the casting of ace Dalek operator John Scott Martin as the protagonist's dad. Mysteriously, nobody much liked that, but by this time the BBC had added Russell T Davies to its wish list. We tell that story in **Why Now? Why Wales?**, but Davies and Red productions went to Cardiff and made *Casanova* whilst working on a new format for *Doctor Who*.

• As mentioned, the press had the usual rather corny ideas about who ought to get the main role. Richard E Grant (later the recurring baddie in

X1.1 Rose

Series Seven, starting with X7.6, "The Snowmen") was mentioned a lot. He'd been in "The Curse of Fatal Death" (see Volume 6) and *The Scream of the Shalka*, the weird online cartoon by Paul Cornell (see X1.8, "Father's Day"). Also in the frame, allegedly, was Bill Nighy (X5.10, "Vincent and the Doctor"), possibly after the costume fittings for his role as Slartibartfast in the long-delayed *Hitchhiker's Guide to the Galaxy* movie. Eccleston sent an email to Davies on spec. So did a number of writers who had worked with Davies on other series. Davies was known to have been a *Doctor Who* fan and had written one of the New Adventures books, *Damaged Goods*. (An everyday tale of a Manchester council estate where alien-infected heroin causes HP Lovecraft-style shenanigans, one of the TARDIS crew has a gay fling and the misheard word "triobiphysics" is muddled up with the science of lubrication; see 13.3, "Pyramids of Mars" and X1.11, "Boom Town". Typical *New Adventures* fare, in fact.)

None of the other NA crowd who'd gone on to write for television was even slightly surprised that Davies had got the gig, after the previous attempt in 2000. What did need to be stated was that certain apparently immutable elements of the previous series were *verboten* in the new regime. This was made abundantly clear in the briefing for the first series given by Davies to executive producers Julie Gardner and Mal Young, BBC1 Controller Lorraine Heggessey and others. This laid out the 13 stories to be told, what the new Doctor would be like and what he would *not* be like. Victoriana was out, as was poshness, feyness, ostentatious eccentricity or linguistic punctilio. The scripts are written as they sound - "gonna" instead of "going to", "yeah" and "for God's sake". This sort of thing was all completely out of character for any previous Doctor, but entirely natural with Eccleston saying these lines. The extent to which Davies had Eccleston in mind from the outset is unclear, but this casting firmly closed off the old style of Doctor.

The old style of companion was also being vetoed: no boyish or whimsical names, no exotic careers and above all no orphans from alien planets. A quick glance at Davies' previous scripts will show that "Rose Tyler" is to him what "Del Tarrant" was to Terry Nation: the statistical average character-name. The obvious way to start a new series was with a story set in the here-and-now. As the title suggests, the first episode was firmly from Rose Tyler's point of view, so her world had to be disrupted after first being made to seem plausible and ordinary. In the BBC scheme of things, "normal" means London, and this allows lots of familiar landmarks to be shown so that children "get" that the whole world is under attack. It was decided early on to re-use the Autons in their shop-dummies-with-attitude manifestation, and to not call them "Autons". The plan was that anyone unfamiliar with the concept (which, they hoped, would be most viewers) would see the story through Rose's eyes and be uncertain whether this was a hoax or a scam. It also meant that the background they had decided to give the new companion contained a reason why the Doctor would meet her. Her boyfriend was to have been called "Mobbsy".

- In the new series, all casting was the responsibility of a dedicated casting director, Andy Prior, rather than the individual directors or the producers. Moving production to Wales had an effect on this, with the majority of professional actors being based in London and the South East. Several people were auditioned for the two semi-regular roles. Camille Coduri scored highly in the scene they chose (confronting the Doctor at the start of "Aliens of London") for intuitively adapting the scripted line to "Stitch this, mate!" Noel Clarke was one of the few who took the scene where Mickey tells Rose about being arrested for her murder and made it reproachful but not angry. By now the series had another producer, this time the one who would actually oversee production day-to-day. This was Phil Collinson, who had hitherto worked on *Sea of Souls* and a series about doctors in rural Yorkshire called *Born and Bred*, which was in no way a knock-off of any other series set in rural Yorkshire (see "Dalek"). His work had also included *Linda Green,* a series for which Davies and Eccleston had both worked (and which will keep coming up in this book).

- Block One, which comprised "Rose" and the two-part 10 Downing Street romp ("Aliens of London" and X1.5, "World War Three"), were allocated to Keith Boak - he was a director with a track record for action and emotional drama (notably *Holby City*, the hospital drama spin-off from the long-running *Casualty*; and *The Bill*, the ITV police series). He had especially come to Davies' attention during work on *The Grand*, on which Davies was a writer. With the first episode needing to sell the series, there was a general feeling that a safe, competent director showing off the script and premise was the optimum starting-point, and that individual directors could add their touches of panache in later episodes. Boak had a few ideas of his own, most of which were vetoed, and accepted that the main thing he could bring to the production was a sense of pace and energy. Many of the decisions a director would ordinarily take were out of his hands, such as the choice of cinematographer, production-designer and music. Eventually, this would result in a well-oiled machine, but in this faltering first step there was a degree of trial-and-error, and Boak has subsequently been singled out for blame for errors both on-set and on the screen.

• Making two stories in the same locations and sets was obviously going to be logistically easier, but switching between stories on the same day made the shoot more tense than it could have been. The production of "Rose" began two days after the first day's shooting of "Aliens of London". There were many reasons for making the two stories set in tourist-London together as a block, the availability of cast being one of the more intractable. Noel Clarke was in Thailand filming the BBC's revival of ITV's 80s comedy-drama *Auf Weidersehen, Pet* and Penelope Wilton (playing Harriet Jones) was making *Match Point* with Woody Allen. It was also worth trying to get summer weather to fit in with the bright, vibrant feel everyone wanted for the episode. Edward Thomas, the production designer for the series, agreed with Boak that the colour scheme for the episodes ought to echo the famous locations and include a few small touches to prevent London and Cardiff-as-London looking too disjointedly separate. (The scene at Clive's for example, has an estate agent's sign outside a house for sale with an 0208 phone number - i.e. outer London - and red bin-bags for refuse, unlike most real residential ones, as a subliminal hint of London-ness, because they'd decided that London is all red.)

The productions of both stories fell into four distinct stages. The latter half of July was split between the set-piece shop-dummy massacre and the obvious London landmarks. The first scene to be shot (we will tend to say "filmed", but this isn't strictly accurate, since it's all done on digital equipment, originally Betacams - see **What Difference Does Field-Removed Video Make?** under X4.15, "Planet of the Dead") was the Auton brides. This was 19th July. As can be seen in the final production, a lot of this sequence was recorded at Queen's Arcade, Cardiff, but much of it (including the first evening's work) was also Working Street, nearby. Rose seeing Henrik's explode was shot on the second night, with the local department store Howell's standing in for the fictional London shop. As the clearances for various real London buildings to be used as the original for Henrik's had been refused or taken too long, the decision had been made to inlay an explosion of a rooftop on a model onto whichever shop was eventually used, rather than construct a model of the entire shop. This scene also saw the debut of the new TARDIS prop, and already the production team were finding it hard to patrol the shoot for camera-wielding fans. A slight retouch was in order as the design team had chosen to emphasise the battering the Ship had received over the centuries, but Gardner wanted to avoid the first sight of the series' icon getting the look of the new show a reputation for cheapness, so insisted on the TARDIS looking impressive.

The first day included two scenes with stunt-driver Paul Kulik, in first the taxi and then the red bus. This was supposedly a No. 22 between Central London and Chelsea (the last stop, as is genuinely the case, is a district called "World's End" - see 2.2, "The Dalek Invasion of Earth"), but was a double-decker, whereas the real 22 route had shifted to Mercedes-Benz "Bendy" buses two years before. Unfortunately, although the production team had alerted the police about the complicated set-up blocking a major road, the announcement on local radio about why this section of Cardiff was to be blocked off for three days mentioned *Doctor Who* and onlookers swarmed in. (A ploy was adopted later of using a fictitious series with the anagrammatical name *Torchwood* as a *Blue Harvest*-style cover-story, but this didn't last long - as we will see, if you didn't already know.) After a third night of mannequin mayhem, the production relocated and the cast got their breath back for six days in London. The first of these was the fake 10 Downing Street location for the other story, but then on Monday, 26th July, Rose and Mickey's lunch-date in Trafalgar Square started a whole slew of scenes in well-known places.

• It wasn't all glamour. The production swapped between famous, exciting postcard-worthy sites and the Brandon Estate, a real London residential area like the fictional Powell Estate. This is in Kennington, just south of the Thames (best known for the Oval cricket ground and its proximity to Brixton). One reason for choosing it was

X1.1 Rose

that it was hard for passing traffic to enter; another was that some of the towers were the same proportions as a police box and had cylindrical cooling-towers on top that looked like the TARDIS light. By day they recorded Rose's normal life, and the Doctor's entry into it, and by night the more exhilarating big-city running-around-ness happened. However, unlike Queen's Arcade, nobody had thought to book a Routemaster bus, and so the chase across Westminster Bridge had to be staggered until they saw real ones coming and could get shots to match each other. The scenes outside the TARDIS on Victoria Embankment - opposite the London Eye - took another two nights in between days in Kennington. (One of these nights became the dawn where Harriet Jones strode out to take charge in episode five.) As the estate looked like a generic "anytown" in Britain, it was easy to insert scenes shot in other, similar areas - this proved helpful later, when the episode was found to be under-running and new scenes were added. One shot that was abandoned was of Rose running into the TARDIS followed by the camera, a composite of location and studio-interior shots edited meticulously.

- Two more days of relocation and there was a return to Cardiff. The University Hospital basement was used for the basement and back room at Henrik's, as well as the Downing Street lift. Work on the two-parter proceeded after this, and it was almost three weeks later that the production of "Rose" resumed at the Q2 studio complex in Newport, east of Cardiff. The set for Jackie's flat was to have the right proportions for a council flat - most television approximations of such places were disproportionately laid out to allow camera-movement. Edward Thomas' team dressed it appropriately, with "realistic" incomplete sets of crockery and furniture, but the finished episodes would be criticised by Davies for the over-use of pink in the rooms and the unconvincing backdrop for behind the front door. This was one reason that there were remounted and reshot scenes. Q2 was inconveniently prone to external noise (jets overhead, police sirens), but very little of this story needed post-production dubbing (the ADR process, generally performed in the historic Abbey Road studio complex, but not the same room the Fabs used). Pestered by nerds, the producers opted to amend the soundtrack to remove the "s" at the end of "dimensions" when the Doctor explained the acronym "TARDIS". In fact, the final sound mix was completed a mere 48 hours before transmission. (The sound had one final glitch on transmission, as we'll see...) The set for Clive's shed was, apparently, right next to the Q2 complex's kitchens.

- There were two more major locations required: the restaurant and the Nestene lair. The former was a composite of a real restaurant in Cardiff (La Fosse) and the now-familiar Cardiff Royal Infirmary where much of the Slitheen story had been made. The first of these locations was used before the bulk of the studio work, the other nearly three weeks later. For the alien Bond-villain-style HQ, the team had found an ideal spot: a disused paper-mill on the old site of the city's Canton Sanatorium. This proved so effective that it became almost as familiar as the TARDIS interior over the next five years (see, for instance, X2.1, "New Earth", where it's the hospital, and lots of Torchwood shooting a few weeks later). After two days there, and another day in the back-alley behind Q2, the next five days (including August Bank Holiday) were spent on the Slitheen assault on Mickey's flat and on 1st September, after Rose went to Mickey's to look up the Doctor on Clive's website, the first scene in the new TARDIS interior was shot. Comic-book artist Bryan Hitch had designed this to seem organic; the later refinements to the design by Colin Richmond took this and made it more mismatched, with bits of machinery and junk from all over grafted into a living entity. Edward Thomas ensured that this and other aspects of the Doctor's life seemed to come from the same place. Dan Walker, an auto engineer by training, supervised the layout of the TARDIS and designed the new sonic screwdriver to look of a piece with this technology; Jenny Bowers, in the graphics department, designed the Gallifreyan script for the new series (based on the collars worn in 14.3, "The Deadly Assassin" et seq, as well as dismantled watches). The finished set had been kept from the press for weeks. One thing people commented on was that the new-style plasma-screen scanner ran on Windows NT.

- The explosion of the roof of Henrik's was one of two model effects for this story, executed between 14th and 16th September along with the work for "Aliens of London". This session also covered the destruction of the Nestene lair, for which purpose Mike Tucker had taken extensive photos of the Paper Mill location and constructed a detailed model. Tucker and his team were veterans of 80s *Doctor Who* and had developed a formidable expertise. Digital effects were handled by a Soho-based company, The Mill, who had an Oscar for *Gladiator* and were very much in demand. As they had all grown up watching *Who*, they came to the project with enthusiasm and a number of ideas for different ways effects could be realised. Alien masks and suchlike were the work of Millennium Effects, and their designer Neill Gorton had a back-catalogue of monstrous bits and pieces (which is how the Hoix - "Love & Monsters" - could be made from leftovers, and why Henry van Statten's museum includes a xenomorph from the *Alien* films; see "Dalek"). Practical effects (explosions, mainly) were the work of Any Effects. These names are going to keep coming up.

- As mentioned, the sequence where Rose asks the Doctor for hints about who he is was expanded and remounted on location in Gabalfa, Cardiff, in October. The sequence of running down the stairs and discussing the world revolving around either of them was one added to make up screen time, and had to be directed by Euros Lyn during the second block. By this stage, Murray Gold had begun work on the music. His opening motif for Rose rushing to work, which occurs in a few later episodes (the pre-credit scenes of "The Long Game" and "New Earth", and "Aliens of London" and "World War Three" for the Previously On... montages) was based loosely on "Cecilia Ann", an old surf instrumental covered by The Pixies in 1990. The episode was still being added to after the first production block ended, with Jackie's bedroom scenes (if you'll forgive the phrase) being remounted and added to in the HTV studios in November, the phone call for the second episode recorded and rewrites for some of the Nestene dialogue (recorded by Nicholas Briggs in early February, just in time for the first press screenings). The Nestene hand-guns and Auton whirrings were among many original Radiophonic Workshop sounds sourced by Mark Ayres (who had provided music in the last two years of the old series). Ayres had taken on the task of cataloguing and archiving all the Workshop's recordings after the BBC closed down this world-beating department in the late 1990s, and was also responsible for cleaning up the sound on some of the DVD releases of old episodes.

- A simple, effective billboard poster showed the Doctor, Rose and the TARDIS, with the date and time of the debut. Critics in the industry giggled, but it worked. There were two main trailers: one had the Doctor asking "D'ya wanna come with me?" and explaining how dangerous it would be, intercut with him running down a tunnel on fire (shot at Newport train station - the flames matted in later, you'll be relieved to hear) and ending with him promising "the journey of a lifetime" as Rose joins him on the TARDIS set; the other was Rose explaining her choice between a job, home, boyfriend and normal life or danger, excitement and so forth. These were made by another department, but with script supervision by the *Doctor Who* office and, unlike the film-look episodes, were really on 35mm film. (They are lit very differently, and the walls seem a lot less brazen and more like concrete.) The official debut of the episode was at a gala launch in Cardiff, although earlier that week a bootleg had emerged online through a leak at Canadian Broadcasting Company's HQ. As the series was part of a rethink of the BBC's online strategy, the old Cult site at BBCi was mothballed and a new-series-specific *Doctor Who* site began, with links to a mock-up of Clive's website and more games.

The juggernaut pressed on, with radio documentaries (*Project Who* was eventually released on CD with extras that had been cut in case of spoilers), press coverage, a vast pull-out section in the *Radio Times* and items on almost every television programme, from *Blue Peter* to *The Culture Show*. (This last was a feature by broadcaster and writer Matthew Sweet, one of many respected figures to announce their lifelong devotion to the series - where were *they* over the previous 20 years? - and was sufficiently fannish to use the Chromophone Band music from 4.7, "The Macra Terror" under footage of him driving to Cardiff to the press screening.) And in each of these interviews, Eccleston was cagy about his long-term commitment to the series, but spoke of his pride at being part of the heritage he was only belatedly discovering (he'd been raised by Trekkies).

BBC1 had planned for *Doctor Who* to vary the pace between talent shows and the results of the (lucrative) phone-in votes, and the first night had a warm-up, with a documentary (*Doctor Who - A New Dimension*) about the making of the series and its history (in reverse order, with Davies describing each Doctor entirely from a fashion point of view). Unlike this year's series of *Doctor Who Confidential* (which began immediately after the episode on BBC3), it was not narrated by Simon Pegg but - with Pegg on holiday and post-

X1.2 The End of the World

production finishing on *Casanova* - by David Tennant, star of Davies' other big production. After this curious programme, which had had a countdown running through the backstage material, came the first edition of *Strictly Dance Fever*. This had a live competitive round, then a pause while the phone votes came in (during which the rest of the country saw *Doctor Who*), then results. During the pause, the studio audience were kept entertained by the host, Graham Norton. However, at this awkward juncture, news broke of the death of former Prime Minister Lord Callaghan. In getting the news-flash on live and then returning to the scheduled transmissions, someone pressed the wrong button and as the nation (except Scotland) saw Rose investigating the deserted basement of Henrik's, we heard Norton geeing up the audience. (A similar flaw afflicted the last trailer before the episode, which made it a lot more intriguing than it could have been.)

Despite Norton's inadvertent intervention (and see X5.4, "The Time of Angels"), there was hardly anyone with a bad word about the episode. The ratings, as anyone who's read the previous *About Time* books will recall, can be a misleading standard of measurement - however many people are recorded as watching, it seems everyone watches. ITV wheeled out its big guns to try to distract people from the main event of Easter Saturday by having its most popular stars, Ant and Dec, interviewing the Prime Minister. Cheapskate commercial station Channel 5 tried to be clever by grabbing the rights to re-show the first season of *Buffy the Vampire Slayer*. Press reaction to "Rose" was hugely favourable, the only slight regret was the music (even former Doctor Sylvester McCoy thought it sounded a bit bedroom-studio-ish). Online reaction was, predictably, more frantic; the British Nationalist Party, who pretend they aren't Nazis, decried the "pollution" of the series with Rose having a black boyfriend. Three days later, both the newspapers and the Internet would have a whole new topic over which to get all aeriated...

X1.2: "The End of the World"

(2nd April, 2005)

Which One is This? We've seen the future and it's blue. The Doctor talks to the trees (but not to the Face), and avoids hitting the fans while Rose gets into an argument with a tanning frame. Oh, and Earth blows up, for real this time we promise, after which our heroes celebrate by going out for chips.

Firsts and Lasts This is the first story to be directed by Euros Lyn, who will direct more minutes of screen-time in the next few years than anyone.

Making their debuts here are two characters who will return: Lady Cassandra O'Brien and the Face of Boe. Of more immediate concern, the Moxx of Balhoon shows up here. Although he was a minor character and a relatively dull one, he is noteworthy partly for being the first recognisably *Doctor Who* monster to receive widespread publicity, and thus proof that it wasn't all going to be worthy stories set in Manchester housing projects. This means it's the first major appearance by actor Jimmy Vee, who's going to be popping up a lot in this volume and the next. (In fact he had been a rather singular alien in a story filmed some months earlier, but as that was a closely-guarded secret, the Moxx is the one that was in the first photos released - see X1.4, "Aliens of London" for the other alien Vee played this year.) And the Hop Pyleen brothers mean the first of Davies' "animal-head-on-a-human-work-related-costume" aliens, like the space pig ["Aliens of London"], the Ood [X2.8, "The Impossible Planet"], the Dalek Pigmen [X3.4, "Daleks in Manhattan"] and the Tritovores [X4.15, "Planet of the Dead"].

The "slightly psychic" paper gets introduced here, as does Rose's Magic Phone, and we have the first pre-credit sequence to blur the lines between a reprise of the end of the previous episode, a "Previously" montage and new material before the titles. It's the first time since 7.1, "Spearhead from Space" that a recent-ish chart hit has been used in the soundtrack.

This story has the first mention that the TARDIS translates everything (well, almost everything) into English, thus setting up the season climax and prompting a whole new essay later in this book. As is Rose's first (ahem) Adventure

RT Phone Home?

In Britain, as with much of Western Europe, the use of mobile phones is so ingrained with anyone under 40 as to be unquestioned. In America and Australia, for example, the vast empty spaces meant that what Americans call "cell phones" began as a largely metropolitan phenomenon. Texting is rarely used (compared to the UK) and smart-phones are only slowly becoming as common as in Europe with the advent of the iPhone. The spread of these habits, even with this innate inertia, has taken on an always-already feel, and by now anyone coming to the first year's episodes of Rose Tyler could be as unaware as most of the children watching the initial BBC 1 broadcasts that the world has ever been different. What's alarming for anyone who has noted the change is how this relationship with one piece of consumer tech has become ingrained in the text of *Doctor Who*, a series hitherto concerned to show other times and places to be different from our own.

Britain, being a small island with 60 million people, isn't like America. Over the last 15 years or so, the idea that anyone can spend any time out of touch with anyone else, voluntarily, has declined. Anyone who does is treated with suspicion, much as any American adult who never bothered to learn to drive might be. A generational gulf exists between people who might own a mobile (a less-than-welcome, politely-accepted gift) that lives in the kitchen drawer with the corkscrews and people from whom they have to be almost surgically removed to get their undivided attention. Mobiles are no longer just for vocal communication; they are MP3 players, games consoles and keyboards. That wasn't universally the case even when the new series began. Smart phones aside (and we'll discuss the way everyone accepts the sonic screwdriver having so many new "apps" shortly[5]), the most basic phones available have engulfed so many other gadgets' functions as to have almost wiped out the Walkman, Kodachrome and wristwatches. Listening to chart music is almost like hearing auditions for the next ubiquitous ringtone[6]. What you notice about the people who have grown up with this as normal is that they are not always as "present" as they could be; they may be physically in the room, but they seem restless if not in touch with friends at all times. Dealing with people face-to-face seems like a chore. People have become used to everyone they encounter knowing everything they have been doing. Part of this is the whole Social Media boom, of which mobiles are one of a number of conduits, but phones were the first and the most, um, mobile.

Obviously, this has an effect on how people engage with television, and once again the generational difference is remarkable. Paradoxically, as the pace of narrative and the complexity of long-term interconnectedness of events has increased, due to a widespread perception among TV professionals that audiences are smarter and paying more attention, the amount of attention people pay to television has diminished. People tweet while watching. They chat through the dialogue. This has been coming for 20 years. Immersion in a story for the duration of the episode has been replaced by low-level engagement augmented by additional material from other sources, including many available on a smart phone. What is noticeable is the way in which the younger audience form a hive-mind and guide each other towards what is significant. Apparently, the proverbial water-cooler moments are happening in real-time as the on-screen events unfold. Older viewers, raised on the expectation that nothing would be repeated and that transmission might be interrupted by a passing car or the set breaking down, are paying attention and, in many cases, find the redundancy of the clues and hints so popular among would-be "cult" shows irritating.

The feedback loop is also noticeable in live programming, where the comments of viewers are now integral to the content. This has mushroomed: just in the Russell T Davies phase of *Doctor Who*, you can see the development of such trends as they emerge. What is noticeable about "Aliens of London" (X1.4) now is that none of the newscasters asked viewers to send in their photos of the crash or reading out comments from "citizen journalists". Instead, the government eventually releases a phone-line for eye-witnesses, as a means to catch the Doctor. Huw Edwards' bibbling about the Olympic Dream (X2.11, "Fear Her") is more noticeable now for the lack of an on-screen request for information from eye-witnesses, and the Doctor's picking up the Torch, apart from the obvious improbability and lack of security agents pinning him down, seems strange because

continued on Page 37...

X1.2 The End of the World

in Time and Space, it's the first occasion where we see the Vortex change colour depending on "direction" (past or future) in which the Ship is travelling, and the first time we see anyone wheel the Ship around like a shopping-trolley.

At the end of this story, we have the first significant mention of the Time War and the fact that the Doctor is the only Time Lord left.

Watch Out For...

• It's *Doctor Who* in space, so we need: kooky-looking aliens (check); futuristic-looking lettering (check); ventilation shafts (in three sizes, humanoid-crawl-though, tiny-vermin-like-robots-skitter-through and stand-upright-on-vast-gantries-with-giant-fans-and-run-through). There's even a space station (Platform One) that looks like it was made from household objects, but it's state-of-the-art computer effects. Sadly, they miss giving us the full set by omitting to include an alien with a hoarse whisper who begins every sentence with "Sssso, Dok-Torr...". But we've relaunched an old tradition in the series of the aliens all being redubbed by one actor. As a sign that these are strange-but-benign beings and not horrid monsters, they aren't voiced by Nick Briggs this time but by Silas Carson, who did that sort of thing in the *Star Wars* prequels.

• Except... one has the voice of Zoe Wanamaker, and the distorted features of the stretched-out membrane are recognisably hers too. Sadly, Cassandra is so obviously the villain that attempts to make the Adherents of the Repeated Meme work as red herrings fail abysmally. Although the other strange-looking beings made great action-figures (as was their function, rather too obviously), the Destroyed Cassandra figure has become a by-word for things not even the most obsessive fans would buy, and had to be re-launched in a set with Chip (X2.1, "New Earth", and see **What Are the Great 21st Century Merchandising Disasters?** under X5.3, "Victory of the Daleks").

• As we all recall ("we" being the British public), Billie Piper's meteoric pop career was torpedoed when she turned 16 and Britney Spears came along with two near-identical smash hit songs in rapid succession. There are two songs in this episode's soundtrack, one of which seems to be the trigger for (or crystallisation of) Rose's sudden realisation that she has jumped into a bizarre new life with an alien she doesn't really know. That song is the version of "Tainted Love" that was a hit here in 1981, and the lyrics match the scene exactly. When it starts, the Doctor goes from merely dressing like the slightly embarrassing social studies teacher who wants you to call him by his first name to dancing like him at the school hop. The second song is "Toxic", the only other song by Britney anyone here can remember, and is used for a sequence when the Earth is being destroyed. (Britney sings and Billie is unable to escape certain doom. Ha bloody ha.) But Murray Gold picks up on that song's distinctive synth-string arrangement and uses it for the spider-robots.

• Talking of which, no sooner have we had the first of multiple mentions in the new series of the Isop galaxy (albeit in a deleted scene), the locale for notorious Hartnell bug-out "The Web Planet" (2.5), than a CGI effect has a (scripted) collision with the camera, like the accidental Zarbi-EMItron interface that is, sadly, the trademark shot of that story. The scene comes just after what is many people's favourite moment: Rose talking to maintenance-worker Rafallo. What few people realise is that this was a last-minute insert, shot several weeks after the rest of the episode, to cover the under-run when the complicated scenes of Cassandra talking to Rose proved too time-consuming to make as written. (Funny how these improvised "filler" scenes stick in the memory more than the planned set pieces: see X1.1, "Rose", and a few more later in this book.)

• Despite the Face of Boe's later returns and significance, it comes as something of a shock to anyone revisiting this episode to find that he doesn't actually do anything. At all. Nobody even comes up and says "I thought you were great in *Dune*." He just sits in his pickle-jar in a corner, as if hoping someone will ask him to dance.

The Continuity

The Doctor When the jukebox (what Cassandra calls an 'iPod') is wheeled on and starts playing Soft Cell's version of "Tainted Love", the Doctor gets well into it and grins, nodding vigorously like someone who wants to dance but knows he's not very good at it [see X1.10, "The Doctor Dances"; X5.13, "The Big Bang"]. He is capable of telling by ear that the pitch of the space station's engines has risen by 30Hz, and he knows what a gravity-pocket feels like. Intriguingly, his reaction on feeling this anomaly is a slight smile, and he says,

RT Phone Home?

continued from Page 35...

nobody's texted in "hes wel fit 100% gorjus". Rose, by the standards of a 19-year-old London girl from 2005, spends remarkably little time on the phone and only uses it for calls (except when she's in the wrong universe; we will pick up on this soon). Mickey (X1.5, "World War Three") uses his to take photos of Slitheen even as his flat is being ransacked. In Evil Parallel London, a variation on Bluetooth is desirable but treacherous (X2.5, "Rise of the Cybermen"). All of Martha Jones' family call her constantly (even though she works in a hospital!), but seem to stop once she starts travelling with the Doctor (possibly because of Mr Saxon's creepy agents, or possibly because this would draw attention to how weird the timeline of events in that series actually is - see **How Long is Harriet In Number 10?** under X2.0, "The Christmas Invasion"). By the time we get to "The End of Time Part One" (X4.17), Wilf and his "Silver Cloud" are using them as a matter of routine. And yet five years earlier, when "Fear Her" was written, they had futuristic-but-spot-on guesses like using her laptop as a TV, but it is never mentioned that any of the kids in the story had phones - especially not Chloe, for whom isolation was enough of a problem for school psychologists to have been called in as a matter of procedure once her father died. As Matthew Graham, that story's author, has a son who was about the same age, this is indicative of how rapidly the situation has changed. Even five years earlier, the Master's use of mobiles to brainwash all of Britain would have been vaguely ridiculous rather than sinister (X3.12, "The Sound of Drums"). At the time of broadcast, only a few people (mainly dodgy ones if the representation in the media were to be believed) had Bluetooth, so the threat to everyone via Lumic's involuntary upgrades was a bit more abstract than it is today ("Rise of the Cybermen").

The BBC obviously believed that the *Doctor Who* audience all had mobiles: for the launch of the tenth Doctor, they began subsidiary content exclusively for phone-viewing. The TARDISodes offered five-minute prequels to each episode of Series Two. As part of a public-service mandate, they have to be offering something to anyone from whom they are accepting money, and this includes exam revision aids and online content for the children of the Licence-Fee payers. It has been suggested that part of the rationale for bringing back *Doctor Who* at all was that it lent itself to this kind of subsidiary activity. (See **Why Now? Why Wales?** under X1.1, "Rose" and **What Were The Best Online Tie-Ins?** under X6.3, "The Curse of the Black Spot") There were three kinds of early-adopters as mobile use spread in the 90s - teenage girls, techno-savvy IT professionals and gay men (episode four of *Queer as Folk* seemed astonishingly up-to-date and the use of phones was seen as a breakthrough in narrative form, but now it's such a period-piece). Once parents started having to have them, mobiles ceased to be a luxury or affectation - the use of the original "bricks" in the 80s by yuppies and meeja berks caused widespread resistance outside London; in some quarters, mobiles of any kind are still associated with shoulder-pads and Perrier. Obsessive phone-use is one of the adult clichés of teenage girls and their socialising, and has been for decades. (See the film *Bye Bye Birdie* for an example as old as the idea of teenagers, or the song "Party on the Phone" from the hit album *Honey to the B* by 90s popstrelle Billie Piper.) In simple audience-identification terms, then, Rose Tyler simply had to have one, and would have complained if she was unable to use it when gollywhacking around time and space.

So, for the audience for whom this iteration of the series is primarily made, there is absolutely no problem about everyone being in constant touch with not only the other TARDIS travellers, but their relatives back home in the early twenty-first century. This, and the info-dump use of smart-phones augmented by sonic screwdriver chicanery, are accelerated storytelling devices as much as psychic paper or perception filters. The only other gadget remotely as handy is the sonic screwdriver itself. This has, like recent phones, become an all-embracing tool. It is significant that younger fans accept this as entirely plausible, whereas anyone who remembers when it took a while even to undo screws (6.7, "The War Games") gags at the increasingly flippant short-cuts the writers are taking. It is also significant that the paradigm has changed from it being a tool the Doctor devised during the ten minutes or so he had between life-threatening scrapes in Season Five to being an

continued on Page 39...

X1.2 The End of the World

'That's not supposed to happen', as if he's relieved that things aren't going to plan. The tree-person Jabe even comments on how his excitement at a potential disaster is the reaction of someone who has nothing else left. [This self-pitying existentialism also comes out in his spat with Rose, where he avoids questions about his past by declaring 'This is who I am, right here, right now.']

He's good at stepping through rapidly spinning giant fans. [At this stage in the series, it's probably meant to be a lingering question as to whether he does this by extremely precise timing, rather like Windy Miller in *Camberwick Green*, or some Time Lord-y ability that lets him (effectively) walk through walls. As nothing else about this is ever said or indicated again, it's likely the former.]

- *Ethics.* He deliberately teleports Cassandra back to the station, presumably knowing that the raised temperature will dry her out and kill her. He tells Rose [referring to Cassandra, but also presumably referencing Earth and his own people] 'Everything has its time, and everything dies', and seems to think that Cassandra clinging pathetically to life when she causes so many deaths is somehow worse than the murders. [As we will see next year in "New Earth", Cassandra herself eventually comes around to this conclusion.] Noticeably, his righteous indignation doesn't start with Jabe's death, but with the sneer with which he points out to Rose that 'the great and good' in this culture means 'the rich'. [And yet, he never castigates the sponsor of this event, the Face of Boe. Nor does he seems to acknowledge the Face of Boe at all, which is inconsistent with later stories; see "New Earth".]

It doesn't occur to him that Rose would mind having her head rewritten, even if it's just for the language conventions. [Given how often this conversation must have come up with previous companions, this is strange. However, the fact that Sarah asked about it - the only recorded instance of companion curiosity on this score - was evidence that she was under someone else's influence (14.1, "The Masque of Mandragora"), so it's possible the Doctor, or the TARDIS, used to condition people not to notice this. Why this should have stopped is another matter.]

- *Background.* Apparently, the Doctor *was* on the *Titanic* [unless there was another 'unsinkable' ship], and wound up clinging to an iceberg as part of the event. He's been to the twenty-second century and thinks it's 'a bit boring'. [Possibly he's just being cheeky with Rose, possibly it is boring compared with other places they could go, or possibly this indicates that the Dalek Invasion of Earth in 2157 has been expunged from history - see **What Happened to Susan?** under X4.18, "The End of Time Part Two". Of course, a lot of the twenty-second century *is* boring: see 17.4, "Nightmare of Eden".]

He's familiar with Jabe's race of tree people [which isn't to say that he's personally met them before now], and his guess about her joy at receiving the 'gift' of the air from his lungs is spot-on. He greets the Moxx of Balhoon as an old friend, but his entire demeanour at this social function is that of an experienced ligger [a Northern term for someone who gets into parties and cushy jobs].

- *Inventory: Sonic Screwdriver.* It can counter malware in the station's mainframe, persuade screens to divulge system schematics and help reverse teleport settings.

- *Inventory: Other.* The Doctor has a wallet, apparently leather and old, that contains a parchment which we are told is 'slightly psychic paper'. At present, it only makes the observer see whatever the Doctor wishes that person to see - such as convincing the Steward that the Doctor and Rose have a proper invite to the Earth's demise. The Doctor's wristwatch has a square dial and roman numerals, and uses hands [so it seems to be analogue, which makes later revelations rather complicated].

He's also carrying a electronic chip [or so it appears from the outside] that, when installed in Rose's mobile phone, enables her to call Jackie in the twenty-first century, and thus proves to be the last word in Universal Roaming [see the accompanying essay].

The TARDIS The Ship telepathically translates whatever is said into English for Rose's benefit. [We had sort of assumed as much before (see Volume 4 and **Can He Read Smells?** under X2.8, "The Impossible Planet"), but this is confirmation on screen for the first time.] It would appear that "linear" time-travel - sticking to the same planet but moving forward or backwards - is controlled by a wheel set into the Console panel [again, using the front door as 6 o'clock, this one is at 9 o'clock], after a few switches in perspex boxes are flicked, and that materialisation is either arranged or denoted by dinging the kind of bell you'd see on old hotel front-desks. A bicycle-pump seems

RT Phone Home?

continued from Page 37...

extension of the TARDIS, explicitly since "The Eleventh Hour" (X5.1), but implicitly in the resemblance of the bone-like handle to the coral-like Console.

This is an exact match for the relationship smart phones tend to have to computers. The TARDIS now has a remote-control facility, when the Doctor remembers (see below), and everyone who has been in it for any length of time is in touch with the Doctor and each other and their relatives. If the Doctor is supposed to be a time-traveller from an alien world, why is his use of technology so bound to that of the viewers? It's alarming, but mobile phones are the one bit of Earth technology he never seems to notice. Anything else is either derided as "quaint" or enthused over like a vintage car or restored steam-train. Mobile phones, whether WAP-enabled, Smart or just for talking to people, are as normal as trousers. Never once, in the whole time Davies was running the show, did the Doctor pass any comment, or anyone else notice that he didn't. The only two times anyone has asked about it was Rose being puzzled that the Doctor could call her from the TARDIS ("World War Three": on a trimphone, like the one the Master uses in 8.2, "The Mind of Evil" to call the Doctor) and Donna noticing Martha's handset (X4.4, "The Sontaran Stratagem"). (In X6.0, "A Christmas Carol", the Doctor seems to have acquired an appropriately steampunk mobile that could plausibly be his own or a local one, but we never see him obtain it.) Looking back on earlier versions of *Doctor Who*, the difference this has made can be seen as more radical and potentially damaging.

Just briefly, let's look at London-made stories that would have been drastically curtailed by such devices being available to earlier Doctors. The most obvious is "Mawdryn Undead" (20.3). Tegan telling the Doctor she's arrived in 1977 and met the Brigadier would save him two episodes' worth of interrogation of his old chum, but would moreover have prevented the 1983-model Brig's amnesia in the first place. It would also have enabled her to prove that Mawdryn wasn't an imperfectly regenerated Doctor and stop him flying the TARDIS back to his spaceship and all the problems that caused. "The Romans" (2.4) would have been a simple one-episode exercise in everyone knowing where everyone else was and just chillin' in da villa. Any story where an imposter or doppelganger turns up, or where a character has gone missing, or they are spread out over time and/or space, is less workable if they can just call each other and ask what's going on. That's almost all of Season Thirteen gone, for a kick-off. If the current production team really wanted to make *Doctor Who* scary for kids, they'd show a world where mobiles don't work. (It's perhaps significant that the use of them to disrupt alien hypnotic signals and the like is almost a cliché in *The Sarah Jane Adventures* and they've had to find ways around it - how many mobiles Clyde's had smashed is a running-gag like Rory Williams getting killed.) As the phones are linked by the TARDIS and trans-temporally tariffed (X5.12, "The Pandorica Opens" has River Song also able to call Churchill, who - as far as we're aware - never travelled in the TARDIS and has a phone that is wired into STD[7], despite it having a weird bell-tone), even the UNIT radios that work when the plot needs them to were never as handy as Doctored mobiles. This also means that when the plot needs someone to not have a phone handy it is really obvious, most notably in X6.10, "The Girl Who Waited". (A story which, perversely, mentions Amy's phone as the reason they become separated, but never uses it and instead has to make play with a giant magnifying glass, a pair of glasses and a lot of doubletalk.)

What this means for the casual viewer is that a character having been given the Doctor's contact details is a form of initiation. There is a definite rite-of-passage feel to Martha being given a TARDIS key and a jimmied phone (X3.6, "The Lazarus Experiment", as if this is when she becomes an official, capital-c Companion. (For a more complex response to this issue, see **Is Arthur the Horse a Companion?** under X2.4, "The Girl in the Fireplace".) A sidelight on this is how Adam's abuse of Rose's "topped-up" phone (X1.7, "The Long Game") both represents and enables his failure to make the grade as a companion. He has to have it explained to him and immediately starts using it to try to alter history to his own advantage. (Yet the method he uses for this indicates that the story was originally written when phones were

continued on Page 41...

to work as some kind of overdrive. Travel into the future is denoted by the Vortex being a deep red with orange flecks [as in the latter half of the title-sequence].

The old girl seems to have acquired castors for being wheeled around by functionaries.

The Supporting Cast

• *Rose*. She has a habit of pointing at the Doctor when mocking him. Her mockery, as in this case, is often grounded in the idea of him behaving like a randy teenager and her being the adult (as when she sets a curfew when he goes off with Jabe). Yet when she buys him chips [he has no money, of course], she refers to it as a 'date'.

She initially seems uncomfortable about the alienness of aliens, but gets over this and starts trying to befriend people, with varying success. Indeed, it's the 'pure' human Cassandra who alienates her most - Rose emphatically claims she'd rather 'die' than become like Cassandra [suggesting she has an innate fear of plastic surgery and prolonged life]. She calls Cassandra 'Michael Jackson' and 'a bitchy trampoline'.

• *Jackie*. On receiving a call from Rose, she asks to be included in the Lottery syndicate. [Jackie says that it's currently 'Wednesday, all day', so if the real-world calender is here applicable, it's presumably a few days *before* Rose meets the Doctor (on a Saturday, prior to leaving in the TARDIS on a Sunday) - see the dating notes on X1.1, "Rose"].

The Supporting Cast (Evil)

• *Lady Cassandra O'Brien.Delta Seventeen* is what's left of a human from Earth. She claims that her father was a Texan, her mother from the Arctic Desert [suggesting that the continental drift was reversed within her lifetime, as it's all ocean there now] and both were the last beings buried on Earth. She has had extreme plastic surgery - 708 operations and counting - with her chin the last bone to be removed. She is now a brain in a tank under a stretched-out skin with eyes, nostrils and a mouth on one side and blood vessels visible through the dermal layers. When she was a boy, she says, her parents had a home carved into the side of the Los Angeles Crevasse.

Cassandra considers herself to be the last true human and all variants are 'mongrels'. In her desire to stay looking 'young', she has spent a fortune and has thus arranged an elaborate [and, indeed, baffling; see **Things That Don't Make Sense**] assassination-cum-con to finance more surgery. She has shares in the rivals of all the companies owned by the other guests, and established the Adherents of the Repeated Meme as patsies for the fatal disaster she wishes to bring upon all of those present. She's been married at least five times.

The Non-Humans [We get several exotic and intriguing species presented to us, but in most cases we only get an individual's name and not a race, so we'll list them that way...]

• *The Face of Boe* is the sponsor of the event aboard Platform One. He [it? she?] is a seven-foot head with what could be tentacles or dreadlocks, with leathery skin and floating in a big glass jar full of liquid. He hails from somewhere called the Silver Devastation [see X3.11, "Utopia"]. Curiously, in the light of later events [X3.13, "Last of the Time Lords"], he shows absolutely no sign of acknowledging the Doctor or Rose.

• *Rafallo* is humanoid and blue-skinned, with markings on her neck resembling a henna tattoo [as used in Hindi weddings]. The majority of the servitors on the Platform have similar skin-colour, although most are considerably shorter. She comes from somewhere called Crespallion (not a planet *per se* but somewhere in the Jaggit Brocade, Convex 56, near the Scarlet Junction). The Steward seems to be of the same species, but has worked on several other platforms - and, unlike Rafallo, is allowed to speak without first being given permission. Both have ophidian eyes, like cats or reptiles.

• *Trees*. These come from the Forest of Cheem. The three we meet are Jabe, who looks human and female, with a low-cut dress and high collar, and her attendants Lute and Cofffa, whose faces are more woody and who wear black, metallic-looking body-armour. These beings are descended from the Rain Forests of Earth and distrust metal technology (although Jabe carries a hand-held scanner/tablet that communicates to her in birdsong). Jabe is incredulous when the scan she conducts on the Doctor first refuses to confirm an answer, then gives one that seems nonsensical - she concludes that he must be one of the mythical Time Lords and consoles him on his loss. Her gift to the other delegates is cuttings from her ancestors (in a pot); the Doctor reciprocates with breath from his lungs, which seems to please her. She has lianas (which she isn't supposed to show in pub-

RT Phone Home?

continued from Page 39...

less sophisticated than they were even in 2005 - let alone 2012 when the story is set, when Adam's mum still has a rather basic tape-based answering machine. Even in 2006 - see "World War Three" - voicemail was the usual method.) In part, this symbolic upgrading of the new girl's phone is a sign of the shift in the Doctor-companion dynamic from pseudo-parental to pseudo-boyfriend. Getting a key to the flat is a serious step, whereas getting someone's phone number is often the first step in asking someone out, even before getting a name or a proper chat. Getting a TARDIS-enabled phone is more of a step; it's like meeting the in-laws.

Earlier companions rarely had relatives, so this wasn't an issue (and when it was, it was messed up - see **Who Went to Aunt Vanessa's Funeral?** under 21.2, "The Awakening"). In the original configuration of the series, anyone who walked into the TARDIS was on a one-way journey unless a handy plot-contrivance got them back to their original place and time. Most of the monochrome-era's companions were, thus, either orphans or desperately homesick. Some were trying to get back to their own time and world, but some had no option but to move into the Doctor's spare room until something better came up. In some ways, a near-perfectly-steerable Ship and the option to phone mum if things get a bit much, or you have a pub-quiz you need her help with (X3.7, "42"), lowers the stakes for anyone who pitches in his or her lot with the Doctor. "Home" was, conceptually, the great unspoken loss at the heart of *Doctor Who*; the Doctor's own home was a mystery, only mentioned as a place from which he and Susan were exiled. Attempts to make the TARDIS a home were as makeshift as Christmas Day in the trenches or a birthday for someone on an Antarctic expedition. The closest we came to domesticity was the beginning of "The Chase" (2.8), and even at the end of that, Ian and Barbara defied the Doctor to grab a potentially fatal chance to return to London in (almost) their original time. The other attempt at this is the notorious end to "The Feast of Steven" (episode seven of 3.4, "The Daleks' Master Plan").

As a consequence of this, the various waifs and strays accompanying the Doctor on his journeys were forced to accept whichever world they were stuck in on that world's own terms, not theirs. And the roster of TARDIS crew could change at any moment, allowing producers to make last-minute changes (see, for example, 4.4, "The Highlanders" or 3.10, "The War Machines"). They might every so often overthrow a regime they found iniquitous, but only as a way of helping locals who were suffering under that regime's yoke - the one time there is a concerted effort to precipitate a coup, it is as an existential act (2.7, "the Space Museum") to resist an apparently immutable fate. Most of the time, especially in visits to Earth's history, the TARDIS crew would accept, and marvel at, wherever they were and engage with whoever they met as if they were going to be there for a while. In "Marco Polo" (1.4), they are in Imperial China for rather longer than the seven weeks' running-time of the story. They are guests, prisoners, allies or companions of Messire Marco depending on where we are in the story. They are emphatically not tourists. When they learn something new about this milieu, it's because they can see that they'll be living out their days there unless something drastically changes. The one time they stay anywhere as long voluntarily is "The Romans" and Barbara teases Ian about how at home they have become. They neither stand outside as observers nor condescend as "superior" twentieth century visitors, and when they draw analogies with their own background, it is generally at the expense of their own smug assumption of progress. (See also **Are We Touring Theme-Park History?** under X2.7, "The Idiot's Lantern".)

Even once the Doctor could steer the TARDIS, this quest for new horizons and a better home characterised the series, as eighties companions became increasingly prone to running away from families and commitments. Every stop could be their last one, and eventually most of them picked a new home to stay in for the rest of their lives rather than carry on travelling hopefully. Rose, on the other hand, only ever has to face this prospect once, in "The Impossible Planet" (X2.8), and only then because the Doctor has forgotten that the sonic screwdriver has a Stattenheim Remote Control app (see Season Twenty-Two). She even sees the apparent loss of the TARDIS as a joke, and

continued on Page 43...

X1.2 The End of the World

lic) with which she can whip objects from a distances of ten metres or more. As the heat rises in the vent system, she burns and dies.

- *The Moxx of Balhoon*. Another blue chap, the colour of Blu-Tak, but this time like a goblin in a motorised wheelchair. He has a bulbous head and a pointed chin, pointy teeth and a pot-belly. He is a lawyer, representing the firm of Jolco and Jolco. Despite the injunction on religion at Platform One, he describes Cassandra as an 'infidel' when she confesses to the murders and sabotage. He dies when the Platform's sun-shield fails, and his chair is left with a smouldering pile in it. His response to the Doctor's gift of air is to spit at Rose.

- *Ambassadors from the City-State of Binding Light*. These chaps are dressed like cardinals, in brocaded satin robes. Their heads are vaguely saurian, with small ears high up on bulbous heads and two sets of nostrils each. They seem in some shots to have skin like felt, a beige colour, with wispy curly hair down their napes, but other shots make them look smoother-skinned. They don't say anything all episode [as they look not entirely unlike the Sensorites - from 1.7, um, "The Sensorites" - this could be a sign of telepathy, or just that they were there to make up the numbers in a "meet the aliens" montage]. Apparently, one cut line suggests that they need strictly monitored oxygen-levels.

- *The Hop Pyleen Brothers*. They invented the Hypo-slip travel system. They look a bit like the "new-improved" Silurians [X5.8, "The Hungry Earth"], but wearing fur mantles over hospital gowns (one black with orange fur, one white with grey fur). [It's claimed that they come from the exalted clifftops of Rex Vox Jax, but the edit in the broadcast version omits this (although that place name is heard when the Doctor is talking to the Moxx of Balhoon).]

- *Mr and Mrs Pacoo*. Assuming the announcements and arrivals to match, these are two tall anthropoid vultures [see *The Sarah Jane Adventures*: "Death of the Doctor" for less convincing ones].

- *Cal Sparkplug*. The two beings that enter when this name is read are rather like the Mogarians [23.3, "Terror of the Vervoids"], but wearing shower-curtains and matching wicker shopping-baskets over their spacesuits. [Trading-cards and tie-in books (and a comic strip about the Moxx's vengeful brother, the Elth) cite the full name of the cyborg film-star as "Cal 'Sparkplug' McNannovitch" - a composite of Scots actor Cal Macaninch (of short-lived spin-off-of-a-spin-off *Holby Blue* and recent hit *Downton Abbey*) and Vin Diesel. Mr Macaninch's comments are not recorded, possibly because the broadcast version is rather clumsily edited as if to avoid legal action. According to the script, Sparky is incognito. Following the tie-in works, we are led to believe that the gold one is Cal and the other is his "Plus One".]

- *Class Fifty Five*. Selected students from that year's cohort from the University of Rago Rago Five Six Rago, steel hemispherical heads with horizontal slots, dressed in white bathrobes. [Similarly headed beings in black bathrobes attended the big end-of-season cosmic flashmob under Stonehenge in X5.12, "The Pandorica Opens".]

- *The Adherents of the Repeated Meme* are dressed in monks' habits, with gold chains like mayors of provincial cities, and give metal balls to each of the guests. These contain the spider-robots that sabotage the Platform. However, the Doctor announces [or discovers] that as a meme is just an idea, they must be fakes and tugs the metal, three-fingered claw off one, whereupon both androids collapse in sparks and smoke. They were concocted by Cassandra to cover her activities. [Nonetheless, they were invited, and announced as belonging to Financial Family 7, so they must have existed and had reputations before this event. Therefore, if Cassandra invented them specifically for this heist/fraud/assassination, it must have been years in the planning (see **Things That Don't Make Sense**).] There are five of them, and only one is heard to speak, in a husky deep voice.

History

- *Dating*. Earth in the year five billion has become the property of the National Trust, and has been restored lovingly to the continental arrangements of our time (a 'classic Earth', the Doctor calls it) and shielded from solar devastation by gravity satellites holding the Sun together until the visiting dignitaries can convene. If Cassandra's claims can be believed, there was an Arctic Desert and a Los Angeles Crevasse, and her father was a Texan [not necessarily denoting the same US state as now]. In the remote past, the humans took various life-forms away, many of which developed intelligence and culture. [One of these, Jabe of the Forest of Cheem, makes this

RT Phone Home?

continued from Page 41...

is more concerned with ribbing the Doctor over him getting a mortgage. The more usual course of events is for her to experience something exciting and pretty, then go home to mum and have chips. All other times and places are overtly judged by our standards, or more specifically, by an assumed audience of teenage girls incapable of contextualising "otherness" except as loserdom. Real teenage girls are more complex, as anyone who deals with them regularly will know.

However, the key points to notice about Rose's first call back to her mum are that: One, it caused a bit of a continuity error, as we've seen in the main episode listing; and Two, it reinforced an idea that's been at the heart of *Doctor Who* since the start but needed to be restated in other terms - namely, that any period of the past or future is, for the people in it, as current as the bit of history we're in. When Rose finally articulates this to Jackie in "The Parting of the Ways" (X1.13), the thought-process of explaining this to anyone stuck in one time triggers her realisation that the phrase "Bad Wolf" is a message to her. Anyone who has had to phone people in other time-zones around the world has had a similar epiphany, as has anyone regularly emailing between the UK and US. This has only recently been a practical part of the lives of anyone in Britain, where the entire nation is in one time-zone. The idea of trans-temporal synchronicity (moment-by-moment events in one time-frame being connected with moment-by-moment events elsewhen) took a while to become ingrained in *Doctor Who* storytelling. You can observe it in Season Nine (the "Blinovitch" conversation in 9.1, "Day of the Daleks" and the sight-gag of Krasis waiting for "the call" from Kronos and the phone ringing in the TOMTIT lab in 9.5, "The Time Monster" - see also the Doctor not being able to answer the phone in 10.5, "The Green Death" because he's on Metebelis 3), but it is only in "Planet of the Spiders" (11.5) that it is accepted and not worth even mentioning. The Doctor's jiggery-pokery with the phone is in part a pretext for a scene setting up the TARDIS telepathic circuits and translation facility (see **Can He Read Smells?** under "The Impossible Planet") and the Bad Wolf plot-line, but it's not really made use of later - in X4.12, "The Stolen Earth", Rose can't call anyone else and join in the group-hug that gets everyone on Earth with a mobile calling the Doctor[8].

And this is the final, most insidious change that this shift in expectations has wrought. People can *call* the Doctor. In the past, the Brigadier was given the special privilege of a Space-Time Telegraph for absolute, Earth-shattering emergencies (12.5, "Revenge of the Cybermen"). Once freed of the responsibility of getting Sarah back to her job every so often, there was little or no reason to make viewer-contemporary Earth at the centre of the series. Now, we have Martha Jones ringing up when UNIT are out of their depth talking to Polish migrant workers ("The Sontaran Stratagem"), Churchill giving him a bell when a relatively minor situation arises in the Cabinet War Rooms (yes, *we* know the Daleks are a bit more significant on the cosmic scale than Dunkirk or Coventry, but he doesn't), and all the recent ex-companions can get in touch if they want. Even "future" companions of the older series, such as Vicki or Zoe, didn't have this facility. "Goodbye" was forever back then.

---

claim, and she resembles a human made of wood, so perhaps humans did this deliberately. It would be improbable for vegetation to naturally adapt to so many worlds and yet spontaneously wind up bipedal, with a head on top, a mouth in the head, fingers, arms and so on.]

The inhabitants of Earth have all left, although several adaptations in the basic human form live elsewhere, including New Humans, Digi-Humans, Proto-Humans and Human-ish. The nearest to the twenty-first century model, it's claimed, is Cassandra. [We have no idea how long she has lived, although she claims to have been the last human born on Earth; the Doctor indicates that the planet has been abandoned for some considerable time. She claims that her latest op left her looking only 'two thousand'.] Humanity has now 'touched every star in the sky'. Teleports have been forbidden since Peace Treaty 5.4/Cup/16.

Earth's sun is permitted to go boom in the year 5.5/apple/26 [circa five billion - the sequels "New Earth" and X3.3, "Gridlock" suggest that it is *exactly* 5,000,000,000 AD] because the 'money's run out'. Earth-death is scheduled for 15.39, followed by drinks in the Manchester Suite [presumably tea, at four pm]. According to the Doctor,

X1.2 The End of the World

those assembled on Platform One are worth 'zillions'.

The Doctor names 12,005 AD as the era of the New Roman Empire.

• *Erroneous History.* Cassandra mis-indentifies a Wurlitzer jukebox as an iPod and plays 'ballads' from ancient times. These are vinyl 45rpm copies of "Tainted Love". [This was written by the future Mrs Marc Bolan, Gloria Jones, who recorded it in 1964, but covered here by pioneering electropop duo Soft Cell (some would say the definitive recording, certainly better than their 1991 remix, hence the 'original version' on the record label).] There is also a vinyl recording of "Toxic" by Britney Spears [which was never actually released on vinyl, but never mind]. Cassandra claims to own the last remaining ostrich egg (a means of concealing Cassandra's teleport device), and cites reports that legends said that such creatures had wingspans of 50 feet and breathed fire through their nostrils.

• *The Time War.* The Doctor says: 'There was a war and we lost.' His people, the Time Lords, were wiped out. The Doctor is the last of his kind, and his race has passed far into legend, so that Jabe is at first unable to believe what her medical scanner tells her - that the Doctor is a representative of this lost race. There was a war against some incredibly powerful enemy [see X1.6, "Dalek", if you couldn't guess], at the end of which the Doctor's homeworld was destroyed: 'It burned like the Earth. It's just rocks and dust, before its time.' [This last statement is curious in the light of what we see in "The End of Time Part Two".]

Catchphrase Counter The Doctor deems the lack of any prospect of outside help as 'fantastic'. Cassandra manages a few 'Moisturise me!'s [she'll get in a couple more before this book's done]. Rose begins her lifelong quest for chips. And the Moxx of Balhoon discusses 'the Bad Wolf scenario' with the Face of Boe. [This starts a whole sequence of stray references for the diligent viewer to spot. See X1.12, "Bad Wolf" and X1.13, "The Parting of the Ways" for why we should be paying attention.]

Deus Ex Machina The Doctor has a hitherto-undisclosed ability to walk through rapidly-rotating fans without becoming coleslaw.

The Analysis

The Big Picture As we have mentioned in the previous story's notes and **What's All This Stuff About Anoraks?** under 24.1, "Time and the Rani", and will return to in **Why is Trinity Wells on Jackie's Telly?** under "Aliens of London": the BBC thought there was a definite "Cult TV" audience, to whom they had to pay lip-service whilst concentrating their efforts on the "mainstream" viewer. Whilst the rival Channel 4 had sucked up most of the various US franchises the station chiefs thought would suffice, BBC2 had selected a handful of them for its 6.25pm slot after *The Simpsons*. Channel 4 had explicitly mocked the people watching *Stargate SG-1* or *Andromeda*, but BBC2 had simply ignored the people voluntarily watching *FarScape*, the assorted *Trek*-derivatives or reruns of Gerry Anderson, *Buck Rogers in the 25th Century* (see 18.1, "The Leisure Hive" for why this was bittersweet) or the original *Battlestar Galactica*.

That was, until they noticed that *Buffy the Vampire Slayer* was starting to get watched by a completely different audience. One aspect of this ghetto mentality was that the "proper" critics were deliberately ignoring something like 20% of prime-time television. Mark Lawson, whose cluelessness is a standing joke amongst teleastes, seriously stated in articles that Brigitte Neilsen was on the cover of *SFX*, the bestselling SF-themed media mag (nobody has the heart to tell him who actually played Seven of Nine). The relaunch of *Doctor Who* allowed this entire buried subculture to be plundered for an audience unaware of it - with the audience-identification figure reacting to it with culture shock. The main thing to observe about the aliens on Platform One is how unlike anything from any of the American series they are. (Well, except one, but we can sort of claim that *FarScape* was Australian.)

This is not to say that they are unfamiliar to anyone aware of television drama outside soaps and Jimmy McGovern. In fact, as with many of what Lawson would later claim to be Davies' most innovative moments, there's a lot of pilfering from late 70s space films and a couple of 90s blockbusters. Specifically, we could point you in the direction of the 1980 *Flash Gordon* (sadly, not for the last time - "Last of the Time Lords" adds this to the *purée* of plundered moments), and the scene where Dale, Flash and Zarkoff first meet

Ming. There's even a big jewelled ostrich egg and little people with blue faces.

However, the main visual reference is from comics - another field where Lawson et al refuse to admit their ignorance. The look of most of the episode is from Jean Giraud, AKA Moebius; mainly from *Le Garage Hermitique*, a mistranslated version of which was published in Britain in the 80s - the translation by our old chum Jean-Marc Lofficier of Mummerset fame (8.3, "The Claws of Axos"; 11.5, "Planet of the Spiders"). Moebius has been a visual source for *Doctor Who* before - "The Sun Makers" (15.4), for example - but since then he had become fashionable and had been a selling-point for a few films. The space-suits and the dead alien in *Alien* had been his work, many of the costumes and nonexistent sets in *Tron* were from his ideas, and most flagrantly *The Fifth Element* had been mainly his designs with a spurious plot to link them. (We'll be talking about that film a lot in the next book, so be advised.) With a bigger budget to allow this book to include screen-grabs and reprints, we could line up a gallery of the Hop Pyleen Brothers, Rafallo, Cassandra's surgeons and many others, and another of Moebius drawings from the 70s, and simply say *LOOK*. It's that obvious to anyone who knows.

But that's rather the point: the BBC were assuming that hardly anyone watching would be the kind of person who'd spot this. Whilst Davies' graphics background means that he could hardly have avoided this even if he'd not seen the films he was plundering (and, again, a chance to reprint his storyboard sketches and some Moebius *Metal Hurlant* panels side-by-side would make our point more forcefully), the objective was to make the aliens odd without seeming generic. Most of his interviews around the time of the launch were about how he thought a lot of the staples of That Kind of Thing were off-putting to the hypothetical "general public" he hoped to attract: the constant harping on about how "colonists" were boring but "pioneers" were sexy is of a piece with this. (See **Is Kylie from Planet Zog?** under X4.0, "Voyage of the Damned".) There is a constant thread through Tone Meeting discussions of sets and aliens to avoid looking - to use the annoying baby-talk term - "Sci-Fi". By this, evidently, he means *Star Trek*. The consequences of this will be felt throughout this book and the next, in embarrassments such as the Space Station 5 branch of Top Shop (X1.7, "The Long Game") and the stream of aliens who have Earth animal heads on top of boiler-suits or armour. Anoraknophobia had set in.

Despite this, the episode is smothered in *Doctor Who* lore, including references to the Isop galaxy ("The Web Planet") - which was overtly mentioned in the cut Cassandra scene [and gets an on-air mention in X1.12, "Bad Wolf"]. The other obvious comparisons are with 3.6, "The Ark" (in which the Earth is also seen to perish), and "The Curse of Peladon" (9.2) - the delegate Arcturus from the latter, in fact, seems to have been the inspiration for the scripted description of the Moxx. It's worth noting that none of these aliens is green. Although that had been standard-issue alien drag since "Doctor Who and the Silurians" (7.2), the simple fact was that the twenty-first century's version of CSO used a green screen instead of blue, so instead we get the start of a New Series cliché: blue-skinned humanoids. One obvious aspect of this story's brief is that - as the second episode - it sets the boundaries for what is possible, logistically as well as conceptually.

A key concept introduced here is the Time War. As we saw in "The War Games" (6.7), the idea of a war between two or more sets of time-travellers, each rewriting history in their favour, has been in print since at least the 1940s (Fritz Leiber and Clifford D Simak did it well enough to still be in print). In *Doctor Who* terms, the reworking of it by Bryan Talbot (in the comic *Luther Arkwright*, later adapted for audio by Big Finish and featuring David Tennant, but itself a reworking of 70s novels by Michael Moorcock) was one of the modish ideas that was latched on to in the tie-in books. (See X2.5, "Rise of the Cybermen" for why all Evil Parallel Londons have to have Zeppelins.) It became especially prominent with BBC Books launching a range to cash in on the Paul McGann TV Movie. In these, the Doctor destroys Gallifrey to save the rest of the universe (with him losing his memory and use of the TARDIS for a century while he lays low on Earth, beginning around 1895). The nature of the Enemy - the Time Lords' main rival in the war leading up to Gallifrey's demise - changed along the way, as the authors of these books shifted their chosen source-material from old books to more recent comics. The consensus seemed to be that, as with comics, it was possible to "reboot" the series with a whole new past to make the Doctor all mysterious an' that. With the series returning, this kind of experiment was no longer viable, but the Time Lords were deemed to be a bit of an embarrassment (see 20.1, "Arc of Infinity"), and the Doctor's status as a

X1.2 The End of the World

Byronic outsider was reinforced by making him the sole survivor. Remember that the 1986 film treatment by Johnny Byrne (author of, um, "Arc of Infinity") was subtitled *The Last Time Lord*.

However, if we're talking about The Big Picture, then the biggest of all is Earth's place in the cosmos. For most of Davies' term, the idea that this planet is insignificant is inadmissible: despite all the Hubble photos of thousands of galaxies and vast stellar nurseries in this one, Earth is central in his version of *Doctor Who*. Spatially, this may be inept, but as far as our temporal position in the life of this solar system goes, there is a case. Earth's sun formed about five billion years ago and will become a supernova in five billion years from now, give or take. Last time we dealt with this idea (21.3, Frontios"), the period was so far into the future as to be beyond the ken of the Time Lords. The time before that ("The Ark") was said to be "ten million years" in one ambiguous line and "the Fifty Seventh Segment of Time" (with Nero and a Dalek invasion two hundred years from now all in the "First"). This time we get a definite and accurate date, and consequences for humanity of this amount of time having elapsed. Trees have evolved legs and the continents have moved (and needed moving back).

The most significant aspect of this is that it needed saying at all: schools have drastically curtailed science teaching and focussed on exam-passes in easily-marked stages, so basic things that used to be assumed to be general knowledge now need to be made concrete through drama. Which returns us to the whole "nerdy" aspect of that unloved Cult television. A lot of this first season of Welsh-made *Doctor Who* is concerned with getting the general public up-to-speed on the broader perspective available to SF. Here, the reference to *Newsround Extra* is the dead giveaway: the BBC's remit to smuggle education into entertainment means that children's television genuinely might have been Rose's main source of information about Continental Drift and stellar gravitational collapse.

English Lessons

- *Ipswich* (n.) Dull port-town on the coast of East Anglia. Literally, the end of the road. (However, it could be argued that if the four Torchwood bases are ports at the compass-points - London, Cardiff, Glasgow and somewhere-on-the-east-coast - then Ipswich is a plausible location. Whitby, some way to the north of Ipswich, is a better bet and is more commonly associated with supernatural events - indeed events of any kind - so the possibility exists that the mystery of Torchwood 4's disappearance would thus be explained by the events in 26.3, "The Curse of Fenric".)

- *The National Trust* (n.) A body dedicated to preserving British (but not Scottish) landscape and buildings. A lot of the fabled stately homes of England were left to this charity in the mid-twentieth century when death duties on estates would otherwise have bankrupted old families. Many nature reserves are run by this body. It's funded by membership subscription, and members get free access to visitor attractions and a pious glow. (Volvos are not a membership perk, nor a pre-requisite, just a statistical likelihood.)

- *The Big Issue* (n.) A magazine designed to be sold on the streets by homeless people (badged for identification in case of scammers) and made to appeal to people on its own merits rather than because it's a worthy cause. Some of the content is by the vendors, who get to keep 60% of the cover-price. (See also "Rise of the Cybermen".)

Welsh Lessons To avoid sounding as if you don't know what you're on about, please note that "Euros" is pronounced almost as "Ayr-ross". Like the love-god. "Lyn" is closer to "Loon".

Oh, Isn't That...?

- *Zoe Wanamaker* (Cassandra). Most recently seen in mechanically-recovered-humour-substitute sitcom *My Family*, Wanamaker has divided her time between well-regarded theatre work and popular television. She was co-star in a massively successful bittersweet drama *Love Hurts* with Adam Faith, and was in the 80s television monument *Edge of Darkness*. As with many of the guest-cast for the first two years, she was in the *Harry Potter* juggernaut (as Miss Hooch). The daughter of expat American actor/director Sam Wanamaker (see X3.2, "The Shakespeare Code"), she had dual US-British citizenship until 2000; upon becoming a full British Subject, she received a CBE for her charity work.

Things That Don't Make Sense Let's just take a moment to consider the design of Platform One. It's up close and personal with a star going nova... and it's cooled by *fans*? Air-cooled systems func-

The End of The World H1.2

tion on planets with air, but unless they are planning to vent all the atmosphere out of the Platform, this is at best impractical. Three sets of fans in close proximity would be turbulent, but wouldn't really affect the air in the rest of the station with that alignment. The most that can happen is that the same heated air will be slightly compressed and thus a tiny bit hotter. (Look, it *could* work if the Platform casts a big enough shadow to keep the differential between the ambient temperature inside the Platform and the near-Absolute Zero of space without sunlight. You compress the air, let it get heated, move it to where there are metal fins to radiate the heat away and decompress - that's how fridges work, more or less, so the technology of Five Billion AD ought to be up to that. But it clearly doesn't cast any such shadow, and besides there's a whole lotta plasma goin 'on - basically, once the containment-field's off, the Platform is inside the sun.) We will return to this when the Jagrafess messes with the air-con for Satellite Five ("The Long Game".)

More to the point, what idiot engineer put the all-important (if there's a crisis) manual force-field override switch *at the end of a gantry with giant fans slicing past*? Why make the fans perpendicular to the gantry *at all*, if you have a vast drop from that gantry, a huge headway above it and only something like ten metres behind or ahead of the fans? (To circulate air, the best way is to have all that space flat on to the blades.) And even setting aside the stupidity of having the blades slice apart anyone who might need to walk that way, a gantry with no handles or bannister is just asking for trouble. How does the Doctor even stand upright, unless these fans are pathetically under-powered? It's as if the whole of this ventilation infrastructure was made so some film-crew could come along and use it to film an action-movie.

Jabe catches fire when the hot air starts venting through the shaft. As an exceptionally agile and mobile tree, we presume that she has a fairly high sap content, but this doesn't seem to help her. If she was part pine, then tar might have exuded from her skin first, but we don't see that. In short, there is no reason for her to burst into flames and not the Doctor. (In fact, as it is her clothes that ignite first, and they seem to be at least partly embroidered with metal, the Doctor's jeans ought to have spontaneously combusted at the same time. If nothing else, the zip in his fly might have started getting uncomfortable.)

Cassandra hasn't especially thought her plan through, has she? She claims that she was hoping to engineer a hostage situation. She also claims to have bought shares in the rival companies for all the celebs on board. But, why stage-manage a situation that would make those rivals look suspicious? Especially as the most likely outcome of so many wealthy entities being threatened and/or dying on the most prestigious Platform in known space would be a major stock-market collapse, making every share in any company worth less. And with Cassandra's scheme putting such suspicion on the Adherents of the Repeated Meme, the investigation to follow (presuming for the moment that her culpability wasn't discovered) would quite possibly result in the Adherents being labelled a notorious terrorist cell, which would make the entire shares market even more volatile. Along those lines, Sparkplug is supposed to be incognito, apparently (not that you'd know from the dialogue that made the cut) - that makes sense, as does incorporating himself as a private company, as some people have done even today. Offering stock in himself is just about plausible too. The snag comes when Cassandra thinks killing him will make her money.

The Steward announces all the kooky aliens we see, and keeps announcing further guests under the dialogue... but we don't see any more guests. In fact, the announcements don't seem to match the visitors: we have listed above the best-guess versions (a Welsh remake of the **Which Sodding Delegate is Which?** puzzle from 3.4, "The Daleks' Master Plan", and we still haven't got that one quite right).

Rafallo is called out to fix a maintenance problem because the Face of Boe can't get hot water. What exactly does he need it *for*? He lives in a giant immersion-heater. (A moment's thought provides the amusing idea of his attendants dropping teabags into his tank at 4.00pm every day. Later on, we have Novice Hame talking about his "smoke", suggesting that it wasn't water in the tank, but it's hard to tell until we get a better look at him and the initial point stands - how does a giant head get into the shower, and where does he put the towel?)

Critique We'll begin at the end.

That scene where the Doctor and Rose decide to go home for chips is either the proof that this new series has "heart" or is a betrayal of what the old series meant to millions of viewers over a quarter of a century. If you are in the latter camp,

47

X1.2 The End of the World

then the scene is a grafted-on "tag" and as smug and trite as Rose's last line. ("Come on then, tightwad, chips are on me. We've only got five billion years 'til the shops close.") If you are in the former, then the whole escapade at Platform One was building up to this moment. If that is the case, then it shows a lack of confidence in the scene immediately before it, which did the same job but without the shock twist that the Doctor is the Last of the Time Lords. That penultimate scene has Rose drawing her own conclusions, whereas the one after it is a sermon from the Doctor. The premise of the scene is fine; Rose steps out of the TARDIS (which they don't even bother to show leaving the Platform or arriving in London) and sees teeming people getting on with their own lives, oblivious to how they are living on a planet with a Best-Before date. It's the dialogue that lets it down.

That's this story in a nutshell. The pictures and the words are pulling in different directions at critical moments. Rose is freaked out by the aliens, but they are obviously men in funny hats. Jabe is allegedly a tree, but she's got a low-cut dress and a slinky walk. As we established in **Things That Don't Make Sense**, the layout of the deadly air-conditioning doesn't, um, make sense (at least, not as described in the dialogue). The story wants to be a whodunnit, but the directing keeps us focussed on the eventual culprit and moves the only other candidate so far down in the mix that they are forgotten. Rather more damagingly, Rose falls rather rapidly into the kind of bog-standard *Doctor Who* girl role from the 60s, existing for most of the story to ask questions and get captured. Already we are meant to be looking at the Doctor and getting swept up as he rushes around investigating and having fun in this freaky-looking exotic locale. Eccleston already looks like he's getting more out of running up and down corridors than explaining technical stuff. Any pretence that this series was about Rose's emotional "journey" is on hold here, as we do 70s-style *Doctor Who* - with a budget for this episode equivalent to a whole year of Jon Pertwee.

But that's why this story, on the whole, works. Although Rose is very judgemental about Cassandra, the main emphasis of this story isn't (as the end scenes seem to want us to think) that other times and cultures are almost as important as ours, but that our usual yardsticks don't apply. It wants to be parochial, but lands up making the bewildering future worlds more interesting and complex than twenty-first century London. For all of Davies' pathological fear of alienating casual viewers by challenging them even slightly, he's gone and made Planet Zog way cooler than chips and *The Big Issue*.

A large part of this is the showcasing of groovy-looking aliens, almost as if advertising action-figure merchandising rather than telling a story. We're encouraged to gawp. They are wheeled on (literally in two cases) as the Steward announces them, so we get identification and a big entrance rolled into one. That ought to be aggravating, but in a story that is a string of set pieces, it's entirely in keeping. However, the problem with that approach is that it's the bits in-between set pieces that stick in the memory. The filler scene with Rose talking with Rafallo is more interesting, more intriguing and more touching than anything in the main plot. We see Rose run away from the kooky aliens, but the real culture shock comes with the inability of this affable functionary to explain her daily life or background. Similarly, the Doctor and Rose just talking at cross purposes about the TARDIS translating everything is more revealing about what they are both like than any explanation of backstory.

Above all, though, this story is so infectiously pleased with itself. They can afford to get clearance for recent hit records (rather than rely on covers, as in the past) and they've got the sheer nerve to have the villain's gloating happen in shot, despite the fact that this villain is very expensive CG animation. It's an episode that simply revels in doing things that no other series could get away with - and above all, that no previous version of *Doctor Who* could really have tried. The only time the effects available to the series were even remotely on a par with anything else being made at the time was in the early 70s and they would have had to have cut corners in other aspects (music, number of speaking parts, number of extras) to have afforded it, even if they had the time to do every element of the story justice. The obvious comparisons are in Season Nine, with a space-station set and models like "The Mutants" (9.4) and comedy aliens plotting against each other in a whodunnit as per "The Curse of Peladon". However, if we continue that analogy, we have to posit a version of 1972 where only that hypothetical composite story, one UNIT adventure and three stories shot on the same sets could be made. "The End of the World" is ebulliently lavish, announcing the new *Who's* ambition and self-confidence by *not* being the showcase episode.

The Facts

Written by Russell T Davies. Directed by Euros Lyn. Viewing figures: (BBC1) 7.97 million, (BBC3 repeat) 0.5 million.

Repeats and Overseas Promotion Le Fin du Mond, Koniec swiata, Das Ende Der Welt.

Production

Almost the first thing the BBC execs asked about when the new series was being planned was whether there would be plenty of merchandisable monsters. The feeling was that if they were going to make a modern *Doctor Who*, it had to be all-out; rather than just people on an inner-city estate talking about aliens, we had to *see* them. By the time of the pitch-meeting in late 2003, the storyline had been more-or-less completely worked out (minus a couple of key details we'll come to presently) and the emphasis on Rose being out of her depth, then accepting, and the ending of her seeing Earth destroyed and then revisiting her own time for chips, were established. This last detail, apparently, was what sold Julie Gardner on the whole series. The final script was signed off on the last day of August the following year, with the tone meeting to match the various departments' contribution four days later, and one small but significant scene shot a few days after this. That scene was Jackie taking the phone call. It was recorded on 7th September, during shooting of Block One, but directed by Euros Lyn, who was in charge of Block Two.

• Lyn's earlier directing highlights include an adaptation of the Welsh-language memoir of 90s rave-culture (*Diwrnod Hollol Mindblowing Hediw*), the obligatory dozen or so episodes of *Casualty*, several episodes of the long-running BBC Wales drama *Belonging* (which is what Eve Myles used to be most famous for doing - see below), and an episode of one of the two-hour filmed detective dramas that were inescapable in the early 90s, each set in a different ITV region, funnily enough. (This one, *A Mind to Kill*, was set in Wales and had Philip Madoc - see Volumes 2 and 4 - as a completely different self-pitying cop in a totally different picturesque country setting, not even slightly like Morse or Wycliffe or Bergerac or Frost or...)

Like most Cardiff-based directors, Lyn had sent emails to the new *Doctor Who* team as soon as the announcement came. Davies had considered him for *Mine, All Mine*. An early suggestion of Lyn's was adopted, namely that the episode should begin immediately after Rose ran aboard the TARDIS, so Davies added the initial TARDIS scene (which also included at one stage a mention of 2500 AD). This scene was grafted into the script on 17th September, a week before the first major sequence. Other changes had been made for practical reasons. The Viewing Gallery would have revolved, tipping up 90 degrees as the unfiltered sunlight approached Rose. The Moxx of Balhoon was scripted as a bowl of blue jelly with eyes floating around in it (and the Steward would have announced that the "standard health warning" applied when talking to the lawyer). The chips sequence was explicitly set at Piccadilly Circus.

• Cassandra was scripted in some detail, as a sarcastic comment on the Botoxed stars at the Oscar ceremony. Will Cohen, the special effects supervisor, was concerned about this, but it became clear that only an elaborate CGI would do. Even after the cuts (see below), she is on screen for four of the episode's 42 minutes. To offset this, and ground the story in real performances where possible, all the other aliens were physically in the set. The Platform was described as resembling a Phillippe Starck hotel and the noted Cardiff venue, the Temple of Peace, was chosen as the main location. (We will see it a lot in later stories and *The Sarah Jane Adventures*; see the essay with X2.3, "School Reunion".) The spider-robots were based on Alessi fruit-juicers and - once his physical form had been decided - the Moxx of Balhoon was described as spitting in Rose's face like Spit, the Punk Dog (a puppet from 70s ATV kid's show *Tiswas* - see 24.1, "Time and the Rani"). There was, apparently, a small problem shortly before the shoot started - every department thought someone else would be making the Face of Boe. This was resolved at the eleventh hour by deciding it was a physical prop and letting Edward Thomas' team make it.

• September 23rd was the day for TARDIS scenes for this and the next story (also made in Block Two - in fact the interiors of Dickens' coach were shot in a coach inside the TARDIS set that day). It was also the day the head of the BBC's exhibitions, Martin Wilkie, and their press officer

49

X1.2 The End of the World

came to "inspect" the aliens. With some observers of the opinion that both Davies and Eccleston were rather too earnest for a children's show, the publicity photos of the Moxx of Balhoon were a welcome demonstration of what was coming. (This is also where the first rumours that the blue lawyer's name might be some obscure innuendo began.)

The next 11 days were spent on the Dickens story and the first day devoted solely to "The End of the World" was 4th October, the day of the Fans. Although Jabe had been planned to resemble a silver birch, the make-up and costume departments agreed on a more autumnal look to tie in with the orange and yellow look of the entire episode. The brocaded coat replaced a planned grey cloak, and her attendants were given a vaguely Florentine look, with breast plates and epaulettes. On the 5th, the sequence of Jabe's arms bursting into flames were begun. Series choreographer Ailsa Altena-Berk supervised the movements of the assorted aliens, including the Forest of Cheem.[4] The following day, the production moved to the Temple of Peace, which was the main location for the Manchester Suite. (An undisclosed alternative venue was tried but proved too small.) This will be seen an awful lot in later episodes, but at the time this one was made, it was mainly noted as an exam hall for the University of Wales.

- The small blue attendants were three adults and two sets of ten children (there are rules about how long a child-actor can work per day; this is why most TV babies are played by twins). The heads were mainly covered by masks, but the chins still needed lengthy make-up sessions, which tried the patience of some of the kids. (The press went with a weird story that the Tim Burton *Willy Wonka* had sucked up the nation's supply of Actors of Restricted Growth, but, as most of you will know, all the Oompa Loompas there were Deep Roy - 14.6, "The Talons of Weng Chiang"; 23.2, "Mindwarp"). Many of the children were relatives of the crew: the one who hands the Doctor a slip for the TARDIS is the nephew of dialogue editor Paul McFadden, for example. The usual backstage coverage was augmented by a crew from the daily children's bulletin *Newsround* (note that the in-depth spin-off *Newsround Extra* is cited as Rose's source for all things astronomical). It was in this that Eccleston first confessed to finding the schedule a bit gruelling.

- For much of this shoot, the lines for Cassandra, which Zoe Wanamaker recorded at the AIR studios in London, were read in by Clare Cage - although on one day Eve Myles performed the role (possibly at the read-through). Although Cassandra is on screen for four minutes in total, the script had longer discussions between her and Rose. This, presumably, is where they planned to use the record *Love Letters* as performed by Alison Moyet in 1985 (it was a cover of the Nat King Cole standard). The non-speaking Trees (if you'll forgive the phrase) were Paul Kasey and Alan Ruscoe. By the end of this book, you'll be saying "of course" when we tell you that such-and-such a monster was one or both of these. In a cost-cutting move, the Moxx's buggy was designed to be pulled along on thin wires. (We refer you to Volumes 4 and 5 for the endless problems with K9, and merely wonder why Davies didn't mention that *before* Lyn found out the hard way why you should always have a decent motor inside these things, especially if you're going to be redubbing all the aliens anyway.) Curiously, the same hand inside the claw that had clouted the Doctor and Rose when they confronted the Adherents of the Repeated Meme (Jamie Edgell) was the one doubling for the Doctor's in rescuing Rose from the sunlight. The maintenance corridor sequences were mainly shot in the cellars of the BBC Wales complex on 14th October. Apart from the readout screen, they really do look like that. One final day of Q2 studio-work, for the Viewing Gallery again, then a few pick-up shots while on location at Headlands School, Penarth (which was Sneed's kitchen as well and will be back a lot in later stories) and that was Block Two done. But not the episode...

- The location for not-Piccadilly-Circus-really, in Queen Street again ("Rose"), was apparently always to have been done in Block Three. However, a preliminary edit of this episode revealed a problem. It was looking as if the longer scene with Rose and Cassandra would not be doable in the time left, and even if they could be completed, this episode was under-running. Lyn was having trouble with the editing facilities at BBC Wales, which were in mid-upgrade. Some of the material with the spiders in the ducts was taking too long (and the ducts themselves were shot later than the rest, on 26th November). As some pick-up shots were still needed and a slot had been cleared for these in February, Davies stepped in with a new sequence to make up the time. This is where Rafallo was brought into the story, and a brief return to the Temple of Peace took place on 19th February, the day after the Doctor's hand-double did some pick-ups of the lever-pull. By this time, many of the alien voices had been added by Silas Carson (not Nicholas Briggs as planned) and some of The Mill's digital malarkey had been completed (the rest followed on 28th February). Murray Gold opted to use a sound like a Theramin for the aliens (he claims to have been inspired by *Donnie Darko* rather than the Treehouse of Horror episodes of *The Simpsons*).

- Perhaps it was asking for trouble making an episode where things hitting fans was a concern, but in the week leading up to broadcast, the series was making the wrong kind of headlines. Easter Saturday night, "Rose" had been the centrepiece of a massive launch effort, the massively favourable press reaction had come in on Sunday, then a Bank Holiday, and on Tuesday the storm broke. *Doctor Who* was now big news... so the leak that Eccleston was leaving made headlines. The BBC's Press Office hastily confirmed that this was the case and cited "typecasting" as the star's reason for leaving a hit show so soon. This was almost immediately retracted (after a word from Eccleston's agent), but the damage was done. The long-running website Outpost Gallifrey, adjusting to the influx of new subscribers, had to close down for a day (see X2.10, "Love & Monsters"). The media warmed over all their old stories from 18 months earlier about Richard E Grant, Bill Nighy and Alan Davies, plus new claims from unnamed "insiders" that David Thewliss was in talks and confirmation that there had been discussions with *Casanova* star David Tennant. Tom Baker confidently predicted that his latest successor would be Eddie Izzard (back then, a bold prediction as Izzard's straight-acting chops hadn't been much in evidence compared to his stream-of-consciousness stand-up). *Newsround* got it most nearly right, and re-used their interview to substantiate the reports that the workload rather than typecasting was behind the shock announcement (and using it as an excuse for an exclusive clip of the Doctor and Rose meeting Jabe). See **Did He Fall or Was He Pushed?** under X1.12, "Bad Wolf" for more on this developing story.

- After the transmission difficulties caused by a news-flash during "Rose", many people wondered if the expected death of Pope John Paul II would affect the broadcast. As it turned out, His Holiness died at the exact moment that the Sun exploded. Later the same week, BBC4 broadcast a live reworking of the 1953 drama *The Quatermass Experiment* (see X1.3, "The Unquiet Dead"). It didn't go entirely to plan, but (despite Jason Flemyng messing up the climax) all eyes were on David Tennant. In one review, it was observed that watching the (probable) end of civilisation with his hands in his pockets was a good sign, if the rumours about him being the next Doctor were true...

X1.3: "The Unquiet Dead"

(9th April, 2005)

Which One is This? This year's selection from the people to be found depicted on bank-notes is Charles Dickens, and so *obviously* he meets ghosts on Christmas Eve.

Firsts and Lasts This is the first story to be partially shot in Swansea, Russell T Davies' home town, and the first of this version of *Doctor Who's* excursions into Earth's past - as such, it's the start of the cycle of "celebrity historicals" where the focal point is less the events, but the famous person from the past whom the Doctor and his chum(s) encounter. This story is the first one to have two non-speaking extras listed as playing "Prostitutes".

It's the first story since "The King's Demons" (20.6) to have the TARDIS land somewhere other than where the Doctor expected without an external influence at work. We see Rose try out the TARDIS wardrobe for the first time (at least, we see her get directions for a place we've not seen and come back in completely new clothes) and the Doctor changes his jumper to prove that we've gone back in time. It's also the start of a new tradition that journeys back into the past entail the Ship rocking and bucking, both parties holding down switches and the materialisation ending with them rolling on the floor, laughing. Also, that the Time Vortex is blue rather than red. (See **What Makes the TARDIS Work?** under 1.3, "Edge of Destruction" for us guessing something similar.)

The cellar scene involves the first of many, many exchanges in which the Doctor bemoans dragging her into danger and Rose insists it was worth it. And it's the first new series story to be written by somebody other than Davies, specifically Mark Gatiss.

X1.3 The Unquiet Dead

Watch Out For...

• With this being the first new series story to be substantially made outside Cardiff, the various digs against the Welsh capital in the script seem oddly heartfelt when delivered. The script is littered with slights against Wales and its residents, although as it's Victorian Cardiff, the cast play it as jokes about nineteenth-century parochial attitudes and not anti-Welsh slurs. Honest. Nevertheless, the location-work makes it seem as though Victorian Cardiff was worth missing Naples to visit.

• And this being a Mark Gatiss script, practically every line, character-name and plot-point is a reference to something else. Virtually the only original line in the entire episode is Dickens saying "What the Shakespeare?" Even the name of the horse is a quote ("Samson" was the dray-horse in *Steptoe and Son* - see Volume 1).

• The sharper-eared amongst you will note that when Rose rounds on the funeral-home owner Sneed for abducting her, she abruptly acquires a West Country accent: "... an' doan't thing oi din feel yur'aands 'avin a quick waaner, you durrdy awl mahn" - sounding for all the world like she's from Swindon.

• We have to mention this... former *About Time* co-writer Lawrence Miles castigated this story for perpetuating in fantasy form the contentious claims that amongst genuine asylum-seekers coming to Britain were spongers, parasites and terrorists planning to abuse our hospitality (see, of course, the accompanying essay). In fact, fringe right-wing parties claimed that *all* asylum-seekers were parasites. This was being stated as fact in some of the less salubrious tabloids, and occasionally came up during the run-up to the 2005 election. (The opposition Conservative Party believed they could regain support by campaigning on this, even though they were then led by the son of a former asylum-seeker who would have been debarred from entering the country under the laws his party had passed when in power.)

Moreover, the story requires the Doctor's humane instincts to be the means by which the fiendish furriners trick him into letting them play dirty. Supporters of Mark Gatiss fell over themselves to deny that this was the intent of his script, and claimed that he was entirely innocent of any such foul thoughts. This was five years before he wrote a story in which Winston Churchill was presented as a sweet, loveable old rogue completely incapable of fire-bombing Dresden or exacerbating a preventable famine in Bengal that killed three million in 1943 (to say nothing of what he got up to as Home Secretary). When you watch this, you can decide for yourself exactly how ingenuous Gatiss really is, and whether it was wise to spend the third story of an entirely new series subverting clichés of the old series when 80% of the viewers wouldn't have seen those episodes.

The Continuity

The Doctor He seems to view the possibility of his being killed in Cardiff as rather more undignified than the thought of dying itself.

He takes two sugars in his tea. [This suggests that he's cut down since the seventies - see, for instance, 11.2, "Invasion of the Dinosaurs". Those who think that he's very recently regenerated might wish to presume that he experimented with what this new body likes whilst buying chips with Rose (X1.2, "The End of the World") or during the night between Henrik's blowing up and him popping in for coffee (X1.1, "Rose") and a quick wrestle with a plastic arm.] Once again, he displays an affection for bad puns ('I love a happy medium'.)

Like Oscar Wilde, he finds the death of Little Nell [*The Old Curiosity Shop*] irresistibly funny [or maybe he doesn't, but is quoting Wilde]. When Rose dresses for the occasion, he claims she looks 'beautiful... considering you're human'. [His smirk might denote that he's just having fun with her, but it's possible that he's trying rather ineptly to avoid an unambiguous compliment, *or* maybe, just maybe, he can see something we can't that makes her obviously a different species - perhaps he can see into the infra-red, and her body-heat makes her look weird to him. He may even be trying to remember how the joke he used in 17.2, "City of Death" went ('You're a beautiful woman, probably').]

• *Ethics*. Here, perhaps more than ever before or since, the Doctor's broader perspective and enhanced sympathies bring him into conflict with conventional [which is to say European, early twenty-first century] morality, as embodied in Rose. He seems to have no issue with, as a temporary measure, the Gelth using human cadavers as holding-bays to prevent the extinction of their entire species. Perhaps goaded by mention that

Is the New Series More Xenophobic?

As we saw towards the end of the last essay, one of the most significant changes in *Doctor Who* since 1963 has been a drift away from the original notion of everything-other-than-present-day-Britain being a source of unending potential, and towards all of that being threatening. To the original viewers, the virtues that Ian and Barbara upheld were self-evidently "right", but had to be proved, time and again, and not simply by force or an assumption of moral superiority. The arguments were won by results: When in Rome, Barbara's refusal to do as the Romans do is how she survives, and Ian's application of twentieth century *mores* transcends the *tempora*. On the one occasion where there is the possibility of actively making people behave "properly", the result would have been a catastrophic change to History and the Doctor forbids it. (Even then, free from fear of whatever would have happened - see **Can You Rewrite History, Even One Line?** under 1.6, "The Aztecs" - his tacit approval of the devastating shock Autloc has been given is significant.)

By and large, though, imposing "our" beliefs (i.e. those of post-War Britain, modified by experience and education) on alien or historical cultures, real or imagined, was frowned upon. Even getting the Thals to fight in self-defence was questionable (1.2, "The Daleks") and the option of rebuilding the Conscience of Marinus was left open, even though the Doctor hinted at strong disapproval (1.5, "The Keys of Marinus"). However much Ian and Barbara wanted to get home, they largely accepted all the other cultures they encountered, and did so *on the terms of those cultures*. Moreover, the moral worth of people they met was clearly indicated to the viewers to be linked to how far they too did this: the First Elder of the Sensorites is benign because he wants to see what people from Earth are like, and the City Guardian is evil - and said to be so - because he wants to rid his planet of a species whose previous visit caused a plague. (We could extend the metaphor of "open mindedness" to telepathy, in which case the source and cure of John's madness makes this linear correlation between xenophobia and "evil" much more complicated. See 1.7, "The Sensorites" for what we mean.) Marco Polo and Kublai Khan are shown as admirable for this (1.4, "Marco Polo", almost the template for Alan Whicker-style travelogue within *Doctor Who* - see below), as is Saladin, whose brother is the villain simply for being against these religious zealot Europeans invading his country. (The leader of those Europeans, Richard I, is similarly open to dialogue in this version of events; see 2.6, "The Crusade".)

Throughout the 60s, we get girls from other backgrounds begging to come aboard the TARDIS to see lives more interesting than their own, while even accidental tourist Polly gamely mucks in. Only Victoria applies her native culture's standards to anywhere she visits, and she's usually teased for this. The black-and-white era of the series was made in a time when the possibilities of communication and travel were widening, and seeing just our own planet was bewildering and exciting. BBC viewers were getting used to live coverage of sporting events in other countries *in real time*, even if this meant going on air at breakfast time (unimaginable in the days when Test Card F took up most of the day's air-time), and exciting foreign places like Tokyo (site of the 1964 Olympics) and America (where they wore stetsons and drove on the right and seemed to be rioting all the time) were suddenly available as more than travellers' tales. A lot of BBC programmes were being made in other countries, with authoritative but open-minded visitors seeing amazing things (Gila Monsters, Ankor Wat, "The Tribe That Hides From Man") and experiencing activities.

Here we have to refer, yet again, to *Doctor Who's* sister-series, *Blue Peter*, where the presenters would be chucked out of aeroplanes or made to spend hours up a pole, fishing in Sri Lanka or visiting the Aztec ruins. The model for this was the *Tonight* programme, one of the first series to be made to fill the "Toddlers' Truce" (see **What Was Children's Television Like Back Then?** under 3.7, "The Celestial Toymaker"). The filmed reports from around Britain were about known personalities (René Cutforth, Fyfe Robertson and Alan Whicker being the "stars") who were experienced, and querulous but keen to see what else was out there that they'd not encountered before. Whicker, who has almost as good a claim as David Frost to be the original for Harold Chorley (5.5, "The Web of Fear"), was latterly the person whose reputation got him exclusive rights to see and meet reclusive people. His encounter with J Paul Getty - who

continued on Page 55...

X1.3 The Unquiet Dead

the Time War caused the entire situation, he is prepared to listen to this proposal, although he draws the line at forcing the psychic Gwyneth - who must facilitate the Rift in Cardiff opening to make this happen - to do anything she doesn't want to.

• *Background.* He pushed boxes off the pier at the Boston Tea Party, was at the fall of Troy [3.3, "The Myth Makers"] and World War V. [We knew from 14.6, "The Talons of Weng Chiang" that there was nearly a WWVI.] He's also read everything Dickens wrote, and - despite qualms about *Martin Chuzzlewit*'s American interlude - considers himself the novelist's 'Number One Fan', and that and that "The Signal Man" is 'the best short story ever written'. [See 17.6, "Shada" and 23.4, "The Ultimate Foe" amongst others.

[More surprisingly, the Doctor claims not have any idea what would have been outside the TARDIS door had he and Rose arrived, as planned, in Naples, 1860. Given that the Risorgimento was at its height and the King of that principality had been evicted from his capital by the once-idealistic army of Giuseppi Garibaldi a couple of months before Christmas, this is *exactly* the sort of event he would ordinarily have lectured Rose about or claimed to have been involved with. (The eleventh Doctor would certainly have been keen to see a conflict that gave its name to two types of biscuit - Garibaldi and Bourbon - and an ice-cream variety. Moreover, if the season had gone as originally planned, the eleventh episode would have seen a different aspect of the Bay of Naples as Vesuvius erupted and destroyed Pompeii.)]

• *Inventory: Other.* He seems to have the right change for an 1860s British newspaper. [What are the odds? This, after he claimed to have 'no money' at the end of the previous episode.]

The TARDIS It flails about wildly when travelling backwards into Earth's history. When making such a journey, the Time Vortex looks blue. The Ship's wardrobe is out from the interior door, first left, second right, third on the left, go straight ahead, under the stairs, past the bins and fifth door on the left.

The Supporting Cast
• *Rose.* She has a strong "ick factor" reaction about the Gelth using the dead. She doesn't give any opinion as to the merits of holding a séance, as opposed to determinedly rational Dickens.

As in "The End of the World", she befriends the help rather than the supposedly "important" people. [Sneed's perviness probably has something to do with this. The script tries to get around this possibly sounding patronising by, erm, having Gwyneth rebuke Rose for being patronising. Unlike next season, when Rose will be increasingly unrecognisable as an ex-shop girl, this is couched in terms of an understandable time-travel rookie error about underestimating the smarts of people who happen to live in a "primitive" period.]

Rose says that she and her mate Shareen [also mentioned in "The End of the World"; X1.4, "Aliens of London"; and X2.3, "School Reunion" - it's odd that this pivotal character never shows up in the series] used to go to shops and look for boys. She's been thinking a lot about her late father recently. [Lending credence to the Doctor's accusation in X1.8, "Father's Day" that Rose only came with him in the hopes of getting to save her father with magical time travel. It's unresolved in that story exactly how premeditated it is, but on a subconscious level, his claim would seem to have some merit. Alternatively, she *has* just started hanging out with a protective middle-aged-looking man who's showing her a world her mum couldn't imagine...]

She doesn't know her Dickens [especially not the eventual outcome of *The Mystery of Edwin Drood*; see **History**], but seems completely unsurprised when the Doctor nonchalantly introduces her to a massively famous author. As much as Rose loves TARDIS-travel, she seems downcast after being told they've landed in Cardiff. Gwyneth sees things in Rose's life that Rose doesn't know about yet, including the 'Bad Wolf' and 'the Darkness'. [We have a pretty good idea of the former, but some might wonder if the latter is the Reality-Bomb from Series Four, about which Rose sounds the alarm with the 'Bad Wolf' trick again.]

The Non-Humans
• *The Gelth* lost their corporeal being in the Time War [see 3.6, "The Ark" for a precedent for this and 4.8, "The Faceless Ones" for something far sillier in a similar vein]. In their new manifestation, they are energy-beings attracted to methane. The decomposition of human bodies makes dead people ideal hosts, although the memories of the recently-deceased seem to affect their behaviour when reanimated. When not hiding inside some-

The Unquiet Dead — X1.3

Is the New Series More Xenophobic?

continued from Page 53...

turned out to have a pay phone in his house for visitors - is rightly remembered as a classic of this style of reporting. *Doctor Who* as originally conceived is clearly in this mould.

However, from Season Four onwards, the centre of gravity shifts and present-day or near-future Earth rapidly becomes the *only* place (or near enough) the TARDIS ever takes us. Even here, the opening episode of each four-parter was a travelogue-style introduction/exploration of the wonders of the new place we'd been brought to, and only after the first cliffhanger was any threat to whichever remote, isolated base we were in this month. We've gone into the implications of this shift (**Was "Yeti-in-a-Loo" the Worst Idea Ever?** under "The Web of Fear"), but it's worth noting that even at its most dogmatically earthbound (seasons Seven and Eight), *Doctor Who* was trying to ridicule parochial attitudes and show encounters with "otherness" to be potentially rewarding. It is perhaps significant that the one Pertwee story that has been tippexed from both the programme's history and the chronology of the UNIT stories vis-à-vis twenty-first century stories is "The Ambassadors of Death" (7.3), even though this and its unofficial sequel (13.4, "The Android Invasion") seem to lead in to Sarah Jane Smith learning about UNIT. This is the story that ends with a successful First Contact - apparently live on air in a global link-up. It also ends with a mad general, who's been trying to prevent this, being locked up. (See X2.3, "School Reunion" and **Was There a Martian Time-Slip?** under X4.16, "The Waters of Mars".) In the BBC Wales scheme of things, General Carrington would have been given a spin-off.

We're setting the scene, possibly a bit laboriously, to firmly establish what long-term fans of *Doctor Who* might have expected of the 2005 series. What we got was shockingly different. With the exception of the Doctor, all alien visitors to Britain are *ipso facto* bad and have to be stopped (and even the Doctor is suspect, hence Torchwood and Harriet Jones' fall from power). Because Russell T Davies was pathologically obsessed with the apparent inability of casual viewers to get worked up about people from Planet Zog, almost all stories this first year are Earthbound. The one Davies story *not* to be about evil aliens is about a camp bigot using fake aliens as a smokescreen, and presents the real extraterrestrials as grotesques, more for display than allowed to have characters of their own (X1.2, "The End of the World"). Other than this, we have one two-part story about misguidedly literal-minded medical software (a story Steven Moffat likes doing at least once a year), one where Time goes wrong and nine episodes where the problem was bloody foreigners coming over here. In three of them, the Slitheen are even taking our jobs.

Closer examination reveals other startling changes. On two occasions, the Doctor wants to help stranded aliens and is tricked. The second of these is a Dalek, and his sympathy runs out rapidly. Rose, however, is shown to be naïve and foolish for doing what in any other circumstances, and any earlier series, would have been demonstrably the right thing to have done. "The Unquiet Dead" (X1.3) notoriously got lambasted for having the Doctor's benign instincts towards asylum-seekers betrayed by nasty scheming abusers of our generosity. The option of putting this story later in the series, which might have worked, wasn't there. The first twenty-first century series had to sell the entire notion of *Doctor Who*, and invasions of present-day Earth, history-with-monsters and humans-on-other-worlds were the most directly graspable aspects of the format. One might expect the later series to play a little less safe, and to begin with they varied the pace by making many of Series Two's threats come indirectly from the Doctor himself, malefactors having designs on his body in all the present-day stories. Not all of these were even alien: Earth, in the shape of Torchwood and the alternate universe's evil Lumic Corporation, provided a more varied set of antagonists. The "Little Englander" attitudes of Torchwood One are supposed to be funny, but the irony of someone hell-bent on keeping out foreign influences with stolen alien tech and causing two invasions in 20 minutes is well down in the mix. What is clear is that the Cybermen are all too keen to invade and just needed someone to open a gateway between universes. The rotters! Preparing an assault on the real Earth just in case the laws of physics went wrong one day. By creating the conditions for such an assault by malicious foreigners, Torchwood

continued on Page 57...

55

X1.3 The Unquiet Dead

one, they are able to travel through the mains gas supply, and the presence of a high concentration of methane in the atmosphere draws them out of their human hosts. When they are occupying a cadaver, they make the bodies supernaturally strong, able to snap necks easily: even a little old lady is able to strangle a fit young man. Most of the times when they exude from a dead person, they appear blue and vaguely angelic. But once they decide to announce that their real plan is to kill every human and take over Earth, they become flame-red and daemonic [see **Things That Don't Make Sense**].

History

- *Dating*. It's Christmas Eve, 1869. Charles Dickens' theatre tour has brought him to Cardiff, of all places, on this of all nights.

There has been a Time Rift in Cardiff for, certainly, all of Gwyneth's life as it's endowed her with psychic ability [for a similar manifestation of such a talent, see **The Big Picture**]. The stories of ghosts and paranormal activities at Sneed's house pre-date even that, and helped keep the price of the building down.

[The obvious question, in the light of the later use of this plotline, is whether the Rift was made by the Time War, or whether the impact of the TARDIS and the Extrapolator actually created the crack that the Doctor sought to exploit, reverberating across time from 2006. The only hint we have about the long-term status of the Rift is that the mechanism to control or close it is destroyed in *Torchwood*: "Children of Earth" and yet Earth is still around - although another crack in spacetime becomes the Doctor's problem from X5.1, "The Eleventh Hour" onwards - assuming it *is* an unconnected phenomenon.]

Dickens had intended that the killer in *The Mystery of Edwin Drood* [unfinished at the time of his death] was Drood's uncle, but here considers that perhaps an extraterrestrial was responsible, and the story should be called *The Mystery of Edwin Drood and the Blue Elementals*.

- *The Time War*. The first time it is named as such is by the Gelth, who announce that, 'The whole universe convulsed. The Time War raged invisible to smaller species, but devastating to higher forms.'

Catchphrase Counter A dead old lady spewing out the angels from *Raiders of the Lost Ark* is 'Fantastic'. So is saying goodbye to Dickens. Gwyneth psychically discerns that Rose has seen 'the darkness, and the Big Bad Wolf'.

Deus Ex Machina Gwyneth manages to hold off an invasion despite being dead.

The Analysis

The Big Picture The big clue is when the Doctor gushes admiration for Dickens' short story "The Signalman". This seems a curious choice to be the story to chill the blood of someone who's faced the Giant Spiders of Metebelis 3, punted through a lake of giant maggots and fought in the Time War. It's not a bad story, but even the most indulgent Dickens scholars would find it hard to differentiate this from dozens of other creepy tales he wrote, except for the biographical details it reveals about the author (of which more in a bit). But the BBC adaptation from 1976, starring Denholm Elliot and shown in the *A Ghost Story for Christmas* slot and as part of the 1991 *A Perfect Christmas* compilation... now *that* is famously creepy. The DVD release was through the British Film Institute, rather than BBC Worldwide - a sign of how far it's become a benchmark for this kind of thing. Anyone (especially anyone a bit bookish) who grew up in 1970 Britain will have a basic grounding in Dickens as much from adaptations in Sunday evenings (especially those produced and script-edited by Barry Letts and Terrance Dicks, who swapped posts at some stage) as from the texts themselves. Similarly, anyone with that kind of background would have stayed up late to watch Hammer films on telly on Friday nights, or various scary and spooky productions made by the regional ITV companies or the BBC, and swapped incidents in the school playground on Monday morning with that week's *Doctor Who*. All of the writers of the first year of BBC Wales' *Doctor Who* are from this cohort. The difference is that Gatiss has made an entire career from pastiching these, adding little or nothing of himself.

This is not necessarily a bad thing. Grounding a story in things the writer knows and loves, and knows worked 30 years ago, saves a lot of effort. When launching a new version of an old series, the risks have to be in production and not content - at least, for the first year or so. Taking elements from a variety of well-remembered sources and stitching them together can work if those sources

Is the New Series More Xenophobic?

continued from Page 55...

"proved" that they were right all along.

However, for a genuinely unpleasant association of ideas, it's hard to beat the way "The Sontaran Stratagem" (X4.4) conflates Polish workers who have the temerity to work harder than anyone born here with alien invasion, pollution and loss of control. This seems, with hindsight, to be the point at which the programme-makers pulled back. When Steven Moffat took over, not only did stories set in real, present-day Earth abruptly reduce, but the ones they did make grindingly switched gears to backtrack on this insularity: Craig Owen (X5.11, "The Lodger") is berated for, then exploited for, his refusal to look beyond his domesticated worldview. Apparently, he talked Sophie out of wanting to travel because we come back to him, still in Colchester and with a baby (X6.12, "Closing Time"). Meanwhile, Mark Gatiss himself has given us a story where everyone is saved by a dad accepting and literally embracing a psychic alien as his son (X6.9, "Night Terrors").

This human-centred view extends to a small but significant piece of thought-control: Davies has repeatedly stated that "colonists" are boring but "pioneers" are exciting. The difference between the two words is significant: a "pioneer" is someone who is the start of something but, more damningly, the word suggests that these people were somehow *meant* to be there. Colonists simply turned up and pitched a tent. A colonist has to deal with whoever was already there on the natives' terms, not their own. (Failure to do this used to be shown as A Bad Thing, as the surprisingly-similar stories 8.4, "Colony in Space" and 19.3, "Kinda" show.) "Pioneers" can simply ignore anyone who is already on a planet, or treat them just as they treat bad weather or volcanoes. Welsh *Doctor Who* has sided with the very imperialists who were always the bad guys in the original series. (We'll return to this in **Is Kylie from Planet Zog?** under X4.0, "Voyage of the Damned".) The situation got so absurd that Davies made a point of writing a story where some humans were turning into monsters and an alien (well, actually, the last surviving original occupant) was sympathetic and cute - and this was presented to us as a brilliant innovation. (X3.11, "Utopia"; Davies' comments in that week's *Confidential* are shameless in their low regard for the audience.)

This comes with a change in emphasis in the presentation of the stories. The style of directing, the music and the pacing of the stories is overtly modelled on action-thrillers, specifically the Hollywood blockbusters that have sought to crystallise America's fear of everyone else. For obvious reasons, the role of "everyone else" in *Doctor Who* cannot, as is usual in Bruce Willis or Mel Gibson films, be someone with a nasty suspicious English accent, but the other generic tropes are all present and correct. The obvious modern starting-point for this sort of film is *Independence Day*, in which all other countries were noises-off[12]. This was a remake, in all but name, of George Pal's rendering (that's "rendering" as in what you do to beef-fat) of *The War of the Worlds*. In that film, there was a fleeting shot of the Martians doing what Hitler had failed to do and destroying London landmarks, as well as the usual shots of the Eiffel Tower in ruins to denote France overthrown and the Taj Mahal to represent an entire sub-continent of about a billion souls. As the whole point of the original book had been an ironic inversion of Victorian Britain's efforts to colonise and exploit Africa, this is especially odd. However, it began the kind of visual shorthand for "the world in ruins and only America left" that was picked up in *Independence Day* and parodied in *Mars Attacks!*. The Slitheen had obviously done their homework, as a spaceship crashing would hit one very obvious London landmark, just as always happened in that kind of film. The only reason for smashing into Big Ben is that it's what the general public think aliens do. It's also what they expect from terrorists. In Britain, we had three decades of the IRA assaulting (or attempting to assault) landmarks. Terrorism is as much as anything about media management, capturing the imagination of the public by making them wonder what else was vulnerable.

As we saw in "Terror of the Autons" (8.1), the public's fears of manipulative, unpredictable foreigners fed on and fed into a whole sub-genre of paranoid fantasies in the late nineteenth century, which in turn provided a vocabulary for conspiracy theorists right up to the present day. The assigned motivation (such as it was) changed

continued on Page 59...

would never ordinarily have met. (Watch any story from Seasons Thirteen, Fourteen and Fifteen, for example. Or, indeed, read any of the *Harry Potter* books, which are a cut 'n' paste of every episode of *Jackanory* from 1968 to 1975, and would have been overly familiar to that bookish teenager mentioned in the last paragraph - especially if s/he had been a member of the Puffin Club[9].)

Similarly, many of the best moments on the films of Joe Dante come when he is allowed *almost* complete liberty to cram every frame and line with references back to a 50s geeky childhood. Steven Spielberg does it too, but he does other things as well. (Given the choice, though, would you rather *Amistad* or *Matinee* was put in a time-capsule to tell future generations what America was like?) Making a densely referential piece about your childhood loves is a tradition going back to Kenneth Graham (especially *The Golden Age* - see also 6.2, "The Mind Robber" and **Did Sergeant Pepper Know the Doctor?** under 5.1, "The Tomb of the Cybermen"). What is often missing in the ones that don't last more than a generation is any commentary on *how* and *why* the influential stories affected the author and what that tells us. We could go though the script of "The Unquiet Dead" listing every reference to every old script by Nigel Kneale, James Sangster or Fay Weldon (yes, really, see below) or indeed old *Doctor Who* writers (one in particular). Indeed, a few significant ones will be cited below, but the bigger matter is what Gatiss does with them and why.

Mark Gatiss was a quarter of the macabre comedy team *The League of Gentlemen*. The name refers to a film from 1959 about a team of ex-army officers who stage a bank job, a film with a cast of the British character-actors who were usually in this sort of film. Gatiss and company grounded their comedy in precisely that kind of half-lost worldview, "collecting" obscure character-actors and out-of-the-way films, and littering the scripts with oblique references and outright quotations from Hammer, Amicus and earlier horror films. A lot of these were recommended in books on the subject that boys tended to get for Christmas (often compiled by Alan Frank or Peter Haining), before working up to Christopher Frayling's more scholarly works explaining the complex interplay of social comment and psychological grounding. It was big coffee-table books about old horror films that salvaged the reputations of a lot of the less successful British 70s output, making these cheap late-night fillers seem intriguing (and appealing to a budding connoisseur - anyone could see why *Alien* was scary, but appreciating and discoursing airily on the subtler merits of *Blood on Satan's Claw* or *The Wicker Man* showed discernment).[10]

These and more orthodox 50s British films that made up afternoon television in the 70s and 80s all blend into one composite drama-generated past against which the present is judged and found wanting, but it is the gaps in what those old "mainstream" films said that the horror flicks exploited. Actual historical detail or fact is occasionally brandished to authenticate or justify the more lurid or alarming details of the fictions, but is generally a distraction.

The point can be made clearer by comparison to three other Victorian-era stories from three earlier phases of the series. In "The Evil of the Daleks" (4.9), the story was predominantly couched in a worldview derived from that era. Whether or not the author, David Whitaker, actually believed in Alchemy is almost irrelevant (and see **What Planet Was David Whitaker On?** under 5.7, "The Wheel in Space" for more on this). He chose, for the purposes of the story, to take this as a starting-point and only offer the opinions of people who *did* think that such things were possible as explanations for what was going on in 1866. The finished story had fewer links to this worldview than what we landed up getting, but the traces of the first draft persist and cause problems. The point is that we know the Daleks and the Doctor, so we have the advantage over Maxtible and Waterfield.

Later, Robert Holmes' hasty salvage job on the abandoned story "A Foe From the Future" managed to purloin the iconography of Sherlock Holmes, Fu Manchu and Jack the Ripper, but again used the misprisions of the locals as both the means by which the fifty-first century war-criminal was getting away with murder and a source of ironic commentary on those kinds of stories from the two outsiders, the Doctor and Leela. (We're talking about "The Talons of Weng Chiang", in case you hadn't guessed.) These two, like us, could plainly see what the bigotry and preconceptions of the Victorian Londoners made them all miss. The racist coppers and cab-drivers see what they expect to see, and ignore the obvi-

Is the New Series More Xenophobic?

continued from Page 57...

from Vampirism to Bolshevist leanings, revenge to greed, Nazi to Soviet to Corporate to Islamic, but the formula was the same. Eventually, these attempts to explain why bad things were being plotted became perfunctory, and soon it became enough simply to say "they're like that" or just to give them green scales and a theramin playing in the background. Being able to blame someone was easier than accepting bad luck or even fault on one's own part. However, when something happens that fits this sort of pattern in real life, it seems to justify all the ugly fantasies it resembles. The attack on Pearl Harbor, not then part of America and geographically about as far from New York as London, is the classic example. Suddenly, all those deranged Fu Manchu stories look plausible, even prophetic. Similarly, with the Soviet Union no longer there to "permit" action-movies, the fad in the 1990s is for aliens to wreak carnage on US cities, just because they can. If aliens are unavailable, or too nerdy, then generic foreigners with equally shaky motives will suffice and need less clever heroes to thwart them. The generic features become increasingly spectacular and silly, matching step with what computers can make appear to happen.

What we're getting at is that when *Doctor Who* returned, suddenly able to bring all of this to bear on the kinds of stories that had occasionally looked a bit crap but had lodged in the memory (for example, 11.2, "Invasion of the Dinosaurs"), it did so with glee, simply because it was now possible. Just as Season Four had exploited Cold War paranoia and existential threats of replacement, brainwashing and surgical intervention, to be resisted in the Churchillian terms of the Doctor's "some corners of the Universe" speech (4.6, "The Moonbase"), and Season Five bit the bullet and actually had present-day London under martial law after an alien incursion, so the new series took what else was on telly and twisted it a bit to play with a familiar sub-genre. It just so happened that a lot of what was on telly was alarmist paranoia about terrorists, because one such group had pulled off a "spectacular" (as the IRA called their bombings) that looked exactly like an especially implausible 90s action movie.

Of course, to say that *all* 2005-style *Doctor Who* is a direct response to Al Qaida is naïve. One US academic tried that and was laughed off the airwaves here. Marc DiPaolo's paper is hilariously ill-informed, as if he only knows about the series from Peter Haining's dismal, cynical 80s coffee-table books. Apparently, mentioning America at all means that the Welsh series is "anti-American" and the "fact" that the Daleks were - he says - predominantly recruited from America in "The Parting of the Ways" (X1.13), plus their religious fanaticism, means that they are an assault on the Midwest values. (DiPaolo is an assistant professor at the University of Oklahoma.) If you want, you could try to link the facts that the last episode of the original series was shown a fortnight before the Velvet Revolution and the demolition of the Berlin Wall, and that the announcement of the return coincided with the Second Gulf War lasting six months after Dubya declared "Mission accomplished". Good luck with that. The more complex truth is that the new series was inflected by many other sources that were themselves changed, or made more popular than they might have been, by the so-called "War on Terror". These include obvious candidates such as *Spooks* (for some reason renamed *MI-5* by the US networks), *24* and *Battlestar Galactica* (the pompous new one), as well as less overt we-always-get-our-man dramas like the *CSI* franchise and its similarly gory-but-reassuring imitators. The rhetoric has returned to the old 50s paranoia of aliens representing whatever "enemy within" is currently fashionable. All that's changed is that the weapons have gone from big cannons and A-bombs to mitochondrial DNA and phone-taps.

Within the expanded *Doctor Who* franchise, this difference is very noticeable. There are two spin-off series about teams of alien-hunters led by former companions. *Torchwood* was explicitly about stopping immigration, and the consequences of letting people from elsewhere come to Wales were depicted as terrorism and corruption, with no upside and no shades of grey. Alien technology was desirable, living aliens weren't. Perhaps stung by criticism (including some from an unlikely quarter - see below), the second series of that show was more nuanced, and even did a story where the advent of an exotic biology was posi-

continued on Page 61...

ous way Li Hsen Chang has been genetically messed-about-with to the point where he no longer even looks Chinese.

Finally, Marc Platt's starting-point for "Ghost Light" (26.2) was doctrinaire cataloguers and an involuted environment which only became Victorian after the first proposal was discarded for giving away too much of the Doctor's background on Gallifrey. It was only after changing Mount Lungbarrow into Gabriel Chase that the reference-games to other Vic-lit, telly adaptations and indeed earlier *Doctor Who* became the story's trademark. This process of stacking-up the references for the viewer to tick-off and feel slightly cleverer for getting was characteristically late-80s, but in "Ghost Light" it was a side-effect of a critique of that very mentality, set against the opposing idea of allowing change, diversity and experimentation. Gatiss, in his *Doctor Who* scripts, his novels (beginning with *The Vesuvius Club*) and his other projects, has made it an end in itself.

So the people in "The Unquiet Dead" all talk and react to events as people in similar stories have: the Welsh are insular, god-fearing and spiritually-minded; Dickens uses stock terms such as " 'pon my soul" and the *Mr Kipling*-commercial standby "exceedingly". (He also name-checks Gatiss's Big Finish audio, "Phantasmagoria".) This story has extras explicitly listed as playing prostitutes - even "Talons" avoided saying out loud what Teresa had been doing to have her coming home at dawn. Yet the two characters who express a worldview akin to that of the viewers are Rose, who is shouted down by the Doctor and undercut by Gwyneth, and, bafflingly, Dickens. His scepticism about things we know to be untrue is shown to be misguided *in this one instance*, but spoken about as if all scepticism is wrong and ghosts really exist - the Doctor doesn't dispute this and the one "impossible" thing he is confronted with (Gwyneth's posthumous rebellion) is held up by Dickens as proof that the Doctor is also wrong to doubt. Gatiss isn't saying that he believes in ghosts, he is simply not having the Doctor say it's wrong because *that doesn't happen in this kind of story*. As the reaction to the accusations that he was pandering to bigots by showing the Gelth to be evil bogus asylum-seekers shows, he is sometimes oblivious to the subtext in his work. What matters is how well he has "recaptured" a period feel or generic tropes, and how many references to his childhood favourites he can cram in without the whole story collapsing in on itself. What the episode lands up saying is less important than how well it says it. ("Well" in the sense of "allusively".)

Everything in this episode is there because it's the kind of thing that "ought" to be in a story of this kind. The TARDIS lands in the wrong time and place because it always used to when the author was a kid; it's a Victorian Britain with séances, snow at Christmas, prostitutes, opium, a horse-drawn hearse and a maid called Gwyneth who's psychic because she grew up next to a time-fissure. That last detail ought to ring bells: it was the key to Martha Tyler's clairvoyance in "Image of the Fendahl" (15.3). That story was a sort of run-through of Nigel Kneale's Greatest Hits, albeit with a different sensibility linking the set pieces. Until very late on, the story would have had an etheric detector based explicitly on the Marconiscope from "Pyramids of Mars" (13.3). But a maid called Gwyneth also turns up in an acknowledged source for Gatiss' story, a 1973 *Upstairs Downstairs* episode written by Fay Weldon (which also had a guest-role for Hammer films leading man Sandor Eles).

As we mentioned in "The Green Death" (10.5), the other cliché at work here is that the Welsh, being all Celtic and wild, are in touch with the Great Beyond. (The theatre where Dickens performs "A Christmas Carol" is, like the Student Union bar at Swansea University, named after the ancient Welsh bard Taliesin - a real sixth-century bard, but better known for his appearances at the end of the Welsh epic *Mabinogion*, as we're sure you all knew.)

Dickens is here presented as a "reformed" sceptic, which is slightly anachronistic. As the script acknowledges, the author of "The Signalman" had a strong interest in the paranormal and premonitions, which had developed after the train-crash that had inspired the short story. This was some five years earlier. Yet even before this, his entire worldview was of a world that was alive, of objects seemingly moving of their own volition and of nature having motivation. Machinery and buildings are described using animal terminology. The Dickens we see in this story is almost performing the role of Harry Houdini in the two near-simultaneous 90s films about the Cottingsley Fairies (*Photographing Fairies* and the better-publicised *Fairytale: A True Story* - the "making of" documentary about which was narrated by Simon Callow).

Is the New Series More Xenophobic?

continued from Page 59...

tive - for humans but not the aliens themselves, allowing Jack to regain moral high ground after an episode where he used torture as a first resort. The *Torchwood* radio episodes were more ambiguous, with Jack belatedly deciding to set up an asylum system for lost human time-travellers. (Err... like himself. Lost aliens, such as the Weevils, have to be interned in dungeons, of course.)

Accusations of thinly veiled racism were countered by showing an ethnically diverse Cardiff and a racially mixed team (although Tosh and Martha being Londoners was more remarked upon) in line with BBC guidelines. In real life, "racially mixed" in Cardiff means having non-Welsh people around. (The joke doing the rounds was that nobody in Wales would mind aliens landing so long as they weren't English.) Historically, Cardiff and Swansea, the major ports, were the most racially mixed parts of Wales and had residents from across the Empire even before the start of mass immigration in the 1950s. Nevertheless, Wales as a whole has been more insular than most parts of Britain, and some towns remained isolated even from other nearby Welsh cities or villages even at the start of this century. Even Cardiff is largely populated by families who have stayed in the same district for generations. As we will see in Volume 8, for Britain as a whole, the racial changes in the population since 1947 are as much as anything a generational shift, and ethnic diversity is just one dimension of a wider debate about stasis and progress. Cardiff, as the location for a team dedicated to keeping Wales (and thus Earth) safe from interference and contamination, is a deeply ironic choice. It's a city built on contact and commerce between peoples from different backgrounds. (Typically, *Torchwood*'s response to this dialectic of metropolitan and progressive vs conservative and insular was to show the people of rural Wales to be inbred cannibalistic serial killers, in the otherwise pointless episode "Countrycide".) Nevertheless, the whole thrust of the first two seasons was to have gun-totin' geeks rounding up any visitor - we don't want their sort round 'ere.

It has been argued that, as much as anything else, the first two seasons of *Torchwood* were replaced by the Davies-written mini-series "Children of Earth" and the odd collaboration "Miracle Day" to correct this tendency. It is certainly true that the next spin-off, *The Sarah Jane Adventures*, began with an explicit critique of the previous spin-off's entire direction and ethos in an episode co-written by Davies. Later episodes wheel on the Brigadier to condemn the "revised" version of UNIT shown in *Torchwood*. This is more complex when *Doctor Who* is brought back into the equation. The reason Earth is being protected, in the spiel at the start of *Torchwood*, is that "the twenty-first century is when it all changes". In X3.13, "Last of the Time Lords", Earth is quarantined and abandoned by all other races. It seems as if the unspoken reason for keeping aliens out of our affairs isn't so much that we need protecting from foreign ideas, but that the "correct" First Contact and its consequences are a Fixed Point in time and must not be allowed to change. It's certainly true that the disaster at Bowie Base 1 was set in stone as a cause of monumental events on the cosmic scale (X4.16, "The Waters of Mars" and see **What Constitutes a "Fixed Point"?** under X4.2, "The Fires of Pompeii"), but then again consider the Doctor's delight at a change in history when the Slitheen send a ship to draw his attention (X1.4, "Aliens of London"). We note that all prospect of aliens coming to Earth at any stage after the expected lifespan of the viewers is couched in terms of small numbers not drawing attention to themselves (such as Mr Copper in X4.0, "Voyage of the Damned", but see X4.12, "The Stolen Earth" for his impact on those in the know). Even the Gelth would be welcomed on a temporary and small-scale basis, so long as Dickens keeps his mouth shut.

However, the problem is that whilst the series as a whole might preach tolerance and "the big picture", individual episodes don't. They are often grounded in entirely the same fears and set pieces that form the basis of alarmist racist tracts and the sort of press reporting that gets formal reprimands without any restitution to the injured parties. And whilst occasional mention of the upsides to visits from other worlds might be made, the stories are, without exception, about the malign effects - usually premeditated and with malice aforethought - of nasty creatures who want to enslave/ destroy/ exploit Earth. The aliens *never*

continued on Page 63...

X1.3 The Unquiet Dead

Dickens' farewell tour of readings was in fact suspended between April 1869 and January 1870 after a stroke. This was on top of various other ailments - the reference to the stage-curtain being "as potent as a pipe" is significant, as Dickens was at the very least getting material from opium dens in the London docks (see "The Talons of Weng Chiang" yet again) and probably self-medicating. If so, it would have been for the same reasons he claimed to prefer theatrical readings of his older works to writing new ones after the rail-crash, as an escape from depression. The precise details of his private life are unclear, but he was separated from his wife, probably living with his mistress and definitely the father of her first child. (By 1869, the surviving eight of his ten legitimate children were alive, and all but two of them were grown up.) The original proposal offered by Davies and selected by Gatiss was set in 1860, when Dickens was more zealous in his refutation of fake mediums. As we will see, little of the rest of Davies' planned story made it to the final version. However, it's rather an obvious idea to have a time-travel-based series meet the man who invented the entire genre. *A Christmas Carol* is the start of the concepts of visiting one's own past and of multiple contingent futures determined by one's actions in the present. This is, in many ways, a development of the Victorian "discovery" of progress (or Progress, as it developed a prominence in the Victorian mind-set worthy of a capital letter), which had informed the relatively recent growth of the Historical novel as a morally uplifting form of adventure. (We will develop this theme in **Are We Touring Theme-Park History?** under X2.7, "The Idiot's Lantern".)

As we'll see in **Production**, Gatiss didn't choose Dickens as a subject out of thin air. The list of 13 episodes Davies presented the BBC Drama bosses had a Dickensian ghost encounter as the third episode right from the outset, and Gatiss picked it as his preferred topic because he "knew" how to do it. In a series you hope to flog overseas, the choice of Victorian London and a famous person seems obvious. In the past, *Doctor Who* had tried to resist being obvious; it seemed needy and desperate. The fourth Doctor narrowly missed meeting Leonardo da Vinci twice (14.1, "The Masque of Mandragora"; 17.2, "City of Death"). American shows never get it right. Television history is littered with American SF/Fantasy shows that tried, for some unfathomable reason, to do a Jack the Ripper episode and cocked it up completely. But as Rose's first trip into History, it was the least risky option - both for production reasons and the audience's ability to follow what was going on. Yet even this is familiar... for all that Davies denied that old *Doctor Who* was really in the business of what he termed "celebrity historicals" (and the choice of wording is significant and frankly worrying), it was a safety-play for production teams facing falling ratings and hoping for a lifeline from the US. Season Twenty-Two, the one conceived as a package to cash in on the overseas success, had two of them (22.3, "The Mark of the Rani"; 22.5, "Timelash"). The extended toy-ad that was 2.8, "The Chase" began with two in one episode (three, if you count the Beatles). After the brief experiment with an adventure in history where the point was that we weren't supposed to know what was about to happen (3.5, "The Massacre"), the incoming team cut their losses and went for a story where practically every character was a household name (3.8, "The Gunfighters"). There are some who would argue that "The Chase", "The Gunfighters" and "Timelash" don't make the happiest precedents, but all three arrested downward slides in ratings and Audience Appreciation indices. (Well, "The Gunfighters" got 30% AIs - remarkably low - but ratings held steady until the end of the following story.)

Finally, it's worth remembering that the address, "Seven, Temperance Court, Llandaff" is a convoluted in-joke: the Temperance Seven were a kitsch novelty act from the 60s who did Rudy Vallee pastiches, but another "seven" associated with Llandaff is *Blake's 7*. Terry Nation, born in that district, also claimed in the publicity the 1965 *Dalek Pocket Book & Space Traveller's Guide* to have discovered the history of the Daleks in a glowing cube that materialised in his garden one day through a rift in space and time. Therefore the whole of this storyline, and sequels, and thus of *Torchwood*, is a massive in-joke about mildly embarrassing merchandising. (And the full story of how a High Court judge's adjudication slagged off "The Chase" in a law-suit about that book and a similar one the BBC launched in 2002 will be told in **What Are the Great 21st Century Merchandising Disasters?** under "Victory of the Daleks".)

Is the New Series More Xenophobic?

continued from Page 61...

have good intentions. Pleas for sympathy and aid are *always* tricks to allow an invasion. The only benefits they bring are leaving behind weapons we can use against the next lot. *The Sarah Jane Adventures* might occasionally have the Judoon or a penitent former adversary acting as the US Cavalry at the end of a story, but the one time *Doctor Who* in its current configuration has hinted at a positive outcome, it was the intolerant Silurians agreeing to come back and talk to the "immigrant" humans about what benefits human technology and culture might have *for them*. (See X5.8, "Cold Blood", but see also **How Does Scotland Have Its Own Spaceship?** under X5.2, "The Beast Below".) Even then, compare this to Malcolm Hulke's original message in 7.2, "Doctor Who and the Silurians" (especially when Barry Letts got his hands on it), and it's a collaboration based purely on a mercantile arrangement - an exchange of goods and services rather than mutual respect as an end in itself.

Then again, as we have been hinting throughout this essay, there are moments of reflection on the less pleasant motives of humans. The set-up of the Canary Wharf Torchwood is a commentary *about* xenophobia rather than an endorsement. X4.10, "Midnight" is *about* mob psychology (although the most paranoid assumption is shown to be the right one, and the solution is to do the one thing the Doctor and most adult viewers have been trying to avoid - turn on the "contaminated" individual and kill/expel her). We would hope that children watching are capable of the nuanced responses these stories seem to expect, just as they are appalled and not excited when Harriet blows up the Sycorax (X2.0, "The Christmas Invasion") and saddened when the Doctor destroys a Sontaran battlefleet (X4.5, "The Poison Sky"). Yeah, right. They all saw that "Talons of Weng Chiang" (14.6) was an excoriation of Victorian racism, didn't they?

There remains one story where the logical and harmonious ending would have been to allow this human-families-rock/aliens-suck rule to be broken. Whereas most of the stories need this sort of conflict to make the plot happen at all, and can use "it's aliens being evil because they're aliens" as the justification for whatever the gimmick is, the confused ending of "Fear Her" (X2.11) could easily have been made to work if Chloe had gone off with the Isolus and joined the big cosmic choir. Aesthetically, this could have been made to seem right. Most children, especially the baffled ones who found the broadcast episode confusing and unsettling in ways that the supposed happy ending couldn't resolve, would find this a more appealing ending. However, the series was focussing on the parent-child relationship (see **Must They All Be "Old Fashioned Cats"?** under X3.3, "Gridlock") and the threat to the domestic sphere is supposedly all that anyone wants to watch. This tension between safety and exploration, between stasis and insecurity, has always been at the heart of *Doctor Who*, and different phases of the series have put the emphasis at different places between those poles. The 2005 relaunch led to the production team playing safe and firmly stressing the familiar as sacred. The next stage, from Series Five onwards, began a move away from this. But for a lot of the viewers who began with the BBC Wales series, the idea has taken root that defending Earth from outsiders is what *Doctor Who* is "about".

English Lessons

- *Innings* (n.) The spell a cricketer spends batting, or that the entire team spends being bowled at. Colloquially, "a good innings" is a long life, or spell doing whatever it is one does. It was not commonly used to refer to the recently deceased until about 1950.
- *Flu* (n): That colloquial abbreviation for influenza was in use a good 40 years before 1869; there were epidemics every 30 years or so from at least the Elizabethan era.
- *Navvy* (n): Navigational engineer, a euphemism for someone who digs ditches. They were first the people who made the canals, laid railway tracks, excavated the tube lines and built the Victorian cities. Many of them were Irish, especially after 1849. They're still in the language in phrases such as "swearing like a navvy".

Welsh Lessons

- *Brecon*. A town about 30 miles north west of Cardiff (as the crow flies) but the other side of a mountain range, the Brecon Beacons (a region now administered by the National Trust, op cit).

X1.3 The Unquiet Dead

Between the mountains and Cardiff is the highest concentration of coal mines, then the basis of Wales' income, which would have been where most visitors to the city would have come from. Brecon would be *terra incognita* to someone like Mr Sneed.

• *Gwyneth* is an interesting name for someone that old in that century - the name would only just have been coming into vogue when she was born and spelling it thus, instead of the Welsh "Gwynedd", would have been a sop to the Anglicising tendency that was forcing the Welsh language to near-extinction. (This indicates that her parents might have been from a slightly higher social echelon than it appears.) It's actually a place-name, meaning "snow-capped", and was a kingdom from the days before Edward I started planting castles everywhere to pacify the newly conquered Welsh marches.

Oh, Isn't That...?

• *Simon Callow* (Charles Dickens) had been playing Dickens on and off for a decade or so. He was by this stage both one of Britain's most distinguished actors, and a critic and biographer of some merit. In between this, he did the odd film. You might have seen him in *Four Weddings and a Funeral* and amongst the bewildering casting decisions in *Street-Fighter* (see X4.0, "Voyage of the Damned"). Amazingly, this most characteristically English of actors first came to public notice as an American cult-leader in the play *Instant Enlightenment Including VAT*. Even more amazingly, he was in a sitcom with Brenda Blethyn that hardly anyone remembers, *Chance In a Million* (some people claim this to be a neglected masterpiece - not true). He makes a return cameo as Dickens in "The Wedding of River Song" (X6.13), allowing Steven Moffat to make an in-joke about "A Christmas Carol" (X6.0).

• *Eve Myles* (Gwyneth). Back then, she was familiar to Welsh viewers from *Belonging*, a long-running series, but we'll take it as read you know she was *Torchwood*'s audience-identification figure (at least, in theory). If you didn't, hang on for "The Stolen Earth" (X4.12), and an explanation (of sorts) in "Journey's End" (X4.13) for why Gwyneth and Gwen Cooper look so similar.

• *Alan David* (Gabriel Sneed). Formerly in 70s comedy *The Squirrels*, 80s sitcom *Foxy Lady* (neither of these is anything like as bad as the titles) and umpteen cop shows. He had more recently played Clement Attleee in *Goodnight, Sweetheart* (see X1.9, "The Empty Child") and Boycie's Welsh rival in *Green Green Grass* (a spin off from *Only Fools and Horses*, op cit).

• *Meic Povey* (Driver) had been an actor for decades, with a long-term role in the Welsh-language soap *Pobol Y Cwm*, another in *Minder* (Taff Jones, the sidekick to the regular police antagonist of our anti-heroes) and several smaller ones, but he also wrote for theatre and television, often in Welsh.

Things That Don't Make Sense To start with, Dickens doesn't leave any footprints in the snow. It's possible that the great author has spontaneously coined the term 'On with the motley' a decade before *Pagliacci* was written, but it's unlikely. The streetlight behind Gwyneth and Sneed when they arrive at Taliesin Lodge is definitely anachronistic. The Doctor is somehow able to see Rose once she's been concealed inside Sneed's hearse and give chase. Sneed's use of the American term 'stiffs' is a bit more Al Capone than Omer and Jorum[11]. We're unsure about that use of 'a good innings' too. And, it must be said, nobody's breath is showing even though there's snow everywhere [see also 24.4, "Dragonfire", and the reverse problem at the end of "The Eleventh Hour"].

Although the overdone Christmas decorations of our day are a long way off, Prince Albert had popularised the habit of a fir-tree with candles on it, and cards from family who couldn't visit in person were common. Except, it seems, in Cardiff. Not even mistletoe or holly.

Surprisingly, it appears that Dickens' comment about catching a mail-train back to London at 4.00am on Christmas morning is accurate, but he has a hotel-room booked and Cardiff is rather well-served for telegraph offices in 1869. He could at least get a hot meal and warn his publishers of these changes rather than risk his frail health in an unheated carriage on a snowy day passing through the sticks. This is even more daft if you think that he is more likely wanting to enfold himself within the family bosom and stop feeling sorry for himself - anyone with a working knowledge of Dickens' biography would have to ask "which family?"

And what of the coach-driver? It would seem that the Taliesin Lodge gave Dickens use of a coach and driver for his stint in Cardiff, but this person took him and the Doctor to Llandaff, then vanished when Dickens was seeking to leg it from Sneed's. Shouldn't he have waited outside? He can't have been a hired hackney-carriage, because Dickens was to have spent a whole evening at the theatre, so he must have been on a contract. It's very improbable that he was on the writer's staff - unless they drove all the way from London to Cardiff by coach rather than take a train, and got there in under a week. And the Doctor, Rose and Dickens get back to the TARDIS somehow, so was it just bad luck that the driver opted to pop off for a cuppa while Dickens was on a mercy-dash to save a maiden in distress?

And if the Time Rift is here found at Llandaff (where Sneed's mortuary is, see **The Big Picture**), how did it get to just next to the Welsh Assembly buildings in Cardiff Bay, where we see it in *Torchwood*? If we're to assume that it's mobile, did Torchwood build their Hub to track it across Wales over 140 years, or did it move once, about ten years after this story, and then stay put until 2011?

"Dicken" being an old euphemism for Satan, the phrase "what the dickens" is in the English language. Cute as it is, nobody, ever, has said 'What the Shakespeare'. Charles Dickens definitely wouldn't have, as he does here. (Depend upon it: if you have a surname that's in a well-known phrase, jokes about that phrase get very old very quickly.) Bakelite light-switches weren't around in 1869, and it seems they've got central heating too. One detail that's very curious is that Gwyneth sees Rose's twenty-first-century world and is alarmed by all the noise: contemporary accounts claim that the horses with iron shoes on cobbled streets, market-traders and street-vendors and light industry in city centres made Victorian England, if anything, louder than today's cities. Cardiff, having docks and several train-lines, would have been a lot louder than the Powell Estate.

The Gelth can bring the dead back to life, so chloroform's not going to be much cop - but why else would an undertaker have some handy, as Sneed does when he renders Rose unconscious? It's not used for embalming. Also, the Gelth manifest themselves through the gas used for lighting. Well and good, we can go along with that, but why then inhabit ex-humans when so many other methane-related conduits are available in Victorian Cardiff? We have the coal mines, from which the town-gas used throughout Britain until 1968 originated (see 5.6, "Fury from the Deep"). Lots of coal-mines in a 30-mile radius, and lots and lots of trains carrying coal from Cardiff, so that would be a good source too (especially if the coal gets snowed on). There are the sewers which, as every British schoolchild knows (even if Russell T doesn't; see X4.14, "The Next Doctor") were the big construction project of the 1850s and 1860s. There are cows (that's a thought - maybe the mythical chupacabra was a lost Gelth), there is horse manure on every street and compost in every garden. Why then, would the Gelth risk discovery and contamination by the dying thoughts of the people who bodies they commandeer? If it is because they need physical form, why not find some way of escaping their dependence on methane?

The Gelth are said to animate the dead via the gasses the human body produces while decomposing, and yet Mr Redpath has probably not been dead long enough to produce such methane before they get him up and walking. Similarly, Mr Sneed is brought back within *seconds* of his being killed. (We might indelicately suggest, by the way, that Dickens' ailments might have made him a more fruitful source than the deceased - but again this story requires us to forget strict biographical details like that, so we'll open a window and move on.)

It's odd that Gwyneth, who's heard the 'angels' singing all her life, has no conception of their plan to occupy Earth, her being telepathic and all that. Neither do the Gelth realise that her preconceptions might allow a more religiously acceptable ruse. She's psychic, hence her utility to them, and it's her mind that allows them through; even if she never twigs their scheme to do the dirty on humanity within seconds, they might have foreseen that she had enough self-will, even posthumously, to blow herself up. The previous Gelth sorties had resulted in at least two old people following their pre-death plans on "autopilot", so this potential flaw can't have been a total surprise, and they have no Plan B. Their plan, such as it was, involved Gwyneth acting as a conduit for them to pass through the Rift - but only after someone with knowledge about life on other worlds happened along and persuaded her to do so.

This *sort of* makes sense if they're that desperate, but then - and here's the most glaring bit of idiocy in this story - they go and make sure everyone knows that they are really an invasion by turning red and husky-voiced imprudently early.

X1.3 The Unquiet Dead

It was all going *really well* until they stupidly opted to look like cartoon devils, gloat in growly voices about taking over the world and generally act as if they've realised that TV's Doctor Who is in the building, so they have to behave like the kinds of things he used to defeat at the end of episode four. This is *especially* odd if they think that they can occupy five billion humans: there must be enough Gelth on their way to overpower a large percentage of the population of Cardiff at least, so is blowing up one house going to stop them? (Yes, it kills Gwyneth, but she's *already dead* - isn't she? The Doctor thinks she's already deceased, but we don't have any actual proof of this; if she has enough self-will to talk to the Doctor and strike a match, we have to ask what "dead" means in this context. See **Why Don't People Die Properly Any More?** under X4.9, "Forest of the Dead".)

Of course, this is before 1967, so the gas in question is town-gas, not North Sea, and thus toxic to humans within rather less time than we see Dickens, Rose and the Doctor breathing it in Sneed's house. It is also a little strange that Dickens believes he can spread the truth about the Blue Elementals in his fiction, given that the use of Spontaneous Human Combustion in *Bleak House* caused him such trouble.

Critique This episode looks gorgeous. That's the single most significant fact here - they have managed to keep faith with the 70s BBC costume-dramas, the cinematic pretentions of the new series, and the technical demands of making a story like this seem like the easiest thing in the world to get right.

The script is wittier than it needs to be, and, whilst it resembles a patchwork of references and half-quotes, it covers all bases. As with the visuals, it has everything you would expect in this kind of television and a bit extra. It just doesn't *quite* match the episodes either side of it in tone or character-development. Seen in isolation, most of the quibbles we've listed above vanish. There's not much actively wrong with this and, when compared to the last nineteenth-century "celebrity historical" (22.3, "The Mark of the Rani"), it seems like a masterpiece. The cast are all enthusiastic and pitch-perfect. The plot follows through on the implications of the initial premise and - barring Gwyneth's apparent posthumous suicide - is free of any overt contortions to make it work out in under 90 minutes. As a shop-window for all the things this series can do that others can't, this is exemplary on its own and, in concert with the two before it, breathtaking.

Why, then, does it ring hollow?

A lot of it is that sheer allusiveness. When Robert Holmes or Terrance Dicks did that sort of thing in the 70s, it was because they'd thought up a story and found excuses to slip in a bit of period detail from a favourite book or something they'd turned up in the research. The same applies, with reservations, to "Ghost Light" (26.2), but the self-regarding references back to *Doctor Who* stories were exciting because it was unprecedented. When the *New Adventures* books started doing it so often, it got wearisome. Gatiss has apparently started with the in-jokes and cribs and put a story together to justify them.

A criticism aimed at Gatiss by experienced fans is that he is essentially writing old-style four-part stories from the 70s, then whittling them down to the bare essentials. A criticism of those self-same stories was that episode three was pretty much redundant in crude plot terms, and was at worst a lot of running up and down corridors. (Bear this taxonomy in mind for when we get to X2.2, "Tooth and Claw", which can be considered to be three episode threes bolted together.) It's also been noted that those third quarters were where the flavour and quirkiness of the stories was most concentrated. Of course, all such rules of thumb are generalisations, but there is a grain of truth in those observations when applied to this story - the narrative abruptly jumps to a climax that comes out of nowhere, as if Gatiss has been ordered to strip out a large chunk of the story to cram it all in and get to the cliffhanger-analogue.

On closer examination, this attempt at a pat explanation is flawed. The events are sequenced as if they follow on logically from one another, true, and they are all there because you need those events in a *Doctor Who* story of the kind Gatiss grew up watching. Nevertheless, they are sequenced differently from an old-style four-parter. Because the Gelth's abrupt (and deeply stupid) decision to reveal themselves to be *Doctor Who* monsters comes where you would expect the end of episode three to fall, it's tempting to map that format onto what came earlier in the story - but where exactly is the cliffhanger for "episode two"? Which of many candidates is the first cliffhanger - the one that looks like it, leading into the titles, is long before the TARDIS has arrived and Dickens hasn't been introduced. This criticism, whilst telling us a fair bit about other scripts by Gatiss, tells us something else about the fans who've made it: they expected a lot more from the author of *Nightshade*. (See "The Idiot's Lantern".)

Looking at what we in fact got, the worrying aspect of the Gelth's abrupt *volte face* is that it shifts the emphasis away from the debate about ethics that ought to have been the real focus of the script, and is where we see glimpses of the kind of drama Eccleston signed up to do. The silly "bogus asylum-seekers" row is a smoke-screen for the real damage done, namely that instead of offering a notion that other times and cultures, even - *especially* - ones we think we know from costume-dramas, had other morals and belief-systems that were valid and made sense to them, it makes all points of view other than Rose's turn out to have been mistaken. This parochialism will become ridiculous when we get to X3.2, "The Shakespeare Code" (see **Are We Touring Theme-Park History?** under "The Idiot's Lantern"). Again, we have hindsight telling us that to avoid this happening, they could have made more of the Doctor's guilt in ending the Time War, but we are only three episodes in to a new series. Were it not for the need to set up the Time Rift as a pretext for doing stories in present-day Cardiff and saving a few bob, "The Unquiet Dead" could have benefitted from being later in the running-order. There would still be the flaw of the gallop to the end, but there are at least three other scripts this year that share that problem. Where the script has *really* run into difficulty is that by focussing so much on the surface details, making everyone talk like fanfic versions of Jago and Litefoot and making the whole episode look like an advert for Quality Street chocolates, the moral debate that would have been the starting-point and motor of a 70s script (especially if during the Pertwee era, with Barry Letts as producer) seems grafted-on to kill time between effects.

Whilst it appears from contemporary accounts that Dickens' readings of his work were rather drab affairs, our *idea* of him is now inextricably linked with Simon Callow's various performances. That he agreed to do it once again is a tremendous vote of confidence in this script and the reborn series (once again, we have to remember that when he agreed, nobody had seen the new version and, for anyone of Callow's generation, it was notoriously cheap and cheerful). Callow gives a nuanced performance, portraying Dickens as a man kept going by a performance of bonhommie who reconnects to his former enthusiasm. It's slightly implausible that he would be so silent on Gwyneth's right to decide her own fate but, as we said, the episode only has 45 minutes to get everything in.

Well, almost. One odd effect of the new production techniques is that what looks like a three-quarter-hour piece on the page lands up under-running. This was the cause of the Next Time clips, and the first two years of the Welsh series are marked by scripts that have been trimmed and then bulked-out. Euros Lyn seems to be especially prone to making scripts clip along without looking especially rushed on the screen. This is his second consecutive story as director, and this and "The End of the World" look so radically different that it's hard to see any points in common other than how expensive they look. Both stories are unapologetically *Doctor Who*, but without feeling like they are speaking exclusively to a niche audience. *Doctor Who* has not been so secure in its appeal to the general public for a quarter-century.

The Facts

Written by Mark Gatiss. Directed by Euros Lyn. Viewing figures: (BBC1) 8.86 million, (BBC3 repeat) 0.4 million.

Repeats and Overseas Promotion Des morts inassouvis, Niespokojni nieboszczycy, Die Rastlosen Toten.

Production

In the Pitch document from 2003, Davies had put in a third story where the Doctor and Rose go to 1860, meet Dickens (in his capacity as debunker of fake spiritualists) and together they defeat Mrs Pendragon and her evil Ectoplasm Machine. The Machine was very like the Marconiscope used by Laurence Scarman in "Pyramids of Mars" (13.3), and the sequence where the Doctor proves to Rose that the world could end 125 years before she was born is also a straight steal from that story.

Mrs Pendragon, on the other hand, was recycled from *Dark Season*, Davies' first solo TV drama series for children (or anyone), where she was a malicious school headmistress combining supernatural forces and a big exoskeleton she plugged herself into - yes, *exactly* like the Cyber King at the

X1.3 The Unquiet Dead

end of "The Next Doctor" (X4.14), but played by Jacqueline Pearce exactly as she played Servalan or Chessene (22.4, "The Two Doctors"). The rest of that series will be back as "School Reunion" (X2.3). When making this pitch, Davies intended that some of the stories would be taken on by selected other writers, but had more idea of which writers he would ask than which stories each would opt to do. Mark Gatiss, who had just written *The Vesuvius Club*, a pastiche Victorian supernatural detective romp, plumped for the Dickens episode but replaced the already rather dated Steampunk elements with an idea he'd had as a small child: gaslight-monsters. The components of the story being so firmly within his comfort-zone, Gatiss was able to submit a workable script before any of the other commissioned writers. His plan was to make the story analogous to *A Christmas Carol* (see, um, X6.0, "A Christmas Carol") and show Dickens recovering his *joi de vivre* after a supernatural adventure with the Doctor. There was a bonus in this, with Davies thinking that perhaps they could wangle a repeat at Christmas. As it turned out, Lorraine Heggessey had a better idea (see X2.0, "The Christmas Invasion").

• It was hardly any secret that Gatiss was a big fan of *Doctor Who*, as he had written books for the Virgin *New Adventures* and BBC Books Past Doctors franchises, contributed three sketches to the BBC2 theme-night in 1999 (one of which dropped him in trouble because it disparaged the lead actors in 1980s *Who,* and so was edited for re-use on the *The Beginnings* DVD box set),written about his love of the Target books and slipped references to the series into the scripts for *The League of Gentlemen* (notably pilfering the plot of the feature film *The League of Gentlemen's Apocalypse* from "The Mind Robber"). And, as mentioned a bit earlier, he had written two *Doctor Who* audio adventures ("Phantasmagoria" and "Invaders from Mars") and acted in a handful of others.

This ready access to fan-lore and a feel for the traditions of the series meant that his first draft needed a bit of tweaking. One scene had the Doctor rummaging around in the wardrobe for Victorian garb and, reportedly, claimed in the stage directions, "He looks like Doctor Who". This, any pre-war locutions such as "my dear" or "now, listen to me" and indeed anything recognisably like Jon Pertwee or Tom Baker were *verboten*

in the new regime. Gatiss originally pitched the story as a rather more grim, *New Adventures*-ish story ("The Crippingwell Horror") where Sneed (a younger man, written with the author's friend David Tennant half-in-mind) was a medium based near a cemetery and the deceased, including Gwyneth's younger brother, came back. Gwyneth herself was due to die much earlier on. The Ectoplasm Machine and the scene where the Doctor takes Rose to a 2005 where the Gelth won in 1869 remained for a few more drafts.

• The read-through for this and the previous episode took place on 8th September (although some scenes were cut about a week later). The recording began on 19th September, 2004, with the Dickens performance. This was in the New Theatre in Cardiff. The authentic-seeming posters had copy written in the script and were placed in the location here and in the street exteriors shot the following night. Although the design team had hoped that the whole stage could have been dressed as if this one-day performance came in the middle of a production of an opera (unlikely on Christmas Eve, one might think, but such things did happen), the ongoing production was contemporary, so the thick red velvet curtains were kept closed. If you look closely, the audience members are a small group of extras duplicated again and again digitally. Simon Callow, who has played Dickens several times in a one-man show, found that the script stepped away from the usual version of the author and at least hinted at the complexities and sadnesses of his last years.

• The downside of the new, exciting go-ahead redevelopment of Cardiff is a lack of Victorian-looking locations. Instead, the production moved 40 miles west to Swansea's Marina for the set-piece nocturnal crowd scene. The main vista was of Cambrian Place, looking towards the Swansea Museum (the big yellowish limestone building at the end of all those red-brick houses) from the junction with Gloucester Place Mews. With eight horsedrawn carriages (and spare horses), dozens of extras, a wind machine and paper-snow to deal with, this was going to be tricky. If anything had gone wrong, it would have happened in front of a lot of journalists. Davies, who grew up just up the hill from the Maritime Quadrant, came to talk to them and watch the spectacle: he later said that it was the way Phil Collinson handled the logistics and kept the over-run to a minimum that first made him think this new series could really work.

- One problem was that the supply of late 1860s dresses was affected by the number of period dramas being made in Britain in 2004. Piper's dress was made from scratch, to suit the black and red theme of the story's look, and she was given slightly anachronistic boots and fishnet tights (at least addressing the perennial problem of Victorian-era *Doctor Who*, how the companion got into period garb unaided - see for example "Ghost Light" for Ace's supernatural ability to do up corsets solo without 12-foot-long arms). There was another small snag: residents of Gloucester Place, especially students, had been told to keep their lights off during the shoot. They had been similarly inconvenienced a few months earlier by the filming of *Mine All Mine*, and weren't especially well-disposed towards Davies making them stumble about in the dark all night yet again. Some of them chose especially awkward moments to illuminate their rooms. The two nights after this were spent in Monmouth, about 45 miles northeast of Cardiff, where both the TARDIS arrival and departure and the explosion at Sneed's were filmed. The latter of these was planned to require a model for the walls and windows blowing out, but the unit managed with simply small charges and Eccleston jumping onto crash-mats. This exterior, Beaufort Arms Court, was also used for the brief scenes of Sneed and Gwyneth giving chase to the late Mrs Peace (with amended dialogue concerning "the Sight").

The following day was spent in the Q2 complex, with some of the TARDIS scenes and the interiors of the coach-chase (Dickens' coach being set up inside the TARDIS set). Between 27th September and 2nd October, the unit went to Headlands School, Penarth (that's five miles due south of Cardiff). This is actually a children's home, and had the cellars, floor-tiles and fittings and overall layout needed for Sneed's. During the cellar scenes, on 29th, new dialogue was added (by Davies) to replace the scene where they go back to the TARDIS so that the Doctor can prove to Rose that it's possible for Earth to be devastated in 1869. This is also where the line where the Doctor rather self-pityingly gripes about being killed in Cardiff was worked in.

- After a trial-run with Charlotte Cottle the day they rode the coach aboard the TARDIS, the effects team made the Gelth Tribune sequence using Zoe Thorne. It was decided that the look of the "angel" should be based on Thorne as well as using her voice and movements, and also more than slightly suggestive of the climax of *Raiders of the Lost Ark*. Most of this material was recorded on October 18th. By now it won't be much of a surprise that the episode was found to be under-running, so two new scenes were devised in the next two weeks and recorded in a two-day return to Headlands and a day aboard the TARDIS in Q2. The Headlands scene was an extension of Rose and Gwyneth in the scullery. By now, Davies had a clearer idea of where the series was heading and added two new ingredients: Rose's father and something Gwyneth called "the big bad wolf". This was the 19th and 20th of October, punctuated by pick-ups for "The End of the World". The 22nd saw the new ending with the Doctor explaining that Dickens was scheduled to die in the following spring.

- In all the kerfuffle over the abrupt exit of the star, the programme was hardly short of publicity that week. As it happened, the fact that Mark Gatiss had just been in the live remount of *The Quatermass Experiment* made him more than usually newsworthy. Once again, the day of first broadcast was one on which other events threatened to impinge on transmission. Prince Charles was getting married that day (it would have been the day before, but he had to go to the Pope's funeral - see last story). As it turned out, the day went pretty much without any snags, and the ceremony and TV coverage thereof were over long before 7.00pm. *Doctor Who* managed to beat the Royal Wedding in the ratings. And immediately afterwards, they ran a trailer for David Tennant in Davies' *Casanova*. Were they trying to tell us something?

X1.4: "Aliens of London"

(16th April, 2005)

Which One is This? Farting Aliens. In 10 Downing Street.

Firsts and Lasts It's the first new series story to be shot, alongside "Rose" (X1.1), and the first Cardiff-based production. The first scene recorded was General Asquith talking to Dr Sato (this giving Tosh from *Torchwood* the first line in Welsh *Doctor Who*), but Eccleston's first scene as the Doctor was here, chasing a pig in a spacesuit down a corridor. It's the first appearance of the Slitheen family, who'll be back less often than it seems, but will be giving Sarah Jane Smith annual

X1.4 Aliens of London

headaches. It's the new-look UNIT's first outing, the first of the annual channel-zap montages using real reporters and the non-real AMNN channel's not-real Trinity Wells. Probably most importantly, it's the first appearance of Harriet Jones, MP for Flydale North.

We get the first "Mickey/Ricky" joke, the first suggestion that Patrick Moore might be the first person the government calls if aliens arrive (see X5.1, "The Eleventh Hour") and the first honest-to-goodness cliffhanger in the new series (although they mess it up with the "throw-forward" coming immediately afterwards and showing that everyone's safe). That's because this is the first story to be explicitly made as a two-parter, which in screen-time terms means the usual four-part story of yore is back.

This is the first of two appearances by Albion Hospital (see X1.9, "The Empty Child"). And, perhaps regrettably, it's the first of many cameos by real-life minor celebrities as themselves.

Watch Out For...

• The trademark shot for this story, and indeed the Eccleston months, is of a spaceship colliding with a national monument. (We might pedantically point out that "Big Ben" is actually the main bell and not the tower it's in, but even the Doctor blurs the distinction[13].) Everyone who remembers 50s monster movies or 90s invasion-of-Earth flicks has seen this shot a hundred times - not always done as well - but the key thing to note here is the handing on of the torch from Mike Tucker's in-house BBC model team (who did the actual collision) to The Mill (who did the splash into the Thames).

• The occupant of this spaceship comes as rather a surprise. The set-up is done almost shot-for-shot like the escape of Paul McGann's Doctor from the morgue, and everyone plays dead straight the scene where UNIT take on a pig in a spacesuit. However, some have claimed that this is the precise moment when Eccleston decides that one year is enough.

• The real aliens are disguised as plump humans. The disguise is perfect enough to fool wives and mistresses, but comes with the problem of periodic gas-release. Quite apart from being precisely the sort of thing Roald Dahl would have done, it's a sidelong glance back at that perennial problem of 70s Doctor Who: that an actor in a latex suit take up more space than an actor would normally, and that "unveiling" the inner monster involves us accepting that they managed to squeeze into a tiny human skin. However, anyone who thinks that fart-gags and Doctor Who don't mix has missed the entire career of the single best writer to have worked on the series (bar none: Davies, Moffat and Adams simply rode in on his coat-tails): Robert Holmes.

• Following on from this... there's always a phrase for each Doctor that sums him up. You probably have a list of your own. There's also a phrase each one says that he maybe shouldn't have - William Hartnell had his many fluffs, Sylvester McCoy had a few OTT moments, and Eccleston drew the short straw with "D'ya mind not fartin' while I'm saving the world?"

• Also note that before we see properly what they look like, the aliens are just fat middle-aged people acting like big kids. Mostly. One is apparently maintaining his human predecessor's active lovelife.

• In all this puerile malarkey, the scene where Jackie is sat alone on her bed as a news broadcast updates us on a bizarre crisis is exactly like what we would expect of the author of The Second Coming. The disjunction between these two registers is the hallmark of this story.

The Continuity

The Doctor He doesn't 'do family' or 'do domestic'.

He first tells Rose, '900 years of time and space, and I've never been slapped by someone's mother', then clarifies that he is, in fact, '900 years old'. [Compare with the tenth Doctor claiming he's 903 in X4.0, "Voyage of the Damned". This resets the Doctor's age where the new series is concerned - the seventh Doctor went out of his way to say he was '953' in 24.1, "Time and the Rani", and by this point, one wonders if so much rewriting of the Doctor's past has gone on that he's lost count. See **The Obvious Question - How Old Is He?** under 16.5, "The Power of Kroll" and updates in Volume 9.]

He initially refuses to use the TARDIS to look at the spaceship that struck the clocktower and fell into the Thames because he's aware of people who'd be keeping an eye out for him [not necessarily Torchwood]. Yet given a chance to sneak in to the alien autopsy, he breaks this rule - albeit after five or more hours of coping with daytime

Aliens of London X1.4

Why is Trinity Wells on Jackie's Telly?

There is a lot in this century's version of *Doctor Who* that didn't need to be said for the first-night audience in the UK, but which flies so far over the heads of overseas viewers as to be almost invisible. It's easy enough for us to answer questions asked by Australian, Russian, French, or American viewers about comments or situations that baffle them, but things they completely miss are harder to second-guess. However, by observing the reactions of foreign fans arriving in London (and the comments of the test-readers of previous books), we have an outline of what our readers might need help getting.

Tug at any one of these threads and a whole lot more come tumbling out. "Aliens of London" has revealed vast chasms between our worldview and that of even English-speaking nations. There are a few aspects of the scene where the Doctor channel-zaps for more information that might need a few lines of further explication. However, when we start explaining the explanations, we get into much bigger topics.

We'll start with the one Americans sort-of spot but don't get: Trinity Wells, a newscaster for the AMNN channel. The use of an American newscaster from a nonexistent US news station is a narrative ploy, nothing more. America is, for plot purposes, "noises off". There's a certain breed of American commentators online who seem to think that any reference to the US that is anything else than entirely complimentary (or uses an English - or more likely Welsh - actor with a vaguely American accent) is somehow proof that the BBC is "anti-American". For the British audience, who, after all, pay for this series to be made (and that's a bigger issue which we'll come to later), it is enough to briefly acknowledge the existence of other countries, especially when the entire planet is being invaded. Trinity is shorthand for "Meanwhile, everywhere else", and is a verbal equivalent of shots of odd things happening in Paris, Rome, Tokyo and, rather improbably, the Taj Mahal. Then we get on with the real story of what's happening in the Powell Estate. What's unlikely to strike anyone not from around here as improbable is that Jackie's TV can get this station and not others from elsewhere.

As we saw in **Why Now, Why Wales?** (under X1.1, "Rose"), there was a profound change in the access to digital television that began shortly after *Doctor Who* ended in 1989. What is worth noting here is that the launch of satellite television was initially the subject of a turf-war between two companies. British Satellite Broadcasting (BSB) had several ambitions and noble aims, but their main objective was to stop Rupert Murdoch getting a monopoly. Murdoch launched Sky TV claiming that he was against monopolies and that offering more choice was his motive, but Sky's actions since call this into question. However, the situation in the 1990s was that Sky and BSB offered a small minority who were willing to pay again for more channels the opportunity to watch additional channels of pop videos, kitsch re-runs, cheaply-made fillers and sport, as well as occasional movie premieres (of Fox films, oddly enough) and occasional exclusive US imports. Both systems allowed other operators aboard, including several owned by other tabloid papers (the *Daily Mirror*'s notorious "L!VE" offered topless darts and bulletins punctuated by the News Bunny, the subsequently notorious Richard Bacon).

The range of content offered by each network was different. Initially, Sky was, obviously, the main outlet for Fox-made US programmes and, by extension (and shameless manipulation of the overseas rights) almost any major US series went out of Sky first before BBC, ITV or Channel 4 got a sniff at it. (In the case of *Buffy the Vampire Slayer*, this was almost three years. *The Simpsons* was available on Sky seven years before the BBC took up Matt Groening's offer[16], but Sky marketed it as a kid's show.) BSB showed programmes it made for itself. There were also re-runs of fondly-remembered (and cheap) shows, including *Doctor Who*. (Indeed, the last producer of the series before the BBC pulled the plug, John Nathan-Turner, was briefly a scheduler for BSB and participated in marathon showings with former stars as studio guests.) Nevertheless, with the exclusive rights to sport, the cachet attached to the US shows it showed (albeit mainly from critics working for Murdoch-owned papers) and the ability to sell packages at a huge loss in ways BSB couldn't manage (not being owned by a tycoon, and by law the BBC was only allowed to donate a small amount), Sky overtook the rival and subsumed it into BSkyB.

continued on Page 73...

television and Jackie's neighbours.

• *Ethics.* Right after having promised Rose that he won't leave her behind, he goes and does that very thing. He dismisses Mickey's irritation about being hauled in by the Met by saying that's just 'domestic'.

• *Background.* He has never seen the kind of spaceship that fell into the Thames, had no idea it was coming and is hugely excited by its appearance on the scene. And yet, he resents the idea of watching on telly like everyone else. David Lloyd-George ["the Welsh Wizard" and Prime Minister in the early twentieth century] used to drink the Doctor under the table. Curiously, the Doctor speculates that these events *might* be humanity's first official contact with extraterrestrials. [The fact that he doesn't *know* the details behind such a major historical event is both curious and alarming; see **He Remembers This *How*?** with the next episode.]

• *Inventory: Sonic Screwdriver.* It undoes locks - in one incident, its squealing noise threatens to alert the guards, so the Doctor shushes it and it squeals more quietly.

• *Inventory: Other.* The TARDIS key that the Doctor gives Rose glows in synch with the Ship's materialisation sound, even at a distance. He just happens to have one on him.

The TARDIS Quite apart from having all the main satellite TV packages, the TARDIS has sensors that can listen in on radar signals from a day or so before. Paint may or may not stay on the exterior shell after dematerialisation/rematerialisation [the 'Bad Wolf' graffiti went when the Doctor relocated the TARDIS to Albion Hospital, but came back when the Ship rematerialised in the same spot as it had been in (see 25.2, "The Happiness Patrol" and others).] The Doctor is able to steer the Ship with pinpoint accuracy once he's got a temporal bearing, but was exactly a year late getting Rose home. [This and X2.2, "Tooth and Claw" indicate that the settings for Earth chronology are in our increments: years, months, hours, centuries, etc. The mistakes are too precise to be caused by external forces.] However, to get to Albion Hospital so precisely entails the Console giving off steam and needing a clout with the rubber mallet.

The Supporting Cast

• *Rose.* She thinks you can use 'gay' as a synonym for "useless". [That was a brief fad around the time she was at school, but you'd think she'd grown out of it.] She's finally changed her clothes, opting for an even pinker T-shirt. She left her passport behind when she spontaneously left with the Doctor [in "Rose", but see X1.11, "Boom Town"]. The missing person adverts for Rose claim that she's 19 years old, 5'4" tall. [In X1.6, "Dalek", Rose says that she will be '26' in 2012 - meaning she was born in 1986, and this advert was placed last year. Piper turned 23 while Series One was being made. Accounts vary as to whether she's actually 5'4", or an inch taller.]

• *Jackie.* She's furious with the Doctor for leading her daughter astray. [Aside from the obvious lack of contact and fears, Rose is about the same age as Jackie was when she started dating an older man - Pete would have been 32 when they met - and we know from X1.8, "Father's Day" and X2.5, "Rise of the Cybermen" that this didn't go as smoothly as it could have.] There is a bicycle and an elaborate hair dryer (a salon model) in the flat, which appears to have been redecorated. She has a lot of friends who pop around to watch her telly and catch up on how Rose is.

When Rose disappeared, Jackie blamed Mickey and started a poison-pen campaign, as well as the usual 'missing' posters.

• *Mickey.* He's surprisingly forgiving towards Jackie considering the nasty letter-writing [perhaps he regarded the police harassment as more or less inevitable, given Rose vanishing on everyone]. He takes a not wholly unjustified delight in informing Rose that the Doctor's left in the TARDIS, and follows up later by asking whether she'll stay with him now - fortunately for Rose, the Doctor manages to blow up something on the Console before she can answer. Mickey has spent the intervening year fossicking online and has a lot of dirt on the Doctor's previous visits to Earth - he seems to know a lot more about UNIT than the general public, for instance. To the Doctor's apparent surprise, he asks the significant question too simple for a Time Lord to think of: why should "invading" aliens draw attention to themselves?

• *UNIT.* The group is here identified, as per the old days, as 'United Nations Intelligence Taskforce'. [This won't last, as the real-life UN decided they weren't as keen on that as they had been in the 60s, but agreed the name UNIT could be used so long as nobody said what the 'UN' bit stood for. See X4.4, "The Sontaran Stratagem" for

Aliens of London X1.4

Why is Trinity Wells on Jackie's Telly?

continued from Page 71...

Murdoch's recent bid to take it over outright was to have been nodded through with only a token resistance from a government that owes him the election, but the scandal over phone-hacking changed all of that at the eleventh hour.

It was easy to tell who had opted for which system, as BSB had "squarials", rhomboid antennae. Sky had parabolic dishes. The aggressive marketing of Sky to people on council estates, especially those on benefits who would be at home more hours of the day, led to a stigma against homes with these dishes for much of the 1990s. For anyone who lived here then, the idea that Jackie Tyler didn't have Sky is absurd. It's even remotely possible that, before Murdoch's launch (and the literal launch of the Marco Polo satellite which enabled all of this), she might have had a cable subscription to one of the earlier systems, such as Superchannel (itself home to the only UK rebroadcasts of 70s *Doctor Who*). It is exactly the sort of scheme Pete Tyler would have tried.

Moreover, as the conversation about where to get cheap SIM cards indicates, the Powell Estate is populated by people who know how to get borderline-illegal deals for this kind of thing. Murdoch aside, the opportunities for access to digital TV were expanded by the advent of set-top boxes, as we'll discuss in a moment, but even if, improbable as it seems, the Tylers weren't early adopters of satellite telly, nothing in their lifestyle rings true for 2006. Jackie spends her days glued to the landline phone, which would make sense if she had some kind of package with digital telly - otherwise she'd be rationing her calls. (Maybe she is; she only seems to call two or three people, possibly on the BT "friends and family'" package.) This highlights how odd it is that she never seems to call Rose, but see **Things That Don't Make Sense** and **RT Phone Home?** under X1.2, "The End of the World" for more on that puzzle.) More curiously, when Mickey wants to plug his computer's dial-up Internet into her line, she reminds him to make a note for her bills. Rose has to go to his flat to look up the Doctor. So Jackie hasn't even got her own Internet address. Sorry, but a single mum with a grown-up daughter, largely absent, would be online at all hours. In fact, with Rose having done GCSEs three or four years earlier, this would have been set up circa 1998. Weirdly, although Mickey's got a laptop, Jackie and Rose couldn't be bothered even to get a second-hand 486 and modem (hardly difficult to come by in Lambeth back then). Cable television offered an alternative, with email via the telly - a briefly fashionable halfway house. They don't even have that in Jackie's flat. In fact, one shot in "World War Three" (X1.5) pans down from outside their window and shows a standard analogue antenna. (It's in the aftermath, just before the Doctor is invited around for shepherd's pie and he makes a counter-offer of a solar flare.)

Clearly, they don't have satellite or cable. So perhaps they'd go for the most popular option of the early 2000s: a set-top digital decoder taking a feed through a conventional aerial. The BBC's mandate is to cater for precisely the audiences that advertisers won't touch. It made sense for the Corporation to invest in dedicated children's channels, their legal obligation towards Parliamentary coverage and more niche material on cable. In order to make sure that this was not taking money that all Licence Fee payers were contributing to pay for the cable-subscribing elite (who would thus be paying twice for BBC programmes that nobody else could see), the digital set-top boxes were launched, and all the terrestrial networks began subsidiaries. The BBC has eight, ITV has four (which is why the original station, formed from the regional franchises as explained in the first essay in this book, is now "ITV1"). One of these was, at the time this story was broadcast, called "News 24" and was part of the earlier Director General's masterplan for the BBC's future as a news-led counter to the encroaching CNN, Sky News, Al Jazeera as well as other unreliable and less well-established rolling news services.[17] After the initial purchase of the machinery, the viewer need not pay any more, so this has been the main method of access for digital television in Britain.

The government stipulated that all broadcast television would have to be digital by 2012, though take-up has been sporadic. Someone in a flat in London would have reasonable reception with a straightforward analogue aerial from a Pound Shop - if that flat faces the Crystal Palace transmitter. However, choosing to pay up to forty quid for a digibox is something Jackie and Rose

continued on Page 75...

X1.4 Aliens of London

the compromise devised later.]

When aliens land and an extraterrestrial body needs to be guarded, obviously UNIT are sent in. They still have the red berets, but seem better-drilled than before. Their investigative team includes Muriel Frost. [A character from the *DWM* comic strip, who also shows up in Big Finish audio "The Fires of Vulcan", although in that she is a captain in 1980 - nobody here is that old. One way to reconcile the age difference is to think there are two Muriel Frosts, possibly mother and daughter.] She and the other experts on extra-terrestrials get killed in an ambush by the Slitheen.

Curiously, the Doctor thinks that few of his former colleagues would accept him in a different body, and fears dissection or worse if he is found to be an alien. Nevertheless, all of the soldiers present fall in behind the Doctor when he shouts 'Defence Plan Delta!' [Either he guessed very lucky, or everyone was just reacting on instinct to Dr Sato's scream, or the Doctor remembers those things from his misspent youth wearing frilly shirts, and thereby persuaded the squaddies that he was an officer from way back].

When the government's emergency protocols on aliens are active, UNIT has a standing order to sniff out references to the Doctor/TARDIS and track him/it down [odd that we never see this used again - at least, not on television], as he's believed to be the 'ultimate expert in extraterrestrial affairs'. In such instances, sophisticated software searches phone and email traffic to check for keywords connected with him and Ship. A Code Nine situation means that UNIT troops can barge in to any situation and take the Doctor and who-ever's with him to where the action is (in this case, 10 Downing Street). The Doctor seems to know about this.

• *Torchwood*. We didn't know it at the time, but that nice Dr Sato who seems so competent and obliging is a ringer: she's working for Torchwood, and isn't really a pathologist as she claims. [We discover in *Torchwood*: "Exit Wounds" that she was covering for the hung-over Dr Owen Harper - see **Things That Don't Make Sense** in the next episode.] She seems happy enough to help the Doctor [possibly just to preserve her cover, or because Captain Jack has had a word with his team where the Doctor is concerned - this, despite Torchwood officially listing him as an enemy; see "Tooth and Claw"].

The Non-Humans

• *The Slitheen*. They've done their homework, and are adept at colloquial English and the processes of the UK's political and Defence systems. They hollow out the corpses of humans and use compression devices to squeeze inside their skins and impersonate them - they even manage to use the same voices and idioms. [This indicates a degree of memory-plundering as well as simple face-theft.] The skins are evidently capable of neural interchange, not just to allow the occupants to smile and blink, but apparently - in the case of the Slitheen masquerading as transport liaison Oliver Charles - have sex with the deceased's usual partner(s) without them noticing any change. Getting out of this skin requires unzipping the forehead, accompanied with a bright bluish glow and a low buzzing sound.

A naked Slitheen is bipedal, with very long arms ending in three-clawed hands. The arms have external tendons. They have long necks and walk with a stoop - their actual height is about three metres, but they are usually at eye-level with most humans. The head is bulbous and has a baby-face, with large eyes that blink. The compressor that lets them squeeze inside human skins is around their necks, and seems to act as a translator - curiously, when they are not disguised, the voices are almost the same as the humans they pretend to be, but with a slight trilling effect. They have vestigial tails in the smalls of their backs. The skin is a pale yellow, and seems like tough leather or bone. [More on this next episode.]

History

• *Dating*. We're a year on from "Rose". [The Prime Minister prior to the one who is here killed by the Slitheen was John Major. Look at the photos on the staircase when Harriet meets Rose. Also, the dead PM kept a Fender Stratocaster in his office at Number 10, so it's unlikely to be Michael Howard or John Prescott (in X2.5, "Rise of the Cybermen", Mickey's example of an alternate universe is Tony Blair never being elected, so it's probably him).] The Prime Minister can be removed from office, and martial law declared, per Section Five of the UK's Emergency Protocols. BBC's news channel is still called 'News 24'.

The UN has taken individual member-nations' nuclear weapons and placed them under a centralised command [cf 12.1, "Robot"; Harriet says she voted against the measure, though, suggesting

Why is Trinity Wells on Jackie's Telly?

continued from Page 73...

might have done simply because they watch a lot of television and don't want to be limited to the five terrestrial channels. (Conceivably, it might have been what Rose bought her mother with her first pay cheque from Hendricks.) When the spaceship zooms over their heads, the Doctor and Rose are on the roof of the tower-block, with a number of analogue aerials but no sign of any dishes for BSkyB. So, despite in many other regards being sold to us as the typical Council estate chav single mum, a broadly familiar stereotype, Jackie is remarkable in not following the almost universal trends of people in her income-bracket, domestic arrangements and lifestyle. (Of course, she's not a single mum, she's a widow, and chavs wouldn't have *Lovely Bones* lying around, but this is another symptom of Davies' uncertainty of who Jackie is other than comic-relief.) No set-top digibox, not even OnDigital, the ITV's version with the amusing ads; no cable, despite the cheap phones and Internet options; no Sky dish. Jackie is, contrary to everything we think we know about her, strictly terrestrial. Five channels, one of which a flat in London would have trouble getting clearly.

In "Army of Ghosts" (X2.12), we get a selection of BBC and ITV fixtures, distorted by the apparent existence of ghosts. So Derek Acorah (then on ITV2 a lot), ITV1's morning talkshow host Trisha Goddard and spoof ads vie with *EastEnders* and a parody of *CrimeWatch* presented by someone usually on either BBC1 or Channel 5 in the mornings. Nothing that isn't available on Freeview (the joint BBC/ITV digital box system that covers the terrestrials and their digital outlets that embraced the failed OnDigital). This is significant. The majority of the assumed first-night audience will be familiar with these faces and formats, and the majority of *that* majority will watch children's programmes. In a lot of ways, the use of *Blue Peter* in "Aliens of London" is entirely natural, as many of the viewers would first have heard of *Doctor Who* on that programme. As we've said, CBBC was integral to the BBC's launch strategy for the new series. The clip of Matt Baker making a spaceship cake is also a note of realism: it's exactly how *Blue Peter* would react if such a thing had happened. (It also gives the casual viewer some kind of temporal framework for how much time has elapsed since

the crash at just after 10.00am - at that stage, *Blue Peter* would have been on live at five-ish, Mondays, Wednesdays and Fridays.) However, Baker and Gethin Jones also did behind-the-scenes features, Jones indeed being one of the Cybermen in "Doomsday". (We will develop this theme when discussing X2.10, "Love & Monsters" and **Has All the Puff "Totally" Changed Things?** under X2.1, "New Earth".) However, this familiarity is also a low-cost tactic: sticking with BBC output slightly distorted keeps it in-house (see **The Big Picture** and **Oh, Isn't That...?** with this episode's listing). Moreover, even a far-future setting (e.g. X4.8, "Silence in the Library") has CBBC cartoons playing on the little girl's telly. This is taken to ludicrous extremes in "Bad Wolf" (X1.12), but we'll deal with this as it arises.

So now you can see why the ability of Jackie's telly to get AMNN is so remarkable. The set she has, and the handset the Doctor wrests from a recalcitrant toddler, are standard late 90s kit, not any souped-up Magpie equipment (see X2.7, "The Idiot's Lantern" et al). It is obviously not the Doctor's doing, as a toddler is able to switch over using the remote control. It's only this one foreign news station, no CNN, no Bloomberg, no France24 (these are available on the Sky digital set-top box among several others). Logically, the Doctor would want as many different sources as possible to make up for not being there in person. If News24 (which is now BBC News Channel) is all that's available and AMNN is the only source of any other information, then ITN, the commercial companies' news company (until Channel 5 took on Sky News some time after this story is set) must be using a live feed from AMNN. This isn't improbable, but generally is done as a change-of-pace in the middle of indigenous coverage, and mediated through commentators in studios in London. It's interesting that we rarely see the full screen when Trinity is acting as Voice of Doom in these two episodes, as if a US company's coverage of a British story shown on British TV would have on-screen graphics, a ticker-tape of updates and an explanatory caption that this is coming from elsewhere. For four-fifths of the viewers, this would be the only way any news coverage other than BBC or ITN would have been visible as anything other

continued on Page 77...

X1.4 Aliens of London

that it was enacted much later than the UNIT era]. The Doctor says that the year Rose missed owing to TARDIS travel was 'middling'.

Catchphrase Counter An unexpected spaceship is, of course, 'fantastic', and a local kid paints 'Bad Wolf' on the side of the TARDIS.

The Analysis

The Big Picture ("Aliens of London" and "World War Three") The story seems like an odd mix; on the one hand, it is in the tradition of screenplays by Russell T Davies where the consequences of an extraordinary event are filtered through media coverage and the intimate lives of the people caught up in it. *The Second Coming* examined the friends of someone who turned out to be the Son of God and the fall-out in their own lives and the mass-hysteria that followed, with real-life TV journalists and well-choreographed crowd scenes and public disorder. This followed on from Davies' participation in earlier projects such as *Springhill* - a series devised by Paul Abbott, produced by Phil Collinson and script-edited by Paul Cornell and Gareth Roberts (of whom more later in this book and the next). Davies' one contribution to the Virgin Books *New Adventures* range, thus his only previous *Doctor Who* writing, had been tale of aliens and drugs in a council estate in Manchester (partly recycled as *Torchwood:* "Children of Earth").

On the other hand, though, the basic concept of giggly alien con-men farting as they planned to take over the world, and by pretending to be the acting Prime Minister and his colleagues, is more akin to his earlier work in series such as *Why Don't You...?*[14], and the kind of gross-out humour, gunk-tanks and underpants that had become the norm in late 90s series, when Davies was still writing for Abbott's *Children's Ward*. On both BBC and ITV in that period, the variety of the programming meant that mundane drama, fantasy drama and slapstick comedy all had bits of education slipped in, whilst educational shows had fart-gags and goo (a tradition upheld by the *Horrible History* books, now a hit BBC series).

In short, this story is exactly what someone who'd not seen *Doctor Who*, but had been told to make a BBC science-fiction serial that children could enjoy, might have devised. It is certainly a mix of the two things such a person might have expected from Davies. In many ways, this can be seen as an attempt to set a benchmark for where to pitch later episodes. What might surprise non-British readers is how close to 2005-style British children's telly it was, not just the fart-gags but the focus on Jackie.

Children's Television in Britain has evolved through a series of accidents, policy-changes and government controls in ways that nobody could have predicted. We have sketched in some of the story in Volume 1 (see **What Was Children's TV Like Back Then?** under 3.7, "The Celestial Toymaker"), but it is a huge topic needing more background than we could find space for[15]. Ask anyone here over 40 and they will all be able to list bizarre and inexplicable programmes we all took for granted. *Doctor Who*, never officially a children's show (it would have been better-funded if it had been, especially in the 80s), existed within a BBC context midway between *I, Claudius* and *Bagpuss* rather than as part of any "cult". Bringing it back meant taking account of what else this large share of the original target audience were watching. They weren't getting anything from the original commercial station. ITV had been phasing out children's television over the previous three years, and by 2006 had ceased altogether. (The usual story is that the £40 million income from advertising for junk food went after the government curtailed the hours when such adverts were permitted, and that's a story for later - X2.3, "School Reunion".) Other commercial terrestrial stations opted for cheap imported shows used to punctuate toy ads. On Satellite and cable (we will use the term "digital" to cover both - the majority of Sky subscribers get the cable channels, whereas cable viewers don't always get access to Sky output), there were umpteen channels given over to rerunning old cartoons or imports - Nickelodeon, Cartoon Network, Disney Channel et al - but precious little for anyone in contemporary Britain. Custom-made series for British children were thus almost the sole preserve of the BBC, and these cost a great deal.

However, the funding arrangement that gave the Corporation a levy for every television set in the country was conditional on providing for all viewers, not just the ones advertisers wanted, and so the BBC was forced by law to make upscale children's programming. When the government refused a rise in revenue, a move widely seen as a punishment for not towing the official line on the

Aliens of London X1.4

Why is Trinity Wells on Jackie's Telly?

continued from Page 75...

than clips (where, for instance, the coverage by other countries was part of the story, or for comic effect). CNN and the rest are known *about* here, but not regularly watched. In most cases, London-based commentators would mediate their feed. (So, for example, when Flight 77 was crashed into the Pentagon, the BBC's Brian Hanrahan - who had been inside the building a few times - was able to offer some idea of how many people worked in the destroyed section.) An American broadcaster appearing on terrestrial UK television with no hint that this is coming from elsewhere is unlikely.

Fake news items by real newsreaders, past or present, have been a staple of fantasy and science-fiction shows and films. The BBC has guidelines on this, which is why when a familiar face appears in a fictional news item, no matter how realistic, there has to be some sort of discrepancy to subliminally suggest that it isn't real. (There was a notorious incident where this went wrong despite diligent precautions - for example, using a cast of actors who had been in drama programmes shown earlier that night - and viewers were disturbed beyond accepted bounds - see "Army of Ghosts" for more about the original *GhostWatch*.) Thus, in "Aliens of London", Andrew Marr is out of the studio and outside 10 Downing Street, as he rarely was; Kirsty Wark presents *Newsnight* and might do headlines, but not as part of a scheduled bulletin (X4.5, "The Poison Sky"); Natasha Kaplinsky wasn't with the BBC in 1999 (as she appeared to be in *Torchwood*).

Verisimilitude and the occasional desire by journalists to appear in a series that they liked as children (or their own children watch) makes such cameos helpful as more than a narrative device for info-dumping. However, even if their roles can be scripted, a regular guest-slot on *Doctor Who* would infringe the guidelines, so an Equity member playing a news anchor is more suitable for a semi-regular slot. That said, Marr was cast for a role originally to have been given to an actor, so it could easily have happened that Lachelle Charles' character (later named "Trinity Wells") would have been played by one of the US news anchors who occasionally do items to be shown on News 24 (and, in the small hours, BBC2). Had this happened, a real-life news outlet would had to have been approached for permission to use name, logo and images, and this would have been costly, protracted and compromised (as what the anchor could be allowed to say would have been vetted by representatives of that company). If they could have afforded it, this might have made these scenes more palatable for the online communities who gripe about *Doctor Who*'s portrayal of Americans, but would have distorted the content and - more to the point - have been utterly lost on the eight to eleven million viewers in the UK on first broadcast, and the hundred or so other nations who buy the series. Later episodes would attempt this, but the effect of such montage scenes diminishes each time they do it, until it becomes just part of what you expect in episode twelve of a series of *Doctor Who*. This first time it is in keeping with how Davies tried to ground extraordinary events in present-day Britain (such as in *The Second Coming*).

Yet we see Trinity in several later stories (and at least once in *The Sarah Jane Adventures*), so evidently AMNN is routinely shown in Britain. From the timings of her broadcasts, it seems that she is in fact based in the UK and broadcasting to America. In "The Christmas Invasion" (X2.0), she talks of the Guinevere 1 probe landing "on Christmas morning", even though 3.00am in London is 10.00pm in New York and earlier further west. If that's the case, then perhaps there is a regular berth for her on UK screens. It would appear that Channel 4 exists in the *Doctor Who* world (hence the Davinadroid in "Bad Wolf"), and there is evidently an ITV even if it is not named as such on a BBC series (although BBC Wales has, for reasons we have discussed in another essay, a more flexible relationship and indeed uses HTV studios on occasion). Channel 5 seems not to exist. (There is a reference in *Torchwood* to its one genuine hit, *CSI*, but that's it.) In our world, it hit financial difficulties and was taken over by another tabloid-owner, Richard Desmond, who also runs the adult digital channels (and a paper that rounds on the BBC for showing "filth"). Perhaps in the *Doctor Who* version, it was wholly subsumed by Americans instead of being bought out by Australians (the Pearson organisation), who sold it on to Desmond and fills its night-time schedules with a feed from

continued on Page 79...

X1.4 Aliens of London

briefings given to Parliament about the alleged Weapons of Mass Destruction in Iraq, the budgets for children's drama shrank, leaving a gap that - some have argued - the return of *Doctor Who* was intended to offset. (It is certainly true that *The Sarah Jane Adventures* has been the biggest in-house drama specifically for children over the last few years.) The BBC was able to have two separate digital children's networks, as well as more hours per day of dedicated output on the terrestrial channels, because of its knack of finding programmes that children wanted to watch and buy merchandising from. *Teletubbies* alone raised enough to fund Cbeebies (the infant channel). CBBC and Cbeebies are, rather confusingly, also the names for the slots on BBC1 or BBC2 for the same programmes in a different order (as with Sky One, first run is on the digital service). The same company behind this, Ragdoll, launched a short-lived series for ITV called *Boobah*, which was trippy and annoying, but which had baby-faced aliens too much like the Slitheen for it to be a coincidence.

(We might also ponder that the pig in the retro-looking pressure-suit is more than slightly reminiscent of *Porco Rosso*, the Studio Ghibli animated film. This is not the last vaguely Ghibli-esque thing we will see in the new series. Of course, the pig air-ace of that film is usually seen wearing a more conventional bomber-jacket, jodhpurs and a Biggles hat, rather like Brannigan in X3.3, "Gridlock".)

In many ways, both this story and "The Sound of Drums" (X3.12) are in the tradition of *The Demon Headmaster*. Gillian Cross' series of books became a phenomenon shortly before the whole JK Rowling bandwagon started. The television adaptations were even bigger, and Terence Hardiman (X5.2, "The Beast Below") seemed not to be off our screens for three years. That the then-Home Secretary looked like him was slightly embarrassing, and Jack Straw had laser eye surgery so as not to need the spectacles that completed the resemblance (the Headmaster's tinted glasses were the key to his hypnotic power). Looking at late 90s children's shows, the main thing that strikes anyone more used to either American kid-fodder or earlier British material is the emphasis on bodily functions. This is entirely in keeping with Cardiff's most famous author, Roald Dahl, and his use of gross-out humour to deflate authority-figures and threatening adults.

This discourse of snot and puke was always there in the school playground, but had entered the mainstream and become, to some extent, commodified. Green slime became a staple of toys, especially the "alien eggs" that were a fad in about 1998 and again in 2007.

However, what makes this unmistakably a BBC take on that trend is that the mum, although still occasionally a grotesque figure of fun, has a life that isn't just a source of problems for the child-protagonist. If anything, she is treated (in CBBC terms) as an honorary kid herself, as the role of ludicrous adult authority-figures has been transferred to the flatulent politicians and soldiers, the stupid police and the rather uptight "good" MP. Jackie gets covered in green glop, but as the punchline to a sequence where she and Mickey become audience-identification figures in the way Rose had been but is increasingly not any more.

Of course, Davies was not unaware of the heritage of *Doctor Who* (at least until 1980, after which his memory goes a bit fuzzy). The whole gimmick of the Slitheen compression-field generators was an affectionate nod back to the convention that aliens played by actors in latex masks were able to somehow squeeze inside human-skin disguises, and thus looked smaller as fake humans than as real aliens. (See, for example, 18.1, "The Leisure Hive" and 17.2, "City of Death".) This was one of those narrative "just go with it" things we sort of accepted, like aliens speaking BBC English and not using contractions, all invasions being targeted specifically at the Home Counties, every planet looking like a quarry and all men over 30 finding Barbara powerfully erotic.

Some took it more seriously than others: David Icke, a former TV sports presenter and goalkeeper for Leicester City, published a number of books in which a curious selection of celebrities were, he claimed, alien lizards in human skins. (Prince Philip might just about be plausible, but Boxcar Willie is a threat to us how, exactly?) He also claims we are stuck in a time-loop and reality is a computational matrix. We're not kidding; he seems genuinely to believe that we are stuck in a mishmash of Tom Baker stories.

If the alien ship flying past notable London landmarks is still an unfolding story while *Blue Peter* is on, and enough time has elapsed for the production team to invent an alien spaceship cake, the story would be current enough to warrant BBC2 giving over slots reserved for its usual

Why is Trinity Wells on Jackie's Telly?

continued from Page 77...

its US-orientated news from London instead of live poker. In this revised world, in a crisis, using this as the basis for its news service in daytime is as plausible as first Pearson and then Desmond's organisation using Sky News.

But that would have caused other, knock-on effects that would have been obvious in this fictitious world. Some of these may indeed have take place between broadcast stories (see **How Come Britain Has a President and America Hasn't?** under X3.12, "The Sound of Drums"). However, if we assume that News 24 is being relayed on BBC1 during the crisis, why not another outlet in the times when nothing much is happening? The simplest explanation is that in addition to the eight digital options and BBC HD (which has now begun - see X4.15, "Planet of the Dead"), there was a BBC News US channel, based in London, that the domestic viewers could get to see in a crisis / if they really couldn't sleep and BBC1 had run out of recent documentaries and current affair programmes to show again with signing for the hard of hearing. One final detail: Trinity is sat behind the unique design of desk used by the various national and regional BBC News studios. The implication is that, for news coverage purposes, the *Doctor Who* version of the BBC treats the US as a region, like the East Midlands, Scotland or Newcastle, and with significantly less autonomy than Wales has.

The broader topic is one that will be a thread throughout this books: Jackie Tyler is written as a stereotype, a single mum on a Council estate who resents her daughter's attempts to look beyond this and who dates a string of unsuitable (and unseen) men. In the circumstances of the stories, however, evidence to support this caricature is either missing or flatly contradicted. She is a widow who has not remarried, even with a daughter now able to leave home, and her attempts to find love are portrayed as grotesque and laughable rather than being played for pathos or plausible motivation. She evidently has a reasonable standard of living, but never seems to go to work and copes when her daughter loses her job and leaves - had she been on Housing Benefit or any other supplementary income, this would have been obvious in both her actions and the incidental details in "Love & Monsters". There is a tension between attempts to get verisimilitude (fake news broadcasts and throwaway lines about compensation claims) and the efforts to make Jackie an instantly recognisable, unchanging stock figure. In the early days of the re-animation of *Doctor Who*, this might have been possible, if you were judging it against the days when Mel (23.3, "The Mysterious Planet" et seq) and Victoria (4.9, "The Evil of the Daleks" et seq) were acceptable as plausible products of their backgrounds and as nuanced as any characters you'd get in the series. By any other modern TV drama standards - the standards by which Davies insisted we judge his version of the series - Jackie is a patronising stick-figure, and anyone who has been to a real household like that would spot her as a summation of stock tropes from 80s soaps rather than a representative of twenty-first century London. As with the selection of info-dump clips on her telly during that afternoon, Jackie exists to speedily get the viewers into the story and setting using slightly distorted versions of familiar items from other TV shows. Tug at any thread, and it all unravels.

late-afternoon schedule of quiz-shows and docu-soaps about workplaces to either BBC1's usual children's programming or News 24 feed (as happened in the aftermath of the July 2005 bombings in London). Such things had indeed been on in those slots during the run-up to and prosecution of the second Gulf War. Anyone who fails to notice the running gags in "World War Three" about "massive weapons of destruction", ready in "45 seconds", and a British source via Downing Street giving the UN questionable intelligence on a threat before the group votes on a resolution to go to war probably slept through the last ten years.

The focus of this story is on doing the one thing previous Yeti-in-the-loo *Doctor Who* stories never really grappled with: how the British government dealt with the unfolding crisis. As is so often the case in this series, the story's starting-point is countering a cliché from the twentieth-century version of *Doctor Who* regardless of whether anyone watching was aware of this being a cliché. Throughout the 1970s, we saw Parliamentary Private Secretaries getting caught up in events beyond their ability to send memos to cope with them, as well as endless ministerial visitors to UNIT, all culminating in two stories in rapid succession (10.5, "The Green Death" and 11.2, "Invasion of the Dinosaurs") where the cabinet minister in charge was working for the bad guys. Here, we see the day-to-day functioning of Downing Street disrupted by, in effect, a terrorist outrage.

As we discovered shortly afterwards, the reality isn't quite like what we see here, but, then again, the Prime Minister didn't disappear. This version of how Downing Street works is noticeably different from any previous televised account, especially the most familiar, the sitcom *Yes, Prime Minister*. By definition, this was about the PM's relationship with the people trying to stop him doing anything with his apparent power (specifically the Civil Service) and the chess-game between these two factions. Neither side of that game is represented here, as the focus is on a back-bencher who would not normally get that close to the PM's office. Like Harriet Jones, there really are MPs who think that the normal operations of Parliament should continue under even these circumstances.

Needless to say, the "Flydale North" that Harriet claims to represent doesn't exist in real life, but the cottage hospitals scheme that she mentions is one of many similar proposals being made as various "initiatives" from central government made the National Health Service more bureaucratic and market-led than doctors would like. Tony Blair, who is evidently the Prime Minister found dead in a broom-cupboard, was elected as leader of New Labour, which - with regard to policies on imposing targets on health, education and policing - was almost indistinguishable from the previous Conservative government. What Blair offered was an idea of engagement with what voters wanted, and the sales-pitch involved being a new generation of potential ministers. These came from similar backgrounds to the not-much-older men they replaced, but more of them were women - the press called them The Blair Babes. Seven years on, the lack of noticeable improvements after all these targets had been set led to rumbling disquiet; a former doctor ran as an independent candidate and became a Member of Parliament specifically because he opposed what many saw as turning hospitals (and schools and police forces) into small businesses and focussing on what met the targets rather than what "customers" needed. Harriet's whole plan to include cottage hospitals within the so-called "Centres of Excellence" scheme is the sort of thing the public would have liked, but which nobody within the Westminster bubble would have thought of. The cabinet weren't permitted to say anything against any agreed policy, but back-bench MPs were allowed to go "off-message" so long as they didn't hope to get promoted. Davies is to some extent indulging in wish fulfilment, showing a likeable MP with a popular cause becoming Prime Minister through pluck and ingenuity rather than playing the political games. It helps that this is a ludicrous situation for such a character to be in.

We have to mention that around the time this was being written, the film *Love, Actually* came out, with more publicity than box-office returns. This completed the creation of an alternate universe, Curtisland, that looks a bit like London but runs on different rules. In this, the Prime Minister gets into the kind of scrape only a Hugh Grant character in a Richard Curtis film ever can. The three episodes in Block One (this two-parter and "Rose") are set largely in Curtisland, as are several others, and the conception of 10 Downing Street in the film is what we see here and in "The Sound of Drums" rather than, say, *Torchwood*: "Children of Earth".

[For **Things That Don't Make Sense**, **Critique**, **The Facts** and **Production**, see the next episode.]

X1.5: "World War Three"

(23rd April, 2005)

Which One is This? The Slitheen one, Part Two.

Firsts and Lasts Err... it's the first time we've had a second half of a story this century, and as far as we know, the first time a character has died in mid swear-word: "Oh, boll—" (Granted, we have no way of knowing what the Nestene was saying, and we could conjecture all day on what the Functionary in 10.2, "Carnival of Monsters" said when he was shot.)

Watch Out For...

• After last week's pre-credit sequence spent 30 seconds on "the story so far" and two minutes leading into the titles, this one manages about 20 seconds of the previous episode and five seconds getting out of the cliffhanger. After the epic-length Steven Moffat mini-episodes before the titles, this now seems almost as quaint as performing the cliffhanger all over again, and then standing still over the new episode title (as in the second episode of 1.7, "The Sensorites").

• Harriet Jones has a knack for this kind of thing, and keeps her head in a crisis. Observe how her response to the Doctor's attempt to bluff the Slitheen with the port decanter is to insist that the port is passed to the left. However grave the situation, one must observe the correct forms.

• Rose is showing companion instincts by knowing in advance how to dress for unexpected eventualities. She's picked out a jacket just like Harriet's for her *Scooby Doo* chase around Number 10.

• The Slitheen run around Number 10 with astonishing grace for such big lumps. When they stand still and talk, they move rather more awkwardly. The mismatch between CG effects and people in suits was widely assumed to have failed, and the design of the Slitheen was criticised in some quarters - a reason why Davies opted for the less-imaginative designs such as the pigs in boiler-suits (X3.4, "Daleks in Manhattan"). They disrobe for the hunt, after a rum scene where two fat middle-aged men in a lift are farting and one tells the other "Your body is magnificent."

• Downing Street security seems to be entirely made up of Welshmen. We hope nobody's going to suggest that this is why they are all so bleedin' thick as to trap the Doctor next to a lift door, and to aim their guns at him in such a way that they'd wind up shooting each other.

The Continuity

The Doctor He identifies the Slitheen homeworld solely by starting off a base of 'five thousand planets' in travel distance of Earth, and capable of supporting life with the Slitheen's basic shape, then narrowing it down as Rose and Harriet cite characteristics of the Slitheen including 'They're green', 'They can smell adrenaline' and 'slipstream engine [technology]'. [Whether he does this because he's *incredibly* knowledgeable, or is able to mentally tap some database - TARDIS or otherwise - with details of extraterrestrials is a subject of much debate. See the accompanying essay and his comparative knowledge of the Slitheen in X1.11, "Boom Town".]

He survives the Slitheen's lethal trap by resisting an electrical jolt that is otherwise 'deadly to humans'. The Slitheen, who seem to hunt by smell, walk straight past the Doctor [suggesting that he doesn't give off any scent, despite wearing a leather jacket]. Here the Doctor gives Mickey a computer virus that, when put online, will eradicate all mention of him [an ongoing concern; see also X6.13, "The Wedding of River Song"; X7.5, "The Angels Take Manhattan" and X7.13, "Nightmare in Silver"]. He continues to be less-than-flattering toward humanity in general, claiming the inability of some people to acknowledge the existence of aliens is because they're 'thick'. He seems sincere in his offer to let Mickey join him and Rose in the TARDIS.

• *Ethics*. He resists using the simplest method of saving the world - blow up 10 Downing Street with a missile - because he promised Jackie that he'd keep Rose safe, but accedes to the strategy after Rose and Harriet goad him to do so. He covers for Mickey's reluctance to go on a voyage in the TARDIS by "refusing" to let him come along.

• *Background*. He claims to have contacts in UNIT, but that the Slitheen killed them all in the ambush at 10 Downing Street [a curious thing to say, considering nobody at the meeting approached the Doctor as an old friend]. He seems to have met Mr Chicken, the owner of 10 Downing Street in 1730, and knows about the facility's 1991 security upgrade with the steel shutters. [In February 1991, the IRA managed to get a van carrying a mortar into the street and fired four projectiles - missing a Cabinet meeting and causing light injuries to passers-by. After that, a large gate blocked off the public, who had hitherto been allowed to get right up to the door. What other precautions may have been taken are unclear, for obvious reasons.]

• *Inventory: Sonic Screwdriver*. The Slitheen think the Doctor is bluffing when he claims he can use his sonic screwdriver to alter the chemical composition of wine to make it more flammable [but watch the grimace when he drinks some later]. The screwdriver also over-rides lift controls.

The TARDIS The Doctor has rigged up his Ship with a 70s-style Trimphone handset that calls people in contemporary Britain. [This, a mere 34 years after the Master did it in 8.2, "The Mind of Evil". We presume the Doctor dials 9 for an outside line.]

X1.5 World War Three

The Supporting Cast

• *Rose.* She's still doing that point-and-laugh thing at the Doctor, and almost entirely ignores Mickey. She packs a rucksack to prove commitment to travelling in the TARDIS [but apparently forgets her passport; see "Boom Town"] and tries to reassure her mum. It's possible that she was planning to resume her TARDIS travels before the Doctor tempted her away with a ride to the Horsehead Nebula, as she looks a bit resigned when Jackie is talking about food. At least one of her grandmothers is alive. In what isn't Rose's most intellectual hour, she speculates as to whether the whole "Slitheen are infiltrating the UK government" problem could be dealt with by launching a nuclear bomb at 'em.

Rose's Magic Phone can get calls from Mickey despite being in the "signal-proof" steel cage surrounding the Cabinet room at Number 10. It has a little police-box graphic when the Doctor calls from the TARDIS.

• *Jackie.* She has a lot of garlic in her kitchen and several specialist utensils. [Another sign that she isn't quite the cliché the scripts make her out to be - a *real* chav would live exclusively on processed, ready-made food and lots of junk food, but there isn't a bag of crisps to be seen. This impression is confirmed in part by her offer to cook for the Doctor, albeit a tried-and-tested shepherd's pie rather than anything fancy or experimental.] Mickey has seen Jackie when she's drinking, and thinks it a bad idea to give her alcohol during a crisis.

Like Rose, she has an idiosyncratic pronunciation of the aliens' name, calling them 'Sligeen'. [This is suggestively Irish-sounding - if Jackie and Pete were courting in South London in the mid-80s, they might have been going to the pretend-Irish clubs that were just starting then.]

• *Mickey.* The Doctor talks to Mickey more this episode, and indeed gets a scene alone with him talking about something other than Rose. Mickey has an improbably large amount of pickled foodstuffs in his cupboards - although in true bloke style, he has less idea of the contents than Rose does.

His computer skills are adequate, with the Doctor's help with passwords, to get himself into the UNIT database and over-ride the security protocols. He also has the presence of mind to take a photo of his assailant and send it tor Rose, and to get the Doctor up to speed on what the Slitheen are telling the world about the "threat" from space. He's brave enough to tell Jackie to run while he attacks the fake policeman with a baseball bat [probably a souvenir of a trip to America, as nobody actually plays it here]. He seems more reasoned in his reluctance to go with the Doctor and Rose than his blind terror last time he travelled in the TARDIS ["Rose"].

The official cover-up and press misreporting of what Mickey knows to be true offends him. [By now, he's has been the victim of half-truths and the reluctance of the authorities to accept aliens as a viable explanation to what had really happened to Rose, and has spent the intervening year uncovering the Doctor's past. As we will see, this investigation will take up a lot more of his time.] His bedroom now looks like Clive's shed, covered in alien-spotting ephemera and a footie scarf or two.

Rather disappointingly, he has a copy of *Battlefield Earth* [unless he is trying to uncover the truth about L Ron Hubbard as well]. He doesn't seem to have finished it. [If anyone has, the Guinness Book of Records would be interested.]

The Non-Humans

• *The Slitheen.* Ah! They aren't a race, they're a family. The surname of each is a long string of (oddly Welsh-sounding) nonce-words ending with 'Slitheen'. They are hunters, but the family seen here is a noted criminal clan. Their scam is to irradiate Earth, get it blown up and sell the fragments as fuel. [This seems improbable, but a very similar operation by the titular characters of 6.1, "The Dominators" was intended to power an entire battlefleet with the aid of a seed-device the size of a rugby ball.]

This family comes from Raxacoricofallapatorius, and are on the run. The human-skin suits are an encumbrance and they enjoy running naked, hunting even indoors when they can. Their sense of smell is particularly acute. [The Doctor is able to put them off the scent with a fire-extinguisher, so they must hunt almost exclusively by smell and not have infra-red sight - the size of their eyes is consistent with this, and might indicate extreme difficulty with close-up focus.] Their skin is calcium-based, and dissolves explosively on contact with acetic acid [rather than just fizzing and dissolving as limescale does when you use vinegar to de-scale a kettle or saucepan, causing speculation that the blood-pressure of a Raxacoricofallapatorian

World War Three X1.5

He Remembers This *How*?

There are two scenes in "World War Three" that show the Doctor performing hitherto unseen feats of recall. We've seen him dredge things up from his past or his background knowledge in extraordinary detail, but here he not only rummages through a database of aliens he's not personally encountered, but somehow recalls events that didn't happen. Not recognising such a prominent historical figure (he says) as Harriet Jones isn't just a temporary absent-mindedness, i.e. forgetting something that would have been handy to recall earlier (as with not recognising the Queen in 25.3, "Silver Nemesis"), but almost seems from the way it is presented here to be a function of her change in historical status.

Let's run with this theory for a bit... we might imagine that had the Pertwee Doctor visited the future from the UNIT lab, he wouldn't have found any record of Harriet Jones' Golden Age following the post-Slitheen reconstruction, *because no such event happened*. (See, by contrast, how time operates per events documented *before* the Doctor arrives on hand in **How Many Cyber-Races are There?** under X2.6, "The Age of Steel".) It's possible that the Doctor's presence "softens" history so that it can be redirected when he has been present at a crucial juncture.

Now that history has been changed, Harriet is destined, apparently, for a three-term stint as Prime Minister which ushers in "Britain's new Golden Age". The Doctor sort-of remembers this, his grasp getting better the closer he is to the events that start this new possibility coming to pass. Those events seem not to be pre-ordained, but form part of a revised timeline (see **How Does Time Work...** under 9.1, "Day of the Daleks"). The oddness of this is compounded by the lack of time he has to have explored the future that can now unfold before he curtails it all again by deposing her (X2.0, "The Christmas Invasion"). He does it again in X1.12, "Bad Wolf", where his day in a timeline he caused but had not visited starts by not making any sense to him, but after a few moments talking to Lynda has details such as the future game show *Bear With Me* surfacing. It's in the next episode that he confesses to Rose-as-Bad-Wolf that knowing what was possibly going to happen as well as all past and future is part of his life ("... and doesn't it drive yer mad?"). It doesn't stop there, as we will see, but the obvious question to ask is how he is doing this.

Two possibilities spring immediately to mind: the TARDIS and the Time Vortex. The Doctor has been initiated as a potential Time Lord by exposure to the Untempered Schism (X3.12, "The Sound of Drums"; X4.18, "The End of Time Part Two") and this could mark the start of his ability not only to manipulate events, but to tell which events are off-limits (**What Constitutes a "Fixed Point"?** under X4.2, "The Fires of Pompeii"). This must entail a sense for what consequences flow from a decision. In that case, how does the Doctor ever make a mistake, a misjudgement or a discovery? In fact, why does he need to go out and discover anything for himself? The only way this ability would avoid contradicting the whole premise or the series is if it is an unreliable, vague, foggy intuition rather than the detailed factual recall we see in those two episodes. The one time the Doctor speaks about a gut-instinct the Time Lords have about time is when trying to excuse his "prejudice" against Jack (X3.11, "Utopia"); even then, he knows he ought not to and rather feebly blames the TARDIS for not rescuing Inn-dee-struct-a-bullll Captain Harkness.

The TARDIS, on the other hand, has known attributes that match some of what we see. It is explicitly stated, and indeed the regeneration follows from this revelation, that the Ship taps into the brain of anyone who travels in her to translate and who knows what else. This obviously means that everyone around is having their thoughts monitored (see **Who Narrates This Series?** under 23.1, "The Mysterious Planet"), and that this somehow extends to long periods before the Ship materialises. (Otherwise, the Matrix account of events on the *Hyperion* would not have been as it is shown in 23.3, "Terror of the Vervoids".) It might be that the TARDIS can access data on wherever the Doctor lands her and download it to the Doctor's head on request; that information perhaps including data from timestreams as-yet uncreated. That makes sense of *some* of what we see, but not all. Once again, if this were an infallible system of data-delivery, the Doctor would never need to ask questions or tap into computers, and would never, ever, intervene. It makes nonsense of the Doctor's curiosity and eagerness to experi

continued on Page 85...

X1.5 World War Three

is higher than that of a human - but the execution method explained in "Boom Town" would seem to contradict this]. The Slitheen posing as Joseph Green says he 'felt' the death of one of his relatives [perhaps the Slitheen have some latent empathy toward their kin, but if so, this talent is never mentioned again]. The collars that control their body-compression can conduct a paralysing electrical charge by remote.

Last episode, the Slitheen pretending to be Margaret Blaine showed off her grasp of phrases such as 'shaking my booty' - now we see that she's surprised that the red phone really *is* red, while 'Joseph Green' dies saying 'Oh, bollocks!' [They *have* done their homework.]

History When all is said and done, *The Evening Standard* [and presumably other media outlets too] airs suspicions that the Slitheen incident was a giant 'hoax'. [Humanity's formal recognition that aliens exist will be an ongoing concern - see in particular X2.0, "The Christmas Invasion"; X2.10, "Love & Monsters"; and X4.12, "The Stolen Earth".]

The Slitheen plot hopes to capitalise on a [galactic? inter-galactic? interstellar?] 'recession' happening 'out there'. The Doctor generalises Earth as having 'five billion' people [a population of six billion was reached in 1999].

Catchphrase Counter Rose tells Harriet that lots of planets have a North [1.1, "Rose"]. Harriet persists in telling everyone who she is ('Harriet Jones, MP for Flydale North').

The Analysis

English Lessons ("Aliens of London" and "World War Three")

• *MP*. Member of Parliament. There are 650 of these, so any party that can muster 326 or more in an election gets to run the country for five years or so. Only 22 of the 326-or-more on the Government's bench (the green seats in the House of Commons don't actually have that many spaces, but "bench" is the usual term for position in the Commons) are on the Cabinet. The Opposition have "Shadow" ministers to match these, making up the Shadow Cabinet (a term which has been taken for granted for centuries, despite sounding like a bad gothic anthology). An MP who isn't any of these is a "back-bencher", like Harriet Jones.

• *Dinner* (n.) *Tea* (n.) It used to be simple - you have a big breakfast, a substantial mid-day meal and a light meal in the evening (and maybe something stodgy just before bed, a "supper"). Then we went and set up colonies in hot countries. In India and Africa and the Caribbean and Australia and South East Asia and all sorts of other places where northern Europeans don't feel comfortable, the local habits prevailed. Big breakfast, of course, but a light lunch, a big tea (or "tiffin" if you were in the Raj) and a more substantial dinner when the sun went down. This set-up came to be associated with those who were "officer class" - or wanted to be thought so - and thus calling the mid-day meal "dinner" was frightfully *declassé*.

• *Sale of the Century* (n) notoriously cheap 70s gameshow, from Norwich, a relative backwater, and presented by Nicholas Parsons (26.3, "The Curse of Fenric"). People competed for lawnmowers and exercise-bikes, as there were laws about the maximum value of prizes on offer in UK television.

• *Viennetta* (n.): a cheap-but-fancy ice-cream cake, made by Walls (the main manufacturer of mass-produced ice-cream in the UK). If Jackie's got one in the fridge without there being a special occasion, she must be doing pretty well. (It's not massively costly, but people who buy them at all do so for celebrations rather than as part of the weekly shop.) Maybe she was saving it for Rose's return.

Oh, Isn't That...? ("Aliens of London" and "World War Three")

• *Matt Baker*. A real-life *Blue Peter* presenter reacting exactly as a real-life *Blue Peter* presenter ought to, by making a spaceship cake. (His then co-hosts get to behave right out of character in the pilot of *The Sarah Jane Adventures*.)

• *Andrew Marr*. Former editor of *The Independent* who became the BBC's chief political correspondent, then the main interviewer for Radio 4's *Start the Week* and his own Sunday morning show. He also gets to do big-ticket documentaries and, bizarrely, covered the inauguration (first time around) of the Large Hadron Collider. What he doesn't do is live coverage to camera from Downing Street, as he is seen to do here (cf. our comments about BBC policy about reporters playing fictional versions of themselves for 9.1, "Day of the Daleks").

World War Three X1.5

He Remembers This *How*?

continued from Page 83...

ence things at first hand if he knows everything in advance and never learns anything. We have to work on the assumption that this ability is an option and not a direct feed. In which case, what exactly is happening?

The readers of the tie-in books will have one idea about this: in one of the other Time Wars in which the Doctor destroyed Gallifrey (don't worry, it grew back), the Matrix - the all-knowing database made of the minds of all dead Time Lords (and the living President) - was popped into his head for safe keeping. At this point, being the Paul McGann Doctor, he lost his memory - again. As the BBC was still publishing this range of books when the first episodes of New *Who* went out, there was reason to suspect that nothing in the broadcast stories would overtly contradict them. Although the "mainframe" of the TARDIS is subsequently referred to as her "matrix" (and "Sexy" and "Idris"; see X6.4, "The Doctor's Wife"), we don't know if it's just another matrix, like the translation matrix (X6.7, "A Good Man Goes to War") or the capital-M Matrix that used to be kept on 2" video-tape (23.4, "The Ultimate Foe").

It's significant that when a new series of books began, the ninth Doctor is rummaging through memorised databases for info stops after this one bravura display. It may also be worth noting that his more gradual info-dump faculty in revised timelines is almost identical to the way Steve Baxter gets prompts from above in Davies' *The Second Coming*. The jibe that Eccleston was going to play the Doctor "like Jesus but brave" is almost true here, but the significant factor is that only *his* Doctor really does this. (As we saw in Volume 1, there have been instances of the original Doctor pulling facts about places he seems not to have visited from some kind of mental Baedeker - notoriously 2.5, "The Web Planet" - but the only precedent for the precise technique of "whittling it down" was in the *Doctor Who Weekly* comic strip "The Iron Legion".)

The matter to settle is whether the information we see the Doctor accessing is from his factual knowledge or seems to him like personal experience. If changing a timeline means rewriting his memory, he might well "recall" events in his past life in this revised timeline. Obviously, as someone who has been present at key moments in any timeline, he's going to have been in whatever past or future is summoned into being by his actions - unless the change is to something massive very early on. (Although this may have happened, or unhappened: see X3.0, "The Runaway Bride" and **Why's He So Freaked Out by a Big Orange Bloke?** under X2.9, "The Satan Pit".) This may also account for the Doctor's ability to visit or know about historical events that have been called into question since the episode in which they are mentioned was written and recorded (see 3.3, "The Myth Makers"; X5.9, "Cold Blood" and **Whom Did They Meet at the Top of the World?** under 1.4, "Marco Polo"). And those events are going to have been part of who he is now, even though he seems remarkably consistent regardless of how much his past has changed. We note that John Smith has a lot of memories of things the TARDIS has invented as part of his biography (X3.8, "Human Nature"), and can foresee an entire future that will never happen.

And here we return to the minority opinion concerning Time-Lord regeneration: as we saw in **What Happens in a Regeneration?** under 11.5, "Planet of the Spiders", it has been suggested that the Doctor's entire past is revised retrospectively by this event (much as seems to have been happening in 22.4, "The Two Doctors", when the second Doctor being turned into a semi-Androgum changes how the sixth Doctor behaves without, it seems, affecting all the incidents his in-between lives have caused). So, for example, we needn't speculate that the Dalek in "The Power of the Daleks" (4.3) only recognised the newly-regenerated Doctor because of an unbroadcast encounter between that incarnation and the Daleks later in his life, on the grounds that those events might have occurred while he looked like William Hartnell, but the event after the regeneration was remodelled so that he had always looked like Patrick Troughton. The only people who remember any different are Ben and Polly (and the Doctor himself). The theory has never been overtly backed up but small details, such as the coat Janis Joplin gave the Doctor before it would have fit him (X3.3, "Gridlock"; X2.0, "The Christmas Invasion") and the number of nonexistent gaps

continued on Page 87...

X1.5 World War Three

- *Penelope Wilton* (Harriet Jones). She had just been in previous Davies project *Bob and Rose* when this was made, and had also been in *Shaun of the Dead* and follow-up *Hot Fuzz*. Before that, she'd been in *The Borrowers* (the BBC version, not the stupidly miscast film) and quintessential suburban sitcom *Ever Decreasing Circles*. More recently, she's been in the ITV hit *Downton Abbey*.
- *Annette Badland* (Margaret Blaine). Her first role was as the omniscient secretary in *Bergerac* (see Volume 5). After playing the manipulative nurse in *Inside Victor Lewis-Smith*, she was all over television like a rash. She's going to be back in "Boom Town" (sorry about the spoiler) and shortly thereafter was Jack Woolley's manipulative daughter in *The Archers*.
- *Naoko Mori* (Dr Sato). She had been Saffie's even geekier friend in *Absolutely Fabulous*, and the hitherto unknown (i.e. fictional) sixth Spice Girl in *Spiceworld: The Movie*. Later, she'd play Yoko opposite Eccleston as Lennon in *Lennon Naked*. You may also have seen her in *Torchwood*.

Things That Don't Make Sense ("Aliens of London" and "World War Three") [There is a huge inexplicable item and several related smaller anomalies about Jackie and Mickey and their domestic arrangements that give us a whole essay's worth of British social history to play with - see **Why is Trinity Wells on Jackie's Telly?** - which you've probably just read, so we'll leave all that to one side for now.]

We'll start with the first title of this two-parter. Specifically, the preposition: why is it "Aliens *of* London" rather than "in", "at", "over", "near"...? The hint seems to be that they are indigenous, and the ruse with the pig was to make people think that standard-issue *Avengers*-style malfeasants were at work hoaxing the authorities (as in that most *Avengers*-ish story, 12.1, "Robot"). Was this what an earlier draft would have revealed? The other possible meaning of this curious title is that it's a riff on Warren Zevon's *Werewolves of London*, and it's true that the Slitheen have a hint of lycanthropy about them. But this is also not really prominent in the finished script, and a lot of other episodes this year have been renamed (including the next one, which began life as "10 Downing Street"), so why not this one?

The operation of Parliament isn't exactly as shown here. If the PM is indisposed, there is a tried-and-tested line of succession that doesn't include a minor DEFRA official in charge of sugar. The Deputy PM was, for all of Tony Blair's term, John Prescott (a stocky enough chap to have been taken for Slitheen use, but too obvious for Davies to risk parodying) and the Chancellor of the Exchequer, Gordon Brown, would have run the country if both of them were unavailable (he's hardly svelte either). For all 22 members of the Cabinet, plus the various Lords, *all* to have been either out of the country or dead is the only possible way the Slitheen posing as 'Joseph Green' could get to be PM. Had this happened, the Opposition would have taken measures to get either emergency powers or a suspension of Parliament. The remarkable thing about General Asquith (the real one) threatening Martial law is that this ought to have been mooted earlier, when a complete nobody like Green got himself promoted beyond his experience.

And from this we come to the single most surprising thing about this story's *donnée* - aliens have arrived, the Prime Minister has vanished and nobody's made the connection. You would think comedians would be on telly making the 'take me to your leader' joke the Doctor makes (or, if it's Tony Blair, wise-cracks about visitors to this planet having more idea what normal people are interested in than him). If the real Margaret Blaine's job was to arrange his diary, and Blon Fel Fotch Passamir Day Slitheen's job was to pose as Margaret to make the PM's disappearance seem unconnected, why is even someone well out of the loop, such as Dr Sato, aware that he's missing? Margaret's arrest ought to have been immediate, and the country would be on an anti-terrorism alert even before the spaceship arrived. All those shots of the public rushing about and blocking roads are completely impossible - everyone would be staying at home and fielding phone calls from relatives. And if 10 Downing Street is a crime-scene, why is the whole alien taskforce thing happening there and not in the more secure offices - COBRA (Cabinet Operations Briefing Room A), for example? How are the Intelligence agencies not vetting all these odd visitors? (That would be the real Margaret Blaine's job, yet nobody's noticed that she's not doing it.) So the PM and up to 22 Cabinet ministers are away from their desks, and not one of the many police officers on the scene has been able to look in the cupboards. Nor have they asked any questions of the staff. Nor have they closed off Downing Street, the obvious first

World War Three

He Remembers This *How*?

continued from Page 85...

between episodes in which that particular Doctor is supposed to have done things (see, for example, 17.6, "Shada" and 14.4, "The Face of Evil"). It covers, perhaps, the way that Clive's record only shows the Eccleston Doctor and LINDA only seem to know about the Tennant version (X1.1, "Rose"; X2.10, "Love & Monsters"). If this theory is correct, had Joan Redfern ever opted to investigate John Smith's past, those details he suddenly "recalls" would all actually have happened as part of a revised timeline with Smith in it from birth. It is certainly true that the Doctor's anecdotes all seem to fall into line with the personality of that specific Doctor. Can this really be what was happening?[18]

The detail about Ben and Polly recalling the previous Doctor chimes with what we see in recent episodes - namely, that TARDIS travellers are able to recall their own experiences in altered timelines. Rose can adjust the circumstances of her father's death and knows both versions (X1.8, "Father's Day"; X1.13, "The Parting of the Ways") and Kazran Sardick has mutually exclusive childhoods vying for his attention (X6.0, "A Christmas Carol"). There is thus a definite link between memory and time-travel. Anyone who has been in the TARDIS has their memories of all timelines they visit copy-protected (except, perhaps, Sarah Jane Smith - we'll discuss what she seems to remember of 12.4, "Genesis of the Daleks" in X4.13, "Journey's End". Also, compare 13.4, "The Android Invasion" with *The Sarah Jane Adventures* story "Warriors of Kudlak", and consider what she thinks the TARDIS key looks like in *SJA*: "Death of the Doctor".) This, to the relief of some of you, means we can (probably) discard the theory about regeneration, as UNIT passes retain the old photos (26.1, "Battlefield") whilst the Brigadier doesn't recognise the newly-regenerated Doctor in "Spearhead from Space" (7.1).

The one apparent anomaly left is that when the idea of altering timelines is first discussed in any more detail than the Doctor saying "Don't!", Steven and Vicki - and the Doctor - seem to think that the second that the Monk (one of the Doctor's people) alters the outcome of the Battle of Hastings, their own memories will be unwritten. The Doctor's belief that this is true suggests that he's never experienced any such thing. (This would follow his own paranoia on the subject, and his subsequent relief at successfully causing history - see 2.9, "The Time Meddler"; 1.6, "The Aztecs"; 2.4, "The Romans"; and **Are We Touring Theme-Park History?** under X2.7, "The Idiot's Lantern".) Yet the prospect of changing the Doctor's past slightly, so that he recalls events as soon as the cause of them has come into being, is still around. As we will see in Volume 9, there is a whole new version of how time can be altered that begins in the Steven Moffat era (see **Is Time Like Bolognese Sauce Now?** under X5.5, "Flesh and Stone"), and which seems to follow a different logic from the stories we are considering now.

However, alterations to the Doctor's own past within this phase of the series (2005-2010) are worth further consideration. Doing it to himself is presented as a top-quality no-no, of the same order as altering a Fixed Point, and only ever proposed as an option when the Daleks are about to destroy humanity ("The Parting of the Ways"). Even then, it is a bluff and the Doctor would literally rather die. Altering Rose's past was tricky enough, as we saw in "Father's Day" - that's such a mess as to warrant its own essay.

If we look at incidents where memories have been removed or blocked, they are almost always TARDIS passengers. Jamie and Zoe (6.7, "The War Games"; 20.7, "The Five Doctors"), the Brigadier (20.3, "Mawdryn Undead"), the Doctor ("The War Games" and 10.1, "The Three Doctors"; 15.6, "The Invasion of Time"), Rose ("The Parting of the Ways", although she seems to get better by X2.2, "Tooth and Claw" and is happily reminiscing about the day she wiped out the Daleks in X2.13, "Doomsday") and Donna ("Journey's End") have events not just scrubbed, but placed behind a firewall until a specific point. Note that in the *Bear With Me* incident, the Doctor was suffering from temporary amnesia after being wrenched out of time - something similar happened at the start of "The Mysterious Planet" and just possibly "The Wheel In Space" (5.7). Presumably each Doctor's memory of the poly-Doctor pile-ups is blocked at regeneration until after the last time he experiences the event (except, apparently, X3.13a, "Time Crash", although the tenth Doctor seems to be recalling it as the events unfold and not in advance

continued on Page 89...

87

move of the police in any emergency.

Not for the last time, we have to posit a special UNIT-issue stealth helicopter that can arrive suddenly without anyone hearing its approach ten minutes earlier (see X4.17, "The End of Time Part One" for a more spectacular version). What makes this more silly is that the chopper arrives while the Doctor and his friends are using the TARDIS sensor array. Doubly silly is the way in which Mickey escapes on foot, despite the number of soldiers that have arrived to surround the TARDIS and round up the Doctor's party.

And UNIT still has a lot to learn about alien incursions: the usual procedure is that they shoot at an alien to no avail until an anonymous squaddie gets zapped or squashed (depending on the size of their antagonist). However, no-one seems to tell them that alien blood would contain things far more deadly than a zap-gun, so even if you *could* harm them with bullets, that might only be the start of your troubles.

The whole time-scale of this story is a bit weird, as days in March aren't that long. And what time are we saying the TARDIS arrived? It's bright sunshine, so we're looking at no later than 8.00am. If the spaceship arrived at 9.50(ish) or not, depending on which shot we go with for the crash, the police must have detained the Doctor for at most one and a half hours. Precisely why they were called is a matter for conjecture. And yet, it took Jackie's phone call in the small hours of the following morning for the Doctor's presence to be noted? Well, maybe the Code Nine software only trips when there's an official emergency, but then what if the Doctor's been around for a while before anyone in authority notices anything untoward (as usually happens)? This system works on the assumption that a crisis arises and *then* the TARDIS lands - it's happened twice in countless contemporary Earth-based stories (5.5, "The Web of Fear"; 11.2, "Invasion of the Dinosaurs"). Alternatively, someone had to have mentioned the Doctor and the TARDIS in reply to the government's plea for information.

But the time's still weird: the Ten O'Clock news is starting when Mickey sees the Doctor, and Mickey rushes to see Rose and tell her the Doctor's 'just left'. Yet between these two events, Dr Sato is discussing the pig 'mermaid' and a clock says five to eleven.

A continuity concern in light of later *Doctor Who* and *Torchwood* stories... what precisely is geekmoppet Toshiko Sato of Torchwood Cardiff doing examining a pig in a spacesuit in London? Here we are, a good year before the Battle of Canary Wharf (X2.13, "Doomsday"), so there are a few hundred equally well-qualified Torchwood staff just a mile away without having to call in someone based in Wales. And most of *them* have also - unlike Toshiko - managed to avoid being locked away in UNIT's very own Guantanamo for stealing ultra-hush secret tech. (Yes, Jack wiped Tosh's official record, but UNIT would still know who she is, as she was their captive less than a year ago and they were going to make an example of her.) We also have the relatively minor problem that Torchwood's *raison d'etre* is to apprehend the Doctor - even allowing that Torchwood Cardiff seems to have been acting independently of the Canary Wharf Mob after 1999 (*Torchwood*: "Fragments"), it just makes it even more improbable that Yvonne Hartman's lot haven't sent anyone once it's registered that the Doctor is in the vicinity.

An anomaly with Rose's age: if she's been gone a year as the missing person posters for her indicate (and those posters don't look like they've been up more than a day - it rains in London, especially in March), then giving her age as '19' now means that she's *actually* only 18. Has she lied to the Doctor, or has Jackie somehow forgotten her missing daughter's birthday? (An early 1987 DOB maybe helps with the apparent goof in X1.8, "Father's Day", but messes up the whole A-Levels and boyfriends backstory, unless we posit something a bit unsavoury about Mickey.)

Once the Slitheen have shed their human skins (because 'victory should be naked'), how do they intend to pick up the phone (when the UN calls) with their giant clawed hands? It's also curious that when the Slitheen masquerading as the police officer who attacks Jackie removes his cap, his forehead actually *has* a zipper off to the side - none of the other Slitheen display this tell-tale sign. And the biggest glitch of all: UNIT's security is so feeble that anyone in possession of the password 'buffalo' (it's not even deliberately misspelled!) can launch a missile from a British *Trafalgar* class sub, and counter-act all efforts to stop it from destroying the United Kingdom's seat of government.

He Remembers This *How*?

continued from Page 87...

– but see that story's essay).

All of this makes Amy Pond's forgetting Rory all the more baffling (although not as baffling as the builders of the Pandorica being able to reconstitute him in plastic from memories she doesn't have - see "Cold Blood"). It does, however, remove the embarrassment of the Doctor apparently living through events he's already seen happen twice before ("Terror of the Vervoids") and travelling with someone who's met him before he met her ("The Ultimate Foe") and who has an eidetic memory. (That last detail is another complication: Mel is yanked out of time to speak as an eye-witness to events that haven't happened yet, despite the process of time-yankage causing the Doctor's memory to cloud even on things he was doing ten minutes earlier.)

However, closer examination of what is on screen, ignoring accreted fan-lore and tie-in works, makes the Doctor's faulty recall more significant. If the impact of altered timelines on memory is a function of TARDIS travel, as it now appears to be, then removal from ambiguous temporal states might "unwrite" memories for companions the way it did for the combatants/specimens in "The War Games". Carstairs, Arturo Villar and the rest had memory blocks not just to enable them to be abducted from their time-zones, but *as a side effect thereof*. The Scientist who adjusts the memories of the new intakes uses what seems to be the same technology that controls the SIDRAT time-machines. Changes to the TARDIS herself also seem to completely efface their own traces (see X7.11, "Journey to the Centre of the TARDIS") and sometimes complete loops that the Doctor only properly recalls after the second iteration (9.1, "Day of the Daleks").

This resolves a few points. First, and most egregiously, Sarah meets the Doctor at Deffry Vale school with no idea that "The Five Doctors" ever happened. Jamie and Zoe forget all but their first meeting with the Doctor as an effect of being replaced in their hitherto "predestined" time-streams, not as a malicious punishment by the Time Lords. Donna's "biological metacrisis" is "biological" because a Time Lord can adjust to it, but is a "metacrisis" perhaps, because so many timelines have been made to converge on her, not because she is the weaker vessel (the monocardial "spare" Doctor is allowed to retain his memories for his curtailed lifespan and stay on as Rose's Doctor-shaped sex-toy). Most pleasingly for readers of these books, Jamie can be told all about the Time Lords ("The Two Doctors") safely because he and the Doctor have been wrenched from "coterminous time" on a mission, which is also why they look so much older (see "Time Crash"), and the only "Season 6B" we need is the latter half of 2011's ration of episodes. We might also mention the TARDIS' curious decision to wipe the memories of the people able to fix the glitch causing impending disaster (1.3, "Edge of Destruction") and to knock out any humans aboard (1.1, "An Unearthly Child").

However, both Donna and Amy are capable of flashbacks... or are they? Is it not perhaps more accurate to say that they are in a state of quantum uncertainty between convergent (or overlapping) but distinct "edits" of their past? (See, amongst others, X2.11, "Fear Her" and **What is the Blinovitch Limitation Effect?** under "Mawdryn Undead", and **What Makes the TARDIS Work?** under "The Edge of Destruction".) As with photons "choosing" to be waves or particles and causing interference-patterns in the Two-Slit experiment, a world-line "next door" can apparently affect the agent of change (Rose, Donna, the Toclafane - X3.13, "Last of the Time Lords" - and maybe others) and lead to two equally "true" sets of facts. Donna's memories of the Doctor aren't triggered by anything reminiscent of her journeys, such as wasps, Agatha Christie novels, weddings, Christmas or togas, so what's different about that day (in X4.17, "The End of Time Part One")? Obviously, the presence of six billion Time Lords on her world and the arrival of Gallifrey from a sealed-off reality. As with the Doctor's growing recognition of the Harriet Jones-as-PM timeline as it approaches certainty, so Donna is less able to withstand the pressure to be what she "ought" to have been in another timeline. If this is true, then what the Doctor did to her when he appeared to be simply hypnotising her into forgetting (X4.13, "Journey's End") is altering her timeline alone, with Wilf's and everyone else's as it was: he is unravelling their past together the way the Crack unwrote Rory Williams from every-

continued on Page 91...

X1.5 World War Three

Critique ("Aliens of London" and "World War Three") The usual thing to say when reviewing this story is to gripe about the "uneven tone" and whinge that farting fat guys aren't in keeping with the kind of serious, emotional drama this story is for most of the time. This is, as Joseph Green would say, bollocks. The entire story is a primary-coloured cartoon, and all the tears and tantrums are bitter-coating a sugar pill. The view of how Parliament works, what life on a Council estate is like and relationships between mothers and daughters is drawn from children's television, not from life. Specifically, Jackie Tyler is a third-generation photocopy of characters from soaps, and not even British ones: she's basically Janelle Timmins from *Neighbours*. The single mum desperate to prove she's still "got it" and denigrating her prettier, cleverer daughter is a regular comic turn in British soaps[18], but it took an Australian series to distil it into an identifiable form (and Janelle was the current incarnation in the most-watched soap among the nation's under-20s). Roald Dahl aliens, Aussie-soap mums and *Demon Headmaster* politics all existed on the same plane for the teenage girls in 2005 Britain, and, as these were the target audience, that's the level at which success or failure was to be judged on first broadcast.

The next routine observation is that the Slitheen were a failure because they don't match the CG sequences to the live-action prosthetics well enough. It's helpful to remember that the Mill got an Oscar for their effects for *Gladiator*, but the tigers and whatever in that don't really match the live-action surroundings. This is the sort of thing that matters to people who watch films *because* of the effects rather than for story, but anyone either raised on old-style *Doctor Who* - or judging this by the standards of the usual fare for teenagers in early twenty-first century Britain - is used to accepting effects as storytelling conventions. The Slitheen keep coming back for a reason. Conceptually, and as characters, they work. Two second-long shots in an episode where Billie Piper isn't running very convincingly either aren't a deal-breaker.

If there is a tension at the heart of this, it is between what Russell T Davies has to say about the scenario he's developing and what he can say on a family show. The starting-point, as with almost everything he wrote up to this point, was to take a pre-existing TV trope and ask "What would *really* happen?" Even *Mine All Mine* can be categorised as this kind of thought-experiment (imagine inheriting Swansea). *Queer as Folk* was colliding the corny soap token-gay storylines against his own experience. In this case, it's the First Contact/Yeti-in-the-loo format of *Doctor Who*. His definition of "reality" is the problem, as we've said, but more for the 7.00pm Saturday Night slot. He is reining in his speculations from the sort of thing he wrote in the *New Adventures* book *Damaged Goods*. What has to be borne in mind when watching this story is the extent to which it is a critique (in the literal sense) of the thinking behind all previous present-day *Doctor Who* stories, and every instance of an actor playing the humanoid disguise of a much bulkier rubber-suit alien.

Once this is taken as the starting-point, a lot of other details become significant and the story is a lot cleverer than it appeared. The Doctor's guesses about the Slitheen being a race are wrong; their intention is only revealed after all the usual reasons for taking over Earth are evaluated and found wanting; and all the things that happen in blockbuster Hollywood films of this kind are tried, shown to be ridiculous and abandoned in favour of asking better questions. It's a script that has its cake (made by a *Blue Peter* presenter) and eats it.

Along the way, we get the by now-standard Davies ploys of real newsreaders, crowds panicking in the streets, fake footage on telly in the background and two or three ordinary people in the eye of the storm. He's had a bit of practice at this, and the two units making this footage get it about right. Broadening out the narrative to a global news event falls a bit flat (as we see in the essay last episode), but that comes with experience later on. Quibbles about the CG Slitheen aside, nothing goes disastrously wrong with the directing as we got to see it, despite all the rumours of tensions on set. A few dud notes, such as Mickey pratfalling as he runs into a garage door, might not work for adults evaluating this (or rather, for over-earnest adolescent boys wanting everything to be lip-bitingly "serious"). However, within minutes of that instance, we have the model for how to watch the new series. The "alien" is a pig in a spacesuit, but it's been made by aliens as bait; something that looks like a sight-gag is a deadly double-bluff.

More crucially, the Doctor, Rose and Harriet defeat the aliens by having occasionally paid attention at school and integrating what they

He Remembers This *How*?

continued from Page 89...

one's life except the Doctor's and (sometimes) Amy's. Amy is somehow able to remember an entire divergent life (X6.13, "The Wedding of River Song", although in that life the details of her "real" existence are muddled and she has no idea she's married to Captain Williams).

As each change to history is made, the recall of other iterations fades a bit more. Thus when Earth is abducted and made part of a Reality Bomb (X4.12, "The Stolen Earth"), it takes the Doctor longer than any old-skool fan watching to figure out that this is a variation on an earlier Dalek ploy (2.2, "The Dalek Invasion of Earth"). This is worrying, because that incident led to him losing his granddaughter. If a memory like *that* can be unwritten, everything else is contingent. (And what precisely befalls any Time Lord stuck in a timeline that now never happened we'll look at in **What Happened to Susan?** under "The End of Time Part Two".) On the other hand, it would seem that the "closer" a timeline comes, the better an idea the Doctor has of how the land lies in this palimpsest. We saw in 18.6, "The Keeper of Traken", that Adric was unable to follow the Doctor's journal of his travels partly because events described on one page then turn out to never have occurred. That the Doctor needed such a record is itself remarkable.

This might therefore be a big clue in one of the biggest puzzles the new series has to offer. We are seeing alterations to the timelines hither and yon, and history is more malleable than ever before, yet there is no possibility of easy travel between parallel universes (explicitly stated in X2.5, "Rise of the Cybermen"). The TARDIS can slip into changed futures on Satellite Five and the Doctor soon "remembers" details - but when stuck in Pete's World, not only does the Ship blow its stack, but the Doctor has no idea who's in charge, how things work or even that there isn't another Rose (at least, not a bipedal one). Bear this in mind for **Bad Wolf - What, How and Why?** under "The Parting of the Ways"; and **How is This Not a Parallel Universe?** under X4.11, "Turn Left".

It is therefore more significant even than it seems that the newly-regenerated Doctor has no sooner regrown his arm ("The Christmas Invasion") than he comprehensively wrecks Earth's history by making the unambiguous First Contact coincide with the end of a seemingly-definite timeline where Harriet Jones gets three terms. The version of early twenty-first century Britain he now revisits has been pushed out of range of his innate/TARDIS-aided info-dump memory. Never again, and definitely not after Jones' apparent place in history is taken by the Master and then that is undone too, can the Doctor sniff out resolving timelines for "memories" of the near-future.

recall in inventive ways. Penelope Wilton in particular sells this scene, and makes Harriet the first genuinely likeable authority-figure since the "good" Borusa (15.6, "The Invasion of Time"), and the most rounded since the Brigadier. Everyone, even the non-actors (especially Andrew Marr), does what they ought to do here, taking it just seriously enough without getting bogged down. The actors playing Slitheen bring a genuine twinkle to the gleeful, infantile behaviour of naughty monsters in positions of power (Davies obviously enjoyed this, as not only did he bring Margaret back that year, he re-used the situation for the Master and the Toclafane in Series Three). In particular, actor David Verrey manages to make Joseph Green funny, menacing and plausibly an alien in a human-skin suit.

What's most clearly visible now is that this is one of the roads not taken. There are so many ways to do *Doctor Who*, and the BBC Wales team opted to restrict themselves to a few obvious and practical ones. They used this story as a test-bed for techniques they would need later and styles of storytelling they could exploit - but they chose not to follow up all the ways they could have progressed from this starting-point. The monsters became more predictable, more obviously men in rubber suits. The relationship between Mickey and Jackie simplified. The mix of topical satire and fart-gags was dropped for either-or, and became mainly digs at celebrity culture. Most significantly, the effects slowly worked their way into the narrative, rather than being something counterpointing the real drama of three people in one room and two in another wresting control of the fate of the world whilst arguing about relationships. For whatever reason (and it wasn't ratings or Audience Appreciation indices), the produc-

X1.5 World War Three

tion team decided that this story was somehow deficient and chose not to do anything quite like it again. An already risk-averse version of *Doctor Who* became more timid as a result. It did make bold stories every so often, and could do so on the back of the goodwill this first phase of the Welsh series generated. But this story marks the furthest limit of a particular style of story, and there would be slightly less of a sense that anything could happen from now on.

The Facts

Written by Russell T Davies. Directed by Keith Boak.

Viewing figures: [From "World War Three" on, there were two BBC3 repeats, one just after midnight and thus on Sunday morning, and a second at 7.00pm that same day.] "Aliens of London": (BBC1) 7.63 million, (BBC3 repeat) 0.6 million. "World War Three": (BBC1) 7.98 million, (BBC3 repeats) 0.2 and 0.6 million.

Alternate Versions Trzecia wojna swiatowa, Der Dritte Weltkrieg, Troisème Guerre Mondiale. The French version, curiously, retains the "lots of planets have a North" gag, even though David Manet, dubbing le Docteur, isn't noticeably more Northern than anyone else in this episode (see X1.9, "Drole de Morte" for an attempt at approximating a regional accent). "Shepherd's pie" becomes "Espagnol", rather cleverly. "Slitheen" is pronounced "Sly teen".

Production

("Aliens of London" and "World War Three"): As with many of Davies' non-*Who* projects, the starting-point was looking at a well-worn scenario and asking "What would *really* happen?". In this case, one option looked at was the set-up for the 1959 serial *Quatermass and the Pit*, wherein archaeologists find a prehistoric ruin with a spaceship in it, and discover that human folklore and prejudices come from alien intervention in our evolution. However, the previous series by the same author, Nigel Kneale, is as pertinent to what we got. In *Quatermass II*, a species manipulates key individuals into using political, military and industrial schemes to their own ends. The conspiracy includes ministers, and a crusading backbench MP is got at just as Bernard Quatermass is getting to the truth. In both stories, the shock revelation is not that aliens are doing the nasty to us, but that it's been going on for a while right in front of us.

As Davies developed the idea, it became more child-friendly, with the conspirators being faintly absurd and gross. At one point, he thought about changing the nature of the disguise, worried that it might make a pretext for bullying fat kids at school, but concluded that it gave such kids a way to play at being *Doctor Who* monsters. As this would be the first new monster added to the series, he thought they had to be big, green and hideous, but also baby-faced and playful. His idea was to add almost stereotypical *Doctor Who* monsters to a political conspiracy thriller and use both to critique each other.

- The final script was submitted shortly before filming began, but three scenes - as we've discussed to some extent - were used as audition-pieces. There was a screen test for Annette Badland (Margaret Blaine) nearer the filming, where Davies stood in as the Doctor. From this, he decided it might be worth sparing her character for a rematch ("Boom Town").

- As we saw in "Rose" (X1.1), the production began with this story and that one simultaneously. The London locations were all to be shot in one week, in July, partly for logistical reasons and partly because two key players, Penelope Wilton (Harriet Jones) and Noel Clarke, were otherwise engaged for large chunks of the summer. Wilton had been in Davies' *Bob & Rose* (see also X4.10, "Midnight"), and needed little persuasion to work of the new series. Neither did Andrew Marr, the BBC's Chief Political Correspondent, who was rather mischievously cast in a role written as just "Reporter #2".

Before all of this, the very first scenes to be made were recorded at Cardiff Royal Infirmary, doubling for Albion Hospital. This was Sunday, 18th July, 2004. They began with the scene of General Asquith meeting Dr Sato, and made all the fake news footage of police and UNIT vehicles arriving. Eccleston's first scene was chasing the pig (played by Jimmy Vee) down the corridor. Vee had already made a commercial with Millennium Effects, and so they had a body-cast of him handy. Davies had asked that the spacesuit not be too shiny and NASA-looking (either because aluminium foil around a pig looks too culinary, or simply because that's what detractors might expect a

Doctor Who alien to look like), so they opted for a 1950s look. Naoko Mori (Dr Sato) confessed to perplexity at some elements of the script, especially what a TARDIS was. The following day was given over to the mortuary scenes for which Eccleston wasn't needed, and publicity interviews for which he was (Piper joined them in the afternoon for this). Eccleston was then released for a week as the crew went on to spend that night and the next two shooting the Nestene mayhem at Queen's Parade for "Rose".

• The grotesque sketch-show *Little Britain* had a thread about a vaguely Blair-like Prime Minister (Anthony Stewart Head, X2.3, "School Reunion") and his creepily adoring aide (David Walliams, X6.11, "The God Complex"). This used the quiet close, John Adam Street, tucked away behind Charing Cross Station. After exhausting all the alternatives in Cardiff, the *Doctor Who* team followed suit. Andrew Marr, who is usually busy on Sunday mornings, came to the shoot on 25th July. This was also where Piper and Eccleston recorded their first scene together. The "clean" shots of the exterior were also taken here for use in the composite shots of the missile attack.

Now it gets complicated. The following day was Monday 26th, and was the day when they recorded all the Trafalgar Square material for "Rose", the spaceship crash and aftermath on Westminster Bridge, then at night the Westminster Bridge scenes from "Rose" and all the Embankment material and, as dawn rose, the exterior in Belvedere Road (just around the corner from the London Eye) where Harriet takes charge and the Doctor remembers her future. Complicated set ups in busy London locations. What could possibly go wrong? To make sure that as little as possible did, producer Phil Collinson was assigned to second-unit duties on the news inserts from the crash-site and cut-away shots of the public jamming the roads. There was a delay when the police noticed a lot of people in official-looking uniforms right next to Parliament, on Westminster Bridge and a launch getting very close. It looked like a security alert. The *real* Westminster security teams arrived and started asking questions.

• Penelope Wilton was working on two other productions at the time, one of which was Woody Allen's *Match Point*. Her only London location scene was (supposedly) around the corner from 10 Downing Street, which was scripted to happen at dawn. That was at around 5:15am, an hour after the Tube network resumed service for the day. A day's sleep later, at 7.00pm, the crew started shooting at the Brandon Estate, about a mile away, for the Powell Estate scenes for both stories in this block. Some of the day was spent dressing the location with the "Missing" posters. Next day was the rooftop and a few other daytime scenes; the last day in London was the 30th and that was the various balcony shots (giving Rose a TARDIS key and so on). As we have seen, this was also the time for recording scenes used in "Rose". The complicated schedule was already causing tensions.

When the crew and cast got back to Cardiff, the over-runs on "Rose" meant delaying scenes intended to be completed on 2nd August (the Monday). The scene in the rubble of Number 10 was salvaged by finding a different location the following day, and then on the 4th, the shoot moved to Hensol Castle for two weeks of work on the interiors for Downing Street. The designers had opted to give an impression of what people think the interior looks like, rather than attempt to research it thoroughly and contradict the public's idea. Apart from the famous check tiles on the floor of the hallway, the main effort at changing the interior of the conference centre where they were filming was to put paintings and photos of former premiers on the staircase walls, and accentuate the red that Boak and designer Edward Thomas had agreed was the visual shorthand for London in Block One. In reality, Downing Street had rather a lot of green inside, but the use of this as the key-out colour for effects made that impractical. Extras in green body-suits and hood were used, for example, to show the Slitheen divesting themselves of the human-skin disguises.

Here, according to most sources, is where the problems arose. The various effects teams were being made to synch without apparently any clear decisions having been made on the proportion of CG to prosthetics for the Slitheen sequences. Neill Gorton's team at Millennium Effects had made costumes for three performers, with animatronic mouths. The blinking eyes were added digitally in post-production. A director handling such sequences has no room to improvise or try things out. Neither is there much leeway for changes of circumstances. The performers inside the suits were effectively blind, so every movement had to be worked out well in advance. Arriving at a location and blocking these moves was a laborious process. The actors playing Slitheens-in-humans recorded most of their scenes in the first week, before a few days in the following week in Cardiff

X1.5 World War Three

doing voice recordings to be dubbed onto the prosthetic Slitheen "streakers". When Gorton arrived at the location, he claims, the paint on the Slitheen suits was still wet.

Eleven of the next 14 days would be spent on shooting the Downing Street sequences, and Eccleston in particular found the process frustrating. It became clear that Boak's idea of how these scenes should look differed from what Davies and Collinson had agreed with the effects teams. (We will note in passing that all the behind-the-scenes accounts that usually list this sort of thing in meticulous, sometimes laborious detail, elide this section. Even the chronology laid out by researcher Andrew Pixley in the Panini *Doctor Who: The Companion Series One* skips a week. Gaps like this allow all sorts of conjecture, much of which you may have read elsewhere.) One problem was that one of the actors playing the humans-with-Slitheen-inside had been on holiday when the castings for the rubber body-suits were made.

- As per "Rose", the Q2 studio complex in Newport was the base for the TARDIS set and the two flats. Sequences of Jackie's room for this and the first episode were made in the week beginning 20th August, with a second unit at the BBC Wales Broadcasting House making the news inserts on the 21st, and a brief scene of UNIT personnel arriving at Heathrow on the 28th. Until very late on, the AMNN newscaster was to have been called "Mal Loup" (bad French for... go on, guess; it's the phrase that keeps repeating throughout Eccleston's run). The Bank Holiday (30th) was the day for starting the scenes in Mickey's bedroom, with the Tuesday off and resuming on Wednesday. Eccleston got first go with the new TARDIS set on Thursday, 2nd September, doing the scene where he sneaks off to Albion Hospital.

- By now, production of Block One ought to have finished. They squeezed in an extra week to pick up the scenes they missed earlier, such as the shot of the lift-shaft, Rose running up the stairs to see her mum after what she thought was a thrill-packed 12 hours, and the TARDIS arriving in a cupboard at Albion Hospital and the Doctor walking into a room full of squaddies. This last location, again at Cardiff Royal Infirmary, seems to have been a late addition because the episode was feared to have been under-running badly.

- With all the emphasis on computer-generated effects, many observers were surprised that the "money shot" of the small spaceship crashing into the clock was a model. Mike Tucker, at the BBC's Model Unit, oversaw many of the effects in Series One. He had been effects supervisor over the last five years of the old series, and in the interregnum had co-written tie-in books with his schoolchum Robert Perry. As you will recall from Volume 6, the models in the last few years were one area where the series could be proud (even if the low reputation persisted among people who'd stopped watching), and the work on *Red Dwarf* had been one of the few popular things about the last few years of that sitcom. Another old boy from that same school in Swansea, Russell T Davies, thus ignored jokes about nepotism and gave Tucker some of the most challenging jobs on the new series. The clock tower (which we persist in pedantically not calling "Big Ben") was a seven-foot high model - look closely and the hands change position on impact because the shot looked more effective when flipped vertically. This was merged with CG splashes into the Thames - water droplets form a minimum size and models splashing always look like models unless isopropyl alcohol is used as a surface layer, which is really only cost-effective if you're doing it a lot. (Even then, it isn't always convincing, as in *Thunderbirds*.) Model filming for both stories in the block was done in mid-September. A fortnight later, on 4th October, the *Blue Peter* insert was recorded. Then a first edit of the episode was compiled and seen to be lacking.

During Block Three, a few new scenes were added, mostly in the gap between the main shoot for "Dalek" (X1.6) and the start of work on "Father's Day" (X1.8). The sets for the Tyler flat had now been moved from the noisy ex-warehouse to HTV's purpose-built studio at Culversehouse Cross, in Cardiff itself. A new scene of Jackie asking Rose where she had been and the "shepherd's pie" scene were shot on 10th November, matching the other end of the phone call from the TARDIS set the previous day. (This in turn was the day after the scenes of the Doctor in Van Statten's office in "Dalek", so Piper had a couple of days off after all that running.) Twelve days later, they added the shot of the Slitheen photo on Rose's phone (in a mock-up of the Cabinet Office set, now at the HTV studios), and two days after that, the public jamming the roads (in Cardiff) and the Doctor and Rose being driven to Downing Street were added. Euros Lyn did some of these, as well as the shots of Jackie in the kitchen he needed for X1.2, "The End of the World" (there were some shots of Jackie in "Rose" recorded on 10th November). Lyn also did one of the TARDIS interior scenes, the one where the Doctor first calls Mickey "Ricky".

• The day before "Aliens of London" aired (in fact, at midnight on 15th April), the BBC came clean and admitted that David Tennant was to be the new Doctor. He had a week to wait before recording his half of the regeneration scene (Eccleston's last day had been 4th April, but we'll come to that), but he was under orders not to discuss *Doctor Who* until the last Eccleston episodes had aired. As we mentioned, this story went out during the campaigning for a real election, so Andrew Marr was hardly off our screens during this fortnight. Indeed, the last trailer before "World War Three" had animated versions of him, Huw Edwards (X2.11, "Fear Her") and Kirsty Wark (X4.5, "The Poison Sky").

X1.6: "Dalek"

(30th April 2005)

Which One is This? The clue is in the title.

Firsts and Lasts There is a school of thought that the most significant "first" here is the use of the underground levels of the Millennium Stadium in Cardiff, which rivals the Cardiff Royal Infirmary and the Paper Mill as the most over-familiar location in the series. However, we ought to mention the return of the new improved Daleks and their formidable new bag of tricks (see **The Non-Humans** for details) and the first appearance of Bruno Langley as Adam.

Then again, it's also the first appearance of the Cybermen (or at least, the severed head of one) in the new series, a fact more significant with hindsight. This is also the first Welsh story to be set in the near future (at least, at the planning stage: "Aliens of London" became near-future when they decided to change the beginning to Rose having been away a year), in America and in the "base under siege" format beloved of producers when Patrick Troughton was the Doctor. Another Troughton throwback, the plot's similarity to 4.3, "The Power of the Daleks" (which worked so well, they did it again in X5.3, "Victory of the Daleks"), is offset by this being the first story to have been reconstituted from a Big Finish audio drama (see **The Big Picture**).

Murray Gold sees fit to give this story the first of his *Omen*-style chants for the Daleks. And this is the first of five episodes this year to be directed by Joe Ahearne.

Watch Out For...

• For about half of the people watching in Britain first time, and most overseas, this was a story about the Doctor acting *way* out of character, being sadistic, using a huge weapon and being prepared to sacrifice Rose to stop an escaped torture-victim out for revenge. As with "The Unquiet Dead" (X1.3), this seems like an exercise in knocking down something that experienced viewers know to be a cliché, at the risk of confusing or annoying anyone not so experienced. As the previous five episodes have been steadfast in avoiding the topic of the single most famous aliens the Doctor has ever encountered - to the extent that Rose has no idea what it is when she meets one of their number - we are supposed to be watching this story from her point of view.

As such, the only way it will ever have the same impact is on someone who has this as their first-ever episode (or watches everything from "Rose" onwards in order with no Internet access). This is an episode designed explicitly to introduce the Daleks to an audience who either know of them vaguely or not at all. It also makes great play of taking everything that third-rate comedians have ever joked about and making Daleks chilling again. So the Doctor calls it a "dustbin", Adam says a "pepperpot"; Rose taunts it when running up stairs, the hapless Simmons sneers at the sink-plunger and something like 50 heavily-armed security guards get killed, including a dozen or so who ignored the Doctor's advice to "aim for the eye-piece". Even the bobbles on its skirt turn out to have a practical use.

• However, the Dalek's main weapon is its mind. It breaks the habits of 40 years and gets all the best lines, especially when taunting the Doctor, and chooses to show its antagonists the contemptuous ease with which it can destroy. In one bravura scene, it eliminates 20 soldiers with three shots. One to set off the sprinklers, then, as it floats above the wet floor, another discharge to kill everyone at ground level and a third to electrocute anyone on the metal balcony.

• Although the Doctor froths at the mouth and yells at the Dalek, that's mainly for show; the one time he *really* gets angry with someone, it's Van Statten, the multi-bulti-billionaire who collects and copyrights anything alien he can grab for his collection. When Rose seems to have been killed, the Doctor blames the human who caused it: "You just want to drag the stars down and stick them underground, underneath tons of sand and dirt, and label them. You're about as far from the stars as you can get. And you took her down with you."

• Davies' flippant suggestion that the character who became "Van Statten" was to be called "William Doors" never made it to the screen, but how does one find character names? Well, if you're writer Robert Shearman, you either find the most American names you can ("Di Maggio", "Van Statten" - all right, not exactly typical American names, but obviously non-English) or you pop a few in-jokes around the place. Shearman's 80s fanzine *Cloister Bell* was co-edited by one Owen Bywater ("Bywater" here being the name of the Cage's security commander); the torturer in the Big Finish audio-play "Jubilee", whence a lot of this story came, was played by Kai Simmons, so his equivalent in the televised version is called "Simmons"; Shearman's wife, whose scepticism about the series as a whole and the scariness of Daleks in particular motivated many of the script's most memorable moments, is Big Finish semi-regular Jane Goddard. And observe the boxes for "Jubilee Pizza" (who have a branch in Cardiff where Torchwood have an account).

• This is the story where Murray Gold's soundtrack switches around wildly between the eighties-style drum-machine patterns and recorded-in-bedroom synths of the first few stories, and the bombastic, orchestral style more familiar later. The sequence where the Dalek shoots soldiers in the corridor is especially schizoid, flipping between the first of those Jerry Goldsmith-ish choral chants we'll hear a lot in later Dalek tales and mid-nineties Junglism. The result sounds like a fight between Darth Maul and the Powerpuff Girls. Since this was broadcast, ersatz-Carl Orff-bellowing choirs (or more likely samples of choirs from real Carl Orff) have become the staple of *The X Factor* and the like, so Gold is having to find other ways to make season finales sound epic.

The Continuity

The Doctor He has two hearts. [Not exactly breaking news for most of the people watching on first broadcast, but we get to see them beating (unlike, for example, 21.6, "The Caves of Androzani") and hear them, in a double-pulse rhythm we'll hear a lot when the Master turns up (X3.11, "Utopia", although it's been there in the theme-tune since the pilot episode).] The hearts are shown to be side by side [in keeping with the likes of 7.1, "Spearhead from Space", "The Caves of Androzani" and 27.0, "The TV Movie", but just wait until X7.4, "The Power of Three" gives us a diagonal presentation.] He also has a belly-button [confirming what's said, strangely enough, in the *New Adventures* books].

He seems more than a little rueful at seeing a Cyberman head in a glass display case. [River Song's comment in X5.4, "The Time of Angels", indicates that - by luck, design or a quirk of the TARDIS - the Doctor invariably finds his way to any significant collection of ancient tech. Consider that within an episode of his first encountering the Slitheen, he sees a claw of a Raxacoricofallopatorian on display and then stumbles, apparently nonchalantly, across evidence of one of his earlier victories.] Not for the first or last time, he feels old. After thinking Rose is about to die, several times in ten minutes, he loses it and makes an uncharacteristic snap at Adam about A-levels.

Unlike some previous encounters [3.10, "The War Machines"; 10.3, "Frontier in Space"; etc], the Doctor's spidey-sense about Daleks isn't working - here, he can walk into a darkened room that has a Dalek present and not know it's there. [Perhaps this is a function of the damage done to the Dalek, or a sign that the Daleks developed some kind of stealth mode during the Time War. Or perhaps it is something that only certain incarnations of the Doctor can do.]

The Dalek plays mind-games with the Doctor, but its accusations of cowardice fail to rile him. The taunt 'you would make a good Dalek', however, hits home. At one point, the Doctor offers the Dalek self-destruction as an order. [Eventually, it appears, the Dalek takes him up on this when the Doctor finally refuses to end its suffering - so was the Doctor simultaneously venting his disgust and offering solace to the only other being who knows what he has been through?]

The Doctor claims he would instinctively know 'in [his mind]' if any of the Time Lords had survived, and that it 'feels like there's no one' [but see "Utopia"].

• *Ethics*. The Doctor is willing to help whatever is trapped in Van Statten's Cage until he identifies it as a Dalek. The Dalek's accusation that the two

What's Happened to the Daleks?

It is obvious that since we last saw them in any detail on TV (25.1, "Remembrance of the Daleks"), the pepperpots have had a bit of an upgrade. So, we will be noting each on-screen manifestation of their enhanced abilities in each story entry from "Dalek" (X1.6) onward, as well as examining the thoroughgoing on-screen rebranding.

Sorry, that should read "reconfiguration"...

This essay, however, is an overview of these changes, with speculation on what happened while the series was off-air to warrant such a startling transformation. On the face of it, the answer is simply "The Last Great Time War", but that's not much help. After all, the Daleks we saw duking it out in Shoreditch in the time of Beatlemania ("Remembrance of the Daleks") were two mighty armies outflanked by one Time Lord and a few squaddies (who were largely window-dressing to make the Doctor's bluff look convincing). Getting from there to the situation described in, for example, X4.18, "The End of Time Part Two", takes a bit of a leap of faith.

If we consider that the Time Lords and the Daleks both wound up contemplating how to destroy the entire Universe at the end of the Time War, then wind back to "Destiny of the Daleks" (17.1), where the Daleks were held to a draw by disco-droids, then it's obvious that Davros performed some considerable tinkering so his errant children could interface with their shells more directly, and had a hope of using Time Lord technology without too much difficulty. Their quest for purity had taken a pragmatic turn - clearly, more has happened to them than just a rethink of what they can do to their shells to make them more battle-ready.

This is where the precise nature of a Time War becomes important. If - as the term is usually understood - this means a war across the whole of time, where each side attempts to travel back and pre-emptively destroy the other, then rewriting their *own* past is a gambit the Daleks would have been more prepared to take than the Time Lords. This might, for instance, explain the curiously semi-restored form Davros has taken when we see him again in "The Stolen Earth" (X4.12). Preventing whatever initially befell him to leave him chair-bound, scarred and blinded would not be an option (at least, not to the Daleks), but he at least has his body back. Both he and Sarah seem to recall the events of their previous meeting differently from what was broadcast in 1975 (12.4, "Genesis of the Daleks"). If so, this is significant, as the final iteration of the Daleks before the New Paradigm (X5.3, "Victory of the Daleks") was an entire race bred from Davros' own cells. If he's now more Dalek than he was in the initial timeline, then their template for purity is also more negotiable. This is also the thinking behind the New Paradigm, even though this in turn assumes that any previous, Davros-designed "paradigm" is less pure, somehow.

Certainly, the nature of their shells is also more complicated than before. Apart from the ability to reconfigure the plating to allow access, and the rotating turret (both demonstrated in "Dalek", with a further option for allowing humans into the skirt, revealed in X3.4, "Daleks in Manhattan"), the plating is now made of a more reactive medium. It is still called "Dalekanium", but - whilst proof against ray-guns, bullets and sprinkler systems - it's notably porous to the genetic material of time-travellers. It's fair to say that this is an unexpected development - even when sort-of explained in "Doomsday" (X2.13), the Doctor only says that the Daleks have the option of using time-energy as a power-source, and that's before he figures out that the Genesis Ark isn't a Dalek-designed doohickey at all. The effect of Rose touching the casing of the wounded survivor in "Dalek" is dramatic. Not only does the shell's entire armoury and capabilities reboot and self-repair, but the occupant undergoes a number of apparent shifts in worldview and self-concept. (We say "apparent", as there are good grounds to presume that the entire enterprise is a scam - see "Dalek" for why - but for now we'll hedge our bets.)

The question then is: what possible use could the Daleks, a race defined by their inability to engage with the world outside their shells except through intimidation, have for such a capability? One possibility is that Dalek-to-Dalek contact has become important. Look at the spectacular effect of one touch from a time-traveller: if a Dalek that badly-damaged can be (there is no other word for it) regenerated and genetically realigned by Rose, a Dalek could heal a fallen comrade despite their touch-taboo. Rose's effect is anomalous, and

continued on Page 99...

of them 'are the same' goads the Doctor into viciously torturing the Dalek with an electrical charge. When push comes to shove, the Doctor *does* lower the vault's bulkheads to keep the Dalek contained, knowing that Rose may not have got clear, and that this act might cost her life. He raises the barricades, however, when the Dalek takes Rose hostage - on the grounds that 'I killed her once. I can't do it again.' [Compare with his similarly fateful decision of whether or not to eliminate the Daleks at the cost of bystanders in X1.13, "The Parting of the Ways."]

Even when the Dalek has (apparently) killed Rose, the Doctor turns his ire on Van Statten for burying the wonders of the Universe in a pit for his own private amusement. [There is a distinct difference between how the Doctor behaves towards the Dalek face-to-face or via screens, and how he discusses its behaviour when talking to Van Statten. However vindictive he seems when matching the Dalek taunt-for-taunt, he considers the Dalek to be 'honest' and acknowledges that it is behaving according to its genetic instructions. Van Statten, by contrast, is the way he is by choice. However, when judged by the same criteria, the Doctor doesn't come out quite as well as usual. Given the opportunity to inflict physical pain on a defenceless Dalek, the Doctor does so with relish.

[There is an argument to be made that the Doctor recognises that the Dalek is, by being 'contaminated', in considerable turmoil and mentally unstable. This understanding seems to come out in the end, when the Doctor - armed and able to destroy the Dalek - sets out to stop it killing not just to save Earth but, in some ways, to save the Dalek itself. As big a threat as the Dalek would have been normally, it was predictable and stopping it was morally justified. A *self-loathing* Dalek is, if anything, more volatile. However, the thing to note is that when the Doctor confirms the Dalek's worst suspicion - that absorbing Rose's DNA has transformed it into 'something new' - he says 'I'm sorry' and means it. Intense as his own grief and anger are, forcing the Dalek to live like this is a line he won't cross.]

• *Background*. The Doctor can identify almost all of the alien technology in Van Statten's collection. He can tell at a glance that various weapons are broken - and that one is actually a hair dryer - and is able to play a metal object resembling a conch-shell that plays pan-pipe muzak. He mentions the creator of the Daleks as 'a genius who was king of his own little world' - meaning that Van Statten would like him. [At this stage, it was unclear whether the programme's past was changed to any great extent - it wouldn't have been the first time the history of the Daleks had been junked for the sake of making a good story - see 2.2, "The Dalek Invasion of Earth"; 12.4, "Genesis of the Daleks" and compare either to 1.2, "The Daleks". But, regarding the Daleks' creator, see X4.12, "The Stolen Earth".] Just after examining the 'hair dryer', he finds a suitable weapon to eliminate the Dalek and exclaims 'now, that's what I'm talking about'. [He may have picked up this phrase from a number of sources, but in context it seems he's quoting Will Smith in *Men in Black* finding a similarly-impressive alien gun.]

The TARDIS The Ship is drawn to the Cage by an SOS signal, which would appear to have been sent by Van Statten's Dalek. [This is, it must be said, remarkable. Not only is it strange that the Ship would pick this time in the Doctor's life to respond to a signal of this kind (a constant problem of stories where a time-machine responds to a distress signal sent out in coterminous time - 13.2, "Planet of Evil", for example), but that this signal is not immediately recognised as being a Dalek message. Logically, there are two likely recipients - a Dalek vessel or a Time Lord one - and in either case, the sender would want the respondent to *know* that it was a Dalek.]

The Supporting Cast

• *Rose*. She immediately rushes down to the Dalek's cage as soon as she realises it's being tortured, without even stopping to think where she is. When running for her life, she displays a strange tendency to stick around and see what the Dalek is up to. [This is almost plausible when she thinks that stairs can stop it. However, in the weapons-testing bay she does it *again*, losing ground and thus getting caught when the Doctor seals the bulkheads.]

Without preconceptions, she's far more accepting towards the Dalek even after it's killed an entire base of personnel, and gets the wonderfully *Doctor Who* line, 'Don't move, it's beginning to question itself'. She rebukes the Doctor at the end for his sudden dip into gun-toting violence, but doesn't push him after the Dalek's dead. When the Dalek asks her for a self-destruct order, she qui-

What's Happened to the Daleks?

continued from Page 97...

there are good reasons to presume that the Dalek was so badly damaged, so desperate and so conniving that it would allow this to happen despite the risk of contamination. If it had been working as designed, the skin's transfer of time energy could also be a reset device for Daleks affected by sabotage. (The Doctor's options in what looks like the opening salvo of the War, the mission brief at the start of "Genesis of the Daleks", includes affecting their gene-code pre-emptively, so this would be one of the first ploys used by the Time Lords.)

It's worth noting that the shell-panels of the Cult of Skaro were used to convert gamma radiation from a solar flare for use in a genetic experiment in 1930 ("Daleks in Manhattan"). Using this source of energy to replenish or replace their depleted reserves, they fused Dalek DNA onto human specimens deemed suitable for one-touch conversion without all the tedious surgery needed for Robo-Men (2.2, "The Dalek Invasion of Earth"). The possibility exists that the Daleks had this feature added to their bonded polycarbide as a means to enslave or convert captives, although if this had been fitted as standard, then the Cult's research programme would not have needed all the practice-runs and pig-human hybrids we see. (Of course, the Cult were imprisoned in their Void Ship some time before the end-game, and so the sole survivor who fell to Earth and was locked in a museum in "Dalek" might have been the result of further R&D on what was, for Thay, Sec, Caan and the Other One, a hypothetical scheme or prototype app.) This might therefore have been a routine method of conquest, just as the use of the sucker-arm for data-retrieval from human brains ("Doomsday" and implicitly, with hindsight, in "Dalek") seems to have been standard procedure. It chimes with the notion of spreading a viral Dalek Factor (4.9, "The Evil of the Daleks"). In which case, what happened when Rose touched the case of the survivor was that this was short-circuited because she was a time-traveller.

There's a problem with that hypothesis, however: in a Time War, many if not most of the people a Dalek would encounter could be assumed to be time-travellers. If this idea is right, then the War could have been ended by TARDIS-loads of indie-kids with "Free Hugs" placards cuddling the Skaroine menace into confused self-destruction. If Rose did this only because the Dalek's force-field generator was damaged, this is still a design-flaw, as the force-field generator is surely the easiest thing in any world for a sonic screwdriver to circumvent. (Here you might be tempted to say, "deadlock seal", and then we'll reply, "So how does a Dalek repair itself in battle?", and a dull debate over which plot-contrivance is stronger ensues.)

So we have to rethink this slightly... why was the effect of Rose touching a Dalek's shell so unexpected, given that the shells appear to have been designed to transfer genetic material (albeit in the rather specialised sense of "genetic" that BBC Wales has developed)? The answer could be that she's both a time-traveller and human. Time Lord DNA (unlike any real deoxyribonucleic acid to be found in any person, animal or plant) can be sent down the wire to lie dormant in Human-Dalek hybrids until activated (see also Donna's rather alarmingly enhanced skill-set in X4.13, "Journey's End"). Perhaps (and we won't know either way unless any new evidence comes to light) human information is more easily assimilated or (more likely under the circumstances) identified and rejected *unless the human is also a time-traveller, which confuses the filter system*. After all, the raw material from which Davros fashioned his first batch of Imperial Daleks (22.6, "Revelation of the Daleks") was selected gifted ex-humans, and a gene-scan of Harry Sullivan showed that he was almost indistinguishable from a Thal ("Genesis of the Daleks"). The new-series Daleks have, as we will shortly see, a drastically different relationship with Time than their original-series counterparts, something that seems at least partially derived from the Time Lords. Is it, therefore, too much to surmise that the casings were designed to soak up time-sensitive abilities from captured Time Lords, and thus "initiate" Daleks into a time-capable elite squad?

The questionable data in "The Two Doctors" (22.4) stands as possible confirmation of this. It's open to debate just how far anything the sixth Doctor told Jamie about the Rassilon Imprimatur can be trusted, but it's notable that the Sontarans and Chessene - not to mention Dastari, one of the greatest geneticists the Doctor ever met, and an

continued on Page 101...

etly confirms it.

- *Adam*. He's unashamedly bright. He accepts that he is a genius and doesn't waste time qualifying this. Aged eight, he hacked military computers and almost caused World War III - something he thinks was fun. Now, harvested by Van Statten, he gets to source and collate alien tech left on Earth, spending vast sums at auction. He is convinced that there's lots of alien involvement in Earth's affairs, but that self-proclaimed abductees are all 'nutters'. The episode ends with the Doctor agreeing - after noting that Rose might be influenced because Adam is 'a bit pretty' - to Rose's request that Adam join them in the TARDIS.

- *Henry Van Statten* has broad knowledge and a good amount of computer programming nous, but no insight. He has the skill and self-control to operate the alien ocarina, but once he realises that it has no commercial worth - or, more flatteringly to him, is no longer a puzzle for him to solve - he hurls it aside. The Dalek recognising the Doctor but not acknowledging *him* is the worst thing that has ever happened to Van Statten. He has a quasi-Vorticist painting of himself over his desk. [A pastiche of Max Beckmann, although it looks as if he's dressed as Tony Hancock. This might be an enormous in-joke - see **Who Really Created the Daleks?** under "The Daleks" - but it's unlikely.] According to Adam, Van Statten owns the entire Internet.

He calls his prize specimen the 'Metaltron'. [This is presumably a deliberate echo of Metatron, the Angel of the Voice of the Lord, which makes his obsession with making it speak to him seem slightly more rational. Or else it's a sly *Transformers* riff on "Megatron", but that's tacky, and everyone else has made that joke.]

The Non-Humans

- *The Dalek*. When it fell to Earth in the 'Ascension Islands' [see **History**], it left a crater and screamed for three days. It's been on Earth for 'fifty years', having been part of different collections in that time.

As is usual for Daleks, this one announces what it is going to do just before doing it; it shouts 'exterminate' and exterminates people, it shouts 'elevate' and levitates up stairs and so on. Normally, when a Dalek self-destructs it shouts "self-destruct", but this one yells 'exterminate'. It then appears to "destroy itself" by sending its bobbles out into a spherical pattern, generating a force field, and then vanishing in a blinding light.

[This has led to speculation that what we saw throughout this episode was a fiendish ploy whereby a contaminated Dalek - wanting orders and a hierarchy, a place to belong above anything else - in fact executed an emergency temporal shift and set about making a new army for itself in Earth's solar system after 200,100 AD (see the next story). This makes sense of a number of seemingly ludicrous features of X1.12, "Bad Wolf". A Dalek well-versed in lousy television from 2012 would have endless scope for lethal variants of the game shows it discovered when trawling the Internet. It would have a reason to spare Rose from the usual fate of losing contestants. And it would, as the Doctor says of the Emperor, hate its own flesh. In fact, Occam's Razor indicates that the odds of *two* Daleks falling through time and escaping the end of the Last Time War are slim - the odds of one of those being the Emperor even slimmer. So the one survivor declaring itself to be Emperor by spawning an empire is possibly more plausible. Some might say that this interpretation weakens the emotional impact of this story, but many would say so does ever having another story with a Dalek in it. Worryingly, this raises the possibility that *the very next location* at which the TARDIS arrives (X1.7, "The Long Game") is chosen because the Ship is trying to show the Doctor the results of the Dalek's interference, perhaps at a stage when he's able to curtail it - and that he fails to do so.]

Other refinements since last time we saw the Daleks include the central gun-turret being able to rotate relative to the base (enabling it to shoot backwards) and a force-field that melt bullets before they reach the skin. This force-field is said to be weakest at the apex, making the old 'aim for the eye-piece' line more valid than ever. The sucker-arm is now a data-retrieval port, able to absorb information from the touch-pad and break codes and capable of digesting the whole of the Internet. It can also interface with devices, and calculate, the Doctor says, 'a thousand billion' combinations per second.

The Dalek can also adapt its shape. This sucker can also create a powerful vacuum and crush a human head, as well as take energy from the mains - enough to bring down the grid on America's west coast - when it smashes a computer screen. Humans who touched the Dalek when it was weakened burst into flame - Rose, as

What's Happened to the Daleks?

continued from Page 99...

astrophysicist in his spare time (suggesting that, for Time Lords and their cohorts, these two disciplines are closely related) - believed it. Moreover, the plan Davros had for replacing the Time Lords with his Daleks needed him to start redesigning his babies' genetic make-up before taking leftover Gallifreyan technology. The grey-cased Rebel faction in "Remembrance of the Daleks" operated a time-corridor, but Davros' Imperial faction not only took a ship through time, they monitored the progress of the Hand of Omega in their native time zone. As we saw in **How Does Time Work...** under 9.1, "Day of the Daleks", **What's the Dalek Timeline?** under 2.8, "The Chase" and **Can You Rewrite History, Even One Line?** under 1.8, "The Aztecs" (and several times in the present volume), most mortals are stuck within time like a train on a track, but Time Lords and a few other exalted species have the ability to move the points. The Daleks, previously able to visit past and future time-periods, but not significantly alter history unaided (whilst participating in it with gusto), were about to join the premier league in "Remembrance". By the time of New *Who*, they'd become the Time Lords' equals to the point that neither race was left.

This returns us to the usual problem when discussing Dalek genetic updates - namely, that they are dead against that sort of thing. However, this might not be quite such a problem if, in the run-up to launching a temporal campaign against all other races, a Dalek subspecies with full time-sensitivity nipped back and altered history so that they and their followers were the only Daleks who had ever existed. This might seem improbable on the face of it, but there are two or three possible pieces of supporting evidence. One is that the tenth Doctor often acts as though he could talk the Cult of Skaro into dropping all hostilities and using their powers for good. The more rigidly orthodox Old Skool Daleks of the pre-1989 stories wouldn't even have listened, but the Doctor seriously believes he has a chance of pushing Dalek evolution down a benign track even after everything that has happened. If these Daleks have been altered so that they can see possibilities such as this, it could be because their "contamination" by Time Lord genes and abilities has left more of a mark than what was necessary to just navigate divergent time-streams. (Along those lines, the Doctor only tries such persuasion on the Cult, a group set up to think the unthinkable. One of the Cult's members, Caan, sees things the Doctor's way sufficiently to manipulate time in order to wipe out Davros' new army. Note also that Sec, when bonded with a human, starts to follow the Doctor's thinking and seems prepared to strike some kind of bargain.)

Perhaps the Cult members are the only extant Daleks with these abilities: they are certainly the only ones who state out loud that they are instigating an "emergency temporal shift". We return, however, to the idea that one of the Dalek "footsoldiers" (a really inappropriate phrase) has the ability to absorb genetic information from Rose, despite all the logical reasons to doubt that a Dalek would do this. It would never have happened in the old days, and this is our second shred of back-up for this unlikely theory.

We also have to consider the Dalek that demonstrates Time Lord-like abilities in flashback in "The Waters of Mars" (X4.16). In the midst of wiping out humanity and constructing a machine to dissolve all created matter in the cosmos, a Dalek opts not to kill young Adelaide because it somehow intuits or divines that she is part and parcel of one of these curious "Fixed Points in Time". Exactly what a Dalek engaged in destroying the Universe has to fear from altering a relatively small part of a history it's trying to prevent ever being possible is a matter for another essay. (See **What Constitutes a "Fixed Point"?** under X4.2, "The Fires of Pompeii".) What concerns us here is that it's able, at a glance, to know that Adelaide is significant. The Doctor seems to have a vestigial version of the same ability (as did Romana in 18.5, "Warriors' Gate"). Similarly, the TARDIS knows that Captain Jack is to be avoided (X3.11, "Utopia"). As we have just seen in the essay with "World War Three", the two most obvious mechanisms for a Dalek to have acquired such a knack are exposure to residual Artron energy from a TARDIS (which we know can't be true, or else they'd've been able to open the Genesis Ark in "Doomsday" as quick as boiled asparagus) or exposure to the Untempered Schism (see X3.12, "The Sound of Drums"). Either

continued on Page 103...

1.6 Dalek

a time-traveller, merely enabled it to regenerate and escape. [See this story's essay and **Is Arthur the Horse a Companion?** under X2.4, "The Girl in the Fireplace".]

Evidently, the word 'pity' is now in its vocabulary-banks [cf "Genesis of the Daleks"].

History

- *Dating*. It's 2012. [Or, at least, *a* 2012. This story's events are rather dependent on nobody knowing anything about Daleks, which is only slightly more plausible if indeed a Crack in the Wall absorbed the events of "The Stolen Earth" et seq, never mind that there were Daleks in the Cabinet War Rooms in 1941 (X5.3, "Victory of the Daleks"). By the way, if the graphic representing the United States when the Dalek brings down the west coast's power grid can be believed and isn't just a rough approximation, the United States seems to have gone through a bit of reorganisation. Five of the New England states have been amalgamated, and top half of Michigan is missing, somehow.]

There was more than one Ascension Island in the early 1960s, apparently. [Unless Goddard misspoke, saying 'the Ascension Islands' but meaning the Aleutian Islands. Because something high-tech falling out of the sky in 1962 - right on the border of the USA and the Soviet Union - would of course have gone completely unnoticed.] Salt Lake City has a population of one million [five times what it currently has].

Van Statten seems to wield enough power and influence to choose presidents. [We have to assume that his ability to select is down to funding campaigns and putting (subliminal) suggestions online to influence routinely scheduled four-yearly elections - 2012 was an election year in the US. This story must therefore be between the Iowa caucuses (3rd January) and the election, mandated by the US Constitution as being the first Tuesday in November - although with so much else weird in this version of America, who knows? See **How Come Britain Has a President and America Hasn't?** under "The Sound of Drums" for more electoral weirdness.]

The UN apparently hushes up alien activities on Earth [that's Adam's view, but he states it as if Rose will know that the UN is influential enough to do this]. The Roswell spaceship left behind the Milometer and the technology behind Broadband [see X6.2, "Day of the Moon"; A7, "Dreamland"; and *The Sarah Jane Adventures*]. The Tunguska meteor left samples that provided a cure for the common cold [see 3.6, "The Ark" - how elephants are involved is a mystery].

Van Statten's collection includes a Cyberman head. [You will frequently hear talk that the text on the front of the head's display case says the item comes from the London sewers in either (accounts vary) 1975 or 1979, but this isn't legible on screen, so it's hard to give the evidence much weight. To *look* at the head, this is a different design from the Cyber-sewer incident in 6.3, "The Invasion", which in any case happened a few years before the mid-70s (see **What is the UNIT Timeline?** under 8.5, "The Daemons" and **What is the Cyberman Timeline?** under 4.2, "The Tenth Planet"). The occupation of London's sewerage did continue - or resume - later on, when a contingent of time-travellers from some time after 2526 (22.1, "Attack of the Cybermen"; 19.6, "Earthshock") were there in 1985. All things being equal, the head seems to come from the time of the Cyber-Wars (12.5, "Revenge of the Cyberman").]

Other exhibits in Van Statten's collection include: something that looks very like a maskless Hath [X4.6, "The Doctor's Daughter"; X5.1, "The Eleventh Hour"]; a Slitheen claw; a meteorite; a hubcap; an anthropoid head; another resembling an orangutan's; a humanoid mechanical exoskeleton; a large ossified carapace; a spherical chamber resembling a bathysphere and at least a dozen other items in display cases.

- *The Time War*. Well, this is a turn-up. It seems that the Time Lords were at war with the Daleks and both races were wiped out. [Last time we saw the Daleks, there were two factions of them and the Doctor outwitted them both (25.1, "Remembrance of the Daleks" - we can't really count their squeaky voice-over in 27.0, "The TV Movie"), so obviously the Skaroine menace got a fairly hefty upgrade while the series was off-air (see the accompanying essay).]

The Doctor was there at the last battle, and seems to have been responsible for wiping out both species while destroying his own homeworld. Ten million Dalek ships - 'the entire Dalek race' - were on fire; the Time Lords 'burnt' with them. He 'made this happen', but only because he 'had no choice'. As the Doctor puts it, 'Everyone lost'. The Doctor taunts the Dalek with the news that the War is over and the Daleks didn't win.

What's Happened to the Daleks?

continued from Page 101...

of these requires the biological Dalek to go skinny-dipping in space-time energy, which we know they simply don't do.

That said, if their polycarbide shells can do more than simply absorb time-energy as a power-source, the Daleks could still have their very own Untempered Schism - or more alarmingly but, given the uniqueness of such a wound in space-time, plausibly - they somehow got access to the same one the Time Lords use. If it's a gap in the fabric of space-time, it doesn't have to manifest itself exclusively at any one point throughout all timelines. (If we're going with this idea, it's worth noting that the Exxilon city in 11.3, "Death to the Daleks" displays many of the same abilities we're here imputing to Dalek shells - it sucked the TARDIS dry of all forms of energy, except oil-lamps and muscles for some reason.) If the Daleks have time-travel capabilities akin to those of Time Lords, then a ploy like the Bad Wolf must have occurred to them at some point. So, did they themselves attempt it? Was this one of the horrors of the Last Great Time War that we've had oblique references to over the years (The Nightmare Child, The Skaro Degradations et al)? The Daleks refer to the Bad Wolf as "The Abomination" (X1.13, "The Parting of the Ways"), as if she/it was expected (see **Bad Wolf - What, How and Why?** under X1.12), so presumably the damage to Dalek DNA would be too great for them to countenance if one of them went the whole hog.

Time-sensitive Daleks have another possible trick up their plungers that might explain something seen here but nowhere else. After the Dalek is touched by Rose, its first act is to reverse all the damage done to its shell. Perhaps this is more than just tiny nanites running around the polycarbide repairing everything, beating out dings and singing "We will fix it, we will fix it" - maybe what we're seeing is a localised reversal of entropy. The Dalek retains its memories - so its mind, like that of the Doctor when negotiating time-reversals (e.g. 11.2, "Invasion of the Dinosaurs") is somehow exempt from such things (as is Captain Jack's), but in reverting to factory-settings, the Dalek seems to be reversing time just around its own machinery. No other Dalek ever seems able to do this - Sec, Thay, Caan and Ringo would have benefitted from such a skill in their off-Broadway romp. This reinforces the idea that the first of all these last, solitary survivors is *more* than just any ordinary Dalek. He can regenerate.

In a lot of ways, all of this simply continues the pattern of the series since 1964. Every time the Daleks have returned, they have been more appropriately Doctor-sized. Originally, he was a slightly amoral scientist - and so were they. Once he had stepped up to be the guy who saves planets, they miraculously came back and were the invaders of Earth (well, London). Then they got time-travel ("The Chase") specifically to stop "our greatest enemy" and went on a *gran turismo* around history and across the cosmos. With each step between the Doctor being just some old fugitive with a time machine to "the Oncoming Storm", the Daleks have matched him. They even gained the ability to traverse alternate timelines 18 months after the Doctor first did it (9.1, "Day of the Daleks"; 7.4, "Inferno").

One option is opened up by the ongoing Melody Pond/River Song storyline (especially given the revelations in X6.7, "A Good Man Goes To War"). If new Daleks were engendered in time vessels in the Vortex, they eventually might develop Time Lord-like abilities. It's difficult to know if this is the case, but it could be part and parcel of an anomaly in the story that introduces the Ikea-style colour-coded Daleks ("Victory of the Daleks") - namely, that Amy can't remember the Daleks invading in either 2007 (the Canary Wharf shindig) or 2010 (the day the stars all went out). This could also explain why Van Statten, in 2012, has a thing in his cellar that he can't identify. The incident with the Matter Bomb ("The Stolen Earth") was the work of a very time-capable Dalek who'd gone mad, and Davros, who was under orders from beings made from his own body. If the Daleks he made to their specs were all time-enabled, then a *whole army* of them is going to make history not just a bit more malleable but almost impossible to settle.

The surprise, then, isn't that Amy can't remember the invasion, but that so many of its consequences remain fixed after the Doctor restores things. (Obviously one of these is his own alleged death, but it remains to be seen how far the

continued on Page 105...

X1.6 Dalek

Catchphrase Counter It's when Adam says 'Fantastic' that Rose starts taking an interest. The Doctor himself thinks an incapacitated Dalek warrants two 'fantastics'. The helicopter arriving just after the titles has the call-sign 'Bad Wolf One'.

The Analysis

The Big Picture When it was announced that *Doctor Who* would be returning, three questions were asked by all the journalists: Why bother? Will the Daleks be in it? Who have you cast as the Doctor? It was usually in that order.

Even though the series was supposed to have been an embarrassment and only loved by a handful of anorak-wearing spods, the Daleks were still iconic. It was easy to use them as all-purpose emblems of inhuman rigidity, alien menace and unreasoning hate. In one of his last public appearances before his death, Dennis Potter - one of the most influential and admired TV writers Britain had produced - referred to then-Prime Minister John Major and then-BBC Director General John Birt as "croak-voiced Daleks" blanching all imagination and joy from the Corporation and the nation.

In the year leading up to the announcement of the programme's return, two large advertising campaigns used the Skaroine terrors for comic effect. In one, the long-running slogan "Have a break, have a Kit-Kat" was left implicit as several celebrities behaved completely out of character; it began with two Daleks in a mall asking passers-by for cuddles and came back to them at the end, joining a Hare Krishna parade and chanting "peace-and-love". The other, for Energiser batteries, was more troublesome. It was a poster of the Dalek Supreme with a "to-do" list including "conquer universe". This was a snag, because the advertisers in this case had assumed that - popular and well-known as they have been for so long - the Daleks were in the public domain. As you will recall from Volume 1 (and the coverage of 6.1, "The Dominators"), the conceptual rights for the Daleks are not held by the BBC (nor the original designer, Ray Cusick), but by the estate of Terry Nation. He had become immensely wealthy on the back of this, but in his lifetime, he had been careful to keep the "brand image" of the Daleks fixed and clear. The agent he hired for this, Roger Hancock, was zealous in maintaining this after Nation's death. Even scurrilous parodies such as Victor Lewis-Smith's notorious "Gay Daleks" sketches were closely monitored and some elements were vetoed. (They could not use actual BBC props, but officially-sanctioned fan-made Daleks, available commercially.) Only two exceptions to this had ever been allowed: Spike Milligan's curiously pointless "Pakistani Dalek" skit (why Pakistanis would wear turbans is only the start of the sheer wrongness of this sketch) and the 1999 *Comic Relief* serial "The Curse of Fatal Death" (see the appendix in Volume 6). In both cases, Nation's earlier involvement with Associated London Scripts, and their former agent, Beryl Vertue, had been the fixer (see **Production** for where this led).

Until March 2005, then, the Daleks were bigger than *Doctor Who* and the British public knew about them in the abstract, as generic robot/alien/fascist figures that third-rate comedians claimed couldn't climb stairs. (Admitting to have watched a 1988 Sylvester McCoy episode in which they did just that was, after all, social death - see 25.1, "Remembrance of the Daleks" and **What's All This Stuff About Anoraks?** under "Attack of the Cybermen.") As the press interest in the returning series began to accumulate, the conflicting accounts of whether or not the Nation estate would permit the BBC to use the Daleks were (mis)reported in various tabloids. Rupert Murdoch's downmarket paper *The Sun* claimed to have "won" when the dispute was settled, while other coverage was less jubilant but no more reliable. The timing of this episode as the potential second launch - if the first faltered for any reason - was thus crucial to Julie Gardner's plans for the series. As it was, this would be the week that ITV's desperate *Celebrity Wrestling* was removed from being an attempt to distract viewers from *Doctor Who*, and that the first reports of who would be writing on Series Two emerged.

(One publicity benefit Gardner and Jane Tranter could not have planned was that a General Election was called for the week after transmission: the *Radio Times* could thus re-mount the famous publicity shot of Daleks on Westminster Bridge - 2.2, "The Dalek Invasion of Earth" - and print this as a fold-out cover with the title "Vote Dalek". An attempt to try this *again* for X5.3, "Victory of the Daleks" with a different cover for each colour of the New Paradigm Daleks was less successful, as it merely alerted viewers that the forthcoming episode would feature the Dalek ver-

What's Happened to the Daleks?

continued from Page 103...

Silence are symptoms of his messing with a Fixed Point.) If the whole Dalek intervention in Earth's history while David Tennant was the Doctor is an aberration from the "orthodox" timeline and was undone, this might all make some kind of sense. However, if both it and the thing that *undid* it were undone, then we're getting into much murkier waters.

sion of New Coke.)

The official line remained as it had been throughout the 70s and 80s: the Daleks would return if there was a story good enough for them. In this case, the story was "Jubilee", an audio drama made by Big Finish in 2003 (see X2.5, "Rise of the Cybermen" for more on this lot). The story was widely accepted by people who bought such things as being one of the "classics", and thus a handy model for a fandom-friendly Dalek story. Aside from the almost obligatory multi-Doctor "Dalek Empire" arc that Big Finish trotted out as soon as they'd got the license (not to be confused with the Doctor-less *Dalek Empire* spin-off series), Shearman's "Jubilee" was the only Dalek audio available as a model for Eccleston's first season. Timing a Dalek story with the fortieth anniversary of the show's founding and naming the result "Jubilee" is an obvious joke, especially when the story goes to the trouble of explicitly setting itself in 2003; the Big Finish version was meant to be an "event" story just as much as "Dalek" was.

What's first noticeable about "Dalek" Version 1.0 to anyone coming to it from the world of 45-minute (and visual) *Doctor Who* is that we open with the Doctor and companion having a philosophical argument in the TARDIS console room, far closer to the old-skool feel of Tom Baker serials than the kinds of stories RTD was putting together.[19] The Doctor in question is the sixth, Colin Baker (who had made a mini-career with these audio adventures), albeit in a contemplative mood that doesn't resemble Eccleston very much at all. Baker's portrayal of the Doctor on audio is a good deal more thoughtful and less shouty than he was back in the 80s, mercifully. His companion by this stage is historian/ college professor/ chocolate-cake-lover Evelyn Smythe (the first new companion Big Finish came up with). Most of her early stories focused in some way on the dynamics between a "professional" historian and the Doctor's amateur smarts as applied to time travel, and Shearman apparently tailors the moral to the companion; Rose gets the nicely straightforward one about accepting others, Evelyn ends up with something rather more complicated about how "History is what we choose to remember" and a lot of *1984*-style rewriting-cum-banality of evil.

The story is yer basic "alternative reality intersects with ours" morality-tale, albeit complicated by two overlapping time periods; essentially a socking great Dalek fleet invades 1903 London, gets obliterated by an alternative Doctor, but accidentally gives Great Britain Dalek tech. (Bear this in mind for when we get to "Rise of the Cybermen".) Then the proper Doctor blunders into this timeline in 2003. Van Statten's stand-in is Rochester - the hereditary President of the British Empire, which now dominates the globe. Intriguingly, there's an America connection in this version too, with Rochester causally cowing the American Prime Minister (yes, really) over the videophone even though the rest of the story involves him being overwhelmed in a position too big for him. The Doctor spends most of the story trying to work out the kinks of this new history and criticizing Rochester for utterly different reasons in very familiar ways, while Evelyn goes off and has the subplot that actually gets turned into "Dalek". She meets the sole survivor of the 1903 battle, who's been kept in the Tower of London for a hundred years.

Some of the story beats make more sense in the original, especially since it's got room to breathe; the first cliffhanger involves Rochester chucking the Doctor in the Dalek's cell to see whether he really is the heroic figure of history, leading into the same "Doctor panics when trapped in the dark with a Dalek" that was the perfect moment for a cut to commercial when this was played on American telly. The Dalek itself acts rather like its televised counterpart; the shock of losing an invasion and then a century of being tortured by xenophobic Englishmen has the same psychological effect that genuinely being the last of its kind does on telly, and its interaction with Evelyn runs along the same lines as the broadcast one's with Rose does.

What the longer version has as an advantage is that it doesn't need to resort to quick 'n' dirty skiffy cheats to make this work. One of the more notorious stereotypes about Big Finish audios is that they're exceptionally talky, and Shearman exploits this tendency - instead of the Artron energy gambit, Evelyn gets several episodes to rationally talk the Dalek into questioning itself and the ethos of hate it's lived by all its life. When the Doctor finally does run into it, he's no happier about seeing a Dalek than he ever is, but restrains himself and tries to keep talking sense into it by pointing out that a Dalek empire is ultimately pointless; once they've obliterated the rest of the universe, Daleks have no function anymore. The intellectual arguments, for a change, actually make sense to the Dalek; it goes and conveniently kills a Dalek fleet before history ever changes, then begs Evelyn to kill it since its self-destruct mechanism was removed. She reluctantly agrees and shoots it with its own gun; presumably someone thought this would be a step too far for pre-watershed BBC drama if Rose did the same. (That's broadly what's done to the story to make it work in the passage from a two-and-a-half hour radio drama into 45 minutes of telly; it's made simpler, shorter, and a lot less scary for the sprogs.)

The dating of the original "Jubilee" CD also makes it unlikely that the common reading of this story by online critics as a commentary on Guantanamo Bay or Abu Ghraib has much validity. This element of the story is largely unchanged, although paradoxically the fact that the humans of 2012 were never at war with the Daleks and have no reason to gloat makes "Jubilee" a closer fit despite the obvious anachronism. Indeed, as we will see, the televised story was at one point to have been about a different kind of alien, one unfamiliar to the audience at this stage, and the huge legacy of the Daleks as the One True *Doctor Who* Monster would not have clouded the issue. The story would, in this formulation, have been what it was for viewers in France or Poland - about the normally humane and broad-minded Doctor apparently going mad and giving in to xenophobic blood-lust. In this light, look again at the Next Time clip at the end of X1.5, "World War Three". The plot elements are introduced succinctly and then, right at the end, the Dalek is revealed, shouting "Exterminate!" The assumption is that everyone watching knows what this thing is; it doesn't need to be shown in action. We are thus assumed to see things the Doctor's way, whereas as written, the story is from Rose's point of view - a tale about a misunderstood being that even the Doctor can't find it in his hearts to leave unmolested.

This element, it must be admitted, is vaguely akin to - and instructively different from - the *Star Trek: The Next Generation* episode "I, Borg". In that, however, each of the regulars sits down and chats with this specimen of the abhorrent former foes, and he becomes jes' like regular folks while they all learn the usual Valuable Life Lesson (to be forgotten by the start of the next episode). Hugh, the loveable Borg, is reassimilated into the Borg Collective and goes back to his former life. But the Dalek in "Dalek" is contaminated and impure, and has to retire from galactic conquest as there is no longer an army for him to rejoin. As befits a series being made in the twenty-first century, the new *Doctor Who* has no reset-button for out-of-sequence reshowing in syndication. The episode has consequences (even if we take the Dalek's apparent self-destruction at face value). The most significant is that we are led to believe that Adam is going to be a permanent addition to the TARDIS crew.

One element that is red-shifting away from us now - so quickly do these things change - is that 2004, when this episode was written, was the height of the public's amusement at the antics of Microsoft and Apple. Bill Gates' inability to imagine any use for the money he was making from other people's ingenuity was the butt of the public's joking, but professional geeks made sport with the increasingly eccentric and dictatorial Steve Jobs. Both men combined to fill a void that Howard Hughes had left in the popular imagination. In Britain, especially, the public believe it to be the responsibility of people who have made vast sums from the public to fritter the money away in full glare of the cameras, so that we can vicariously enjoy this insane wealth. Whereas rappers and sports stars can be "allowed" to enjoy their rags-to-nouveau-riches conspicuous consumption, the one thing worse than bad taste is secrecy. If someone is only suspected of being obscenely comfortably off, that person slips into the realm of conspiracy-theory "them"-ness, one of the shadowy people that "explain" the theorist's misfortune. Computer millionaires fill this space nicely, as the motives and operations of clever kids are automatically suspect - whereas everyone could see what (say) Michael Jackson was up to, even if they couldn't quite see what he did to earn that much. The overlapping narrative on display here is the traditional "good with computers = bad with people" compensatory fantasy, and Van Statten hiding in a hole in the ground - surrounded by yes-men, a private army and trinkets he doesn't understand - ticks all the boxes for the British view of Americans generally and computer millionaires specifically. (Britain's computer millionaires are more overt, more down-to-Earth and more prone to make prats of themselves in public. Look up "Sinclair C5".) Our mental image of these people has changed now that Google and Facebook have become the main public notions of what computers do, and the people behind those are a new kind of annoying idiot (see X4.4, "The Sontaran Stratagem").

English Lessons

• *Spooning* (v) A courting couple couldn't be left alone unchaperoned, but if they wanted privacy with no suspicion of shenanigans, parents would equip the young swain with a block of wood and a knife to keep his hands busy and provide evidence that he'd been behaving himself. These were more innocent, and apparently unimaginative, times. The tradition of carving elaborate lovespoons had an implication that low-level intimacy might be occurring and provided the couple with a keepsake - a large and impractical kitchen-utensil to put on the mantelpiece and show their own children what standard of workmanship was expected as and when they themselves started sparkin'.

• *Milometer* (n) Obviously, a thing on a car that measures how many miles it's travelled. (Apparently Americans call it an "odometer". We'd think that was for measuring smells.) In the event of Britain adopting metric for distances over the height of a house, everyone will still probably call it "the clock".

Oh, Isn't That…?

• *Bruno Langley* (Adam Mitchell). By now, it won't be much of a surprise that he was in *Linda Green* as the sarcastic kid brother, but shortly thereafter he got a gig as one of the first uncomplicatedly gay teens in a British soap (i.e., just there as a character who happened to be gay rather than this being a huge "problem" that motivated months of screen-time given over to the routine reactions of the family and friends) and, officially, the first openly gay character in *Coronation Street* (although we had our suspicions about Minnie Caldwell…). If there was anyone who could convincingly look to the casual viewer like the optimum casting for the next male companion, it was him.

Things That Don't Make Sense You've captured an alien that survived falling from space hard enough to leave a crater. People who touch it burst into flames. So you keep it in a room next to a storage facility with tanks marked 'Liquid Oxygen' and 'Flammable'. Lucky you've got a sprinkler system, eh? (Err, except that chucking water on burning LOX makes Hydrogen Peroxide, which will take it from an inferno to a massive explosion. Talk about a blonde bombshell…) Then Van Statten places someone who knows about aliens in that vault with his prize exhibit and locks him in, because he wants to know what will happen. So he monitors the situation closely with CCTV… and then switches the lights off in the cell. But he leaves the controls of the Metaltron-torturing equipment functional, in case the mysterious Doctor might wish to damage the rare treasure from the stars.

Speaking of Van Statten, he recognises Rose's accent as English, but not the Doctor's. [All right, this is plausible, as (pardon our pointing it out) Americans can be a bit slow about these things.] It's even more remarkable that Van Statten is a leading authority on extraterrestrials, and yet he doesn't know who the Doctor is. Not even the virus the Doctor deployed to erase all mention of him (X1.5, "World War Three") can fully explain this one, given that Van Statten owns the Internet and hires genii with the kind of research skills that almost start wars. Are we to believe that Clive (X1.1, "Rose") and Mickey (in "Aliens of London") are smarter than these guys?

Moreover, Van Statten is well connected enough to obtain a Cyberman head, and yet seems unable to find any record of the Daleks. (It's not sufficient to claim that the Time War meant that all Dalek incursions into even twentieth-century history were erased, because then presumably the crew of the *Mary Celeste* never perished - 2.8, "The Chase" - and the public should have never heard of the ship, and yet references to it keep being made, even in *The Sarah Jane Adventures*. Even if we invoke the get-out-of-jail-free card of the Crack in the Wall in Season Five, X5.3, "Victory of the Daleks" especially, it's hard to see how anyone in 2012 can fail to know about the Battle of Canary Wharf. So this story *has* to come from a closed-off timeline... except that doesn't work, because it has obvious consequences in the main narrative of the series from now on.)

Oh, and the Dalek's been passed around from collection to collection with auctions every few years for five decades, and nobody from UNIT knew about it? (The BBC's UNIT website has a bizarre reference, dated 28/08 but no year, to their not being able to afford it.)

We mentioned above the various cartogrrrraphical anomalies (after 25.1, "Remembrance of the Daleks"; it's compulsory to spell it that way) under **History**, but one that needs mentioning here is that a Dalek in a base in Utah draws all its power from the West Coast. If this was in Britain, we could surmise that it has shopped around for the cheapest supplier. (Perhaps after seeing online adverts, especially the annoying Sly Stone clone who told us "Youuuuu gotta switch". Exterminating him would have been a public service.) As far as we know, the only way someone Way Out West - even someone who's swallowed the Internet and can switch things around - would do this rather than just take a more local route is if they are deliberately depriving Washington state, Oregon and California of energy. It might be that there's a military need for this, and that all those silos nearer to Utah have been emptied of their missiles (and that's maybe how Van Statten built this base without anyone noticing - he took over a bunker built by Uncle Sam), but that doesn't work either. The Dalek would simply adore to have America become the kind of post-apocalyptic radioactive wilderness he grew up in. Unless it got so bored that the idea of killing everyone on Earth, one by one (possibly in alphabetical order), was what kept it going, there seems to be no reason why the Dalek is re-enacting the Enron scam. Quite *how* he's doing it, with nobody on the outside taking steps to stop it like manually switching off the supply (or the fuses at the various sub-stations blowing with the unprecedented and sudden demand) can be filed with "Where's Vermont?" and "How many Acension Islands are there now?" (see **History**).

The moment when the Dalek is seemingly daunted by stairs and then levitates is fine and dandy, but it has a gun capable of pointing up at the assembled taunting humans. And the bulkhead that stops the Dalek... it's a bit flimsy, isn't it? This thing later *blows a hole in the ceiling*. It also knows how to switch the video cameras on and off by remote, so presumably it can over-ride the systems that Van Statten's just ploughed through in a hurry.

What actually happens between the Dalek doing indoor fireworks and the tag-scene, in which Adam informs the Doctor and Rose that the base is to be filled with concrete? We get Van Statten deposed, but no effort is made to evacuate the people doing the deposing. We hear no alarms and, even with the lifts not working, the Doctor and Rose can't have taken longer to get down to the TARDIS than it takes to move 200 bodies and mix up that much cement. More to the point, how are they going to get that much concrete there in a hurry? (Maybe it was always there as a precaution, but the only places that do that are nuclear power stations, so we're back to the Dalek switching supplier for no good reason.)

A plane to Heathrow from Utah? (It turns out, actually, that there is a flight to Paris from Salt Lake City. But not to London.)

Critique The episode had an unfair advantage on first broadcast: everyone who had ever heard of the series before had high hopes, and simply not making a mess of it would be enough to get a good response. For the newer viewers, this story has the crafty deployment of all the possible jokes about the Daleks just before each one is systematically rubbished. For everyone, the story had the big extra point that at last we got the background on the Time War.

Watched now that the dust has settled and we know more about the Time War than perhaps is sensible, the thing that strikes one about "Dalek" is how relatively slow it is. At the time, it was taking no chances, cutting no corners and methodically re-establishing the Daleks as the Doctor's worst nightmare. Now, this has been done. We get that. However, there are still things to enjoy here. There are moments when the script, directing and technical aspects combine to make moments of savage beauty out of the potentially routine material. The Dalek destroying troops *en masse* with a sprinkler and one shot to the floor is a smart idea that any director could have made work, but Joe Ahearne makes it worth lingering over; it's not going too far to say that it's a tiny moment of Kurosawa[20], filtered most likely through Ridley Scott[21]. It might not be consciously echoing either director, but the effect is similar enough to draw the comparison. Likewise, the oddly balletic sequence of the Dalek rotating its central gun-turret to pick off individuals takes a good scene and makes it sing.

More impressive now, with later stories sending in legions of the beggars, is that one chained-up Dalek with no power is such a threat. They play the scene where the Doctor first confronts the Dalek as *Silence of the Lambs*, and show the two of them pressing each other's buttons in a way that we won't ever get again. They later tried, in another bunker ("Victory of the Daleks"), but Matt Smith simply isn't up to it. This is where Eccleston, playing to his familiar type, comes into his own. Once the chains shatter, the Dalek is able to do a lot of things we've never seen before (we've *heard* about a few of these facilities in Annuals, but it's not the same) and - crucially - don't need to see again. The subsequent appearances work better because we know of the hitherto-unmentioned tricks displayed here.

Which is our first snag. This story would have worked pretty well if it had been a new alien we'd not heard of, and it works better if you forget any subsequent Dalek story. However, because it exists in a context with a very long-running storyline and annual reappearances of a race, this story needs us to think that the Daleks are almost extinct. The Dalek seen here goes through desperation, revenge, isolation, anguish and self-loathing, whereas all later Daleks are simply one of a species and following (or giving) orders. Whether you buy that this Dalek really self-destructed - or that it was manipulating Rose again and really bracing itself for a temporal shift and setting up Satellite Five and building an army (see **The Non-Humans**) - the ending works as a discussion of whether to apply our values to a race designed to hate. Even the botched revisiting of this in "Evolution of the Daleks" (X3.5) never does as much in ten minutes as this scene does in two.

A large part of that is that this episode is planned as one 45-minute piece. The pacing of this episode is - at last - spot-on for the new format. The debates come at moments where they can draw examples from what's just been happening. This is a rebuttal of the old "show, don't tell" saw, because the showing relies on the telling to provide context, and the telling comes when it is unavoidably needed. The logic of the story needs a showdown between an armed Doctor and a reborn Dalek, but this ends up with Rose caught between the two warring aliens. We've become so used to people (especially Davies) telling us how important it is to have an emotional content, in terms that equate "emotion" to "Billie blubbing her eyes out and Murray Gold doing a piano moment", that a situation engineered to make us feel sympathy for a Dalek isn't usually included in any list on *Doctor Who Confidential*. The Dalek is suffering *because* it has emotions. The situation forces first the Doctor, then Rose, to make choices between two almost equal moral positions apiece. Rose is trying to do what she thinks the Doctor would, but the Doctor is becoming more like he claims the Daleks were. This isn't "emotion" plastered over a science-fiction premise as if the two were antithetical, it grows *out of* the situation.

Whilst that situation has evident resemblances to real-world events, it is not a clunkingly obvious *Galactica*-style allegory. This isn't "really" about anything, it is a story that exists on its own terms. Eccleston may have wanted the series to be about capital-I issues, but, wisely, the script and directing move too fast for anyone to pin it down and say "Aha! This is like Camp X-Ray!" or "Oho! This is Rudolph Hess." Even if Shearman's script had been that crass, Ahearne has written comics and a TV serial, so he can spot how to broaden out a single-issue script. Fortunately he didn't need to, but instead makes maximum use of what the script gives him. Another director might have shifted the emphasis, making the switches from action to rhetorical conflict more alarming, whilst a third might have tried to make *RoboCop* in Cardiff and relegated the arguments to brief asides between shoot-outs and black humour. Shearman, originally a theatre writer who has worked in radio, has made a very visual story with long set-piece arguments (a comparison with Ahearne's next story as director is illuminating - see X1.8, "Father's Day").

The central problem is Van Statten. Corey Johnson's not *bad* in the role, he's just underpowered as a threat in a story with a Dalek in it. Once again, if the story had been in episodes along the lines of the old series, this might not have been a problem. The character is complex enough to be a full-scale antagonist of the Doctor's in his own right, but as soon as the Dalek arrives, he's relegated to a supporting role. If they'd kept him around for further development, this might have been interesting; if someone capable of suggesting more was going on than the dialogue intimated had played the part, it might also have worked. Then again, if the part hadn't been built up and then trimmed back (see **Production**), the character might have had more gravitas after the Dalek awakens. As things stand, Van Statten's last scene is marred mainly by his underling not ever showing any concern for the two hundred dead she uses as a pretext for retconning him into oblivion. It just seems like a grim screwball comedy, perhaps echoing the oddly *West Wing* scene of Van Statten's arrival. It has no real link to the fact that the Doctor has ever been there, or that Rose has just saved the world. If Van Statten had been the Charles Foster Kane they want to suggest, this might have been an appropriately callous way to show him suffering by even threatening him with being nobody, and a good way to foreshadow Adam's eventual fate - but nothing is done with it. In any other story this might have worked but, once again, the Dalek overtopples everything. Van Statten's downfall is a bit of accounting, a loose end in the story dealt with in passing.

So, it's not *entirely* flawless. But nothing's egregiously wrong, which is a start. *Doctor Who* is playing with the big boys now, making an episode that looks like a bigger-budget American series, or a mini-feature-film, whilst digging into its core iconography and basic tenets, all the things that made it work before the johnny-come-lately yank shows were even thought of, and still finding new things to do with the single most over-used monster of them all. Last week it was doing something else entirely; next week it'll go somewhere else and start from scratch again. That's how this series works, and now everyone's along for the ride.

The Facts

Written by Robert Shearman. Directed by Joe Ahearne. Viewing figures: (BBC1) 8.63 million, (BBC3 repeats) 0.2 and 0.5 million.

Alternate Versions The French version, also called "Dalek" but with equal stress on both syllables, has an approximation of the Dalek voice effect with the Ring-Modulator; the verbs "exterminate" and "elevate" become nouns, "Ex-ter-mi-na-ti-on" and "E-le-va-ti-on". More damningly than in the original, the Dalek switches between the familiar/patronising "tu" and the respectful/distant "vous" when talking to the Doctor about how similar they are.

Production

Looking back, it seems odd to think that there was ever any doubt that the Daleks would be returning. However, the estate of Terry Nation made the BBC jump through a few hoops. For the reasons sketched in under **The Big Picture** above, they calculated that *Doctor Who* needed Daleks more than the Daleks needed what might have been an embarrassing dud revamp.

To recap: the deal Terry Nation struck for the rights to the Daleks was unlike that for any other writer's creations for the series. Whereas the merchandising and copyright for some of the other monsters were owned by the BBC and these beasties were available for any writer who wished to use them in a *Doctor Who* script (with only a nominal fee and, these days, a credit for the original writer), Nation and the Daleks were different. Anyone writing a Dalek script would get 40% of the fee, the rest going to Nation (or his estate). His agent, Roger Hancock, had zealously patrolled the media for the potential misuse of the Daleks (see **Who Really Created the Daleks?** under "The Daleks"). The BBC Drama department was, by 2003, staffed with people unaware of this anomaly. When the return of the series was announced, they blithely stated that of course, the Daleks would be back. Nation was dead and the responsibility was now with Tim Hancock. The BBC's arrogance led to an exchange of letters, beginning with Hancock suggesting that it would have been better to check that the rights for the Daleks were available before shooting their mouths off. The full story is still emerging piecemeal, but this seems to have become a stand-off, albeit not to the extent that the tabloids made out.

The sad irony is that there was nobody in fandom who couldn't have seen this coming. Certainly those fans now writing the scripts all knew it, and the one writing episodes nine and ten was well aware of the situation. Steven Moffat's mother-in-law, Beryl Vertue, had been in the agency that employed Nation when he first came to London, Associated London Scripts. (This was set up by Galton and Simpson, writers of *Hancock's Half Hour* and *Steptoe and Son*, and Spike Milligan, whose influence of British culture is inestimable but start with *The Goon Show*; he soon became the nexus of comedy writing in Britain.) Vertue began by typing up the scripts, but by the time the agency was sold to Robert Stigwood, she was managing director and had become a formidable player. Few Americans appreciate that *All in the Family* and *Sanford and Son* were re-workings of BBC shows. Vertue had learned to play hardball with US TV executives, so when Moffat wanted Daleks in his *Comic Relief* skit (see "The Curse of Fatal Death" in the appendix to Volume 6), Nation's people simply let him. As soon as the relaunch of *Doctor Who* began, it looked as if this would happen again, but the new generation of BBC suits declined the offer of the mother-in-law of one of the writers having a word with the people handling the BBC's most famous monster. Accounts vary about precisely how patronising the wording of this was. The BBC's case wasn't helped by the unauthorised (according to Tim Hancock) use of a couple of Daleks in the "Area 52" scene from *Looney Tunes: Back in Action* (2003). (It being a Joe Dante film, this comes in between Robbie the Robot, a Metalunan from *This Island Earth* and Kevin McCarthy carrying a giant seed-pod.)

So for six months, the press reported the will-they-wont-they story of the Daleks' rematch with the Doctor. Behind the scenes, the plan to rework Robert Shearman's "Jubilee" audio kept changing, and a Plan B was needed. Shearman had all the right credentials to do this. Apart from "Jubilee", he had written three Big Finish audio dramas for various Doctors, and had worked on a series called *Born and Bred* (one of many Sunday night series where people in Barbour jackets drive Land Rovers around Yorkshire, or sometimes Scotland), which was produced by Phil Collinson. He had written dark and strange stage plays and Radio Four dramas, had been a protégé of Sir Alan Aykbourne and used to co-edit a *Doctor Who* fanzine before renouncing fandom and going to university. He knew Moffat and Paul Cornell socially - as you will have realised from Volume 6, he's firmly back in the fold - but had not met Davies before. Their first meeting was awkward. This, and the prolonged uncertainty over whether the story's *raison d'etre* - the Daleks - would even be in it, made for a difficult genesis.

As we will see, one option that was seriously discussed was a new arch-enemy, a different antagonist for the Time Lords in the Time War. The race that was developed was a breed of psychopathic giggly children, who were built into armoured, heavily-armed suits and treated killing the way real children behave when on a sugar-rush. Some of you might be thinking of the Quarks when reading this (6.1, "The Dominators"), but most will have worked out that this new foe for the Doctor was substantially recycled as the Toclafane (X3.12, "The Sound of Drums" - see also **Was Series Two Supposed to be Like This?** under X2.11, "Fear Her"). A version with one of these new creatures in Van Statten's cage was written (Shearman referred to this as "Absence of the Daleks"). Another way to fill the void was to build up Van Statten's role, making him the principal antagonist and exploring his motivation. Possible additional impetus for this was the reported prospect, which waxed and waned in plausibility, of Christian Slater (or, at least, that's the name being bandied about) being available and interested in the part. Van Statten as the focus of the story rather than a monster from the programme's past made the relationships between him and his staff more complex: the characters who became Adam and Goddard as we saw them were briefly moved to being his son and wife, and - in a reversion to "Jubilee" - it was Mrs Van Statten's frustration with her husband's obsession that led to whatever-it-was-in-the-cage being tortured. At around this point, the news that Shearman was writing something that was to have been a Dalek story emerged on the Jade Pagoda fan website.

• Eventually, the rather infantile stand-off over the rights to the Daleks was resolved, and production on a story that Julie Gardner suggested should just be called "Dalek" could begin properly. Once again, Mike Tucker's crew were given a high-profile assignment, making a Dalek that looked like we all imagined they did when we were small. He had built the last Daleks used in the series (25.1, "Remembrance of the Daleks"), and used two of the remaining shells as reference. The discussions of what needed changing (or, in most cases, changing back) began with production designer Edward Thomas, concept designer Matt Savage and Russell T Davies. The latter had a long list of things he didn't want from the 80s designs, and was insistent on copper and bronze as the basic "look". He brought a Dapol model from the 1980s to show what he didn't want (see **Why Did They Think We'd Buy This Crap?** under 22.5, "Timelash"). The base of the shells had to be more pointed, as with the original design by Ray Cusick in 1963, and the lights on the dome were to be like those from the Peter

Cushing films (see Appendices 1 and 2 in Volume 6). A new element was the "bar-code" under the eye-stalk, making every Dalek unique (sort of - see X1.12, "Bad Wolf"). With three weeks to build both the damaged "prisoner" Dalek and the "regenerated" one, Tucker borrowed two replicas owned by Andrew Beech, convention organiser and so much more (see Volume 6), and took them to bits to see how to make the new ones. This saved about a week's work. Meanwhile, Neill Gorton's team at Millennium Effects began work on the occupant, making it both consistent with the various ideas of what a Kaled mutant might look like and recognisably ex-human enough for pathos.

Unlike before, the head mechanisms - with lights illuminating in synch with the dialogue, a powerful blue light in the eye-stalk and the dome rotating to observe through 360 degrees - was operated by radio control rather than the occupant. There was a small problem with the animatronics being on a frequency that made the ring-modulator used for the voice (performed "live" on set by Nicholas Briggs) leap up an octave if the two units were too close. During the BBC's botched celebrations for *Doctor Who*'s thirtieth anniversary, the indulgent documentary *Thirty Years in the TARDIS* was eventually broadcast - but was cut down from what was made. In making this, any fans with Equity cards who could be in London early on a Sunday morning were pressed into service to dress as monsters and recreate well-known scenes. So it was that David Hankinson, Nicholas Pegg and Barnaby Edwards were on a list of potential Dalek operators over a decade later. (By this stage, the previous main Dalek operator - John Scott Martin - was rather too frail, although he had been in Davies' last ITV production, *Mine All Mine*, a few months before.) Edwards was the pioneer for this, and there was a trial run for the practical details of moving the prop around the location on the first day of the shoot. This showed up one potential problem: the chosen location, the basement of the Millennium Stadium in Cardiff, had very narrow corridors, with about an inch of clearance in some places. Edwards was almost completely unable to see either side of him in the shell.

• Block Three was originally to have included "The Long Game" (X1.7), but this was moved later down the schedule, eventually getting its own mini-block. Instead, "Dalek" and "Father's Day" (X1.8) were made almost back-to-back, with additional scenes for "Rose" (X1.1), "Aliens of London" (X1.4) and "World War Three" (X1.5) slotted in on what were to have been days off. The read-through for both episodes took place on 18th October, 1994, with Briggs talking through his ring-modulator. Director Joe Ahearne's track-record was formidable. He had written and directed the 90s series *Ultraviolet*, a thriller that neatly avoided ever using the word "vampire", but was about how the authorities would handle such a situation. He had then directed a few episodes of the under-performing supernatural chiller *Strange*. His methodical approach to directing a complicated piece impressed the crew and cast.

Eccleston in particular came to trust Ahearne; on the second day of the shoot, in the cell where the Doctor confronts the Dalek, Ahearne offered to retake the scene to remove the froth from Eccleston's mouth, but this was declined because it was agreed that it simply looked better. This was shot in the Broadcast Suite of the Stadium, the first actual scene recorded there. The previous day had seen the crew in an unused section of the National Museum of Wales for the opening and closing scenes. Julie Gardner had been keen for a Cyberman to be one of the exhibits; others came from Neill Gorton's Van-Statten-style collection of aliens from various previous film projects (including *Alien3*). However, for the first day at the Millennium Stadium (26th October), the *Doctor Who* team were joined by a press that was keen to see the new-look Dalek. For the scenes with the chained Dalek, Mike Tucker operated the radio-control head. Eventually the three operators (Edwards inside, Briggs on voice and one of Thomas' crew taking over from Tucker) would become so closely in synch as to be able to ad-lib when things went wrong. There were slight delays when the sound of gunfire in a public arena caused terrorist alerts.

• On October 29th, the corridors of the Stadium approaching the so-called "Dragon's Mouth" (the atrium leading onto the pitch) got used for the first of what would be many times over the next few years, for the massacre of the troops by the newly-restored Dalek. This continued for the next day, with a bulkhead (built by the BBC, not a fixture) closing. (Some of this sequence was remounted at the Q2 complex almost a month later.) The next day, Sunday, was Hallowe'en; no work was done that day (a relief for those on the crew with children going back to school the next day). There is some conjecture that there were logistical problems with the originally-scripted climax, and that the Dalek self-destruction was a compromise worked out to cover for difficulties getting Eccleston and Piper on set at the same time. There is no proof of this. Monday, however, was the day the sprinklers went on. Other scenes in the Stadium (notably the corridor walks at the beginning and end of the episode and the stairwell sequence) were shot over the next two days and then on Thursday the 4th, the unit relocated to Q2 for Van Statten's office. This used inserted video-feed material from the Stadium to allow Johnson and Eccleston to react to Piper and the Dalek as if conversing. The following week had a few scenes from "Father's Day" and the Block One salvage-work, so the work on "Dalek" resumed, appropriately, on 23rd November (Ahearne's birthday - he's exactly as old as the series, being born in 1963), with the remounted Bulkhead shots and Adam's den. The latter was Clive's shed from "Rose". With the rights to the Daleks secured, Davies could go ahead with planning the season finale.

• Some time later, Eccleston feted Shearman for his script. The consensus was that the writer should work again on the series, but to date this has not happened (although there was, by all accounts, a near-miss with Series Six). Nonetheless, any subsequent project, for radio in particular, has had him identified as "*Doctor Who* author Robert Shearman". The episode went out the week of a General Election, as we mentioned last time: the *Radio Times* cover played on this with a remount of the publicity shots for "The Dalek Invasion of Earth" (2.2) on Westminster Bridge and the caption "Vote Dalek"... although one reader objected to the way the Dalek became "soft", the episode made something of an impression and confirmed that the reborn series was on a roll.

X1.7: "The Long Game"

(7th May, 2005)

Which One is This? The one no-one ever remembers. The one with Simon Pegg in it, if that helps. An alien media mogul has enslaved humanity by setting up a news corporation that tells lies (the very idea!). In other news, Adam, the companion nobody remembers, fails his audition.

Firsts and Lasts At risk of a spoiler, this is our first visit to Satellite Five (we're going to get to know these sets almost as well as the basement of the Millennium Stadium). And it's Adam's second and final appearance. He gets a surname just in time to be booted out of the TARDIS (almost literally). And that's about it, except that this is the first time Rose tries to use the sonic screwdriver and she can't quite figure it out.

Watch Out For...

• The episode's title refers to the fact that what happens in this week's story only really becomes important six weeks later. What actually occurs *now* is, apparently, a routine space-monster-enslaves-humanity-by-exaggerating-something-contemporary tale (6.4, "The Krotons"; 15.4, "The Sun Makers"; and 23.1, "The Mysterious Planet", all by Robert Holmes), but this is a ruse. In "saving" Earth, the Doctor may have created the necessary conditions for a much nastier trap that will lead to his death at the season finale.

• Yet those Holmes stories, and others like them by other writers, were set in futures that looked like The Future (a sort of consensus of designers and directors, especially noticeable in 1960s BBC science-fiction plays - *Doctor Who* is just the tip of the iceberg). This story's version of 200,000 AD seems to have a branch of *Top Shop* supplying low-cost couture, and a space station that looks like a warehouse-scale DIY outlet. Whilst the script indicates that this station is based on a real place quite unlike *Homebase* or *Do-It-All* (see **The Big Picture**), the look is resolutely prosaic. Even the freaky-looking extras who show up to buy Kronkburgers - accompanied by music almost identical to that for those *kerrAYzee* aliens in "The End of the World" (X1.2) - are the sort of people you'd see running market-stalls at Camden Lock in the 90s.

• The starting-point for this story is that Adam has to be shown to be wanting compared to Rose. The original season outline Davies presented simply had this one idea as the subject of the episode. So we can hardly complain that the Doctor overthrows a corrupt system by telling people off for not asking questions and then letting the Editor - the Bond-Villain-style mouthpiece for the alien foe behind it all - gloat within earshot of a disgruntled employee. However, the finished episode relegated Adam to a subplot, and his best moments come in two brief scenes with a nurse selling him some upgrades involving brain surgery.

X1.7 The Long Game

- This is the second story in a row to have the Doctor manacled while a tycoon threatens to take and abuse his powers, but it at least keeps him fully clothed. It's as if they *want* people to write torture-porn fan-fic.
- A deft edit at the end removes the need for a TARDIS dematerialisation by having an angry Doctor shove Adam in through the Ship's door left-to-right and then out, again left-to-right into his own living-room. Less noticeably, the establishing shot of the Mitchell residence is an outtake from "Rose" (X1.1). Apparently, Adam's mum lives next door to Clive Finch and family.
- This week's important life-lesson: "Never underestimate plumbing."

The Continuity

The Doctor He will hug anyone.

In response to Rose's concern that the Doctor's knowledge of this era isn't as sharp as he thinks, he says: 'My history's perfect.' [Compare with his fumbling attempts to identify one of the most successful Prime Ministers ever in X1.4, "Aliens of London".] No records of either the Doctor nor Rose can be found in this era [possibly the result of the "delete all references to the Doctor" virus that was deployed in "Aliens of London," or a similar data purge the eleventh Doctor performs in the wake of X6.13, "The Wedding of River Song"]. He refers to humanity of this period as 'stupid little slaves', but as a means of goading Cathica to take action and become something more. [It's akin to the reverse-psychology he uses with Sarah in 12.2, "The Ark in Space."] With the Jagrafess dead and no longer influencing mankind, the Doctor predicts that humanity's development should 'accelerate back to normal'. [See X1.12, "Bad Wolf", for how well that turns out.]

- *Ethics*. Having divined that this culture is 'wrong' compared to what he historically knows to be true about it, he sets about investigating, sending Rose and Adam off to have fun without him. He asks questions and, more pointedly, rounds on anyone who doesn't. [In this regard, he is at his most manipulative since Season Twenty-Six. Noticeably, his opposition to alien interference in Earth's affair not only includes a belief that them keeping aliens at arm's length is a mistake, but refusing to give answers or lead a rebellion himself. His treatment of Adam is, conversely, manipulating him into *not* doing anything.]

- *Background*. He describes visiting Paris as: 'You can't just read the guidebook, you've got to throw yourself in. Eat the food, use the wrong verbs, get charged double and end up kissing complete strangers. Or is that just me?' [This is usually taken as the Doctor reminiscing, but as we know (from the *Doctor Who Annual 2006*) that Rose and Shareen played hookey on a school trip there, he may be teasing her. He knows a few odd things about her childhood, actually - see X1.10, "The Doctor Dances" for his surprising knowledge of her twelfth Christmas.]

He appears to know a great deal about the Fourth Great and Bountiful Human Empire and is alarmed at how this version of 200,000 differs from what he expects.

- *Inventory: Sonic Screwdriver*. The Doctor waves the sonic screwdriver at a cash-dispenser, and gives Adam the resulting metal bar of spending money. [This turns out to be a *lot* of spending-money, and Adam misuses it. Maybe the Doctor is setting him a test, but this is unusual, and more likely a mistake caused by the change in currency from the timeline he knew.]

- *Inventory: Other*. The journalist Cathica concludes that the Doctor is management setting her a test, and a flash of the psychic paper seems to confirm this to her and Suki, her co-worker.

The Doctor checks his wristwatch to make sure he's in the right year. [This looks like a sight-gag but later stories will confirm that he can align it to local chronology with a tap to the glass; see X1.9, "The Empty Child".]

The TARDIS It manages not to blow anything around [compare with "Rose", etc] when arriving at either the space station or Adam's front room.

The Supporting Cast

- *Rose* has had time to change into her Punky Fish top and rather tighter trousers, as if expecting to be an action-heroine. She's still doing the point-and-laugh thing towards the Doctor [observe how this diminishes in frequency after his regeneration], threatening him with a slap for teasing her about Adam. She takes the basic information the Doctor has given her about the station and embroiders it plausibly to pretend that she's a lot more experienced in time travel. When Adam faints, she replies to the Doctor's 'He's your boyfriend' with 'not any more'. The Doctor compliments her on spotting the obvious anomaly about

Why Doesn't Anyone Read Any More?

If you glanced at **How Important Were the Books?** under 2.6, "The Crusade", you'll have seen a first attempt to equate fannishness with bookishness. The first merchandising for *Doctor Who* was three novels wrought from scripts that were made into television plays, but were worlds away from the later Target novelisations of *Doctor Who* stories, which frequently resorted to transcribing their sources and added "he said" or "she said" every so often.

It's hard to understate the cultural impact of these books. In the pre-video age, the presence of Target novelisations in every school library and bookshop in the country was not only a source of fan-lore, it was the first significant reading-matter for a generation. Apart from the novelisations providing expanded scenes and background, and prolepsis giving motivation and sympathy for antagonists who were simplistic villains on screen (not to mention and a diligent campaign to expand the vocabulary of Britain's ten year olds), the sets, effects and acting were so much better on page. Even better, some stories made slightly more sense when transmogrified into prose - the end of "The Dalek Invasion of Earth" (2.2) is a mess, but Terrance Dicks rationalises it; this at the peak of his notoriety for perfunctoriness. Malcolm Hulke sometimes took this to extremes - "The War Games" (6.7) was ten episodes long, but Hulke got it to 126 pages *and still* added more details, even though he was dying when he wrote it.

Educationalists at the time praised Dicks for his clarity and pace, as it was precisely the sort of thing that could get a young reader into the action while making them reflect on the processes of storytelling and language-use. Also, this being *Doctor Who*, each book was *different* from the others in the series, with a central character who was subject to abrupt changes in appearance, and had to be introduced from book to book. It was still a *series* of books, but not quite as redundant as its contemporaries.

In short, this is almost-perfect material for developing reading-muscles. Here we've just touched upon a big subject that changes almost constantly, but the current state-of-the-art account - using PET scans, NMR and all that malarkey - is Stanislas Dehaene's work. In brief, the adolescent reader abruptly jumps from working out individual sentences and words to second-guessing; skipping laborious neural links formerly used to make prose intelligible means that brain is now free to make connections with personal experience, rather than just attempting to make sense of marks on a page or screen. Crudely put, this means that once a critical level of *experience* has been reached, the reader uses both hemispheres to do two or three different things with the text. He or she "inhabits" a book rather than just piecing the sentences together word-by-word. (See **Can He Read Smells?** under X2.8, "The Impossible Planet".)

One consequence of this is that the quantity of previous reading is as important as the quality, although in the run-up to this breakthrough, the ability to figure out meanings of unfamiliar words from context or similarity to other words - "syntactic bootstrapping" as it's called in the trade - is the most important skill to pick up. Adventures on made-up worlds or in curious places and times are ideal training-grounds for this. So if a team of modern-day educational psychologists and neurologists had worked out the optimum preparation for full literacy among 12-year-olds, it would be a collectable set of books with a lot of redundant features (stock phrases, recurring characters), but unfamiliar vocabulary and word-use in each individual book - plus a lot of sequences where unique and exotic places and situations are evoked, but the precise details left to the reader's ability to infer from cues in the text.

In short, Target novelisations. A whole generation in Britain grew to literacy via 80 or so Terrance Dicks novelisations of lost or unseen space/historical adventure tales, plus variations on this formula by Malcolm Hulke, Ian Marter, Donald Cotton, et al...

Now, we have New *Who* and a new generation of fans, many of whom discovered the series from the heirs of Target: Virgin Books and their *New Adventures* (*NAs*) franchise. This, and the BBC Books rivals/successors after the McGann incident in 1996, took the Doctor's adventures out of the limits of what the BBC could do on VT with a small budget and children watching. The *NAs* were launched in 1991 with the slogan "stories too broad and deep for the small screen", and some of them indeed were. Notably, several key writers of the BBC Wales series started there. The only prose

continued on Page 117...

X1.7 The Long Game

the heating system when nobody else has.

• *Adam Mitchell* occasionally surprises the Doctor by asking good questions, but generally annoys him. He lies to Rose about being freaked out by this whole "travelling in time and space" thing in order to steal her phone and abscond with the TARDIS key, whilst using the money-bar the Doctor gave him to pay for a surgical upgrade to access the station's database and ring home in 2012. He thereby hopes to give himself the low-down on the next few years' technological advances [apart from anything else, this is rather an unimaginative scam]. His reaction on seeing Earth from space is to faint [so his subsequent claim to be queasy might not be entirely a ruse]. Adam assesses that it's going to take 'a better man than me' to get between the Doctor and Rose.

Adam's selfish betrayal angers the Doctor, and the resultant punishment is Adam being consigned to lead an inconspicuous life - to 'be average' - in his native time.

The Non-Humans

• *The Mighty Jagrafess of the Holy Hadrojassic Maxarodenfoe* is a big dollop of toffee with teeth. It hangs from the ceiling of Level 500, which is refrigerated to keep him cool. The species lives for three thousand years and gives off a lot of heat, which is vented throughout the rest of the station. It talks in a guttural growl, which the Editor - its human agent - can understand (although he speaks *to* it in what we perceive as English). The Jagrafess has, through a consortium of banks, taken control of Satellite Five and thereby the human race. Chips inside the head of every human enable complete control and identification of potential troublemakers, and enable corpses with the chips to serve as the Editor's minions.

History

• *Dating.* It's the year 200 000. The Doctor says that Earth is covered in megacities, and its population is 96 billion. [Note, however, that he states this before he finds that things aren't as they should be.] The planet now has five moons. In the unadulterated timeline, the Doctor claims, Earth is at the centre of the Fourth Great and Bountiful Human Empire: 'a million planets, a million species'. This ought to be an age of elegance and harmony, with humans interacting with all manner of species to the benefit of all.

However, in *this* version... Satellite Five started broadcasting 91 years ago, and its transmissions (now encompassing 600 channels) have been used to stunt humankind's development about the same duration of time. Extraterrestrials are not outright banned, but a 'climate of fear' has been perpetrated to seal Earth's borders and keep alien species out. The price of spacewarp, rightly or wrongly, is said to have doubled. Earth's influence barely extends across the Solar System. There are water-riots in Glasgow [not *the* Glasgow but one on New Caledonia, wherever that is], deadly sandstorms in the New Venus Archipelago and the University of Mars has cut its subsidies. The government of Chavic Fice has collapsed, meaning a reduction in visitors to Earth. Sunspot activity has closed Space Lane 27 and Lane 5,5,6 and the price of space-warping has recently doubled. There is an Independent Republic of Morocco.

The entire population have chips in their heads to access computers. This allows the Editor to isolate dissent and remove doubts. To get around this, Eva St Julienne - as the only surviving member of the anarchist Freedom 15 group - has been equipped with a genetic graft to create a false identity, and infiltrated Satellite Five under the name 'Suki McCrae Cantrell'.

Although the staff of Level 139 all seem regular, the traditional greeting seems to be, as Cathica says, 'Ladies, Gentlemen, Multisex, Undecided or Robots'. Those who work in the newsrooms place their hands on metal dishes with finger-shaped indentations and commune with the compute; the main operator (such as Cathica) sits in a barber's chair and counts down to 'spike', at which point a four-hinged circular door opens in the forehead and light - a data-stream - pours in, allowing that person to be a conduit for editing all the Empire's information into bulletins. The main output goes via a similar process with the chips of dead people sent to Level 500 ('non-entities' get promoted). Once basic surgery is carried out on Level 16, everyone stays on their assigned level until (or unless) sent for, and then takes a one-way journey in the lift to Level 500, where the walls are allegedly covered in gold.

As an optional extra, those who get the ten-minute upgrade to Type Two chip (the hole in the head option) have 'nanotermites' implanted in their throats to freeze-dry vomit. This costs 10,000 'credits'; the Type One chipping costs only 100 'credits'.

The Face of Boe [X1.2, "The End of the World"]

Why Doesn't Anyone Read Any More?

continued from Page 115...

fiction Steven Moffat has written has been short stories for anthologies in the range (and one for *Doctor Who Annual 2006*; see X3.10, "Blink"). Russell T Davies has also restricted himself to one novel (*Damaged Goods*, one of the *New Adventures*) and two books of his emails. Many other writers, however, combined their desire to become novelists and their affection for the series that shaped them, and took the opportunity to write for a living in print rather than for television.

This is odd, when you think about it. The cachet afforded TV writers in Britain has never been higher, and it's harder to make a full-time living in prose than in screenplays. But fans and ex-fans have it in mind that writing means *novels*. Also, that reading - not just fan-fic or SF or TV spin-offs but *absolutely bloody everything* - is what makes a *Doctor Who* fan different from many other TV aficionados.

You would think, therefore, that the process of reading, the business of writing and the moral superiority of the literate would be as loudly proclaimed in New *Who* as it was in the pre-1989 stories. Alas, looking at the evidence, not a bit of it. Books are still held up as important, true, but they are *only* held up, never opened. They have been relegated to being props.

Consider this... a two-part tale is set in a Library (X4.8, "Silence in the Library" and X4.9, "Forest of the Dead", if you'd not guessed) that contains every book, ever. And yet, apart from a mysterious message on the Doctor's psychic paper, nobody is seen to read anything, at all, in the story's 90 minutes. There's a girl whose brain has been wired into the database so she can read any book she wants, and yet she's more interested in watching CBBC and painting Bad Wolf pictures. There's an enormously helpful book lying round at the end - River Song's Benny Summerfield-like diary - but the Doctor refuses to glance at it. The physical books in the library are both sources of darkness (set against the Mediaeval idea of books as beacons of light - hence, perhaps, the family name "Lux"), and are violently hurled at the archaeologists when the girl flips her TV remote. Even the central conceit of people becoming documents is couched in the terms of computer files (with the punning use of "saved") rather than the older idea of Recording Angels with scrolls and quill-pens. (Do they use their own feathers?)

Books-as-objects are a theme with Donna Noble. She boasts of how she learned the Dewey Decimal System in three days as a temp librarian (X4.6, "The Doctor's Daughter"), but never mentions *reading* anything. She prompts Wilf and the Doctor towards the Master with a mysteriously well-chosen celebrity biography (X4.17, "The End of Time Part One"), but still doesn't seem to have dipped in for herself. Donna's fiancé Lance (X3.0, "The Runaway Bride") ridicules her small-scale ambitions and horizons, and mentions *Heat* magazine but no other reading. It's the first thing we see the Doctor reading in the new series, and he gives it more attention than a novel in the same scene. (Which is almost the last thing he reads unless there's an info-dump due – see X1.4, "Aliens of London" and X5.4, "The Time of Angels". The next time the Doctor is seen to read something for fun, it's *Knitting for Girls* while he's waiting for Gantox in X6.13, "The Wedding of River Song".) Donna's one encounter with a Famous Author (Agatha Christie; X4.7, "The Unicorn and the Wasp") is marked by her only knowing the TV adaptations of Christie's books. In fact, the meeting with Christie is singular, because it is only the second time in New *Who* that anyone having read fiction is germane to the plot, and even then it's precisely the formulaic nature of Christie's books that motivates the villain. (The first time was Gareth Roberts' previous script, "The Shakespeare Code", and it's Martha having read Harry sodding Potter that makes the difference.) Yet Donna is unsurprised when a physical paperback of a Christie novel from the year five billion is handed to her. However gratifying it is to see reprinted 70s Pan editions outlasting Kindles or iPads, there's no discussion of the text itself, just the cover and date. The BBC Wales series seems to treat the lives and reputations of authors as more important than what those authors actually wrote and why, and yet they keep cropping up as characters.

When we recall that Churchill won the Nobel Prize for Literature (for History of the English-Speaking Peoples), the stats get more fearsome. The only Celebrities-of-Yesteryear *not* to have been professional authors appeared in Series Two:

continued on Page 119...

is expecting a Baby Boemina. This appears to be the only story running on the Bad Wolf channel. The water riots are being covered on McB News. Kronkburgers [first mentioned in the *DWM* comic "The Iron Legion", which was an alternate history] cost two credits twenty and are served with Pajartos; Zaffich is a beef-flavoured slush-puppie.

The Single Molecule Transcription process superceded the microprocessor [possibly developed by Adam Mitchell] from 2019 onwards.

Catchphrase Counter The Fourth Great and Bountiful Human Empire is, inevitably, 'a fantastic period of history'. News of the Face of Boe's pregnancy is on Bad Wolf TV.

The Analysis

The Big Picture It's theoretically possible that someone could watch this and not spot that it's a satire on media ownership. The Jagrafess is called "Max" by the Editor - maybe notorious former *Evening Standard* editor Max Hastings or spinmeister Max Clifford, but much more in keeping was Robert Maxwell: the corpulent, flamboyant, ludicrous, dictatorial and ultimately deeply sinister Czech mogul who bought *The Daily Mirror* in the 1980s and used it to further his business interests. (These included diverting the pensions of his employees into a complex money-laundering scheme connected with arms deals for the Mossad, Israel's secret service. In 1991, Maxwell mysteriously walked off the side of his yacht and his body was dragged out of the Mediterranean a few days later. Then all the dirt started to emerge about his crimes.)

Maxwell, however, never really branched out into satellite television, which is why the real subject of "The Long Game" has to be Rupert Murdoch - owner of News International, NewsCorp, Fox, Sky, *The Times*, *The Sun* and, until it was shut down after the scandals concerning the criminal actions of its reporters, *The News of the World*. The clues aren't exactly obscure: the Editor's line "Gotcha!" refers to a spectacularly tasteless headline in his tabloid *The Sun* about the illegal sinking of the Argentine warship *General Belgrano* (see X2.0, "The Christmas Invasion"). This line has come back to haunt Murdoch recently as allegations concerning his papers' criminal activities, police bribing and attempts to influence politics at a deeper level than hitherto suspected have emerged. Cathica clams that it is company policy to be "open, honest and beyond bias", a close approximation of the mendacious slogan used by Murdoch's Fox News. The Doctor's tirade against the Editor is almost exactly what people say about Murdoch's cynical manipulation of fears and prejudices. In the mid-1980s, when the young Russell T Davies submitted this story to the *Doctor Who* office, it was less subtle and more all-embracing: saying it was braver simply because the lies had been repeated often enough to become self-evident to a majority of people. (What changed? A lot of small things happened at once, and the turning point was *The Sun* making outrageous claims about the actions of Liverpool supporters during the Hillsborough disaster that were untrue, insulting to their next-of-kin and easy to prove wrong.)

It is, in all fairness, what people have been saying about press barons since the 1890s. Lords Northcliffe and Beaverbrook were, in their day, just as powerful and are now accepted to have been as poisonous as detractors claim Murdoch to be. It's more obviously true of Silvio Berlusconi, who owned all the non-government-owned media outlets in Italy until he got to be President... and then got the rest too. It was the substance of Orson Welles' *Citizen Kane*. It was what George Orwell observed as both a journalist and an observer of how working people lived. It became, after a Wartime stint at the BBC trying to keep the news substantively accurate without giving anything away, the theme of *1984*. Keeping the public in constant terror and amnesia is, in this, a means to keep the economy buoyant by making everyone think there was a war on and that dissent was treason. The language was changed to prevent certain thoughts, surveillance was constant and so routine as to be almost invisible, and former heroes were turned into the subjects of the "Two Minutes' Hate". This is almost so well-known that it is ignored: the name "Big Brother" became the title of a prurient "reality" show (see "Bad Wolf"). So what else links this story directly to Murdoch and his kind?

An obvious item is the design of Satellite Five. The heat is funnelled through a big long structure from a forbidden top floor, nobody ever leaves their floor and the plumbing is secret. This sounds familiar: although we still use "Fleet Street" as a cover-all term for the newspapers, most of the papers moved to Wapping at Murdoch's behest.

Why Doesn't Anyone Read Any More?

continued from Page 117...

Queen Victoria and Madame de Pompadour (and they both had diaries that were published). Prior to 1989, the only famous authors ever to appear on screen (discounting the controversial Marco Polo, who was in any case not the author of the book that Rusticello of Pisa made of his reminiscences; see 1.4, "Marco Polo" and accompanying essay) had been Shakespeare (2.8, "The Chase"), who turned out not to have an original thought in his head, and someone purporting to be HG Wells (22.5, "Timelash"). Oh, and Wyatt Earp, who gave his name to ghost-written books about the West (3.8, "The Gunfighters").

The point is that writers, whilst now disproportionately represented as Big Names from History compared to artists or engineers, have come out of it rather badly. Only one painter has actually appeared in New *Who*, and is rather sanitised compared to his biographical details (X5.10, "Vincent and the Doctor"). Compared to the merciless way Dickens' behind-the-scenes torment and ambiguous marital status are brought into the light in "The Unquiet Dead" (X1.3), or the relentless debunking of Shakespeare ("The Chase"; 13.2, "Planet of Evil"; 17.2, "City of Death"; "The Shakespeare Code" and the various books and audios that have him up to no good), Van Gogh is sanctified and the perpetually-absent Leonardo da Vinci is a paragon (2.9, "The Time Meddler", et al). One real-life author, Bracebridge Hemyng, became an all-out monster (**Who is the Master of the Land of Fiction?** under 6.2, "The Mind Robber"). The only time the programme's authors show someone writing for a living who is above reproach, it's Sarah Jane Smith. And, considering the lousy time other journalists get in the series (eg X4.1, "Partners in Crime"), it's hardly surprising that we only see Sarah file copy once (13.1, "Terror of the Zygons"), and even then have no idea if it gets into print.

And yet, if writers seem to have a low opinion of their chosen profession, look at how they see the potential customers... most people shown watching television in New *Who* are too busy watching reality shows or clearly inaccurate news bulletins. *EastEnders* is referred to twice, once disparagingly by the Doctor ("The Impossible Planet") and - surprise surprise! - enthusiastically by Jackie (X2.12, "Army of Ghosts"). Sensationalist news is presented in "The Long Game" (X1.7) as a method of enslavement, and *Big Brother* and *The Weakest Link* are tools of the Daleks in "Bad Wolf" (X1.12). The only significant stories are word-of-mouth and all factual. The one person writing a fiction is John Smith - and we the audience know that his tales are the truth and *he* is a lie. (The only other non-historical writer of fiction in the series, Shardovan, in 19.1, "Castrovalva", is in a similar ontological predicament.)

It gets worse when the process of reading is examined. In "Rose" (X1.1), the Doctor can flick through *The Lovely Bones* in seconds, whereas reading it takes 40 minutes at the very least. (As we will see, Rose's chosen form of voice-over in her last two "official" episodes is taken from that book, so maybe she'd read it too: see "Army of Ghosts"). There is barely a single instance in the post-2005 series of anyone reading except as a form of downloading. This Time Lord ability is shared by Daleks, who can even do it with your head (and by Toshiko Sato, with some alien tech she stole from the Torchwood Hub). This is presented as admirable, even desirable. Get to know all the stuff that's in these books without wasting precious viewing time - kewl! Adam thinks that visiting the year 200,000 is valuable because he can get an implant to beam information directly into his brain ("The Long Game"). Nobody wants to invest any time in processing, digesting and assimilating text, even though neurologists are increasingly discovering that this is the source of the human ability to empathise and conceptualise. Nobody actually enjoys reading as an act in itself, everyone just likes having read things.

Of course, the lack of time to read things and the ability of technology to provide alternatives is something older people grumble about, and have done since radio caught on. What's intriguing is that, despite the perceived reluctance of anyone under 40 to devote any time to reading, the consequences of not doing it are still shown as mainly bad in New *Who*. The super-advanced upgraded Bluetooth (X2.5, "Rise of the Cybermen") is a prelude to converting millions of people into machines. Two episodes earlier, by-passing conventional learning by means of chip-fat is a

continued on Page 121...

X1.7 The Long Game

Many of them, including those not owned by NewsCorp, each took a floor of the tower at 1, Canada Square, colloquially known by the tube-station name Canary Wharf - and known in *Doctor Who* as Torchwood 1 (X2.12, "Army of Ghosts"). The tower was claimed by some to be an obvious target for a 9/11-style assault, and the plumbing was declared a secret in case of terrorist poisoning, piranhas or whatever. Oddly, this wasn't a consideration with the other famous 80s tower in London, the Lloyds building (seen in the abysmal film version of *The Avengers*), which famously has all its infrastructure on the outside. Moreover, when the Canary Wharf thing was first built, before anyone wanted to move in, the air-conditioning was a major publicity point. Plumes of vapour issuing from the pyramid at the top are a familiar sight in East London and on any shots of the tower.

That's the subject-matter, but the approach is familiar too. Davies claims to have had the basic idea some 20 years before the broadcast version (but then, so did everyone else - Maxwell and Murdoch were establishing themselves at Wapping at around the time 22.2, "Vengeance on Varos" was shown, so half of fandom wrote stories like this). It seems that he had, like a lot of up-and-coming writers in the late 80s, approached Andrew Cartmel with a view towards writing for *Doctor Who* in its last few years. Precisely when this happened is unclear, and neither party offers any hint of how far this got (probably not very). It's hard to see how a version of this with Ace in would have worked - even Rose in the finished story is uncharacteristically prone to simply follow the Doctor around asking questions. The Doctor here is as aloof and manipulative as Sylvester McCoy's, though, and the plot very clearly follows a three-part structure, with Suki's death from above and the first sight of the Jagrafess being obvious cliffhangers for a three-parter (this would have been the all-studio half of a six-episode block, sure as eggs is eggs). It's no stretch to see this story belonging in a tradition with "Paradise Towers" (24.2) and "The Happiness Patrol" (25.2): grotesque dystopian satires with character-actors and *ingenues* sent into a tizzy by the Doctor asking questions. (One of which might well have been "Mel, you're the computer expert: how does this central heating work?")

Rupert Murdoch's move into television began after *Doctor Who* ended in 1989, so the accretion of details about TV news that seems so over-familiar in the transmitted story would have been an extrapolation. It's interesting that although we see output with pictures, and observe the incoming data-stream being digested by Cathica and her team, we don't see any actual camera-crews, and the only cameras on the station are internal security. The story still treats news-gathering as a textual process.

Other small anomalies might be resolved if we assume that Davies only lightly reworked a story he'd had on a back-burner for a while. The charred skeletons in the abandoned Spike-room were obviously intended to feature more prominently. There's been speculation that this story was reworked and submitted to Virgin Books for their *New Adventures* range - this seems less likely, especially as so few opportunities that a book version of this story (or a later, more expensive, TV version as might be made in the twenty-first century) would have offered are explored. It was, however, perfectly able to fit in with the vaguely satirical, vaguely dystopian trend in the range (a good indication of how it might have come out is Gareth Roberts' second book for Virgin, *Tragedy Day*).

Little things might confirm this: the big clue to what's occurring is that it's hot. Even though nothing on screen indicates this (nobody's sweating, Rose keeps her tight fleece zipped up), the plot needs this to be stated twice. Had this been conceived of as a television play right from the outset, something more obviously visual might have been the telltale sign that the residents ignore but our identification-figure confirms for us. The Kronkburgers, a reference back to the comic strip "The Iron Legion" in *Doctor Who Monthly*, are exactly the kind of detail you'd get in the early *New Adventures*. (One version of the creation of this script is that Davies first had the idea when he was 17 - around the time "The Iron Legion" appeared. That strip's resemblance to early editions of *2000AD* suggests another line of enquiry for the overall feel and look of this episode, but all of that seems to come from production designer Edward Thomas and director Brian Grant via *Blade Runner*.) We will be returning to the impact of the *New Adventures* on the Welsh series in the next volume (especially **How Many Times Has This Story Happened?** under X3.8, "Human Nature").

The Long Game X1.7

Why Doesn't Anyone Read Any More?

continued from Page 119...

definite no-no (X2.3, "School Reunion"). Adam's upgrade leads to him being dismissed as a potential companion.

There is also the issue that many of the writers have taken *Star Trek: The Next Generation* as their template. In that series, books often exist to be adapted (or, more accurately, plundered) into Holodeck games, or as a source of facts for bravura displays of recall, as in a pub-quiz. This is ultimately about control: reading a novel by an adept author entails the reader (to some extent) surrendering control of part of his or her consciousness, becoming both a passenger in a plot and a sort of receptacle for the focal character's emotions and opinions. Knowing facts *about* that author but not allowing yourself any time out from being yourself might seem to be preferable - if you are so shallow as to be unable to cope with having someone else in your head for a few hours. Being able to see how another perceives the world was the key to many of the Doctor's most satisfying victories, but was also part of the reason he travelled. It was held to be how mature societies work. The Leisure Hive on Argolis (18.1, "The Leisure Hive") offered an "experiential grid", a process of being someone else from another species for a few hours. This was a parting gift to the universe when the Argolin believed they had less than a generation to live after a pointless war. Wise cultures are often shown to be like literate individuals, so secure in their self-hood as to allow and encourage contact with outside influences and otherness. (See also **Does Plot Matter?** under 6.4, "The Krotons".)

Ponder the uses of literacy[23] in pre-1989 *Doctor Who* - societies that had stamped out reading were, of course, evil and had to be deposed. In the real world, dictatorships don't just deny access to facts; the ability to envisage alternatives is also a threat to totalitarian regimes (hence the Chinese government's ban of fiction involving time travel). Moreover, the experienced reader's tendency towards inwardness - a by-product of the changes reading does to the brain during one's teens - makes individuals more awkwardly, er, individual. It also makes it possible to empathise with other people in written-about situations, to walk a mile in someone else's shoes. All in all, it's harder to go to war against people if you can imagine being them.

Many repressive regimes use exaggerated or confected hate of "the other" as a tool of control. Now look at the non-literary societies where reading is possible - but not widespread - in *Doctor Who* pre-1989. Right back to the start of the series (or near enough), the Thals have their history and culture in tea-tray form and would rather die than give it up. Conversely, the Daleks can't even use pens. Which side do *you* want to win? Even such self-awareness as the Daleks have in this story is later removed, and their extremely brittle regime is finally brought down by the risk of reflection on their lifestyle choices (4.9, "The Evil of the Daleks"). In "The Chase", Ian takes time out from adventures with aliens to read a book of adventures with aliens. The most alarming paradox is in "The Mind Robber", where the capacity inculcated by reading fiction is exactly what separates real people from fictitious characters.

By the time Tom Baker has become the Doctor, this notion has become the whole grain of the series. Scholars are always outsiders, always right. Stultification as a tool of government is almost always the sign of a dictator, and most of those dictators are so small-minded and parochial that anyone with any idea of how big the outside universe is gets either punished or killed. The twin pillars of this narrowing of the mind are banning books and imposing a geocentric (or Ribosocentric, or Xanakocentric or Chrlorisocentric or anonymous-planet-in-E-Space-ruled-by-Great-Vampirocentric) dogma (see 16.1, The Ribos Operation"; 16.2, "The Pirate Planet"; 17.3, "The Creature from the Pit"; and 18.4, "State of Decay"). Note also that in this phase of the series, the Doctor is seen to read and enjoy reading more than at any other time. He even gets K9 to read Peter Rabbit to him at the start of "The Creature from the Pit", which underscores the difference between him and the unimaginative Chlorisians. He has other books on his person but, like all textbooks in this phase of the series, these are at best unedifying (see 17.1, "Destiny of the Daleks"). Treating books as objects to be collected is what the Baddies do, in both "City of Death" and "Shada" (and, implicitly, 17.4, "Nightmare of Eden", where places and life-forms

continued on Page 123...

X1.7 The Long Game

English Lessons

• *Mutt and Jeff*. All right, this is an American comic strip, but it's been adopted here as rhyming-slang for "deaf". (There's no other reason for the Doctor to refer to Rose and Adam like this, as there's not much of a height difference between them and they aren't keen on horse-racing.) Weirdly, it turns out Adam's dad is called "Geoff".

• *Me Old Mate* is how people from outside London like to pretend people from London address one another, and is thus a handy way of saying "I'm going to pretend to be your friend for the moment", especially when spoken with a Salford accent.

• *That'll do nicely* was the tag-line when American Express launched in the UK in 1980, and thus the punch-line from a sketch on *Not the Nine O'Clock News* that more people here know than have ever even seen an AmEx card. (Shops here tend to refuse them because the company's processing charges far exceed the cost of the majority of goods and services people try to use it to buy.)

Oh, Isn't That...?

• *Tamsin Grieg* (Nurse). In a curious career-shift, Grieg went from being most famous as the voice of Debbie Aldridge in Radio 4's *The Archers* to appearing in sitcoms, sketch-shows and strange adverts. In particular, she had been in *Big Train* (see below), *Green Wing* and *Black Books* - the same network of actors, writers and directors all seem to work with each other. Most recently, she was the mum in *Friday Night Dinner*. You might also have caught her in *Neverwhere*, making the lead even more lifeless than usual.

• *Anna Maxwell-Martin* (Suki). Well, to be honest, only theatre-goers would have known who she was when this was first shown. That changed with the transmission, later that year, of the BBC's frantic, soap-like adaptation of *Bleak House*. She was the pivotal Esther, potentially a sickeningly good character (because the book is part-narrated by her and omits uncomfortable details). As such, she was one of only three major cast-members not to already be famous - the others were Carey Mulligan (X3.10, "Blink") and future *Torchwood* star Burn Gorman. Maxwell-Martin has tended towards really earnest dramas, but did a comic cameo in the most recent TV version of *The Wind in the Willows*.

• *Simon Pegg* (the Editor). As we have just mentioned, there was a clique that can be said to have been centred around peculiar sketch-show *Big Train*. (See also "Army of Ghosts" and "Doomsday".) Pegg was in this, and went from co-writing and starring in *Spaced* (see "Human Nature"). This was the crystallisation of a geek/stoner nexus and led to films such as *Shaun of the Dead*, *Hot Fuzz* and *Paul*. Pegg somehow became a big-ish film star and wound up as Scotty in the rebooted *Star Trek* flicks - but at this stage, he was small-fry enough to be narrating *Doctor Who Confidential* and doing tiny guest-spots on *Look Around You* (18.1, "The Leisure Hive"). Basically, Simon Pegg being in *Doctor Who* was as surprising as a Dalek, a police box or a ventilator shaft.

Things That Don't Make Sense To begin with, as trivial a point as we can make: in Billie Piper's video diary, it emerges that the monitor that Suki is in front of when frozen is showing "The Leisure Hive". Either this is a news item about tachyonics from c.2250 (that's one heck of an archive they have), or Satellite Five is showing old *Doctor Who* episodes. Some people have wondered if perhaps the signal from Argolis has taken 98,750 years to reach Satellite Five, meaning that Argolis is 98,750 light years from Earth. (Not only does this not quite match what we're told in "The Leisure Hive", it would mean that the tachyonics experiments never came to anything, otherwise the signals would have been a lot brisker.) Of course, it *could* just be a costume-drama set on Argolis...

Now, about the physics of refrigeration - let's not get too technical, let's just point out that Satellite Five is a satellite and thus in space, where it's very cold. Without knowing anything about the Jagrafess biology, anything that lives for three thousand years and chucks out heat at that rate must eat, um, like a fire. Generally, long-lived species tend to be cold-blooded, but if a totally alien biochemistry is involved, providing food for the slug on the ceiling would be even more complex. The thing doesn't eat any of the people it wants rid of and, despite those huge teeth, doesn't seem to eat at all. It could be that the creature has a food-supply (and toilet) built in to its lair at the top of the shop - but if so, how hard would it have been to rig the air-conditioning to work properly?

It's not just that nobody notices how hot it is, or ever mops their brows, or asks for something cooler than a freshly-cooked Kronkburger (we note a few 2005-vintage water bottles around, and

Why Doesn't Anyone Read Any More?

continued from Page 121...

are turned into data). Season Eighteen sees the start of a change, where books are there solely to be used for factual education and admired for their scholarship.

The transition is noticeable in the first story to be written that year, the leftover Season Fifteen script reworked as "State of Decay". In this, reading is banned by a regime that would seem ridiculous to anyone looking at it from a perspective other than fealty and dread. The way to avoid anyone imagining what the Three Who Rule would seem like to anyone from the outside would be to remove the concept of "outside". As with the Chin Dynasty, the Three begin their regime by destroying all records - although being in a tiny universe, they have no need to construct a Great Wall, they only need to harp on about "protecting" the villagers. Rebel scientists have computers with documents that reveal the truth, but the Doctor's reaction is horror even before this aspect of the book-ban is apparent. Appropriately, Terrance Dicks expands on this in the story's novelisation - as the champion of children's literacy, he could do no other. He was, after all, someone who went from hardcore cockney East Ham to Downing College, Cambridge, through a love of reading.[24] Less appropriately, this was the first book to be adapted for cassette, so Tom Baker's voice tells us that the Doctor is appalled that people don't read habitually while we drive, do the washing up or work out at the gym. Crucially, it's not what can be learned factually from books that matters, it's how reading transforms the reader and makes them harder to control.

Still unsure what we're getting at? Consider a different library, from "Tooth and Claw". We have a brave speech about books being weapons and a library being an arsenal, but what's altogether more important is that the shelves and walls are coated with werewolf-repelling mistletoe oil. The books contain facts about the Earth-landing of the cell that turns people into werewolves, but if those facts had been on a teatowel or a smartphone, they would be the same facts. (Indeed, the significant finding is a woodcut, rather than the text.) "Hitting the books" for the way to defeat a supernatural being is more than just another symptom of Russell T Davies wanting to be Joss Whedon so bad it hurts, it's another effect of trying to do the work of four 25 minute episodes in three-quarters of an hour. This is especially noticeable as so much of the story resembles "Horror of Fang Rock" (15.1), the first story where the Doctor openly acknowledged the source-text and proved that his reading was a significant factor in how he prevailed. He knew not only that he was in a known and knowable situation - he cites an Act of Parliament - but how to behave according to the character he would be in a tale of this genre, i.e. how everyone here would expect him to behave. The previous story (14.6, "The Talons of Weng Chiang") made this overt. In both of those stories, the Doctor and Leela noticeably adjusted to the situation in episode-length increments, as the situation itself changed with every cliffhanger. Here, by contrast, the Doctor and Rose hide in a library to punctuate the wolf's attacks with a skim-reading montage as the story develops in a different direction. Obviously, sitting reading is less visual than chucking the Koh-I-Nor around, but the use of books as mere source-material rather than a means of benign self-transformation is quite distinct from how *Doctor Who* used to treat reading.

the beefy-slushies), it's that nobody going from this sultry environment to Level 500 seems to feel the chill. Suki is wearing a flimsy blouse with no sleeves, but doesn't react to the abrupt thermocline. (She's got two bags of her belongings and gets a torch out, but not a jumper or even a longer-sleeved shirt or cardie.) Nobody's breath mists. Rose, conversely, keeps her warm, snug sports-fleece tightly zipped and just tells us she's too warm.

The story begins with a report of major sunspot activity - a century later ("Bad Wolf"), this will be enough to blot out all transmissions and allow the Controller to warn the Doctor about the Daleks. Nevertheless, the 'backward' technology they have here is able to keep broadcasting. The only television not affected by this would be the internal CCTV, which seems to cover everywhere - and yet fails to tell the Editor about a big blue box materialising on Level 39.

X1.7 The Long Game

If the population really is 96 billion on Earth, and they never go anywhere, and there are a mere 600 channels (not so many more than BSkyB customers can get), then how is a drought killing 200 people on Venus newsworthy? Even if this is 600 *news* channels and Satellite 4 is doing cookery and so on, this is a bit poor. It might be a "Don't bother leaving Earth, the rest of the Universe is dangerous" ploy, but there are sunspots stopping space travel anyway. They could have made up anything and nobody would have been able to verify or asseverate this - why not go for a bigger, more audience-friendly lie?

As with "Day of the Daleks" (9.1) and "The Time Warrior" (11.1), there is an assumption here of a linear and pre-arranged order for technology to progress. The Doctor observes that the equipment on Satellite Five is about 90 years behind where it ought to be. He also states that humans have - or ought to have at this date - an empire crossing a million worlds and mixing with hundreds of other species. The point being: an empire *that* big and diverse wouldn't be quite so prone to fads and fashions as to be dateable with such precision. (In fact, if they were an expanding empire, and the hint from the name 'Fourth Great and Bountiful' indicates several expansionist stages, then uniformity and reliability when sending emissaries to new worlds to (re)claim them would be a more sensible policy. And his "great discovery" that the technology of Satellite Five is where it would have been at when the satellite was built is hardly a surprise.)

The skull-hatch link has a default setting to open when the user clicks his or her fingers. Or, as it turns out, if anyone else clicks their fingers within earshot. The first of these makes a bit of sense... if it was the *action* of clicking that set up a neural relay, but not if it is the sound of the click. Lots of things make similar clicks, especially in a big space station with dilapidated and held-back technology. If this sound is the 'default', then presumably a lot of people have it (taking the precedent of mobile phone ringtones), so a room full of top executives could be embarrassing.

Cathica's skull-link opens with a snap... but doesn't when the Editor snaps his fingers within earshot. She's in the convenient abandoned infospike bay next to the lift door on Level 500, the one with all the desiccated corpses to welcome the lucky winners. (Presumably this has made none of them, including Suki, run for it - and yet the Doctor says everyone's had their curiosity removed.)

If the anarchist Freedom 15 managed such a good graft of a new personality that Suki herself didn't know she wasn't Suki (until, it appears, the Editor told her), why is she then trusted to be put into the grid controlling everything? Her chip must be compromised, so even dead, she is a risk. And if all of the Editor's minions are so immobile and useless as they appear during the Jagrafess' downfall, how does Suki's corpse suddenly grip the Editor to prevent his escape?

Why exactly does sending the sound of a neural download to a 90s answerphone make Adam's mum's machine pour out blue plasma? Wouldn't this magnetic flux wipe the tiny cassette on which the messages are being kept? (We'll leave aside the idea that someone so tech-savvy as to have been head-hunted by Henry Van Statten could let his mum use an old Binatone machine in 2012, or conversely how someone growing up in such a household got to be an ace hacker and expert in alien tech.) We also have the worry of how an acoustic recording of this data could be translated by Adam if he's also recording himself going 'Aah! Argh!' His mum seems to almost notice the TARDIS dematerialisation, but not the strong smell of germanium and solder that would fill the house when the Doctor makes her phone explode. And the Doctor's punishment for Adam isn't much, as he knows at least one useful forthcoming attraction (Single Molecule Transcription - just seven years into his future), so he could at the very least make a killing on the Stock Exchange.

One of the stations has a logo of a smiley face and '+1'. It's another news channel. But '+1' is what digital stations have as a catch-up service, rebroadcasting their output exactly an hour later. Who needs a repeat of a news service that's on a constant loop anyway?

And the big one: if everyone, all 96 billion people, have chips in their head that the Editor can monitor for dissent and doubt, *and* if the Editor's claim that they can snuff out any such mental misgivings is even slightly accurate (and Suki/Eva's fake personality seems like too baroque a precaution if it isn't), why do they bother with editing the news at all?

Critique Following "Dalek" was going to be a thankless task. Following it with a satire so obvious that BBC1 Continuity Announcers mentioned it before the episode started might have been a daft move, although we now know that this was an exercise in hiding a big development in plain sight. Perhaps they wanted this one to slip past almost unnoticed.

That's a two-edged sword, if it's true. It relies on nothing going wrong. At the very least, this is something we can say in this story's favour. Directors are like plumbers (to use an apt analogy from this story's dialogue). If you can't help noticing their work, then something's gone massively wrong. Close analysis reveals that director Brian Grant has made some canny choices, but with so much of the script, design and casting out of his hands, it's unavoidable that the look of the episode is a bit weird. Not to put too fine a point on it, this is what a 1990 episode of *Doctor Who* would have looked like. Even Murray Gold is impersonating Keff McCulloch (see Volume 6). Although the script hints that there is a retrogressive force afflicting humanity, the "retro" look of this future is almost embarrassing. The air is heavy with Fuller's Earth, that off-the-shelf look of 80s dystopian futures (*Brazil*, the Apple Mac launch ad, *Max Headroom*), and even the readers of the *Radio Times* noted the lack of imagination in the costumes.

And yet, that conservatism is one thing that makes this story resilient. It's not hard to see how the relative lack of effects, the small speaking-cast, the plot relying on mechanical answer-phones and perennially-topical "issues" could have worked in any period of the programme's past. Indeed, with the Doctor essentially talking the Jagrafess to death and Rose asking the right questions, it's a story that could have been made in the 80s with any of that decade's three Doctors (indeed, four - the empiricism might have made this an unusually interesting Season Eighteen story and Adam is basically Adric, if he'd liked girls or vice versa).

For experienced fans, however, the plot is rather too by-the-book. It's all grindingly obvious and thus a bit preachy. If this had been shown in 1990, everyone would have been joining in with half the dialogue. If "The Unquiet Dead" and "Aliens of London" were busily subverting clichés that most people watching didn't know existed, "The Long Game" treats one we all knew as a blindingly original observation. And whilst it may have been novel and innovative to a seven-year-old, that notional child-viewer wouldn't really have been very enthralled by the process of getting there.

So if this episode had been broadcast in the early 90s, it would have been familiar enough not to alienate casual viewers, but just kooky-looking enough to keep them watching. But it wasn't - it was shown in 2005 and barely caused a ripple. It deserves to be remembered for more than setting up "Bad Wolf", though. There were favourable comments about some of the performances (and while Pegg is too obviously "Look at me, I'm a *Doctor Who* villain", Tamsin Greig is precise as the surgical nurse - observe her double-take when seeing what Adam's been eating). It's amusing when it needs to be, and most of the cast make it seem that the jokes are their characters' rather than the writer's.

What's wrong with this episode is what the public spotted - or, rather, that is a symptom of the main problem. This over-cautious future has nothing in it that looks futuristic, because they've heard someone (probably on BBC4) saying that nothing dates as fast as television depictions of "the future". Nobody believes in "the future" any more, and certainly any hint that people will be different as a result of growing up under different circumstances is *verboten* under the new regime. (See **Are We Touring Theme-Park History?** under X2.7, "The Idiot's Lantern", **Is Kylie from Planet Zog?** under X4.0, "Voyage of the Damned" and **RT Phone Home?** under X1.2, "The End of the World".) Any potentially silly-looking clothes or props are ruled out, along with wobbly sets or science that makes any sense. This is pointless, as even by the time of writing this review, those clothes look horribly dated and the whole thing looks cheap (and not in a good way). Grant avoids this spilling over into the rest of the episode's aesthetic, but there's very little here to make anyone go "Ooh!"

Making viewers go "Ooh!" is the whole point of the series. *Doctor Who* can scare them, inspire them or make clever jokes, but these are side-effects of the programme's primary function. Nobody has nightmares about a programme that they aren't watching. Nobody reminisces decades later about an episode they switched off or talked through. Whilst professional reviewers note that Grant's directing is salvaging scares and thrills from a dull set and a flat-looking palette, the overall effect of this episode is as background for a better one six weeks from now. With a more interesting story and better dialogue, this might have been enough, just as getting the designers to re-do

X1.7 The Long Game

everything to look more exotic might have allowed them to get away with the script they had. But this is the story where everyone was relying on everyone else to save their bacon, and nobody excelled enough to retrieve the episode.

The Facts

Written by Russell T Davies. Directed by Brian Grant. Viewing figures: (BBC1) 8.01 million, (BBC3 repeats) 0.2 and 0.6 million.

Repeats and Overseas Promotion Langzeitstrategie, Długi mecz, Un jeu interminable

Production

As mentioned above, the origins of this story's setting and message were in a proposal submitted to Andrew Cartmel in the late 1980s. The outline document from late 2003 had a proposed seventh episode called "The Companion Who Couldn't", with the emphasis on Adam's inadequacies, but with a brief suggestion that the system devised to eliminate bias had, by 8299, been corrupted by a yellow leech who was secretly manipulating humanity. One of Adam's failings was terror when confronted with friendly aliens, but the absence of aliens became a clue (and a budgetary consideration). The date was moved forwards because Davies believed it sounded better (yes, really) and to suggest a cyclic rise and fall in the fortunes of the Human Race. The missing reporters on Floor 500 were euphemistically called "Freelance" and the entire episode was now about Rose's qualities, the ones Adam conspicuously lacks - the idea being to suggest that the Doctor doesn't just pick up teenage girls because he fancies them. (Something else Davies later questioned - he really ought to go with his first instincts.) By this time, Davies himself was in a position to mentor young wannabes like he had been when he sent this in: a few years earlier, he had taken an interest in a promising writer, Tom Macrae (see X2.5, "Rise of the Cybermen") and had slyly given Suki his surname.

As a further budgetary precaution, the different floors of the Satellite were, except for Floor 500, all the same basic set redressed and with grafted-in floor-numbers added in post-production. It became apparent fairly early on that the sets for both this episode and the two-part finale would be the same ones, redressed. It was also becoming clear that, as Joe Ahearne had established a good rapport with the cast and crew and had handled two very distinct types of story with equal facility (X1.6, "Dalek" and X1.8, "Father's Day"), he would be the one to direct the climactic story. What was less predictable was that he would also be given the as-yet-unwritten "cheap" episode eleven.

The result was that episode seven became its own mini-block, 4A, and was given to Brian Grant to direct. Grant's track record was formidable. In the 70s, he'd been a cameraman for ATV and worked on historical dramas and *The Muppet Show*. In 1980, he had been one of the first directors to specialise in pop videos; a quick trawl through his early successes is like a core-sample through the development of the medium[22]. He had been the first recipient of a Grammy for a promo ("Physical": the high-camp Olivia Newton-John comeback). After 1990 and about 200 of these, he moved into "proper" television, often involving choreography and crowd-scenes. His television work was varied, but he'd come out unscathed from making *Bugs*. Crucially for the Davies team, he had directed a few episodes of *Clocking Off*, a series devised and mainly written by Paul Abbott.

• Almost all of this story was to be made in the Q2 facility, with the Spike Room(s) being a set in the disused British Telecom building in Coryton. Production designer Edward Thomas opted to make the sets grimy and functional, comparing the Station to a tug-boat - partly to make it less immediately obvious that the Doctor had been abducted and brought to same station a century later ("Bad Wolf"). This also made the Spike Room more conspicuously out-of-keeping with the rest of the technology. Grant used a different team for practical effects; MTFX provided the steam, explosions and Jagrafess slop instead of Any Effects as per usual.

• It had been decided that, as part of showing Rose to have the "right stuff", she would dress less casually in this episode and wear tighter, more action-heroine clothing. The red-and-black look was a stark contrast with everyone else around her, but this had unforeseen consequences. The BBC guidelines on promoting specific ranges were stretched almost to breaking point (unwittingly) by the prominence that the "Punky Fish" range would receive from now on, and the denizens of

Satellite Five, in not looking too "futuristic", were ridiculed in the letters page of *Radio Times* for having branches of high-street retailers doing a 2005-themed retro sale. The extras were outfitted with slightly outlandish accessories to contrast with the "professional" look of the staff, and it was decided that the nurses should be in blood-red to show how far medicine has altered (white was a futuristic cliché, blue was being used for the Editor and green is usually a no-no in *Doctor Who* because of the green screen effects).

- The shoot began on the last day of November 2004, with the Observation deck and some of the crowd-scenes for Level 139. Grant shot these with a long lens from a distance, so that the picture-frame was crowded and compaced with layers (you will see that some shots have out-of-focus dangly things between the camera and the people talking). One effect of this approach was that the dozens of extras in futuristic/ 90s indie-band get-ups never all appear in any one shot, so that the broadcast scenes seem more chaotic but less densely-populated. Grant augmented a lot of these with a second, hand-held camera he operated himself. Much of the lighting was from units that had been design-features of the set, making the picture that bit murkier and more variable in colour. The Level 139 shoot went on until Friday, 3rd December, after which - for a change - they all took the weekend off. (It was a long weekend for the two stars.) The set was then reworked into Floor 500.

Monday morning was the first day at the BT building, for the cold, corpse-strewn version of the Spike Room. Due to a misunderstanding, Thomas had envisaged this as being shrink-wrapped for storage, and Phil Collinson had been annoyed, on arriving on set, that the line of communication had broken down. There was a delay while the PVC sheeting was removed and a distressed-looking series of fragments put on the set, with mummified corpses borrowed from another film. Meanwhile, Bruno Langley (as Adam) was being photographed for the family portrait on the phone-table (his house being a set in the BT building too). This was the day all the scenes with his family's dog were shot. On Tuesday, the aftermath of the Jagrafess' death was recorded back at Q2. Having spent six months teaching aliens to move, series choreographer Ailsa Atena-Berk finally got some orthodox choreography, and coached Eccleston in his lunch-hour for the end of "The Doctor Dances" (X1.10).

By the next day the schedule was a bit off, so most of the Spike Room scenes were Adam's. The rest were shot the following day, along with experimental make-up for Simon Pegg. This proved workable, so the next day saw work begin on the Control Room scenes. As this was a BBC production, footage from documentaries was easy to find and clear, so the screens were always busy. Each had a small DVD player feeding it (a process re-used in "The Idiot's Lantern") and two had old *Doctor Who* adventures on - "The Leisure Hive" and "The Ark in Space" (12.2). With Sunday 12th off, the recording in this set went from Friday to Tuesday. Most of Pegg's conversations with "Max" were made with a locked-off camera. The wrap party was on Tuesday night, complete with the first showing of "Rose". Although Eccleston was allowed to go home for Christmas, Piper had work to do later in the week (dancing with Captain Jack on Thursday, and then falling from a barrage balloon from which she'd been dangling - "The Empty Child"). Moreover, the shoot on "The Long Game" needed an extra day. For this, they needed a different crew (the main unit being on a recce for the next story). All that was missing was the first scene of Adam going to Floor 16 to talk to the nurse and a spot more work with the dog, the answerphone (including the insert of it exploding). The Q2 set was mothballed for use in Block Six. (Block Five, X1.11, "Boom Town", was all locations except for the TARDIS interior.)

- Unlike previous episodes, very little had gone wrong and there was enough material to fill an episode without any new scenes needing to be written, recorded later and worked in. Post-production was more elaborate than originally planned. Grant's choice of lenses meant that depth-of-field had to be restored for long shots, while the Jagrafess became more elaborate as The Mill became more confident. The voice for the Jagrafess was also a problem: dialogue editor Paul McFadden decided that the voice Nicholas Briggs had given it was too much like the Nestene, so he added wallpaper-paste slops and retimed the interjections to seem to be replying to the Editor rather than just fulminating ad lib. Several scenes were trimmed, many of them between the Doctor and Cathica. After broadcast, Davies apologised to Piper for giving her so few lines that weren't info-dump questions; Piper was actually pleased to have less to learn.

- A subplot that didn't make the final cut is that Adam's motive for trying to send futuristic tech back in time was to help his ailing father. This may have been altered because of the constant changes to "Dalek" and Adam being, in some drafts, Van Statten's son.

• Grant has not returned to the series, but this is largely because he was busy. He worked on the now-forgotten *Hex* (yet another attempt at a British *Buffy*) and launched the hapless *Britannia High*, which got to the screens just in time to get adverse comparisons with *High School Musical*.

X1.8: "Father's Day"

(14th May, 2005)

Which One is This? City on the Edge of the Oval. The Doctor and Rose crash two weddings, the second leading to a bewildering chain of events surrounding time-dragons.

Firsts and Lasts This is where we first meet Pete Tyler, in the first of many stories wherein resolving a time-paradox entails inviting somebody to go and have a fatal accident (see also X4.11, "Turn Left" and a trilogy of Gareth Roberts scripts in *The Sarah Jane Adventures*).

Of more long-term significance, perhaps, this is the story that introduces the voice-over narrative from a character other than the Doctor. There had been previous incidents where things like this had been attempted (1.4, "Marco Polo" being the most sustained, apparently read from Polo's journal), but in general this was a narratological ploy kept in reserve for trailers. At the start of "The Deadly Assassin" (14.3), Tom Baker reads aloud a screen-crawl that might have come from an as-yet unwritten history of Gallifrey, but this is the first time a character - namely Rose - is talking to the viewers directly from within the story. (See **Who Narrates This Programme?** under 23.1, "The Mysterious Planet" and **How Messed Up Can Narrative Get?** under X3.10, "Blink".) And as we'll see in a sec, this is the first time a record used in the soundtrack is followed years later by a cameo by the artist.

Watch Out For...
• The set dressers have had fun with Pete and Jackie's flat. Anyone who was around in the 80s will cringe at the naff fittings, many of which were considered a bit tacky even then (Tretchikoff's Green Lady was a national joke in 1987, and wasn't even ironically reclaimed until about 1990). In fact, some of the kitchenware is the same as in *Only Fools and Horses*.

• Our first hint that "time is of affliction" is when Pete's radio picks up a rap track from the twenty-first century. The one the director chose was "Don't Mug Yourself", a recent (at time of broadcast) hit by The Streets. Anyone who is unaware of what British acts have done with this American form won't have experienced a Brummie-accented lyrical flow, but that's the tip of the iceberg. More to the point, The Streets is basically Mike Skinner, who gave it up after three successful albums and turned to acting - he's the first person you see in "The Time of Angels" (X5.4), perhaps appropriately off his face in a field.

• It became a cliché of 80s news reporting on disasters that the camera would close in on a child's shoe or toy left behind: newsroom sitcom *Drop the Dead Donkey* had a running gag about a cynical cameraman who travelled with a supply of teddies and shoes. This story's strenuous efforts not to leave any tear unjerked means that this ploy is back. Let's agree to call it a period detail.

• In 1987, if we take this episode and "Rise of the Cybermen" (X2.5) as authoritative, Jackie is 19 and Pete's 33. In Series Two, Jackie will celebrate her 40th, making Pete 53. Neither of them looks any different. That Vitex is amazing stuff!

• This isn't *quite* the first time a child actor has played a younger version of a companion - that precedent was, unfortunately, "Mawdryn Undead" (20.3). However, Julie Joyce is the first non-embarrassing one, and played a young Billie Piper in two other productions (*Ruby in the Smoke* and *Mansfield Park*). She's also one of Frobisher's doomed kids in *Torchwood*: "Children of Earth". (That's Frobisher the corrupt civil servant, not the shapeshifting penguin.)

The Continuity

The Doctor He gets coldly angry with Rose when she betrays his trust; he expected better of her. He wanted to share seeing the Universe, but 'it's all about what the Universe can do for you' [there's tinges in this of Adam's actions last episode]. Once again, he talks of humans as 'stupid apes'.

Crucially, it would seem that he can deny Rose nothing. She asks to go to see her dad, he does it (with a warning: 'be careful what you wish for').

Reapers - Errr... *What*?

Now that the once-vexed question of UNIT Dating has been definitively resolved (we were right, everyone else was wrong and the only way their dates work is if they pretend *The Sarah Jane Adventures* doesn't exist, so *nyerrr*), we need other things to worry at. The good news is that the new version of *Doctor Who* is stuffed with riddles, but the bad news is that these are often trivial: the authors knowingly put them there to keep us watching. Ultimately, it doesn't do any good wondering who Mr Saxon or River Song are, how the Doctor retrieved a jacket he'd lost to the Weeping Angels or what happened to the pirate who vanished between scenes (X5.5, "Flesh and Stone"; X6.3, "The Curse of the Black Spot"), because the answer came *first* and the show-runner strategically deployed these apparent anomalies as clever-clever clues to that year's Big Bad. Sit patiently, tolerate the occasional necessity of re-watching an episode you didn't much enjoy because it explains one coming up soon, and all will be revealed. Or not, in the case of the pirate.

No, for a true fan of the series, the kind of puzzle that really satisfies is where two or more authors have contradicted each other. Alas, with hard-core fans of the old series running the new one and micromanaging every tiny detail, this isn't going to happen very often.

Or so one would think.

You will have noticed from the **Things That Don't Make Sense** entry with this episode that the activities of the Reapers are inconsistent and hard to resolve. The attempts to make sense of their actions founder when nothing that can tentatively be put forward as a theory fits all of the available data from *even this one story*. Reconciling it to any theory of how Time works in *Doctor Who* from before 2005 is hard, and making sense of their actions in the light of all the subsequent stories about time-paradoxes is impossible. The bulk of those later stories form a sort of consensus (which we'll elaborate on in Volume 8), at least until 2010, when what comes out of Steven Moffat's crack messes it all up again. We'll deal with that in Volume 9 (**Is Time Like Bolognese Sauce Now?** under "Flesh and Stone").

Just on the evidence in this one episode, it's difficult to resolve what exactly is going on, but let's at least look at that for clues as to which questions to ask when we widen the search.

We begin with the Doctor's comments about the Reapers. These are confusing: one minute, the Reapers are attracted to the time-rupture, like "bacteria"; the next, they are "sterilising" a wound in time. Let's assume for the moment that he misspoke and meant "antibodies". If the Reapers respond to damage to the timelines exactly as antibodies respond to infection, they would adapt themselves specifically to the kind of irritant or contamination causing trouble. A guided, intelligent sort of agency would therefore have targeted either Pete (the anomalously-alive man), or the Doctor and Rose (the time-travellers who caused him to be alive). The Doctor admits that having two of him and two Roses (and we presume two TARDISes) close by was weakening the fabric of time. Pete remains stubbornly unkilled for pretty much the whole episode, and the Reapers ignore Rose even when she's touched her younger self. The Doctor is removed from time when shielding everyone else. He had hitherto claimed that "older" things were better able to resist the Reapers - but suddenly, they're attracted to him. An instinctive antibody-like agency would be drawn to the same sort of "scent" that attracted them to the Powell Estate in November 1987.

Notably, their actions aren't indiscriminate. They pick and choose between people, ignoring a screaming bride for an older, calmer vicar. Nonetheless, they seem to steadfastly refuse to attack the three people who have *created* this rupture (until the Doctor forces their hand) and can be seen in one shot flying around being a bit menacing and completely ignoring this Peugeot that keeps winking in and out of existence.

What logic governs their choice of victims? The first three of these - a housewife, a gardener and a dosser - aren't especially close to either the incident or Rose and Pete's current location. Later, the Reapers assault the church but leave Pete and Rose alone. The Doctor claims that the older something is the stronger it is, but they grab Stuart's dad shortly after taking children, and their biggest scalp is the TARDIS, which was arguably ancient even before the Doctor stole it. So are they taking things that are big threats? No, because the Doctor acts as a shield long after he has started making moves to undo this situation.

continued on Page 131...

X1.8 Father's Day

She asks for a do-over with regards seeing her father's death, he gives it.

Somehow he's aware that after the second iteration of him and Rose being present during her father's death, they don't get a third go. However, he seems woefully out of his depth once the crisis develops - eventually his guesses prove to be right, and he maintains a show of knowledgeable confidence to avoid a panic. He seems to redouble his efforts after the bride and groom petition him, on the grounds that he never had a life like theirs. [This is perhaps disingenuous: there are enough stray comments about him having had a few tentative relationships and a family.] He seems to actively enjoy ordering Jackie to shut up and go away. Pete's goof over Jackie's name at their wedding amuses him greatly.

Once again, he seems very good with babies [18.1, "The Leisure Hive"; 26.3, "The Curse of Fenric"]. Jackie trusts him with baby Rose. Adult Rose is another matter, and he is furious with her until she says she is sorry, but this reconciliation comes when it seems too late to learn anything useful from the mistake.

• *Ethics.* Once again, this Doctor proceeds by identifying the problem, working out what needs to be done, dropping heavy hints to the person he wants to do it and then, indirectly, engineering a crisis so that person follows the recommended path to save everyone. Except, this time, he knows that there's an easy solution (send Pete out to be killed by the oncoming car) that would hurt Rose and struggles to find an alternative.

• *Inventory: Sonic Screwdriver.* It's here used to power-up a mobile phone battery [a facility that will be useful later on - see, for example, "The Time of Angels"].

• *Inventory: Other.* Rose's TARDIS key heats up and glows when the Ship wants to attract the Doctor's attention. It also provides a homing signal/template for the displaced TARDIS to regrow around, somehow.

The TARDIS As the temporal anomaly concerning Pete's survival continues, the TARDIS' interior disappears, and it's reduced to being just an empty wooden box, battered and a bit loose at the seams. Later, when Rose's TARDIS key glows, the Doctor is able to make the police box manifest itself around the key in mid-air, and the exterior is translucent [allowing us to read the backwards lettering on the panel from behind]. The Reapers sever this link, making the Ship disappear again until Pete dies and time is put back on track.

The Supporting Cast

• *Rose* used to hear the details pertaining to her father's death whenever Jackie was a bit drunk, so memorised the details. She shuts down any and all flirtation that Pete (a result of his not knowing they're related) might be directing her way, going on at length on the theme of 'don't go there' (and oblivious to how recent that turn of phrase is). She's utterly sick of the assumption that she and the Doctor are a couple. It doesn't occur to her that checking her messages on the phone is in any way anachronistic or pointless [see **RT Phone Home?** under X1.2, "The End of the World"]. Apparently, she can drive.

[As veteran *Doctor Who* fans doubtless noticed, Rose's physical contact with her younger self doesn't trigger a burst of energy per the Blinovitch Limitation Effect - see "Mawdryn Undead" - which is something we're going to encounter again, in X5.13, "The Big Bang" and X6.0, "A Christmas Carol".]

• *Jackie.* Her full name is 'Jacqueline Andrea Suzette Prentice' [see X2.12, "Army of Ghosts"]. She instinctively assumes the worst about anything Pete does or says. Although later she would tell Rose a slightly idealised version of Pete's clever plans, in 1987 he's a 'useless article' and a philandering chancer who might have fooled around with a cloak room attendant. She claims to not be stressed by Pete's getting her middle names wrong during their wedding vows, saying that it was 'good enough for Lady Di' [although Di actually only got 'Charles Philip Arthur George' in the wrong order]. She takes charge of events as soon as she arrives at the wedding, and attempts to browbeat the Doctor even when it is obvious that what's going on is his field of expertise.

• *Mickey.* He's four or five years old here, and his reaction to being the sole survivor of a mass-disappearance from the playground - itself possibly significant - is to run screaming into the church claiming that aliens are attacking. Everyone indulges this, as if that's what he says when he stubs his toe, loses his socks or whatever, and they laugh at his obsession even despite everything else that's been happening. He runs instinctively to grown-up Rose; she claims he's imprinted on her like a hatchling chick. [The Doctor claims that nobody but he and Rose recalls anything of the

Father's Day X1.8

Reapers - Errr... *What*?

continued from Page 129...

So, we can fairly conclusively rule out the antibody theory. One option is that, like the Weeping Angels (before their mission-creep in Series Five), these beasties feed on the potential lifespan of the people they remove. This would make a bit more sense: an ability to tell by scent or whatever who was going to live longest would be logical for such predators and would therefore explain why Pete (who ought to be dead already) and the Doctor (who has five more episodes before he regenerates) are less tasty than toddlers, youngish housewives and an abstemious vicar. This is bad news for the happy couple, as Stuart's dad was "scheduled" to out-live him, apparently, and the Vicar is more appealing than Sarah. It's frankly terrifying news for young Mickey.

Or is it? Because if Mickey Smith, someone we know for a fact is alive in 2006, doesn't have enough future to make him tempting even as a snack, then everyone else in that church is destined to keep going for decades to come - but less than some old tramp necking cider in a gutter. However, if the Reapers know Mickey's future, then they might know that at some point in the original timeline he was going to get a ride in the TARDIS and land up taking over the place of his counterpart Ricky in Evil Parallel Universe of the Cybermen (X2.6, "The Age of Steel"). This might be enough to protect him from the attack that takes everyone else in the same playground. But if that's the case, then Rose, the Doctor, Jackie (and, for all we know, Martha Jones, Donna Noble and Wilf Mott) may also be standing around wondering where everyone else went. But what about Pete? Well, a version of him *does* belong in what the Doctor later terms "Pete's World". He never goes in the TARDIS, so the usual exemption to temporal shenanigans might not be in play here (see **Is Arthur the Horse a Companion?** under X2.4, "The Girl in the Fireplace" and **He Remembers This *How*?** under X1.5, "World War Three").

If, on the other hand, the Reapers feed on the temporal potential of change, then people for whom a number of almost identical variant futures are possible might be appetising. Admittedly, any multiple of infinity is infinity, but the wider the "nearby" alternatives are, the stronger someone might be. Whilst at first sight the logical suggestion would be that someone with a stark choice (such as running out into oncoming traffic ten minutes from now or not) might be *more* fruitful a snack for the Reapers, what we actually see in the story suggests otherwise. Stuart's dad was probably going to spend every day much like every other, whereas Stuart and Sarah were about to get married (or not). Baby Rose is going to run into a time machine in 19 or so years, or not.

So let's remove Wilf from the list of people potentially standing around in an empty London (something he's rather good at - X4.0, "Voyage of the Damned"), but look again at Donna and Martha. They both spend time in altered timelines. "Last of the Time Lords" (X3.13) is about Martha's "gap year" travels, "Turn Left" (X4.11) is about Donna creating a whole new world (and then uncreating it). The latter is suggestive. The bug on her back that feeds off time energy is able to alter one person's timeline to make a whole different history, and Donna's choice made a world so different that it revived the Bad Wolf. There's a potential to salvage this story's claim to hold together, but it needs a slight detour.

We begin with the way that the first iteration of the Doctor and Rose in "Father's Day" just snark out when their later selves materialise around the corner. Let's pretend that what's happening is the opening up of a new timeline where they aren't involved, and that what we see is them stay put while we and the whole world leave them behind in the unedited chronology. Well and good, and it makes an intuitive, aesthetic sense, but then... why aren't there Reapers around every time someone tosses a coin or makes a choice? Indeed, if we're going with this quantum stuff, anything requiring light to be both wave and particle is going to cause trouble, which means anything using a laser (bar-code readers, CD players, DVDs... we're doomed). It must be the significance of the alteration that attracts Reaper-action. (We'll come on to that old standby of signal-to-noise ratios shortly, but it won't make your heads hurt much this time.) So, all right, just for this one story, we'll assume there is the one and only, truly original timeline, and all deviations therefrom are wicked and sinful and cause Reapers. (See also **How is**

continued on Page 133...

131

X1.8 Father's Day

anomalous hour, but given the change in Jackie's reaction to him, perhaps people who are *going to* travel in the TARDIS are partially exempt. Given that Donna's peculiar ability to generate fluky coincidences resonates back through her life from her contamination with the Doctor's DNA, this is at least arguable. See **He Remembers This *How?*** under X1.5, "World War Three".] Mickey doesn't find the disappearance of his mum any more distressing than that of his playmates.

• *Pete Tyler* was born 15th September, 1954. During his wedding vows, he spectacularly botched his recitation of Jackie's middle names ('Suzanne... Anita...'). He seems to get by with a few small-time deals and distribution for risky products, including solar power, Vitex energy-drink, cut price detergent and - late as it is - Betamax tapes. He came third in the bowling championship and has several trophies on display. He and Jackie seem to have gone to Spain at some point and brought home a straw donkey and a glass flagon. There are exercise gadgets lying around [whether his to sell or Jackie's to lose baby-fat is unclear]. He seems to spend his waking hours thinking up potential nice little earners.

The speed with which he pieces together what is going on and the truth about Rose's identity is impressive, but doesn't follow through to being genre-savvy: he puts his baby daughter in the lap of her adult self and causes the final crisis. Nonetheless, he is a jump ahead of her and sees through the Doctor's attempted euphemisms about him.

When not dressed for a wedding, he goes in for leather jackets and collarless tops open at the neck [sound familiar?] with a gold necklace. He has ginger hair, cut unfashionably short, possibly to cover his receding hairline. His charm seems to get him deals from small businessmen he meets at the pub, but also seems to lead Jackie to suspect he tries it on with any woman he meets.

The Non-Humans

• *The Reapers* [not actually named on screen] are flying creatures, about ten feet from head to tail and with a wingspan half that again. They have savage teeth in their abdomens. When attacking or ingesting a human victim, they glow light orange [that same shade used for time-energy in other stories] and the rim of the "mouth" a dark red. They make a screaming sound as they attack. They have three-taloned claws which are not enough to destroy wood, but can make limestone crumble. The age of something repels them, normally [so they never smash the stained-glass windows]. Once the 'paradox' of Rose touching her younger self empowers them, however, and lets them materialise inside the church that had hitherto been too old for them to penetrate, the opposite seems to be true: they seem to target the Doctor because he's the oldest thing in the vicinity.

The Reapers seem to travel silently when they are stalking, and their point-of-view shots from above are red, broken up into cells and have multiple images. They manifest in mid-air over time anomalies, so that they have to stalk their prey from where they arrived to where the people are.

History

• *Dating*. We're told that this is 7th November, 1987 [a Sunday in our world] - the day Pete Tyler died. The couple getting married that day were Stuart Hoskins and Sarah Clarke.

• *The Time War*. Apparently, the reason stories like this never happened before the 2005 series is that the Time Lords were zealous in patrolling the consequences of injuries to Time. The Doctor's whole world was destroyed and, he claims, his entire family were killed. [See **What Happened to Susan?** under X4.18, "The End of Time Part Two".]

Catchphrase Counter A mobile phone battery warrants a 'Fantastic!' The fly-posted ads for 'Energise' [which looks to be one of the warehouse raves starting around that time, rather than a rival glucose-rich drink] include one with 'Bad Wolf' scrawled on it.

Deus Ex Machina [As we'll discuss in the essay and **Things That Don't Make Sense**, there is a lot about this story that seems like writerly *fiat*, but one obvious one is a Peugeot. The car that keeps appearing and disappearing - as if controlled by Fate itself - until it kills Pete is hard to explain *even when* the rest of it is almost resolved. We also have the Doctor's apparent belief that once the TARDIS is restored, Pete will be able to remain alive, and the fact that he and Rose remember everything about this incident even when he had been consumed by a Reaper.]

Reapers - Errr... *What*?

continued from Page 131...

This Not a Parallel Universe? under "Turn Left", **What Constitutes a "Fixed Point"?** under X4.2, "The Fires of Pompeii" and **Bad Wolf - What, How and Why?** under X1.13, "The Parting of the Ways".) And we'll also take as gospel the Doctor's speculation that the two Roses and Doctors simultaneously caused a weakening of some kind of boundary, allowing the Reapers in from outside. Does this clear up any of the Reaper madness?

The biggest anomaly in this story as it stands is the car that is orbiting though time, re-running the crash with nobody to hit. Apart from providing a neat ending for the story, how is this happening? If this, rather than overlapping Roses, is the weak-point between realities, then its perpetual re-run through the hour or so that the Reapers wreak havoc is only explicable as them wedging open a doorway, so to speak. But the Pete who runs in front of this rather slow-moving vehicle is an hour older than he ought to have been and dressed differently. How much can change before this ceases to be the same event and before re-staging the death closes this rupture? If it's Pete's consciousness that's significant, would this have worked if he'd had a nap? If it's his physical body, would a meal, a few ciggies or a haircut have made any difference? This sounds footling, maybe, but if we assume, as earlier stories have, that consciousness is what makes things like this happen (see 20.3, "Mawdryn Undead" and 22.4, "The Two Doctors" and the attached essays), then once again it's hard to see how a sleeping baby Rose being held by an adult version who doesn't have any real link with this version of her self would make any difference. (Because the baby comes from an altered time-line anyway - "our" Rose doesn't suddenly remember Pete having been in her childhood. This is how Amy Pond can pat the head of an Amelia who never met the Doctor, because *that* Amelia could never grow up into her - X5.13, "Big Bang".) The significance of this Pete is his similarity to Parallel Pete, around whom the entire alt-London has apparently been formed.

This story's Pete has the potential to become "Gemini" and a tycoon on the back of Evil Parallel Red Bull (X2.5, "Rise of the Cybermen"). That potential grows the longer he is alive, but this would create an alternate universe and apparently those aren't allowed any more. We see one where John Lumic creates the Cybermen, but that appears to have been brought into being by the Bad Wolf Rose as a result of this meeting. This time, when Rose lacks any supernatural abilities, Pete's survival is the last straw for a patch of space-time that's been worn through by coexistent Time Lords, companions and TARDISes. But the very thing that makes him so important in the other narrative is what seems to be keeping him safe here: his potential for making a big change to the world.

Pete Tyler matters. His death matters. As the Doctor says, he is "... an ordinary man, that's the most important thing in creation". As is so often the case in *Doctor Who* stories where time is messed up, the centre of the messed-up-ness is the last to be destroyed. However, this isn't another "eye of the hurricane" effect, but appears to be a process whereby the people with the closest proximity to their counterparts in the pre-existent one parallel universe that can exist are going to have the strongest hold on the "forbidden" alternate timeline that has been made. People who seem to die as a result of the Reapers are simply being removed from the narrative. They are "noise" and not "signal" because, it would seem, they lack the anchoring with other versions of themselves who make a "sanctioned" parallel universe happen. Except that there isn't a Rose in Pete's World, and there are two of them in this one.

And here we have to remark on what we mentioned earlier: when the "revised" Rose saves Pete, the "original" Rose and Doctor softly and suddenly vanish away. The obvious precedent for that is at the first cliffhanger in "The Space Museum" (2.7), where the TARDIS has jumped a time-track and sent versions of our heroes into a near-future where they can see but not hear, and where (when?) they have been captured, stuffed and mounted as exhibits. When the anomaly resolves, we see the potential future TARDIS crew vanish and the footprints they should have been leaving all episode fade into being. In this instance it is a *potential* future, which they pre-empt and forestall by the usual expedient of starting a revolution and overthrowing an alien invasion. But in "Father's Day", it is a definite past that is undone and it's the whole world that's skipped a time-track, not the

continued on Page 135...

X1.8 Father's Day

The Analysis

The Big Picture The knee-jerk reaction is that this is a simple reworking of the *Star Trek* episode "City on the Edge of Forever" by Harlan Ellison. This might work at a very basic conceptual level, but examination of either teleplay in any detail shows big differences. Ellison is coming from a literary SF background and is compromising for television: his starting point is the dilemma of letting people you care for (after however brief an acquaintance) be sacrificed to the rigorous and predictable rules of the universe - compare it to, say, "The Cold Equations" by Tom Godwin[25], where a pilot has to chuck a stowaway out of an airlock because her weight will affect the ship's orbit and kill them both, and the point is clear. Ellison games his story so that a nice lady has to die - because if she lives, Hitler will win and the USS *Enterprise* will never have been built.

The effort of contorting what is essentially a *Twilight Zone* episode into *Star Trek*'s constraints is obvious. Cornell, though, is doing the exact opposite: Pete has to die because the rules of the universe *have ceased to work*. Pete is not someone who is going to provide a turning point in history in a couple of years - his significance is that he wasn't around. The focus of the story is a girl getting to know her father, not Kirk trying to cop off with Joan Collins in soft focus. The visitor to the past is someone from our time going back to the 1980s, not twenty-second century military types (one an alien) going to the author's childhood. Going back a bit further, the idea of an alternate universe with a better version of one's domestic arrangements can be traced to John Wyndham's story "Random Quest", filmed as *Somewhere in Time* and starring - blimey! - Joan Collins. (It's another anomalous timeline resolved by traffic accidents, by the bye.)

Closer to home, the story is evidently indebted to "Mawdryn Undead", where the time differential between two chronologically distinct Brigadiers discharges in a providentially timed burst of Artron Energy according to the Blinovitch Limitation Effect. This was, in the pre-Davies era, the archetypal *deus ex machina* cheat ending - after four episodes of the Black Guardian hinting that if it should happen, the Universe would end, a lot of fans wrote variants where the effects were more interesting than simply mercy-killing a few men in frocks and pasta-strewn baldy-wigs. One of these was the quantum-physics/metatextual prizewinner "Lackaday Express" by Paul D Cornell (middle initials were "in" back then). Although most UK fanzines were analytical and research-based (when they weren't bitching about each other), there was a strand of them that ran fan fiction and Cornell was usually to be found there.

Once the BBC disowned *Doctor Who* and let Virgin Books play with it, Cornell was among those first in the queue. His debut novel, the seventh Doctor book *Timewyrm: Revelation*, went beyond trying to be a Terrance Dicks-style novelisation of an unbroadcast story and was something only possible in prose. It obviously made a big impression on Steven Moffat, who is re-using vast chunks of it now he is in charge. More cogently here, it is the end of a four-part sequence about a parasite messing with time, and in this story uses something in Ace's childhood to open up a wound; the characters take refuge in an intelligent, self-aware church. (Just. Don't. Ask.) By this time, Cornell had also been involved in a new writers' scheme for television and had got a 15-minute play, "Kingdom Come", made. For budgetary reasons, this had the end of civilisation as noises-off during a stagey series of conversations and monologues to camera in a café in Cromer.

Thereafter, Cornell worked on soaps and Paul Abbott's *Children's Ward* - which is where Davies enters the story. Davies and Abbott created an apocalypse-themed soap, *Springhill*, which in its second and final series was script-edited by Cornell and Gareth Roberts. Cornell got a solo children's ITV series, *Wavelength*, which was sort of like *Press Gang* but in a radio station - a bit like the one he'd worked at a few years earlier.

You're getting the idea: if ever *Doctor Who* came back, Cornell would be in the front line of available writers. Indeed, that was the case - the BBC promoted its new online services with a 40th-anniversary relaunch, *The Scream of the Shalka*, starring Richard E Grant and Sophie Okenedu (X5.2, "The Beast Below") and written by Cornell. This was somewhat overshadowed by the near-simultaneous announcement of the return of a television version of *Doctor Who* produced by that bloke who did *Queer as Folk*.

English Lessons
• *Del-Boy*. The anti-hero of long-running BBC sitcom *Only Fools and Horses* (see "The Mysterious

Father's Day X1.8

Reapers - Errr... *What*?

continued from Page 133...

Doctor or Rose. (At least, not the Doctor or Rose from the revised timeline.)

Where similar things have happened in the wider BBC Wales scheme of things, it has usually been done to Sarah Jane Smith and her chums. In those instances, a changed history leaves the crucial figures languishing in a white void (see 6.2, "The Mind Robber" and possibly more cogently 18.5, "Warriors' Gate"). This tends to be the work of something called the Trickster (not that bloke from *Grange Hill* in a loin-cloth - 19.3, "Kinda"), who may or may not be the Black Guardian, but is definitely the employer of the beetle-thing from "Turn Left". The Trickster is a representative of the Pantheon of Chaos, and is set on undoing nice orderly history in favour of entropy - it keeps trying to remove Sarah from the scene because it knows how much she is going to contribute in the near future. (See also **What Do the Guardians Do?** under 16.1, "The Ribos Operation".) This allows us to at least attempt a reconciliation between "Father's Day" and the rest of *Doctor Who*. The Reapers would appear to be busily making one of those voids for Pete, Jackie, Mickey and the Roses by removing anyone else. The Graske (see *The Sarah Jane Adventures*: "Whatever Happened to Sarah Jane?") probably wasn't up to the job.

In fannish circles, a storyline is often spoken of loosely as a "Universe". It appears that in this case, the converse is true: the people who make the story happen, or could change it materially, are the ones that the Reapers leave. As far as we can tell, the person telling this story is the person we hear telling the story at the beginning and end: Rose. This is why the second most important man in her life, the one who could undo it, is also a victim. The Doctor is obviously key to this story-world, but that's "key" in the sense of "unlocking and letting people in". Once that's done, he can be written out of the story. But when Pete decides it's not really his story, the Doctor is back, unaffected.

Jackie isn't: Pete's still dead in the revised timeline, but his death has become, for Rose, a story of a heroic father sacrificing his life rather than a random traffic accident. Jackie knows that the driver of the Peugeot stopped and gave his details, so there's at least one other person whose future is different.

Planet", as well as 13.6, "The Seeds of Doom" and "Rise of the Cybermen"), who lived in a flat in South London, made a precarious living on dodgy deals while expecting the Next Big Thing to fall into his lap, and had boxes of unsellable "bargain" goods stacked up around the place. Sound familiar?

• *'Er Indoors*. How Del-Boy's TV rival, Arthur Daley from ITV's *Minder*, always referred to his wife. Terry, Arthur's eponymous minder, seems to be Pete's fashion guru.

• *Didcot* is a small town in Oxfordshire near where Cornell lives, and is noted for its historic links with the Victorian railway system, its supremely ugly power station and some nearby scenic views. It's somewhere a lot of people have been through, rather than to. (Actually, if you've got a car, it's not a bad base for a holiday spent in the area - see the White Horse at Uffington, for example - but not the obvious place to offer as a first prize.)

Oh, Isn't That...?

• *Shaun Dingwall* (Pete Tyler) usually plays soldiers or cops. He had been in the majority of such dramas in the late 90s and after, including *Soldier Soldier* and *Touching Evil*. About the only non-service role he'd had for a while was in *In a Land of Plenty*. He'd actually been in *Minder* (see above), but after this landed up as Del-Boy's dad in the prequel *Rock and Chips*. After this he was in *The Long Firm*, a rather perplexing 60s crime-drama. He now has a second career doing video-game voices.

Things That Don't Make Sense Any of it. The whole of the accompanying essay deals with the difficulties of reconciling this story's premise to the notions of how Time functions to be found in any other BBC Wales episode, let alone previous versions of *Doctor Who* lore. So here, we will limit this to the moments when the consequences of the time-mangling contradict other things *within the same story*...

The two biggest and juiciest causality violations are the radios and phones getting weird signals from other time periods, and that the car destined to kill Pete keeps winking in and out of existence on a perpetual loop. It's *just* about plausible that a clear Radio 1 transmission from 2005 might make it to 1987 and Pete's car-radio and that, against the odds, the frequency is so perfectly aligned that an undistorted Mike Skinner should come through on 88-91 FM simply because it was transmitted on the same frequency (or will be transmitted). However, a mobile phone is essentially a radio receiver, and the message is encrypted in a very specific way. An earlier phone message sent on a wire as simple impulses has no business being picked up on a modulated carrier-wave. But it happened, and thus Alexander Graham Bell's spoken message from 1871 ('Watson, come here, I need you') became, whilst it repeated over the phone, the oldest thing around. Why not use *this* to ward off Reapers? If the argument is that a pattern of impulses isn't an object (and that doesn't hold at the subatomic level, but never mind), then how are those patterns being transported intact across time and no others?

Now let's discuss the Doctor's strategy that everyone should take refuge in the church because it's the oldest thing around, and to the Reapers, the 'older [something] is, the stronger it is'. To be fair, perhaps he just wants to bundle everyone inside, and they're closest to the church when the Reapers appear. All things being equal, though, it looks as if he means that the Reapers can distinguish between a late nineteenth-century building from other buildings on the same street built at around the same time. (Actually, the whole street looks Edwardian, including a church that is in a retro design but probably slightly younger than the rest of the neighbourhood. Never mind that being taller than most other buildings in London then, churches were disproportionately damaged in the Blitz, and so this may have been substantially rebuilt in the 1950s.)

Or, does he mean that the stone from which the church was made is older than the bricks of the terraced houses and shops? Well, the church seems to be made of limestone, from dead-critter deposits laid down in the Cretaceous era - but the clay brick houses have slate or lead on their rooves, so might "smell" even older. But he specifies that the windows and doors of the building are old, when they really aren't: the doors are wood in all cases, so no more than a century old.

(Here's another thought, then: maybe, despite what he says aloud as a shorthand, he thinks the Reapers are alert to the age of the church *as an institution*. It was a Church of England wedding, so the start-date is 1536 at the earliest - on that logic, the Doctor would have been better urging everyone to head for the nearest Synagogue or Hindu temple - Divali was a fortnight earlier, during school Half-term, so they'd know where it was - or flagging down the Number 3 bus to South Norwood, the HQ of the World Zoroastrian Organisation and conveniently close to where the Powell Estate is supposed to be. If we're playing ecclesiastical Top Trumps, faiths older than writing beat the local brand.)

Regardless of whether any other stories (eg 18.7, "Logopolis" or 22.1, "Attack of the Cybermen") contradict it, the scene where the TARDIS is reduced to being a real Police Box is effective. So is the scene where the Ship manifests itself around the key. The problem is that making *both* phenomena work in the same story is tricky. Somehow, the Reapers severed the link between the TARDIS dimension and its outer plasmic shell (the bit that looks like a Police Box) - and yet this link is active and makes Rose's key glow and heat up. Why did the Reapers not take the box as well? Putting the key in would be hard, even if the Doctor has guessed the precise bit of church air to place it, as he left his own key in the lock when he ran off to protect Rose.

The TARDIS' interior disappears for quite a long time before Rose's TARDIS key starts warming up and glowing noticeably - why does it pick that precise moment to do so? If it was simply that the Doctor had been carrying a red hot lump of metal in his inside jacket pocket but failed to realise until Rose hugged him, that's silly enough - but the alternative is that the Ship dithered around in a numinous dimension letting people get killed, and then decided to whistle for help after about an hour.

Why should big grown-up Rose holding the basket with Baby Rose cause a 'paradox' (as the word is typically defined), let alone a paradoxical rupture that empowers the Reapers? (Even if there *had* been skin-to-skin contact, if we're assuming that different clothes touching isn't a time-crime, isn't this a continuation of the previous paradox rather than a whole new one?) And why, exactly, does the Doctor think that he can both eliminate the Reapers and create a timeline in which Pete lives if he can just get the TARDIS back? Does he actually have such a plan, or is he just lying?

Lesser snags: the production team has, more or less, got the right period details but... the car-radio Pete has would have been worth more than the car itself back then. (That's just about plausible as a character-detail, but suggests that it fell off the back of a lorry, and that he has friends with better deals going from whom he could have learned.) He would have removed it and taken it into the church, with the inevitable argument to follow. Jackie, born in 1968 ("Rise of the Cybermen"), looks even more raddled than a mother of a small baby would have at 19. Pete's line about 'mixed signals' is as anachronistic as Rose's 'don't go there' aria. The "How_____ is that?"/ "How ___ am I?" formulation is mid-90s too. How Rose's two blue-eyed parents had a brown-eyed daughter is another matter for another day.

The Doctor needs a power-source, and is given a mobile-phone battery which he promptly powers-up with the sonic screwdriver. Why not just use the screwdriver?

Why are Stuart and Sarah getting married on a Sunday (as "our" 7th November, 1987, actually was)? Why was the vicar available, especially as this seems to be a pretty last-minute arrangement and a bit shambolic?

One for old-school fans: The Doctor tells Stuart and Sarah that he never once had a night at a club that ended with a taxi home at 2.00am. Actually, this was significant to the plot of "The War Machines" (3.10).

Critique Shamelessly manipulative, overly familiar, utterly predictable - and yet, it just about works. It's the dialogue and performances that enable the story to avoid staleness, even as the music, monsters and some of the directorial flourishes threaten to drag it back to cliché. Especially crass is the red-tinted, distorted aerial shots of potential victims with the naff screechy synth music. It almost looks as if they are trying to kid long-in-the-tooth fans that we're due for a return of the Cheetah People (26.4, "Survival").

Where this story scores, therefore, is in the things that could have been done on stage. This is very much an ensemble piece - the Doctor is removed for much of the story, and his addressing people from a pulpit seems more natural than when he talks to them face-to-face. Instead, it's Shaun Dingwall (as Pete) who is centre-stage here. Piper is more or less his straight man for most of the episode, only really getting the spotlight when, once again, called upon to blub and hug everyone. Fortunately, Dingwall is pitch-perfect and his timing makes many of the lines funnier or more revealing than they could have been. But where this is most important is with the longer scenes where, as with theatre, everyone is listening to everyone else.

This is, however, a story where having an experienced director of photography tells. There are a few shots that would simply not have worked in old-style VT in a studio, nor yet on location with the OB rigs used in the late 80s. One in particular stands out: Pete decides to die and swigs the Communion wine before saying goodbye to Rose. There are any number of ways to have done this, but director Joe Ahearne has Piper in close up, in profile, on the extreme left of the frame, as Dingwall enters from the right some 30 feet away at the back of the church and approaches her and us. There is a barely-perceptible shift of focus as he starts to speak. Using digital cameras inclines the shots towards deeper focus that is now commonplace (because the "target" of the lens is a small chip rather than a frame of 16mm film), but not so much that it could have kept both Piper and Dingwall in focus at once. Instead, most directors would have cut between this set-up and a few other shots, or made a more elaborate lighting plan and used a longer lens to make this one shot crisp at all levels. Ahearne instead sticks to his guns and allows the shot enough time without cutting away so that we get the picture, literally and figuratively, and avoids the potential side-effect of Pete's approach looking like Azal growing to 50 feet high (8.5, "The Daemons") against a static church interior backdrop. This also means that he doesn't need to flood the church location with lights, as would have been the case with film. Touches such as this are potentially flamboyant, but here it is in the service of the dialogue to come.

This stateliness comes at a price, however. While the storytelling opts, probably rightly, to emphasise the people going through the situation rather than what this situation actually is, there's so little attention paid to clearly and concisely setting out what's happening that the logical sequence of events goes right out of the window. We are told, as viewers, simply to sit back and *accept* what we see. *Doctor Who* has never been as brazenly anti-rational as this; even the McGann movie's incomprehensible ending made vague gestures towards explanation, and even

X1.8 Father's Day

"Dimensions in Time" *believed* itself to be making sense. This story resists any coherent account of the things we see, and even the Doctor can't make up his mind what's going on

It was invariably the case that *Doctor Who* resolved situations by one or more main character asking questions. This was even true last week (X1.7, "The Long Game"), and the attitude spilled over into the people watching - they would often get little rewards for wondering things that characters might have wondered, and were enticed into watching by being given small puzzles to solve. The easy thrills of action sequences or groovy-looking special effects (especially early on when the *Top of the Pops* aesthetic prevailed) came as treats after the story had clicked into place. "Father's Day" expects - indeed, demands - that viewers supinely gaze at the screen and look at the pretty pictures. Asking what's going on is being a killjoy.

This is as true of the characters as of the viewers. The moral of this story is "Don't question or resist your fate - accept it." Only once has this been tried before, in the enigmatic-but-visually-appealing "Warriors' Gate" (18.5). That story featured beings who were more clued-up than the Doctor or Romana, had already figured the whole thing out and wanted to prevent the two of them from messing with their neat plan. *This* story is resolved by Pete, the go-getter, the man who looked into possibilities, going along with what Time had in store for him all along. The Doctor's bid to fix everything with Pete still alive afterwards may or may not have been viable - it's shown as a last throw of the dice. The usual comment made about this is that it is making the story "richer" by concentrating on the characters - there would be some kind of statement in *Doctor Who Confidential* along the lines of "You need that *emotion*" (Davies would always stress that last word). Well, true, but delight in things fitting together and a puzzle being solved is also an emotion. So are anger and frustration when the resolution is blitheringly stupid or a cop-out (as we will see in later volumes, usually in episode thirteen of a series). They are working on some weird eighteenth-century model of human behaviour that has intellect and emotion as opposites. The BBC Wales series is mainly concerned with a constricted definition of "emotion" that can be measured in fluid ounces - teenage girls sobbing buckets or small children peeing their pants. As we said, "Father's Day" just about avoids being too stupid to engage any viewer with the right amount of curiosity and imagination to have been watching *Doctor Who* in the first place, but it set a dangerous precedent.

The Facts

Written by Paul Cornell. Directed by Joe Ahearne. Viewing figures: (BBC1) 8.06 million, (BBC3 repeats) 0.2 and 0.6 million.

Repeats and Overseas Promotion Dzien ojca, Vatertag, Fete des peres.

Production

Just as the Victorian ghost story with Dickens was a natural fit for Mark Gatiss, and Robert Shearman would be given first refusal on the re-write of "Jubilee", so the low-budget, effects-light tearjerker would most likely have Paul Cornell's name on it. Davies' initial brief was a sort of *Rashomon* story, with Pete dying over and over, but different people from his life telling different versions of his past. The Doctor would hear the story from "Judy" (later renamed "Jackie") in the present day, and permitted Rose to try to change the past in order to find out how resistant Time is to being changed. This would have kept the Doctor's involvement to maybe one day's shooting, allowing a holiday, maybe.

Cornell attempted to make this a story where each iteration revealed a slightly different Pete with a different timeline. The earliest versions had everyone hiding in the pub; as the Reapers attacked and altered the past, so the pub's décor moved backwards in time. (Many older pubs have photos of the interior as it was - Cornell was in particular familiar with the celebrity photos of the Fitzroy Tavern in London during World War II and the 1950s.) Davies proposed moving the story to the church and using a wedding as a means to bring back characters from Jackie's life (Bao and Ru, from X1.4, "Aliens of London", for example - they were dropped, but Mickey was shown as a child already obsessed by aliens). With this in place, Cornell could re-examine the central premise and make the story about Pete's ordinariness, rather than having him turn out to have been a secret agent or whatever, and having him *not* dying as the central problem for the Doctor.

This allowed the Doctor, who was partly responsible through not "getting" humans, to be removed from the story halfway through - they still had ambitions of making this a double-banked episode (see X2.10, "Love & Monsters"). They also hoped to make it free from complicated (and costly) effects. Jane Tranter had other ideas and insisted on a monster in every story, so the Reapers came in.

- Several ideas were proposed for the Reapers: the obvious Ingmar Bergman-style Grim Reaper with a cowl and a skeletal hand was one, Cornell suggested a mouth on legs (see 19.6, "Earthshock"), various permutations of vampires with cloaks were mooted and something akin to the Gravelings from *Dead Like Me* seemed like a goer. The cloak idea seemed like a good way to avoid anything visually distressing, but there was still the problem of vampires or monks wandering around South London in 1987 in broad daylight. Eventually, making the cloaks wings and having dragon-like Reapers emerged as the front-runner, although obviously this had budget implications. Suddenly, there were fewer wedding-guests. That could be made to work with the plot, though.

- Some of the details of Pete's life were autobiographical. Cornell's dad had spent a lot of time trying various ways to make a living, the difference being that one had worked. Once the wedding setting and date were agreed upon, Cornell's wife - then training to be a vicar - checked the details of the service as it would have been then, including the right prayer-book. The Tylers' wedding was dated in the script as 1982, which would make Jackie older than she claims in Series Two. It is reported that one planned anachronism in the script was the use of a mid-90s song, "Hobart Paving" by Saint Etienne, which had been used at the Cornell wedding (and sung for them by the band's Sarah Cracknell, which was nice). Contrary to some reports, at no time were the Isley Brothers to have been heard in the episode (this being a running gag in Cornell's *New Adventures* books). Apart from "Don't Mug Yourself" by The Streets (whose subsequent album *A Grand Don't Come for Free* had been inescapable when this story was being written), the soundtrack eventually had "I Never Can Say Goodbye", a hit for the Communards in late 87 (their previous single had been No. 1 when Sylvester McCoy made his debut, so went in every fan's book of pop trivia) and, inevitably, "Never Gonna Give You Up" by Rick Astley.

- Recording began on 11th November at a church in Cardiff, St Paul's; this was redressed with 80s ribbons and detailing. On the noticeboard are photos from Clive's garage, and the hymn-numbers on the board near the pulpit are the same as the bus-numbers on the fake London Transport bus-stop outside (both of these details were circulated in behind-the-scenes material and hinted to be Huge Clues). Rather than use boom-mics inside, microphones were strategically placed inside the church to add resonance to the timbres of everyone's voices and a sense of scale and age to the church. The police closed the road off for almost a week, and faux London street-signs and 1987-vintage details were put up. They even made an authentic-seeming cider bottle label for the wino (it's supposed to resemble Diamond White, a popular cheap brand then). On Saturday morning, Shaun Dingwall made a detour to the car-park of a furniture warehouse to have his photo taken for the pre-credit scene. The actor playing the father of the groom, Sonny, has been claimed to be the Doctor's legs in some of the dance scenes at the end of "The Doctor Dances" (X1.10).

Although the weather stayed mercifully dry for most of the shoot, the cold got to many of the cast - Eccleston got the flu during this story. Those of the cast who were smokers used the tacky vase prop as an ashtray. As is usual, baby Rose was a pair of twins (whose first birthday it was during the shoot). There would have been a scene where Pete and Rose break into the communion wine - look carefully at the shot where Rose is in profile in close-up as Pete decides to jump under the car, and you'll see him take a last swig. The sequence where she accuses him of being "a bit of a Del-Boy" would have been longer, but the car was bouncing on the traffic-calming lumps in the road too much for a clear shot. The scene where the Doctor paraphrases *The Go-Between* ("The past is another country - they do things differently there") was added late on.

After a week at St Paul's (except Sunday, obviously), the unit went to the HTV studios for the registry-office scenes and the redressed Tyler flat on the Friday and returned the following Monday (we're now at 22nd November). The following day was split between the opening TARDIS scene and the work in Adam's cubby-hole in "Dalek" (which, as we stated then, was actually Clive's shed). November 23rd is always a special day for old-school fans, and Cornell got to celebrate the

X1.9 The Empty Child

Doctor's birthday by being interviewed on the TARDIS. The last two days of the shoot were in the Butetown district of Cardiff, for the terraced street and then finally the playground.

• It was at around this time that Eccleston's father had become gravely ill, which affected the working relations he had with the other cast and crew. Piper, whose own domestic problems had caused her to have to avoid tabloid journalists, had been close to her co-star - but this became increasingly strained. The shooting schedule for the next story in line, "The Long Game", was affected by this.

• The digitally-realised Reapers were an amalgam of scorpions, mantises, vultures and sharks, with bat-wings. The sound began as a recording of a vulture, and the flapping was Paul Jeffries rapidly opening and shutting a brolly. Joe Ahearne was the original voice of Alexander Graham Bell, but it was redone as he got the line slightly wrong.

X1.9: "The Empty Child"

(21st May, 2005)

Which One is This? "Are you my Mummy?" Blitz-era capers as a whole new generation finally "gets" *Doctor Who*.

Firsts and Lasts Steven Moffat's first "legitimate" script for the series, after several non-skeddo *Who*-adjacent projects, features the first use of the phone in the TARDIS' police box exterior to make a call. For the first time since... ooh... 11.1, "The Time Warrior", the Doctor uses the pseudonym "Dr John Smith" (although we don't know what was on his ID in 26.1, "Battlefield" or 26.3, "The Curse of Fenric"). Perhaps surprisingly, it's the first time anyone (in this case, Rose) asks "Doctor Who?" to Our Hero's face. This comes in a scene where the existence of *Star Trek* in the *Doctor Who* universe is acknowledged (see also X2.11, "Fear Her"). In passing, we have the first hint in the new series that the Doctor had something like a childhood (and not a happy one).

With the introductory info-dump about nanogenes, we get the first of many, many orange, sparkly fairy-dust-like events. In the pre-credit scene, we have the first instance of this title-sequence being used within the story to depict the space-time Vortex. (Something that has happened, on and off, since the very first episode, regardless of the precise nature of the titles - it has also been used, often shortly afterwards, to depict the Doctor's mind. We will return to this odd conjunction of narrative conventions in two episodes from now.) Although *Doctor Who* had steadfastly avoided World War II until "The Curse of Fenric" (1989), this story marks the first of Moffat's campaign to keep doing it until he gets it right (X5.3, "Victory of the Daleks"; X6.8, "Let's Kill Hitler"; and X7.0, "The Doctor, the Widow and the Wardrobe").

Most of all, it's the debut of shy, retiring John Barrowman as Captain Jack Harkness...

Watch Out For...

• Steven Moffat is another of those writers whose dialogue has its own particular rhythm and idiom. For some actors, especially those well-versed in 30s screwball comedies and US sitcoms, this comes naturally and does most of the work for them. Others have to find a way to work around it. Eccleston is in the latter category and, most noticeably in the opening TARDIS sequence, seems ill-at-ease trying to sound like Matthew Perry. (Curiously, and suggestively, the only Scottish-accented cast-member, Richard Wilson, is flawless when delivering this Scots writer's lines.)

However, once Eccleston figures out how to add this style to his Doctor - such as in the dinner sequence with Nancy and her young charges - the result is something entirely Doctor-ish that no other Doctor has ever quite done. As a corollary of this, the Doctor becomes an avatar of one of Moffat's stock sitcom types: the nerdy best-friend of the cocky male lead. Moffat had tried this type of Doctor before, with Jim Broadbent's clumsy, girl-shy northern one in "The Curse of Fatal Death" (see Volume 6 and **Production** with the next episode), but now, and especially next week, Moffat will be editorialising about the programme's past within the dialogue.

• Anyone hoping for a gritty, authentic fly-on-the-wall examination of London in 1941 will be sadly disappointed. Everyone involved has opted for the impression of the Blitz as a romantic period with moody ruins lit starkly. It raised eyebrows on first transmission, even among children. What's really obvious is that the music was chosen to really make the point that this was an *idea* of 1941 and not how it seemed at the time. The *Singing Detective*-style nightclub has a chantoosie

What's So Great About the 51st Century?

Doctor Who initially went 14 years without mentioning the fifty-first century at all, then two stories in the space of six months involved people from this period. In "The Talons of Weng Chiang" (14.6), Magnus Greel is a future war criminal hiding in Victorian London and fearing discovery by Time Agents. Then in "The Invisible Enemy" (15.2), we discover that humanity finally starts migrating from the Solar System in earnest in AD 5000, during "The Great Break-Out", and that all sorts of wonders, including the Kilbracken technique of cellular photocopying, space hospitals in the asteroid belt and computerised dogs are commonplace. Hitherto, only one story even *seemed* to be from that era, and even that had a controversial dating. "The Ice Warriors" (5.3) mentions "five thousand years of civilisation", which would perhaps mean that the story is set in the same Ice Age that Greel and the Doctor knew from the Battle of Reykjavik. (The alternative dating, 3000 AD, also has its problems when other stories known to be set there are taken into account.)

So, fast-forward to 2005 and Captain Jack Harkness. Rose, whilst drunk, concludes that he's a former Time Agent from the fifty-first century, and older fans latched on to this as proof that Steven Moffat is One Of Us. The trouble is, Moffat got the details slightly wrong. Yes, Greel is a fugitive from World War VI, and, yes, he *seems* to think that Time Agents will be on his trail, but he never actually says that these people are from his time. In fact, as the Doctor points out (and the plot of "Talons" rather depends on this), Greel's time technology is dangerously primitive. Greel's Zygma Beam is a "cul-de-sac" and doesn't lead to any worthwhile temporal displacement. All it does is whisk the subject back in time in such a way as to cause genetic damage, necessitating Greel's absorption of the life-essence of local women. So when Jack Harkness - whoever he really is - turns out to be a former Time Agent *and* born in the fifty-first century, these two facts are not necessarily connected.

Nevertheless, this connection has been maintained by everyone writing for the BBC Wales series. Moffat himself has gave us Professor River Song, an archaeologist (she says) from... ah, well, there's some glitches here. The on-screen date we have for her adventures after she obtains a dubiously-acquired Vortex Manipulator (X5.12, "The Pandorica Opens") is 5145, i.e. the *fifty-second* century, but when we first meet her, just before her death (X4.8, "Silence in the Library"), she clearly states, repeatedly, that she is from the fifty-first century, which is when that story takes place. Moreover, in 5145 she was still "Doctor" Song - so as far as everyone else is concerned, it's before her visit to the Library. Not to worry, temporal ambiguity is very much River's schtick, but it gives us lots more on-screen visits to this period to date (we also have X5.4-5.5, "The Time of Angels" / "Flesh and Stone", and the coda to X6.8, "Let's Kill Hitler") and adds to the off-screen reports of this colourful phase in human history.

Jack, meanwhile, got his own spin-off series - and, in *Torchwood* Series Two, Cardiff became the stopping-off point for three other visitors from this time. Just to add to the jollity, Moffat prior to this had performed another exercise in time-malarkey, as a spaceship from this period used advanced hardware and bonkers software to provide us an accelerated biography of Mme de Pompadour (X2.4, "The Girl in the Fireplace"). Although some other periods of history also get repeat visits (the year five billion, starting with X1.2, "The End of the World"; and the forty-second century, starting with X2.8, "The Impossible Planet"), this is the one for which we have more contradictory reports. The society of the forty-second century seems little changed from our own, but nine hundred years later than that, it is all transformed.

Sifting through all of this confusing evidence and inference to get a clear idea of what's happening/will happen/will have happened between 5001 and 5100 is tricky, and one does worry that this text will have been contradicted on screen by the time it gets into print. Nonetheless, we feel obliged to make the attempt anyway. Here we are making the usual assumption that, unless definitively stated, it's all one timeline and everyone's telling the truth. The overall picture divides, for our purposes here, into Earth, Space, Time and Sex.

• **Earth**, In the 1970s TV stories set in the fifty-first century, the planet is still inhabited and inhabitable. Professor Marius is returning there soon, so bequeaths his tin dog K9 to the Doctor and Leela.

continued on Page 143...

X1.9 The Empty Child

doing "It Had to Be You" in a very obviously 80s torch-song manner, and the song was probably chosen because of *When Harry Met Sally* or *Annie Hall* rather than to suggest World War II. Similarly, the two Glenn Miller recordings used are the ones that made it back into the UK charts just before Punk, when clubbers in Essex and East London opted to go for the demob/GI look because there was nothing else to do in early 1976. (Think about it: how old was Steven Moffat in early 1976...)

• And as the name "Captain Jack Harkness" seems a little over-familiar to many of us old-skool *Who* fans, consider that Russell T Davies' original name for the character was "Jax". (Or maybe "Jaxx": he would have been making plans around the time Basement Jaxx released their second album, *Rooty*.) This means that, as well as a "Jackie" (called "Jacks" by her late husband and potential son-in-law), we could have had a "Jax" in the TARDIS. Instead, we get an epic romance between an American called "Jack" and an English girl called "Rose". Davis isn't letting this Kate Winslett thing go, is he? (See X1.1, "Rose" for the origins of this, plus X1.2, "The End of the World"; X4.0, "Voyage of the Damned" and the first ten minutes of *Queer as Folk*.) In real life, however, there was a noted rose-grower called Jack Harkness who bred a variety called "Compassion"...

• After the debacle with the "Next Time..." segment in "Aliens of London" (X1.4) giving away much of the resolution to the cliffhanger, they here go to great lengths to keep the potential give-aways about the next episode until after the end-credits. This was something Moffat insisted upon. What anyone watching this episode now will miss is that the BBC1 Continuity Announcer made a point of telling anyone watching that, if they want to avoid spoilers, they should leave the room for 30 seconds.

The Continuity

The Doctor He's stealthy enough to sit down at a table where Nancy and her gang are eating without any of them noticing.

• *Ethics*. The Doctor expresses nothing but admiration for Nancy's scheme of sneaking into people's homes and stealing food for the street-living children she's taken under her wing. [Rationing was set up at least in part to instil a sense of being all in the War Effort together, so anyone obviously fiddling the system - such as Arthur Lloyd, whose larder Nancy targets - deserves to have their excess redistributed to children who have fallen though the cracks. This point will be amplified in the next episode.]

• *Background*. He responds to Dr Constantine's comments about losing children and grandchildren in the War, but remaining a doctor, with 'I know the feeling' [see also 26.3, "The Curse of Fenric"].

If we take his comment to a stray cat about the duration of his adventures ('Nine hundred years of phone-box travel') and his remark to Rose about if he gets tired of just being called 'Doctor' ('Nine centuries in, I'm coping') at face value, it would appear that he's been travelling in the TARDIS *and* called 'Doctor' for the same length of time. [This is peculiar: the *nom-de-travaille* of 'Doctor' appears to have been one he had been using long before the TARDIS chameleon circuit broke down (right back at the end of the first episode, see 1.1, "An Unearthly Child"). Nevertheless, if we go with this hint and take the nine hundred years as at least an approximate guide to how long has elapsed since Ian and Barbara barged into his Ship, and factor in all the other details we've had over the previous 40 years or so, we can guess that this means that he is about 1300 years old. This would be a good match for other comments about how long he was travelling and how old he was when he started - *except* that in X4.0, "Voyage of the Damned", we get a definite statement from the tenth Doctor, backed up by all subsequent mentions, that he is a mere stripling of 903 summers. (See 25.1, "Remembrance of the Daleks"; 16.2, "The Pirate Planet"; and **The Obvious Question: How Old is He?** under 16.5, "The Power of Kroll".) So either he stole the TARDIS when he was a time-toddler and it was already Police Box-shaped, or he's lying about his age. (Or maybe he's a bit confused by where "he" begins - see **What Happens in a Regeneration?** under 11.5, "Planet of the Spiders" and **Who Are All Those Strange Men in Wigs?** under 13.5, "The Brain of Morbius".) X6.4, "The Doctor's Wife" contradicts all of this by (more reasonably, given the available evidence) saying that the Doctor made off with the Ship about 'seven hundred' years ago.

[Another curious feature of this episode is that - mainly to allow Moffat to set up jokes - the Doctor goes to great lengths to avoid identifying

What's So Great About the 51st Century?

continued from Page 141...

Shuttle flights between the worlds of the solar system are routine (an asteroid dash is a "milk-run", despite the huge expenditure of delta-V). 5000AD, a conveniently round number, is the year of The Great Break Out, when humanity swarmed across the system. And yet - sometimes in stories by the same authors as "The Invisible Enemy"! - Earth two thousand years earlier had a galactic empire (see, for instance, 9.4, "The Mutants"). At the end of that phase, people were talking about returning to the over-developed, over-populated Earth with its concrete sky-cities and submarine nations; London had been subsumed into a Southern England megalopolis (1.7, "The Sensorites"). However, there's now reason to believe that Earth was abandoned around 3000 AD because of solar flares (X5.2, "The Beast Below" and possibly others). Three hundred years later, Starship UK is still ferrying most of Britain's populace across the stars in a self-consciously nostalgic version of pre-spaceflight blighty. (Once again, this *appears* at first blush to chime with pre-existing continuity - notably 12.2, "The Ark in Space" - but it gravely fails to make sense when that and two follow-up stories, 12.3, "The Sontaran Experiment" and 12.5, "Revenge of the Cybermen" are looked at closely.) All other nations fled first.

But come the time of World War VI, as described in "The Talons of Weng-Chiang", everyone *else* is back. There's a Philippino Army fighting in Rekjavik against the Butcher of Brisbane. Bejing is now called "Peking" again and makes homicidal dolls with the brains of pigs. Notice anyone missing? This cosmopolitan future omits any mention of Britain or mainland Europe. We now know that Elizabeth X is still on the throne 1,940 years after meeting the Doctor ("The Pandorica Opens"), but where that throne is remains unclear. We do, however, know that WWVI takes place during an Ice Age. So is this when Britannicus Base is lain siege by Ice Warriors? Well, the internal evidence there is confusing. Europe is one of five blocs, all more-or-less holding back the ice with ionisers (hardly the advanced tech of "The Time of Angels" or even "The Invisible Enemy"). There's no hint of any political shenanigans that might lead to a global war, although there is an "Australasia" Zone which might support the rise of someone like Greel or his party. The regimented society we see in this story is far closer to what we hear about in "Terror of the Vervoids" (23.3) and see in "The Mutants". On the other hand, Ireland is still inhabitable in "The Invisible Enemy", so we can't simply assume a Europe-less fifty-first century Earth and boot "The Ice Warriors" back to 3000 on this alone. Although the Zones system sounds suspiciously like the near-future set-ups of "The Enemy of the World" (5.4) and "Warriors of the Deep" (21.1), the retro names of cities and countries is more in keeping with a Reconstruction after the Empire falls than the self-consciously utilitarian place-names of late third-millennium urban sprawl. If nothing else, we know that the old names are back by 4000 AD (3.4, "The Daleks' Master Plan").

Perhaps the way out of this impasse is to stop assuming that the terms "human" and "Earth" are interchangeable. Just try to imagine the culture that produced Miss Garrett ("The Ice Warriors") making clockwork robots and a time-corridor disguised as a fireplace. Obviously, different parts of human space are progressing at different speeds. Human technology seems to include a lot of things unavailable on Earth. If there's a mass evacuation by people with the money and skills to get off a planet rapidly hurtling into environmental and political deep-freeze, then this socio-technological apartheid makes a sort of sense. In 5000 AD, it is still possible for "spaceniks" to bum around the solar system, possibly emigrating from Ireland, but ten or 20 years later, the planet is a no-go area. Even chancers like Findecker ("Talons") seem scientifically advanced by Earth standards, despite the fact that on the galactic stage, his double-nexus particle is a joke and real time-travel technology is, if not taken for granted, at least accepted as possible.

(Incidentally, this solves one of the real puzzles of "Talons": why Greel thought that fleeing in a risky time machine that had apparently never been tested - he claims to have been the *first* man to travel back in time - and pretending to be a figure from Oriental mythology seemed like a better option just than buying a wig and moving to Venus. A blockade of Earth would also explain the apparent lack of off-world participants - one Time Lord aside - in the impending World War VI.)

continued on Page 145...

X1.9 The Empty Child

himself as such; even when asked outright, 'are you a doctor?' by Dr Constantine, he evasively replies 'I have my moments'. He's less circumspect when telling Nancy that the Empty Child, shunned by others and left in the cold, has his sympathy. In stories from the 1970s, the implication that the Doctor was born, had a childhood and grew up was repeatedly reinforced (see, *inter alia*, 13.5, "The Brain of Morbius"; 17.3, "The Creature from the Pit"; 9.3, "The Sea Devils"; 9.5, "The Time Monster"; and 18.4, "State of Decay"). It was emphatically avoided in the 1980s stories, to the extent that the TV Movie's claim (in 1996) that he had two parents seemed mildly shocking. The *New Adventures* novels made sure that the Doctor was freed from all of the squelchy stuff by invoking the Gallifreyan 'Looms' and stating that Time Lords are born grown-up. The BBC Wales version reopens discussion of the Doctor's childhood and marital status from this point on (see **Who Was That Terrible Woman?** under X4.17, "The End of Time Part One", **Does He, You Know... Dance?** under X3.4, "Daleks in Manhattan", **Gay Agenda? What Gay Agenda?** with this story and - most of all - X3.13, "Last of the Time Lords" and "The End of Time Part One".)]

The Doctor is mildly vexed about milk ('Of all the species in all the universe, it has to come out of a cow'). [Has he never been to Greece? Or had Soya Milk? His gripe suggests that he has another issue with cows - odd for a man in a leather jacket.] He knows his Louis Jordan, almost [see above] and paraphrases Wellington's comments about his troops ['Dunno what you do to Hitler...'].

• *Inventory: Sonic Screwdriver.* In such a heavily *Trek*-inflected script, it is perhaps no surprise that the sonic screwdriver can be used as a Medical Tricorder [see also stories such as X6.7, "A Good Man Goes to War"]. Nevertheless, the Doctor pointedly doesn't use the screwdriver to scan for alien technology. More conventionally, it can open padlocks, although the one in question snaps open loudly and smoulders a bit.

• *Inventory: Other.* This time around, the psychic paper claims that the Doctor is 'Dr John Smith, Ministry of Asteroids'. Jack's got psychic paper too [so it must be technology either available from the fifty-first century on, or made available to Time Agents, or something Jack stole from another era].

The Doctor is carrying a small pad and a pencil, with which he rapidly sketches the mystery object he's looking for. He also has opera-glasses which appear to be brass and Victorian but, as seen from a POV shot, have electronic calibration and some kind of infra-red facility. [These seem to be the same ones the eleventh Doctor routinely uses in Series Five.] Curiously, when sitting at table with the children, he glances at his wristwatch and says 'I make it 1941'. [See also X1.7, "The Long Game". If this is something he can do with a similarly retrofitted device to the opera-glasses or the pen-torch that became the original sonic screwdriver (see 5.6, "Fury from the Deep" and the various uses of that same prop as a torch throughout the Hartnell era), then why he didn't do it earlier is a puzzle. Series Five suggests that this is indeed a feature of his wristwatch. (The last two years of the original *Who* had the seventh Doctor use his pocket-watch for many of the things the sonic screwdriver now does - pocket-watches now have other uses, as in X3.8, "Human Nature" et seq.)]

The TARDIS When the Chula ship crosses time-tracks and the Doctor gives chase in the TARDIS, the Console explodes. [A clue to this otherwise puzzling event is in that curious turn of phrase, 'jumping time-tracks', especially in light of the only other use of this term in 2.7, "The Space Museum". In that story, a malfunction on the Console - a stuck spring, would you believe - led to ghost-like events as the TARDIS crew wandered around a place they would soon visit once the Ship "really" arrived, and seeing a potential future with themselves incarcerated as museum exhibits. Similar incidents occur during the third Doctor's attempts to repair the Console, notably at the start of 9.1, "Day of the Daleks"; 7.3, "The Ambassadors of Death"; and 7.4, "Inferno".] The Doctor is able to slave the Console to the errant vessel's flight computer, and thus knows that it is heading for London - even though he has no idea what year he's in when he arrives. The telephone in the door is a 1920s model, even though the Police Box is post-war.

The TARDIS' materialisation [as has now become the norm] isn't accompanied by gusts of wind. Presuming that Rose isn't just joking around with the Doctor, the Ship does, from time to time, run out of milk. [If so, they presumably don't have any kind of lacto-synthesizer on board, but purchase dairy products as we all do (the use of

The Empty Child — X1.9

What's So Great About the 51st Century?

continued from Page 143...

Nonetheless, it would appear that the Luna University ("Let's Kill Hitler") is worthy of River Song. Maybe this is part of Earth (and thus a sufficient backwater for her to study less diligently than anywhere else would stipulate), but not so closely tied to that world as to be beyond the pale as and when she needs to use her doctorate to pull rank.

One anomaly remains. On Earth and the surrounding solar system, and despite growing competition for limited resources - especially land, once the glaciers start encroaching - nobody seems to care about money. All food and life-support facilities come free of charge, and a machine for dialling up any chemical combination comes as standard in Britannicus. You would expect that ration-tokens of some kind, either credit-units (coins and notes) or electronic debit, would ensure that everyone earns what they consume - why else would the scavengers and spaceniks be so despised? But even as American-seeming an institution as the Bi-Al Foundation is a not-for-profit, NHS-style free service. Volunteers and conscripts staff Britannicus. Money is never mentioned, and is so conceptually remote that viewers never ask about it.

Yet out in the unlimited galaxies, with amazing nanotechnology and treeborgs, people still need to take packed lunches when exploring abandoned city/planet libraries. Classical supply-and-demand economics persists even with infinite supply and various grubby deals are made by con men, traders and megacorporations. Perhaps because the writers of the BBC Wales series all want to be Robert Holmes when they grow up (see Volumes 2-6), the assumption that capitalism will persist even when everyone has almost everything they want (and absolutely everything they need) is unquestioned, even when something as influential as *Star Trek* shot that one down in flames about 40 years ago.

- **Space**. So humanity had, by Jack's time, spread "across half the galaxy" (X1.10, "The Doctor Dances"), and yet in the forty-second century, there were humans in at least *three* galaxies. Surely some mistake. Well, not necessarily. In "The Girl in the Fireplace", there are ships that have reached the Dagmar Cluster (this is said to be "two and a half galaxies" away, so maybe it's a Magellanic Cloud). Just because humans have visited places, it doesn't automatically follow that they dominate there. A galaxy is a big place and there are lots of potential worlds that simply aren't suitable for us - either because they are too big, too hot, too cold or already occupied. Even today, people have been to the South Pole, but we haven't exactly "spread" across Antarctica.

This spreading, we're told, has been partially achieved by interbreeding. The assumption seems to have been: if you can't beat them, conjoin with them. This apparently began with Adelaide Stone's great-granddaughter (X4.16, "The Waters of Mars"), and by the fifty-first century is seemingly the standard human response to anything. Yet as late as 5000 in "The Invisible Enemy", there is a hospital in the Asteroid Belt dedicated to keeping humans free from disease. What is a disease but a non-human form of DNA making itself part of a human? What Professor Marius and his team see as "infection" might be seen as a romance on the molecular level. So where humans draw the line is, apparently, consent. We'll come back to this.

And yet, the on-screen evidence for any large-scale miscegenation has been scant. You get the odd blue humanoid, but you get lots of humanoid species with no obvious genetic connection with Earth's bipedal mammals, even after the BBC Wales embargo on any non-Earth humans. (See **Is Kylie from Planet Zog?** under X4.0, "Voyage of the Damned".) What we have are lots and lots of planets colonised by humans, either for habitation or to turn into giant libraries ("Silence in the Library") or what have you. Jack can refer to his home planet as a "tiny little place" (X3.13, "Last of the Time Lords").

Here we have to pay attention to the most obvious thing about Jack: he's got a funny accent. So has his ex-partner, Captain John Hart (see below)[27]. Jack's brother Gray, in fact, has an accent that defies all attempts at rationalisation (*Torchwood*: "Exit Wounds"). Other than one Data-Node in the Library ("Silence in the Library"), nobody else in this century seems to sound American. The whole galaxy, and others nearby, seem to have been colonised by Britain. (This is, of course, entirely

continued on Page 147...

145

The Supporting Cast

• *Rose*. She unwittingly gives details of her relationship status (she's still sort-of dating Mickey, but considers herself '*very* available') when handed Jack's psychic paper, and yet divulges nothing at all about time-travel with a man she trusts with her life on almost an hourly basis. Indeed, her treatment of the Doctor throughout this episode is quite odd, almost resentful. She berates him for not using flashy technology when investigating the crashed object and thinks he's an amateur, insufficiently 'Spock'. [Like she's met so many alien time-travellers before him!] Jack is (in her words) 'finally, a professional', and she is charmed by his spectacular rescue of her, his markedly *Star Trek*-like ship and his [possibly drugged] Champagne. She's had some kind of dance lessons before as, even when pretty much out of it, she can slow-dance to Glenn Miller on top of an invisible spaceship moored next to the Palace of Westminster. She fails to listen when Jack's explaining the plot, and says a lot of silly things people only ever say in sitcoms by Steven Moffat ('You're not even in focus', she says perfectly clearly before fainting). In this light, her lack of complaint when a strange man binds her wrists is downright alarming, as is her lack of curiosity about nanogenes.

The reason she needed rescuing from a barrage-balloon floating westward over London during a bombing-raid? She saw a child in what looked like a dangerous situation and rushed to his aid without consulting (or even telling) the Doctor. [The Doctor would hardly have complained - he does that sort of thing himself (X5.2, "The Beast Below" is a good example by the same author). It's presented as if she's learned nothing in her TARDIS travels, although in fact this is the first time she has ever wandered off (until now, this year has entailed the Doctor leaving her behind or - as in X1.7, "The Long Game" and X1.8, "Father's Day" - virtually ordering her to go and explore.)]

• *Jack Harkness*. Whoever this person really is, he has adopted the identity of Captain Jack Harkness, 133 Squadron, and is not from the twentieth century. [He also hasn't spent much time in the latter part of it, as he doesn't know who 'Spock' is.] He has researched the period in which he is operating reasonably well, and has managed to persuade senior Army officials of his bona fides. He knows the precise time of the explosion at Limehouse Green station. It seems not to surprise him that another time-traveller would be suspended from a drifting barrage-balloon, and he is appreciative of male and female bottoms (or so he says). He seems very certain of his ability to charm any Time Agent he encounters. [This further complicates the idea that all of these people would be from his own century - if his biochemical "tricks" are commonplace and everyone from his time is constantly flirtatious, this would not really work and he would have to make a more substantial pitch. Perhaps he overdoes it with Rose simply because he doesn't realise that she lacks the experience a real Time Agent would of coping with sixth-millennium sluts like him.] Rose somehow deduces that he is from the fifty-first century and a former Time Agent. He is proud of his ability to blend in [despite all the obvious flaws we can see in his disguise] and compares himself favourably to the Doctor and Rose in that regard.

His con job relies upon Time Agents to make a bid for the Chula technology. [Why anyone with time-travel facilities would not be able to obtain it for themselves is a mystery, so perhaps he thinks they want it in order to remove it from history.] He was able to track the TARDIS well enough to see its exterior in the Vortex. His con is one of which he was immensely proud, and its failure to attract 'professionals' (with big bucks) annoys him. [In the next episode, Jack says he isn't here motivated by the money, but because he wants a bit of revenge against the Time Agency for removing two years of his memories. Exactly how damaging this con would be to the Agency's finances is, of course, another question - see **What's So Great About the 51st Century?**.]

Jack's leather wrist-strap [later identified as a Vortex Manipulator] can project computer-generated holograms, detect alien technology and scan patients for medical anomalies. He also carries a small silver lenticular device, rather like a car-key fob, that operates the ship's stereo, illuminates national monuments and deactivates the cloaking device on the stolen spaceship [although none of the ground-installations open fire on this obviously non-British flying object hovering over Parliament in an air-raid - exactly how effective is the ship's cloaking device?]. He tries never to do

What's So Great About the 51st Century?

continued from Page 145...

logical. Torchwood collared all the alien goodies after the persistent attempts by nefarious off-worlders to invade these islands *and no other part of Earth* throughout the 1970s and again in the early twenty-first century. The existence of a time-rift in Cardiff might be partly to do with this, but at least five assaults on London were inspired by the Doctor being there.) Jack's accent is neither part of his disguise as a member of 133 Squadron (which is daft anyway, as this story's notes prove) nor a translation convention. River Song and the various other people from this time we meet in her adventures are galactic-normal, and Jack is the anomaly. Evidently, therefore, some planets were colonised by non-British humans. If, as we hear, all other nations fled Earth long before the British ("The Beast Below"), then something may have befallen any spaceships not powered by a tortured space-whale.

• **Time.** In the *Torchwood* episode "Kiss Kiss Bang Bang", Jack's ex-partner, using the name "Captain John Hart" (see 9.3, "The Sea Devils" for why this is amusing), hints that he and Jack were both recruited in their original time - the late fifty-first century, to judge by Hart's comment that Jack was "Rear of the Year 5094" - and that the Time Agents are now ("now"?) almost extinct. Jack himself talks about being recruiting-poster material ("Last of the Time Lords"). But, does this mean that the Time Agency was based in Jack's time? Not necessarily.

The comments about the space-time engines of the vessels of this era are intriguing. In "The Girl in the Fireplace", the spaceship *Madame de Pompadour* has a drive that can "punch a hole" in space-time. Note, however, that organic crew-members don't use this to escape being converted into spares. Clockwork robots can skip through the various tableaux of Reinette's life, as can the Doctor, but Rose and Mickey are under strict orders to remain on the ship. Controlled time-journeys are still beyond the ship's capacities and Reinette is only able to traverse into the future and back with the Doctor's aid. If this is the same sort of time-travel that wrought so much harm to Greel, then nothing has changed. However, with events like this increasingly possible, it would make sense for any future Time Agency to make its presence felt, letting everyone in the fifty-first century know that their past and the fabric of space-time is being looked after. We know of at least one other vessel of approximately this period that got lost in the past (11.5, "Planet of the Spiders", from 5433 or thereabouts).

So, the Time Agents visit this period often enough to be known about, but use a technology rather more advanced than anything "local". Even if a Vortex Manipulator can be wrested from the body of an Agent[28], nobody in this period knows how to safely dismantle it to see how it works or even operate it without instruction (River Song, by contrast, already knows how to fly a TARDIS). Jack knows an awful lot more about temporal matters than people of this era seem to ordinarily - he can identify at a glance that the TARDIS has been turned into a Paradox Machine; he is aware of the Daleks' abrupt removal from history; he can figure out technology from the year 200,100; and he can do clever things with the Cardiff time-rift. If the fifty-first century is the earliest date from which the Agency can openly recruit, and this recruitment even extends to backwaters like the Boeshane Peninsula where Jack lived, news of their existence must have travelled far and fast.

However, that isn't the only possible interpretation of Jack's comments about his background. Yes, he was poster-boy (assuming he isn't just winding the Doctor and Martha up about his being the Face of Boe; see "Last of the Time Lords"); and yes, he and a friend volunteered to fight "the worst creatures imaginable" some time after his brother Gray was abducted from Boeshane (*Torchwood*: "Adam"). Yes, Jack, or whatever he was originally called, was recruited into the Time Agency after he was captured and his friend was killed. So he was a poster-boy *and* recruited to the Agency; but he wasn't necessarily a poster-boy *for* the Agency. An analogy might be this: just because so many Soviet spies went to Cambridge University, it doesn't follow that the KGB is based in East Anglia. For all we know, likely candidates from earlier periods might be offered work with the Agency if their lives have been messed up by time travel. This might be what happened to Ace (see 26.4, "Survival").

One of the most interesting things about "The

continued on Page 149...

X1.9 The Empty Child

business with a clear head and would rather be thought of as a 'criminal' or 'con-man' than merely a "rogue agent". He has psychic paper, and can control what appears on it better than Rose can.

The Non-Humans
• *Chula*. They're a race of warriors. [The fact that Jack claims to have the 'last (Chula) warship in existence' might suggest that they've been wiped out. Certainly, their surviving ambulance/battleship must fetch a high enough price on the open market for Jack to risk all the potential consequences that go with pulling a con job on the Time Agency.] Their Scout ships, one of which Jack has commandeered for his own use, have cloaking devices, tractor beams, talking computers (female in this case) and teleports [a bit like, um, *Star Trek*]. But, the ship is cramped, cluttered with wiring and graphic displays and with a seat culled from a WWII bomber [a bit like, um, the *Millennium Falcon*]. Apart from the pilot's seat, the only concession to human occupancy is an inset bed. [These seem to be standard fixtures, so we can conjecture that the Chula are humanoid, but a bit shorter than Jack.] This vessel has onboard nanogenes for first aid; these only operate when the hull is secured. The Doctor is unaware of this race, as the TARDIS scanner fails to identify the species, even when the vessel's [basic] flight computer is slaved to the Ship's.

History
• *Dating*. Gordon Bennett! Well, it's during the Blitz, so between September 1940 and May 1941. It's a full moon [but that might not be helpful - see the essay with X2.0, "The Christmas Invasion" for why not, but they tended to be towards the middle of the month during this period]. Mr Lloyd's garden has roses in full bloom and some freshly pulled-up carrots. Jack and his bait arrived a month earlier, give or take a few days, although it is far from clear that this is his first visit to that time. [If we assume that the name 'Captain Jack Harkness' was taken from the dead US airman we meet in the *Torchwood* episode called, um, "Captain Jack Harkness" (1.12), who died on 21st January, 1941, then the earliest we can date this story is the beginning of March. So, let's go with 13th March, 1941; a bit early for roses and carrots but in keeping with everybody's breath misting, the full moon and the night lasting so long. Of course, for someone to have been in 133 Squadron during the Blitz is ludicrous - see **Things That Don't Make Sense** next episode - but this has now been established in two different hit BBC Wales series, so we're into damage-limitation here.]

The Chula warship fell next to Limehouse Green station [which, of course, doesn't really exist] and near Albion Hospital. History records that the same site was destroyed in a bombing raid at around 11.30pm.

On the Galactic stage, the universally-recognised way to denote danger is 'Mauve Alert'; red [to which human eyes respond better] is widely seen as being 'camp'. [Before you ask, yes, Holly mentioned a 'mauve alert' in the *Red Dwarf* episode "Dimension Jump", but he was conjecturing from it being too bad for blue but not a full red alert. Any crossover fiction you want to write will require a better basis than this.]

The Analysis

The Big Picture ("The Empty Child" and "The Doctor Dances") Not for the first or last time, the date of first transmission gives the big clue. May 2005 was the 60th anniversary of VE Day, and the news coverage of memorials and events to mark this were relentless. Similarly, this was thought to be a good time for dramas and documentaries on the subject of World War II (not that schedulers don't think that every day is a good time for these, but they kept some big ones for the occasion).

More to the point, every schoolchild in Britain - certainly those who had gone through the English Key Stage II - would have spent a term on this, knowing the conditions under which people lived through novels such as *Carrie's War* and *Goodnight, Mister Tom* (note that Nancy says "Goodnight, Mister" to the Doctor) and trips to the Imperial War Museum to try hunkering down in an Anderson Shelter. The schools packages for this age-group (8-11) is focussed on the domestic aspects of the War rather than the causes or details of specific battles - so gas-masks, black-outs and rationing would have been a subject that the ostensible target audience for *Doctor Who* would have been guaranteed to have known all about (unlike the writer, it seems, but lots more on that later).

Within popular culture, the Wartime conditions were a given for sitcoms, including the per-

The Empty Child — X1.9

What's So Great About the 51st Century?

continued from Page 147...

Girl in the Fireplace" is that the Doctor refuses to land the TARDIS anywhere in Reintte's life because it would destabilise established history. And yet, the machinery being used to send the clockwork robots back is obviously "traditional" time-corridor equipment as used by the Daleks and others for limited investigations and hiding in the past. Actively changing the past needs more than this (see **How Does Time Work...** under 9.1, "Day of the Daleks"). It has been established in the series that full-blown time travel, of the kind used by the Time Lords and "interval" Daleks, can unfix time within certain parameters (see **What Constitutes a "Fixed Point"?** under X4.2, "The Fires of Pompeii"). However, the removal of the Time Lords from the cosmic arena seems to have made this a little more complicated. After all, what else is a Time Agency for if not to do a job a bit like what the Time Lords did? The two must have been concurrent (sorry, but we have to persist in using temporally-inexact language for this situation) for such Agents to be at work when Greel was on the lam, and yet neither seems to have noticed that thousands of troops from the American Civil War, World War I, the Thirty Years' War and elsewhere have been vanishing to an alien world and getting their memories messed with (6.7, "The War Games"). It would make sense if the Agency existed solely to monitor human intervention in the past, perhaps as a "franchise" established by the Time Lords but exempt from whatever sealed off the Time War. Perhaps, paradoxically, it's an extension of Torchwood's activities on other worlds (X2.8, "The Impossible Planet") and a result of the Cardiff team's rift-monitoring.

• **Sex**. The population of Alfalva Metraxis reaches six billion in two centuries ("The Time of Angels"). All we see of this planet is a beach and some caves, so we have no way of knowing how much like current-model humans they all are. Everyone we've seen from this century - other than a brief scene on the Maldovarium in "The Pandorica Opens" - looks and acts human. Clients at the Library are requested to respect one another's species and hygiene-code, but they all seem to be human and wearing black T-shirts. So our only real guide to whether the Doctor's description of fifty-first century pansexuality is real is what Jack says. He appears to have seduced the previous owner of the Chula ship ("The Doctor Dances"), although we have no idea what they look like. What this means is that the Doctor's explanation actually makes no sense as a causal relationship - people from the fifty-first century are more self-confidently flirtatious with more varied potential partners, but this is in no way connected with their fecundity. Captain John lusts after poodles ("Kiss Kiss, Bang Bang"). River Song dated a Nestene duplicate (X5.13, "The Big Bang") and an android ("Silence in the Library"). Neither of them seems to have had any children. Jack hasn't fared much better, although he has a daughter (*Torchwood*: "Children of Earth") and - assuming he will become the Face of Boe - will give birth to baby Boemina in 200,000 AD (X1.7, "The Long Game"). In an odd way, their attitude is nothing new: conceiving (sorry) of oneself as merely a receptacle for the next generation's genes, in whichever combination they manifest themselves, is what royalty have always done. All that has changed, apparently, is that everyone is royalty now. (Yet, curiously, there is only evidence of Jack having just one child in all the 130 years he was stuck in Cardiff.)

There's certainly no suggestion that Leader Clent ("The Ice Warriors") is, shall we say, as broad-minded as Captain Jack (although Penley and Storr do act like a married couple). Similarly, everyone on the Bi-Al Foundation seems utterly professional (despite those tight PVC nurse's uniforms). It is, of course, possible that after finding ways to expand desire, the "antidote" is also available and an effective libido-suppressant is available to people in stressful jobs. This would, however, make Miss Garrett's actions toward Penley a little harder to fathom than hitherto. On the other hand, it makes a sort of sense for the church militant ("The Time of Angels") to function in its "expanded" capacity as the militia if its soldiers are immune to the various biochemical lures available to the rest of society.

And that's another odd thing: the three people who seem to have aids to their conquest are all time-travellers. Jack has souped-up pheromones (*Torchwood*: "Fragments"), whilst John and River

continued on Page 151...

X1.9 The Empty Child

ennially-repeated *Dad's Army* (see "The Curse of Fenric"), and the more recent *Goodnight, Sweetheart*. In the latter, a man finds a short cut from the 1990s to the Blitz and manages to keep two relationships going, aided by his ability to pass off Paul McCartney's songs as his own and find buyers for mint-condition Wartime memorabilia in the present-day. Later episodes play up the time-paradox potential in a way congenial for the average sitcom viewer, something Moffat's *Doctor Who* episodes have sought to emulate. (A more oblique connection is that the author of this had earlier written a goofy series called *Nightingales*, which had used the line "Ain't nobody here but us chickens" as a catch-phrase. The show appears only to have been seen by Cult TV enthusiasts, as it was put on in a late-night ghetto slot after reruns of *The Prisoner*. The line is, of course, a paraphrase of one of Louis Jordan's big hits of the late 1940s: "There Ain't Nobody Here but Us Chickens.")

Among the generation who lived through the 1939-45 War, gratitude and admiration for the American forces is tempered with the resentment at how they treated their hosts and the fact that they were, once again, late for a World War. The usual gripe among those men stuck in England not fighting (especially those whose girlfriends were more impressed by the Yanks because the doughboys were issued with desirable items and had eaten properly within living memory) was that they were "over-paid, over-sexed and over here". This has given local filmmakers endless scope for casting American leading men, usually in romances where they woo frightfully decent English gels. Ronald Reagan co-starred with Richard Todd (19.3, "Kinda") in *The Hasty Heart*, for instance.

Anglo-American rivalry usually manifests itself on screen as disputes over girls (witness all those 60s ITC adventure shows). In the 80s, when our film industry was fairly buoyant, this led to flicks like *Yanks*, *Memphis Belle* and the one that launched this mini-genre: Harrison Ford's first starring vehicle, *Hanover Street*. This was a weepie from 1979 wherein archetypal English Rose Lesley-Anne Down has to choose between dashing American airman and a worthy-but-dull husband, forcing said husband to volunteer for a dangerous mission to prove himself, as usually happens in these stories. Significantly, it was an early example of a film about the War made by people too young to have experienced it at firsthand. Whereas 50s War movies were mainly true-life tales of pluck and ingenuity and tended to downplay emotional complexity (not avoid it altogether, just put the focus elsewhere - see, for instance, *The Dambusters* or *Ice Cold in Alex*), and 60s films were revisionist and tended to have everyone die at the end (see, for example, *633 Squadron*, *Tora! Tora! Tora!* or *Operation Crossbow*), by the late 70s the war was the backdrop for three-hankie love-stories. *Hanover Street* starts with an annoying "cute" meeting between a GI with 70s hair and an English girl who apparently reads *Cosmopolitan*. This is irrelevant, as "The Empty Child" is so obviously a romance in the modern (then) idiom, using the backdrop of the War to justify cranking the drama up several notches beyond what you could get away with otherwise. Davies told the Tone Meeting that this episode and "The Doctor Dances" should have the key-word "Romantic". And it is films and books like this, where the general impression of World War II London is more important than the details, that he has in mind. (Although we could cite the first fantasy-romance film set then, Powell and Pressburger's *A Matter of Life and Death* - the US title was *Stairway to Heaven* - as a sort of precedent but for one detail which we'll come to shortly.)

However, if we're thinking of Captain Jack as a Harrison Ford avatar, two other obvious roles spring to mind. Jack's a scoundrel with a spaceship, the cockpit of which that looks a bit like a WWII bomber's. He has lapsed from pure study and is throwing himself into scams for "fortune and glory". It's possible to overstate this, especially when discussing how the character developed, but in these two episodes Dr Jones and Captain Solo are obvious touchstones. It's not as if Moffat's averse to pilfering from Indiana Jones films, especially when he has a season finale to write.

... but not nearly as much as 60s-style James T Kirk. All of Rose's "Spock" comments have an ulterior motive in this script, to play up the whole galactic lothario element. It's not difficult to find traces of *Trek* in the spaceship design and the off-the-shelf gadgetry. (Although most of the terminology - tractor beams, force-fields and so on - was itself culled from earlier sources: see **Is This Any Way to Run a Galactic Empire?** under 9.4, "The Mutants" for Asimov and the *Lensman* books.) More cogently, the invisible, winged spaceship - one that is borrowed from aliens and

What's So Great About the 51st Century?

continued from Page 149...

use mind-altering lipsticks ("Kiss Kiss, Bang Bang", "The Time of Angels"). So far as we're told, nobody else has access to these (although the authorities seem to know River's tricks). However, one piece of technology on offer to the expedition to the Library and, implicitly, to the Clergy-squaddies is a technologically-mediated afterlife. This might seem a little out of the overall theme of "sex", but the point is that the boundaries of selfhood, biological or cognitive are a little more fluid than in our culture. (See **Where Have All the Monsters Gone?** under X3.6, "The Lazarus Experiment".) This extends to literacy (the Doctor mentions holovids, direct-to-brain downloads and something called "fiction-mist"). This is the only on-screen confirmation of any new cultural tendency towards hybridity, and is clearly not in place in the forty-second century.

So the fifty-first century is more complex off-screen than what we actually see. This makes sense. The writers (Moffat in particular) have used it as a vague background for Jack, John and River that allows any wild one-liner they think might be amusing - even if those one-liners rely for their effect on slightly contradicting expectations. For budgetary reasons, this has to be pretty much all talk, but "Silence in the Library" relies on us thinking that Cal is a child from the present day. Thus, the only domestic scene we have from this century is an early twenty-first century childhood - with, rather damagingly for the story's premise, no books - and a subset of this is so convincing to Donna that she doesn't realise she has been "saved". In this way, the fifty-first century is like St Olaf's in *The Golden Girls*: only plausible if glimpsed briefly, and referred to often.

used for a time-travelling American to woo a local girl whilst on a mission - is flagrantly *Star Trek IV: The Voyage Home* with the serial numbers filed off. A cut line from the end of the first episode, just after Jack has met "Mr Spock", has the Doctor tell Rose "I prefer 'Doctor Who' to *Star Trek*". Don't forget, *Star Trek: The Next Generation* only came to UK screens a year after *Doctor Who* left, so this is the first time that all the new toys that this and the other spin-offs had introduced were available for *Who* writers to play with (although in the case of the Cybermen, it was recovering stolen property). However, nanotechnology was hardly obscure or fringe by this point: Prince Charles was making headline-grabbing (and ill-informed and downright loopy) speeches about the threat of this latest hubristic development; car manufacturers were even describing the paint-finishes of their vehicles as "smart paint" and calling this small-scale self-adjustment "nano-tech" (literal go-faster stripes, who'd've thought it?). The whole notion of Time Agents being humans from a fixed point a nice round number of years in our future is very *Trek*, with Captains Sisko, Janeway and Archer getting visits from thirtieth-century G-Men.

On the other hand, the script's initial description of Jack reminds us of something: he has "the jawline of Dan Dare, the smile of a bastard". And when you see a dashing dark-haired man in RAF uniform with a spaceship parked by Parliament, it is hard *not* to think of Colonel Dare (see **What Kind of Future Did We Expect?** under 2.3, "The Rescue"). Directly or subtly, the 1950s comic hero from *The Eagle* has influenced *Doctor Who* since Terry Nation, shall we say, "took a generous amount of inspiration" when writing 1.2, "The Daleks". (See that story's essay for several other sources.) We're going to see an awful lot more of this over the next few years (see, for instance, X2.0, "The Christmas Invasion"; X4.3, "Planet of the Ood"; and Evil Parallel London in X2.5, "Rise of the Cybermen"). Those who read the *New Adventures* tie-in books in the 90s have also suggested that Jack, at least in this configuration of him, is an amalgam of companion Chris Cwej and Bernice Summerfield's husband Jason Kane. (This is patently absurd - doing that would be like combining Bernice with Iris Wildthyme to produce a future archaeologist who can fly the TARDIS, drink a lot and act like the Doctor's ex-wife.)

However, all of the comparisons and probable sources we've mentioned so far have one drawback: they are all very primary-coloured. The myth of London in the Blitz, borne out to some extent by contemporary sources, was how drab everything was. There were practical reasons for this: paint manufacturing was downscaled so that the companies doing it, mainly major chemical firms, could devote their resources to medical and military materiel; camouflage and matte-finishes were *de rigeur* in time of air-raids; and the entire make-do-and-mend philosophy putting practicality over aesthetics. However, a lot of this is because of the combination of dim lighting, such colour film-stock as there was being requisitioned, and the posters and photos fading at different rates for different inks. Recent advances in digital recovery, and the colour films that were made at the time[26], tell a slightly more complicated story.

But the version we all "remember" is sepia-tinted. And it is true that a lot of the Austerity furniture and all of the bakelite domestic fittings were brown. Set against this is a desire by the director of these episodes to emulate both the pre-War Expressionist lighting - consciously deployed and configured for mood and effect - and the immediate post-War *film noir* look, using faster film stock and better portable lights to shoot on location at night to save on extras and remounts. Obvious comparison-points would be *The Third Man*, which used stark and downright theatrical lighting on its bomb-site locations in Vienna; *The Singing Detective*, which set pulp-thriller clichés and mood inside a writer's wartime childhood memories; and Powell and Pressberger's *The Small Back Room*, a heavily Expressionist-influenced film about an alcoholic bomb-disposal expert. Attempting both fidelity to the Blitz era and *chiaroscuro* lighting caused no end of technical problems and created anachronisms that every ten-year-old in Britain spotted (see **Things That Don't Make Sense**). In that regard, the running joke in the second episode about bananas is apt, because these were the emblematic unavailable item during the blockades and rationing.

We have to remember, however, Moffat's previous form as a writer of not-quite *Doctor Who* and of various half-hour farces in his sitcom career. He grew up with *Doctor Who* as something that scares children and - however much he disowns his comments - had been very dismissive of the technical aspects and the judgement-calls of the programme's makers. He developed a very particular "take" on what *Doctor Who* should and shouldn't do or be, and it is hard not to see this story as a rebuke to previous administrations. On the one hand, he is clearly influenced by the Philip Hinchcliffe style of production (Seasons Twelve to Fourteen, 1975-77) and references 14.6, "Talons of Weng Chiang" overtly in the idea of Time Agents from the fifty-first century (although we think he got this wrong - see the accompanying essay). Equally obviously, director David Maloney had a tendency to work gas-masks into everything he could (see **Who are the Auteur Directors?** under 18.5, "Warriors' Gate"). On the other, his conception of the Doctor's relationship with female companions was rather singular. We will return to this in the essay with the next episode.

One of the techniques of farce most useful in writing *Doctor Who* is the disguising of info-dumps as character-points or apparently stand-alone gags. Both formats need the writer to keep a close eye on details, and set up situations without it *looking* like a set-up. That a sudden and unexpected development is the logical result of a situation or event elsewhere in the plot ought to be a given; whether that "elsewhere" is before or after in the narrative is a decision only people playing with time-paradoxes have to worry about. It is, however, the fruit of the same tree that orthodox farce-plot sitcoms come from. (We might at this point mention an earlier meticulous plotter of outlandish farces, Joe Orton: there are a few similarities of subject-matter, but it is really the idiosyncratic use of language that makes it seem that Moffat has learned from Orton. Although many of the Doctor's lines have an Ortonesque formality at odds with the subject matter and the usual ninth Doctor style, Dr Constantine's line to Mrs Harcourt *re* her regrown leg is the most obvious: "There is a war on: is it possible you may have miscounted?". Note that Richard Wilson - playing Constantine - had just starred in a revival of Orton's *What the Butler Saw*, playing a doctor with a very odd set of priorities. Of course, both writers were looking back towards Oscar Wilde, but Orton was a more diligent plotter and thus a better match for early Moffat.)

In passing, it's worth noting that "Captain Jack Harkness" is another of those recycled names. On the one hand, we have Captain Jack Harkaway, hero of an adventure serial in the late nineteenth century and - in the *Doctor Who* universe - the work of a hack writer who became Master of the Land of Fiction (see 6.2, "The Mind Robber" and its associated essay). However, Davies' children's serial *Dark Season* had a creepy old woman called Esme Harkness who filled many of the same plot functions that Martha Tyler had served in 15.3, "Image of the Fendahl". (See also X1.3, "The Unquiet Dead" and most of Series Five.) And Ma Tyler's grandson was called Jack.

[For **Things That Don't Make Sense**, **Critique**, **The Facts** and **Production**, see next episode.]

X1.10: "The Doctor Dances"

(28th May, 2005)

Which One is This? "Everybody lives!" The Doctor makes the best of Blitz-era London and gains another new TARDIS crewmember.

Firsts and Lasts Despite what the tie-in books had said, this was the first time we saw that the Console of the TARDIS has a built-in music system (rather than the Dansette used in the TV Movie). This is also the first time since the Hartnell era that the Ship has been able to materialise in some kind of "stealth" mode without the traditional wheezing groaning sound (see X5.4, "The Time of Angels" for a sidelight on this, and 2.6, "The Crusade" for the last known previous silent materialisation).

After disarming a man pointing a banana at him, the Doctor proposes eating the banana. We've had *Monty Python* references in the books, but this is the first obvious and deliberate one on screen. Moffat obviously liked that joke, because it came back in the "Banana of Reasonable Comfort" scene in X6.8, "Let's Kill Hitler". Talking of River Song, this episode introduces the Squareness Gun (see X4.8, "Silence in the Library", but the term is here coined by Rose). And we get a definite idea of how many additional features the new sonic screwdriver has with the first numbered setting (unsurprisingly, it's a big number).

Watch Out For...
• And so after a textbook cliffhanger, we get a complicated fusion of the modern "Previously On..." montage and a standard old-fashioned cliffhanger-reprise from 1963-89, which takes us up to the last shot of the previous episode and then turns the situation on its head in one line ("Go to your room!"). The Doctor applies lateral thinking to a situation that, if we'd thought of it, we could have resolved the same way. And then, just to show Moffat's mastery of this new format, he ends the scene with a punch-line ("I'm really glad that worked - those would have been terrible last words.") that takes us into the titles *still* wanting to know what happens next.

• Anyone who's encountered Steven Moffat for more than the half-life of Beryllium 11 (look it up) will realise that he is just about the most relentlessly heterosexual man in the Western hemisphere. And yet... until now, this new series has accepted relationships and lust to be entirely boy-meets-girl, but now in the space of this one episode, we get two scenes where the twist is that an apparently straight man is gay. In the first, although there is a less innocent, merely criminal explanation on offer if you squint at the precise form of words, Nancy is unflappably callous in threatening Mr Lloyd. In the second, it's worth noting that Rose is mildly freaked, but the Doctor hasn't been this happy since Adam failed to impress her.

• As you may have heard (and if not, **Production** will give you the rest), the sequence with the kids and the typewriter made to type "are you my mummy?" by the Empty Child is a late addition to fill two minutes, using the only available cast-members and vintage props they had a fortnight after the rest of the episode had been recorded and roughly edited. Whilst the precise workings of how the Om-Com system operates a keyboard by remote are unclear (see **Things That Don't Make Sense**), what is worth noting here is that the whole "but if Ernie's there, who's typing?" pay-off is almost identical to the "but if the tape's run out, who's talking?" scene ten minutes earlier. But because everyone involved does what they do so well, hardly anyone spots this - and those that do rarely care.

• As a potential plot for later writers to explore, Moffat threw in the fascinating detail that Jack, whoever he really is, has two years of his memory missing through the actions of the Time Agency. Jack has been in eight more episodes of *Doctor Who* and (to date) 41 episodes of *Torchwood* (plus several tie-in books and seven radio episodes) and nobody has bothered with this, one of the most intriguing aspects of the character.

The Continuity

The Doctor He has a tendency to insult entire species when stressed. Rose claims that when he cuts himself shaving, he launches into half-hour tirades. [She says this as though it's a regular occurrence. The tirades may be, but he surely

X1.10 The Doctor Dances

can't cut himself shaving too often, unless he has some kind of regenerative property analogous to an alum stick. That the Doctor needs to shave is - contrary to the books - a given. We saw a shaving mirror fitted as standard in the old Console Room in 14.1, "The Masque of Mandragora" and have seen facial-hair experiments and fluctuations over the course of a few episodes. See 6.5, "The Seeds of Death" for an obvious example and Season Twenty for many peculiar shifts over the course of what, in script terms, is a few days. And, in the new series, see X6.13, "The Wedding of River Song". Why Rose is *present* when he's shaving is, of course, another matter for conjecture.]

The Doctor is a bit put out that nobody thinks he can or would 'dance'. [Eventually, everyone involved stops trying to be subtle and admits that 'dance' is a euphemism, but along the way, he seems genuinely hurt that Rose doesn't appear to think of him as male. This, despite some very overt signs that he finds Jack's swagger at best distasteful and possibly a bit threatening.] There is a lot of competition between the Doctor and Jack over the size of various sonic devices, and Rose suspects that the Doctor has 'Captain envy'. [So the Doctor is male enough for it to be joked about, but not - as we saw last episode - for Rose to even subconsciously mention him when Jack's psychic paper asks her about Mickey.]

The Doctor later gets more than a little conceited when trumping Jack with 'moves' that only a Time Lord could do [see **Things That Don't Make Sense**] and then attempts to slow-dance with Rose - awkwardly at first, despite several centuries' experience (he claims), then suddenly it clicks and this incarnation is as twinkle-toed as his fourth. ["The Masque of Mandragora" again. You can bet we'll return to this (see, just for example, **Does He, You Know... Dance?** under X3.4, "Daleks in Manhattan").]

When the Chula nanogenes have realigned their DNA template for 'human' by comparing Nancy and what they've made from her son Jamie, the Doctor is able to allow them to touch him, then rewrite their programming [somehow] and shoot them off to cure all the zombified patients and staff, fixing even amputated legs in a matter of seconds. [He calls this 'emailing the software patch', but it's clearly more than that. Given that we later see a markedly similar effect associated with regenerations, it is possible that Time Lords have inbuilt nanogenes, but in that case the effect is scripted as being Artron Energy that just happens to *look* like nanogenes. See also X4.6, "The Doctor's Daughter".]

In a curious development, he asks someone to 'give me a day like this [in which everyone lives]'. [This comes after he has been talking to the 'clever little nanogenes', but it seems almost like a prayer to an unseen higher power - unless he's just a big fan of Mancunian rock band Elbow.]

His enthusiasms include bananas, pop music and the Welfare State.

• *Ethics.* The Doctor's treatment of Jack is, to say the least, curious. He swaps Jack's sonic disruptor/cannon/squareness gun for a banana to prevent Jack shooting civilians. Later, using 'psychology', he effectively bullies Jack into making a suicidal decision to take the bomb away, only to "reward" him with a show-offy rescue. He also forces Nancy to make what, for the time, would have been a shameful confession in order to save the entire human race [so presumably World War II isn't a Fixed Point].

• *Background.* He reiterates [see the notes on **The Doctor** last episode] that he's 'nine hundred years old'. Somehow, he knows that Rose got a red bicycle for Christmas when she was 12. [He states this in reply to her accusation that he's acting like he was Father Christmas. Given that the same writer introduced the eleventh Doctor by having him crash in the garden of a girl who had just prayed to Santa Claus, we can't entirely rule out this possibility, try as we might. This would, of course, cause problems for anyone who thinks that Bill Mevin's 1960s *TV Comic* strips are canonical.]

He has been to the Weapon factories of Villengard, once, apparently destroying it. He claims that it is 'now' a banana-grove. [What 'now' means when he's talking to a fifty-first century fugitive ex-Time Agent is anyone's guess, but Jack didn't know this, so the Doctor probably means after his rival's original time.]

• *Inventory: Sonic Screwdriver.* The sonic screwdriver setting No. 2,428-D mends severed barbed wire. [Not just welding it back together, oh, no; we see it making metal "heal" and grow back over gaps of up to an inch. Hitherto, the only scripted label for a setting was 'theta-omega' in 13.4, "The Android Invasion".] Despite this alarming development, the Doctor claims that the screwdriver's primary use is putting up cabinets. It takes a long time for the screwdriver to set up resonance pat-

Gay Agenda? What Gay Agenda?

To state the blindingly obvious, there really is an awful lot of nonsense on the Internet. Anything that moves gets people appending their ill-informed comments and writing badly-spelled addenda, often using the word "methinks" (a sure sign of garbled thinking) and making knee-jerk comments regardless of relevance to the initial topic. Journalists, increasingly pushed for time and under-resourced, will often use this in lieu of research, and soon one person's slightly odd observation takes on the status of fact.

So it was that, in the late 1990s, one self-publicist preacher derided *Teletubbies* for corrupting young minds - not for the usual reasons of baby-talk or letting Toyah Willcox use a sentence with a lot of sibilants in, despite her much-parodied lisp, but because - get this - apparently it was "obvious" that Tinky Winky was gay. The alleged evidence for this was that he carried a handbag (um, they don't have pockets), he kissed Po (Po is a girl, don't you know *anything*?) and he is purple. Apparently purple is "code" for gay (nobody told Prince, or all those Roman emperors). This was proof, this loon claimed, that the BBC were following some kind of "gay agenda". Those words started attaching themselves to anything not under the control of Midwestern TV evangelists.[31]

News that *Doctor Who* was returning under the aegis of *Queer as Folk* creator Russell T Davies was, therefore, the starting-point for a flurry of speculation, innuendo and terrible jokes. Many of the latter were the work of Nev Fountain, fanboy and gag-writer for *Dead Ringers*, a radio series based on the cast's ability to do about three impressions each. The idea of Graham Norton (see X1.1, "Rose") being cast as the Doctor and Daleks running a beauty-salon ("Ex-fo-li-ate") was moderately amusing the first time, but these gags did the rounds for about three years afterwards in the run-up to the new series.

Among more informed fans, the announcement reminded people of Davies' one *New Adventures* novel, *Damaged Goods*. In amongst the many odd ideas (see X1.11, "Boom Town" for more on this) is a subplot about the Doctor's companion Chris Cwej and a gay present-day lad from a Manchester housing estate (yes, just like Nathan from *Queer*, but not as conniving). The Doctor seems to approve and - in an appendix afterwards involving Harry Sullivan from Season Twelve - something entered David's blood that potentially cures AIDS.

But that was the *New Adventures* for you: Bernice Summerfield was at the very least bi-curious and non-species-specific, as was her errant husband Jason Kane (of whom more later). Meanwhile, former TV companions Steven Taylor and Captain Mike Yates were retroactively shown to be more, um, versatile than there had been any on-screen evidence to suppose, but this varied with individual authors. These books formed the basis for online flame-wars but, by the standards of the present feverish and apparently universal interest in *Doctor Who*, they are a tiny fringe activity. As such, they are a bellwether of how hardcore fandom and the new influx differed in their reaction to what was shown in 2005.

Something to bear in mind in all of this: the majority of the British public were unaware of everything we've just mentioned. For them, *Doctor Who* was a fond childhood memory - or an embarrassing one - and belonged in a different time when things were, apparently, a lot simpler. It was straightforward adventures, with no angst, no messy emotions and utterly chaste characters. Any hint of twenty-first century life creeping into this idyll would upset some of the more rigidly minded viewers, just as the 1980s stories sought to resist any hint that Britain wasn't exactly as it had been shown to be in *The Avengers*. (Yes, the last two years were a bit different, but hardly anyone was watching by then. See Volume 6.)

On the bulletin-board of the sad extreme right-wing British National Party, the advent of Mickey and the placing of the episodes before a series hosted by Graham Norton caused splutterings of fury. But Davies had pitched the revival of the series in terms that made it clear he was not interested in nostalgia. He was thinking right from the start that this was a series for teenage girls, and what was now suitable for them was very different from what a series starting in 1963 would have allowed if it had run uninterrupted. The series' founders - especially David Whitaker, the original story editor - had worked hard to remove any hint of sexuality from the format. Susan was made the Doctor's granddaughter (which only raised *more* questions about the Doctor's past loves) and the

continued on Page 157...

X1.10 The Doctor Dances

terns in concrete [presuming this is even possible].

• *Inventory: Other.* He's packing a banana from the groves of Villengard, on the off-chance that he's going to run into someone with a fifty-first century sonic weapon and feel the need to make a point.

The TARDIS It can not only play Glenn Miller records with a flip of a switch on the Console (on the panel opposite the door), but the internal lighting - in the roundels, under the floor and on the Console - pulsate in time to it [that green light is, mercifully, off]. Moreover, the Doctor is able to steer his Ship into a moving spaceship and make it materialise silently. Just to be even more flash, the Doctor somehow persuades the exterior door to open whilst he is ten feet away, dancing with Rose on the rostrum. [In every other story using this TARDIS set, the doors have to be opened manually from inside - although from X4.9, "Forest of the Dead" onwards it is hinted that he has figured out how to open the door from outside with either a snap of his fingers or a central-locking feature on the key - see X4.18, "The End of Time Part One".]

The Supporting Cast

• *Rose.* Compared with the Doctor's previous companions, she's 'setting new records for jeopardy-friendly'. [A lot of her behaviour in this episode could easily be explained as the side-effects of the upgraded pheromones Jack's people have (as explained in *Torchwood*[29]). After the let-down of Adam, finding that Jack isn't so much interested in her specifically so much as in *anything with a pulse* seems to affect her relationship with the Doctor for the remainder of his ninth life. In this light, her sudden interest in his lovelife, however inappropriate it might be in a life-threatening situation, makes a lot more sense. Note that her next move is to call Mickey on a flimsy pretext and try to get him alone in a hotel room in Cardiff (X1.11, "Boom Town").]

Once the subject has been raised, her frustration with the Doctor's rather sensible set of priorities is obvious - but, once they are alone and out of danger, she teases him for being full of himself and then immediately brings up the subject of Jack. When we next see them, the Doctor and Rose are attempting to dance - a verb she's taken to using as a sexual euphemism. [Indeed, for a lot of this episode, she is an inbuilt critique of previous versions of the series, voicing what appear to be authorial comments about earlier Doctors and production teams: 'doesn't the Universe implode or something if you dance?']

Having her life saved is 'bloke-wise... up there with flossing'.

• *Jack Harkness.* [We'll accept this as his name from now on, because even the computer aboard a stolen Chula spaceship calls him 'Captain Jack Harkness'.]

It emerges that he has had two years'-worth of his memories removed. He blames the Time Agency for this, and has embarked upon his criminal career as a form of revenge. [What he did to warrant this is, so far, unexplained.] Like most people in the fifty-first century [or so the Doctor says - see **What's So Great About the 51st Century?** under the previous episode], this charming man is omnisexual, and will happily miscegenate with any life-form going. This seems to include the Chula ship's real owner [described in passing as 'gorgeous', even though we never see any of her species].

Jack feels he has to work to earn the Doctor's trust [perhaps because his souped-up pheromones don't work on Time Lords]. His misguided scam has caused a threat to humanity three thousand years in his past. [We will revisit this, but see for now **Can You Rewrite History, Even One Line?** under 1.6, "The Aztecs", and **How Does Time Work...** under 9.1, "Day of the Daleks".] He is therefore keen to do whatever it takes to repair the situation and meekly accepts the Doctor's barrage of criticism.

He's been sentenced to death often enough to calmly reminisce about 'last time' - an incident wherein, with the aid of four hypervodkas, he wound up in bed with both his executioners ('nice couple', Jack says).

His gun can convert into a sonic cannon, a sonic disruptor or a 'squareness' gun; in this final mode, it has a digital rewind so that it can seamlessly replace any square of brickwork, door or metal it has erased. [This seems remarkably like the Continuous Event Transmitter from 17.4, "Nightmare of Eden".] These features use up the batteries quickly. [Intriguingly, the gun makes a very Dalek-like noise: Jack has heard all about the Daleks, as we later discover, and River Song, who allegedly "inherits" Jack's weapon, may possibly have met them in a Doctorless encounter - see

The Doctor Dances X1.10

Gay Agenda? What Gay Agenda?

continued from Page 155...

two schoolteachers remained chummy, like work-colleagues, in almost every situation they were in. This is not to say that Barbara was "outside" sex, as just about every middle-aged man they encountered tried it on with her, but it was never her doing. Similarly, Bennett (2.3, "The Rescue") had to be "defused" to make his keeping Vicki alive seem somehow above board, or as much so as killing everyone else and pretending to be paralysed so he could impersonate a monster and boss her about could be. *Doctor Who* began in the tradition of Victorian adventures, where explorers and other arrested adolescents went off and got into exciting scrapes until responsibility - in the shape of girls, family and earning a living - dragged them down.

Davies tore up that bit of the rulebook. His original pitch makes it clear that the Doctor has to be sexy, compassionate and dangerous. "Let's move on from that neutered, posh, public-school fancy-dress frock-coat image." Even if we leave aside a Welshman's characteristic assumption that only people with regional accents get laid, this is an odd association of ideas. The Doctor was, in this reading, neutered *because* he was dressed like an Edwardian gentleman, and because he affected a "posh" accent (as we saw in **What Are the Dodgiest Accents in the Series?** under 4.1, "The Smugglers", all but one of the first seven Doctors was "passing" for southern and middle-class, and even McCoy toned down his natural accent). But in another way, it is exactly the right set of assumptions to make for his long-term aim of making the Doctor every schoolgirl's dream man work. Anyone who knows adolescent girls will know that they want romance rather than sex: an unavailable or damaged fantasy boyfriend is so much more alluring. The Byronic cliches of Mr Darcy, Mr Rochester and various vampires rely on a girl's idea that she might be The One to cure his malaise. Pop stars have traded on this - the British Invasion of the early 60s was partly about the music (fab though most of it was), but mainly because these ambivalent boys who didn't fit any available stereotype were just what America's teenage girls wanted. In romantic fiction down the centuries, the unapproachable, moody man who isn't trying to get into every woman's pants has been a winner. In real life, teenage girls have always latched on to gay boys to get all the fun and intense emotional bonding with none of the squelching and mundane practicality of an orthodox relationship. In making his version of *Doctor Who* primarily for the *Buffy* market (and thus recognisably about the lives British teenagers live), boyfriends, parents, jobs and dreams of escape all have to be balanced. Having a strange man come into Rose's life and bond with her immediately without, shall we say, "dancing" requires him to take seriously the things UK teenagers know. So we have a Doctor who reads *Heat* magazine, loves pop music and isn't that interested in sport. The Doctor's persona hasn't actually changed all that much since the 60s - Hartnell was more into the Beatles than Barbara was (2.8, "The Chase") and he didn't then know anything about cricket (3.4, "The Daleks' Master Plan", but cricket isn't really "sport", as we will explore in a later essay). What has changed is the context in which he is depicted on screen.

In 1963, even words like "divorce" were never heard in family-orientated drama. As mentioned above, the 1980s version of *Doctor Who* persisted in pretending that this was still the case, and removed all "taint" of emotional attachment, sexuality or dirt. It became knowingly, deliberately, kitsch. As an accidental bi-product (so to speak), the Camp elements and gay sensibility of the series, always threatening to sneak in from just out of the corner of the screen, took over. (See **Is *Doctor Who* Camp?** under 6.5, "The Seeds of Death"; **What's All This Stuff About Anoraks?** under 24.1, "Time and the Rani" and - you knew this was coming - **What Are the Gayest Things In *Doctor Who*?** under 25.2, "The Happiness Patrol", which, if nothing else, proves that if you put your mind to it, you can find a "gay agenda" absolutely anywhere.) In many ways, the series began to mimic those "mega-soaps" coming from across the Atlantic, where relationships consisted entirely of point-scoring; this feature is one singled out by media theorists as a reason for the huge gay following for *Dynasty* and *Dallas*. In this regard, if no other, "The Mark of the Rani" (22.3) is worth a look. Three Time Lords and characters from a bad schools documentary about the birth of the

continued on Page 159...

X1.10 The Doctor Dances

X4.9, "Forest of the Dead", and X5.13, "The Big Bang".] Jack can rewire the Chula ship's transmat to rescue the Doctor and Rose. He implements 'Emergency Code 417', which makes a martini appear [but it's not entirely to his taste, so this may be a preset].

Jack suggests that one of his earlier 'self-cleaning cons' was in Pompeii. [This is said in such a way that he might just be joking about it. Still, see X4.2, "The Fires of Pompeii" and its accompanying essay, **What Constitutes a "Fixed Point"?** for why this is curious.]

The Non-Humans The *Chula* ship, surprisingly, has a 'sink' [or that's how it sounds when Jack says it - it could be a heat-sink for re-entry, or it could be a "synch" of some kind]. Less surprisingly, the ship has a *Trek*-style replicator (which makes slightly substandard martinis) and a literal-minded computer. It has no escape pods [at least, not now] and using the teleport would detonate the bomb that Jack disposes of. [That's got to be a design flaw.]

Chula warriors use a system called 'Om-Com', which interfaces with anything with a speaker-grille to communicate. [Hence the TARDIS phone, the radios and, um, the typewriter all conveying the question 'Are you my mummy?'] Jack's ship also has this [as, apparently, does the Atraxi vessel in X5.1, "The Eleventh Hour"].

The nanogenes on board the ambulance ship access the casualty's genetic blueprint to repair injuries swiftly, thus getting the maximum number of battle-ready soldiers into action without having to convey them away from the battlefield. [So the onboard version in Jack's ship, which only works when the hull is secure, must be slightly different. These are able to heal the Doctor's burnt hand, whereas the battlefield edit are somehow able to rewrite themselves first to undo the changes they made to Jamie, and then to accept the Doctor's reprogramming without making him human.] On finding Jamie's corpse and in the absence of data on humans [see **Things That Don't Make Sense**], they conflate his genes and the gas-mask and take his last thoughts as a mission-brief. This fusion is then taken as a template and applied to every human the micro-bots encounter, causing a plague of zombies with ingrown gas-masks all looking for mummy. The Doctor's revised edition restores the victims to how they were, and as a side-effect fixes any defects - up to and including amputated legs.

History By the fifty-first century, humanity will be spread across 'half the galaxy'. [Odd, as in the forty-second century, we were sprawling over three separate galaxies, according to X4.3, "Planet of the Ood". The Doctor must be using the word 'galaxy' as loosely as he used to use 'constellation' or will from now on use 'DNA'.]

Travel evidently broadens the mind, as humans will now mate with anything. Or, as Rose puts it [cementing Jack's status as a marginally more plausible James T Kirk]: 'Our mission - we seek out new life and... "dance" '.

Catchphrase Counter We get a 'fantastic' in the TARDIS when the Doctor is rather full of himself, and the phrase 'everybody lives!' gets a right old pounding during the climax. The euphemism 'dance' crops up here and seems to follow the Doctor around [if the production team had been on the ball, they could have used the contemporaneous 1941 hit "Dancing in the Dark", which exploits the same ambiguity about the verb, instead of leading people to think that the Doctor was a big fan of Billy Idol and was citing "Dancing With Myself" by Generation X, Idol's old band.]

The bomb that Jack straddles has the words 'Schlechter Wolf' chalked on it. [For further wonky German, see X4.13, "Journey's End".]

Deus Ex Machina Although we'd seen the nanogenes in action briefly in the previous episode, here their status as the first in what will be a very long list of miraculous orange, sparkly, fairy-dust-like plot contrivances is brought to the fore.

The Analysis

English Lessons ("The Empty Child" and "The Doctor Dances") *Living Rough* is an odd phrase: "sleeping rough" is simply not having a roof over one's head at night, but this extension isn't common. "Roughing It" was a term in use in America (and the title of one of Mark Twain's memoirs of life on the road).

• "Live by the sweat of our brows" is a version of Genesis 3:19 favoured by the Diggers, a movement led by Gerrard Winstanley who held property-owning to be ungodly (this was in the Interregnum after the Civil War, c.1650) and which spread through the pamphlets printed by

Gay Agenda? What Gay Agenda?

continued from Page 157...

Steam Age do their stuff, but two women from a pit-village have lost their husbands - where would anyone seeking to do actual drama about this situation put the emphasis? Even the (at times uncomfortably Pip 'n' Jane-like) X1.3, "The Unquiet Dead" manages to keep the human victims at the heart of the story.

By letting the genie of sexuality and relationships back out of the bottle (as it had been an occasional feature in the black and white era - see, or instance, 3.5, "The Massacre" or 5.4, "The Enemy of the World"), the new series was bound to upset viewers who hadn't actually wanted *Doctor Who* back so much as their own childhoods. And the idea of childhood being under threat from consumerism, sexuality and politically-motivated malfeasants with "agendas" is always contentious, but especially when the BBC is under fire from the right-wing press and the government. The *New Adventures* having swearing and explicit sex had been a mildly amusing small filler item in some tabloids ten years earlier, but now *Doctor Who* was big news and anything about it, especially a controversy, was guaranteed to sell papers. Curiously enough, the first derogatory comments about homosexuality in the 2005 series were accusing Davies of being homophobic (!!!). Rose called the Doctor "gay" in the word's current school-playground meaning of "a bit feeble", just as a character like that would have done. It may not be right, but it's accurate, and - compared to the downright offensive language some of Davies' characters used in *Queer as Folk* - justified after the event as "in character", it's pretty mild. However, as is so often the case, a small matter fed into the infinite feedback-loop of the Internet turned into an out-of-control event. Soon, the Slitheen pretending to be a minister who had been having affairs with people of both sexes was somehow demeaning to gays. And then people who said it wasn't were joined by people who said it wasn't demeaning enough.

Anyone looking for overt homosexuality in the BBC Wales series can find it, but what's offensive to the bigots is that it is treated as normal - or, at least, as normal as any other kind of desire. This is at the heart of the Davies approach to television drama: the workings of human desire to upset neat, orderly plans and social hierarchies has been a theme of his work right from the start, and most obviously in his BBC 3 three-part series about the most heterosexual man not to have written *Press Gang*, namely *Casanova*. Those hierarchies and systems are precious to certain control-freaks and vested interests, notably newspaper proprietors, TV evangelists and right-wing politicians. Discrediting any opposition they face is obviously going to be high on their agenda, so claiming that there is a "natural" form of desire and then anything else is "fringe" and "wrong" has always been the first resort. The tabloids will happily print pictures of Billie Piper not wearing much, but if John Barrowman is anything but apologetic about his orientation - fat chance! - they will react with contempt and fury. Unless it's his wedding, in which the number of famous people attending means they'll fight over the photo-rights. There is always the risk that, in presenting sexuality as a matter of preferences rather than innate core identity, the writers of *Doctor Who* and other such series are playing into the hands of the zealots who wish to present gay relationships as a "lifestyle choice", as though it were a carpet or career. This devalues the suffering of many people over several generations, but when this aspect of the past is mentioned, it too is dismissed as "propaganda". Shortly after the original *Doctor Who* went off the air, a tabloid furore over school books led to the notorious Clause 28 of the 1994 Education Act (now repealed) forbidding teachers from "promoting" homosexuality - because teachers' attempts to promote road safety, better diet and the correct use of apostrophes had been so conspicuously successful. The idea that sex of any kind can be a "fashion" is one of many curious ones held by tabloid editors.

The problem now is that, in presenting sexuality as a spectrum, anything else - the chastity that was the default assumption in *Doctor Who* up to 1989 - is now deemed to be odd. One of the most refreshing things about the show in the post-*Star Trek* TV environment was that, unlike every other hero on the screen, the Doctor was saving the world because it was the right thing to do, not to get the girl/boy/robot dog. Anyone not quite fitting the tabloid assumptions of "normality" could

continued on Page 161...

X1.10 The Doctor Dances

the associated group, which went on to become the Quakers. (The King James Bible has "the sweat of thy face".) It's completely inappropriate here as everyone had ration books, so boasting about paying for food was admitting to being a black-market customer or worse.

Oh, Isn't That...? ("The Empty Child" and "The Doctor Dances")

• *Richard Wilson* (Dr Constantine). Until 1990, he was one of those classic "Oh, isn't that..." faces you sort-of recognised, in such comedy-dramas *Tutti-Frutti*, *Whoops Apocalypse* and *Hot Metal*; the sitcom *Only When I Laugh*; and various straight dramas (including the final, colour episode/s of *Secret Agent/Danger Man*). Then came Victor Meldrew. *One Foot in the Grave* exploited his precise diction and hangdog expression to great effect, as Victor dealt with the idiocies of modern life, and the astonishing bad luck that assails people in David Renwick sitcoms, with rococo tirades that only prompted tradesmen to extract humiliating revenge on him. Meldrew said all the things we wish we'd been able to think of when stuck in traffic-jams on Bank Holidays, dealing with snooty neighbours or watching gimmicky documentaries. That it was a combination of script and performance is indicated by the failure of the US version, starring Bill Cosby.

Wilson has also directed and - after years of schoolkids running after him saying "I don't be*lieve* it" - returned to theatre, including revivals of Joe Orton. Moreover, as interviews revealed how unlike Victor he really is, he has appeared as himself in many places, including a memorable *Father Ted* episode and a series of documentaries where he has belatedly learned to drive and taken vintage vehicles on tours of Scotland. Most recently, he's been the Obi-Wan figure in *Merlin*.

(Oh, yes, and he was in dire sitcom *Duck Patrol*, which would have slipped into let-us-never-speak-of-this-again-dom but for the then-unknown David Tennant's involvement, which has raised the DVD's eBay price.)

• *John Barrowman* (Jack Harkness). Hard as it is to remember now, especially if you've been in Britain over the last five years, there were people unaware of his existence when this story was first broadcast. For TV viewers with long memories, especially those who had been children or parents in the early 90s, he was the American one-off *Live and Kicking*, one of many seemingly interchange-able Saturday Morning TV shows to feature boy-bands and puppets. (Actually, despite growing up in Illinois from the age of four, he's a native Glaswegian.) But on the West End stage, he was something of a fixture, which caused complications when casting him for a regular TV role (see **Production** next episode). Then, with Captain Jack raising his profile the way the Long March raised Mao Xedung's, he got just a bit *too* ubiquitous. Now, after *Torchwood* and a stint on *Desperate Housewives* and *Arrow*, he's big in the US and it is finally possible to turn on a telly in Britain without coming across Barrowman singing, judging other people's singing, hosting gameshows, plugging his CDs, talking about musicals or simply talking about himself.

• *Florence Hoath* (Nancy). Fans who spent the late 90s doggedly watching everything with Paul McGann in will remember her as one of the girls behind the Cottingsley Fairies hoax in *Fairytale: A True Story*. Everyone else was trying to place her from the various other small roles she'd had in the year or so leading up to these episodes.

• *Cheryl Fergison* (housewife Mrs Lloyd). As with a number of this year's supporting cast, anyone watching *EastEnders* over the following five years will recognise Mrs Lloyd as a future Albert Square regular, to whit Heather (pron. "Ev-vah"), the comic-relief character whose mysterious pregnancy provided one of the few relatively plausible plot-twists.

Things That Don't Make Sense ("The Empty Child" and "The Doctor Dances")

Anachronisms ahoy! Nearly everyone knows by now about the reel-to-reel tape recorder being a Nazi invention, so we'll just ask if anyone involved in making this story knew what the term "black-out" actually entails. In real-life London, in the genuine Blitz, the Air Raid Patrols - staffed by volunteers and not all as power-crazed as folklore suggests - would have been risking their own lives running around from building to building insisting that all of these brightly-lit rooms with open windows and no curtains should be obscured. If we're in 1941, then this would have been habitual for at least three months and everyone would have known someone killed in an air raid, so it's not something you just neglect one day. Just one example: Jack is standing in a well-lit room with the curtains open during an air-raid and, and like everyone else in that room (all senior officers, mind you) is hap-

Gay Agenda? What Gay Agenda?

continued from Page 159...

to some extent identify with his outsider status, whether they were gay, shy, genuinely asexual or just a bit bookish. Unlike Spock, he was perfectly good at social interactions and had a full range of emotions, but a bit old to be starting anything, especially with anyone he was likely to outlive. Davies, and more especially Steven Moffat, have confined the Doctor and the series into a more orthodox, restrictive and limiting formula. It is as though all television aspires to the condition of RomCom. Even the Doctor is now rethought as either slightly girl-shy and undergoing an 800-year dry spell or - as Davies' parting gift to a series he'd allegedly asked the BBC to cancel when he left - not just written and played by David Tennant exactly as Casanova was, but shagging Elizabeth I. (Or not: see **Does He, You Know... Dance?** under X3.4, "Daleks in Manhattan".) Moffat's earlier work might have led us to expect more of the same, but his overall notion of the character is rather different. In "The Curse of Fatal Death" (see the Appendix, Volume 6), it is apparently simply that he's not met the right girl until now. In interviews, Moffat cites the end of "The Green Death" (10.5) as proof that, alien though he is, the Doctor is more than parentally fond of his "fledgling", Jo Grant. It is hard to justify this simply from watching that episode, but, as script-writer and now executive producer, Moffat has sought to bolster this formerly minority view and establish that the Doctor's reticence with women is simply because he's shy and a bit nerdy.

This makes the Time Lord akin to the standard-issue Moffat male-lead's-best-friend character. Beginning with school-based screwball romcom *Press Gang*, continuing through supposedly more adult series *Joking Apart* and *Chalk*, and culminating in *Friends*-for-grown-ups series *Coupling*, Moffat has consistently shown a worldview where the sole motive for any action is impressing girls. (Women who try to achieve anything in his scripts usually land up neurotic, most spectacularly in the last episode of *Press Gang*.) Doing anything at all for any other reasons is just sad, apparently. This Hetero Agenda is at work in self-contradictory ways, such as "The Lodger" (X5.11). In this, the Doctor has to ensure that the shy bloke gets the girl and makes babies even though there are already six billion humans - which is why the girl is working to save endangered species threatened by all these humans making babies left, right and centre. Allowing her to do her self-imposed duty - or live her dream - is not an option, not when there's a fat shy bloke who works with her in a call-centre and doesn't want her to do anything else. This would all be fine if the story ended with them eloping to somewhere with endangered species to save, but the plot relies on the shy bloke not wanting to leave (which somehow blows up a home-made TARDIS). Deciding *not* to have adventures - to instead settle down and raise a family - used to be the equivalent of death in *Doctor Who* (especially when a companion needed to be written out in a hurry). Between Series One and Five were four years with the most self-confident and flirtatious Doctor ever, someone so secure in his appeal to women and men that he can ignore Martha's huge crush on him. And Jack's. And Shakespeare's. And the Master's. In fact, Donna is something of a relief after all of this adoration.

Once this point had been made, repeatedly, the use of a sudden revelation that a character wasn't vanilla ceased to even be amusingly unexpected. Instead, the 2010 series opted for what might be called an Embarrassment Agenda, where the characteristic human response to sexuality is a feeling of slight inadequacy and awkwardness. This is enough to make a walking bomb revert to being human-but-gifted (X5.3, "Victory of the Daleks") and a completely different android-who-thought-he-was-real spend two thousand years making it up to his girlfriend for killing her (X5.13, "The Big Bang"). It also makes the new Doctor sufficiently different from his cocky predecessor to avoid direct comparisons.

So there's an emphasis on relationships, a Gooey Agenda which, on the plus side, makes something like "Father's Day" (X1.8) worth watching even though the plot makes a minus quantity of sense. There is less reticence about making characters either actively homosexual, polysexual or doing things stereotypically ascribed to gay men (e.g the Master's trashy taste in music). Is there anything that might be conceived of as a gay aesthetic running through the BBC Wales series? It is hard to pin down anything that isn't

continued on Page 163...

X1.10 The Doctor Dances

pily watching the bombs fall rather than making his way to an air-raid shelter. Also, the Limehouse Green site has a dirty great searchlight pointing down at the mysterious object (see **Production** for why at least one person making this story must have thought it a silly idea). A hospital might also be expected to observe such precautions, and there is no way that street lighting would be switched on. And there are an awful lot of candles being used in both the Officers' Club (which also has electric lighting) and the night-club, despite rationing of alcohol and the paraffin from which the candles would be made. Also, Jack shows Rose the time by illuminating Big Ben behind them, making it a huge target for the attacking airplanes. Or, is this hidden behind the same shrouding effect that we might hope conceals Jack's spaceship from detection (but which we're never told about)?

(By the way, Moffat was obviously sensitive to criticism regarding war-time lighting, as much of what passes for the plot of X5.3, "Victory of the Daleks" is about the effectiveness of blackouts, with a hapless ARP warden as the nearest we get to a member of the public. But even if we assume that both stories are set on the same day - which might account for some of the street-lights and domestic fittings being switched on for an hour or so when the Daleks over-ride every light-switch in London - we have to posit an additional improbable device that makes everyone forget to draw curtains. And doesn't activate Jack's scan for alien tech that finds one set of opera-glasses in Limehouse and not Daleks in the Cabinet War Rooms, an Oblivion Continuum with a Scots accent device and two versions of the same TARDIS. There's a potential get-out clause for this last snag, see **Is Time Like Bolognese Sauce Now?** under X5.5, "Flesh and Stone", but you're not going to like it and it most likely reverts us to the initial problem. Furthermore, any attempt to make these two bombing raids the same one has to deal with the fact that, yes, the clock says 9.20pm when the Daleks illuminate the city, but it *still* says it after Bracewell has been talked out of suicide, adapted his plans for gravity-bubbles to a real-life machine, equipped Spitfires with space-drives and launched them into a dogfight in orbit. We conclude, therefore, that the Daleks didn't need to develop a specific Forget To Draw Curtains hypno-ray, and that everyone who did so the night the Chula ambulance was blown up did so spontaneously. And simultaneously.)

Talking of rations, when the TARDIS phone rings, some reasonably fresh cauliflowers are left in a box of rubbish, despite all the make-do recipes for leftovers; unless these greens were actively toxic, they would have made their way into a Woolton Pie or some other eke-out "Victory" dish. Or, indeed, with eggs becoming almost a currency in themselves, fed to chickens. (There was a Ministry of Food film about the need to save scraps for chicken-feed in which the Minister, Lord Woolton, is interviewed by a hen.) Anyone with things like these going begging would be trading them for other groceries or services. Similarly, Mr Lloyd's garden has some freshly-pulled-out carrots just lying there. We know he's fiddling the rations, but anyone with an asset like that would be capitalising on it. (Contrary to what has been written elsewhere, the cake we see Nancy steal is possible even without eggs: some recipes used vinegar instead, some used the reconstituted egg powder available on ration and others just skipped eggs altogether.[30]) What's *really* odd is that, for all his interest in food (and how to obtain it), Mr Lloyd has bucked the national trend and - unpatriotically, some might say - persists is growing flowers rather than "digging for victory" and growing his own turnips and spuds.

Something else the nation's sprogs asked when comparing this story's version of Blitz-era London with what they knew: where are all the sandbags? A hospital, at least, might have been expected to have observed the usual blast precautions.

Jack's gun (the Webley revolver, not the sonic-squareness pistol) is the wrong one for that period. More importantly, he claims to be a US serviceman working for the British prior to Pearl Harbor. There was a 133 Squadron of this kind, founded in August 1941 - i.e. five months *after* the Blitz - but entrance was very limited. American civilians could join the RAF if they wanted (some did it by means of a brief stint in the Canadian forces), but becoming a captain that way took ages (if he *is* a captain: the most likely rank for someone with those stripes is Flight Lieutenant). He couldn't have been a captain beforehand, because active or recent American servicemen were barred from joining any other force. Either he or the real Captain Jack (whom our Jack meets and snogs in *Torchwood* some time later) is breaking the law or possibly blackmailing superior officers to get such

Gay Agenda? What Gay Agenda?

continued from Page 161...

also an aspect of trying to pitch the new version of the series to small children who've grown up on Roald Dahl and Jacqueline Wilson, teenage girls who conceive of all drama being about who got off with whom, and parents who are slightly phobic about anything that looks too much like *Star Trek*. The new series' assumption that all time-periods are peopled with folks who are "just like us" (see **Are We Touring Theme-Park History?** under X2.7, "The Idiot's Lantern") in their attitudes and - in non-historical yarns - their *Top Shop* wardrobe seems like the ahistorical, postmodern, essentialist worldview sometimes associated with gay literature, but it's also what children's books have been doing for decades. (See **Did Sergeant Pepper Know the Doctor?** under 5.1, "The Tomb of the Cybermen".) Indeed, the only thing that complicated Gatiss's slightly *Daily Mail* view that civilisation ended in 1956 is the idea that homophobia was A Bad Thing and The Wrong Answer. Having contemporary reality shows in the year 200,100 (X1.12, "Bad Wolf") is Camp, but not intrinsically gay. Indeed, it forms part of the overall "Zogophobia" that was part of Davies' initial pitch (see **Is Kylie from Planet Zog?** under X4.0, "The Voyage of the Damned"). The celebrity cameos, usually in episode twelve of a series, often have a sort of "aura" of gay-friendliness, especially in "The Sound of Drums" (X3.12), but they are almost always people small children will recognise. If anything there's a Populist Agenda at work, making sure that the biggest possible spread of sub-cultures and the general public can get something out of any given episode, instead of it being made exclusively by and for a coterie.

And the basic audience for *Doctor Who*, now, is teenage girls. They watch *Hollyoaks* and *Skins*, so nothing really shocks them. Most of them assume that a fair percentage of the interesting or pretty boys they encounter won't actually want to shag them. Having a *Doctor Who* that looks like contemporary Britain might have been a wrench after a quarter-century, when it existed in its own little bubble and the nearest they got to a "normal" girl character was Bonnie Langford as a computer programmer with an eidetic memory and a love of CP Snow, but here it is. Reflecting a Britain that some people would rather pretend was a media creation might not go down well with some vocal critics, but the alternative was a series that (comparatively speaking) only gays, and a few nerds, and masochistic hardcore fans, were watching. That got cancelled.

Next they'll be saying that two references in "Gridlock" (X3.3), an ambiguous flag in "Dalek" (X1.6) and a brummie whose biography is a bit odd in "The Waters of Mars" (X4.16) constitute an Iowa Agenda.

rapid promotion. (Not to worry, the dismal film *Pearl Harbor* made the same error more obviouly.)

More annoying is the way Nancy knows the American tune to "Rock a Bye Baby" (she may, possibly, have heard this once or twice in *Tom and Jerry* - assuming a young single mum could go to the pictures at all) and her use of the American term 'use your bathroom' is hopelessly wrong. It's especially out of keeping as we (and she) have already seen that Mr Lloyd has an outside privy, and a tin bath is seen hanging on the wall. We might voice similar quibbles about Dr Constantine's phrasing 'the exact same injuries'. (We may also ask how someone from the fifty-first century knows the term 'cell phone' rather than "mobile", and yet doesn't know who Mr Spock is. On the other hand, it seems like an encouraging sign that *Star Trek* doesn't last as long as Dickens or *The Weakest Link*.) Similarly, the phone in the Lloyd house rings like an American one, with the wrong type of bell and the wrong pattern of rings for a London exchange. (Even if it's bypassing the exchange via Om-Com, it wouldn't change the shape of the bells. "Victory of the Daleks" makes the same error.) Even Rose is at it, saying 'tell 'em thanks' when discussing nanogenes (even today, this isn't a habit that's crossed the Atlantic - we "say" thanks and goodbye, and she'd be more likely to say "thank them from me"). Then there's the rather twenty-first century handle tagged on corrugated iron seen behind the Doctor at 8.24 in "The Empty Child" - we could make a "graffiti's rainbow" joke, but you'd not thank us.

Onto more prosaic problems: the script seems to be working on the assumption that Rose's Union Jack T-shirt makes her more of a target than any girl hanging off a barrage-balloon during an air-raid would normally be. (Maybe she thinks

X1.10 The Doctor Dances

Nazis don't shoot blondes. Or maybe her real fear is all those carrot-eating RAF chaps who could see a pattern on a T-Shirt while flying at 120 mph, at night, from a mile away.) Later, after illuminating the clock-face - there's still an air raid happening, remember - and revealing his spaceship, Jack and Rose dance and yet some minutes later, it's *still* 9.30. And if it was 9.30 when they started dancing, they could have been mildly concussed when the half-hour chimed (assuming they could hear any music over the sound of people being killed in bombing raids, they would have been way too close to the actual bells which, unlike church bells, didn't stop for a war). And wasn't it raining a few minutes earlier? They must have had a lot of faith in the grip on their shoes to risk dancing on a slippery sloping spaceship over the Thames. (Yes, all right, there's probably some kind of magical *Trek* style force field, but Rose would need a bit of persuading, so this should have come up in the conversation.) Jack's monitor has that TARDIS facility of showing the view from somewhere else, showing Rose suspended by his tractor beam as someone across the river would have seen her. Why was his ship tethered to a landmark so far from where he needed to be anyway - why not Tower Bridge, which is closer to Limehouse? It's not like he'd be able to get a taxi.

The Doctor is amazingly obtuse as to the fact that he's in Wartime London this evening. He fails, for a start, to spot sticky-tape on the windows (maybe he thinks the Master's around messing with a nuclear power station; see 8.3, "The Claws of Axos"). Even if this, the chaps with Brylcreem and tuxedoes and the (admittedly perfunctory) black-out precautions don't tip him off as to his location, the barrage-balloons might have been a clue. If even *these* failed, the fact that he's able to track this mauve-alert-worthy Chula vessel through time and already knows which city he's going to be in before it lands (and that it arrived up to a month earlier) ought to have given him a vague hint. Ten minutes later, miraculously, he's able to look at his wristwatch and know what year it is. But we might allow that he's not feeling well - after he repels the scarily powerful spooky kid with his 'Go to your room!' stunt, his next move is to head straight for... the scarily powerful spooky kid's room.

And in that room, apart from the stolen German tape-recorder with anachronistic plastic tape instead of a band of steel, we have lots and lots of wax crayon drawings of Mummy. Yes, wax crayons and paper were rationed too, but the point is this: if the Child could do *that*, then why is he less self-aware now? In fact, why is he only now worried about finding his mummy when - for as long as he can remember - he's not had one, just an older sister and no parents at all? It *ought* to be going around asking, "Where's my sister Nancy?".

The effects of Om-Com system are a bit random, too: verbal communication (in English) via anything with a speaker-grille is fine and dandy, but shutting doors by pointing at them, making clockwork monkeys go hyper, typing by remote control (when Jamie couldn't even read, still less figure out a QWERTY keyboard without having seen one) and - apparently - teleporting to wherever Nancy is are all beyond this. Occasionally, the Child steps outside his mission-brief of finding Mummy and taunts the Doctor for no good reason, also pointing out that Rose is about to do something silly with a barrage-balloon. (Which is itself a bit strange as she starts off at street-level, next to a door that the Doctor finds leads to a cellar, then is on a platform about 30 feet in the air *before* the balloon rises and takes her away.)

Come to think of it, with Nancy raising Jamie alone, on the run (a different house every night, as she says), and him being at most six years old, the 'Go to your room' stunt shouldn't have worked at all. He's never *had* a room since he could speak, and all the other zombies just go to bed - even Dr Constantine, who wasn't *in* bed when he converted. The Child has spent a lot of time in Room 802, but never voluntarily left there, so being told to return to it is still pointless.

Rose, meanwhile, is alarmingly insightful, deducing from virtually no evidence that Jack used to be a Time Agent - this, while she's tipsy and otherwise incapable of saying or doing the right thing. She is, however, more sure than she ought to be that someone in 1941 who fails to recognise the name 'Spock' isn't a local boy. Although she seems to think of herself as 'very available', the ring that's been wandering around her hand from story to story has now settled on the ring finger of her left hand. In spite of all she's seen, and the Doctor's ire when the timeline has been tampered with (X1.7, "The Long Game"; X1.3, "The Unquiet Dead" and especially X1.8, "Father's Day"), she claims that the Doctor is 'usually... first in line' when it comes to arguing with

The Doctor Dances X1.10

history. Jack's also very quick to announce that he's a con-artist, even though it must have occurred to him that the Doctor and Rose might still have enough money for him to at least break even in the absence of real Time Agents. Nancy's ability to whistle with her fingers whilst wearing woolly gloves is impressive - as is her ability to find a household in London with more food than the ration books allow for a family that size, and also more place-settings (indeed, there are enough for all her posse, a new member plus an unexpected Time Lord).

Precisely why the full moon should be in the West some time before 9.30pm is another of those lunar anomalies we get from time to time. (Maybe Churchill and Professor Bracewell - "Victory of the Daleks" again - rigged up a giant mirror over Chelsea to confuse Jerry. Don't sneer: the Allies did something very like this in North Africa a couple of years later, and it was Jasper Maskelyne, grandson of our old chum John Neville Maskelyne - see, amongst others, 5.7, "The Wheel in Space" and 16.1, "The Ribos Operation" - who devised the magnificently daft scheme to make the Nile vanish.) How the moon knows which camera-angle the director is using so it is always hiding behind the clock tower when Jack and Rose are having a shiptop shuffle-bop is a mystery unique to this story. Meanwhile, Albion Hospital was 'closest to the River' in "Aliens of London", but is now right next to Limehouse Basin, quite a way away from Westminster Bridge. (On second thoughts, this is more likely right as we know for a fact that, when the Slitheen hoax crashed, the reporters on the bridge had Guy's Hospital visible over their shoulders - and in the *Doctor Who* universe, this is where the Royal Hope Hospital was; X3.1, "Smith and Jones".) Either way, it was only five episodes ago, so they ought to have been more on the ball.

As with real *Star Trek* scripts, the ideas on display here about cellular biology are curious, to say the least. The nanogenes take the patient's DNA and use it to fix any deviations from this pattern. All right, but Dr Constantine is still bald, so it can't *just* be that. Moreover, the "wrong" version they get from Jamie's corpse is fused with the gas-mask he was wearing. This includes the metal and glass (notably lacking in chromosomes) and the leather and rubber are gasmask-shaped, rather than taking the DNA from the cow and rubber-tree or whatever Jamie had just eaten (this being wartime, that might include horse or whale-meat) and making a *Quatermass*-style mutant hybrid. And why stop at his gas-mask? Why aren't all the patients wearing serge shorts and knee-length socks? Meanwhile, one of the "zombies" is a heavily pregnant woman, but even this isn't enough to tip off the nanogenes about how humans work. If it's not Jamie but the Chula tech asking 'Are you my mummy...' in the sense of "Do you have the same mitochondrial DNA as our original specimen, so we can work up a functional comparative analysis and reconfigure our blueprint?", then why would the nanogenes carry on spreading their version of "corrected" human to anyone apparently working and healthy whilst they/he were out looking?

Because a lot was cut from the bomb-site sequence, the stuff about using the German bomb to destroy the nanogenes was removed, but the line 'Change of plan - don't need the bomb' wasn't. Rose tells Nancy she's from London in the future, but when she says 'Oi'm fraam 'ere', her accent shifts westward again.

Jack claims that he checked the Chula ambulance and found it was empty. So either he would have been assaulted by nanogenes or - assuming this was long before dropping it on London - the Chula would have his DNA as a template and you wouldn't be able to move in 1941 London without seeing John Barrowman (a bit like 2007 London, then). So maybe he scanned it from outside, using his otherwise omniscient wrist-device or the apparatus on a Chula spaceship, either of which would say "achtung - nanogenes".

There's a bit of a problem with Jack's backstory and behaviour. If he's from a future where humanity is 'dancing' with every species and is completely upfront about desire, his tendency towards innuendo wouldn't be so pronounced. He might here be using it as part of his disguise, coding references to sex for comic effect whilst in 1941, but from his position (!), it's about as much fun as making up "naughty" code-names for food or furniture.

Although the scam with the Chula ambulance is one Jack sprung on the TARDIS crew in the belief that they were Time Agents, this version of it not only leaves a bit of alien tech in the hands of the War Office (or Torchwood, in which case Jack will one day clean all this mess up - but he doesn't know that yet), it means there are probably some real Time Agents wandering around the Blitz (hoping Connie Willis isn't taking notes).

Schlechter Wolf, which is written on the side of

165

X1.10 The Doctor Dances

the bomb that Jack deals with, doesn't actually mean "Bad Wolf" so much as "Worse at wolfing."

Critique ("The Empty Child" and "The Doctor Dances") The pre-publicity made a big play of this being "The Doctor's scariest adventure yet", but it actually presents a very sanitised view of World War II and a fairly routine catalogue of things that have been in other spooky films. Most of the tricks used here were beaten into the ground by re-use in later Moffat scripts and other stories in Seasons Five and Six. One gets used twice in the same episode here, as we saw. That doesn't seem to matter, however. Rose goes completely out of character, acting like the libidinously driven female characters in Moffat's *Coupling*, and offering snide comments on the conventions of *Doctor Who*. The Doctor undergoes moments of complete stultification when the plot needs him to forget everything he knows about the situation. Jack is profoundly annoying right from the start. None of *that* really matters either. It's not even that much of a problem that the script and direction contains historical howlers that every schoolchild in Britain spotted.

What is really going on here is that two distinct genres, the *Trek*-derived space opera and the World War II romance, are being turned inside out in a way that only *Doctor Who* can do and made into something stronger than either. Whatever the ratings say, this story is one everyone in Britain seems to have watched.

The thing we have to bear in mind is that what appealed to people over these two episodes seems to have alienated casual viewers when spread over two whole series. Moffat has a knack of making one riddle the answer to the others, so long as everyone remembers all of them well enough for the pay-off to make sense ("everyone" in this case includes the author). What people took way from this adventure, apart from the spooky moments and one-liners, is that the entire story came together in the end in ways that should have been obvious. Every episode of every sitcom Moffat wrote was an exercise in selling viewers a pup, with a few simple tricks and a lot of pace. Here, the pace is restrained, but that's because he's making the most brazen pup-sale of his career to date: a Blitz story with no casualties and a rom-com with no romance. The director exploits this relatively tentative pace to add menace to the Empty Child's non-sequitur abilities (he can close doors, operate a typewriter and make toy monkeys start up - a lot of the plot would be different if these Jedi tricks were used consistently). It also draws attention to the biggest risk the story takes.

Because every child in Britain has had to study this period before they were ten, the emphasis in schools has been on what it *felt* like to be evacuated, how you would feel about having to live on the scant rations and whether you could cope with having to hide in a cupboard every night not knowing if your family or friends would be all right, let alone yourself or your house. Empathy is in short supply in this story, though, because it is using the Blitz as a reservoir of pretty pictures. This is a Wartime London derived entirely from film clichés by someone who wasn't taught it at school, because it wasn't history back then. It's all surfaces, and gets even these wrong. Those surfaces are collaged with the outward symbols of space opera. Because this is a cut-and-paste of images, using a real and painful experience within living memory as an evocative backdrop for yet another story about Rose's hormones - even death, the single most important aspect of a war conducted against civilians, is negligible and reversible. So the *real* achievement of the story is in skating over this parlously thin ice without leaving a crack.

This is as good a time as any to mention John Barrowman. In this version of Captain Jack, it's hard to see any discrepancy between his public persona and the part he's playing. Later on, as we all know, he seems incredibly against-the-grain in a series created specifically for him. Here, though, he is doing what he does best and obviously enjoying every second. His arrival makes the two regulars have to keep up, and the result is a screwball comedy with the cascade of zippy lines converting even running up and down lots of corridors into *Doctor Who* as Billy Wilder might have made it. (Watching "The Doctor Dances" in other languages, it is obvious that the "shape" of a Moffat line withstands translation.) There is a different form of farce performance at work when Richard Wilson (Dr Constantine) is on set - a precise, measured matter-of-fact delivery of lines that suggest completely different priorities. This works as well in the "creepy" scenes as in outright comedy, but is the same procedure applied to the dialogue to make it jar with the circumstances.

It's in the performances and how the cast make the script's carefully engineered cause-and-effect seem real that these episodes come to life. Moffat has spent the intervening years trying to make lightning strike twice by taking what he thought were the reasons it worked and doing them again and again in different combinations. Sometimes the results have been interesting, and in some ways even *better*, but this is the one where it all comes together - and, sadly, it came first. What we have here is a two-part story that you can sit anyone in front of and say "This is why *Doctor Who* had to come back and why it's a global hit." Very few BBC Wales episodes have all of the programme's strongest suits as well-displayed all in one package.

The Facts

Written by Steven Moffat. Directed by James Hawes. Viewing figures: "The Empty Child": (BBC1) 7.11 million, (BBC3 repeats) 0.2 and 0.8 million. "The Doctor Dances": (BBC1) 6.86 million, (BBC3 repeats) 0.2 and 0.5 million.

Overseas promotion

• *France:* Drôle de Mort (a pun on *Drôle de guerre*, or "Phony War"), Le Docteur Dance.

• *Germany* (!): Das Leere Kind, Der Doktor Tanzt. (Remember, during the Sylvester McCoy years, the deal the BBC had signed with RTL - Radio-Television Luxembourg - for German-language transmissions meant that the Wagner-loving baddies in 25.3, "Silver Nemesis" could not be stated as being Nazis and 26.3, "The Curse of Fenric" saw World War II skirmishes between British and Russian troops...)

• *Poland*: Dziecko bez Wnetrza, Doktor Tanczy.

Alternate Versions These episodes seem to have escaped relatively unscathed: Canadian and some US edits have a sound drop-out in "The Empty Child" when Jack is explaining nanobots. Listening to the French version of "The Empty Child", it appears that the cracking noise for Dr Constantine's transformation was dubbed on and later removed for the UK. The thinking seems to have been that we could either see a metamorphosis or hear it, so the sickening sound is used for Algy's (off-screen) change in "The Doctor Dances".

Production

("The Empty Child" and "The Doctor Dances"): Stop us if you've heard this one before... the name "Chula" is the Indian restaurant in Hammersmith, about a quarter-hour's journey from Television Centre, where Steven Moffat, Paul Cornell, Robert Shearman and Mark Gatiss convened to celebrate getting commissions for the revived series. (Don't go looking for it, it's not there any more.) That was at the end of February 2004. Four months earlier, when the return of *Doctor Who* was announced, Moffat had contacted Davies congratulating him and been informally told that, should the series be longer than six episodes, there would be a job for him. Moffat had been writing for television for 15 years and had always been in total control of his scripts and production - the one exception being the *Comic Relief* 1999 sketch "The Curse of Fatal Death" (see Appendix 2, Volume 6). If there was one series where he would have been prepared to be a "hired gun", it was a Davies-led *Doctor Who*. A contract had been sent by December, although Moffat was hard at work on *Coupling*. By the beginning of March, Moffat had a plan, which he explained to the production team over a Chinese meal - his description of this event is a little *ben trovato*, but it is certainly the case that Davies was lukewarm about this pitch and they worked on a fresh idea.

• Davies instructed Moffat on the new character to be introduced in this slot (still called "Jax" at this stage), who was a soldier from the future to be used in the big battle in the last episode. The idea originally was that he'd get on so well with the Doctor that Rose would feel a bit threatened. One detail, not really important, he said, was that the man had to be pansexual. Notions that Moffat introduced as the story developed was that Jack's mission in London was a con, that Jack was human (to contrast with the Doctor better), and that Jack was missing two years of memories. As the rewrites continued (Moffat suggests that there were 17 drafts), it emerged that Jack would be played by John Barrowman, an actor Julie Gardner had wanted to work with - no others were even considered for the role. By late August, Barrowman was doing pre-publicity for the series, in-between parts in major West End musicals. As Moffat continued to refine his scripts, Phil Collinson contacted James Hawes, a director with whom he had worked on *Sea of Souls* to manage these two episodes as Block Four of the production.

X1.10 The Doctor Dances

- In an early draft, the mysterious object was in fact Jack's own ship from his personal future. It was obvious from the start that whatever the antagonist, it had to be something that would not distract from the Blitz setting, and instead use it as an asset. A photo of a schoolboy in a gas-mask seemed to convey the right air of menace and suggest a world with distorted priorities. All children in Britain were coached in how to put on a gas-mask quickly, even though - unlike in World War I - toxic gas was never used as a front-line weapon. One idea that persisted until almost the last draft was that Jamie's father was German, hence the shame that led Nancy to raise her son as a brother. In earlier versions, a mysterious mute beggar would be following people around (to be revealed as the father), and Nancy would voice a belief that Jamie's zombie state was a curse caused by her "treacherous" union. Script editor Helen Raynor suggested that "nanites" might be copyrighted by someone and the bugs were renamed "nanogenes".

- Aware of the restrictions on the hours that child actors can work, Nancy's "gang" had their scenes rationed, meaning that the Doctor met Nancy herself earlier in each draft. (Indeed, when it came to filming, the scenes with a whole lot of kids were shot first, which is why the exchanges between the Doctor and Nancy are tight close-ups to conceal the youngsters' absence from shots done later in the evening.) It was originally planned that they too would fall victim to the Chula nanogenes and not get dialogue in "The Doctor Dances", but this changed (see below). As the rewriting proceeded, the Doctor's fury at Jack's blundering was rethought as frustration, although some tirades were only reworked in location recording.

- Hawes and Davies agreed that the look of the story ought to emphasise the mood rather than the practical accuracy of the London-in-Wartime setting. At the Tone Meeting in early November, the key-word was "romantic". Hawes opted for an amalgam of *film noir* and later films with wartime themes; his touchstone was the 1986 musical fantasy-drama *The Singing Detective* (see Volume 6), and the night-club scenes in "The Empty Child" are markedly similar. (Although, as Kate Harvey sings live, in a noticeably modern phrasing style rather than lip-synching to old records as had happened in the Dennis Potter series, the resemblance isn't exact.) As we have seen in the notes earlier, the main "casualty" of this decision from the point-of-view of verisimilitude is the moody lighting flatly contradicting what every schoolchild knows about blackouts - but there were other, practical reasons for this, as we will see.

- Mike Tucker's model unit set to work making barrage balloons and small-scale burning buildings to augment The Mill's digital models - the flames from the miniatures were matted into the CG shots. He already had a model Big Ben clock tower from "Aliens of London", which was easier to dirty-up to Wartime pollution-levels than the real thing. But the balloon needed to be a detailed model to billow slightly in the breeze and have all the requisite wires (a nightmare to do on a computer in that timescale). Jenny Bowers made all the fake wartime posters ("Hitler Will Send No Warning" was, surprisingly, not a genuine slogan), as well as devising a graphic style for the Chula display screens. This was based loosely on Maori tattoos and predominantly in red and orange to match the story's overall look.

- The gas-masks are nothing like real wartime children's-issue ones. The glass eye-pieces are much bigger and would have given away the plot too soon. Some good-looking Russian army-surplus gas-masks were tried, but had asbestos in, so only the eye-pieces of these were used. Instead, the prostheses had the airfilters made from baked-bean tins, hurriedly constructed in the days before the Christmas break began.

- Shooting began on 17th December, 2004 - two days after that for "The Long Game" ended - with Jack and Rose dancing on top of a spaceship. Predictably, this is all green-screen work and required regular monster-choreographer Ailsa Berk to do some actual dance-coaching. Barrowman's costume needed to be carefully selected, as he has a wool allergy. By this time, it had been decided that Jack would not be faking an English accent. The next day, Piper went to the nearby RAF hanger to be suspended on wires over a big green floor and shot from above, clutching a rope. (They completed this about a month later.) Then everyone got a fortnight off for Christmas. Eccleston rejoined the unit on 4th January as they returned to Cardiff Royal Infirmary, AKA Albion Hospital (see X1.4, "Aliens of London") for the slightly amended "resonating concrete" scenes. Richard Wilson joined them for the next two days, long enough to perform his main scene with

Eccleston and record the taped conversation between him and the Child. In many later scenes, he is doubled for by someone in a gas-mask, although a few scenes of Wilson in the prosthesis made for him were shot around now. He then left (as he is very much in demand), to return three weeks later when the railway location scenes were recorded. The weekend of the 9th and 10th were for the street-scenes, once again around the Millennium Stadium (Womanby Street, if you're looking for it). During the course of this long night, the crew went to Penarth, to the same children's home used in "The Unquiet Dead" for the funeral parlour, to record the night-club scenes, then back for the cat and phone-call sequence. The following afternoon, after Eccleston had had a few hours' kip, they were back in hospital for the "squareness gun" malarkey. The rest of the hospital stuff took the next four days.

- Incidentally, there were three Empty Children. Albert Valentine is the main one. In some scenes, because of the same child-actor laws, he is doubled by Luke Perry (no, not *that* one), who is also Mr Lloyd's son in "The Doctor Dances". But Valentine's voice was just slightly too endearing for "Are you my mummy?" to be scary: after a false start with Zoe Thorne (the voice of the Gelth), the son of a friend of Hawes' dubbed Jamie's dialogue.

- Jack's cockpit had to be built to abut the TARDIS set and was, consequently, smaller on the inside. Standby art-director Arwel Jones, identified in the DVD commentary as "Arwel the Cowardly Lion", had to hold Jack's chair still whenever Barrowman stood up or sat down. (see 13.3, "Pyramids of Mars" for a less discreet version of the same task). Now the shooting schedule went into the now-familiar "double banked" situation, as the scenes with Jack and Rose discussing nanogenes and psychic paper were shot whilst Eccleston was off taking Margaret Slitheen for steak and chips (X1.11, "Boom Town").

One problem with filming wartime London in go-ahead twenty-first century Cardiff is the lack of derelict sites. (As viewers of *Torchwood* will know, modern-day Cardiff is like a little patch of Barcelona dropped into South Wales, all new and costly, so no area of waste-ground more than the size of a station-wagon gets left un-built-on for long.) The Limehouse Green locations were out-of-town, in Barry Island. If that name rings a bell, the precise location was literally across the road from the derelict holiday camp used for 24.3, "Delta and the Bannermen". The Vale of Glamorgan Railway, a steam-preservation society, had been there for seven years and had vintage (if *slightly* anachronistically-liveried) rolling stock, leading a slight rewrite to make the bomb-site a railway siding. To illuminate the night-shoot, director of photography Ernie Vincze opted originally for a floodlight on top of a pylon. This avoided the problem of moving lighting rigs and generators across uneven terrain, leaving cables in shot and complicating the effects explosion shots. However, it shone brightly into the windows of practically everyone in the district, and was rapidly becoming a traffic-hazard, especially for the trains relying on coloured lights for safety warnings. Phil Collinson, on arrival at the shoot, said he could see it four miles away. Instead, therefore, the scene was lit from numerous small lights at floor-level, illuminating faces from below and looking marginally more authentically Blitz-y.

- In some interviews given in the run-up to the launch, Eccleston admitted that some scenes were hard because he was doing something similar to an earlier episode. One, he claims, was such a "Groundhog Day" that he froze and forgot his lines. The most reported instance of this we've found is the "software patch" technobabble from this sequence, although it is hard to see any similarity between this and anything in previously recorded episodes.

- The bulk of the recording after this was in the studios at Unit Q2 (although the outside privy was in Bargoed Street, Grangetown), and the balcony where Jack and Algy discussed bottoms was Glamorgan House, where they were simultaneously shooting the Council sequences of "Boom Town". The last major sequences to be shot were the material in the Lloyd house, which allowed Piper time off (she attended the Brit awards and did a lot of press interviews), and, for the final day's work, on 11th February, only Florence Hoath (as Nancy) and the children were needed. Well, *almost* the final day...

- Davies always told the press that Moffat's scripts were the only ones where he never needed to change a single line. This is slightly disingenuous: "The Doctor Dances" required a significant alteration. Here, if anywhere, is evidence for the rumour that Davies was contractually prevented from altering Moffat's scripts; when the finished episode was found to be under-running by two minutes, a new scene was added some months later. Some reports claim that Davies attempted to build a scene out of the one set and handful of

X1.11 Boom Town

actors still available (Nancy's "gang" and an air-aid shelter) and failed, but the broadcast version - the "typewriter" sequence - was hastily written by Moffat whilst he was in Australia accompanying his wife on business (she and her mum were producers on the ambitious but mildly disappointing Anglo-Australian Rob Brydon vehicle *Supernova*). Moffat claims in interviews - as always, these stories come with an embroidery health-warning - that she had such a low opinion of *Doctor Who* that he had to pretend to be doing something else.

- The two episodes suffered a small dip in initial ratings: "The Empty Child" was moved half an hour earlier to make way for the Eurovision Song Contest, whilst "The Doctor Dances" was on in a Bank Holiday weekend (fewer people watched any television at all, so *Doctor Who*'s audience share made it the most-watched programme of the day). Nevertheless, the press were increasingly enthusiastic, and it was during this story's two-week run that the betting-shops began offering odds on what the Bad Wolf would turn out to be.

X1.11: "Boom Town"

(4th June, 2005)

Which One is This? Margaret Slitheen tries to blow up Cardiff and gets turned into a root vegetable.

Firsts and Lasts After Cardiff-pretending-to-be-London and Swansea-pretending-to-be-Victorian-Cardiff, we finally get the first story set entirely in present-day Cardiff. We get to see all the landmarks we'll come to know so well in *Torchwood* and the locations for so many *Doctor Who* stories appearing as themselves (the first aerial shot gives us the Millennium Stadium and National Museum of Wales, and later the Cardiff Royal Infirmary shows up).

As we indicated in Volume 6, William Thomas (appearing here as Mr Cleaver, a nuclear engineer) is the first actor to have appeared in the revamped *Doctor Who* who'd been in the twentieth-century version (as the funeral director given custody of the Hand of Omega in 25.1, "Remembrance of the Daleks"). He's killed by the first returning monster of the new series (unless you count the Nestenes, but they aren't returning within this year's series).

Although on-screen visits to other worlds don't begin until X2.1, "New Earth" (and even here, the title suggests a lack of real alien-ness), we get the first suggestion that Rose has been to other planets when there weren't cameras rolling. Typically for BBC Wales' *Doctor Who*, one of these is a deserted beach (even though, as Woman Wept exists only as dialogue, the budget for effects is infinite) and another, Justicia, is cross-promotion with the re-launched tie-in novels (specifically, *The Monsters Inside*).

The means by which the Ship is *supposed* to disguise itself - the Chameleon Circuit [first named in 18.7, "Logopolis"] - gets mentioned at last in the new series, correcting Rose's description of it as a 'cloaking device' [see the McGann Movie for why this is satisfying].

This story introduces the surfboard-like Tribophysical Waveform Macro-kinetic Extrapolator, with which many force-field-related hi-jinks with the TARDIS become possible (see, X1.13, "The Parting of the Ways", but similar things happen in X3.0, "The Runaway Bride" and X5.2, "The Beast Below") and the TARDIS energy-source, a *slightly* different form of orange, sparkly light which we will be seeing an awful lot from now on. And, in a curious foreshadowing of "The Doctor's Wife" (X6.4), we see the "soul" of the TARDIS and meet a character called "Idris".

Watch Out For...

- This episode is primarily a love-letter to Cardiff. As such, it lets itself linger over the new cityscape and the idiosyncratic details. It's hardly unrequited love, though, as the city's former main municipal building is given over to this series (remember, nobody had seen a single episode yet, so this was an enormous act of faith on the part of the good burghers) and the local paper, the *Western Mail*, allows them to fake up a front-cover. Of course, this means that when they are depicting a local journalist being fobbed off with feeble excuses, she has to work for a made-up rival publication. Even the usual supervillain gloating (typical, when a fiendish plan involving a nuclear power-station is outlined) gets a piece of local colour, as Margaret explains how she got away with doing something so evil so publicly: "We're in Cardiff; London doesn't care. The South Welsh coast could fall into the sea and they wouldn't notice. Oh, I sound like a Welshman. God help me, I've gone native."

- All this diligent verisimilitude is in aid of the old theory that people are more scared by anoma-

Does Being Made in Wales Matter?

At the start of every episode, if you were watching in Wales in the first few years of the new series, the local announcers proudly proclaimed: "And now, made in Wales, *Doctor Who*."

It was not only a flagship of the nation's pride in making something that was shown across Britain and worldwide, it was one of the most high-profile employers in Cardiff. There was a subtext, lost on anyone under 30. As one of the old centres of manufacturing industry, South Wales had gained prestige in the late nineteenth and early twentieth centuries as an economic powerhouse and a reliable source of quality goods. When this fell apart, and especially in the late 1970s, there was a concerted attempt to remind everyone of this heritage. In 1980, there was a big advertising campaign with the slogan "Made in Wales". (The television adverts had a Male Voice Choir, of the kind associated with South Wales coal-mining communities, listing famous brand-names to the tune of traditional Welsh hymn - and Rugby-match favourite - *Bread of Heaven* and a voice-over by Philip Madoc; it was relentlessly parodied). The announcers (and the set-designers of *Torchwood*, if you look closely) were consciously and pointedly associating a globally successful television "brand" with the foundries, shipyards and coal mines that had been a big part of what it had meant to be Welsh.

If this seems like a bit of a stretch, consider the whole regeneration of Cardiff Docks. The economic benefits of the leisure, tourism and media industries are stressed in all of the promotional literature and websites. However much the rest of Wales may seethe at Cardiff getting all the attention, anything that complicates the stereotypes that still persist (see 10.5, "The Green Death") is grudgingly welcomed. This pays off in the goodwill of the public for having their lives disrupted by almost constant location-work. *Doctor Who* in particular is able to get into places simply by asking nicely, giving a bit of advance notice and offering a few autographs and photo-ops for small children.

As we have said, the only way to make a series with such a variable budget (even though this budget is far in excess, per minute of screen-time, of what either old *Doctor Who* or a lot of BBC drama made now can command) is by using locations where possible. This makes retaining the goodwill of the public absolutely imperative. The use of both "Boom Town" and *Torchwood* to show off the city to the best advantage helped, but anyone who's had their lives disrupted by filming knows that the novelty wears off fast. So whilst there are some locations that have become very familiar to regular viewers (especially if those viewers also watch *Torchwood*, *The Sarah Jane Adventures*, *Life on Mars* or *Sherlock*), a large part of the effort of finding suitable places is to minimise the inconvenience or hostility, especially at night (see X1.3, "The Unquiet Dead"). This often translates into finding a suitable area that hasn't been used before by any of the Cardiff-based BBC dramas, so that the thrill and novelty is intact. (See **What Are the Most Over-Familiar Locations?** under X2.12, "Army of Ghosts".) The transformation of local spaces into alien worlds or historical settings is also newsworthy, and both the regional press and the BBC Wales section of the BBC website often made a point of playing up the "little-Cardiff-takes-on-Hollywood" aspect of the story.

Press management was especially delicate when the first series was being made in Cardiff. With little experience of anything on this scale, the BBC Wales Press Office made some understandable errors, especially handling the rumours concerning Eccleston's abrupt departure (see **Did He Fall or Was He Pushed?** under X1.12, "Bad Wolf"). The mainstream media, especially the tabloids, weren't used to sending showbiz reporters to Cardiff and often made stories from fragmentary reports from local "stringers" or press-releases-with-added-speculation. With Billie Piper's marital difficulties, and the rather zealous policing of the set for fans with cameras or anyone who might be a source for spoilers, that slight sense of isolation on the location shoots or in the various studio complexes used in Series One was heightened. Some cast members and production staff not originally from Wales felt a long way from home. It was important to be amenable to the public, not least because this was a BBC production (so the public were paying for it, whether they liked *Doctor Who* or not), but the use of public spaces as though they were part of the secure studio complex led to miscalculations and awkward moments, as we have seen. On the other hand, this sense of public ownership of the series was some

continued on Page 173...

X1.11 Boom Town

lous aliens in domestic or well-known real settings. We saw this tried in X1.1, "Rose" and X1.4 "Aliens of London". The usual description of this thought-process is Jon Pertwee's well-worn phrase about a Yeti in a Loo in Tooting Bec. Well, Cardiff's Glamorgan Building (home of the city Council until 1979) isn't everyone's idea of a well-known setting, but we do at least get a giant, man-eating space-monster on the toilet…

• … a scene that entails a mournful oboe providing the music as Blon Fel Fotch Pasameer Day Slitheen (AKA Margaret Blaine) gurgles and frets over whether to kill a nosy journalist who is about to get married and have a baby. You really aren't going to get that in any other series.

Mind you, the music and the directing are already streets away from the last time we saw the Slitheen. However, Murray Gold has apparently decided that the appropriate measure for a comedy episode is a tango, something that will cause problems once the one-off novelty companion he does it to next (X3.0, "The Runaway Bride") becomes the companion in Series Four. Although most of the best sound effects these days are samples of things Brian Hodgson bodged together in the 60s using sticky-tape, milk-bottles and abused pianos, this story benefits from one perfectly-judged tinkle. The Doctor asks Idris the gopher to announce him, then the music stops, there is the sound of a dropped tea-cup, and then the Doctor says, "She's climbing out the window, isn't she?"

• The dynamic aboard the TARDIS is also considerably different from earlier this year. We not only get the Doctor trading innuendoes with Captain Jack, but Mickey seriously suggesting that he and Rose get a hotel room together even though he's supposedly seeing Trisha Delaney now. Which brings us to the most curious feature of this story…. since narrating X1.8, "Father's Day", Rose has ceased being the audience-identification character. She has spent the last two episodes being the mouthpiece through which Steven Moffat slags off all previous *Doctor Who*, and now she's so completely in the Doctor's world that Mickey looks on in disgust at the team's sheer smugness. Mickey is nevertheless pining for her like Greyfriar's Bobby, and is simply too needy to have our sympathy. So the viewpoint character for this episode is a flatulent reptile who is trying to blow up the world. Margaret is given the chance to comment on the Doctor's lifestyle and self-justification, and there is never a satisfactory answer.

The Continuity

The Doctor He's now become outright flirtatious, matching Jack line-for-line. However, he does bristle, just a little, at the implication that he's not handsome [see the less-than-flattering insinuations he endured last episode]. He takes Margaret out for what can only be described as a dinner-date and, although denying any prior knowledge of her species, anticipates all her ploys to kill him. His choice of meal is steak and chips. [This is the first time we've seen him eat since 20.4, "Enlightenment", unless we count one jelly-baby in the TV Movie; he was supposedly vegetarian from 22.4, "The Two Doctors" onward.]

It's more noteworthy what he doesn't do. Margaret/Blon gets in a number of stinging barbs (metaphorical, after the real ones fail) about the Doctor's *modus operandi*, how he flees responsibility and appeases his conscience by letting a few of his opponents live. She has a degree of authority, being the sole survivor of his last encounter with her clan. The Doctor lets her continue; he makes a few comments about her morals, but never excuses his own. [It's as if having someone obviously debased making these accusations for him removes their force. It could also have another motive (see **Ethics**).]

[Interestingly, this is both the first and last time that this Doctor lets his guard down and simply relaxes in a strange city with his mates. It seems normal until you look at how short a time ago it was that this Doctor had a death-wish that hurled him into bizarre and dangerous situations just to feel alive and worthwhile (X1.2, "The End of the World"), or got fidgety when surrounded by ordinary people ("Aliens of London").]

He spectacularly fails to comprehend that the number of references to a "Bad Wolf" they've been seeing lately isn't a coincidence [see the next two episodes].

• *Ethics.* [Precisely how benign the Doctor is in this story depends on whether you think that he anticipated Blon's double-bluff and knew that the TARDIS would react as it did, by transforming her into an egg to live her life anew. If so, he is allowing Blon a second chance after she proves that she might have the capacity for redemption. If not, he is prevaricating over returning her to be executed in the vague hope that something will turn up and absolve him of this responsibility. In either case, he is apparently letting her accuse him of being

Does Being Made in Wales Matter?

continued from Page 171...

thing the BBC Wales website encouraged, with people texting in sightings of the cast and crew (subtly redacted when there was a spoiler afoot) and with details of what those locations were in real life.

This tension between the need for security, secrecy (especially lately) and uninterrupted shooting and the sense of ownership that the people of Cardiff have for the *Doctor Who* projects was most clearly demonstrated during the making of the *Torchwood* episode "Sleeper". This was about aliens planting bombs in key locations around Cardiff and, as such, needed the city centre to be the site of a fake explosion. The police put out bulletins to the effects that this wasn't a terrorist attack and everyone should avoid the area if possible, but of course this made people want to come and watch. And not everyone got the memos. Similar problems beset any attempt to use central Cardiff after dark, as there are a lot of pubs and nightclubs in a relatively small area (as you'll know from *Torchwood*). Any attempt to record dialogue at chucking-out time is doomed to failure (or redubbing - see X3.1, "Smith and Jones").

Central Cardiff also has the problem that it isn't London. Nevertheless, the series has traditionally assumed that the public are more familiar with even the suburbs of London than the relatively recently promoted touristy bits of Cardiff. This has meant a lot of grafting on of London landmarks in scenes shot in St Mary Street or the docks, with varying degrees of success (especially in *The Sarah Jane Adventures*, which purports to be set in Ealing). It also means that set-dressers have to be diligent in providing signage with London phone numbers and avoiding street-signs in Welsh. Outside the redeveloped central area are lots of generic "anytown" districts, some 1930s terraces, some concrete 1960s builds and a lot of Victorian streets, but redeveloped over the years and looking like the rest of Britain. Unlike many older towns, there have been very few preservation orders put on buildings that aren't castles or streets that aren't award-winning new developments. With the new-look Cardiff comes a paucity of period locations. Fortunately, there are a lot of small towns in the 50-mile radius that is a reasonable daily drive from Cardiff, and many of them are well-preserved from various eras. As the series has progressed, the number of space-ish places has slightly increased, but the degree of lateral thinking and audience indulgence has also had to rise. We land up with peculiar back-stories and scripted explanations of why the planet in "The Doctor's Daughter" (X4.6) has a military base resembling a school hall buried in soil, why acid is being pumped from beneath the North Sea into a castle (X6.5, "The Rebel Flesh") and why the Tower of London, transposed onto a spaceship, looks like a church crypt (X5.2, "The Beast Below", and the same one is in X5.10, "Vincent and the Doctor"). So far, no attempt has been made to explain why nearly every alien world seems to be entirely made up of beaches.

(Talking of which, for anyone who's not been there, South Wales is a crinkly part of the UK, with hills and valleys and above all a lot of coastline. This is why Cardiff, Newport and Swansea exist, but they are at the point where the Bristol Channel starts to narrow. So, on a clear day, one can see Devon on the other side of that channel. Getting a clear day is another matter as the Irish Sea, off to the west of the funnel-shaped Channel, is a bit turbulent. Torrential rain is a definite risk for any production in that area, although with the city itself forming a micro-climate, it's not even predictable. Of course, when they need it to be overcast and wintry looking - X3.0, "The Runaway Bride" - there's a record-breaking heat-wave and brilliant sunshine.)

One thing that cannot escape your notice (unless BBC America has cut straight to Graham Norton) is the sheer length of the end-credits. There are about 105 people listed, along with the cast for each episode and organisations such as Any Effects, BBC Wales Graphics and Millennium Effects. Most of those people are the same week after week, and are based in Cardiff. From Series Two onwards, there was a purpose-built complex for these big projects, the Upper Boat studios. Series One utilised three studios: one, at Culverhouse Cross owned by HTV (still used occasionally afterwards - it was Jackie's flat in Series Two and Gallifrey in X4.17, "The End of Time Part One"); the original BBC Wales studios in the heart

continued on Page 175...

X1.11 Boom Town

morally bankrupt as a means to assess her capacity for making judgements - he is looking at whether these are mere debating-points or signs of a conscience troubling her. And we are left to guess whether the Doctor thinks that a damaged TARDIS can look into Blon and see sufficient worth to have her reverted rather than evaporated. Similarly, whether you think that his monitoring of Rose and Mickey's date-oid is creepy or protective depends on what you think he is looking for: he glances at the screen and they are on it, but there's no sign that he tuned the scanner to them.]

He claims that Blon letting *one* of her victims go from time to time doesn't mean anything, and she responds with 'Only a killer would know that'.

• *Background.* He still doesn't know much about the planet Raxacoricofallapatorius beyond what he's read. [So it would seem that all that stuff he dredged from his memory in 10 Downing Street was just from background reading (see **He Remembers This *How*?** under X1.5, "World War Three") rather than from direct experience or a cerebral download of some kind - unless he's just lying to Blon to not tip his hand.] He does, at least, know the different biological methods by which Blon might try to kill him.

He and Rose have been to Justicia, the Glass Pyramid of San Kaloon and Woman Wept.

• *Inventory: Sonic Screwdriver.* It can over-ride and reverse teleport settings [as with "The End of the World"] - this time, the Doctor does it just by waving his little tool in the air [as with the transtemporal phone-calls, this is a facility that could have prevented 20.3, "Mawdryn Undead" from needing more than 90 seconds of screen-time].

• *Inventory: Other.* He's got a bog-standard mobile phone. [It's the sort of thing he might have bought in a shop.] The dialogue suggests that he pays for dinner with Margaret [so he has present-day sterling currency on his person, unlike "The End of the World"]. And against all the odds [or perhaps not, if he prepared in advance], he has an antidote to Raxacoricofallapatorian toxic halitosis in breath-spray form.

The TARDIS A brief, almost accurate description of police boxes is given by the Doctor's party. [They miss the rather obvious point that the phone was routed directly to the police station, rather than needing the kind of switchboard in use then - see 2.1, "Planet of Giants" for what a less-direct line would have been like.]

The TARDIS can soak up the imperceptible time-energy from the Rift under Cardiff [X1.3, "The Unquiet Dead"] and use it for fuel. This would, at the normal rate, take 48 hours. Blon's Extrapolator speeds this process up, but in so doing re-opens the Rift - causing lightning, small earthquakes and, if left unchecked, the implosion of Earth and a tidal wave of pure energy that can be surfed on by anyone using the Extrapolator.

The 'heart' of the TARDIS transforms Blon into an egg, and the Doctor assesses that this happens because the Ship is telepathic and the energy it here exudes can 'translate all sorts of thoughts'. [See, of course, "The Parting of the Ways."]

The Supporting Cast

• *Rose* has a long stripey scarf, but not the right kind [see Volume 4 if you really don't get it]. Notably, she seems wiling to spend the night in a hotel with Mickey, deeming it 'none of [the Doctor's] business'. She's taken to using words like 'lamenting' in everyday conversation with Mickey. She left her passport at home when she left with the Doctor. [As established in "Aliens of London". It's notable that she *has* a passport, though, which contradicts the version of her life-story Davies gave us in the Panini Annual - if her only trip abroad was a school trip, then a full adult passport would have been a costly and unnecessary upgrade. She must therefore have been further afield than Tenby in the last 18 months.] The Doctor offers her a chance to go and check on Mickey, but she declines.

• *Jack* has some idea of early twenty-first century slang and gestures [the "what-evah" W, 'cheesy' and 'bad' meaning 'good' - well, alright, that's 1970s, but close enough]. To judge by his attire, he appears to have spent some of his furlough in Cardiff at Top Shop [see X1.12, "Bad Wolf", although this must have been before Mickey arrived]. He carries potentially lethal electro-handcuffs around [just in case?], and tells the story of some event involving 15 naked people and a tusked creature that woke up suddenly. Like the Doctor, Rose and Mickey, Jack is armed with a mobile.

• *Mickey* claims to have been dating Trisha Delany. Rose seems to correctly assess that Mickey doesn't even *like* Trisha, to which he can only retort that at least he knows where she is. He tells Rose that her leaving made him feel like 'nothing'.

Does Being Made in Wales Matter?

continued from Page 173...

of Cardiff - briefly visible in "Boom Town" and used specially for fake news reports; and the Q2 complex, a converted factory with terrible acoustics. Meanwhile, the editing facilities and general production amenities were slowly being bolstered up to the standard needed for twenty-first century, internationally-exported fantasy-drama.

This becomes a lot more cost-effective if the studios are in constant use and the production staff were retained all year. Having to pay for part-timers or freelances would have been costlier than having permanent staff. To some extent, the two spin-off dramas and the two "making of" series accompanying the first two series made at Upper Boat were commissioned to make optimum use of this capacity and keep the wages bill manageable. It's not just that finally they could commit resources to *The Sarah Jane Adventures*, *Doctor Who Confidential*, *Torchwood*, *Totally Doctor Who* and *Torchwood Declassified*, it was more that they *had* to, simply to keep *Doctor Who* viable until other long-running series relocated or begin in Cardiff. Three series with standing-sets made more efficient use of the studios than one alone could. The two spin-off dramas were for very different audiences and premiered on different digital BBC channels. (To begin with, at least. *Torchwood* was explicitly targeted at the 16-24 age-range and made for BBC3, with BBC2 repeats. However, its growing success led to BBC2 getting first dibs on the second series - until scheduling problems arose later in the run - and BBC1 getting both "Children of Earth" and "Miracle Day".)

As we will see in **Has All the Puff "Totally" Changed Things?** under X2.1, "New Earth", there were strategic reasons for the BBC to be moving in this direction, and *Doctor Who* and its derivatives were deployed cold-bloodedly to reposition the Corporation in the global marketplace. However, from the point of view of how this affected the on-screen material in any given episode of *Doctor Who*, the main effect was economies of scale. When the series had been made in London, they had whatever sets and props, costumes and monsters were lying around in Television Centre, as well as any specially constructed materials (which would themselves vanish into this pool of resources, to be re-used on comedy shows or *Blake's 7* - assuming you don't bracket that as comedy too). After seven years and three not-quite separate series and a few totally unrelated ones, the BBC Wales complex is now almost up to this strength-in-depth. The drawback was that, of all of these series, *Doctor Who* was the one most likely to have been seen by viewers or one or more of the others, so whereas a CG alien effect from *Torchwood* could be re-used in *The Sarah Jane Adventures* on the grounds that most viewers of the latter would have been forbidden to watch the former (and not all of the former's fans would bother with the latter), for *Doctor Who* the main benefit was experience and expertise was retained and honed. Locations used in the subsidiary series could be re-used and occasionally items in *Doctor Who* were tried out in the other shows. The thriller aspects of "The Sound of Drums" (X3.12) were things that *Torchwood* had already got off pat.

With the government-enforced cuts in the Corporation's income forcing London-based productions out of that city and into new regional centres, Cardiff is going to be the main home of BBC drama. This is something *Doctor Who* pioneered seven years earlier. It will, presumably, become a lot easier for productions using guest-artists to ferry them between shows if both are being made in the Welsh capital. Getting this started back in 2003 was harder by far. Not only is there the problem of their other work-commitments, but they have to get across to Wales and stay there for however long it takes, with the knock-on effect that reshoots or pick-up shots are that bit more difficult if needed at short notice. Very few big-name actors are based within easy commuting-distance of Cardiff. This isn't always a problem; Maureen Lipman (X2.7, "The Idiot's Lantern") was only free for a few hours in one week, but as her part only required her to be on a television screen, they were able to record these in a nearby smaller studio (in fact, the BBC's original studio in Alexandra Palace). However, with television production distributed around Britain - both with regional power-bases amongst the BBC and the independent companies using former ITV studios - it isn't unusual for the shooting-schedule of *Doctor Who* to be worked out around when an actor can physically get there. The making of

continued on Page 177...

X1.11 Boom Town

He's saved a little money, and could afford a night in a hotel room for him and Rose if necessary. [We have to wonder whether he thought he'd be going home immediately after handing over the passport. If he can get an open-ended return train fare from London to Cardiff at short notice, he must have more than a little money.] He still reacts badly to being called 'Ricky' [as if he's forgotten this trick]. When an earthquake hits and Rose runs off to the TARDIS, Mickey's first thought seems to be of his relationship with her rather than the crisis at hand.

• *Torchwood*. [As we later discover in the first *Torchwood* episode, "Everything Changes", the opening of the Rift left a low-level perception-filter around the square metre or so where the TARDIS had been standing. As Torchwood 3 has been under this square for over 130 years by this stage, it's not the ideal place for the Doctor to have parked, but it left the Torchwood staff with an invisible entrance - they built a lift from the Torchwood Hub to that square metre-and-a-bit, and can exit without the public seeing them. It seems reasonable to presume, therefore, that Jack-in-the-future - who's been in Cardiff since the 1880s and working for this sinister organisation for about a century (see *Torchwood*: "Fragments") - arranged for his little team to take today off and leave the city undefended against the alien they knowingly let become Lord Mayor as she tries to blow it up. Given that *Torchwood* wasn't in anyone's mind when they made this episode, the fact that Margaret indicates that she lives in the same block of flats where we see Owen Harper's pad is an unfortunate coincidence, and not a slur on his alien-detecting abilities. She might even be lying.]

The Supporting Cast (Probably Evil)

• Blon Fel Fotch Pasimir Day Slitheen. Although keen to leave Earth, and apparently dismissive of the humans, Blon has started to get comfortable in someone else's skin. She has become interested in cooked food and even catches herself starting to 'sound like a Welshman'. It would appear that she drinks tea when nobody's watching [so it isn't just part of her disguise]. Although she is given to slightly Victorian turns of phrase ('with child', 'take sup'), she's able to use current idioms ('dinner and bondage - works for me') and knows which buttons to push when manipulating humans.

Planet Notes

• Raxacoricofallapatorius has the death penalty and can sentence entire families *in absentia*. Nonetheless, there are thousands of the Slitheen clan on other worlds. [Most of them will be showing up in Bannerman Road, Ealing.] They are raised from birth to obey their blood-lust, and Blon seems typical in that she made her first kill at age 13. [We have no idea how long their year is, but this seems young to her.] Criminals are thrown to the Venom Grubs [yes, the same ones from 2.5, "The Web Planet" - this seems to indicate that Raxacoricofallapatorius is in the Isop galaxy, and that the Venom Grubs are not confined to Vortis]. The executions are public and entail weak acetic acid - the convict remains conscious and in pain as a pool of liquid. The dominant species grow from large eggs that have tentacles, look like tubers and are hatched in cubicles. The females can fire poison darts or, *in extremis*, exhale toxic dust.

• *Woman Wept* froze in an instant, leaving the waves and foam in an icy snapshot. This creates hundred-foot breakers that people can walk under, except that there are no people for thousands of miles on the beaches. The world gets its name from a continent that, when seen from space, resembles a bowed, lacrymose female figure. [Precisely who gave it that name if nobody's there is another matter. We will hear of this world again in X4.12, "The Stolen Earth".]

History

• *Dating*. It's 'six months' on from the attack on 10 Downing Street in March 2006, so it's presumably September 2006. Cardiff has a Lord Mayor [an appointed post rather than elected, and the title applies to women too - "Lady Mayoress" is the Lord Mayor's wife], and somehow Margaret Blaine secured this post despite neither being Welsh nor having been to Cardiff before the election [still less actually being Margaret Blaine any more]. Such is the new Mayor's clout with the burghers of the city that she has secured a deal to demolish Cardiff Castle and put a nuclear power plant in the heart of the Welsh capital. She has got the green light for this despite the "unfortunate" accidents that befell the European Commission's safety regulators, the Cardiff Heritage Committee, the chief architect of the site and Mr Cleaver, the nuclear expert who has posted online notes about some design flaws.

Does Being Made in Wales Matter?

continued from Page 175...

"Boom Town" required complex negotiations for Annette Badland to be freed from *Cutting It*, made in Manchester. (American or Australian readers please note: flying from city to city is just not possible here unless you are stupidly rich and live in a city with a regular scheduled shuttle-service. Manchester and Cardiff are close enough for this not to be viable, but not so close that a train or car journey is something you do nonchalantly. Indeed, sometimes an unexpected train journey is costlier than flying, and renting a flat there for a week might be cheaper than either.)

This is compounded when there is a long location shoot somewhere else as well as work in Cardiff. "Vincent and the Doctor" was a nightmare because they cast Tony Curran, now a resident of Los Angeles, as Vincent and had to ferry him first to Croatia, then home for Christmas, then back to Cardiff for the interiors (where he was hurled about on a Kirby wire whilst jet-lagged). One thing the guest-cast regularly commented upon was that the tight-knit unit were friendlier and more efficient than most crews they had worked with. This is remarkable, as efficiency often comes at the expense of friendliness and vice versa. (Although the majority of these reports come from Series Two. One of the more plausible stories about Eccleston's departure suggests that the gruelling schedule may have caused tempers to fray, as we will see in the next essay.) It's certainly true that the regular cast got to know the majority of the production team by name and could tease them (and vice versa). And a lot of the smaller parts went to locals: just as British viewers thought of *Xena: Warrior Princess* and *FarScape* as the retirement plans for any Australian actor trying to get away from *Neighbours* or *Home and Away*, so *Doctor Who*, especially early in the new version, looked like the *Pobol Y Cwm* escape-committee.

It's possible that a different city might have got the nod back in 2003. Manchester or Birmingham, both localised centres of types of television and both used by the BBC, could have done the job. Birmingham, as base of the training unit and the daily *Doctors*, a production line for new writers and directors and the pet project of original executive producer Mal Young, might well have become the base for *Doctor Who*. However, with the BBC already committed to investment in the Cardiff studios, not least as part of the deal for the Welsh-language broadcasting stipulated by law, it was easier to upgrade the facilities there to the point where they could make a world-class, effects-driven series as part of rolling improvements already under way. Cardiff got *Doctor Who* dropped on it, and the difficulties of getting it up and running were substantial enough. The lack of alien planets was noted even by the BBC's Director General, Greg Dyke. There were jokes, especially amongst comedians old enough to remember what *Doctor Who* had been like in the 70s, to the effect that this was a series about an alien with a time machine able to travel the length and breadth of Cardiff. It's significant that we wait until the second series before we get to see a different planet and that's called New Earth, populated by familiar-looking aliens and two characters we've already met. Without the equipment, local support, motivated staff and relative isolation that BBC Wales had in the first year, even this much would have been impossible.

The Time Rift in Cardiff ["The Unquiet Dead"] has been sealed since 1869, but left a scar from which temporal energy seeps, harmlessly and undetectably, in sufficient quantities for the TARDIS to refuel in 24 hours. [This isn't *quite* the impression we get from *Torchwood*. In that series, the Rift has been open across history and allowing slippage from across the cosmos and all through time. If what the Doctor, Rose and Jack tell Mickey is taken at face value, then aircraft from 1953, Roman centurions and Weevils couldn't have come to present-day Cardiff; neither could Jack and Tosh have gone to 1941. And that's just three episodes from Series One.]

Blon suggests that second-hand, contraband or black-market space technology can be picked up at airlock sales [presumably, a bit like a car-boot sale].

Catchphrase Counter Blon's Extrapolator-surfboard - the means by which she intends to escape after destroying Earth - gets one 'fantastic' from the Doctor, and Rose gets one from Mickey. [Is he subconsciously emulating her hero?]

Deus Ex Machina This is the story where the Doctor is spared an icky ethical dilemma by the TARDIS magically turning a war-criminal whom the Doctor rather likes into a tuberous egg with dreadlocks, so that he can return her to Raxacoricofallapatorius without sending her to be painfully executed and allow her to start all over again as a literally new person.

The Analysis

The Big Picture As we mentioned in the revised Volume 3, Wales periodically gets very assertively self-confident. 1973 was a high point, where the combination of cultural kudos, political clout (during periods when coal-miners managed to exert influence over a government that had lost control of the economy) and unapologetically Welsh public figures were keeping attention on the principality.

1996 was another. Many of the young, popular and articulate Welsh rock-stars, broadcasters and opinion-makers were children of the early seventies flowering. It helped their cause that the increasingly unpopular Tory government had imposed a succession of accident-prone Englishmen as Welsh Secretary - if Welsh independence had not seemed like a good idea before John Redwood had been parachuted in from London, it certainly did afterwards. Economically, Wales had suffered greatly and disproportionately over the previous two decades: coal-mining had been wiped out almost completely by Margaret Thatcher's government (see 22.3, "The Mark of the Rani") and entire towns which had been built around the pits were devastated. One of the traditional solutions to such deprivation was investment in big showcase rebuilding schemes, using money from the European Union, to change the image of a region and thus supposedly attract employers and long-term redevelopment. Cardiff, like Liverpool, London's Docklands (X2.12, "Army of Ghosts"), Newcastle and others received EU Schedule One loans, in sums reckoned by experts to run to "shedloads", for redevelopment in the mid-90s. Then, once an election was finally called and New Labour won an unprecedented landslide victory, Wales and Scotland were given the chance to vote in referenda on increased independence. Although the terms were not the full sovereignty that the Scottish Nationalist Party and Plaid Cymru (the Welsh separatists) would have wanted, what was on offer was far more than the Tories had ever contemplated and voted for resoundingly in both cases. This caused even more investment in Cardiff, as a new Assembly for the nation was needed, with its own civil service and so on and a shiny new building (the gold-roofed tortoise-shaped thing you can see in helicopter shots of the city whenever Captain Jack feels like standing on a tall roof like Angel).

Meanwhile, the proud heritage of Cardiff Arms Park, the spiritual home of Rugby (although residents of Twickenham might disagree) was to be continued in a new, vast complex: the Millennium Stadium. In 1999, this was firmly put on the map when it hosted the event of New Year's Eve that a lot of people forced to attend the pompous event in the Dome at Greenwich would rather have been at: the Manic Street Preachers' massive gig. This band had been one of the many successful Welsh acts of the previous five years (although they never performed in the Welsh language - Super Furry Animals had bagged that niche). The Stadium would later be used for the FA Cup Finals while the Wembley Stadium was rebuilt over several years, so football fans from across the world got to know it well. The immediate practical effect of this is that the rest of Britain may have continued to make snide comments about Wales in general, but they all had to deal with Cardiff differently. Whether any of this investment had trickled down to those former mining towns is a moot point: anyone who could was probably planning to move to Cardiff, leaving the rest of South Wales even worse off. The visibility of the new city was part of a political rhetoric of a changed, twenty-first century Britain (just count all the uses of "Millennium" in the dock redevelopment). As we have seen (not least in **Why Now? Why Wales?** under X1.1, "Rose"), both Welsh-language broadcasting and Cardiff-made drama for local and national consumption ("national" in this case meaning Britain, not just Wales) was on the increase, and this had allowed the executives at S4C and BBC Wales to do a bit of empire-building.

So with the new-look Cardiff in the foreground, as a city rather than as a set of new buildings being opened on news reports, the old-style provincial city was relegated to being used as locations standing in for other places (usually London). Nevertheless, the script for this episode makes it clear that bulldozing the past was something the Bad Guys did. The plan to build a nuclear power plant on the site of Cardiff Castle was a *reductio ad absurdum* of the redevelopment frenzy this regeneration project had spawned over the previous decade. Politicians were mainly wary of supporting nuclear power, although the Enron scandal and the Gulf War had led to a lot of them making efforts to avoid seeming to be in the pockets of the oil lobby.

What we're getting at, in short, is that Cardiff was now a recognisable and desirable "brand". All the effort into reconfiguring both the Welsh economic and political structure and the image of Wales in the rest of Britain had been focussed on Cardiff (with a bit of "me-too" in Swansea). It was not just "iconic", it was *totemic*. The existence of this image was supposed to have power in itself. However much the rest of Wales was still thought of as rural, derelict, resentful, insular, unhealthy and damp (see 10.5, "The Green Death", a compendium of London-based writers' prejudices), Cardiff was young, sexy, affluent and slightly exotic. (At least, that square mile of it was... see the essay with this story.)

As we will see in **Production**, the script for this episode was the last to be begun and came as a replacement for a much costlier project. In keeping the locations largely untouched and making Cardiff the focus of the story, it was possible that they could have launched a whole new phase of the series (if it were to be re-commissioned) based there rather than London, and avoid having to go to the capital for location-work. As it turned out, a spin-off set entirely in Cardiff came shortly afterwards and it is hard, with hindsight, not to see this episode as a set-up for *Torchwood*. Certainly, the name (an anagram of *Doctor Who*) attributed to the "guerrilla" filming of New *Who* by this stage, to help conceal from prying eyes which show was *really* being worked on. Apart from re-using Margaret Blaine (or, more to the point, Annette Badland) and introducing the idea of the "heart" of the TARDIS to set up the regeneration/season ending, this episode is diligent in establishing present-day Cardiff as a place where any number of (low-budget) adventures could plausibly happen as a result of the Time Rift.

English Lessons *Isle of Dogs* (n): About a mile and a half east of Westminster, but almost another world. It's opposite Greenwich on the north of the Thames, and isn't really an island. And there aren't that many more dogs than anywhere else. It was the bit of Docklands that was used by Sir Joseph Bazalgette for sewage treatment (see X4.14, "The Next Doctor"), and the last to be given any attention during the 1980s attempt to turn the various quays into ersatz Manhattan ("Army of Ghosts"). The Vietnam scenes from *Full Metal Jacket* were made there, but it's not like that now; they've got a Tesco and everything.

Welsh Lessons
- *Heddlu* is, obviously, "Police". In case you somehow missed Volumes 6 and 3b, the "dd" is pronounced as a "th" and the "u" is closer to an "eo". (Quite why not all of the police-cars in this episode had this on is a puzzle.)
- *Cymru*. Wales itself - but it sounds more like "comree".

Oh, Isn't That...?
- *William Thomas* (Mr Cleaver). As we indicated above, he's been in the old series (25.1, "Remembrance of the Daleks"). He was also Gwen's dad Geraint in *Torchwood*, and Welsh viewers will have seen him in shedloads of things. *Belonging*, for example.

Things That Don't Make Sense All right, Margaret is Lord Mayor, but surely an up-market restaurant like Bistro 10 would have learned to keep their notoriously flatulent regular a bit further away from the rest of the customers. How often have the staff offered her "a waffer theen meent"? (That's a point: how come she suddenly learns to control her botty-burps once the Doctor shows up?)

Margaret seems to have become Lord Mayor without any publicity, and the fact that the first photo of her makes the front page - and shows her looking shifty - is apparently unremarkable. If she's managed to secure this job with a word in the right ear (and rivals having unfortunate accidents), well and good, but why stage and attend a press conference? And the original excuse for her to be in charge of the PM's security ("Aliens of London") was that the real Margaret worked for MI5. This would ordinarily debarr her from holding any public office, especially a mere six months after witnesses saw her in Downing Street moments before a missile hit, and then suddenly she was in the Isle of Dogs. There would have

1.11 Boom Town

been an enquiry running for months, and thus Margaret would have been out of the running for Mayor for that year at least.

It's also on record that she drove the car that killed an architect affiliated with her nuclear power project, and yet (as far as we're told) there was no inquest or even the slightest hint of suspension whilst the police investigated this convenient tragedy. (We know from *Torchwood* that the police in Cardiff are a bit dense, but this looks a lot more suspect than Cathy - the *remarkably* incurious journalist - has realised.) There is also the small matter of her being implicated in the murder of a Prime Minister and a "hoax" alien invasion ("Aliens of London"). If nothing else, we are given to understand that this story takes place in the early days of Harriet Jones' term of office - that's the same Harriet Jones that Margaret threatened in the Cabinet office whilst in her human skin. Even if the general public are unaware of this, the PM has the intelligence services at her disposal and might, perhaps, have been alerted to their former employee, responsible for the safety of her deceased predecessor, getting a high-profile job in one of the capital cities of Britain.

Getting clearance for a nuclear power station even in a remote corner of Wales is a process that takes five to ten years of consultation and public meetings, surveyors' results and lots of lawyers. Getting one on the site of a national monument in the middle of the Welsh capital - and nobody complaining - is as impossible as getting all this approved by the Welsh Assembly and Westminster. London might not care what happens in Cardiff, but the Assembly Members who meet in that big building with the gold-coloured roof would be a bit upset. Especially if they had apartments in the city centre and property values plummeted. They have jobs for five years at a stretch, depending on how well they do in elections. The Lord Mayor is an appointed post and lasts for one year.

There's also the problem that if a nuclear power-station next to the Rift is such a catastrophically bad idea, then Turnmills, the one that's been up and running for about 30 years in the *Torchwood* episode "Exit Wounds", was a monumentally stupid notion, and one Torchwood/Captain Jack was in a position to have prevented.

The provenance of the Extrapolator hardly matters, except that the logic of the story means that it must have come into Margaret's hands after the Downing Street caper. If she had such a handy (and potentially lucrative) bit of kit *before* that, why risk it being blown up with Earth? It can't have been in the Slitheen's spaceship, because she's stuck on Earth. And it wasn't the planned escape-route of the half-dozen Slitheen who were killed in "World War Three", because it's only big enough for one. (We'll assume that the basic plan was to teleport to a mothership as Earth went kablooey, and that a glitch sent Margaret to Beckton.) If she had it as a Plan B for the possible failure of the scheme to destroy Earth, then she must have had a fairly advanced plan to become Lord Mayor of Cardiff before murdering the real Margaret.

We'll buy that Rose needs the words on the poster translated into English despite the plot relying on us remembering that the TARDIS translates everything, but even when the Doctor speaks the words 'Blaidd Drwg', she has to be told it means 'Bad Wolf'. The ominousness of this name seems to have also slipped past all the many, many Welsh-speakers who live in Cardiff.

Mickey's got a train from London to Cardiff, responding almost immediately to Rose's call. He doesn't seem to be going home any time before midnight, so he must have planned for a hotel stay. It's September, probably, so the sun sets at eight, making it about ten when he suggests it to Rose, as if he's just thought of it. If he was planning to get back to London that day, he'd've had to have left by then. Anyone planning a rail journey from London to Cardiff and back has to either plan better than this or have a week's wages for a motor-mechanic just lying around. You don't do it on a whim, and definitely not on someone else's whims. We're not saying that he doesn't carry enough of a torch for Rose to make this plausible, but she's relying on him being able to do this simply because she feels a bit guilty, and wants to see him again to get absolution.

Rose runs across the square, ignoring the huge rents and clefts that have opened in the ground. (It's almost as if she thinks they've just been drawn on in post-production.) Her method for finding Mickey at story's end entails her asking the police some derivation of, "Have you seen a bloke in a parka, probably scowling?", as opposed to just calling him on her mobile. (Is all the Rift energy in the area disrupting communications?)

The TARDIS opening is an unprecedented catastrophe - but there's a switch on the console to fix it afterwards.

Critique Bloody typical! No sooner does Eccleston get the hang of this Doctoring thing than he's off the show. In fact, all but three of the speaking roles are people who've done this before, just not in this combination. The effects team(s) have worked out how *not* to do Slitheen, and Davies has seen what works before writing this. A small point worth making again is that, after the toilet scene, Margaret/ Blon doesn't make any sounds that aren't speech. Once we've been reminded of (or introduced to) the idea of aliens squeezed into human skins, the joke isn't needed any more and we can get on with a character-piece.

Davies has kept in sight his original main objective: to use the *Doctor Who* format to tell stories that can be watched collectively by a whole family and could never happen otherwise. This is a risky venture. Over the decade and a half when the series was off the air, television had fragmented into niches and "demographics" (when the word "demographic" became a noun is unclear, but that day was where future historians will date the start of the collapse of Western civilisation). This is something to be borne in mind at all times - that we are watching the first television drama for ages to be intended for general consumption rather than targeted after careful research and testing. There may be a lot of people who enjoy it more than anything else currently being made, but no one section of the British public owns it, and *certainly* nobody outside Britain. So if one or more element of a given episode isn't precisely what one individual likes, that person can rant online or make suggestions to the producers... but there will most likely be an equal number of viewers who thought it was the best bit. As it happens, very little in "Boom Town" actively offended the clingy fans, but not a lot made anyone's heart beat faster. It did the job.

Is that enough, though? "Aliens of London" and "World War Three" had significant flaws and teething troubles, but lodged in the public's memory far more than this. Is the lack of any major goofs with the Slitheen costume a problem with this episode? Was playing safe and bringing back elements that had already been tried in a slightly different context making this a "routine" *Doctor Who* episode, something we were led to think couldn't exist? Obviously not: as we just said, this is almost the only time we see a non-angsty Eccleston. Most significantly, he shows a remarkable calm in the face of Blon's accusations of the Doctor's callous nature. This isn't just screensaver-face, it's an active effort to let her talk and not rise to the bait.

This story is the flip-side of "The Long Game" (X1.7). There, the discovery that this was really just part of a bigger story led people to re-evaluate the episode upwards with hindsight. Now, with the consequences of this story overshadowing it, we lose sight of its original job of making full use of what this version of *Doctor Who* has to play with that earlier iterations and other TV shows don't. Even more so than the next episode's run-through of affectionately parodied gameshows, this looks like channel-zapping. We've got a grotesque satire on the Welsh Development Agency (trashing the city centre and historic monuments to build a nuclear reactor and getting applauded for it by simply saying "It'll bring jobs") that's straight out of *Spitting Image* or *The New Statesman* (the sitcom, not the august magazine); the Mickey-Rose soap is getting a bit *Hollyoaks*; the Doctor's dinner with Blon begins like *The Princess Bride* and ends like Harold Pinter; and the climax is like a freakish episode of *Stargate SG-1* that they've set in Wales rather than Canada-pretending-to-be-America-or-another-planet. Not only does this all hang together, but every scene seems like a logical consequence of what's gone before rather than just what they could afford to do or felt like doing.

Fundamentally, this is an excuse to give the Doctor and Blon more screen-time together. Mickey and Rose are mercifully relegated to being the B-plot, where she belongs, frankly, as Rose has long since ceased to be any kind of audience-identification figure. In her treatment of Mickey, we get what has to be seen as a concerted effort to remove any sympathy casual viewers might have for her. This comes at a price: a lot of what is to follow depends on us seeing why all these men are so concerned about her. Instead, we now see things through the Doctor's eyes as much as anyone's.

But given that the only major costs are an effect of the energy ripping through the TARDIS to the sky, a sheet of shatter-glass and a re-use of an alien costume and one guest artist, this episode ought to have been more perfunctory than it is. It is considerably more than the sum of its parts, and the first sign of a new form of *Doctor Who* waiting to be born - one about the consequences of the big show-offy effects and set pieces of earlier episodes, rather than just setting these up.

X1.11 Boom Town

The Facts

Written by Russell T Davies. Directed by Joe Ahearne. Viewing figures: (BBC1) 7.68 million, (BBC3 repeats) 0.2 and 0.5 million.

Repeats and Overseas Promotion L'exlosion de Cardiff, Der Spalt, Atomowe miasto.

Production

This story was given a whole production block to itself. There needed to be a gap between "The Long Game" and the two-part season finale made substantially on the same sets, redressed. The only use of the studio at Unit Q2 in "The Empty Child"/ "The Doctor Dances" (X1.9/10) had been Jack's ship (although after production on "Boom Town" had begun, the scenes in Mr Lloyd's house and the "extra" scenes at the Den were made there). Most of the World War II story and all but the TARDIS scenes in "Boom Town" were made on location. This allowed both the small but significant changes to Satellite Five, and the rewrites of the climax to allow for the regeneration. It was also a means to consolidate the revised TARDIS crew, making new character "Jax" seem more than just a contrivance for the finale.

The precise nature of the story was decided long after this cost-cutting, team-building exercise was planned. One reason for this was that they had a Cunning Plan - call in Paul Abbott, Davies' mentor and currently the hottest writer in British television, and let him do whatever he wanted. This has led to all manner of rumours about unsuitable story proposals, but he was flat-out busy on the first of many series of *Shameless*. One idea Davies had proposed was a story about the eruption of Pompeii (see X4.2, "The Fires of Pompeii" and the comment in "The Empty Child" about "volcano day"). As we now know, making a story of that kind required Cinecitta in Rome. Davies, with a bit of prompting from Julie Gardner, opted for something they could make in the new-look, exciting Cardiff. Showing off the city that was *Doctor Who*'s new home was making a virtue of a necessity and, it has to be admitted, a chance to see a city not often shown off to this extent (see **The Big Picture**).

- By now, Davies had worked out/decided/been told that Eccleston was on his way out at the end of the season. He had also decided that, after paying so much for the suits and realising how little he had given Annette Badland to do, the Slitheen (or one of them) deserved a second chance. The two-part Downing Street story had already been made and largely edited by the time Davies had to begin writing this, the last script to be begun for Series One. A story which introduced the TARDIS energy-source as a conscious entity, was set in present-day Cardiff and reworked the Time Rift from "The Unquiet Dead", showed the new team having "the Right Stuff" (even Mickey) and allowed the Doctor to finally notice the words "Bad Wolf" stalking him all crystallised around the idea of Margaret Slitheen being captured and taken to her death. The storyline for "Dining with Monsters" (as it was briefly called) also left open the potential for the rough idea for Series Two that was developing. One of the production team had devised the anagram "Torchwood" to prevent the kind of public spectacle that accompanied the shooting of the Nestene massacre in X1.1, "Rose", and the name began to develop a life of its own, first being mentioned as an answer in *The Weakest Link* (X1.12, "Bad Wolf").

- At first, this story was to be a completely effects-less episode. With five of the eight speaking-roles being returning characters, less time was needed to establish them all, but instead the focus was on how they interact. This opened up a potential problem with timing: Badland was filming in Manchester for another series (hairdressing-themed bitchfest *Cutting It* - see X3.0, "The Runaway Bride"). Eccleston was also unavailable for some days due to a family bereavement. The director chosen for this story was Joe Ahearne, who had already been rostered on to do the two-part finale and had earlier directed Block Three (X1.6, "Dalek"; "Father's Day"). His calm, methodical approach had gone down well with Eccleston and Piper. The first-draft script was ready in late November and, with a few small tweaks, was practically what we saw (the name of one planet the Doctor and Rose visited was changed to "Justicia" to tie in with the forthcoming novel *The Monsters Inside*). Permission was sought from the *Western Mail* to use their masthead for a fake edition. The Tone Meeting was on 12th January, and the first shooting was a week later, the day after Ahearne finished editing his previous two episodes.

- The timetabling of Badland's trips to Cardiff meant that the dinner sequence needed to be recorded on a night during Block Four, so Eccleston and Badland went to Bistro 10 on 19th January. Barrowman and Piper spent that day in Q2 for the scenes on Jack's ship. A lot of redubbing and editing was needed for this, as the dolly for the camera made hefty clunking noises. Bistro 10 is a real restaurant (although there's no food being eaten in this sequence), and so the sheet of glass that was to shatter needed to be replaced with a fake (lacking the logo). The woman closest to that window, Kim Garrity, also doubled for Piper in some of the later long shots in this episode.

Almost two weeks later, another building owned by the University of Wales, the Glamorgan Building (which, on broadcast, viewers had just seen as the Officers' Club in "The Empty Child") played itself as Noel Clarke returned to the fold for the first time since pick-up shots for episode four in early November. This was the start of the chase in the corridors (and thus didn't need Eccleston, who was given a day off). By night they went to Mermaid Quay, just around the corner, to record scenes with Piper and Clarke (including the stuff seen on the TARDIS monitor two days later back at Q2). The following day was more of the same, with the exteriors. Badland and Eccleston were back, and did the frantic running back to the TARDIS from the restaurant. Thursday was the day of the first TARDIS scenes, whilst Friday, back on location, had Mr Cleaver's death and Margaret's bid to escape the "gang". Ahearne took advantage of Alan Ruscoe's experience with the Slitheen costume to work out what was possible, and rehearsed thoroughly. Badland was on-set, so where dialogue for the original Blon back in July had been dubbed onto footage of an animatronic head worked in synch to a floor-assistant saying the lines, this time the dialogue was faster and more in-character as a smoother "performance" from Neill Gorton's Millennium Effects team was possible. The head was used predominantly in close-up, and CG for full-frontal Slitheen action was now the preferred option.

• Everyone recalls the location shooting as being bitterly cold, which had the benefit of keeping low the number of onlookers and members of the general public. On one night the fountain stopped, as it was programmed not to run when the temperature got below 3 degrees Celsius. Most days, the noise of the water meant a lot of post-synching in ADR. As Saturday *would* be a busy day for the locations, the TARDIS scenes with Blon's claw were recorded next. The egg prop was one of the ostrich eggs made for "The End of the World".

The next work on this episode was on the Tuesday, in the morning, for the Bosphorus Restaurant sequence. This week's production was interspersed with work on Block Four, including Barrowman returning to the Glamorgan Building for the "excellent bottom" sequence of "The Empty Child" later that night. That shoot occupied the regulars for the next day, and more TARDIS scenes were completed the day after that, so it was on Valentine's Day (the following Monday) that Badland did her scenes with the press-launch for Blaidd Drwg. Mali Harries, playing journalist Cathy Salt, had in real life just become a mother, and was anxious on her first working day away from the baby. The next day was the toilet scene (actually the Gentlemen's convenience at the Glamorgan Building), Mickey arriving in Cardiff and Rose running after him as the city trembled. In fact, Piper was off sick and, this being mainly long shots, was replaced by doubles. Clarke got a short train-ride from Newport (the original Welsh one, not Rhode Island - about five miles away). His arrival at the TARDIS was the next daytime shoot, before the effects team made fake neon lights start exploding. Apart from Barrowman opening the TARDIS door back at Q2 later that week, it was all done.

• If you've been counting during this and the last two episodes, you'll notice that Eccleston has had a week off since doing the TARDIS scenes on 10th February. According to some sources, this is when he received confirmation that he was being written out.

• By the time this was broadcast, the speculation on what exactly the Bad Wolf would turn out to be was getting ridiculous. Not quite as ridiculous as the truth turned out to be, though - the theories about Anubis, Adam's bid to change history and Fenris (see 26.3, "The Curse of Fenric") all fit the broadcast episodes better than what we got (see **Bad Wolf: What, Why and How?** under X1.13, "The Parting of the Ways"). Bookmakers were offering odds on it being Jackie. Some even seriously suggested that the prominent "Punky Fish" decal on Rose's tops might be a clue.

X1.12: "Bad Wolf"

(11th June, 2005)

Which One is This? It starts off as every major "reality" TV hit parodied, with the voices of the actual presenters and a couple of the real sets, then in the closing minutes it all kicks off - and 40 years on, *Doctor Who* finally looks like the *TV21* comic strips.

Firsts and Lasts There were on-screen dating captions in "Silver Nemesis" (25.3), but this is the first time we've had a minute-long synopsis of an earlier episode (1.7, "The Long Game") and then a black screen and an update ("100 years later"). The new-series introduction of the all-purpose sonic screwdriver here necessitates an all-purpose countermeasure: the Deadlock Seal. This is the first time the Time Vortex/end credits is used to denote "I'm having a flashback", as Rose remembers the times people have said "Bad Wolf" (regardless of whether she was there when they said it).

It's the first-ever mention of the name "Torchwood", although it's here spoken of as a place, not an organisation. Jack gets to do the first overt knob-joke in the programme's history: glancing down at his nakedness, he quips, "Ladies, your viewing figures just went up." (We might point out a few salacious double-entendres in the Troughton era and any number of stray remarks amenable to this sort of innuendo - but this is scripted.) Although there have been oblique references to the comic strips from *Doctor Who Monthly/Weekly/Magazine* in recent episodes (including a character-name in X1.4, "Aliens of London"), this is the first time the Doctor quotes a notorious panel from one... when declaring that he was "Gonna wipe every stinking Dalek out of the sky", he was repeating a boast by Absalom Daak, the Mad Max/Judge Dredd composite from the early 80s whom Marvel UK hoped would get a spin-off (they even had a flexi-disc single as a cover-mount[32]).

And the "heartbeat" sound effect from "The Daleks" (1.2) and all but one of the twentieth-century Dalek stories makes a long-awaited return. That makes this the first Welsh-made story where the cliffhanger hinges on us finding out who'd been behind everything we've seen so far, and the first time the hints are there to excite rather than mystify small viewers.

A small thing but pleasing for long-term fans: the word "transmat" makes a welcome return (12.2, "The Ark In Space" et seq; 20.7, "The Five Doctors"; 22.4, "The Two Doctors"). "Teleport" sounds like a town in South Wales.

Watch Out For...

• Leading into the credits is a spot-on recreation of the Channel 4 version of *Big Brother*, with the set, logo (slightly amended by Channel 4's staff - see **Production**), theme tune (instantly recognisable even if you've never seen the series, as it was a hit single and used in all the endless parodies of the series) and the voice of Davina McCall using a lot of the catch-phrases. One of these, "I'm coming ta get ya", is quoted by the Doctor at the end of the episode. The routine announcement "You are live, please do not swear" would have been redundant for any previous Doctor - but Eccleston, one suspects, might have said something that would have cross-faded into the theme-tune sting.

• The pre-credits sequence begins, however, with a lengthy montage of clips from "The Long Game", which might be considered a bit of a giveaway for one of the two big plot-twists here. As the other (the return of the Daleks) was proclaimed loudly in the Next Time trailer at the end of the previous episode, it would seem that the BBC Wales team have very little faith in the intelligence or attention-span of the average viewer. More charitably, we have chosen to think of this as a *homage* to Terry Nation, having the Controller talking cryptically about "My Masters" and "Them" for a whole episode (in amongst all sorts of teasing hints about who might be exterminating the Controller, what sucker-armed menace is gliding towards an incredulous Rose, and what kind of vicious, inhuman creatures might have sponsored *The Weakest Link*) before the big reveal of the shocking truth we've known for a whole week (see 10.4, "Planet of the Daleks"; 17.1, "Destiny of the Daleks").

• Rose's arrival at the studio for *The Weakest Link* is directed as if she thinks she's dreaming. Indeed, the entire game seems to be like those nightmares where you're sitting a test you haven't prepared for. Rose, however, is fully clothed...

• ... unlike John Barrowman, who is only the second person to have appeared naked in *Doctor Who*[33], and whose rear view was trimmed by the BBC before transmission. His modesty in frontal

Did He Fall or Was He Pushed?

As many of you will recall, the abrupt departure of Christopher Eccleston caused Outpost Gallifrey (as it was called then) to have to shut down for a day rather than melt the Internet. The posted comments veer from the hilarious to the deranged, and one frequently repeated line, asserting that "*Doctor Who* died today", has been used as a punchline by anyone with a low opinion of online fandom and any new development from BBC Wales.

The press release and subsequent clarifications and desperate back-pedalling added to the general hilarity. Eccleston himself has recently begun to open up about this, but doesn't name names and his answers are veiled in cryptic references to leaving taints on his soul and family. It's going to be a long time before the full story emerges, but so many wild and, frankly, loopy theories are still in circulation despite crucial facts disproving these being in the public domain that we can at least evaluate these. So all that follows is, if nothing else, *informed* guesswork.

Theory One: Typecasting

The BBC's initial press release suggested that Eccleston's decision to walk away from such a high-profile role was because he was concerned about the effect this would have on his future career. To be fair, being associated with playing the Doctor had damaged some of his predecessors' employment prospects - but it had, on the other hand, kept some of them in work.

If we look closely at this - and despite, as David Tennant said, having the first line of an actor's obituary pre-written for the rest of his life if he's been the Doctor - the only ones who, after a decent interval (call it five years) had not made an entirely new career were Tom Baker and Sylvester McCoy (William Hartnell is a different case). Neither would have had much of a career on television without *Doctor Who*, and theatre was their first love in both cases. However, the thing that created the impression that an ex-Doctor was doomed was Tom Baker's new career as professional self-parody as the voice of *Little Britain* and Mr Wyvern in *Randall & Hopkirk (Deceased)*, as reworked by Charlie Higson in 2000.

Was Eccleston realistic in thinking that, as a film star, iconic TV actor and known celebrity-advocate for causes, he would be consigned to always playing aliens with Salford accents? If anything, he had taken on the role to escape always being thought of as "intense" and "humourless". After playing the Son of God (in *The Second Coming*), there's only so much more anguish you can muster on screen before becoming a standing joke. Moreover, his next high-profile role was as the Invisible Man in *Heroes*[36] - not the actions of someone whose agent would get sacked if any more geek-friendly telly was offered. Look at the films he did in the next five years and many if not all (*The Dark is Rising*, etc.) were broadly Fantasy faff.

We come back to the basic fact that, as someone who grew up in the North of England in the 1980s, Eccleston views unemployment as a big worry - every time he does an interview for any of the many, diverse roles he's taken on since 2005, he mentions how long it had been since he last worked. (As we will see, he offers this as proof of integrity - "it's easy to find a job when you've got no morals", as he recently said.) Typecasting is not plausibly a worry for someone with this mentality. If he'd found a job that didn't compromise him, he would have stuck with it. If he was worried about offers not coming his way - if he was known to be handcuffed to a part that would take up nine months of each year for however long the contract ran - that's different. (As we will see in Volume 8, Tennant's offer to play Hamlet caused - or maybe allowed - the production to more or less shut down for six months.)

Films, however, could be to some extent scheduled to fit Eccleston's availability, and any low-budget, almost hit-and-run projects from Michael Winterbottom might have offered unannounced cameos in British-made films (along the lines of his scene-stealing bit-part as the Boethius-quoting beggar in *24 Hour Party People*) might have appealed to him. There's one persistent rumour that he quit specifically to be free for the part of the Albino in the film version of *The Da Vinci Code*. On the face of it, this is unlikely, especially if the near-certainty of *Doctor Who* running for several years was set against the possibility of the film bombing at the box-office. (Yes, it looks like a sure thing with hindsight... but so did *The Lovely Bones* and *The Golden Compass*.) Quitting just on the off-chance that the role would be offered to him and

continued on Page 187...

X1.12 Bad Wolf

shots is preserved by a gun-turret, which says it all.

• There is a school of thought that the first 39 minutes of this episode is prevaricating until the main event, but even when you know it's coming, the one big expensive shot of kerjillions of Daleks yelling "Ex-ter-min-ate" and levitating around for the benefit of anyone just joining after 20 years looks as though they are simply doing it *because they can*. The episode leading up to this could have made any monster perpetrating this scheme seem evil and devious and, frankly, the big pull-back-and-reveal would have been dramatically justified with just the three Dalek props they really had in the studio.

The Continuity

The Doctor He seems to know a lot about a timeline that shouldn't exist: He can preach about the world's population being 'sheep' and 'half the world too fat, half the world too thin', even as he is being introduced to the revised Earth by one of the *Big Brother* contestants, Lynda Moss. He also 'remembers' the Celebrity edition of *Bear With Me* where the bear gets into the bath [see **He Remembers This How?** under X1.5, "World War Three"]. His opinion of Reality TV is reassuringly low, and before he realises that the games are fatal, he is sardonic about the motives of contestants. He seems to think that Lynda is companion material.

When the Doctor believes Rose to be dead, he seems to go into a stupor, barely registering the outside world. He recovers to lead an assault on the security guards and then Level 500 - but, apart from sidestepping an oncoming guard and hurling him towards a wall, isn't violent about it. He is much more aggressive towards a recalcitrant computer that won't tell him Rose's location.

Strangely, he claims he just wants a quiet life.

• *Ethics*. After using a huge gun to get an appointment with the people on the top floor, he chucks it to one of the people he was threatening and says, 'like I was ever gonna shoot'.

• *Background*. Immediately prior to this, the Doctor, Rose and Jack were at Raxacoricofallapatorius [following events last episode], then Kyoto in 1336 [a much more interesting place and time than Cardiff 2006, but we don't know what happened on this occasion except that they only just escaped with their lives]. The Doctor knows that this particular *Big Brother* house in 2005 had a garden behind the black-glass windows that are impenetrable in the 200,100 version.

• *Inventory: Sonic Screwdriver*. It can zap the *Big Brother* cameras and get information out of monitors as per usual, but it can't open anything that's been Deadlock sealed. The Doctor can get energy readings by holding it vertically.

The TARDIS It appears that to penetrate the Ship's defences when it's in flight, a transmat beam has to be 15 million times stronger than usual. The Ship's onboard systems figure out the transmat scam and tell Jack what's going on. It doesn't have a garden [cf 15.6, "The Invasion of Time"].

The Supporting Cast

• *Rose* spends the first round of *The Weakest Link* convinced that she is dreaming / in a hoax / just playing a silly game. She takes it seriously when it turns out that the game-losers are (seemingly) killed, but she laughs insouciantly when she doesn't know an answer, and is nonchalant about voting other people off. Once it becomes real to her, she *still* thinks that it doesn't matter because the Doctor will arrive and sort things out. Once awake on the Dalek ship, she is incredulous [apparently assuming that the Dalek approaching must be the one she pitied in X1.6, "Dalek"].

• *Jack* tells the robots he's just deactivated with extreme intent, 'the pleasure was all mine, which is the only thing that matters in the end'. He manages this piece of vandalism with a 'Compact Laser Deluxe' [which the robots cite by name, so it's closer to the tech of this era than not] he had somehow secreted on his person whilst naked. Prior to this, his vanity allowed him to go along with the sartorial suggestions and be seen naked by millions. He'd considered a facelift [he will soon get a rather more extreme anti-ageing treatment] and resents being called an 'Oklahoma farm-boy'. He needs no command beyond 'let's do it' from the Doctor to assault and overpower guards and, once armed, takes control of the defence of Level 500 - 'do I look like an out-of-bounds kind of guy?' he jeers, holding up two sub-machine guns. All in all, he settles into the role of taking orders from the Doctor - of accepting that there's a chain of command in the TARDIS travellers - very well. His wrist-device can first locate the Doctor by a double-heartbeat and then,

Did He Fall or Was He Pushed?

continued from Page 185...

that the film would pay his bills for three or four years looks like a gamble. If, however, he was already planning to leave or thought he would be booted off the show, he might have lined up a few safety nets.

What we *can* say is that after Eccleston refuted the claim in subsequent interviews and the BBC hastily retracted the original statement, the theory that he left simply to avoid typecasting ought to have been dead in the water.

Theory Two: Workload

When the series returned, Russell T Davies justified his preference for younger Doctors by pointing out how punishing the relentless shooting-schedule was. Eccleston runs marathons for fun, so the physical demands on him may not have been the issue. However, Eccleston made similar comments after an eight-month stint where he had had little time to think about anything else.

It's noticeable that Eccleston's subsequent television roles have been for shorter-run series or projects where he is not the lead. One-off dramas such as *Lennon Naked*, brief series such as *The Shadow Line*, and not-quite guest roles, such as the aforementioned *Heroes*, have interspersed lucrative but relatively undemanding parts in dodgy blockbusters. Eccleston has veered away from theatre simply because the monotony of the same performance night after night for a long period frustrates him. He is certainly not alone in finding long production schedules on TV drama wearying - this is why John Simm only did two series of *Life on Mars*, and the writers had to reboot *Ashes to Ashes* to finish telling their story.

Modern television production, especially with BBC series being made in Cardiff, is a protracted period away from normal life and the usual support-network an actor can rely on (especially if that actor has finally bought a home in London to be near these people and most of the available work). These days, so much BBC drama is made in Cardiff that there is a fairly close-knit long-term "colony", but this wasn't the case in 2004. The only people anyone working on *Doctor Who* would see regularly would be colleagues. If they are of roughly the same generation, interests and temperament, this can be exhilarating - as the David Tennant-Catherine Tate partnership has shown when they have reunited for other projects, and the Smith/Gillan/Darvill team demonstrated in coping with the added burdens of US location filming. Before them, however, Piper was going through a traumatic divorce and Eccleston isn't known as a particularly affable, easygoing chap. Whilst it is sometimes reported that he acted as a support for Piper and helped shield her from tabloid intrusion, this would simply have reinforced the sense that being the Doctor was a full-time job.

During the production notes on the series so far in this book, you will have seen how few days off there were, and that Eccleston was taken ill during the making of the last five episodes. This, a family bereavement just before Christmas and the bout of flu caught during filming in a church (X1.8, "Father's Day") would have coincided with the window of opportunity for either signing on for a second series or bowing out in time for a regeneration or cliffhanger (depending on whether the series was renewed). After six months of 14-hour days, with Billie crying on your shoulder between takes, bad news from home and your holiday wrecked by coughing up lumps, you're hardly going to think "Yes, I want another year of this", are you? Well... maybe. As we will see in a while, it's a good reason to delay making a decision until you're on your feet and in a more even mood.

In a *Radio Times* interview to launch the Lennon play, Eccleston comes as close as he seems likely to confirming that this was at least a big contributory factor in his departure. He was quoted as saying, "I was open-minded, but I decided after my experience on the first series that I didn't want to do any more... I didn't enjoy the environment and the culture that we, the cast and crew, had to work in...." This can also cited as evidence for other theories, as we will see.

Theory Three: It was Only Supposed to be a Year

As we've been saying throughout this book, bringing back *Doctor Who* was a gamble. In the spring of 2004, it might have seemed like a one-off project, good for the CV and easy to recover from if it failed. If it succeeded, being able to walk away

continued on Page 189...

X1.12 Bad Wolf

more intriguingly, can isolate Rose out of thousands of humans on the Station.

He knows Dalek ships by sight and is aware of their reputation. Notably, Jack has a TARDIS key.

• *Torchwood*. The Anne-Droid asks: 'the Great Cobalt Pyramid is built on the remains of which famous old Earth institute?' and the answer is 'Torchwood'. [The question remains whether it's Canary Wharf, Plass Roald Dahl or Inverness that's got a thumping great carcinogenic monument slapped onto it.]

The Non-Humans

• *Daleks*. So, it was they who installed the Jagrafess. ["The Long Game". That's not their usual style, but the plan was initiated 190 years ago, and they're only ready to bring it to fruition now. The Controller alternatively claims that it took 'hundreds and hundreds of years'.] The Daleks seem to have been in rather desperate straights when the scheme began: It's a plan that involves forcing randomly-selected humans to compete and then letting the winners go, whilst transmatting the losers to a base of operations on the edge of the Solar System [somewhere in the general direction of the Horsehead Nebula, it seems]. There are now 200 Dalek ships, each containing something like 2000 Daleks. The ships are saucer-shaped, with hemispherical lumps on the base [see 2.2, "The Dalek Invasion of Earth", but more overtly the 60s TV 21 comic strip] and inside them are cylindrical tunnels with hexagonal, golden plates [like a honeycomb, or the Welsh Assembly building's roof... or the current configuration of the TARDIS].

With hindsight, a lot of their plan seems familiar... They have taken a five-year-old girl and plugged her into their computer to run the Games Station [cf 25.1, Remembrance of the Daleks"], but conditioned her adult self not to be able to think of their name. They have also taken advantage of an alteration of history to create a nightmarish future 200 or so years on where Earth is too weak to resist [9.1, "Day of the Daleks"].

[Two things seem slightly odd here. One is that when Rose loses *The Weakest Link*, she is zapped but sent straight to the Dalek mother-ship and used as a hostage in negotiations with the Doctor. The other is that, despite the sheer number of Daleks here and the sheer number of Time Lords they must have faced, the name 'Doctor' chimes with the Controller and is an especial fear of her Masters. So they must know that he survived the Time War. (See "Dalek" for speculation on this, and why they've got 2005 British game shows off pat.)]

Planet Notes *Mars* has Drones who get Default Social Security payments.

• They eat Gaffabeque on *Lucifer* [the *New Adventures* novel *Lucifer Rising*].

History

• *Dating*. The Doctor says it's 200,100 - a century on from his intervention in deposing the Jagrafess ["The Long Game"; the caption that opens the story concurs that it is now '100 years later']. In the wake of the Doctor's last visit, the government and economy of the Fourth Great and Bountiful Human Empire collapsed. Satellite Five became the Game Station, and is now run by the Bad Wolf Corporation. The extra moons seen above Earth are now absent.

Earth is now dangerously polluted, so the population have to stay indoors and watch game shows. Randomly selected members of the public are transmatted to the Game Station, in orbit above, and made to compete in fatal programmes [for a list of these, see **English Lessons**]. Failure to pay the telly tax can incur the death penalty. The continents are aligned almost as we remember them, with the Atlantic slightly smaller and more toxic. The Great Atlantic Smog Storm has been going for 20 years. Pola Ventura, Iceland, hosted Murder Spree 20. There is a Lunar Penal Colony [cf 10.3, "Frontier in Space"; X6.8, "Let's Kill Hitler"]. The Grand Central Ravine is named after Sheffield [an 'ancient' city, so it might not still be there].

Technology on Earth is still fairly stunted after the setbacks of "The Long Game"... Average life-expectancy is about what it is today, apparently, although nobody on the Game Station seems to be any older than 35. There are 'defabricators' that can remove clothing with a single blast, various weapons that are actually transmats [and which leave dusty deposits - see 21.7, "The Twin Dilemma" - but not Rice Krispies as in *The Sarah Jane Adventures*] and ordinary-looking submachine guns that fire Bastic bullets [22.6, "Revelation of the Daleks"].

Hoshbin Frane was President of the Red Velvets and Stella Pok Baint is a milliner. Pandoff comes after Hoob in the Pan Traffic Calendar (Clavadoe

Did He Fall or Was He Pushed?

continued from Page 187...

without the series ending is a good way for the glory to rub off on you (especially if the new guy doesn't catch on and the show ends there). You will always be remembered as "the man who saved *Doctor Who* from oblivion" (well, you and Davies). If you've played the role completely your own way, and changed what people expected, even better. So agreeing to come on board for one year only, with a surprise twist at the end when either the series ends with Rose terminally ill (see **Production**) or an unexpected transformation into a different leading man would make sure you could get all the benefits of this role in the space of one year. This would have made any amount of hardship or loneliness tolerable. Eccleston maintains to this day that he's proud of the year he did.

A variant of this theory was that Davies had wanted Tennant all along but, until he was available, the *Doctor Who* juggernaut got underway with Eccleston as a sort of place-holder. However plausible you find this, the deal would have suited Eccleston if he was reluctant to commit to anything for more than a year. In this reading, the real villain is whoever leaked the story that Eccleston had left nearly three months before this was to have been revealed on screen. The BBC's press release is, thus, even more of a botch.

Theory Four: Personality Clashes

Here we get into murkier waters, in which the boundaries between gossip, actual information and speculation get porous.

The knowable facts are: Joe Ahearne directed three blocks, five out of 13 episodes; his next major project also starred Eccleston; and he never returned to *Doctor Who* despite being an obvious choice and rather good at it. Two of the other four directors didn't return either, and everyone who worked with *both* Eccleston and Tennant comments on the very different atmosphere making the later episodes (Eccleston is not known for keeping his opinions to himself). On top of this, there are any number of incidents reported via Chinese Whispers (actors, in particular, being notorious gossips) and stories that have the ring of truth. Few of these, for obvious reasons, have made it into print. We may never know whether the star genuinely threatened violence against any of the directors. (If any violence had *happened*, as is sometimes alleged, the BBC's lawyers, good as they are, could never have kept it quiet with so much location work in public places, even if the supposed victim had opted not to bring charges - one frequently-hinted-at tale would, if true, have caused the alleged victim to sue for defamation of character and loss of earnings and this person is still in work, often with the BBC, so it's massively improbable.)

One obvious aspect of the production that has been the source of a lot of speculation is Eccleston's relationship with Billie Piper. People have tried reading the tealeaves and finding significance in the fact that they never did interviews together, that there were no photos of the pair of them that both artists authorised for use (which is supposedly why the publicity material, DVD covers and the like, is almost all photoshopped from solo photos) and didn't really talk about each other. After Eccleston had gone, Piper commented on the different atmosphere on set, but was careful to praise Tennant without denigrating Eccleston. Quite the reverse: She was scrupulously respectful about Eccleston, never teasing him publicly the way she would Tennant and always commending his professionalism. Both of them were going through rough patches that year, and neither was really the type to socialise with the other's crowd - Piper was more usually to be seen out with Cardiff's own superstar Charlotte Church, with whom she had rather more in common.

Then there is the management. Eccleston always singled out Davies as the key reason he took the role in the first place. They had worked together on *The Second Coming*, so it's unlikely that either would have considered working with the other if this had not gone well. However, there were two other executive producers, a producer running things day-to-day, a head of drama and a head of BBC1 in the mix, and there are accusations that *at least* one of these people had somehow rubbed Eccleston up the wrong way, or maybe vice versa. Almost all of these people stayed around for five years, and the only people to leave their posts were promoted. It's hard to see them *all* merely tolerating each other for that long a period. If only one person had actively angered

continued on Page 191...

seems to be another month). The Face of Boe [X1.2, "The End of the World" and others] is the oldest inhabitant of the Isop galaxy [2.5, "The Web Planet" and others].

The fashion robots with Jack make mention of a "President Schwarzenegger". [This presumably means Arnold Schwarzenegger, who was then governor of California. He wasn't born in America, however, so a Constitutional amendment would be required for him to become president.]

• *The Time War.* The Daleks somehow survived and fear the Doctor.

Catchphrase Counter [Um, did you note the episode's title? It's mentioned rather a lot in the dialogue.]

The Analysis

The Big Picture ("Bad Wolf" and "The Parting of the Ways") Now that the tide of makeovers, docu-soaps and ruthless game shows has receded, it's hard to remember just how big a threat they seemed to (overtly) scripted television drama.

In Britain, the low-cost "reality" shows had, over the previous decade, dominated prime-time, and people on them had been brief sensations in the tabloids before receding into oblivion. What's strange is that, for all that he protested that he loved them and thought they were the true state-of-the-nation dramas of the UK, Russell T Davies has here bracketed three distinct genres together in a way that only their sternest critics ever did. Few people who voluntarily watched *The Weakest Link* thought of it in the same category as *Big Brother*, and certainly none of the makeover programmes seemed to be similar (nobody, public or contestants, got to vote anyone off those). There was an element of bullying in all of them, especially the most grotesque makeovers, *Ten Years Younger* and *Would Like to Meet* (to do with shaming people into surgically removing any distinctiveness and being conditioned to become Stepford-like nobodies, ostensibly for their own good). Nonetheless, there were elements of bullying in a lot of other programmes.

Significantly, what's missing in this run-through of the biggest shows is any element of ritual humiliation (the Walk of Shame from *The Weakest Link* is removed, and there is nothing even approaching the sorts of ordeals visited on the non-entities on *I'm A Celebrity - Get Me Out Of Here!*[34]), and anything that makes the contestants agents of their own or each other's fates. There is some tactical voting in *The Weakest Link*, but no option to actively sabotage each other. Davies isn't doing satire. Indeed, he had at one stage been asked to participate in one[35]. A genuine satire on this kind of television would have been crueller and - possibly because he wanted the makers of real shows to give him freebies, but more probably because he genuinely enjoys that sort of programme - Davies pulls every possible punch.

This is most evident when we consider the throwaway detail of Murder Spree 20 (a fictional event in Iceland, mentioned in one of *The Weakest Link* questions). Had the rights to the various shows being exaggerated not been available, a story where the contestants *were* trying to kill each other would have been the most likely fall-back. Davies had this in his back pocket if his original plan to do *The Weakest Link* had fallen through (he had the naff joke about the "Anne Droid" ready from the 2001 meetings when he first pitched his idea of a low-budget *Doctor Who*). Lethal manhunt game shows were an idea dating back to the 1950s. (Robert Sheckley's short story "The Seventh Victim", later expanded into *The Tenth Victim*, was filmed in 1965, and there had been numerous dystopian flicks such as *Rollerball* and *Running Man* - it had even been done as an episode of *Blake's 7*, which officially makes it a cliché.) One twist on the idea was linking this to politics by having voting on a bill a matter of life or death for the leadership - hey, guess what? That was one of ours (22.2, "Vengeance on Varos").

It's customary at this point to mention Nigel Kneale's embarrassing 1968 play *The Year of the Sex Olympics*, in which a public jaded by live sex get excited by the prospect of real death, and tune in to a live feed from a remote island where a family try to get by - unaware of a serial-killer introduced to spice up the ratings. Kneale's contempt for the viewers is evident, but at least they are mentioned - Davies, at least in the broadcast story here, has the over-populated Earth as noises-off. That's a vital omission. Most of the series he shows us *mutatis mutandis* are ones where the host gets to decide what happens, and although we hear rumours of a public vote for *Big Brother*, we only have the Davinadroid's word for any of it. No attempt is made to show what the people on the receiving end are getting from the shows. For Davies, they exist only as numbers. After so many

Did He Fall or Was He Pushed?

continued from Page 189...

the star, the entire production team would have closed ranks - this would have been worse than any one incident or tendency.

With Eccleston's most recent pronouncements on this topic, it becomes a bit clearer. Whilst some of what he says consolidates the "Making a Stand" theory (see his comments for the *Radio Times* below), it seems more likely that it was disagreements with a person or persons higher up the management that made an incident with a specific (and still un-named) director seem like the shape of things to come. He speaks of an entire culture of management dismaying him. "I left *Doctor Who* because I could not get along with the senior people. I left because of politics... I didn't agree with the way things were being run."

Theory Five: Disappointment

There's a story going around that, during the making of "Father's Day" (X1.8), Eccleston turned to Davies and said, "Why can't you write something this good?" Even if this happened, it's a comment that could be a misjudged backhanded complement, a joke or a challenge. It doesn't *have* to have been an insult, and even if it *had* been, Davies wasn't inevitably going to go home and plot a regeneration story there and then. But, as we stated above, Eccleston never hesitated to comment on Davies' scripts as the motivation for taking what looked like the biggest gamble of his career. Moreover, the point he made next was usually about making sure quality drama was available to younger viewers who would grow up demanding better. He knew full well that this was to be at least accessible to children, if not exclusively for them. So whatever qualms he may have had about some aspects of the early episodes, they wouldn't have been deal-breakers.

That said, he commented later on the surprise of his first full day of shooting being chasing Jimmy Vee in a pig-mask and spacesuit, in a story about farting fatties who were aliens in 10 Downing Street. Nevertheless, with all the things that have annoyed Eccleston about current TV drama, especially in Britain, being expressed forcefully whenever he's given a chance in public, something like this alleged sense of being cheated might have come up. He's not exactly reticent on such topics. In interviews, even after he'd (secretly) filmed his last scenes, he spoke proudly of being part of a tradition, and working on a series that had led to so many ground-breaking developments (he was especially enthusiastic about the Radiophonic Workshop and Tristan Cary, pioneering electronica in the 60s). Above all, the opportunity to act for children was one he embraced, and seeing an audience grow up with his character might have been enough for him to stay with a part.

Theory Six: Making A Stand

Here's another of those "well, *I* heard it was..." stories that actors pass around like bon-bons, one that has been stated as fact by people in a position to know but unsubstantiated by anyone who wants to go on record.

In short, Eccleston found out about some kind of bullying or malpractice affecting the lower end of the production, runners, costume and wardrobe support or somesuch, and threatened to quit if they didn't stop. The obvious question there is that making a stand like this is pointless unless you are going to use the opportunity to blow the whistle on such abuse - so why protest in secret? It's like carrying a placard around in your living room. With all the publicity hoo-hah and people wanting to know what made him leave (once he was allowed to say anything without committing the mother of all spoilers), he had a platform to make a principled and very public stand against something that, if unchecked, would ruin the business he's in and threaten his and every other actor's livelihood. Whilst it's entirely in keeping with his public persona for Eccleston to have quit rather than let such things continue, it's completely out of character to then not mention this, or to side with management against employees. Until broadcast of the first episode, Eccleston was bigger than the series, so it was entirely his decision whether to go public with something like this and, as we've said, he's not normally given to holding anything back.

Understandably, the BBC never mentioned anything like this. Possibly understandably, nobody else involved and no other actors in the series, or working for Equity in any other capacity, has ever

continued on Page 193...

X1.12 Bad Wolf

years working for ITV and Channel 4, his criteria for a success or failure isn't memorability or public comment but the (largely notional) overnight ratings. (See **Should *Doctor Who* be Appointment Television?** under X4.14, "The Next Doctor".)

More fundamentally, the plan was always for this run of 13 episodes to end with something from that earlier adventure on Satellite Five to come back and bite the Doctor. Davies had the series ready to be pitched to the BBC as a story in 13 parts, and the overall shape of the series was one with a two-part climax - the first half of which was a feint to disguise the return of the Daleks. Then, when the estate of Terry Nation kicked up trouble (X1.6, "Dalek"), it became maybe the Cybermen, perhaps. The point is, there was a definite season finale, at the end of which everything would be different. If this were to be all the *Doctor Who* this century ever got, this would be a good end-point, if not, it could lead in a number of fresh directions. Rather like the first season of *Buffy*, in fact - or *Firefly*, if they were less lucky.

The key point is that this is an explicitly American-styled format, applied to British television for almost the first time. And, as such, it needed some kind of foreshadowing to make the surprise solution to the problem seem both obvious-with-hindsight and appropriate, rather than a grafted-on cop-out. This was standard practice in those American series, and had been since *Babylon 5*, but was presented here as something new and innovative because the majority of the target audience (and TV critics) wouldn't have been seen dead watching those series (except *Buffy*, which was ostensibly for teenage girls and thus daringly *outré* for trendmongers, rather than risking ridicule for watching something not a soap or cop-show). So the Bad Wolf maguffin began in the scripts for episode four and got dropped in as this year's Big Bad. Making the first half of the story about familiar TV fixtures disguised this, and kept the family audience who would not have been expecting the ending on their toes. (At least, that was the theory when they were making it.) Even then, in many ways this style of seeded reference working back from the ending and giving tantalising hints is one that long-term *Doctor Who* viewers would have known. The main difference between the Bad Wolf and the Watcher (18.7, "Logopolis") is that the latter only appears at the start of the final story, even though references to entropy and the Master had been dropped into earlier stories

that year. More pertinently, "Planet of the Spiders" (the story where "regeneration" is first mentioned and shown to be something all Time Lords can do) ties up storylines from up to two years earlier.

Even in the pitch document, the title for the last episode is "The Parting of the Ways". It was intentionally ambiguous right from the start which of the two leads was to leave here. It is unclear exactly how early on the decision to end with a regeneration was taken - the same document explicitly says that such a concept would only be reintroduced if necessary. The leak of Eccleston's departure makes a lot of this story's curious features redundant in practice. It's noticeable that the build-up to the last episode, including the sneak-previews each day after "Bad Wolf", had to emphasise the "What will cause the Doctor's death?" aspect of the story, even though there was one screamingly obvious answer, and another they couldn't possibly mention without blowing the whole Bad Wolf mystery (which, by then, was being bet on and discussed in the press). The publicity could have made more of the pretty-looking effects if they'd simply been pushing the "How will he get out of this?" elements. The two endings were recorded and one of them kept less secret than the other. Originally, the plan was for the press to see the "fake" ending with Rose made fatally ill by the Vortex energy, and only include the regeneration on transmission. Rose had, to some extent, outlived her usefulness as a character. The idea was always that the viewers would (re)discover the core concepts of *Doctor Who* through her eyes. Here is where the strategy to demolish the wall between "cult" and "mainstream" was at work most obviously, using tricks developed in the programmes the critics don't watch to maximum effect by deploying them inside a story - beginning with the most popular and talked-about programmes currently on being parodied, albeit too affectionately to actually draw blood.

English Lessons As not all of the shows parodied here are still running in Britain or have ever run (at least under those names) in all of the many countries where *Doctor Who* is shown, we'll begin with those:

• *Big Brother* began as a Dutch format where ordinary people were stuck in a house together under constant surveillance, as in *1984*. The people applying in the local version here became

Did He Fall or Was He Pushed?

continued from Page 191...

said that anything like this took place - who would risk it with the BBC still the major employer of actors in Britain? The most recent statement by Eccleston specifies a director bullying a propsman, but in such terms that this might be a *hypothetical* example of how a director would lose his trust. The culture that grew up around the series (and that's a phrase he used a lot in this context) seems to have involved a tight-knit community who all agree not to rock the boat. This may have been one of the key strengths of the series (see **Does Being Made in Wales Matter?** under X1.11, "Boom Town"), but if, as he puts it, "my face didn't fit", then it would be alienating.

It's also true that the same code of silence that sought to keep a lid of spoilers has prevented dissent and disquiet emerging (until the whistle-blower who contacted *Private Eye* magazine around the time that two executive producers abruptly left between the two half-seasons in 2011). However, returning to that *Radio Times* interview (ironically, the issue that had the launch of Series Five as the cover feature), he was quoted as saying: "I thought if I stay in this job, I'm going to have to blind myself to certain things that I thought were wrong." This and the "culture" comment could be about this sort of alleged bullying (but why not say so?). Or it could be about the use of the series as a "franchise" and the overall risk-averse culture of BBC drama post-Hutton? Or simply that he was unprepared to engage in the whole promotion rigmarole of *Doctor Who Confidential* and publicity photos? Again, the comments are more useful in limiting the more lurid speculation than in supporting any one interpretation.

Theory Seven: Misunderstanding(s)

In some ways, the saddest and most believable of all the theories: Eccleston, due to one or a combination of the above, delayed making a firm commitment to Series Two until after Julie Gardner, as Head of Drama, would have had to have issued a new contract. So, no sooner had he decided to give it another year than he was told they were replacing him. (One *ben trovato* version has him only finding out when he read it in the papers like the rest of us. The dates don't work for that.)

This is oddly familiar. In some ways, it's a cruel inversion of the way William Hartnell was accidentally retained for six months after producer John Wiles had engineered a way to replace him (see 3.7, "The Celestial Toymaker"). In others, it's similar to the way the BBC called Jon Pertwee's bluff after he threatened to quit if he wasn't given a pay-rise beyond what the series could afford.

One possible clue is that the decision would have to have been made at exactly the time Eccleston was dealing with a bereavement, at the end of 2004, during work on "The Long Game". If the paperwork and negotiations came at him when he was preoccupied and at a low ebb, he may have simply missed the deadline even though the management wanted him to stay.

Supporting evidence for this comes from the sheer volume of tie-in merchandising with Eccleston and Piper depicted on it. Had they been planning from the outset to replace the lead, no 2006 calendars or costly high-tech electronic games would have been sanctioned by the BBC - and certainly not an Easter egg with the Moxx of Balhoon on the foil wrapper for the day after X2.1, "New Earth". The BBC's entire Christmas schedule was orientated around the new Doctor, and the presence of so many toys and games with the previous Doctor depicted thereupon was a mild embarrassment. The BBC's first-ever Annual seemed to have been commissioned on the understanding that Eccleston would be back for another year and Davies wrote much of the content, hinting at forthcoming developments but never once saying, "Actually, the Doctor's face changed after Rose became the Bad Wolf" (see **Was Series Two Supposed to be Like This?** under X2.11, "Fear Her"). Even a surprise regeneration as a planned plot-point would have been discussed with the people making the decisions about commissioning Chinese manufacturers under license from Character Options. (See **What Were the Great 21st Century Merchandising Disasters?** under X5.3, "Victory of the Daleks".)

It would appear, again using the *Radio Times* interview as evidence, that it was Eccleston's decision to leave and that some degree of financial inducement was offered to retain him. It would

continued on Page 195...

1.12 Bad Wolf

increasingly fame-hungry and clueless, and it was a twenty-first century version of rich people paying to see the lunatics in Bedlam (X3.2, "The Shakespeare Code"). It paid all Channel 4's bills, so live infra-red coverage of people asleep filled the schedules every summer for ten years. Desperate newcomer Channel 5 bought the rights and in 2011 used it to fill time between *CSI* reruns. In a curious life-imitating-art situation (assuming that the words "life" and "art" apply), they borrowed *Doctor Who*'s idea and did *Bear With Me*, but with a gorilla. Still hardly anybody watched.

- *Call My Bluff* had three definitions for an allegedly recondite word, two of which were mendacious. In its original 60s/70s incarnation, it was presented by the sesquipedalian Robert Robinson and rapidly became a parody of itself. The two team-captains were humourists with speech-impediments, which would simply not happen today. The guests would often be loquacious actors, including Tom Baker. (A regular was the "other" Russell Davies, so it would stick in the memory of "our" Russell.) They revived it as a daytime filler in the late 90s, with different captains and presenters.

- *Countdown* was the first programme shown on Channel 4 in November 1982. Contestants have 30 seconds to either make as long a legitimate word as possible from nine randomly selected letters (they can choose from the pile of vowels or the pile of consonants) or combine six randomly-selected numbers in order to approximate a computer-selected random three-figure total. This is leavened with anecdotes from studio guests and the lame jokes of the host. The jingle for the 30 seconds is instantly memorable. (Oddly, this show is adapted from a very staid French original which has stayed true to its roots and is now almost unrecognisable as the same show.)

- *Ground Force* was a garden makeover show where the presenters come in while you're out and rebuild your entire garden. There was a celebrity edition where they fixed up Nelson Mandela's back yard. Sturdily-built trowel-wrangler Charlie Dimmock had a certain appeal for elderly men.

- *Stars in their Eyes*. Before the resistible rise of Simon Cowell, this was the ITV Saturday-night freakshow that was held by otherwise sensible folk to signal the End of Civilisation. People would dress up as and try to sing like major recording artists, usually Marti Pellow of Wet Wet Wet. (Exactly.) Matthew Kelly, the host, would attempt to summon up enthusiasm as the choice of artiste was announced with the ritual "Tonight, Matthew, I'm going to be..." and the viewers got to vote for them using the name of the star, not the contestant. Cat Deeley took over, but "Tonight, Cat..." didn't catch on and it was dropped.

- *The Weakest Link* was a quiz where at the end of each round the contestants were encouraged to make like jackals and pick on the one they thought was most vulnerable. To make it more venal, the questions were insultingly easy (for anyone not under the spotlight), so viewers were only focussing on the nastiness and stress-related mistakes. The bullying was led by the host - Anne Robinson, in the UK original - who under normal circumstances would be facing legal action for what she said.

- *What Not to Wear* had irritating snobs Trinny and Susannah sneering at poor people and offering completely wrong fashion advice.

- *Wipeout* was the retirement plan of conjurer Paul Daniels. The game itself was an accumulator where the first wrong answer lost you the lot in each round. Nobody remembers that - it was his insecurely attached wig that kept people on the edges of their seats.

On to other matters...

- *Does exactly what it says on the tin* was the slogan for Ronseal wood varnish, and then drifted into a sardonic comment on unimaginative names for products or websites. Jack must have heard Rose or Mickey use the phrase (or maybe the Doctor, as the bloke in the advert is from up north).

- *Top Shop* is mainly women's-wear, with *Top Man* upstairs. Everyone on the Game Station (except the Controller) seems to have bought their clothes there. (Futuristic robots calling their rather run-of-the-mill clothes "a design classic" is the same joke as thinking of Jackie Collins as "literature".)

- *Bonkers* (adj.) Insane. A big hit for Dizzee Rascal has spread this rather dated word worldwide since this episode aired.

- *TV Licence*: How television is paid for in the UK (except for the johnny-come-lately commercial stations, but even to watch them you need to have paid the Licence Fee). There are historical and legal reasons why this persists, and after 75 years of BBC television, the evidence seems to be that it works (despite governments using it to

Did He Fall or Was He Pushed?

continued from Page 193...

also appear that his departure wasn't heartbreaking news to those who remained on the series. The integrity he brought to the role, and which caused him to depart and remain true to himself (he says now) may also have made it impossible for others to work with him.

However, that interview made one point clear: Eccleston was proud of his year as the Doctor, and for breaking the mould so that almost any actor good enough could be imagined as a future casting. The key point, he said, wasn't how or why he left but that he took the role at all.

---

punish the Corporation for not doing their bidding). Without it, no *Doctor Who*. The penalty for being caught without one is a £400 fine or six months in prison.

[For **Things That Don't Make Sense**, **Critique**, **The Facts** and **Production**, see the next episode.]

X1.13: "The Parting of the Ways"

(18th June, 2005)

Which One is This? Eccleston's Last Stand.

Firsts and Lasts The first unambiguous Doctor-companion kiss of the new series occurs. It's with Captain Jack. Later, Rose's life and the fate of the cosmos absolutely depends on the Doctor snogging her, honest.

This is also Jack's last appearance, as he dies. Then he gets better, and eventually he becomes the first companion to be written out for real and written back in (Tegan - 19.7, "Time Flight" doesn't count, because it was a bluff). In the meantime, he goes off into another series, itself a first (18.7a, "K9 & Company" doesn't count either, because that wasn't a series, thank goodness). And, incredibly, despite a paralysis within seconds of the Daleks' first-ever appearance (1.2, "The Daleks"), this is the first time a companion has been Exterminated.

This is the first overt, self-proclaimed Season Finale, although episode ten of 6.7, "The War Games" has as good a claim as this, as does episode six of 11.5, "Planet of the Spiders" and in many ways episode six of 16.6, "The Armageddon Factor". It ends with the first regeneration to be performed standing up (as far as we know: two have taken place off-screen), in what will become the standard effect for this.

This is the first time the credits have had the Bond-style message: "*Doctor Who* will return in..." and then the name of the Christmas episode (in this case, "The Christmas Invasion").

And, of course, it's the first appearance of David Tennant - who, in about a dozen words, completely takes over the role of the Doctor.

Watch Out For...

• The whole of this story is, obviously, forcing a crisis for the Doctor. The BBC goofed and let slip that this was to be a regeneration episode, so that element of suspense is replaced with "How is it going to happen?", but we do get some other ingenious feints. Jack is killed before our eyes and then... recovers (and that caused no end of trouble - see X3.11, "Utopia" and, if you didn't know, *Torchwood*). The script and promotion make it seem as though this Doctor will die when outnumbered by Daleks. The prophesied threat passes, and then the Doctor is felled by something relatively quiet and a consequence of helping a friend - exactly what will happen next time (X4.18, "The End of Time Part Two"). And the Doctor's sweet little friend Lynda looks as if she might be replacing Rose... and then is not only killed, but slain in one of the most self-confident ways the series has ever managed. Seconds prior to Lynda's demise, we see Daleks in space and the lights on the head pulse in time to an (unheard, for obvious reasons) "ex-ter-min-ate" and the glass protecting her shatters.

• Emergency Programme One is an override for the TARDIS to take Rose home to safety, with a hologram message as to what's happening. At the end of this, the image of the Doctor turns to *look directly at her*, and the timbre of the recording changes as he orders her to "have a fantastic life". It's a glimpse of how good a second year of Eccleston's Doctor might have been, as he effortlessly pulls off a moment many of his predecessors would have struggled to make work.

X1.13 The Parting of the Ways

- This episode, the Doctor snogs both of his companions, as first Jack says goodbye to the Doctor and Rose as only he can, and then the Doctor kisses Rose on the brow for suggesting a handy time-paradox (actually not practical, and he's really saying goodbye to her), and later still when he absorbs the Time Vortex from Rose-as-Bad Wolf in a method indistinguishable from getting the girl. He's a lot more awkward seeing off Lynda, so maybe she was never meant to come with him at the end of this.

- However, the Doctor pashing his lady-friend is the sort of thing that brings back unfortunate memories of Paul McGann's hour or so as the TV Movie Doctor. Obviously the Emperor Dalek hated this escapade, which is apparently why the words "half-human" are regarded as "blasphemy".

- Because there was a gap between Eccleston finishing work on the series and Tennant being cast, this regeneration can't be the hitherto-normal cross-fade of two actors lying on the same bit of floor. Instead, it's another "Look-at-what-we-can-do-that-Barry-Letts-couldn't" shot.

The Continuity

The Doctor He dies as a result of absorbing the Vortex from Rose. His last line/s, delivered to her: 'You were fantastic. Absolutely fantastic. And, d'yknow what? So was I.'

His regeneration this time [and every time anyone does it from now on; we've seen the effect eight times more to date - nine, if you count the different POV of the Doctor's "death" in X6.13, "The Wedding of River Song"] is for raw [Artron] energy to pour from his cuffs and collar while he remains standing. The process of regeneration is, he says beforehand, 'a bit dodgy'. The Doctor speculates that it could result in his having two heads, or none. [The option to not look humanoid is something hinted at in some of the books. Terrance Dicks makes it a feature of *Timewyrm: Exodus*.]

Prior to all this, he manages to get information by landing the TARDIS in the Dalek fleet and - protected by the Extrapolator's force field [see X1.11, "Boom Town"] - talking at them. He scares the Daleks just by being so fearless and unbowed. His cockiness remains until he decides it's time to leave - when he offers them a cheeky grin before closing the doors and, head bowed against them, listens to the alternate cries of 'exterminate' and 'worship him' in anguish.

His plan to stop the Daleks is to use the Game Station's transmitter to emit heavy-duty Delta waves, which - as he's no time to calibrate it properly - will kill Daleks and humans alike in the vicinity of Earth. [To clarify - in real life, this is a *shape* of wave-form, not a substance. The Delta waves mentioned in 19.3, "Kinda" seem to be the ones the sleeping human brain generates, and those are a pattern of electrical activity. Even if Dalek brains are like those of humans and Traken princesses, Earth would not be saved with lullabies. The Delta waves generated by synthesizers, which were the characteristic sound of late 80s Rave records, would be just as ineffective against an army of Daleks.] These waves are of Van Cassedyne energy, and will deracinate any conscious organism in their path [he would need two weeks to tune it just for use on Daleks]. Much to his surprise, he completes the task with a few minutes to spare, and uses that time to satisfy his curiosity [or try to] about the Emperor's role in the 'Bad Wolf' situation.

Once the Daleks arrive, he continues to try to bluff them that he will use the Delta Wave and when it becomes obvious that he will not, he accepts death - 'maybe it's time', he says before bracing himself for extermination.

When discussing with Rose the prospect of legging it and leaving Earth to the Daleks, he sardonically suggests Marbella, 1989, as an alternative. [Whether this is to appeal to Rose's tastes or to live up to his apparent age, accent and style - or even from personal experience in a previous life (somehow the thought of Hartnell in cycling shorts, wigging out on Balieric beats whilst necking disco biscuits or largein' it at an Ibiza foam party, is oddly appealing[37]) - we can't tell.]

Apparently, being able to see all of time, past present and possible, is how he goes about his business. When Rose is in a similar state, he asks, 'doesn't it drive yer mad?'

He says he's 'got' five billion languages. [That's a suspiciously-familiar number (X1.2,"The End of the World"), but plausible nonetheless - note he says he's 'got' them, not "speaks" - see **Can He Read Smells?** under X2.8, "The Impossible Planet" for why this distinction might matter.]

- *Ethics*. Faced with the prospect of saving the Universe and sparing the people of Earth from Dalek conquest and conversion, he hesitates and eventually steps back. If the Daleks consider him

The Parting of the Ways — X1.13

Bad Wolf - What, How and Why?

In the beginning, or at least the third episode of the new series, the Bad Wolf was just a throwaway phrase given to Gwyneth the maid to make her eldritch power sound more spooky. It came back, and filled exactly the same purpose as all the season-long hinted menaces that have befallen heroes of American fantasy shows since *Babylon 5* - the sort of thing that in *Buffy the Vampire Slayer* was called a "Big Bad". Eventually, it became the all-purpose clue-phrase for whatever it was that was causing the Doctor and Rose such trouble when visiting the Fourth Great and Bountiful Human Empire (or the time when this should have been happening). Then, eventually, we got an explanation - but even for people who were able to follow this (and that wasn't everybody, so we'll spell it out again just in case, in a mo), that's where the real problems began. Whilst it made sense at the time, the explanation given doesn't account for later manifestations of Bad Wolf phenomena.

What might be happening is that the TARDIS grants a boon to anyone who survives looking into the core. Margaret Slitheen gets a second childhood, Rose gets to rescue the Doctor. But that's not *all* that Rose causes to happen. She evaporates the attacking Daleks from (apparently) all of time. Then she resurrects Captain Jack. This isn't just a get-out-of-jail-free card, this is the agency of something much more powerful manifesting itself through Rose and hurting her, probably fatally if the Doctor hadn't snogged the energy out of her. That's not the same as simply giving someone her heart's desire.

The Bad Wolf's wishes aren't just Rose's need to rescue the Doctor. Rose has temporarily allowed the Time Vortex to pass through her consciousness. She doesn't absorb it, because that's too much even for the Doctor to survive - she is a conduit, but one whose desires are capable of influencing the Vortex energy. As such, the composite being Bad Wolf says some very interesting things. She speaks of defending "my Doctor". She can see time synoptically, as if laid out in front of her spatially. When the TARDIS is briefly corporeal (X6.4, "The Doctor's Wife"), she says similar things. The difference between Idris as "Sexy" and Rose as the Bad Wolf, though, is that Rose is still in there. In attempting to resolve all the implications of this act and the otherwise inexplicable details in later stories, it becomes clear that Rose Tyler is a bigger monster than Davros and a greater threat to the Universe than whatever it was in the Satan Pit. This is a perfect time-paradox: Rose saw the messages from her future self and decided, once she had the power, to send them back along her life so far. "I create myself", she says. Looked at in detail, this becomes the kind of thing that Steven Moffat is hauled over the coals for doing by less nimble TV critics and online fans.

Another cryptic comment is that she (whichever "she" we mean) claims to be able to see all time, past, present and potential. The Doctor sympathises, but he simply (simply!) means that he has an ability to navigate, to sense out these troublesome "fixed points" and situations where history is in flux. (See **He Remembers This *How*?** under X1.5, "World War Three" and **What Constitutes a "Fixed Point"?** under X4.2, "The Fires of Pompeii".) Here's where the problems arise. Rose gets custody of the power of the space-time Vortex, but not full control. She accidentally (it seems) makes Jack immortal, with all that this entails. None of the other victims on the Game Station seem to have been resurrected, just the one she fancies. What other unexpected side-effects of a 19-year-old girl with cosmic awareness might there have been?

Well, almost immediately after (X2.2, "Tooth and Claw"), there is an encounter with another wolf, one who recognises Rose as kindred. This entity plans to make a new future. Shortly after the Doctor and Rose thwart this, they find themselves in a parallel universe, rather like the Empire of the Wolf as prophesied (X2.5, "Rise of the Cybermen"). The Doctor tells us that parallel universes can no longer be visited, or indeed sustained, without the Time Lords - and yet here we are with monsters the Doctor admitted to sort-of missing (in X1.6, "Dalek", he tells Rose that he feels old because the Cybermen aren't around), a president of Britain (eventually, Rose's mate Harriet Jones gets the job) and airships everywhere. In this altered world, Rose's dad is alive and wealthy, Mickey is called "Ricky" (exactly as the Doctor used to pretend to think he was called) and is in a long-term relationship - and yet almost everything else is familiar.

Suspiciously familiar. An infinite - literally, infinite - number of possible alternate Earths that could exist and yet the only one that is actually created

continued on Page 199...

X1.13 The Parting of the Ways

a coward for not destroying two races to prevent a worse fate (again), so be it. [It's hard to judge how much his gambit with the Delta waves is a bluff from the start. It's possible that he hoped the Daleks would retreat, or perhaps he genuinely thought it best to do *something* and give the people on the Station a chance to go down fighting rather than be processed. The end result, however, is that Jack and his band of volunteers are sent out to be slaughtered while the Doctor refrains from killing the enemy that is sure to eradicate/convert all the humans on Earth. Either way, perhaps this should be read as his simply being too *tired*, after his actions in the Last Great Time War, to again throw the switch that dooms everyone present.]

He tricks Rose into leaving him, and his workrate increases once she's not there for him to worry about.

- *Background*. Apparently, the Daleks know the Doctor as 'The Oncoming Storm'. [This is an odd coincidence, as the Draconians (10.3, "Frontier in Space") used to call him that, according to Paul Cornell's *New Adventures* novel *Love and War*.]

- *Inventory: Sonic Screwdriver*. Although the development of any kind of remote control for a TARDIS was treated by the Doctor as a remote possibility until "The Mark of the Rani" (22.3), the most remarkable new use for the sonic screwdriver is exactly that. By sending out a quick bleep, he can close the doors from afar [see also X4.9, "Forest of the Dead"] and operate Emergency Programme One [see **The TARDIS**].

The TARDIS It can, in fact, die. The process seems to take a while [and it's suggested that the prolonged absence of the Doctor prompts it; cf X4.11, "Turn Left"]. We learn this as Emergency Programme One's holographic "Read This" runs: this appears to be a pre-recorded message from the Doctor telling Rose that the autopilot is taking her home to Jackie, and that the Ship can't be allowed to fall into enemy hands. [We say "appears to be" for two reasons: one is that later stories have the TARDIS tell the occupants things they need to know in the form of someone trustworthy: the Doctor in X3.10, "Blink", a whole menu ending in Amelia in X6.8, "Let's Kill Hitler". Moreover, this time, the message turns to look *at* Rose. If this is the TARDIS pretending to be the Doctor, then the degree of overlap between his consciousness and the Ship's is negotiable. It seems more likely to be something like an avatar on a computer, scripted by the Doctor but animated by the TARDIS and manipulated according to local circumstances. What this projection says is sufficiently all-purpose for this to have been recorded some time after X1.5, "World War Three", as it mentions promising to keep Rose safe.]

The same panel that accidentally opened last time ["Boom Town"] and put Blon back in touch with her inner child proves remarkably difficult to prise open with machinery. Once this is done, Rose is contacted through her eyes and the doors close of their own volition. The Ship races through space and time even faster than it took Rose home. Once there, Rose is conjoined with the TARDIS to produce the Bad Wolf: a self-creating entity capable of seeing all of time and unravelling the molecules of the Dalek fleet. It then sends the words 'Bad Wolf' back across Rose's journeys to guide her into realising that what has just happened to her is possible and resurrects Captain Jack after he is exterminated. [This last is significant: in "Utopia", the Doctor tells Jack that they left him behind because the TARDIS rejected him as 'wrong', and seems to be shifting the blame onto the same auto-pilot that got Rose to Satellite Five. If the TARDIS is conscious and created Bad Wolf, then this is untenable as an excuse.]

Other odd TARDIS features include: in crossing to the Dalek mothership, the Ship spins in real-space [see 13.2, "Planet of Evil", etc], only dematerialising as normal once a missile appears to hit. The blast doesn't affect them because the Extrapolator ["Boom Town"] is wired in. This allows a cordon sanitaire where the Doctor can walk outside the TARDIS and not be exterminated, at least until Jack removes the Extrapolator to build it into Satellite Five's defence grid. The Ship materialises around Rose (and a Dalek), so that she (and it) appear inside the Console Room as if they are materialising [see 18.7, "Logopolis"; 19.7, "Time Flight" for similar precise landings]. Jack then blows up the Dalek [proving that the Ship's 'temporal grace' feature still isn't working (see 14.2, "The Hand of Fear"; 20.1, "Arc of Infinity"; several 80s stories where Cybermen and others get zapped; and X6.8, "Let's Kill Hitler")].

The Supporting Cast

- *Rose*. As the Doctor points out, it never occurs to her to bail - she is so loyal to him that she has to be tricked into being sent back to 2006. Once there, her old life seems like a living death, with

Bad Wolf - What, How and Why?

continued from Page 197...

is one that matches Rose's wish-fulfilment criteria exactly? And they get to see what it's like on the same day they left "real" Earth? This isn't a coincidence.

There is a small problem with making this linear relationship work: the most likely turning point in history is the one that an entire episode was given over to thwarting, the attempted infection of Queen Victoria in 1879. The projected alternate future is explicitly called "the Empire of the Wolf" and combines the worst elements of Torchwood's remit and naff 80s steampunk comics. It's *not* the one we see in the Cybermen two-parter. If anything, some of the technology in the flashbacks in *Torchwood* is closer to this warmed-over Moorcock. So the evil parallel universe where John Lumic created the Cybermen is possibly what *should* have happened and the "change" to established history has created Rose's ordinary world, a nightmarish distorted reality where Derek Acorah still has a career. Rose and the Doctor have somehow summoned up a compromise between antithetical realities, from a starting-point where Queen Victoria is affected a *bit* - because she's met them and is not amused. So perhaps the originally-scheduled timeline ends up in Rose's ideal situation, with no monarchy at all, whereas the werewolf wanted something a bit more Captain Nemo and the Doctor thinks that the latter is a threat but the former is impossible. That doesn't work. So, perhaps the Doctor is concerned about the potential future the werewolf wants because *that's* how history was "supposed" to go, and it was one of the changes he fought to undo in the Time War. But, as we've just pointed out, three episodes later he says that alternate universes are inaccessible. Only two things have changed since the Time War: there are no Time Lords left to supervise this sort of thing, and Rose has been temporarily turned into the Time Vortex in baggy jeans.

(One obvious point to consider here is that Pete's World still has homelessness. If this is a universe constructed from ironic reversal, then this isn't such a problem. If Rose made a world where Pete is as rich and successful as she thinks he deserved to be, maybe these derelicts who get turned into Cybermen are people who, in our world, are wealthy celebrities despite lacking any discernible talent. Somehow, it's easier thinking that the people being killed and re-deployed as shock-troops by Mr Crane are Simon Cowell, Ricky Gervais, Katie Price, Chris Moyles...)

Could things have been different if Jack had gazed into the abyss and become an omnipotent being? Obviously, the phrase that alerted him to the possibility would have been something less innocuous than "Bad Wolf", and the whole of creation would have become a bad *Round the Horne* sketch, but the point seems to be that Rose is on a path from ordinary shopgirl recognisably like the majority of the viewers to the indispensable "other half" the Doctor needs. Exposure to the Vortex didn't make Blon Fel Fotch Passamir Day Slitheen Mistress of all Space and Time. It turned her into an ostrich-egg with dreadlocks. There was something in Rose that the Vortex, or the TARDIS, sought to protect and empower to rescue the Doctor. She was, in short, recruited and exploited.

The phrase "Bad Wolf" is one that she spots (eventually) because it's more than two randomly selected words. We are led to assume, perhaps because of her tendency to wear red hoodies, that she came up with the phrase from her own childhood. It's not quite the Big Bad Wolf from *The Three Pigs*, and not quite the wolf who impersonates grandma or the one from *Peter and the Wolf*, but it could be any of those. (We can imagine how these old cautionary tales would have meant a lot more to Jackie - herself trying to keep the wolf from the door, financially, once Pete died - and how much Rose would have identified with those slightly reckless little girls who wander off, get captured and get told off when they get home late.) So, however common the phrase is, especially with manipulation of time and space to seed them across the Doctor's travels, it is tailored for Rose to pick up on. It is never quite explained how the various people who decided to use those two words made their choice. Margaret Slitheen claims the name "Blaidd Drwg" just came to her one day (X1.11, "Boom Town"). We presume the Nazi bomber with the chalk, the person who allocates call-signals for Geocomtex's helicopters, a few graffiti artists in Kennington and the Daleks (or their TV exec lackeys) all had similar rushes of blood to the head and picked the same two-word

continued on Page 201...

X1.13 The Parting of the Ways

chips. She tells Mickey 'there's nothing left for me here', which is as callous as she ever gets. When talking to Jackie, she says that the most important thing about being with the Doctor is making a stand. She then runs out on her mother. At this point, the graffiti 'Bad Wolf' messages suddenly seem more important and she decides that it's a signal for her and her alone. [It turns out she's right, but even so...]

When Rose tries to bust open the TARDIS console, it seems as if she has become obsessed. Jackie and Mickey offer some support, but with reminders that success will be most likely fatal. Rose eventually resorts to invoking Pete Tyler [and the Doctor's rewrite of history to make Rose part of his death; X1.8, "Father's Day"]. The end result of all this manipulative behaviour is that she gets their help, manages to access the power-source of the TARDIS and becomes...

- *Rose as Bad Wolf.* This is a composite of the TARDIS core and Rose [probably: see the accompanying essay]. It manifests itself as Rose with gold skin and glowing eyes [see 15.3, "Image of the Fendahl"], a halo of [Artron] energy and a slightly posher accent [although still saying "th" as 'v']. Occasionally the glow in her eyes recedes and Rose can come out to ask for help. This being can reverse Dalek weapon-fire, annihilate a fleet of ships, reduce the Dalek Emperor to atoms and revive Jack rather more thoroughly than planned. It speaks of seeing all of time, but that experiencing this causes pain for Rose. It tells the Daleks and the Doctor that all things must 'come to dust' [all cosmic entities can quote Shakespeare - *Cymbeline*, in this case] and can paraphrase Nietzsche [the stuff about looking into the void and it looks into you, which is interesting when we get to next year's season-ender]. Most importantly, it speaks of protecting 'my Doctor'.

- *Jack.* Knowing full well there is no chance of survival, he ruefully admits that he would have been better off as a coward, and then kisses Rose and the Doctor, but later defiantly tells the Emperor that he 'Never doubted [the Doctor], never will'. He is aware of how the Van Cassedyne energy works (that it fries brains), but doesn't seem to know that the Doctor's lash-up will result in the deaths of *everyone* on the Game Station and Earth until the Dalek Emperor mentions it. So informed, Jack nonetheless rouses the few unevacuated staff and civilians on the station to battle. It would appear [either to buy the Doctor time, or to let those present go down fighting] that he knowingly lies to his volunteers that the 'Bastic bullets' they're armed with can destroy the Daleks, when in fact such weaponry is all-but useless.

Jack knows that aiming for the eyepiece works, eventually. He accepts that the Doctor has removed Rose and the TARDIS as a sign that this really is their last stand. He faces the Daleks down to his last bullet and goes out with a one-liner: they shout 'Exterminate', he replies 'Kinda figured that'. He is shown reviving from death owing to Bad Wolf-Rose's power. [This endows him with the immortality he will repeatedly demonstrate in future. Jack next appears in the debut *Torchwood* episode, "Everything Changes". *Torchwood*: "Fragments" details how he spent the time between "The Parting of the Ways" and his next meeting with the Doctor, in "Utopia".]

- *Mickey* has exceptional hearing, running to the TARDIS landing-site after hearing it from Clifton Parade. Conveniently, he's traded his yellow Beetle for a Mini Cooper, which is capable of having a chain attached. Once he accepts that Rose is determined to try, even at risk of her own life, to open the TARDIS and return to the Doctor, he gives his total support. He can figure out the complicated gearing on a car-haulage lorry.

- *Jackie* is surprised that the new Pizza place sells pizza [if you've been to the low-rent bits of London, this is less surprising] and thinks that the coleslaw at her usual tastes 'clinical' [probably too much cabbage-heart and celery]. The notion of Rose having ambitions beyond this is taking time to sink in.

Jackie is also reluctant to accept that Rose knew her father well enough to predict how he would respond to such a situation ["Father's Day"]. She is supportive of the Doctor's decision to protect Rose at all costs, but once the thought of what Pete would have done develops she calls in an (unspecified) favour from Rodrigo, the local car-haulage specialist, and borrows his tow-truck [she apparently has an HGV 3 licence and can drive such a vehicle].

The Non-Humans

- *Daleks.* The Emperor claims that these new Daleks were cultivated from human flesh, that was sifted until 'one cell in a billion' was harvested as ideal. The result, it says, is that everything human has been purged to create a more 'pure and blessed Dalek'. [However, the next model of

The Parting of the Ways X1.13

Bad Wolf - What, How and Why?

continued from Page 199...

phrase (or dodgy translations of it) out of the air.

As we know, the phrase recurs even after Rose has been a goddess for a few minutes, so the information about her is corrupted by the "Bad Wolf virus" (X2.10, "Love & Monsters"), Cal has paintings of a blonde girl in pink and a wolf on her imaginary wall (X4.8, "Silence in the Library") and Rose apparently manages to revive this power (somehow) along with her hitherto-impossible ability to jump between universes at the end of Series Four. The problem then arises of what happened next. After she had taken a few moments from her busy schedule as a teenage girl to become the conduit for the will of the spacetime Vortex, Rose forgot all of what had happened to her... for two episodes. The clouds had lifted by the time she met a werewolf whom she acknowledged as vaguely connected to her. By the time she met the Cult of Skaro (X2.13, "Doomsday"), she had perfect recall of her stint as a goddess and knew that she had annihilated the Dalek Emperor and his fleet. This is curious, as she had no idea what had happened to her in "The Christmas Invasion" (X2.0).

It gets more perplexing as she finds her way (we are never told how this happens) to a weakness between universes at Bad Wolf Bay in Norway, to get a farewell message from the Doctor. A year later, this same location is the site of the Toclafane's arrival on Earth. Then it gets *really* confusing as the same words are used by Rose to warn the Doctor that the cosmos is being eradicated and, for some reason, every form of text on an entire planet is rewritten (X4.11, "Turn Left"). This might, of course, be a side-effect of the TARDIS language-system panicking (see **Can He Read Smells?** under X2.8, "The Impossible Planet"). Although she has seeded the phrase across space and time and then forgotten it when she goes back to being just Rose, some features of Rose's relationship with the two universes remain. We note, for example, that when she returns to help the Doctor fight Davros and his I Hate Everything device, Mickey and Jackie - who belong here - can come too but not Pete. Rose can visit Donna in an unreal history. Indeed, most of Series Four can be read as the walls of reality being rent asunder by Rose to get back with the Doctor at all costs, and Davros taking advantage of this. This makes her the single most destructively needy woman in history. Any history. (This is the only motivation for X4.13, "Journey's End" not following the logic of the series so far and making Rose, rather than Donna, the half-Doctor hybrid but instead locking her away in Evil Parallel Norway with a David Tennant-shaped sex-toy, to stop her doing anything like that again.)

On the other hand, who said that Rose was the *only* Bad Wolf? The next two episodes show us that there was at least one other being whose exposure to the Time Vortex had caused freak effects: the same Dalek Caan who was in the room when Rose told the Cult of Skaro all about vaporising the Emperor. Caan obviously knows something about the effect of Artron Energy on time-travellers (the Cult's cunning plan relied on it somewhat), and so we can't help wondering if their remit for thinking the unthinkable included a scheme for one of them to do what Rose had done, absorbing the Vortex to become an ultimate weapon far beyond even Davros' Matter-Bomb. It is obvious that they had been experimenting with something of this sort (see **What's Happened to the Daleks?** under X1.6, "Dalek"). It's also a good bet that the Void Ship punched a hole between our universe and Pete's World. (More than a good bet, it was stated in a cut scene in "Doomsday", but we're sticking as far as possible to what was broadcast for our evidence.) Neither is it a coincidence that *this* is where the Cult of Skaro made their escape-hatch from reality. We don't know what effect that arrival had on the "intended" timeline of that world. (This does offer the entertaining possibility that this is actually the alternative universe's Daleks fresh off their own Time War. Except that would tend to require an alternative Doctor as well, and considering the heartache that the production staff went to creating Rose's blue-suited version, the production staff seem to have been very keen on avoiding that. Rose would have made a universe without the unique Doctor, because his uniqueness was part of his appeal.)

So the term "Bad Wolf" applies to both Rose-as-TARDIS-incarnate and Caan-as-Destroyer-of-his-own-kind-by-means-of-stage-managed-flukey-coincidences. They have the ability to unlock "sealed" universes, including the one where the

continued on Page 203...

X1.13 The Parting of the Ways

Daleks - see X5.3, "Victory of the Daleks" - will still see these Daleks as genetically inferior.]

Exo-glass that can withstand a nuclear bomb is no match for a single blast from a Dalek gun. They seem less adept at cracking the code on door locks [see X1.6, "Dalek"], and have one member who is specially equipped to burn through metal doors, very slowly. [This is the fine old tradition of the 60s stories. No sign of the specialist I-can-hold-a-piece-of-paper Dalek from 1.2, "The Daleks"; 10.4, "Planet of the Daleks"; and others.] Aiming for the eye-piece pays off, and the victim declares [all together now] 'My vision is impaired, I cannot see'. Bastic rounds are [just about] unable to damage their shells, and for real devastation you need the Anne Droid. [Which, of course, the Daleks themselves built. But see **Things That Don't Make Sense**.] The base has a central circular blue energy outlet, with smaller surrounding circles, for levitation and manoeuvring.

Three big revelations to report, though: they can levitate up lift-shafts and staircases (and even propel themselves through space), they've found God, and the Doctor claims that they have one remaining emotion: fear. [Last time, it was hate.]

• *The Dalek Emperor* claims to have been in a shipwreck that fell out of the end of the Time War [so he is either *another* sole survivor of the Time War - see "Dalek" - or the same one after giving himself a promotion and faking his death]. Over the ensuing centuries, he insinuated Dalek influence into Earth's affairs, installing the Jagrafess [X1.7, "The Long Game"] and siphoning the dispossessed into his extreme makeover programme. All the half-million or so Daleks in this fleet are the end-product of selecting suitable human tissue. One cell in a billion is appropriate [a lower strike-rate than the cryo-morgue in 22.6, "Revelation of the Daleks"]. Over the centuries, the trauma of the Time War has festered and the Emperor believes himself to be a god.

His casing is substantially bigger than any normal Dalek's and exposes his biological body in a glass tank. It is still broadly conical, but has three shield-like plates with gaps between them. The space below his tank is big enough for a pair of orthodox "guard" Daleks. [To give some sense of scale, the spherical bobbles on the shell, normally the size of tennis balls, are the size of beachballs on this casing.] His voice, as with the previous "real" Emperor [4.9, "The Evil of the Daleks"] is more modulated and resonant.

Planet Notes

• *Barcelona*. This planet has dogs without noses. [We presume the customs officials have trained pigs.]

History

• *Dating*. There's no mention of Howard from the Market, which might suggest that it's at least two months before "The Christmas Invasion" (X2.0). Either way, it's after X1.11, "Boom Town", because Mickey remembers Cardiff.

Roderick claims that the Daleks disappeared 'thousands of years' prior to 200,1000. The continents of Earth in this era, shown as physically warping under a barrage from the Dalek fleet, are: Europa, Pacifica, the New American Alliance and Australasia.

• *The Time War*. Jack says that the Daleks were 'the greatest threat in the universe', but that they all up and disappeared one day - an event the Doctor attributes to their departing to fight the Time War. [This most likely refers to the "contemporary" Daleks (the ones that follow on from 25.1, "Remembrance of the Daleks") all vanishing, and shouldn't be construed to say that every single Dalek story prior to this never happened. Even in a "summon every Dalek to fight" scenario, they're hardly going to call upon their comparatively primitive forefathers ("The Daleks", etc.), and they're *certainly* not going to want to wholly eradicate their own history in such a fashion.]

The Emperor says that the Daleks died in the Doctor's 'inferno', but that his ship fell into the 'dark spaces'. With the ship ruined and him alone, the Emperor began manipulating humanity to give him suitable genetic material for a new army. He tries to resume the conflict, but Rose-as-Bad-Wolf waves her hand and reduces the ships and Daleks to dust.

Rose-Bad Wolf claims that the Time War here 'ends'. [See, however, X2.13, "Doomsday" et al.]

Catchphrase Counter Well, we get to find out what 'Bad Wolf' means [not that it's entirely helpful as an explanation, see the essay with this episode], but we get three 'fantastics' - two of them in the Doctor's dying words; the other, as we mentioned, is his instruction to Rose on what kind of life to have.

Deus Ex Machina The biggest one since regeneration: the Bad Wolf itself.

Bad Wolf - What, How and Why?

continued from Page 201...

Time War is still always being waged. Observe that it's after Rose has made a reappearance and Caan has rescued Davros that first the Cyber-King (X4.14, "The Next Doctor") and then Gallifrey (X4.18, "The End of Time Part Two") pop over to say hello. The Emperor identifies glow-in-the-dark-Rose as "The Abomination" ("The Parting of the Ways"). Note the definite article. She was expected.

One odd development that seems to connect this to later stories is that there has been a tendency of late for people to speak of Time as if it were a conscious entity, a player in the story rather than the location. The strangely unspecified nature of the sealing-off of the Time War is a matter for a later essay (**What Happened to Susan?** under "The End of Time Part Two"), but it's worth noting that the High Council, and especially the lady who may or may not be Chancellor Flavia or the Doctor's mother, say that "Time" is resurrecting everyone to die again and again. The rather puzzling ending to "The Wedding of River Song" (X6.13) requires there to be a universal observer of some kind to witness first this otherwise pointless wedding and then the Doctor's apparent death. This is all getting a bit *Sapphire and Steel*, and we will resume this story under "The Fires of Pompeii" (X4.2) and its essay.

What we're getting at is that raw Vortex power, combined with a consciousness, seems to have abilities almost entirely identical to whatever improbable coincidences a writer thinks he or she can get away with. Dalek Caan stage-manages flukes around Donna Noble left, right and centre and admits as much. Rose arranged for the clues she needed to be able to arrange those clues to be visible to her younger, non-angelic self. (Except... half of them happen when she's not around.) Rassilon plants a message to himself inside the Master's head via the Untempered Schism ("The End of Time Part Two"). Just as every movie-goer over the age of seven realises that in *Star Wars* the phrase "The Force" can be replaced with "The Plot" without changing the meaning of any line or incident, so "Bad Wolf" is cognate with "Deus ex machina". The bigger question is whether this kind of story arc is something the series should do every single year, or over even longer periods. (See **Should *Who* be Afraid of the Big Bads?** under X6.2, "Day of the Moon".)

And there is one last feat this being seems to have engineered. The next thing to happen to do with Artron energy and the TARDIS is the Doctor's regeneration. Within moments of having been fused to Rose's mind, the Ship helps its operator change into someone else. Someone with Rose's accent. Someone we later hear she finds "foxy" (X2.1, "New Earth"). The Doctor goes from Byronic, damaged, inaccessible surrogate father to Rose's ideal boyfriend with super-powers. Are you saying *that*'s a coincidence?

The Analysis

English Lessons

• *Nul Points* (n. Fr.): Obviously, it's French for "no points", but has a cultural connotation for anyone who grew up with the cosmopolitan cheese-fest of the Eurovision Song Contest. For a song to be so unappealing to voters of other nations as to not get anything is odd enough, but given the block-vote tendencies of various clusters of countries to give their neighbours top marks, a song has to be actively offensive and bad to not have a knee-jerk loyalty vote. The first to get this was Norway in 1978: traditionally, Sweden, Denmark and Finland *always* vote for Norwegian songs, no matter how deranged (see, for instance, "Saami Ednan", the 1980 entry). So Jahn Tiegans getting the first-ever *nul points* for the not-unappealing "Mil Etta Mil" was a shock and a turning point. Great Britain repeatedly getting it this century is usually seen as a comment on Tony Blair supporting the War against Iraq rather than anything to do with the lousy choices of song.

• *Marbella* (n. Sp): Island resort in Spain which, in the late 80s, was home to new forms of electronic dance music and a less intimidatingly hipper-than-thou club culture. The medium-term results of this more inclusive, less categorised scene was that austere Indie bands, especially from Manchester, loosened up and became dance-friendly whilst the Hip-Hop purists started sampling from a broader range of older music. A couple of years later, the Hacienda club in Manchester became the springboard for this to conquer the UK - "Madchester" - and an entire

X1.13 The Parting of the Ways

chapter of British Social History happened (albeit not one as sellable overseas as Punk or "Swinging London" had been). This incarnation of the Doctor looks and sounds as if he went there and inhaled.

Oh, Isn't That...? ("Bad Wolf" and "The Parting of the Ways")

• *David Tennant* first came to many people's attention in the 1996 comedy-drama *Taking Over the Asylum*, about a hospital radio service with a difference. One episode in particular got him noticed, when he upstaged not only main star Ken Stott but guest-star Spike Milligan. (See Volumes 1 and 2 for why this is a big deal - or simply look at the episode of *The Muppet Show* where Spike out-does the entire cast.) Many medium-sized roles followed, and eventually the two that cemented his status: as the policeman in the curious musical drama *Blackpool* (opposite David Morrissey, X4.14, "The Next Doctor"; and Sarah Parish, X3.0, "The Runaway Bride") and in the title role of *Casanova*, which was written by Russell T Davies and made by BBC Wales. As Casanova, Tennant had to be not only a plausible match for Peter O'Toole as his older self, but convincingly winning as the ultimate ladies' man. For this role, he dropped his usual scots accent and adopted a sort of all-purpose Estuary (see **What Are the Dodgiest Accents in the Programme?** under 4.1, "The Smugglers") and a trademark "Oh yes", sounding like WORR-Yuss. We'll hear that a lot over the next four years. (We'll also pick the bones of his career in the next "proper" episode.)

• *Jo Joyner* (Lynda Moss) was shortly afterwards one of the mainstays of *EastEnders* as Tanya Branning. There had been a lot of small but significant roles before this, including one in Davies' *The Second Coming*, a regular role in Toby Whithouse's *No Angels* (see X2.5, "Rise of the Cybermen") and sketch-show *Swinging* for which Gareth Roberts had contributed pieces.

• *Nisha Nayar* (Female Programmer). With *Doctor Who* being watched by the same audience as *The Story of Tracy Beaker*, a large percentage of the viewers will have been thinking "That's Elaine the Pain", the clueless social-worker. If you were watching "Paradise Towers" (24.2) more closely than even Mark Gatiss, you might have seen her as a Blue Kang.

• *Jo Stone-Fewing* (Male Programmer) was in *Mine All Mine*, so you can be forgiven for not having seen him.

• *Paterson Joseph* (Rodrick, a game contestant). One of the better casting decisions in *Neverwhere* (see X6.4, "The Doctor's Wife") was the camp, enigmatic Marquis de Carabas. Then Joseph was in peculiar medical sitcom *Green Wing* with Tamsin Grieg (X1.7, "The Long Game"). He has more recently been in the remake of Terry Nation's *Survivors*. At the time that series was shown, he was the bookies' favourite to replace David Tennant as the Doctor. The jury's still out on whether Matt Smith was a better choice...

• *Anne Robinson* (voice of Anne Droid). Originally a journalist, and the public face of the *Daily Mirror* during the period when Robert Maxwell was fleecing it ("The Long Game"), Robinson landed up as a cult figure for the bullying-themed game show *The Weakest Link*. She had hitherto been the host of consumer-protection show *Watchdog* and viewer-opinion outlet *Points of View*, notoriously winking rather stiffly at the viewers at the end.

• *Davina McCall* (voice of Davinadroid). The host of *Big Brother* when it had been on Channel 4, she had been the presenter of a great many less fondly-remembered series before that - and a shockingly poor chat-show shortly before the return of *Doctor Who*. She retained a lot of popularity, and has been largely forgiven for these because she is very good at live television.

• *Trinny and Susannah* (voices of Trine-E and Zu-Zana). Annoying posh women (surnames Woodall and Constantine) who presented *What Not to Wear* and patronised anyone not on an expense account for daring to do things that made practical clothing necessary. The website that made them famous in the first place collapsed, leaving investors £10 million in a hole, but they walked away unscathed. They then moved into relationship counselling (basically, getting people to take their clothes off in front of the cameras), and a number of increasingly unpopular follow-up series once the BBC had let them go (shortly after this episode was aired). They persist on minority cable channels and advertisements.

Things That Don't Make Sense ("Bad Wolf" and "The Parting of the Ways") [See the accompanying essay for the gulf between what we're told the Bad Wolf is, and what Rose-as-Bad-Wolf actually does.]

A continuity problem (if we're permitted to

The Parting of the Ways — X1.13

look ahead)... we last see the Extrapolator when it's outside the TARDIS and wired into the force field of the Game Station, and there is no opportunity to undo this before the TARDIS leaves (either time). So how has the Doctor got it back by the time of "The Runaway Bride" (X3.0)? They break off in *The Weakest Link* for adverts, and yet there is a License Fee. And what is there to advertise in the hellish world Lynda describes? Why have they cut back on the number of *Big Brother* shows running? Why does Lynda think she and the Doctor are the first-ever escapees, when ten minutes earlier she was telling him about an earlier mass-exodus that prompted the exo-glass windows? If there's only ten thousand channels as Lynda claims, why is her *Big Brother* series being shown on 'Channel 44000'?

The Doctor seems to think that a cloaked spaceship out beyond Pluto might be detected by Sonar. Maybe he's trying to prove to Jack that he's *not* a U-Boat commander (X1.9, "The Empty Child") by pretending he doesn't know you can't use sound-echoes in the vacuum of space. Radar isn't much use either, as 'the edge of the Solar System' is presumably the Kuiper Belt, and this is about a third of a light year off - you *might* just detect something that big, but you wouldn't know for eight months. Also, the Anne Droid appears to destroy three Daleks, but its "gun blast" is really a teleport beam, and the teleports have been disabled with the transmitters cranked up. So they've just sent a trio of quite angry Daleks somewhere else on the Game Station. Nice going.

And *now* no-one can see the Time Vortex and survive without help? What about the occasions when the Doctor has been out there "naked"? (7.4, "Inferno"; 9.1, "Day of the Daleks"; 9.5, "The Time Monster"; and most egregiously 17.6, "Shada".) In one of those stories, Jo Grant went skinny-dipping in spacetime - but the Daleks remained stoically unevaporated, even if their voices went funny. (Maybe it's the TARDIS power-supply aspect of it, in which case the Doctor's DIY project in 17.5, "The Horns of Nimon" ought to have been less inconsequential.)

The end credits say 'And introducing David Tennant as the Doctor'. We know what they *mean*, but the convention is that "introducing" indicates it's that person's first screen appearance ever.

Critique ("Bad Wolf" and "The Parting of the Ways") The conventional line is that this is two rather disjointed episodes, with the last five minutes of each having all the "good stuff". Fiddlesticks and flapdoodle! This is a 90-minute play with an awkward 167-hour intermission, and the pacing is designed to escalate the situation until Rose is sent packing, making each abrupt change or moment of *wha?* do its job. That job is to stop people from feeling that they know what's going on and what will happen. Retaining viewers on first transmission was the basic requirement, but watching it again as part of a complete work - knowing what's going to happen - makes the range of this story more apparent.

Let's start with the basics. Director Joe Ahearne and effects-man Mike Tucker's team managed to make one Dalek look as if it was a credible threat, whilst the script for "Dalek" made the creature inside the real focus of the story. On the back of this, they manage to make half a million of them look impressive without diluting this effect. In the original and current meanings of the word, the Daleks are *awesome*.

Juxtaposed against this is a set-up parodying popular shows. It has its cake and eats it, with the Doctor ranting about how these series work in our world as a pablum to stop anything worthwhile happening, but as guilty as anyone of enjoying the shows. An angry dig at the whole Society of the Spectacle and anything attacking the participants in these shows isn't going to happen here. If the parody is too affectionate for many, it exists and got on to prime time to an audience young enough to find criticism of it novel in itself. So that's space opera and social satire.

Into this mix they throw the single best moments of Eccleston's performance as the Doctor: his numbness on being arrested after Rose is zapped, his turn-on-a-sixpence switches of tone and mood in conversations, his hologram message, his abrupt capitulation as he realises that "cowardice" (in the eyes of the Dalek Emperor) takes more guts than crass heroism at the expense of all life on Earth... The rest of the cast come up to this level, led from the front. Piper isn't *quite* up to playing an omniscient goddess, but she manages to convey an impression that it isn't just Rose in there any more. Even for those not overly keen on John Barrowman's acting, it's remarkable to see how he justifies Jack's swagger by putting more energy into the scenes where he's facing insurmountable odds - Jack now makes sense as a character who makes the most of opportunities to pull because he spent a lot of his life genuinely expecting to be killed at any moment. Piper's

205

X1.13 The Parting of the Ways

wobbly theophany aside, there isn't a dud note in the whole enterprise. So they've ticked the boxes for space opera, social satire and straightforward drama.

And as all three of these have been pushed as far as they will go, we abruptly get cold water flung in our faces as Rose is back in the Powell Estate, forced to live in a world where the quality of coleslaw in a pizza place is the most urgent issue. All the things *Doctor Who* can now do better than anyone else are being done at once for the first time. Seen as a complete unit, these two episodes show not only the range of the series, but all the *combinations* of things that no other series can even think of attempting. As a package to sell the idea of *Doctor Who* to either overseas markets or the British Public, this is a story that has the lot. And that's rather the point.

BBC Wales now spent eight months, 13 episodes and an estimated £10 million getting rid of preconceptions. This is not a series with visible corner-cutting or substandard effects relying on an indulgent coterie audience who'll accept the unspoken message of "Look, just accept that it's not by, for and about geeks." You don't need to have studied the programme's past to degree level to work out what's going on. The main character isn't some posh twonk surrounded by vacuous eye-candy who get captured and never learn from one story to the next. Viewers whose favourite programme is *Hollyoaks* can get something out of this, viewers whose favourite programme is *Gardener's World* can follow it and, above all, the audiences who watch *Big Brother* and *The Weakest Link* won't be put off by the spaceships and council estate stuff.

Series One is essentially an exercise in teaching the non-cult audience how to watch *Doctor Who*. The whole Bad Wolf storyline was a simple exercise in getting people used to paying attention to apparently incidental details. The Doctor's relationship with Rose was an exercise in taking a wounded outsider who has lived for centuries and known the whole universe and turning him into something recognisably like the old series Doctors, but from the inside out - not making him wear a silly costume and talk continuity-soaked gibberish and hoping this will do the trick. He finally gets absolution for whatever he did to end the Time War and, against the odds, lives to tell the tale, at the cost of this particular incarnation. With all of these warm-up exercises done, they can start again with an audience ready for anything.

The audience who came in knowing that this quality was possible in a series treated as a national joke for a quarter century get bonuses too. The Dalek spaceships are overtly based on the *TV21* strips from the 60s. Nicholas Briggs gets to shout "My vision is impaired, I cannot see", the Doctor identifies himself as "The Oncoming Storm" and there's even a nod to Absalom Daak, Dalek Killer.

Davies promised Eccleston the biggest send-off imaginable. He delivered it. Nothing else would have been appropriate. The real achievement of the script and the people making it is that they throw the kitchen sink at us... and it all works. Daleks, Anne Robinson, the end of a complicated storyline, tears, jokes, action, more Daleks, romance, pathos, satire, an outrageous cheat and more Daleks than we have ever seen even in drawings we did as eight year olds. And then David Tennant shows up, and we realise we ain't seen nothing yet.

The Facts

Written by Russell T Davies. Directed by Joe Ahearne. Viewing figures: "Bad Wolf": (BBC1) 6.81 million, (BBC3 repeats) 0.3, 0.7 and 0.2 million [there was an extra "catch up" just before the next episode]. "The Parting of the Ways": (BBC1) 6.91 million, (BBC3 repeats) 0.3 and 0.7 million.

Overseas Promotion Boser Wolf, Le grand mechant loup, Zły wilk; Getrennte Wege, Rozstanie. (We can't find a French title for "The Parting of the Ways", so perhaps they used the same title for both episodes).

Production

("Bad Wolf" and "The Parting of the Ways") Back in 2001, when the first conversations between Davies and the BBC about *Doctor Who* began, he had suggested the idea of a lethal *Weakest Link* and come up with the gag about the Anne Droid. While other ideas proposed to then-Head of Drama Laura Mackie had fallen by the wayside (including, apparently, dinosaurs in London - see 11.2, "Invasion of the Dinosaurs" for why nobody had done this since 1974, and **What Are the Lousiest Cash-In Series?** under X4.10, "Midnight" for why nobody should have bothered), this one was still thought viable. *The*

The Parting of the Ways X1.13

Weakest Link was a BBC property and a worldwide hit, so it gave a parody global appeal that sending up, say, *Bargain Hunt* would lack. If this had not panned out, Plan B was the concept of live manhunts and killings, hinted at in the Anne Droid's question about "Murder Spree 20".

However, the Pitch document from 2003 included references to *The Weakest Link* and *Big Brother*, and it was soon after this meeting that the horse-trading began over the latter. Endemol, the company that was making the series, needed to be approached very early on in the production of the new series for clearances for the logo, music and format-specific details (obviously the name "Big Brother" isn't theirs, but the estate of George Orwell has a better claim if it ever leaves the public domain). James Dundas, the BBC Wales clearances negotiator, is said to have taken 11 months of patient talks with Endemol before a final green light was given. The final agreement to allow Paul Oakenfold's distinctive theme-tune came through very late on in the proceedings. Endemol threw themselves in to the idea, even amending their usual "eye" logo to include a spinning galaxy.

That first storyline had the control of the Station given over to a 14-year-old boy called "Edward", who was wired into all of the games. The look of Martha Cope's Controller was inspired the original Dalek Emperor (4.9, "The Evil of the Daleks"), a picture of which Gardner had seen in a book being used by Davies to sell the new series to possible co-production partners in America. The version of "The Parting of the Ways" (and it was always going to be called that) stopped with Rose stuck on Earth, unable to help the Doctor but determined to do something.

There are various stories of what the original end was supposed to have been, or if there was only one planned. It is known that a version of the script for the end did the rounds (and indeed was recorded), with Rose fatally affected by the Artron energy and the TARDIS monitor indicating "Life Form Dying". This might have been a genuine option if they had only got the one series of 13 episodes, although the decision to commission Series Two and Three had been made before that scene was shot. It may have been a conscious "dummy" to throw people off the scent: one plan was, apparently, to have included this in the version of the episode shown to the press in advance and then switch it for the real ending and spring a surprise regeneration on the public. Obviously, this was not an option when the series aired.

By the time Davies started writing these two episodes in November 2004, it was unclear whether the series would return after the climax of episode thirteen, but it was almost certain by this stage that Eccleston would be leaving. (It's reported that the last word, "Barcelona", was intended, in the event of non-renewal of the series, to be left at the "B" - as with 22.6, "Revelation of the Daleks" and the word "Blackpool".) Retaining him and losing Piper may have been an option, but that seems not to have been in anyone's game-plan.

The other elements needed for this episode were lined up in the two stories preceding it, so that the military character "Jax" who would actively fight the Daleks was introduced in the two-part World War II story, and then both the enhancement to the TARDIS force-field and the energy of the Ship allowing Rose to stage a rescue were in the cheap episode that followed. Davies had also made sure that the stories after "The Long Game" (X1.7) in production were almost all location shoots, so that the Game Station could be made from Satellite Five over the two months between the end of that shoot and the beginning of work on the finale. By this stage, the name of the entity had popped out from a stray line of dialogue he had added to X1.3, "The Unquiet Dead" about "the Bad Wolf", and this replaced "Gameshow World" as the title of the first half. Davies began writing episode twelve before getting clearance from the second show on his wish list, *Big Brother*.

• With his proven ability to wrangle Daleks, tug heartstrings and keep the cast enthusiastic, director Joe Ahearne was probably the optimum choice for these two episodes, even though he would still be making the previous episode. The script for the final episode was being written as "Boom Town" was on location, and the sequence of the Big Brother house (actually a flat in Canton, a bit of Cardiff they used a lot and which would get a one-story companion named after it in Series Six) was recorded two days before the end of recording for the Cardiff-based episode. This was 16th February, the day that the two new Dalek operators, Nicholas Pegg and David Hankinson, took their proficiency test over in Q2. They finished this the next day and got on with bits from other episodes; the hologram message was recorded on the 18th.

Then the material for Floor 500 began; as many of these scenes were when Rose seemed to be dead or was in 2006, Piper was able to pop to the

207

X1.13 The Parting of the Ways

year Five Billion for her newly-written chat with Rafallo (X1.2, "The End of the World"). Next day, there was a brief scene at the Temple of Peace for the same episode, now edited and found to be under-running, before more of Eccleston and Barrowman's visit to the top floor was shot. They did a bit more on Saturday and then on Monday a bit more, with Piper finally starting work on this episode on Tuesday and Nicholas Briggs (voicing the Emperor) on Wednesday and Thursday. The voice Briggs used was one he'd employed in his own *Dalek Empire* audio adventures for Big Finish, and was closely modelled on Peter Hawkins in "The Evil of the Daleks". This seems to have been when the Bad Wolf Rose arrived, and Piper was treated to an 80s-style makeover, with gold paint and industrial-strength hairspray to withstand the effects of the wind-machine. A day off, during which script revisions were made, then to the Newport City Live Arena, a former Bingo hall converted into a TV studio, for *The Weakest Link*. As would be the case a lot from now on, not everyone got all the script - a fact that vexed Paterson Joseph (playing Roderick).

• Anne Robinson had angered almost the entire population of Wales by listing it as a pet hate In the TV series *Room 101* (another Orwell-derived title). So, Ahearne, Davies, Collinson and sound recordist Paul McFadden went to the recording of her voice-overs in a studio in Berwick Street, Soho, in some trepidation. In fact, it was all fine and she was charming - Davies read the contestant's lines and helped with pronunciation of his made-up spacey names (most of which are half-Welsh). The amendations to episode thirteen made on 24th February included building up the Makeover series for Jack to resemble *What Not to Wear*. Trinny and Susannah were, it appears, double-booked for this and *Comic Relief* (see A4, "The Curse of Fatal Death" and "Time/Space" in Volume 9). Eventually, their scenes were slightly reworked and made somewhat shorter. (And then, a lot of what was recorded was dropped.) Davina McCall's material was done in one 15-minute session during the frantic lead in to *Big Brother 6*. In fact, the Anne Droid got some new line added and Robinson emailed these to the crew some time later.

• By this time, the transmission of "Rose" was settled for Easter Saturday, a month away, and the publicity machine started getting in the way of production. The weekend was given over to Eccleston and Piper recording trailers, including the one of the Newport rail-tunnel apparently on fire and the Doctor running down it. There was a press-launch in Brighton on the Monday evening (after more *Weakest Link* stuff and Rose's "death") that needed Briggs and Barnaby Edwards to do Dalek shenanigans. March began with the battle of Floor 499 and other sequences only needing Barrowman. He burned his arm slightly on shell-casings (there was a pair of professional armourers for this sequence). The next two days would see the same big set become Floor 56; the holding area for Jack, Lynda and the Doctor; and Floor 407. The scene of Lynda and the Doctor discussing other game shows was a late addition to make up the timing. Piper was back on the 4th to record both the real end of the story and the alternative ending. Some of the set-ups required stand-ins, who were given dummy scripts. The end of the regeneration was not recorded until some time later, after a new Doctor had been cast (which is another reason for doing it standing up rather than the supine cross-faded shots of the old series, only possible when both actors are on set at once).

• The design for the Dalek Emperor was a variation on one of the concept drawings for "Dalek", where they had tried out the idea of the shell rear-ranging itself like the Roman "Testudo" (turtle) formation of centurions' shields. The eventual effect was a composite of computer imaging and a model by Mike Tucker's team. Dan Walker, formerly an industrial designer, devised the final shape of the shell, whilst Neill Gorton supervised the occupant. The designs for this were part of the plan for the Dalek Ship set, although the models were nearly the last piece of this story to be recorded. The Ship set as physically realised was in the Enfys Television studios in another of the many industrial estates around Cardiff. The first day of this was the 5th, Eccleston's final day on the series. Eccleston had his photo taken with the entire crew, did press interviews and pieces for *Doctor Who Confidential* and then recorded the "Nul Points" scene. All of the scenes with Daleks were written to be made with multiples of three, because that's how many shells they had. Only two of these had radio-controlled heads, so Hankinson had to operate his the old-fashioned way. The shot of the Daleks recoiling from the Doctor's shout was improvised on the set. A gag that didn't make it past rehearsals was the Doctor sticking his middle finger up at the Emperor as he leaves. Instead, the shot of him stepping into the TARDIS was his last work on the series.

• It was now three weeks until the first episode was due to be transmitted, and already a copy was online. The press launch was three days later, and Eccleston began a series of interviews where he used the gruelling recording schedule to evade questions on how long he would stay in the role.

• The production team still had a lot to do, however. Another day on the Dalek ship had Piper alone with the pepperpots (and a sneak preview of the Emperor effect for the crew). Next day, she was at the press launch (a bigger news item than anyone who remembered the series limping off-screen in 1989 would have imagined) and Barrowman was on set doing more heroics, and there was the death of Lynda. Wednesday was TARDIS interiors with Piper, Camille Coduri and Noel Clarke and second-unit Dalek chicanery, including the Anne Droid zapping a Dalek before finally being made to shut up. At a pub in Cardiff, the Paddle Steamer (the locations for the TARDIS landing), the Trin-E and Zu-Zana costume/props were shown to the team. The design was partly based on the real women (one stocky, one skinny) and partly on 1960s food-mixers. In the morning, a nearby chip shop was used to represent… a chip shop. In the afternoon, the chains coming from inside the TARDIS prop were pulled first by Mickey's mini (the script had asked whether there was a tow-bar on a VW) and then the recovery vehicle. Coduri had to sit on the real driver's lap for some scenes. Finally, the shot of Mickey running up the road as he hears the TARDIS land were committed to tape, ending Piper's work on Series One. The wrap party was that night, but Barrowman had two more days to do, starting bright and early next morning.

• Barrowman's penultimate day was his birthday - he got a radio-controlled Dalek - and the day he was in his birthday suit. It was only just before transmission that the decision was taken higher up in the BBC to trim the shots of his buttocks; this mildly annoyed both Barrowman and Davies. Two days later, the 14th, was his last day of the series. This was back at Q2, and was Jack's death and resurrection. Just over a week later, in London, Tucker's crew began filming the Dalek Emperor. The designers thought that, with all the religious overtones of the character, his spindly arms would be in a position of prayer. On 23rd March, this was completed.

• Just under a month later, with a skeleton crew, David Tennant finished off the regeneration scene. He had not seen the lead-in to the Doctor's death, and wasn't anxious to, believing that every new Doctor gets a clean slate. It was decided that he would use the same accent as in *Casanova*, although he had teased the press that he would be the first kilt-wearing Doctor. As a hardcore, *DWM*-reading fan whose earliest memories included Jon Pertwee turning into Tom Baker, he had immediately bonded with Davies, joking that the way to account for his brown eyes turning into Peter O'Toole's famously blue ones in *Casanova* might involve a spaceship, a lighthouse and a diamond (15.1, "Horror of Fang Rock"). In the final dub for the Doctor's last/first scene, McFadden recorded a blowtorch to make the "volcanic" effect of the regeneration more punchy. Just this once, Tennant was credited as "Doctor Who" (see 18.7, "Logopolis").

• Once the biggest surprise had been blown, the emphasis for the publicity was on "how" rather than "what". In the week between the two episodes, there were trailers, each containing a different sneak preview of "The Parting of the Ways". Meanwhile, the online speculation about the true nature of Bad Wolf was itself a news item. And then the fact that this had become a news item became another news item, and so on. In Britain, more people remember this fact than what the answer was - much as "Who Shot JR?" had been a bigger story than the eventual answer. (Apparently, the one person unaware of all of this was the BBC1 Continuity Announcer, a Scottish woman who seemed convinced it was called "Doctor Woo".) Whatever the official ratings say, the simple fact was that there was simply no other television anyone was talking about that week. Not even *Big Brother 6*, which that year was mainly notable for an idiot rapper who called himself "Science".

X1.13a: "Pudsey Cutaway"

(18th November, 2005)

Which One is This? The *Children in Need* vignette about what happened just before X2.0, "The Christmas Invasion".

Firsts and Lasts The 1:56-long "Previously On…" has Eccleston's last appearance other than as a flashback clip, leading into the first time Tennant's name has been in the titles, at the start of the first

X1.13a Pudsey Cutaway

custom-made mini-episode for *Children in Need* (unless you are prepared to countenance "Dimensions in Time" as canonical, and you might be alone in that - not least because that will never *ever* be released commercially).

In this story, we have the first use of the "Artron Burp", wherein the miraculous orange sparkly pixie-dust of the Time Lords eructates from the Doctor's mouth as proof that his regeneration is a work-in-progress. And although it's not mentioned in the rather sparse end-credits, the music now has full orchestral back-up, even though it seems mainly to be re-used from the next few episodes in transmission order.

This is also the first episode to be broadcast without a title: the name "Pudsey Cutaway" was one used semi-seriously by the production team as a joke reference to the official designation of the ambiguously-titled X3.2, "Mission to the Unknown" (see **What Are These Stories Really Called?** under that episode/story, and the massive essay accompanying this slight installment, **What Constitutes a "Story" Now?**). It's named "Children in Need Special" on the DVD menus, whereas *Doctor Who Adventures* and *Doctor Who: The Encyclopedia* call it "Born Again".

And for those watching in November 2005 on BBC1, it's the first time this century that the Cloister Bell (18.7, "Logopolis" and frequently thereafter) sounds to ward that the TARDIS is in trouble. (For those watching on disc, it isn't.)

Watch Out For...

• The total running-time is a whisker over eight minutes. With the credits, the actual episode/scene starts two minutes and thirty-eight seconds in. If the set-up seems disproportionate, note that the ratings for this clip/bonus/episode/story were three and a half million up on those for "The Parting of the Ways" (X1.13), so the circumstances of the regeneration stood repeating for those just joining us. Besides, a lot of those viewers, and many in the studio audience, wouldn't have seen *any* of the series so far, not being entirely the kind of people who watch *Doctor Who* or any television on Saturday nights.

• If you compare the lighting in the TARDIS in the pre-credits reprise to the scenes in the actual... let's agree to call it a "vignette"... there is a marked change. As was usual in Series One, the regeneration was lit and set-up by cinematographer Ernie Vincz and makes full use of the green underlighting from the Console to make the Ship look all spooky like. This time, although nobody is credited, it looks more like the work of Euros Lyn's lighting cameraman for Block Four, Rory Taylor. There *is* a green light from above, which is on Rose until the line "and we never stopped running". Whatever the case, this is a definite shift in tone towards the TARDIS seeming like home and the new Doctor being the only weird thing in it.

The Continuity

The Doctor This new one speaks a lot faster, and tends to turn a simple 'no' into a machine-gun reiteration [rather as the Paul McGann model did]. He skips about the Console, at one point jumping like a four-year-old, and is rather puppyish. This becomes a full manic episode as his regeneration starts going wrong. He flips between being coherent and concerned and ebulliently pushing the TARDIS to go faster. He also offers Rose the chance to decide whether to stay by sending the TARDIS to the Powell Estate at Christmas Eve.

He can feel the presence of a mole on his back. This seems to please him. His right wrist seems to be a slight concern. [Still, it's not as if he's going to be wielding a broadsword around in the next few hours - see "The Christmas Invasion", where he reveals an alarming method of bulking up his sword-arm. See also **Things That Don't Make Sense**.] He's delighted to have more hair, and sideys, and is perplexed at being thinner. He's not happy about his complexion. He's so concerned, in fact, about listing all the things about his new body we can't see, for once he is remarkably unconcerned with what he looks like. [This is, obviously, so that the previously recorded scene where he demands to know if he's ginger isn't redundant (since that episode will be shown overseas and repeated a lot more than this one-off).]

• *Background.* Apparently, there was an unseen adventure where the Doctor and a companion [probably not Rose, as she shows no sign of remembering this incident] had to hop for their lives. [Could this be the incident with the Terrible Zodin? If so, the Doctor's muddled up Rose with the post-retirement Brigadier - see 20.7, "The Five Doctors"; 22.1, "Attack of the Cybermen"; and a mention in *The Sarah Jane Adventures*.]

What's a "Story" Now?

As part of the publicity build-up for "Dragonfire" (24.4), it was proclaimed that this would be the 150th *Doctor Who* story. Twenty-two years later, in the hype for "Planet of the Dead" (X4.15), this episode was proclaimed to be No. 200, and the bus in which the Doctor and his chums crossed the cosmos was given that number. Anyone trying to make both of these true has a problem.

The problem has been compounded by the BBC Wales series making each episode appear to be distinct, giving all of them different titles, even if this means including "Part One" and "Part Two" in the names of the Christmas and New Year specials for 2010. The curious accounting that gave "Planet of the Dead" the No. 200 was in a poll organised by *Doctor Who Magazine*, and this had some odd decisions. It counted Season Twenty-Three not only as one story, given the overall title *The Trial of a Time Lord*, but also the four individual stories under that heading (23.1, "The Mysterious Planet"; 23.2, "Mindwarp"; 23.3, "Terror of the Vervoids"; and 23.4, "The Ultimate Foe"), making *five* stories in their tally. They counted the Paul McGann TV movie (not made by the BBC, strictly speaking), but not the *Children in Need* specials, made by the *Doctor Who* team in Cardiff, starring David Tennant and written by Russell T Davies and Steven Moffat respectively. They counted "Utopia" (X3.11) as the start of a three-part story, despite the fact that it was made in a different recording block, set in a different time and planet, with a different director and with only the regular cast in common (John Simm never appears with them as the Master, the regeneration being filmed on a different day and happening inside the locked TARDIS). Even Russell T Davies doesn't think of it as one story.

One thing that was notable was a separate vote for a selection labelled "And Just For The Pedants..." that included 17.6, "Shada" (made - almost - as part of Season Seventeen and released on a BBC video; the Region 1 DVDs include the story in their back-cover numbering); 18.7a, "K9 & Company" (acknowledged in 20.7, "The Five Doctors"; X2.3, "School Reunion" and a whole spin-off series - possibly two, if you count the Australian thing), the *Children in Need* mini-episodes and "The Infinite Quest" (see Volume 8, Appendix 1). This sub-section also incorporated definite no-nos such as "A Fix With Sontarans" (see 22.4, "The Two Doctors"), the two Peter Cushing movies and 90s charity freakshows "Dimensions in Time" and "The Curse of Fatal Death" (see the appendices to Volume 6). There is no mention of the radio episodes ("Slipback", etc.), but the webcast "Scream of the Shalka" is included. They also got the names of the first three stories wrong, but that's another matter (see **What Are These Stories Called?** under 3.2, "Mission to the Unknown").

Evidently, this is a more complicated matter than it appears. What are the criteria for calling any collection of episodes "a story"? In the earliest days of the series, it was all one long narrative, each adventure beginning at the end of an episode. As a production, there was a budget allocation for a group of episodes written by the same person, but if we go with production rather than reception, then Season One ends with "The Dalek Invasion of Earth" (2.2) and "Carnival of Monsters" (10.2) belongs with Season Nine. What viewers were expected to *perceive* as a self-contained story is quite another matter. The very first episode ends with the start of what is, for most practical purposes, a totally separate adventure in prehistoric times after an elaborate set-up for the programme's premise and protagonists. Some people treat episodes two, three and four of "An Unearthly Child" (1.1) as "The Tribe of Gum". Yet they are all written by Anthony Coburn and directed by Waris Hussain. They all have incidental music by Norman Kay. The change in writer, director and composer marks the start of a new story (1.2, "The Daleks"), but even then it's muddy, because three of the seven episodes are directed by Richard Martin and the rest by Christopher Barry.

Clearly, the boundaries are porous; if we decide that the credited writer is the distinguishing mark of a story in this early phase, we have a reliable rule-of-thumb until we get to "The Daleks' Master Plan" (3.4), when Dennis Spooner comes in to flesh out Terry Nation's back-of-an-envelope notion for where the story ought to go after episode four of this 12-part epic. Making this our guideline helps us resolve the problem of "Mission to the Unknown", made as part of the same production as the previous story (3.1, "Galaxy 4") with the same director and about 1/5th of the budget allotted for the five episodes spent on this stand-alone episode on a different planet with different

continued on Page 213...

X1.13a Pudsey Cutaway

The Supporting Cast

• *Rose* isn't convinced that the Doctor being replaced by this new fellow is not an alien trick. She lists various previous antagonists, warning this stranger that she's not easily fooled. Being reminded of their first meeting does the trick. She doesn't remember hopping for her life. She wants the Doctor to change back, but doesn't say she wants to leave.

• *Jack*. The Doctor tells Rose that the Captain is busy rebuilding Earth. [This seems odd, especially as an excuse for not going back. What's really odd is not that the Doctor claims to know what Jack's doing, but that Rose - who only a few moments earlier had forgotten everything about being Mistress of the Universe - knows that Jack's alive.]

The TARDIS There is a small switch on one of the coral-like braces that the Doctor hasn't used in years; it accelerates the passage through the Vortex. The Doctor speaks, when not at his most coherent, of breaking the Time limit.

Planet Notes The planet *Barcelona* is apparently most visitable in October 5006. On a Tuesday.

The Analysis

The Big Picture After a year of benefitting from BBC internal politics, it was time for Russell T Davies to pay the Corporation back. As you will recall from "The Five Doctors", the BBC's annual *Children in Need* appeal had been running since 1928 and had been the big telethon a month before Christmas since the late 70s. When the 1993 show had the theme of 3D, the organisers sanctioned a brief 30th anniversary *Doctor Who* playlet, a cross-over with *EastEnders* that was even worse than that sounds (A3, "Dimensions in Time"). Where the broadcast of "The Five Doctors" had been overlaid with on-screen messages about the pledging process, the things people had done and so on, this was specifically to be shown with only the phone-number or website address in a corner. Davies was insistent that no audience reaction (laughter, applause, booing) was to be included and that the plot was to have no links to the appeal. The BBC tried to get a Pudsey Bear toy onto the Console, but this didn't happen either.

Instead, the suggestion came from Julie Gardner that a gap existed between the regeneration and the start of "The Christmas Invasion" that she wanted to see. The format of a scene - emphatically not a "sketch" - for the appeal telethon made this possible. As we will see (**Has All the Puff "Totally" Changed Things?** under X2.1, "New Earth"), the BBC were very committed to establishing *Doctor Who* as a "brand" and promoting it in its other activities whilst using it to promote services and facilities. *Children in Need* is characterised by all aspects of the BBC being shown letting their hair down, even the most solemn and worthy. As used only to be the case when Morecambe and Wise did their Christmas extravaganzas, the staid newsreaders, stodgy sports commentators and "serious" actors all stepped out of character, with decreasing returns as it became expected of them. The *Doctor Who* production team were keen to establish the series as here to stay, so the potential element of self-parody was nipped in the bud. In order not to make the show's team seem like party-poopers, a lot of the inserts from Piper and Tennant for how to donate were done jokily (they did various, including special ones for Wales and Scotland). It's worth noting that subsequent "specials" for *Children in Need* have been sneak previews of the forthcoming Christmas episode (or similar - see X4.16, "The Waters of Mars"). Instead, all specifically written mini-episodes have been for the two-yearly *Comic Relief* telethons in spring (see A4, "The Curse of Fatal Death" and the appendices to Volume 8).

Children in Need has a long lead-in, during which the public get to perform their various fundraising stunts and events. So announcing this episode four weeks before transmission was a gamble, especially as this was two weeks before they shot the scene.

English Lessons *Nut Loaf* (n): What people who don't know any vegetarians think vegetarians eat all the time: a sort of loaf of mixed nuts and oil, to be baked alongside or instead of whatever meat is in the Sunday roast (see X2.4, "The Girl in the Fireplace" for this faded tradition). Most actual vegetarians would rather have a Christmas dinner of something using filo pastry, spinach and ricotta (for some reason this combination has caught on, even among people who wouldn't eat either alone) or at a pinch some myco-protein, such as Quorn (see 10.5, "The Green Death" for the fictional precursor of this).

What's a "Story" Now?

continued from Page 211...

characters. Except... "Mission to the Unknown" is a one-off episode that serves as the prelude for the epic "Master Plan" that follows a month later, making it effectively a 13-part story. Except... the middle of the 12-week Dalek story has an episode going out on Christmas Day with no Daleks and no connection with the previous or subsequent episodes, *but*, as part of the same production, with the same director and budget allocation. So do we differentiate on grounds of what the BBC financiers thought was "a story" or what the viewers at home perceived?

Well, if the latter, the end of the episode "The Plague" would have been an eye-opener. It has all the hallmarks of being the end of a two-part story and then... it isn't, it's halfway through "The Ark" (3.6) as we now call it. The *Radio Times* may have given the game away, but most viewers would have been sold a dummy. Is this really two stories on the same set? The TARDIS crew are the only actors in all four episodes, as the humans on the Ark in the latter half are the descendants of the earlier characters and the Monoids were non-speaking roles in the first half, so even if the same actors are in the suits, it's as different people. Shortly after this, the BBC got fed up with giving each individual episode a title and told everyone at home that 3.9, Story AA was called "The Savages" and was subdivided into episodes (four, as it turned out). The viewers got used to everything having a story-title and episode-number, and the *Radio Times* would tell the readers how many to expect and all this Hartnell malarkey seemed irrelevant. Then, in 2005, episodes got individual titles again and it all got messier than ever.

The same rule that made "'The Ark" one story makes "Rose" (X1.1), "Aliens of London" (X1.4) and "World War Three" (X1.5) all one story. They have the same writer, director, semi-regular performers and location and were made in the same recording block. (This is so obvious that the awkwardness of referring to what is obviously one story by two titles has led to people inventing shorthand, such as "Bad Parting" for the last two Eccleston episodes.) Obviously, "Rose" is intended to be a stand-alone one-part story, the first since "Mission to the Unknown" forty years earlier. (The precise nature of 20.7, "The Five Doctors" is a legal mine-field as well as everything else that complicates it. Keep reading.)

But what about the other two episodes made in Block One? They are presented to us as continuous - but so are "Rose" and "The End of the World" (X1.2). The clear intention is for the two episodes to be treated as halves of a two-part story, but what makes that obvious? The main difference is that it appears at the end of the second half that we have closure; the story has left the main characters and the world in which they are active at some kind of equilibrium. The earth is safe, the Slitheen thwarted and dead, Harriet Jones has a job to do worthy of her pluck and ingenuity, Mickey and the Doctor have reached an understanding, and Rose has asked her mother's permission to resume her adventuring (even if this is only given grudgingly). Sorted! Except... six weeks later (X1.11, "Boom Town"), Mickey will be lying to Rose about how well he's coped and one of the Slitheen is out for revenge. Six months after *that*, Harriet has to be deposed after she annoys the Doctor and his relationship with Mickey and Jackie is altered (X2.0, "The Christmas Invasion"). These could be seen as extraneous to the story told in the two episodes in 10 Downing Street and the Powell Estate, but another way of looking at it - Davies' preferred interpretation - is that this incident is part of the bigger story of the Doctor and Rose's extended family, one that also includes "Father's Day" (X1.8), and many others in Series Two and beyond. This had happened, after a fashion, in earlier phases of the series. In the later stretches of Jon Pertwee's term, having a script-editor and producer who had worked in soaps made the medium-term planning of the characters' destinies a key part of the programme. The last few years before the series went away, there was a messy attempt to hint of forthcoming developments for the Doctor and Ace and big shocking revelations that never quite came. (See **Did Cartmel Have Any Plan At All?** under 25.3, "Silver Nemesis" and **Is Continuity a Pointless Waste of Time?** under 22.1, "Attack of the Cybermen".) Davies had plans for the characters and destination-points for the situations, in keeping with many of the customs and practices of cult TV.

continued on Page 215...

X1.13a Pudsey Cutaway

Things That Don't Make Sense The Doctor's convulsions apparently make the entire TARDIS shake (or maybe just the camera, as Rose stays remarkably still).

The Doctor flexes his right wrist and then checks it with his left thumb and forefinger, detecting what he calls a 'slight weakness in the dorsal tubercule'. What he's actually examining is his flexor carpi ulnaris (the muscle) and ulnar styloid (the bone, see X3.8, "Human Nature") - the dorsal tubercule, which of course isn't to be found in healthy humans, would be a growth on one of the bones in his back, a rib or vertebra. (Just let's remember, the author's dad is a Latin teacher. Let's also remember that the Doctor traditionally talks cobblers when he's just regenerated.)

Critique There's always a risk of damning with faint praise when looking at such vignettes, but there's not much option here. It's adequate for its purpose, watchable when not in the middle of an evening's variety and sob stories, and doesn't cause big continuity errors. Robbed of the curiosity-value of being our first proper glimpse of the new Doctor, what we have is something that doesn't fit into either of the bigger episodes that surround it. This is worth a look, but hardly much more. What stands out revisiting it now is that the theme-tune plays under a shot of the TARDIS in vortex, and it still seems like as plausible an end as the scene that follows. There's no plot progression until the regeneration starts failing, and even that is a sort of warning for what will follow in the "proper" episode. Tennant going mental, it turns out, isn't much different from the performance he'll give for the next four years.

The Facts

Written by Russell T Davies. Directed by Euros Lyn. Although the official viewing figures for that section of *Children in Need* containing the six-minute mini-episode are about nine million, the recorded peak for this episode is 10.8 million. There being no repeat or online catch-up facility, this has to be taken at face value. The episode was scheduled to miss *Coronation Street*, and so the main opposition was *Gardeners' World* and a re-run of *Ghostbusters*.

Repeats and Overseas Promotion For obvious reasons, this has never been repeated, nor was it on the original DVD releases. It is included as an extra on the Series Two box set.

Alternate Versions The DVD edition in the Series Two box set has a conventional alarm-bell instead of the Cloister Bell.

Production

As is usual for *Children in Need*, everyone gave their time for free. Time was a concern, as the only slot free was in the middle of making the four episodes in Block Three of Series Two, the Graeme Harper-directed Cybermen two-parters. Euros Lyn, who had directed Block Two and was going to do another later that series, was available. Tennant and Piper were the only cast needed, and only the TARDIS set at Q2 was required. The shoot was over a five-hour period on 3rd November, just over two weeks before transmission on Friday 18th. The two leads had by this stage been working together for five months, and Tennant found getting back into Eccleston's costume a bit strange.

- The timing was handy, as a start for the pre-publicity for "The Christmas Invasion". Although there was a risk of the episode-ette defusing some of the surprise, it was hoped that the delay would help this fade and the previously recorded episode would still be surprising. It was also hoped that the occasion and the performances would offset the fact that it was just two people talking for five minutes. The episode was trimmed of one line before broadcast, where the Doctor comments on the lack of reflective surfaces.

- The episode was introduced by the appeal's main host, Sir Terry Wogan, and John Barrowman (who sang later in the evening). It came ahead of performances in that segment of the show by Madonna and Rod Stewart, but the overall ratings for this half-hour were one and a half million viewers fewer than for this eight minutes. £17 million was pledged just on that night.

What's a "Story" Now?

Pudsey Cutaway   X1.13a

continued from Page 213...

While *Doctor Who* was off air from 1989 to 2005, the majority of the shows herded together into the "cult" ghetto had such forward planning as standard. As we discussed in Volume 6, the starting-points for this were the "novel for television" *Babylon 5* and the "comic for grown-ups" *Sandman*. (Arguably, though, both were influenced by the 70s BBC space-soap *Blake's 7* - which could thus be considered the single most influential thing Terry Nation ever did, even though Chris Boucher did most of it.) Both of these, and the many, many TV shows that followed in their wake, deliberately teased the audience with hints of what was to come and artfully deployed clues and red-herrings. These were discussed online, and attempting to figure out in advance what was planned became part of how you watched. In cases such as *Lost* and *Heroes*, the effort may have been misplaced; in the new *Battlestar Galactica*, there was widespread anger when the extent to which the makers were making it up as they went along was revealed, and the ending turned out to be the hoariest cliché imaginable. Individual episodes, no matter how entertaining or self-contained, were no longer the basic unit of plotting.

The most obvious example, *Buffy the Vampire Slayer*, gave us the terminology to discuss the season-length revelation of the major antagonist: the "Big Bad". *Doctor Who* in its new formation followed this template exactly. In its first year, with no guarantee of its renewal after 13 weeks, the individual episodes were all leading towards one end. The surprise of the year (after the one they had planned for us was blown) was that "The Long Game" (X1.7) was less of a throwaway than as at first appeared. As an episode and story in its own right, it was relatively insubstantial - but as a tile in the mosaic, it gained with hindsight. This meant that *Doctor Who* was finally detached from its original conception, planned before they even knew it was to be about time travel, of being a series of serials. It was now *one* serial, with individual episodes having their own self-contained plots (paradoxically, the same could be said of the first and last black and white episodes). This moved the focus simultaneously inward and outward from the previous state of affairs, when after the last episode of a story it was possible to proceed as though that story had not happened. There had been a clear distinction between stories that were somehow part of the grand scheme of things and those that had no significance beyond themselves - even though between "Full Circle" (18.3) and "Time and the Rani" (24.1), there had only been one story that had been planned as a "stand-alone" (22.2, "Vengeance on Varos") and even that spawned a sequel that was part of the over-arching saga. The new regime made each 45-minute episode, if not entirely self-contained, certainly self-sufficient as entertainment. The pre-credit sequences could be adjusted to include recaps of the situation so far, not necessarily a straightforward reprise of the cliffhanger as had been the case before.

So it was that for the 2005 *Children in Need* telethon, the BBC broadcast an eight-minute episode, made as part of Series Two, showing what happened to Rose and the newly regenerated Doctor between the end of "The Parting of the Ways" and the start of "The Christmas Invasion". Is this a story? It has the formal properties of an episode, a pre-credit reprise of the regeneration, titles, the two stars, the TARDIS set, music, a script by the main writer and end titles (of sorts). What it lacks is any dramatic development. "The Christmas Invasion" had been written, shot and edited before the decision to make this vignette was taken, so the plot had to run on the spot, not changing anything about the Doctor and Rose, whilst keeping viewers watching. As a part of the bigger story, it's intriguing and provides details we didn't have (and one that might be significant about the Doctor's right arm), but the dead giveaway is the face of Sir Terry Wogan just after it was broadcast as part of his telethon: *Is that it?*, he seems to be about to ask. When the DVDs came out, this was not included in the "vanilla" set, but relegated to being an extra on the box set (with the sound slightly messed up). Wogan calls it "a special extra scene..." and the consensus is that this is a side-salad to the "real" episodes. Is that the case? For anyone used to stories split into episodes, there is nothing objectionable about the format of this piece, but the notion of self-contained 45-minute "segments" (an American term some commentators have taken to using, even though it is singu-

continued on Page 216...

X1.13a Pudsey Cutaway
What's a "Story" Now?

continued from Page 215...

larly inappropriate in this connexion) has taken root. So much so that when a season-opener ends with the Doctor not even having met the aliens yet (X6.1, "The Impossible Astronaut") after three-quarters of an hour of setting up riddles, and not giving the slightest comfort for people who want instant answers, it is treated by the press as a deliberate insult to the viewers.

It could be countered that this ignores the use to which the episodes (and mini-episodes) are put by viewers and the BBC, not simply as narrative but as events. The first broadcast of any one piece is something to talk about and experience communally, but repeated transmission, online access, DVD sales and widespread discussion make any episode of *Doctor Who* made this century something that will be endlessly re-encountered (see **Should *Doctor Who* be Appointment Television?** under X4.14, "The Next Doctor") and, on stumbling across a re-run episode on a digital station, the viewer has to figure out where in the longer-term narrative that episode sits. The publicity for each new episode has had to be about mysteries and clues, moments to watch out for and memorable images. In the commentary surrounding it, there would be a great deal of discussion about what it means for the regular characters. Again, the parallel with 80s stories that tried this is uncomfortable - something like "Planet of Fire" (21.5) existed as part of the Doctor/Master bitchfest, but with a different backdrop, as did "The King's Demons" (20.6) and "The Mark of the Rani" (22.3). The intrinsic merits (if any) of these stories and historical/exotic settings were so far down in the mix, viewers wondered why they had bothered. We are now in a position where entire 45-minute episodes exist to set up longer stories ("The Long Game" and "Boom Town", for example) and where a split-second incident in an otherwise forgettable episode seems to be the only reason for watching (e.g. Madam Kovarian's cameo in X6.3, "The Curse of the Black Spot", which led to lots of speculation on whether a character simply vanishing was a devious clue or simply inept direction).

In many ways, this seems like an attempt to return us to the programme's roots as a series of serials, with individual stories partaking of bigger ones (will Ian and Barbara get home? Will the Daleks be back?) whilst remaining distinct. It does so in a more planned and controlled manner, and with the same production designers and composer across entire series and usually the same lighting cameraman - so that all those stories filmed in disused castles or churches look interchangeable and the same murky, oily look pervades every planet and time visited in the first half of Series Six. Individual episodes are judged on what they bring to the longer story more than what they are like as episodes or stories. Again, this is vaguely familiar to long-term fans, as both "The Almost People" (X6.6) and "The War Games" (6.7) are seen by many as lengthy preambles to the "real" point, what happens at the end. However, the closing moments of any new episode are deliberate disruptions to any sense of equilibrium that the story's innate tendency towards an ending might have brought. We have the "throw-forwards" (or "trailers" in old money) or a Simon Cowell-style slamming of big silver letters saying To. Be. Continued. We also have tag-scenes that re-open questions the viewers might have forgotten - near enough the last ten minutes of "Day of the Moon" (X6.2) is given over to these - and we have little verbal hints that any balance or harmony is short-lived. Series Two seems to end every episode with people asking how long the Doctor and Rose can get away with it. Again, this endless deferral of a place to pause was normal once, to the extent that when the broadcast season ended before the production series, they would add a little temporary ending on the close of the last episode to be shown before the summer holiday (1.8, "The Reign of Terror"; 2.9, "The Time Meddler"; and most curiously 5.7, "The Wheel in Space").

Something else that used to be a common part of the programme's wobbly boundaries was the use of specially made trailers. Season Five had scripted scenes using elements of the story starting next week for three stories. "The Ice Warriors" (5.3) was introduced with a short spoken introduction by Leader Clent explaining the global plan to stop the glaciers, and then Penley contradicting it. More alarmingly, the end of "The Enemy of the World" had the Doctor running down a tube tunnel and, seeing the children watching, telling them that the Yeti would be back next week (5.5, "The Web of Fear") but looking scarier, so it might be an idea to hold mummy and daddy's hands in

Pudsey Cutaway   X1.13a

What's a "Story" Now?

case they're scared. The end of "The Wheel in Space" had an on-screen introduction to a repeat of "The Evil of the Daleks" (4.9), and the first episode of this, when repeated, had a voice-over by the Doctor explaining the end of "The Faceless Ones" (4.8) to Zoe and, thereby, anyone else watching who hadn't seen that story. Zoe was used as the pretext for the Doctor talking to us. In various episodes made this century, we have been "eavesdroppers" on a character, usually the companion of the day, telling a story to... *someone*, but not "really" us. Nothing like the prologue to 14.3, "The Deadly Assassin" - explicitly addressing the viewers - occurs in the new series (although asides to camera from Clara seem to be hinting at a change in this policy), and so these can't be counted as part of the episodes any more than the Doctor apparently skipping the chance to rush to the Brigadier's aid long enough to watch Disney films on August Bank Holiday 1975 can be counted as part of "Terror of the Zygons" (13.1)[38]. However, look at what now happens online. Series Two had "TARDISodes" for each episode, and three of the first chunk of Series Six had "prequels" on the BBC's website. None of the material in these was germane to the broadcast episodes, or added much to our understanding, but they set the mood for the following adventure. (Indeed, our decision to put **What Are the Best Online Spin-Offs?** under "The Curse of the Black Spot" is motivated partly because the prequel clip was so much better-received by fans than anything in the episode itself.)

Perhaps the most peculiar instance of the series having boundary issues is that the cliffhangers to "Last of the Time Lords" (X3.13) and "Time Crash" (X3.13a), are the same: the TARDIS being ruptured by the *Titanic*. The second *Children in Need* special is inserted into the narrative between Martha leaving and the collision so that anyone who missed or ignored the one-scene story can go from the end of the series proper to the Christmas Special as originally intended, and those who *did* see the double-Doctor vignette can have a better idea of why the shields were down and a ruddy great space-faring ocean-liner smashed its way through the walls of a normally impenetrable time machine. But when individual viewers are left to choose what bits of the whole run of *Doctor Who* "really" happened, it gets horribly messy. (See **Where Does "Canon" End?** under 26.1, "Battlefield" and weep, then look at **Was There a Martian Time-Slip?** under X4.16, "The Waters of Mars" for the apparent decision at the highest level that 7.3, "The Ambassadors of Death" never happened at all.)

series 2

X2.0: "The Christmas Invasion"
(25th December, 2005)

Which One is This? Does exactly what it says on the tin. Robot Santas, killer Christmas trees, that sort of thing. And the new Doctor figures out who he is by taking on alien swordsmen single-handed (literally, at one point).

Firsts and Lasts Whilst this isn't the first purpose-built Christmas episode (that was precisely 40 years before; see 3.4, "The Daleks' Master Plan"), this was the first time a complete story, independent of the main series, was commissioned to go out on 25th December. So this was the first time an episode got its first showing on a Sunday. And despite X1.13a, "Pudsey Cutaway" (commissioned and made after this), it's really our first look at the new Doctor.

This is the first episode to be exactly one hour long, at least in its natural state. We hear the revised theme tune, using the BBC Wales Orchestra to give it some welly, including the major-key "middle eight". Murray Gold also sets a new precedent by having the first specifically composed pop song on the soundtrack (the Phil Spector pastiche "Song for Ten", heard as the Doctor selects his new wardrobe), something that will also happen in the next two Christmas specials. This story has the first of five uses to date of Slade's definitive Christmas single, "Merry Xmas Everybody". (Non-British readers who don't know this have our sympathy - forget Dickens, this is what Christmas is like here, and anything else is a feeble substitute.)

We have the first of two appearances by the Robot Santas (the second being X3.0, "The Runaway Bride"), the first mention of an *organisation* called "Torchwood" (as opposed to it being a monument; see X1.12, "Bad Wolf"), and the first time that humans across the world have unequivocal proof of aliens with evil intent and Britain's ability to defend Earth. We see the Doctor decide to wreck established history simply because he can (see X4.16, "The Waters of Mars" for where this leads), and, according to some fan-lore, it's the first mention of Martha Jones (as she is occa-

Series 2 Cast/Crew

- David Tennant (the Doctor)
- Billie Piper (Rose Tyler)

- Russell T Davies (Executive Producer)

sionally claimed to have been the med student staying with Tina the Cleaner; Jackie nicks a stethoscope from this unseen character). UNIT get a *seriously* hi-tech HQ underneath - get this - the Tower of London (see **The Big Picture** for why this and much else here was a bit familiar to hardcore fans). Also, the British Rocket Group (not named aloud, but clearly the idea behind Daniel Llewellyn's space-probe organisation, as evidenced by a screen behind Llewellyn during his press conference, his badge and the BBC's website material) finally make an on-screen appearance (unless you count 7.3, "The Ambassadors of Death", and reconciling these two stories will take rather a lot of doing).

Whilst the newscaster Trinity Wells has been shorthand for worldwide opinion before (X1.4, "Aliens of London"), this is the first time that a global crisis of this scale has been outlined by her. It's also the first time that the public have been possessed en masse in the new series (see X2.5, "Rise of the Cybermen" for more - and indeed, it will happen about once a year in *The Sarah Jane Adventures* until the last story, where Clyde comments on this).

This was the first time that the coveted *Radio Times* Christmas cover went to *Doctor Who*, and a 16-page behind-the-scenes feature was also included (with a couple of hefty spoilers). And in the final seconds, we have the first season-trailer grafted on to the end of the Christmas episode (Ooh! Werewolves, robots in wigs, cats in wimples and... surely it can't be... K9? Oh, and a Cyberman.) and the credit thanking the Canadian Broadcasting Corporation.

And this was the first time that English Heritage allowed a lot of actors and film-crew to walk on the roof of the Tower of London to make a TV show. *That's* how much goodwill *Doctor Who* had by then. And, to gladden the hearts of old-time fans, the interior and hull of the Sycorax space-

How Long is Harriet in Number 10?

As we mentioned in **Things That Don't Make Sense**, for Harriet Jones to go from being the most popular Prime Minister in living memory to oblivion in a week is unlikely - and to do so over the Christmas holidays, when there is no Parliament to depose her, is impossible. There is also the small matter of her seeming (to any outside observer) to have single-handedly saved Earth from alien Witch-Doctors - a guaranteed vote-winner. The impression Davies wanted to give is that the Doctor's high-handed behaviour caused the Master to get in to Number 10 (X3.12, "The Sound of Drums"), but not only is this not actually possible under UK constitutional law, it doesn't even fit the facts established in his other scripts.

Moreover, looked at from the other direction, the Master's plan requires him to twiddle his thumbs for a lot longer than is plausible, even though we later discover that he also created a pseudo-religious cult around himself just in case he was cremated (X4.17, "The End of Time Part One"). All right, so stupidly over-complicated and risky fiendish schemes are his thing, but even compared to hiding in a Jurassic ziggurat, dressing up as Ali Bongo and stealing Concorde (19.7, "Time-Flight"), this is ludicrous. This version of the Master isn't someone who would have the patience for the scheme we're told about unless there is no alternative.

In "The Sound of Drums", the journalist Vivian Rook refers to Harriet's "downfall", which could mean almost anything. Given how popular Mrs Jones was *before* the Sycorax ship was shot down - never mind that this isn't exactly something that would alienate a large contingent of the British electorate - any slide in support would be an event. Some political commentators use the word "downfall" in connexion with Tony Blair, who never lost an election and survived a colossal dent in his popularity after 2003 through the lack of any coherent opposition. He still won his last election with a landslide, but the shine had come off his halo. The version of British politics in this version of *Doctor Who* is so bizarre, we've got a whole essay on it in Volume 8. For now, we'll just focus on when the Saxon landslide happened, what exactly this "downfall" said to have happened "18 months" earlier was, and whether or not there's an anonymous Prime Minister between these two events.

An earlier draft of this essay went on for twelve thousand words while trying to work out the dates of the new *Doctor Who*, *Torchwood* and *The Sarah Jane Adventures* based on internal evidence, and came to the conclusion that the on-screen details in *Torchwood* are either a complete pack of lies or the result of the Time Rift messing up everyone's calendars. However, the *sequence* of events is still helpful. We've decanted the list of evidence into two other essays, one under X2.3, "School Reunion" dating *The Sarah Jane Adventures* vis-à-vis *Doctor Who* and trying to fit *Torchwood* into this, and another under "The Stolen Earth" (X4.12) about *Torchwood* dating as an end in itself, and whether we can legitimately use any of it for conjectures about *Doctor Who*. The present piece will simply focus on the possible sequence of events between our two visits to Downing Street, and what evidence we have on screen and when compared to real life to bolster this up.

It's tempting to date "The Stolen Earth" to July 2009. This might be why Captain Jack has noticed Sarah Jane's work enough to congratulate her without ever mentioning her to Gwen Cooper. All of *Torchwood* Series One and much of Series Two have happened before *The Sarah Jane Adventures* begins. Sarah definitely knows about Torchwood and the new-style UNIT. And Harriet Jones has not exactly been idle this last year or so. She's used Mr Copper's network to circumvent the Daleks' monitoring of all frequencies. We can work backwards from this.

A Prime Minister has the choice of when an election can be held and, unless there is a massive hypnotic signal sent out on the first Parliamentary working day after Christmas, a No-Confidence vote would actually reinforce Harriet's position. Nobody's in a position to do this, except the Doctor. Quite apart from her position as Saviour of Humanity and worker of an economic miracle in her first six months, it's fairly quickly established in "The Christmas Invasion" that she knows an awful lot more than she ought to. Quite simply, she knows where the bodies are buried. With judicious use of the Parliamentary Whips (employees of the major political parties whose job is to enforce discipline and make sure every MP turns out to vote in line with the leadership's wishes on any measure), even a tarnished saint is going to withstand Opposition calls for an election. The effects of such a vote would be to undo the Doctor's whispering campaign and show up flaws in the Opposition. Her "downfall", whatever it was, wasn't in January 2007.

Further clues come when we start looking at

continued on Page 221...

X2.0 The Christmas Invasion

ship are the first bits of Welsh *Doctor Who* to have been filmed in a quarry. The windows shattering around the Powell Estate is the last major work by the BBC's long-established Visual Effects Unit (see 5.1, "The Tomb of the Cybermen" and 1.1, "An Unearthly Child" for comments on their pre-*Doctor Who* period). Mike Tucker and his crew will be back, but in a different guise (X2.2, "Tooth and Claw").

It's the first time we see any of this version of the TARDIS other than the Console Room (when the new Doctor changes his attire in the Ship's Costume Room), and the first time any content deliberately made for a medium other than television was made as part of the production and promoted after the episode.

Watch Out For...

• No matter how often we mention it, nothing quite prepares you for the scene with the radio-controlled Christmas tree that trashes Jackie's flat. Nor the way a brass band assaults a market stall and fells a real tree. Every festive cliché is present and correct, including brussels sprouts, the Queen's Speech and the thick snow we haven't actually had in London on Christmas Day since 1895 (although this last is, of course, sarcastically undercut within seconds). If you look carefully, the card next to the one Jackie is hanging up when she hears the TARDIS is made from a screen-grab from X1.3, "The Unquiet Dead".

• She was one of a lot of newscasters when the Slitheen scammed Earth to the brink of Armageddon (X1.5, "World War Three"), but now Lachelle Charles as AMNN newscaster Trinity Wells returns - as she will every time present-day Earth is in peril - to become the RTD era's official Voice of Impending Doom. As usual, she's among real-life journalists, in this case BBC Wales' very own Jason Mohammed (who simply asked Davies if he could be in it when they were at a telethon). It's entirely plausible that a regional announcer such as he would be doing the national news in the small hours on Christmas Day - but as he turns up a few more times, it would seem that, in the *Doctor Who* universe, he is given UK-wide exposure and moves to London. (This wouldn't be so remarkable if it had been an isolated incident, but the careers of many genuine BBC journalists are subtly different in the series and its spin-offs, as we will see in later stories.)

• Last time Harriet Jones helped defeat an alien invasion of London, the rotters crashed a spaceship into Parliament in what was that episode's calling-card shot ("Aliens of London"). How do you top that? Well, you shatter every single window in the city, including the thousands of individually made triangular ones on the most famous new building in the metropolis, the Swiss Re "Gherkin". This distinctive space-age/rude-looking edifice is also seen from the unique vantage-point of the roof of the most famous really old building here, the Tower of London.

• The rule used to be: no more than three aliens in shot except for long shots. Now, with fewer TV sets confined to 4:3 ratio, they can do things like introduce the Sycorax with a tableau deliberately intended to remind us of the video for Queen's "Bohemian Rhapsody" (the out-takes on the DVD include a faltering attempt to perform this). Later, we get to see a vast gladiatorial arena full of the beggars.

• Six words to bring down a Government... and he walks off without looking back.

The Continuity

The Doctor He can apparently identify Type A Rh+ human blood by taste [compare with his similar predilection for licking things in "Tooth and Claw"]. He can quote from *The Lion King*, and is familiar with the Sycorax 'sanctified rules of combat'. He seems happy to go along with the Sycorax leader's description of him as 'this world's Champion'.

This new Doctor seems upset that he isn't ginger [for reasons we will elaborate upon later] and is unsure of his impact on people. He is even more uncertain about his own traits and preferences. It is only really when Harriet and, more especially, Rose accept him that he comes into focus. The crucial difference between this Doctor and his immediate predecessor is that he emphatically *does* "do domestic" [compare with X1.4, "Aliens of London"]. He even lets Jackie hug him. As he observes, he's got a gob on him: he simply won't stop talking.

The aftermath of this regeneration is different, yet again, from any before: the Doctor burps orange sparkly time-energy. [This is enough to draw power-hungry parasites towards Earth; from the way this is shown, it is an excess of this stuff that is causing the regenerative failure and synaptic 'implosion' of which the Doctor complains in

How Long is Harriet in Number 10?

continued from Page 219...

the career of Harold Saxon, and the way he insinuates himself into power. His first significant job is as Defence Secretary, apparently, but as he has so much say in the design of HMS *Valiant*, it looks more likely that he began in Defence Procurement - a more powerful if less glamorous job and one where he would be meeting and taking in bids from major industrial and military outfits. He also gets his hands on the Archangel satellite system, globally: a conflict of interest that would have had him debarred and possibly jailed under UK law. The last thing he needs is a General Election putting the spotlight on government projects to do with space, aliens, military hardware and so on, the things that caused Harriet so much (alleged) hassle. Until Archangel is up and running, the Master needs Harriet exactly where she is. If she was thinking of quitting, he'd prevail upon her to stay put. As we will see in the essay with "The Sound of Drums", Saxon's career makes a lot more sense if, instead of Prime Minister, he is Mayor of London (and the biographical details and obvious lies about his past are in keeping with the life and career - real and self-proclaimed - of Jeffrey Archer, whose Mayoralty campaign was curtailed by being Detained at Her Majesty's Pleasure[42]). If he has had to become an MP, then hold two separate ministerial posts (one at Cabinet level), then force an election (as well as writing a novel), he needs a few months under cover beforehand while he sets up Archangel and influences *Valiant*, before he finally emerges to start climbing the greasy pole. His first public act (in the sense of getting headlines) is shooting down the Racnoss (X3.0, "The Runaway Bride"). We can date that pretty accurately, to Christmas 2007. But how long does it take him to get to this position, and how long does he need to go from there to the top job? And what else happened in Britain during that period?

That last one's the killer: with all his apparent flair for fool-proof plans (err... this is *the Master* we're talking about), Saxon's biggest worry is, as Harold MacMillan (Prime Minister 1956-62) said, "Events, dear boy, events." The Master is not in control of what's going on in Cardiff, for starters. With crises and calamities abounding, the easy way for anyone seeking to criticise this man who appeared out of nowhere is to compare his lack of experience to the maturity of the incumbent. This is why we've been so diligent in looking at every-thing happening in Britain and globally during the critical period. George W Bush defeated John Kerry, a more plausible candidate in many people's eyes, simply by saying "There's a war on" and appealing to the nation not to change horses in mid-stream. With The Battle of Canary Wharf (X2.13, "Doomsday") and the Racnoss ("The Runaway Bride") in rapid succession, the Master would avoid forcing an election for a few months simply to let the public's fears subside. Anything more assertive risks the delicate balance of his subliminal suggestion.

That poll in summer (seen on the Abzorbaloff's newspaper in X2.10, "Love & Monsters") is interesting. Unlike America, the polling of the electorate here is pretty sporadic. It comes whenever there's been a big event, or a political crisis, or when there is a news organisation stirring up trouble to sell papers. This one comes amid other headlines in the usually staid *Daily Telegraph* claiming "Four more months of government paralysis" and "Fourth minister resigns - so who's running the country". There's also an odd photo of silhouettes in front of a giant, back-to-front poster saying "Election". (We can't read the date, but we managed the Sudoku in a few minutes.) Most intriguingly, it has a red strap-line saying "Election Countdown". Ministers resigning en masse, Saxon ahead in some poll or other and it's summer 2007. (Of course it's summer: the banner headline is about Fantasy Football and the word "previews" is prominent, making it July or early August if the pre-season friendlies haven't even started yet. The weather-map looks like confirmation too.) The obvious linear narrative Vivian Rook outlined doesn't work.

We can think of four or five scenarios that allow Saxon to get to lead the country without leading a party, and we'll outline those in Volume 8. What we can say in the meantime is that if the situation in summer 2007 looks as if it will drag on for four months before an election, that election isn't the one that gets the Master into power. Eighteen months before that date, Harriet is still a backbencher. However, those headline-writers don't know that the Daleks and Cybermen will be arriving shortly before the time they expect an election. Saxon's headline news in July, with no explanation or photos needed, which gives us a latest *possible* date for the Toclafane around November 2008. Traditionally, people date the election to

continued on Page 223...

X2.0 The Christmas Invasion

his few lucid moments (cf 19.1, "Castrovalva").] Tea, containing tannin and free-radicals, is the optimum restorative agent. [Whether this is simply because he inhales it as a vapour, or because it first enters the TARDIS systems directly, is unclear. We note that in 15.6, "The Invasion of Time", Chancellor Borusa knows all about genus *camilla* and that in the next story, 16.1, "The Ribos Operation", it is the first "useful" thing the Doctor thinks of for Romana to do. There are many, *many* other examples, but then we'd get into the uses of a nice cup of rosie lee in 9.5, "The Time Monster", and that way madness lies.] Once fully recovered, the Doctor has enough residual cellular energy for dismemberment not to be insurmountable - when his hand is cut off, bloodlessly [or so it seems], he's able to regrow it in seconds. [Presumably this is how his brain can melt hours into his new life with no discernible ill-effects, neural implosions being an occupational hazard, it seems - see "Castrovalva". For further details on the Doctor's severed hand, see **Deus Ex Machina**.]

Eschewing the pith-helmet, jockey-silks or pierrot outfits also seen in the TARDIS wardrobe, the Doctor finally selects a narrow, brown, pin-stripe suit with high, thin lapels [the sort of thing a mid-90s Britpop band-member might have worn, specifically Pulp's guitarist/violinist Russell Senior or Kasabian lead vocalist Alex Kapranos], a shirt and tie, white plimsolls and a long brown coat with no lapels. [Maybe he's a big fan of *Firefly*. The net effect is rather like Phil Daniels in the poster for *Quadrophenia*, the definitive Mod film (see **Which Are the Most Mod Stories?** under 4.6, "The Moonbase" and X2.7, "The Idiot's Lantern" for the requisite Vespa scooter).] He also seems to have decided to try hair-gel.

[Something newer fans picked up on that was too obvious for more experienced ones to see: this Doctor is one who takes action himself. His immediate predecessor was given to stating what the problem was and strongly hinting that someone local ought to take responsibility and do what was needed. This one not only makes the moves, he stands in as Earth's 'champion' and wields a thumping great broadsword on the planet's behalf. This is such basic Doctor-ish activity that it's only when it returned in this episode that anyone noticed that Eccleston's Doctor was any different.]

• *Ethics*. Erk! This Doctor is shaping up to be a bigger git than the first two combined. Quite aside from destroying a friend's life out of pique - over-throwing Harriet when she disappoints him - he is someone who decides early on in his new life not to give anyone a second chance. He does both with a quiet, calm resolve that's far more unnerving than his immediate predecessor's angsty anger. He shows signs of being scared by what humans do en masse when encountering other races [see, for example, 15.2, "The Invisible Enemy" and then several examples in this new Doctor's life]. He seems to have no issue with allowing these Sycorax, seemingly slavers by trade, to go off into space and presumably enslave someone *else*, so long as they steer clear of Earth.

• *Background*. Not much, unless you count a reference to him having met Arthur Dent from *The Hitchhiker's Guide to the Galaxy*. He seems to know something about the Roboforms, calling them 'Pilot Fish' and saying that they want him as a power-source [but it's not clear that he isn't guessing]. And he knows something about the rules of challenge that the Sycorax will accept, and how to insult them in [to human ears] an untranslatable fashion.

• *Inventory: Sonic Screwdriver*. The Doctor can literally use the sonic screwdriver in his sleep. It's able to blow up the lethal Christmas tree in Jackie's flat, and simply pointing it at the Roboforms causes them to flee.

• *Inventory: Other*. Although it slipped his mind when doing a quick inventory of his new self [in the vignette for *Children in Need*], the Doctor apparently needs glasses to watch television. [This chimes with the reference in "Castrovalva" to hypermetropia in his right eye and the *pince nez* and/or monocles used by Doctors One and Three for close-up electronics (eg 9.2, "The Curse of Peladon"). Later, in the *Comic Relief* vignette "Time Crash" (X3.13a), the tenth Doctor will claim that neither he nor his fifth self actually needed them.]

The TARDIS seems to have gone into shutdown automatically on landing. [Unsurprising, given that it has just had a violent regeneration followed by a strenuous ride through time at top whack, followed by a bumpy real-space flight across South London.] Rose and Mickey reactivate the Ship by accident, alerting the Sycorax to its presence. Beneath the Console, under the gantry section near where the ramp to the door joins, is a blue-green toroidal element which, when soused in tea, restores the Doctor's synapses and reboots the Ship's telepathic translation system. [We've

How Long is Harriet in Number 10?

continued from Page 221...

June, on the assumption that Harriet Jones fell from power in January 07. Untenable as that seems, the disarray we hear about in summer 07 has to begin somewhere.

One obvious possibility is that Harriet precipitated the collapse by resigning *despite* her popularity. We don't know who was in her Cabinet, but if we take the many hints that she was New Labour and this is early 2007, there are lots of familiar names available. We know from recent history what happened when they tried to get leadership of the party. If Harriet so much as hinted at quitting, the results could have been catastrophic, with internecine bickering and the wobbles on share values. A General Election before a suitable leader is selected would be suicidal. Is Saxon the leader they settle on? That wouldn't make a lot of sense: with the polls in the summer of 2007 so favourable, they'd pick him, go to the country and get re-elected for another five years. Saxon has to be in the Opposition (presumably the Tories, at least to begin with, until he can form a nucleus around his personality cult and undertake his peculiar rise to power). The forces that might have been expected to try to engineer her downfall, or profit from the Doctor's bid to unsettle her, would in this scenario be trying to persuade her to stay.

That word "paralysis" in the headlines suggests a situation where whatever lead the government had at the last election has been whittled away and none of the smaller parties want to do a deal. This might actually explain a lot of the anomalous information. Saxon's personal popularity doesn't get him the keys to Number 10 until a lot later, but he has a Cabinet post and attracts all-party support for whatever platform he's running on when the election comes. This is looking like a coalition government or even a hung parliament[43] before the election, whose one achievement is rewriting the rules on electoral procedure to allow the situation we see in "The Sound of Drums" and the Master taking over after this Parliament has ground to a halt. So there may well have been an election *before* July 2007, in which Saxon got his first Parliamentary seat (probably by arranging a nasty accident for someone in a safe constituency), then a meteoric career built on his invented track-record and the amendments he'd made to Archangel before standing for Parliament.

Whether the timing of the Election was his design to get into power exactly when the Doctor returned, and the Paradox Machine was charged-up, depends on whether he expected this lame-duck Parliament to stay in power for 16 months or so. Or it was one of several. It could be that everyone expected an election in autumn, after this interim caretaker coalition had allowed the parties to elect plausible leaders - but events, dear boy, in the shape of Cybermen and Daleks ("Doomsday"), kept this bodged-together alliance in place longer than anticipated.

In case it isn't clear, what we're getting at is that, contrary to what we are supposed to conclude, it's not the Doctor who deposes Harriet Jones, it's the Master. How he does it is unclear, but anyone with his gifts could manipulate the media or have a word in the right ear. He's befriended the daughter of a noted peer (whom he marries as part of his disguise). Any number of real-life scandals could have been arranged to break simultaneously, removing the PM's more trusted advisors. It suits his purposes for a popular Prime Minister to abruptly depart and leave a weak Opposition and a factional Government in such disarray that they land up forming a self-destructive alliance until he's ready to force an election he can't lose. He can't do this immediately after Christmas, when she's bulletproof. If he arrives in March or April, when she's more vulnerable (and may have decided to go, having accepted the popular will for exactly a year and set things right, as she sees it), then 18 months later is September 2008, which works nicely with the *Torchwood* dates we've laboriously worked out, misses any significant events in *Doctor Who* other than the ones surrounding Tish and Martha's Mad Week.

So, finally, to answer the original question. Harriet Jones is a back-bencher until the events of March 2006 ("Aliens of London" / "World War Three") leave Britain without a Prime Minister. Given how long a leadership election takes when the party's in power, we can assume another month (especially with a lot of rebuilding needing doing and several MPs now dead). This leaves us with the small problem of her as Prime Minister when Margaret Blaine becomes Mayor of Cardiff (X1.11, "Boom Town"), but we can ju-u-ust about live with that. Eight months later, she is popularly assumed to have saved Earth from aliens and has already caused a mini economic boom in the UK

continued on Page 225...

X2.0 The Christmas Invasion

previously seen occasions when the Doctor being rendered unconscious doesn't impede the Ship's translation abilities - see, for instance, 1.8, "The Reign of Terror" - so this must be a special convergence of the Doctor having recently swapped bodies, his being comatose and the TARDIS babelfish being solely required for the participants to understand one another. "Castrovalva" would have been more fun if Nyssa and Tegan had been forced to point or draw pictures - yet this story, as with 24.1, "Time and the Rani" (the only other comparable situation), had another Time Lord in proximity, and all parties had been in the presence of a fully-functioning Doctor when they met.]

The Ship's wardrobe is another cupola like the Console Room, and contains a vast spiral staircase. Several familiar old styles of clothing can be seen [velvet jackets, long, stripey scarves, straw hats, Hawaiian shirts...] as well as a suit of armour with a feather boa on it and apparently hundreds of other garments.

The Supporting Cast

• *Rose* veers wildly from being distraught about the Doctor to being domestic and nosy about her mum's love-life. As opposed to what she told Jackie and Mickey the last time they met [X1.13, "The Parting of the Ways"] about taking a stand, here she's inclined to take the comatose Doctor and hide in the TARDIS. [To be fair, there isn't much else she can do during the crisis, unless she's inclined to gaze into the TARDIS heart again (1.13, "The Parting of the Ways").] She tells Mickey that she's now unable to pilot the TARDIS [as with last episode], as the knowledge as 'sort of been wiped out of my head, like it's forbidden'. [This immediately brings to mind the mental blocks placed on the third Doctor during his time with UNIT, but with the Time Lords dead and the Doctor largely incapacitated after Rose's previous spin with the Ship, the most likely suspect to have imposed such knowledge-walls is the TARDIS itself. Compare with Rose having at least *some* memories of what occurred last episode in X2.13, "Doomsday".]

Forced by circumstances to take a stand after all, she tries the Doctor's preferred tactic of talking tough. Using what she can remember of previous confrontations with aliens, she invokes Article 15 of the Shadow Proclamation and sounds reasonably convincing until she turns her affidavits into a list of any alien names she can remember [even if she can't pronounce a few]. Once she's overplayed that hand, she remains sufficiently calm to work out the significance of abruptly understanding Sycorax without Harriet's assistant Alex translating for the humans.

Perhaps her most characteristic trait here is that, with the world under threat and the Doctor apparently dying after saving her from the effects of the Time Vortex, she blubs and wails that 'he's left *me*'.

• *Jackie* wrapped a present for Rose, just in case. Her forethought didn't extend to food, apparently - as even with Christmas dinner being an unavoidable event, she claims not to have anything to eat in the house. [This is probably exaggeration, but she lives in the kind of area that would have shops open even on Christmas Day. Later, when evacuating to the TARDIS, she brings laundry-bags full of stuff, including food.] She seems to admire Harriet and, being £18 a week better-off, thinks that the talk of Britain enjoying a 'Golden Age' hype is justified [see X4.17, "The End of Time Part One"].

Jackie's been letting Howard from the market stay over some nights, and he left pyjamas and a dressing gown (with fruit in the pockets, cos he gets peckish at night). This has been going on a couple of months. As always, Jackie knows a neighbour who can lend her something useful, in this case a stethoscope.

• *Mickey*. Bored as he is by being told about Rose's adventures with the Doctor, he tolerates this because she's back. He heard the TARDIS engines over metalwork and Noddy Holder, from streets away [as with last episode, he must have some kind of dog-whistle hearing]. He's keen to stop Rose brooding on the Doctor's condition and takes her shopping.

Later, when he has tried to defend everyone from a tree with a chair [he's getting the hang of this life], he brings his computer to Jackie's to look up 'pilot fish' and get into some secret sites. Jackie makes him take a note of his use of her phone line for this, in a way that indicates that it must be a fairly common occurrence. He's scornful of the idea of hiding inside the TARDIS and of simply drinking tea and waiting for something to happen. He seems to be the Doctor's biggest admirer after he orders the Sycorax to leave.

He's still able to hack into UNIT computer systems ["World War Three"]. Mickey makes a right mess of carving the turkey. [That's more significant

The Christmas Invasion   X2.0

How Long is Harriet in Number 10?

continued from Page 223...

("The Christmas Invasion"). Her work done, she carries on for another few months until a combination of her own lack of ambition and a back-bench revolt or Cabinet back-stabbing leads to her departure despite the lack of an obvious successor. She's Prime Minister for exactly a year, but (drum-roll) she never gets into 10 Downing Street because, as Mr Saxon says to his soon-to-be-dead Cabinet ("The Sound of Drums"), they spent all that time rebuilding it after some jug-eared goon fired a missile at it.

Now see **Why the Great Powell Estate Date Debate?** under X2.3, "School Reunion", **How Come Britain Has a President and America Doesn't?** under X3.12, "The Sound of Drums", and **Must All Three Series Correlate?** under X4.4, "The Sontaran Stratagem".

---

than it appears - it means Jackie's accepted him as de facto man-of-the-house and he's accepted the role despite Rose not being around most of the time. As we will see in X2.5, "Rise of the Cybermen", Mickey's own family situation has changed enough recently for even a messed-up "traditional" Christmas to be welcome. In X2.10, "Love & Monsters", Jackie claims that Mickey was a 'little mate' who would fix things in her apartment as a handyman.]

* *Harriet Jones, Prime Minister* has an Act of Parliament forbidding her to write her memoirs. She is solicitous of everyone around her, and isn't above making coffee to make people feel welcome. It still hasn't sunk in that she is known to people without her telling them she's PM. She knows about Torchwood, somehow, and UNIT protocol. As Prime Minister, she is able to speak for Earth [and to tell the US President to butt out - see **The Big Picture**; X3.12, "The Sound of Drums"; and accompanying essay]. In every other regard, she is at UNIT HQ in her capacity as someone with experience of aliens and especially the Doctor. Despite her alleged 'Golden Age', there are people questioning the worth of the Guinevere space-probe project, and she speaks up for it in news conferences.

Harriet willingly defies the Sycorax leader, despite seeing people killed for less. [This may be why, in spite of the Doctor's victory, she tells Torchwood to fire at will at the departing ship. She looks heartbroken as she gives the order, and seems more scared of the Doctor's response than of anything else that she's seen that day. Nonetheless, she has seen the Sycorax leader go back on his promise by attempting to attack the Doctor after surrendering.]

* UNIT. As mentioned, they have a snazzy *pied a terre* under the Tower of London, with big Mission Control-style monitors and consoles, lots of glass with their logo engraved thereon and a kitchenette where the Prime Minister makes coffee for the staff. As soon as Guinevere One goes AWOL and the Sycorax snarl for the cameras, UNIT assumes complete, unquestioned, control of the situation and allows the PM and rocket-group manager Danny Llewellyn and some of his staff to participate. [Major Blake is also able to order the PM's right-hand man Adam to start translation software, and Adam complies with no question or need for instruction - it would appear that Adam is a UNIT operative within the political infrastructure, an impression confirmed when Llewellyn speaks to Adam of 'records on file for all your staff'. This is something that would have made *Torchwood:* "Children of Earth" a lot more complicated and politically murky than it already was. It also makes Adam's role in Harriet's downfall - as patient zero of the reputation-destroying meme that the Doctor deploys - all the more alarming.]

The top UNIT operative seen here, Major Blake, has not met the Doctor but is, of course, familiar with the files. [It seems that Harriet's previous contact with the Time Lord is what persuades Blake to trust this particular politician, against all precedent in the Lethbridge-Stewart era.] He is surprised that Harriet knows about Torchwood, but seems reluctant to involve this organisation, whatever it might be. Blake is killed for protesting at the Sycorax murdering a civilian (Llewellyn).

When Llewellyn asks if the Sycorax are Martians, Blake nonchalantly says, 'Of course not, Martians look completely different'. [If UNIT have met Ice Warriors, it was in an unbroadcast story - possibly the one alluded to in "Castrovalva", if the fifth Doctor's murky memories can be trusted. (See also **The Big Picture** for the tie-in novel involving Ice Warriors that springs to mind.) Or,

225

X2.0 The Christmas Invasion

can it be that UNIT managed to fend off an invasion without help from the Doctor? It's amusing to imagine the Season Nine *Dad's Army*-style UNIT seeing off vicious, inhuman killers from the Red Planet and avoiding the public ever hearing about it, but we have no evidence.]

• *Torchwood*. Aha! Our first real clues about this mysterious outfit [it was a place when the Anne Droid asked about it in X1.12, "Bad Wolf"]. They're so secretive that neither the UK Prime Minister nor the United Nations is supposed to know about them, and UNIT have only a hazy idea about their activities. They collect alien technology, in this case a hefty ship-zapper from a ship that crashed about ten years before, and use it to defend Earth (or maybe just Britain) from undesirable offworlders. The PM is able to get in touch with them through Alex, her PA, and order a strike to remove the Sycorax threat and any others that arise when the Doctor is unavailable.

The Non-Humans

• *Sycorax*. The race identifies themselves as such in their own language, refusing to translate for human 'cattle'. They consider the Earth theirs simply because they have arrived here [which is curious, in the light of later episodes where Earth is off-limits because it's classified as a 'Level Five' world]. Unlike most other would-be invaders, they resort to simple intimidation rather than stealth. This includes a display of eldritch powers, putting anyone with Type A blood into a trance and making them stand on the edge of any tall building nearby. [This is convenient, as they stumble across a phial of human blood on a probe sent to Mars, when they are near that planet for some unspecified reason (possibly homing in on the Doctor's energy-coughs). What technique they would have used had this not dropped into their laps is uncertain.] Anyone in the thrall of the blood-hypnosis cannot be made to commit suicide, as the survival impulse is too strong.

The Sycorax are basically humanoid, with metallic armour and long red velvet cloaks. Under their bone-like masks are faces resembling diagrams of facial musculature. They have red eyes. Their leader wields a whip that glows with a blue light, which is attached to [or generated by, it's not clear] a long staff that could be wood or bone. The Doctor is able to snap this over his knee, but the whip kills Danny Llewellyn and Major Blake instantly, reducing them to piles of bones.

Their ship resembles a vast floating mountain, with wings, shaped like a spear-head [the actual design was based on a conch-shell]. Inside is a vast cavern, with hundreds of Sycorax in tiers. The exterior is rocky and has a variable-geometry wing. This, like the doors and the blood-control system, are operated by big red hemispherical buttons. The ship is so huge that its arrival in Earth's atmosphere sends out a shockwave sufficient to shatter every window in London.

Although they seem unconcerned that Earth is off-limits, the Sycorax are sufficiently honourable that their leader being defeated in single combat (using broadswords) is enough for them to retreat. They do exactly as the Doctor commands, apparently because he was victorious.

Their language is harsh and full of Ks and SHs, long vowels and monosyllables. [It's not at all like Klingon, honest. See **Aren't Alien Names Inevitably a Bit Silly?** under 9.2, "The Curse of Peladon".]

• *"Pilot Fish"*. [They're identified as 'Roboforms' when they return ("The Runaway Bride").] These robots have dressed as Santa and homed in on the Doctor's exhaled [Artron] energy. The parallel with Earth-style pilot fish is made by the Doctor when in crisis, and seems to be a warning that the Sycorax are the main attraction. The Doctor believes the Pilot Fish can run their 'batteries' [personal or spaceship?] off his energy for 'a couple of years'. They can play brass instruments, although as these later turn out to be guns and flamethrowers fiendishly disguised as trombones and cornets, it's possible their rendition of "God Rest Ye Merry, Gentlemen"[39] is a recording. [How anyone thinks men in metal masks can develop the *embouchure* for brass is another matter.] They also have a remote-control tree that turns into a flying buzzsaw. Once scared off with the sonic screwdriver, they teleport away [using the same system as the Sycorax, suggesting a similar origin].

[We later discover that these robots are mercenaries and can be slaved to a remote control - apparently contradictory facts - but we have no indication here who has employed them, or whether they are freelancing to get power for their ship and reduce their dependence on races such as the Sycorax. What either species was doing around Mars is never clarified.]

The Christmas Invasion X2.0

Planet Notes
• **Mars.** The import of the Guinevere One space programme suggests that the Red Planet has yet to be explored by humans. [This is confirmed in *The Sarah Jane Adventures* 1.3, "Warriors of Kudlak", despite the contradiction with "The Ambassadors of Death" - this wouldn't be such a problem had a) Sarah's first encounter with UNIT not been in a sort-of sequel to this (13.4, "The Android Invasion", when she covered the story of Guy Crayford's disappearance and must therefore have had security clearance to enter the base), and b) her spin-off series given us many dates that make it obvious that all the 70s UNIT stories were set around the time of transmission (see **What's the UNIT Timeline?** under 8.5, "The Daemons"). We will explore this in this story's essay; see also **Was There a Martian Time-Slip?** under X4.16, "The Waters of Mars".]

History
• **Dating.** It's 24th and 25th December, 2006. [At the earliest. Harriet Jones has been Prime Minister long enough to have a beneficial effect on the UK economy. Realistically, this might have been cause to assume 2007 or 2008, but with later stories and two spin-off series giving complications, this is the nearest we can get to any of it working. See the essay with this story.] The damage to the clock tower containing Big Ben has almost been repaired - see "Aliens of London" - and scaffolding is up around the clock-faces. One third of the Earth's population is said to be 'two billion'.

[There are a few wrinkles in the timeline of this episode that need to be resolved, however, so please bear with us...

[The TARDIS arrives in daylight, which in late December in London means before 3.00pm (even allowing for camera apertures to have been adjusted if this had been a documentary, the streetlights would come on at around then). Rose and Mickey go for a wander past a street-market, which puts the Robot Santa scene at some time before 5.00pm (Christmas Eve is usually pretty busy, but shops in Central London, which is where this purports to be - see **Things That Don't Make Sense** - would start closing from 4.30 to allow staff to get home despite the usually heavy traffic that evening). Christmas Eve in 2006 was a Sunday, although Mickey was working at the garage as normal. (It's possible that Davies forgot that Rose had skipped a year and wrote it as 2005. Even so, a car-mechanic working on the weekend, especially on Christmas Eve, is a bit much.) Dawn would be at about 8.20am (at least, that's when the lights would go off again), and so this gives us an earliest time for the Sycorax ship to arrive.

[Llewellyn and Sally estimate that the time between the first Sycorax sighting and their arrival is five hours, which puts the "Bohemian Rhapsody" shot at around 3.30am. The ship is over Westminster at 8.35 (assuming the clock's working; a shot that in screen-time is seconds later shows another clock on the Big Ben tower apparently ten minutes later). Minutes later, the clock at UNIT HQ shows a weird time of 00:22:24:54 when Harriet is teleported, so presumably this is an "elapsed time" count for the crisis. BBC News 24, for once, doesn't have a time-check on the tickertape at the bottom of the screen. A week after the Winter Solstice, there is about six hours of full daylight in London. The Sycorax crisis is resolved, twice, during broad daylight, but it's thoroughly dark by the time the spaceship pieces start burning up on re-entry. Jackie's had time to change, do her hair and lay on a Christmas dinner for four and - it's a safe bet - had intended it for the usual 3.00pm Queen's Speech, which had previously been cancelled (most families in Britain time their turkeys or spinach and ricotta filo for this deadline). There is, however, a live news-flash about Harriet's leadership crisis, which Rose reacts to as if not expecting it, so they must not have been watching a news channel by then. (In the mood of national euphoria, perhaps the scheduled wrist-slittingly depressing *EastEnders* Christmas episode was postponed - see X2.9, "The Satan Pit" for a comment on this ritual.)

[The conclusion we have to draw is that the sword-fight and zapping the Sycorax ship all take place before noon. (This makes the Doctor's return in time for dinner more significant than it appeared on transmission, because he has chosen not to leave without Rose.) However, it must be even earlier than that if this new Doctor is less than 15 hours old.]

Additional Sources. In the BBC's online back-up for this, the UNIT site had a background feature claiming that the Sycorax were scavengers, based on an asteroid in the JX82 system.

227

X2.0 The Christmas Invasion

Catchphrase Counter The newborn Doctor has one final 'fantastic'. [In the episode as broadcast, that is. A cut scene has the Doctor finding himself unable to say it with his new mouth, and trying synonyms including a David Banks-style 'excellent' (see 19.6, "Earthshock" and every subsequent 80s Cyberman story), a Russell T Davies-ish 'marvellous', the 'molto bene' which would later crop up a lot and finally 'very, very good' in a Hugh Grant/Richard Curtis way.]

Harriet Jones persists in holding up her ID and identifying herself, even though everyone knows who she is now. The UNIT CO, Major Blake, is the first of many people to describe the Doctor as 'the stuff of legend'.

Deus Ex Machina Apparently, in the first 15 hours of a new life, a Time Lord can regrow severed limbs if they have enough 'residual cellular energy'. [That's convenient! Not only is the Doctor's regrown hand free of the slight wrist-kink noted in X1.13a, "Pudsey Cutaway" (it's 'a fightin' hand'), but the severed one - which survives its fall from the Sycorax ship intact and is later collected by Captain Jack as a Doctor-detector (see *Torchwood* Series One and X3.11, "Utopia") - provides plot get-outs in "The Sound of Drums" (X3.12), "The Poison Sky" (X4.5) and "The Doctor's Daughter" (X4.6) *and* gives us a whole 'nother Doctor for Rose to snog in "Journey's End" (X4.13). It really is the gift that keeps on giving. The 15-hour thing will later (X6.8, "Let's Kill Hitler") allow River Song to face a dozen Stormtroopers, get shot with machine-guns and still wipe the floor with them, so we got off lightly here. It might also retroactively explain Romana's otherwise bewildering regeneration in "Destiny of the Daleks" (17.1).]

The Analysis

The Big Picture Christmas Specials had altered since the last time *Doctor Who* was regularly on. The notion of a longer episode of a series that incorporated a major plot-development was one that television writer John Sullivan had taken to phenomenal heights of popularity, and then diminishing returns, during the 1990s. He had begun with *Just Good Friends* and *Dear John*, but it was with *Only Fools and Horses* (his most famous series) that this had become a staple of the festive schedules, and the makers of other series had followed in his footsteps. The Christmas-ness of any individual special varied, but the special-ness (a major character departing, a wedding, a revelation and so forth) was part of the deal.

Some of this was practical: if you've got a long-running series, you want everyone to be up-to-speed on the developments, so you make them happen in the *one* episode anyone who might want to watch will be watching. It saves a lot of repeated explanations. People are more indulgent of Christmas episodes, so if a development is one they want to try out and then press the reset button, they can because it can be a one-off. On the other hand, complicated long-running storylines can be abandoned, as they are in real life, if everyone's just calling a truce for the day. We will see Russell T Davies exploit all of these features in later Christmas episodes, but here he is (under orders from Lorraine Heggessey) following the first requirement and making Event Television. The Doctor quoting *The Lion King* is a deliberate hint - Davies was watching a family watching this together when formulating his final pitch for *Doctor Who,* and was keen to get that kind of multi-level appeal into his series. Heggessey, in making a Christmas *Doctor Who* a regular part of the schedule, was consciously positioning the series as the replacement for *Jonathan Creek* or *Morecambe and Wise* - or, indeed, *Only Fools...*

Strategically, then, this is a sign that the BBC thinks of *Doctor Who* as something more than a means to fill 45 minutes of a Saturday. The promotion of it (including a *Radio Times* cover - the first for a specific programme at Christmas since 1990 and with 16 pages of material on the episode) made sure that this was as big a part of the day's schedule as the Queen's Speech or misery in Walford. For *Doctor Who*, it was an opportunity to complete the changes needed so that anyone in future who was dipping a toe in to the series without much background knew what was what - there was a new Doctor, people in present-day Earth knew about aliens now and Jackie and Mickey liked having a Time Lord around on occasion. Moreover, they knew full well that for a lot of the casual viewers, "normal" is beside the point. After a whole month of Christmas build-up, they wanted a change - so the story included all the hoariest clichés turned inside out. They get that element of the story out of the way early on, so from the moment the Sycorax ship smashes every window, we are rid of the festive stuff until the

The Christmas Invasion X2.0

dinner and crackers. However, they made a large plot point reminiscent of the Christmas before last.

In 2003, the European Space Agency sent a small probe to Mars on the back of a larger orbiter. Beagle 2 was made by a consortium of universities, private firms and unlikely individuals. With the weight penalties, the equipment needed to be versatile and ingenious. The leader of the group putting this together was Professor Colin Pillinger, from the Open University (a body specialising in mature students, and which had used television as the lecture-hall for students across the country with jobs and families). He looked and sounded so unlike NASA that the public warmed to the idea. So did the art-rock band Blur - they promoted, fundraised and contributed a call sign, and got their mate, controversial artist Damian Hurst, to produce the test-pattern for the cameras. The engineering was co-ordinated by the University of Leicester (the nearest we have to a real British Rocket Group) and the robot arm was designed and built by the University of Wales, Aberystwyth (making a project leader called "Llewellyn" for Guinevere One very plausible). There was government support for about half the cost, but almost everything about the project seemed like it came from a 50s Ealing Comedy. Yet it was a serious bid to land a probe on Mars and do some proper science. The Mars Express probe of the ESA was due to reach Mars orbit on Christmas Day and release Beagle 2, which would land in the early hours of Boxing Day, GMT. There was one snag: the parachutes (made in America) failed, so the vessel became interplanetary graffiti - another victim of the so-called Great Galactic Ghoul. Just about half of all missions to Mars go wrong at some stage; the most notorious was NASA's Mars Climate Orbiter, which failed because half the measurements were in metric, the others in imperial. The orbital part of the Mars Express mission, which sent Beagle 2, is still going strong but everyone forgets that. Instead, the sense of inevitability about a British space launch falling at the last hurdle and the idea of there being some "curse" or enemy activity making Mars probes go wrong is what remains.

This makes Guinevere One a reset device. Llewellyn's comment about struggling for funding while UNIT have their own Mission Control under the Tower of London allows the real, known world to coexist with the routine *Doctor Who* set up of ray-guns and Faster Than Light drives. However, the ability of the viewing British Public to tolerate endless amnesia on the part of the (fictional) British Public was at breaking point, so a clear-out was needed. (See **How Believeable is the British Space Programme?** under "The Ambassadors of Death", **Is "Yeti-in-a-Loo" the Worst Idea Ever?** under 5.5, "The Web of Fear" and **Was There a Martian Time-Slip?** under X4.16, "The Waters of Mars"). Anyone watching *Doctor Who* from now on could watch with the same basic knowledge of where Earth was with regard to aliens as any hardened A5 fanzine editor from the 80s.

There was one thing those more experienced fans would identify, and that was the episode's debt to the tie-in books. Whilst some might see the *voudon* elements of the Sycorax's blood-control, bone masks and stone spaceships and be thinking of Lawrence Miles, a lot more would be pondering another story where Britain - and *only* Britain - is invaded by warriors from Mars who take up residence in, of all places, the Tower of London and are brought here by the activities of the British Rocket Group. UNIT are powerless and the Doctor appears dead. All of this was in Lance Parkin's *The Dying Days* (1997), the anomalous Virgin Books *New Adventures* finale with the McGann Doctor and Benny Summerfield, overtly using tourist-friendly London landmarks as a hypothetical second episode of a series beginning with the TV Movie might have done. As this book was something of a collector's item, the text was available as an ebook on the BBC's Cult website, which was being mothballed as this episode aired. Another is the whole business of the tenth Doctor being ginger. Apart from any possible reference to Billie's ex, this sounds like a wink at the *New Adventures* range and the suggestion, beginning in the novelisation of 26.1, "Battlefield", that a future incarnation of the Doctor with red hair and an Afghan coat was the Merlyn who buried Arthur, as well as popping back to help his seventh incarnation out of a few jams.

To British politics (again), the Doctor's "don't you think she looks tired?" quip was something said of Tony Blair after the heart arrhythmia that had him hospitalised in 2003. (Except they didn't call him "she".) It was also how the grandees of the Conservative Party seeking to depose Margaret Thatcher in 1990 undermined her "Iron Lady" image. The 2005 Election in the *Doctor Who* universe had thrown up the interesting fact that, according to surveys, the most popular politician in the country was the MP for Flydale North, Harriet Jones. Part of the appeal was that, unlike Blair, she had been prepared to stand up to the US President. Here she is, as Prime Minister, doing a lot of the things viewers would love to think a Prime Minister would do. And then they make her throw it all away on a morally ambiguous act that earns her the Doctor's scorn and revenge. The circumstances of shooting down the Sycorax ship are obvious to any British viewer over 30 as a reworking of the *General Belgrano*'s sinking. Briefly, and as uncontentiously as possible, an Argentine warship was sailing away from a battle in the Falklands War in 1982, and a British sub was ordered to destroy it, even though it was by now in neutral waters. (X1.7, "The Long Game" has a comment on *The Sun*'s headline "Gotcha!"). Margaret Thatcher, the Prime Minister, was consulted on the decision (the only time a nuclear submarine has brought down a battleship), and when asked about it by the press, she simply repeated "rejoice!" Over 300 mariners died.

The point here isn't satire *per se*, but familiarity. Everything about this episode has to be exactly just-so. This is an entertainment for Christmas Night and intended to be watched by as broad a spread of the population as possible. If you like Christmas, it's got everything there, even a song (but not the one they planned). If you don't, everything's sent up. If you just want to see aliens attack London, then the Swiss Re building - universally known as the "Gherkin" - explodes and the Tower of London has a top-secret base under it. Choosing the Gherkin as the landmark to get shattered this time around was a calculated move. It represented twenty-first century London in the same way that the Canary Wharf tower at Canada Square had been the emblem of the 1990s, and the Lloyds Building had been the 80s. In the 1960s, we'd had the Post Office Tower (3.10, "The War Machines"). The Gherkin was something everyone in Britain knew, and its complex construction and ingenious energy-saving design became familiar very quickly and, like the London Eye (X1.1, "Rose"), had soon started to seem as if it had always been there. The real surprise was that it wasn't revealed to be a spaceship. This is emphatically the kind of epic, cinematic production that usually has Britain as noises off, but here America is a nuisance and the story centres on us.

One small detail those of you who've read Volume 6 might have spotted: the cover story for the Sycorax is that it's students or hoaxers with masks who've hijacked the signal and claim to be aliens. This actually happened in Chicago in 1987 during a rerun of 15.1, "Horror of Fang Rock" (see 24.4, "Dragonfire").

English Lessons

• *Satsumas* (n.): Small citrus fruit, analogous to clementines, mandarins or small oranges. It used to be traditional to use an orange, a walnut and an apple to make the "toe" of a Christmas stocking, but satsumas have become fashionable because they can be peeled more easily and the pips can be removed whilst eating. (Actually, the thing the Doctor finds in his pocket is a clementine, but don't tell anyone.)

• *Gob* (n. coll.): Mouth. Also a verb meaning to spit, as in punk concerts.

• *Jim-Jams* (n. coll.) Pyjamas.

• *Christmas Crackers* (n.): The paper tubes with small explosives that people pull with each other around the table during the traditional Christmas Dinner. They contain crepe-paper crowns, a bad joke or riddle, and a small pointless plastic toy.

• *Sprouts* (n.): The traditional joke with brussels sprouts is that you have to start boiling them before dawn for them to be ready to go with the meal at ten past three (because families usually wait until after the Queen's Speech), but anyone with any taste or savvy roasts them with the potatoes and parsnips in a tray underneath the turkey. They have to be laboriously peeled and small cruciform incisions made in the base so that they cook evenly, and this was always the job for the lowliest member of the family.

• *Chipolatas* (n.): The second-most popular kind of sausage here (and we love our sausages). Britain has a different kind of sausage for everyday use, the traditional pork-based "banger", but chipolatas are skinnier and often used as a side dish with turkey. Like the bangers, they come in links, each about 10cm long, and can be shallow-fried, grilled or popped in with the roasting vegetables or bird. Not a full meal, even for students.

Things That Don't Make Sense We flagged a lot of this up for discussion in **History**, but there are still odd features of this story's timeline. If it's still light when the TARDIS arrives in the Powell Estate, then there is no way the Doctor is anything less than 17 hours old when his hand gets amputated and magically gets better, even though he says he's 'less than 15 hours' into his regeneration. And despite a police box appearing in mid air and doing structural damage to nearby buildings, there's no Code 9 sighting (i.e. "the Doctor is here" - see "Aliens of London") for Harriet to use. (And why is there a post office van collecting mail late on Christmas Eve?)

Rose and Mickey decide to go out for a stroll and wind up at Henricks' department store. Several points arise. One, how did they get there so fast when anyone who's tried using any form of public transport - or worse yet, driving - around London at sunset on Christmas Eve will know it's virtually impossible? Two, if, as we were led to believe in "Rose" (X1.1), the store is located on or around Regent's Street, where are all the lights? Even without any long shots or glances upwards, the reflections and shadows would have made this scene look very different. In fact, how is it possible that the whole road is pedestrianised (they *do* put astroturf down and forbid traffic, but that's for one day a year in September). So, maybe it's a different branch, perhaps nearby in Kennington (possibly to visit Howard from the Market and ask to hang on to his dressing-gown). In which case... Three, why do they need a taxi to get home, and in either case how can they find one empty in Central London on Christmas Eve just as the shops are closing? Come to London and try it. (Furthermore, hindsight makes us wonder why these apparently savvy and culturally-aware carol-playing robots didn't anticipate this and have a taxi-driving droid as they would a year later - "The Runaway Bride".) Oh, and Four, because of edits for timing, nobody tells the driver where to go.

It was dawn in London about 20 minutes before the A-Positives started climbing to the rooftops, although in Paris the sun still hasn't properly come up, despite them being an hour ahead of London. Then the very huge spaceship sends out a sonic boom that shatters every window in London, but doesn't knock a single one of the hypnotised people off the edge. (Does nobody think to put mattresses or cardboard boxes down, as you would for a stunt fall? Or tie those afflicted to the railings with skipping ropes, or the cords from their dressing-gowns?) No car-alarms sound or water-mains burst when this concussive wave hits town. The leaves all stay on the trees, despite it being December (and they don't usually look quite that green, even though global warming means we start getting blossom in November these days). A sonic wave that big would also cause a bit of a tidal surge in the Thames and probably flood a lot of Central London, as well as getting rid of all those clouds we see. Nobody even gets a nosebleed. Sewers don't gush.

So, Danny Llewellyn's team have sent a probe (whose name changes spelling depending on which screen you're looking at) to Mars. One of its goals, presumably, would be to look for life there (never mind that UNIT, at least, know already what Martians look like) - and yet there it goes, with a plaque in case it misses Mars and flies off into the depths of interstellar space and a few gifts for any aliens who might intercept it. Let's get this straight, then: you launch a probe to seek out tiny traces of organic by-products from micro-organisms, and you construct this device in sterile conditions, but then you pop in a vial of human blood, tap water and some wheat-seeds. Not even the slightest chance of these spilling in a bumpy landing and contaminating the tests, is there? And human blood has all sorts of potentially toxic things for anything sufficiently like us to register on these tests. It could accidentally wipe out alien life-forms (especially the ones so fragile that it needs a sophisticated probe like this to find where they've been). How did this brilliant plan get past the many oversight committees a probe of this nature takes to get literally and figuratively off the ground? (This is an even bigger worry if this is the same British Rocket Group that Bernard Quatermass led in the 50s - see 25.1, "Remembrance of the Daleks" and **Is This the Quatermass Continuum?** under 15.3, "Image of the Fendahl" - as they have very good reasons to be wary of cross-planetary contamination.)

And isn't it helpful that they equipped a Mars probe with microphones? We'll assume that the "Hubble Array" that Sally uses for computer-generated graphics of the Sycorax ship approaching isn't the large optical telescope that takes months to collect one image from the edge of the observable cosmos and takes weeks to realign. Similarly, we can work with Trinity Wells announcing that the First Contact on 'December 25th' was for dramatic effect to "sell" the story - as if it needed it - as she was speaking at what has to be 3.30am GMT and so, for her US viewers, would be 10.30pm on the 24th at the earliest.

UNIT's snazzy base is underneath the Tower of London. Excavating this, which is not only an archaeological site and a listed building, but right next to a river on fairly sandy soil, must have been hard to keep secret. Wouldn't the sheer volume of

X2.0 The Christmas Invasion

tourists make this unwise as the base of a top-secret paramilitary organisation? Especially as the press would be right across the river, in clear view, at the new Greater London Assembly building on the opposite bank. *Especially* as building a tower on soil like that required a lot of Normans to bully a lot of Saxons into lugging a lot of rock to make foundations, which you don't remove just any old how without making a terribly famous building go lopsided. The other point here is... precisely how big is this base? In some scenes, you'd think they'd managed to squeeze a vast complex into a relatively small mound of damp earth - something the size of, oh, the Millennium Stadium in Cardiff. And why does a worldwide organisation have to have so many Union Flags?

We'll overlook the Doctor's suggestion that Arthur Dent might have been a real person (in which case, all attempts at dating stories set in the future are pointless as Earth is doomed - although see "Destiny of the Daleks" before dismissing the idea completely) and just ponder how hard it is to operate a control by chucking a satsuma at it. Anyone who wants to test this with the neighbour's doorbell might want to try freezing the fruit first, but that just brings up the problem of why people can stand on a spaceship so high over London and not have goosebumps - if it's engine heat or the result of the ship entering Earth's atmosphere a few hours ago, there would be a lot more wind than even what you'd expect on any platform a mile over London (such a breeze is itself conspicuously absent). Unless, of course, there's a force field. But if there were, it would prevent the Sycorax leader from falling into the Thames. Whether a dead alien bleeding into the water supply is a worse threat than slavery or making people stand on things is another problem: the Doctor's hand found its way to a pickle-jar in Cardiff, so we hope that the good people at Canary Wharf woke up in time to go trawling before any serious threat of contamination. (And anyway, as we said, the Doctor doesn't wield a satsuma, it's a clementine.)

Torchwood can zap an alien ship in what appears to be a low Earth orbit, yet even two years later, the US President seems not to take Britain seriously ("The Sound of Drums"). And despite all the A-Positives coming down off the rooftops, nobody's looking at this big vessel as it leaves, so apparently the team manage to turn London into the Death Star without affecting TV signals. (As we'll see later, apparently nobody saw it.) If you woke up on a roof with no idea how you got there, wouldn't the presence of a mountain in mid-air over London seem like the only thing that made sense?

Once again, the timing's weird; it's still light when the Sycorax ship is zapped, but the ash takes until after dark to fall, although the main worry is how someone with allegedly no food in the house (Jackie) manages to find a full Christmas dinner for four when all the shops are shut (except the ones that wouldn't stock turkey and sage-and-onion, in any case[40]). What if we just assume that the Doctor had a Christmas dinner lying around in the Ship's fridge? Well, Rose's immediate thought when holing up in the TARDIS was for Jackie to bring food in case they were stuck there for more than a day, and you'd think she'd know where the contemporary equivalent of the TARDIS food machine (1.2, "The Daleks") is by now. It's also doubtful that Jackie could cook a turkey in the time it takes for the Doctor to change his clothes and the ash from the Sycorax ship to settle down to Earth. (The turkey's too big for her microwave, so it must have needed a decent amount of time in the oven even if it had been pre-cooked.) She's even had time to do sprouts, and you usually have to start peeling them around breakfast time.

So Rose loses all hope after seeing Harriet Jones put out a query for the Doctor, and gives up to go hide in the TARDIS. She could have *at least* called that very number to explain that the Doctor definitely isn't coming, which gets her in touch with the one other woman who she knows has coped with an alien invasion.

Why, exactly, is the Queen's Speech cancelled? It's always pre-recorded, and in times of crisis people like having something familiar and stereotypical to cling to. (We might presume that when the Queen got down off the roof of Balmoral - the family go there or to Sandringham for Christmas, and usually attend the local church, in which case she and the Duke of Edinburgh would have had to have been very nimble to get onto a slate roof with a steep slope - she did a live broadcast. Maybe she also thanked the Doctor live in front of millions of viewers. See X4.0, "Voyage of the Damned" and X5.2, "The Beast Below" before rejecting the idea.)

A few perverse points arise from Harriet's abrupt fall from grace (and here we're elaborating on some of the point in the accompanying essay, **How Long is Harriet in Number 10?**). As far as anyone in Britain is concerned, she is single-handedly responsible for saving Earth from a very big, very public invasion by horrible space monsters. Obviously, you need to replace someone like that forthwith. Moreover, she's done it with the aid of very noticeable green rays from five locations in London, something never mentioned again (even the following Christmas when a big star hangs over the city, zapping people). Parliament, in calling for Harriet's resignation, evidently don't think that her knowing of the existence of such handy materiel might either mean that she knows about lots of *other* useful (and/or compromising) stuff, or that she is better suited to handling the apparently regular extraterrestrial threats that afflict London and Cardiff these days. If there's a specific Act of Parliament preventing her memoirs (something other than simply the Official Secrets Act), then presumably there is a widespread fear of what else she knows about that she's not allowed to. Who do they have lined up to succeed who is remotely in the same league as her (bearing in mind that the dates don't work for Harry Saxon to be around just yet)?

And why exactly does Adam, Harriet's liaison with UNIT, start briefing against her? He's the only person the Doctor said those words to ('Don't you think she looks tired?'), and yet suddenly, the meme is all over the media. (Some fans have speculated that the Doctor here deploys a "super-meme" guaranteed to end Harriet's rule, but that's an unworkable idea in the long-term. Just as 20.3, "Mawdryn Undead" would be over in seconds if anyone present had Rose's phone and the sonic screwdriver had a reverse teleport setting, so for instance X3.3, "Gridlock" and X5.1, "The Eleventh Hour" would be impossible if the Doctor had this ability.) Assuming any of the Opposition are around in Westminster to start action against the PM on Christmas Day, why would any of them have any contact with anyone he'd be talking to? The ticker-tape under the news of her press conference suggests a Whitehall "mole" and a human rights group have conspired - to be honest, anyone like Amnesty International would be against the enslavement of humanity, and if there were any working journalists to whom any moles could slip information they'd be a bit busy with the alien spaceship, a third of the planet threatening to jump and Harriet *saving the world*. Even on as slow a news day as Christmas usually is, a story about the PM's health would take a few days to make the headlines.

There is also, arguably, the problem of why a ship going back to tell the rest of the cosmos that Earth isn't worth attacking should be prevented from doing this. Does she *want* a load of invasions? As it happens, all the next half-dozen threats to Earth are either locally sourced baddies (including a couple of alternate-universe horrors that Torchwood bring here), an old chum of the Doctor's and some lost tourists on a collision-course with Buckingham Palace. The next *actual* invasion (with spaceships in the sky and everything) is the Sontarans three years on, and somehow Torchwood's big zapper used against the Sycorax is out of action by then. But the Sycorax weren't an invasion, they were coming here because the Doctor was burping out orange sparkly pixie-dust. Except that they weren't aware that he was here and act surprised when they discover the TARDIS. So were they following the Pilot Fish? Basically, what were they doing here and, if it was an invasion all along, did they have a plan that didn't rely on someone stupidly including a vial of human blood in a space-probe?

Critique It might be damning it with faint praise to call this the best Christmas Special so far, but it's certainly the least lazily written of any that have been made up to 2012's effort. It has the obvious advantage of going first, and having the full repertoire of a British contemporary Christmas to parody or celebrate. As a consequence, it feels as if it has an hour's worth of material. Being set at Christmas is germane to the plot. Any casual viewer can find something entertaining here.

These all ought to be minimum requirements, but comparison to later Christmas offerings shows how important it is that these are all at least attempted. We can't *not* make that comparison now. Although there were other merits that this story had in abundance at the time of broadcast, the main one - that this was our first glimpse of the new Doctor in action and the first time they'd done a specific hour-long Christmas episode - are lost to us after that first broadcast. It's almost impossible to look at it afresh.

If we *try*, though, one thing stands out immediately: they took a huge gamble on keeping the Doctor out of the story for so long. Admittedly, they make his occasional lucid moments occur at critical junctures (for the impatient viewer as well as the plot mechanics), but as we'll see in double-

X2.0 The Christmas Invasion

banked episodes later, the story is largely about his absence. This allows Mickey and Jackie to move closer to centre-stage than they've been for a while, and as such it allows these characters to be subtly remodelled, written for the actors rather than as background for Rose. The scene of them at the dinner table at the end is largely improvised, and the four of them seem comfortable - Mickey's done some heroing (so Noel Clarke is obviously happier with where the character's going) and they know they've got a hit show. That self-confidence, the sense of the *rightness* of things, is the secret of this story's success just as it undoes later season-finales and festive offerings. Davies, director James Hawes and the cast know what they're doing, and judge to a nicety precisely how far they can go with things. This is the one time that a specially commissioned song seems appropriate. It's the only time that having the Doctor mentioned on a supposedly "real world" BBC broadcast is tolerable. They can even mutilate the lead character and have him recover in seconds. Get the tone right, and anything like this is acceptable. Do things like this any time other than Christmas, or become over-reliant on an indulgent, slightly bloated or sozzled audience, and the results are horrible.

There are things only *Doctor Who* can do, and things only a Christmas *Doctor Who* can do. This story does all the ones worth doing in the latter category. Where *else* will you see robot Santas, a buzz-saw Christmas tree, a man defending Earth against aliens while still in his pyjamas and people walking on the roof of the Tower of London? The means by which these sundry delights have been made to work is simply pacing. Everything happens just when it ought. It's all motivated logically, rather than seeming to occur when a story like this needs something like that happening (see, for example, X2.8-2.9, "The Impossible Planet"/"The Satan Pit" for generic tropes and set pieces cropping up apparently at random), and above all it keeps the mood changing. There would have been a lot of bored six-year-olds just hoping that *something* would come along to relieve yet another scene of Jackie comforting a blubbing Rose... and then the windows explode.

Some stories feel like Christmas despite the lack of the trite signifiers of snow, carols or spouts. "Shada" (17.6) ends with possibly the most festive moment ever, the Doctor reading Dickens - but not *that* one - as everyone eats muffins and drinks tea in a book-lined study. "The Three Doctors" (10.1) not only has an embarrassing family reunion and petty squabbling, but gives us monsters and a castle that look like they're made of *Quality Street* wrappers. You can smell the mince pies and cherry brandy. Other stories lard the screen with every conceivable off-the-shelf trick; snow, top hats, horse-drawn carriages, cockernee urchins, turkey, Noddy Holder... yet they feel about as Yuletide as *Grease* or *High Noon*. "The Unquiet Dead" (1.3) even has Charles Dickens and ghosts, on Christmas Eve, but fails to make the grade. It's just too Perry Como, as if someone's decided to tell us what our Christmas ought to be like from the comfort of Beverly Hills. "The Christmas Invasion" gets it right on both scores. It has the trappings of Christmas as we know it here, albeit messed with for comic effect, but it actually *feels* like Christmas, with a family agreeing to a truce after earning a good time.

It's not entirely flawless: Rose is getting so erratic that it's hard to say what's "out of character" any more, but giving up and hiding in the TARDIS feels so contradictory even when compared to the last complete episode - by the same author - as to be irritating. Piper's doing her best with this material, but over the next year, we'll see Clarke and Coduri (and indeed Tennant) take over the whole audience-identification brief. The rights and wrongs of Harriet Jones blowing up the Sycorax ship as it leaves can be debated endlessly, but it's a bum note for this kind of story and - worse - out of keeping. It's as if Davies has decided to start the Torchwood storyline with her instead of Queen Victoria and then changed his mind. The logic of the Sycorax assault doesn't bear examination.

Yet as this review has indicated, by unfavourable comments about near-misses rather than singling anything out for especial praise here, the overall sense is of an episode firing on all four cylinders. By the end of it, Tennant is obviously the Doctor - possibly *the* Doctor - despite something like 15 minutes of actual screen-time out of an hour, and... well, it's hard to say anything more without making it seem as if Eccleston's casting was a mistake, but Tennant's obvious ease with the role is of a piece with the general sense of rightness, the *of course*-ness of everything else here. The whole of the last year was about proving that *Doctor Who* could be made to work again on Saturday nights on BBC1. From now on, the question is how the BBC could ever manage without it.

The Christmas Invasion X2.0

The Facts

Written by Russell T Davies. Directed by James Hawes. Viewing figures: (BBC1) 9.81 million (the second most-watched thing in Britain that day, after *EastEnders*). A week later on BBC3, it added another 0.5 million. AIs for first transmission were 84%.

Repeats and overseas promotion As this episode is made to be an hour without ads, those overseas networks that include commercial breaks have been faced with either making this a 90-minute special or dropping the episode entirely. Other foreign broadcasters, notably the US not-for-profit PBS regional stations, have deployed it as a treat for telethons and pledge drives.

Reruns in the UK on commercial cable stations (and BBC3) have been sporadic, as it doesn't fit in with the routine daily transmissions in whatever format they have for 45-minute episodes. The BBC showed it many times on BBC3, but as the first of these was on New Year's Day, i.e. over a week later, it cannot be counted as part of the figures. AI figures were in the mid 80s for every episode where these were recorded, except one. (We'll tell you about that when we get there.)

It was shown uncut in Germany, under the title "Die Weihnachtsinvasion". As far as we can find out, the French network France4 has only shown it in VO (i.e. untranslated from English).

Alternate Versions BBC America has apparently chosen to trim out these scenes: Harriet asking for her reply to the (un-named) US President to be relayed verbatim; Harriet on live TV begging for any information about the Doctor's whereabouts; the new Doctor selecting his new clothes in the TARDIS wardrobe, accompanied by a song about waking up and running. The DVD includes a longer version of the "miss me?" scene where the Doctor tries out synonyms for "fantastic" after hearing about Harriet's victory at the polls.

Additional Sources Immediately after this episode, the BBC's digital viewers had the chance to play an interactive game, "Attack of the Graske", using their remote controls and a facility called the Red Button. This was written by Gareth Roberts (X3.2, "The Shakespeare Code") and had especially-filmed sequences starring Tennant talking to the players, and Jimmy Vee (X1.2, "The End of the World" and many others) as the eponymous time-bothering scamp. We will discuss this in more detail in the Appendix to Volume 8.

Production

On being told that he had to make a Christmas Special, Russell T Davies was delighted. Later, he discovered that this was *on top of* making 13 regular episodes and the various TARDISodes and an interactive adventure. Nonetheless, it was a chance to give the new Doctor the biggest possible launch and make him noticeably unlike Eccleston's portrayal by choosing to spend the day with the Tylers after saving the world. When writing the story, Davies invented a Sycoractic language (with declensions and vowel-changes, a bit like Welsh), but he binned the sheet of A4 with the entire language on it - so there's no chance of University courses in it or translations of Shakespeare into Sycorax. (This would be apt - the name came from *The Tempest*, as we hope you knew. It was Caliban's mum, the "blue-eyed hag", and we'll see the Bard get the idea from the Doctor in "The Shakespeare Code".)

This also seemed the optimum way to introduce the new Doctor (and the idea that there could *be* a new Doctor) to as wide an audience as possible. Although he had been in a number of high-profile roles over the last three or four years, David Tennant was an unknown quantity. Born David McDonald in 1971 (during 8.3, "The Claws of Axos"), he had joined the agitprop theatre company 7:84 (the name denotes the 7% of the population of Britain who owned 84% of the country's assets when the group was founded) simply because they offered him work. He'd decided to be an actor around the same time he realised *Doctor Who* was made-up stories. Under Equity rules, he had to find a different surname and selected "Tennant" from that of Pet Shop Boys front man Neil Tennant (although he claims his all-time favourite band was Scots twins The Proclaimers, and tells the camera in the bits fast-forwarded by Martha in X3.8, "Human Nature" that the best gig he went to was The Housemartins). The theatre work expanded into television, where he carved a bit of a niche as intense, charming criminals (as would be his last pre-*Who* role in the two-part ITV play *Secret Smile*), but went through the gamut of bad sitcoms (see X1.9, "The Empty Child") and a part in *The Bill* as was apparently mandatory for any actor in the UK (playing an intense, charming criminal) and several radio

235

plays and Big Finish audios (including one with his friend and former landlady Arabella Weir, where she'd been an alternate universe Doctor - see also X7.0, "The Doctor, the Widow and the Wardrobe") and "The Scream of the Shalka" until, in rapid succession, he got the role of the conflicted policeman Carlisle in *Blackpool*, and then the titular role in *Casanova* (see last story's notes). When *Blackpool* was on, Steven Moffat texted Davies saying that he'd just seen the tenth Doctor. However, when the part was offered to him, a rather daunted Tennant hesitated. A day or so later he gleefully accepted, knowing that, as he would later say, that was the first line of his obituary written in advance.

- Other casting decisions were pressing. Penelope Wilton was asked over a dinner whether she would be prepared to return as Harriet Jones. It turned out she would, and would be free when needed. Playing Danny Llewellyn was Daniel Evans, whom Davies had cast once before, at the very start of both their careers, in *Why Don't You..?* He's now Artistic Director of the Sheffield Crucible theatre. Chu Omambala, as Major Blake, had auditioned to play a Sycorax, and the policeman trying to cope with an apparent mass-suicide was Big Finish veteran Sean Carlsen.

- As he had been reading *Doctor Who Magazine* since the first issue, Tennant knew that it would be prudent if the Doctor had a decent thick coat for location shoots in winter. He specified a long one and mentioned to Louise Page, the chief costume designer, that brown was a good colour for him. In discussions with Davies, it was argued that such a coat needed big lapels, otherwise the skinny lead actor would resemble "a big pencil". Eventually, they decided that this was a distinctive enough look to go with anyway. The coat was made of a fabric usually used for furniture. The material for the suit was a thin cotton to give the crumpled, informal look Tennant and Davies wanted without actually crumpling; the cut of the jacket was intended to look old without being specifically of a period. Nobody wanted the Doctor to wear a costume, as had been a misguided policy in the 1980s, so the details - such as shirt, tie, how many buttons would be done up and the colour of plimsolls - would vary from story to story. The Doctor was to have worn Japanese army boots, but Tennant decided that a Paul McCartney-style suit and plimsolls combo was not only in character but could allow children to dress as the Doctor. The first pair of Converse worn in this episode were the star's own.

- Block One, which comprised this special, "New Earth" (X2.1) and "School Reunion" (X2.3), was to be directed by James Hawes. He was initially nonplussed by how long the Doctor was unconscious. The read-through for all three was done in one session, attended by other writers keen to see how the new Doctor would sound. (One of these was Stephen Fry, rostered on for the eleventh episode - see **Was Series Two Supposed to be Like This?** under X2.11, "Fear Her"). This was Tuesday, 19th July. The shoot began without the regulars, at Tredegar House, on 22nd. (The last shot completed was on 10th November, and the last use of the regulars on this episode was on 8th October - the timeline for the three stories in this block and the next two get a bit tangled.) This first day was material to appear on televisions in the rest of the episode, concerning Llewellyn's rocket group and Harriet's two press conferences. It was also the day they recorded the Prime Minister's plea for the Doctor to help. As part of the episode's attempt to reassure younger viewers that the new person really was the same Doctor, familiar characters Jackie, Mickey and Harriet all come around to the idea even though they had not seen the regeneration happen.

- Tennant joined the shoot on 25th, at the start of a week in London. Tom Baker and Peter Davison had sent him good luck messages. His first task was to show the press his new outfit, then actual recording began. They began toward the end, with the "six words" sequence in a part of Brentford not previously used as a location by the series (behind the old Beecham's Powders factory). At the end of this, Tennant gleefully announced that they couldn't get rid of him now, and that any plans to cast Wee Jimmy Krankie as the Doctor would have to be dropped.[41] The crew returned to the Brandon Estate the following day - almost exactly a year after their original visit (X1.1, "Rose"; X1.4, "Aliens of London"; X1.5, "World War Three"). That time, they had been left pretty much alone, as *Doctor Who* wasn't such a big deal to most residents. Now, it was a rather more public event. One or two annoying locals caused a few delays, as did flash photography and the back of the TARDIS falling off, but the main problem was the rain. This was the day they recorded the end of the pre-credit sequence, and a lot of the time was spent carefully playing conkers with the

The Christmas Invasion   X2.0

lower half of a TARDIS prop hung from a crane. By day they recorded the crashing TARDIS, and at night they saw off the Santa robots. Next day, in filthy weather quite apt for December but disappointing for July, they finished this and, as the sky cleared at sunset, recorded the last scene with the not-quite snow and the Doctor in his suit.

In the months since the last episode was shot, Piper had got a haircut, so extensions were attached while they waited for it to grow back to the right length for continuity purposes. Next day, although most of the regulars got time off, was more remarkable as the crew took reference and background shots for the Sycorax ship and then went to the Tower of London. They were given unprecedented access to the roof of the White Tower. Tennant, meanwhile, was rehearsing his broadsword fight with Sean Gilder (the Sycorax leader), choreographed by Kevin McCurdy. This needed care not only to avoid the Doctor seeming too aggressive, but because Gilder would be in a heavy costume and wearing contact lenses inside a mask that reduced peripheral vision. One last day in London had the Brandon Estate sequences completed. Tennant arrived in the afternoon, as did Peter Davison, who lived nearby. Davison's younger children were more impressed by Piper (see X3.13a, "Time Crash"; X4.6, "The Doctor's Daughter"). Then a weekend off and back to Cardiff... but they hadn't left the Powell Estate, because the first scenes of this episode shot on 1st August were in the same part of Loudon Square, Gabalfa, that had been used in X1.13, "The Parting of the Ways". (Actually, the earlier part of the day was spent at a dim-sum restaurant filming Cassandra's death for X2.1, "New Earth".) This Gabalfa shoot was scheduled to include the pre-credit scene of "New Earth" and the TARDIS interior that followed at Q2, but they were already running late. Thus the TARDIS interiors were begun the following day at Q2 and the planned start of work at the HTV studios, where Jackie's flat had been moved started a day later. These three days at HTV were mainly taken up with killer Christmas tree action. Clarke was glad that Mickey was finally taking the initiative and being brave. Piper and Clarke did night location work in central Cardiff (again, hampered by rowdy drunks) for the Christmas shopping scene with the robot santas, the falling tree (which took until 3.00am to get right) and a decorated street (the local council put up the lights for these two nights).

• It had been decided that the Sycorax were to use full-face masks and contact lenses (although only their leader would have functioning prostheses and dentures). Their look was partly determined by the script's insistence on "real" eyes and masks like horse's skulls, but also by a plan to make them look vaguely Masai (hence the staves) and also a thought that - it being Christmas - red velvet would be nice. Beneath this were rugby pads and adapted Wellington boots, on top were jewellery from a film set in Papua New Guinea. Ed Thomas, who had been a designer on a film using Clearwell Caves (a disused ochre mine) in Gloucestershire had suggested this as the interior for the vast Sycorax ship. The shoot went there from 10th Wednesday (Tennant's driver apparently getting lost) and, as they were going to be in an airless hole in the ground, naturally the weather got hot. Logistically, getting equipment down to the location was tricky, and once in the caves, radios and phones stopped working properly. This location was in use until 15th, although the last day was the material before the TARDIS arrived. The shots of Mickey in the garage were done back at Cardiff that day. Hawes took the crew back to Barry Island next day (X1.9, "The Empty Child"; X1.10, "The Doctor Dances"), because nowhere in Cardiff had a clear enough skyline to pass for the wing of a spaceship. (A clear blue sky, ideal for matting, made it look very un-Decemberish.) Tennant mooned a passing yacht. Meanwhile, the second unit got the shots of people standing on ledges and rooves. After this, the UNIT HQ scenes, which didn't need the regulars, were recorded under the Millennium Stadium. Most of the regulars got the rest of the week off, but Tennant went to the *Blue Peter* studios on the Wednesday to pick a monster for Davies to write into "Love & Monsters" (X2.10) and then do a live webchat with the programme's viewers.

• The design of the Sycorax ship was based originally on a conch-shell. The decision to make the vessel seem to be made of stone came from the script rather than looking for locations that weren't conventional spaceship interiors. It was realised fairly early on that the shot of the Gherkin shattering wouldn't be practical as a model - the number of panes and their shape would have made the model as big as a house to look plausible. The windows of the Powell Estate, however, could be done physically by Mike Tucker's group. This took place in the second week of September.

X2.1: "New Earth"

The over-runs and some changes and additions requested by Jane Tranter meant that this episode was incomplete long after the projected end of Block One. Some extra scenes were added at the beginning of Block Two, along with the missing parts of "School Reunion" and "New Earth". An additional day was found for one scene Tennant believed was crucial: the new Doctor selecting his clothes. For the Costume Room scene, the main shots were done as normal, staying away from the Console, and the spiral staircase was matted in later. Amongst the many, many in-jokes in the clothing were Tennant's *Casanova* costume and a Hogwarts uniform (see X2.5, "Rise of the Cybermen"). The Tom Baker-style scarf had been knitted for Phil Collinson in the 70s. This was Tennant's last scene of the shoot, the rest of the crew also doing some pick-ups of the wing of the spaceship. Two days later, the various news reports were recorded. Jason Mohammed, of BBC Wales, had met Davies at a charity function and asked to be in the series.

- With all the other Christmas clichés in place, the rough edit used two obvious records: Slade's "Merry Xmas Everybody" and the version of "The Bells of St. Mary's" by Bob B Soxx and the Blue Jeans on Phil Spector's *A Christmas Gift for You*. From bitter experience, Murray Gold knew that even ten seconds of the latter would cost more to clear than the rest of the episode put together, so he knocked together a pastiche with the same chime motif and roped in occasional collaborator Tim Phillips to help with vocals. The result was supposed to be a place-holder until a better idea (or a better recording) came along, but it was used. Gold's anxiety about the sound quality meant that he re-recorded it for the soundtrack album with Neil Hannon of art-rockers The Divine Comedy (not everyone prefers this). The melody (it's become known as "Song for Ten") crops up again in the tag-scenes for "School Reunion" and X2.7, "The Idiot's Lantern".

- With the profile of the series rising, the expectation surrounding this episode was immense. The *Children in Need* promotion launched a series of trailers themed around the line "Something is coming" and using the Santa Robots. Tennant was interviewed for the *Radio Times* to promote *The Secret Smile*, and then the Christmas edition came out. Whereas most covers are generic festive images twisted to include television, this time there was a painting of a snow-globe: inside this were a police box covered in snow, a snowman with Tom Baker's hat and scarf and a snow-Dalek. Other than a shot of a choirboy to depict the King's College Cambridge service on Christmas Eve, 1989, the last one to illustrate a specific television programme was the not-terribly-jolly 1986 *EastEnders* episode.

X2.1: "New Earth"

(8th April, 2006)

Which One is This? Carry On, Doctor. The inevitable "body-swap" farce episode, but in a futuristic city with cat-nuns, zombies and a couple of familiar faces. But no grapes.

Firsts and Lasts Finally! An alien planet. It looks a bit like Swansea - but it's got humanoid cat-people, a race too expensive to only appear once (X3.3, "Gridlock"). This is the first time the Face of Boe speaks, but the last time we meet Cassandra.

There's a new script editor: as the bulk of the work that people with this title used to do is now Davies' responsibility, this is less noteworthy than it was in earlier times (see Volume 6 - or indeed any previous volume, but that's the one where it really mattered). The new bug is Simon Winstone, who is the first one to have come from editing the Virgin *New Adventures*.

Watch Out For...

- Those of you noting the re-use of locations will have something to play with in the Intensive Care scenes and Cassandra's hidey-hole, but this episode is just about the only one *not* to use Cardiff Royal Infirmary. Given the nature of the script, this was possibly a tactful move.

- Talking of re-use, there's a gag here when they rapidly cut from Cassandra calling Rose a "little bit—" to Rose saying "Bit rich". Ooh, they almost said something Americans think is rude (although Rose got away with calling Cassandra "a bitchy trampoline" last year). Then in the next sequence, Rose identifies that Cassandra is talking out of her "Ask not!".

- So, they thought, there's an award-winning beauty spot not far from Swansea, where the show-runner used to live. It's got a majestic clifftop overlooking a bay. Why not make this the location for the first properly alien world Rose visits? Why not? Because it's late September 2005

Has All the Puff "Totally" Changed Things?

Series Two of the BBC Wales *Doctor Who* is very probably the most relentlessly "revealed" television series of all time. As well as every story having behind-the-scenes features and interviews for *Doctor Who Magazine, SFX, Starburst, Radio Times* and occasional local press on location, there were two separate sets of commentary (one on the box set DVDs and another on the podcast), the BBC's *Doctor Who* website and even David Tennant's home movies. And on top of all of this, we had the launch of *Doctor Who Adventures* (a BBC-produced comic rather like the original Marvel *Doctor Who Weekly* from the 70s) and two different TV shows about this TV show. Some stories topped even this, with *Blue Peter* following the progress of William Grantham's creation, the Abzorbaloff, from prize-winning entry to design, to filming and eventually to the transmission of "Love & Monsters" (X2.10). The *Blue Peter* connection was a significant factor in *Totally Doctor Who*, but this came a year after the launch, with the new series itself, of *Doctor Who Confidential*.

Confidential served several masters. At a very basic level, it was there to draw a young, dedicated audience towards BBC3, the unloved digital service that was at the time trying to compete with commercial digital 16-24-friendly stations such as Channel 4's T4. BBC3 was the first-run home of *Torchwood* Series One, which should give you some idea of its usual output. Putting *Confidential* on immediately after each *Doctor Who* episode had aired on BBC1 allowed seasoned fans to watch something other than Graham Norton, but also served to introduce a Saturday Night line-up that they hoped people would stick with. (Often re-runs of popular shows that had had the episode in question premiered during the week, making Saturday the night to show the station at its best. This meant *Top Gear* reruns and *Horne and Corden* - see X5.11, "The Lodger". Unsurprisingly, the station's viewing-figures peaked for 45 minutes for *Confidential*, then sagged again.)

A second function was to get new fans to appreciate exactly how much the episodes rested on the 40-plus years' heritage of *Doctor Who*, so there would be montage clips edited to current hit records trying to reinforce the idea of *Doctor Who* as a continuum. Anyone anxious to see what the Macra looked like first time around could hang on after "Gridlock" (X3.3) and see the only extant footage from "The Macra Terror" (4.7). This became less prominent as the series proper gained the rights to show clips in the narrative (X4.14, "The Next Doctor"), but remained a good way to fill three quarters of an hour when the episode that's just been on is the first half of a two-parter and they want to avoid too much behind-the-scenes stuff - partly to avoid spoilers, but mainly because that's about all they have for next week.

Sometimes, this is a blessing: the restrictions on what they could reveal in "The Hungry Earth" (X5.9) made this an ideal opportunity to simply show how all the specialist departments that had been highlighted over the previous five years dovetailed in making an episode. As there is a finite number of times Danny Hargreaves, the operator of the physical effects, can show us how to blow things up, the series became increasingly more useful as a method of filling in the background. Thus the making of "The Fires of Pompeii" (X4.2) allotted a day off so that David Tennant and the camera crew could visit the real ruins and be told about the devastating effects of Vesuvius erupting. Tony Curran, who played Vincent in "Vincent and the Doctor" (X5.10), lives in Los Angeles, so was on hand to be given a tour of the Getty Museum and shown the real Vincent's work. There are times in these episodes when it's hard to escape the feeling that if *Doctor Who*'s main creator, Sydney Newman, were alive and watching, he would have preferred *Confidential* to what they were doing to his baby.

However, the bulk of the episodes is given over to the practicalities of making an episode and the thinking behind writing it. Russell T Davies was, of course, on hand for most episodes to talk it up, and seasoned viewers started to spot certain stock phrases: "How could we not do it?", "big, iconic" and most notoriously "marvellous!" The cast did the kind of interviews now familiar from the DVD extras of movies, and the writers (when it wasn't Davies) would explain how many rewrites it took to give the producer what he wanted. All of this, plus all the green-screen stuff, chats with The Mill and so on, would be narrated with laboured puns and occasional shafts of wit. The first series had commentary spoken by Simon Pegg (see X1.7, "The Long Game"); Series Two's episodes had Mark Gatiss (see X1.3, "the Unquiet Dead" and others);

continued on Page 241...

X2.1 New Earth

and the weather's decided to be horrible, that's why not. The Doctor and Rose are lying in the apple-grass not because it's dead romantic or anything, just that any higher off the ground and Billie's hair was going everywhere at once. At least two scenes were lost because the digital cameras simply wouldn't record in that weather, and a number of others were reworked from the original plan because by mid-afternoon it was just too dark. Production difficulties beset what was supposed to be a 12-day shoot for this episode, with some shots completed three months later. If you find the result a bit dull, you can always look at Tennant's hair to see when the various inserts were shot.

• When Cassandra possesses Rose, the obvious behavioural changes are compounded by her mysteriously acquiring a padded bra and different-coloured lipstick. When Cassandra occupies the Doctor's body, it just makes him seem even more like Kenneth Williams than usual. (We're struggling to think of an equivalent for impatient US readers who can't be bothered to google Kenneth Williams - the best we can come up with is Paul Lynde, but that's not quite right.) As both this story and "Partners in Crime" (X4.1) feature characters addressed as "Matron", this may have been deliberate[44]. It is now *de rigueur* around these parts for any lightly suggestive or easily misconstrued comment to be met by a slightly plummy, slightly adenoidal cry of "Ooh... MmmAY-tron!", based loosely on Williams' performance in *Carry On Doctor*. (See 5.3, "The Ice Warriors" for comments on this landmark cultural icon.) Tennant's fake Estuary accent and face-pulling had already garnered unfavourable comparisons with Williams (especially the latter's camply irate histrionics in *Just a Minute* and *Round the Horne* - and see 10.2, "Carnival of Monsters" for *that*). So see if you can spot moments that may have been scripted that way until wiser council prevailed in rehearsals.

The Continuity

The Doctor He doesn't like hospitals, but is, quite uncharacteristically, enthusiastic about little shops found there. He knows a lot about the medicine of this period, and is able to adapt the cures developed from the human "specimens" to cure those same people. He knows Petrifold Regression to be incurable, and can identify this and other diseases at a glance. When Cassandra tries to occupy his mind, he shuts off all his thoughts.

• *Ethics*. The Doctor judges the proposal that Chip should allow Cassandra to occupy him as unethical because, even though Chip is a 'half-life', he has the right to a life of his own. [This is congruent with the Doctor's stance on the specifically created bodies used to develop the cures. Had they not developed consciousness, they might have been grudgingly sanctioned, but the Doctor's comments suggest that even this was unlikely. Further taking us into ethically complex territory is the development that the dying Chip *volunteers* to spend his last few hours as host to his mistress - the Doctor finds this appalling, when there is no reason why he should. Chip's own choice in the matter is either valid, since he is an individual, or not, because he was made to be a servant. If the latter, the Doctor has no right to make someone go against their nature, any more than he would have if Rose became a genius or a Dalek felt compassion and self-doubt.]

He acts as final arbiter in the discussion of what to do with the test subjects, arguing that he is the 'highest' authority. [What's worrying is that, for all the reasons in favour of his shutting down the cat-nuns' operation, one does wonder if it might have quelled the plague that has overtaken New New York by "Gridlock", making the Doctor more responsible for that status quo than might initially be evident.]

• *Background*. He claims to have met the Face of Boe 'just the once' [X1.2, "The End of the World"].

• *Inventory: Sonic Screwdriver*. It can access the subframe of the hospital's systems to reveal a whole area to explore. It also opens and closes pods, lifts and stuff and adapts the Duke of Manhattan's winch.

• *Inventory: Other*. The Doctor carries glasses, which he here uses to read the notes on a patient's bed. The psychic paper can receive cryptic messages from specially attuned people - the Face of Boe turns out to be one of those gifted/privileged individuals [and we only know of one other, see X4.8, "Silence in the Library"].

The TARDIS It appears to need a more elaborate start-up procedure than normal for this trip.

The Supporting Cast

• *Rose* has done a lot of laundry and packed her rucksack for a long journey. She's wearing a little

New Earth X2.1

Has All the Puff "Totally" Changed Things?

continued from Page 239...

Series Three, Series Four and the Tennant specials had Anthony Head (X2.3, "School Reunion"), with Noel Clarke on some of the specials; Alex Price (X5.6, "Vampires in Venice") did Series Five; and Series Six was Russell Tovey (X4.0, "Voyage of the Damned"). In many cases, these actors were on hand in Cardiff for something else - when Pegg was unavailable for the launch programme on BBC1 (itself a sort of pilot for *Confidential*), the star of *Casanova* was handy. David Tennant narrated Davies explaining that Eccleston was a marvellous choice for an iconic new Doctor. Only by comparison with Davies could Steven Moffat be called camera-shy, but he has stepped back and presented a more collegiate approach to making the series. At the same time, the new cast have worked out ways to work around the constant presence of the *Confidential* crew. "The Rebel Flesh" (X6.5) was notable for a making-of that consisted mainly of the TARDIS crew sat in a tent talking cobblers while waiting for the weather to improve.

Confidential was the last remnant of BBC3's previous incarnation as BBC Choice. This had been a digital-only back-up station and had been the broadcast equivalent of DVD extras, with occasional re-runs (the promotional material had host Pauline Quirk dressed as Tom Baker, but actual *Doctor Who* was restricted to another semi-BBC-run digital channel, UK Gold). They did behind-the-scenes stuff about *EastEnders* and the like, which persisted when the relaunched BBC3 began. With the spread of digital television, much of the original point of BBC Choice was the kind of thing better catered-for with the red button on the remote control, opting-in to additional material or alternative events. The full-length *Confidential* material was often bulked out with those montages to recent hits, so a 15-minute version was also shown and is an occasional extra on the bumper-de-luxe DVDs. It was often noticeable when they had under 30 minutes'-worth of material. The episode for "The Waters of Mars" (X4.16) was bulked out with the same four or five sequences over and again, and that for "The Pandorica Opens" (X5.12) milked the director's rather coals-to-Newcastle use of the incidental music from *Raiders of the Lost Ark* for all it was worth. And then another few minutes.[47]

However, executive producer Julie Gardner believed that a second puff-show was needed, specifically for children and on BBC1, the main terrestrial channel and home of *Doctor Who*. This needed to be an extended teaser for the episode to come rather than the one that had just been on. *Totally Doctor Who* was made in a studio in Cardiff re-using the tunnel set from "The Impossible Planet" (X2.8) and had an ex-*Blue Peter* presenter, Liz Barker, teamed with a future one. (Barney Harwood has just joined the long-running series after a career coming in at the end of other children's staples, so if *Blue Peter* is cancelled after leaving London for Salford, we'll know who to blame.) It also had kids. They sent in their paintings, they competed in "Companion Academy" (see 22.5, "Timelash") and they went head-to-head with the cast of the series in quizzes. Much of it was "how-to" material, with stunt arrangers showing how to pretend-fight safely, Barker helping out on the Foley dub for Cybermen stomping, Harwood becoming an extra (in "Love & Monsters" - it's lucky the two stars were hardly in that episode; the canteen would have been stuffed, what with *Blue Peter* there as well) and monster-choreographer Ailsa Berk showing kids how to walk like scarecrows (X3.8, "Human Nature"). The second series replaced Barker with Kirsten O'Brien, who had been one of the in-vision continuity presenters for CBBC (see X2.6, "The Age of Steel") and swapped competitions between individual kids for a pair of teams, Team TARDIS and Team Time Lord, attempting to perform various aspects of making an episode. (Set-dressing, storyboarding and so on. There is no truth to the rumour that the prize was to make Series One of *Torchwood*.) Best of all, there was an animated serial running through the series, which was later collated into a 45-minute episode shown the morning of X3.13, "Last of the Time Lords". (See **Is Animation the Way Forward?** under "The Infinite Quest" in the Appendix to Volume 8.)

You will notice that this is completely unlike anything any other SF series has ever had. Even in the late seventies, when child-friendly space-opera was in vogue, no attempt was made to yoke a children's educational show to, say, *Buck Rogers in the 25th Century*. It was noticeable that a lot of

continued on Page 243...

241

X2.1 New Earth

peaked cap when she steps into the TARDIS.

According to Cassandra, Rose considers the new Doctor 'a little bit foxy' and it's 'hormone city' inside her head. She refers to her first trip in the TARDIS - going to the year five billion to see the Earth perish ["The End of the World"] - as a 'date', possibly just to see how the new Doctor reacts; his reaction is to mention chips again. She feels obliged to state all over again how much she 'loves' travelling with the Doctor, just in case anyone missed it. Whereas a departing Rose repeatedly tells her mother, 'Love you', her response to Mickey's 'Love you' is just 'Bye'.

She reiterates her point from "The End of the World" about evolution to Cassandra, and is immediately taken far more seriously than she was expecting. She's impressed by the futuristic hospital, and apple-grass. After unexpectedly arriving alone on a floor that looks like it's been taken from level one of a horror video game, she picks a hefty piece of piping to use as a weapon and threatens to use it, until identifying Cassandra on the cine-projector.

- *Mickey* is a bit sullen at Rose's departure, but seems resigned to this being his life from now on.
- *Jackie*. Rose urges her to get back in touch with cousin Mo [the person they thought about hiding with when the Sycorax ship arrived last episode].

The Supporting Cast (Evil)

- *Cassandra*. The turning-point in her human life seems to be the combination, in rapid succession, of a) being told she is beautiful by a stranger who has no reason to suck up to her and is about to die, and b) losing faith in humanity when nobody else lifts a finger to help her with the dead Chip/Cassandra. [The surgery and callous use of others all date from this moment - which the Doctor has facilitated.] There is hope for her, though, as the Doctor observes when she has spent time in other people's bodies and seen the world through their eyes, especially one of the human lab-rats who has never been touched. After assisting in the creation of a new form of humanity, she becomes resigned to her own mortality, although she contemplates the hat she could wear at her trial.

Before all of that, however, she is her old malicious, waspish self. She shows no concern that her original brain-tissue has died as her mental engrams have survived, and uses people as taxis with no regard for their potential fates after their own memories/personas undergo mental compression. She has mixed feelings about being inside Rose, liking some of the body's features but expressing contempt for Rose herself. After decades in the cellars of the hospital, she is aware that something is amiss and potentially blackmail material.

Chip has been stealing medicine [including, we suppose, the knock-out perfume Cassandra wields] on Cassandra's behalf. He is a force-grown clone, her favourite model - because he resembles the one who she met at the Ambassador of Thrace's party who had such a big impact on her. Cassandra still drops in occasional French tags, but her knowledge of 'Old Earth Cockney' is, whilst surprisingly close, a bit rubbish, really. [So she can't be getting it from Rose, which makes Cassandra's knowledge of the term 'chav' mysterious.]

- *The Face of Boe*. He [it?] spends a lot of time sleeping, is variously said to be 'thousands... some say millions [of years old]', and is purportedly 'dying of old age'. He [it?] appears to have been suffering from ennui more than anything else, ending this story invigorated because the Doctor has taught him to 'look at [the universe] anew'. It's rumoured that the Face of Boe will import a great secret to a 'wanderer, a man without a home, the lonely god' - and he [it?] says he [it?] will do so to the Doctor, at their third and final meeting [see, of course, "Gridlock"].

Planet Notes

- *New Earth* is in the M87 galaxy [so fairly nearby, at 53.5 million light years away], and was selected because it has the same mass, rotation, atmosphere and type of sun as Old Earth. [This is apparently very rare - see 23.1, "The Mysterious Planet".] It was apparently occupied by the Cat race before humans came. They have apple-grass. The bit where the TARDIS lands is a coastline, overlooking a bay with the city of New New York and a hospital on the outskirts.

One of the major cities, New New York, is actually the 'fifteenth' New York since the original; it's actually New-New-New-New-New-New-New-New-New-New-New-[gasp...]-New-New-New-New-New York. There is a Duke of Manhattan and an Ambassador of Thrace. [These could be more of those planets named after cities, as with 'Barcelona' in X1.13, "The Parting of the Ways".]

Has All the Puff "Totally" Changed Things?

continued from Page 241...

the emphasis was on showing artwork made by the young viewers, in the tradition of *Vision On* (24.1, "Time and the Rani"). O'Brien later took over as host of *smART* (sic). If the "education" remit went a bit askew, such as the episode linked to "The Idiot's Lantern" (X2.7) getting not only the dates of the Coronation wrong but the names of two previous Doctors, it was still closer to the BBC's Charter commitment to "Inform, Educate and Entertain" than any DVD extra. That notion was taken a step further in the last-ever episode of *Confidential*, when an episode-ette, written by a class of schoolkids and shown being storyboarded, cast, shot and edited, was shown. (See the mini-episode "Death is the Only Answer" in Volume 9.) This was supervised by the Head of BBC Learning, Saul Nassé, whose fan credentials include running the Bedfordshire Local Group of the Doctor Who Appreciation Society in the 80s.

This came at an interesting juncture in the Corporation's history. During Greg Dyke's spell as Director General, the emphasis shifted towards greater inclusivity. The BBC was paid for by the public, so they owned the Corporation's output as much as anyone else did. Thus the archive material ought to be more widely available. This was becoming possible with the increased use of broadband in the UK, and the BBC was shifting its ground from radio and television to any form of dissemination. Admittedly, there were still costs, especially for anything using copyrighted music or actors who had not been dead long enough, but Dyke saw the BBC as a curator of the television heritage as much as it was a news organisation and source of entertainment. However, Tony Blair's chief spin-doctor, Alistair Campbell, hounded Dyke from office over the reporting of the questions raised on the accuracy of what Parliament was told over WMDs in Iraq. Dyke's deputy, Mark Thompson, was promoted and his emphasis, especially with the government not agreeing to a funding raise for the BBC, was capitalising on those archival resources and the popularity of particular "brands" such as *Doctor Who*. DVD distribution, like the *Doctor Who* tie-in novels after 1996, were under the aegis of BBC Worldwide (BBCW), formerly BBC Enterprises, and formed part of the cost-defraying overseas sales operation that was helping keep the BBC afloat. Polarising Thompson and Dyke this way is rather simplistic, but it will help clarify the conflicting demands on the BBC for public service and financial viability.

It also makes clear that any asset the Corporation owned would be made to earn its keep as much as possible without losing the very things that made it popular. BBCW had made a deal with Woolworth's to form 2|Entertain (sic) and, as many of you will know, their lovingly-crafted DVDs of old *Doctor Who* stories contain as much effort and care as some new programmes (naming no names, but see X2.11, "Fear Her" and think "archaeology"). It would be cynical to suppose that the main reason they went to all the time and expense to make animated visual coverage for the soundtracks of the missing episodes of "The Invasion" (6.3) was because the BBC Wales series was bringing back the Cybermen a few months before the release-date, just as it would be silly to presume that they made the Cybermen Series Two's big relaunched old monster because they had a Troughton DVD coming out with them in. Instead, think of the 90s management-ese floating around the BBC at the time, with words like "synergy" and phrases such as "360 degree cross-promotion" and "multi-platform". If the BBC now has eight TV channels (two of which anyone can get), almost a dozen national radio stations (five of which were available without buying a digital gizmo) and a website with clips and back-up material, it was ridiculous not to have something on these for people who liked one or other of the popular programmes.

Thus *Doctor Who Confidential* was not promoting *Doctor Who* on BBC3, it used *Doctor Who* expressly to promote BBC3. In another of its clever plans, the government announced that from 2010 to 2012, all the analogue TV signals would be closed down so everyone would have to have digital. The BBC, as a publicly funded body, had to meet the cost of this technical and logistical feat without extra funds, so enticing people onto digital was part of a long-term strategy for survival. *Confidential* also served as a point of access for the public to see how their money was being spent. With reports of the budget for the relaunch of

continued on Page 245...

X2.1 New Earth

History

• *Dating*. [When the episode opens, some time seems to have elapsed since the Doctor and Rose were deciding which star to visit at the end of the last episode. It's daylight, there have been changes of clothes, and the ash/snow from Christmas Night has all gone. The TARDIS seems to have moved from Bloxom Road, too. Everyone's got new windows. That can't have been easy, in the week between Christmas and New Year. In the light of what we learn in X2.10, "Love & Monsters", this is worth bearing in mind. It's also obviously summer, but that can't be helped. Turning to the bulk of the story...]

It's the year five billion and twenty-three [so, about 20 years since the Earth was evaporated in "The End of the World"]. Green crescent moons are universally recognised as denoting hospitals.

The main hospital in New New York is run by Cats, specifically Sisters of the Order of Plenitude. They worship a goddess called Santori [and possibly others]. They have developed remarkably potent cures for apparently terminal and untreatable conditions that have developed over the aeons, such as Petrifold Regression (slowly turning to stone), Marconi's Syndrome (which seems to involve bleeping in Morse whilst levitating) and Pallidome Pancrosis [what this might be is unclear; the patient is bone-white, but that might be normal for him]. They're still using nanodentistry [cf X1.7, "The Long Game"].

The Face of Boe has become the source of legends, mainly concerning his [alleged] great age and a big secret he will only impart to a wanderer. He is the last of Boekind [note that he was pregnant in "The Long Game"] and identifies the Doctor as the last of an even older race. He can send messages via telepathy and psychic paper, and can apparently teleport himself by sheer mental effort. Others, notably Novice Hame, can hear his ancient songs in their minds.

For other mental projection, the kind of transference Cassandra exploits is banned in every civilised galaxy. Meanwhile, some kind of thought-transference and activation of consciousness and language is at work in the specimens kept in 'intensive care'. Whilst force-grown clones such as Cassandra's factotum, Chip, seem to be permitted - and clone-meat, biocattle and other cellular agglomerations are legal but too slow - the manufacture of human bodies for experimentation seems to lead to those bodies developing thought-processes, awareness and language.

Catchphrase Counter Here's where we get the start of the Doctor's 'I'm sorry, I'm so sorry' routine when people can't be helped. Cassandra gets a couple of 'moisturise me's in - one as her old self, and once in Rose's body.

Deus Ex Machina The Doctor cures everybody of everything by having them lay hands on one another [with this episode first going out at Easter, that looks distinctly odd]. More to the point, the Doctor creates a temporal paradox by setting Cassandra on the path to becoming self-obsessed [see below] and creating Chip to look like, um, Chip.

The Analysis

The Big Picture In any long-running fantasy/SF series, you get body-swap episodes. It's a way of preventing the regular cast from getting too bored with the usual things they have to do. Other ploys for the same purpose include parallel universes (see X2.5, "Rise of the Cybermen"), possession, hypnosis, mind-altering drugs, amnesia and doppelgängers. We saw an awful lot of those in the Troughton episodes, and a fair amount of possession in the early Tom Baker years, but it's the US series of the 90s that really went to town on them. In particular, *Star Trek: Deep Space Nine* did it to such an extent that it was difficult to get to know what the characters were like normally, so often were they under the influence of alien mind-parasites or locked into holodeck games of Bond clichés. Another handy use for this is to allow someone else to take over a character when the star is away or ill, and this covers *The Prisoner* letting Nigel Stock be Number Six for a bit while Patrick McGoohan's off making *Ice Station Zebra*, or Hudson Leick playing Xena for a few weeks when Lucy Lawless fractured her pelvis (and, of course, all the fun and games with Autolycus in Xena's body). Quite apart from all of this, it is an opportunity to do farce, and especially for Billie Piper to do something other than suffer and bawl her eyes out.

Equally inevitable, given Russell T Davies' early work on Paul Abbott's *Children's Ward*, was the use of a hospital setting. As a specific reference, Michael Crichton's film of Robin Cook's medical paranoia shocker *Coma* is worth noting, not least

Has All the Puff "Totally" Changed Things?

continued from Page 243...

Doctor Who being flung about with no authoritative answer from BBC Wales, the behind-the-scenes material was reassuring about how homespun the glossy-looking episodes really were. Similarly, *Totally Doctor Who* was about connecting the child viewers to the making of the series and getting their homemade pictures and monster-costumes appraised by the experts. Just as BBC Wales encouraged a sense of ownership amongst the people of Cardiff (see **Does Being Made in Wales Matter?** under X1.11, "Boom Town"), so *Totally* (or *Totely*, to older fans a bit cynical about all this puff) was about a proprietorial sense that Britain's children were the real owners of this series.

The paradox is that this glasnost came at precisely the time when the makers of the new series were beginning to have to issue dummy scripts and shoot whole fake scenes to preserve secrets and surprises. The solution was to use this secrecy to plant teasers. When the BBC's website was revamped, the links to sneak previews and bonus scenes (including some specifically shot for the online service) became a part of the countdown to a new episode. "Voyage of the Damned" (X4.0) had an advent calendar of games and puzzles, with stills, pages of script or even clips as prizes. Some of the special scenes for telethons were rewatchable only on the website (as was the "making of" for X3.13a, "Time Crash"). "Voyage of the Damned" was the first main piece of BBC programming (or "content", as those managementoids would call it) available on the BBC's mischievously named "iPlayer". Almost anything transmitted on BBC can be accessed by anyone in Britain with a suitable computer link for up to a week after. (Overseas, there is sporadically available iPad app coverage for this too.) This has messed up collating the ratings and forced the commercial channels to follow suit. Before this, there were the TARDISodes, brief vignettes (usually prequels to the forthcoming adventures) available on smart phones, and an interactive game, "Attack of the Graske", that launched minutes after "The Christmas Invasion" (X2.0) and promoted in a trailer immediately after the episode's debut. All of this has to be made somehow consonant with the broadcast episodes of all three drama series in the stable, even if one of those series seemed to be going out of its way to mess up the other two (see **Why the Great Powell Estate Date Debate?** under X2.3, "School Reunion" and **Must All Three Series Correlate Properly?** under X4.4, "The Sontaran Stratagem"). More recently, executive producer Piers Wenger insisted that the online computer-games for the eleventh Doctor were entirely canonical adventures and as valid as any broadcast Pertwee story, let alone the books or comics. The Graske became a recurring character in *The Sarah Jane Adventures* - but, as we will see in forthcoming episodes, some of the material in the TARDISodes is problematic.

Meanwhile, at the newsagent's, there was a new arrival. The BBC seemed not to have noticed that Panini's *Doctor Who Magazine* was repositioning itself to cater for a whole new readership who weren't up to speed on Drashigs and Drahvins (see 10.2, "Carnival of Monsters", and 3.1, "Galaxy 4", if you're one of those people). It took on a new set of behind-the-scenes interviewers and embedded them at Q2, filling the gaps where they couldn't say anything with a return to explaining the basics. With the magazine a commercial success during the long period with no programme to promote it, the impending rebirth of the series made it worth retaining. So Panini, and their new commercial agency Orange 20, weren't going to simply drop this. The BBC's magazine wing was itself buoyant at that time, with spin-offs for everything from *Gardener's World* to *Top Gear* and endless cookery and lifestyle titles (and obviously *Radio Times*) all run by BBC Worldwide. Rather than get into a turf-war with Panini, the obvious solution was a child-friendly magazine, *Doctor Who Adventures*. This arrived at the same time as Series Two and *Totally*. It was fortnightly and each issue had a cover-mount toy (starting with a pencil-case, then a Slitheen Whoopie-Cushion, then a TARDIS alarm-clock). It had a strip that was almost like *TV Comic* reborn (see Volume 2 and **Why Did We Countdown to TV Action?** under 8.3, "The Claws of Axos"). The two magazines rubbed along amicably for five years until the imposition of further cuts on the BBC in 2011. Worldwide was, at this stage, still publishing the tie-in novels - until 2007, when Random House was sold the rights.

continued on Page 247...

X2.1 New Earth

for the shots in the broadcast episode of patients suspended on wires in the wards. The plot was that people with relatively minor ailments were being pronounced brain-dead and harvested for organs in a vast warehouse. They were kept hanging on wires, in the same position as the person with Marconi's Syndrome (but the cables were more visible). More generally, the film and novel were about the exploitation of medical technology for making vast sums of money out of people. We'll come back to that in a second, but consider the ways in which this story tries to be as unlike orthodox British TV dramas about hospitals as possible. *Children's Ward* focussed on the patients and their distress at being uprooted from the usual family, even if the family is what caused them to be in hospital. *Casualty* (see Volume 6) was about the over-worked staff at a provincial Accident and Emergency unit; its spin-off *Holby City* was about nurses and surgeons. In both cases, the point was that despite every outside influence, they kept going. As various recessions took hold and successive incoming Health Ministers took it upon themselves to make their mark with whatever fashionable managerial system had come along since the last Cabinet reshuffle, the hospitals had to run. Being set in an A&E unit allowed whatever emotional turmoil or dispute that was happening to be abruptly ended just before everyone got bored by it, with a new ambulance crew coming in and starting a fresh storyline. Every so often there would be a set-piece catastrophe, a plane crash or explosion. Eventually, an American series, *ER*, did something similar but - for reasons which will become clear - with less inclination to rebuke government dogma and its bureaucratic aftermath. US television about doctors has to appeal to advertisers, many of which have connections to the pharmacological industry, so it has to pull punches and present all American hospitals as staffed by quirky miracle-workers who will take on any patient, rich or poor. To British eyes, this looks like propaganda.

There are people in Britain who can pay for private medical treatment, in clinics and hospitals staffed by doctors and nurses trained on taxpayers' money within the National Health Service, but the principle since 1945 has been that treatment is free at the point of use unless you opt out. Even the Queen has had NHS treatment. No politician, even on the far right of UK politics, would ever dare to say out loud that this is wrong. (Oddly, America, where criticism of this has itself become a cottage industry, spends 17.4% of its GDP on healthcare compared to 9.8% in the "inefficient" UK.) This system, an expansion of the National Insurance scheme that gave everyone over 65 an old age pension, regardless of prior income, after 1908 (see X1.4, "Aliens of London" for more on David Lloyd George), has been tinkered with and diluted from its original aims and, in some regards, drastically compromised. Nonetheless, attempts to discredit it (usually in election campaigns, such as the one running when this story was being drafted) invariably flounder when the factual inaccuracies are revealed. Note how, when seeking to present Harriet Jones as likeable, she was given a pet topic connected with healthcare being made more inclusive (X1.4, "Aliens of London"). As with X2.3, "School Reunion", the topical impetus for this story is to be found in the attempts by the political parties in 2005 to grab the headlines on an emotive subject, in this case each party claiming to be the only one able to protect the NHS from the political interference of the others. (Thus the BBC tactfully avoided showing *Casualty* during an election campaign.) And, as is so often the case, the threat is that the other side will drag things down to the state they are in over in the US. American health-care provision, even after Obama, is presented in Britain as a Dickensian nightmare. If it hasn't become clear, the set-up in "New Earth", with a few mega-wealthy clients being treated in luxury because an entire species is being tortured, is a grotesque parody of what America's healthcare system seems like to us.

Independently of the election-fuelled concerns about the role of private companies in health-care, a debate about the ethics of testing has been running for centuries. Back in the 1860s, Lewis Carroll - of all people - was questioning the use of animals in pharmacological tests (not just white rabbits), but in the late 1980s this took a violent turn as the Animal Liberation Front not only broke into labs and released diseased animals into the wild, but planted bombs under the cars of anyone suspected of working in such places. Most medical scientists are frustrated that, because of laws passed over a century ago, anything to be ingested or applied to human tissue has to be tested on animals regardless of whether this tells them anything useful about their possible side-

Has All the Puff "Totally" Changed Things?

continued from Page 245...

But, once again, the emphasis of *Adventures* was child involvement, sending in pictures (either drawings of monsters or photos of themselves in costume).

What did all of this cross-promotion do to the original basic programme? Does *Doctor Who* benefit or suffer from all of this malarkey? The obvious point to make is that Series Two had both of the stars not only crossing the country to make the series and promote it on other programmes, but also making video-diaries, doing interviews for the promotional series and on occasion going off to do mini-documentaries for *Confidential*. It's hard to see Tennant's video diary without wondering if he slept at all in the whole eight months. By Series Five, we were getting Toby Whithouse - author of X5.6, "Vampires in Venice" - getting a tour of Venice and narrating half the episode, the rest of which was devoted to explaining that they didn't make it in Venice at all but Croatia. One might think that the commissioning process was "Will this episode make a cool *Confidential*?" Series Six took this to extremes, with half of one episode looking like *Jim'll Fix It* (22.4, "The Two Doctors"), but as with most of this, the main question is how the cast managed to fit all of this in.

There is, of course, one obvious aspect of the impact of all this on the series we have to consider. As we saw in **Did He Fall or Was He Pushed?** (X1.12, "Bad Wolf"), the delphic comments made by Christopher Eccleston about the workload and "culture" associated with the part are the main hints as to why he left after one series. Tennant, who was essentially living out his childhood fantasies, always appeared far more enthusiastic about this aspect of the job. And in many ways, it was a return to the conditions of the 1960s, when five and a half days in any week were given over to making the episode to be recorded on Friday or Saturday, and the one day off the cast got was spent opening fetes, visiting hospitals or giving interviews. The proportions of time spent on promotional activities is slightly lower now, but it is spread across the whole week for 35 weeks of the year. However, factor in the distance from London to Cardiff, and this peculiar goldfish-bowl life must have an effect on the stars. The effect of being a major part of a strategic realignment of BBC output, both moving most Drama to Wales and promoting every service using every resource, makes this version of *Doctor Who* uniquely complex and stressful.

But it isn't remote. The most important effect of all of this, and the one Moffat took pains to encourage in *Confidential*, was that making a complex and ambitious television series was an extension of what kids do when they make up stories, or draw their favourite (or imagined) monsters. Indeed, one side-effect of the double-banking on X3.10, "Blink" was that Tennant got to direct a whole *Confidential* himself, looking at how old-school fans such as himself, Davies, Moffat and Nicholas Briggs were now making the series that got them writing or acting. Rather than being passive, supine consumers (or active consumers, buying *DWM*, the child-orientated *Doctor Who Adventures* or the assorted action-figures and books), the youngest viewers were empowered as potential future producers. It was emphasised that everyone writing Series One came up through organised fandom[48] (as did the Dalek operators and voice-man Briggs, model supremo Mike Tucker, sound archivist Mark Ayres and dozens more since). Others who'd been *DWM* readers in the past included Tennant, production designer Ed Thomas and executive producer Phil Collinson. Even if it never returns to our screens, *Doctor Who Confidential* - and maybe *Totally Doctor Who* - will probably be cited 30 years from now as the starting-point for a whole generation of writers, actors, directors and designers.

effects. One arena in which the NHS has been cooperating with private medical companies and pharmacological concerns is the recruitment of human volunteers for new drugs. In some high-profile cases, this has been injurious to the volunteer. It can, however, be lucrative. Nonetheless, it is closely monitored by a number of government bodies and the changes to all aspects of medical testing are debated in Parliament, with the usual party divisions on where the profiteering / state interference divide comes. Thus the whole matter of medical testing is one made fresh in the British media almost every month. As we saw in "Planet of Giants" (2.1), the mythologised lone inventor

X2.1 New Earth

in a shed was a story we needed to hear in wartime, and helped cover the fact that penicillin had to be taken to America to be developed on a suitably big scale. Post-war, the major chemical companies were more keen on developing wonder-drugs (see, obliquely, 4.2, "The Tenth Planet") and some of these are among the nation's biggest exporters, albeit that the NHS takes the proprietary versions and has been forced over the years to make cost-benefit analyses of some of the more expensive medicines being developed.

The whole point of New Earth, we're told, is that it represents a New and Exciting frontier that has all the best of the old Earth but better. Even grass has to be special "apple-grass". This doesn't stop New Earth from having most of the problems the old one had (they haven't even got rid of polluting exhaust fumes, as we'll see in this story's sequel) and a whole host of new ones all their own. These don't fit the shining, pristine image - one imagines that the Doctor landed the TARDIS on exactly the bit of coastline from which they shoot promotional brochures - but are too useful to be done away with, so they're chucked in the basement and kept safely hidden away instead. (The wilful societal forgetfulness pattern is still going in "Gridlock" right in front of the Doctor's face, and if there's anything that explains his anger then, it's that his intervention last time didn't have any effect on this.) By contrast, X3.1, "Smith and Jones" has a present-day London hospital that has everything more-or-less as it should be until the crisis arises.

One of the many set ideas (they're too well-established to even be clichés any more) about the NHS is that patients in hospital should always be given grapes by visitors. It was certainly the custom post-War, especially when grateful nations with vineyards donated shiploads to wounded soldiers, and medically it's a much better idea than chocolates or flowers. (Anti-oxidants and vitamins, no sorbitol, no mess and they used to be a high-status item.) It's the subject of jokes long after it ceased to be real. It has the same status now as snow on Christmas Day or, more precisely, giving gift-boxes to tradesmen the day after. Nobody actually does it, but everyone thinks everyone else does.

As noted, Davies had written for one medical drama, but James Hawes, the director of this episode, had worked on two others: *Casualty* and the ITV knock-off *Always & Everyone* ("A&E": see what they did there?). The usual grammar of these shows is that the camera is pseudo-documentary, hand-held where possible, and the corridors are always tight so that action and bustle and apparent chaos are established with only a handful of extras[45]. What you will notice, if you watch this episode with that in mind, that the space between people in the wards and the foyer is emphasised - and that there are lots of shots from above, with the whiteness of the walls and floors and the vast window-effect green-screens making individuals seem to exist in the abstract. With every decision like this, the makers of this episode were working against the expectations of both conventional, clichéd UK hospital dramas and conventional, clichéd US Space Opera shows. Davies is clearly besotted with the latter, but aware that many people (including the TV professionals with whom he consorts and who say such nice things about him) aren't, so he never missed an opportunity to slag these things off. Above all, he is still insecure at this stage on whether the mass audience in the UK is ready for a drama set on another planet. The tentative nature of his moves towards making the kind of programme he himself would watch is something that this volume and the next will chart, but observe how he defuses the "alien" nature of New Earth by making it not only "new Earth" but specifically the futuristic avatar of the one city everyone thinks is already futuristic. It's emphatically not New London, or New New Cross, and despite the fact that only one person there has an American accent (he's a Duke, though, but absolutely nothing to do with "The Duke of Queens" in Michael Moorcock's *Dancers at the End of Time* - who would pilfer Moorcock's ideas for *Doctor Who*?), this is explicitly the Big Apple. Even the grass agrees. It's the America that Dennis Spooner and Terry Nation dreamed of in Season Two, rather than any genuine extant country of the same name, but that's how New York tends to think of itself.

Of course, when you are resisting cliché, the problem comes when you resist it the same way as everyone else. In avoiding little green men, Davies has given us brick-red bald men, bone-white bald men and so on. As with much of the other two visits to Five Billion-and-change, he's chosen to do just the same brave, innovative bold visuals as *The Fifth Element*, i.e, defrost a few ideas from 70s Moebius comics, and add in a few other exciting visuals from late 70s / early 80s films he enjoyed as a lad. (A possible reference not often cited is Polish Posters. The film posters for US and British flicks on release in translated versions were often innovative, despite having no bearing on the content. The 1978 British-made drama *The Legacy* certainly didn't contain any cats in wimples last time it was on telly.) One cliché appropriate to mention here is the "clone grown to provide spares for rich person" thing, which, a few years later, Kazuo Ishiguro "invented" for *Never Let Me Go* - one of those "it isn't science fiction because I'm a famous author" books which was made into a trite film with TV's Carey Mulligan (X3.10, "Blink").

English Lessons

• *Chav* (n. Perj.): It's *almost* the same as the Australian "Bogan" and the American "trailer trash", but not quite. The main thing that offends anyone using this word isn't class or education so much as the stunted ambition of these expensively-badly dressed youths. Whole books have been written on the distinction.

• *Bouncy Castle* (n.): Inflatable castle on which one bounces. In America, they're apparently called "spacewalks", which would have made the joke so much more complicated. (Davies has used this joke before, in *Queer as Folk*, about sex with over-muscular men.)

• *Wotcha* (int.): "Hello." (It might derive from "what are you doing?", but more plausibly the older "what cheer".) As used in Albert Chevalier's Music Hall song "Wot Cher" ("Knocked 'Em in the Old Kent Road"), memorably performed by Fozzie Bear as well as Bernard Cribbins, Brian Cant, Marlene Dietrich (!) and many others. Knowing this makes Adric's response at the end of 18.7, "Logopolis" slightly less awe-struck.

• *Apples and Pears* (n. coll.): Victorian cockney rhyming slang[46], and the textbook example. Nobody in living memory has called "stairs" this.

• *Boat Race* (n. coll.): Another piece of this rhyming-slang, one that nobody has used seriously since 1930, this denotes "face", as in "nice legs, shame about the boat-race". (That was in a minor hit song in 1979, the last known use.)

• *Guvnor* (n. inf.): "Sir" (as in "Governor", the head of a prison), used to refer to anyone in charge but not *too* in charge. Particularly associated with 70s thick-ear cop shows (*The Sweeney*, *Life on Mars*). Compare Mickey's colloquial use of "Boss" or some aspects of the US use of "Dude".

Oh, Isn't That...?

• *Zoe Wanamaker*. She's in person this time - that's her as Cassandra at the end. The wig's not hers (she usually goes for a slightly punk-ish spikey do, as she sported in the first *Harry Potter* film. She had also been in *Edge of Darkness*, the unforgettable 1986 drama that inspired the already-forgotten 2010 film.

• *Lucy Robinson* (Frau Clovis, the Duke of Manhattan's assistant) had been in one of Davies' less-publicised earlier projects, the deranged ecclesiastical soap *Revelations*.

Things That Don't Make Sense Let's think about this "cure for everything" business that the Cats are perpetrating for a minute. They obviously mean everything *infectious*: people don't develop immunities to broken legs. The analogy is with plague-carriers not getting plague until everyone else has succumbed. All right, but that's not something the plague does to the carrier (unless Lavinia Smith's paper on *The Teleological Response of the Virus* is a breakthrough in our understanding and the Nucleus of the Swarm is only distinctive by its vocabulary - see 11.1, "The Time Warrior" and 15.2, "The Invisible Enemy"). Instead, a plague carrier is *naturally* less prone to immediate symptoms, and thus gets to transfer the infection; had Typhoid Mary not been constitutionally able to pass unnoticed among healthy people, then there wouldn't have been an epidemic and she'd just have been a person who died of typhoid. Nobody would have heard of her.

But anyway, let's go with the idea that people with longer incubation times aren't just better carriers and *thus* spread a disease, but are kept from developing symptoms *in order* to spread it. How would immunity to a specific disease protect anyone against another one? Well, maybe along the lines of penicillin, one pathogen destroys a less tenacious but more deadly one. But that just means you'd get someone with one dreadful and nameless futuristic disease, not all of them at once. The Cats' plan is just about plausible if each individual specimen is a test of a combination of two diseases to see which one prevails out of each possible permutation, but giving every zombie every disease in one go is just going to make a very big pile of diseased carcasses.

Similarly, the Doctor's brilliant plan to cure them of everything by soaking them in virus-rich coloured water (and then personally hugging the younger, female zombies) looks dubious, as a cocktail of viruses, bacteria and whatever doesn't work for whatever genetic or environmentally triggered complaints the hospital might be called upon to treat.

And if these pouches contain inoculations against diseases the Doctor himself doesn't have, he's in trouble anyway. It's also quite remarkable that he can look at someone for half a second and - being unable to touch that person - diagnose that he's been infected with 'everything'.

We're also a little unclear on the difference between Chip, a 'half-life', and the similarly force-grown ICU 'patients'. The patients can formulate arguments coherently, and in English, despite no experience or training beyond standing around in cupboards all their lives (they are presumably born adult). This, despite a ban on the sort of psychic transference Cassandra does. Then again, if it has to be banned, it must be possible, and there seem to be many ways of doing this. So whatever consciousness inhabits the patients may, as the Cats speculate, be residual patterns from other people. Do none of the half-lives have this capacity? Evidently, Chip can and does accept a download of Cassandra's mind, an option that has never occurred to anyone before. Also, the Doctor seems to think that Cassandra can exist as particles floating around in the air, but he doesn't think she can continue inside a person who has been bred to endure all illnesses, who is now immune to every single one of them and who has next to no preexisting personality. Weirdly, neither does she.

Rose seems to swap lifts in mid-journey. Later, Cassandra seems surprised to be inside a male body - presuming anything she says in "The End of the World" can be believed, wasn't she a boy to begin with? We can overlook her use of a cine-projector (after all, she had a Wurlitzer "iPod" last time we saw her), but quite why she chooses the moment when she has decided to steal Rose's body to go on a trip down memory lane is another matter. (It might be that she knows her original "brain-meat" is dying. In which case, why not use whatever technology is being used for the ICU zombies or Chip to make a new one? It might have to be flattened out later, but if she's squatting in a dank cellar under a hospital, she's already resigned to being in this for the long haul. Indeed, as a fugitive from justice and registered dead, a totally new look might be a good option. It would surely be less effort than growing a new skin and keeping her brain in a jar, with Chip stealing medicine to keep that from dying until a temporary host can be found.)

The TARDIS lands across the bay from New New York, on the side with the hospital, and yet the applegrass scene shows the Doctor and Rose looking across the bay from the New New York side. It's a good ten miles as the crow flies, and across water. And why does Cassandra have spider-robots patrolling odd patches of grassland? Possibly, they respond to the arrival of the TARDIS and get to that specific bit of beach post-haste for a snoop - but what did they *think* the event was? Why, then, does Cassandra need to process Rose at all, instead of just popping into Chip, going upstairs, grabbing the first passing humanoid and investigating the hospital that way? We can only presume that a plan was at work that the Doctor's arrival interrupted and complicated. It's not impossible that Cassandra didn't want to possess anyone who she didn't find "pure" enough by her standards, as per her dialogue in "New Earth", but given how fast her skin-form burns out, she's risking death for the sake of genetic snobbishness.

Critique As a production, it is bold, experimental and ambitious. As a piece of television, it's curiously timid. Whilst the technicalities and horrible weather led to endless complications (as you will shortly read), the script leaves so little to chance, and is so by-the-book, that it's almost not worth them having bothered. Almost.

The real problem is one represented by, but not limited to, the cat-nuns. Apart from their claws in one shot, there's nothing about them that isn't simply humans-with-animal-masks, and no reason why they have to be cats other than it looking kooky. If they evolved from cats, why are they being so servile towards humans? Why not make them dogs and make the point more effectively? If the point is that they're supposed to be untrustworthy, why not make them snakes (a creature with a lot of prior medical associations)? The same problem is there in the whole premise of NewX15 York - it's supposed to be familiar to us as New York-but-changed, but why bother? Why not call it New Cardiff? Davies has given us a collage of quasi-familiar things, but no real reason for them to be the way they are other than that he felt like it. We therefore have no reason to be all that interested. After all, anyone can make collages. The entire point of New Earth (the planet) and "New

Earth" is that it's not too unfamiliar, so no thought has to be exerted by viewers who might be put off by anything that makes you wonder. Anoraknophobia - i.e. the fear of making *Doctor Who* too much like science fiction for the soap audience - boils away any flavour this story might have had. As director, James Hawes does what he can, but all the decisions about the look of the episode, the style of the city and the colour-scheme of the sets have been taken out of his hands long before. What he's left with is managing the set-piece action sequences and making the comedy less irritating than it ought to have been.

They've solved the problem of Cassandra being such an interesting character that they had to bring her back, despite the complexities of the CG effects for her, by the simple judo-throw of having five people play her. Three of them do it well, and Sean Gallagher makes both Cassandra-in-Chip and Chip himself the most likeable characters here. However, Cassandra's body-swapping gets old a long time before Davies thinks it does.

Still, Piper's evidently relieved to be doing something other than blubbing, and Zoe Wanamaker's clearly enjoying being both versions of Cassandra. That's the most positive thing to be found in this episode - that everyone seems, despite the arduous production, to be having a good time. It comes through the screen and makes it hard to actively dislike anything here. It's a season opener, so it has to be a bit frothy, and if the ending's irritatingly nonsensical and out of the blue, and if it does look as if they have simply bolted set pieces together and hoped nobody would notice, we can live with that this once. Even the overt admission that the story is three-quarters of an hour of set-up for something that now won't happen for another year, and thus the whole thing's been a wild goose chase, doesn't dampen this.

And they *do* solve some formidable technical problems. The entire lift-shaft sequence is a *tour de force* that any other programme would have made more of. They manage to make an all-white set interesting visually with the digital video film-look trickery almost militating against this. The cat-masks are majestic and their lack of plot-purpose makes this and the primary-coloured humanoids almost profligately spectacular - they don't *need* to be this good. There are other production companies as good, but they make nothing else, and every episode is set in the same period or world. BBC Wales is making a lot of other programmes and *Doctor Who* is doing something different every week.

So that's it: they've taken us to a different planet without frightening the horses. It's an amiable episode, with admirable technical qualities, but not much else. It's as innocuous as hospital grapes.

The Facts

Written by Russell T Davies. Directed by James Hawes. Viewing figures: (BBC1) 8.62 million (and an 85% AI), (BBC3 repeats) 0.4 and 0.5 million.

Repeats and overseas promotion Die Neue Erde, Une nouvelle terre.

The **TARDISode** for this story was a promotional video for the Hospital, with Novice Hame showing a miracle cure for Hawtrey's Syndrome; this is interrupted by someone off-screen screaming "help me" and prefaced with some of the effects shots from the actual episode. (We presume that "Hawtrey's Syndrome", pronounced "haw-tray" here, isn't what Charles Hawtrey's character had in *Carry On Doctor* - he was a husband having sympathetic pregnancy.)

Production

Before we go any further, here's a quick run-down of the production blocks for Series Two, so it's written down somewhere in this book. Block One was X2.0, "The Christmas Invasion", then on to X2.3, "School Reunion" and then X2.1, "New Earth", although the precise running-order was still unclear very late on. Block Two, directed by Euros Lyn, was the two celebrity historicals: X2.4, "The Girl in the Fireplace" and X2.2, "Tooth and Claw". Block Three was the marathon, in which Graeme Harper directed both of the two-part Cyberman stories, "Rise of the Cybermen", X2.6, "The Age of Steel", X2.12, "Army of Ghosts" and X2.13, "Doomsday". Block Four was, as it turned out, Lyn again, doing two other "historical" stories (counting a near-future London as a period rather than a planet): X2.11, "Fear Her" and X2.7, "The Idiot's Lantern". Lyn was, however, originally rostered to do Block Five, X2.8, "The Impossible Planet" and X2.09, "The Satan Pit", but James Strong got that gig and, concurrently with this, Dan Zeff was directing X2.10, "Love & Monsters". Got that? Good. Let's proceed...

X2.1: New Earth

- After the positive reception "The End of the World" (X1.2) got, it seemed obvious that this set-up had some juice in it still. Piper was asking to be given more comedy and several commentators, notably Steven Moffat (who had scored a big hit with a story where "everybody lives!") were noting that Davies tended to bump off all his most interesting characters. Cassandra's escape was explained by her hitherto unseen sidekick Zaggit (later renamed "Chip") stowing away on the Face of Boe's vehicle. The plan was to allow the Doctor to do all the things a Doctor ought to - up to and including healing people - to reassure the audience that it was the same character as before.

- Still terrified of scaring away a mainstream audience by making anything that looked too much like *Star Trek* or the many other series tucked away in "Cult" slots, Davies planned his first proper alien world adventure to be as unthreatening as possible. His long list of things to avoid included pseudo-mediaeval villages where scared people in hessian hoodies ran to tell everyone that the Visitors from the Skies had returned, quarries, complicated backstories and anyone green. The world had to be *almost* familiar, and so New Earth's main difference from Earth was that the grass smelled different (so much easier to show on television). The rest of the plot followed from this; re-establishing the scenario from "The End of the World" allowed the audience to get to grips with the body-swap plot because Rose had already been there and only the face of the Doctor was changed (since a large chunk of the audience had never had to get used to a new Doctor before) and this inexorably led to bringing back the Face of Boe and, if possible, Cassandra. Phil Collinson checked Zoe Wanamaker's availability and she was free to do one day's shooting in Cardiff. In the latter, as before, her facial moves were videotaped for a reference for The Mill to do composite a digital face. The script reduced the amount of time the "bitchy trampoline" was on screen this time, and The Mill had worked out a more sophisticated method of making this happen. The first draft of the script had two significant differences: the Doctor's "cure" for the ICU patients was to kill them mercifully (and indeed a lot of other characters died in this version, including the Face of Boe and the Duke of Manhattan), and the Face of Boe delivered his message at the end. It was while writing this draft that confirmation came that there would be at least one more series of *Doctor Who* after the one just about to start shooting, so a familiar face, so to speak, would be helpful to make yet another trip to Five Billion-and-some-odd AD worth doing (see "Gridlock"). This was also intended, with so many effects written as being re-used from "The End of the World", to be a relatively low-cost and uncomplicated episode. That didn't quite pan out.

- The design for the Hospital was a rare instance of a last-minute change of plan: the finished effect by The Mill was a replacement for the original when Collinson decided against the agreed-on shots. Most of the rest of the design was as conceived. Louise Page saw the name "Novice Hame" and opted for a nun-like look for the cats, using starched paper-like linen and purple beads bought from a high-street chain. The décor was planned to work with white, for the nurses' habits and the walls, and green, a pale shade as per University College Hospital, London, or the scrubs worn in present-day hospitals (and more to the point, hospital dramas). Stronger, bilious green was used for the ICU. Everything else, including the skins of many of the patients, was themed in primary colours. With a pre-existing location chosen for the first scenes in the complex to be recorded, the designers had a starting-point for the rest of the design, with the wood panelling and steel piping of the Millennium Centre being expanded upon in the built sets of the hospital interior.

- The shoot began on the morning of 1st August, in the middle of making "The Christmas Invasion", as this was the one day Wanamaker could get to Cardiff in the midst of shooting an episode of *Poirot*. This party sequence was made at the Bar Orient, which can just be glimpsed in X1.11, "Boom Town" and was a regular haunt for some of the technical crew on the series. Tennant finally got to act in his suit instead of being photographed in it. Wanamaker asked for a "Jessica Rabbit" wig as corporeal Cassandra; other make-up requirements included stencilling Chip's markings and putting Piper's hair up to cover the change in length. For the next scene made, the departure from the Powell Estate (remounted from a week or so earlier), she wore a hat for the same reason. While this was being staged, Wanamaker stayed on to record Cassandra's dialogue, with a video camera monitoring her facial movements for reference when The Mill did their stuff. Effects manager Will Cohen supervised this, with Phil Collinson reading Rose's lines. Then a three-week gap while "The Christmas Invasion" was sort-of-finished and back to the HTV studios for some green-screen work for the lift-shaft scenes (especially Casp's death) and the infected patients emerging from their "Borg Ship" (yes, the script was that explicit) ICU booths and shuffling about (by now you will have guessed that Ailsa Berk was on hand to supervise that bit). Then another two weeks to try to get X2.3, "School Reunion" made on an even tighter schedule, and then the one day they had to shoot the Foyer scenes at the Millennium Centre. (That's the building with the gold hexagons on the roof that you can see in every episode of *Torchwood*, and next to the fountain where the TARDIS refuels. The Foyer was also used for a different medical unit in X6.10, "The Girl Who Waited".)

• The introduction of the Duke of Manhattan was also a lot longer, and an earlier version of this was to be shot that night at the Millennium Centre - but as they only had a few hours before the next day began and they had to be out, this was reworked for use in the studio set. The revised script had the Doctor fixing his misbehaving winch (and that's how he becomes the Duke's good luck charm). In either case, this is why the Cats took against the Doctor, although neither scene was ever made as it turned out.

• This episode required ten regular make-up artists and then a few more on some days. Although the close-up cat prostheses were detailed and designed to look individual, many of the extras had Hallowe'en masks of cats under veils, to give the right shape without spending three hours per performer. It had been decided to cast actors who already had the right bone-structure and small noses, so that the feline profile was augmented rather than overlaid on the actors' faces. The decisions on how the cats should look were mainly practical, giving them human eyes to avoid the complications when smoke effects, contact-lenses and odd lighting combine and opting for individual looks for each character to prevent the homogeneity that occurred in 26.4, "Survival". That was Monday, 5th September, and the rest of the week was given over to "School Reunion" (and a TARDIS scene for "The Christmas Invasion") until 9th Friday (although the BBC's Visual Effects Department did a bit of smoke-effect inlay for later on the Wednesday, alongside the window-shatter from the Christmas episode) and the original plan was to do the TARDIS interior scene on the Tuesday). Friday's big event was the start of the ICU shoot proper, at that now-familiar Paper Mill on Sanatorium Road, which is where things started getting complicated.

• There were considerable delays, especially after one of the green CGI screens fell off the wall. Rather a lot of the intended material for the first day was remounted. The rest was abandoned or rewritten to be done in summary at a different location. Six whole scenes were sacrificed to try to make the deadline. The sequence with Cassandra-in-Rose confronting Matron Jast was longer; the palm-pilot she was consulting in the broadcast version was used when Cassandra, tiring of the impersonation, reveals her identity and the Matron, seeing that she is officially listed as dead, states that shooting her is thus not murder and she wouldn't be breaking her vows. An early attempt to do the shot of the cat's claws springing forth, using a dummy arm instead of CG onto the actor's hand, was abandoned as risibly ineffective. Much of the material about the "Echo of Life" theory was reworked for a later shoot. The shot of the Doctor regaining consciousness, seen through the grimy perspex bubble, was improvised on set. There were only nine of the booths built, and never more than eleven extras as the ICU patients. (The later scene, shot earlier at the Millennium Centre, has about 20, doubled up digitally.)

• From the Monday to Friday of the next week, they were at Q2, at the set built for the Wards. The design team had tried to make the whiteness of the walls and fittings a positive rather than simply an absence of colour. Michael Fitzgerald, as the Duke of Manhattan, was plumbed in to a set of cooling pipes; an already large man, he was padded out considerably and then had hefty make-up for his scenes when ill. (As with all the "cures", the before and after make-up took time.) His inbuilt fridge couldn't be used during takes, though, and his fans were switched off too. The unit's runner, Sarah Davies, deputised for an extra who didn't show up (although that person can be seen wiggling her toes a lot in the early shot of the Face of Boe). The Face of Boe was a new prop, using the same cast for the rubber exterior, but more levers and pumps for the movements and lip-synch. This all broke as Piper's then-boyfriend had a go between takes.

However, some time was being made up as eventually two units filmed the same episode, with pick-up scenes and a remount of the cats'

X2.1 New Earth

claws shot for The Mill to augment, and Chip hiding in the ICU pod. Cassandra-as-Chip leaving with the Doctor and Rose was a shot that had not been planned but was thought necessary. Similarly, the Duke teleporting away, as scripted, was dropped from the schedule here. Later, the events leading up to Frau Clovis leaving his service and attempting to take charge of the emergency were curtailed. His butler now had no dialogue. (There would have been a scene where he attempts to close off the service elevator, and later he and Clovis tip the Duke out of bed. Stuart Ashman was credited as an extra since he eventually had no lines.) Thus Cassandra-in-Rose never got to ask the butler for champagne by asking "Moisturise me". The Ward set was used for scenes in two different wards, although it's not always obvious on screen that they *are* supposed to be different places. Boe's coy refusal to deliver his last secret was recorded, to be dubbed later (eventually they hired Struan Rogers, with whom Collinson had worked on *Sea of Souls*) and after more lift-shaft business, on Friday, a third, successful, attempt got the TARDIS interior scene in the can. Apparently, many of the team took to stroking the faces of the cat-nuns as stress-relief. The scene of Frau Clovis attacking the Doctor and Cassandra-Rose with a chair was split up, as the Hospital set had been struck by the time the reaction shots of Tennant and Piper were done, long after Lucy Robinson (as Clovis) had left the shoot. Her component was the very end of the main Hospital set shoot, as the set had to be removed to make way for Versailles. Hawes doubled for her in the remount.

- As Tennant took a few days off after two months, Piper came back on the following Monday (19th September) to the cellar of Tredegar House, the nicer bits of which had been Harriet Jones' official residence and the HQ of Llewellyn's rocket group's in "The Christmas Invasion". Unlike last time, Cassandra's dialogue was pre-recorded by Zoe Wanamaker and could be played back. They completed these scenes on Wednesday and Thursday, the latter being when Tennant rejoined and - supposedly - the end of shooting for Block One. Work began on converting New New York into Versailles for the next story to be made, "The Girl in the Fireplace", although some of the set elements were kept on hand because there was still a lot to do on this story.

Tennant did a few pick-ups of ICU stuff back at Q2 and they had the wrap party, but on the following Monday, the opening scenes of arriving on New Earth were to be shot at a noted beauty spot. That had originally been timetabled for a few weeks earlier, in August (when, as you will recall from the swordfight on the Sycorax spaceship shot at roughly the time they had planned to do this, there was a heat-wave and clear blue skies, as there had also been when the TARDIS left the Powell Estate in, um, December). September 2005 wasn't pleasant. High wind and torrential rain, heavy cloud-cover reducing the available light and rainwater shorting the lights were only the obvious problems. It later turned out that one of the cameras used in the close-ups simply had not worked. Some scenes were salvaged, by the ploy of having Piper and Tennant lie down on the grass (not apple-scented in reality) and discuss their first "date" in the lee of the TARDIS prop, to avoid Piper's hair going "like the Dulux dog" (an Old English sheepdog used in the paint ads). The TARDIS itself blew over later on. An entire sequence of Cassandra-in-Chip was abandoned. In short, this had them all watching a sunset and the Doctor explaining that a billion years hence humanity would leave for yet another Earth, possibly ad infinitum; although the deaths she caused couldn't be forgiven, as Chip's heart slowed, the Doctor decided to take "him" to a party. The long-shot of Chip/Cassandra being led away from the Hospital was used, redubbed, to cover this, and the ADR system was used on the entire "we had chips" scene. (We should state, for the record, that most days in Rhossili are a lot better and that the Gower Peninsula as a whole is worth a look if you've got a picnic planned, whenever you're spending a week in Swansea. The Mumbles is better if you want chips, though.)

There was one last major sequence to record: the showers. The water was warm, to begin with, and the first few takes were agreeable, although as the end of the scene required Tennant to get into wet clothes after drying from the previous take, this got less fun as the day went on (that day being 7th October). The following day was yet more lift-shaft malarkey, and there was a remount of the Doctor looking out of the TARDIS in the bar, shot during the *Children in Need* vignette a month later, but that was pretty much a wrap.

... at least, for the stars. The pick-up shots were still being completed as and when possible, right up until the end of Block Three in December. The last shots were the first patient being cured after getting a hug from the Doctor some three months earlier, and the replacement of the extra in the first booth the Doctor and Cassandra open. This was 9th December, the afternoon they recorded Rose and the Doctor being separated at the end of episode thirteen. As we suggested earlier, the effects for the view of the Hospital and the two flying police cars were, almost uniquely, changed after the original edit had been signed off on; rather than being a lone monolithic block, it was now part of a complex, looking more like the "Sail" tower in Dubai, or a 1930s Deco design (a thread which will return: see "Rise of the Cybermen"; "Gridlock"; X3.4, "Daleks in Manhattan" and others).

• The "chav" joke not only got noticed by all the UK reviewers, but seemed to go down well with foreign buyers who saw this episode. The debut was - as with the previous year's - on Easter Saturday, and did better than the various items on the other four terrestrial channels (including the TV premiere of a Harry Potter film). "Petrifold regression" made a comeback in the tie-in book *The Stone Rose* by Jac Rayner, and the cat-nuns and Frau Clovis were featured in the newly-launched *Doctor Who Adventures* issue #2, which came out that week (see the essay with this episode). Already, Davies was planning a comeback for Novice Hame and the Face of Boe, but Sister Jatt (or rather, Adjoa Andoh) would also be back next year. James Hawes, despite the nightmare of this production block, considered but eventually declined the opportunity to become producer on *Torchwood*. Instead, he directed Tennant in a docu-drama about the obscenity trial of *Lady Chatterley's Lover* and then made new versions of *Fanny Hill* and *The 39 Steps* and a biography of Enid Blyton as well as being the original lead director on *Merlin* (see X4.10, "Midnight").

X2.2: "Tooth and Claw"

(22nd April, 2006)

Which One is This? Crouching Fido, Hidden Sporran: Kung-Fu monks, a werewolf, a braw, bricht moonlicht nicht, Queen Victoria, Ian Dury and the Blockheads... and a remake of "Horror of Fang Rock" (15.1), but with nice oak-panelled corridors to run up and down. At length.

Firsts and Lasts This is the story where the word "Torchwood" stops being a stray bit of colour, like the Isop galaxy or the Shadow Proclamation, and becomes significant. It's also, with the Doctor's choice of the pseudonym "James McCrimmon", the first hint that, far from being a whole new continuity with its own rules, this is the same series we've been following from 1963.

Following the BBC's decision to close down the Visual Effects Department that Jack Kine founded for *Quatermass* in 1953 (just after they'd won an award for X1.4, "Aliens of London"), this is the first story to have the same personnel working as the BBC Models Unit. The only real change is that they have cool T-shirts and a logo (and the change happened before the credits for X2.0, "The Christmas Invasion", so they get called the new name there). The interior view of the telescope is their calling-card here. And this is the first BBC Wales episode to reach the screen to have someone other than Ernie Vincze as director of photography.

Watch Out For...

• The pre-credit sequence with the Kung Fu Monks may well have been intended to cash in on the Kirby-Wire-ballet epics we'd had recently (*Hero*; *Crouching Tiger, Hidden Dragon*; *House of Flying Daggers*; and the inevitable Hollywood cash-in, *Kill Bill* Vols. 1 and 2), but because it's a castle in Scotland (well, all right, Wales) and red-clad Caucasians doing improbable acrobatics to vaguely oriental music, the look is almost exactly like the BBC 1 station idents that were then just coming to the end of their five-year run. Unfortunately, after their bravura pre-credits calisthenics, the Brethren don't really do a lot. Their main purpose is to stand around trying to look well-'ard whilst wearing pyjamas and garlands around their necks. Their plot-function is to stop anyone leaving Torchwood House, leaving Our Heroes locked in with a shape-shifting alien killer. As we mentioned, this *donnée* and the resolution are remarkably similar to "Horror of Fang Rock", with local legend fitting in with the activities of the Rutan in the lighthouse (referred to by the Doctor as having "the chameleon factor, otherwise called lycanthropy", although Tom Baker's pronunciation of "chameleon" is a bit odd). That being the case, the "Tooth and Claw" equivalent of the aristocrat whose main contribution was to die and leave a large handy diamond is Queen Victoria, and the monks serve the same essential purpose as... fog. With all that effort put into opening the episode exuberantly, the next 40 minutes or so might seem a bit unimaginative and anti-climactic. Stick with it, though, because in the last scene something is going to happen that changes everything.

- But inert as the Brethren are for much of the episode, they're good for a cheap joke. As one of the first episodes to be written after all the kerfuffle about the series' alleged "Gay Agenda", there's a gag about all these athletic, shaven-headed men that's flagrantly there to get a reaction, but everyone ignores it.
- The opening TARDIS scene has Rose changing her clothes - even while they were shooting, nobody was sure if this or X2.1, "New Earth" would be the season-opener, so they planned the pre-credit scene for that to be mix-and-matchable with either episode. Imagine if they had put that farewell to the Powell Estate and *then* the Kung-Fu Monks and *then* Ian Dury and the Blockheads - what would a first-time viewer have made of this series?
- If you were watching a lot of series with computer-generated beasties at the time, it's hard to avoid the sense that a lot of the shots of the werewolf are presented to us as *Look, everyone - we've worked out how to do fur!*
- Rory Taylor comes in as director of photography in Series Two's episodes directed by Euros Lyn. Here, he lights everything beautifully and makes the TARDIS seem more honeyed than hokey-green-lit-alien. However, he struggles against the curious changes in the weather between takes, and in particular he makes a bold but forlorn attempt to make a blue sky and white fluffy clouds go away in the scene where the Queen makes her entrance. All the digital grading effects and careful lighting can't make this look like the same day as the miserable wet shoot of the next scene at the MacLeish estate, but it does make David Tennant's skin look spectacularly mottled and blotchy.

The Continuity

The Doctor He loves: Ian Dury and the Blockheads, books, *The Muppet Movie* and stories about werewolves. He hates: being shot at, Margaret Thatcher. 1979 seems to be a year he's warmed to [since calling it a 'table wine' in 17.2, "City of Death"], and he even refers to the Brethren as 'Monkey monk-monks'. [This suggests another bit of late-70s pop-culture: *Monkey*, a Japanese TV adaptation of a Chinese Buddhist parable, played for laughs and with lots of slapstick martial-arts mayhem. This is what we all thought of when *Hercules* and *Xena* were presented to us as the New Big Thing from the States.]

Corny attempts at accents and idioms embarrass him. [We can only conclude that Americans sound fundamentally different in the *Doctor Who* universe, but see **What Are the Dodgiest Accents in the Series?** under 4.1, "The Smugglers" and **Whatever Happened to the USA?** under 4.6, "The Moonbase" for more on that.] He tends to shout at people who he knows are putting their lives in danger for no reason. He also seems concerned at the nightmarish vision of the twentieth-century on offer if the Wolf wins. [It seems more an ontological terror of altered history than simply fatigue at the 80s comic-book clichés on the menu - see X2.5, "Rise of the Cybermen" for more on steampunk.]

His enthusiasm about meeting Queen Victoria is almost schoolboy-ish. [Although he claimed to have attended her coronation in 9.2, "The Curse of Peladon", and to have been chummy with the Prince of Wales, we never had any firm indication that the Doctor had actually met the Queen-Empress before now.] It's an opportunity to add another name-drop to his collection, but not such a good one that he immediately bounces in and announces himself as an alien time-traveller. Instead, he makes up an identity on the spot ('James McCrimmon from the township of Balamory'), and drops into a Scots accent. [It's not really like the one he acquired mysteriously in 24.1, "Time and the Rani". The idea that there's a single "Scottish accent" is as misguided as there being just one for London, or Wales, or Manchester or the whole of the UK.] For once, he sticks around long enough to be thanked (and knighted). [The extent to which this goes wrong afterwards is a great example of why this is usually such a bad idea.]

Despite having a perfectly good Scottish accent, he drops it when he starts panicking about Rose's fate. He thinks the werewolf is 'beautiful', something he'll come to say fairly often just before the whatever-it-is in question lunges at him [see also X2.4, "The Girl In The Fireplace" and many others].

Stunt-Casting: What Are the Dos and Dont's?

It's a cultural thing: when viewers in Britain see any of those effects-led shows made in America (or, more likely, Canada), we just see the same dozen or so guest actors over and over again, and consider how many unemployed actors they could have got who don't come tainted with associations from other shows. America seems to have a special category of Science Fiction Acting, and a select few specialists who are considered capable of donning latex or fatigues and spinning out a few anecdotes into a career of orbiting the convention circuit. They embody Science Fiction-ness for casual viewers. Even if nobody has exploded or no CG spaceships have arrived, we can tell even with the sound off if the show we're watching is likely to have these simply because Brad Dourif, Summer Glau, John De Lancie, Nicole de Boer, Tracey Walter, Claudia Black, Dwight Schultz or Marina Sirtis have shown up. Whilst the barriers seem to be coming down now, and there is now a sitcom, *How I Met Your Mother*, that functions as a rehab for ex-Joss Whedon regulars, America still seems to shove the same small pool of talent into all the guest roles and keep out anyone with any other kind of expertise or exposure.

So anyone coming to *Doctor Who* and trying to fit it into this mind-set is going to come unstuck, simply because it has a different target audience who have different expectations. This series is made for a wide cross-section of the British Public rather than a self-selecting coterie who only watch That Sort of Show. This, inevitably, feeds into the casting decisions. There are respected, popular actors with a number of varied roles under their belts who would gnaw their arms off at the elbow before doing a Vulcan salute, but who drop everything when *Doctor Who* comes a-calling. Some do it because they want to do something with no swearing or overt violence that their kids (or mums) can watch, just once in their careers. Some do it because it's a good way to remind people they aren't dead and work for an audience who may not remember the seemingly-career-ending part they've been associated with for decades. Some do it because *Doctor Who* is what made them want to be actors. For whatever reason, over the decades *Doctor Who* has been a series that has cast its net wide and netted a widely diverse cast. In particular, the 1980s was a strange period where the decision-making process of who to get for which role seems at times to have been determined by what headlines it would get rather than, you know, ability to play the part.

We've flagged it up by having a section in each story since 1980 called **Oh, Isn't That...?**, which indicates when a cast-member is supposed to elicit exactly that type of response from mum or dad while the kids are trying to watch. At times, it drifted from getting an actor who was simply right for a role to someone with a halo of associations from elsewhere. It's silly to pretend this never happened before, but from 18.1, "The Leisure Hive" onwards, it became a much bigger weapon in the show's armoury, and one the showbiz-minded producer allocated some of the budget - the so-called "knicker-elastic fund" - to cover.

These days, it's one of a number of such ploys, and yet there is still the sense that they could have got absolutely anyone to play the cowardly alien Gibbis (X6.11, "The God Complex") and just *told* everyone it was David Walliams - and that they really should have got absolutely anyone else, at all, to play the UNIT scientist Malcolm in X4.15, "Planet of the Dead" rather than Lee Evans. Knowing the cast from elsewhere is an entire aspect of the experience of watching *Doctor Who* that anyone not living in the UK completely misses - but it's an essential part of what the people making the series think they're doing. If the appearance of Sir Patrick Moore isn't the single most exciting thing in X5.1, "The Eleventh Hour", you're simply not seeing the same things we saw in that episode. Similarly, nobody who wasn't over 12 and watching telly in Britain in 1977 can *quite* apprehend the sheer number of associations that Henry Woolf brings to the role of the Collector in "The Sun Makers" (15.4).

It's possible that the earliest example of what we now call stunt-casting was the original Doctor. If you look at William Hartnell's career up to that point, nothing stood out as saying "this is the man to play an ageless, cantankerous scientist from a far-off world who's met various historical figures". He had a radically different reputation from films, either as the perennial no-nonsense Sergeant-Major or Chief Petty Officer, with time as a hoodlum in *Brighton Rock* and a rugby coach in *This Sporting Life*. Instead, announcing that he was in a

continued on Page 259...

X2.2 Tooth and Claw

After the wolf reveals itself to be unfriendly, he labels it a 'lupine wavelength haemovariform'. [This is really just stating the obvious in fancier words for Her Majesty.] He seems to think that finding a werewolf is more impressive and exciting than meeting Queen Victoria.

He loves the Observatory [enough to have an exact replica aboard his Ship later (see X7.11, "Journey to the Centre of the TARDIS")].

• *Ethics*. He regards betting about a historical joke as abusing his time travel privileges, but promptly abandons this principled stance when Rose increases the bet. [Maybe this is why he doesn't mind mentioning the Elephant Man years before Joseph Merrick became famous.] Along with Rose, he's able to delight in the experience of seeing a werewolf only moments after Captain Reynolds has been brutally killed while giving them time to escape. The prospect of blowing up the werewolf with explosive apparently excites him, and he readily turns up the light to lethal levels when the Wolf asks to be 'released'.

He's actively trying to be less rude than he was in his last regeneration, to the extent of checking with Rose when he's being obnoxious.

• *Background*. The Doctor nearly ripped his thumb off redirecting the falling Skylab. In fact, 1979 seems to have been a busy year for him.

[In case anyone reading this was unaware, the name 'James McCrimmon' is that of a former companion (see Volume 2, et al), so those people who were loudly proclaiming that the Time War had ruled out all adventures pre-"Rose" looked a bit silly, but not as silly as they would a week later (X2.3, "School Reunion"). Thus, strictly speaking, we could include every broadcast adventure up to this point in *Background* for this episode. In terms of episodes, Jamie is still the longest-serving companion, with 113 weeks aboard the TARDIS and two return engagements. Sarah, K9 and the Brigadier are all in double-figures.]

Now, here's an interesting turn up: in his sales-pitch to Captain Reynolds, the Doctor claims to have studied medicine at Edinburgh under Joseph Bell. [As you'll recall from Volumes 2 and 4, his medical qualifications from Victorian Scotland are a bit muddled. He claims in "The Moonbase" to have studied under Lister in Glasgow in 1888, but Lister wasnae there then. Bell was in Edinburgh Royal Infirmary and taught his students to spot the patient's trade, habits and possible aetiology of diseases by close observation of small details - one of his students, Arthur Conan-Doyle, adapted this technique and invented Sherlock Holmes. But, as we saw in **Is He Really a Doctor?** in 13.6, "The Seeds of Doom", this whole aspect of his background is clouded in mystery, and it appears that seven years in 1880s Scotland has slipped his mind - despite several hints that he has spent some considerable time in this era and country and has famous friends who all knew Conan-Doyle as well. Muddling up Lister and Bell is an impressive feat for anyone who's met either or both.]

• *Inventory: Other*. The psychic paper reveals the Doctor to have been appointed by the Lord Provost of Scotland as Queen Victoria's protector, which comes as news to him [see also X2.7, "The Idiot's Lantern"]. His glasses are whipped out as a "let's get serious" signal when he announces that the next minute or so will be a montage scene of people reading. [This also seems to make the room tilt alarmingly to the left.]

The TARDIS Misses the intended target by exactly one hundred years [which suggests the Doctor has calibrated the controls on Earth measurements and in Base 10 - see also X1.4, "Aliens of London"]. There's a sound-system in the Console [as per X1.10, "The Doctor Dances"], this time playing "Hit Me With Your Rhythm Stick" [UK No. 1 during 16.5, "The Power of Kroll"]. As is usual at the start of a Celebrity Historical, the Ship pitches around as the Doctor and Rose travel, causing peals of laughter and rolling on the floor.

The Supporting Cast

• *Rose* seems oddly motivated by a £10 bet with the Doctor, and thus spends the whole episode trying to trick Queen Victoria into saying 'we are not amused'. She has a rather disrespectful attitude towards the Royal Family of 2006, and finds it oddly plausible that they're all werewolves [see also X2.4, "The Girl in the Fireplace" and **Bad Wolf - How, What and Why?** under X1.13, "The Parting of the Ways" for why an omnipotent Rose might have created a People's Republic of Britain for her daddy]. This doesn't stop her looking abashed when the Queen gives her and the Doctor a good scolding. She identifies herself to the Host as a reformed Wolf, and she offers help to the Host before the Wolf inside him rather stupidly starts ranting about biting Queen Victoria. [It's becoming a basic rule: anything that

Stunt-Casting: What Are the Dos and Dont's?

continued from Page 257...

series with William Russell (TV's *Sir Lancelot*) and it was "an Adventure in Time and Space" just made people curious. However, this wasn't part of the publicity build-up the same way as later announcements, simply because nobody knew what *Doctor Who* was until an episode had been shown. Therefore, the first time they could do the inevitable "Look Who's..." headline was when *Crackerjack* (you know what to do... thank you...) star Peter Glaze donned the romper suit and mask to play the City Administrator in "The Sensorites" (1.7).

This is important. Peter Glaze was cast partly because he was short and tubby and could carry off the role of a pompous, xenophobic alien, but mainly *because he was Peter Glaze off the telly*. It is quite unmistakeably *him*. For the majority of the viewers, *Crackerjack* (... and again...) was a weekly ritual. Anyone watching "The Sensorites" on first broadcast knew who he was, and that he was the eternal straight-man to a succession of taller comedians. (He also has a better claim than Homer Simpson to have popularised "D'oh!", usually when getting wet.) Those viewers who never saw his more famous series[50] won't pick up on this.

A lot of what the first-night audience of any *Doctor Who* episode see is conditioned by the guest cast. Admittedly, for the majority of stories made in the 60s and 70s, it was largely a matter of who was available to play a specific role, regardless (almost) of what else they were known for amongst the adult viewers. Then, in 1979, a new sort of casting policy began with "City of Death" (17.2). In this, there was a deliberate decision to freak viewers out by abruptly cutting from the Doctor and his chums running through Paris to John Cleese and Eleanor Bron indoors somewhere. It turns out they're in an art gallery admiring what seems to be a Mark Wallinger installation of a London police box, but the split-second when the edit comes is purposely intended to bring viewers up short. This was deliberately not publicised. However, the effect is one that the BBC Wales series has sought to replicate once a year, usually in episode twelve. The most spectacular example was the end of "Doomsday" (X2.13), when Catherine Tate - *Catherine bleedin' Tate!* - arrived unannounced in the TARDIS. Anyone who can't see the significance of this has missed the point of the entire programme and should rewatch everything from scratch armed with these books. (See **Why Weren't We Bovvered?** under X3.0, "The Runaway Bride.)

So, with one eye on what casting director Andy Prior has managed with BBC Wales, and another on the egregious failures of John Nathan-Turner in the 80s, we'll look at *Doctor Who* casting from the point of view of how to balance pre-publicity and sensible casting of difficult-to-fill roles.

DO: Get Someone Who's Up to the Job

As opposed to, say, Lee Evans ("Planet of the Dead"), Roger Lloyd-Pack (X2.5, "Rise of the Cybermen" / X2.6, "The Age of Steel"), Ingrid Pitt (9.5, "The Time Monster"; 21.1, "Warriors of the Deep")... all of these outlived their utility once the press had gone home. There is a special type of wrongness about these performances, because in all cases their inability to say the lines convincingly was nothing to do with their acting ability *per se*, it's just that they weren't giving the performance that role needed. However, getting rid of them would have been a costly and very public admission of error. Lee Evans is especially odd; for a comic actor from Bristol to decide to play the character as Welsh in a production being made in Cardiff was not just perverse, it was insulting to his hosts. A spectacularly unconvincing accent didn't help his cause.

A more peculiar kind of miscasting comes when it's blindingly obvious that the writer or director were pilfering from a hit film, but the person making the casting decisions doesn't twig and gets a celebrity who is never going to match up to the original. We all rather admire the wilful, defiant wrongness of slotting Beryl Reid into a part flagrantly intended to be Ripley from *Alien* (19.6, "Earthshock"), and Joan Sims is at least plausible as a futuristic iron-age matriarch, even if she is obviously not Tina Turner from *Mad Max: Beyond Thunderdome* (23.1, "The Mysterious Planet"). However, young viewers unaware of these films were left simply wondering what these characters were supposed to be and why any of their underlings listened to them. In any article about bad casting decisions in *Doctor Who*, it is inevitable we'll be talking about "Voyage of the Damned"

continued on Page 261...

X2.2 Tooth and Claw

Rose offers to help should be destroyed before the casualties get into double figures.]

She's got her "make friends with the lowly servant-girl" routine down to a fine art [even though this also tends to end badly for the other party: see X1.2, "The End of the World"; X1.3, "The Unquiet Dead"; X2.8, "The Impossible Planet"]. Of course, she has to be more pro-active and spunky than the Victorian maids when chained up in the cellar, and is almost dismissive of the Doctor's arrival just as she's almost led a break-out.

Despite making light of the Doctor's Punk tendencies, she gets more excited about Ian Dury than Horatio Nelson, Caesar or anti-grav Olympics.

- *Torchwood.* Well, it took a while, but we're getting the picture. The estate where this all takes place is Torchwood House, and Her Maj has decided that she doesn't like smart-alec aliens treating extraterrestrial incursions onto her patch as a lark. So, as soon as the Doctor goes, he's made Imperial Enemy No. 1 and an Institute is set up, named after the estate, to deal with all such visitors to the Empire. ["The Torchwood Institute" is a strangely prosaic name for a royal-founded organization; the Queen must very much want it to stay under the radar. Anybody who's been to tourist London will be acquainted with the many, many places that start with "the Royal Albert" - even if the name "Torchwood Institute" is still a memorial to Lady Isobel's husband, the MacLeish Institute would really be more in line with her usual style of nomenclature.]

The Queen pledges that should the Doctor return, Torchwood 'will be waiting'. [This is often interpreted to mean that the group's No. 1 goal is to *kill* the Doctor, but that's not expressly stated here, and their relationship will become more complicated than that - see especially X2.12, "Army of Ghosts". Victoria even 'rewards' the Doctor with a knighthood before sending him into exile, although - to be fair - she might feel that she simply doesn't have the means to terminate him at this juncture. We've already discussed the problem of what Torchwood were playing throughout the twentieth century, including where the Doctor is concerned, in Volume 3b (**All Right Then... Where Were Torchwood?** under 9.3, "The Sea Devils").]

The Non-Humans

- *The Werewolf* is a modulated wavelength of light [conveniently, it's the precise colour of moonlight in Scotland] which uses that light to trigger a bodily change in its Host. [The nearest analogy we have for this is - although it's not the happiest of comparisons - is 18.2, "Meglos". In this, Meglos is a waveform of green light that had bonded with a xerophyte but is able, with a human Host, to impersonate the Doctor, occasionally reverting when the Earthling rebels and becoming Tom Baker made up as a cactus in a scarf. See also X7.8, "The Rings of Akhaten", where we hear of a 'Hooloovoo', the name being a "superintelligent shade of the colour blue" from *The Hitchhiker's Guide to the Galaxy*.]

When it inhabits a human, it first makes the eyes turn completely black - then, on receiving a booster-shot of a full moon, it transforms the Host into an eight-foot bipedal wolf, with fangs and fur. This Wolf is impervious to bullets or swords. It can detect trace elements of mistletoe oil (*Viscum Album*, containing lectins and viscotoxins, the Doctor helpfully says to Rose) and avoids any wood varnished with this, or anyone wearing a garland of the berries and sap-bearing twigs. A boiled infusion of mistletoe injures it. The Doctor speculates that the monks have conditioned this as a psychosomatic reaction in the Host, whom they have raised since boyhood, abducting him as they have every one since the original Host in 1552. Once the Host has reached the equivalent of critical mass, and transformed, they have no other means of controlling it or differentiating themselves from the other humans on whom it preys.

The Wolf is carnivorous, and seems to devour any assailant completely. It can be killed by the correct use of modulate moonlight, dispersing the alien 'lupiform' wavelength and freeing the human Host (who dissolves, neatly). Shortly before his transformation, the Host identifies something of the Wolf in Rose [per her becoming the Bad Wolf in "The Parting of the Ways"]. It has, apparently, picked this moment as the most propitious to intervene and alter Britain's destiny, forging an 'Empire of the Wolf' by transferring to Queen Victoria. [This might suggest that it's aware of potential changes in the timeline. It's alternatively possible that the Wolf has simply required the centuries since its arrival on Earth as a single cell to achieve a critical mass, but, certainly, it's been

Stunt-Casting: What Are the Dos and Dont's?

continued from Page 259...

(X4.0) an awful lot, so let's just point out how little of the middle of the episode works if you don't realise that Debbie Chazen is supposed to be Shelley Winters in *The Poseidon Adventure* rather than Jessie Robins from *Magical Mystery Tour*.

DON'T: Get Someone Whose "Baggage" Distorts Everything Around It

It's a tenet of film theory that a "star" is a performer whose off-screen persona (real or perceived) influences how we interpret any role they're in. So, for instance, all those dismal Robin Williams films of the 90s had the basic plot of an uptight adult who finds his inner child and becomes That Loveable Robin Williams. Any actor who's become known for one big part or a lot of small similar ones will have a similar set of associations, especially if their off-screen activities feed into this perception. The problem comes when these get in the way of the role that actor has been cast in now. There have been many odd examples in *Who*, but the most mystifying recently was Kylie Minogue in "Voyage of the Damned".

Because they'd decided to make the Doctor enthusiastic about British popular culture of the early twenty-first century, we know that he knew full well that Astrid Peth closely resembled a huge star. He'd even quoted her in "The Idiot's Lantern" (X2.7). Moreover, Wilfred Mott didn't say "Blimey! It's Kylie - wait there, I'll get me camera". The Doctor being oblivious to Rose's strong resemblance to Billie Piper or Donna's to Catherine Tate were explicable, because he never once showed any sign of having listened to Piper's "Because We Want To" and has clearly never seen *The Catherine Tate Show* (otherwise, he would have gone up to Davros and said "How very dare you?"[51]), but Kylie is in another league. The fact that this was part of her comeback after cancer made a lot of viewers ignore her dialogue and just look at her closely to see if she was all right.

Far sadder, though, was the fate of Bonnie Langford. The production team devised a fascinating character for her, but the writers they got in decided to write Mel as a version of the pre-existing Violet Elizabeth persona, but with computer skills and no friends. Nicholas Parsons just about gets away from his game-show past to make a convincing vicar (26.3, "The Curse of Fenric"), but there was no way that Simon Pegg (X1.7, "The Long Game") was going to be anything other than Simon Pegg pretending to be a *Doctor Who* villain. You can just feel the smugness coming through the screen (although as this is pretty much what the character needs, it's not a problem).

Conversely, a bit of fun can be had by bowing to the inevitable and getting the most famous deputy-headmaster on television to play the Head of Coal Hill School (25.1, "Remembrance of the Daleks"), the archetypal TV cop of the previous generation to be a Victorian policeman (26.2, "Ghost Light") and Peggy Mount to play what must surely have been sent out to casting agents as "a Peggy Mount kind of part" (25.4, "The Greatest Show in the Galaxy"). Anyone else would have been second-best in each case.

Even though he was anachronistically old for the part, having Alexander Armstrong as the pilot of a Lancaster bomber (X7.0, "The Doctor, the Widow and the Wardrobe") comes under this heading, because of the series of sketches he and Ben Miller had done parodying World War II pilots by having them speak twenty-first century teenage slang, innit doh? Had anyone else got the part, everyone in Britain would have thought they were the first to redub the scenes with dialogue from those sketches.

DO: Check Their Availability

Had Brian Blessed not been around - or willing - to make "Mindwarp" (23.2), the whole thing would have been a worse fiasco than the rest of that year. The part was so obviously written with him in mind that getting someone else is literally inconceivable. There is only one actor who could stand in for Blessed, and he'd spent seven years playing the Doctor, so getting him in as another character was a non-starter. As we have seen earlier in this volume, the time-tabling of the shoots for Series One was compromised by both Penelope Wilton (Harriet Jones, Prime Minister) and Annette Badland (Margaret Blaine) having lots of other things to do, and Noel Clarke being in Thailand. Moreover, the content of "Dalek" (X1.6), was messed about with in endless rewrites because there was the option of getting a Big

continued on Page 263...

X2.2 Tooth and Claw

seen in Wolf form enough before now to prompt stories about itself.] The transfer is achieved by the wolf-form biting someone.

History
• *Dating*. It's 1879, and a full moon. [If we go from the TARDIS' intended destination-date, it may be 21st November. Ian Dury and the Blockheads were nowhere near the Top Rank, Sheffield that night. In fact, the two gigs either side of that date are with the Clash at the Hammersmith Palais just after Christmas, and at the legendary gig at the Gant's Hill Odeon, Ilford, Essex, in August. That was the one where the stomping fans broke through a concrete floor. Of course, "Lucky Number" by Lene Lovich was the original selection in the script for the record they played in this scene, so perhaps it was her band they were going to see. Either way, it was Stiff Records getting the money.]

Hellier and Carew are the Royal jewellers, based in Hazlehead, near the Glen of St Catherine (location of both the monastery and Torchwood House). The Queen takes the Koh-i-Noor on an annual pilgrimage to get it recut to Prince Albert's specifications. [This is flying in the face of various established facts, including Albert's displeasure at the way over-zealous Amsterdam diamond-cutters had reduced the gem by 40%.] The Prince Consort was close to Sir Robert MacLeish's father, who had built an observatory at his mansion, Torchwood, with various eccentrically aligned prisms. It appears that they were aware of the Brethren's plan and devised a counter-plot.

Catchphrase Counter Once a year from now on, the companion - as Rose does here - will have a go at a local idiom or accent and be told "No, don't do - don't, *don't* do that" by a flustered Doctor.

Deus Ex Machina You thought we'd heard the last of Bad Wolf but here it is again, and the whole of this series will be the ramifications of this [again, see **Bad Wolf - What Why and How?** under X1.13, "The Parting of the Ways"]. The Koh-i-Noor appears out of nowhere in the script, although director Euros Lyn sneaks in shots of its case being carried to minimise the extent to which it's pulled out of a hat half an hour in.

An entire library full of books, and they just happen to find the one page that talks about the meteorite landing - just in time to show it to everyone before the werewolf decides it's given them enough time for plot exposition. Isn't that lucky?

The Analysis

The Big Picture You may remember that we noted in Volume 6 that every so often the person in charge of the series decides that it's time to do a werewolf story, because "they've never been done in *Doctor Who* before". John Nathan-Turner managed to do it for the first time ever *twice* (23.2, "Mindwarp"; 25.4, "The Greatest Show in the Galaxy"), although we could point to instances as long ago as 1970 (7.4, "Inferno"). Davies, admittedly, has only the sketchiest memory of anything after K9 left, but even he has 13.1, "Terror of the Zygons" committed to memory well enough to re-use the stories Angus told Sarah as backstory here, and we've already mentioned the more-than-passing similarity this script has to "Horror of Fang Rock". One more recent memory is the chase around 10 Downing Street in X1.5, "World War Three", which this was consciously intended to rectify. We'd obviously have to mention the basic source of all recent werewolf stories, John Landis' *An American Werewolf in London*, not least for the then-ground-breaking transformation scene. We'd also have to allude to *Alien* for the shot of the Ghillie being hoisted out of shot from the ceiling (actually, more like Brian Glover's death in *Alien3*) and the POV shots. We can take the *Buffy* similarities almost as read by now.

As we will see in **Production**, Davies was very insistent that this story should include four ingredients: a werewolf; a lot of Shaolin monks; Queen Victoria and Scotland. For anyone raised in 70s Britain, the combination of an attempted assassination of Queen Victoria and a lot of Scots repeatedly saying "1879'" can mean only one thing: William Topaz McGonagall, Poet and Tragedian. Whilst modern scholars are finding hints that he was somewhere on the autism spectrum and comparing his versifying with rappers freestyling, associating words by sound more than meaning, he is famous for not accepting that he was anything less than a genius (despite 200 or more poems that prove otherwise) and not giving up even when pelted with rotten vegetables at his recitals. His most celebrated piece is "The Tay Bridge Disaster", supposedly the worst poem in the English language[49], which has the repeated refrain "... on the last Sabbath day of Eighteen

Stunt-Casting: What Are the Dos and Dont's?

continued from Page 261...

Name Star to play Henry Van Statten.

A simple rule is, if you don't think that performer will be around to come back, kill the character. This causes obvious problems with plotting, especially when the character has been a one-off companion-surrogate. Again, Kylie is the most flagrant example. Nobody watching thought Astrid would be allowed to survive the episode, and any suspense was about how exactly she'd die. Similarly, the episode that puts the stunt-casting at the foreground in the very title, "The Doctor's Daughter" (X4.6), made it so obvious that Jenny was going to make a noble sacrifice that the script conferences were about how to avoid this cliché - so they rewrote the episode to borrow not just the Genesis Device from *Star Trek II: The Wrath of Khan* but its cop-out sequel-hunting ending.

DON'T: Force Square Pegs Into Round Holes

... but if the hole is squarer than the public thinks, a square peg can challenge preconceptions. To some extent, the Doctor is the most spectacular form of stunt-casting possible. With one or two exceptions, when the new one is announced, the public reacts with surprise because they'd got used to a particular idea of what the character's limits were. Hartnell, we've touched on; Troughton, simply the idea that you could recast on screen was shocking; Pertwee was a comedy actor who did funny voices; Who on Earth is Tom Baker?; Davison was "too young"... It's possible, though, that the most overt and cynical decision was getting Eccleston in for one year just to change how people thought of the Doctor and the series - and then jettisoning him like the launch-rockets on the space shuttle once the job was done. Meanwhile, his sidekick was a faded pop star: anyone not boggled by Eccleston getting the part would have been mildly freaked out by Billie Piper being his co-star. It would be like Debbie Gibson and Sean Penn doing a film together.

Just occasionally, an ingeniously "wrong" piece of guest-casting can raise the whole tone of the proceedings. Martin Jarvis is too young to play the Governor as written (22.2, "Vengeance on Varos"), but makes the corruption of this regime more obvious by being relatively untainted while crushed by the weight of the mess the planet's in.

DO: Mix and Match

Although some people were muttering about a sort of all-purpose *Doctor Who* acting-style as early as its second year, one of the reasons the series stayed fresh for so long was the sheer promiscuity of influences; like nothing else on television (or stage, or film), it took writers, directors and actors from a variety of different sub-categories and shoved them together at short notice to make a story set in an unfamiliar environment. You watch something like "Kinda" (19.3) or "The Seeds of Death" (6.5) and boggle at such an unlikely cast all working together and (more or less) making it happen despite their alarmingly different styles of acting. In the case of "Kinda", we have a 40s film-star (Richard Todd), a 70s sitcom star (Nerys Hughes), a stage-actor who'd been doing the odd film or TV role almost as a hobby (Mary Morris)... and three actors who later became famous in *The Bill*. Throw in a stand-up comic who later got a gig in *Grange Hill* (Lee Cornes[52]) and retire to a safe distance. The only performers (other than two of the regular cast) who don't seem at ease are a small child and the guy playing Aris, who drifted from acting to presenting a consumer-advice show. The thing that stands out about this story, even when the New Romantic pop-video stylings have stopped looking so charmingly period, is that everyone's watching and listening to each other rather than waiting for their cues.

Conversely, a most bizarre collage of actors appears in "The End of Time" (X4.17-X4.18), and rarely did any particular team-up get more than a few moments in the same scene. A cast with June Whitfield and Timothy Dalton, Catherine Tate and Claire Bloom, John Simm and John Barrowman simply doesn't happen every day. Bernard Cribbins gets scenes with almost all of these, though.[53]

It is impossible to allow for subsequent events. At the time of broadcast, "Human Nature" (X3.8) had only one obvious potential distorting influence: Jessica Hynes as John Smith's love interest. However, with hindsight, the same people who knew her as Daisy from *Spaced* are more likely than the general public in the UK to know Thomas Sangster as the voice of Ferb Fletcher, since *Phineas and Ferb* is only shown on minority-interest digital channels here. Thus it was possible back

continued on Page 265...

X2.2 Tooth and Claw

Seventy-Nine/ Which will be remembered for a very long time" (and though his memorable, if not actually *good*, verse, it is). Another, "Attempted Assassination of the Queen", described the final attempt on Victoria's life (by Roderick McLean, agreed by the press to have been insane - but they would say that, as this was 1882). Apart from the bathos of McGonagall's faltering attempts at praising Her Majesty, there are details of her habits he knew from his attempt to get royal patronage, which culminated in walking to Balmoral and being told to go away by the guards. And, once again, because of this earwormy gibberish, an entire side of Victoria's reign - her stoicism when held up at gunpoint on a Scottish heath - has become part of the collective memory of her, but probably wouldn't have otherwise.

However, the collective impression we have of Queen Victoria has changed markedly just in the time since the actress here playing her, Pauline Collins, was last in *Doctor Who* (4.8, "The Faceless Ones"). The publication of Victoria's diaries indicates how little she resembled the usual pre-existing connotations of the word "Victorian". She and Albert didn't produce nine children simply out of patriotic duty. There's some evidence that she smoked cannabis, possibly "just" to ease the pain of childbirth. The caricature of the dumpy little old lady saying "we are not amused" is largely a combination of her unwillingness to participate in public life when Prince Albert died and partly a bit of image-making by Prime Minister Benjamin D'Israeli, establishing an iconography of the Queen-Empress as a focal figure (mainly for his own political ends). There was a degree of obsessive morbidity to her behaviour, possibly because his death in 1861 didn't make sense. (If it was typhoid, as the coroner said, why was he, a relatively fit adult, the only victim at Balmoral Castle?)

Nature, red in tooth and claw is a line from one of Queen Victoria's favourite poems, Tennyson's *In Memoriam AHH*. It's very long, but has quite a few memorable lines, including "Ring out the old, ring in the new" (and, curiously, "dust and ashes", as per 13.3, "Pyramids of Mars"). The view of nature as brutal and pointless is a common Victorian motif, making all things done by humans seem that bit more elevated; a few lines later, the length question in which that line is a parenthesis ends. It is, basically, do we just become meat when we die? Is there a soul and what becomes of it - all the problems we see Queen Victoria wrestle with here. We could go on about this for hours (and indeed the poem seems to), but in short, Tennyson was mourning a friend at around the time that Charles Lyell (see 7.2, "Doctor Who and the Silurians") was proving how much older the Earth was than hitherto thought and palaeontologists were figuring out that the dinosaurs had existed. Tennyson's optimistic conclusion is that both the theological argument for hope (the existence of a soul) and the scientific one (that so many tumultuous changes have happened but life persists, and improves rather than blindly repeating) are tenable. It was a view that Prince Albert shared. (The poem also has several allusions to the Moon, to the afterlife and to technological progress, as if they are the same thing. This offsets a theme that every Christmas that passes is the same as the last without the deceased.) We'll assume that Davies knew what he was doing using this as the title rather than "The Empire of the Wolf". He may even have remembered the line "Farewell! We lose ourselves in light".

But Queen Victoria is here because this is an exercise in revamping the "pseudo-historical" story, and she's the most obvious character on which to perform this operation. Davies' stated aim was to "kick the historicals up the arse". He sought to get away from tales such as "The Unquiet Dead", where looking like an old-fashioned BBC costume drama was the object of the exercise, and the TARDIS landing there and monsters arriving was subverting the format from within. This story's script made it clear that the directing style should follow on from the pre-credits sequence in editing, composition and pace. This was to be modern-looking television (i.e. made to look like mid-90s MTV or a late-90s action movie), with items of period costume and lots of mud inserted within. It was all about surfaces. Most period pieces made in the previous ten years had been like this; since the rash of deliberately anachronistic romps, beginning with *Plunkett & Macleane* (1999), *A Knight's Tale* (2001) and the accidentally hilarious "serious" drama *Elizabeth* (1999). We should also note that these attempts at a "fresh" approach to adapted novels led to a misguided BBC serialisation of *Vanity Fair* in which every scene seemed to end with someone getting pig-dung on them. At the same time, Baz Lurhmann had been attempting to apply the same thinking to Shakespeare and musicals (*William

Stunt-Casting: What Are the Dos and Dont's?

continued from Page 263...

in 2007 to hear Tim's monologue about how the Doctor "burns at the centre of time" without giggling or expecting Daughter of Mine to come in and ask "Whatcha Doooooo-in?"

DON'T: Get Someone Who's Only In It For the Money

Because it shows. Anton Diffring's motives for doing "Silver Nemesis" were slightly different (he wanted to be in London for Wimbledon fortnight), as were Richard Briers' (he claims he wanted an opportunity to "act badly", or at least to lose the restraint for which he was almost too well-known). However, Paul Darrow (22.5, "Timelash") is on record as claiming to be simply after a fat paycheque before Christmas, and absolutely not to pay back Colin Baker for upstaging him in *Blake's 7*. One wonders what Lord Olivier would have been like (see 22.6, "Revelation of the Daleks"). Anyone who was in *Triangle* (other than Kate O'Mara) comes into this category. One in particular stands out - see if you can guess who we mean.

If Casting People as Themselves, DO Make It Plausible

However much fun the Episode Twelve Guest Montage might be for the people making the first four series of Welsh *Who*, the problem viewers had was that sometimes they were a bit gratuitous. McFly, Anne Widdicombe and Sharon Osbourne are *just about* believable as willing dupes of Harry Saxon (X3.12, "The Sound of Drums"), but would they have done a TV endorsement like this at all? Probably not, because such things don't really happen here. It's obviously a visual shorthand, like the news-from-around-the-world thing they do in this kind of episode, but it's there to get across that this person is now famous even though we know he doesn't exist. The clip isn't on long enough for us to ask the obvious question of why nobody thinks it's odd.

On the other hand, the following year included an interview with Richard Dawkins about the Earth moving (X4.12, "The Stolen Earth"). Which begs the question: When exactly did the most famous evolutionary biologist in Britain become an expert in astrophysics? It's not as if they couldn't get Patrick Moore. You will have seen the way we tied ourselves in knots trying to justify the voices of the Davinadroid, the Anne Droid and Trine-E and Zu-Zana (X1.12, "Bad Wolf") on plot-logic alone. Similarly, the trouble with Barbara Windsor as Peggy Mitchell in a fake *EastEnders* (X2.12, "Army of Ghosts") is that, as with the spoof ad just before it, you realise that the television companies can fake ghosts as convincing as the ones we see in the rest of the episode.

Newsreaders have their own pitfalls. The BBC's tendency to hire respected journalists and authoritative correspondents means that they have to be careful not only to avoid breaching internal guidelines on fake bulletins, but also of devaluing their cachet when meeting world leaders or experts. There is usually a deliberate wrongness about their use in *Doctor Who*, with interviewers reading bulletins from behind desks, specialists in one field supposedly reporting on another, and visual cues such as close-ups of screens showing the phosphor dots or the on-screen graphics being off-kilter somehow. One exception to this was Nicholas Witchell's spot in "Voyage of the Damned", which worked on the assumption, it seems, that everyone knew it was *Doctor Who* because it was Christmas Day and nobody would accidentally switch over in mid-episode. (Because you don't on Christmas Day in Britain.)

DON'T: Write a Character Just as a Reason For Stunt-Casting

When you look at the list of who they had asked to play the DJ in "Revelation of the Daleks", you realise very soon that the whole point of this character was to be cast purely for publicity. It's safe to say that Ringo Starr or Roger Daltrey would have given a less interesting performance than Alexei Sayle. However, apart from giving Peri a side-plot unconnected with the body-snatchers (who were clearly intended to meet her at some point), this character has no bearing on events as anything other than padding, and yet is for that very reason more watchable than any of the routine figures you get in this kind of story. All his bits could easily have been recorded on another date and given to any visiting celeb. Had anyone but Graeme Harper directed this, the effect would have been profoundly naff.

continued on Page 267...

X2.2 Tooth and Claw

Shakespeare's *Romeo+Juliet* and *Moulin Rouge!* - the latter looking to us suspiciously like the end sketches of *Crackerjack*). "Tooth and Claw" is more clearly in this tradition than in the usual *Doctor Who* approach to stories set in identifiable periods of British history. The real surprise is that the Ian Dury record is in the TARDIS and not playing under one of the many chase-scenes (the rough-cut used surf-guitar rock under the pre-credit fight, Tarantino-style). Davies had, after all, availed himself of the cost-cutting advantages of premeditatedly ahistorical costume drama for *Casanova*, covering himself with the framing sequences that this was how the older Casanova remembered his life rather than how it actually was. *Casanova* was made to be shown on BBC3, a digital "yoof" station whose target audience are less forgiving of anything that doesn't look like everything else.

At around the same time that this was made, BBC1 had launched a bravura reworking of Dickens' *Bleak House* with lots of show-offy editing and a cast drawn from so many unlikely sources as to be even more distracting than the direction. (See X1.7, "The Long Game" and X3.10, "Blink" for two of the three "unknowns" in big parts - the third being Burn Gorman, later of *Torchwood*.) Pauline Collins was in it, and indeed uses the same wig as she sports as Victoria here (see **Production**). What is curious about such projects is the belief that they need to be so "radical" with the visual style to get away from a manner of television costume drama that hasn't been made since the 1980s. Each of these projects rebels against the perceived "norm" in exactly the same way. If anything, the *Bleak House* adaptation was innovative in going back to half-hour episodes, like the old Barry Letts-produced Classic Novels on Sundays. Most costume dramas made now are shot to look like they happened in a thunderstorm, have blood, dung and nudity as often as possible and, if adapted by Andrew Davies, they find a way to squeeze some lesbians in somehow.

As we will see in **Are We Touring Theme-Park History?** under X2.7, "The Idiot's Lantern", the supposedly novel approach to "celebrity historicals" was one that was par for the course in the mid-1980s, using space-monsters as a means of focussing attention on a character-study of a complex person from the past. Such was their inopportune selection of famous dead people that the simplified versions of them capable of being shown before the 9.00pm watershed made them as unremarkable and vacuous as people in "celebrity" gossip-mags. In many ways, Queen Victoria serves the same function here that the London Eye did in "Rose" (X1.1) or the Tower of London did in "The Christmas Invasion" (X2.0). She is, in essence, a spectacle, like the werewolf. She is there to be gawped at, and to do stereotypical Queen Victoria-type things. Even Rose, who's always held up as being the Doctor's conscience and able to relate to people, expects the Queen to perform for her and say her catch-phrase.

Scottish Lessons

• *Balamory* was a children's series just ending its original run on CBBC when this aired. It was set in a relentlessly cheery, improbably racially diverse Hebridean village. Older, genre-savvy viewers were never sure whether they expected to see Patrick McGoohan being chased by a balloon or Edward Woodward being burned alive in a wicker man.

• *Hoots Mon* translates to "Hey, man!" and was famously the name of a smash single in 1958. (It was a twist version of *Wi A Hundred Pipers And A'* and credited to "Lord Rockingham's XI". The perpetrator of this later went on to co-write and score the engagingly naff sword 'n' sorcery flick *Hawk the Slayer* and did the haunting string arrangements on Nick Drake's bedsit classic *River Man*.)

• *Wee Sleekit Cow'rin' Tim'rous Beastie* is the first line of Robert Burns' poem *To a Field Mouse* (that's the one with the line about "the best-laid scheme o' mice or men", which Steinbeck lifted because everyone had heard of it in 1936). Bear this in mind for X4.14, "The Next Doctor".

German Lessons

• *Saxe-Coburg*. For the benefit of Rose and British viewers, the Doctor notes that it's now called Bavaria. For the benefit of anyone who, as Lance derides Donna (X3.0, "The Runaway Bride"), can't point to Germany on a map, it's the bit north of the Alps, just next to Austria. If you can't find *those* on a map, just watch *Chitty Chitty Bang Bang*. It's all oompah bands, forests and bears in Victoria's time (Jakob and Wilhelm Grimm collected old stories from there). More to the point, she calls it superstitious because she's head of the Church of England and Bavaria's the bit of what became Germany that was unaffected by the

Stunt-Casting: What Are the Dos and Dont's?

continued from Page 265...

Worse yet, if you've decided on such a part, make sure whoever you do get is a big enough name to justify it. Otherwise, you waste your limited screen-time in a climactic episode that's supposed to answer the great mystery on a pointless interlude - as happened in "Silver Nemesis" with the Dolores Gray Incident. Or, in the case of "The End of Time", you get someone who was a *huge* name once showing up in a pointless part, so that anyone savvy enough to realise that Claire Bloom's character must be someone pretty important just *because she's Claire Bloom* is left wondering why yet another set of mystical prophesies was added over the Ood and the Mad Old Lady on the Bus. (See "Planet of the Dead" and **Who Was That Terrible Woman?** under X4.18, "The End of Time Part Two".)

Because of the peculiar nature of the character's creation, we can absolve the Abzorbaloff ("Love & Monsters") from this, just about.

DO: Get Someone Who Can Play the Publicity Game

So you have a story called "The Next Doctor" (X4.14), and an announcement due on who's going to replace David Tennant. Obviously, all the build-up will focus on whether David Morrissey is actually *the* next Doctor. Morrissey plays a blinder! He is clearly having a great time teasing everyone, on any chat show going, knowing that the smart money's on Paterson Joseph and that the current head of the show has nominated Russell Tovey ("Voyage of the Damned", "The End of Time") as who he'd pick if it were still his decision.

On the other hand, Clive Swift is only the most spectacular of the many examples of self-important luvvies who revile anyone who brings up their appearances in the series. He notoriously slagged off the readers of the magazine for which he was being interviewed and has almost vanished since (we'll pick up this story under "Voyage of the Damned"). When the reputation of the series was at low ebb, shortly before the revival was announced, Sheila Hancock would routinely bitch about anyone who reminded her about "The Happiness Patrol" (25.2). We await the backlash against Carey Mulligan (Sally Sparrow in X3.10, "Blink") with unalloyed glee.

DON'T: Fish From the Same Pool Too Often

The oddest things start happening when you get a run of actors who've all been in one hit series cropping up in *Doctor Who* in rapid succession. There was a period in the early 80s when everyone in the universe seemed to have been in *Triangle*, *Tenko* or *Blake's 7*, and then immediately afterwards any actor who'd been in *Doctor Who* lately and hadn't done one of these three shows was in the cast for the first episodes of *EastEnders*. A lot of this is down to casting directors using the same agents. (To be fair, this saves a lot of explanations, and a good rapport with one or two out of hundreds is worth five days of phone-calls. Besides, becoming an agent is often the best career-route for retired *Doctor Who* companions. At least two Doctors have had ex *Who*-girls handling their careers.) One problem is that everyone slumps into a comfortable relationship with everyone else and they all just say their lines instead of playing their parts. Another, when the *Blake's 7* crowd all showed up in rapid succession, is that the casual viewer stopped paying attention - it was just another of That Kind of Show rather than something anyone normal would voluntarily watch.

And when *Doctor Who* was on in the *Triangle* slot, that same casual viewer would wonder what possessed everyone on a North Sea ferry to put on velour frocks and pixy hats to start talking cobblers whilst posing amid formica shelving units.

Of course, all of this applies to actors who are on set when the rest of the story's being made. Voice-overs are another matter entirely. For an afternoon's work in a studio in West London, an actor can get a bit of *Doctor Who* kudos without needing to wear rubber or a boiler-suit - or even learn lines. You can mess with people's heads by having a bigger name in the story than anyone making it realised would be involved (X6.4, "The Doctor's Wife"; X6.10, "The Girl Who Waited") and even completely change what people think the story is going to be like (X2.8, "The Impossible Planet"). If you're *really* lucky, you can get to do some actual acting in the sequel (X2.1, "New Earth").

We would still rather have had Roy Skelton do the Ood Priest ("The End of Time"), but Brian Cox was all right.

Reformation and stayed pretty much uniformly Catholic. Albert was Prince of the House of Saxe-Coburg Gotha (see also 26.2, "Ghost Light").

Oh, Isn't That...?

• *Pauline Collins* (Queen Victoria). Since her appearance on *Doctor Who* in 1967 as non-companion Sam Briggs, she's only gone and got herself famous, hasn't she? First there was *The Liver Birds* (although everyone forgets this because she was in the first series, made in black and white, and Nerys Hughes replaced her), then *Upstairs, Downstairs* (Sarah, the mendacious maid who becomes a Music Hall star and has a fling with James after many episodes sharing a bed with Rose) and spin-off *Thomas and Sarah* before more sitcoms and *Wodehouse Playhouse* and then *Shirley Valentine*. She got a Tony for the Broadway version and an Oscar nomination for the film. Since then she's been everywhere and, just before this episode, was Miss Flyte in *Bleak House*.

• *Derek Riddell* (Sir Robert) had, as the script alludes, just played Sir Walter Raleigh in BBC's *The Virgin Queen* (which is why he caught the script's goof about "Sir Francis Drake"). He was also the senior doctor in *No Angels*, about which we'll have more in the next episode.

Things That Don't Make Sense As we mentioned above, Queen Victoria's behaviour is written with an eye to how the audience watching will perceive it rather than a documentary representation of how she actually behaved. Much of the time, they'll get round this problem by writing about authors who are conscious of the nature of their stories (compare Dickens' dry incredulity about ghosts in "The Unquiet Dead" or Shakespeare asking about witches in X3.2 "The Shakespeare Code"). This time, however, it results in a version of Queen Victoria who feels she has to explain that her late husband was from Saxe-Coburg. Even allowing for obsession, this is a little silly. And it's a minor point, but everyone knows the Koh-i-noor is only unlucky to its *male* possessors. Someone as superstitious as she's portrayed in this story would at least be consistent about it.

Moreso than usual, this story causes us to wonder where all the corpses go between scenes; this werewolf is usually in too much of a hurry to stop and eat up every scrap. Moreso than usual in historical stories (eg "Ghost Light"), Rose being allocated a selection of Victorian dresses and nobody to help her squeeze into them, lace up the corsets or do up the umpteen hooks and eyes is silly - and when she *does* find a maid, it's a shock to both of them. And why is there the same pair of engravings of armillary spheres in every single room of the house?

You don't often get mistletoe in Scotland. And even if it were plentiful, or imported at enormous expense, the logic of the mistletoe-slathered library scene is as questionable as its message. Mistletoe is established as a substance that gives a modulated-light-embodied-in-a-human-and-thus-looking-like-a-wolf the screaming abdabs. That substance can be turned into a varnish that, being toxic to humans, would probably kill anyone spending any amount of time in the library (not immediately, but over repeated exposures, like Napoleon's wallpaper). So, the library's walls deter a werewolf. (This must have been an act of faith on the part of MacLeish and Prince Albert, there not being any other werewolves on which to test it.) This would make the library an admirable cage for the werewolf... but instead they use it as a moderately effective sanctuary. They stupidly forgot the ceiling, though, and so the werewolf enters without there being a trap-door or escape hatch in the wooden panelling for the fugitives. The Doctor only just fails to lock it in after him, but surely a trap so elaborately conceived must have had a method for springing it? For that matter, wouldn't a smaller door have been a good idea?

During their hiatus in the library, the Doctor sees pictures of mistletoe, licks the walls coated with this toxic substance and then gets everyone to look for anything handy in the many, many books in the library. MacLeish Senior didn't believe in making it easy for his son, did he? No special shelf of books on local folklore with bookmarks or handy list of "Helpful Hints For Those Sequestered In a Library Through the Machinations of Malefacent Monks and Lycanthropic Assailants". Not even a diagram of the telescope with the direction "Insert legendary jewel A in slot B". Sir Robert's father and the Prince Consort have hatched a fiendish plan that rather depends on there being a Time Lord stuck in the house on that day to deduce the correct relationship between moonlight, the observatory, the Koh-i-Noor and the Brethren's even fiendisher plan to create a Steampunk Empire. It also means that they've correctly guessed, years beforehand, that the

Brethren will attempt to capture the Queen and infect her with the wolf taint at the Torchwood Estate, and not any other location.

Nonetheless, Our Heroes find the very book they need, and it opens automatically, as might be expected, on the right page. Then, in a pleasing inversion of the usual cliché, Rose thinks it's a crashed spaceship but Sir Robert corrects her, saying that it's a 'shooting star'. And yet it left a crater, something light doesn't usually do. So that's a waveform of light colliding with Earth, somehow, and infecting a human, somehow, to turn that person into… a wolf. Of course! Because a consciousness modulated on a frequency of light turning a human into anything *else* would be silly. (And, let's face it, this script is daft enough without Queen Victoria being menaced by Shaolin Scotsmen and a were-cactus.)

Now we turn our attention to Scottish Shaolin monks. Who had their monastery when Scotland was still stoutly Catholic (except the Calvinist bits). We'll buy a Scottish order avoiding the Dissolution of the Monasteries in 1536 - but it's still going, unmolested, from 1552 (when the meteor landed) through Unification and the Highland Clearances (4.4, "The Highlanders")? This only works if they are so remote and well-defended already, nobody can approach. So where did they pick up these fancy fighting moves? Moves, incidentally, that their leader - Father Angelo - doesn't seem to have in the slightest, as he's shot dead in close quarters by a 60-year-old with a pistol. And where's all the red cloth coming from? We'll just about accept that they're a mad cult of werewolf-worshipers, because that's how *Doctor Who* stories work (though given Father Angelo's bout of conscience at the start, even this is questionable), but does this sound remotely like any Catholic monastery you've ever heard of? And that's even before trying to figure out what they think the werewolf's plan is, and why they'd want to help it in the first place.

Ah, yes, the werewolf's plan. It's to infect Queen Victoria and (presumably) accelerate the Industrial Age towards coal-fired space-travel - so how did it pitch *that* to monks in the 1550s? We have to accept that there have been lots of visits by Queen Victoria to this bit of Scotland on days without a full moon that the Monks thought better than to sabotage, even if this sort of supposes that they have an agent within the royal household with access to travel plans. There would be a few signs that colleagues might spot, but more importantly, how could they insinuate such a person without finding out that Prince Albert had been in cahoots with MacLeish and had made a weird telescope and odd alterations to the Koh-i-Noor? All right, they might not be as quick to figure out the connection as the Doctor, but the penny might have dropped eventually. We also have to accept that the similarity of this visitor to our planet to a piece of middle-European folklore is either the result of this werewolf inspiring Germanic lore or of there having been a few others. If the former, why has it been visible but inactive all this time? If the latter, why did none of these succeed in altering history? (Assuming that they all had the same ambitions for wherever they landed that this one had for Britain; they could, of course, have had ambitions to make France the nation with the largest number of cheeses.) And the plan this Haemovariform has hatched obviously needed to wait until after the Industrial Revolution, rather than, for example, deciding that circa 1550 they had more chance of getting to where they want to be by biting the Pope or Emperor Rudolph II of Bavaria. Or, to be frank, why not infect Prince Albert, thus making their plan seem like a perfectly natural extension of his interests? He'd been at Torchwood House alone often enough, it seems, so nobody would have noticed any difference if he returned with a new loony enthusiasm.

And… the Queen naming Rose as 'Dame Rose'? In 1879, she could only get to be "Lady" Rose, and even then only if she had been married to someone who was knighted. Inherited female titles were a whole tier of nobility higher than a mere knight, and appointed ones had to wait for Victoria's son to be King. (Aggravatingly, there are a whole lot of these details that they asked experts about and then decided to go with the more picturesque anachronisms: Debrett's, the regal protocol consultants, explained to the script editor that a Victorian knighting ceremony would have been rather less pompous than the business with the sword we see here. And the Koh-i-Noor wasn't much like this then.)

Critique We'll begin with the positives. Rory Taylor, as director of photography, has made all of the interior sequences look like Rembrandts, with rich browns and limpid dark blues. The Mill have surpassed themselves with the matte paintings, werewolf effects and the seamless alterations to Torchwood House. Pauline Collins is perfectly cast. Derek Riddell, as Sir Robert, has made a thankless role seem to make sense. The pre-credit sequence is sensational and way beyond anything we've seen on British television. Unfortunately...

Give any ten-year-old the task of writing a *Doctor Who* story with Queen Victoria, a werewolf and Kung Fu, and they'd make a more interesting story than this. It might have made even less sense, but it would have had fewer *longeurs*. Once the werewolf-transformation happens, it really is like the caricature of 80s stories, running up and down corridors to kill time until the next cliffhanger. It's frantic but unenthralling, much as the previous episode's zombie-evading had been. How can you even *have* a dull moment in a story about Queen Victoria, a werewolf and Kung Fu? It's almost as perversely impressive a non-achievement as making pirates, a ghost and a spaceship boring (X6.3, "The Curse of the Black Spot").

Then there's the library sequence. For all the bold speeches about books being an "arsenal" rather than a "gym" or anything more uplifting, the main point of this scene - as with so many others in *Buffy* - is to info-dump. The Doctor has already divined, somehow, what he needs to know to fight the werewolf (that it is some kind of modulated light, which he seemed to guess when he first saw the Host transforming), or is later told it by Queen Victoria. The entire library sequence is for our benefit, not the Doctor's. In a story set in the present day or future, the Doctor would do this sequence in seconds, waving his sonic screwdriver over someone's phone ("The Runaway Bride") or a terminal, as he did last week. The most important thing is - as with 13.1, "Terror of the Zygons", oddly enough - the physical nature of the library *as a room* not the books themselves. It might just as well have been a boot-cupboard in plot terms.

Also, this is the episode where Rose goes from being slightly annoying to downright irritating - we're not *supposed* to be rooting for the werewolf, or Queen Victoria. Granted, the idea of doing a radical rethink of the supposedly traditional "celebrity historical" was, in some ways, worth attempting, but it needs more than this. If we must only have stories with people familiar from banknotes, as if anyone else from the past is too alien for the general public, they need to be considered as part of their world. If, on the other hand, the idea is to make the past "relevant" by making it just like the present but with funny hats - or if, as with Sofia Coppola's explanation of her dreadful *Marie Antoinette*, you use contemporary music to "humanise" people from the past - you should follow-through and be more brazen about the anachronisms. This story falls between two stools. There's a hint in the request for more aggressively "wrong" music in the pre-credit scene that Davies started with the idea of going for the latter approach, but pulled back.

The most frustrating part of the whole project is that it *almost* comes together. A lot of the dialogue is clever, some of it witty, some just as it should be for the characters from that time. Many of the pictures are gorgeous, and the action is, if seen scene-by-scene in isolation, effective. It's just a bit repetitive, relentless and oppressive. After that bravura opening, the Brethren are shockingly under-used, and instead it's a dozen or so interchangeable scenes of being chased by a werewolf around a castle. There ought to have been more variety of threats, or types of scene. This episode is a lot less fun than it thinks it is.

The Facts

Written by Russell T Davies. Directed by Euros Lyn. Viewing figures: (BBC1) 9.24 million, (BBC3 repeats) 0.6 and 0.4 million. (AIs at 83%).

Repeats and overseas promotion Mit Zahnen und Klauen, Un Loup-Garou Royal.

TARDISode Something falls from the sky, after passing the Moon (never mind that the light on the Moon in space makes it impossible to be a full moon seen from Earth, as it is in the next shot); 300 years later, a caption tells us, an auld crofter on the moors is stalked and then attacked by a gigantic hound.

Production

Annoyed at the way the chase had gone in X1.5, "World War Three" and intrigued by the possibilities of the "celebrity historical", Davies decided he wanted to move things on a bit - "give the historicals a kick up the arse", as he put it - and suggested an idea of Queen Victoria and a werewolf, and a proper chase around a big house with something fast pursuing the humans (and Time Lord). This was a notion he had on the back burner until it became obvious that his episode six plotline "The Runaway Bride" would work if he was forced to make another Christmas special and he needed something else. He thought that having people from the past interacting with a new Doctor helped sell the idea that he was rooted in time, part of events we all knew from history. He touted the idea around, specifying Queen Victoria, a werewolf, Scotland and Kung Fu. The writer who got the gig came up with a possibly more intriguing idea, of the queen getting an alien insect stuck in her eye and seeing the world differently, needing the Doctor to operate in ways that Victorian physicians couldn't. The writer, whom Davies refuses to name (see **Are Writers Just Hired Hands?** under X2.5, "Rise of the Cybermen") simply gave up when asked "where wolf?", saying that he couldn't "get" *Doctor Who* as Davies envisioned it. Davies took on the job himself, just after transmission of the last episode of Series One. With a Scot aboard the TARDIS, the idea of the Doctor slipping into an authentic accent was too good to miss; Tennant was sounded out about possible Caledonian pseudonyms other than "John Smith", but was up a gumtree - one idea he suggested was from a phrase analogous to "we are all God's children" (a preacher called "John Thompson" became "Jock Tamson", hence "we're all Jock Tamson's bairns"). Davies gave up and went for the obvious joke of Jamie McCrimmon. Phil Collinson added the idea of the Koh-i-Noor as the key to defeating the werewolf. Davies' script was filled with impressionistic descriptions of how a scene should behave, with the fight at the start seeming to be almost all sound-effects like the fights in 60s *Batman* episodes and a request for wailing guitars on the soundtrack.

• Block Two was given to Euros Lyn, who had impressed everyone with his Victorian episode last year and his versatility in doing this and a gonzo space story in the same block ("The End of the World", "The Unquiet Dead"). The production schedule was revised as Block One dragged on. An early decision on how to execute the wolf effects was needed, and both The Mill and Millennium Effects were plausible, but it would be entirely digital or entirely prosthetic largely because of time. Lyn was aware that it was possible to combine the two effects teams on werewolves (as they had done on *Hex* a year earlier). However, with the plan to make the episode more contemporary-looking, the mobility of the camera on location or in the studio was thought to militate against elaborate mechanical effects and inclined everyone more towards adding them in post-production. Although some parts of the script had the wolf as a quadruped, the design team worked on the idea of a humanoid gait, possibly with a furry "sporran" to make it suitable for teatime.

• Queen Victoria was difficult to cast: she had to look as everyone imagined her, and yet run up and down corridors and staircases and occasionally twinkle mischievously. The delays while the part was filled caused anxiety for costume designer Louise Page, amongst others. During the read-through, the part was read by Helen Griffin, later to play Mrs Moore in the two-part Cyberman story. (Captain Reynolds and Lady Isobel were read in by Tennant's parents, who were around and had the right accents. And Tennant's mum and dad were, he says, disappointed that they didn't get to play the parts for real.) The design for the royal dress was kept as vague as possible until the last possible moment; the Friday before the Monday when the dress would first be used. On receiving confirmation that it was Pauline Collins, Page went to Collins' house (only a short distance from her own home) and asked her husband, John Alderton, for measurements. (Collins was away for the weekend, presumably learning lines in a hurry.) Meanwhile, Sheelagh Wells, the make-up designer, found that the wig Collins had been using in *Bleak House* was available, even if its owner was himself on holiday. (She rang him when he was up a mountain in Scotland.) Collins listened to a few speeches of Victoria's, more to get used to her rhythms than as meticulous research. Wells also consulted contemporary sources, looking at photos of the Queen visiting Scotland at around the time the story is set.

• On the same day that Collins' involvement was announced, the news was released that there was to be a spin-off from *Doctor Who*, featuring Captain Jack in Cardiff fighting aliens in a "*This Life* meets *X-Files*" series called *Torchwood*. This was supposedly the "adult" counterpart to *Doctor Who*, and Davies and Gardner would again be executive producers.

• The filthy weather that had led to over-runs on "The Christmas Invasion" and slapstick on the Gower Peninsula ("New Earth") continued. Indeed, the first day's shooting - at Penllyn House, for the pre-credit flying-harness stuff - was on the same day that the disastrous Worm's Head location was afflicted. This was Monday, 26th September, 2005, after a day's preparation and setting-up. Members of the Korean Kick-Boxing Association of Wales and the United Tai-Kwon-Do Association of Wales had been asked to shave their heads to play these roles. Unusually, the whole day was given over to one page of script. The fight-arranger for this scene was David Forman, who had begun in the Hong Kong street-fighting films and had just worked on *Batman Begins*. He used *Wushu* techniques for the stick-work and a composite of martial arts for the rest. Lyn used a high-speed camera to capture the flight of the monks with a flickery picture-quality he'd liked in *28 Days Later*.

The weather was equally capricious the following day, with the regulars and Pauline Collins recording the first meeting of the Doctor and Rose with Queen Victoria. September just outside Bargoed felt like January. Here, as for much of the shoot, Collins wore trainers under Queen Victoria's widow's weeds. Apparently she swore a lot, in costume. The clouds weren't as thick as necessary to fit in with the lowered colour-tones needed for the story, and indeed whilst the wind was strong and there were threats of rain all day there was a blue sky for some shots and fast-moving clouds. (Indeed, the shot of Her Majesty inside her carriage was redone in the studio because the drapery flapped about distractingly.) The snowy mountains in the background are later matting by The Mill. As had happened in the "New Earth" location, the crew managed to get some shots in just before sunset, notably of the Doctor and Rose returning to the TARDIS. This was also the day Tennant and Piper got the scripts for the four Cybermen episodes and found out Rose's eventual fate.

Wednesday, 28th September was the day at Craig-Y-Nos, a castle just north of Swansea, for the exterior sequences of the front of Torchwood House. This building was commissioned by one of Queen Victoria's favourite sopranos, but was by this time owned by an industrial cleaning agency. The Celtic cross was matted in later, to disguise an anachronistic well, and obviously the observatory was a digital extension. As might be expected, the weather was different again that day, with heavy rain, and not all of the horses followed the script. A scene cut from the broadcast episode was shot here, of Sir Doctor and Dame Rose trying to keep straight faces as they set off back to the TARDIS in exile from the British Empire. The following day was a return to a location Lyn had used last year,

Headlands School. This had been Mr Sneed's funeral parlour in most of the scenes there in "The Unquiet Dead". Tennant and Piper were away, but making a first appearance were drama student Josh Green and his "Ultra-Lupine Stunt Hat", as the werewolf-place-maker onto whom the digital effects could be added. For this, Green wore a series of tight lycra body-stockings, with muscula-ture drawn on in marker-pen, and said hat, a converted cycle-helmet with a stick and a ball on top for the wolf's eyeline. Not all of the cast could look the wolf in the eye: Green's physique was distracting (and, to male cast-members, a bit intimidating...).

Meanwhile, the wolf's other half was Tom Smith, who had been a couple of years above Tennant in the same drama school. He was inside the cage for much of the time, although when the transformation came, the cage would be removed from the set (by this time remounted in a studio) and replicated digitally along with the changing wolf-image. Another take of Green in a leotard (a green one, to be matted out as per the green screens) knocking the pieces of the cage flying was composited into this, to smash it when the computer-generated wolf took over the role. Smith adopted a scary voice for the part, and this was apparently a bit of a surprise to some of the cast who'd not been present earlier. On the second day, a few of the scenes in the corridor below stairs were shot, alongside the part of the wolf's trans-formation that needed Smith. He wore a flesh-coloured thong, contact lenses and a bit of make-up on his teeth.

• Dinner was served at Llansannor on Saturday, 1st October. The dining-room scene was explained in a cut line as being possible because the Queen had brought a cold collation with her in a hamper. Piper was off that day. Tennant was finding it difficult to remember when he was supposed to sound like himself and when he slipped into Doctorese. A new week began with two days at the Q2 complex, beginning with hallways and the observatory. Piper and Tennant had to make moving the telescope seem harder than it actually was. A day at Treowen House, Dingestow, Monmouth was spent using their seventeenth-century staircase and a window. (This was where Derek Riddell, who had occasion to know, commented about the line where Sir Robert is called "Sir Francis Drake" and not Sir Walter Raleigh.) Here, Collins tripped a few times and in some shots was doubled by Colleen Quinn. That was 5th October. The crew and cast then relocated to the HTV studios, which had the advantage of decent soundproofing when it rained. The other advantages of the purpose-built corridor sets included the ability to winch actors into the rafters as if grabbed from above by a wolf, the safe firing of guns towards cameras (shielded by Perspex) and a handy green screen for lupine transformations, and for hand-held cameras. This was where the shot of the farm-hand having his face thrust into a bucket of water was done. They made a few scenes of "The Girl in the Fireplace" here on the same day. Next day, just for a change, they did some location work at Tredegar House, which had hitherto been Cassandra's hideaway ("New Earth"), Harriet Jones' HQ and the base of Llewellyn's rocket group ("The Christmas Invasion") and would a week later be Versailles. Here, it would be the kitchens, library and study of Torchwood. For the first day there, 7th October, the two stars were absent, spending the day at Q2 frantically making up time for Block One. During the following weekend, the crew would attempt to complete the lift scenes for "New Earth" and the cyber-cafe for "School Reunion", whilst Smith's measurements were taken by The Mill for digital jiggery-pokery. Then on Monday, it was back to the location for three more days, but only two involving the main cast, as the shoot for "The Girl in the Fireplace" at the same location included a bit of second-unit material for this story. One of the doors in the library was replaced by a prop door with the mistletoe carving. A longer scene of Tennant trying three times to shut the door behind him and being yanked back was trimmed, as it looked a bit silent-movie comedy. Tennant and Riddell had to be careful of the genuine antique furniture and the props brought in to be apparently hastily piled against the doors. (One prop they brought was the suit of armour we saw aboard the TARDIS at the end of "The Christmas Invasion".) The prop for the Koh-i-Noor was a straightforward glass jewel used in decorating, said to have come from a normal hardware store such as Homebase or B&Q.

They were back at Q2 for the spaceship interiors in episode four on Thursday, and this story's work resumed on the 20th, with a cutaway of Lady Isobel looking out of the window at the monks - this was included in the schedule for the crew's first at day at Dyffryn, doubling for a different bit of Versailles. Finally, there were two days in the studios (26th and 27th October) - one for the TARDIS scene and then one for the model telescope interior (while the other story's TARDIS scenes were being shot nearby). Due to a last-minute glitch on clearances, the originally scripted use of "Lucky Number" by Lene Lovich was replaced by "Hit Me With Your Rhythm Stick" by Ian Dury and the Blockheads, although the date and venue of the gig seem to have been unchanged. (The Lovich song is clearly a lawyer's dream, as even advertisers with limitless funds have to use substandard covers for car commercials. Nobody knows why, as Lovich was on the same UK label, Stiff, as Dury and was born in Yorkshire.) The rough edit of the pre-credit fight was cut to up-tempo surf-guitars, although a relatively straightforward score by Murray Gold, using themes he'd re-use later in the series, was added later. Everyone was impressed by the end-result and there was talk of beginning the new series with this episode instead of "New Earth".

X2.3: "School Reunion"

(26th April, 2006)

Which One is This? The pilot episode of *The Sarah Jane Adventures*. Sort of.

Firsts and Lasts Well, obviously it's the first appearance this century of Sarah Jane Smith and thus of anyone from the old days - but, more significantly at the time, it's the first time that *events* in the old series were acknowledged to have happened to this Doctor. Look back to X1.1, "Rose" and the way the Nestenes try the whole shop-dummies-attacking-shoppers thing as though it had never failed before and the difference is stark.

Meanwhile, this is the adventure where Mickey steps up to the plate and becomes TARDIS-worthy. So, contrary to what the tabloid press believed, he becomes the first non-Caucasian companion, and - depending on your interpretation of Rose and Mickey's status as girlfriend / boyfriend - part of the first official couple aboard the Ship. (See **Was There Any Hanky-Panky Aboard the TARDIS?** under 6.6, "The Space Pirates".) On the other hand, this is where the Doctor's "curse of the Time Lords" whinging about getting old and watching the rest of the universe go by starts. You'll be hearing a lot more of it in later seasons.

This is the first episode this century to have

X2.3 School Reunion

been written by someone who didn't come up through the ranks of fanzines and/or Virgin Books.

Watch Out For...

• For anyone under 35 watching this episode, it was a story about Rose coming to terms with the Doctor discarding old sidekicks like worn-out shoes. But, for that audience, the entire series was about a romance between a teenage shopgirl and a Byronic alien, so *obviously* Rose would prove to be different. For anyone over 35, this was about the return of Sarah Jane Smith but written by someone too young to comprehend why that character, out of all of the officially sanctioned Companions-with-a-capital-C, is the one the whole of Britain remembered most fondly. The whole point was that her travels with the Doctor were punctuated by a proper job, and that of all of them, she was the one with a life beyond the TARDIS - the one who travelled with him in between her real adventures as a solo reporter in the sexist world of Fleet Street in the 70s. She left the Doctor as much as he left her. See if you can spot the moments when Elisabeth Sladen is having to grit her teeth and rewrite the past while claiming that Sarah was just like Rose back then.

• Because, originally, Sarah's role was supposed to have been what Mickey is doing in this story. This is the episode where he is most obviously the audience-identification character, finding out mysteries slightly too big to take on alone and calling in the Doctor and Rose as reinforcements, crashing a car through a school door, offering sarcastic comments about the storyline and character-developments and finding a brilliantly simple and obvious solution to a problem that the other characters would have resolved with high explosives or alien technology.

• Those who suspect that this iteration of *Doctor Who* wants to be *Buffy the Vampire Slayer* when it grows up can consider the guest-villain here (Anthony Stewart Head) as Exhibit A, although, once again, there's an age-differential at work as most parents would be thinking "It's the posh bloke from those annoying instant coffee ads in the 80s" rather than "It's Giles from *Buffy*". Tony Head is icily precise as Mr Finch, but after years of topping fan-polls of "person who ought to be the Doctor if they ever bring the show back", he is most effective as the anti-Tennant. In their set-piece confrontation at the school swimming-pool, a scene written as a sort of Spaghetti Western stand-off becomes an exercise in how unlike previous Doctors Tennant really is.

• Even those who claim never to have liked K9 admit that in this story he gets some fairly impressive moments, holding off the Krillitanes and getting in sardonic rejoinders. He also has a heroic sacrifice, followed by a regeneration of his own. However, he is largely there as a rebuke to Mickey, making him step up and become a fully-fledged companion.

• You know that old cliché about the Doctor's lady companions twisting their ankles at key moments? Well, Sarah Jane never did it, but Elisabeth Sladen did: a lot of the running up and down corridors in this episode has the second assistant director doubling for her, hence the knee-high cameras and long-shots from behind.

The Continuity

The Doctor He apparently fondles the Console when he thinks nobody's looking. He is remarkably definite about promising Rose that he'd never leave her behind. He refuses to be guilt-tripped about leaving Sarah behind, although her version of events does seem at odds with the last time she claims to have seen him and everything leading up to it.

[This is downright curious: when Sarah asks the Doctor why he didn't return for her after whatever detained him on Gallifrey (see 14.2, "The Hand of Fear" and 14.3, "The Deadly Assassin"), he simply states 'I couldn't'. And yet, this was only the last in a long line of instances where he drops her off in her time and place, gets on with his life, leaves her to get on with hers and then offers her another ride some time later. Do we know how long elapses between 11.4, "The Monster of Peladon" and 11.5, "Planet of the Spiders"? Or how long they were in London before Sir Colin got on the phone in the run-up to 13.6, "The Seeds of Doom"? We do not. All that is different about the end of "The Hand of Fear" is that both parties treat it as exactly the sort of definite farewell that Sarah spends this episode gripping that she never got.

[Nonetheless, we have to acknowledge that something other than the potentially awkward meeting of Sarah and Leela prevented the Doctor from looking up an old friend, just as he chose not to pop in on the Brigadier. The explanation the

Why the Great Powell Estate Date Debate?

Unavoidably, the bulk of this essay is going to be an attempt to get the chronology of the "present-day" stories to make sense, despite BBC Wales' strenuous efforts at times to prevent this.

Because the all-new Welsh version of *Doctor Who* was written, produced and run by people who'd been fans during the most fervid period of the after-the-fact attempts to get everything into order, it was inevitable that there would be a lot of energy put into avoiding the type of vagueness and mistakes that peeved them. Having Sarah Jane Smith claim "I'm from 1980" (13.3, "Pyramids of Mars"), then returning to her aunt's five years later in December 1981 (18.7a, "K9 and Company") whilst her boss, Brigadier Lethbridge-Stewart, had left UNIT in 1976 (20.3, "Mawdryn Undead") but was in charge even after Sarah had returned to "1980"... surely this kind of insanity was unworthy of the new-style *Doctor Who* and could be consigned to the same scrapheap as putting "The Power of the Daleks" (4.3) at 2020, only 20 years after the *Radio Times* claimed the Daleks had invaded Earth (2.2, "The Dalek Invasion of Earth", actually dated in the story as 2157). No, this time it would be different; there were professional fans-turned-script-advisors to look into it, and they'd worked out a chronology, with measuring and everything. Everything was going to be fine.

Except that it wasn't. The arguments began within weeks, especially as not everyone involved seemed to remember that Rose skipped a year and returned to her mum's in March 2006 (X1.4, "Aliens of London"). (Neither did whichever eight-year-olds compiled the Chronology on Wikipedia.) In fact, they'd messed it all up by the second episode, with Jackie Tyler getting a phone call from Rose even though it was established two episodes later (in a sequence already filmed when this bit was rewritten and reshot) that Rose was away for a year with Jackie having no idea where her daughter was (see **The Supporting Cast** under X1.2, "The End of the World" for more). But the plan was for it all to work out and all the on-screen details, designed by a graphics department briefed from the same big book of dates that the writers were using, were intended to fit together perfectly. Anyone paying attention could figure it all out, and there would be no repeat of the UNIT Dating controversy.

While no discontinuity the BBC Wales series have produced are arguably of *that* magnitude, ironing out a cohesive timeline for the new *Doctor Who* is all the more challenging because there's two spin-off series that have to be accommodated, and they aren't always in agreement with their parent show. *Torchwood* contains a few internal glitches, and while *The Sarah Jane Adventures* is less of a worry, it steadfastly provides six more alien invasions/ celestial anomalies/ mass hysteria incidents per annum to include in the list of things everyone pretends not to remember. The two spin-off shows allude to events in *Doctor Who* every so often, but the converse isn't always true - strangely, none of the events in *Torchwood*: "Children of Earth" seem to have affected Rani's dad, a school head, nor the teenage protagonists who would surely have noticed and asked Mr Smith for an explanation. (Nor does anyone in "Children of Earth" refer back to all the similar things that happened worldwide that seem to start in Ealing, many of them involving vast numbers of children acting as though hypnotised.) The problem becomes magnified with the impossible-to-ignore events of *Torchwood*: "Miracle Day", which aren't mentioned, not once, in New *Who*.

Just at a very basic level, trying to resolve the three series isn't without its stumbling blocks. Series One of *Torchwood* seems, all other things being equal, to obey the "Year Ahead of Broadcast" rule started in "Aliens of London" (so, should occur in 2007) - and yet a CIA file *TW*: "Miracle Day" (in an episode written by Russell T Davies, even!) names "2006" as the year that Gwen Cooper joined Torchwood (in *Torchwood*: "Everything Changes"). This would be the same CIA, however, that sent Bill Filer to catch the Master (9.3, "The Claws of Axos" - at least in the early scripts and the novelisation), so clearly isn't the highly efficient real-life CIA then. *Torchwood* Series Two gets tricky in that it *mostly* takes place in 2008, but ends in 2009. (There's a seeming error in that Jack is dug up in 1901 - *TW*: "Exit Wounds" - and demands to be frozen for "107 years", although he could just be rounding down from "107 years and a few months".) Even without matching these dates with Martha Jones' med-school finals and her sister Tish's extraordinarily busy week (starting two high-profile jobs in three days, and not mentioning either to her family during the run-up to dad's birthday party and Martha's exciting afternoon on the Moon), we have got problems. The first series of *Torchwood* ends with "Vote Saxon" posters up everywhere (in *Torchwood*: "Captain Jack Harkness"), just after Christmas (*Torchwood*: "Out of Time"), and the

continued on Page 277...

X2.3 School Reunion

Doctor offers to Rose is that, given his expected lifespan, he can't bear to see a human spending their entire life growing old and dying with him while he lives on. He calls this 'the curse of the Time Lords' - which is rather insulting to loads of people who have, in fact, watched a loved one grow old and expire, and so can relate perfectly well to the issue from the vantage point of being human.

[An alternative argument - although nothing on screen is said about this - is that the old problem of interfering with his own timeline comes into play. It's possible that, some time before the start of, say, 14.4, "The Face of Evil", the Doctor visited a point in the future where an older Sarah reminisced about there being a long gap before she saw him again and thus avoided any contact, just as reading Reinette's note made a final visit before she died impossible (X2.4, "The Girl in the Fireplace"), or being told that the Brigadier never saw him again meant that this one last hurrah was denied them (X6.13, "The Wedding of River Song"). If we follow this reasoning through, it might indicate that the Doctor knew in advance that K9 was coming with him (15.2, "The Invisible Enemy"), that there would be other Doctors, and that Sarah would eventually acquire a posse of plucky teenagers and an alien super-computer - but this is no more of a problem than anything involving River Song or multi-Doctor stories. (See **Was There a Season 6B?** under 22.4, "The Two Doctors", **Why Not Warn Him About the Time War?** under X3.13a, "Time Crash" and **Is Arthur the Horse a Companion?** under "The Girl in the Fireplace".)]

He tells Sarah that he has regenerated 'half a dozen times' since they last met. [Not for the last time, this raises the question of whether Sarah remembers - or didn't get a proper explanation for - her trip to Rassilon's Tomb (X20.7, "The Five Doctors"). See **The Supporting Cast** for more.]

The Doctor has K9 identify the Krillitane oil. [Possibly just to show him off, as he was first on his way to have the TARDIS do it. Either way, it's another strong indication that the "whittling-down" technique he used in X1.5, "World War Three" is gone for good.]

He's keeping up the 'I used to have mercy' schtick [see X2.0, "The Christmas Invasion"], as part of the sense of himself being too old for this sort of thing. Since Mickey's around again, he has a go at Captain Jack-style commanding [see X1.11, "Boom Town"]. It's not what he's good at. He teases Mickey for screaming when the rats fall on him [in a sexist and out-of-character manner more like Spike from *Buffy* than anything].

He has been able to secure school jobs for himself and Rose on remarkably short notice. [As anyone who's worked in a school in any capacity will know, were it not *the Doctor* that we're talking about here, the speed at which this happens would be massively improbable. The usual procedure is for the applicants for any vacancy (especially one filled through a supply teaching agency) to have been registered for work in the area and offered it at short notice that very morning. These agencies will see to it that anyone seeking work in the UK has tax, National Insurance and a work-permit (as many of the staff are visiting Australians) and a clean check from the Criminal Records Bureau. That last detail can take four or five months. All things being equal, Rose and the Doctor both appearing magically on the system and getting to the head of the queue so quickly *at the same school on the same day* would be a matter for a detailed investigation, not least if they used any chicanery like making someone win the Lotto despite not playing. Mickey goes to look at the school's background online, but Torchwood are blocking much of what he does, so they obviously know all about it and yet fail to spot - or *do* spot, if Captain Jack is covering for his friends - a 'Dr John Smith' and a 'Rose Tyler' showing up at a school they are either keeping under surveillance or sponsoring as a pet project. The 'Bad Wolf Virus' pertaining to Rose (X2.10, "Love & Monsters") might also be in play here.]

He can touch Krillitane Oil, which otherwise is corrosive enough to incinerate dinner ladies, and eat the oil-laced chips with seemingly no effect. He's now referring to Mickey as '[Rose's] boyfriend'.

• *Ethics*. The prospect of using the Krillitane oil and a school full of children's souls to stop the Time War seriously tempts him; it takes Sarah Jane giving him what-for before he pulls himself together. He's mocking Mickey as much as ever, but needs only the slightest prompting from Sarah to welcome him aboard the TARDIS.

Oh, and using time travel to cheat at the lottery doesn't seem to bother him as much as it did once [see 2.9, "The Time Meddler", and also X4.18, "The End of Time Part Two"].

Why the Great Powell Estate Date Debate?

continued from Page 275...

last scene of Series One leads into "Utopia" (X3.11). Harry Saxon's meteoric rise to power is said to have started 18 months before that - if we don't do something to untangle all this, we'll have Harriet Jones being deposed six months before she gets into office and Rose not believing in aliens even after the President of the USA is assassinated by one live on air (X3.12, "The Sound of Drums").

Okay, so let's pretend for a moment that we could magic away all the impossible on-screen dates for *Torchwood*. What we're left with is that *Torchwood* Series One, where everyone talks about the Battle of Canary Wharf as a past event (but not the recent-past, like within the last month) has to be Autumn 2007 at the very latest. By Christmas, Gwen Cooper has learned how to shoot straight, had an affair, befriended an amateur alien-hunter and learned how to use quite a lot of hi-tech and acquired devices. The events between Christmas and Jack's tussle with the hundred-foot-high behemoth that everyone forgets are telescoped into a few days, the only wriggle-room being how long Owen sulks over Diana dumping him for a Cessna (*TW*: "Out of Time") before deciding to open the Rift. Tosh and Jack are hurled back to January 1941 (*TW*: "Captain Jack Harkness"), but that doesn't mean they *have* to have left in a January. (The number of years is asymmetrical whatever number it is: if the month is constant, why not a neater number of years like 70 or a square/cube like 64?) A similar weighting of aesthetics over logic makes some commentators want Jack's defeat of Abaddon (*TW*: "End of Days") to be on Good Friday and the comeback and assumption into time and space to be three days later (with Gwen presumably washing his feet with her hair or something). In real life, someone would have commented on it - the news reports at the start if nothing else.

This is starting to get confusing, so let's start again with the one rock-solid(ish) date we have: the destruction of Henrik's and Rose's disappearance. If the missing-persons poster for Rose seen in "Aliens of London" is to be believed - and it's on screen and in close up specifically for us to see it - she was last seen on 5th March, 2005. This makes the explosion at Henrik's in "Rose" approximately 6.30pm on 4th March. Ah, but the website to promote the series, supposedly started by Clive and carried on by Mickey (if the BBC's *Doctor Who* website can be believed), has it as 26th March, Easter Saturday (the day of the episode's first transmission). Rose is up at 7.30 next morning and there's no Easter egg and no reason to suppose she has the day off, because it's a Sunday and a Bank Holiday. The poster claims that Rose is 19. In 1987 (X1.8, "Father's Day"), she was a baby, not a toddler. What if the poster had a typo and Rose vanished in 2004? This gets rid of some anomalies in the later dates, especially the Christmas episodes, and resolves a few apparent contradictions with *Torchwood* details. That said, few people would want to get rid of the only cast-iron certainty concerning the near-present-day stories, so we'll keep this ploy as an emergency measure for now.

A few odd details might give us some leeway: the ending of the first series of *Torchwood* ("End of Days") has the 50-foot-high being Abaddon stomping around Cardiff killing anyone who is where its shadow falls. Curiously, this isn't mentioned again, ever. However, three or four days after being killed so often that he drained Abaddon's nastiness (yes, really), Captain Jack wakes up, hugs everyone, then legs it (pausing only to pick up the hand-in-a-jar he keeps as a Doctor-detector), and is whisked away from his subterranean lair by something unseen that makes a mysterious wheezing groaning sound. This doesn't exactly match what we see at the start of "Utopia" - in this, the TARDIS has camped on top of the Torchwood secret magic invisible lift (so Jack can't have got out that way) and he is running towards it and clings on as the Ship dematerialises. (Watch "End of Days", and there is no way Jack can have got out of the Hub unless the TARDIS actually materialised inside it; the emergency exit is the very paving-slab where we see the TARDIS, and the rest of Jack's Scooby Gang are coming in through the main entrance, carrying pizzas.) Then, after the whole year (pre-temporal reversal)/ morning (post-temporal reversal) when Jack is chained up aboard Cloudbase (X3.13, "Last of the Time Lords"), he decides to go back to his little crew, whom Saxon had previously sent off on a wild goose chase to the Himalayas ("The Sound of Drums"). The next time we see them, they are griping that he's been gone for months (*TW*: "Kiss Kiss, Bang Bang"). There's a potential get-out clause here, if the TARDIS arrived to refuel in

continued on Page 279...

X2.3 School Reunion

- *Background.* He's met the Krillitanes when they were in an earlier phase and had giraffe-like necks, which is why he doesn't immediately spot them here. He seems to know about the cultures they absorbed and want to revive, including Perganon. [The associated website, a mock-up of a Deffry Vale school webpage from the same time as this adventure, notes that new teacher Mr. Smith taught physics at Shoreditch. There is a different, probably better, story behind that if we believe "An Unearthly Child" (1.1), "Remembrance of the Daleks" (25.1) and what we're told at the end of Appendix 3, *The Sarah Jane Adventures*: "Death of the Doctor".]
- *Inventory: Sonic Screwdriver.* Once again, the Deadlock Seal crops up to thwart the sonic screwdriver [and thus stop the episode under-running, providing an excuse for an explosion - the Krillitane oil is inside a vat with an unlockable lid]. The Krillitanes must have been expecting visitors with this sort of apparatus, since the computers are deadlocked as well.
- *Inventory: Other.* [The psychic paper almost certainly gets used offstage to get the Doctor and Rose their entirely-too-convenient jobs, but there's nothing on-screen.]

The TARDIS Sarah's not keen on the redecoration. It appears the Doctor can dematerialise and leave a passenger behind, in this case with K9. [There is a hint that this was possible in 19.1, "Castrovalva", but that version of Adric was a projected computation generated by the Master's TARDIS.]

The Supporting Cast
- *Rose* is very catty to Sarah about her age, relevance to the Doctor and knowledge of what happens in schools these days. She gets inordinately irritated about working as a dinner lady, before starting to tease Mickey and coming off rather the worse there. She finds the investigating as nostalgic as anything else. As a child, she used to think all teachers slept in the school. She still likes chips, and is very keen on the school ones. The discovery that they've augmented her arithmetic skills alarms her. The prospect of being left behind, like Sarah Jane, terrifies her.

She is oddly unimpressed by the idea of Mickey coming along on their journeys.

- *Mickey* has got himself a niche finding weirdness in the press and filtering out anything that is worthy of the Doctor's time. His ability with computers is helpful in filtering out the hype and finding something sinister in Deffry Vale. When even he runs into an insurmountable firewall, he sends for the Doctor [this provides the **TARDISode** for the episode].

In many ways, this is Mickey's finest hour; he's the one responsible for correctly identifying a Doctor-worthy situation, saves a school full of kids, and finally decides it's time to step up and see what's out there. [He's come a lot farther since X1.1, "Rose" than Rose herself has. He's blokey enough to tease both the Doctor and Rose about their relationship vis-à-vis Sarah Jane.]

- *Sarah Jane Smith* is working for the *Sunday Times* now. [Or so she claims. She might be using that paper's former prestige to get a foot in the door. In the light of later disclosures about her career, it appears she still has contacts within UNIT and is a respected freelance journalist and quite comfortably-off.]

She's obviously older, but not as much as perhaps she ought to be [a fact later glossed as being residual Artron Energy from TARDIS travel]. Sarah is still a journalist, still single and still looking into peculiar events. She resents the Doctor's apparent abandonment of her. [At the end of "The Hand of Fear" - this, despite getting a tin dog from him in 18.7a, "K9 and Company". Since we see that particular K9 here, that much still has to have happened.

[An odd sidelight on all of this is that Sarah has no memory of the events in "The Five Doctors". When sorting out her own life in her very own spin-off show, it appears that she checked on anyone who might have been a former companion - possibly without any idea that she met Tegan, at least, in Rassilon's Tomb. See the Appendix to Volume 8.]

Apparently, the TARDIS left her in Aberdeen, not South Croydon as intended, at what she recalls as their last meeting ["The Hand of Fear"]. She evidently expected the Doctor to come back and ask her to accompany him again. [So their on-off relationship must have had longer gaps than was implied in the transmission of those adventures. This explains how she had a job to return to after so long away, although it is possible that a few of the Earth-based adventures were out-of-synch with calendar time, which helps with dating the Brigadier's departure from UNIT (see 20.3, "Mawdryn Undead" and 13.6, "The Seeds of Doom" for one apparent contradiction that goes

Why the Great Powell Estate Date Debate?

continued from Page 277...

"Utopia" some time in the past relative to Martha's family and their eventful week (meaning Jack skipped a few months that year because he was off in the far future, returning in "The Sound of Drums"), and that the "18 months" gap is stretchier than the Doctor thinks. (Why should waiting 18 months be such a theme with Davies? See 22.6, "Revelation of the Daleks".) On closer inspection, this doesn't help much, as we will see.

The Cardiff MIBs' next batch of adventures (*Torchwood* Series Two) include a newly qualified Martha joining them and two members dying. Those deaths are mentioned by Gwen Cooper just after she and Ianto finally encounter the Doctor (X4.12, "The Stolen Earth"). The same day, it is explained to us that Luke Smith is still at school, and Series Two onward of *The Sarah Jane Adventures* mentions the Daleks as a historical incident that everyone knows about (see especially *SJA*: "The Mark of the Berserker"). The first episode of *The Sarah Jane Adventures* offers the detail that K9 Mk IV has been used to block up a black hole for (here it is again) 18 months, but Maria's clock suggests that this episode happens in early January. "School Reunion" (X2.3) happens some time between Christmas and 1st February. (Mickey provides the latter date when he reads the front page of Evil Parallel *Evening Standard* in X2.5, "Rise of the Cybermen" - the paper may of course have been yesterday's, but he says it's "bang on" when they left "their" London.) Taking all of this at face value becomes rather difficult - favouring Maria's clock means that the "18 month" gap is actually something like two years, and overlooks all the other clues that *The Sarah Jane Adventures* Series One occur in 2008. *Torchwood*, meanwhile, explicitly begins some time after the Canary Wharf incident. Jack expressly mentions the destruction of Torchwood One in that battle (X2.13, "Doomsday") in conversation with Gwen Cooper, and the Hub's tourist information-booth front even has a faded newspaper clipping of Margaret Blaine from "Boom Town" (X1.11).

Mentioning that tag scene and the beginning of "New Earth" (X2.1) brings in other evidence: the trees. Whenever the Doctor and Rose take their leave of Mickey and Jackie, it's at the very latest spring, and the same weather and foliage occur in that park with K9 Mk IV ("School Reunion"). But then, the dating clues given in *The Sarah Jane Adventures* are routinely at odds with the foliage seen (note especially *SJA*: "Sky", which should occur in early March, despite the trees being relatively lush and Sky herself commenting on all the green plants about the place). We'll try to avoid inferring too much from such details, unless there really is no other on-screen hint about when things are happening.

While we're about it, a quick note on "Turn Left" (X4.11). This shows us all of the horrid things that befall Earth in the two years after "The Runaway Bride" (X.3.0) in a Doctorless universe and thus gives us a sequence. It doesn't tell us a lot we wouldn't have known otherwise, but the existence of this story removes any potential leeway with shuffling the running-order - two of the three yuletide disasters *do*, really, take place on successive Christmases. On top of all this, Series Five strongly hints that the Dalek-Cybermen tussle ("Doomsday"), the Matter Bomb incident ("The Stolen Earth"; X4.13, "Journey's End") and the Cyber-King (X4.14, "The Next Doctor") were removed from history by the Cracks in Time. Whether these are restored when the Doctor restarts the Universe (X5.13, "The Big Bang") is, at present, conjectural. Those people most likely to have large holes in their pasts were TARDIS travellers and may remember these things, even if they now no longer happened (see **He Remembers This How?** under X1.5, "World War III", and **Is Time Like Bolognese Sauce Now?** under X5.5, "Flesh and Stone").

Here we go, then. First, we'll note the rock-solid dates and the reasons to treat other dates as suspect, whilst giving our reasons to put some things within reasonably well-defined parameters. Anything with a **TW** next to it is a *Torchwood* dating, **SJA** for *The Sarah Jane Adventures* and **!** is an apparent anomaly.

4th March, 2005: Rose meets the Doctor ("Rose").

5th March, 2005: Rose leaves with the Doctor ("Rose" again; unless, as the website claimed, it was 26th March, in which case Mickey had better renew his car tax pronto).

TW 2005 Owen Harper encounters Jack Harkness when an alien parasite kills his fiancée ("four years" before the modern-day portion of

continued on Page 281...

X2.3 School Reunion

away if the latter is actually *before* 13.4, "The Android Invasion").]

She is apparently a bit flummoxed by the redesign of the sonic screwdriver. And the Doctor's new appearance. And the TARDIS. And, apparently, Rose, but eventually the two bond over mutual mockery of the Doctor. Sarah Jane suggests that Rose come find her when she's done travelling. Mickey's request to come on board the TARDIS meets with her enthusiastic support, and possible connivance [some might see the conversation ending with 'Oh my God, I'm the tin dog!' as being her slyly nudging him].

She's driving an old silver hatchback [rather than a yellow VW Beetle or a jade-green Figaro as seen in *The Sarah Jane Adventures*]. This gets rather damaged when Mickey drives it into a doorway. [Presumably Mickey gives her his old Beetle by way of an apology, which suggests he was thinking ahead even before a better opportunity presents itself two stories later.]

For those just joining us, those prior adventures and alien encounters that Sarah mentions to Rose are:

Mummies. "Pyramids of Mars" (13.3), although the god-like alien Sutekh was the real threat and the mummies come under the heading of...

Robots, lots of robots as in "The Time Warrior" (11.1), "Robot" (12.1), "The Sontaran Experiment" (12.3), "The Android Invasion" and of course "K9 and Company".

Daleks. "Death to the Daleks" (11.3), "Genesis of the Daleks" (12.4).

Anti-Matter Monsters. "Planet of Evil" (13.2).

Real, Living Dinosaurs. "Invasion of the Dinosaurs" (11.2).

The. Loch Ness. MONSTAH. "Terror of the Zygons" (13.1).

[Sarah neglects to mention Morbius, Cybermen, the Giant Spiders of Metebelis III and several others. Fortunately, she also omits any hint that Barry Letts' radio plays "Paradise of Death" and "The Ghosts of N-Space" are admissible as canon.]

- *K9.* Just as loveable as he was in the 70s [precisely *how* loveable that is remains a matter of personal taste], but working even less well this time. He's quite willing to let himself be blown up for Sarah's sake, and objects to being called 'shooty-dog thing'. The revised K9 has omniflexible hyperlink facilities.

Here K9 Mk III [first seen in "K9 and Company"] is blown up while eradicating the Krillitanes. At story's end, Sarah is given a new model, who tells her that the Doctor 'rebuilt me'. [This suggests that the Doctor rapidly refurbished the destroyed one, but as this scene was originally scripted to be immediately after the explosion in the ruins of the school, we'll assume he had a new one handy. This suggests that he knew he could let the previous one get blown up, which is a bit callous and less daddy's-got-something-in-his-eye. (In the online material, it appears that the sonic lipstick and scanner-watch were hidden somewhere on the new K9's person in case Sarah wanted to maybe resume alien-hunting and get her own show. The new K9 and Sarah next appear in *The Sarah Jane Adventures* pilot, "Invasion of the Bane".]

- *Torchwood* seem to be blocking Mickey's attempts to hack into army records related to the Krillitanes' activities. [Quite why they would be doing this is baffling, as it's not as if anyone else who might be interested is going to survive investigating for themselves (unless they're professionals like Our Heroes). Maybe they think they can cut a deal with the aliens, just as the Department of Education seems to have done.

[One possibility is that this is Captain Jack trying to warn the Doctor, who he knows will only respond to a clue like this if he is hit over the head with it week after week ("Boom Town"). In which case, it may only be Mickey that's getting this message...]

The Non-Humans

- *Krillitanes.* A species who collect the genes of their conquests and add anything they fancy from them to their own phenotype. Since invading Bessan, ten generations back, they have had the vaguely bat-like form. Mr Finch introduces himself as 'Brother Lassa' and refers to the other Krillitanes as his brothers [though it's not clear whether this is a biological or social reference]. In a previous encounter with the Doctor, they were roughly humanoid, but with giraffe-like necks. Now, their essential shape is as eight-foot gargoyles, with leathery wings, claws and hippo-like lower jaws. They tend to be pale, although the one masquerading as 'Mr Wagner' is noticeably darker [just as in human form, he presents as Afro-Carribean]. They can spend long periods disguised as humans, with sharp suits (for the teachers) and the appropriate overalls (for dinnerladies). They normally have to drop the pretence

School Reunion

Why the Great Powell Estate Date Debate?

continued from Page 279...

TW: "Fragments"), but the two don't formalise their relationship until...

TW 2006 Owen Harper is recruited to Torchwood Cardiff (*TW*: "Fragments") a mere two weeks before...

March(ish) 2006: Rose returns home a year after she left, and the Slitheen crash a spaceship into Westminster ("Aliens of London").

September/October 2006: "Margaret Blaine" causes the time-rift to open in Cardiff ("Boom Town").

Christmas 2006: The Guinevere 1 probe reaches Mars, causing everyone with A+ blood to stand on a roof. A spaceship arrives over London and Harriet Jones is eventually deposed after opening fire on it with secret weapons ("The Christmas Invasion"). Her fall from power is protracted (see **How Long is Harriet in Number 10?** under X2.0, "The Christmas Invasion".

Late January 2007: Deffry Vale School explodes. K9 Mk IV arrives. If not for Mickey's "same date" comment concerning 1st February in "Rise of the Cybermen" (X2.5), we could place "School Reunion" at any date before July except school holidays. However, the line is there and reinforced later, so we have to assume that it's early 2007. (This makes Sarah's "last Christmas" comment concerning the Sycorax incident a bit odd, if it's under a month ago, but we have to live with this.)

1st February, 2007: Parallel-Jackie's "40th" birthday, so presumably "our" Jackie's 40th. This makes "The Christmas Invasion" 2006. ("Rise of the Cybermen"/ X2.6, "The Age of Steel")

March 2007: LINDA infiltrated by Victor Kennedy ("Love & Monsters"). Some months later, a Hoix lands in Deptford, Elton Pope approaches Jackie, and Mr Saxon is ahead by a hefty margin in a poll of some kind. (A lot of circumstantial evidence, much of it on the same front page, confirms a summer date for this.) Rose doesn't see Jackie again for at least two months, during which time "ghosts" start appearing (the run-up to X2.12, "Army of Ghosts").

Sally Sparrow and Kathy Nightingale encounter Weeping Angels, and a series of messages on DVD extras help Sally locate the Doctor (X3.10, "Blink"). Oddly, Larry Nightingale doesn't encounter any hint that the man in the extras is the same "Doctor" that LINDA have been following, that the website set up by Clive (then fostered by Mickey and now tended by a kid at Deffry Vale) is dedicated to tracking, or is the same individual that the Prime Minister pleaded for assistance from on-air during "The Christmas Invasion".

September-ish 2007: The Battle of Canary Wharf ("Army of Ghosts"/ "Doomsday"). Ianto Jones sort-of loses his girlfriend and attempts to join the Cardiff-based Torchwood 3. (As seen in *TW*: "Fragments", which would strongly imply that the incidental details suggesting that *TW*: "Random Shoes" and "Out of Time" occur in 2006 - 29th December is a Friday in the latter, which was true in 2006 but not 2007 - are even wronger than the rest.)

Autumn / Winter 2007: Jack recruits Gwen Cooper to join Torchwood (*TW*: "Everything Changes").

December 2007: A light aircraft from 1953 returns to Cardiff (*TW*: "Out of Time").

Christmas 2007: The Racnoss Queen is defeated by draining the Thames into a hole dug by Torchwood (X3.0, "The Runaway Bride"). By now, Mr Saxon is well placed in the Ministry of Defence.

And now we come to Martha Jones, and more especially the peculiar CV of her sister Tish. The week starts with their dad's birthday and Martha's visit to the Moon (X3.1, "Smith and Jones"). There's no mention of Tish having any work. Twelve hours later, she's employed by Professor Lazarus (X3.6, "The Lazarus Experiment"), and the whole family's invited to the slap-up do to launch his sonic botox. The following day (apparently) their mum gets a phone-call from Martha about Beatles records and Mr Saxon's goons are at her shoulder (X3.7, "42"). That's the day of the election, which has to be a Thursday. So, either the phone isn't quite working right and routing a call from the forty-second century to the twenty-first gets it there a

continued on Page 283...

X2.3 School Reunion

in order to feed. They snack on vacuum-packed rats (as sold at pet shops for snakes) and occasionally eat any schoolkids they think won't be missed, as well as the human teaching staff [and, according to a cut scene, an OFSTED inspector]. They sleep suspended from the ceiling of the staffroom, undisguised.

The oil they secrete [somehow] is the secret of their ability to put go-faster stripes on the minds of children who eat the chips. They have, however, evolved so rapidly that they are themselves intolerant to this [see **Things That Don't Make Sense**].

Somehow, they know about Time Lords and the general lack thereof, though no one specifically mentions the Time War [they probably don't know about it, or they wouldn't think Time Lords were 'peaceful to the point of indolence']. Nevertheless, Mr. Finch is clever enough to play on exactly the right psychological notes that are troubling the Doctor at the time.

History

• *Dating*. It appears to be not long after they last saw Mickey [X2.1, "New Earth"]. The Doctor and Rose have got school-jobs in very little time, but this must have taken a day or so [even with the TARDIS, and they're getting perilously close to messing with their own timelines here]. They were there for two days before the episode starts, and stick around for another morning. [If we go with the strong hint from Mickey in X2.5, "Rise of the Cybermen" that it's the same day they left but in a different London, then the last scene of this could be 1st February, 2007. They may well have come back for Jackie's birthday and agreed to rendezvous with Sarah then. It's not long before that when the bulk of the episode happened.]

• *The Time War*. Sarah enables the Doctor to resist temptation and not 'stop the war' [or retroactively prevent it from starting] by joining the Krillitanes' plan to rewrite reality with their "godmaker" Paradigm - the fallen Perganon and Ascinta, as well as the Time Lords themselves, could potentially have been restored had he succumbed. Mr Finch, who speaks of the Time Lords as 'dusty senators', at the very least knows that the Time Lords are 'all but extinct'.

Catchphrase Counter Once again, the Doctor's in Paul McGann repeat mode. [He says 'physics' 13 times in a row, since you ask. Just be glad no one thought 'correctamundo' was funny enough to revisit.]

Deus Ex Machina It would appear that the Doctor has a spare K9 lying around that he didn't bother building for his own amusement or company [see **The Supporting Cast**].

This is where we have to put the improbable development of a fatal intolerance towards an oil the Krillitanes themselves secrete. At best, this is like an anaphylactic reaction to tears - at worst, it's like being allergic to your own blood. Happily, though, the oil is so toxic that even a small drop kills a Krillitane, so the ones at the back of the hall are just as dead as the ones who cop a bucketload in the face.

The Analysis

The Big Picture As we saw with "New Earth", a lot of people expected the 2005 General Election to be fought on the issue of the NHS. In fact, the main issue that grabbed the public's imagination was school dinners. After decades as a national joke, the quality of food served for children - and particularly the amount of carbohydrate and saturated fat - had become a matter for debate due, in part, to celebrity chef and TV star Jamie Oliver. In the usual way of these things, he had made a series where he tried to change a bad habit he thought everyone else had picked up and turned it into something of a crusade, by attempting to show children what they were putting into their bodies and suggesting healthier alternatives (which, of course, the kids didn't like as much, but that made better telly). It just so happened that this reached the screens as the campaigning started, and the carefully planned "narratives" the politicians wanted to get across weren't what people wanted to hear.

The reason the meals had deteriorated from the legendarily low standards of the 1970 was...? Delete according to taste: A) the catering budgets had been slashed as part of a concerted, doctrinaire programme of privatisation and put out to competitive tender so that the low-cost, bulk-bought chips and mechanically-recovered meat could be used (the notorious "Turkey Twizzlers" that became the emblem of Oliver's antagonism), moves introduced by the previous administration or; B) an earlier government that had been committed to increasing choice for the consumer had

Why the Great Powell Estate Date Debate?

continued from Page 281...

few weeks or months late, or there's a gap of several weeks between "The Lazarus Experiment" and "42". That hardly seems likely. If the phones reliably call at periods as long for the recipients as for the caller, this is a way to resolve this, but we know from "The End of the World" that this isn't always the case. So, therefore, Martha called her mum three times in one day, but maybe that day was longer since they last met for mum than it was for Martha. Luckily, all three of those calls arrived in sequence and on the same day.

However, the dialogue suggests that it's only four days since Martha met the Doctor. Martha's time in the TARDIS has been considerably longer than that: months in 1913 (X3.8, "Human Nature" / X3.9, "The Family of Blood"), weeks in 1969 (X3.10, "Blink") and three days in New York alone (X3.4, "Daleks in Manhattan" / X3.5, "Evolution of the Daleks"). That puts the Doctor's trip to hospital ("Smith and Jones") as a Monday, the Lazarus press-launch ("The Lazarus Experiment") as a Tuesday, Martha's flat exploding on a Friday and the assassination of President Winters on a Saturday. The morning after the election, Martha, Captain Jack and the Doctor arrive in London (or somewhere like it) and find that her telly's been booby-trapped ("The Sound of Drums").

Here we run into another problem: Martha remembers an earthquake that happened in Cardiff "a couple of years ago" ("Boom Town"), but (evidently) not Abaddon arising from beneath the Rift and killing thousands, trampling office-blocks and so on, and somehow the Election campaign has been the main focus of everyone's attention despite the various, plague outbreaks, Centurions, Roundheads, UFOs over the Taj Mahal and other fairly hefty Signs and Portents (*TW*: "End of Days"). These were all on News 24, so we can't even pretend that Cardiff was under a D-notice to block reporting. There's also a government hounding Jack for answers, despite the election.

Once again, we run into a possible snag with one line of dialogue: Winters calls himself "president elect" ("The Sound of Drums"). For an American to do that, he has to have won an election but not been sworn in (per the US Constitution) - a convergence can only happen in a period of November, December and the first three weeks of January. Why the President-elect, and not the incumbent, is sent to negotiate with the Toclafane is another matter. (See **How Come Britain Has a President and America Hasn't?** under "The Sound of Drums" for a possible way out of that.) Martha comments on the Racnoss spaceship, shot down on Saxon's orders ("The Runaway Bride"), when she first meets the Doctor, but not as if it was that recent. Jack talks about it later as something that was the start of Saxon's rise, so it can't be mere weeks ago. But if we take this at face value, then the available dates for Harry Saxon's brief term of office are shrunk to a Thursday and Friday in early January 2009. Even the bizarre election where we seem to have a president in Number 10 (because he makes a government out of members of various parties, so a proper General Election seems not to have happened) would need at least three weeks. This almost makes sense of the "Vote Saxon" posters up just after Christmas in *Torchwood*, but not if that's early 2007.

(If we squint at it and hold our breath, it's *ju-u-ust* possible to pretend that the Racnoss arrived on the same day as the Sycorax and thus shave a year off the timetable. We then only have to worry about how Saxon managed to run a campaign against a massively popular Prime Minister and cause a vote of no-confidence on Christmas Day. And why America had a "president-elect" in 2006, but that last is almost trivial by comparison with the constitutional mess of Parliament first sitting during the holidays and then starting an Election campaign for a Prime Minister with no party in under a fortnight.)

Let's assume, therefore, that Winters is just being pretentious, and that by telling the Toclafane he's the "president-elect", he means that he's "the duly elected representative of the American people". When during the year does all of this take place? Freed from the necessity of making both of Tish's pointless jobs happen in the space of a week, we could have had a period about the length of an election campaign. The longest recently was 1997, which dragged on for seven weeks despite everyone knowing in advance what the result would be (and the incumbent Prime Minister, John Major, had been hinting for four months before the official start that the campaign was on in all but name). The shortest ever was the first of two in 1974 (see **Who's Running the Country?** under 10.5, "The Green Death"), which was 20 days. Let's call it a month for now. As a junior doctor, Martha can plausibly go for weeks

continued on Page 285...

X2.3 School Reunion

not anticipated that when "choice" is between two cheap options, one bland and not very filling, the other stodgy and greasy, improperly-raised children will opt for the latter, especially on cold days. Or C) both of these, because the then-government had come to power in 1997, when the previous lot had had nearly a generation in power, and not done a single thing to fix any of it. Guess which side claimed A or B. So childhood obesity was on the rise, and the long-term health of the kids was looking shaky after a century of consistent improvement. The solution? Well, a few posters up in school canteens with the slogan "Eat Less Bread". Now look at the "Eat More Chips" posters in Deffry Vale.

It became part of a debate on the whole tenor of schooling, with whoever was in opposition claiming that the annually rising percentage of good exam passes was proof of either easier exams or coaching strictly for that test and nothing else, and whoever was in power stating that it was just rising standards unlike the other lot's shoddy record. This mattered after the then-government had spent the 1980s making schooling a market and allocating funding according to results. (The contradiction between behaving as though schools were in a Darwinian zero-sum struggle for money and parental support and being in control of at least one of these resources is one both main parties pretended wasn't there when they were running education.) These results were often misleading, or easy to "game", but with more money coming as wealthier parents (with better resources at home) picked that school and brighter kids from poorer homes getting stipends it became, according to critics, a self-fulfilling prophesy that a school with a good reputation got good results. The schools nobody wanted to send their kids to got fewer resources and a rapid turnover of temporary staff, and as *that* prophesy self-fulfilled, local authorities turned to private sponsors who imposed new schemes and high-profile head teachers. Mr Finch looks, acts and speaks exactly like one of these "super-heads" (they were always on television) until he thinks nobody's looking. Their job was PR rather than teaching, and few of them had orthodox educational backgrounds. As it turned out, in the medium term the results of these so-called "Academies" weren't outstanding: the proportion of good exam passes per £1000 of taxpayers' money wasn't much better than in the "sink" schools.

Part of the 1980s programme of reforms was the imposition on schools of a new kind of inspectorate, under the classically John Majorish acronym "OFSTED", which meant that on top of all the other demands on a teacher's time (with increased paperwork and endless tests instead of actual lessons) came a wholesale audit conducted during teaching hours. Mysteriously, this was unpopular with many in the profession, especially the experienced teachers, so the government tried to retain staff by forbidding any teacher from taking early retirement. Thus the Krillitanes eating an OFSTED inspector was guaranteed to cheer up any teachers, families or friends of teachers or anyone with a child at school (whilst the children themselves get proof of their worst suspicions about the staff).

But this is *Doctor Who*, so obviously the view of school has to be from the child's perspective. In all of this kerfuffle about "standards" and "targets" and the whole Jamie Oliver malarkey, there was an undertone of contempt for today's children. The Doctor's gag about "happy-slapping hoodies with ASBOs and ringtones" is exactly the sort of thing old people say about other people's children (their own are, of course, gifted and need individual attention). What's noticeable about the Deffry Vale kids is that they are almost all Caucasian (so this is, contrary to the fake website on the BBC's "Cult" site, emphatically not South London, Croydon or even Cardiff) and, when under the influence of the chip-fat from hell, very obedient and smart. Kenny, of course, is naturally clever and an outsider - there may be a whole new audience, but this is *Doctor Who*, and it's the unusual kids who'll prevail. As we saw in the first two volumes, especially in "An Unearthly Child" (1.1) and "The Wheel in Space" (5.7), fear of calm, clever children is something we saw a lot of in the 1960s. Kenny is, of course, calm and clever in a different way, good in a crisis and innovative. A lot of his material was cut before this went before the cameras, but a cut after shooting is interesting here: as scripted, he spends a long time laboriously reasoning that the Krillitanes would hate bells. Apart from slowing down the action and showing the regulars and Sarah Jane getting annoyed with him, it made him seem a bit useless. Instead, the final cut has him simply walking past the Doctor, who is trying to think of what to do about giant bats, and nonchalantly breaking the glass. It's classic companion activity but, more importantly, it

Why the Great Powell Estate Date Debate?

continued from Page 283...

without calling her annoyingly persistent mum, especially with Tish's meteoric career and a baby grandson taking up so much of Francine's time. Maybe not a whole month, though, so we're looking at a date for "Smith and Jones" when the campaign has been going for a while, and a date for "The Lazarus Experiment" where everyone is in awe of Saxon despite him not only not being Prime Minister yet, but there being an election on, during which he isn't even an MP or Minister. We're stuck with the "four days" comment, but this process helps us narrow down when during the year we might be looking at. (There's some evidence that the year in question is 2007, but we then have to wonder why the election everyone's been waiting for isn't being linked to ghosts, zombie-like consumers forcing Bubbleshock on everyone else, ATMOS or the various attempts to destroy Cardiff.)

Another consideration; that whole storyline starts with the TARDIS in Cardiff for refuelling ("Utopia"), apparently days after Abaddon arrived and killed everyone in its shadow. (That was caused partly by opening the Time Rift and loosing all sorts of anachronisms, so we can excuse posters for impending lectures in 2006 as freak side-effects if we have to.) If, as we are clearly supposed to, we assume that the take-off and trip to one hundred trillion AD comes hours, if not minutes, after Jack returns from the dead (*TW*: "End of Days"), then Saxon's been on Earth for 18 months or so before that date. Whenever it is. That's if Jack, Martha and the Doctor have got back to London on the same day they left Cardiff, using a wonky Vortex Manipulator ("The Sound of Drums"), which they presumably haven't.

But Jack is away from his desk for weeks if not months, apparently. Some time after Jack's return, Martha - now qualified and working as a UNIT medical officer - is seconded to Cardiff (*Torchwood* Series Two). She is also able to get the Doctor to come in and investigate ATMOS (X4.4, "The Sontaran Experiment"). There is nothing much in the dialogue in either series to give us a sequence of events here - she could go to Torchwood after the Sontaran incursion, for all we know. (She tells Jack she doesn't miss "him" much, so maybe she's not seen the Doctor recently, but that's about it.) The main reason to assume that the Torchwood gig comes before the ATMOS incident is that in the former, she tells Owen she's got a boyfriend,

and when she meets Donna in the latter, she says she's engaged to Tom Milligan - this assumes that the "boyfriend" is also Milligan, not a rebound thing with Mickey Smith. Of course, this is *Owen Harper* we're talking about, so she could be politely letting him down. (He finally agrees to a date with Tosh later the same episode, after which you can start the countdown to one or both of them dying.)

Perhaps it's worth looking at the dog that doesn't bark: the President of the USA is assassinated live on air by the British Prime Minister, who himself vanishes two minutes later, two days after a landslide victory. The murder-weapons are aliens. Nobody ever mentions this, and a lot of peculiar events that look like terrorist attacks or alien incursions take place in Cardiff without comparisons being drawn by the public. Even if the public have swallowed an amazingly good cover story, the first few weeks after the election would see endless discussion of it. The mysterious stranger briefly identified by the PM as the most dangerous fugitive in Britain, who was seen on the *Valiant* being attacked with a laser screwdriver (because all of this went out live before 8.02am) isn't recognised. One possibility is Jack hijacked the Archangel network for one last broadcast - *forget everything you saw, aliens aren't real, keep calm and carry on, no, the impossibly handsome chap you saw get shot twice wasn't TV's John Barrowman* - but this would have taken a while to set up, especially with Torchwood's technical expert, Toshiko, off in Tibet ("The Sound of Drums"). The Doctor only immobilises the Vortex Manipulator just before Jack goes back to work ("Last of the Time Lords"), so presumably the whole funeral and rebuilding the TARDIS took a bit of time and hitched rides. That gives everyone else time to get back from the Himalayas, get the Mystery Machine out of mothballs and go chasing blowfish around Penarth before Jack can make an entrance (at the start of *Torchwood* Series Two).

(Confirmation of this, in the dialogue, is that the sun comes up in Norway about an hour before 8.00am in London - Saxon tells Winters that he can be aboard *Valiant* within the hour and Martha, on being teleported there, is surprised that the sun's up. Some of you might be thinking that this is within the Arctic Circle and might thus be Midnight Sun territory, but the details of "Doomsday" - where Rose goes to the same place

continued on Page 287...

X2.3 School Reunion

shows that director James Hawes thinks viewers can be trusted to make the link, but writer Toby Whithouse thinks everyone needs it to be spelled out. The first edit patronises Kenny, the broadcast one celebrates his savvy. That's a tension running throughout this story and indeed the whole debate on education in Britain.

Here we remember *Dark Season*: one of the earliest solo dramas by Russell T Davies, in which a chubby kid (female, this time, and very like Sylvester McCoy's Doctor) unearthed a conspiracy by a new managerial team imposed on her school and got two other kids, one played by the unknown (and horrifically early-90s-looking) Kate Winslett, to help her save the world. The new leader was Miss Pendragon. (Jacqueline Pearce in a turban, absolutely not playing Servalan again - the very idea! - and her followers were all blonde and had mittel-European accents, catch our drift?) Anyway, the point was that the kids weren't being listened to as an ancient cult exploited an abandoned wartime prototype of the Cyber-King (X4.14, "The Next Doctor") and so wasted valuable time making over-wrought speeches about how the imaginations of children were a resource for teachers and not a distraction from learning. (Did we mention Davies' dad being a Latin master?) But, predictably, it was precisely this mental flexibility that the Bad Guys were seeking to harness and use as a fuel-source for their "Behemoth". This thread was irritating at the time, even though it was the main thing preventing this six-part serial being just a medley of Andrew Cartmel's Greatest Hits (see Volume 6 and specifically 25.1, "Remembrance of the Daleks").

This is worth exploring: as we mentioned under X1.4, "Aliens of London", most of this episode is pretty much par for the course of children's TV drama 1985-2012. Joss Whedon didn't invent any of this. Programmes like *MI High* and *The Demon Headmaster* made weird events at a normal school escalating to national and even global significance (and being thwarted by kids and, sometimes, one super-capable uncle/aunt surrogate that they couldn't tell their parents about) the common currency. It was the usual pattern of the schools early-reading series *Look and Read* (which is a fairly good indication of what an early 1990s *Doctor Who* would have been like, and certainly more likely as a template for a series than the TV Movie). It was a common thread in the kids' comics IPC was putting out in the 80s (see X2.13, "Doomsday" for the reference for *Shiver and Shake*), which all seemed to have at least one strip about a sinister school run by aliens/vampires etc. However, we have to admit that Davies, who is known to have reviewed *The Demon Headmaster* unfavourably in *TV Zone* at the time, was probably thinking as much of Sunnydale High as Bash Street, specifically "Earshot", the *Buffy* episode where she gets telepathy for a week (just like Toshiko in the *Torchwood* episode "Greeks Bearing Gifts", which was written by Whithouse). Until ITV stopped commissioning children's television, they kept having similar formats for fantasy adventure shows; the reconfigured 1992 Australian co-production of *The Tomorrow People* was just the most successful. Into this context came Davies' proposed *Doctor Who 2000* (see **Why Now? Why Wales?** under X1.1, "Rose") and thus *The Sarah Jane Adventures*.

It's not as if they'd not *tried* to give Sarah her own series (18.7a, "K9 and Company" tells that sorry story). There had been no end of re-appearances in the various novel franchises, with curious ideas about what she did afterwards. (In Lawrence Miles' books, she appears to marry Paul Morley, the real-life music journalist who devised all of Frankie Goes to Hollywood's merchandising and publicity, and who brought Derridean Deconstructionism to the reviews column of *NME*. See X4.0, "Voyage of the Damned" for more about Morley's antics.) The once-bottomless market for audio adventures that was curtailed when the TV series came back had included a set of Sarah Jane adventures by Big Finish, with the usual cast of that kind of project augmented by Sadie Miller, Sladen's daughter.

A couple of stray points: remembering what we said under 18.7, "Logopolis" about the Lurianic Kabbalah, it's worth considering the upsurge in interest in this subject after Madonna started whittering on about it, and then looking at the symbols used in the Skasis Paradigm. A system of ancient symbols enabling the "enlightened" to rewrite the machine-code of creation was a big enough threat to write out the most popular Doctor ever, so it'll do as a background detail for a story about Rose sulking. Oh, and the Doctor's lesson beginning with naming the subject a dozen times while thinking of something to say... again, *Monty Python's The Meaning of Life* is an irresistible comparison, with John Cleese as a Mr Chips-style schoolmaster[54] doing a practical lesson for bored

School Reunion

Why the Great Powell Estate Date Debate?

continued from Page 285...

in what has to be November, but it's daylight for quite a while - rule that out. The sunrise makes it seem that this story is in early spring or late autumn.)

TW One unequivocal date we get, over and over again, is 1918 at the start of the *Torchwood* Series Two story "To the Last Man". Torchwood defrosts Tommy Brockhurst once a year on the same day (they don't tell us which month) and states his date of birth as 7th February, 1894. He's either 24 or 114, because he's been on ice for 90 years. They say this a few times too. Hooray! So, *Torchwood* Series Two begins in 2008.

For info-dump purposes, Gwen has to ask all the viewer's questions, which means that she's not acquainted with Tommy. If he's brought out of cryo-freeze on the same day every year, it must be that Gwen hasn't been with Torchwood a whole year yet. If Canary Wharf was early September, and Gwen joined Cardiff's rump in October-ish, we have a reasonable latest date for this, the third episode of the series and thus probably not long after Jack's return. Two episodes later, Jack asks Martha how her family are coping with the effects of their year aboard HMS *Valiant*, so we might well have a fairly short gap between "Last of the Time Lords" and Martha's arrival at the Hub in *TW*: "Reset".

2008's other big events are the Atraxi threatening to boil the Earth (in what looks like spring; X5.1, "The Eleventh Hour") and the tag-scene from "Blink". This, and the pit-stop in Cardiff, happen without Martha bothering to call home. They may be chronologically before she left on that Monday.

T! 2008 When Martha comes to Cardiff with a mystery (*TW*: "Reset"), one of the patients is cited as being "45" years old, and has a date of birth in January 1962. (Unless Jack was responsible for the dating 11/1/62, and it's actually November on Tosh's screen.) Either way, this puts her arrival at 2007.

SJA! 2008/2009: Luke Smith "born" (in *SJA*: "Invasion of the Bane"), but the dating of this is tricky. K9 has been keeping the black hole in check for "18 months" since "School Reunion" - as we've said, that story probably takes place in late January 2007, so it's presumably now 2008. Contradicting that, Maria Jackson's clock gives the say as 11.1, which is a plausible date (the time is accurately set, so it's not a glitch), although it's still light out at 6pm, which isn't right for January. Moreover, Maria is starting at a new school in what seems to be the start of term (her father Alan says "next week"). However, *Blue Peter* is still being presented by Konnie Hug, suggesting that this is before late January 2008, when she ended her ten-year stint.

Further complicating matters is the alternate history in "Turn Left" where Sarah, Luke and Maria are killed in the Judoon ploy to isolate the Plasmavore that - in the "correct" version - introduced Martha Jones to the Doctor ("Smith and Jones"). There are four possible ways to resolve this: one is to discard the "18 months" line and have K9's stint as a cosmic bathplug last a year less than we thought; another is that perhaps the Judoon were delayed by a year in the altered timeline by some other side-effect of the Doctor's absence - maybe it was Harry Saxon who tipped them off to arrange Martha's meeting with the Doctor and thus his own creation; the third is to ignore the date on Maria's clock; the fourth is to whistle nonchalantly, point over the reader's shoulder and then run while your back is turned.

Christmas 2008: The *Titanic* almost falls onto Buckingham Palace and the Doctor meets Wilf. A lot of Londoners have taken the hint and deserted the city. Mr Copper takes up residence and starts quietly making a difference (X4.0, "Voyage of the Damned").

TW So if the absolute latest date for Earth's jaunt to the Medusa Cascade ("The Stolen Earth") is May 2010, we can work backwards to fix Martha's three-episode stint in the Cardiff Hub (ending with *TW*: "A Day in the Death"). This is - if we go with the dating evidence provided by *The Sarah Jane Adventures* and the subsequent *Torchwood* episodes - before March 2009. Her medical qualifications were fast-tracked by UNIT ("The Sontaran Stratagem") after she was approached out of the blue; in *Torchwood*, Martha seems to think that the Doctor recommended her to the group. At the end of "The Doctor's Daughter" (X4.6), Martha *seems* to be returning to the same flat that was blown up by the Master, which might suggest a period of rebuilding. That might have made a stint

continued on Page 289...

boys (but this is the sex education class, being treated as if it were Latin declensions). So he gives a brief, incomprehensible spiel about chits (permission-slips) before beginning: "Now, Sex... sex, sex, sex... So where were we?" We're going to come back to this (Mr Chips, not so much Cleese shagging in the classroom) in X3.8, "Human Nature".

English Lessons
• *OFSTED* (n): Office of Standards in Education. Its most notorious head was Chris Woodhead, whose own standards were questionable.
• *Happy-Slapping* (v., ger.): A brief fad for using cameras in phones to record and distribute online minor assaults on innocent passers-by. The idiots who did this failed to realise that distributing such clips was essentially admission of guilt if charges were brought (see ASBO, below).
• *Hoodies* (n): Originally the fleece tops with unnecessary hoods worn by children, adults with no self-respect and anyone attempting to remain anonymous on CCTV or happy-slapping clips. Thereafter, the people who wear these garments. David Cameron, as Leader of the opposition, was ridiculed for attempting to suggest that the kids were more in need of sympathy than punishment (a view he abandoned pronto as Prime Minister), a policy dubbed "hug a hoodie" by his critics.
• *ASBOs* (n): Anti Social Behaviour Order. A policing tool introduced under Tony Blair, allowing prosecutions and monitoring of anyone being a bad neighbour, making a nuisance, doing anything the curtain-twitchers or police didn't like but couldn't otherwise punish, and, in essence, being under 30 in a public area. The move backfired as disaffected youth began to take getting an ASBO as a status-symbol among their peers. These control orders were issued on increasingly spurious and frivolous grounds until judges and police began to criticise their over-use. One notorious instance was a woman forbidden from making "excessive" noise during sex, anywhere in England or Wales. Another was an attempted ban on suicide attempts. These orders were widely criticised as symptomatic of the Blair/Brown government's perceived control-freakery, and were rapidly abandoned by the incoming Coalition government in 2010.
• *Are you all sitting comfortably? Then we'll begin* was how Daphne Oxenford (24.4, "Dragonfire"; X4.7, "The Unicorn and the Wasp") began the story on *Listen with Mother*, the radio programme for under-fives that ran from 1950 to 1982 (the last presenter was Nerys Hughes, 19.3, "Kinda"). We'll hear it again in X2.7, "The Idiot's Lantern".

Oh, Isn't That...?
• *Anthony Head* (Mr Finch). In the 1980s, he was Tony Head, the male half of a "will-they-won't-they" couple in a series of ads for instant coffee. Perhaps through typecasting as posh eye-candy, he sought work in America as Anthony Stewart Head, taking on the role of Doctor-surrogate Rupert Giles in *Buffy the Vampire Slayer*. Returning to the UK midway through the series, he became sought-after as a voice-over artist and appeared in a number of comedy-dramas about middle-aged men trying to prove they'd still "got it". In the pilot for *Jonathan Creek*, he was the original Adam Kraus (the role being taken over for the series by Stuart Milligan - X6.1, "The Impossible Astronaut"). He was also the Prime Minster in *Little Britain*, in a set of sketches about his aide (David Walliams, see X6.11, "The God Complex") having a hopeless crush on him (the location was the one used in X1.4, "Aliens of London"). More recently, he was a regular on *Merlin*, and also appeared in the dodgy-accent-athon *The Iron Lady* as Sir Geoffrey Howe, about whom it was said that being attacked by him was like being savaged by a dead sheep. Head's a sucker for a *Doctor Who* tie-in project, narrating Radio Two's documentary *Project Who* and Series Three and Four of *Doctor Who Confidential*. He'd also been in the misbegotten *Death Comes to Time*, and the Big Finish *Excelis* series. We'll return to him in the appendix for Volume 8 ("The Infinite Quest", where he played the villain). Shortly before the official announcement of the return of *Doctor Who*, the *Radio Times* polled readers for who ought to be the next Doctor and Head won. Had the public remembered 90s ITV children's series *Woof!*, this might not have been the case.
• *Caroline Berry*. If you were a Russell T Davies completist, you might have watched *Breakfast Serial*, something he virtually improvised in the early 90s, and know that Berry's Dinner Lady seen here was a quarter of the cast of this knowingly cheap show, supposedly narrated by crockery.

Things That Don't Make Sense When "Logopolis" (18.7) did the "pure mathematics can literally reshape the universe" storyline, it was in the con-

Why the Great Powell Estate Date Debate?

continued from Page 287...

in another city more appealing. (Even Cardiff.)

Although it *looks* as if the Adipose event and the ATMOS problem (respectively X4.1, "Partners in Crime" and "The Sontaran Stratagem") happen in autumn, it could also be very early spring. The plants in Wilf's garden support this. Everyone in "The Sontaran Stratagem" says Donna's been away "a few days". That might be why Martha's phone call arrives at this precise moment in the Doctor's life; it's been as long since his last visit to Donna's time as it seems for Donna. The TARDIS likes doing that sort of thing (26.4, "Survival", for example).

TW 2009 Owen Harper finally dies properly (*TW*: "Exit Wounds"). Toshiko Sato also dies on the same day. Their passing is referred to in "The Stolen Earth". Ianto has now been with Torchwood Cardiff for 21 months (*TW*: "Fragments").

SJA 2009 A Sontaran left behind after "The Poison Sky" (X4.5) is the last foe Maria Jackson faces before leaving Bannerman Road (*SJA*: "The Last Sontaran"), so all *Sarah Jane Adventures* stories featuring Rani Chandra (everything from *SJA*: "Day of the Clown" on) have to be after this. Maria is referred to in "The Stolen Earth". The indications are that "The Last Sontaran" is during the school holidays, and Maria moves six weeks later, a convenient school hols-size gap. Rani's family move into Maria's house almost immediately (October, to go by the date on Maria's email in that story to Luke). But why should a new head - Rani's dad - be taking over a month into the school year? And why does nobody know who he is until he arrives? He'd be an obvious alien malfeasant in any other situation, but this isn't the case, so we just have to accept that Park Vale School was slow in replacing a head who vanished mysteriously (*SJA*: "Revenge of the Slitheen"). That all just about fits, making Series One of *SJA* an eventful six months for Maria and the gang.

2009 Adelaide Brooke (X4.16, "The Waters of Mars") was born May 12th, 1999, and was ten when the Daleks teleported Earth into a different part of space ("The Stolen Earth" / "Journey's End"). So, we have an earliest and latest date for that event. (The way "The Waters of Mars" is directed strongly suggests that we take the on-screen data readouts as accurate and part of the narrative, rather than an additional detail like the DOB in *TW*: "Reset" or whatever.)

26th June, 2010: Amy Pond marries Rory Williams ("The Big Bang"). Assuming that the Doctor's vagueness about dates where Amy is concerned was only a post-regenerative glitch, and that he knew by the time he went to see Churchill when Amy was from (and he gets the date right three times later that season), we have a two-year wait until this date from when the Atraxi arrived ("The Eleventh Hour").

---

text of a handful of trained, monastic professionals whom even the Doctor respected. This time around, it takes an intelligence booster, a chip-pan and a couple of busloads of school children. So why doesn't every other reasonably bright super-villain have a go at this?

But the Krillitanes are themselves, it turns out, unable to tolerate the oil they secrete. This is like a fatal allergy to earwax, or saliva-poisoning. It rather suggests that they have no clue what aspect of which conquered race they are going to acquire. That can't be much help. After all, unless the entire Krillitane race is this one party of, um, let's say a dozen, they aren't going to get back to their homeworld looking anything like the people they left behind. It could be easy to infect the whole race, which might be how this awkward allergy arose (a race sacrificed itself to destroy their tormentors). If it's an involuntary response to the planet they've attacked rather than a conscious choice, the chances are that - rather than photocopying the official boss-species of any world - they'd acquire characteristics of the most populous species. So an attack on Earth will result in them becoming like beetles or algae or blades of grass. Within the context of *Doctor Who*, this might just about get in under the wire on precedent (see **What Were Josiah's "Blasphemous" Theories?** under 26.2, "Ghost Light" and **How Does "Evolution" Work?** under 18.3, "Full Circle") rather than logic or science, but it's a serious setback for wannabe conquerors. They would seem, on the evidence presented here, to have genes that can identify technologically advanced races as the only ones with useful traits. (Then again, the technologically advanced ones would

X2.3 School Reunion

tend to rely less on their genes than their machines or culture.)

Also, precisely how many of these Kritters are there? The numbers from scene to scene don't tally properly. There are more sleeping in the staff-room than we see get killed, but fewer than we know are in the story.

Given the manner in which the Doctor and Rose obtain their school jobs, why isn't Sarah Jane Smith investigating the odd coincidences of these abruptly-hired staff-members appearing out of nowhere the day after a teacher wins a lottery she didn't enter? (Maybe she is: the scene of her meeting 'Dr John Smith' can be read as her expecting to see Tom Baker, but she doesn't react as one might expect if that were the case. But then, the Doctor isn't exactly whipping out a stethoscope and saying "Count the hearts, kid".)

Mickey's happily looking up the Deffry Vale website, as any parent might, but when he cross-references it with flying saucer sightings, a big flashing screen tells him 'access Denied' and plasters the word 'Torchwood' in red capitals. If anyone was looking into such things, being told to go away like that is exactly the sort of confirmation they'd want, and has the added bonus of telling the wannabe Mulder the name of the officially non-existent organisation in charge of that kind of thing. (Nice going, Yvonne.)

Most versions of GCSE Biology have the option of doing dissections, so it's not as ancient and neglected a practice as Rose seems to think. It's just not compulsory these days. Two days as a dinner lady, and Rose knows the entire layout of the school. (Some teachers take months.) After a whole day with chips, she goes off with the Doctor and Sarah and eats... chips. (No wonder the Doctor suspects she might be pregnant at the end of "Doomsday".)

An old standby, but one that will persist until viewers protest en masse: how exactly does chucking a chair at a screen destroy an evil super-computer?

Why does Mickey's cyber café have a copy of Jacob Bronowski's *The Ascent of Man*? It's a perfectly fine book (and the original TV series was magnificent), but why's it there? It appears that nobody involved in making this episode has been to a London cyber-café. Almost all of these will have plywood booths, posters for cheap international calls (which was the stock-in-trade of most of these places until mobiles caught on and the Internet became fashionable), overpriced chocolates and soft drinks and a clientele of lary teenagers who would steal anything not nailed down. Even books.

The finale makes less sense than the rest of it put together. This school's doing terrible things to children, making them all brainy and well-behaved. When the school blows up, all these Stepford Sprogs get really excited and praise Kenny to the skies for engineering the fatal explosion that's killed the entire staff. If they think he's so cool suddenly, shouldn't they be using what's left of their super-smarts to hide him from the police rather than jumping up and down like four year olds and chanting his name? If the argument is that the kids are free of an evil enchantment that made them good at maths (heaven forbid!), then what is there in the explosion that undoes a chemical reaction to oil in chipfat affecting their brains?

Finally, to judge by Sarah's memories, apparently "The Five Doctors" (20.7) is no longer in the canon, but "K9 and Company: A Girl's Best Friend" is. As the tin dog once said, "Your silliness is noted".

Critique Maybe it's significant that the most memorable sequences were rethought on location almost on the spot: the confrontation at the pool; Sarah's first glimpse of the TARDIS in the gym; the farewell in the park. It might be important that the bad guys in this story, who seem to see children as a resource or occasional snack, get more lines than the children - as if the author of the script agrees that they should be seen and not heard. It might be worth noting that the Doctor takes Sarah's hand rather than Rose's when they are running for their lives. All of these things, and the cut mentioned in **The Big Picture** seem to suggest the same thing: director James Hawes has a very different idea about what this story's about than the writer did. Toby Whithouse, for all the research he did watching a few old episodes, thinks that this is about Rose facing up to the Doctor discarding her rather than about Sarah getting back into the swing of things or Kenny seeing further than the grown-ups. Hawes, with the finished script (now containing Mickey) as his starting-point, thinks that this is about the Doctor taking responsibility for everyone's lives, if not always as carefully as he might.

This is what redeems the episode. In the commentaries and back-up literature, there is a sense that everyone else involved in making this thinks that Mickey's quip about "the missus and the ex" is the heart of the story. They honestly think that *Doctor Who* aspires towards being *Dynasty* and ought to have cat-fights in wet mud once a year. And they think that they can misrepresent the 70s episodes in that light. On screen, we get a different approach, with the Doctor acting as father-confessor to his present and past companions, despite being simultaneously the problem they face and the person they go to with it. Tennant's beaming pride in the shot (again, added on the day and not scripted) of the Doctor in the corridor watching Sarah as she leaves is the hallmark. She disappoints him later by having not got on with her life, and he shows her how to resume her old ways. *That* is the happy ending, not Rose and Sarah buddying up or Mickey finally coming aboard the TARDIS full-time (for a bit). It's why we landed up with the only TV series to have a middle-aged woman as an action-hero, made explicitly for children and in many ways being more like *Doctor Who* as it used to be than the Welsh version. It removes the Doctor from the category of "boyfriend" to that of "lifestyle", where he belongs.

Set against this augmented team is Brother Lassa and his gang. Anthony Head makes the most of the inspiration to move like a predator, with that curious turn-on-his-toes movement and the erect squatting on the balcony. He is quietly assured, making Tennant return his serve in the pool scene. Eugene Washington (as a Krillitane / Mr Wagner) follows suit and is if anything more sinister. This just makes the dinner-ladies seem more peculiar, as they move and talk like, er, dinner-ladies. Everyone else - at least everyone over 15 - is pitch-perfect, especially the older teacher in the brief scene in the staff room. This brings with it one huge problem.

With Mickey coming to the fore, K9 saving the day, Sarah standing up to Mr Finch and Kenny becoming a hero, what is there for Rose to do but sulk? Her plot function vanishes once Sarah's in the story and, catty remarks aside, she is utterly redundant. Mickey's been the audience-identification character at least since Christmas, and for some viewers since "Boom Town", so Rose simply gets to say all the nasty things Whithouse thinks it would be funny for her to say and, at the end, grudgingly accepts that she can't stop Mickey joining them on their travels. Add Mr Finch to this, and it's hard to see what they thought Rose would be doing other than lurking in the background of scenes. She's barely missed. On top of this, Tennant's fannish enthusiasm for scenes with Sladen make it seem as though the Doctor's relieved to have a grown-up to talk to. This wasn't what Whithouse had in mind. He has so little invested in the returning characters that he bumped off K9 in the early drafts. The dialogue may *say* that Rose wouldn't just be left behind (unlike Sarah or Jo or Leela), but the whole of the rest of the story makes her seem like Generic Companion Girl - the one thing Davies said would never happen. It's not Billie Piper's fault - who else could make going undercover as a dinner-lady seem exciting? - but Whithouse underestimated how much Tennant and Sladen would look like a long-established team.

What else? Oh yes, the plot. A scheme such as this, to rewrite the cosmic machine-code using the stolen brilliance of illegally augmented children, is a season-finale-worthy idea, not to be frittered away as background to a throwaway episode. The Doctor walking into a classroom as a supply teacher is a start of a better story about a class of kids saving the Earth (imagine what Matt Smith could do with a scenario like that). K9 is used as much as they dare, but should either have been back properly or not included at all. If they've removed "The Five Doctors" from Sarah's past, and rewritten her opinion of the Doctor to retroactively turn her into Rose but from the 70s, they could easily have removed "K9 and Company" too.

So far this year, they've not made an outstanding episode, but they've made competent ones that differ from each other enough to make the series as a whole special. Oddly, this is very like Sladen's first year in the series. Then, it was a policy of putting *Doctor Who* on autopilot while the producer and script-editor set up their escape-plan, *Moonbase 3*. Now, this caution is trying to get the series re-established as a staple for the long haul, after a first year when they thought they might only get the one shot at it. But if they didn't do something spectacular and brave soon, they wouldn't deserve a third series. Apart from the slightly wonky balcony scene, nothing goes really wrong here, and Hawes has made a fairly routine script work a lot better than it ought to have done, but...

.... sorry, but it has to be done...

B Minus - Must Try Harder.

X2.3 School Reunion

The Facts

Written by Toby Whithouse. Directed by James Hawes. Viewing figures: (BBC1) 8.31 million, (BBC3 repeats) 0.6 and 0.4 million. BBC1 had AIs of 85%, but on BBC3 this was up a notch, at 89%. BBC3 viewers are notoriously easily pleased, though.

Repeats and overseas promotion Klassentreffen, L'ecole des retrouvailles.

TARDISode Mickey's in a cyber-café and looking into UFO sightings over a comprehensive school. Suddenly, his access is blocked and a big red flashing sign says TORCHWOOD. So he rings Rose.

Production

More by luck than judgement, all three stories to be made in Block One saw the return of popular female characters. However, whilst Davies had created Harriet Jones and Cassandra - and they had been in Series One, so were known to virtually everyone watching Series Two - Sarah Jane Smith was the first character to be brought in from pre-2005. However, this story was not originally to have been part of Block One. Neither was it set in a school. And Mickey wasn't in it at all.

It was also touch and go if K9 would be in the finished episode. Although Davies and Collinson were desperate to have the robot in the story, the rights were a minefield. Bob Baker and Dave Martin, authors of K9's first appearance in "The Invisible Enemy", had retained the copyright and had been touting a series for children about their character. Just as it looked as if they had a glimmer of interest, Doctor Who had come back and clouded the issue. Baker had, by this time, co-written the scripts for three of the Oscar-winning Wallace and Gromit shorts animations (one of which, A Close Shave, had a cyber-dog called Preston). Although he and Martin (who died in 2007) had agreed to the design of the robot being used for commercially available radio-control replicas (one features as Vince's birthday present in Queer as Folk, and is seen ferrying a drinks-tray later), the negotiations were ongoing. Perhaps for this reason, the early drafts of the script all ended with K9 being blown up.

• Elisabeth Sladen had been appearing as Sarah Jane Smith in a series of Big Finish audio adventures, so her cooperation was rather easier to secure. Enough time and other jobs had come and gone for fears of typecasting to be largely irrelevant. Indeed, when Collinson and Davies asked her to dinner, Sladen wasn't sure if they intended a cameo or a different role entirely. By now, there was a working version of the storyline that they could pitch her, although the specifics were still being worked out. The scene where Sarah trumps Rose with the Loch Ness Monster ("Terror of the Zygons") was the result of conversations Whithouse, Collinson and Davies had later on. It would originally have continued with Sarah adding the detail of the Skarasen's halitosis.

• Toby Whithouse had written Attachments (archetypally modish BBC2 twentysomething series, a bit like This Life - this time with computers instead of lawsuits, hence the title) and had created a hospital-based drama, No Angels. As the title suggests, this was both a rebuttal of the usual nurses-with-emotional-problems format (as in the 70s BBC soap Angels, see Volume 5) and shifted the emphasis onto their off-duty misbehaviour, with a soundtrack of obscure 60s Soul records. Jo Joyner (X1.12, "Bad Wolf") had been one of the four nurses and Derek Riddell (X2.2, "Tooth and Claw") was the doctor they all seemed to land up chasing. Whithouse had also been an actor, with a part in Bridget Jones' Diary, a semi-regular gig in House of Elliott and playing what can only be described as a Time Lord in Goodnight Sweetheart. His first idea for a story was an isolated station of some sort that Sarah and the Doctor's party would investigate; an army base, a remote village or somesuch. Collinson pitched in with the idea of Rose and Sarah acting as if the Doctor was romantically involved with them both and feuding for most of the story. Davies, for reasons we spelled out in **The Big Picture**, was attracted to the idea of making it a seemingly ordinary school and tying it to the debate on healthier school dinners. This seemed to make everything else work, but caused one logistical problem and one extra requirement...

• The best place to shoot a story set in a school is a school. While it was unclear how the flying aliens would be achieved, the option remained that they would rig harnesses for the actors on location - so schools with high, wide, long corridors were a priority. The most suitable locations were only free for use during the six weeks between mid-July and the first week of September.

Making an episode in the school holidays moved production to Block One. Therefore, Mickey had to be in the story because Noel Clarke had films to make and an episode of *Torchwood* to write. It would have been weird had Mickey not been in a story set in the present-day before his apparent departure in the Cyberman story, and the scripts for the later blocks were in gestation (or unwritten in two cases). "School Reunion" thus became the story that brought Mickey aboard the TARDIS and was timetabled to be shot between "The Christmas Invasion" and "New Earth". Whithouse delivered the script and a few small changes needed to be made. The name "Krillians" had already been taken for computer games, there was a real headmaster called "Hector Finch" and the matter of how the aliens transform (and what it does to their sharp "New Laboury" suits) was a matter for later clarification. Mr Finch was going to transform along with his colleagues. Incoming script-editor Helen Raynor added the name "Deffry Vale". The read-through for all three Block One stories was done in July, and Collinson lived out a childhood dream by reading in for K9. (One problem in earlier drafts was that everyone, including Bob Baker, was dismayed that the dog-bot blew up at the end, but when the revised ending was added is unclear. It was probably around now.)

- The look of the alien teachers was to be sharp, in contrast to the real ones who were to be suitably functional and a bit shabby. Louise Page took the actors shopping, spending two days on a suit for Eugene Washington as Mr Wagner. In fact, two suits: each of the costumes had to be duplicated as the first day of the shoot would include the gunking in Krillitane oil, after which the suit worn in that shot would be unwearable. That first day was 23rd August, and was warm enough without the need to keep the windows closed to keep out the noise. This would be a problem later. As Collinson had finally got a holiday, Julie Gardner stood in as a regular producer, at almost the worst possible moment as the budget and time-pressure escalated. Fitzalan School was one of two nearby schools chosen, to make the school look generic whilst having all the facilities needed for every scripted scene. Fitzalan was bigger and accommodating, but Deffryn High School, Newport, was more atmospheric and slightly retro. The design team worked on a blue and green colour-scheme to make it all seem like the same building. That first day saw the first deviation from the script as the crew had made two discoveries in the recce: the school gym, originally to be the scene of the confrontation between the Doctor and Finch, looked good as the place to park the TARDIS (instead of the stationery cupboard as written), and the pool looked like a better bet for the gym-showdown, making the scene look more like the kind of thing that would happen in a 70s cop-show (*Shoestring* or *The Sweeney*) at a gangster's mansion. Tennant was the only regular needed on that first day. The other school selected, Duffryn, had provided 50 child extras. These and the three principal child-actors were restricted in the hours they could work, complicating James Hawes' direction timetable. Even by this first day of recording, the plan had been altered to put the cyber-café scene safely after the school locations were in the can.

- Tennant, now a long-standing *Doctor Who* fan in his mid-30s, was very excited at working with Sladen. On the second day, his joy doubled as K9 joined the crew. This was mainly the remaining kitchen scenes. In Season Eighteen, there had been two main K9 props, the 1977 one with all of the elaborate radio-controlled workings and a lighter fibre-glass one to be carried around and - on occasion - hurled across the set (see, for example, 18.5, "Warriors' Gate"). Mike Tucker had kept the latter, Mat Irvine the former. Tucker's team used this as the basis for a shell to put new mechanisms inside, to make a viable, beaten-up looking prop. Everyone wanted a go. The official operator mistakenly flashed the eyes in time to the syllables of dialogue, which was usually read by 1st AD Jon Older. Being an old school kitchen, the floor was tiled and the traditional problem of K9 action came back. This day went on into the night. Sladen was slightly injured, which affected the amount of running she could be seen to do: her part in the fight in the dinner-hall was reduced to rolling on the floor seeking cover, and we see her get up as K9 says "engage running mode", but not actually running (the second assistant director doubled for her in some shots). Next morning, the second school, Duffryn, became the base of operations for almost all of the rest of the shoot. They began with the science labs and Sarah's break in at night (well, under cover of a blackout curtain). The detail of the rats falling out of a cupboard was based on something that happened to Helen Raynor's sister. These two nights didn't need Piper, and the Saturday didn't require Tennant.

X2.3 School Reunion

- This being the middle story in a block of three being made in one go by one director, any over-runs on the previous episode made would be trouble and would have to be made up on the shoot for the last one, because time for this episode was tighter than usual. Of course, this is exactly what happened. As you may just have read, "The Christmas Invasion" went drastically over its allotted time. An additional problem had arisen, when the fake front of the school was being added for Mickey to drive through - asbestos (again). There was a lot of frantic rescheduling and, when Collinson returned from his holiday, he found the production in trouble. (He also vetoed flashing K9's eyes.) The computer monitor the Doctor reads from and smashes was a greenscreen. Another, in the car park, would later be used for Finch on the rooftop and other such effects. In the Maths room on 31st August, Hawes had Tennant enter wearing a drawn-on silly moustache to get Sladen and Piper to laugh at the Doctor in the "Loch Ness" scene. Next day, everyone was chased up and down corridors by poles with balls on the top, as it had been decided that the Krillitanes (as they were now called) would be CG monsters and not actors on flying-harnesses. Friday, 2nd September, the original end of the shoot, was the first time they had been to Duffryn by day, for the exteriors. The building-site across the road (another reason to have windows shut) hung a sheet with "We Love You Billy" on it as the explosion and car-crash were shot. They did one take of the fake front being trashed by the car, with Maurice Lee driving and usual stunt supervisor Peter Brayham overseeing, and shot it with three cameras. The "right stuff" sequence of the TARDIS gang (minus Mickey and K9, plus Sarah) was slightly marred when Tennant couldn't open the car door.

To complete the Duffryn shoot even though term had started, they returned on the following Tuesday night instead of a session of deferred scenes for "The Christmas Invasion". As the episode was thought to be under-running, a new scene of Finch apparently befriending a girl with no family who'd miss her was added. Meanwhile, British Telecom had completed demolishing their old Cardiff base. This was awkward, as the semi-demolished building was to have been the remains of Deffry Vale with the TARDIS in, for the last scene. The scene was moved to a nearby park in Newport on Wednesday. Fortunately, it was a bright, sunny day; unfortunately, this meant a lot of onlookers. Here, Irvine's original K9 prop was brought on. Later, the crew relocated to Da Vinci's Coffee Shop, also in Newport, for the café scene. On this day, Collinson read K9 on the take, grinning for most of the evening. They returned for the exteriors next night (after a day in the TARDIS). Almost all of the dialogue needed redubbing as loud drunks were in plentiful supply. The next day was the model work for the explosion, with other models for Block One (notably the set-piece window-shatter in "The Christmas Invasion"), the last to be done by Tucker under the aegis of the old-style Visual Effects Unit, disbanded formally a week later.

The only scenes left to do were the cyber-café sequence in the episode proper and the TARDISode. These were made over a month later, on 8th October, by which time Clarke had undergone a severe haircut, hence the hat. This set was a hastily constructed flat in a corner of the Q2 studio. The dubbing sessions in February included John Leeson returning as the voice of K9. The line "forget the shooty dog thing" had to be composited out of various takes and bits from other scenes. The digital effects were intended to resemble the Harpies from the 1963 Ray Harryhausen *Jason and the Argonauts* (which had assailed Patrick Troughton), but anyone familiar with the *DWM* comic strips for the eighth Doctor would recognise the Krillitanes as looking suspiciously like the entities that assailed him when he met Destrii in "Bad Blood".

- A few trims were made to scenes, but only two major scenes were removed. One was the reason Milo was said to have "failed" Mr Wagner. After being asked a question about Simple Harmonic Motion (which used to be A-Level Physics, for 16+), he froze and slumped onto the desk. The Doctor took him to the school nurse, who slammed the door in the Doctor's face. The other big cut, missed by Eugene Washington but on the DVD in the box set, is of Wagner being offered a frozen rat and declining, because he was going organic. Asked if there was any of the kid left from yesterday, he is told there's a bit of an OFSTED inspector, "behind the Yakult" (a yoghurt health-drink). Other than this, most of the cuts were to Kenny's subplot with Melissa teasing him and Luke, who now doesn't have any lines, trying to impress her at Kenny's expense. Rose tries to reassure Kenny that the weirdness he's just experienced shouldn't upset him and he replies that he used to live on the Isle of Man, which apparently explains everything to Rose. (It's an odd place, an island between Liverpool and Ireland, with tax-exiles and antiquated views.)

• As we saw in the last story's notes, by now the idea of a *Doctor Who* spin-off was well on the way to coming off. They'd tried it before, as we mentioned above, but the Children's television department of the BBC, CBBC, now had a whole digital channel to fill and, crucially, no competition from ITV (see **Why Now? Why Wales?** under X1.1, "Rose", **The Big Picture** for X1.4, "Aliens of London" and that story's essay). One idea floated was the breathtakingly unoriginal notion of a *Harry Potter*-style series about the Doctor as a boy on Gallifrey; Davies had to deflect the idea tactfully when the BBC suits proposed it. (And see **What Were the Lousiest Knock-Off Series?** under X4.10, "Midnight" for another version of this idea.) Instead, his original *Doctor Who 2000* pitch, a relatively inexpensive series about an old ex-time-traveller in an attic and some kids who helped him/her to save the world from Yeti in loos was blended with "K9 and Company" to become *The Sarah Jane Adventures*. But that's another story. Or 27 other stories, to be accurate (see the appendix in Volume 8 for three of them).

X2.4: "The Girl in the Fireplace"

(6th May, 2006)

Which One is This? Clockwork Robots.

Firsts and Lasts This is the TV debut of Steven Moffat Standard Plot #2: a girl encounters the Doctor and grows up sporadically meeting him out-of-synch with his chronology (see also X4.8, "Silence in the Library", plus all of Series Five and Six, the end of X3.10, "Blink" and the earlier short stories "What I Did on My Christmas Holidays by Sally Sparrow" (sic) and - to some extent - "Continuity Errors", as well as A4, "The Curse of Fatal Death" and Series 7). Some of you might be thinking *The Time Traveller's Wife*, but it's older than that (see **The Big Picture**). This is the first story to use whole lines from *New Adventures* novels from the 90s, letting the Doctor claim to be what monsters have nightmares about. We also see the first overt suggestion that a child's nighttime anxieties are going to be the mainstay of a story (by the time we get to Series Six, this will get

deeply annoying and repetitive). For legal reasons, it's the last time the ugly word "droids" is applied to automata: George Lucas apparently doesn't care about reminding everyone of the terrible cartoon series of the mid-80s. (As you will recall, we had the Anne Droid and Davinadroid in X1.12, "Bad Wolf" et seq, but the only other use was in 21.6, "The Caves of Androzani".)

After neatly avoiding it for nearly three decades, the Doctor does the Vulcan Mind-Meld.

Watch Out For...

• The write-up for this story in the *Radio Times* promised us "Clockwork Druids". To date, this has yet to happen, but the lethal wind-up automata are both a design triumph and a perfect evocation of the Age of Enlightenment. Cogs, powdered wigs, Carnival masks and precise moves... they fit in with the *ancien regime* vibe almost perfectly, and yet are just wrong enough to be effective.

• And at the root of all this trouble is literal-minded repair software. If you liked that idea in X1.10, "The Doctor Dances", you'll love it here. (And in X4.9, "Forest of the Dead". And X6.10, "The Girl Who Waited". And X6.3, "The Curse of the Black Spot". Well, maybe not in that one so much...) However, the rationale for this week's baroque time-paradox-cum-surgical-intervention is withheld from us until the very last shot of the episode, making it hard for less alert viewers (TV critics, say) to see the rigorous logic of the story.

• Rose seems really happy to have Mickey along at last. It's almost as if nobody told Steven Moffat or Euros Lyn about the end of the last episode.

• In the past, the programme's makers would be careful to avoid showing children doing anything imitable and dangerous. Here, because they think nobody has grates any more, it's perfectly fine for a little girl with long hair to stick her head into a roaring fireplace and converse with the Doctor (see **Things That Don't Make Sense**).

• The Doctor rides a horse through a mirror into a ballroom. It's obviously not David Tennant in the saddle, and when he's in close-up it's obviously not a horse.

• Unlike most modern *Doctor Who*, this story requires hardly any green-screen work. The scenes of people walking from a spaceship to Versailles are done by walking from the bit of the set with a spaceship in to the adjacent bit with Versailles in it. As a result, the costume department have the chance to use any frocks they fancy, especially on

X2.4 The Girl in the Fireplace

location. As with the sets, these are as much as anything to give a sense of the time and place, even though strictly speaking they are good copies of the re-vamped look *after* Madame de Pompadour had sold her jewels and gowns to build the Military Academy, and her various houses were redecorated to stamp the new owner's taste for yellow and gilt on what had hitherto been pastel décor. (As many of these were demolished, we only have the evidence of a few incidental details in portraits and hints in letters.) But it's pretty dresses, a horse and a palace: it's as if they were ordered to make an episode for an eight-year-old girl without having ever met one.

The Continuity

The Doctor He can tell if a clockwork robot is scanning a girl's brain. He adores the French, seems to have invented the Banana Daquiri [in a country with no access to bananas] and seems to want to rub his closeness with Madame de Pompadour in Rose's face. [Of all the songs to perform when pretending to be drunk, "I Could Have Danced All Night" is the most tactless - see X1.10, "The Doctor Dances" for why. Whether he did "dance" with Reinette in that sense is another matter: Moffat says no, and it really doesn't make a lot of sense to assume that he picked her out of all of her species. We'll get to this in **The Critique**.] He can persuade a horse he's only just met to make extravagant leaps through mirrors and, most alarmingly of all, has learned to do the Vulcan Mind-Meld. [This, despite *Star Trek* being just a made-up TV show in the *Doctor Who* universe - or is it? See X6.4, "The Doctor's Daughter" for the evidence.] He seems befuddled as to how one acquires money [see also X2.8, "The Impossible Planet"].

He's fine with being alone with a little girl in her bedroom, but finds it rather embarrassing to be in the same position with a young woman. The idea of lingering in seventeenth-century France *sans* TARDIS seems to appeal to him [of course this would strand Mickey and Rose on a spaceship in the far future, which perhaps clarifies the otherwise completely inexplicable error of his rushing back through the time portal without realising that he'll be desynched from Reinette again; belated anxiety about his companions means he's not thinking things through], although Reinette knows he'll figure out an escape route and offers him it to spare herself from forlorn hope. In the Age of Enlightenment, he quips to Reinette that she should never listen to reason. [That she was a chum of Voltaire and Diderot just makes this equivalent to telling George Washington that a little white lie every now and then isn't going to harm anyone.] Right after admiring one of the Droids' camouflage and clockwork mechanism and declaiming that disassembling it would be a crime of vandalism, he announces he intends to do it anyway. Reinette's contact with the Doctor's mind leads her to conclude [literally or figuratively] that he knows 'the name of every star' in the sky.

• *Ethics*. Forced into a Mind-Meld with Reinette, the Doctor gives a preamble about consent, what sanctions she can use against him prying and the clearly demarked parameters of his investigation. He says that he doesn't make a habit out of using this technique. [Which suggests that he's done this with humans before. He has not hitherto demonstrated this facility, although there have been instances of him reluctantly treading on the thoughts of others (3.10, "The War Machines"; 5.2, "The Abominable Snowmen"; and 26.1, "Battlefield", mainly to undo the harm done by others. We might also consider the posthumous mind-reading of the Wirrn Queen in 12.2, "The Ark in Space" as a trial run for this.] This time, the Doctor is investigating a spaceship 'stalking' [his word] the Marquise de Pompadour, and so his own interventions are, to him, an exercise in damage-limitation. [He will use similar justifications for the way he influences the childhoods of Amelia Pond and her daughter in Series Five and Six, although after it happens again with Rose (X4.18, "The End of Time Part Two") and Sally Sparrow ("Blink"), it's all looking a bit suspect. By the same token, the Mind-Meld technique becomes a bit more flexible and less consentual (X5.11, "The Lodger").]

• *Background*. He was 'such a lonely little boy' - and is even 'lonelier' now - and apparently his lack of a name is more than a lifestyle choice. [See "Silence in the Library" et seq, especially X6.13, "The Wedding of River Song" and **Is His Name Really "Who"?** under "The War Machines".] He seems to have been rather fond of Cleopatra [see 14.1, "The Masque of Mandragora"], and calls her 'Cleo'. Paris, 1727, is 'one of his favourite' years, although he thinks that August was 'rubbish' [rainy].

The Girl in the Fireplace X2.4

Is Arthur the Horse a Companion?

In "The Girl in the Fireplace" (X2.4), Rose seems slightly offended that the Doctor wants to take a horse aboard the TARDIS. The Doctor deflects her criticism with a gag about Mickey, but this masks a more serious question: from the Doctor's point of view, *is* there any difference between Rose and Arthur?

The one that immediately springs to mind is that Rose can talk, but this isn't as significant as it seems, now that we know that the Doctor can speak Horse. This was made explicit in 7.3, "A Town Called Mercy", but was first intimated in a scene cut from "The Girl in the Fireplace" (but is on the DVD). In this, within seconds of the Doctor ruefully muttering (again) about his chums and their inability to comprehend "don't wander off", a horse diligently starts following him around a spaceship. The horse in question - Arthur - met the Doctor by blundering into a time-corridor and going from Versailles to a fifty-first century spaceship; the stable-keeper, in another cut scene, threatens to punish the missing horse. So, Arthur has an unpleasant home-life, curiosity, acceptance by the Doctor and a journey in time. All good qualities for travelling with him, and enough for the Doctor to put his faith in his new friend and expect him to do something extraordinary to save someone from monsters. That's how the episode ends up sealing the deal, with a time-window shattering as the Doctor and Arthur charge to the rescue. It could be concluded from this that there's little to choose between Arthur and, say, Dodo, Kamelion or Katarina.

Evidently, this isn't going to work. It's not just a bias that the Doctor's inner-circle must all be humanoid (there's at least one tin dog who makes everyone's list) or the viewer-identification figure (on that score, most people in Britain would take Jackie over Amy and Wilf over Martha). Drawing clear lines between characters in a way that matches their status in the title-sequence (and the BBC's pay scale for the cast) with the on-screen narrative and apparent significance to the Doctor of each character is tricky. Sometimes, the stories make illogical leaps of faith to make these two match: there is no real reason why Parallel-Pete should accept a Jackie *he doesn't know* as a replacement wife, nor that she should pretend that the 20-odd years of flings and single-parenthood didn't happen (see X2.13, "Doomsday" and **Must They All be Old-Fashioned Sort of Cats?** under X3.3, "Gridlock"). There is absolutely no reason why the Doctor's response to Amy getting all smoochy is to take her and Rory to Venice rather than simply leg it and avoid Leadworth, if not all of Earth, for the period after June 2010 (X5.5, "Flesh and Stone"; X5.6, "Vampires in Venice"). With Mickey, the formal acceptance of a semi-regular character as a proper companion came after that character had clocked up more screen-time than the doomed Katarina (3.3, "The Myth Makers"; 3.4, "The Daleks' Master Plan") - and more different stories, taking a longer narrative time, than Harry Sullivan. The days of a higher authority (the Brigadier, the Time Lords or the BBC management) simply ordaining that such-and-such a person was now assigned to the Doctor were a brief blip, however much the programme's publicity suggests otherwise.

This was a problem even back when the *Doctor Who Monthly* of the early 80s ran new-readers-start-here profiles of the approved list of companions (and indeed the use of that word, with capital C, rather than "assistants" or "*Doctor Who* girls"). Why was Bret Vyon ("The Daleks' Master Plan") not on the list? Well, his visit to the TARDIS didn't involve any travel in time or space. (The Doctor, though, seems not to make that distinction in the story's final episode, mourning Vyon's cold-blooded execution as much as Katarina's suicide.) But what about Sara Kingdom (also "Master Plan")? Her only "fault", as far as any tick-box of criteria was concerned, was that she was only in one story. That simply means that the artificial distinction between any group of episodes as perceived by the viewers was the key. (See **What is a "Story" Now?** under X1.13a, "Pudsey Cutaway".)

"Companion" is a word with a curious history: it literally derives from the idea of breaking bread with someone. It has been used as a euphemism for "mistress" or "nurse" ("paid companion" was a live-in minder of roughly the same age, especially in Agatha Christie books), and as a polite way of suggesting putting up with someone on a long journey. It also has a vague sense of old army-buddies, brothers-in-arms and so on. This covers pretty much all bases with regards to *Doctor Who*, but finding any one character who has these

continued on Page 299...

297

X2.4 The Girl in the Fireplace

- *Inventory: Sonic Screwdriver.* It can light candles. It can also repair shoddy workmanship on time-portals hidden in revolving fireplaces, and detect holograms.
- *Inventory: Other.* The Doctor is packing Zeus Plugs [for the first time since 14.2, "The Hand of Fear"], but is using them as castanets. He has multi-grade anti-oil on his person, for some reason, and as he was in 1745 in a palace on the outskirts of Paris, he must have had his own supply of bananas [again, see "The Doctor Dances"] to have made Daquiris. His glasses are pulled out for close-up inspection of the Droids, and whipped off again when a pretty girl wonders into the room. He seems to have brought a set of normal sunglasses to the party as well, rounded ones with more curve than his standard glasses [by X4.15, "Planet of the Dead", he'll just be altering his normal ones to get this effect].

The TARDIS can't be used to go back and change Reinette's history as 'we're part of events now'. [We had a go at this one in the revised Volume 3 with **How Does Time Work...** under 9.1, "Day of the Daleks", but it still contradicts other time-corridor malarkey, such as 22.5, "Timelash" and 21.4, "Resurrection of the Daleks".]

The Doctor can use the Ship to close down the time windows, but only after all the Droids have shut down.

The Supporting Cast

- *Rose.* As before [X2.0, "The Christmas Invasion"], she uses what she's heard the Doctor say to try to intimidate the aliens holding her hostage, citing the Daleks' name for him [X1.13, "The Parting of the Ways"] as 'The Oncoming Storm'. She's got yet another haircut, and a slightly more vampish look. [This may be because Mickey's aboard, a fact that caused her to sulk last episode, but is now fine and dandy.] It does amuse her to explain the TARDIS translation systems to an incredulous Mickey in a slightly toned-down version of the way she treated Adam in "The Long Game" (X1.7). [Even though she's already had that conversation with Mickey in "The Christmas Invasion".] The end of the episode is the closest she comes to losing faith in the Doctor. On being told not to go looking for the robots, she picks up a fire-extinguisher and goes looking for them. The Doctor seems to have anticipated this. She also appears to really like carrying around a big hefty weapon [see X4.12, "The Stolen Earth"]. Rose acts as his intermediary when Reinette needs warning, and guides her around the spaceship. Although Reinette's attempt to engage her in discussion about the Doctor meets with a notable lack of response, she does ask her usual "are you all right" line for tormented girls.

- *Mickey* is still occasionally the butt of the Doctor's jokes - he claims Rose keeps Mickey as a pet when she objects to Arthur joining them, but Mickey returns the favour by ridiculing the Doctor's apparent womanising. The Doctor seems awkward hugging Mickey, instead resorting to a handshake. It is Mickey who sees that the Doctor needs to be alone to read Reinette's letter, and makes up an excuse for Rose to give him the tour of the TARDIS.

This is the first place Mickey has gone to in the TARDIS [apart from a lift home in "Rose" and an accidental ride in "The Christmas Invasion"] and he considers getting a spaceship on the first go a 'result'. He claims it's 'realistic' [he may be ironically quoting the USAF bomber pilot from Desert Storm]. He is wearing a limited-edition Nintendo T-Shirt [unchanged from the end of the last episode]. He's slightly less convinced that the Doctor will show up in time when he and Rose have been running around the spaceship fighting off droids for hours. Alone in a creepy, *Nostromo*-like spaceship, armed with a fire-extinguisher and hunting clockwork robots, he does action-hero rolls and quotes Travis Bickle when a scanner-eye follows his movements ['You lookin' at me?' - maybe Mickey has plans to go into movies, perhaps as stunt-double for Noel Clarke of *Kidulthood* fame.]

The Non-Humans (Severely Misguided) This is an odd one, as the principal antagonist for the Doctor is actually [ahem, spoiler alert]...

- *S.S. Madame de Pompadour*, a spaceship from the fifty-first century [there's a surprise] that has withstood severe damage in an ion storm. In its befuddled state, it has decided to use the human crew as a source of spare parts. However, being aware of its own name and the lack of a functioning operating system, it has opted to harvest the historical Madame de Pompadour for her brain when she is the same age as the ship, i.e. 37 [and would entail killing Reinette five years before history says she died]. Not having the precise control needed to get to 1759 on the first try, it has made crude temporal gateways to intersect with her life

Is Arthur the Horse a Companion?

continued from Page 297...

attributes in the same proportion as any other is tricky. We used to accept that there were rules about what a capital-c Companion was. There was a list, memorised by all novice fans. The characters the *Doctor Who* production team told us were on this list were officially "true" companions. Liz Shaw made the cut despite never stepping aboard the TARDIS and only being in four stories; Sergeant Benton, with 20 stories with three different Doctors (four, if you count Hartnell on the Scanner) and a jaunt to a different universe (10.1, "The Three Doctors") isn't counted. Mike Yates, who was with Benton in most of those stories, but never once set foot in the Ship on TV, is. The fact that no single feature (within the programme's narrative) linked these characters without potentially including a lot of others was of no consequence, the list had the status of Fact and acted as a night-club bouncer for importunate second-string characters - if your name's not down, you're not coming in.

In **Who Decides What Makes a Companion?** under "Planet of Fire" (21.5), we discussed possible reasons for this and adopted a working hypothesis that the most likely agency for this is the TARDIS herself. (Liz Shaw squeaks through this criterion by having been flung across time by the Doctor's attempts to fix the Time Vector Generator in 7.3, "The Ambassadors of Death". She was kept safe rather than being scattered to dust, lost in the Vortex or any number of potentially nasty fates - see 5.4, "The Enemy of the World" for a possible comparison directed by the future producer of the later story.) At first sight, the twenty-first century episodes have confirmed this and made it a plot-point. There's a side effect of TARDIS travel, in that passengers soak up what Rose called "background radiation" ("Doomsday") and was identified as Artron energy (in *The Sarah Jane Adventures* stories "Invasion of the Bane" and "Death of the Doctor" - significantly, these are the two episodes that Russell T Davies has his name on as writer). We've been coming across this stuff by name since the 70s (it was first mentioned as a mental force of which the Doctor has an unusually high reserve, in 14.3, "The Deadly Assassin", and as the fuel for the TARDIS in 19.2, "Four to Doomsday"). In **What is the Blinovitch Limitation Effect?** under 20.3, "Mawdryn Undead", we attempted to make sense of several apparently daft plot-contrivances and in **What Makes the TARDIS Work?** under 1.3, "The Edge of Destruction", we used this to account for a lot else. We are pleased to report that nothing broadcast since then has significantly made us change our views, and indeed on-screen confirmation has been plentiful. Yay us!

So we can reasonably authoritatively sum up our tentative Grand Unified Theory of *Doctor Who*. Conscious observers, as anyone who's had a bore at a party try to explain the Copenhagen Interpretation of Quantum Theory to them may already know, "collapse'" all sorts of other overlapping potential states at a sub-atomic level (but this has ramifications up to the level of history changing - see **How is This Not a Parallel Universe?** under X4.11, "Turn Left"). The energy released as these might-be quantum states resolve into certainties is what we're notionally saying powers the TARDIS and psychic phenomena, as well as regenerations and - apparently - Sycorax spaceships (X2.0, "The Christmas Invasion"). Travelling forward in time allows the TARDIS to absorb it, travelling back requires it to be expended. (The colour-difference in the Vortex in the 2005-2010 era seems to indicate an analogy with doppler-shift. Quite how this connects with the colour of Doctor's bow-ties is unclear, but this could be why the all-purpose orange-sparkly-pixie-dust effect for regenerations and sundry magical events turned into blue fizzy energy when Clyde Langer grabbed the TARDIS in *SJA*: "The Wedding of Sarah Jane Smith", and soaked up enough Artron to make himself a doorway for the Doctor in "Death of the Doctor"). Apart from making at least one aspect of "Mawdryn Undead" seem to make sense, this seems to combine the automatic translation facility of the TARDIS with the time-travel, and gives us a way to account for a lot of odd things that happen to Rose, Mickey, Martha et al.

Apparent confirmation of this comes in the *Torchwood* episode "Reset", where not only is the effect on Martha's leucocytes observable by evil government-backed medical research corporations, but the cause is correctly identified by Jim from *Neighbours*. The point being: TARDIS travel upgrades one's immune system in ways that can

continued on Page 301...

X2.4 The Girl in the Fireplace

at various points, including one on the day she died in 1764. As part of its camoflague routine, the ship has constructed robots using roughly contemporary techniques and available machinery. The time-windows are linked to physical locations in the ship and at Versailles, Paris and surrounding region. When the link is severed, the scout-robots are unable to return to the ship for winding-up. The ship has enormously powerful warp engines, capable of taking it to the fringe of known space or making time-corridors.

• *Clockwork Robots* are androids, with glass bowl heads revealing their clockwork operating system, when the period wigs and carnival masks come off. The wrists contain hypodermic needles. They are capable of speech [possibly relaying communications from the ship, but they seem to keep going after their transmat link has gone]. The machines have worked out that to hide their presence, they need to break the clocks in the rooms they hide in. Their power-source is a big mainspring, which needs winding up.

Planet Notes

• *Dagmar Cluster*. This is two and a half galaxies away from Earth and, some time in the fifty-first century, a ship there was caught in an ion storm and suffered 88% damage.

History

• *Dating*. The future segments are variously said to occur (in a caption) "3000 years later" after the crisis in 1764, and (by the Doctor) "about three thousand years [after Rose's time]". The historical timezones seen in this story are as follows:

1727: Jeanne-Antoinette Poisson [daughter of a financier, and born in late December 1721] is 'seven' years old when she converses with a strange man in her bedroom fireplace, in a year she identifies as '1727'. She has a revolving fireplace in her bedroom, for some reason.

Months later, clockwork robots first pay her a visit, as does the Doctor. It's snowing.

Some time before March 1741: Mlle Poisson has not yet married Normant d'Etoiles, nephew of her *de facto* stepfather, when she pounces on her imaginary friend, the Fireplace Man. [The script clams that she is 19, so it must be spring of that year.]

1744: [When the King's previous mistress, Madame de Chateauroux, dies and the apparent obvious next-in-line fails to make an impression - it being Madame de Lauraguais, the fourth sister in a row from the family of one of the Queen's ladies-in-waiting - his neighbour, Mme d'Etoiles, manages to cross the class divide by wooing the King at his son's wedding bash. Practically the whole of Paris was there, but she had a cunning plan. Therefore, the Doctor's afternoon hiding in the bushes and talking to a horse was about three months before the Ball of the Clipped Yew Trees, which was in February 1745. She was presented to the Court, formally, on 14th September, and managed to charm the Queen and avoid the *faux pas* everyone else was hoping for. Presumably, this is the day the Doctor dances with her and does things with bananas and Zeus Plugs.]

1754: Rose has a chat with Reinette, who follows her aboard the spaceship to hear a sneak preview of her future.

1759: Reinette is 37 years old, and the robots come to collect her brain whilst she is giving a ball. The Doctor saves her by leaping through a mirror atop Arthur the horse, then returns to the future.

15th April, 1764: The day before Palm Sunday, Reinette died after a long illness. As befits protocol, the King could not attend the funeral, nor accompany the body, but he could watch the hearse as far as the heavy rain would allow.

Catchphrase Counter Once again, the Doctor grumbles that the phrase 'don't wander off' has fallen on deaf ears. Rose asks how he is after Reinette dies; he responds that he's always all right. [Moffat will turn this into a gag in "Forest of the Dead," or we wouldn't mention it.]

Deus Ex Machina Apparently, the TARDIS can't go in to Reinette's life because the Doctor and his chums are now part of established history.

The Analysis

The Big Picture Come with us to dismal rainy Saturday afternoons in 70s Britain. There's only sport on the two main channels, but BBC2 has a lot of old films to while away a few hours while we wait for *Doctor Who*. One of these is the 1947 adaptation of the 1940 hit novel *A Portrait of Jennie*, which had been one of those books everyone was reading a few years earlier but - as with *Lovely Bones*, *Captain Corelli's Mandolin*, *The Time-Traveller's Wife* and *One Day* - was killed stone

The Girl in the Fireplace X2.4

Is Arthur the Horse a Companion?

continued from Page 299...

be seen with a microscope. But where do we draw the line? Because the official companions list now has a lot of also-rans who ought to have had the actors playing them getting *their* names in big sliver blocks in the titles (imagine that: X4.13, "Journey's End" could have been even longer if the credits had gone on for ten minutes). From the point of view of the production team, Jackie Tyler is a regular. She's been in the TARDIS, twice. She's saved the world and, like almost all of the BBC Wales companions, wound up working for Torchwood. But she isn't counted as a companion, even though she's got a poseable action-figure.

Just to make matters worse, if you want to say that absorption of Artron energy, hearing aliens talking English and having travelled in time makes someone a companion, then the whole population of Cardiff, who live on a time-rift powerful enough to recharge the TARDIS and who went through the whole year-that-never-was incident (X3.13, "Last of the Time Lords"), count. They might in some cases hear the aliens speaking Welsh, but that oughtn't to be a problem - it might even explain a little about *Torchwood*.

Perhaps the criterion is who is invited aboard and who isn't. This makes Adam Mitchell more plausible a candidate than Jackie, and also allows us to make cases for the following: Ida Scott (X2.9, "The Satan Pit"); Caecullius and family (X4.2, "The Fires of Pompeii"; Luke, Clyde and Rani (at least two *Sarah Jane Adventures* stories); Vincent Van Gogh (X5.10, "Vincent and the Doctor"); Nasreen Chaudhry (X5.8, "The Hungry Earth"); Kazran Sardick and Abigail (X6.0, "A Christmas Carol"); Canton Delaware III (X6.1, "The Impossible Astronaut"); and a huge motley army of aliens, pirates and Victorian lesbian samurai reptiles (X6.7, "A Good Man Goes To War"). And that's just this century - Peter Davison's Doctor ran the TARDIS like a taxi service. These people have all travelled in time and space at the Doctor's invitation, but only Adam, as far as we know, planned to move in. However, this distinction means that Martha Jones wasn't a capital-c Companion until the end of "The Lazarus Experiment" (X3.6), which strongly implies that you don't make the list until your mother has clouted the Doctor.

It also comes with the obvious problem that any list of companions that skips Ian and Barbara, Sarah and Tegan has to be considered flawed. For at least the first ten years, the TARDIS was a sort of cosmic orphanage, combined with a trans-temporal dating-agency. Before regaining the degree of control needed to steer back to a companion's starting-point, the only person who voluntarily left a stable home environment to see the universe was Zoe, and other than her only Vicki was ever offered time to think about it. Otherwise, the TARDIS has been populated by people who had lost their homes or had wandered in by accident. Well, them, and Harry Sullivan. Harry's an interesting case because he is the only time the Doctor has tricked someone into becoming a companion and not actively wanted that person to stick around. The trip that starts at the end of "Robot" (12.1) was intended to be a quick flip to shut the UNIT medic up. Acquiring a companion with malice aforethought makes the later decision to allow Turlough aboard ("Mawdryn Undead") seem utterly logical by comparison ("Keep your friends close and your enemies closer"). Conversely, a few people have declined the offer - Donna originally chose to stay at home despite the embarrassing fall-out from her wedding (X3.0, "The Runaway Bride"); Sam Briggs (4.8, "The Faceless Ones") and notoriously Grace Holloway (27.0, "The TV Movie") had every reason to go, but didn't bother. Craig Owens (X5.11, "The Lodger"; X6.12, "Closing Time") made a point of not going - the Doctor, nonetheless, considers the use of the C-word before apparently deciding that "partner" has more scope for comic misunderstandings.

So we return to a slightly sinister interpretation of the facts we posited in the "Planet of Fire" essay, and which "The Doctor's Wife" (X6.4) seems to confirm. The TARDIS chooses the level to which the various beings who travel in her are accepted. We speculated (**Are Stephen and Dodo Related?** under 3.5, "The Massacre") that Dodo Chaplet might have been an experiment in creating an ideal companion. The Doctor's giddy enthusiasm for taking this total stranger for a one-way jaunt across creation rather than letting her call the police to report a car-crash is extraordinary, but his abrupt irritation with her, and the fact that he successfully drops her off at her own time and place

continued on Page 303...

X2.4 The Girl in the Fireplace

dead by a less-than-successful film. The film isn't *bad* as such, although Joseph Cotton is arguably miscast and Jenny Jones is unconvincing as a pre-teen, but the sententiousness of the first-person narrator of Robert Nathan's lean novel is transferred awkwardly into a pseudo-religious voice-over (and it's hard now to believe that the special effects got an Oscar).

The story is simple: a struggling artist meets a small girl in old-fashioned clothes. He meets her again a few weeks later and she's a lot older, but talks about the Kaiser as a current concern. A few weeks after that, she's older still and discusses her parents' job in a theatre that closed down ages ago. You get the picture. He paints her and makes his fortune, then marries her and loses her (almost) in a drowning accident like the one he painted - except that the newspapers say she died a long time earlier. (Unlike in the film, other people can see her, so it's a time paradox and not a ghost story.) Nat King Cole had a hit with a song about the story, so the title might be naggingly familiar even if the book and film eluded you.

The film was a staple of Saturday matinees and the book was reprinted in 1998, just in time for people to point out that *The Time Traveller's Wife* is the same story less well told and four times the word-length. Moffat's acknowledged starting-point for this story, however, was the children's book *Tom's Midnight Garden*. (An adaptation of this by the BBC in 1974 was enormously successful and repeated the following summer, but the original book came out in 1958. It was done again in 1989, around the time work on *Press Gang* started.) In this, Tom Long is staying at a dingy flat and finds that late at night, the door leads him into 1911 and the garden of a large country house. He meets a plucky girl called Hatty who calls him "Long Tom" (a French pun) and seems never to be the same age two nights running. Eventually, she gets old enough to discover boys and can't see Tom any more. Finally, she turns out to be the little old lady who owns the property. Phillipa Pearce, the author, was influenced by JW Dunne (see 2.7, "The Space Museum"). We might also mention *Slaughterhouse 5* and *The Sirens of Titan* by Kurt Vonnegut, in which Tralfamadorians, aliens who see all time synoptically, mess with humans and rearrange the running-orders of their lives. (*Slaughterhouse 5* has someone who is doing this spontaneously attracting their attention rather than being manipulated, but you get the idea.)

This was one of the few plundered sources Douglas Adams was prepared to admit to having read when interviewed about *The Hitch-Hiker's Guide to the Galaxy* (although see 3.4, "The Daleks' Master Plan" and 17.1, "Destiny of the Daleks" for more obvious pilfering). Even at the most extreme phase of his public denouncements of all *Doctor Who* as embarrassing rubbish[55], Moffat worshipped at the temple of Adams. He may also have been dealing with the snag that, just when he was officially "too old" for this series, along came "Warriors' Gate" (18.5), a story a lot more sophisticated in its approach to time-paradoxes than hitherto, and with robots walking through mirrors into the past to disrupt a party. The main thing this has in common with "The Girl in the Fireplace" that's rare in *Doctor Who* is a notion of time as navigable spatially whilst still being potentially malleable (see **Are We Touring Theme-Park History?** under X2.7, "The Idiot's Lantern").

Underneath all of this is something simpler: Davies had done some reading as preparation for *Casanova* (despite how it seemed on screen) and was fascinated by Mme de Pompadour, so he put a story about her in the proposal document for Series Two and Moffat drew the short straw. Quite why Moffat, of all people, was entrusted with a story about a courtesan (intended for an audience too young to know what that meant) is another matter. The fact remains that he did some research and found the anecdote about the revolving fireplace. The clearest account we've found is in Nancy Mitford's biography of Mme de Pompadour (as might be imagined, we've read several books on the topic, especially in the last seven years). In this, she comes across as what would now be called "frigid", and in fear of losing her beloved king through not pleasing him in bed. She also comes across as having influenced many of the poor decisions that led to French humiliation in the Seven Years' War, something that Moffat is able to sidestep by presenting her in snapshots when her true skill was in negotiating the tiny shifts in influence on a day-to-day basis. Indeed, the version of her in the episode is a whitewash compared to even this most sympathetic of biographies. The more common attitude towards her is that she, more even than the more famous and interesting Madame Du Barry, pretty much made the French Revolution inevitable. Moreover, except for a cut sight-gag about Voltaire, none of her more colourful friends and protégés in the

Is Arthur the Horse a Companion?

continued from Page 301...

and leaves without saying goodbye requires more explanation than we got (3.10, "The War Machines").

A look across the whole series with this in mind indicates that there are more companions that the TARDIS likes, but whom the Doctor merely tolerates, than any other sort. Why should she do this? Apart from her own possible agenda as a complex space-time event with psychic powers, one who seemed to like Leela's mental emanations (15.3, "Image of the Fendahl"), it could be that she opts for people the Doctor needs in his life. When we floated the idea in the earlier essay on this topic, this was a side-issue, but now we find ("The Doctor's Wife") that the TARDIS manipulated the Doctor into stealing her rather than any other time capsule in better condition because she was as bored as he was. She overtly states that she over-rides his commands to take him to where he needs to be rather than where he wants. She also took rather a shine to Rory, which may be very significant in the light of what happens in the rest of that series. More significantly, she has a panic attack when Captain Jack is turned into Captain Scarlet, and runs away rather than help him (X1.13, The Parting of the Ways) and tries to scarper to the last syllable of recorded time to shake him off (X3.11, "Utopia"). The Doctor likes Jack - sort of - but his Ship is terrified of him. (They seem to have patched up their differences when X4.13, "Journey's End" happens.) So is the capricious Ship allowing strangers to wander in past a triple-curtain trimonic lock whenever she thinks the Doctor needs a special someone?

The evidence of "Turn Left" indicates that this might be the case. Donna's apparently arbitrary choice of direction seems to have been guided by Dalek Caan (who had become a sort of Bad Wolf) and Rose (who had been one), both of whom were manifestations of the will of the space-time Vortex - as are, it appears, the Time Lords via the Untempered Schism (X3.12, "The Sound of Drums"; "A Good Man Goes to War") and the TARDIS herself. We previously mentioned as a wild-card the idea that the Ship knows which people will make a significant contribution to history, despite not having been born in that time or world. Now, with at least two speaking characters (we'll leave "Sexy" Idris out of it for the moment) acting as Agents of Providence through the same mechanism that drives the TARDIS, this looks likelier with every passing episode.

That the conception of Melody Pond was allowed (indeed, connived at) seems to be definite - the idea that every other couple to have travelled in the Ship put bromide in their tea isn't likely (see **Oh, Very Well...** *Was* **There Any Hanky-Panky in the TARDIS?** under 6.6, "The Space Pirates"), and we can hardly imagine that the Ship only allows begetting within wedlock (especially if Dodo is descended from Anne Chaplet), so there has to be a reason for Amy and Rory to be unique. They are only the second heterogamous couple to have been aboard since the Time War ended, and the first is Rose and Mickey. The TARDIS had plans for Rose and may well have facilitated the whole parallel-universe and Oddbod Junior (**Bad Wolf - What, How and Why?** under "The Parting of the Ways"). Rory gets a hint about his daughter's future from the TARDIS in person. If the Ship is exploiting the temporal discontinuity that used to prevent people from harm whilst in flight (the "state of temporal grace" mentioned in 14.2, "The Hand of Fear", suggested to be merely the work of a "circuit" in 20.1, "Arc of Infinity", and clung to as the only possible explanation for the end of "The TV Movie" before being alarmingly, discounted completely in X6.8, "Let's Kill Hitler"), it may be that the TARDIS is - usually - a contraceptive. We might get a straight answer on this eventually, but we note that this only happens once the adult River Song has been aboard a couple of times. We also note that this is only after the Doctor has knowingly altered a Fixed Point (X4.16, "The Waters of Mars") and all sorts of freak events have started (**Is Time Like Bolognese Sauce Now?** under "Flesh and Stone"). Although there seem to be at least three other malign forces manipulating events for the eleventh Doctor, the logic of the episodes broadcast so far is that Amy and Rory have been vouchsafed a time-sensitive baby specifically to make the earlier stories come out right. (Allowing a small temporal paradox to prevent a far greater and more destructive one seems to be the definition of "wibbly-wobbly-timey-wimey" - see 3.10, "Blink".)

continued on Page 305...

X2.4 The Girl in the Fireplace

court get a look-in. One aspect of her life that comes across again and again in the books is that she never seems to have had a moment alone, and only when consorting with Louis does she not have an entourage of three or more visitors. Yet the version we get here is of her constantly on her own, whenever the Doctor arrives, and not just because the Droids have found windows in time that match these rare instances. If they've managed to isolate these few instances, when everything else about their scheme is so haphazard and ill-thought-out, it makes the whole story seem just that bit sillier.

(What's odd about this is that the rest of Mitford's book - the most available and readable book just on Pompadour in the UK - not only gives different dates for the events in Reinette's life, but goes into great detail about the character of the King. Louis XV, especially from Mitford's account, is the sort of character that Moffat would have put at the centre of the story if he had been given a totally free hand. The script, where he calls the king "bumptious" - in interviews the word he uses is "megalomaniac" - gives no sign of this. Because all his male relatives died, leaving him heir to the throne in childhood, he was raised in fear of his own life; a bookish, shy boy who as an adult covered it with a jack-the-lad swagger and who felt obliged to take mistresses despite loving his rather prosaic wife, simply for the sake of appearances. A war-hero whose first act after an improbable victory is to take his young son around the battlefield to see the human cost of the triumph for which everyone in Paris would be throwing parties. Mitford's characterisation of Mme de Pompadour is radically at odds with the version we see in Moffat's script, but we cannot find the fireplace anecdote in any of the books that fit with his conception of her or Louis. And before anyone asks, the Wikipedia entry that would have been available when Moffat was writing this was three paragraphs, mostly about her taste in furniture.)

Yes, the revolving fireplace really existed. It was the means by which the Duc de Richelieu (one of Reniette's adversaries in the court) used to execute trysts with the wife of his next-door neighbour, La Popelinière. It didn't end well for anyone, and was a scandal largely because her husband evicted her from her home, which was not quite *comme il faut* with the Versailles set. Being a book by Nancy Mitford, this "Non-U"[56] behaviour was unsympathetically considered and the court's view that it was worse than treason is semi-ironically accepted. That was in 1956 in a book for sophisticated adults; in 2006 for a family audience, they have to be more circumspect, hence Rose's brief mention of "Camilla" and then moving swiftly away (see **English Lessons**).

Some seven years after Reinette's death (a slow, lingering unglamorous one that makes lousy children's television), a courtier whose own grief had led him to Science as a comfort presented the latest and most sophisticated in a number of automata. Wolfgang von Kempelen's Chess-Playing Turk was the subject of a popular book in 2002, but that came at the end of an upsurge in interest in Enlightenment androids. Before this mechanical Grand Master, the French court had been presented with a flute-playing metal boy by Vaucason, whose most notorious creation was a clockwork duck. That duck was a running gag in Thomas Pynchon's long-awaited *Mason & Dixon*, published in 1997 to tremendous media interest, big sales and widespread exhaustion and bewilderment by less-self-disciplined readers. Enlightenment-era automata seemed to catch the mood of the last few years of the twentieth century, with increasingly sophisticated software making it harder to tell real people from machines, and were often the prize items of *Antiques Roadshow*. They were a visual metaphor for a knowable universe and human nature and the alleged folly of such opinions, often in pop-science documentaries about Chaos Theory or Freud. At the same time, the writings of Walter Benjamin (one of those 30s Germans in vogue again in the 80s and 90s - see Volume 6) had made a comeback and thus his use of the Chess-Playing Turk as a metaphor became current all over again. (What he used it for is a long story.) The 1770 Chess-Paying Turk was supposedly really a boy inside a machine, just as the 1730 Harpsichord-Playing Automaton had been a girl. Its true significance is that people trying to figure out how it might have really worked were spurred on to make advances in engineering and social science. (Tom Standage's 2002 book makes big claims for everyone from Ben Franklin to Charles Babbage being inspired to greatness, Poe and Goethe being taken in and our old chum Charles Nevil Maskelyne deriving his automata "Zoe" and "Psycho" from the popularity of the idea - see 5.7, "The Wheel in Space".)

Is Arthur the Horse a Companion?

continued from Page 303...

Even this isn't enough to clear up our question about who makes the list. If the three criteria are making a journey in the TARDIS, saving history from going wrong and saving/being saved by the Doctor even if he didn't want it, then Duggan (17.2, "City of Death") has to count. Besides, history's in flux. The TARDIS can't base her decisions solely on who is going to "matter" in one version of events. We have to rethink the extent to which the Doctor is the TARDIS' companion and all others are taken in by some kind of mutual agreement. He claims at the end of "The Long Game" (X1.7) to have picked Rose and discards Adam for disappointing him. Yes, obviously he likes her and is impressed by the kinds of questions she asks, but this is true of many other minor characters who don't return. If we stop looking at the series through the eyes of the official Companion, the choices seem a lot less inevitable. Lynda (X1.12, "Bad Wolf") seems to be passing the audition and Rose is annoyed; nonetheless, Jack had passed a similar test, while the jury was still out on Mickey. At the end of "The Runaway Bride", Donna and the Doctor have decided not to bother. The obvious question, though, is why the presence of Huon particles in Donna made the TARDIS pick her up from Christmas Day 2008 within seconds of the Doctor saying a "final" goodbye to Rose. The Doctor looks for certain features in people he's going to offer to take, but this is far from the whole story. The one time he ran into someone with all the requisite features, apparently ticking every box (and repeatedly saying so) was Lady Christina De Souza (X4.15, "Planet of the Dead"), and he turned her in to the police rather than let her come with him (before apparently relenting and giving her a nice inconspicuous flying bus). Did he suspect a trap? If so, that didn't stop him acquiring - some might say "grooming" - Amelia Pond, then Clara Oswald. They might as well have had T-shirts bearing the words "I am the Lure in a Fiendish Alien Conspiracy".

The BBC Wales series has set up a sliding-scale of Companionicity, from bringing your own clothes, toothbrush and stuffed owl aboard, getting your own key and officially passing the "get a phone upgrade" level of world-saving ability, down to being a relative or work-colleague of one of these exalted ones who may or may not be brought along for the ride one day. Just behind these are people who might have been anointed as worthy had they not only been in a Christmas or Easter Special, or killed in the story, or both (X4.0, "Voyage of the Damned"). The precise level of any character on this scale - from getting an upgrade the way Rose temporarily did and Melody was born with, to just being taken home after what looked like certain death - would appear to be the subject of negotiations between the Doctor and the TARDIS. This seems to be the answer to another problem. Because Blon Fel Fotch Passerine Day Slitheen never actually travelled across time or space in her, the TARDIS doesn't recognise the entity staring into her "heart" as a companion *per se* (X1.11, "Boom Town"). Thus the Ship chooses to go to work on an egg, reverting "Margaret" to infancy to begin again. Rose, on the other hand, is permitted to become a goddess and absorb the space-time Vortex because she's earned her place.

Arthur, meanwhile, is never seen again after the Doctor rides him around a ballroom. If he is a companion now, he presumably speaks English (although they would hear it as French). History does not record any such thing, although neither does it mention clockwork assassins and a man appearing on horseback from inside a mirror.

We ought to note that the Doctor's fake-drunken rant at the robots includes calling one "Mr Thick Thickety Thickface from Thicktown Thickania", a riff taken almost wholesale from later episodes of *Black Adder*. Still in retro sitcom mode, the whole robots and periwigs, *Star Trek/Alien*/Jane Austen thing is more than slightly reminiscent of *Red Dwarf* episodes, especially "Meltdown" and "Beyond a Joke". Of course, what everyone's trying not to say out loud is that the spaceship is the *Nostromo* from *Alien*, and everything else is the video for "Prince Charming" by Adam and the Ants, right down to the arm-movements of the robots. But if we're talking early 80s pop videos, it's worth dredging up half-forgotten disco-baroque wallpaper Rondo Veneziano, whose bland track *La Serenissima* (by co-writer of the memorable soundtrack to the French TV

X2.4: The Girl in the Fireplace

Robinson Crusoe that haunted 70s BBC children's television like the smell of paraffin lamps) was used a lot as background for regional TV trailers. It had a longer half-life as the music for being put on hold by electricity companies, but was soon superceded by Michael Nyman's soundtrack for *The Draughtsman's Contract* (see X2.13, "Doomsday"). The point is that the cartoon video was lots of egg-shaped steel heads of robots in powdered wigs, Venetian Carnival masks and 1780s garb playing their cellos and violas as a visiting astronaut, with no face visible through the space-suit (all-purpose Moffat Trope 4B) raises the sunken city of Venice from under poorly animated waves. This video was shown everywhere that pop videos got shown in 1981-2, but nobody seems to have bought the single. They had other attempts, and session musicians in robotic masks and embroidered waistcoats did the rounds of children's TV well into the decade (showing up on *The Rod and Emu Show* - we're not even going to try to explain that reference). The mask is said by some to look like the protagonist's in the dated graphic novel *V for Vendetta* (later adapted into a film), but is much closer to the make-up worn by Gene Simmons of Kiss - the action-figures for which were a staple of Pound Shops in the UK, where nobody really listens to that band.

Just in case you'd forgotten, the Sofia Coppola film *Marie Antoinette* came out at around the same time, after a lot of hype. It has a ridiculous cast and soundtrack and died a slow, painful death, but seems to have ended the fad for deliberately anachronistic historical dramas (see X2.2, "Tooth and Claw"). It's theoretically possible that Davies gave Moffat this job hoping to get something to cash in on this anticipated hit, but more likely not.

English Lessons

- *Cowboys* (n): dodgy, unregistered builders, plumbers, car-mechanics... an accusation of shoddy workmanship usually offered as a reason why fixing everything will be a longer, more costly job than originally anticipated.
- *Fag* (n.): A cigarette. It only applies to a person if it is a younger boy who is semi-officially a servant of an older one at a Public School (see X3.8, "Human Nature").
- *Sunday Roast* (n): Roast beef, roast potatoes, cabbage, Yorkshire Puddings and gravy. A mum will judge a prospective daughter-in-law on the quality of her Yorkshires. The scares of the late 80s, and Britain being a small island, means that our beef is now safer than American or French cuts. Mickey is more likely to have smelled this in a pub when watching a Sunday afternoon football match than at Rita-Anne's. Unless, of course, he did it for her, but then he'd've made a better job of carving the turkey in "The Christmas Invasion"...
- *Camilla*. HRH the Duchess of Cornwall. As heir to the throne, Prince Charles couldn't marry just anyone, so they had to find either a foreign princess who wasn't Catholic (there are, amazingly, still laws against that, so Princess Caroline of Monaco was out) or someone local, relatively well-established and free of any previous boyfriends. His own views on the matter were never made public, but it's significant that Diana Spencer was introduced to him by Mrs Parker-Bowles, someone in whom the Prince had a lot of trust. As it turned out, Charles and Di had very little in common so, once the succession was assured, both parties went off and had affairs. In an early example of tabloid phone-hacking, Charles' calls to Camilla were made public and those same tabloids made her out to be a vile home-wrecker and so on. It's now widely accepted that they're a contended couple - rare for royalty these days - and their rather low-key wedding got lower ratings than X1.3, "The Unquiet Dead" the same day.
- *Wind Up* (v. sl.): to tease, hoax or mislead. It can also be a noun, as in "Bonnie Langford's going to be the new girl in *Doctor Who*? This is a wind-up, isn't it?" Therefore, the Doctor telling Repair Droid 7 "I'm not winding you up" is literally true, but also means "you can trust me on this".

Oh, Isn't That...?

- *Sophia Myles* (Reinette, a.k.a. Madame de Pompadour). Universally accepted as the one good thing in the rancid live-action *Thunderbirds* film (as Lady Penelope), she had also been in the original *Underworld* film, *From Hell* and the rather less embarrassing *Hallam Foe*. Soon after this episode, she was Lucy to Marc Warren's Dracula in a TV movie version. She had also been in the gossip pages when, after this, she was seen to be dating Tennant. (There's a clip in his Series Two video diary where he has to explain to her what a Dalek is, so maybe not *that* close a relationship...) It is customary to point out that the name is pronounced to rhyme with "pariah".
- *Angel Coulby* (Katherine) is now mainly

The Girl in the Fireplace X2.4

known for playing Guinevere in *Merlin*. She'd worked on Davies' *The Second Coming* as a cop, and had made her TV debut in the notorious sitcom *'Orrible*.

Things That Don't Make Sense One thing common to all the biographies of Madame de Pompadour is that no two portraits of her look quite the same and none supposedly captured her to anyone's satisfaction. It is remarkable, therefore, that the rather more angular features of the "real" Reinette we see here not only differ from the only things any of the paintings agreed on, but show up in an otherwise rather undistinguished portrait of her aboard a spaceship three thousand years later. Evidently, the fifty-first century crew had already popped into her timeline to take photos, before naming the ship after her and starting off all the problems we see here.

We're not saying that someone close to Reinette couldn't have escaped the histories and gossip of the age, especially before she became the infamous Marquise de Pompadour, but most of the people who were good to her before she was anyone special were rewarded afterwards. So precisely who her friend 'Katherine' might be is a puzzle. Similarly, we're not saying that the BBC's policy of colour-blind casting is historically invalid, even for eighteenth-century France, but a person of colour making it that high up the social scale would have left traces. They were, after all, exciting technical challenges for the fashionable portraitists and often used as examples of meritocratic advancement by the *philosophes* whom "Pom-Pom" encouraged at court once she had her feet under the table. Which brings us to a bigger problem - this is a *Doctor Who* story set in Versailles in the 1750s... *so where's Voltaire?* Not just him, what happened to Diderot, surely the kind of person the Doctor would look up the second he found he was stuck there for a while? With these guys and their circle of chums around, making the whole story about Madame de Pompadour is like doing X3.2, "The Shakespeare Code" about Bess of Hardwick and skipping Shakespeare altogether.

We'll also tread carefully around the fact that if the dates given are right, the seven-year-old little girl with something nasty under her bed is calling herself 'Reinette' a good two years before that name is given to her. (A fortune teller said she'd rule a king, hence the nickname, but that was actually when she was nine.) And the curiously rugged, under-dressed King who at story's end is looking very good for 54, despite a suntan that would have had him ridiculed as looking like a peasant (and the lack of the jaundiced look Reinette saw it as her lot in life to dispel, signifying as it did displeasure or boredom). We know from bitter experience that Steven Moffat's response to accusations of slipshod history is to keep revisiting that period less interestingly until we shut up about it (see X1.9, "The Empty Child"; X5.3, "Victory of the Daleks"; X5.12, "The Pandorica Opens"; X6.13, "The Wedding of River Song"; X6.14, "The Doctor, the Widow and the Wardrobe"; and counting...). That said, anyone comparing this story to the historical facts and then to the messed-up transmission-order of Series Six may want to speculate on whether the sonic screwdriver has a "make her forget she has a daughter" setting. (Actually, the roll-call of missing persons not even mentioned in the script would have to include Reinette's *husband* and daughter... Alexandrine D'Etoiles died aged ten, around the time her mother stopped sleeping with the king.)

Instead, we'll consider the story's title. Reinette is able to talk to the Doctor through a double-sided revolving fireplace. So air from the two time-streams is mixing. They are talking in real time; neither party perceives the other to be going faster or slower. Yet as soon as the Doctor's back is turned, the situation on the other side switches to a few months later, with no change in air-temperature or anything. So the time-corridor somehow *knows* when the Doctor is going to chat. It does the same thing at the end. (This isn't just any old chat, then; *c'est le chat du Schrodinger*.) More proof that this fireplace is Doctor-sensitive: when the reverse situation applies, time in the 1750s flows slower than in the fifty-first century, so the Doctor experiences a few minutes and Rose observes him to be gone for five and a half hours. Why should this fireplace be a constantly open link, when so many other time-portals are specifically linked to one day in Reinette's life? The exit teleport works at some remove from the point of entry, so the ship can bring home any scouts who've wandered off or been sold to scrap-dealers.

There's a portal to the day Reinette died. The logic - bizarre though it is - of the ship's attempts to harvest her brain has been kept to for most of the story, but once they've been to the day when she is the same age as the ship, there isn't any purpose in expending all that energy unless the

307

X2.4 The Girl in the Fireplace

ship has been programmed with a "poignant ending scene for a kid's show" algorithm. Alternatively, if this was a ranging shot on the way to finding the correct date, wouldn't the fact that their target had out-lived the specified 37 years tip them off that they weren't destined to succeed? (Yes, the computer is fried and confused, but if it can make time-windows and clockwork robots, it can figure out that the windows must only get them into established history - and that if they alter it, the computer's data will be altered. The dates it has for her are about all it has to go on, so it wouldn't risk that even in its befuddled state.) Besides, *what kind of programming must this ship have had to do what it does?* Kill the crew, punch holes through history... if all fifty-first century vessels have the capacity to do this when something goes wrong with them, it's a wonder that history isn't in shreds.

That jump through the mirror: look at it from the point of view of Arthur. He was happily chomping on grass in Paris and then he was in a metal box that smells of burning flesh. Someone talks to him, and soon afterwards, he is making a leap through a time-portal into what seems to him to be a room full of people ten feet below him. Even if he's unaware of the pane of glass he has to break, and the lack of smell from the humans would be unsettling enough, this isn't a jump for a practiced steeplechase horse, let alone one trained for hunting in the open fields (Louis kept a few thousand for that) or for pulling a carriage. There's also the slippery floor on which he manages to stay upright after a long run-up and a leap down twice his own height. There isn't room for him to slow down in that ballroom, so he and the Doctor would collide with the opposite wall, unless a press of people in posh frocks slow them down. (We'd give Moffat the benefit of the doubt here, except that this scenario was the subject of a joke in the first episode of *Knowing Me... Knowing You With Alan Partridge*, and he would have known all about that.) If he is lame, he might well have been shot.

But the shock of shattering this time-link (which, a few minutes ago, needed a truck to be driven though it, but never mind) sends a feedback pulse that wrecks all the other links. The Doctor is able to return because the Fireplace was off-line from when Reinette moved it from her old house, damaging a connection that the Doctor can fix. So how is she using it in the pre-credit scene, earlier that evening? We know she got through to the ship because we (and she) can hear her voice when she steps aboard.

One obvious question is left. Why is everyone at the ball fleeing in terror from such elaborate and fascinating machines? This is Versailles in the 1750s. They'd seen automata before, hence the whole "clockwork robots won't be noticed" ploy. They were mainly soldiers[57] and a few scholars, what would today be called "scientists". Most of the women at this sort of event were trying to supplant Reinette, so they'd want to show off their resourcefulness and unflappability. Even, *especially*, if the imaginary friend of an aristocrat comes crashing through a mirror, leaving an intact brick wall in his wake, they would be keen to assert the rule of reason. The rest would be entranced and curious, and wary of traps. Effectively, the stampede of screaming courtiers is as if the Chumbleys (3.1, "Galaxy 4"), had landed aboard HMS *Valiant* (X3.12, "The Sound of Drums" et seq) and Colonel Mace and his team had messed themselves and run away. As killing-machines, these tick-tock men are about as much use as the IMC robot from 8.4, "Colony in Space", and unless you let yourself be strapped to a gurney, they are really easy to overpower. Or knock over. Or sabotage with melted candle-wax. Or melt the brass workings. Let's face it, the average wristwatch can be damaged by leaving it on when you do the washing-up, so a bucket of water, or sand, both of which would be on hand in a wooden building with lots of candles and fireplaces, could take these things out. In fact, why not close the circle and use the fireplace itself? About the only thing that wouldn't work on them is a fire-extinguisher.

Critique To return to a theme from the last review, this is an episode that's different if you came to *Doctor Who* with "Rose" (X1.1) or have some previous exposure. For the former, it's sold to us as the Doctor in lurrrve with someone who isn't Rose, and then losing her because Time is horrible and malicious. For anyone else, it's about a historical personage figuring out the format of *Doctor Who* and getting briefly involved, just as Dickens or HG Wells or Marco Polo had done, but with the added complication of a Vulcan mind meld.

Either of these is a misreading. What this is about is predestination. As a *farceur*, Moffat is prone to conceiving of events as mechanisms. He begins at the end, with the root cause, then works backwards into the more arresting consequences and presents them to us first. It's a world-view that has little room for individual choice or volition, and that's such a close match for the clockwork of the robots and the Enlightenment world-view that the story seems natural, obvious with hindsight. There was no other way it could have been. As we will see, there *were* a number of options and blind-alleys along the way, and a critical detail (why the robots are clockwork) is lost in the edit. Nonetheless, the lack of free will in the way things pan out as they "ought" is completely characteristic of Moffat's work, but utterly antithetical to doing a love story. Moffat appears not to believe in love, but thinks of people as motivated by desire and anxiety to impress potential mates. At least, this is the thread common to his sitcoms and *Sherlock*, his *Doctor Who* scripts and *Jekyll*. Any other interest, he seems to be saying, is "sad". Nonetheless, Davies got him in to write romances.

But the script is the cake at the base of a trifle. On top of it is the jelly and custard and cream and sprinkles. Like Moffat, director Euros Lyn knows exactly what he wants to do and has a plan to do it as efficiently as possible. Everyone on the production nudges their contributions slightly further than was necessary and makes this look and sound unique. Even if there had ever been another story of clockwork robots from a fifty-first century spaceship chasing Madame de Pompadour, this would have been the best one. It's a design triumph. Costumes, sets, props, effects, music and cinematography all make this special.

So why doesn't it stand up to repeated viewings as well as others this year? Part of it may be that precise match of the literal-minded computer and the Age of Reason. Even the Doctor coming out of Reinette's nightmares and through a mirror on horseback isn't enough of a disruption to this neat, all-embracing, inescapable mesh. Moffat is on the side of the clockwork. Once you know why everything happens, the result is like a crossword puzzle someone's already done, or hearing a joke the second time. The episode is made to unfold in time, but is planned almost like a building. The same metaphor is at work in the very nature of the story, with Reinette's life being navigable. Other stories this year have odd turnings and cul de sacs, so they still have surprises and items of interest on later viewings. This story, once seen, has fewer toe-holds. It's entirely self-contained. On a return engagement, you see this story the way Moffat did when writing it, and reviewing seems oddly like marking his homework.

There are other oddities. Rose, as with Moffat's last story, seems to be there not so much as audience-identification but as author's commentary. She has no real purpose other than encouraging Mickey to disobey the Doctor and wander off, thus getting captured so she can make more sarcastic comments and get rescued. She briefly serves as a foil to make Reinette seem formidably sharp, and then to throw around lines about how brilliant the Doctor is. Part of this may be another result of being ordered to make a story about a one-off encounter with the smart guy's dream-woman, but coming straight after *another* story where the Doctor sidelined Rose for someone more interesting and three episodes after Rose was possessed by someone more fun, it makes every scene in subsequent episodes where she and the Doctor go on about what a great team they are seem like the writers trying to persuade us everything's all right.

There's a thin line between being clever and being clever-clever. This story is just on the right side of that line, and the production is sumptuous enough, with only the King miscast and one or two set pieces that work each time, but it's best left alone for long periods between rewatches. It won awards, but it's one to admire rather than like.

The Facts

Written by Steven Moffatt. Directed by Euros Lyn. Viewing figures: (BBC1) 7.9 million, (BBC3 repeats) 0.7 and 0.4 million. AIs 84%, and one point higher on BBC3.

Repeats and overseas promotion La cheminée du temps, Das Madchen im Kamin.

TARDISode Solar flare activity in the Dagmar Cluster leaves a ship paralysed. Something stalks up on the crew as they try to send an SOS. Then we cut to an ormolu clock on a marble mantlepiece.

Production

In the Tone Meetings for "The Empty Child" and its sequel, the key word was "Romantic". Steven Moffat instead wrote a farce riddled with anachronism and scary moments, but no deaths.

X2.4 The Girl in the Fireplace

Hope triumphed over experience as Davies gave Moffat what was billed as "*Doctor Who*'s first love story", rather than anything with cool monsters like werewolves or Cybermen. Given the task of writing a story where the Doctor meets Madame de Pompadour, Moffat hit the books. Apart from the details of the revolving fireplace and the Chess Playing Turk (Davies' contribution, although Moffat was under orders not to make the story all about these), his starting-point was that the Doctor was perfectly capable of falling in love but not necessarily lust; the historical Reinette was less keen on sex than might have been expected of a courtesan, but had been trained to beguile a King. She thus had exactly the accomplishments and outlook to provide Rose with severe competition. But, being aware that a lot of the target audience would be bored silly by a love-story with posh frocks, Moffat put in a spaceship, a horse and time paradoxes. He also claimed that he wrote it with a vague impression that Sophia Myles could be cast (his rather drooling descriptions of 19-year-old Reinette could be read that way). It was, he said, the *Glenn Miller Story* approach to biographical drama.

There were amendations along the way. It was impressed upon Moffat that Rose wasn't as keen on Mickey coming along in the TARDIS as the early drafts said, and a whole set-up of Reinette remembering a visit that, for the Doctor, hadn't happened yet was dropped. Rose was to have offered Reinette a gemstone that could remove the anachronistic visits of the robots and Doctor from her memory. Instead of us simply hearing that the TARDIS had closed all the time-windows, the Doctor was to have used his key, as per 13.3, "Pyramids of Mars". The Doctor was to have been genuinely drunk when he rescued Rose and Mickey, until Davies requested that this be changed. One issue that was debated at length was whether the Mind-Meld affected Reinette and made her "ready" for the Droids to harvest.

- The decision to go for a fully CG werewolf in the other Block Two story, X2.2, "Tooth and Claw", made it obvious that the androids would have to be physical, containing actors. Until fairly late on, the machines were to have been faceless, with wigs over the glass heads or simply a dark void. Neill Gorton thought that a slightly-too-large leering mask would be more effective, and Collinson believed that the lack of a mask made the robots-with-wigs look like Cousin It from *The Addams Family*. Peter McKinstry's design for the spaceship exterior emphasised the similarity to a giant key turning.

- The shoot was efficient and almost faultless. It took three weeks, from 6th to 27th October, 2005, running concurrently with some of "Tooth and Claw". The first item to be shot was rain, against a black screen, to add to the high shot of the funeral cortege. This was in the day at HTV studios for werewolf transformations and gunshots, 6th October. Almost a week later, on 12th, Myles joined on a day on location at (guess where) Tredegar House. Her first scene was the two-hander with Piper. (There was a notion for Rose to go undercover in a period dress.) Meanwhile, the POV shot of the Doctor watching the hearse was taken upstairs, to have that rain added in post-production. (The window wasn't real either.) The day after, Jessica Atkins (as the young Reinette) went, with Tennant, to Q2 to record the earliest meetings of Reinette and the Fireplace Man. The Q2 sets, as mentioned above, were both the spaceship interior and the various rooms where Reinette lived, and so many of the individual components had to be struck and moved around to make different parts of both venues. (Bear this in mind for later.)

The hours Atkins could work were, of course, limited, so a lot of this day was concentrating on her scenes first and then as much as possible of the tussle with the Clockwork Man (Paul Kasey, predictably). This involved safely spinning around on the fireplace, as well as the complexities of switching between Kasey in costume and prop clockwork droids from Millennium Effects. It was a physical fireplace as part of the combined spaceship/France set. The revolve was done by stagehands, but Tennant managed to make it look as if the Doctor was doing it. The CO_2 pumps were among the most costly things in the shoot. They completed the young Reinette scenes the next day and introduced the 19-year-old version to the Doctor.

- Tennant had worked with Myles once before, on an episode of the wartime crime drama *Foyle's War*, and she had seemed to him a bit stand-offish. (She had been doing an intense scene that day.) Piper reassured him that she was all right, really, and so he and Myles snogged on camera. Also that day were the TARDIS arrival scenes and thus Noel Clarke's first work on this episode. For continuity, as they were *still* working on Block

One, he had to keep his hair as it had been. That was Friday, and there were various *Children in Need* events over the weekend, so on Monday, some of the small over-runs on the spaceship scenes were taken care of before handling the freezing of Repair Droid Seven. This took a lot of hair-gel and time, and required both Kasey in costume and the prop-droid again. Tuesday was the Doctor's day to pretend to be drunk: this was debated long and hard by all concerned. Moffat wrote it as the Doctor genuinely drunk, but Davies wasn't keen. Tennant did both at once; either the Doctor was *acting* drunk or he genuinely was but had the ability to sober up in seconds. Here is where the end scene of the time-windows being shut down were to have been made, and the Doctor would have read the letter on the bridge of the ship. Sophia Myles and Ben Turner (as King Louis) were at Sixth Form college together, and he knew Noel Clarke socially. He had been called in earlier to do make-up tests for ageing. Back on location on 20th, the crew went to Dyffryn Gardens for the exterior. Here, the scene with Arthur's owner (Phylip Harries, who was paid for his work even though it was cut) was shot along with the material of Katherine and Reinette discussing the latter's chances with the King. This was also the day Lady Isobel looked out of her kitchen window at Torchwood House to see monks (in "Tooth and Claw", the scene shot at Dyffryn) and, in case the weather turned and the planned sequences weren't possible, Clarke and Piper were along to salvage something from the day if they landed up going indoors. (The scene they had in mind was the shot of the TARDIS crew observing Reinette in peril and confronting the female droid. This was made on the following Monday.) The next two days were spent at the ballroom, where Myles continued to wear the gold dress sourced by Louise Page, previously worn by Helen Mirren in *The Madness of King George*.

• There are obvious problems with getting a horse into a ballroom, quite apart from making one jump through a mirror into such a space. The team had found a real ballroom in a genuine stately home (Ragley Hall, Warwickshire) which had a no horses policy. Strangely, it was only in the final preparations for recording this episode that anyone had any doubts about the horse-through-the-mirror sequence. Moffat hastily compiled alternatives, including the Doctor alone somersaulting through the mirror and discussing good and bad times for horses to shy. In this revised version, the horse ran into the TARDIS in fright and Mickey had to fetch a shovel. Moffat rather warmed to the idea of the horse as a semi-regular feature, along the lines of Kamelion (see Volume 5) and cited the scooter in "The Idiot's Lantern" as a comparison. Instead, they went with the original idea. An ingenious compromise was thought up involving a trolley with a saddle for Tennant in close-up, a green-screen shot of a horse jumping, matting Tennant's face onto the professional rider and making all of this work against footage of the ballroom. (To Moffat's annoyance, the *Radio Times* published their behind-the-scenes photos before transmission of the episode.) The choreography for the ball was handled by Ailsa Berk, and the number of extras was bulked out by multiple shots with a locked-off camera.

• The Dyffryn House location interior for the castle room was reconstructed in Q2 for some of the mirror sequences. This was also where they used the revolving fireplace into a different bedroom. Because by now some of the Versailles and Paris sets had been struck and bits re-used elsewhere, the end meeting with the King was remounted and set in the castle room. The graphics department had translated Reinette's last letter to the Doctor into French and written it in copperplate for Tennant to be holding. It was decided to allow us to know what the message said fairly late on, and the scene of the Doctor reading it had been moved from the bedroom with the fireplace to aboard the TARDIS, with Myles (who had recorded it as her last work on the episode) played back over the speakers in the set. That TARDIS scene would come later, but first there was the business of the horse in the spaceship and finishing off the mirror-jump...

• The first of the two horses used really was called Arthur. He was a show-jumper and was used for a location green-screen version of the mirror-jump (shot at Chepstow, on the Welsh border, at a facility owned by former Olympian David Broom). This was a problem for Tennant, as horses set off his allergies. His stunt-rider was Peter Miles (no, not *that* one... 12.4, "Genesis of the Daleks" et al). This was Wednesday 26th, and apparently Myles was needed for an unused scene of Reinette riding off with the Doctor on Arthur. The following day, in amongst finishing the TARDIS scene, an Arthur look-alike, Bolero, was used in the studio (being better at handling confined spaces). Tennant had sugar-lumps in his pockets, so the horse followed him happily. Relatively happily. It took a lot of takes, although the shot of Tennant holding his hand up to stop the horse was fine; that's the way Bolero was trained to halt. This was at the end of the shoot, on 27th October. Also that day, the reverse of the mirror sequence, with Tennant, Piper and Clarke (and Bolero) were made, shot from almost side-on so we can't see the absence of Myles and Turner. The following week, the huge Block Three began in London, so everyone took time out. Clarke finally got his hair cut, Tennant and Myles went to the theatre. By now, the gossip columns were taking interest in the new Doctor, over a month before his official debut.

• In the post-production, a lot of effort went into covering the absence of the "Have you seen a horse?" scene. A few trims for timing were made, notably one where, after literally crashing the ball, the Doctor mistakes someone in a wig for Reinette and finds that it's Voltaire. (Even as scripted, the great wit and scholar never got a line in this story.) Davies did most of the promotional stuff for this episode, and after the success of "Are You My Mummy" attempted to suggest that "Tick Tock" would be a catch-phrase in school laygrounds (it wasn't). His pitch was now that Moffat was the king of scary. That's going to cause problems later on...

X2.5: "Rise of the Cybermen"

(13th May, 2006)

Which One is This? An entirely new creation-story for the second-most-iconic *Doctor Who* monsters is used as a backdrop for Rose whining about her dad again. London's got Zeppelins and oak-trees have leaves on 1st February - so someone's obviously decided that after 20 episodes, it was time to do a parallel universe story.

Firsts and Lasts This sees the debut of the new-look Cybus Industries Cybermen. And this is the first time a director from the old days comes back to play with all the new toys. This is also the first episode this century not to have a "Next Time" instalment (because it was already over-running). The cover of the *Radio Times* was given over to the returning monsters as part of a promotional push for magazine and programme alike that resulted in (drum-roll, please) the first-ever ITV commercial for the *Radio Times*, and thus the first legitimate *Doctor Who*-themed advert since the glory days of Weetabix cards of the 70s.

Watch Out For...

• Tom MacRae, this story's writer, was 24 when this was made. His only clear memory of *Doctor Who* was "Silver Nemesis" (25.3). All the various people who were in a position to say something about his scripts seem to have clasped their hands, tilted their heads and sighed "aww... *bless*" when he proposed a deranged, wheelchair-bound creator for the Cybermen. Nobody, not even director Graeme Harper (whose last work on the series was, um, 22.6, "Revelation of the Daleks"), had the heart to tell him about Davros.

• Inevitably, the *plus-ca-change* parallel universe story has fun with the regular cast playing variants of their usual selves. Jackie's a right cow, Pete's a dodgy tycoon, Mickey's an action-hero and Rose is Toto. The TARDIS even goes over the rainbow. As you might have guessed, tin men are in plentiful supply.

• ... as are cowardly lions, in the shape(s) of Mickey and his parallel-universe self, Ricky. The revised edition of Mickey is London's Most Wanted and walks around with a permanent scowl and snarl. The original is given moments of being the comic foil (again) and others where he is the forgotten hanger-on (still), but he also gets to do some info-dumps about parallel worlds (which he knows from comics). Noel Clarke is possibly overdoing the differences, making Mickey's eyes pop out like Tom Baker's and clenching his jaw for every line as Ricky, but we only have to watch "The Chase" (2.8) to see how badly wrong this could have gone.

• Impending Companion Departure Alert: two things used to signify a character leaving the series. One was suddenly acting as if s/he was in lurve, the other was becoming indispensible at short notice. Davies and his gang have added a third: name-checking the source of the script, with Mickey starting the countdown by shouting "I'm just a spare part" (see **The Big Picture** and **Production** for Marc Platt's Big Finish audio about the creation of the Cybermen, *Spare Parts*).

• For some reason, the music selected to drown out the screams of men being converted is the 1982 chart-topper by Tight Fit, a cover of "The Lion Sleeps Tonight" by Karl Denver. Their follow-up, "Fantasy Island", might have made peo-

Are Credited Authors Just Hired Hands?

Through various comments - both official or unguarded - many people outside the loop of the BBC Wales Lubianka have picked up on an idea that Russell T Davies used to tell people what to write and, if they didn't do it as he asked, wrote it all himself again. Others have picked up the impression that he only selected writers he trusted to give him exactly what he wanted, so he didn't need to do this. Another school of thought is that he rewrote everything in the last camerascript to make it cohesive. There may not be one overall pattern at work.

It is apparent, though, that the Cyberman two-parter went through a lot of stages between a vague notion of "let's do *Spare Parts* on telly" to what we got. The author of that Big Finish audio, Marc Platt (26.2, "Ghost Light") was thanked in the end-roll for both episodes and did indeed receive a small payment, alongside the estates of Kit Pedler and Gerry Davis. Writer Tom MacRae was from a soap background. The conspiracy theorists ask, "Why pay Marc Platt *not* to write something and get some kid to bodge something together out of Big Finish leftovers?" One possible answer is that Davies wanted someone inexperienced and malleable but, as regards breadth of types of television he'd written for, MacRae had already far outstripped Platt. All of Platt's credited work is for *Doctor Who* in some form or another, whereas MacRae had a couple of other (ignominious but exacting) gigs to his name. He had to be given a crash-course in *Doctor Who* lore, and now claims that he only "got" the series later, although this was in the build-up to broadcast of his second attempt, "The Girl Who Waited" (X6.10). Why not get someone with a sense of the series *and* television experience? There were several of those who had risen though the ranks of fandom, and parlayed writing for the Virgin *New Adventures* books into jobs on the major soaps (and *Emmerdale* - we'll come back to this one in a mo). In fact, Davies *did* take on one of these per annum in his first three years, but they were mainly hired for other skills and experience. Paul Cornell, Gareth Roberts and Matt Jones had all worked with Davies on earlier projects, notably the scouse-satanic curio *Springhill*.

It's been reported that the average Welsh-*Who* script goes through eight drafts. This has been greeted with derision by Terrance Dicks, who had bitter experience of nursing "The Ambassadors of Death" (7.3) through six iterations and still having things fall through the gaps. With the current trend towards Big Bads and seeded hints, the last of these drafts would be the main writer including whatever was needed for the series-long storyline. Those storylines were decided in advance of signing up writers and, at least for the first two years, pitched to the BBC1 executives as a package and then farmed out to writers. The series, at this stage, was explicitly an "authored" work by Davies, with help from others.

However, the details were negotiable. Close examination of the four stories in Series One not by the ostensible "show-runner" reveals that they all wandered away from what was pitched to suit not only the individual authors' own tendencies but the character dynamics. The Pete Tyler we get in Series Two is one plausibly derived from what Cornell wrote in X1.8, "Father's Day", but that character isn't quite what the original brief suggested. The Doctor in "The Unquiet Dead" (X1.3) is oddly different to the character in the episodes either side of it. Jaxx, the future soldier needed to fight the Daleks and to bond with the Doctor in a way that threatens Rose, becomes Captain Jack: conman, rogue and ladykiller whom the Doctor mistrusts and Rose falls for in a way that wouldn't have happened in another episode by another writer. Most spectacularly, "Dalek" (X1.6) is recognisably the Big Finish audio *Jubilee* amended to suit the conditions of recording, but with changes made and unmade along the way for contractual reasons.

Taking all of that into account, Davies hasn't just farmed out the scripts to reliable sock-puppets who'll give him what he asks for - he has let the writers do what they do best and incorporated what they gave into what he did next. Then he has added a veneer of his own where necessary to make it more closely fit the overall pattern of the series. This is no more or less than what old-series script editors did, and considerably less amendation than Tom Baker used to do to the scripts in rehearsal. However, the more clueless critics assumed that Davies did everything and the BBC was keen to promote this as his work with a few other writers as stabiliser-wheels. It would seem that this is the main reason he is credited as co-

continued on Page 315...

ple volunteer to be processed. Unlike, say, "The Impossible Planet" (X2.8), there seems to be no clever cryptic hint in the choice of record. Look closely, and it's obvious that Mr Crane is bopping to a completely different tune.

• For most of this episode, the Cybermen are kept out of focus, or only seen as feet or fists. The first time the Doctor sees them is the first time we see them properly, and they come into focus before our eyes. Unfortunately, the press had got photos and the *Radio Times* had the Cyber Controller on the front cover that week (just over a month after their last cover, which had one in a peculiar conga-line with a cat-nun, a clockwork robot and Sarah Jane on the fold-out).

The Continuity

The Doctor Here he literally breathes ten years of his life into a fuel cell to bump-start the TARDIS after a cosmic prang. The TARDIS shutdown makes him thoroughly depressed [much like 22.2, "Vengeance on Varos"].

He finally manages to get Mickey's name right after seeing two of him, only to receive the crushing response from one of them that, 'It's Ricky!' When the Cybermen show up, the Doctor tries to get Rose away from them immediately. Then when they're all caught anyway, he attempts to surrender [although possibly as a bluff, giving him a slim chance of saving everyone rather than none].

He's very concerned about Rose running around looking for her father in a parallel reality, trying everything from arguments to pleading to flat out ordering her not to meet him. When forced to choose between his two companions, he follows Rose on her exploration of the parallel world rather than Mickey. [He doesn't know anything about Mickey's family life, but knows full well what damage Rose can cause - see X1.8, "Father's Day". Still, he could have explained this to Mickey better.]

Later on, in disguise, he shows off about having picked up some of the local gossip by chatting with the other catering staff.

• *Ethics*. He offers an unconvincing protest when Mickey points out he was 'forgotten' - this is when Mickey's been left holding a button down for a half-hour longer than needed. The second time the Doctor forgets Mickey, he doesn't even attempt a justification. When Rose tries to run into the house to save alt-Jackie, he sharply reminds her that this woman isn't her mother and pulls her away.

• *Background*. At some point, he and Rose were on this asteroid thing and that goblin-lady blew fire from her mouth. You 'had to be there', evidently. He seems to have had training in how to be a butler [or can at least fake it convincingly].

• *Inventory: Sonic Screwdriver*. It's no match for brute force when fixing a broken TARDIS.

• *Inventory: Other*. The psychic paper, it seems, provides a complete fake CV for Rose and the Doctor, aiding them in getting catering jobs in a high-security prestige event.

The TARDIS Has a button (on one of the struts) that Mickey was told to hold down. They later tell him that he could have let go half an hour earlier... but as soon as he does release it, everything goes wrong.

The Ship needs the space-time Vortex to move in [apparently as both a fuel-source and as something on which to gain some kind of traction]. When removed from this context, the TARDIS 'dies'. [The gap in the Vortex seems like coloured smoke and flames - remarkably like the Matt Smith title sequence. This also raises the question of how the TARDIS moved without the Vortex in X6.4, "The Doctor's Wife". If, as we are told, the absence of the outside universe-of-origin is like trying to run a petrol engine on diesel, we have to ask what it was the Time Lords did that allowed TARDISes to make such journeys before (see, for instance, 26.1, "Battlefield"). There seems to be something qualitatively different about spacetime in Pete's World that makes it unlike the altered timelines of other stories (see **How is This Not a Parallel Universe?** under X4.11, "Turn Left"). If simply altering history were enough to make a whole new universe and this made the TARDIS not work, then hypothetically no period of Earth's future after X1.5, "World War Three" and *definitely* not the changed future(s) of Satellite Five (X1.7, "The Long Game"; X1.12, "Bad Wolf") would be visitable.]

However, one fuel-cell persists and, charged up by the Doctor breathing on it (not the usual orange sparkly pixie-dust, but a green glow) can, given time to run through its recharge cycle, give five minutes' flight after 24 hours. As the crisis develops, breathing masks on tubes fall from the ceiling [there's three of them, either indicating the original intended number of crew - X4.13,

Are Credited Authors Just Hired Hands?

continued from Page 313...

author on "Planet of the Dead" and "The Waters of Mars" (X4.15-4.16), even though these are apparently only as rewritten by him as any other script credited to another author. (At least, in the latter case, until the last ten minutes, which laboriously sets up a big plot-line that never *quite* materialises in the two-part regeneration story.)

Another gobbet gleefully pounced upon by tealeaf-readers is the werewolf that didn't bark in the night. Davies makes a point of not naming the original author of "Tooth and Claw" (X2.2), but is very clear that he gave that author a shopping-list of elements to include and took over the project himself when the anonymous scribe omitted Scotland and werewolves. The whole Monster Shopping List approach has been a matter for some debate, and Helen Raynor in particular has been given two-part stories with the kind of brief John Nathan-Turner used to deliver from on high in the 80s, which resulted in such gems as "Time Flight" (19.7) and "The King's Demons" (20.6).

More on Raynor in a minute, but the riddle of who exactly Davies asked to write the Queen Victoria episode persists, and might have been instructive if we'd had a name. It matters, because rather than crack a whip and say "Do this again", Davies chose to rework the entire episode from scratch himself. Given that he sets most of his writers endless redrafting regimes (a bone of contention with a couple of them), it suggests that this was someone close to or above Davies in the television-writing pecking-order. We can be reasonably sure it's a "he" as Davies said, and is "a very good writer". With all the speculation about the never-was Paul Abbot Vesuvius story (see X1.11, "Boom Town"), this would be a talking-point. (Anyone with a working knowledge of British TV drama c.2005 can play: Jimmy McGovern; Frank Cottrell Boyce; Peter Flannery; Andrew Davies; Phil Redmond... place your bets and wait for Davies to name names, if ever.[61]) It might make sense if this was one of the calibre of writers that Eccleston would have come to work for and who might have been attracted because he was involved. The point is, it seems unlikely that a relative unknown would have been treated this way rather than be told to do it again and again until it was right.

One curious detail can be heard on the online commentary for "The Sontaran Stratagem" (X4.4): Julie Gardner praises Russell for how the episode is written and Helen Raynor, the accredited author and another participant in the session, says nothing. Another is the often-cited observation that Davies never needed to rewrite a line of a Steven Moffat script. Given the industry clout Moffat could bring to bear on the contract negotiations, it's possible he couldn't have even if he'd wanted to. It's certainly true that Moffat had to add the typewriter scene in "The Doctor Dances" (X1.10) whilst in Australia, because Davies apparently couldn't come up with anything. This was, however, during the writing of the final three episodes. It does seem to some observers that as far as the executive producer's willingness to rework their material is concerned, some writers are more equal than others.

However, Raynor is a textbook example of Davies making a list and forgetting the most important ingredient, as he had stipulated 1930s New York and Daleks, but the small matter of the Great Depression seemed to have slipped his mind. (This is cited as evidence that the whole project was damage-limitation after commissioning props for the Stephen Fry episode that never happened - see **Was Series Two Supposed to be Like This?** under X2.11, "Fear Her".) Several other Davies pet projects were farmed out to other writers who didn't make any noticeable contributions. James Moran (X4.2, "The Fires of Pompeii") has written many other thrillers, but the broadcast episode bears no trace of his usual concerns, being heavily continuity-led (the debate on "Fixed Points") and only different from the Big Finish audio *The Fires of Vulcan* in being more colloquial and littered with Latin O-Level jokes and gags about the Welsh - and having very perfunctory aliens. It's hard not to see these as Davies' contributions. The next story was credited to the archetypal writer-for-hire on soaps and churn-em-out drama, Keith Temple (X4.3, "Planet of the Ood"). He's not been able to escape this typecasting and went back to *Casualty* and the like.

The other big name recruited from outside fandom for Series Two, Matthew Graham, was asked for ideas and told to keep coming up with them until he delivered something they liked. The

continued on Page 317...

X2.5 Rise of the Cybermen

"Journey's End" - or detecting the number of occupants at that time].

The Supporting Cast

• *Rose* finds a London sky full of zeppelins to be 'beautiful'. When the Doctor starts a rant about technological upgrading, she attempts to point out that it isn't actually her world.

As is becoming a trend this season, she's frustrated about working as a waitress and complains to the Doctor about being a server to get into the party. [The Doctor argues that the kitchens are a far more useful place to find things out, which might work better if we ever actually saw them in the kitchen.] She's even huffier when it emerges that Pete and Jackie's 'Rose' in this reality is a Yorkshire Terrier.

As soon as she realises that she's in an alternative universe where her father's alive, she wants to go meet him and does the necessary research to find out how best to go about it, then keeps talking about him until the Doctor's natural curiosity takes over.

Mickey's told her a rundown on his family situation; for some reason, she found the memory of his gran slapping him to be hilarious. She admits that she takes Mickey's presence for granted, then looks at the Doctor and corrects it to 'we'.

Rose's Magic Phone is able to pick up Lumic transmissions and get data on Pete Tyler's business empire. It also taps into the downloads people get in their ear-pieces, but not in enough detail to possess Rose [or tell us what the joke everyone else laughs at was].

• *Mickey* has, or had, a gran who was blind and who looked after him after his dad left and his mum was unable to cope. [This seems to contradict what we learned about him last year, but there's a long enough gap between him being set up as Rose's boyfriend (who tells her everything) and Christmas Day (when he spends all his time at Jackie's) for Rose's account of his past to fit what he actually does.]

He's patient as ever, apparently willing to listen to an endless number of Rose/Doctor adventuring stories without comment. When the Doctor starts panicking about Rose wandering off, he's mildly sympathetic while pointing out that there are items of interest for him in this reality. He sardonically repeats the 'never going to be me' line when the Doctor leaves him to chase off after Rose, before going off to find his alt-reality gran.

In "our" world, she died by tripping down a staircase about five years ago, when Rose was still in school. [For this to make any sense, we have to assume that Rose is now comfortable with the idea that more time has elapsed for Mickey than for her, so Mickey's gran, Rita-Anne, died circa 2000, and his father Jackson Smith did a bunk in 1990, which is when a lot of people fled to Spain to escape their problems. If Rita-Anne died shortly before X1.1, "Rose", then Mickey's moving into a flat by himself may only have been very recent, hence Rose not moving in with him and him spending his second Christmas without relatives, but with someone who was only a few months earlier accusing him of murdering her daughter.] When confronted with "his" gran (who oscillates between being concerned and whacking him with a stick), Mickey is understandably concerned by the worn staircase carpet.

He's familiar with the concept of parallel universes from films, as he says to Rose - later on, when it's only the Doctor's around, he brings up comics. Oddly, when this guy-talk is happening, the Doctor seems glad to have him around [maybe the business of wrenching up the TARDIS floorplates is more like garage-work].

When the Preachers kidnap Mickey, he has enough presence of mind to realise that he's been mistaken for his alt-self, and string it out for as long as possible until actually confronted by his parallel self. It's in this context that he says 'cool' about being London's Most Wanted before doing a double-take. Even with a nervous group of rebels ready to take him out, he can't resist quipping. He doesn't seem to overly mind being strapped to a chair and stripped to his briefs.

• *Ricky*. Both versions of Mickey had a father named Jackson Smith, who worked at the key cutters in Clifton's Parade, and eventually went to Spain and disappeared. [It's widely assumed that 'Ricky' is a diminutive of "Richard", but he's the right age and background for his dad to have named him after Ricardo Tubbs from *Miami Vice* - or it could be he's a slightly embarrassed "Eric". A deleted scene in the next episode would have explicitly stated that Ricky was Jake's boyfriend.]

• *Pete-through-the-looking-glass*. He's somewhat more hard-edged compared to "our" Pete [last seen in "Father's Day"], having succeeded with one of the dodgy Del-Boy schemes we saw then - Vitex, a purported health drink that is actually just pop. Lumic buying his corporation doesn't

Are Credited Authors Just Hired Hands?

continued from Page 315...

most cited rejected idea, like the one eventually used ("Fear Her") is rather familiar from children's fantasy (indeed both the "colour-being-stolen" and "people-being-trapped-inside-crayon-drawings" conceits have been used as episodes of *The Powerpuff Girls*), but it was his Matthew Graham-ness that was what they wanted, his approach to potentially-hackneyed material, and - let's be frank - the kudos attached to his name. His script was brought forward to replace one by a writer who was manifestly there as the scriptorial equivalent of stunt-casting, Stephen Fry. The announcement of Fry's involvement in Series Two made headlines, and it still gets column-inches whenever he gives little crumbs about what he had in mind. Fry and, arguably, Graham by this stage were too big within the industry to have substantial rewrites to anything with their names attached.

It's worth noting that among his few regrets about being put in charge of *Doctor Who* was that Davies couldn't bring new writers to television (he can be heard voicing this opinion at the end of the BBC Radio *Project Who* documentary, but never again). The BBC's deal was that only writers with previous television experience could be entrusted with this enormous and relatively risky project. This is the exact opposite of the terms of Andrew Cartmel's stint as script editor in the late 80s, the period when Davies himself was attempting to get a toehold into writing (see X1.7, "The Long Game"). In some ways, it can seem that the only reason *Doctor Who* was broadcast at all after "The Trial of a Time Lord" was as a nursery for potential writers. After the series ended in 1989, the BBC had a few small schemes and eventually an online project called The Writers' Room, but the main point of entry into television scripting was a daily lunchtime series (probably best not to call it a soap) called *Doctors*, produced and nurtured by Mal Young. The same Mal Young was executive producer on the first series of BBC Wales' *Doctor Who*, so this stipulation probably didn't come from him. In this light, Davies' decision to give the two non-fan writers on Series Two the stories that involved the return of something with a lot of backstory was perhaps a form of mentoring. Toby Whithouse and MacRae were lent DVDs, comics and books to get up to speed on the details, but after they were brought on board for what else they had to offer as writers. The hardcore fans writing the rest of the series had a sense for the programme's traditions, but might not have been the right people to sell the old material to the new viewers. (Whether Whithouse got Sarah Jane Smith right is another matter, but MacRae was explicitly told to abandon all previous Cyber-lore and start again from scratch.)

MacRae's "added value" was simply that he wasn't hidebound by 40 years of previous Cyberman adventures, but was encouraged to pick and choose what he thought would work for an audience coming to them completely fresh. He was, in that sense, more of a hired-gun than most other writers on the series, but his relative "outsider" status was his principle asset. Paradoxically, when he returned in Series Six, he did so with a whole story he had devised and presented to Steven Moffat on spec. Other writers have stated that they came to him with ideas rather than getting delegated to add tiles to a mosaic planned in advance. The Davies pattern of planning an entire series and distributing episodes as subcontracted tasks was gone, even though Moffat was, if anything, more prone to having long-running plotlines that needed micro-management and rewrites.

However, his main emphasis has been on the use of incoming writers as "names" to get publicity - with the obvious message that nobody as famous as Neil Gaiman (X6.4, "The Doctor's Wife') or Richard Curtis (X5.10, "Vincent and the Doctor") gets used as a "sock-puppet", and nobody with as distinctive a style as Simon Nye (X5.7, "Amy's Choice") can comfortably be made to synch with a season-long plot. Moffat's collegiate policy has, paradoxically, led to more homogeneity, as Series Six gave us several almost-identical scripts by different writers that had to be forcibly differentiated by the visuals overlaid on them.

X2.5 Rise of the Cybermen

bother him enough for him to have made any public protest. In fact, off the record, it allows him access to the inner circle. He's chummy with the President.

At first, it seems Pete is willing to put up with any amount of complaining from his wife when she's on edge about her age, which may or may not have anything to do with her accusations that he's been playing around. He fondly remembers taking Jackie out for her 21st birthday, having cider at a pub, then shifts into talking about how he's moved out of the mansion and is keeping it quiet mainly because it's bad for business. [Of course, that would give him rather more time to spend on other projects - see next episode for what these might be.] To Rose's joy, he innately trusts her for no reason he can ascertain.

• *Jackie-through-the-looking-glass* delights in ostentatious wealth and conspicuous consumption. She gets flowers from Iceland [the country, not the frozen-food shop] in February, has an authorised biography that fudges her age, and is calm about getting personalised gifts from John Lumic himself. There's a strong undercurrent that she's worried about being replaced by a trophy wife, as most of her dialogue relates either to putting down Pete or worrying about her reputation. In front of a room full of potentates, though, she's gracious and charming.

She's friendly with Rose until Pete comes up in the conversation, whereupon she blows her top about the mere idea of giving him a second chance and insists she'll dock Rose's wages. [This is after Rose has said she was talking to Pete, so it's possible that Jackie's seeing this as a painfully roundabout message from her estranged husband.]

She calls her dog 'Rose'. [If, as is sometimes stated, that was her mother's name, then the argument in "Father's Day" about Pete picking girls with that name makes even less sense than calling a dog that.]

The Supporting Cast (Evil)

• *John Lumic*. The leader of Cybus Industries was apparently born in Great Britain, but has been living abroad [in his zeppelin, one presumes] for years before the story opens. His creation of 'high-content metal' is what's mentioned first in newscasts about him. His wide-ranging conglomerate has purchased any number of businesses, including Vitex.

He suggests to the President that his main goal for the Cybus industry upgrades is to enable his own life to be lengthened. He seems to expect to be refused permission for trials on living specimens, so launches an obviously well-prepared plan for upgrading the whole of the UK. [There's plenty of references to other locations and factories, but he refers to Britain as 'the homeland' and returns to take charge of matters there personally.] This may have been his aim all along, but he's on life-support and unable to leave his throne/commode/workstation. He needs an oxygen mask for most of the day.

The Non-Humans

• *Cybermen*. This lot are the creation of Cybus Industries, created by Lumic's special projects team under his personal supervision. In outline they're largely akin to the Telos versions - jug-ears, blank faces with eye-pieces perforated to resemble teardrops [as in 6.3, "The Invasion"], external cables and an articulated armour around the hands [yes, just like *RoboCop*]. They speak like the "Invasion" model, and when they do so, blue LEDs light up, up to eight of them according to the volume [yes, just like KITT in *Knight Rider*]. The bodywork is more overtly armoured, with a carapace over an inner core of wiring and pipes [yes, just like C3PO] and, in place of the traditional exterior chest-unit, there is simply a Batman-style plate with the Lumic logo. The overall effect is as if they had been made in 1930s Germany, in Art Deco style. [Or, with an eye to 18.6, "The Keeper of Traken", *Melkur: The Street-Mime Years*.]

Their main twenty-first century innovation is verbal: instead of "destroy" or "convert", they speak of suitable victims being 'upgraded' and unsuitable ones 'deleted'. Methods of deletion include electrocution by clamping those hands on people's heads or shoulders. They don't use the karate-chops so popular in the 60s. They march in strict, mechanical formation. [You might think this was a given, but watch the cliffhanger to episode six of "The Invasion", supposedly their most militaristic sortée to date.] They make impressive stomping noises as they do so, like industrial jackhammers [except when they sneak up on Mrs Moore in the next episode - see X4.14, "The Next Doctor" for them possibly having a silent mode].

The initial batch that's sent out to kill everyone at Pete's party has been recruited from the home-

Rise of the Cybermen X2.5

less population of London; Cybus Industries, under the guise of 'International Electromatics' [the evil megacorp in "The Invasion"] has been sending around food trucks to entice and then kidnap people off the streets. It's been happening for a while, as even Mickey's grandmother knows about it.

• *Torchwood*, in this London, is well-known enough to be mentioned in news broadcasts, and for Pete to ask about it openly at a party where the President and his security detail [at least, we assume he didn't come alone] are present.

History (Alternate)

• *Dating*. Err... Mickey reads a newspaper and says that it's 'first of February' - the same day as the one that he, the Doctor and Rose were aiming for in the real universe. Rose later confirms that 'February the first' is her mum's birthday. [Confusing matters, Jackie says that her biography claims that she was born the same day as Cuba Gooding Jr, and that they're "both" supposed to be turning 39 today - for Gooding, that actually happened on 2nd January, 2007. One theory is that Jackie and / or her biographers misread the American dating convention, swapping the day and the month (because Americans do it month-day-year, for some reason).] No Christmas decorations are around and nobody wishes anyone Happy New Year. Lumic gives the date of the party as 1st February.

In this world, most of technology seems to have gone down the same path as ours despite various social and economic changes that might have made this difficult. Britain has a President, Europe is rather more federal than in our dimension and there seems to be a co-ordinated Europe-wide government. Jackie suggests that all of her rich friends own airships [it's possible that the elite live in zeppelins, enabling them to avoid local tax], although land-based oligarchs such as Pete Tyler can afford mansions]. Video billboards are activated by touch and have speakers.

Cybus Industries makes consumer electronics, including the implanted 'pod' earpieces. They also do home insurance and personal finance. John Lumic owns [by the Doctor's estimation] 'just about every company' in Britain, including a dummy corporation called 'International Electromatics' [again, see "The Invasion"].

There is a New Germany and a Geneva-based government that implements a Bio-Convention restricting the creation of new species. There is also a New South America, where Cybus Industries have been up to no good. ['New Germany' might be a political construct, formed after re-unification, but South America is a whole continent, so there's a possibility that this is like "New South Wales" or "New Jersey", or maybe an off-world colony. The TARDISode suggests otherwise, and we can think of one other possibility which we'll mention next episode.]

This version of London has all the landmarks as per the real one, but Battersea Power Station [2.2, "The Dalek Invasion of Earth"; 3.10, "The War Machines; 18.7, "Logopolis"] is owned and run by Lumic as a processing-plant and airship-dock. In this London, Blackfriars is a wasteland within sight of the Millennium Dome [so they built the Dome exactly as it was, but on the site of the Festival of Britain and our South Bank complex, for some reason]. Homelessness is a far bigger problem in this London, but the *Big Issue* is on sale, and there are lots of derelict sites owned by Cybus. A 10.00pm curfew is in place in London, except for guests at Pete Tyler's mansion.

[By the way, the alteration from our world may not be as far back as all that. Tight Fit apparently had a hit with "The Lion Sleeps Tonight" as they did in our Britain in 1982, and Jackie's 21st was a pint of cider at a pub called the George, rather than any black market whisky.]

• *The Time War*. Apparently, the removal of the Time Lords from the cosmic stage means that there can be no access to and from parallel universes. [Something fairly drastic, then, has to have happened for the TARDIS to have been stranded in the wrong reality.]

Catchphrase Counter Oddly, the Doctor's usual line ('I'm sorry, I'm so sorry') is spoken by the President of Britain to someone who has been puréed into a Cyberman. [As it was his government's policies that made the ex-human homeless and allowed Lumic to go unchecked, he is quite right to apologise.] The Cybermen get a couple of new ones: 'Delete' and 'You will be upgraded'.

Deus Ex Machina As we've explored in detail in an earlier essay, what seems like a massive coincidence - the one accessible parallel universe is one where everything is how Rose would have wanted it - might not actually be a coincidence at all. [See **Bad Wolf: What, Why and How?** under X1.13, "The Parting of the Ways".] As with "Boom Town" (X1.11), the fact that the TARDIS takes exactly 24

319

X2.5 Rise of the Cybermen

hours to refuel is suspiciously convenient. There are problems about the Doctor refuelling the TARDIS with his mojo too, but we'll come to those [see **Things That Don't Make Sense**].

The Analysis

The Big Picture ("Rise of the Cybermen" and "The Age of Steel") As we saw under "Inferno" (7.4), Alternate Histories were a fad in the 1930s that took on increased urgency in Britain after 1939, for obvious reasons. It's a form of speculation that doesn't require much practice and allows people to wallow in the period details (thus allowing men to write Historical Romance without adopting feminine pseudonyms). Among the literati, the fact that Churchill did one means that it isn't tainted with the usual associations of Science Fiction (and thus doesn't require as much skill to sell to that more specialised and experienced readership who're more likely to spot shoddy worldbuilding), and made it seem scholarly. However, the SF fraternity had got bored with "time wars" some time around 1953[58], and the idea was soon only useable as a springboard for other notions (e.g. Philip K Dick's *The Man in the High Castle*, which was a meditation on the *I Ching* disguised as an America conquered by the Axis powers, but not noticeably much different from the Eisenhower era).

Then it underwent a revival through the regular writers at *New Worlds* magazine in the late 60s. Keith Roberts wrought a series of delphic short stories about an England that had not had a Reformation (collected under the title *Pavane*). In these, the Industrial Revolution was a rumour about some foreign craftsmen. The magazine's editor, Michael Moorcock, was busily writing a whole slew of fantasy sagas, social satires and stylistic experiments and brought them together through the contrivance of a "multiverse", enabling characters to meet in each other's stories. In one of these series, supposedly dictated to his grandfather, one Oswald Bastable[59] related his experiences in an alternate history where steam, zeppelins and elegant brass contraptions created a 1970s resembling the engravings of late nineteenth-century French illustrator Grandville, a world following the uninterrupted trajectory of the 1893 Paris *Prevoyants del'Avenir* exhibition with no awkward World Wars. (And, if you haven't already read it, we refer you to X2.2,

"Tooth and Claw" for more on this.) In this, half the fun was spotting real historical figures transfigured into minor characters. Harry Harrison continued in this vein with his 1974 book *A Transatlantic Tunnel, Hurrah!* (in which descendants of George Washington and Isambard Kingdom Brunel run into cameos by Kingsley Amis and Arthur C Clarke). Amis killed this sub-genre by doing it badly for the benefit of the literary establishment, presenting *The Alteration* (a book about, um, the Reformation never having happened) as a blindingly original conceit.

By now, the "many worlds" conception of quantum physics was being taken seriously. This was originally proposed as a resolution to the paradoxes of the front-runner, the so-called Copenhagen Interpretation (see **What is the Blinovitch Limitation Effect?** under 20.3, "Mawdryn Undead" and **How Does the TARDIS Work?** under 1.3, "The Edge of Destruction"). It proposed, simply, that each tiny choice, from the decisions people make down to photons opting to pass through one slit or another, offered alternatives that "somewhere" were the actual result: the two-slit experiment showed not particle-wave duality being affected by the consciousness of the observer (a photon behaving according to what the researcher is looking for at that moment), but overlapping universes where the photon chose both options and adjacent realities interfered with each other slightly. This seemed more sensible to many scientists, which shows how messy subatomic physics is once you start studying it thoroughly. So rather than "parallel" universes, we have forking paths (and, yes, Jorge Luis Borges got there first in the 1940s, so writing about it was "literature" and not greasy kid's stuff). Writers and historians could deal with that, whereas the maths and counter-intuitive terminology of hard physics was off-putting unless you were making a statement about how parochial other novelists and historians were. In particular, there was a great deal of research into "euchronia", a sort of compensatory fantasy used by oppressed peoples that began with "If only..." instead of "What if..." Bereavement, and the potential careers of dead celebrities who were thought to have died too young, provide rich pickings for anyone investigating these avenues.

Meanwhile, the multiverse idea allowed comics writers to resolve continuity errors (see "Battlefield") and to play with different visual styles. Moebius (see X1.2, "The End of the World") was up-front about his sources until Moorcock's lawyers made him stop using the name "Jerry Cornelius". But the most overtly Moorcockean comic was Bryan Talbot's 80s mini-series *The Adventures of Luther Arkwright*, about a sort of agent who skips between realities, most of them containing zeppelins and steam-driven computers. (Fritz Leiber, who, as we saw in 6.7, "The War Games", more or less created the idea of time wars and battles to rewrite history back in the 40s, alerted the SF reading world to this cliché in a story actually called "Catch That Zeppelin".) So, as Mickey points out, by the time Marvel, DC and the independent comics had turned the idea into a staple, anyone could do it under a "fair use" policy that also covers EE "Doc" Smith and his "tractor beams" and "force fields".

And so everyone *was* using it. The scholarly ones called them "Counterfactual History" and it became a sort of parlour game for historians, especially the ones with lucrative TV tie-in book deals. Corny TV series used them as a way to keep the cast happy by giving them a break from saying their usual lines (and when *Friends* uses an SF conceit better than *Deep Space Nine*, you know things are going wrong). Some of Phil Dick's friends started doing them again in book form, but, this being the 1980s, it had to be rebranded so some idiot decided that things like Harrison's squib were now "steampunk" (see *The Digging Leviathan* by James Blaylock, *Infernal Devices* by KW Jeter and *The Anubis Gates* by Tim Powers, for a start). Oddly, when the TV show that seems to have inspired these, *The Wild Wild West*, was made into a very dull film, it looked less steampunk than the film that blew it away at the box office, *Star Wars Episode 1: The Phantom Menace*. Because whilst it is easy to make a collage of Victorian machinery having space-age results, suggesting a world that made this happen is harder than it looks. When William Gibson and Bruce Sterling served notice on this being done to death, they did so in a book that required the readers to have actually read some Victorian literature. and know about the mathematics of computing (which is why *The Difference Engine* is one of the great unread bestsellers). Most clued-up SF writers moved the change back to the early seventeenth century, but the publishers haven't thought of a sales-pitch for that stuff yet.

Within pop-culture, stories about travel between universes tended to have the same people knowing each other, for budgetary reasons, and all having more than shared experience binding them together with people who look like their friends but have different pasts. (As we have said, the "Human Nature" series is beloved of advertisers.) Within Young Adult reading, the then-current most favoured series was Philip Pullman's *His Dark Materials* trilogy, which was massively popular in the UK until the first book was adapted into a dreadful film. This made the process of navigating alternate worlds the thing that separated children from adults, by means of a numinous material called "Dust" that was somehow connected to both life-force and the gaps between realities. Davies was entirely within his rights to capitalise on this parent-friendly fantasy, but wholesale plundering of the ending was another matter (see X2.13, "Doomsday", if you don't know what we mean). However, Pullman was in many ways reworking earlier children's books, notably those of Joan Aiken. From the mid-60s on, she wrote a set of stories, beginning with *The Wolves of Willoughby Chase* (see X4.14, "The Next Doctor") in a world where the 1688 coup, the "Glorious Revolution", had no lasting effect and a century later, London and other cities were like an exaggerated version of Dickens. What's impressive coming back to the 13-book series now is that no real effort is made to set up the backstory through a lecture - children were assumed to be able to discern the differences between this colourful world and genuine history (see 22.3, "The Mark of the Rani" for how that period was usually taught in the 70s). Once again, the linkage between altered history, lurid crimes, child-slavery and steam-driven machinery is a given and it is spunky pre-teen girls who make change happen[60].

Going back to "Inferno", you will recall how laboriously the Doctor had to figure out where he was and explain it all to two different Brigadiers across four episodes. It was easier, when audiences were still new to all of this, to simply have another planet exactly like Earth in an orbit that meant we never saw it. You will recall from Volume 1 that everyone in Britain had this brilliantly original idea when the gas bill needed paying and pitched it to *Doctor Who*. Ultimately, Innes Lloyd, forced into producing the series, opted to do it once and for all and thus allowed Kit Pedler to air a few pet peeves (4.2, "The Tenth Planet"). Whilst the Cybermen were, for Pedler, a manifestation of body-horror and personality under the influence of psychoactive compounds (especially the tranquillisers and anti-depressants he thought were turning people into zombies), the BBC Wales team believed these fears to be too abstract for kids today. Instead, they went for something they believed to be universal: mobile phones. The language used for the new-look Cybermen was entirely technical and communications-based, "upgrade", "delete", "interface", "download" and so on. It is entirely a matter for individual consumers to choose to have Lumic machinery on their persons, although peer-pressure and government contracts make it an act of defiance to avoid it.

This is a small but significant change from the source-text: *Spare Parts*, Marc Platt's Big Finish drama about the creation of the Cybermen, in which the progress made by citizens of Mondas towards becoming the first Cybermen comes from the compromises of people offered a commercial / medical way out of intolerable conditions. As with "The Tenth Planet", the Cybermen were formerly people pushed to extreme measures, and in the original story they are scrupulously offering their solution to Earth-humans who will otherwise die. Unlike that story, and in marked contrast to *Spare Parts*, the people forced into making these choices are not presented sympathetically and their removal of choice for later subjects of the conversion process is less complicatedly shown. This is something we will address in **Things That Don't Make Sense**, but there is less a sense of the complicity of the viewers in having made similar decisions about consumer technology - the parallel universe setting makes even the shock of everyone being controlled by their phones into laughing at an unheard joke whilst stupefied in a street less potent than it ought to have been. This is not a plausible exaggeration of a current trend, but a safely unfamiliar situation.

This is one reason why the *frisson* that masses of people sleepwalking into a slaughterhouse in the cosily familiar Battersea Power Station ought to have had is missing. Compared to earlier alternate histories, especially those of Nazi-occupied London so popular a generation or so back (see "The Dalek Invasion of Earth"), this changed world is too changed to be uncomfortable, and so the activities of its citizens have a "can't happen here" distancing effect. Even the sympathetic characters are changed beyond all that much sympathy. No resistance movement in Britain would be exactly like the Preachers (although that they picked this name, oblivious to any idea that for a lot of people elsewhere this would make them out as religious zealots and thus no better than the Cybermen, is very English).

But if we're looking for an alternate universe, *It's A Wonderful Life*-style reallocation of roles because one character's life was different, a foe from the past making a giant machine for processing captured humans into slaves and a food-supply, and a rag-tag army of embittered versions of old chums fighting a losing battle, we're looking at *Buffy the Vampire Slayer*, specifically the Season Three episode "The Wish". That even has Evil-Parallel Willow dying in mid swear-word. (Just to prove that the borrowing wasn't one-way, the villain who lands up not killed in this reality was called "The Master".)

[For **Things That Don't Make Sense**, **Critique**, **The Facts** and **Production**, see the next episode.]

X2.6: "The Age of Steel"

(20th May, 2006)

Which One is This? Enslave all of London? There's an app for that.

Firsts and Lasts Well, Mickey's stint as a full-blown companion was brief. He's staying in Evil Parallel London to fight Cybermen and look after Ricky's nan (and what else he gets up to with Ricky's boyfriend Jake is a matter for conjecture and fan-fic). It's also the first time the TARDIS has materialised in Jackie's front room. She must have been asked to keep a space clear on the off-chance.

This is also the first episode this year not to start at 7.00pm; it was moved 25 minutes forward to make way for the Eurovision Song Contest. (It was won by Finnish metal band Lordi, who performed apparently dressed as the Sycorax.). And after Matt Baker's cameo as himself in X1.4, "Aliens of London", we have the first instance of a *Blue Peter* presenter being inside a monster-costume in a broadcast episode, as one of the Cybermen is Gethin Jones. (And the sound of them marching in one scene is partially performed by a former host of the show, as we explained in **Has All the Puff *Totally* Changed Things?** under X2.1, "New Earth".)

The Age of Steel X2.6

How Many Cyber-Races Are There?

The chronology of the Cybermen is messy and self-contradictory. We knew this even when examining the Cybermen's early years in *About Time 2*, but we had no idea that the situation would be messed up further by the then-current production team complicating their own revised timeline, and after that ignoring it completely.

Even though one of these stories is unique in being the only time a recently-broadcast episode has been denounced on-screen as too stupid to be allowed into the canon (X4.14, "The Next Doctor", slagged off in X5.5, "Flesh and Stone", although the attempted disavowal of 6.2, "The Mind Robber" as a bad dream might also count), we have to include this and three other Cyberman adventures in any attempt to resolve BBC Wales' Cyberman chronology with that of twentieth-century *Who*. They said as much even before the new costumes for the second-best monsters had been designed. In "Dalek" (X1.6), we have a botched continuity reference back to either "The Invasion" (6.3) or "Attack of the Cybermen" (22.1), with a thirtieth-century Cyberman head (12.5, "Revenge of the Cybermen") dated to "1975". However, "Dalek" is set in a 2012, where not only is the Dalek attempt to drag Earth across the galaxy and rain down on humanity in assault-squads (X4.12, "The Stolen Earth") not remembered, but neither the Battle of Canary Wharf (X2.13, "Doomsday") nor the existence of Torchwood seems to have affected Van Statten's activities. (See also **What Happened in 1972?** under A7, "Dreamland".)

So the situation is this: in addition to Pete's parents, Jackie's parents, Mickey's parents and so on all having met and produced identical kids who all knew each other despite wildly different biographies, the Parallel Universe seen in "Rise of the Cybermen" (X2.5) has produced its own-brand Cybermen. Cybermen that, against all odds, are exactly like the ones from Mondas who colonised Telos and were, briefly, the scourge of a small bit of this galaxy, but who are treated by the Time Lords as being a far bigger menace than Wirrn (12.2, "The Ark in Space"). Indeed, after a while it became very hard to tell fugitives from John Lumic's factories in Evil Parallel Battersea from Telosian veterans of the Cyber-Wars some time in the latter half of the third millennium. As we've seen, this level of coincidence drops down to near-inevitability if you assume that Rose, when incarnating the Time Vortex, selected this out of the infinite possibilities (**Bad Wolf - What, How and Why?** under X1.13, "The Parting of the Ways"), but it leaves us with another problem as a sort of epistemological tidemark. Has the pre-existing continuity, shaky as it was after classic *Who*, been affected by the influxes of Lumic-model Cybermen - or was it in fact caused by this?

(All right, let's go through all of this again: just because the cause of a piece of history only runs into the Doctor's personal biography later doesn't mean that it hadn't happened until the Doctor was there at the start. The Great Fire of London was an established historical fact in every piece of subsequent Earth history the Doctor had already visited before "The Visitation" (19.4). As we mentioned in **All Right Then... Where Were Torchwood?** under 9.3, "The Sea Devils", the version of St Paul's Cathedral in "The Invasion" and other stories made before "The Visitation" is that made by Sir Christopher Wren after the Great Fire. Queen Victoria's creation of Torchwood in 1879 happens after she's appalled by the Doctor, but it only occurs because the Doctor has reaffirmed a history where she *wasn't* turned into a werewolf in that year. Rose had heard about Torchwood in *The Weakest Link* a whole four episodes earlier (X1.12, "Bad Wolf"), and - incredibly hard to ignore, this - Torchwood obliterated the Sycorax ship with a super-cannon two episodes earlier in "The Christmas Invasion" (X2.0). Elizabeth I was angry with the Doctor (X3.2, "The Shakespeare Code") *before* he caused her to be angry (X4.17, "The End of Time Part One"). Only a Time Lord and / or (apparently) Time War-enabled Daleks can change events - everyone else has to participate in them, even if they have been brought back in some form of time corridor to a point before they were born. However, not every event caused by a Time Lord (or Dalek) is contingent. If that Time Lord (or Dalek) has already encountered the consequences, it seems to be firmer, if not a rock-solid Fixed Point (and we'll get into all of *that* in **What Constitutes a "Fixed Point"?** under X4.2, "The Fires of Pompeii"). See also **How Does Time Work...** under 9.1, "Day of the Daleks" and **What's Happened to the Daleks?** under "Dalek".)

continued on Page 325...

323

X2.6 The Age of Steel

Watch Out For...

• After Joseph Green (X1.5, "World War Three"), Mr Crane continues the trend for dying halfway through saying something naughty. This time, the sentence is "Die, you bugg—" and is addressed to Lumic.

• Fanwank alert! Not only does Mickey get to quote the Doctor quoting Davina (X1.12, "Bad Wolf") by telling Rose "I'm coming to get ya", but the Doctor manages to contrive a way to compare Battersea Power Station to the Tomb of Rassilon ("Above, between, below"; see 20.7, "The Five Doctors"). To keep the 1983 theme, we get a Cyberman freaking out until his head explodes. A less premeditated similarity comes when Mrs Moore is spared from her scripted death in a ladder to a hatch in a tunnel so that she can be given a few more bits of heroism and audience-sympathy before a more brutal and unexpected death, rather as Griffiths was in 22.1, "Attack of the Cybermen".

• Anyone who's played *Lego Star Wars* will know of the detail where opening the wrong door leads into a Stormtrooper sauna. Anyone who's played *Lego Batman* will recall the disco where the various characters can have a temporary truce. Well, in escaping a burning building, the Doctor and Rose open a door to find three Cybermen shaking about with a pulsing red light behind them. Draw your own conclusions.

• Just as Vila Restal in *Blake's 7* had a suspiciously handy knack of revealing unexpected skills whenever the need for a comic relief stooge came into question, so Mickey abruptly demonstrates companion ability and a remarkable aptitude for steering dirigibles. When asked how he learned to fly an airship, he says, "PlayStation."

The Continuity

The Doctor He's uncharacteristically terse in this one, insisting that everyone be heroic and forget about anyone who fell victim to the Cybermen. When the Preachers threaten Pete, he promptly jumps to the defence even before knowing the situation. He thinks at first that shutting down Cybus Industries will require nothing more than alerting the authorities that something's wrong [it turns out that they're attuned enough to the situation to warn everyone to take off their earpods, though we don't know if the Preachers warn them about this off screen; a few references suggest that the Doctor and company must have contacted them when we aren't looking]. He says that he'd call Lumic a genius if he himself wasn't in the room.

He shouts at Rose to keep her from trying to take the earpieces off a person, then complains about how susceptible humans are to control. When she insists that she's going after other-Jackie, he doesn't bother arguing. When Mrs Moore asks if he has any relatives, he replies, 'Who needs family? I've got the whole world on my shoulders.' And yet, the first place he takes Rose after they land back in "normal" reality is the kitchen of Jackie's flat, where he stands around awkwardly while she sobs into her mother's shoulder.

He's nonplussed by Mickey's decision to stay in the alternate reality, but quickly acquiesces to the situation without much overt concern. His plan to thwart Lumic seems always to have hinged on Mickey overhearing him boast to the Cybermen, and he uses the code-phrase 'An idiot could find that code' [see especially X1.5, "World War Three"] as a clue for Mickey to act on this information. When our Jackie asks where Mickey went, the Doctor quietly says, 'He's gone home'. [This being one of those parallel universes where people land up friends with the same people they would in ours, he must assume that Jake needs Mickey around and that Mickey needs a place to be heroic without the Doctor stealing his thunder. As with the end of "World War Three", there may be an element of face-saving, the Doctor seeming to reject Mickey to cover the latter's emotional inarticulacy.]

This incarnation has a fondness for hot dogs and contriving ghastly jokes about them.

• *Ethics*. This episode marks a new low for the Doctor. His brilliant plan for overthrowing Lumic and stopping the mass homogenisation of Londoners is, in effect, to torture those people already converted until they either commit suicide or get killed by insanely wandering into lethal situations caused by other deranged and heavily armed victims. [Whilst this may well have prevented worse atrocities, it's not exactly the punch-the-air moment the script and directing want us to think.] The Doctor discovers that there is an override code for the emotional inhibitors in Cybermen by talking to an injured one, then mercy-killing his specimen. [He doesn't find a simple off-switch, but if he can kill "Sally" just by flipping a switch

How Many Cyber-Races Are There?

continued from Page 323...

The obvious problem with assigning any upgrades to normal-universe Mondasians to the influence of visitors from Zeppelinland is that everything the "ghosts" brought with them was sucked into the Void along with Dalek POWs and Rose Tyler ("Doomsday"). Well, almost everything. Not only is Rose able to pop across the Void under extreme circumstances, but there is the awkward *Torchwood* episode "Cyberwoman". In this, we learn that Ianto's girlfriend Lisa was halfway through being converted when the Doctor solved the two invasions afflicting Canary Wharf and the rest of the world. So, after he was transferred to Torchwood 3 in Cardiff, Ianto smuggled Lisa into the basement of the Hub and secretly hired experts to either finish the job or unpick all the alterations. For this, he had a conversion cradle and life-support system apparently using Lumic tech. Why Lisa wasn't simply a sloppy pile of body-parts when the metal bits of her were returned to sender is glossed as being because the Cybermen in Canary Wharf were adapting local machinery for conversions.

This raises a procedural point about the Doctor's apparent solution - is someone from "normal" London who is converted into a Cyberman going to be affected by the "background radiation" and dragged into the Void along with the two invasion forces? (This also applies to the kerjillions of Daleks who emerge from within a TARDIS-like prison-ship that was itself within a Void Ship and thus unaffected by said irradiation, but that's a can of worms for later.) If you copy a design of a machine from something that originated in the other realm, does it become somehow connected to that realm? Is there a copyright lawyer ensuring that ideas, notions or phrases from the Alternate Universe have to be returned there? We have to consider that the Void is somehow connected to the space-time Vortex we all know and love - the end of "The Next Doctor" rather depends on this link. So the ploy to drag the "ghost" Cybermen back to "hell" worked the first time because of the way they arrived, whereas the accidental advent of Cybermen in 1851 was a side-effect of the Daleks cracking open the walls between universes and so they and the Cyber-King had to be pushed back into the "orthodox" Vortex. As a result, they could have wound up anywhere in "our" space and time. Or not. So that's one option.

The Cybermen fleeing the Void are, however, unable to successfully navigate in space-time and wind up in 1851 London. Even at the time, the Doctor is unconcerned about whether posterity will have a record of that night's events. (We will pick up on this in Volume 8.) The Cybermen are able to travel as such because of the weakening of the boundaries between realities caused by the Daleks' crazed scheme to destroy all matter ("The Stolen Earth"), the same weakness that allows Rose to flit around checking up on Donna (X4.1, "Partners in Crime"; X4.11, "Turn Left"). Rose, however, has a base-camp in a definite reality and can request particular stopping-off points. The Cybermen are stuck in the Void and - somehow - get Dalek technology to work for them. Maybe the ones in 1851 were a lost patrol and others made it to other times and worlds.

Such as Mondas in prehistory, perhaps?

There is a lot to be said for this as a cause for the whole saga. It has to be admitted that the technology for the Cybermen in "The Tenth Planet" (4.2) is markedly less advanced than anything the Lumic-model conversions have, but they seem to have been working with scant resources over a period of thousands of years. Indeed, austerity seems to be their watchword: rather than kill, where possible they immobilise their opponents and conserve energy and resources. The one exception to this rule is in their bizarre plan to invade Earth and steal our energy rather than just rig up solar panels. The one plausible reason to do this is if they think of Earth as "theirs", and this becomes more sensible if the Cybermen originated on a version of Earth rather than a nearby planet that looks like it, a bit.

The account of their origins is rather at odds with this theory. The leader, Krang, explains that they were already on Mondas when it started moving and turned to "our sibbernetic scientists" to fix their shrinking lifespan. (Let's assume that it was Roy Skelton not knowing the word "Cybernetic".) Is this a clue that the scientists weren't just specialists in cybernetics, but were literally cybernetic scientists, themselves machine-based? It would only take one or two stranded,

continued on Page 327...

X2.6 The Age of Steel

on his sonic screwdriver, there must be one.]

In the more overt [and well-publicised] moral lapse, the Doctor's treatment of Mickey here has gone from neglect and ignorance to outright manipulation. [It's possible that he has cleverly got Mickey to "volunteer" to keep Jake from doing anything suicidally heroic, knowing that apparent neglect of Mickey is the button to press to get him to step up to the plate and be the hero the Doctor suspects he ought to be.]

The one time he seems genuinely angry about anything that's happened here is when Mrs Moore, someone with whom he's had some time to show off and chat, is killed. The only thing he has to say to anyone in the alternative universe before leaving is a request that her husband and children be found and told of her bravery.

- *Inventory: Sonic Screwdriver.* The sonic screwdriver can, apparently, send out a "Turn right and ignore me" signal to Cybermen. It's also handy for tracing transmitters in airships, burning through ropes, locking doors and switching off emotional inhibitors (and later a whole Cyberman). Pete seems able to use it without training.

- *Inventory: Other.* The TARDIS cell that the Doctor is carrying discharges a lot of energy that immobilises Cybermen - this jolt leaps from one Cyberman to the others, but somehow knows to ignore humans. Mickey finds the Doctor's discarded suit [it survived the ruckus at Pete's mansion?] and returns it to him. [It would also appear, on the strength of the next episode, that the Doctor kept Mrs Moore's torch.]

The TARDIS Twenty-four hours and a recharge restores the diminished Ship to normal, but the return to the "proper" universe has a limited launch-window. [This recharge-cycle, as with the soaking-up of Artron energy when in Cardiff (X1.11, "Boom Town"), seems oddly neat for a ship not from Earth - unless it is affected by solar activity.] The Doctor considers parking the Ship anywhere "a good policy". When they return to "our" universe, he closes the trans-universe crack so they won't be able to return. He still claims that it's an accident they landed here.

The Supporting Cast

- *Rose* considers going back inside the house to rescue Jackie from the invading Cybermen, but doesn't need much persuasion to leave. She stridently defends Pete - to the confusion of everyone including him - with only momentary doubt. When Pete asks why she's walked into Battersea Power Station to rescue his wife, she can't resist saying it's for her mum and dad.

She remembers previously seeing the handlebar Cyberman head. [In X1.6 "Dalek". As we've noted before, this might be significant - the Doctor seemed forlorn to be without his old foes, so if Rose-as-Bad-Wolf *did* create or select this out of all the potential other universes, she did it for him as well. How thoughtful!]

When Rose sees that Jackie has been turned into a Cyberman, she decides that Jackie is dead and tells Pete so.

She tries to invite Pete into the TARDIS for a trip, though this is before she knows the Doctor doesn't plan to ever return to this reality. She's far more shocked by Mickey leaving than the Doctor is, and protests that she might need him one day. Even after she and the Doctor return to their universe, she's still sobby and is very relieved to find her mother still alive. [There's no hint that Rose wants to pair up this newly widowed version of her father with her mother, for what that's worth. On the other hand, she conceals her background until the end of the story, so she and Pete never really come to terms with their peculiar relationship. At risk of spoilers, this will go some way towards being resolved in X2.13, "Doomsday".]

The Doctor confiscates Rose's phone and gives it to Mickey to use the emotional inhibitor codes for all the rest of the Cybermen.

- *Mickey.* He's impressed by his parallel self's status as London's Most Wanted, and chooses to stick with him rather than go with Rose the first time the group splits up. He thinks that Ricky is braver than he is, and is distraught by his parallel self's death [as much over having to tell Jake as anything else; he's careful with the phrasing in an attempt to make it sound as heroic a death as possible].

He's frustrated by the Doctor's lack of planning, and is even more put out when the Doctor comes up with a plan that fails to include him. He says his days of being 'the tin dog' are over, and in Ricky's absence goes with Jake - and gets downright angry when Jake calls him an idiot. His hacking skills enable him to transmit the emotional codes to the Cybermen - a ploy he figures out when the Doctor tips him off with the word 'idiot'. Faced with the prospect of killing human guards to get on board the zeppelin, he insists that

How Many Cyber-Races Are There?

continued from Page 325...

injured Cybermen from Pete's World to give the people of Mondas a fighting chance at survival. Perhaps, then, the relative humanity and individuality of the Mondas mob is because they are all volunteers and only partially processed, using elements of the design rather than wholesale conversion. This could also be why they seem not to have access to the data-stamps ("The Next Doctor") and thus don't recognise the first Doctor when they meet him at the South Pole (or maybe they do - he is singled out for taking to their ship, with Polly brought along to ensure his cooperation). The Mondasians are the last Cybermen to be able to immobilise or kill by touch, even though their hands seem unchanged, until the Lumic branded ones start electrocution.

All of this is plausible, but what about other points where the fugitives from the Void may have impacted on established continuity rather than rewritten it? After all, when we see some Cybermen in "A Good Man Goes To War" (X6.7), they have ships exactly like those in "The Invasion" and "Silver Nemesis" (25.3) and are apparently active in the fifty-first century, long after their last recorded appearance hitherto. (Please note the strategic use of "apparently" in that last sentence. The chronology for River Song is something we'll have to sort out later.) Apart from the missing Lumic badge, these ones are identical to the ones from Pete's World. So were the ones in the Flashmob of Doom (X5.12, "The Pandorica Opens") and the ones whose spaceship crashed in Colchester 300 years ago without anyone noticing (X6.12, "Closing Time").

An intriguing discrepancy arises when these last two are compared, one which explains a lot. The Colchester ones have Cybermats, a tool only really used by them in their most depleted state. Their conversion equipment is remarkably basic, and fails to even damage Craig's chain-store jeans. The snap-on heads are part of a totally different conversion system from the one in the Lumic factory, but one refined far beyond that initial stage when the one under Stonehenge attempts to recruit Amy. (The conversion process in "Cyberwoman" is so unlike anything else connected to the Lumic process as to be almost a different species. It seems to be based on a painting by Pete Wallbank, called *Cyberwoman*, which was a grubby piece of torture-porn inspired by Lytton's death in "Attack of the Cybermen" and featured on the back of an issue of *The Frame* in 1989.) Yet at Stonehenge, the Cybermen were playing with the big boys: they had a scout whose dismembered limbs and head were semi-autonomous and capable of firing knockout darts. For them to be more advanced in 102 AD than in 1711 is improbable. The one that attacks Amy has Lumic markings. The ones that attack Essex shop-workers don't.

So Lumic-model Cybermen have made a home somewhere in our universe, despite the Doctor twice sluicing them into "hell". Those ones are in the proverbial loop about keeping space and time safe by locking the Doctor in a box under Stonehenge. Admittedly, the aliens named and shown who are also in the posse include a number of second-string foes (see **Wot? No Chelonians?** under "The Pandorica Opens"), but there's a Cyberman (or what's left of one) on sentry duty, rather than a Dalek or a Drahvin (3.1, "Galaxy 4"). Yes, that was probably a ruse to make the Doctor feel as though he'd defeated his antagonists when they were tricking him, but the key point is that this lot know that he is a Time Lord and connected with a threat big enough to make the Daleks team up with the Zygons, the Sontarans and, er, the Hoix (X2.10, "Love & Monsters"). This sounds as if they've been playing with those naughty Dalek data-stamps again. And that might make a lot of things about 80s Cyberman stories suddenly almost make sense. A bit.

There is a good case to be made that "Silver Nemesis" is only possible if the Cybermen have access to information about the Doctor's murky past from beings who experienced it at first hand. Admittedly, this information is post-Time War, but who is to say that the opening salvo of this conflict had not already happened (25.1, "Remembrance of the Daleks" or indeed 12.4, "Genesis of the Daleks"). The Cyberleader in "Earthshock" (19.6) has been briefed thoroughly, and his Lieutenant knows of the Time Lords and their current policy on non-intervention. They seem to think, however, that their accidental trip back to 65 million years before affords them a chance to alter history,

continued on Page 329...

X2.6 The Age of Steel

they avoid murder if possible. He's clever enough to realise that the Cyberman on board the vessel is a robot, then figures out how to fake it into destroying the transmitter mechanism for them. He risks himself and Jake to rescue Rose and the Doctor, but seems adept at flying an airship *and* operating the PA system to stage a rescue. He claims this to be the result of diligent gaming.

At some point, he decides to stay and fight the Cybermen, even if this means he won't see his home universe ever again. He justifies this to Rose by pointing out his gran's still alive and needs him. He's come to terms with Rose being with the Doctor, sounding not so much regretful as adult about the way the two of them have moved on. The first thing he decides to do after leaving the TARDIS for good is to go liberate Paris with his alternative self's boyfriend. [Mickey next appears in X2.12, "Army of Ghosts".]

• *Pete Tyler.* Secretly, he's been a high-ranking level of the Preacher resistance movement, code-named 'Gemini'. [This could be something simple such as birth date, but having this as a codename in a story that's all about odd parallels is a bit rich to be a coincidence.]

When Jake and Ricky want to kill him, he stays fairly calm when explaining that he's Gemini. He believed the Preachers to be better organised and more numerous than 'Scooby Doo' and their van / Mystery Machine [so Evil Parallel BBC1 shows Hanna-Barbera cartoons]. He's picked up a few things about Cybus Industries, enough to know Battersea is where the action is and that the Cybus technology was focused on preserving the brain without worrying about the rest of the body. What's more, he knows the code for the emotional inhibitor - and when the Doctor hints about needing it, immediately catches on and says it. When he kills the Lumic Cyber Controller by dropping him to his death, he says it's for Jackie Tyler. He decides he'd rather not look inside the TARDIS, telling Rose that someone needs to work on the cleanup operations [but also while looking for an excuse to leave after Rose reveals her parentage].

Intriguingly, he seems aware of the theory of parallel universes, as if he was somehow expecting something like this to happen. [Bear this in mind for when the Cybermen return at the end of this season.] He thinks of Rose as his dog [though she seemed to be rather more Jackie's]. When our Rose calls him 'Dad', he tells her 'Don't'.

The Supporting Cast (Evil)

• *John Lumic.* He seems genuinely curious to hear what the Cybermen are thinking, and calls them his children rather a lot. He does seem to genuinely want a Cyber upgrade eventually, but panics when his creations force the issue. They retain enough sentiment and admiration for their creator to make him Cyber Controller [after all, what's the point of using him in particular if uniformity is such a blessing?], and upgrade him as such after Mr Crane badly injures his life-support systems. The Lumic Cyber Controller acts rather like the pre-converted version, and is still conscious and alive enough to threaten Pete even after the codes have been sent. It seemingly dies by being dropped into a burning factory from a great height. To denote his status, they leave his brain showing through a transparent case [see 13.5, "The Brain of Morbius"] and give him black coating on his tubes and face-plate [see 12.5, "Revenge of the Cybermen"]. Although he is mainly plumbed into his throne, he is not part of any collective; his voice retains some of Lumic's timbre and he is able to yell 'No-o-o-o-o-o-o' when things go pear-shaped.

The Non-Humans

• *Cybermen.* They remember their previous lives, but a small chip - the Doctor dubs it an 'emotional inhibitor' - prevents any emotional reaction. Battersea Power Station has a large number of Cybermen who have been converted, but are 'paralysed'. [So presumably are kept in some sort of deep sleep for later operations. The tunnel is identified as 'Deepcold Six', but, despite Mrs Moore's comments about the chill, it is not *cryogenically* cold, or else she wouldn't be there to complain.] They're interested by a binary vascular system and decide to analyse the Doctor rather than shooting him [so there's some sense of curiosity remaining where biological improvements are concerned]. The rest of the converted Cybermen die in torment when their emotional inhibitions are cancelled.

When the transmitter blows up, the formerly enthralled people marching into the factory are terrified, but alive and capable of running away [so the Doctor's sniffy warning about deactivating the ear-pods might have been unreasonable, although see "Army of Ghosts" for a rather unpleasant counter-argument].

There are factories on every continent (all

The Age of Steel X2.6

How Many Cyber-Races Are There?

continued from Page 327...

whereas their limited time-corridor abilities mean they can only participate in pre-set events. This extends to the attempt to save Mondas ("Attack of the Cybermen"). Thus the ones in the sewers in 1985 are the leftovers from 1970-ish, but given plans for how to upgrade themselves to the same level as the state-of-the-art ones sending them the info. There is no need for them to ferry vast armies around in their tiny time machine, if they can simply smuggle back information on how to do the upgrades and knowledge of what is going to happen in December 1986 to the stragglers from 1970-ish.

(Sorry to digress here, but... one way to resolve the hopeless mess that is "Attack of the Cybermen" is to assume that the business on Telos is happening, as Flast says, "at this very moment" and that the time machine has come to them from future-Telos. Otherwise, the Cryons have a magic radio that sends replies to Lytton's signals back a thousand years. If they can do that, much of their sorry story could have been prevented. Maybe the Cryons are behaving themselves on orders from above not to rewrite history (even one line). The idea that the Cybermen can themselves operate a time machine with no ill-effects seems to contradict 22.4, "The Two Doctors", so we will go for the simplest version, that they use the specs of the captured machine to construct time-corridors, not full-blown time-travel. Anyone can do that, apparently.)

So the three main Cyberman stories from the 1980s ("Earthshock", "Attack of the Cybermen", "Silver Nemesis") could all be the result of a stray data-stamp allowing the Cybermen to mess about with limited time-travel and give themselves an upgrade to the model we see in those stories. It's not quite the Lumic design, but it may be a compromise between that and their available resources after the Cyber War. Had they had the abilities we see in "The Pandorica Opens", a large chunk of history might have been very different, though, so it might *only* be data-stamps that made the trip. The Lumic model, amended, seems to have been less adept at time-travel than the ones who go around saying "Excellent!" - possibly because it has less organic matter and thus less scope for the DNA amendations that we now hear are essential to time-travel.

That the "Attack" Cybermen think of Mondas as their ancestral home seems to count against this theory. With all that they know, maybe re-opening the Void might have seemed like a better idea than fiddling with an earlier Doctor and their own history, if it were at all practicable. Let's face it, the old-style Cybermen barely seemed capable of faster-than-light travel (although they must have had a bit of this, or else the plan to invade using a far-off star going nova on cue is utterly stupid rather than just very, very silly - see 5.7, "The Wheel in Space"). We've no real evidence that any others have; the Cybermen in "The Invasion" and "Silver Nemesis" both have vast fleets in nearby space, hiding and the only other planet we see them on is Telos. The ones in "A Good Man Goes To War" have long-range scanners able to pick up whatever's going on in fifty-first century space, but they aren't invited along to the party on Demons Run. There's no evidence that they are time-travellers.

As a most-parsimonious theory, we could say that one souped-up Lumic model might be all that was needed, landing on Mondas to give hints to the eager and desperate masses before going to Stonehenge to be killed by an angry Celt and leaving behind a data-stamp waiting to be read by a later, compatible model. The Mondasians go to Telos, as we all thought. This doesn't explain why the fifty-first century ones are the apparently less developed ones we also see in a crashed spaceship in Colchester, unless it's one that left Mondas three hundred years ago. Of course, if they can't travel faster than light, the possibility of a lost ship not showing up for thousands of years might be a simple relativistic effect. As and when it arrives, the Cyber-War (some time between "Earthshock" and "Revenge of the Cybermen") has come and gone and they can start converting people in a whole new area of space.

seven), and the Lumic Cyber Controller indicates that they've been activated as well. [We don't know how much market saturation there's been for ear-pods on other continents, so how many people have been converted and what's happened to transmitters on other continents is anyone's guess.] They appear to have been kept in storage, deactivated and ready for use, pending a successful takeover of London; Mickey and Jake believe that Paris would subsequently have been assaulted. [The update the Doctor gets from Pete in "Doomsday" seems to confirm this.]

History

• *Dating*. [We have to assume that the finale - with the Doctor and Rose visiting Jackie in her kitchen - was on Jackie's birthday. (No doubt there was some comment about a lack of presents, hence the gift in "Army of Ghosts".) We're led to think that the whole stay in the alternative universe takes a bit over 24 hours, with most of the action taking place in one night. As Mickey commented last episode on the date being the same when they arrived as when they were expecting to be in London after a trip to the Dagmar Cluster in the future, we'll assume that the return without Mickey was timed for that day. In later stories, we're told that the time-flow between universes is unsteady, but what this means when at least one of them has time-travel is perplexing at best.]

Lumic has bases on 'seven continents'. [If Pete is to be believed in "Doomsday", the world has got so warm that the ice caps are melting, suggesting that Antarctica is inhabitable (maybe this is the 'New South America' we heard about last week).] Mrs Moore, while employed at Cybus Industries in '95', accidentally read a file so classified, she was forced to go on the run [possibly suggesting that this programme has been in the works for at least a dozen years].

Alternative London [not to be confused with the 70s guide-book of the same name - see 16.6, "Shada"] has a superstition about it being unlucky to see a bride the night before her wedding, just like the proper version. And *Scooby Doo* is common to both universes. There's a force called the Security Services, whom 'Gemini' still trusts despite Lumic's coercion of the government and most institutions. When the Cyberman invasion becomes obvious, London is placed under martial law and everyone is urged to stay in their homes.

Catchphrase Counter A couple more 'I'm sorry, I'm so sorry' incidents. One is to the former Sally Phelan, another to an anonymous Cyberman looking in a mirror. There's an unexpectedly enthusiastic 'WorYesss' when the Cyber-Controller asks the Doctor if he's ever felt pain or grief. Thankfully it won't be used much, but since the Doctor repeats the 'This ends tonight' phrasing in later seasons, we're required to note that he uses it here in reference to his plan to take down all the Cybermen.

Deus Ex Machina Handily, the codes for switching off the emotion-suppressor are readily accessible. Precisely why they had one installed is another matter. And the TARDIS battery somehow manages to zap Cybermen without affecting any nearby humans. Mrs Moore is killed by a stealth Cyberman wearing slippers.

The Analysis

English Lessons ("Rise of the Cybermen" and "The Age of Steel")

• *Honk* (v.) To smell bad.

• *Pop* (n.) Apparently, other countries have more specific rules for what's "pop" and what's "soda" (we used to use "soda" to do laundry, unless you mean bicarb), but here all fizzy non-alcoholic drinks are deemed "pop". (The curious term "mineral" - as in "mineral water" - was used until about 1975, but became too confusing once people started selling water in bottles.)

• *Cider* (n.) Fermented apple-juice. Unlike America, the rule is that apple-juice on its own is never called this, because "cider" is not only stronger than most beers on sale, it is often more laden with hangover-inducing histamines and likely to trigger weak stomachs into revolt. For this reason, it's usually seen as a younger person's drink, the staple of teenage parties. The home-brewed version, "scrumpy", is more potent still and common in the West of England (see 8.5, "The Daemons"; 4.1, "The Smugglers" and comments in Volume 3b about "Pigbin Josh" and his ilk). This has been the cue for endless fan-jokes about drunken robotic "Cidermen" talking like characters from *The Archers* and failing to take over Earth.

• *"Your father had a bike"*: a late-Victorian term, popularised by Music-Hall, for promiscuity.

- *Jack the Lad*: Another Victorian term, for someone who believes himself to be charming and gifted, a self-confident chancer. Del-Boy (op cit) began as one. It has connotations of being a bit of a hit with the ladies (or other lads in some circles). Rose would obviously have this as part of the legend of Pete Tyler, but had spent some time with one who apparently really was called "Jack". (Of course, "Jack" was often shorthand for a sailor, as in "Jolly Jack Tar".)
- *Toffs* (n.) Aristocrats, oligarchs, etc. Not, as is often thought, derived from "toffee-nosed" but "tuft", as in the tassels on the mortar-boards Oxford students wore. (It's recorded at least a century before "toffee-nosed".)
- *Mrs Moore* (n): A character from *A Passage to India* by EM Forster. She posthumously started a human-rights protest during a rather pointless trial caused by her own son's small-mindedness. She herself was rather more open, and found even the fearsome wasps in India to be enchanting (cf X4.7, "The Unicorn and the Wasp").
- *Tariff* (n.) The agreement and payment-plan for a particular mobile phone network, generally pay-as-you-go or monthly fixed fees.

Oh, Isn't That...? ("Rise of the Cybermen" and "The Age of Steel")

- *Roger Lloyd Pack* (John Lumic) is, of course, the roadsweeper Trigger from *Only Fools and Horses*. He spent nearly 30 years as a petty criminal so dim even Del-Boy (op cit) can outwit him - the leg-man for Boycie (see 13.6, "The Seeds of Doom"). He has pretty much mined that seam in various other roles too, including a stint in *The Vicar of Dibley* and as Barty Crouch Snr in the *Harry Potter* cash cow. The upshot of this is that everyone in Britain sees him in the Potter flicks or as Roger Lumic and says "It's Trigger!".
- *Don Warrington* (the President). Another sitcom veteran, this time from ITV and *Rising Damp*, as one of the tenants in the grotty house let by Rigsby - the pilot, derived from the stage-play *The Banana Box*, revolved around Rigsby believing that Philip (Warrington) was an African prince. After this, Warrington tended to be cast as bosses - notably in odd cop-show *C.A.T.S. Eyes*. By the time this story was broadcast, he was appearing as himself in the BBC2 I-don't-know-kids-today-jeremiad-fest *Grumpy Old Men*. (In fact, he'd been in a BBC1 trailer for *New Street Law*, where he played a judge, seconds before the episode began.) Big Finish cast him as Rassilon (14.3, "The Deadly Assassin" and others) in some of their audios.
- *Andrew Hayden-Smith* (resistance member Jake Simmonds). Like any teenage actor in Newcastle, he had been in *Byker Grove*, which was like *Grange Hill* with Geordie accents (and produced by Matthew Robinson - 21.4, "Resurrection of the Daleks"; 22.1, "Attack of the Cybermen"). Then he had been one of the main presenters for the CBBC programming on BBC1 in the afternoons. His departure from that provided handy pre-publicity for this story.
- *Mona Hammond OBE* (Rita-Anne, Mickey's gran) has done the triple of British soaps, with three years as Blossom in *EastEnders*, a semi-regular gig on *The Archers* and a stint in *Coronation Street*. She's done all the usual cop shows and ethnic-based sitcoms (notably *Desmonds*). All of this helped keep her theatre company going.
- *Colin Spaull* (Mr Crane, Lumic's assistant). A child-actor at the same drama-school where Graeme Harper trained as a boy, Spaull has been in many things Harper directed (including 22.6, "Revelation of the Daleks") and all over the place.

Things That Don't Make Sense ("Rise of the Cybermen" and "The Age of Steel") There's a recurrent problem with people echoing back comments from conversations they weren't in. Ricky seems to know that he's London's Most Wanted despite the fact that Jake broke the news to Mickey. Rose is expected to remember a conversation the Doctor had with Mickey about gingerbread houses while she was off looking up her "dad".

The TARDIS lands at Lambeth Palace at what the clock says is 11.55am. And yet, two or three hours later, Rose's magic phone says it's 11.35. Mickey apparently walks from the Embankment to the Powell Estate (half a mile, tops), but when he gets there, he's told that he can go past an army roadblock because it's before the 10.00pm curfew. Even if the soldier does mean that it's ages until 10.00, the imposition of a curfew five hours after nightfall is abnormal. And why this conversation means that Mickey can just walk past the roadblock when the person before him had a full check on his ID is another matter.

Beggars actually *can* be choosers. Mr Crane shows up with a van, promising food and, more importantly, tea... and a crowd of young-ish men who have been living on their wits for at least a month each are fooled despite the disappearances of their friends. (Anyone who has any experience

X2.6 The Age of Steel

of London's homeless would be horrified by this automatic assumption that they are all stupid. Some are, mainly as a result of long-term drug or alcohol dependency or mental illness that's often the initial cause of their homelessness. Worse, because we have earlier seen a *Big Issue* seller with an ear-pod, we can assume that anyone who hasn't got one must *really* have fallen though the cracks despite efforts to help - or exploit - them. Those not on some kind of programme or in a shelter are somehow still alive despite armed soldiers enforcing a curfew. So Lumic's elite troops are either brain-damaged, insane or feral.)

They've moved Blackfriars, apparently. For the Dome (presumably the "Lumic Arena" in this reality) to be visible from this wasteland, there must not be any buildings at all in or around Bermondsey - although we know from later episodes that Evil Parallel London has its own Canary Wharf development run by Benign Parallel Torchwood. Maybe, as a geordie lad lost in That Lunnon, Jake is confused and means Blackheath. In that case, it's been flattened out quite a bit and Lewisham's been demolished to make way for a devastated wilderness. (No, that *would* actually be a change.) Similarly, when they are opposite Battersea Power Station, there seems to be a hill in front of an industrial wasteland, with a dirty great gasometer behind them. If we map this on to the real-world location of the Lumic base, this means that this hill is where Pimlico Public Library ought to be and the blue-lit gasworks is right on top of, er, Buckingham Palace. They've taken this Republic thing to heart, obviously. Maybe building a giant mound of earth was a job-creation scheme.

The Doctor concludes from Rose's Magic Phone that Pete Tyler is very well-connected in this reality. All right, it turns out that actually he *is*, but the leap from soft-drink-manufacture to total world domination is one even Coca-Cola have failed to make. Maybe this is Evil Parallel Virgin Cola, in a form that actually caught on, and Pete's got Richard Branson's life in this reality (hmm... did he get to publish the *New Adventures*?[62]). And what on earth was he thinking when he, as 'Gemini', he fed the Preachers information that Pete Tyler was working for Lumic? If it was all a clever double-bluff in case Lumic tapped into Gemini's broadcasts, you think he'd mention that as well. And the information he got doesn't seem to have been as reliable as all that, if he didn't even know that his own house would be the key point in the plan.

And where *is* Pete's home? It's close enough to London for Jackie to get over-ridden along with everyone else and be almost first in the queue to be canned, but it's also far enough away for Lumic to not be able to pop in on a winch from his blimp. It's handily close for Mickey to rush off and retrieve the Doctor's suit (and apparently Rose's clothes too), but a long drive for the Prez. The Doctor and Rose take hours to get there (assuming the 11.35 time is right, it wouldn't have been dark before 5.00pm). The Doctor tells the Preachers to get him back to the city, but Jackie is there before them and in enough time to be converted, despite going on foot. Moreover, how does the whole population of London get to Battersea Power Station? We'll assume that the curfew is suspended (because the regular army all had ear-pods too), but somehow the Preachers get from the TARDIS (south of the river, opposite Parliament) to a handy vantage-point north of the river, opposite Battersea, without being caught in a logjam of marching canning-fodder and Cybermen on either bridge. Why not cut half an hour (or probably more, with the whole city walking there slowly) off the journey time by walking down the Albert Embankment and heading along Nine Elms Lane or the many side streets along the same route (which, as local residents, Rose and Mickey would know even if Pete's forgotten them)? Despite earlier comments we've made about London topography, Mickey is able to rendezvous with Ricky, so the streets can't have changed that much. Rita-Anne still lives at her address from the other London.

Lumic's homecoming is said to cause shares in Cybus Industries to *double*, defying most conventional laws of economics if the company is as established and huge as it otherwise appears to be. (Stop for a moment to think about the incredible surge in buying it would take for Apple - estimated in September 2012 with a worth of $626 billion US - to similarly double in price overnight.) And it seems rather curious that the President can go to a party and no security personnel are around, nobody has a radio and a code-word for a terrorist assault or insurrection (which is essentially what Lumic is doing) and London's subsequent paralysis isn't the prompt for a national - indeed pan-European - military assault. Basically, there's been a coup and nobody comments. Admittedly, the media are all run by Cybus (and a cut line from Mr Crane seeing Jake filming would have confirmed this), but a society so fixated and dependant upon this sort of thing must have contingency plans for viral attacks or other systemic failures. The over-ride on Jackie reveals merely that her own domestic security is run by Cybus, with full-body scans on entry (odd that the Doctor gets past these without his coronary abnormality showing), nothing about the President's personal guard. If there's a need for a curfew, then someone somewhere must have realised that putting military and commercial comms on the same network was asking for trouble - it'd be the first thing Mrs Moore would have thought of, surely?

And the Cybermen arrive, looking to recruit the nation's top people... as always, though, the logic of shooting dead people they ought to have added to their data-store, if not their work-force, is shaky. (Maybe, as these Cybermen were dossers a few hours ago, this is a form of class warfare - in which case, *not* killing the filthy plutocrat who tortured them into becoming like this is a strange move.) Yet from then on, they adopt a new strategy of allowing anyone who might be a regular character in *Doctor Who* off the hook. Ricky is killed by Cybermen who just stand there glaring at Mickey until he rather belatedly runs away; the Doctor is recognised as biologically odd, and so is taken to Cyber Control to talk for ages, unimpeded; Rose and Pete are spared because Pete is famous and Rose, er...

Speaking of whom, Rose has just been told she's trapped in the wrong universe because the TARDIS has died, then seen two Mickeys (one of whom is killed by terrifying metal men who wanted to kill her), and seen her late father alive and rich, and become angry with her mum (who's a right cow in this universe), and was threatened with execution by her boyfriend's evil twin - who was then revealed to be the Scarlet Pimpernel - and *now* she and her long-lost daddy voluntarily go into a slaughterhouse to try to rescue her mum. This, after the Doctor stresses, 'You'd have to show *no* emotion. None at all. *Any* sign of emotion would give you away.' For pity's sake... this is *Rose Tyler* we're talking about. A woman who bursts into floods of snotty tears when confronted with rotisserie chickens (X1.13, "The Parting of the Ways"). And what are Rose and Pete going to *do* with an earbudded Jackie, assuming they can find one individual amongst the entire population of London, since the Doctor's told them that they can't take off the earbuds? And if Pete knows the file that contains the code for the emotional inhibitor (and thus, presumably, quite a bit more detail about how the Cybermen tick if he has an obscure bit of data like that), you think he'd be able to contribute a little more directly to the 'above between below' plan. Considering what's going to happen to the rest of the world if they don't save *London* tonight, his determination to find his estranged wife at a time like this seems strange.

We'll buy the idea of Mickey and Ricky having the same tattoos, but not Ricky having two identical outfits and thinking that dressing his deeply suspect doppelganger in the spare set and taking him along, explaining everything to him as they go, is a good idea. Later in the Preachers' van, the Doctor disables some earpieces because 'Lumic could be listening' to their conversation - a better idea, surely, would have been to turn off those devices at the *start*, rather than the *end*, of that chat?

So... before adopting the name 'Mrs Moore', Angela Price was a secretary at Cybus Industries who had to go on the run and adopt a new identity when she opened the wrong file. Somehow, hiding out with the Preachers (whose numbers were never that large) allowed her to learn chemistry up to degree-level and develop weapons, hacking skills and a TARDIS-like bag full of gadgetry. They called Donna Noble 'Supertemp', but this is a learning-curve only Batman villains have ever undergone. Mrs Moore seems to have Googled her way from Miss Moneypenny to Q, without Cybus finding her. And these are the guys who are anti-technology? (Maybe she's one hell of a fast reader and had access to a lab she could carry with her in that satchel, as well as a very up-to-date technical library.)

If a magnetic mine sticks to a Cyberman, then all this stuff about 'steel' is more than just picturesque. Why, then, don't the Preachers just go to a scrapyard and drive off with one of those giant magnets, picking Cybermen off the streets and dropping them into the Thames to sink and rust? (Or just magnetise one of them thoroughly and let all the others who come to help stick to him.) Why are they allowed out in the rain? Sentiment aside, Lumic might have picked a better place to start than London in February - if Geneva's giving him gyp, why not attack them first?

Other design-flaws would have to include:

X2.6 The Age of Steel

heads that explode when presented with anomalous information (which gets worse when their own data-stamps can be used to confuse them into bursting in "The Next Doctor"); a cancellation code for the emotion-suppressor, fitted as standard and remotely triggered by a phone call; and visible cerebral hemispheres for the Cyber Controller protected by a bit of glass. That emotional suppressor has to be repressing a lot besides emotions; the Cybermen all seem conscious and can reason, so why are they blindly obeying Lumic's orders? It's certainly convenient for the plot that all the converted Londoners spontaneously implode when the emotional inhibitor code is cancelled. (Why the Doctor thinks this is going to work at all, given that the one whose inhibitor broke is asking sensible questions and very much *not dying* until he points the sonic screwdriver at it, is another question altogether.)

More to the point, why is there an invasion at all? Lumic's fear of death/fear of cyberisation is set up well enough, but that's a long way from deciding to turn the entire London into Cybermen, and we never get a sense of why he's even bothering. There is only one solution to these last two problems that works, and that's if a newly converted Cyberman gets some kind of loyalty bonus if s/he can persuade a friend to join, rather like signing up for a satellite dish and getting £50 for everyone else you get to do likewise. But this just means that when they are talking about compulsory upgrades for everyone at Pete's party, they have even less reason to abruptly decide that electrocuting everyone is a better idea. (Although, of course, as the second-best *Doctor Who* monsters, they must have the innate ability to know when a cliffhanger's coming...)

Critique ("Rise of the Cybermen" and "The Age of Steel") A lot of people were worried that this would be a gamble too far. They'd just about managed to get away with relaunching the series and bringing back the Daleks, but if they messed up the Cybermen, or reminded anyone unfamiliar with the programme's history of the elephant in the room, the Borg, this could be the end. The overwhelming sense that this story gave on first transmission was relief. As a script and production there are flaws, but in general they got away with it. Anything else is a bonus. There are a lot of bonuses here.

Getting Graeme Harper out of mothballs has paid off. Faced with what ought to have been a daunting technical challenge of multiple Mickeys, armies of Cybermen and a subtly-different world - not to mention a script that could have come out looking hackneyed - he has managed to inject pace, warmth, tension, menace and, above all (the word that keeps coming up when he is discussed), *energy*. He has ensured that this model of Cybermen belong in the world that spawned them just as much as the Skaro that housed the Daleks (1.2, "The Daleks") was an extension of its inhabitants. As is well-documented, everyone had an idea what the Cybermen should look like, what the Alternate Universe scenario should have been and how dystopian this world ought to be. Harper was able to impose a cohesion onto this, picking what he thought would work together and would fit the backstory for this world. A less-respected, less secure director might not have got his own way over all the other interested parties. His decisions, from the Art Deco/ engine-block look to the sound the Cybermen make as they stomp and even the bizarre choice of record used by Mr Crane to drown out the screams and the lingering shots of the factory that follow, raise this story above its raw materials.

They have to, because the script's all over the place. There are a lot of good moments when characters get to talk like real people (especially Mickey and Mrs Moore), but a lot of the dialogue has to convey complex information and amend earlier-shot scenes. A number of sequences have people saying things that seem to have Post-It notes all over them. Lumic and Jake are the worst casualties here, but the Doctor and Rose get caught by this too. Tom McRae's script occasionally has its own voice, but for a lot of the time the dialogue is purely functional, the sort of expository lumps we had in the mid-80s. Nobody here actually *says*, "This is madness" (the stock line that came whenever Eric Saward had "improved" a script), but it seems horribly likely at times. The pre-credit scene is especially clunky, although MacRae can be exonerated from that. Another apparent 80s throwback is the way that so much of the end of the first episode is prevarication to get the cliffhanger to work. In fact, there are moments halfway through each episode when the entire plot changes and someone's in peril, so the whole thing seems oddly retro. (It might have needed a bit of rejigging to make Mickey being bundled into a van by strangers a full-blown cliff-

The Age of Steel X2.6

hanger - maybe meeting Ricky would have been it - but the Cybermen waking up while the Doctor and Mrs Moore are in a tunnel is classic end-of-episode stuff.) As broadcast, the pacing is all out of whack for 45-minute episodes. The story builds up momentum then squanders it, or rushes through scenes that need more time to breathe. Harper's almost on top of this, but he's not a miracle worker.

What's most noticeable here is that we learn more about how this world works and where it differs from ours in visual signs than dialogue. Most of these are scripted. There are sequences like the mass halting in the street to get the downloads that tell us more about what's happened and how people were *persuaded* to let it happen than the inconsistent lines about "New South America" or "signals from Venuzuela". It's things like the shot of Battersea Power Station at night, with airships over it, that sell this as a viable world. What the newsreader tells us is less significant than him appearing on a phone, with an "E24" logo behind him (we're already in danger of forgetting that this facility wasn't around in Britain when this episode was shown). The moral of the tale isn't rammed down our throats, but in amongst all the thinking that viewers are being encouraged to do about the links between technology, society and choices people made that shaped this world differently from ours, there's a clear line of reasoning available. Sydney Newman would have approved: this is what *Doctor Who* was invented to do.

They come close to laying it on a bit too thick with Mickey and Ricky. It might have helped if they'd ever bothered with his backstory or as anything but an appendage to Rose before now. One problem we'll have a lot with this run of episodes is that all of the writers have seen Series One but not each other's scripts. They have been chopping and changing script editors, and Davies has been too busy with his own work to pay that much attention to getting everyone to agree who Mickey is. Everyone but Davies is writing as if the most recent episode is X1.8, "Father's Day". What they've missed, because they are all starting from the same place, is that Mickey has long since replaced Rose as the "ordinary" character in the Doctor's life. Even though they've put him in an anorak and given him computer-skills and an obsessive interest in the Doctor, he's more than the comic foil they seem to want him to be. A lot of this is down to Noel Clarke, who shows with Ricky how much Mickey is acting rather than just performing, but it's mainly because Rose has used up almost all the goodwill the public had towards her. *Billie Piper* is still massively popular, but Rose Tyler is a pain. For some commentators, the last straw is the end of the "Daily Download" scene where she tries to simper the Doctor into submission. Piper's doing her best, but this is creepy: any girl over seven who tries this is probably cajoling a sugar-daddy. It's icky enough that she's doing it to a centuries-old alien, but then we remember why she's doing it, and what her interest in the billionaire Pete Tyler is, and it's downright unhealthy. Mickey's meeting with Ruth-Anne is more effective for being understated (even though we can see the camera crew reflected in her glasses). The story needs more of this, drip-fed over a longer period. Just transposing Rose's "all about Mickey" spiel into X2.3, "School Reunion" would have helped both stories. (Rose needed to have more to do in the latter half of "School Reunion", and talking to Sarah about Mickey might have paved the way for Sarah's out-of-the-blue suggestion that the Doctor needs a Smith in his life.) Yes, this is backseat driving, and yes, we're quibbling to stop this review being too gushy.

Most of the casting decisions pay off, although it's hard to see what they thought Roger Lloyd Pack would bring to the part of Lumic other than making everyone at home say "it's Trigger!" If it was an attempt to cash in on the *Harry Potter* link, then the fact that Pack never gets a scene with Tennant was perverse, however welcome it might be for everyone else. Helen Griffin (as Mrs Moore) is especially helpful in rooting this story in a kind of plausibility. However, once again Shaun Dingwall stands out as the one to watch. This is a plausible extension of the Pete Tyler we saw in 1987 last year, but different enough to be untrustworthy.

If we had to have a parallel universe story at all, it's probably best we had this one. It's not a simplistic dystopia, not an implausible utopia, just a lived-in world like ours could have been. In it, those most pointless of monsters, the Cybermen, have a reason to have come into existence after all. All the accumulated dead wood of continuity is gone without offending the people who like all the continuity. They make sense for the first time since their return in 4.6, "The Moonbase" (in 1967!) and are properly scary again. They are a physical threat - no longer susceptible to radiation, gold, hot ice or, er, jazz - as well as an exis-

… tential one. As with all evil parallel universe stories, they are the "there but for the grace of God" warning. Yet they are created out of a basic fear of mortality. For once, a world made out of borrowed trappings from other allegedly-SF TV shows makes sense on its own terms and does things no other form of drama could do, but for more than just making pretty pictures and exciting action happen on a screen for 45 minutes. If they could just invent entirely new worlds from first principles, rather than hand-me-downs, they'd be using the *Doctor Who* format to its utmost. As things stand, this and "Father's Day" are as close as the twenty-first century iteration has got yet.

The Facts

Written by Tom MacRae. Directed by Graeme Harper. Viewing figures: "Rise of the Cybermen": (BBC1) 9.22 million, (BBC3 repeats) 0.6 and 0.3 million. (AIs at 83%). "The Age of Steel": (BBC1) 7.63 million, (BBC3 repeats) 0.6 and 0.1 million. (AIs at 83%).

The initial broadcast of "The Age of Steel" began at 6.35pm. AIs were at 86% for both.

Repeats and overseas promotion Die Aufstehung der Cybermen, Die Ara des Stahl, Le Regne des Cybermans 1&2.

TARDISodes Attention Preachers: a message from Gemini (with a different voice) detailing Lumic's rise to power (a £78 billion fortune between 1982 and 2001) and the apparently related fact of a quarter of a million missing people in South America. Then what looks like Mickey driving a van away as the message is interrupted by Cybus Industries, telling us that the "ultimate upgrade" is coming.

An Order From Lumic: worldwide upgrading to begin, incompatible versions - delete. (Illustrated by a computer graphic of a brain going into a Cyberman head, a Lumic logo being stamped on the chest, then footage of Lumic and the Cybermen in the tunnel from the episode.)

Production

("Rise of the Cybermen" and "The Age of Steel") As soon as a second series was granted, Davies knew how it had to end and began making plans. As the second run was being planned, he had explained to Noel Clarke his hope that Mickey would develop from stooge to everyman to action-hero, apparently leaving and then returning as a self-confident secret agent, and that Rose would be separated from the Doctor by something vast, potentially a whole universe. As we will see (**Was Series Two Supposed to be Like This?** under X2.11, "Fear Her"), the plans were flexible, but there would probably be Cybermen and almost definitely an alternate universe. When it came to making the more detailed plans, he left the last two episodes vague in the proposal, but was very clear on what he had in mind for the parallel-world two-parter that was to re-introduce the Cybermen, evidently planning to give this pair of scripts to someone else to write.

Precisely *who* got this gig was a surprise to everyone. Tom MacRae had thrust a script at Davies during a 1999 signing of the *Queer as Folk* book, and the elder writer had unofficially mentored the tyro thereafter. MacRae had wound up on Sky One's soap *Mile High* and written for *No Angels* - see "School Reunion" - but Davies offering him such a substantial part in the high-profile *Doctor Who* relaunch was unexpected. Davies autographed and dated a copy of his *New Adventures* novel *Damaged Goods* to mark the event. Knowing a little of the series (mainly Sylvester McCoy's stories), the 25-year-old, as MacRae was by then, was more confident writing about the Cybermen than making up a new foe from scratch, but was given reference material including the *DWM* comic strip "The Flood" (see "Army of Ghosts" for why this is significant) and the Big Finish audio *Spare Parts* (which examined the early days of the classic-series Cybermen). He also watched a number of the earlier Cybermen episodes.

By this time, Davies had sounded out Shaun Dingwall about coming back as a slightly different Pete Tyler, and the notion of the Cybermen origin story taking place in an alternate Earth grew. MacRae wanted to explore the alterations to society (he studied Anthropology) and took the first few scripts into this area. Instead of the cliché where everyone in a parallel world is an evil alternate of their "usual" selves, MacRae wrote in a twist that Pete's surrogate was secretly a hero ("Puck", who became "Gemini") and revealed that Ricky and Mickey were more similar than they pretended. Davies thought that the ideas were stronger if the world in which they happened was almost fingerprint-identical to ours, and wanted the emphasis to be on a movement like the wartime French Resistance. Permission was sought to use the name "Body Shop", a high-street brand of ethical cosmetics, for places where people could trade in flesh limbs and organs for the latest models. Eventually, this idea and the whole premise of *Spare Parts* was sidelined for a new approach equating personality to software and "downloading" minds. Whilst the starting-point for Kit Pedler in 1966 had been anxiety about medical intrusion into personality, Davies thought that anyone writing about that now would explore genetics rather than big metal men stomping around. Thus to make the Cybermen work in the twenty-first century, without a lot of explanations and flashbacks, they had to not be decaying or diseased, but tricked into this living death through consumerism. MacRae was given a sneak preview of the as-yet unbroadcast "Father's Day", to get a feel for the characters of Pete, Jackie and Rose. (He clearly didn't pay too much attention to the details as, in post-production, the dialogue in "Rise of the Cybermen" about Mickey's mum dying when he was six had to be redubbed to avoid contradicting the Cornell script. Then again, nobody else spotted this until long after recording.) Davies prevailed upon him to make the alternate versions of the semi-regulars closer to the "originals" than MacRae originally intended. This also shifted the focus of the story to the phones and related consumer electronics, with everyone wearing Bluetooth-style earpieces. This decision caused problems with actors not hearing each other or the director, and delays when the earpods popped out, especially when this gave Noel Clarke and Andrew Hayden-Smith the giggles on a fraught night-shoot.

• A less unexpected decision was the director. Graeme Harper had been active since his previous *Doctor Who* work (21.6, "The Caves of Androzani"; 22.6, "Revelation of the Daleks") and had simply not been available to direct any episodes in the 2005 series. He had been in touch with Davies right from the moment the return of the show was announced, and their paths had crossed on a couple of earlier projects. Davies was confident that someone who had worked on the series since the early 1970s and who had been trained by Douglas Camfield (to date, still the most prolific director ever to have worked on *Who* and one whose decisions and approach changed the direction of the series in countless ways) was able to handle a three-month slog through four episodes in one production block. Tennant also hugely admired Harper's work, and was impressed by the veteran director's boundless energy and invention.

• Sorry, but things get complicated at this point. Block Three was two two-part stories made concurrently, but shown two months apart. In fact, counting the news bulletins in "Army of Ghosts", shooting went from 1st November to 11th April. They never did anything as gruelling or complex again, but telling this story will require a bit of duplication when we get to the end of the book...

The shoot began on 1st November, with the scenes of the TARDIS arrival in on the Embankment. The main location for the actors was just in front of Lambeth Palace, official residence of the Archbishop of Canterbury, opposite the Houses of Parliament and fairly near Battersea Power Station. Another nearby landmark, the 80s ziggurat of the security service, MI5, was in some shots, having now officially been acknowledged to exist after almost a century. The following day, the TARDIS arrived in the Powell Estate again, as the crew went to the Brandon Estate for the beginning of "Army of Ghosts". Thursday 3rd and Friday 4th were the days when Jake observed Mr Crane's "recruitment drive" at the docks in Cardiff and Ricky met Mickey in an abandoned mansion (Tal-Y-Garn), whilst Tennant and Piper returned to Q2 to make the mini-episode for *Children in Need* (X1.13a, "Pudsey Cutaway"). Louise Page's costume for Ricky (and later Mickey) used test-designs from sportswear manufacturers that weren't made into commercial product; after the hassle over the Punky Fish motif on Rose's clothes last year, they had to not have Nike swooshes or Adidas stripes. Later the second night, Tennant and Piper went with the others from that day to shoot material of the Preachers' van (which stalled several times: one of the props men fashioned an L plate for Clarke). Officially, everyone had the weekend off, but Tennant had to go to the premiere of the latest *Harry Potter* in London, as he was in it. Monday was the day for the TARDIS scenes and Tuesday was the day Newport's Riverfront Arts Centre was to have doubled for Lambeth Palace Road for the scenes of Rose with her phone looking up Pete's bio and Mickey storming off to see his nan. They didn't get much work done, because of rain.

• There had been dozens of potential designs for the Cybermen, veering from rotting corpses in

X2.6 The Age of Steel

steel exoskeletons to lightly reworked versions of the 80s "Earthshock" design. The Lumic logo in place of the traditional chest-unit was one of MacRae's suggestions. It was generally agreed that real actors would have to be inside physical costume/props rather than CG Cybermen throughout (although one sequence in "The Age of Steel" shows that it might have worked if they'd had time and money). Davies emphasised the industrial look, making sure everyone thought "steel" instead of "silver" (cf. the "copper and bronze" mantra when giving the Daleks their "Mini Cooper" makeover; X1.6, "Dalek"). Harper had, in his initial meetings with the team, suggested "Art Deco" as a theme for this entire world, and that the Cybermen could look like prewar carbonnet figurines. Neill Gorton had one suitably *Metropolis*-esque design out of 30 possible options, and the rest of the world took elements from this.

Unlike most episodes, this one had meetings specifically about the creature design, because all else spun off from this. There were three elements from older designs that were explicitly retained: the tear-drop from "The Wheel in Space" and the jug-ears and flexible neck from "The Tenth Planet". Although the "metal" casings were plastic or glass-fibre, there was an aluminium powder mixed into the resin and the resulting pieces were rubbed with grate-polish. The light in the mouth, after attempts to work out radio-control, was chin-operated. The finalised design was based on the measurements of Paul Kasey, one of the main monster-men of the BBC Wales era, and individual costumes had to be customised to fit other performers whilst still looking uniform (everyone had memories of 20.7, "The Five Doctors", when Welsh extras of various sizes tried to look menacing and machine-like). After an original request for 40, only ten suits were made. Harper and choreographer Ailsa Berk had worked out ways to make the actors march in synch and look mechanical whilst unable to see what they were doing - some days, they were joined at the wrist by elastic bands. Harper's stated aim was to make the implacable march like the fascistic hammers in the animated clip from Pink Floyd's video "Another Brick in the Wall". There had been an attempt at drilling them in V-formation so that only one needed to see where he was going, but eventually they found ways to move in a line without too much difficulty.

However, before all of that, the first use of the costume in front of a camera was the one in the Zeppelin (Ruari Mears, with a stuntman doing the punch through the deck). This and some of the boardroom sequence took up 9th and 10th November. At around this time, the first photos of the revised Cybermen were released - to devalue any leaks - and it seems that the episode title "Parallel World" was long-gone. (The title for episode six was only decided upon later, but various permutations of "Rise of the Cybermen" were in use from October on.) As fittings for the other dozen or so Cyber-suits continued, Roger Lloyd Pack recorded the dialogue for post-conversion Lumic and an attempt was made to shoot POV shots with a camera on the wheelchair. That didn't go as planned, and the chair collided with a wall. Contrary to reports in the tabloids, Lumic was always intended to be in a motorised wheelchair. It was pure coincidence that Roger Lloyd Pack broke his ankle shortly before production began. One early draft had made Lumic the son of a dying millionaire, trying to save his father to finally earn respect, but the two characters were eventually combined, inadvertently becoming more like Davros than originally planned. Pack thought the character had similarities with Donald Rumsfeld, although this isn't apparent in his performance. Two units were used on the next day, with one lot back at Newport for an attempt at recovering Tuesday's lost scenes and the other going to a nearby power-station, doubling as Battersea in close-up. This is where they needed ten Cybermen in formation, and the problems of shooting precision-drilled Cybermen in darkness became more obvious. As there was a cold spell, the power station had to work more than they had planned so the shoot was rethought on the fly. (Tennant, meanwhile, was at Q2 for the interactive episode "Attack of the Graske", and astounded the crew by having learned all of his lines for this as well as the "real" episodes being made.)

- After a weekend off, the shoot resumed at Veritair, the Cardiff heliport used for Rose's balloon-flight in X1.9, The Empty Child". This would be used for some of the factory roof scenes, and a few months later for the climb up Alexandra Palace aerial (X2.7, "The Idiot's Lantern"). This was mainly the day of the rope-ladder scenes with Clarke and Hayden-Smith. Next day, another familiar location, the Paper Mill at Sanatorium Road, was used for the burning factory interior; the exterior can also be seen in the scene where

Mickey is stopped by soldiers (the train on the bridge was serendipity). A last go at the Riverside scenes was squeezed in to a photo-shoot and recording shot the interview with Derek Acorah for "Army of Ghosts" and the police briefing the following day before the start of a week at the Tylers' mansion. This was a private home on the outskirts of Cardiff, so the crew were obliged to wear plastic overshoes. Harper had ten weeks to prepare for the shoot, and the location was found on week eight; the owners, who live there, were very obliging. The kitchen of that house was used for the advert for ghost polish in episode twelve, and the third day of the shoot required the use of a land-rover for the end of episode thirteen, but the main use of the house was at night, for the party and massacre. The location had only been discovered and agreed with the owners a few days before the crew arrived. On one of the days there, the daughters of Gerry Davis, co-creator of the Cybermen, attended the recording (some versions claim that they were recruited to swell the numbers of party-guests, but this doesn't seem to be true).

• Nick Briggs was on set to provide Cyberman voices, as he had for the Daleks. There was some debate on how to pitch the voices, with Harper veering toward Darth Vader-ish delivery, Briggs preferring the 60s Peter Hawkins versions (see Volume 2) and Davies receiving 11 almost-indistinguishable suggested voices from Briggs and being unable to choose. On location, Briggs went with something like "The Moonbase", until in post-production his guide-vocal was sped up and something close to 6.3, "The Invasion" was agreed upon as a compromise. He also read in for Lumic arguing with the President.

• The shoot continued through snow, drizzle and thick mist; the thin plastic casings, with a high metal content to conduct heat away from the body, over a tight rubber suit made the Cybermen actors freeze (one got a cold and sneezed gooily inside his helmet). Between takes, they huddled around an electric heater, thawing out during an unscheduled three-quarter hour break when snow prevented recording altogether. Tennant and Piper were whizzing back and forth between the various extra-mural requirements of their roles. As Christmas drew nearer and the launch of X2.0, "The Christmas Invasion" caused them to drum up publicity, they were going to be spending more and more time in London, often to receive awards, although during this bit of the shoot they also did the switching-on of Cardiff's Christmas lights and Tennant recorded messages for two charities on-set. Piper helped soon-to-be-ex-husband Chris Evans launch his new Sunday night chat-show, *OFI Sunday*, describing her action-figure as looking like Master Splinter from *Teenage Mutant Ninja Turtles*.

By the time they left this location, the weather was forcing changes to the schedule. Sally/ Kerry Phelan's death (in one early version, the Cyberman remembered having been a small boy) was to have been in the open air, to be shot in Victoria Park. The rewrite used Mrs Moore, as they had decided to retain Helen Griffin after the character's original death in the tunnels. As it was, much of the 24th was spent back at Veritair, this time actually appearing as an airstrip for the President's chat with Pete, and back on wasteland for the Preachers escaping from the mansion (planned to have a dodge 'em sequence with Cybermen). The next day, as revised scripts were produced, the Cyber Control Centre scenes were shot in Treforest. Due to availability, Pack and Tennant were never on set at the same time, as by the time the Doctor was in Lumic's presence, the conversion had been completed and Lumic - now converted into the Cyber-Controller - was played by Kasey and Briggs. On the Saturday, the death of Mr Crane and Lumic's voice-overs were the main activity, with Tennant and Griffin going to the tunnel entrance on the same industrial estate. On Monday, the Preachers picked up Mickey from a street in Grangemouth (Compton Street, at the corner of Court Road and with Ninian Park rail sheds in the background, was transformed into Waterton St, Southwark, SE15 via road-sign, and a few "For Sale" signs).

The next four days were spent at Q2 on the Torchwood scenes for episodes twelve and thirteen, then two days off, so it was on 5th December when the team went to the streets around the Hamadryad Health Centre, near the bay, to record more scenes of the Cybermen marching around a terraced street and the exterior of Battersea Power Station. (If you are wondering how the posh bit of London where they have to be to see it from that angle acquired a big old industrial gasometer, the scene of the Doctor's party observing the Lumic factory was shot at the top of a hill near Cardiff Bay Industrial Park, still in Grangemouth; Mickey is actually heading towards Pizza Hut.) In the early stages of the evening, one of the Cybermen was Gethin Jones of *Blue Peter* (being tall and from Cardiff, it was inevitable he'd be recruited), making yet another behind-the-scenes piece.

The next day was the day Tennant and Griffin headed for the hills, to a former atomic bunker near Bridgend that was now the tunnel; the second unit were nearby, making Brackla stand in for Norway in "Doomsday". The tunnel was nowhere near as long as the careful editing and remounting makes it seem, and there were only a handful of Cybermen needed. That evening saw the premiere of "The Christmas Invasion", with the teaser at the end concluding with a glimpse of a Cyberman. The next few days were given over to the season finale, and so it was on 15th December, after the rest of the cast had gone home, that Ricky was killed and the split-screen conversations and chase were made, mainly at Q2. Some of the shopping street scenes with the extras only were recorded the following day, including the night scene of everyone being "overridden", along with more work with the International Electromatics pantechnicon out in Newport docks. Although work on this block resumed on 3rd January, the next piece of this story to be made was a rescheduled attempt at the Doctor and Rose in that same shopping-street scene (you will observe slight differences in the weather). This was in Cardiff Bay, with St Paul's Cathedral matted in some time later. Piper and Dingwall spent the night of the 11th at the Stella Artois brewery for the rescheduled Cyber-conversion scenes. The last day for Noel Clarke on Series Two was on the 13th, at the RAF base at St Athan's previously used in X1.9, "The Empty Child", completing the factory roof scenes. Finally, on 18th, Jackie's flat at Q2 was the last scene on the original plan. (Something to bear in mind from now on: Piper had already filmed her departure from the series by this stage, but it was a closely guarded secret.)

- And that was supposedly that. The next month was spent finishing the two-part story at the end of the season, but in the meantime two new scenes had been devised. One was the pre-credit sequence of Lumic and an out-of-focus Cyberman, with the new character of Dr Kendrick; the other was the news bulletin in episode six. This was all shot by a second unit as "The Idiot's Lantern" was being made nearby on 18th February. Some additions and amendations to the dialogue were made in late March in the ADR session, so that the Doctor warned Mrs Moore about trip-systems rather than simply traipsing down a tunnel full of dormant Cybermen. The sound of the Cybermen stomping was augmented by, amongst other things, the kind of date-stamp used in libraries. Despite all the trims, the broadcast version of "Rise of the Cybermen" was almost 47 minutes long, and so the "Next Time" trailer was dropped. This was a popular move, as the cliffhangers were rare but welcome, and "spoilers" were considered a pain. However...

- As mentioned, the *Radio Times* for the week of episode five had a starkly-lit Cyber Controller on the front. Inside, stapled into the centrefold, was a free copy of the Panini sticker-album and two packets of the randomly-assorted stickers depicting everything from X1.1, "Rose" to X2.4, "The Girl in the Fireplace". As a consequence of this cross-promotion, the BBC's listings magazine had a television advert on the commercial stations, with a child playing at being a Dalek with a cardboard box and being chased by something after the *Radio Times* plopped onto the doormat. Episode six was moved from the now well-established 7.00pm slot to make way for the Eurovision Song Contest finals. That week's *Doctor Who Confidential* focused on Mickey's transition ("Zero to Hero", as they imaginatively put it).

X2.7: "The Idiot's Lantern"

(27th May, 2006)

Which One is This? *Quatermass and the Telly.*

Firsts and Lasts For only the second and final time, Rose wears a dress (the other instance being in the previous Mark Gatiss story, X1.3, "The Unquiet Dead", unless you count the mini in X2.2, "Tooth and Claw"). That's about it - although, if you really want to make something of it, the use of Magpie Electricals as the supplier of all television sets and monitors when BBC Wales are trying to avoid product-placement begins here and extends throughout *Torchwood* and well into the future (X5.2, "The Beast Below", and Martha's set from X3.12, "The Sound of Drums" to cite really obvious examples).

Watch Out For...

- This being a Mark Gatiss script, it's a pastiche of old cult-ish stuff, mainly the kinds of shows a small boy would feel slightly daring for watching circa 1978 while his parents were out or in bed. It's primarily a compilation of *Sapphire and Steel*'s

The Idiot's Lantern X2.7

greatest hits, but with a setting that lends itself to *Quatermass* pilfering (mainly the dubious Hammer Films cinematic remakes of the original TV serials) and a purée of nostalgia documentaries about the history of British television (so obviously *Muffin the Mule* has to pop up, as he did in Gatiss' sketch about the creation of *Doctor Who*). As we'll see in **Production**, Gatiss and David Tennant had just worked on a remake of *The Quatermass Experiment* and - perhaps for this reason - the script team were keen to root out all the in-joke references they could find. One made the final cut (see if you can spot it before we point it out). Even the name "Florizel Street" is an obvious gag. (Obvious to anyone here, anyway - see **The Big Picture** for what British viewers would have brought to the party.)

- This week, Cardiff is pretending to be North London in the era of trams and ten-bob notes. There are a few small flaws, such as the matte shot of Alexandra Palace (AKA Ally Pally) being flipped so that we see a side of this Victorian edifice that is facing away from Muswell Hill, but the main problem is that, with clever digital jiggery-pokery, they triple the attendance of the street-party at the end. Not really a problem as such, except that they don't change the costumes and the one Indian family in this street (just about plausible for 1953) becomes a statistically improbable number of such individuals for any part of London pre-1970. And Ally Pally, in close-up, has very different brickwork from what anyone who's been there would recognise - if we didn't know better we'd swear it was, ooh, maybe a hospital in Cardiff or something.

- For only the second time, a vehicle is seen to exit the police box exterior of the TARDIS. The first time was a bewildered motorcycle cop in the McGann TV Movie, shown exactly ten years to the day before this episode premiered, but this is the first hint that the Doctor has a garage aboard. (Other than in the tie-in books, in which the eighth Doctor kept a VW Beetle in the Ship - not a Morris Minor, you'll note, but a Nazi vehicle supposedly fuelled on Weetabix. We could stretch a point and include Bessie's interdimensional journey in 7.4, "Inferno", but that isn't *quite* the same thing. See also X7.7, "The Bells of Saint John".) They could have got the scooter through the doors by editing, in the traditional "come along, K9" manner (see Volume 4), but they fiddled about with digital effects and building a little ramp for the scooter to hop over the lintel. If you look closely, the majority of scooter scenes use a slightly chubbier stunt-driver in the Doctor's costume.

- Back in the far-off days of Volume 6, we proposed the notion that "Paradise Towers" (24.2) is best watched as an unofficial pilot episode of *The League of Gentlemen*. We mentioned the more-than-passing similarity of this story to that (executed criminal becomes a psychic entity that shouts "Hung-gree" in a city resembling 50s Britain gone wrong), but we had no idea how often this pattern would be repeated afterwards. Far from being the "oddball" story the self-appointed custodians of the programme's morals claimed, "Paradise Towers" is the template for "The Beast Below" (X5.2), "Gridlock" (X3.2) and arguably elements of "The Long Game" (X1.7), "Amy's Choice" (X5.7) and the Silver Cloak from "The End of Time Part One" (X4.17). Most recently, and obviously, the latter half of Series Six had two stories markedly similar to it, one by Gatiss (X6.9, "Night Terrors"). "The Idiot's Lantern" is really the story that established the Sylvester McCoy adventure as an integral part of the programme's heritage. If you think it's coincidental, watch the scene where the Doctor turns being interrogated by DI Bishop into his own quest for answers, and compare it to how McCoy and Richard Briers handled a remarkably similar set-up.

- Talking of over-familiarity, this story was moved up the broadcast order at short notice, a fact that does it a huge favour. If this had been shown ninth as planned, there would have been two consecutive stories about an alien that absorbs people and keeps a "scrapbook" of their faces, pleading for help (X2.10, "Love & Monsters"), and then another story where an iconic, televised London event makes the unexplained disappearances of people from an ordinary street something to be hushed-up (X.2.11, "Fear Her"). To make it worse, this story and "Fear Her" are both directed by Euros Lyn, and both end with street-parties.

The Continuity

The Doctor He knows at least one Kylie Minogue song, as he cites her as the origin of the phrase 'It's never too late'. [He calls her just 'Kylie', as most people would in 2006 Britain. See X4.0, "Voyage of the Damned" and **Stunt Casting: What are the Dos and Don'ts?** under "Tooth and Claw" for why this is deeply odd.] He's perversely stubborn

341

X2.7 The Idiot's Lantern

in not admitting that they haven't landed in New York, and oddly insistent that the Vespa is a good idea. [He seems rather desperate to be thought of as "cool".] He wears a helmet even before it's compulsory, and messes up his elaborate - and anachronistic - DA hairdo[63]. He regards 1953 as a 'brilliant' year, a 'classic!'

- *Ethics.* Once Rose has been abandoned in the street, faceless and brain-dead, the Doctor takes the Wire's activities personally and vows no power on this Earth can stop him. [So was he prepared to let the populace get deracinated and shoved in warehouses until this point?]

- *Inventory: Sonic Screwdriver.* As usual, the sonic screwdriver opens padlocks, scans for medical information [neurological this time] and detects power-sources, but it also does something unspecified to stop the Wire sucking the Doctor's face off.

- *Inventory: Other.* Here the psychic paper proclaims the Doctor to be the King of Belgium. [The significant thing about this is not that anyone on duty at Alexandra Palace is unaware of what this regal chap really looks like (and they were well-used to royal visitors from across the globe by then), but that the Doctor doesn't know what it said until he himself caught a glance at it. This seems, though, in keeping with his presenting the paper to Queen Victoria in "Tooth and Claw" and only knowing the results after-the-fact. Earlier, the Doctor evaluates the Connolleys' household (out loud) and then decides what sort of fake ID to use to impress Eddie.]

The Doctor is carrying a small chunky torch [it may have been Mrs Moore's; see last story]. He has a Betamax video recorder.

The TARDIS Aboard the Ship, somewhere, is a late 50s Vespa scooter [possibly with a supply of helmets in many sizes and shades, which is why Rose gets one to match her outfit]. The Doctor feels able to give this to Tommy at the end [suggesting he must have a few more similar vehicles around the place - a Lambretta would be more his style anyway]. He somehow gets this vehicle to drive up the Console Room ramp at enough speed to get over the lintel of the exterior door. [So he must have revved up somehow - let's hope the TARDIS has decent air-conditioning to remove the fumes.]

The Supporting Cast

- *Rose* seems to have spent her youth watching Cliff Richard films on telly with her mum, and listening to Jackie's sailor boyfriend explaining the old saw about the Union Jack being the flag when on a boat. [It appears she had a different mother during this part of her childhood.] She is enthusiastic about the Doctor's scooter and the chance to dress up a bit, and remembers being told all about the Coronation and television catching on. She uses her smile as an offensive weapon when ducking out from under Eddie Connolly's arm, and investigates the televisions and Mr Magpie's role in the "infection" off her own bat. [Basically, she seems to be auditioning to be Sarah Jane Smith this week.] She has no compunction in asserting her authority over Eddie, even shouting orders at him.

When reduced to being a face on a screen, she is clearly shouting 'Doctor' instead of asking where she is, as every other victim does.

- *UNIT/Torchwood.* Not a sausage. [At least, in the broadcast version. A cut scene implies that Torchwood are supervising the investigation.]

The Non-Humans

- *The Wire.* [As anyone familiar with pre-1989 *Doctor Who* will almost be able to recite...] The Wire was executed by its own people, but escaped as an incorporeal electrical/psychic field, made contact with a human who was dabbling in such matters, reworked a familiar twentieth-century form of technology, and got him to build alien tech because it needs to harvest the mental energy of humans to manifest itself and take over Earth. [See 5.2, "The Abominable Snowmen"; 5.5, "The Web of Fear"; 6.2, "The Mind Robber"; 7.1, "Spearhead from Space"; 13.3, "Pyramids of Mars"; 14.1, "The Masque of Mandragora"; 14.2, "The Hand of Fear"; 15.2, "The Invisible Enemy"; 15.3, "Image of the Fendahl"; 19.3, "Kinda"; 20.2, "Snakedance"; 26.3, "The Curse of Fenric"; about 20 *New Adventures* books and alternate episodes of *The Sarah Jane Adventures*.]

In this specific case, it has chosen to appear on television sets as the lady who did the closedown announcement, and has learned a lot of 50s broadcasting idioms and phrases appropriate to a lady of that apparent age and upbringing. It exerts a pink lightning-like force that bends the image and absorbs both the neural impulses and the actual physiognomy of each victim, preserving an

Are We Touring Theme-Park History?

We commented in the notes for "Tooth and Claw" (X2.2) that there was a mini-genre of deliberately silly and self-consciously anachronistic costume-drama romps, and a broader tendency to try to make anything set pre-1940 look "contemporary" and "earthy", with lots of mud and shagging. Film producers and television executives had no faith in the ability of audiences to accept anything else. Within the context of *Doctor Who*, this compounded, or facilitated, a shift away from Adventures in History (the staple of the original set-up in 1963) towards using an all-purpose setting of Da Olden Days as a backdrop for the same old *Doctor Who* schtick of monsters, explosions and sparkly-orange-pixy-dust. This period was a homogeneous mass of common folk in wigs, cloaks and Mummerset accents, ruled by posh types who talked in such wise, enunciating divers arcane locutions the better to establish their suzereinty. Prior to 2005, the lowest reach of this tendency had been whenever Anthony Ainley had travelled to Historyland (20.6, "The King's Demons"; 22.3, "The Mark of the Rani") and potentially interesting or exciting set-ups had been squandered on yet more Time Lord name-calling. Rather than showing history as a process, this was just using it as a location, a genre or an excuse. As we will see, the idea of travel in space equating to travel in time is stubborn and unhelpful.

It might be significant that the most forceful iteration that our own time will be history one day, and that decisions made in the past shaped our present, was a time-paradox story written by a former university History don, Louis Marks (9.1, "Day of the Daleks"). The process of change, of one time being different from the periods before and after it, is what distinguishes fiction that can be called "Historical" and the more popular (in style and intention, if not in actual readership) stories set in a version of a past period. In adapting books either set in or written in a particular time, the makers of films and television have each chosen where they pitch their work on this sliding scale. Just as writers setting stories in "The Future" or another planet have the choice of devising all the rules, systems and customs of a world from first principles or nicking it all from other people's work, so anyone using an earlier time on Earth has a choice of taking the hats and words from earlier bodice-rippers or actually researching the period and its *mores*. Television production always has some degree of compromise, based on what sets and costumes they can afford or borrow. (A bigger worry if you have to do each one from scratch rather than, as with the Hollywood studio-system or the pre-John Birt BBC, having warehouses full of handy things left over.) Freed, as much as possible, from such practical concerns, a writer could choose how far to use any time and place as just a reservoir of pretty frocks and heightened passions. Now, there is little option.

There's a word used, almost always insultingly, that needs to be more carefully explained. "Escapism" simply means any work where the audience is invited to contemplate a lack of consequences for tempting-but-forbidden actions. James Bond has a Licence to Kill and can drive as fast and recklessly as he likes; Robin Hood evades taxes and traffic; *Grand Theft Auto* rewards players for actions that would get most people a prison sentence; Superman can fly and see through girls' clothes. The converse of this is that in most other ways the stakes were higher - no fussing about mortgages or motor insurance, but getting hanged or flogged if the Bad Guys (because History is all Bad Guys and Good Guys in this version) catch you, or shame, ruin, pregnancy and death if it's a female-led tale. Many of these books were in long series, so the evasion of consequences was not only the plot of each one, but the appeal of the whole set. The absurdities of some of the popular series of the 50s are well documented, and later bestsellers made sure they aged the characters and reflected small alterations in the technical details of military hardware, surgical techniques and millinery. Yet once the Historical genre was kicked off in earnest by Sir Walter Scott's *Waverley* (1814), there was a strong urge to use the past as a model for a more "authentic" style of living where people (well, white men) were free of most modern constraints and the stakes were higher and more uncomplicatedly settled with violence and cunning. That's where Alexandre Dumas and Raphael Sabatini come in, buckling swashes for pleasure and profit.

However, altering the recorded sequence of events was a no-no; Hollywood could make stupid errors (deliberately, in the case of *Braveheart* or The

continued on Page 345...

X2.7 The Idiot's Lantern

impression of each on a screen as a disembodied face silently begging for help. [This must surely expend a lot of that precious energy, so it must have a practical function - possibly intimidation to get panicking victims thinking faster and more "juicily".] The Wire can somehow make itself turn the right colour on the screen and has cajoled Magpie into building a simple, elegant portable set in which to store itself.

The faceless victims have their features replaced with blank skin rather than being left gaping, and are left 'ticking over' with barely any neural activity. They compulsively clench and unclench their hands [how they breathe is another question].

History
• *Dating.* Well, *durr*, it's the day before the Coronation, then Coronation Day itself [1st and 2nd June, 1953], although significantly drier than everyone remembers. Magpie receives the Wire into his home [so to speak] some time before this [although the sequence of events is confused in the broadcast version].

Catchphrase Counter Mr Magpie tells Rose: "I'm sorry, so sorry".

Deus Ex Machina Whatever the Wire's power is, it resembles electricity enough for the Doctor's plimsolls to afford him protection. Lucky it wasn't raining, eh? [See **Things That Don't Make Sense**.]

The Analysis

The Big Picture As we mentioned under "Delta and the Bannermen" (24.3), the British film industry (back when we still had one) spent most of the 1980s and 90s making acerbic dramas about life in 1950s Britain. Films made in the 50s were governed by laws which, whilst laxer than Hollywood's Hays Code, still meant that anything seamy was discussed in code. The gulf between what life was really like when rationing and the ready availability of war-surplus weapons led to the black marketeers replacing Nazis as the villains of contemporary dramas and the inability of these dramas to say outright what the sharp-dressed spivs were up to was the theme of those 80s films. The men with quiffs and hair-oil were pimps and murderers; that everyone with families to feed was somehow implicated in their activities was the great unsayable of the last years of George VI's reign. Contemporary sensibilities amongst 80s movie-makers meant that being able to say that conditions in living memory were so alien seemed to turn into an obligation to keep saying so. True-life dramas from the 50s were filmed in the Thatcher era with the sales-pitch that a Britain where racism, sexism, homophobia and the death-penalty were accepted is more than just an abstract horror for most people in this country today, but the source of real-life misery for people whose relatives were still alive and campaigning.

Audiences seemed to want to keep being told this. Much of the Conservative party's appeal was to people who accepted the 50s films as being true-to-life and desirable, both in 1951 and the 1980s (and more explicitly under John Major from 1990). Just as contemporary comedies and dramas under Clement Attlee's government had been coded rebukes at how things hadn't magically returned to pre-War conditions (or what people fondly imagined it had been like), so the various biopics made by Film Four were critical of the double standards in their historical era and the use of this period by politicians on all sides. *Let Him Have It,* released in 1991, takes place mainly in 1952 and made strenuous efforts to keep faith with the day-to-day life of people then - this cost a lot and required a lot of promotion, so the campaigning nature of the script became the sales pitch (because the two leads were unknowns, Paul Reynolds from *Press Gang* and some gawky bloke called Eccleston). Like the earlier *Dance with a Stranger*, it told the story of one of the last people to be hanged, and made society out to be the source of the wrongs. However, a dispassionate eye might observe that the unspoken villain is cinema itself, and specifically the attempts by young people in Britain to live up to how Hollywood presented America. This attempt was also the subject of the notorious *Absolute Beginners*, which presented late 50s Soho as gawdy and hep, when films made there at the time were all stark monochrome and pseudo-documentary, often "exposées" of the prostitution, drugs and black-mailing of gay men that somehow they never actually got around to exposing. (See **Things That Don't Make Sense** for the early careers of Adam Faith and Cliff Richard. Or watch the films they made then... if you dare.)

So, life in Coronation-era Britain wasn't as wholesome as even the Ealing Comedies made it

Are We Touring Theme-Park History?

continued from Page 343...

Patriot, because Mel Gibson could be prejudiced against the English on studio time and money, and nobody cared back then), but in books you can't change the facts. If you remove the underpinning of these stories all being in "true" periods, you may as well have dragons and supernatural jewellery. The appeal of the historical romance (that's "romance" in its original meaning of "story without a moral attached to it") was that this daydreaming was somehow connected to how people once really lived. Factual research, however slight and nonchalantly deployed, was the pizza-base for the tasty stuff on top. As originally formulated, Doctor Who was similarly constrained. Whilst it had the ultimate evasion of consequences - never being able to return to any place or time once they'd left - they maintained a curious double-standard about overthrowing terrible monsters and oppressive regimes on alien worlds, but scrupulously avoiding any change to Earth's sequence of events. Stories set in Earth's past were, therefore, all about *avoiding* having consequences. This persists as late as X5.10, "Vincent and the Doctor" (we'll draw a veil over X6.8, "Let's Kill Hitler"), and it is in these stories that the concept of the Fixed Point comes in to play. More particularly, the fact that well-known figures can be put in jeopardy and, therefore, all of History will go wrong as a result is one rehearsed in "The Unicorn and the Wasp" (X4.7), despite the apparent inconsequentiality of the events. The Vespiform is about to either die or leave Earth, so the only real threat to the Causal Nexus is whether Agatha Christie is going to die in 1922, a matter that will only be of concern to Angela Lansbury's agent. Nonetheless, The Past is sacrosanct in ways that The Future apparently isn't, and other planets can never be. Since "Day of the Daleks", this kind of doublethink has been addressed within the stories themselves (see **What Constitutes a "Fixed Point"?** under X4.2, "The Fires of Pompeii" and our notes on X4.16, "The Waters of Mars").

The more thoughtful novels that followed Scott developed the idea of vast changes affecting representative families over decades, and relegated the Great Men of History to off-stage or minor roles. Perhaps significantly, the one time *Doctor Who* has even come close to attempting this was the "wrong" chronology in "Turn Left" (X4.11), and this is telescoped into half an hour rather than given four to six episodes. Other than this, only "The Dalek Invasion of Earth" (2.2) can be shoehorned into this category. Finally, and largely untapped as a source in *Doctor Who* for reasons we'll discuss later, there is a whole tradition where the forces that used to prevent people with ambitions to live as we do in some regard are dramatised and given form as character-motivations. Traditionally, this was how women characterised history (George Eliot did it very well, but Thomas Hardy was considered "immoral" for trying something similar). The best approximation in *Doctor Who* is "The Idiot's Lantern" (X2.7), but this ran into problems in the attempt.

The image of previous *Doctor Who* Adventures in History that Russell T Davies was purposefully countering is one that is harder to find when you go looking for it. There is a perception that the Hartnell Doctor spent any time he had not fighting Daleks meeting famous people, but his autograph book is actually pretty sparse: Marco Polo and Kublai Khan (1.4, "Marco Polo"), Nero (2.4, "The Romans"), Richard I (2.6, "The Crusade"), Robespierre (1.8, "The Reign of Terror"), Bing Crosby (3.4, "The Daleks' Master Plan"), a few mythical characters (3.3, "The Myth Makers") and most of the antagonists in the Gunfight at the OK Corral (3.8, "The Gunfighters"). And in almost all of these cases, the characters were there almost as landmarks, not influenced by the Doctor and certainly not inspired by him. The model for the supposedly "traditional" Celebrity Historical is in fact the Colin Baker Doctor, who in the space of five episodes had met George Stephenson (22.3, "The Mark of the Rani") and someone claiming to be HG Wells (22.5, "Timelash"). In both instances, these were people helping the Doctor and Peri in some routine space-opera shenanigans rather than something normal for their own time, as had been the case in all those Hartnell adventures. More usual, from 1.6, "The Aztecs" on, was meeting people at the bottom-end of the fame-scale, reacting to changes occurring in historical periods - or not occurring. We may have seen Richard the Lionheart and Saladin plotting things we read about in textbooks (back when these things were

continued on Page 347...

X2.7 The Idiot's Lantern

out to be. Hardly ground-breaking, even for *Doctor Who*. The point is that those 80s films and a dozen more like them had turned domestic tragedy in early 50s Britain into a mini-genre, with a cottage-industry of period billboards, magazines, radios, tea-cups and wallpaper to support it. By the time we get to films such as *Buster* or *The Krays*, the attempts to pass judgement on violent thugs who were being turned into folk-heroes was secondary to the "ohh-look-we-had-a-teapot-like-that" sensibility. (This is a large part of the success of *Life on Mars* - the real one, not the American version - and *Ashes to Ashes*.)

Meanwhile, the ownership of the well-known and dearly loved films that these were opposing, the Rank and Ealing films whole generations grew up watching as afternoon TV, was now divided between Carlton and Granada, the two ITV giants. For these companies, the DVD rights were more important than allowing BBC or Channel 4 to keep showing them all once a year until the crack of doom. (ITV1 wouldn't show black and white films in daytime now it was a national concern, although the regional stations it had subsumed had done so when they were cheap.) As a result, TV companies were more inclined to show the other British-made films of the period from smaller companies, which meant that the public's impression of the 50s started to conform closely with what had been the "revisionist" view taken by Film Four. The "Quota Quickies" (intended to keep the studios in line with protectionist moves to stop our screens being filled with Hollywood product back when film was a significant employer in the UK) were a sort of London *film noir*.

This period was also, as you've probably gathered by now, the dawn of television as a mass medium and so a lot of capacity was kept in use by the studios making cheap film series. An early hit was former police-chief Edgar Lustgarten (yes, really) putting his name and face to anthology series of slightly sanitised shockers (see 2.1, "Planet of Giants"). These were re-run for kitsch value by Channel 4 in its early days, usually as a double bill with either 40s US *noirs* or *The Avengers* (amazingly, getting its first repeat on our screens in late 1982). The trouble with early television, as most of you have probably figured out, is that 90% of it went out live with no option for recording; what we have left, such as was recorded and not destroyed in line with Equity agreements or technical difficulties (see **What Was the**

BBC **Thinking**? under 3.1, "Galaxy 4") is hardly representative. The filmed series and items that were telerecorded for export or the potential historical importance bosses at the time thought they might have are what our collective folk-memory of television is now grounded in. The anniversaries and themed seasons have put undue emphasis on specific figures who later became officially "important", in time for preservation orders to be put on the tapes or film-reels - most of the time.

Which brings us to Nigel Kneale and Rudolph Cartier. Cartier was the director who tried to turn Lime Grove into Hollywood. Kneale was the writer who combined folklore, conspiracy theories and SF tropes and whose contempt for the masses made his choice of television as a preferred medium all the more perplexing. It is our sad duty to confess that the scripts for the lost episodes of *The Quatermass Experiment* reveal a rather routine Cold War / police-procedural thriller for the middle two episodes, followed by a knee-jerk sneer at American science fiction and its devotees, and then the climax where television and its makers were both an obstacle to the hero and the source of his victory over what we would probably find a rather disappointing monster. The film version, made by the then obscure Hammer company, makes the story more coherent and exciting, but even this is a routine thriller for the middle 20 minutes.

However, the most shocking element of the TV original is that the three things every viewer would have known about - wartime bombing, the conventions of live television and Westminster Abbey (location of the Coronation a mere two months earlier) - were being subverted. The creepy monster from space was placed within the familiar, and the people dealing with it (the government boffin Bernard Quatermass, the police chief, the ace reporter and the "comical" ordinary folk) were all from central casting. It is the start of the "Yeti-in-the-Loo" theory of British television science fiction. (See **Was "Yeti-in-a-Loo" the Worst Idea Ever?** under 5.5, "The Web of Fear", and **Is This the *Quatermass* Continuum?** under 15.3, "Image of the Fendahl", although the answer is manifestly "No." If it were, everyone would have foreseen the events in *Torchwood*: "Children of Earth" from last time they happened.)

The Quatermass Experiment was made and shown (live) in August 1953, as a summer filler just after demand for television had exploded

Are We Touring Theme-Park History?

continued from Page 345...

taught in schools), but the focus of our sympathy was the family Barbara encountered, whilst the sneaking admiration the Doctor had for Ben Daheer - and Ian for Ibrahim - was more memorable. "The Massacre" (3.5) similarly cuts between cause (Catherine de Medici and her court) and effect (Steven and Anne) without the two sides ever getting a scene together.

Because of the way the subject of The Historical Novel has been treated in literature classes, there's a hierarchy of "good" ones that follow the proscribed pattern, commercial "trash" and - worst of all - ones written by women before Sir Walter Scott supposedly invented the form. *Doctor Who* went across all of these forms willy-nilly, but we'll stick with the theoretical taxonomy now because it'll help in a bit. The root of the difference is the idea of progress. The Victorian era was the first time any culture had been forced to adjust to continual change rather than odd catastrophes that could all be written off as unique. The past being different from the present was a novel idea. Look at paintings: prior to the Pre-Raphaelite fetish for "authenticity" (sending Holman Hunt on fact-finding tours of Palestine to get the details of his Nativity paintings right), each generation had depicted Biblical or Classical themes in the seemingly unchanging styles and settings they knew. Breughel may have been joking when he had visitors to the Epiphany wearing glasses, but he was far from being the only Dutchman to assume that Roman-occupied Judea was just like the Netherlands and had the same style of barns and hats. Even visiting other countries in the present day was done largely on the terms of the visitors. Even more intractable is the idea that people in other times thought and felt differently. The notion of a universal, unchanging Human Nature is still ingrained and useful to advertisers and politicians, but it had never been challenged until the twentieth century. Within *Doctor Who*, there were attempts to depict known "alien" cultures on their own terms, at least in the first year, but this was patchy. Imperial China was largely reported to us through intermediaries, notably Marco Polo himself, but Ping-Cho's problems began when she was shown to be influenced by Susan, who in this story is "us".

Nobody sat down and invented that hierarchy before the Historical novel became popular, nor did any of the Victorian authors consult this taxonomy before starting work. Neither the authors of the novels nor the *Doctor Who* hacks ever consciously considered where what they were writing sat on some chart or consulted a tick-box, but it's perfectly possible to infer the intent in each case by looking at the hoped-for impact on the desired audience. It comes down to two considerations: is the use of a specific time and location simply a backdrop with heightened melodramatic potential, or does the period's difference from the reader's time and culture go deeper than funny hats and recognisable villains? And is History a location or a process? If we had time, we could illustrate this by comparing Victor Hugo's novel *Notre Dame de Paris* (about how the Mediaeval mindset was forced to confront changes that made it untenable by examining the actions of people locked into it on sympathetic victims whose "crimes" are inability to fit in with those beliefs) and the Disney cartoon version *The Hunchback of Notre Dame* (in which the relatively minor character Quasimodo is pushed to the fore and made cute). The intermediate stage is the 1933 film, the Charles Laughton one that was such a gift to bad impressionists, which is all spectacle and pageant, but might as well have been set in 1933 India for all it tells us about the impact of the printing press on human rights in fifteenth-century Paris. But you can do that in your own time.[70]

If the model for all Historical fiction is Tolstoy rather than Scott, as mid-twentieth century critics held, then all deviations from that norm were inevitably a falling-off. *War and Peace*, despite its many virtues, has long dull passages where Tolstoy spells out his theory of history. It also makes Napoleon close to being a pantomime villain. But at least Bonaparte is there: the theories said that this would be a flaw and that it was the vast, impersonal forces of economics, social change and technology that were the real motors of the plots. This works in novels better than on screen. Dialectical Materialism is harder to depict than getting a short actor to shove his hand in his waistcoat. Now we've brought in the Little General, we can bring in a debate that *Doctor Who* had that

continued on Page 349...

with the Coronation. It was made in a tiny studio on the third floor of Alexandra Palace (the tower by the side of the main concourse is where television was based; the rest of the building was still for functions, concerts and ice-skating). The two BBC sequels, *Quatermass II* and *Quatermass and the Pit*, form the ur-text of Jon Pertwee's time on *Doctor Who* (as well as at least two stories in Season Fifteen). They were made in Lime Grove, the BBC's next home for drama and current affairs (see Volume 1) and the ratio of filmed inserts to studio drama is far higher. What is noticeable about both of these slick, pacy productions as regards content rather than style, is that nobody talks about television, even though they are set in a near-future where the fad for coffee-bars has come and gone and Britain is sending men into space (see **How Realistic is the British Space Programme?** under 7.3, "Ambassadors of Death"). The original play's novelty was in laying bare the function of this new medium. Television, which had brought the Queen's procession through London and all but one minute of her crowning by the Archbishop of Canterbury into the homes of millions[64], had seemed to be involving viewers in both the arrival of a monstrous being from space and the efforts of the troubled scientist who had responsibility for its murderous course across London to stop it before the whole world was consumed. The Outside Broadcast team, the invisible back-room boys who brought live sport and the Coronation to the living rooms of the land, were shown to be bitchy, small-minded and intransigent, but also technically adept and professional. Apart from the climactic image of Kneale's hand in a rubber-glove covered in twigs sticking through a photo of Westminster Abbey (the height of 1953 special effects technology, but scary enough for people who'd never seen anything like it on their small screens in their darkened front parlours), the entire last episode is one long in-joke at the expense of the very people allowing Kneale's script to get on air.

Caught unawares by the success of a drama intended to fill air-time in summer when nobody usually watched, the BBC was forced to pre-empt criticism for scaring the public by prefacing later episodes with the now-famous announcement that the programme was "unsuitable for children and people of a nervous disposition". As with most such introductions, this was done by an on-screen announcer in evening dress. BBC had begun television transmissions in 1936, for a small, well-to-do, metropolitan audience. The Alexandra Palace transmitter barely covered all of London. However ludicrously formal the presentation style seems now, it was exactly what that audience knew from theatre, cabaret, public meetings and any radio broadcast conducted before an audience. The novelty of television was, to begin with, television itself, not the things it showed. Moreover their enunciation was, whilst out-of-fashion now, tailored to be comprehensible across the whole of Britain. The standards being applied were those for radio, the first-ever national, instant medium. Received Pronunciation ("BBC English") was devised to avoid unintelligible accents, *especially* the "refined" aristocratic vowels, alienating any sector of the audience. Sylvia Peters, who can be seen at the end of episode two of *Quatermass*[65] warning viewers that next week it got really scary, was hired by the Queen to coach her in sounding (relatively) relaxed and un-snooty when making her annual Christmas Message to the Commonwealth. (Another from this period was Alex McIntosh - see 9.1, "Day of the Daleks"- who was the voice of the first advert shown on ITV in 1955.) Peters and Mary Malcolm are the originals for the lady whom the Wire is impersonating, and both ladies came back for BBC Television's 50th Anniversary celebrations in 1986 (see 23.3, "Terror of the Vervoids"). Such nostalgic events, originally fairly rare, increasingly took the clips collated for the previous ones and a sort of Authorised Version of television history in Britain has emerged, as pernicious in its way as the mythologised 1950s in film and its now-commonplace counterpart.

It is this, rather than the factual details and nuanced complexities, that Gatiss is using as his source-material. Significantly, the same 405-line monochrome images and séance-like viewing conditions that made *Quatermass* so successfully scary are why telerecordings of the Coronation look so much sunnier than the real event - EMItron cameras couldn't capture small, fast-moving raindrops. As with Dickens and Churchill, Gatiss has chosen to "print the legend". No wonder his idea of a typical street is given the name "Florizel": the archetypal every-town street from a generic North of England is *Coronation Street*, but that name was a last-minute change from *Florizel Street*. We're lucky the Connelly family weren't called "The Groves" (the UK's first TV soap - see

Are We Touring Theme-Park History?

continued from Page 347...

ran athwart this literary squabble. David Whitaker, the show's original story editor, had very fixed ideas about history as both a subject in the abstract and a source of potential adventures. Dennis Spooner, his successor, had very *different* ideas, close to those current in the series now and the wider culture this century. Spooner wrote stories where Time was malleable: "The Romans" (2.4) broke the stern rule Whitaker set that the Doctor should not cause historical events, and "The Time Meddler" (2.9) introduced what was then the shocking idea that a change in the past would have consequences and nobody in the present would know any better. Whitaker had a conception of History as a force that tended towards the order we know. His introduction to the novelisation of "The Crusade" discusses this at length, with the Doctor furnishing instances from the history books of Great Men who tried to resist their inevitable fate. This argument is rehearsed at the end of "The Reign of Terror" (1.8), when the Doctor, Ian, Barbara and Susan discuss how close they came (or didn't) to preventing Robespierre's death. Spooner wrote "The Reign of Terror", but Whitaker was in charge and seems to have added the final scenes. The consequences of the tug-of-war between Spooner and Whitaker are a matter we've touched on before and will again (**Can You Rewrite History, Even One Line?** under 1.6, "The Aztecs" and **Is Time Like Bolognese Sauce Now?** under X5.5, "Flesh and Stone").

Meanwhile, another opposition between these two founding fathers of the series is the one we were discussing with regard to novels. Spooner tended to depict people in the past as being just like people now, and struggled to get the ideological battles of the French Revolution to work as motivation because they were grounded in such alien thought-processes. The period-details and trappings were all there as per, but it was a conventional spy-drama with cribs from Dickens and a convenient trunk of clothes for the companions to dress up in, rather than a story about how history happened. Whitaker, even when writing futuristic adventures, thought like a historical novelist and tried to convey other ways of thinking or reacting to circumstances. In many ways, "The Enemy of the World" (5.4) is a historical story set in a period that hasn't happened yet. It's pitched on the fault-line between Victor Hugo and Jules Verne (writers with more in common than you'd think from screen adaptations).

This is very curious indeed. If you were to believe the theorists, the attitudes of Whitaker and Spooner to character and circumstance are the opposite of the ones writers with their respective views on the contingent nature of history ought to have. We would expect Whitaker, who thinks of time as a roller-coaster and people as passengers, unable to change course, to have Spooner's attitude of personality and attitudes being constant; or we would expect someone with a notion of history as potentially malleable and dependent on incidents that could have gone a number of different ways to think of people as palimpsests - rewritable, with their ideas and motives just as influenced by outside circumstances. But it's Spooner who conceived of present-day beliefs and styles as constant and read other times and cultures in the light of 1965. A possible clue is in how each writer came to television. Whitaker had an idea of being a novelist and drifted into screenplays. Spooner had a background in comedy and a love of comics. Television is a duel between words and pictures.

Spooner's approach is one that came in and out of vogue over the decades of *Doctor Who* being made in London. It's one that treats history as a set of pictures, as befits someone who worked for Lew Grade's ITC. It was the era before people started talking like Americans or cockneys. Anything slightly formal was old-fashioned (this was the 60s, he was from Tottenham), therefore, apparently, anything old-fashioned sounded like people in 30s films. The style of delivery and stiff postures used by both the other Shakespeare and Lincoln (2.8, "The Chase") makes it seem as if "the past" is an undifferentiated period of about ten years, not unlike the afterlife, where all the people who ever lived rub shoulders regardless of how many centuries divide them. But then they immediately mess this up by having the Beatles as a "historical" period for Vicki.

Nevertheless, the child's-eye-view of "da olden days" when Shakespeare was at school with Dickens and hardly anyone had mobile phones is

continued on Page 351...

X2.7 The Idiot's Lantern

Volume 2 for Peter Bryant's later career after his brief stardom in this in the mid-50s).

Of course, sometimes the clichés are true. Parthian Productions' *Muffin the Mule*, one of the first pre-filmed series and thus one of the first to be repeatable, was quite staggeringly popular amongst that proportion of the public to have had televisions before 1953; it was the first merchandising bonanza, and TV retailers had enamelled plates to put over the screens depicting Muffin and his chums[66], because that, for a lot of people, was what television was *for*. Similarly, *What's My Line* was the first American-format game show to catch on and made "sagger-maker's bottom-knocker" a familiar job-description and Gilbert Harding (see 8.5, "The Daemons") famous simply for being famous. Muffin and Harding were the first stars created by television.

So, whilst the majority of what look like specific *Quatermass* details are half-remembered from the film (or the 2005 remake with Gatiss and Tennant) and many of these didn't make the final edit anyway, the compulsive clutching of fists by the victims is the thing anyone who saw the 1953 episodes recalled Victor Caroon doing. Caroon's wife in the original is the female lead, another scientist and thus Quatermass's confidante, despite her having an affair with the team's medical chief Gordon Briscoe. This was the part played by Tennant in the remake, but that element of the story was given less emphasis - partly to get the running-time down to two hours, but mainly because leaving one's husband is nowhere near as hard, legally or socially, as it was in the early 50s. That last consideration must have been in Gatiss' mind as he wrote this episode. What now seems rather a trite subplot about an astronaut's wife agonising over whether she can leave him while he's turning into a cactus would have been the emotional core of the serial for many viewers who were unaware that this was going to turn out to be science fiction (the British public's perception of "genre" is something that developed over time, and was very different from America's, which explains a lot about early *Doctor Who* and what Davies was trying to achieve in 2005). We're at the start of the sub-genre that John Wyndham made all his own in the late 50s, where the institutions of Britain cope with outlandish threats in the same way that they had coped with Nazis and post-war austerity. (See **What Kind of Future Were We Expecting?** under 2.2, "The Dalek Invasion of Earth".) Again, a number of the less-successful films of the 50s that were now coming to the fore, once the Ealing Comedies and Rank war-movies were being sidelined, had this tone. A number of flicks began as police procedurals or military *verite* and then introduced a space creature. Gatiss regularly turns up as an "expert" in documentaries about these, so we presume he's seen at least some of them.

The other element of the Wire's capture of victims is the face-removal. Ultimately this must be traced back to Rene Magritte's paintings, but more directly to Adventure Four of *Sapphire and Steel*, ITV's last attempt before *Primeval* to make something like *Doctor Who*. The author of this story, PJ Hammond, wrote a sort-of sequel which was the *Torchwood* episode "From Out of the Rain". The Man-With-No-Face was that person in old photos who you never quite recognise, and he had the ability to trap people in any photo ever taken. There's more than a hint of *Poltergeist* about the eventual effect, but this seems not to be how it was written. Trapping a media-entity in a defunct format was common to both Hammond stories and "The Idiot's Lantern", but the latter's use of Betamax as the means of imprisonment might, at a pinch, be linked to "The Priest and the Beast", an episode of *The Mighty Boosh* broadcast in August 2005, i.e. during the writing of this episode. We could try to explain the plot and style of this series, and specifically this episode, but it would make even less sense as a summary. Just accept that it was about the only comedy on BBC3 that year that Gatiss or his circle weren't in, so he's likely to have caught it. The abstracted faces on TV screens resembles some of the films and photographs by Man Ray (the 30s artist, not Mer-Man's arch-nemesis in *Spongebob Squarepants*), but also seems to recall the more experimental strand of BBC television drama pioneered by the non-mimetic directors from 1936 to the early 60s. Because none of this exists in the archives, and because drama head Val Gielgud opted to follow the Cartier style of mini-cinema instead of all the other alternatives to theatre-on-screen or radio-with-pictures that Michael Barry and others thought were worth trying with a new medium, the only glimpses of this sort of thing extant are attempted reconstructions for documentaries which, by definition, emphasise how weird the road not taken looks to us. (There was a small coterie of directors looking into alternatives to the

Are We Touring Theme-Park History?

continued from Page 349...

the standard one for Welsh *Who*, and was a running-gag in earlier periods of the series. It was of a piece with Ben's assertion that Polly can "talk foreign" (4.5, "The Underwater Menace") and that everyone not from 1966 was as backward as everyone not from London. The parochial aspect of the spatialising metaphor of time as a place is that everyone so ill-mannered as to be born before one's parents is as backward as a foreigner. Thinking of "otherness" as "inferiority" was always a no-no in the series, but a certain small degree of irony was always accepted - often the same way that out-of-towners or anyone unfamiliar with the Doctor's way of life were the subjects of amused tolerance and coded remarks.

Spooner did have one advantage that later periods lacked. In those phases when "history" has been a set of generic markers, and an acting-style, there is usually a homogeneity of visual style and production values as well. Spooner was lucky in that in the 1960s, each individual story was almost a different series. In "The Crusade", we had an orchestral score by Dudley Simpson, Barry Newbery's sets making intriguing shadows and Douglas Camfield moving the action sequence set pieces to filmed inserts so that they could be edited faster and shot with hand-held cameras. This was in between "The Web Planet" (2.5) and "The Space Museum" (2.7), with very different types of music, different set-designers and lighting, and a different ratio of film-to-studio and use of effects and peculiar lenses. By contrast, Series Three was all scored by Murray Gold, lit and shot by Ernie Vinzce or Rory Taylor and designed by Ed Thomas. (See **What Constitutes a "Story" Now?** under X1.13a, "Pudsey Cutaway".) This is nothing new, as we saw in Volume 5. "The Visitation" (19.4) and "Black Orchid" (19.5) are more similar than different, with the big twist of the latter being the absence of aliens. They are also very similar-looking to everything else in Season Nineteen (except 19.3, "Kinda", which aims at a modishly distorted look in some scenes). All times and places sounded like the BBC Radiophonic Workshop.

In other phases of the series' development, there has been more of a push towards making the motives and perspectives of people from elsewhere and elsewhen the main thrust of the plot, rather than crashed spaceships or silly men going "heh-heh-heh" and trying to wreck history. Paradoxically, and perversely, the most pro-literacy period of the series only once, almost accidentally, made a story set in Earth's past (15.1, "Horror of Fang Rock"), but in general the points when comprehending "otherness" has been at the forefront of the programme's agenda have been the ones where people from different times not all being "just like us" has been most clearly stated. Oddly enough (although not if you've read **Is Doctor Who Camp?** under 6.5, "The Seeds of Death"), the idea that "personality" is less rigidly pre-determined than popularly imagined, and that to some extent it is a sort of performance (even to sexuality and self-image), is one that comes to the fore when people have read a lot. Reading entails empathy, a sort of "trying on" of being another person for a while. This shift in perspectives, as we've seen (**Why Doesn't Anyone Read Any More?** under X1.7, "The Long Game") is usually a hint that the programme-makers don't just see books as "sources" for visual works. And, as far as we can rely on the Ratings measurements for anything, it doesn't seem that this approach alienated viewers. Letting viewers see how other people thought is possible in a visual medium. Indeed, some of the biggest and most successful TV dramas have been about precisely that.

The problems of adapting historical novels for the screen are most obvious when you have a period that specifically written television drama has also handled. Any ambition beyond simply doing soap in fancy-dress has to be either foregrounded in ways that make a watchable analogue of the narrator's interjections and voice, or abandoned altogether in the hope that the visible incidents still make some kind of sense. Now that the 1970s have become a historical period and Britain's social turmoil then is sufficiently odd-looking to younger eyes for there to be something worth saying, there's been a bit of a boom in both original dramas and book adaptations on this subject. Around 2001, it was impossible to turn on your telly without seeing faked-up 8mm home-movies of Raleigh Choppers and patterned flock wallpaper. (We could explain these terms, but you need to see them for yourselves.) Starting with the

continued on Page 353...

mainstream, the so-called Langham Group, of whom *Doctor Who*'s original associate producer, Mervyn Pinfield, was a protégée; their only lasting impact is the original title sequences for *Doctor Who*.) In fact, attempted reconstructions of John Logie Baird's 1920s experiments into what would eventually become television all tend to land up looking like the faces in the dark we see in this story, although the first face was a vent-dummy called Skooky Bill.

We'd be remiss in our duty to explain all the references and allusions if we neglected at this point to mention Evil Edna, the witch imprisoned/incarnated in a television in *Willo the Wisp*, a five-minute cartoon shown in the *Magic Roundabout* slot (see **What Was Children's Television Like Back Then?** under 3.7, "The Celestial Toymaker") and narrated by Kenneth Williams. Gatiss may not have had it in mind, but everyone over 30 watching this episode did. And whilst the Admiralty is less insistent than pub-quiz judges on the distinction between "Union Jack" (officially the small pole on which the flag is mounted on a ship rather than the flag itself) and the Union Flag, there is an asymmetry about the width of stripes that means that Rose is right to shout at Mr Connelly... but would have to yell at every single household in the street for the same reason. If anyone cares, it means that the top left corner should have the thicker white diagonal stripe uppermost.

English Lessons

- *Goodnight, children, everywhere* was how Uncle Mac ended *Children's Hour*, the radio programme for under-15s.
- *Epilogue* (n): The last programme shown, a homily from a priest of some kind. By 1970, everyone was so embarrassed about religion that these were disguised under trendy names and seemed almost like an ecumenical version of *Just a Minute*, where the speaker had to see how far he could get before mentioning Jesus, God or prayer. It was followed by the Closedown, which was a recording of the National Anthem followed by a quick announcement about unplugging the set in case of fires, and then the picture would go black and there would be a continuous test-tone for half an hour.

Oh, Isn't That...?

- *Maureen Lipman* (the Wire). Well, she's Maureen Lipman. Isn't that enough? We'll pick up on some of her past in **Production**, but from hit 70s sitcom *Agony* onwards, she'd been in constant work - either in drama, as a regular, reliably witty chat-show guest or advertising British Telecom in a long-running series of commercials playing Beattie, the eternally optimistic *yiddischer momma*, North London-style. (These monologues were eventually published in book form, as *You've Got an Ology*.) Her husband, Jack Rosenthal, was one of the most successful TV dramatists of the last 40 years; they met when she was in a *Coronation Street* episode he'd written. Shortly after he died, just before her *Doctor Who* appearance, a major former character was re-introduced but the person playing her had fallen ill, so Lipman, as an emergency measure and a mark of gratitude, stepped in as a similar character at short notice for a standard fee. These days, it is odd to see older work where she was still mainly a straight actress, such as *The Knowledge*, and even rarer to see this in things not written by Rosenthal, such as *Smiley's People*. By 2006, she was more famous for who she was than for any one role, so much so that a mobile phone company cheekily cashed in on her past ads by showing her trying to go unrecognised when "defecting" from BT.

- *Margaret John* (Grandma Connolly) died just as we were finishing this book. The last decade of her life was her busiest. She had just been in *Game of Thrones*, although for British audiences this was a minor detail compared to her memorable performance as Doris, the randy granny in *Gavin and Stacey* (see X5.11, "The Lodger" et seq). As a native of Swansea, she had been in many, many Welsh dramas over the decades and was also instantly recognisable in sketch-shows, sitcoms and films. For our purposes, it's worth mentioning that she had played Megan Jones (as Welsh a name as you can get) in 5.6, "Fury from the Deep".

- *Jamie Foreman* (Eddie Connolly) has just taken over someone else's role in *EastEnders* and is kind of the go-to guy for East End villains when they can't get Hywel Bennett or Bob Hoskins (unlike them, he's from there and observed real gangsters from close up as a kid, although it has to be said that his *'Stenders* performance hasn't bowled anyone over with its authenticity). Outside the UK, he's mainly noted for film roles,

Are We Touring Theme-Park History?

continued from Page 351...

earliest, *In a Land of Plenty*, the most obvious thing is the use of different filmstocks and digital grading to establish differing perspectives on the action. The novel is as much as anything about perceptions. With the digital image-manipulation making Betacam video look almost like film, this was an option open to Welsh *Doctor Who*, but it has largely been ignored - except in the one story to be "authored" by someone outside the TARDIS crew. "Love & Monsters" (X2.10) plays with both fake webcam footage and mock home movies of Elton's mum apparently going to Heaven, accompanied by an ELO song not written for another five years. (See **Who Narrates This Programme?** under 23.1,"The Mysterious Planet" and **How Messed Up Can Narrative Get?** under X3.10, "Blink".) By the time we get to *Life on Mars* (the BBC one, not the embarrassing American remake), the look of the episodes is muted, to suit the faded 16mm news footage that makes up the misremembered version that's now commonplace. The set design was carefully considered (moreso than the scripts) and again veered towards browns and yellows to suit the clichés of those Saturday night clips-shows where B-List celebrities waxed nostalgically about things before they were born. Even though anyone with relatives alive at the time will have seen over-coloured living-rooms in Kodakchrome, and anyone watching BBC will have seen 625-line PAL video footage of the lurid clothing and décor of the era, *Life on Mars* clung to the "standard" account, sanctioned by endless repetition and self-reference.

Underneath these stylistic differences, the sequence of events is instructive. *In a Land of Plenty* was a generational family saga and followed a set of characters through slow changes (following in the same path as *Our Friends from the North* seven years earlier). *Life on Mars* took the *Upstairs, Downstairs* approach to extremes, and did one week about Pakistani immigrants, the next about the IRA, the next about wife-swapping, the next about the coal strikes, blah blah blah... Each week had a "theme" that was introduced, discussed, "sorted" and then forgotten.

Between these poles came an adaptation of Jonathan Coe's *The Rotters Club*, which almost completely lost the novel's narrative voice and thus reduced all the plot-items to a sort of tick-box of Things You Need in a Seventies British School Novel. In attempting some kind of narrative objectivity, unlike the source novel, this went to the opposite extreme from *Life on Mars*, which, unlike the sequel/continuation *Ashes to Ashes*, was entirely told from one character's point of view. Sam Tyler is in every scene, and the choices of incidental music are all motivated by how he reacts to situations. (This workload was one reason why John Simm left after two years - X3.12, "The Sound of Drums" will pick up on this.)

Our last specimen (out of dozens) is *Fear of Fanny*[71], one of a seemingly endless stream of biographical dramas on BBC4 that all seem to have Mark Gatiss in. Here, the challenge was accurate recreation of existing video and film clips of Fanny and Johnny Craddock (termagant TV chef and her wine-expert husband and stooge), but organised around a conception of the protagonists at odds with their public personae. The events are all vouchsafed to have happened exactly as shown, and if we don't believe it, it's because this period of history was so much weirder than the accepted consensus. So where the TV version of *The Rotters Club* lost all of Coe's satirical intent and simply became a pageant of stuff from the 70s, presented to us as we passed by as if we were on a tour-bus, *Fear of Fanny* was intended to unsettle us by showing how far we have come within the memory of most BBC4 viewers. To resume the spatial metaphor, her peculiar life was a place we went on a tour of, unlike fictional characters whose passage through social history we observed from a safe distance.

And this metaphor is literally what happens in "The Girl in the Fireplace" (X2.4). Reinette actually speaks of the Doctor walking through incidents in her life as if from room to room. As a known, historical figure (and with some double-talk explanation for not using the TARDIS), Mme de Pompadour is treated as a stately home. In this one instance, this is appropriate: Reinette Poisson was bred and trained for a specific purpose - on which topic they can't elaborate because there are children watching - and her options were constrained almost to non-existence. Where much historical fiction considers the choices made by (and avail-

continued on Page 355...

X2.7 The Idiot's Lantern

including Bill Sikes in Roman Polanki's *Oliver Twist*, the Earl of Sussex in *Elizabeth*, assorted parts in *Saving Grace, Nil By Mouth, The Football Factory* and so on.

Things That Don't Make Sense Just to get this out of the way, everyone (except Mark Gatiss, apparently) knows that it was raining bucketloads all over London during the Coronation. Street-parties were washed out, which is a large part of the reason that the collective memory of the event is of holing up in the living-room of anyone with a television set who was willing to show it off.

And, as we've also stated earlier, because the street-party used the same extras three times over (many of whom were also the faces on the screens), Muswell Hill seems a lot more racially-mixed than a snooty area like that would have been in 1953. (There were some affluent Indians in London, but Muswell Hill would have been downmarket for them - it was traditionally *nouveau riche* until the 90s.) However, the day after the news broke that Mount Everest had been climbed by Commonwealth citizens, representatives of the former Empire were perhaps more welcome at street-parties than would usually have been the case, assuming that there were any around. (The history of mass immigration in postwar England is very complicated - see the essay we have for X3.2, "The Shakespeare Code" - but we're looking here at something no London borough would have had until 1960 at the earliest.) But where were the headlines and photos about *that* iconic event? Tensing and Hillary and the euphoria they added to the festivity is another thing people who were there always mention.

Straight from the Fridge, Dad is the title of a book of period teen-argot, so many more people know that it comes from the hilariously lurid 1959 shocker *Beat Girl* (starring Adam Faith, who was sort of the Anti-Cliff) than have actually sat through *Beat Girl*. (We have seen it a few times, as you may recall from "Paradise Towers".) Nobody - as Rose claims here - says it in any Cliff Richard film. If Rose knew the term at all, it would be from *Beat Girl* (and we can't imagine Jackie sitting patiently through dreadful songs like "Made You"[67] or even being that amused by trying to spot the then-unknown Oliver Reed) or from that book. And why the Doctor thinks that driving around Manhattan on a Vespa would look even remotely cool in 1958 - or any year - is a mystery.

That entire scene only works if they were aiming for London 1956-1965, possibly to attend *Ready, Steady, Go!*

Just in case anyone's forgotten, this story is set in 1953, just as sweet rationing is being phased out - but almost every other kind of rationing is still in place, hence the meagre fare at the street party... oh. (It's a long story, but Harry Truman put the screws on us for daring to elect a government he didn't approve of after the War. Britain was making the last payment as this story was being broadcast.) Obviously, anyone who was a child in the early 50s remembers the end of sweet rationing as the point when things started looking up - no more carrots on sticks as makeshift lollies - but the rationing of meat continued for another year. The Points system, in place since late 1941, ended in 1950, which is when most adults believed things started improving. And a mere eight years after the War, everyone's voluntarily putting huge Swastika-style TV aerials on their rooves (you'd not get that even today) and *nobody comments on this*. You'd expect at least a brick through Magpie's window.

Magpie's business-plan is a bit odd for the period, meaning that this is another of those stories (like 4.8, "The Faceless Ones") where you have to imagine a plan to take over the world that required an indulgent bank-manager or an amazingly unobservant venture-capitalist. The overdraft that Magpie mentions is about £12,000 in today's terms, which given his line of work and the prospects for television taking off in the next few months is not insurmountable: a bank in affluent Muswell Hill would have seen this as a potential goldmine, so Magpie's anxiety at the start of the story is rather implausible. He simply would not have got into that big a mess without an offer of a takeover or a substantial investment. The only way a bank would have sanctioned that hefty an overdraft is if they were confident that he could repay it promptly. Given the press coverage of television sales in London, this is entirely reasonable, but only as a sideline for his main business. If he'd marched into the bank announcing "I've seen the future and it's 405 lines", he would have been offered money on condition that he maintains his core business as it had been to date, not blown it all on umpteen new sets without pre-orders and certainly not on making his own model of TV set in his shed or wherever (see below). Once the Wire arrives, money is suddenly

Are We Touring Theme-Park History?

continued from Page 353...

able to) the protagonists, there is a strong strand that looks at how the desires and ambitions of people (especially women) are thwarted by social convention. (This is coming close to claiming Steven Moffat to be a feminist, which is so untrue, it's not funny. "The Girl in the Fireplace" has Reinette's situation shown to be part of the Laws of the Universe, and only the intervention of freaky anachronistic robots - who, of course, have to be stopped at all costs - calls this into question. And they are also following the historically sanctioned "script" and waiting until she is ready to be harvested for their needs. The only critical voice is Mickey the Idiot, and the Doctor info-dumps him into submission.)

The point is that, unless you are trained as the royal courtesan, nobody in any period has a pre-planned future. Everyone experiences their life as if it could go in a number of different directions at almost any moment. This was another big Victorian innovation in fiction: Keats saw the figures of what he thought was an ancient Greek urn as all caught in the middle of doing things, captured in the moment of being just about to do things and always in the middle of uncompleted doings-of-things. Our old chum Bulwer-Lytton (7.2, "Doctor Who and the Silurians") milked this for a novel, *The Last Days of Pompeii* (see, of course, "The Fires of Pompeii"). Nobody thought they were in history. The Victorian discovery of the past as another country allowed them to imagine different possible futures, hence the whole Utopia boom, and to imagine what future ages would think of *them*. The future was contingent, the past no longer pre-ordained to go the way we know now it was about to, so the present also became less set in stone. If our customs and beliefs aren't necessarily "right" but just local habits, maybe they weren't at work in the past after all. So what changed? Asking that is the start of serious historical fiction, according to the standard view.

As we said, "The Idiot's Lantern" comes closest to looking at history in this light. Imagining a Doctorless version is easier than with a lot of stories that year. Tommy is shown to have technical expertise and could have helped Bishop (and maybe Magpie) defeat the Wire. (Given his interest in electronics and Eddie's determination to get his boy into a trade, he could have been one of Magpie's sorely needed apprentices and landed up taking over the firm at the end.) The other element of Tommy's story is even more satisfying without visitors from our time encouraging him. It's strongly hinted that Tommy's gay, and that all his ambitions and fears are connected to a tyrannical paternalistic culture, exemplified by Eddie. But when Tommy finally stands up to his father, it is in a tirade that makes it clear that World War II has changed everything. No time-travellers were needed for this strand to work out as it did on screen. From this perspective, the Doctor and Rose were there to explain to the children watching that there was a time before television, and to speed up the story so that it could be squeezed into 45 minutes. And there's the rub: history-as-process requires there to be consequences for every action or decision. Tommy might as well be painted on the side of that Grecian urn after the credits roll. "The Idiot's Lantern" is a snapshot of a period that is presented to us almost entirely from bits seen in other dramas set in 1950s England.

(This is actually moderately embarrassing: after spending a whole essay denouncing the idea that the Welsh series has an overt Gay Agenda - see, ahem, **Gay Agenda? What Gay Agenda?** under X1.10, "The Doctor Dances" - here we are observing that, alone, out of all the various "issues" might that get routinely discussed, homosexuality is singled out for repeated mention. Other people remind Martha about what colour she is, but it only matters in one story, X3.8, "Human Nature". Nonetheless, the repressive attitudes of past periods is cause for Donna's scorn in "The Unicorn and the Wasp", the Doctor's sly jokes in X3.2, "The Shakespeare Code", and several other allusions along the way - and a lengthy speech by a character, in code, in "The Idiot's Lantern". The reason this is noteworthy is that the idea of things having been different, not just materially but with regard to attitudes, in living memory is one never normally countenanced in the BBC Wales series. We will pick up on another aspect of the new series' attempts to project present attitudes onto the past, as if all the recent battles were won before they began, in **Fun with Colourblind Casting!** under "The Shakespeare Code".)

continued on Page 357...

X2.7 The Idiot's Lantern

no object, and Magpie can mass-produce sets for the income-bracket who had not been able to afford anything like this before - but he hasn't obtained a bigger shop. A bargain deal like his would have either brought people flocking from all over London or ruined him in weeks when he couldn't meet demand. Yet nobody had been buying these wondrous devices even when they could see Ally Pally from their bedroom windows, knew that television was the coming thing and ascertained that the Coronation would be the big spectacle of the year. In short, *prior* to the Wire, what was the point of specialising in television and not having radios, gramophones or fridges as his main source of income, with a few desirable walnut-finished sets on display for people to come in to drool at and leave with a packet of record-needles or Mullard valves? This was, after all, how every other electrical retailer in Britain made a mint out of television before people started buying the sets. But no, when we first see him, he has a showroom full of unsellable tellies. Then, *suddenly*, everyone in the street has one (although they all, for some reason, piled into Eddie's front room to watch the Coronation). How would the bank have known that this reckless policy would pay off?

Five quid for a telly isn't exactly 'practically giving them away' as is claimed, even if they are apparently being bought outright. Average income was £8 a week. £5 in 1953 is approximately £300 now (or $500 US, more or less). The cost of a set would be something like £50 before tax, plus perhaps £10 to have the aeriel mounted on the roof. (We've seen an ad for a top-of-the-range 1954 model GEC set that "eliminated Halation" and had a Baretta Interrupter to prevent power-surges - much the same selling-points laptops are now using to differentiate themselves - for 65 guineas. Let's call that $4,100 today.) In the run-up to the Coronation, many people recall supply-and-demand pushing this up, as deliveries of new sets continued into the late evening on 1st June. (That's a point: Where are all of Magpie's employees, if *he's* driving the van? Who's minding the store?) Consumer electricals like this would generally be bought on Hire Purchase agreements right up into the age of satellite television. Most people would have made a down-payment of maybe ten shillings and then monthly payments of 7/6 over a few years.[68] (By which time, ITV had started, so everyone already owning a set had to pay for a conversion and an aeriel-adjustment - *ker-chinggg*.) This is how Sky made a killing with the apparently loss-making satellite service. (See **Why is Trinity Wells on Jackie's Telly?** under X1.4, "Aliens of London".)

Which brings us to another problem: if Magpie is in retail, it makes sense in this period that he has a degree of technical nous and can repair and keep spares for all major models (Fergusons, Pyes, Ekcos...), but suddenly he's able to build sets from scratch, from a corner-shop with no manufacturing facilities. All of these different makes had slightly different designs of CRT, so were incompatible. Only by making his own, with a factory capable of glass-blowing and caesium-coating the inside of a vacuum tube, is this possible. The Wire's portable also causes problems in this way - the tube is just about possible if he retrofitted an oscilloscope, but the custom-made bakelite casing must have been commissioned from an outside specialist. It's not just that he's paid off a massive £200 overdraft, but he's bought a factory and outsourced very specialised moulding *and* been able to go up every chimney in Florizel Street to mount his (again, custom made) aerials and run a shop with just two delivery boys, neither of whom he trusts to drive his van.

The Doctor is able to tell that the hand-held set is bakelite - not by its distinctive smell, and not by the fact that it's a brown, moulded material exactly like all the light-fittings, plugs and television sets made from the universally-used bakelite, but by licking it and evaluating its iron content. For 1953, this is like deducing that DI Bishop's shoes are made of leather by eating a bit of one. And rather anachronistically, he proves a point by asking Mr Connolly what 'gender' the Queen is, and is told, 'She's a female.' They *mean* to say "sex" and "lady", as anyone born before 1980 ought to remember.

There's a big logical flaw that opens up when comparing this story - and Mr Magpie's death therein - to subsequent appearances of Magpie Electricals product / logos (see "The Sound of Drums", et al). How is a consumer media tech empire created when Magpie dies, still almost penniless, with no children, apprentices or other outlets? Compare the situation we have in later episodes (and *Torchwood*) with how a real-life British electrical company such as Murphy or Bush fell victim to foreign competitors simply because the latter had better infrastructure, and you start to see what we mean. Even companies

Are We Touring Theme-Park History?

continued from Page 355...

Mark Gatiss, in discussing his next script (X5.3, "Victory of the Daleks"), quoted the end of *The Man Who Shot Liberty Valance*. Given the choice between the truth and the legend, the old newspaperman said in the film, "Print the legend". This was part of his excuse for deliberately ducking any unpleasant aspects of Winston Churchill and portraying him as a cuddly old teddy bear. It was a problem he had encountered before: the admirable aspect of "The Unquiet Dead" was that, for once, the alien menace were a magnifying-glass through which they could do a character-study of Charles Dickens at the end of his life. However, the causes of Dickens' *weltschmerz* were things not suitable for 7.00pm on a Saturday night when kids were watching. Dickens was part of the deal, as Davies had planned the stories in advance when making his pitch to BBC1. Similarly, Steven Moffat was given Madame de Pompadour as a starting-point. Davies was allocating tasks he knew could not be done adequately in the time-slot and for that audience. Yet in both cases, the writers managed to make plausible character-studies almost as side-effects of the routine *Doctor Who* stuff.

Everyone used to discuss the "magic" of *Doctor Who* by using a stock phrase: "the flexibility of the format". But since 1967, there has not been a trip into history that hasn't had an alien messing things up. No, not even "Black Orchid" (19.5), which was all about Nyssa's unexpected effects on things and wherein the Doctor took everyone on a trip in the TARDIS. Every single historically set adventure of the 80s had the same parpy music as every single space-based yarn. And the same over-emphatic pseudo-Shakespearean dialogue. So when Shakespeare himself shows up, he has to be "modern" and sound like a rock star from Manchester, because that whole "they must think us fools" thing won't wash any more. An interesting comparison is between the Big Finish audio *The Fires of Vulcan* and "The Fires of Pompeii", set on the same day in the same doomed city. Steve Lyons' audio is written and performed in a heightened manner. Apart from the seventh Doctor and Mel (and UNIT finding the TARDIS in 1980, buried in pumice), there is nothing in the story from outside Roman times, or at least the traditional representation of those times in other kinds of drama. Whereas with the TV story, James Moran is under orders to make the 72AD lifestyle as familiar and "nothing really changes"-ish as possible, and has the one established, historically valid but unfamiliar part of their lives - the Sybils - turn out to be the work of (guess what?!) aliens messing with history.

To some extent, *Doctor Who* has always presented bits of the past as clusters of generic expectations. As we saw in **Whom Did They Meet at the Top of the World?** with "Marco Polo" (1.4), the history we had presented to us as fact was as reliable as the knowingly debunked version of the Trojan Wars in "The Myth Makers" (3.3). When the third production team came in and opted to play safe, they went for "history" as the settings for variants on well-known novels or films - or, indeed, films of novels (see 3.8, "The Gunfighters", plus 4.4, "The Highlanders", and 4.1, "The Smugglers"). Yet this was because in all cases the period setting was the starting point, a known and partially known-about agreed beginning for exploration of the new world they were in. The starting-point for the writers and production was that children would be curious about what this world was really like, and have enough of an understanding that it was different from their world to make the connections unaided. A sign of the trust they had was that "The Massacre" is largely Doctor-less and Steven's assumed connections to one side or another put him and those around him in danger, but with no clue as to what the outcome will be. A few of the viewers might know where this is headed, but until the Doctor gives the date and decides to leg it, most people are as unaware as Steven was what would happen at the end of episode four. They would, however, know all about conspiracies, Tudor-era intrigues, religious sectarianism and what can happen if a lone gunman shoots a noted leader.

The fashionable alternative to this is the knowingly anachronistic attempts to make history "relevant" to kids by having it all presented as being just-like-us. Anything that might have come from a 1970s BBC costume drama is rejected, and instead it's all rock music, fast-editing and shagging. The worst excess of this is Showtime's *The Tudors*, which is like *A Knight's Tale* without the wit. Unsurprisingly, Russell T Davies has had a go, with

continued on Page 359...

X2.7 The Idiot's Lantern

that were employing hundreds of manufacturing and design staff in the 1950s and managed to cash in nationally to the growth of enthusiasm for television fell by the wayside in the early 80s, or were swallowed whole by overseas companies. A household name like Marconi-GEC was only viable into the 1990s by government defence contracts (and, in a few cases, board-members who were also ex-Cabinet ministers). By contrast, Mr Magpie's newfound wealth and influence extends the length and breadth of Florizel Street and dies with him: he doesn't seem to have had the time or energy to leave a will or *even buy a second van and hire someone to drive it*. (Even if he's got his act together to leave circuit-diagrams behind, having apparently invented the transistor six months before Shockley published his famous paper, there is no reason that his name and logo would be on any subsequent equipment made using these - and if he took out the patent, he didn't live to see it pay off and had no-one to supervise it for him.) We would also have to conjecture that, by the standards of alien fiends offering Faustean deals, the Wire was a remarkably generous employer and gave him time off from being possessed in order to pursue his other interests and buy a new suit - but she doesn't even give him time to shave regularly, so this can't be true.

Then again, perhaps the source of Magpie's posthumous wealth is that he appears to have invented the UV fly-zapper 40 years early (watch carefully in his exchanges with Rose). He's definitely doing something very clever for the Wire to manifest herself in colour on a monochrome phosphor-dot cathode-ray tube. Even allowing for the potential of a technical advance so pointless until / unless anyone figures out a compatible system of transmission for the set to decode and show, we can't help wondering how a disembodied alien intelligence which is manifesting as an image it perceived via monochrome modulated UHF transmission even knows what colour hair, skin and make-up to use. (This is especially puzzling as its knowledge of local idioms seems to come exclusively from radio programmes.)

However, the *big* problem with this story is that it seems sometimes to be that only Magpie's sets are of use to the Wire, and sometimes that it is *any* TV receiver. The Wire wants as many faces in front of tellies as it can get, so why is it piddling about with Magpie when it could easily have infiltrated one of the big-scale retailers? Magpie's bargain-price sets deliver at most 500 people who wouldn't have been in front of a set on the big day. The problem of why it chose his tiny little aerial instead of the thumping great Ally Pally tower a mile away is almost trivial compared to this. (If, as a transmitter rather than a receiver, it repelled the alien, then why did that being not go further away? The dialogue makes it seem as if the Wire researched all the TV retailers in London to find one with the most peculiar financial arrangements - see above - and knew him already.)

If, as we do, you visit Muswell Hill from time to time, you'll wonder how Ally Pally has rotated around to present the side it shows if you're looking from Crouch End. And it is as it has been rebuilt after the fire in the late 1980s, not as it was in 1953. (The brickwork is more like the original in the scenes shot in Cardiff - you can see the join in some of the matte shots.) This is also the place to point out the usual 90s railings, 80s stonecladding and the lack of tramlines - since even though these wouldn't have been so frequent in such a hilly area, and the trams had been phased out by then, roadworks were still in progress - but they've done a better-than-usual job of recreating 50s Haringay, which only makes it more stupid that the Doctor mistakes it for New York despite all the bunting and terraced houses.

Rose's Union Jack-Union Flag upside-down comments are only partially true, as we've discussed, but it highlights a curious feature of Eddie's reactions to an obviously authoritative figure such as the Doctor. Acting as he does as man-of-the-house in a home not actually his, it is plausible that he might exploit the sudden absence of his mother-in-law/host to establish his authority, but he does so with reference to a military background; the Doctor evidently has some sort of authority beyond this, and someone like Eddie might be expected to align himself with this to strengthen his claim, just as he had done when the police were called in. The production team were diligent in ensuring that none of Eddie's medals suggested any heroism or active combat (consigning him to the "forgotten" Burma campaign, which isn't quite as clear-cut as they thought) and this would make his desire to be associated with service and duty keener, if anything. Anyone of his age would, in wartime service, have encountered mysterious hush-hush War Office types, often accompanied by overqualified "secretaries", so he would have been less

Are We Touring Theme-Park History?

continued from Page 357...

Casanova. Here, it was obvious that the anachronisms were as much as anything a cost-cutting device. (See, if you haven't, **The Big Picture** for "Tooth and Claw".) This approach works (to some extent) if you know the originals, so to speak. Anyone with a reasonable grounding in the facts of the period in question can enjoy what they've done with the material. The danger is that so few people these days *do* know anything beforehand. A story such as "The Crusade" relies on everyone at home having the basics off pat (possibly via Ladybird books - see "Marco Polo"). By the time of "The Shakespeare Code", the BBC cannot assume even the most rudimentary knowledge of Elizabethan England or the works of the single most famous writer ever. What is most striking if you watch both stories back-to-back (or what's left of "The Crusade", at least) is the trust the writers, director and performers have that viewers will be able to follow all of this and comprehend even the existence of other points of view. It helps that the makers of "The Crusade" are, to some extent, following the conventions of other genres of 60s television. But observe the effort the Hartnell tale puts in to making Vicki "invisible" as a clever girl. The Doctor steals period clothing for her and himself (his gold-embroidered hoodie makes him look like a deeply odd rapper), and the disclosure that Vicki isn't a pageboy is a big chunk of episode three. This foreshadows the entire plot of Joanna's enforced marriage to Saphadin and the sub-plot of Barbara and Safiya escaping El Akir. It's hard not to get the message that patriarchy is a bummer, but what we sometimes miss is that Joanna's objection to an arranged marriage (which is, after all, what princesses were *for*) is grounded in religious objections rather than it being a bad idea per se. We get an entire world-view sketched in with remarkably few lectures or hints from the Doctor. The conversations are all conducted on their terms, not ours, and Ian and Barbara run into trouble trying to make the locals see that any other view is even possible.

"The Shakespeare Code" is at the other extreme (despite including a quotation from "The Crusade" as one of the lines of the play: 'The eye should have contentment where it rests.'). The Doctor and Martha stay in their usual togs - a short-haired woman in trousers not getting a single mention - and the Doctor spouts off background whilst making it seem, rather laboriously, that nothing in 1599 is different from 2007 except the fashions. This isn't maintained for long, and the sequence where Shakespeare says the efficacy of Bedlam in scaring him out of grief is exemplary. Nonetheless, Martha's role in this, until the climax, is as a TV presenter asking the questions and observing what's on offer, not as an audience-identification figure in the old sense. She never experiences what it would be like to be stuck there for life. We learn more about the rules governing Carrionites than we do about 1599 London. The BBC Wales writers don't have that trust in their viewers. Gareth Roberts, pressed on the apparent obviousness of "The Shakespeare Code", made a sweeping statement about "today's kids" being different somehow and that "nobody would be interested in a story about the Defenestration of Prague". This has never really been put to the test. Not specifically 1612 mobs in a city run by a fanatical occultist who collected scholars and objects that could each or collectively keep *Doctor Who* going for years (John Dee, Tycho Brahe, Rabbi Loewe), but there's never really been any attempt to go beyond only doing stories in the bits of the past that are already on the comparatively restricted school syllabus, or with people who've been on banknotes. And they even get that wrong. Anyone with experience of "today's kids" knows that they are less well-informed, but more able to investigate for themselves if they can be made to care.

Two things bear mentioning here: one is that Gareth Roberts wrote a note-perfect pastiche of a Season Two historical, the Missing Adventure *The Plotters*, in which Vicki had to cross-dress again. (It was a staple of black and white Historicals, with Polly commenting on not having to do it in 4.4, "The Highlanders".) It must have been a conscious decision to skip all that here. The other is more damning: far from being someone at home in all times and places, the Doctor has become a tourist from our time gawking at the attractions of The Past as if visiting a city with a sight-seeing checklist. That's a side effect of Roberts playing for what he thinks the mass audience wants. For Gatiss, it's an end in itself, and one he's built a career doing with cut-and-paste Victoriana and Hammer/Tigon/Amicus horror films.

X2.7 The Idiot's Lantern

inclined to doubt the Doctor's affidavits or Rose's right to be there (and shame him in front of his family) than anyone else.

Moreover, Eddie's haircut, along with almost everyone else's in this story, is anachronistically shaggy and long for 1953, military service or not. The Doctor, with his suit, haircut and accent making him seem slightly more like a black marketeer than a government agent, is unlikely enough to have caught Eddie off-guard long enough to establish his credentials as an expert. But anyone looking like that, with a girl dressed the way Rose was, hanging around an area where people had disappeared mysteriously days before a major public event, would have been rounded up by the rozzers long before Detective Inspector Bishop busted him. And even if Bishop's name had been written on his collar visibly (which it isn't), would it have had his rank marked there by the laundry? Does his wife call him that? However, with so much official pressure to make a breakthrough, how is it that he hasn't spotted how many TV aerials there are in the street with the peak number of faceless sightings?

DI Bishop comments that the sun has come up on the Great Day, and we go to the Connolly house to see everyone watching the procession. It's June. Ergo, the sun came up at around 4.00am, whereas the Outside Broadcast began at 10.17 and went on until 5pm - the procession arrived at Westminster Abbey at around 11, so the piece of commentary by Richard Dimbleby (which the BBC have churned out again every time there's a Jubilee or something) is presumably at around 10.30. We could excuse this with the Wire knocking the Doctor and Tommy out for three hours, but that's not the sequence of events shown here. We also have to explain how Magpie's drive to Ally Pally took ages in a van when the Doctor and Tommy got there - apparently on foot, up a *very* steep hill - in almost the same time. (Maybe they used the scooter, but the roads up the hill to the transmitter would be tough on a Vespa's gears and would make it pull wheelies, even assuming all the street-parties and obstacles on the route from Muswell Hill, down through Wood Green and back up Alexandra Park were magicked away by the Coronation. It might have been easier to cut through the park, but even then, you've got a school, two railway lines and a gasworks in the way.)

Everyone in the house stays seated when "God Save the Queen" is played. When this is played at the end of a night at the pictures (which everyone would have done twice a week, even in wartime), the rule is that you stood to attention. Surely someone would have made the effort? Eddie would have insisted upon it.

Finally, as was the case with Season Twenty-Five, we have to ask how two nearly identical stories (this and "Fear Her") wound up being written by authors who were supervised so closely, plus another by the person doing the supervision. And these two stories about Big Events in London had the same director. In fact, with its emphasis on mass-possession of Londoners through consumer electronics, it's not a million miles away from the two-part Cyberman story we've just had either.

(And we'll leave aside the starkly monochrome BBC Television "Batwing" design on the screens throughout this story, which wasn't launched until December 1953, because it's a much cooler design than the previous grey Lion and Unicorn thing.)

Critique We've established that there's little point expecting anything original from Mark Gatiss. Pastiche is what he does. Here, he's been given a chance to emulate and synthesize a lot of his favourite things, so the result is at least warm and loving, if a bit by-the-numbers. There are a few unexpected, funny lines, but a lot of the dialogue is straight out of schools television, as if we're watching *How We Used to Live* about the Coronation. Allowing him to do a full-blown *Quatermass* reworking would have been pointless, as he'd already done that definitively in his New Adventures book *Nightshade*. No, more than ever, this episode's script is a pretext for the visuals. Fortunately, they are generally wonderful. The design has moved from the general to the specific, taking Gatiss' hints and exploring a number of options to get the precisely right wallpaper, delivery van, mock-up TV set or frock.

Getting things like that right is half the battle, but what's going on here is more intricate than that. Compare this story to 25.1, "Remembrance of the Daleks". In that case, all of the details were right too, but they chose to make a very contemporary looking (for 1988) piece. It was as if they had taken the Outside Broadcast crew to 1963, but then carried on as normal. Here, by contrast, Euros Lyn and director of photography Rory Taylor have opted to make something that looks as if it might have been made in 1953. The tilted cameras, use of light-sources in the shot, the grading and colour scheme all make the episode look like a cheap thriller. This isn't intended as an insult. One of the main reasons those films are still being watched now, when so much of the big-budget product has slid down off the film-buff's list, is that the low-budget films were resourceful in using what they had to best effect. Everyone's now familiar with the term *film noir*, but the quick, cheap fillers that got bracketed together after the event aren't entirely interchangeable, and the material that used the same techniques isn't restricted to crime dramas set in Los Angeles. That aesthetic of faster monochrome 35mm film and longer lenses you can use with this - night-shooting with crisp, stark lighting and shadows and peculiar camera-angles because they were using real locations that weren't always accessible any other way - is common to Jack Arnold's monster films (do you ever see *The Incredible Shrinking Man* listed as *film noir* though?) and several dozen B-movies made in London, often by Merton Park Studios. French theory and American documentaries have ignored these, but they're the main source of a lot of our ideas about that time (see **The Big Picture**), so Lyn and Taylor have good reason to shoot this story that way. Taylor is also thinking of Edward Hopper's paintings, not something Gatiss had in mind. He wrote it as the drab, faded Britain to be found in old photos and memories clouded by what happened later. That allows the characters a bit of depth, but the visuals complicate this trite pageant of shabby. The contrast between shabby and *noir*, that sense of a knife-edge between postwar and new Elizabethan, is 1953 Britain's defining trait rather than either one of these options. Lyn absolutely gets that.

Into this comes a cast who all know what they're doing. Look at even a tiny part such as Crabtree (Ieuan Rhys); when the Doctor tells Bishop that you can't close your fingers around your elbow and make a fist, Crabtree's quietly trying it for the rest of the scene. Margaret John takes a small and fairly thankless character, Gran, and makes her vivid enough for Tommy's concern to ring true. Tommy is less a character than a point-of-view, one we're supposed to share. Gatiss has dramatised the pull of past and future as a family row and loaded the dice, but it makes Tommy almost absent as a person. Jamie Foreman's Eddie is far more dynamic and memorable, even though he's a panto villain complete with a little moustache to twirl. Rory Jennings, although much older than he appears, fails to make Tommy young enough to get away with this sort of behaviour. Any older than 14, he'd've been sent out to work by now. Gatiss would have known this (*Hue and Cry*: Ealing Studios, 1949). This doesn't entirely detract from the story, but it makes that aspect of the episode more like a sermon; unfortunately, this seems to lead up to an implicit moral that the nuclear family is so valuable that it must be cherished even when the dad's abusive, something that sat uncomfortably with a lot of people. As we've established, Gatiss isn't great with subtext.

The problem we identified with Mickey's characterisation in the last story is an asset here. Rose is written as the likeable girl from last series, but with more experience and initiative - in short, as Sarah Jane Smith. Making her disappear for the latter half is supposed to motivate the Doctor, but in fact doesn't change him appreciably. He makes jokes and is clearly having a good time defeating heinous space-monsters in 1950s London. What it does is put Tommy, someone who understands valve radios, in Rose's place and spares us a long explanation of what he does to save the Doctor. Another problem from 2005 is that there isn't quite 45 minutes' worth of material here. Shifting the emphasis from the official climax to the end scene at the Street Party was wise, but they take slightly too long over the set-up, and don't seem to trust us to get the idea that Eddie's a bully.

Sandwiched between two self-consciously "epic" two-parters, this story was always going to seem a bit lightweight. In isolation, it's *still* lightweight, but less frustratingly so. A lot of love and care has been lavished on something insubstantial, but now we know what the rest of the year had in store, we can look at this episode squarely and be thankful that they bothered. If only Gatiss had bothered a bit more, it would have been entirely satisfying.

X2.7 The Idiot's Lantern

The Facts

Written by Mark Gatiss. Directed by Euros Lyn. Viewing figures: (BBC1) 6.76 million, (BBC3 repeats) 0.6 and 0.4 million. AIs at 84%.

TARDISode A television set is delivered to the Connollys. The set appears to break down; Gran goes to hit it, and is assailed by pink lightning. She vanishes as the announcer reminds viewers of the Coronation tomorrow morning.

Production

Mark Gatiss was asked by Russell T Davies to write the 1950s story. The plan was originally to do London at the birth of Rock 'n' Roll: "Mr Sandman", as it is called in the Pitch document, was a story about a piece of music that stole people's souls in the era of Soho coffee-bars and Bebop. Gatiss was aware that the original period setting was too easy to get wrong, and too many people would see the mistakes. As the proposed title suggests, the version of the 1950s on offer is one derived entirely from other nostalgic recreations (the song, originally by the Chordettes, appeared in 24.3, "Delta and the Bannermen", but was used as the first sign that something was wrong when Marty McFly enters the drug-store in *Back to the Future*). Gatiss opted to move further into his comfort-zone and set a story in a land of pullovers and orange squash. Thus, this script morphed into a story about the birth of mass-audience television. (Although it appears that Alexandra Palace was somewhere in even this first notion.) His original opening was for the TARDIS to arrive and the Doctor to only notice something amiss when a red bus passed with a suitably vintage ad on the side. Once the Vespa had been written in to the story, Gatiss tried writing a long chase through the London Underground. He did, however, realise that making a Vespa go from South London to Alexandra Palace was implausible, so Powell Street (i.e. the future Powell Estate) became "Florizel Street", N8. Another change was that the grandad who got absorbed by the Wire became a much more iconic/ clichéd Grandma, who had more dialogue reminiscing about the 1902 Coronation. Rose didn't lose her face in the first version, then in a later one was shown wandering, faceless, around the back streets. Most significantly, Tommy was originally older, slightly cockier and more assertively gay: Gatiss toned this down when he saw Captain Jack. Later edits also removed a lot of in-joke references to *The Quatermass Experiment*.

An early version was in the works when the production blocks were rearranged. Instead of three months to finish his script, Gatiss had three weeks. He was about to go on tour with the League of Gentlemen, before recording a whole string of BBC4 dramas, so only had a slim margin for getting the completed script in to BBC Wales. Another consequence of this change was that Euros Lyn was assigned to this story, as he had been for Gatiss' last script (X1.3, "The Unquiet Dead"). Lyn's conception of 1953 London was more vibrant than the impression of drabness Gatiss had derived from watching black and white TV and films; Davies concurred, as this episode was now likely to follow the two-part Cyberman story (which had been purposefully colourless).

• During the 50th Anniversary celebrations for BBC television, a play about the launch of the service, *The Fools on the Hill*, had been shown. This was by Jack Rosenthal. Unusually for a Rosenthal play, there wasn't a part for his wife, Maureen Lipman, but at around this time they became involved in the efforts to restore the dilapidated site and, after his death, she was often involved in promotions for the appeal. She had also carved a small niche for herself performing material written by the comedienne Joyce Grenfell, for which she had acquired 1950s frocks. Her home has a good view of Ally Pally (as could be seen when, in her capacity as advocate for the restoration, she was interviewed for a documentary, *And Then There was Television*, shortly after this and using clips from the episode in the finished version). This made her an obvious choice for the Wire, although as she was on stage in the West End at the time, it took a bit of planning. Eventually, they managed to get her scenes down to one day's recording in London (as with Zoe Wanamaker's part in X2.1, "New Earth") and arranged to make all of the scenes actually in the studio where it all began. (It is in the process of restoration, having been used by the Open University until the 1990s.)

• Shooting began on Block Four with that one day at Alexandra Palace, on 23rd January, before returning to start "Fear Her" back in Cardiff. Gatiss was available to observe the recording (and, as he was the focus of that week's episode of

The Idiot's Lantern K2.7

Confidential, got to interview Lipman). She wore one of the dresses she had used in *Re:Joyce*, although for most scenes she did not bother to lace up it completely. If you have been reading the production details sequentially, you'll realise that it was freezing cold that week, and the studio was draughty. Lipman found ranting alone with no other cast exhausting. The make-up wasn't quite authentic; monochrome TV make-up for presenters was garish (although the earlier use of blue lipstick for male presenters had long gone) and Sheelagh Wells had to find a plausible compromise.

- On 7th February, the location work at Florentia Street began. This had been retrofitted to look more like 1953 (although a few modern railings and windows slipped past them until they saw the footage later). For the street-party, mainly shot on the 9th, the playback used, amongst others, Tommy Steele's 1957 cover of "Singin' the Blues" and Lonnie Donegan's "Putting on the Style", redubbed by Gold in the final edit with a rearranged "Song for Ten". One of the residents of Florentia Street showed photos of the real street-party they'd had on the Coronation day, with herself as a small girl. (It looked almost exactly like what Lyn and production designer Edward Thomas had guessed for the episode.) Gatiss had been keen for the Doctor to stick around for the "real history" after the end of the story. As we mentioned, the extras doubled and tripled up for some of the long-shots. Thomas had made sure that all anachronistic street-furniture, including the lights, had been replaced, so the pillar-box has George VI markings (obviously, nobody had manufactured "Elizabeth II" ones yet). For most of their time in this road, Lyn was careful only to change what would be in shot on any given day, to minimise disruption to the residents and avoid wasting time.

- Ron Cook (Mr Magpie) and Debra Gillett (Rita Connolly) had both worked with Tennant before, on stage playing in a Gorky play ten years before. Cook had also been in *Casanova*. Rory Jennings, as Tommy, was actually 23 when this was shot. Jamie Foreman, who grew his moustache specifically for the role of Eddie, wore a period watch his wife had just bought him for Christmas.

- There were worries about Piper wearing pink as Rose, but it was concluded that it was in-character for her to be dressed up for a trip to Elvis or Ed Sullivan. Louise Page found the shoes in Camden and, after showing them to Piper, the rest of the costume was devised to match (to the extent of spray-painting the helmet). They tried to find her "Lolita" sunglasses. Although they were given permission to not use helmets, it being before 1972, when they became compulsory, the cast decided to set a good example. It also helped disguise the three stunt drivers and Piper's double. The main problem was that taking the helmets off messed up the elaborate hairdos the cast were sporting (Tennant had made a point of growing his hair during "Fear Her" because this story was coming up). The anachronistic scooter was tricky to drive, although Tennant felt better when he saw professional stunt-drivers also having trouble with the top-heavy vehicle. To get it to come out of the TARDIS prop, they built a little incline over the door lintel at the base.

- On the 10th, they relocated to Blenheim Road, the location for Mr Magpie's shop. The building had been a shop, but was currently converted into an artist's studio. The white-painted woodwork for the exterior was given a temporary black overlay and appropriate period fittings. The location was opposite a school, so Cook had a big audience whenever the van stalled. They also did a few shots for "Fear Her" while they were there. Although an early draft ended with all the sets exploding, destroying the shop, this was considered pointless. Rory Taylor, as director of photography, decided to make the episode look like the *chiaroscuro* paintings of Edward Hopper, specifically his famous *Nighthawks*. (Hopper had just been the subject of a major retrospective at Tate Modern, which had broken attendance records.) Ed Thomas had found a 1950s telly in a skip[69] and based the Magpie design on it, making most of the cases in MDF with vacuum-moulded bulbous screens.

From 13th February, they began to shoot the two main interiors: the Connolly house and Mr Magpie's shop. When designing the house, the crew sourced the last remaining rolls of various patterns of "Utility" wallpaper from the period, which they scanned and copied for later use. The warehouse that supplies television with period wallpaper and props was the one that also supplied *Life on Mars* with authentic Wagon Wheels wrappers and Trimphones. Each roll of paper cost about £100. The subliminal impression they wanted to give was that this was not Eddie's natural environment, but Gran's choice of décor. (Historically, this is likely: after the Blitz, a lot of

X2.8: The Impossible Planet

families "temporarily" moved back in with the in-laws while waiting for new houses to be built, making the paterfamilias more defensive and territorial - hence the spread of mother-in-law jokes in postwar Britain.) Margaret John was pleased to be back on *Doctor Who*, and Tennant was especially pleased to see photos of "Fury from the Deep" she had kept. For the shop, there were banks of DVD players feeding into replica period TV sets. The meeting between Rose and Magpie was rewritten at the last minute, to allow the sets with the Wire to be in the front of the shop rather than behind the tricky bead curtain. Obviously, the Wire's dialogue couldn't be rewritten. Apart from the extras, Piper and Margaret John, a few of the production staff had donated faces for the test-run, but only two appear in the finished take. The decision was taken to use the slightly anachronistic "Batwing" BBC Television logo, introduced a few months after the Coronation. The studio work continued until the 15th, without the stars (off doing a read-through of X2.9-2.10) and then on 16th, they briefly returned to Florentia Street. Operation Market Garden was actually at the end of the same road as the Street Party, but with period removal vans to obscure where residents had parked twenty-first century vehicles. The fruit-stall was the last of several suggested disguises for the secret holding-bay; Gatiss had written it as a newspaper vendor and a man in a bowler hat - just like the start of *Quatermass and the Pit*, in fact.

The 17th had them using the back entrance to Cardiff Royal Infirmary as Alexandra Palace. Gatiss had scripted a sight gag of scene shifters moving parts of the *Quatermass* spaceship in the background. Another line was cut from around here, although not a *Quatermass* in-joke so much as a "Logopolis" one (18.7): the Doctor was wary of climbing up a radio transmitter after last time... Next day entailed another familiar setting, the Vertair helipad used three times already, most recently in the Cybermen two-parter a month earlier. This had a clear skyline, making it better than anywhere else nearby for faking a climb up the Ally Pally transmitter tower. The day had a moderate breeze, but was mostly clear and chilly - especially with hands on bare metal. The actual tower set was only a dozen feet tall, but raised on a dais so that it was about 20 feet in the air. It was decided not to give either actor a safety harness (although there was a crash-mat below them for some scenes, but not the ones where they were shot from above over a green screen). The Wire got an unscripted extra go at stopping the Doctor, to delay the climax. Both actors were covered in bruises next day. They had decided that Tennant should be wearing the coat, to look good on a windswept tower, so they devised the short scene of the Doctor returning to the TARDIS and filling his pockets with odds and ends to justify it. Cook wasn't allowed a coat.

After this they got a weekend off, and a day in Q2 before the most unpleasant part of the shoot, the night filming in the docks. Quite apart from the cold and the smell, this was the day when the faceless extras had to be herded around. The prostheses drastically reduced their sight and hearing, so some of the runners became zombie-wranglers, escorting them slowly up and down stairs (such as on the trailers used for make-up) and taking them on and off set. Most of the extras were cheerful about this enforced sensory deprivation, as at least they were marginally warmer than the rest of the cast. Any scene where someone has to touch where a face used to be required digital matting rather than prostheses. Black crosses were drawn on the face of the actor for reference, a fact that caused trouble when Tennant and Piper got the giggles. For Margaret John's face-ectomy, The Mill added wrinkles to her blank skin.

Two more days at Q2, again concurrent with "Fear Her", and that was the block in the can. For future reference, it was during the studio sessions for this that the first tests of HD cameras took place (see X4.15, "Planet of the Dead") and a few pick-ups for the Cybermen stories were added. Gatiss, by this time, was free again and, in addition to narrating every episode this year, was the focus of the seventh *Doctor Who Confidential* of the year, catchily entitled "The Writer's Tale". In the run-up to broadcast, Maureen Lipman enthusiastically promoted the episode, saying that her street-cred with the local kids had shot up.

X2.8: "The Impossible Planet"

(3rd June, 2006)

Which One is This? Black Holes and Revelations. The TARDIS is apparently destroyed and Rose reacts to being stuck two thousand years in the future in orbit around a black hole by teasing the Doctor about getting a mortgage. His later decision to shove her into a parallel universe at the next available opportunity seems oddly merciful.

Firsts and Lasts It's the first of many visits to the forty-second century. The Doctor dons his orange *Dan Dare* spacesuit for the first time. After a season and a half of the TARDIS crew not landing on a properly alien planet, The Mill pulled out all the stops for the "gravity globe" scene (see also X5.4, "The Time of Angels") to make it look as beautiful and alien as possible. Nevertheless, it's a quarry doubling for an alien world, just like they said they'd never do.

Most importantly, the alien Ood, largely the Welsh series equivalent of the Ogrons (9.1, "Day of the Daleks"), are introduced in this story. They'll have several more appearances before the Davies era is over, and have popped up in the Moffat era as well. Strictly speaking, they're the only recurring sympathetic alien race since the revival, not that you'd expect that from their appearance here.

Watch Out For...

• The good people at The Mill spent ages researching what a black hole ought to look and making a photogenic, scientifically accurate digital image for the showcase effect of the episode. Then BBC Wales took a look at it and told them to do it again to look more like the poster for the 1979 Disney dud *The Black Hole*. Mercifully V.I.N.CENT isn't around - one 70s-style cutesy robot per year is enough (X2.3, "School Reunion", but just wait for X4.16, "The Waters of Mars"). However, if you've seen this film you will recall that the crew of the *Palomino* huddle around the holo-projector (identical to the one in this story) to get their first glimpse of the eponymous stellar event: one of the astronauts calls it "right out of Dante's *Inferno*" and another says, "Every time I see one of those things, I expect to spot some guy in red with horns and a pitchfork". Disney declined to actually go down that route in their Captain-Nemo-in-Space snoozefest. Would BBC Wales show similar restraint? As if...

• In case you didn't get the hint from that, we have the Doctor rapidly calculating an amount of energy in units that come out as a lot of sixes, and the base switches over to night-time with a spot of light-classical, like a holiday camp (see 4.7, "The Macra Terror") and very like the odd juxtaposition of Mozart and monsters in *Alien*. Tonight's selection is Ravel's *Bolero*, used by Torville and Dean in the 1984 Winter Olympics for an ice-dance routine that was the first ever to get top marks across the board, i.e. a lot of sixes. Still, they ought to be given a little credit for not calling Toby Zed "Damien Baal".

• The Beast sounds *very* like Sutekh the Destroyer from the rather good 1975 story "Pyramids of Mars" (13.3). (The Ood sound like Jedi Master Coati Mundi or whatever it was from the naff *Star Wars* prequels.) The voices were dubbed after the shooting, so it must be considered to be premeditated. There was a lot of speculation about the Beast's relationship with Sutekh (see **Are All These "Gods" Related?** under 26.3, "The Curse of Fenric"), but we can't help noticing that Series Four of *The Sarah Jane Adventures* referred back to "Pyramids" three times, and there was another running gag in X6.0, "A Christmas Carol" and a mis-quote in X1.11, "Boom Town", plus a scripted reference in X2.12, "Army of Ghosts", so this is not one of those stories that's fallen into the cracks like "The Ambassadors of Death" (7.3). And to rub it in, the possession scene comes at exactly where a cliffhanger would be if this was in four 25-minute episodes.

• Zack's full name is "Zachary Cross Flane", but a lot of people misheard it as "flame". The production team don't think about what associations American viewers will bring to a series not actually made for them, so the casting of a black actor when you have a name that - accidentally - suggests Klan meets is unfortunate and not (um) inflammatory. In a station that has a "Toby Zed" and "Scutari Manista" as well, you have to wonder what could be so embarrassing about Mr Jefferson's first name that he never uses it. (Actually, it's "Johnny".)

The Continuity

The Doctor He and Rose think that the idea of leaving a planet before the trouble starts is laughable. In keeping with his penchant for analogies that depend on anachronisms, he compares a spacebase kit to building a flat-pack wardrobe.

He's terrified by the untranslatable writing and not hiding it very well, which might explain the cynical mood he's in all story [we'll pick this up further in next story's essay]; he immediately jumps to the conclusion that a massive new power source might be used to start a war, then tells the expedition that they should leave right away. [Considering this is exactly what he was just

X2.8 The Impossible Planet

giggling over not doing with Rose, this is peculiar at best.] The TARDIS disappearing in a earthquake at least presents some reason to look horrified, and after an outburst of pleading for the drilling to divert to rescue his Ship, he quickly switches the subject to Rose's fate. The prospect of settling down in this era with a house and mortgage horrifies him. [For some reason, neither of them think of any of the modifiers that might ease their current situation, such as a sonic screwdriver proven capable of hacking infinite amounts of cash, the possibility of hailing down other time travellers, or indeed the fact that they're in an era with space travel that extends through three galaxies. There's hardly a need for all the emoting.] As soon as Rose demonstrates having picked up on some of the local terminology, he says she's 'gone native'. He mentions having promised Jackie that he'd bring Rose back. When Danny calls them a couple, he doesn't object.

When challenged to explain a rock orbiting a black hole, he instead gives Rose the Cliff Notes explanation for what a black hole is, although only after she'd indicated she knows nothing about them. He has a way of ascertaining the characteristics of a black hole, enough to tell that this one isn't any kind of Einstein-Rosen wormhole, and doesn't do anything but consume matter. [As he had no idea when he stepped out of the TARDIS that there was such an object nearby, this must be an innate time-sensitivity alerting him to an anomalous lack of the correct amount of bending of spacetime that gives a black hole its name. If it's 'just' consuming matter, it isn't really a black hole. Simplistic errors like this will persist (see X3.13a, "Time Crash"). We'll assume he's patronising Rose with a really bad explanation.]

Trapdoors aren't a favourite. When confronted with Ood proclaiming, "We must feed", he assumes they're about to attack him and Rose. He seems slightly claustrophobic after losing the TARDIS. He's not fond of the view of the black hole, but asks that the window shutters stay open anyway, to properly mourn the Pallushi race from the Scarlet system.

• *Background*. He's concerned about having 'gone beyond the reach of the TARDIS' knowledge' [which smacks of 21.3, "Frontios"]. He hasn't worn a spacesuit in a long time, and certainly not this model. [He will dust it off a few more times before he regenerates. And his knowledge of black holes extends beyond the five on-screen encounters with them back in 625-lines.] He seems familiar with the type of Sanctuary Base seen here.

• *Ethics*. He utterly ignores the whole question of keeping the Ood as slaves. [When Rose Tyler is getting into a debate on morality in front of your face, you'd think the Doctor of all people would pay attention. However, as she's wearing a jacket probably made in a Shanghai sweat-shop, he could have called her out on this - see X4.3, "Planet of the Ood", and our comments on Character Options in **What Are the Great 21st Merchandising Disasters?** under X5.3, "Victory of the Daleks".]

• *Inventory: Sonic Screwdriver*. The Doctor waves the sonic screwdriver at an Ood when he thinks they're making threats.

The TARDIS Gets 'queasy' when they land, and makes peculiar noises. [Given the relationship of the Time Lords to black holes, it seems unlikely that the peculiar local physics can be all that's troubling her; it's possibly just the type of events they've getting into, considering the number of times the TARDIS has landed in far more problematic situations.]

The Doctor says that TARDISes are grown rather than built [thus confirming a long-running fan theory previously seen in the *New Adventures*]. He doesn't think he'll be able to construct one now that Gallifrey's gone. The Doctor's offhand comment about being forced to live in a proper house hints that the TARDIS may not have any carpets [as one has never been shown on screen, except in the McGann TV Movie, this is quite possible].

The Supporting Cast
• *Rose*. Immediately identifies the peculiar star as a black hole, but when there's a need for an info-dump later, she seems to know absolutely nothing about black holes, or, apparently, astronomy in general. Later still, she says she's seen films in which black holes are gateways to other universes. [Is she thinking of the one this story's designers have plundered for the look of Zack's workstation, perhaps? Or maybe *Event Horizon*, with Sean Pertwee.] She gets appropriately angry about Danny defending Ood slavery, and tries to talk to them [her attempts are frustrated by other members of the crew/ possession/ the scriptwriter, so she doesn't get very far].

The Impossible Planet

Can He Read Smells?

Back in the heady days of *About Time 4*, we reviewed the on-screen evidence for three theories of how language functions in *Doctor Who*. That essay, **Does Everyone in the Universe Speak English?**, summed up the situation in all broadcast episodes up to 2004. There have been a few more since then, and they don't take us much closer to a Grand Unified Theory. Where once we might have accepted that speech was being translated, but writing was presented as being in English as a narrative convention, we are now confronted with on-screen evidence and spoken dialogue to the contrary. This seems to settle the matter. In fact, it messes things up no end.

The clear, stated facts in the new version are simple enough. Everyone speaks their own language and hears replies in the same language, most of the time. The TARDIS does an imperceptible telepathic upgrade, so that all who've been in her get their perceptions adjusted accordingly. The Doctor is the Ship's source for all the grammar and vocabulary, local turns of phrase and British-English approximations. He speaks almost every known language, but had to learn them all the hard way. Locals hear whatever he and his companion-of-the-day say as their own language, or a suitable nearby one for some purposes. Written text can also be translated, although this often takes longer, and a few - mainly the ones Time Lords use - are untranslatable.

So far, so good - and pleasingly in keeping with what we wrote then. Unpacking all of that brings problems, though, when we step away from the assumption that even all Earth languages have interchangeable concepts, tenses and conventions for how to denote spoken utterances as marks on a surface. The assumption that English is the One True Language and all others are deviations doesn't even hold true as far away as Wales, a country where "w" is a vowel. If English covered all bases, we'd have no need for loan-words.

With the programme now being made in a city where the street-signs are in two languages, it is inevitable that everyone involved is thinking about all this a lot more than they used to. Welsh provides us with handy examples across the board: Mickey's first visit to Cardiff (X1.11, "Boom Town") is an opportunity to display the sheer foreign-ness of this relatively anglicised, cosmopolitan Welsh city (maybe not as Eastward-looking as Swansea, but certainly moreso than Lampeter). Yet the street-signs and the writing on the side of the Assembly Building stay defiantly foreign (to anyone not Welsh-speaking) even when the point-of-view character is supposed to be Rose. This gets really odd when she needs the term "Blaidd Drwg" translated. If we take this and the running-gag in "The Fires of Pompeii" (X4.2) together, she might be thinking it's Latin. As Donna discovered in 72 AD, if she says a word in a language not her own, it comes across to others as a word in a language they've heard but don't speak, even when, as in this case, she's talking Latin to Romans. The Romans can't hear words in their own language as sounding familiar and think she's Welsh.

This provides us with a clue: it's intent that matters, rather than delivery. This could account for why Lorna Bucket's attempt to write the name "Melody Pond" in "A Good Man Goes to War" (X6.7) came out as "River Song" and not "Sea Shanty", "Aqua Boogie", "River Dance", "Orinoco Flow", "Song of the Volga Boatmen" or "Water Music"[72]; most European languages have "melody" and "song" as opposites, or at least distinctly different things. The key scene in that story shows us the physical stitches on the cloth changing position in real time to become the Roman letters E, G, I, N. O, R, S and V. Similarly, we may have reason to assume that the Doctor's cryptanalysis of the signal broadcast as Horus' "away-from-my-desk" message (13.3, "Pyramids of Mars") merely seems *to Sarah* to involve the most common letter in this signal being E, and every other letter following the statistical average for mid-nineteenth century English. (Just since the process was described in the Sherlock Holmes story "The Yellow Man", the proportions have changed. The same calculations were used to plan the layout of the QWERTY keyboard and in France, even back then, this was wrong, hence their AZERTY set-up.) The stitches probably didn't really change place, any more than the words in every language all became "Bad Wolf" at the end of "Turn Left" (X4.11). It was the abilities of the characters (and thereby anyone watching) that changed. Similarly, Goddess-Rose didn't really scatter the letters from the logo of Bad Wolf TV across the universe (X1.13, "The Parting of the Ways"), she seeded the idea of those

continued on Page 369...

X2.8 The Impossible Planet

She's less worried about the TARDIS disappearing then the Doctor is, and first insists that she's all right, then realises how worried *he* actually is and shifts to showing her concern so that he can comfort her instead. She lightly teases him about settling down, and has a go at the vexed question of their relationship, but quickly relegates that to the category of "let's sort the details out later". She just stops short of asking him to move in with her in this notional house she'll have to get. The prospect of being stuck in the forty-second century for good doesn't bother her so much as long as the Doctor's around, and she quickly picks up on the terminology and mixing that makes the gloopy-looking rations edible. She's never quite come to terms with space travel not being an easy matter of teleports and anti-gravity [considering her usual mode of transport, this is more forgivable than it might have been]. Basically, she's freaked out by reality not being like *Star Trek*.

When the Doctor throws himself down a ten-mile shaft, she sees him off reasonably enough and only starts wibbling about deep breathing when he's past the oxygen field. She has enough sense to query people who shoot guns in space bases surrounded by vacuum.

Rose's Magic Phone can't get a signal [possibly because the TARDIS is out of commission], but it *can* get calls from the Beast whenever it decides long enough has elapsed since leaving a threatening message. [Presumably it's a new phone, as Mickey's still got her old one to deprogramme Cybermen - see X2.6, "The Age of Steel".]

The Non-Humans

• *The Ood* are a bipedal race with heads resembling cephalopods. They have tentacles that writhe, where a mouth would be on a human. They speak through glowing hand-held spheres, connected via a cable to their necks, which only leaves their left hand free for their various duties. The hands are humanoid, but in black cotton gloves at all times. They wear grey Nehru-suits, with a breast sigil denoting status [in Greek letters, but not as big as those in their next story]. When possessed, their eyes glow red [yes, exactly like the robots in 14.5, "The Robots of Death"]. They all share the same calm voice, even when talking about killing humans [again, those Sandminer robots spring to mind]. They can use the translator spheres to electrocute humans from a distance.

They're presented as a low-level telepathic species used for grunt work such as drilling and mining, and treatment of them as a 'slave race' is considered normal in this society. When a blonde space tourist asks them if they're happy in front of the very people who enthusiastically enslave them, they say they have no other purpose in life. [Anyone who has studied the dynamics of slavery in real life will be aware that professing acceptance of the situation is generally part and parcel of the instigators' demands; since Rose clearly isn't aware of any of this, we'll take up the discussion again in the next volume.] To all appearances, they pine away and die when deprived of any useful work. Danny Bartok, the wrangler for the Ood, is officially designated as a member of the 'Ethics Committee' and seems as concerned that they are suffering as that they are disobeying him. [Well, until they start killing the anonymous security people around him.] They avoid telling their overseers when they're ill. The telepathic field can be monitored by machinery.

Everyone thinks that the Ood's telepathic field makes them peculiarly susceptible to possession by the Beast. [This doesn't precisely follow, since with power levels in excess of Basic 100, it should really be capable of taking over humans as well. And there's an endless number of stories in which humans demonstrate telepathic powers of one sort or another, including most of the stories that this one's referencing.] When the crisis begins, all 'non-essential' Ood are ordered back to their pen, suggesting a hierarchy [the Greek letters seem to confirm this, as all the ones Danny counts back in have the prefix 'Gamma'].

• *The Beast.* Glimpsed briefly on the scanner, the Beast is a lurid orange image of a muscular humanoid torso with horns on its head, one of which is broken. At the same time, the Ood begin chanting 'He is awake... and you will worship him' and Toby Zed is afflicted by first a seductive smooth voice cajoling him for his sloth in translating the runes. Then the marks leave the pages and manifest themselves on his skin, with his eyes glowing Ood red. Thereafter, Toby begins toying with people, luring Scooti to her doom by standing, smiling, outside the airlock and then shattering the windows, leaving her dead (but bodily intact) floating above the base.

The Beast tells Toby that to look on him is to die, but it keeps appearing on the scanners anyway.

The Impossible Planet — X2.8

Can He Read Smells?

continued from Page 367...

words back along her path to lie dormant until her earlier self developed the ability to piece them together as a message.

Ah, but, ah, but... if a message somehow "wants" to be read and there's a pool of available minds from which to source the ground-rules, it ought to be possible to interpret anything at all that was meant to be interpreted by someone. All codes would be redundant. Everyone in Revolutionary France would have known that Prison Governer "LeMaitre" was British agent James Stirling (1.8, "The Reign of Terror"). It seems that we have yet another instance of the all-purpose cop-out, the Perception Filter, with the same caveats about how they don't work if you are really concentrating or if something happens to disrupt the unreflective acceptance of what you're seeing and hearing. (That way madness lies, as we will see in **How Much of This is Happening?** under X5.6, "Vampires of Venice", and **How Messed Up Can Narrative Get?** under X3.10, "Blink" - once Perception Filters have been invoked, it's possible that all of *Doctor Who* is the result of Ian Chesterton inhaling something he shouldn't've in the lab at Coal Hill School.)

Whatever the agreed relationship between uttered sounds or marks on a surface and the ideas the combinations of these convey, once that language is understood, it will be there for the Doctor and his chums to think they can hear or read. This also appears to include anyone within telepathic "earshot" of the TARDIS. (2.6, "The Crusade", would have us believe that Saladin and Richard I would have understood each other had they met while the Doctor was around - and so would their troops. Imagine the change to history if this had been true.) Moreover, once the system for interpreting an alphabet, sound-arrangement, eyebrow-wiggle (7.1, "Spearhead from Space") or anything else (A4, "The Curse of Fatal Death") was in place, any manifestation of that type of language would be open to interpretation, whether intentionally put there or not.

It's a big step from hearing a language to reading one. Apart from the visual manifestations of writing apparently changing into English (or whichever language), the relationship between that symbolic system and speech might not be as simple as an alphabetical representation of sound. It might be a pictogrammatical language. The human brain has an extraordinary ability to adapt itself. One effect of this is that once you have learned to read a specific type of written language, it becomes hard to imagine that any other kind could work, the first one becoming so "natural". Even among European languages, there is a remarkable degree of difference. Human languages have many features that seem specific to the one species, but closer examination with computers is showing that even birdsong has a grammatical structure. Vocabulary and grammar are the main features of most recognised languages. Pictograms have tended to resist being strictly sequential, making it harder to infer a syntax from documents where nobody alive is speaking the language. The tendency in alphabet-based writing has been for the writing to approximate fairly closely the verbal language, to the extent that brain-scans have shown people to be reading English or French by relaying signals from the character-recognition centres at the back of the brain to the speech and hearing sites, Broca's Area and Wernicke's Area, on the left hemisphere just above the ear. (See **Why Doesn't Anyone Read Any More?** under X1.7, "The Long Game".) This isn't universal even among human languages, and neither, as far as anyone can tell, is the activation of the right hemisphere on "autopilot" after sufficient practice at reading in other types of writing. (So far, the only substantial tests have been with Arabic, and so much depends on such tiny differences that this script appears to need more close attention than English or Italian.) Even if the Ship's translation matrix is able to figure out (the phrase is doubly apt here) the written version of a language, the TARDIS then has to interfere with three separate sections of the human brain to make words appear to be written in English *and* make sense *and* not need to be sounded out word-by-work as a small child would. If this is the case, it's lucky for the series that the TARDIS has tended to pick almost-English-speaking aliens with experience of alphabetically encoded writing and to have landed in places where this is commonplace. The Daleks write in a language that it is easy to convert into roman lettering (except, apparently,

continued on Page 371...

X2.8 The Impossible Planet

Planet Notes According to the chief scientific officer, the idea of the planet they're on having a name is apparently 'stupid'. Five minutes later, she explains it was named 'Krop Tor' in the scriptures of the Faltino; and that the name translates to 'the bitter pill'. [This is later given as one of the names of the Beast.] It maintains a 'perpetual geostationary orbit' [sic] around a black hole. The planet maintains a gravity funnel that makes it possible to fly from open space to the planet surface; this requires a tremendous power source that's to be found ten miles below the surface. The planet supported life at some point, but this was eons before humanity evolved. [According to the TARDISode, the race that did this left traces and legends across that galaxy, so they may have gone to this world specifically to chain up the Beast as a farewell gift for the rest of us.]

The black hole is officially designated 'K36 Gem 5'. In and of itself there seems to be nothing unusual about it whatsoever. [Except, apparently, that time and space aren't so badly affected that the expedition members seen here will have no home to return to, and that there's a force-field capable of holding the planet at arm's length, and that there was a civilisation there that could do all that and then got wiped out. You know, minor details like that.]

The Doctor repeatedly states that they are amazingly far out, on the edge of known space [and implicitly of the local group of galaxies; see **How Many Significant Galaxies are There?** under 2.5, "The Web Planet" and **How Can the Universe Have an Edge?** under 13.2, "Planet of Evil"] and that to get to Earth from here would take 500 years. Nonetheless, he seems to accept that the humans on this world are all from Earth.

History

- *Dating.* Err... the date is given as 43K 2.1, apparently. [As the Ood are here established as slaves and were liberated in X4.3, "Planet of the Ood", set in the forty-second century, we seem to have a latest date of 4199. The Ood-sphere is right next door to Sense-Sphere (1.8, "The Sensorites"), and that was visited by humans in the twenty-eighth century, so we have an earliest date and a latest possible date. Except... they're in orbit around a black hole, with all the relativistic effects that will have had. But as far as the humans are concerned, they left home some time in those 1600 years and have been there what seems like a few months. The spaceship is the same as the one in "Planet of the Ood", but is similar to the one in "The Sensorites"; the space-suit is the same model used in X3.7, "42". Then again, it also looks like the one the Doctor wore in 10.3, "Frontier in Space", set in 2540.

[The TARDISode for the episodes gives a vague hint of an Earth Empire in collapse. It's tempting to put this at the thirtieth century, as per the Pertwee era's future-history and the way later stories followed this (see **What is the Timeline of the Earth Empire?** under 8.4, "Colony in Space" and **Is This Any Way to Run a Galactic Empire?** under "Frontier in Space"; plus 23.3, "Terror of the Vervoids"; 9.5, "The Mutants"; and 12.5, "Revenge of the Cybermen"), but the new series might not be playing by the same rules. Then again, so little else about "Planet of the Ood" makes sense, it's tempting to consign that and the Ood involvement in the regeneration story that followed to the crack in Amy's wall and just stick with the 70s chronology.]

The people sent to this world represent an 'Empire' of some sort. It appears to be at least partially centred on Earth. The Empire is in trouble and needs this new, semi-legendary power-source, even though [logically, and see **Things That Don't Make Sense**] the elapsed time for anyone *not* orbiting a black hole will be measured in centuries rather than days. Captain Walker was dispatched to investigate; he was killed on arrival and Zack unsteadily assumed his place.

The idea of slavery is so common that it's possible to refer to various species as being fitted for it. There's at least one organization against this practice, the Friends of the Ood [akin to the 'Sons of Earth' from 16.5, "The Power of Kroll", perhaps]. The expression 'FYI' has persisted to shortly before this story is set, and Thomas Babington Macaulay is still being quoted.

There's a power ratings system called the Blazen Scale, with units given in 'Stats'. 'Ninety' is a potentially revolutionary level. Another scale exists to measure telepathy; 'Basic Five' is tangible but low, while '30' is equivalent to mental screaming; '100', like so much of the rest of this episode, is simply impossible and ought to mean that any unfortunate Ood who are at that level should be dead. Contrary to what Rose thinks, there does seem to be a practical use for anti-gravity, but not much of a one. [This has to be what the 'gravity globe' that lights up the cavern uses. Then again,

Can He Read Smells?

continued from Page 369...

"J"), which is why the radiation-counter the Doctor and Ian find (1.2, "The Daleks") has a clear label in marker-pen, despite the Daleks not being able to use such pens even two episodes later, and the Sensorites seem to be adept at copperplate, despite telepathy presumably making writing fairly redundant (1.7, "The Sensorites").

While we're in Hartnell mood, how about a look at a story where translation is significant? In "The Ark" (3.6), the spoken English of the humans (as far as we hear it) is denied to the Monoids, who are mute and thus communicate in signing. The humans have sometimes tried to learn this and there seem not to be any problems, but we are denied their input until they develop handy speech-boxes in the second pair of episodes. The TARDIS doesn't bother to give us even subtitles. It might be that what they are signing is significantly different from what we gather they are saying. (If we go with the simplistic misreading of this story as being about slavery and race, the Monoids might have unpleasant names for humans - rather as we are occasionally told that "Kimo Sabe" doesn't really mean "Great White Brother", and Tonto's meek acceptance of the Lone Ranger's commands isn't all it seems.) Withholding this information from us and the first Doctor might be part of preventing a big change in history - after all, the TARDIS returns to the same spaceship seven hundred years later at the end of the second episode - but it may just be that such non-verbal encoding is invisible to the TARDIS translators. The Ship has no difficulty with vastly more alien beings who are nothing *but* spoken language when they reach Refusis. And we've seen, far more alien languages than something like English delivered in gestures, and the TARDIS has managed to make them legible. If it can translate writing, why not signing? It must be, as with the pictograms the Doctor is sent to deliver to Solos (9.4, "The Mutants") or the runes on the walls of various buildings (11.3, "Death to the Daleks"; 26.3, "The Curse of Fenric") that the act of translation and its effect on the person making this effort is the transformative moment in a crisis. The analogy would be with moments when the Doctor's ability to speak a language his friends cannot is important (8.2, "The Mind of Evil"; 11.5, "Planet of the Spiders"; 14.6, "The Talons of Weng-Chiang"; and others; and, conversely, 7.3, "The Ambassadors of Death"). We're left with the human assumption that speech is the "real" language and writing or any other kind of symbolism is secondary, an approximation. What if that's not the case?

After all, it's a commonplace (especially among proper-written-down-grown-up-SF novels, and occasional linguistics textbooks) that speech is itself an approximation to the subtleties of thought. It could be argued that words are supplementary to pointing at things; it has often been argued that language introduces artificial binary oppositions to define one thing in terms of another (the foundation of most present-day Linguistics was Saussure's attempt to analyse precisely that pattern of system-building and people have spent about a century trying to find an alternative - don't let's get into all of that again now). Just because our species has taken grunts to a level of sophistication where pigment on 2D surfaces denoting those grunts is now the most common use for neural processes previously specialised for hunting, selecting the right fruits and recognising faces, that doesn't make speech and writing inevitably "the" language-system. If the TARDIS is telepathically translating, why not cut out the middle-man and send thoughts directly without words getting in the way?

Well... that might not work if people are expecting words. The Doctor's newfound ability to mind-meld needs explanation and permission - or a head-butt (X5.11, "The Lodger"). Introducing an unfamiliar communications system takes time; let's not forget that the TARDIS' first attempt to talk to the Doctor took two episodes and a couple of attempted murders to decode (1.3, "The Edge of Destruction"). Victorian literature, paintings and courtship had a well-developed set of associations between different varieties of flowers and different signals sent to potential suitors. Anyone alert to this can see coded signals in all sorts of unexpected places, and a lot of effort can be fruitlessly expended assuming that a more recent author is aware of this, or that a photo of an unweeded garden is a carefully contrived insult. Similarly, Henry V invaded France because - so Shakespeare and Holinshead tell us - the French

continued on Page 373...

X2.8 The Impossible Planet

they're all orbiting a black hole without being spaghettified, so presumably some kind of anti-grav is at work, as well as the spaceship that got the crew there needing it.]

The Scarlet system here undergoes its final death-throes, having previously been home of the Pallushi - a 'mighty civilisation spanning a billion years'.

Catchphrase Counter Scooti gets a posthumous 'Sorry, I'm so sorry'. The Doctor cajoles Zack into letting him go investigate the ship by saying 'look me in the eye'. [It was rather more effective the last time that a Scottish Doctor tried this; see 25.2, "The Happiness Patrol", but also 26.1, "Battlefield".]

Deus Ex Machina As we will see, the entire bloody planet, the whole premise and the ancient race that built this anomalous gap in the laws of physics makes everything in this and the next episode one big deus ex machina. Or "diabolo in profundis".

The Analysis

The Big Picture ("The Impossible Planet" and "The Satan Pit") As we've noted many times in earlier volumes, *Doctor Who* is cheerfully secular and routinely shows almost all religions (real or made-up) to be at best misunderstood alien interventions and at worst massive cons. This allows them to use iconography from all faiths, current or past, as source-material. Whilst it's unlikely that there would be any Vikings watching who would complain about misrepresenting their beliefs in 20.4, "Terminus" (and if they did, nothing so polite as a strongly worded phone call would have followed), the one time a specific, current belief-system was shown in a positive - not to say vaguely propagandist - light (11.5, "Planet of the Spiders"), practicing Buddhists wrote in and complained. Whilst angels can be shown elevating the Doctor to safety (X4.0, "Voyage of the Damned"), they are robots with jet-packs and have been trying to kill everyone. The bulk of the programme's use of Christianity is as a period detail, such as in "The Massacre" (3.5). In this, sectarian schisms were the pretext for attempted genocide, manipulated for political ends; this is the majority view in the UK (outside Northern Ireland, where belief really *was* enough to make people plant bombs and shoot at their neighbours, albeit with some murky politics behind it all). It's noticeable that the only times a religious belief has shown to have functional validity, it's been presented as a massive coincidence (1.6, "The Aztecs", where the rains fall as the Perfect Victim kills himself; 16.1, "The Ribos Operation", where the Seer prophesies accurately and there really is a war between an Ice-god and a Fire-god, or the Guardians as the Doctor calls them). So whilst old beliefs such as Cartesean Dualism and Sympathetic Magic are routinely evoked as a way of making a story happen in a familiar way (**How Does "Evil" Work?** under 8.2, "The Mind of Evil", **Does This Universe Have an Ethical Standard?** under 12.1, "Robot", and **How Does Hypnosis Work?** under 8.1, "Terror of the Autons"), there are usually given the same kind of doubletalk "explanation" as werewolves (13.1, "Terror of the Zygons"; 15.1, "Horror of Fang Rock"; X2.2, "Tooth and Claw"). If it makes a Fu Manchu pastiche work better if they revive the old idea of a "life-force" that can be drained, so be it (14.6, "The Talons of Weng-Chiang"): similarly disembodied consciousness is a "higher" plane (so many to choose from, but let's take X4.18, "The End of Time Part Two" because the story began in a church). For *Doctor Who* scriptwriters, religions are simply a fund of useable images and plot-devices, much as *Star Trek*, Sherlock Holmes or 30s horror movies are.

Consider "The Daemons" (8.5) in the light of the BBC's guidelines about avoiding causing deliberate offence to any faith-group. Christianity is almost wholly avoided, in a story mainly set in a church. The real vicar is long-gone and the Master is using this post as a cover for his activities: other than that, the only practicing clergyman mentioned is Matthew Hopkins, the notorious "Witchfinder General", hardly a positive role-model for trendy vicars. But look closer: no attempt is made, as would happen in an American series, to equate paganism with devil-worship. It's a very old set of practices and beliefs and Johnny-come-lately Christianity is largely irrelevant to actual pagans, as is the Judeo-Christian devil. Miss Hawthorne is partly comic relief, partly info-dump central, but she is the only genuine pagan in the story and she's on the Doctor's side. The coven summoned by the local vicar are largely there for their own ends, more like Freemasonry than satanism, and only when it starts to look serious does one break hypnotic conditioning and

The Impossible Planet — X2.8

Can He Read Smells?

continued from Page 371...

king sent a gift of tennis-balls. This was an insult because both parties knew that it was, and each knew that the other knew. However, a language can be intended for one person: Leonardo da Vinci's mirror-writing and Samuel Pepys' cypher were intended to keep secrets, but were still a system of preserving thoughts on paper and amenable to (eventual) reading by others. (The Doctor managed to crack Leonardo's puzzles almost without effort, but he seems to have been let into the not-too-difficult secret in an unscreened adventure. See **When Did the Doctor Meet Lenoardo?** under, obviously, 17.2, "City of Death".)

One person having tried some sort of private language might be enough to make the TARDIS able to see or hear it in any context, at any time and among any species. We're just a short step away from the paranoid delusions that signals are being put in records played backwards or cartoons on TV[73]. Yet, in a series where the Doctor is shown to have mastered various semiotic systems and structures of signification that regular folks see as just random, it's worth looking at where the ability to read words and worlds ends for him. Can he unlock messages in pheromones? Do bees dancing tell him anything? (See X4.12, "The Stolen Earth" before answering.) Can he read what bar codes tell the machines and a few dedicated (or profoundly sad) humans? Hypothetically, if someone encrypted a message by the numerical values of measurements (using binary notation and thousandths of an inch) so that a very precisely-executed scratch in a door could be read and translated, then once the Doctor had found this out, every single scratch in every single surface would be legible and a high proportion of them would mean something, whether or not the maker of the scratch was "writing".

If the Doctor speaks Baby ("A Good Man Goes to War"; X6.12, "Closing Time"), Horse (X7.3, "A Town Called Mercy") and possibly Cat ("The Lodger"), then all pre-syntactical utterances by intelligent, not-quite-self-aware entities (dolphins, chimps, anthills) would be open to him with a little effort. Information encrypted in physical form is, thus, all waiting to be decoded. This includes the sugars and amino acids that make up deoxiribonucleic acid (we're using the long form because

"DNA" stopped meaning anything in *Doctor Who* when X3.5, "Evolution of the Daleks" was broadcast). The Doctor is able to tell human Type A blood by taste (X2.0, "The Christmas Invasion"), so is he able to sniff dust and work out who was in a room thousands of years ago? What other information might be encrypted in even human chromosomes? We have some hints that exposure to Artron energy makes changes over time (see **Is Arthur the Horse a Companion?** under X2.4, "The Girl in the Fireplace" and **What Happened to the Daleks?** under X1.6, "Dalek"), so maybe the metaphor of "rewriting" isn't just a figure of speech. What else might the Doctor be "reading" while we see the things the companions see and hear what they hear? It seems obvious that he spotted the Flesh fraud version of Amy right from the start (X6.6, "The Rebel Flesh"; X6.9, "Night Terrors"), but the story as broadcast declined to let us in on this secret.[74] Fair enough that he *didn't* spot the flesh baby double (X6.7, "A Good Man Goes to War"), but perhaps that's because he knows Amy better.

Pheromones are a method of communication used by a large number of species on Earth. Most of this is simple territorial marking and the occasional mating call or distress signal. Anyone who keeps cats will know that rubbing scent on any passing object is something a cat will do if awake, under any circumstances. There's no intent there. Similarly, individual insects don't have any volition, but taken as a collective, with the bees or ants treated as "bits" in a "program" or "cells" in a "brain", it's a different matter. Again, the parochial assumption that intelligence has to be housed in each individual, or that an "individual" is something other than a lot of cells co-operating, might be leading us astray. Any self-regulating system can be considered, in a limited sense, "intelligent" if it has the ability to adapt; whether it can be treated as conscious is another matter. A rain forest is a homeostatic system, but expecting a message from one is probably a sign of madness (19.3, "Kinda", but then again there's X7.0, "The Doctor, the Widow and the Wardrobe"). On the other hand, at the beginning of "The Ice Warriors" (5.3), the Doctor is able to hear information nobody else can in a system he's obviously never encountered before, and gets the notion that everything will go

continued on Page 375...

2.8 The Impossible Planet

protest, with unfortunate results. Azal isn't the devil, he's a very naughty boy. The BBC were at pains to avoid offending the Church of England, pagan groups and even rugby supporters. (Morris dancers are casually insulted, but sod them.)

With this in mind, observe the way that writer Matt Jones and everyone else associated with "The Satan Pit" gleefully borrowed all the trappings of those 70s schlock Satan flicks and then spent the last half-episode frantically back-pedalling to avoid accidentally ruling out the existence of an actual devil in case any American viewers firebomb Television Centre. Whilst the series is made by and for people in Britain, where just under 3% of the population attend church regularly (at least, across the entire country - localised centres of ethnic minorities have far higher attendance at mosques and gurdwalas, but spread out of the nation as a whole, the ratio stands), there is no sense in starting a fight. Especially not with BBC Wales eyeing up a lucrative new global market. The result is that the series walks a tightrope between reflecting Britain as it is and not appalling the US networks (see **Gay Agenda? What Gay Agenda?** under X1.10, "The Doctor Dances" and **Must They All be Old-Fashioned Cats?** under X3.3, "Gridlock"). During the making of this story, a flurry of emails and memos went around to establish how far they should go to avoid suggesting that this either was or wasn't the character from the Bible. Prior to BBC Wales touting around for co-production money, this simply wouldn't have been an issue.

After all, the accredited author was a veteran of the Virgin *New Adventures*, a range which had consolidated all its theological concerns into one manageable monthly package (see **Are All These "Gods" Related?** under 26.3, "The Curse of Fenric") and had then spun off into the non-copyright-infringing adventures of Bernice Summerfield. Matt Jones was in the loop for these (writing the third release, *Beyond the Sun*), making this story's outward similarity to another book in the range - *Down* by Lawrence Miles - look a little suspicious. In this book, an affectionate pastiche of 30s chapterplays (specifically *Undersea Kingdom* and *The Phantom Empire*), a journey to the centre of a planet reveals a bigger-on-the-inside sphere of reality containing a demonic force: said force was created by God. Not *that* God, silly, but the magical vast computer of the People, operating a Dyson Sphere full of powerful entities (first encountered by the Doctor in *The Also People* by Ben Aaronovitch, which owes absolutely nothing at all to Iain M Banks). God sent Benny Summerfield on missions exactly the way the Time Lords used to get the Doctor into odd situations. This God-complex had created the dark overlord as a means of motivating the People, and was trying to escape into our reality as a meme.

And we ought to acknowledge that the word "meme" was coined by Richard Dawkins to denote a habit or idea that self-replicates. There are lots of examples of these, including LOLcats, which in and of itself is proof of the existence of Satan.

But, as we said, the real starting-point for this story and the source of the plot-beats and overall "shape" of the script is that rash of horror movies about summoning the Devil. Specifically, John Carpenter's *Prince of Darkness* is an obvious source, as it was for "The Curse of Fenric", since in all cases the Devil is summoned by decoding information and expresses itself physically after being stored as text. Jones' script is at pains to deny that the McCoy-era story ever happened or was indeed possible (see this story's essay). This is, again, an odd thing for someone steeped in the *New Adventures* to do. Both stories use the removal of writing from an article to somewhere else as a plot-point. Both have the story resolved by the "devil" being incarnated in a killable human who is killed. We can also mention *The Omen* and *The Exorcist* and several dozen Hammer films (but start with *Blood on Satan's Claw*). However, the simple fact is that anyone looking for sources of inspiration for this story should simply consult *About Time* Volumes 3b and 4. This is overtly an attempt to evoke the same thrill amongst 2006 eight-year-olds that "The Daemons" did in 1971, and consciously echoes many of Tom Baker's early adventures. There is even one line (The Beast to Jefferson: "Did your wife ever forgive you?") taken wholesale from "The Daemons" (the Master: "Has your wife come back from her sister's yet? Will she ever come back, do you suppose?").

[For **Things That Don't Make Sense**, **Critique**, **The Facts** and **Production**, see the next episode.]

Can He Read Smells?

continued from Page 373...

bang in two minutes thirty-eight apparently by listening to how "wrong" the system sounds. The read-outs and speaking computer are busy giving requested information to the staff, but eventually deliver the same dire prognosis to Leader Clent. The system is designed by humans to be understood, but nobody was listening.

If we carry on like this, we get into whether the messages dogs leave for each other on lampposts are open to interpretation, so the safest course back to useful speculation is to look at the lapses. The TARDIS cannot interpret the writing on the walls of the base on Krop Tor (X2.8, "The Impossible Planet") because it is "too old". The three, count 'em, three scripts the Time Lord have used over the last 40 years of the series are impossible to translate (and yet Adric could read the Doctor's old journals, 18.6, "The Keeper of Traken", so presumably he wrote them in a different language again). The runes written on the walls of St Jude's church ("The Curse of Fenric") were translatable, but the system of logical relations between the individual figures was part of the code-sequence for unlocking Fenric, which it wouldn't have been in English. A few alien species have languages that viewers can't understand but some characters can (X4.6, "The Doctor's Daughter", shows us Martha understanding the bubbly Hath language, and them understanding her, but during a war between humans and Hath caused by misunderstandings). Much of X7.8, "The Rings of Akhaten", follows the same procedure, and the plot needs people to sing lullabies to a star; the Doctor barking at Do'reen is the least of this story's problems in this regard and many others.

Let's mention Foamasi. The main difficulty with translating their language to whatever everyone else in "The Leisure Hive" (18.1) was speaking is that the squeaks and chirrups were beyond even Time Lord hearing. The mechanics of making words with mouths unlike ours is occasionally touched upon (notoriously in 2.5, "The Web Planet"), but incidents like this are rare. More commonly, we encounter the secondary signification-system of English accents. We hear Anne Chaplet (3.5, "The Massacre") as sounding West Country because that's the English equivalent of whatever accent she would have spoken French in, but the various personae adopted by Garron (16.1, "The Ribos Operation") are perceived by the Doctor to come from bits of the UK that come with connotations of different value-systems. (It's a can of worms we opened in **What Are the Dodgiest Accents in the Series?** under 4.1, "The Smugglers" - lots of planets have a North, and a great many have a Dorset, apparently.) It is a well-worn joke that most 70s monsters seemed to have laryngitis, but the vocal delivery of aliens speaking something we hear as English is a complicating factor - yes, we hear a lot of them as speaking BBC-standard Received Pronunciation English, but without contractions and with hisses, clacking noises and grunts ad lib. The real puzzle of how the Sycorax speak isn't their own language translated by UNIT technology, but how they sound when the Doctor wakes up ("The Christmas Invasion"). Even with the TARDIS translating normally, we hear them sounding like the caricature baddies in the translated version of *Monkey* (see 14.1, "The Masque of Mandragora"). It might be that this distortion is the alien thought-processes interfering with the translation. The question then arises as to why the translated Sycorax grunting didn't get misinterpreted as Haitian Creole or somesuch. (This is a deeply weird situation: the TARDIS is out of the game, for the moment, so the Sycorax are telling the humans what to do in their own language, which the humans are remarkably able to convert into idiomatic English - "Sycorax rock!" - and the only real interpretation problem is the import of their threats. Yet the Sycorax can follow Harriet and Rose perfectly well. That's not such a good strategy for being accepted as masters of a world. If it is a calculated insult, it suggests a lot more research into the situation on Earth, so why pick the one nation with the technology to beat them as its base of operations?).

As we saw in **Aren't Alien Names Inevitably a Bit Silly?** under 9.2, "The Curse of Peladon", the entire series seems to require the cosmos as a whole to conform to the tiny nuances of British English 1963 to date, especially with regard to what's a language and what isn't. But as we saw in **Who Narrates This Series?** under 23.1, "The Mysterious Planet", what we're being shown might not be the whole story anyway. We might be missing lots of other stories happening at the same time under the Doctor's nose. Or in it.

X2.9: "The Satan Pit"

(10th June, 2006)

Which One is This? Evil, evil since the Dawn of T-i-i-i-ime (again). Something purporting to be the ultimate force of evil in the cosmos is defeated by Rose opening the window. That's after a lot of crawling through ventilation shafts, running up and down corridors and mollicking about in a quarry. Other Tom Baker-era throwbacks, of which there are dozens, are less welcome.

Firsts and Lasts The scene with the Doctor and Rose claiming to be "the stuff of legend" was the last Billie Piper recorded as full-time companion. It was also the last scene to be made at the Q2 studio before relocating to the new permanent home of Upper Boat. This was the last story for Series Two to be completed, and the final edit of the sound and effects was completed with just over a day before transmission.

This episode has the first of several hints over the next three episodes that the Doctor and Rose are skating on thin ice, as the Beast prophesies that Rose will die in battle. That makes this the first of rather a lot of misleading prolepses.

Oddly enough, the shots of the TARDIS spinning in space - which used to be the standard establishing shot when the Tom Baker Doctor was about to enter the story (beginning with, oh look! - 13.3, "Pyramids of Mars") - hadn't been used in the Welsh series until the rocket seen here needs a tow.

Watch Out For...

• To paraphrase Anton Chekhov, if you have a bolt-gun with precisely one bolt in the first act, you have to use it in the third act. Similar handy lines of dialogue include Danny telling us that the Ood have gone berserk: "all 50 of them!" (see 22.5, "Timelash") and Rose helpfully comparing Jefferson's escape-route to a "ventilator shaft", allowing him to acknowledge the cliché and correct it, tipping the wink to the viewers that there is a slight change because of the oxygen-bubble plot-device. And then doing exactly what people have been doing to kill time in *Doctor Who* since 4.2, "The Tenth Planet".

• It's rather hard to figure out the layout of this base, so it's entirely possible that the route they take through these metal tubes in some way follows the corridors we saw this time last week. However, the exterior shots of the base show that they planned the sinuous linked rooms and corridors to look like the alien lettering, so *someone* was paying attention, just not the people in charge of the script.

• In fact, though, the whole ventilator shaft chase is just one of the ways this story betrays its roots as a composite of 70s movies and Hinchcliffe-era *Doctor Who*. To the experienced viewer, Zack's sudden realisation that the rocket has its own generator and can power the whole complex looks as if he's remembering having watched "The Ark in Space" (12.2) as a kid. The politely voiced Ood with red eyes going on a primly unflappable killing-spree is very like 14.5, "The Robots of Death" (although not as flagrant as X4.0, "Voyage of the Damned"). We've already mentioned Sutekh's guest-appearance last episode, so watch the end of the story and wonder whether Matt Jones and Chris Chibnall (X3.7, "42") were having a contest over who could pilfer 13.2, "Planet of Evil" most brazenly.

• The final edit of this episode - sound effects, CGI and all - was completed hours before transmission. This two-parter was the end of the second series' production, and all of the money had been allocated. As such, you will note that nearly all of the music is recycled from earlier in the series and that the Doctor's confrontation with the Beast is very strangely edited. It chops about in the scene where he works out the puzzle, in the manner that was in vogue in the mid-90s (series such as *Homicide: Life on the Streets* used it a lot). We have a sneaking suspicion that this is a side effect of Tennant's performance being trimmed to fit pre-edited computerised big-scary-orange-man-going-*Raaar*! footage, because the tight deadline meant they had to sign off on The Mill's contribution before the final edit was complete.

The Continuity

The Doctor He's unwilling to rule out the possibility of a devil, but thinks that the only practical definition is equating it with 'the things that men do'. For once in his life, he thinks it'd be a good idea to retreat from the unknown [this is admittedly at the bottom of a miles-deep hole on an expedition with no backup systems, lots of earthquakes and no TARDIS, so he mayn't be at his best right now; we'll discuss this more in the attached

The Satan Pit — X2.9
Why's the Doctor So Freaked Out by a Big Orange Bloke?

The Doctor's alarm at what the Beast is telling him comes not from seeing a being that looks like the caricature of Evil Incarnate (big horns and all, just like in *South Park*), but through something it says. It claims to come from "before time", which unsettles the Doctor more than any preposition ought to. He himself says that "outside" or "beyond" would have been acceptable.

We might argue the philology, that "before" implies the existence of time whilst simultaneously denying it, but it's not the Beast's grammar that is causing the Doctor such existential heebie-jeebies. What he's denying is the existence of anything older than the Universe.

And this is odd because, as we've seen, there have been many indications that this is not the first Universe, and a whole story (20.4, "Terminus") about the events leading up to Event One, a.k.a. the Big Bang, that had rather disappointingly drab consequences later on. Moreover, you may have read the essay with "The Curse of Fenric" (26.3) on this topic (**Are All These "Gods" Related?**) and know more than you ever thought you'd need to on how the *New Adventures* attempted a Grand Unified Theory of Preposterously Powerful Entities and God-Like Thingies, yoking all such beings from broadcast episodes into the HP Lovecraft "mythos"[77]. In brief, things like the Great Intelligence (5.2, "The Abominable Snowmen" et seq) or the Nestene Consciousness (7.1, "Spearhead from Space", et al) were hangovers from the previous Universe, possibly that cosmos' very own Time Lords, and their interference in our realm's affairs was at best awkward, at worst a severely traumatic experience for any "local" Time Lords who were outclassed. Because, as a result of having originated somewhere with different physical laws, they found conditions here magnified their powers and made them immune to attempts to contain them. That's handy!

This provided a climax (of sorts) to the Bernice Summerfield-only, post-*Doctor Who* version of the *New Adventures*, as well as an explanation (of sorts) for the odd physics-defying properties of the Menoptra (in two separate novels called *Twilight of the Gods*; neither, sadly, much cop). It would be possible, even desirable, for the return of broadcast episodes of *Doctor Who* to have consigned this notion to limbo were it not for an embarrassing detail: there was an episode of *The Sarah Jane Adventures* written by Gareth Roberts, the author of "The Shakespeare Code" (X3.2), that proposed and required the existence of pre-Big Bang forces within the Universe. (This was *SJA*: "Secrets of the Stars", which was sort of like 14.1, "The Masque of Mandragora", but with daytime TV instead of the Renaissance.) "The Shakespeare Code", and before it "The Runaway Bride" (X3.0), made much play of the fact that the Doctor's antagonists were beings from a time before the Universe was thoroughly cooked, when the rules were slightly different. That's not the same as "before" time, but bear it in mind for later.

A couple of episodes after this alarming exchange between Time Lord and spooky voice-over, we encounter a Void Ship (X2.12, "Army of Ghosts", but more pertinently X2.13, "Doomsday"). Two things are worthy of our attention here: the Doctor casually mentions beings called the Eternals (20.5, "Enlightenment" and several *Sarah Jane* episodes, but we'll come to those); he equally nonchalantly declares that a Void Ship can outsit eternity and carry on past the end of this universe and into the next. So there's a next, is there?

Well, that's one popular theory: that if the Universe has enough mass, it'll stop expanding and gravity will slam everything into reverse, possibly making time go backwards. Ultimately, everything will end in a Big Crunch which is simultaneously the Big Bang for the revised edition of creation. For the Doctor to be so blasé about there being "after time" makes his screaming ab-dabs about "before time" seem a bit silly. This so-called "Concertina Universe" has a lot going for it as a source of stories, and until anyone proves that there isn't enough Dark Matter to make it viable, it seems to fit the physics.

There's just one problem: We've been to the year one hundred trillion (in X3.11, "Utopia"), and there wasn't. The Universe petered out, leaving Professor Yana and the last few humans killing time with DIY projects. However, this is just a small problem, because that entire future was paradoxical and may have been forestalled by the subsequent actions of the Doctor, the Master and the TARDIS. The earlier volumes of *About Time* commented on the possibility that the observed red-shift of expanding galaxies and the other results

continued on Page 379...

essay]. He says now he knows he's getting old. [A better sign of that might be the absurd number of speeches he's making this story - after the fourth Doctor-ish speech about the excitement of space travel last episode, he witters on about the joys of adventure, a pep talk on communal spirit, several bouts of comparative religion analysis...]

Nevertheless, when it's a matter of him or Ida going down to investigate the hole, he demands first go. After they've run out of cable, he insists on going on rather than coming back up to comfort her. Uncharacteristically, he asks if she has any religious faith.

Before cutting the hearable, he pauses to give Scott a message for Rose, but trails off saying, 'Oh, she knows'. Predictably, Rose gets on the comms ten seconds later and is distraught about not getting a chance to talk. If he believes in anything, it's that Rose isn't just a victim.

- *Background*. His people invented black holes. [See, if you have the stamina, 10.1, "The Three Doctors"; 14.3, "The Deadly Assassin"; and the essays with both of these; then 15.6, "The Invasion of Time"; 17.5, "The Horns of Nimon"; and sundry other references.]

He rattles off a list of religions, including the Archphets, Qualdonity, Christianity, Pash-Pash, New Judaism, Sanclar and the Church of the Tin Vagabond. [This last one sounds as though it might have something to do with the Patriarchs of the Tin Vagabond that Sarah Jane mentions in *SJA*: "Whatever Happened to Sarah Jane?".] In similar vein, he's aware that Earth, Draconia [10.3, "Frontier in Space"], Vel Consadine [that one's new], Daemos [8.5, "The Daemons"] and the Kaled [12.4, "Genesis of the Daleks"] God of War all invoke a concept of a Horned Beast. He speculates that this particular Beast might have been the inspiration for all the legends, but refuses to commit himself to that.

He's adamantly against the idea of anything existing before the start of Time and the Universe [which runs against a fairly significant plot thread in the *New Adventures*, for which Matt Jones actually wrote]. This is despite him being perfectly fine with the idea of something coming from *beyond* the universe. [The script, at least, has the sense to note this has the feel of an arbitrary distinction. Again, see this story's essay for further complications here, not least an outright contradiction in four episodes' time in a story already recorded and written by Jones' boss.]

- *Ethics*. When put to the choice, he rescues the plummeting spaceship with Rose Tyler and two other people aboard rather than 50 Ood. He does at least apologise for this.

- *The TARDIS*. Evidently, the Ship's force-field generator [for what we'll follow eighty years of tradition and call a "tractor beam"; see Volume 3b for more on E.E. "Doc" Smith] has had a bit of an upgrade lately. [In 24.3, "Delta and the Bannermen", it struggled to pull a space-time charabanc to safety after a ding from a tiny US satellite. Now, it can pull a hefty spaceship out of the gravity-well of a black hole, no bother.]

The Doctor isn't remotely surprised that the TARDIS handled an earthquake and ten-mile drop without sustaining a scratch.

- *Inventory: Other*. He keeps the spacesuit for use in later adventures [before finally losing the helmet in X4.16, "The Waters of Mars"].

The Supporting Cast

- *Rose*. Almost calls the Doctor something presumably rude when they lose contact over the cliffhanger, for which he scolds her. She's very perturbed by the idea that the devil might be real, and asks the Doctor to say that it can't possibly exist. Understandably, the Beast's claim that she is valiant and will soon die in battle has her concerned. [What no one seems to notice is that, of all the secrets the Beast airs about those present, its claim about Rose is the only one that hasn't already happened; the rest is something that anything capable of telepathically overwhelming minds could have picked up easily. Of course, given Rose's lifestyle, it's not an unfair guess. If it really is basing this in something factual, we can guess that exiting the universe reads as "death" for your average prophecy anyhow. See, of course, the "fulfilment" of this in X2.13, "Doomsday".]

Depending how you look at it, Rose is responsible either for saving a life or getting most of the expedition killed when she stops Jefferson from killing the possessed Toby. She doesn't mind hugging a bloke who's in shock from being possessed, but objects to having her bum stared at.

After the Doctor and Ida lose contact, Rose rises to the occasion and efficiently kicks the numbed expedition members into gear, encouraging them to do their jobs properly. It isn't until Ida tells her that the Doctor has vanished and not responding to the comm that she loses it and insists she'll wait it out on the planet until he turns up, and would

The Satan Pit X2.9
Why's the Doctor So Freaked Out by a Big Orange Bloke?

continued from Page 377...

that give a date for the Big Bang don't entirely match, that somehow the amount of mass in the Universe has increased at some point and thus gravitational force has strengthened. And Lo... in "The Runaway Bride", we find that the Time Lords apparently had the ability to remove a type of energy from the menu (although, thinking about it, subtracting Huons is like creating one-sided coins or one-ended pieces of string). If they could do that, then adding mass, despite the Law of Conservation of Energy, ought to be easy. In fact, we've seen it happen (18.7, "Logopolis").

So there are two possible ways to resolve that contradiction. One is that the future that led to "Utopia" is one where someone removed a large chunk of mass, the other is that the one that *didn't* had, at some point pre-one hundred trillion AD, a period where humans were able to take delivery of hitherto unsuspected mass in sufficient quantities to "close" the Universe; this phase only happening as a result of a Time Lord - or suitably equipped Dalek - altering the timelines in an as-yet unmade adventure[78]. Thus, the TARDIS panics and takes refuge in a possible future, because she's trying to shake off the anomalous Captain Jack... and who should they meet there, but someone hiding from the Time War in a future that can't happen if either side gets an outright victory. Until the Paradox Machine is taken out of commission (X3.13, "Last of the Time Lords"), the potential future ending in the Toclafane and Heat Death is more probable than the one where the missing mass is found (under the cushions?) and the Universe gets a sequel. Just as well, because time-travel rather relies on the Universe having this kind of enclosed nature.

So we've removed the one on-screen objection to the Concertina Universe. We're not much closer to resolving why the Doctor was so panic-stricken about the idea of "before time" and, a mere four episodes later, so cheery about the next Universe. Whilst it's possible that abducting mass from next door allows this to be the first of an infinite sequence, it doesn't resolve the contractions with earlier stories. "Terminus" might, at a pinch, be a tale of how this one was made by an accident in an "outer" universe, along the model of Russian dolls (17.4, "Nightmare of Eden"). If the one a level up is inaccessible and the creation of this one came with our own unique physical laws, then time began right at the start and there is no "before" that we can meaningfully visit.

But then we have to wonder why nothing from a technology capable of making bubble-universes can visit those bubbles. The answer, as far as anyone contemplating doing it here can say, is that any bubble-universe has to be considered to be, effectively, a black hole. (NB this is not to say that all black holes contain bubble universes. But how would we know?) The Doctor nonchalantly mentions that his people invented these, so the beings who made this planet-sized puzzle-box can surely hold no terrors for him. Nonetheless, it's stretching a point to call someone from the Garm's universe ("Terminus") a being from "before time", so much as "outside" or "beyond" or any other term the Doctor would accept. Indeed, the Doctor was quite pally with the Big Bang Dog so what, apart from it talking like Sutekh ("Pyramids of Mars") and looking like Tim Curry in *Legend*, was so offensive about the Beast?

Well, maybe the problem is that the Universe-creating explosion we learn about in "Terminus" seems to have taken place in a spaceship from somewhere quite unlike wherever the Beast comes from. The Doctor had no difficulty reading the operator's manual for the spaceship controls, and talking to the Garm wasn't such a problem either. Reading the inscriptions at Krop Tor was beyond the TARDIS' translation capacity and several elements of the physics of gazing at a black hole were said to be "impossible". Repeatedly. The Doctor is not freaked out by the Beast, but by his unseen, anonymous gaolers. They have bent the laws of the Universe to imprison a creature less scary than they were.

Such as who? These mysterious Eternals? They get mentioned a few times in later stories (and *The Sarah Jane Adventures*). There are also a set of beings called the Pantheon of Chaos, whose most common manifestation is the annual altered-timelines-to-trap-Miss-Smith-but-resolved-through-traffic-incidents instigator, the Trickster. (See **Should the Trickster Have a Dead Bird on His Head?** under "The Wedding of Sarah Jane Smith" in the Appendix to Volume 8, and the

continued on Page 381...

X2.9 The Satan Pit

stay even if he did die. The crew decide to short-cut an emotional conversation and forcibly drug her instead. [Fortunately, she's too young to have seen *The A-Team*.] When she awakens on the spaceship, she has a go at threatening Zach with the bolt-firing tool to make him turn back, but admits it's a bluff when she's called on it. Simple logic after that enables her to work out that the escape has all been too easy, and she is therefore mentally prepared to shoot out the window of the rocket when the still-possessed Toby starts gibbering and breathing fire.

The Non-Humans

• *The Beast*. As manifested in the Pit, we have yer basic Devil model, as tattooed badly on countless bikers' arms. It is orange, and has chains connecting hoops around its horns to the walls, with a similar arrangement on the wrists. It's something like a hundred feet tall. It cannot speak when confronted with the Doctor. This is because it has downloaded its mind into Toby [in keeping with the programme's traditional views on Cartesean Dualism], but when Toby is killed, the Beast's mind is unable to escape into, say, Rose and just gets killed by falling into a black hole [thus calling into question the entire premise of the story].

The Beast is physically kept in this cosmic oubliette by a force-field generated by two Etruscan-looking vases that glow when approached. [A cut scene elaborates on this with cave-paintings (all of which assume visitors of a certain height with the ability to decode markings in the visible spectrum, but never mind).] The Beast claims that the Disciples of the Light rose up against it and imprisoned it there 'before time', before the 'cataclysm' of Event One.

[We should probably note that "End of Days", the *Torchwood* Series One finale, referred to this episode. The name of the giant killer horned beast in *that* story was Abaddon, which - if you were paying attention - is cited as an alias of this one as well. There's even a bit of dialogue indicating that the *Torchwood* version is the "son" of the Beast seen here, however that might be expected to work. Certainly, this entity, which slaughters thousands in present-day Cardiff and is never mentioned again, is the same basic pattern (by which we mean "programming") that The Mill devised for the nasty-orange-thing-going-RAAAR!, except it's grey, it walks around Cardiff like Godzilla, its left horn is intact and anyone in its shadow drops dead[75]. Destroying this is what kills Captain Jack so badly, it takes him a suitably messianic three days to recover.]

• *The Ood*. Apparently, their owners have the ability to convert a software virus into an actual airborne contagion [a technology that would have been supremely useful for a number of other plot contingencies in this tale, such as teaching Rose how to fly a starship in a few minutes]. Flipping a monitor can broadcast a flare capable of giving the Ood a brainstorm that'll destroy them all. [Why this stuff isn't as mocked as "megabyte modem" - see 23.4, "The Ultimate Foe" - is a question we're not going to figure out here.] As might be expected of a slaveholding society, there are polite euphemisms for killing the victims, such as 'tanking' [though it's hard to tell whether this is a general term, or refers only to death by telepathic overload]. The computer doesn't register the Ood as 'proper' life-forms, but Zack mentions them in dispatches, ahead of the four anonymous humans also killed. They are each identified with a Greek letter and a number.

Planet Notes Ten miles down is a cave with vast statues and a vast disc concealing another pit. The precise depth of this is unclear, but the Doctor is in almost total darkness when his cable runs out [this is, presumably, ten miles long] and he decides to drop the rest of the journey. At the base [handily] is a bubble of Earth-type air and an alcove leading to a cliff-edge, surrounded by cave-paintings and two pillars holding vases. Over the cliff is the Pit, containing the Beast. Nonetheless, from however far down he is, the Doctor can hear and feel the rocket launch.

History

• *Dating*. Zack says that Jefferson dies '43K2.1'. [This is the same date as he gave for Scooti last episode, so it must be a day rather than a time.]

The expedition turns out to have been sent by the Torchwood Archive. [So something going by the name is still active in this time zone. Considering how the expedition is equipped, it may still be a relatively small organization - and there's no indication that they know to remain on the alert for an enigmatic, time-hopping meddler named "the Doctor". The TARDISode makes it seem as if they have Imperial sanction for their activities.]

The escape vessel is the first ship ever to fly

Why's the Doctor So Freaked Out by a Big Orange Bloke?

continued from Page 379...

remarkably similar X4.11, "Turn Left".) The Doctor seems happy about their existence, and possibly that of the Shopkeeper (a.k.a. the Guy With the Parrot, who keeps giving Sarah and the gang things to do in *The Sarah Jane Adventures*). He even manages to be condescending to the Shadow Proclamation (X4.12, "The Stolen Earth").

Or it might just be lazy scripting. You no doubt feel by now that you've exerted more thought on the matter than the author did. Imagine how we feel.

away from a black hole, and then they are the first people to fall into one: Zack even says that's 'History'.

Religiously, Ida was brought up Neo Classical, congregational [her comments make it sound like the forty-second century's version of Anglicanism]. A central tenet is that the 'Devil' is 'the things that men do'. [So it's Anglican Existentialism. Rev Magister would be amused - see "The Daemons", again. Both Scutari Manista and John Maynard Jefferson have the suffix 'PKD' after their names - maybe that's why the Beast appears through the Scanner, darkly. ("Scutari" was the battle where Florence Nightingale distinguished herself; 'John Maynard' could be a reference to economist John Maynard Keynes, back in the news these days, or evolutionary biologist John Maynard Smith.]

Catchphrase Counter [The Doctor's comment of 'gravity-schmavity', trying to sound all Noo Yawk and cocky, prefigures the 'timey-wimey' quote from X3.10, "Blink". This turn of phrase will be driven into the ground by both this Doctor and the next one, especially in Moffat scripts.]

Deus Ex Machina The rocket doesn't depressurize and kill everyone when Rose shoots out the window at point-blank range. Handy, that. So is the TARDIS landing right next to where the Doctor needs it to escape.

The Analysis

English Lessons ("The Impossible Planet" and "The Satan Pit")

• *Walford*. Fictional location of the BBC's main TV soap *EastEnders*, which is a diligent attempt to rid the world of the stereotype of chirpy cockneys. In particular, it is almost guaranteed that at least three characters will die horribly during the Christmas episodes (see A2, "Dimensions in Time"; X3.7, "42"; and X2.11, "Fear Her").

• *Flat-pack*. In the context that the Doctor's using it, a non-copyright reference to IKEA furniture.

• *Friends of the Ood* is obviously a reference to pioneering environmental pressure-group Friends of the Earth, who have been around long enough to be part of the political process, like Oxfam or Amnesty International.

• *Tesco's*. The original "pile it high, sell it cheap" supermarket, Tesco was a market stall selling groceries on Hackney market in 1919, but is now, globally, bigger than Walmart. Indeed, the expansion just in the last 20 years has looked terrifying to anyone not an employee or shareholder, with small "Tesco Direct" outlets filling any shop left unattended for more than 15 minutes, it seems.

Oh, Isn't That...? ("The Impossible Planet" and "The Satan Pit")

• *Claire Rushbrook* (science officer Ida Scott). Inevitably, perhaps, another regular from *Linda Green* shows up as potential-regular-that-wasn't Ida Scott. Rushbrook's character had come centre-stage in an episode written by Davies. *Linda Green* was script-edited by Matt Jones. (You'd be forgiven for asking why, after Linda's best mate was here, Linda herself, Lisa Tarbuck, hasn't been in *Doctor Who*. See "The Infinite Quest" next volume.)

• *Gabriel Woolf* (Voice of the Beast). Well, obviously, he'd been Sutekh in 1975, but he got that on the back of years of radio and voice-over work. Back when BBC used to source children's television from Europe and the Soviet Bloc by the mile rather than per minute, he would often narrate film series rather than anyone paying for a whole cast of voice-over artists to redub every character.

• *Will Thorp* (possessed archaeologist Toby Zed). Formerly a regular on *Casualty* as paramedic Paul Joyner, AKA Woody, he'd most recently been in the 2005 series of *Strictly Come Dancing* (which spawned an American version, the more sensibly named *Dancing With the Stars*).

• **Danny Webb** (security officer Mr Jefferson) would have had *déjà vu* during the tunnel-crawl, although last time he did it, he was the one who survived *Alien3*. He's also been in *Brookside*.

• **Shaun Parkes** (base commander Zachary Cross Flane). The last time most British viewers would have seen him was as David Tennant's cellmate / amanuensis in *Casanova*.

• **MyAnna Buring** (maintenance trainee Scooti Manista). Well, recently you might have come across her in *Breaking Dawn*, but before then she was the girl dating a dinosaur in *The Wrong Door*, and was in *The Descent* and *The Descent Part 2*, so had previous experience of pits, tanks of water and so on. If you bothered with James Corden's film *Lesbian Vampire Killers*, you might have seen her again (see X5.11, "The Lodger" et seq).

Things That Don't Make Sense ("The Impossible Planet" and "The Satan Pit") (If we go comparing what this story calls a 'black hole' to the real astronomical bodies, we'll be here for months. We could point out that there's one effects shot that makes it look as if the image they see when Ida opens the roof is just painted on the ceiling, and as the word 'impossible' turns up six times in an episode called "The Impossible Planet", they are deliberately ignoring basic science, so we'll concentrate on the internal contradictions and logic-lapses...)

To explain our annoyance at a regular occurrence in films made by people with little or no common sense (eg *Outlands*) and which will be back to bug us in later Tennant stories, let's conduct a little experiment. Wait until dark. Open the curtains and look outside. What can you see? Now switch your lights on. Can you see anything other than your own reflection? No, and this is with a flat pane, so imagine how much worse it is with curved glass. This is why people don't drive with the interior lights of their cars on after dark. So any time you see a space-helmet with little lights inside to illuminate the faces of the actors, ask yourself how they avoid walking into furniture.

In "The Impossible Planet", the Doctor reckons that it would take Rose five hundred years in a spaceship to get to Earth - but the very next week, the survivors are in a rocket looking forward to getting to Earth itself. The rocket has five seats, so whether *everyone* at the base would have been able to evacuate is a moot point (there's talk of a Hold, where the TARDIS lands, and maybe five seats in the cockpit is for the five people needed to fly the ship - but they end up with just three survivors). One aspect of the story that falls apart from this perspective (and is the sort of thing that might have made a more interesting two episodes than what we get) is that proximity to a genuine black hole without spagettification (see the essay with 10.1, "The Three Doctors") makes everything in this story take centuries, from the standpoint of people anywhere else. Time on Earth, or anywhere else, would pass faster from the perspective of people near the Event Horizon. Something almost like this is stated in the first episode, then left forgotten in their attempts to make the Beast more scary than something genuinely unsettling that really exists. So for the team sent to this world, it's effectively a one-way journey because they'll never see anyone they knew again. (This was the basic premise of afternoon-filler *Andromeda*, and if Gene bloody Roddenberry can get the science right, how hard can it be?)

The Beast offends the Doctor's sensibilities by claiming to pre-date time and come from an earlier universe. We've picked up on this for this episode's essay, but one obvious thing to ask here is what exactly the builders of this baroque prison-world hoped to achieve. They have the biggest, meanest black hole in the known universe (outside the supermassive ones that form the hearts of the various galaxies in Earth's sphere of influence, which we later discover - X4.3, "Planet of the Ood" - to be three whole galaxies and counting), and instead of just shoving this monstrosity into the Event Horizon, they pervert the laws of physics to *leave it accessible for anyone with a spaceship and a thirst for knowledge / power to pop in and see*, with a handy reality-defying gravity funnel and a planet in what is described - in a contortion of semantics and reason - as a 'perpetual geostationary orbit'. (The 'geo' bit is definitely wrong, but the nucleus of a black hole rotates on its axis several thousand times a second, so a planet orbiting over one point on that surface would have to be tough to withstand tidal forces - no wonder drilling ten miles took so long.) Assuming Ida actually means "stasis" - when you have a gravity funnel, this is only as impossible as anything else in this story and not drastically more as her description would entail - it's obviously a "come and get me" signal for any life-form big and brave enough to notice it on long-range surveys and risk sending people to probable oblivion. The ancient race who built this thing did so to trap what makes itself out to be the ultimate force of evil in the cosmos... and allow anyone who came looking in so they could un-trap it again. And they took out an ad, with a big physics-busting neon sign saying "here be things beyond comprehension" and rigged it so that the doorway into the Pit vanished as soon as anyone went to look at it. Given that at least one character in this story belongs to a church that thinks of the Devil as a meme rather than a physical entity, the thought must have occurred to the makers of this pointless and ostentatiously impossible trap. And if Rose can kill "Satan" once and for all by chucking him into an Event Horizon, why couldn't they?

And what are we to make of the decision of the Torchwood Archive to send such a half-baked party? This planet screams alien technology beyond anything reasonable, offering unlimited power and abilities to any race that can unlock its ancient mysteries. Yet they send one - count 'em - *one* archaeologist. Not even a cryptologist. You can do that if it's a small expedition to a remote bit of the same planet you're on (see **The Big Picture**), but on a mission to a region where communication with the outside universe is at best haphazard, you either send a large team or you don't go at all. Or, you could send robots and have the archaeologist(s) a long way away watching a feed - if there isn't a reliable feed, then nobody will ever know what *any* party that went there would have found, so as a source of information it's worthless.

And Scooti is said to be a 'trainee maintenance engineer' - on a mission like this, they only had a *trainee* for life-support? When was she supposed to qualify? Who was supposed to train her, given that the only other people we see or hear about are a dead captain, a couple of non-speaking extras who get zapped by the Ood and have no apparent function worth Ida even mentioning them when introducing the speaking-part characters (and yet, they still need someone for laundry)? Zack, the only other person whose original function is unclear, doesn't seem to know which button does what or how things work generally.

The Doctor works out the power-requirement for the raspberry infundibulum (the gravity-funnel has that late 80s rave vibe) as six to the sixth power every six seconds. Leaving aside that this requires parochial Earth time-measurements to be suitably supernatural-sounding, the Doctor works this out *in seconds* when it took the humans present months... and yet Ida thinks he and Rose can best help out in the laundry. The obvious next question is: if the Doctor *hadn't* come along, who would have gone down in the lift with Ida? Toby seems not to be considered for the mission-as-it-happened (and this is before they find out he's contaminated with graffiti), so we're left with the trainee plumber Scooti, the anonymous couple killed by Ood before they can get any dialogue, the two people who die in the TARDISode and aren't mentioned as casualties, or either the Captain (who seems sufficiently indispensible that Zack is at full-stretch filling the great man's shoes) or Zack, who may have been specifically trained for this kind of job. If that's the case, then him sending anyone underqualified would not have been an option, and the only logical course would have been to suspend operations until a new captain arrived. Why stay there if they couldn't fulfil the job they were sent to do?

(Oh, and the possibility of leaving with Toby unwittingly infected seems not to have occurred to the builders of the planet, Matt Jones, Russell T Davies or anyone. This "trap" is only viable if the thing in the pit deliberately shouts "I am too dangerous to be let out!", but the visitors to Krop Tor make a deliberate decision *not* to leave until they know they are carrying something evil-evil-since-the-dawn-of-time-ish. Other scenarios, such as a possession-detector to alert the gravity-funnel to the potential of a jail-break and send the whole planet on a one-way trip into the Schwartzschild radius, would be far more practical and sensible - unless you think that beings playing with space-time like it was Playdoh and capable of imprisoning Satan have no way of telling when someone is under the influence.)

Coming back to the anonymous Oodzapped screamers (why not give them red Starfleet jerseys and have done with it?), the lack of mention of them in a story where everyone's so keen to establish how tight-knit this team is seems peculiar, but starting the obituary column with the Ood and skipping these fallen colleagues (we can *almost* overlook the people from the TARDISode) is downright insulting. And Scooti comes to see Toby to give him a form about 'expenditure'... of what, exactly? If this project is a commercial concern, then the pay-scale is going to be huge or non-existent. Never mind that quite aside from the time-dilation effect and the 500-year journey

X2.9 The Satan Pit

to Earth, what is there on this planet that they didn't bring with them? Any costs will be one-off at the start, because they've no way of getting fresh supplies; we have to assume that oxygen and so on is recycled and power is the only non-renewable resource (right next to a black hole stripping matter to its bare essentials, a big enough power-source for the Time Lords).

The ability of "possessed Toby" to survive exposure to vacuum would just about follow if he had been rendered immune (and his skin does seem to be the medium for possession), but him then spending most of the next episode behaving and breathing normally seems to put the kibosh on that. Then again, it's hard to tell; Rose thinks that Toby is restored once the Ood start revolting, but, by this point, deliberately killing anyone else would be unnecessary to get aboard the ship. Really, why is it even possessing the Ood in the first place, driving Toby mad and all that hassle, instead of being patient for a little longer when it's already spent eons stuck in a rock? The best gloss possible is that the initial Ood translator malfunctions are genuine accidents, the Beast can't actually possess anything until Toby's read enough of the text to be possessed by it, and it starts a massive Ood riot so the team will leave right away instead of heading down to investigate the vases.

So, the oxygen in the not-a-ventilation-shaft-at-all is being moved from chamber to chamber and needs air-locks to keep it in. This is fine when the metal crawlway you're in has two solid walls, a solid ceiling and a solid floor - but when the ceiling *is a mesh*, the whole scene seems a bit silly. Besides, these tunnels were airless because they were designed for machines to use - so why not send a machine down them with the Ood 'virus'? Jefferson's death is shown by a light on the schematic going off, but when Scooti died, her implanted chip continued to register when she was floating in space after being killed several minutes before. The descent of the pod with the Doctor and Ida is shown on the monitor to be at a rate of a mile every three seconds - that's 20 miles a minute, 120 miles an hour, so it's lucky neither of them had a full stomach. But it still takes several minutes to make a ten-mile journey. And 20 miles plus however far he fell is apparently close enough for the Doctor to feel the rocket take-off. Speaking of which, a spaceship with breakable glass windows is just at the limits of plausibility in the forty-second century, but shields that have to wait for Zach to flip a switch before raising and sealing the air in... not so much.

The Beast is evidently, one of those supernatural entities that waits until people with amusingly appropriate names have arrived before launching the fiendish plan (see also 15.3, "Image of the Fendahl"). Why else pick someone as a vessel whose first name is a character from the Apocrypha who wrestles an angel and whose surname is the last letter of the alphabet? And someone called 'Scott' for an (apparently) doomed exploration. The planet, though, is said by Ida to not have a name ('How can it have a name?'), but the very next scene entails her telling the Doctor that it was called 'Krop Tor' in ancient writings of the Veltino.

And it just keeps going - it's not only stupid but against the norms of a slaveholding society to not use technology for constant surveillance just to guard against the type of uprising that we actually see. The worst possible thing you can do when hiring slaves is get telepathic ones. And yet, given that the base members have basic, standard precautions in case of an Ood uprising, and are aware of a pro-Ood sympathy lobby back home, they let these beings prepare and serve their food. Even apart from the risk of deliberate poisoning, the Ood drip slime from their snotty tentacles. And, just at a basic design level, not only is making the Ood handle their translator units - making them really unhelpful as slave labour - very silly (but not as silly as their origin - see X4.3, "Planet of the Ood" and weep), but making an alien race that looks so much like Dr Zoidberg from *Futurama* is idiotic.

Critique ("The Impossible Planet" and "The Satan Pit") A lot of times, there is no correlation between the length and ferocity of the **Things That Don't Make Sense** section and the general impression the story gives. Neither is there any real connection between how the **Production** went and the outcome. This time, however, those sections tell the story. They abandoned anything that didn't look like films they saw as kids in the seventies, putting in "borrowed" visuals because they thought it would look cool rather than for any practical or coherent reason to do with the world they were creating. They made a story about a fiendish alien intelligence building a devious trap that has the logic of a six-year-old making it up as she goes along, "and then the Ood all

The Satan Pit X2.9

woke up and went crazy, and then the Doctor fell down a big big hole and then they all got in a spaceship and then there was this big orange thing going RAAAAAARRR! and then Toby was the Devil and..."

If this had been ineptly made or as forgettable as X6.3, "The Curse of the Black Spot", there wouldn't be a problem, but director James Strong has done a good job of keeping it watchable. He made a point of keeping the survey team together for more rehearsals than was usual, and getting them to think up backstories for their characters, and makes the team feel like a unit who've been together since before the TARDIS arrived. Corny as the Ood are, they are accepted as almost furniture by the team, which makes this world they come from that little bit more real. The set, equally hackneyed, looks a lot bigger than it was. Lumbered with idiotic decisions by the producers to have inaccurate black hole effects and the most embarrassing spaceship in the programme's history (and we include 6.1, "The Dominators", which was an attempt at something new, not a "this'll do" cliché), he's done his best. It's hard to build up suspense when the whole first episode is random outbreaks of spooky-looking gibberish, but he does it. Watched in one 90-minute burst, it's a bit more tolerable, simply because anything a viewer thought would happen as a consequence of what took place in the first half would have been (and, anecdotally, *was*) more interesting and satisfying that what we eventually got after 167 hours of speculation. Seen again with no hope of surprises, one simply accepts and follows the pretty pictures and kooky characters.

What we've got here is more like a pop music video that parodies a genre by inserting Things You Need In This Sort of Movie in time to the lyrics of the song rather than in the order they would come if they *were* in a movie with a plot. It's all arbitrary, with no cause-and-effect. The way the story (if we can even use that word here) is presented, the initiating action is the arrival of the Doctor, who is shown what the viewers need to know despite not having explained how passing strangers could get there. It's a display, for us, rather than a world with real people investigating it. In any properly-thought-out film in that whole "Satan Rises - He's Real, You Know" genre the start of everyone's troubles would have been breaking the seal (or possibly seven of them) and yet loads of bad stuff's already happened by that point. Making whatever-it-is (and we'll accede to the episode title and call it "Satan" for now) perform party-tricks that look like what the Devil does in that ludicrous Schwarzenegger film or having Toby-Possessed do what Linda Blair did better in *The Exorcist* just because it looked kinda cool in those films turns this alleged ultimate force of evil into a poodle at a dog-show. In a story that keeps hitting us over the head with words like "clever" and "intelligence", it has made Satan literally and figuratively dumb. It gets away with it because the good guys are even stupider and do things for even less reason. The crawl through the (soddit) ventilation shafts happens because they want to release a software virus into the air. The builders of this world wanted to stop the *idea* of Satan from getting out, so they arranged for it to be physically present and killable so that someone could come along, release this killer meme, then destroy the Beast and the planet and get out to tell everyone at home how clever they are... and the Doctor says that this race were "brilliant". And then they have the nerve to show us Rose sitting in a *Tintin* spaceship escaping a black hole and saying, "This doesn't make sense..."

There aren't any bad performances here, but the only outstanding one is the voice-over by Gabriel Woolf - one which caused more forlorn hope between episodes than anything else. For anyone who remembered the Tom Baker stories that were also in this script's DNA, the whole enterprise seemed even more tired. However, the episode wasn't made for middle-aged parents or fanboys (except for the ones who wrote and produced it, who seem to be the only people happy with this), it was made for a family audience. Obviously, the Ood were a hit. They're this century's equivalent of the delegate from Alpha Centauri (9.2, "The Curse of Peladon"; 11.4, "The Monster of Peladon" and various other shows), standing in as an emblem of freaky-looking aliens from *Doctor Who*, the first-thought creations of people parodying science fiction films from a previous generation. The difference is that the people making the Pertwee story half-knew they were doing a parody. Even last year (X1.2, "The End of the World"), the new team were playing this sort of thing for laughs. Now, they think the Ood are to be taken seriously. They really want us to believe in servitors who can only use one hand and drip snot into your dinner as they dish it up.

Matthew Jones is paid to edit other people's scripts. Surely, he and Davies and Collinson and Strong and the hundred or so other people

385

X2.9 The Satan Pit

involved in getting this to the screen could have taken a moment to say, "Hang on..." In umpty-zillion rewrites, a lot of the point of this story seems to have vanished. The story acts as if there's a moment it's leading up to where they whole situation becomes clear and viewers think "of course!" What do we get at the point where this is supposed to be happening? The Doctor "realises" that he has faith in Rose. That's it. The fiendish plan for stopping Satan in his tracks is to stop worrying about his sidekick and break some crockery. Once they'd committed to making this story at all, they should either have had one more rewrite or eight fewer.

You'd be better off rewatching 26.3, "The Curse of Fenric". So would Jones have been.

The Facts

Written by Matt Jones. Directed by James Strong. Viewing figures: "The Impossible Planet": (BBC1) 6.32 million, (BBC3 repeats) 0.7 and 0.3 million. (This was the most-watched thing on BBC3 that week, although the AI of 85% put it 1% lower than "The Satan Pit".) "The Satan Pit": (BBC1) 6.08 million, (BBC3 repeats) 0.7 and 0.3 million.

Repeats and overseas promotion Der unmögliche Plane, Der Hollenschlund, La planête du diable 1 & 2.

TARDISodes ("The Impossible Planet"): Captain Walker being hired to investigate K37Jan5, and shown a notebook full of runes from the Geddes Expedition, on the other side of the galaxy. Then his Ood servitor calmly announces, "... and the Beast shall rise from the Pit".

("The Satan Pit"): Some guy we've never seen is given Walker's belongings by an Ood, and the female computer voice repeats, "He shall awake." The book we saw in the last TARDISode then bursts into flames and someone else not in the actual episodes walks in and sees the chap who was holding the book with runes on his face. (This makes four crewmembers not introduced by Ida or noted as killed in action by Zack.)

Production

("The Impossible Planet" and "The Satan Pit"): As with X2.1, "New Earth", Davies' pathological fear of the audience suspecting that *Doctor Who* might be Science Fiction meant that when they decided to do a story on an *Alien*-style base in the far future, they felt obliged to pop in a mythological figure and a shedload of horror-movie tropes to sweeten the pill. The emphasis on the story was on the humans as "pioneers" rather than "colonists", this being, to Davies, a more positive word. Thus the story was about a frontier planet far from anywhere, and people there to explore rather than live. Moreover, he wanted to test the Doctor by showing him out of his depth, unable to definitively say what it was he was confronting. Matt Jones had been script-editor on *Queer as Folk* and executive producer on *Shameless*, so even if he'd never seen a single episode of *Doctor Who*, he would have been brought in. However, he had also written for the *New Adventures* range and contributed think pieces to *DWM* in the 90s, in a column called "Fluid Links". He began a tentative script in January 2005, while Davies waited for confirmation of a second series. In his initial storyline, Jones thought that a tangible monster in the base with the humans as evil as an intangible threat elsewhere would be easier for children and less alert adults to follow and, as he had seen a rough edit of X1.4, "Aliens of London", wrote in the Slitheen clan. The story was that they had fallen on hard times and were indentured servants of the humans, but were also adherents of a faith based on whatever was in the Pit. In one account, there was a sympathetic non-believer called Janine Slitheen.

- Since originally that this story was to be the fourth block to be made, and thus the money would be tight, the cast was kept small. The Slitheen recycling seemed like a good idea and the true nature of the force of ultimate evil was agreed to be something fairly cheap. Ideas kicked around included a big glowing eye at the base of the Pit (exactly like at the end of 25.4, "The Greatest Show in the Galaxy"), a creepy little girl (exactly like 25.1, "Remembrance of the Daleks", as well as some bits of "Greatest Show" and the Test Card Girl from *Life on Mars*), and a sinister old man (exactly like the end of Series One of *Torchwood*). The creepy girl idea hung around until it became obvious that X2.11, "Fear Her" was going to be pulled forward from Series Three.

• Care was taken in the scripts to make the Doctor's relationship with Rose the key to defeating the Beast and to avoid Rose actively shooting at Toby whilst still killing him by indirect means. The beginning of the second episode got a line about there being one bolt in the gun left. Meanwhile, the Slitheen subplot looked like taking on a life of its own, and the costumes were going to need to be upgraded to cope with what they would be doing. Even though the computer-generated Slitheen in "Attack of the Graske" seemed to have worked, the budget for this two-part story would not stretch that far. It was calculated that the cost of refurbishing the Slitheen costumes was only marginally less than making half a dozen new alien heads, if it was just one animatronic one and a few masks. After getting ribbed about the tongue-twister names he gave things, Davies called his new creatures "Ood", and opted to give them hand-held voice-boxes as a sly nod towards his point of reference, the Sensorites (1.7, "The Sensorites"), telling anyone who'd listen that they came from "Ood-Sphere, near Sense-Sphere".

• Davies had been following James Strong's progress since they were both at Granada and decided that by now he was up to doing a *Who*. By this time, the production had been moved about with an additional episode to come later, shot alongside this two-parter, but no costly Stephen Fry episode to worry about. "The Satan Pit", as the two-parter was collectively known, was to be Block Five - right at the end of the production year. There would be no leeway, as not only did the BBC Wales employees all come to the ends of their contracts the day after the projected end of the shoot, but the whole production was moving to custom-build studios, and so there would be no TARDIS set and nothing else would be available. The result of the trade-off was that with "Love & Monsters" (X2.10) and "Fear Her" both being relatively quick, cheap and easy, they could afford a proper CG effect of the Beast. The Mill put their best men on it. And their other staff. And the girl who delivered pizzas, by the sound of it. The eventual winner was a rough sketch by one of their dispatch riders. The production team had suggested that Simon Bisley's designs from *Slaine*, the strip in *2000 AD* (see Volume 6) should be the template[76], but also Tim Curry in Ridley Scott's *Legend* (on the grounds, presumably, that so much else in this story was from Scott films and he

could only sue the once). The "Tough" look for the episode was agreed on, with an industrial-style base (a mine, oil-rig or factory) and a claustrophobic look like the film / mini-series *Das Boot*. The base would be a computer image rather than a model (although the Model Unit did get a look-in right at the end of production).

After discussions about shooting in various factories, it became obvious that the bulk of the base would be achieved in the studios, albeit with one or two easily redressable, reusable sets. But, with gritted teeth, Phil Collinson agreed that the planet's surface and the "Valley of the Kings" had to be a quarry shoot. Quite apart from being the worst *Doctor Who* cliché, it was going to be at night, in Wales, in February. They had looked at one in Wenvoe (on the borders of Cardiff) for an earlier story, but it was in use during the day; for a night-shoot, it was possible to utilise the location so long as they left at dawn. They had scripts ready for any meteorological occasion, explaining rain on an airless world, snow, fog or whatever and commenting on these being toxic.

• The shoot began on 28th February 2006, the first of three nights in the quarry with just Tennant and Claire Rushbrook (Ida Scott). In one take it did indeed snow, but not enough settled for the continuity with other shots to allow it (and the special dialogue) to be used. At one point, it looked as if the vehicles would be stuck there. On another night, it rained heavily and it was feared that the location would flood. The crew had to wear hard-hats. As only these two characters would need spacesuits, and one was the Doctor (whose measurements Louise Page, the costume designer, already had), the suits were available on time despite being almost the last thing to be commissioned. The helmets eventually had small earpieces installed so that they could hear the director and each other, after a lot of problems and gesticulation. The night of 2nd March was when most of the abseiling scenes were shot, although the Doctor's drop into darkness was done the following day at the HTV studio before returning to the quarry for the last night. They noticed that the Land Rover parked on site had a registration number ending "OOD".

Over in Q2, they had built the set for the base, including the corridor that would be re-used for different bits of the same station (and eventually, *Totally Doctor Who*). Monday the 6th was the first day for this, and Piper joined the production along with the Ood (mostly the same old monster-

X2.9 The Satan Pit

men, Paul Kasey, Ruari Mears et al, and of course Ailsa Berk to coach them). Unusually, Strong had given the guest cast a week's extra rehearsal to get used to each other and devise their characters' histories. Danny Webb, as Mr Jefferson, had been auditioning for something else when Strong met him, and asked if he could do a *Doctor Who*. In contrast to his rather austere character, Webb brought his little dog, Mabel, onto the set most days. On the 8th with Tennant away, the crawl through the access tunnels began, and the make-up and lenses for Will Thorp were used for the first time (after a lot of testing earlier). This carried on for another day and on the 10th, Tennant returned to Clearwell Caves (see X2.0, "The Christmas Invasion") for his confrontation with a big green sheet. By now, the Beast designs were being finalised and he had some idea what it was the Doctor was seeing. It was planned to remove the fake cave-paintings, but the owner of the caves asked for them to be retained.

Next day, a Saturday, allowed more shooting at Wenvoe, for Scooti in a spacesuit and Toby rather alarmingly not. (They also got some pick-up shots of Ida in the same spacesuit, ending at 3.55am as dawn broke and the mine crew arrived.) Enfys Television was where Toby's room and the spaceship were built. The spaceship set was on hydraulic jacks, to give access for a variety of shots and to make it feel and look as if the occupants were accelerating. It was considered to be a little too antiseptic-looking, and so the walls were given a sort of caramel-coloured overlay in post-production. Once again, Thorp needed to spend a great deal of time in make-up. Wednesday the 15th was back at Q2 for lunch, with baked beans and mashed potato dyed to look futuristic (and a visit from a competition winner). More of the same Thursday, and on Friday, it was back at Enfys for more work in utter blackness and spacesuits and a few capsule interior close-ups of Piper. Saturday was back to Q2 for the stars to record the Series Two trailer, with the TARDIS set, an ice-world location (done in the studio rather than Iceland, as the directors had hoped), a SteadiCam and trippy editing. The next Monday saw a trip to a hastily rethought location. The Bore Room and Ood Pen were to have been shot at a chemical plant that was found to have asbestos (see X2.3, "School Reunion" and 25.4, "The Greatest Show in the Galaxy"), but they found an alternative in Pontypool. It was, apparently, even colder than the quarry. The Ood were shot in such a way that they could multiply the numbers, although the time this took annoyed Collinson. On the second day, Tennant left early to shoot some of his scenes for "Love & Monsters". On Wednesday, they made the capsule descend by putting it on a forklift truck. That bit of the shoot ended on the Saturday, but Tennant wasn't needed for the last two days.

By this time, the Q2 sets had been redressed as the Command Centre, and the next week began with Shaun Parkes (Zachary Cross Flane) and James Strong recording Zack's responses to radio messages from everyone else. Strong got quite into doing all the characters. He had hitherto read the Ood parts and had a go at the Beast until the cast stopped taking it seriously. Tennant and Piper came back from "Love & Monsters" on the Wednesday, as the "earthquake" scenes came up (Piper accidentally wrenched a bit of the set loose). If you've lost count, this is 29th March, the day of the press-launch of "New Earth" and perilously close to the end of the production block. They had three crews at work the next day, covering the walkway and Command Centre, Toby's Room and the Seal at the Cavern. The following day, Piper's last, covered some Bore Room material, the Habitation #3 area and, the very last shot of Rose, the ending TARDIS scene and Ida's rescue.

And so we bid a fond farewell to Q2, its pigeons, canaries, ferrets and rats, with the wrap party that night (from which Tennant sneaked away to record the end scene of "Doomsday" with Catherine Tate, but don't tell anyone), and, early next morning (back in Pinewood Studios near London), a hung-over MyAnna Buring and Will Thorp jumping fully-clothed into a pool to be filmed underwater for their space-floating scenes.

- As it turned out, the Model Unit was needed after all, for various dust, smoke, fire and shadow components of effects shots, so they spent a couple of days at Ealing Studios. As can be imagined, a lot of post-production and effects work needed to be added after the shoot (which actually ended a couple of weeks later, with an insert shot of Toby's seat-buckle being undone, shot at Enfys on 11th April).

- Decisions finalised after the shoot included the look of the spaceship exterior (sort of based on George Pal's *Destination Moon* by way of Herge's *Tintin*), casting the voice of the Beast (a slam-dunk, Gabriel Woolf) and the Ood (Nicholas

Briggs was unavailable, so Silas Carson got the nod), whether to include the Beast in the "Next Time" clip (Davies opted not to) and a few trims for timing. Notable cuts include the Doctor trying to sweet-talk the Ood into not reporting strangers by saying, "We're just friends you haven't met yet", the Ood repeating this to Jefferson, and a scene where the Doctor tricks Ida into letting him go first down the pit. (He challenges her to scissors, paper, stone after earlier using worlds like "rock" and "stone" in conversation, then tells her how he did it because he likes showing off.) The map of the base was altered after the shoot, because the set had been changed since the BBC Wales Graphics team had made it. Other cuts in the dialogue before shooting removed comments about Curt and Chenna, the hapless victims in the second TARDISode.

As mentioned, The Mill initially tried to get a scientifically accurate black hole into the episode before being told to go away and do it like Disney. The effects were completed at the end of May, and the pre-shot Doctor scenes in the Pit had to be edited to the digitally created Beast. The final sound-edit and music dub was completed very close to transmission. The door voice was Ceres Doyle, who may well tie with Murray Gold as most-credited person since Dick Mills, having been an editor of some kind on every episode from X1.1, "Rose" to X7.14, "The Name of the Doctor". (We would need to see all the missing episodes to assess whether Ron Grainer or Brian Hodgson were credited more often.)

X2.10: "Love & Monsters"

(17th June, 2006)

Which One is This? That Peter Kay Thing.

Firsts and Lasts The production team calls them "double-banked" episodes, the online fans call them "Doctor-lite", but for the first time since 6.5, "The Seeds of Death", we have scripted and planned absences for the regular cast. Even though the episodes are now recorded much further in advance than in the monochrome days, the punishing production schedule requires at least one a year where one or both regulars will only be needed for a day. (See also X3.10, "Blink"; X4.10, "Midnight"; X4.11, "Turn Left"; X5.11, "The Lodger"; X6.10, "The Girl Who Waited"; X6.12, "Closing Time" - and also all of Volumes 1 and 2.)

This is, more significantly, the first time ever that a monster designed for a *Blue Peter* competition was actually used in the broadcast episodes (see 5.2, "The Abominable Snowmen" for a near-miss). David Tennant came into the studio, live, and picked the winner with the arrangement that Davies was to write whatever he and the panel selected into an episode. (Sadly, the lucky winner was slightly nonplussed by the result.) They could do this because this episode was written right at the end of the recording block, making it almost the last piece of the season to be made (the very last being the tag scene at the end of X2.13, "Doomsday", because they were keeping that secret). The big "reveal" of the Abzorbaloff comes 31 minutes into the episode, and because all eyes are on *that*, few people notice until it's pointed out that the *Daily Telegraph* that Victor Kennedy is reading has an intriguing headline - it's the first of many references to someone called "Mr Saxon". (Actually, this is the only episode to have references to that, Bad Wolf, Torchwood and planet Clom - one of the missing worlds in Series Four - all at once. Just have someone knocking four times, and we'd have the set.)

If you're *really* sharp-eyed, you will also see a reference to something only available on one of the unofficial websites... This is the only mention in the series of near-forgotten Ragga nuisances Chaka Demus and Pliers, whose one hit, "Tease Me", was 12 years in the past when this was shown. (The line everyone *thinks* is about them in 19.7, "Time-Flight" is actually Anthony Ainley with false teeth trying to say "cacodaemons".)

This is the first and, to date, only story to have an ampersand in the title instead of "and".

Watch Out For...

• Such was the kudos attached to making a major ratings-winner from a formerly derided show, Russell T Davies was allowed to do almost anything he felt like. Thus the BBC, at the expense of the TV License-Fee payers, donated three-quarters of an hour to a thinly-disguised love-letter to fan groups and a full-blown slagging-off of a certain type of fan who exploits such a network of people with shared values and experiences, and derides anything other than the ostensible focus of their meeting as irrelevant mush. Did Davies have anyone in particular in mind? Well, if you've not read Volumes 4, 5 and 6, be patient until we get to **The Big Picture**. However, if we take the story's moral at face-value, and accept that fandom was fun and friendship until people started making out that obsessing over the details of *Doctor Who* was all there was to it, then it could be argued that the man who brought the series back and closed off so much of what we'd been doing as "Off Topic" was the real villain - the Abzorbaloff was Davies himself. (See this story's essay for more.)

- As we have just said, this was the final episode to be written for Series Two and, as such, afforded Davies the opportunity to remedy any perceived lacks in the series so far. Therefore, this one is the episode where Jackie Tyler comes to the fore.

- The pieces to camera by Marc Warren, as Elton, are the core of the story but were all executed in the first two days of a 12-day shoot. Most of this was taken up with costume-changes, as Elton wears a total of 35 different outfits in what was supposed to be the cheap, quick episode. Other not-as-inexpensive-as-planned details include a remount of the shop-dummy massacre from X1.1, "Rose" (the original took three days to film, this version took three hours), the digital remount of the animatronic faces inside the Abzorbaloff skin and the last-minute addition of the carnivorous Hoix that runs around with the Doctor and Rose. This, we're told, was made from odds and ends Neill Gorton had lying around at Millennium Effects. Does it show?

- After 30 years of *Star Trek* trying to kid us that aliens have American accents, we follow a year of a Salford-accented Time Lord with a story where only the regular cast don't sound like they come from north of the Watford Gap. Most noticeable is Victor Kennedy, who sounds like he's trying to avoid sounding provincial. When he lets the mask slip, it turns out that Clom is one of those planets that has a North, specifically a Bolton.

- And, while the spooky music for Victor Kennedy sounds suspiciously like the theme from *The X-Files*, the main musical thread in this story is big-haired Brummies ELO and a selection of their 70s hits. This is fine, if you like ELO. Davies was amazed to discover, once he'd got the LINDA band murdering "Don't Bring Me Down", that the word in the chorus is *Gruß*, pronounced "Groos", and not "Bruce" as everyone thinks.

- Apart from the prudish outrage about Elton and Ursula's "bit of a love-life" (one of those things that's only rude if you already know what they mean, and nothing like as risque as the things Tom Baker used to smuggle into scripts), pay close attention to the shot of her talking to him from within her slab. This is the one part of this episode that is not either narrated (possibly erroneously) by Elton as a flashback or relayed to us via his video diary: it's happening in real-time and brought to us via whatever mechanism gives us any other episode of *Doctor Who*. As such, it's our only guarantee that any of what we've seen really happened.

The Continuity

The Doctor He needs to ask, rather than already knowing, the name of the twin planet of Raxacoricofallapatorius. [Once again, compare this with his "searchable database" ability concerning the latter in X1.5, "World War Three".]

- *Background.* At some point in his current life, he has dealt not only with the Elemental Shade that killed Mrs Pope [we'll assume that was her name], but the grieving son who stumbled upon the assault.

- *Inventory: Sonic Screwdriver.* The sonic screwdriver is identified at last (by Elton) as the Doctor's 'magic wand'. It can key into the Abzorbaloff's absorbtion matrix and manages to filter Ursula out from the rest of the goo, although she still needs to be preserved as a paving slab.

The Supporting Cast

- *Rose* has been experimenting with hairstyles, apparently. She's very annoyed with Elton for upsetting her mum, but sympathetic when he's mourning Ursula.

- *Jackie* lives at 48 Bucknall Place. She gets phone calls from Rose every so often, and misses having Mickey around to do odd jobs. She pops on a CD of Il Divo [the bored housewives' favourite of the era] when planning an assignation. She does the pub quiz at the Spinning Wheel. Her neighbour, Mrs Croot, knows where to find her. [Jackie was sort-of dating a 'Billy Croot' in X1.4, "Aliens of London", although given RTD's habit of recycling names, this could mean anything or nothing.]

- *LINDA.* A loose collective of Doctor-spotters, meeting every Tuesday under the library in Macateer Street. The group was centred around Colin Skinner, struggling author, and Ursula Blake, who ran a blog on the topic. Other members include Bliss and Brigit, no surnames given,

Is *Doctor Who* Fandom Off-Topic?

The idea of "fandom" has entirely different connotations depending which side of the Atlantic you're on and how old you are, which has led to a lot of confusion about how it works in *Doctor Who*.

Look at the people who came through our original version of fandom to make the new series. Consider Mark Gatiss, Steven Moffat or Gareth Roberts - *Doctor Who* runs through them like the lettering in seaside rock, but they would chew off their own legs rather than behave like the usual attendees at ComiCon. Russell T Davies was always pleased when it turned out that one of the staff with whom he was working knew what a Drashig was, but could be offensively vituperative about online fans. We've been over some of the groundwork in Volume 6 (**What's All This Stuff About Anoraks?** and **The Semiotic Thickness of What?**), but to recap: the idea on the Internet is that *Doctor Who* fans are science fiction fans keen on self-proclaimed "cult" shows, but for most of the history of the show, that wasn't how it worked.

As we saw in **Where Does All of This Come From?** under 1.1, "An Unearthly Child", the committee set up in 1962 to look into the possible use of Science Fiction as a means to make a mainstream drama for the whole family had resulted in *Out of the Unknown*, a set of adapted stories for the new up-market, experimental BBC2 and a Saturday evening show to go on between *Juke Box Jury* and *The Telegoons*[79] and aimed at the widest audience possible. *Doctor Who* was always child-friendly. As it turned out, it was especially popular with children, and marketable worldwide as such. And as it became, in the phrase quoted on the back of early Target novelisations, "The Children's Own Programme That Adults Adore", the occasional "lapses" where it was a mainstream drama with aliens and guns earned it the reputation as "the thing that scares kids" (see **When Was *Doctor Who* Scary?** under 15.1, "Horror of Fang Rock"). Simply for that, it got a bit of cachet from enthusiasts of British-made horror movies. It was in a magazine about these that the advertisement that launched the Doctor Who Appreciation Society was first run. However, this kind of fannishness was unlike old-school SF clans of London and Brighton, who ran monthly meetings in pubs (origin of the One Tun meetings, later transferred to the Fitzroy Tavern and latterly dispersed across five pubs). It became obvious very quickly that fans of *Star Trek* didn't get the idea. They left.

This was also the era of Punk, and that movement's DIY aesthetic informed how *Who* fans made fanzines; sarcastic, cheap and referring to all the other things fans had in common. Perhaps most important, the *Doctor Who* fans had a programme still being made - one that everyone in the country watched and one where the producers weren't remote deities to be idolised, but real people they could meet at a pub and tell to their faces what was going wrong. Graham Williams and Douglas Adams, producer and script-editor of Season Seventeen, might have thought they were in for a night of worship and free drinks, but they came away wondering why they were bothering. Those meetings at the One Tun were piggy-backed on proper-written-down-grown-up-SF meetings that had been going since the 1940s (Arthur C Clarke's *Tales from the White Hart* is based on the early days), simply because here was a bit of overlap between the memberships of the two groups at one stage. After all, the people who had been at school when *Doctor Who* began were now pushing 30; not every *Doctor Who* viewer became an SF reader, but all SF readers in Britain watched *Doctor Who*. So did all taxi drivers, History teachers, factory workers, left-handed people... the idea that it would ever be a minority-interest "cult" would have been risible in 1975.

However, by the time things moved on, the template was set: monthly meetings, and exchange of views via idiosyncratic fanzines. Once a large-scale, paid-up fandom emerged in the crucial years between 1978 and 1983, this happened on a larger scale but along precisely those lines (see **Did *DWM* Change Everything?** under 18.2, "Meglos" and **What Happened at Longleat?** under 20.6, "The King's Demons"). Don't imagine it was just the one pub. The pattern repeated in all major cities and in the DWAS Local Groups across the nation. *Doctor Who Monthly*, the Target books and (later) the videos and DVDs weren't confined to lonely specialist shops, they were in every high street. UK fandom achieved critical mass, in every sense. The establishment of, well, an establishment - a party-line combining fact and opinion almost indiscriminately - meant that everyone joining the party had ready-made opinions on

continued on Page 393...

X2.10 Love & Monsters

and Elton Pope, who devised the acronym London Investigation N Detective Agency (something he'd had in mind for a book he wanted to write). Their ostensible purpose was to collate and log sightings of the Doctor and, while this remained the core of their meetings, it soon ceased to be the whole of their connections to one another. Unlike Clive Finch ["Rose"], they have deduced that the Doctor has had more than one face and that the blue box is more of a constant in his manifestations throughout history and mythology.

[A question that has bothered some observers is: how much does the Doctor know about this? In X3.13a, "Time Crash", we learn that the fifth Doctor knew about LINDA. The current Doctor, who had recently run into Elton twice (once in the 1970s, then again in Rotherhite just before the Jackie-stalking), would presumably have known from Jackie's description (and the unlikely name 'Elton') who this was, and eventually tracked him down to near Macateer Street on a Tuesday. It's not *such* a feat for someone of the Doctor's resources, although the pinpoint accuracy of the TARDIS's arrival is possibly the Ship adding a grace-note, or the Doctor homing in on an alien presence (the Abzorbaloff).]

• *Torchwood* have vast files on the Doctor, but Rose is apparently harder for them to find out about because of something called 'the Bad Wolf Virus' [the result of her subconsciously covering her tracks while she was briefly "Bad Wolf Rose" in X1.13, "The Parting of the Ways"?] corrupting the data.

The Non-Humans

• *The Abzorbaloff* is not its real name, but one that Elton and the Doctor independently devise for it, to the creature's apparent delight. It stands about six feet tall but is rather portly, with a pot-belly. It has oily skin the colour of pea-soup, with nodules and flaps, on which the faces of his victims manifest themselves, apparently at random locations. Although mainly humanoid it has three-clawed hands - as Rose points out, it looks 'a bit sliveen'. [See, as if you needed telling, "Aliens of London" et seq.] Clom, its home planet, is indeed the twin of Raxacoricofallapatorius [and therefore, as far as these things have any logic, produces similar species - see X4.3, "Planet of the Ood" and 1.7, "The Sensorites"]. The entity calling itself the Abzorbaloff is hairless except for a mane running across the top of its head, down the nape and into its shoulders, like a bad 80s hairdo. It can spring with surprising speed, and chases Elton vigorously despite its bulk and jockstrap.

The ability to consume humans and their knowledge is governed by the silver-topped cane it carries, which has a clasped fist that unclenches when releasing the energy to soak up a victim. The process of absorption is done by direct touch. When disguised as the human tycoon Victor Kennedy, it refuses to allow anyone to touch him, claiming as an excuse 'exseema'. [We never see how he converts between 'Kennedy' and 'Abzorbaloff', but the inference is that this is more of a "glamour" or perception-filter than a human skin hollowed out as per the Slitheen. Whilst 'Kennedy' affects a less easily localised manner of speech, the Abzorbaloff sounds as if he is from Lancashire, specifically Bolton.]

• *The Hoix*. It's big, it eats raw meat, there's something it fears that comes in liquid form and sloshes around in steamy buckets, it has big teeth, a crested head, wears some kind of body-armour with tubes, it's bipedal and hairless and salmon-pink and it's easily confused. That's about it. [We don't even get to hear it identified as a "Hoix" on screen, nor find out if that's a name, a species or a title. Then, in X5.12, "The Pandorica Opens", it turns up as one of the time-travelling superpowers in the Flashmob of Doom, so there must be a bit more to it/them than that.]

• *Elemental Shades*. They are living shadows and can escape from the Howling Halls. Apparently. [On no account to be confused with the Vashta Narada - X4.8, "Silence in the Library" - which are living things that pretend to be shadows.]

Planet Notes

• *Clom*. Twin planet of Raxacoricofallapatorius, with whom the natives seem to have a rivalry. [See X4.12, "The Stolen Earth" for a tiny bit more background than this scant detail.]

History

• *Dating*. Elton meets Ursula a couple of months after "The Christmas Invasion" (X2.0); Kennedy attaches himself to LINDA 'that day in March' [see **Things That Don't Make Sense** for more on the improbable number of Tuesdays they have in what we assume is 2007]. We are obviously some time away from the first appearance of 'ghosts' [X2.12, "Army of Ghosts"], which were

Is *Doctor Who* Fandom Off-Topic?

continued from Page 391...

stories they had little chance of ever actually seeing, or seeing again as adults. However, the influx of new hardcore fans in 1983 meant that the Local Group network soon had access to the older episodes and made up their own minds, as groups or individuals, and wrote their own narrative. Although co-ordinated centrally, the LGs all developed their own tendencies and habits. They tended to retain members with a "halo" of similar (possibly unrelated) enthusiasms. UK *Doctor Who* fandom was, as we've mentioned, a safe place for exploring sexuality. More often than not, though, it was an opportunity to meet people with two or three similar interests to yours and a lot of others you would never have voluntarily considered. Unlike the self-selecting membership of online groups, you had a good chance of meeting and befriending someone with whom you actually had very little else in common.

Once you have a regular meeting with the same people, and have bonded over something in your childhood(s), you can discuss anything. Outside the London-based foundation of DWAS, the various Local Groups developed their own collective identities in each other's front-rooms, with sandwiches and, later, grotty fourth-generation VHS copies of episodes not seen since transmission (another difference between us and the Trekkies, who had a series in syndicated re-run on BBC1 for nearly 20 years). Then, copies of other old television series from friends-of-friends-of-friends who worked in regional ITV stations or had somehow got jobs at the BBC. Not just so-called "cult" shows, but old kid's programmes, ancient drama shows and obscure factual series that would never be rerun in a million years. We covered what happened next in volumes 5 and 6, but you can see from the above why trying to fit UK *Doctor Who* fandom into a *Trek*-shaped hole wasn't going to work.

You can also see why when the series itself fell from grace in the 1980s, it almost didn't matter to a lot of the fans. The cancellation didn't kill *Doctor Who* fandom (obviously), but it did crystallise some of these tendencies. Even so, though, 90s fandom represented something pretty much unique in the history of programming; a group with a well-established enough history that the way the fans related to each other could be at a remove from the very reason they had all got together in the first place. The result was that the fanzine culture that had been developing through the 80s was now flourishing - not least because fandom was now something you did in secret. It was the Trekkies again. The press got the idea that all *Doctor Who* fans wear Doctor costumes to conventions, and so anything that didn't fit that narrative was ignored. Anoraknophobia set in. This was partly self-protection, but mainly because by this stage there was very little point in rehashing old arguments about *Doctor Who* when there was so much else to exchange. Anything worth saying about *Doctor Who* was worth saying properly in a fanzine article rather than wasting time that could be spent reminiscing about Hammer Films, *Pogle's Wood* or the "Sunny Smiles" Catalogue. (No, really, there's no point asking if you don't already know.) Younger participants generally came to *Doctor Who* via nostalgia, being fans of, say, 60s music or 70s TV drama who had found that the *Who* fans (nobody ever called us "Whovians" and lived to tell the tale) had all the best stuff and were more fun to be with than the hardcore *afficionadoes* of such things. And from that it was a small step to being just friends who meet regularly. For someone who denied ever having been inside that world, Davies captured it exactly in X2.10, "Love & Monsters".

Soon anyone new to fandom in the 80s was immediately obvious and, to some extent, to be avoided until proof of non-dorkishness was offered. Essentially, it was a complete stranger dressing like an idiot, sitting next to you in public, uninvited, and saying "can I be your friend?" Anyone who approached in plain-clothes but then started asking "who's your favourite Doctor?" was similarly cold-shouldered. That wasn't as important as the big question: "What *else* interests you?" Because the series had always been so promiscuous in its sources, influences, subject-matter and relations to other television, it was as much a starting-point for other things as an end in itself. Assuming you could get to know someone from a check-list of "favourites" was insulting as much as it was very, very annoying. (Oddly, though, a repeat visit by someone who'd made this mistake once allowed everyone to start again from scratch and

continued on Page 395...

X2.10 Love & Monsters

two months before the Battle of Canary Wharf. Nevertheless, Mr Saxon is already prominent enough not to need the press to explain who he is, or why him being 64% ahead in a poll is significant. Other clues on that newspaper, which the Abzorbaloff reads, make a summer date likely [see **How Long is Harriet in Number 10?** under "The Christmas Invasion"].

Deus Ex Machina Well, there's the Doctor's last-minute ability to resurrect Ursula as a paving slab. The new version of Ursula has her personality and memories, her voice and her face... and her glasses. [Another possible plot-contrivance is the TARDIS turning up in the patch of wasteground where the Abzorbaloff was menacing Elton, but we will deal with this shortly.]

The Analysis

The Big Picture In Volume 4, we had an essay about the impact and significance of the long-running BBC children's series *Blue Peter* (**Cultural Primer #2: Why *Blue Peter*?**). As you will have seen in "Aliens of London" (X1.4), this series was used as a "realistic" detail in the nation's reaction to aliens crashing into the Thames, but was the main conduit by which *Doctor Who* was relaunched to its target audience of children. The series editor, Richard Marson, had been editor of Marvel's *Doctor Who Monthly* in the 1980s and had sought to keep the memory of the Doctor green during the wilderness years of the 90s, promoting the BBC2 repeats. Before the announcement of the Doctor's return, his choice of celebrity guests on *Blue Peter* had been cannily aimed at who this audience would like, so both Billie Piper and Catherine Tate had been on long before being cast as companions. (Contrary to what older viewers "remember", Billie, in her capacity as pop star, had been on far more often than either Musical Youth or Precious McKenzie, the legendarily "always on" guests.)

Inevitably, therefore, Russell T Davies kept the *Blue Peter* production team in the loop when promoting his series. The spin-off *Doctor Who Confidential* was co-hosted by a former *Blue Peter* presenter, Liz Barker, and a future one, Barney Harwood (who can be seen as an extra in the market scene where Elton is asking Mrs Croop where Rose lives, and less obviously when the Slitheen spaceship powers over London). A then-current presenter, Gethin Jones, is tall and Welsh and thus a shoo-in for both a stint as a Cyberman and a behind-the-scenes feature for his series. A Design-a-Monster competition was exactly the sort of classic *Blue Peter* crossover with *Doctor Who* that had always worked but, whereas the prize in 1967 was meeting Patrick Troughton (a rare privilege), seeing the Visual Effects Department make it for *Blue Peter* alone and hearing Brian Hodgson make radiophonic noises for it, this time it was going to be the focus of a whole story.

The timing was important. David Tennant had been cast as the Doctor a few months earlier, but between his fleeting appearance at the end of "The Parting of the Ways" (X1.13) and this point, he had been out of the public eye making the programme. Then the location filming for "The Christmas Invasion" had provided an opportunity for a photo-shoot for the new costume and a week's discussion in the fashion-pages, the first cheerful story of July 2005 after the bombings and concerns over the Olympics (see next story). So on 19th July, *Blue Peter* launched the contest with a Dalek coming into the studio, and four weeks later Tennant selected an outright winner from the three selected by Davies, Marson and Jones. For the record, the other two were a football monster (Tennant teased the soccer-averse Davies that he might pick this) and something called a Xerconian (which, curiously, resembles the head of the Dragon from 24.4, "Dragonfire" on top of a suit like the Silence in Series Six). The chosen beast, the Abzorbaloff, was invented by a nine-year-old, William Grantham. This allowed the *Blue Peter* cameras to go behind-the-scenes and follow Grantham seeing the making of the episode, where he expressed slight chagrin since, in his drawing, the alien had been the size of a double-decker bus. Other *Blue Peter* competitions followed: the small Glaswegian boy who meets Martha in "Utopia" (X3.11) and is later revealed to be the Toclafane she helps dissect (X3.13, "The Last of the Time Lords"), won an acting competition they ran. The TARDIS console built by the Doctor and Idris in "The Doctor's Wife" (X6.4) was another competition entry.

Davies was able to incorporate this winning entry into this story because, as they used to say on *Blue Peter*, he could hold up the storyline for what was originally called "I Love the Doctor" and say "here's one I prepared earlier". This solved

Is *Doctor Who* Fandom Off-Topic?

continued from Page 393...

often worked out fine.) It got like *Fight Club*. The first rule of *Doctor Who* fandom is... you don't talk about *Doctor Who*.

Now, slam that set of unwritten rules and gag-reactions against the standard netiquette of American-style, *Trek*-inflected online fandom, and you know there's going to be trouble.

The self-perceived point of much of American cult fandom, especially on the Internet, is to talk about the Thing You're There For. Members of a group are likely to be fervent about the Thing and perhaps mildly interested in a few things other members are mildly interested in. (The obvious example is the well-hashed story of Bjo Trimble and her friends going on a letter-writing campaign to save the original iteration of *Star Trek* for another season - in retrospect the results weren't much, but that's someone else's story.) At some level, this is all logistics; if there wasn't such a thing as organizing by content, fishing through the sea of people with computer access would be absurd. Of course, "off-topic" depends on your choice of topic. If you've created a niche that allows crossovers, or joined one where the borders have become porous through accepted practice, there's leeway.

In some ways, this is perfectly natural. Internet fandom emerged with the mass-migration online after 1993, when the main action as regards *Doctor Who* as an ongoing story was the *New Adventures*. Virgin Books' open-door policy made some users into commissioned novel-writers. This could have made for democratic fan grouping, since everyone is theoretically coming to it on a level playing field. In practice, the Usenet heroes were the same people who were making names for themselves in offline circles; the likes of Paul Cornell and Jonathan Blum held a currency in terms of fan interest. What's more to the point is that the very ability to get online was still rather more costly and complicated than getting together with fans in real life - certainly in Britain. This isn't the intuitive storyline in the circles of serious computer geeks, of course; to them, the 1993 Eternal September was when AOL suddenly gave access to the masses and things were never the same after that. America's experience is almost the exact inverse of Britain's, while Australia's is a combination of the more awkward features of both.

The best example of the overlap between this new Internet-based fandom and the *New Adventures* in the US might be the *Doctor Who Novel Rankings*, run for most of its existence by Shannon Patrick Sullivan. Actual participation was quite low, with perhaps 200 or 300 people responding in its heyday. This was a project that defined its purpose solely as a function of the community-defined objective and was inherently only for those people who were self-selected as geeks already (it was originally a set of polls on rec.arts.doctorwho, and some of the participants are still studiously adding to the *Doctor Who* Ratings Guide, which has archived hundreds of *Doctor Who* reviews from the Usenet group, but nothing else from that community). Its demise in 2006, as the BBC killed its ongoing *Eighth Doctor Adventures* and *Past Doctor Adventures* series, and made it clear that the novels were now for the new childhood audience, was the final kibosh on this version of fandom, but this all laid the foundation for the influx of new Internet fans in the RTD era. About a month before the announcement of the return of *Doctor Who*, a fiction-based group called "Teaspoon and An Open Mind" began (the name comes from 17.3, "The Creature from the Pit" - NB this group is not connected with the opportunistic popular-science book of the same name we ridiculed in Volume 3b). Depending on your interpretation, this is either the *Doctor Who* version of the Gossamer Project[80], one of the basic foundations of your fandom experience, or where the Trekkie fanfic started "invading our culture". An entire subculture now exists around *Doctor Who* fanfiction (and yes, *Doctor Who* slash, redundant as that is[81]).

From a number of disparate sources, we can put together a snapshot of current Internet fandom. Despite that being the BBC's usual term, America doesn't use the word "cult" in quite the same way (in America they've had Charles Manson, Jonestown and Scientology). So there are basic standard-issue American geeks who like things like *Star Trek* and *Battlestar Galactica* and perceive *Doctor Who* to be on the continuum of "geeky sci-fi/fantasy shows" they enjoy. (*Den of Geek*, despite being British and strictly commercial, tends

continued on Page 397...

several problems the production team were confronting. One big one was that Lorraine Heggarty, head of BBC1, had ordered a Christmas episode. This meant that they had the time and budget they had used for 13 episodes in Series One to make 14 episodes, one of which had to go to air on 25th December, three months before the start-date they were expecting. Double-banked episodes are common in the big-budget American series, where 22 or 26 episodes a year is usual, but it was an additional problem on top of the other logistical nightmares of the shoot, at a relatively late stage.

His judo-throw was to write a story about the effect of *Doctor Who* on anyone who lets it get under their skin. Perhaps the most obvious symbol that this is the true focus of the story is the apparently random detail of Elton being a fan of the most unfashionable band imaginable: the Electric Light Orchestra. This is an act who were massive in the 1970s, embarrassing in the 80s and not-talked-about until about a year before this story was written, when a lot of high-profile trendsetters admitted to a sneaking affection for the poodle-permed Brummies. (Anyone under 30 just didn't know about them, because they were so unmentionable for so long.) The same style-mags that had said that Jeff Lynn's look and sound was beyond the pale (if you've seen photos of 80s *Doctor Who* producer John Nathan-Turner, you've got some idea) went hog-wild over briefly-fashionable band/cult The Polyphonic Spree, who were an amalgam of ELO, The Pixies and the Eisteddfod. Then the Orchestra's "Mr. Blue Sky" started being used in adverts and film trailers. This was also the beginning of the "Guilty Pleasures" nights at various hip clubs. ELO went from being a punchline to a band suddenly everyone claimed to have always liked, really. Those of you unable to make the imaginative leap to *Doctor Who* should examine **What's All This Stuff About Anoraks?** under 22.1, "Attack of the Cybermen" and **The Semiotic Thickness of What?** under "Dragonfire".

This story's essay will pick up the story from there but many, many people within Old-Skool fandom have seen the fat northerner co-opting a gang's fun hobby to further his own ends in this story and thought "Ian Levine". LINDA is very like fandom in the 80s and more especially the 1990s, when the lack of an actual programme wasn't going to distract anyone from the combination of shared childhood, common interests outside the series and a siege mentality against the outside world's skewed values that made *Doctor Who* not something you admitted to liking. 90s fanzines had a conspiratorial feel and were more fun than any other aspect of fandom, ever. Part of the merriment was knowing that the acquisitive fans had as hard a time "getting" it as the Not-We. Levine was not part of the fanzine culture except as the butt of jokes.

To quickly recap: Levine had retrieved a great many telerecorded episodes due to have been destroyed (see **What Was the BBC** *Thinking*? under 3.1, "Galaxy 4") and had parlayed this, along with and his persistence with the *Doctor Who* production office in the late 70s, into a position as "superfan". When the new production team of John Nathan-Turner and Christopher H Bidmead was installed at short notice, Levine became a special advisor on the sort of continuity references the previous regime hadn't cared about. This began with advice on tiny details, and escalated to impossibly unlikely dialogue and "team-up" storylines such as "Attack of the Cybermen". This fans-only tendency, as much as anything, contributed to the series being cancelled in 1989. All the while, Levine and his chums were discovering hitherto lost episodes in strange far-off places.

This, for Levine and others, was what fandom was "for", and all that fun and friendship was irrelevant. In his "proper" career, Levine spent the 90s inflicting Boy Bands on the nation and was, financially, able to indulge in his interest. He was recently reported to be travelling to Russia in search of 1.4, "Marco Polo". However, he became emblematic within fandom for the attitude that status was down to what you could obtain, not what you could give or create or what kind of person you were. (That said, he *did* give something back with the release of "Doctor in Distress", his charity single from 1985. See 22.6, "Revelation of the Daleks".) His website was entertaining for a while, as the series returned and fandom moved on. His seething at apparent ingratitude (not entirely baseless) was compounded when, in 2010, the BBC did a radio documentary about the recovery of old episodes and didn't mention him once. (Interestingly enough, Levine has commented on the episode itself, saying that he hated it on initial broadcast before deciding that he loved it after all.)

Is *Doctor Who* Fandom Off-Topic?

continued from Page 395...

towards this mould. It's full of "news" items such as the "prison planet of the Amazons" story from Season Six being suppressed because it was "too subversive'"; see **What Else Wasn't Made?** under 17.6, "Shada" for the real reason, but here's a synopsis - it was crap!) These tend to gather on news websites, in which a few people write the main content and the communal communication is the sort of short, immediate commenting that's not conducive to considered correspondence. This is Internet default mode, and this is the audience that is likely to be captured by BBC America the more they push *Doctor Who*; in a sense this is a good thing, because the young bloke demographic is exactly who you want to target in America when you're advertising stuff, so everyone pays attention to them. However, the female fans who have already attached themselves to the series might be slightly off-putting to this market.

The most famous newspost/forum site was Outpost Gallifrey (in **What Are the Best Online Extras?** in an upcoming volume, we'll talk more about how relatively new this concept was even in 2005 and how close the BBC came to doing something similiar), but this collapsed under the strain of the new intake of news - especially the day Eccleston's "resignation" broke - and a replacement, Gallifrey Base, began. It's widely perceived as being of less use. There's still a version of rec.arts.doctorwho limping along to this day. Then there's the selection of BNFs (big name fans) who have shifted from Usenet to blogging, although many of them don't talk about *Doctor Who* that often unless they've just been paid to write about it. Several used to be involved with the Livejournal communities, which took off around the same time *Doctor Who* fan fiction did and have declined commensurately (the high point was perhaps the week "Last of the Time Lords" aired - guess why). In addition to general news and reviews, LJ fandom featured cross-Atlantic discourse on how to go about writing UK-based stories, and the making and distribution of fan art and fic; there was a group just for recommending fics posted to Teaspoon (Fanfiction.net has a somewhat younger selections of enthusiasts doing much the same). LJ *DW* fandom being mostly by and for women, what discussion continues is still more conscious of "isms" than anywhere else on the Internet. Lately these women have been going to "An Archive of Our Own" (the Virginia Woolf reference is undoubtedly deliberate), but that's not where conversations take place. And there are *DW* Internet fanzines; some of them are the UK Tavern crowd, one is the New Zealand, one of the big ones is *Enlightenment* from Canada. (They have their own Tavern and call it such. In Toronto.) You might notice that like the NZ one, this Canadian production is *Doctor Who*-only. And there are podcasters; they're their own little subculture.

In this new context, *Doctor Who* becomes just one of many favoured platforms to communicate about writing. One of the defining characteristics of the *New Adventures*-crowd is a fondness for discussing the technicalities of authorship, while "amateur" fan fiction writers have developed the art of creation into the real motivational force behind their interactions; fan fiction is meant to be read, and to be commented upon. The access is multiple-level. Someone equipped with a basic grasp of grammar, a spell check, and a reasonable understanding of the characters can now be accepted into a group with almost as much ease as wandering into a pub. The currency becomes how well you can write, how much you can help out your fellow writers with reviews or beta reading, and (sometimes) how cleverly you've rehashed overworked tropes.[82]

But in the UK, subject matter needn't equate to form. The online-ness of whatever was happening online with fans was less significant than the pre-existing fan-mentality manifesting itself in a new manner. For starters, we have the fact that *Doctor Who* is conceived of and made as a family show, one meant to appeal to everyone over teatime before *Basil Brush* or, these days, some phone-in talent thing with Graham Norton and John Barrowman. This is something most Internet fans are at least vaguely aware of, but that's a long way from understanding the implications at a gut level. When something is watched by over half the people who own televisions, the term "cult" is doubly ridiculous. This series is made to be watched by everyone, and thus refers to things we all know. What "things we all know" entails even a year after broadcast, or in another country, is another matter.

continued on Page 399...

X2.10: Love & Monsters

Davies, for what it's worth, claims that he managed to not know anything about South Wales Local Group, nor their fanzine *Muck and Devastation*, but had observed the self-appointed "superfans" draining the joy from many other enthusiasms and concluded that it was a general rule of such groups. But nobody as chummy with Paul Cornell as he was could have avoided knowing about fanzine culture, not least through Virgin's collection of fanzine material: *Licence Denied* (1997).

In what was *probably* a coincidence, the digital "upmarket" channel BBC4 re-played a 1978 ELO concert the same night this episode was first shown. The gig was introduced by Tony Curtis, and the announcer on BBC4 made reference to the *Doctor Who* episode as if it was all cleverly planned.

English Lessons *Pub Quiz*. Something that, prior to smart phones, was a staple of most people's week. You'd be in a team of about four, with a whimsical name, and would once a week answer sets of questions on a sheet of paper, asked by an MC (usually the pub landlord) who didn't understand the long words. Each round would be a different type of trivia, and the overall winners each night would win a pizza or free beer. A complex system of hand-signals allowed teammates to collude without giving hints to other teams. (As she's presented in *Doctor Who*, Jackie is an unlikely enthusiast for this sort of thing, but a real-life Jackie might well do this and be a member of a book-club.)

Oh, Isn't That...?

• *Marc Warren* (Elton Pope). Star of comedy-drama *Hustle* and a regular of crime dramas for well over seven years by this stage. He had been in the noteworthy drama *State of Play* by Paul Abbott (see X1.11, "Boom Town"). If you see him in any detective series, he did it. (In one, *A Touch of Frost*, he was that week's killer and strangled Camille Coduri.) Shortly after this, he played Count Dracula in a BBC adaptation of Stoker's novel, and the murderous Mr Teatime in the first Discworld drama to be made by Sky One, *Hogfather* (a lavish Terry Pratchett adaptation that annoyed as many purists as it pleased).

• *Shirley Henderson* (Ursula Blake). One of the most ubiquitous of British performers, Henderson had recently been in one of the *Harry Potter* films alongside Tennant and Trigg... sorry, Roger Lloyd Pack (X2.5, "Rise of the Cybermen"), but she was also in Mike Leigh's *Topsy Turvy* (playing the person who originally played Yum-Yum in *The Mikado*, and singing "The Sun Whose Rays" on the soundtrack), Michael Winterbottom's *24 Hour Party People* (as was almost everyone, but she got an award nomination), *Trainspotting* and *Bridget Jones: The Edge of Reason*, plus lots of neat stuff that wasn't internationally released. Her breakthrough role was in *Hamish Macbeth*, a cop show that defines "wilfully quirky" to many people. She's actually very Scottish indeed, but hides it when necessary.

• *Peter Kay* (Victor Kennedy / the Abzorbaloff). The list of performers who have had a UK number One single and a *Doctor Who* role includes Kay, whose team-up with Tony Christie for *Comic Relief* was at the top of the charts when "Rose" was broadcast. Since coming apparently from nowhere in the late 1990s with *That Peter Kay Thing* (a series of *faux* documentaries about people in Bolton, mainly played by Kay), he had dominated British television comedy and was, at the time of "Love & Monsters", at the peak of his success. His stand-up tour was released and became the nation's top-selling DVD. His autobiography, *The Sound of Laughter*, was a bestseller that Christmas and was, unlike most of these, well reviewed and rarely given away to charity shops. Perhaps aware of the risk of over-exposure, he downplayed his availability after playing the Abzorbaloff, making one last series (*Max and Paddy's Roadshow*, a spin-off from *Phoenix Nights*, itself a spin-off from the first *Thing*) and only emerging for a satire on Simon Cowell-style talent shows and the biannual *Comic Relief* singles. Guess what... he'd been in *24 Hour Party People* too.

• *Moya Brady* (Bridget) is one of those faces you've always seen somewhere, but you're not sure where. Her highest-profile gig had been as the (fictional) wife of the narrator in odd TV satire *Inside Victor Lewis-Smith* (almost everyone in this turned up in *Doctor Who* - Annette Badland, Roger Lloyd Pack, Tim Barlow... the main exception was Nikolas Grace, who was Sheriff in *Robin of Sherwood* and Einstein in "Death is the Only Answer" - see Volume 9). She's also one of eight (*eight!*) people who've been in *Doctor Who* and were in Woody Allen's *Scoop*.

• *Bella Emberg* (Mrs Croot). Since her two non-speaking roles in Pertwee stories (see Volume 3b),

Is *Doctor Who* Fandom Off-Topic?

continued from Page 397...

Much of what we have been obliged to explain in the *About Time* books is what hardly needed to be said when the episode in question was first aired. Those commonly-assumed links to everything else are why the old skool fans appear to be veering around randomly between topics to anyone who wasn't the original target audience. The boundary of what's "off-topic" to us is nebulous and negotiable.

Where old-skool British fandom saw the television episodes as the primary text and discuss it as the work of writers, actors and producers, for the fan-fic enthusiasts the stories exist in some idealised state, free from earthly contamination by practical considerations of being made almost-live in Lime Grove. Often, the Doctors aren't identified by actor but by capitalised numbers, so the original Doctor is "One", his replacement is "Two" and so on. In Britain, it's surname or a sardonic nickname ("Twerpee", "Eccles", "Ferret-Boy"). This reminds us of a significant detail. For a sizeable minority of the British fans, and certainly the founders who provided the basic narrative of the series to date when *Doctor Who Weekly* began in 1979, the series developed over time, responding to outside events. It didn't happen all at once. We've spent seven books and counting explaining this, but for anyone coming cold to *Doctor Who* in 2005 or after, the whole prior series exists as a complete, closed object (and nowadays to be tackled, if at all, only after investigating the shiny new stories). Older American fans had already experienced this, assuming that the concept of Regeneration was there in some "series Bible" in 1963 (see **When Was Regeneration Invented?** under 11.5, "Planet of the Spiders"). When the Eccleston episodes showed up at almost the same time that *Star Trek* had its mercy-killing, a chorus of woe went up as people realised they had 26 years of backstory to learn, some of it not there in the archives. Many instinctively looked it up online, and here a familiar problem returned.

Since 2005, phylogeny has recapitulated ontogeny and the development of these online groups has been a small-scale replay of this original developmental process. But, being online, it was faster, louder and less subtle. The online resources also often copy from one another, with far-from-enough fact-checking or first-hand experience of actual episodes or books. There's a real risk of the unwary fan falling into a hall of mirrors. There are people parroting other people's offhand comments as though they were sacred writings; one woman at a convention was convinced that there was a race of aliens called "Gunfighters" (see 3.8, "The Gunfighters") and that these were so offensive that they should never be brought back (as though someone would resurrect the dead Clanton brothers to invade present-day London somehow). This is so like the phase in between the start of *DWM* and the rise of the Local Group network, it's almost endearing. Almost. For someone who'd paid dues back in the day and watched actual episodes, it can be a bewildering nest of connections. Online, it's thousands of individuals going it alone and stating their case in easily-misunderstood gobbets. Basically, the version of fandom we see in X3.10, "Blink" - a socially-maladroit loser arguing with other loners online and missing the point - is the nightmare vision of fandom. Moffat was never in a Local Group, and had little to do with fanzines. He was, however, a regular on computer-based newsgroups and fan-sites in the 90s.

Internet fandom has a pernicious effect on the mode of debate. Quite apart from militating against long, closely-argued and nuanced statements (the basic unit of fanzine discourse), it equates the writer's identity with a one-line description of everything that person thinks on this central topic. Other users clump that person in with other views that could be summarised the same way and it quickly gets tribal, whether you as an individual believe yourself to belong in the tribe consensus has placed you in. Attempts to qualify or contour your new reputation are seen as back-tracking or hypocrisy. It becomes treacherously easy to play up to this ascribed identity/position instead of calmly stating your more complex viewpoint as you would in person. This is characteristic of teenagers, who attempt to conform to group identities and prefer all-embracing systems that (apparently) explain and control everything neatly. Online debate tends towards curtness, so attempts to explain why things are more complicated than they might seem get

continued on Page 401...

X2.10: Love & Monsters

Bella Emberg had been a household name - admittedly, usually small boys were using it to insult each other with "she's your girlfriend, she is" taunts. Russ Abbott's Saturday Night shows, first on ITV then BBC1, had made great play of her weight and homely looks (both exaggerated with make-up) for what passed for comic effect in those dark years. Then came years on stage and now a cameo that reminded the public (and casting directors) that she was still around. She was due to have another appearance as the same old lady in "The Runaway Bride" (X3.0).

- *Kathryn Drysdale* (Bliss) is probably going to spend her entire career as "her off *Two Pints of Lager and a Packet of Crisps*, not Sheridan Smith, not the other one, but the other other one". At time of writing, she's in the "is that still going?" ITV sitcom *Benidorm*.
- *Simon Greenall* (Mr Skinner). On screen, he is best remembered as the near-incomprehensible Geordie doorman in *I'm Alan Partridge*. Currently, he is the voice of one of Aleksandr Orlov, the Russian-accented meerkat who sells car insurance. No, really...

Things That Don't Make Sense To whom is Elton talking throughout this story? More to the point (and we're going to elaborate on this in an essay in the next volume), when? Ursula's there in scenes with a zoom-lens, so evidently after the majority of the to-camera stuff. But in that apparently earlier material, he alludes to realising 'the truth' about seeing the Doctor as a child, something that only dawns on him after LINDA has been (literally) dispersed. So Elton's visit to his childhood home, which is apparently sutured into his account, either has help from a paving-slab on a trolley operating a camera or is, like the clips of the rest of the story, edited in by someone using this found footage to make an episode of *Doctor Who*, but from "inside" the story's fictional universe. In which case, who is shooting the one "conventional" shot from over Elton's shoulder, of Ursula as a paving-slab?

It seems odd that everyone in LINDA is from oop north; if the story had been set in another city, this would be unremarkable, but they make a point of plastering signs for a (non-existent) 'London Library Service' outside the depot where they meet and use 'London' as the first letter of their acronym; the TARDIS lands in Woolwich and Kennedy equips them all with the London A-Z book. Brigit comes down to London from an unspecified location 'far up North', but all of them are from outside the Capital - meaning that Elton, whose accent varies as though he has been in London for a few years but grew up in the East Midlands, must have left and come back, since he is able to take Ursula to his former home before he's had the nerve to buy her a Chinese. (She lives half a mile from his current home, i.e. in London, so for her to accompany him after so short an acquaintance, it probably means the old house is close by.) Her accent is from further north than Brigit's. Of Victor's accent as 'Victor' and as the Abzorbaloff, we shall simply assume that his more recognisably Peter Kay-like voice when green and scary is more likely to be the real one. But, why does the Abzorbaloff keep consuming the LINDA members - thus reducing the ranks of his foot-lackeys - rather than satiate himself by absorbing random strangers? Has the scant knowledge the LINDA members have gained about the Doctor made them irresistible to the Abzorbaloff, somehow?

And, they are supposed to be meeting below a library, but nothing in the location shots indicates that this is a public thoroughfare. It looks like docklands and there's no toilet (they have to use the pub on the corner), unlike any library in the UK (well, every library's *basement* - not all libraries allow the public to use their loos, but they have some for the staff). And whoever runs this public space allows Kennedy to festoon it with his own equipment. Nine times out of ten, the space below a library would be a shop or council offices, and the tenth time it would be a reserve for that very library.

Elton claims that it was 'Quarter to eight' when the windows shattered as the Sycorax ship hit the atmosphere, which isn't quite the time-scale we saw in "The Christmas Invasion". His employers must be very obliging, if he's getting time off from running a haulage depot in order to pretend to need his shirt laundering. And why is Elton still carrying a picture of Rose some days / weeks after establishing 'contact' with Jackie? There are enough pictures of her dotted around the flat as it is (although one seems to be a *Smash Hits* publicity photo of former popstrelle Billie).

Chaka Demus and Pliers don't use the contraction 'n'.

Is *Doctor Who* Fandom Off-Topic?

continued from Page 399...

ignored, shot down or forgotten as one-liners fly thick and fast (mainly thick). One prominent London-based online commentator has stopped watching *Doctor Who* out of sheer exasperation with Matt Smith and Steven Moffat, but will not admit this simply because the "performance" online has become too much a part of that person's self-image. We have been asked not to name names (don't worry - it's nobody connected with *About Time*), but this individual is frequently maintaining a line adopted early on despite no longer holding those opinions. To some extent, anyone who posts regularly to any forum, or blogs "instinctively", becomes a self-parody.

If some of the older British fans feel slighted, it's because the decline of the series' popularity and (subject of intense debate, this; see volumes 5 and 6) quality under John Nathan-Turner was something they experienced as it happened - to many of these fans, each new story felt like a fresh test of faith. Then the 16 years of the programme's absence was in some ways a trial. Many of those who struggled to retain optimism and enthusiasm feel (rightly or wrongly) as if they've "earned" the new series in ways that others have not. (This is also the place to mention that UK fans pay for the series to be made via the TV Licence, and some of the more established US fans pay for the PBS stations that showed it with the telethons, so some viewers have always felt as if they're more equal than others even without organised fandom.) Moreover, the unshakeable fans were the ones who nurtured the people who brought it back. The *New Adventures* and BBC Books tie-ins, the Big Finish audios and *DWM* all had to be bought and responded to by someone. Most of the writers came through the fanzine culture of the 80s and 90s, and those that didn't knew the people who did. It is more than mere propinquity that makes the bigger players in this fan culture, the ones who never got the call from Cardiff, act as though they have special privilege. Anyone coming to the series cold in 2005 would not have known this, and might have seen any old-time fan online griping and saying how else the "faulty" episode, story or character could have been developed, as an entitlement queen. In the polarised, all-or-nothing world-view of online debate, anyone who has any complaint with an aspect of a new episode is frequently shouted down and asked why s/he claims to be a fan of something when all s/he does is complain and why not go away and like some other show. The idea that the veteran fan really *does* know better (sometimes), and has been a fan longer than the complainer has been alive, is inadmissible. And, to be fair, those veterans who are active online have occasionally made spectacular idiots of themselves.

Where this all comes to a head is the advent of Twitter, which has accentuated trends in online *Doctor Who* fandom just as it amplified everything else on the Internet. The simplicity of an online presence that requires only single sentences has attracted an astonishing range of people associated with the show; even those BNFs who never bothered with the Internet before have taken one-liners to heart, and they all use it now to chat with each other and receive flattering kudos from Americans who have sought out cult artefacts and want to commend them. (In an inverse of online normality, arguments are generally semi-comic in-fighting by people who already know each other.) The actors have embraced this fashion of interacting with the fans, and while the current production team's attempts to interact with the general public are regarded as fair game for trolls, Colin Baker gets to bask in universal acclaim. (Oddly enough, Steven Moffat deleted his account shortly after "Asylum of the Daleks", for "family reasons". Really.) But it's the opposite of fanzine discourse; you'll know who liked something and possibly why, but there's nothing considered enough to build a self-sustaining community upon.

Because we have been mainly looking at US online fandom and UK old-timers, a third and much larger group has not been mentioned. In Britain, there is now a vast cross-section of the public who think their opinions are as valid as anyone's, even those who bought *New Adventures* books, and who consider themselves "fans" despite not watching anything pre-2005 and apparently not paying much attention to what they did watch. Every newspaper now realises that running a controversial piece on *Doctor Who* is an easy way to get traffic and half-thought-out opinions for

continued on Page 403...

Critique There's a school of thought that this was a mistake. But, the people who thought so really liked the previous two episodes, so their opinion is suspect at best. One shot - of the Abzorbaloff lumbering after Elton - is almost like everyone's impression of 80s *Doctor Who* and why it had to be cancelled, but anyone who doesn't see *why* this is in the episode ought to think more carefully about what this story's telling us. More to the point, they should think about *how* it's telling us this. We have no guarantee that this isn't just how Elton remembers the incident rather than what, if anything, really happened. Since "Father's Day" (X1.8), they've been tentatively messing with the whole narrative habit of this series and now they've tried something a bit more overtly subjective than just having Rose do a voice-over.

Being playful and trying new things isn't always going to go down well with the unimaginative obsessives. These are precisely the kinds of people being parodied as a silly-looking monster. However much fun it was seeing the point-missing tirades online, all of which read as if they were written by Comic-Book Guy from *The Simpsons*, what offended these people wasn't ridicule of themselves (they didn't get it), but having a story without the Doctor in and with an on-screen narrator talking to us. None of what they are criticising is what could be considered a "flaw" or "defect", just not what they're used to.

The flaws and defects come from trying to do both of these things at once, and for doing it at the end of production whilst planning a move from the usual studio. It's rushed. An on-screen narrator telling us about his meetings with the Doctor could have worked a lot better. We know that stories where the Doctor-shaped void is the main point can go down well with the same people who criticised this one. Apart from this, having Marc Warren as a narrator is a big mistake. His is not a voice designed for voice-overs. It was only a last-minute decision, based on the number of other women whose lives the Doctor has wrecked this year, that Elton became male. It would only have taken a small tweak to have Elton as protagonist and Ursula as narrator, or interviewer. (Or got Craig Kelly from *Queer as Folk* - Elton's basically a straight Vince Tyler, even down to having the same job.) And not everyone can stand that much ELO in an episode of anything.

But what we got is, if you go along with the premise, generally well-done. The remounts of earlier episodes are a bit better than the originals. Warren on screen is better than Warren telling the story, and the rest of the cast are picked judiciously. Yes, even Peter Kay. It's hard to convey just how big he was when this went out. He's carefully limited his exposure since the high-water mark of *Amarillo* and *Phoenix Nights*, but his autobiography outsold *Harry Potter* that year. What other star of that magnitude would have put himself through that long a make-up process?

The other huge plus is that, at last, Jackie stops being comic-relief soap-opera mum and becomes a character. She has a life beyond Rose. Indeed, people thinking of her as an adjunct to her daughter is what goes wrong here. For a long period of the story, there's nothing overtly *Doctor Who*ish about her scenes with Elton. That's another thing that offended the less nimble-minded critics, but this is a situation that couldn't have happened without the story's initial premise. This is all about the consequences of the Doctor, and about what price Jackie's been paying for Rose's selfish behaviour. To anyone thinking this was the Doctor-and-Rose show, it has been just about possible to ignore what a brat she's been since the regeneration. This is the story that rubs our noses in it. That's not comfortable for people who hold Rose up as some kind of model of what a companion should be like.

One mark against it from the point of view of the obsessives: although the Abzorbaloff was designed by a child, this isn't a particularly child-friendly episode. The threats come from the idea of being absorbed, but this is only revealed late on. Before that, there's the grown-up stuff, tiresome to about half the BBC1 audience. As with next week's story, the concept is scarier than what we get on screen. And, these days, the idea that every episode has to have a scary monster in it - ideally one replicable in plastic - has become part of the BBC Wales sales-pitch. The most terrifying idea is the unseen thing that kills Elton's mum when he's small. Other than that, there's the Hoix. As with "The Androids of Tara" (16.4), they put a token, self-consciously joky monster in the first five minutes, but then get on with a better, cleverer story. What we've got here is what we were told "The Girl in the Fireplace" (X2.4) was going to be: a story about how the Doctor's lifestyle makes romance almost impossible, but all the more worth trying for. It's actually rather more romantic than the cold, mechanical Moffat script.

Is *Doctor Who* Fandom Off-Topic?

continued from Page 401...

page after page. Once again, considered argument, factual knowledge or accurate typing aren't obligatory. If the BBC lost patience with Moffat and axed *Doctor Who* tomorrow, a small percentage of these people would keep thinking about the series years later and the whole pattern would repeat - maybe not with fanzines, but somehow. One difference is that access to old television is easier than it was in the early 80s. Another is that physical proximity to other vaguely like-minded people (who are the only ones you'll've met) doesn't mean you get exposed to opinions other than your own (or one you read as "fact") articulated clearly and patiently. But at the moment, there are millions of people in Britain keen on *Doctor Who* who don't give a toss about *Star Trek* and many are teenage girls. This, as you will have guessed from Clive's wife's comments (X1.1, "Rose"), is new.

But it will be their childhoods, their subtly-altered perspective on history, science, social activism or just shop-dummies that will fire them, and the actual old Eccleston, Tennant or Smith episodes will seem as cheesy to their friends as blue-screen CSO, Roger Limb's synthesizers or Yartek, Leader of the Alien Voord do to ours. And us.

(In the next volume, we're going to broaden our scope: with an American publisher and an English author, it's easy to assume that there are only two countries doing anything with *Doctor Who*. Just wait until you see what Russian and Japanese TV companies do with it, and the viewers. And this may be the time to finally open the Pandora's Box of Australian fandom, after looking at the subject with a view to an essay in Volume 5 and thinking "strewth!")

The argument that this must be a duff story because the ratings fell is bogus: the ratings indicate who switched on, and are thus determined by what was on the previous week. By that argument, "The Satan Pit" (X2.9) was the turkey. The AIs dropped, mainly because the under-tens (and emotionally stunted over-tens) were a bit nonplussed by putting Elton's romances in where there should have been more explosions and things. But having the same thing week after week would have killed the series stone dead. The hype for the new-style *Doctor Who* was that it was going to be all about "emotions" and "personal journeys" and make the relationships more important than the special effects. Here we have a story that lives up to that description, and people say "Worst. Episode. Ever." They think it ought to be "Love *or* Monsters".

But we're not reviewing the online mouthbreathers' comments, we're looking at the episode. This is one with more nooks and crannies with odd little surprises than any other. It is one to revisit once a year, when more celebrated adventures have used up their flavour like chewing gum. It's one that gets funnier the more about contemporary Britain you know. It's one for anyone who's ever been a genuine enthusiast about anything. And it's got Bella Emberg in it, which means a great deal to a lot of people here.

Obviously, it's a Marmite episode, one that will prompt extreme reactions and little in the middle, but the joke is on the people who hate this story. And without stories as bold as this, there wouldn't be a *Doctor Who*.

The Facts

Written by Russell T Davies. Directed by Dan Zeff. Viewing figures: (BBC1) 6.6 million, (BBC3 repeats) 0.7 and 0.2 million. AI was 76%.

Repeats and overseas promotion Liebe und Monster, L.I.N.D.A.

TARDISode The LINDA website is being investigated by someone with a silver-topped cane. It has lots of dead-ends, refusing to reveal their location, but has drawings of the Doctor and refers to an "Elton" who got to him first. (It also has a page devoted to Jeff Lynne, including The Idle Race and The Move, as well as ELO.) The person watching uses a metallic disc with a red jewel at the centre to over-ride the firewalls and gets the address, causing a green glow and making his gurgling snarls louder, as a lady comes in with a tray of tea things. The lady is assaulted by whatever it is (and whatever it was isn't played by Peter Kay).

X2.10 Love & Monsters

Production

Part of the "I Love the Doctor" storyline had been in Russell T Davies' mind since he devised a comic-strip for *Doctor Who Magazine* (never used). This told the story of an innocent bystander who had always been on the receiving end of alien attacks of London, beginning with being evacuated from Coal Hill School in 1963 (25.1, "Remembrance of the Daleks") and continuing with his mother's death from an Auton daffodil (8.1, "Terror of the Autons"). When Series Two was pitched to the BBC Drama heads shortly before the broadcast of the first series, the story was still nebulous; Elton only became male when it became obvious that this new Doctor was travelling across time breaking female hearts all season. It was apparent very early on that this would be the double-banked episode and would, in effect, be a different production in isolation from the main episodes being made then. Once the dust had settled concerning Mark Gatiss' availability to complete the script for what became "The Idiot's Lantern (X2.7), it was agreed that the two-part Matt Jones story and this episode would be made concurrently as blocks Five and Six.

It would also, in theory, be the low-cost option, with minimal effects and a small cast. Tennant and Piper would be freed from making X2.8-2.9, "The Impossible Planet"/"The Satan Pit" for a couple of days. This didn't work out either. One element that did go to plan was the use of a monster suggested by a *Blue Peter* viewer. As the double-banked episode would be the last to be written by Davies, they had time to work out the rest of the script around whatever was selected on 19th August. Just under six months later, director Dan Zeff formally began work on the episode. By now, you will not be surprised that he was another alumnus of *Linda Green*. He had also worked with Peter Davison on *At Home With the Braithwaites*.

• The script was diligent in both avoiding making LINDA risible and trying to get the time-frame nailed down. The descriptions of the characters are careful to make sure that Elton is not "a twat" or "silly", and kept it ambiguous whether he lived alone, with his family or elsewhere (a female voice was to have been heard, turning out at the end to be the landlady). A great deal was cut before transmission, including a scene where Jackie mentions naming Rose after her own mother and not mentioning Pete's death, simply agreeing with Elton's assumption that he left and that she's better off without him. Elton also tells whoever's watching about the inept government attempts to deny that the Slitheen, Nestene and Sycorax assaults on the capital were the work of extraterrestrials. The acronym LINDA was one used by Davies in *Why Don't You*, as the title of a rival kid's gang (Liverpool instead of London), with a small girl in combat gear claiming, "We're the Men from LINDA".

• With the exception of Jackie's flat, the episode was made in Cardiff locations. The first sequence to be recorded was the webcam material and everything in Elton's flat. This was made at what had been the Corona fizzy-drinks factory. Warren spent two days recording the pieces to camera and changing clothes. There was a sequence about picking his way across the glass-strewn floor on Christmas morning. This was cut for timing reasons, but executive producer Julie Gardner insisted that the line about "a rudimentary pulley system" was reinstated in ADR during the final edit. The second day, 20th March, was when Henderson came in to perform with her head sticking through a paving-slab. Although her body is removed in post-production, she really did kneel below Warren and perform with the prosthesis. Next day the park scenes were done, around the corner from the BBC Wales complex in Llandaff. Later, they went to Elton's childhood home: the interior was really like that, an almost perfect 1973 time-bubble, and only needed a few old *Reader's Digests* to complete the illusion.

Tennant made his first appearance towards the end of this, after a hard day at the Ood holding pen. Next morning, Zeff discovered that his proposed location at the Cardiff Docks, doubling for Woolwich (originally scripted as "Dulwich", which is a very different place despite both being pronounced to almost rhyme with "village") was in use. A vast consignment of steel cable was being offloaded, so an alternative around the corner was found. The piece of newspaper blowing across the shot as if on cue was a pure fluke.

This was also the day of the crowd-scenes. Bella Emberg was standing where the TARDIS had taken Rose and left Mickey in "Rose" and *Totally Doctor Who*'s Barney Harwood spent a day as an extra. Next day, Thursday 23rd, was the launderette. This was a real one, with faked-up nonexistent detergent boxes and "out of order" posters stuck over any recognisable promotional material in keeping with BBC guidelines. The sequence of Jackie telling Elton to go was filmed amid a lot of public interest, including, apparently, distracting youths on pogo-sticks (these came back in vogue, briefly, that year). This was also the day that four-year-old Thomas Coleman played young Elton in the final flashback. He was a bit put out not to meet the Doctor.

• Peter Kay had contacted Davies about possibly being in the forthcoming series of *Doctor Who*. When the part of Elton was suggested, he declined, as it was almost the same as his cameo in an episode of *Coronation Street* in early 2004. However, when he saw the Abzorbaloff, he was interested. Indeed, as phone calls between him and Davies continued, Kay simply asked, "Are you in Manchester right now?", and half an hour later showed up at Davies' door to do a reading. (Davies reports, regretfully, that none of his neighbours were at home to see this.) Although keen to play the part as an acting role, and concerned about where to draw the line with the monster's accent, Kay added a few comic touches, such as mispronouncing "Eczema".

• Kay and LINDA's other members began their shoot at the basement of an antique shop in the Cardiff Wharf on the Sunday. It began with Kay as the Abzorbaloff. The make-up took five hours to put on, so Kay's day began at 4.30am. Millennium Effects already had a cast of his head from his appearance in *The Catherine Tate Show*. It was planned to use animatronic inserted human faces where possible, edited together with close-ups of the actors in prostheses like the slab Henderson had already used. When the rushes were seen, the amount of digital infill and pick-up shots had to increase, and in the event only one scene really uses the animatronic face of Ursula as it is looking the right way and the prosthetic cutaway shot isn't. The location was chosen to fit Davies' idea of a drab, colourless world that LINDA made, temporarily, more appealing. The lift was an unexpected bonus and Ed Thomas, the production designer, sought to make it less like a garage and more nest-like.

Next morning *Blue Peter* returned, and Kay greeted William Grantham with "Hello, I'm Green Peter". By now, Grantham was very excited about his creation (what he called "a Sumo Monster") being on screen and slightly improved from his drawing, despite it being smaller than a bus. The day of the Abzorbaloff chase and death was miserably wet, and the latex skin made Kay feel as if he were inside a giant bathsponge. This was the first day when Tennant and Piper were available, and they recorded this and interviews for *Blue Peter* and *Doctor Who Confidential*. Meanwhile, Neill Gorton and the Millennium team were turning odds and ends from other productions into a monster costume for Paul Casey. Next morning, at Newport Docks, this being would confront the Doctor and Rose (and Elton) at a pumping station where seven doors had been installed in a corridor for the *Scooby Doo* chase with the buckets.

• Murray Gold re-used a lot of cues from earlier in the series, such as the chase music from "The Idiot's Lantern" in the pre-credit sequence, and exactly the same music for Elton finding the TARDIS that had accompanied Rose's first visit, but one piece he recorded in advance for this episode was a deliberately rough instrumental of ELO's 1979 hit "Don't Bring Me Down" for the cast to sing to during the last three days of recording. In looking up the lyrics, he found the word "Groos" and queried it: the production team contacted Jeff Lynn - apparently this was an in-joke about the German word used by a recording engineer (and spelt *grüß*). Lynn asked to see the completed episode. His comments are not recorded.

• At one stage, Davies apparently considered bringing back Elton as the co-ordinating agency for the "Children of Time" ("The Stolen Earth"). His role eventually went to Harriet Jones.

• The episode went out during that absurdly hot summer of 2006, with temperatures that week approaching 40 °C. The ratings were respectable, but the pre-publicity about Kay's appearance led to many people who didn't see the whole broadcast assuming that the episode was entirely like the chase at the end. Talent-vacuum Ricky Gervais certainly did, and had appearing as a lumpy latex *Doctor Who* monster as the final indignity for the protagonist of his alleged comedy *Extras*. Tennant misguidedly appeared in this episode.

• The name "Hoix" was hastily improvised by Davies when the credits were being written and they realised that the monster hadn't got a name.

X2.11: "Fear Her"

(24th June, 2006)

Which One is This? People turn into drawings, Huw Edwards turns into a gibbering wreck and the TARDIS turns around in Dame Kelly Holmes Place.

Firsts and Lasts This is usually cited as the first time they've done the "TARDIS-materialising-facing-the-wrong-way" sight gag, but just look at 26.2, "Ghost Light". (Precisely what happens at the start of 5.7, "The Wheel in Space" is open to discussion, and there are at least eight other stories where this could have happened, for all we know.) It is, however, the first time the Doctor has been able to fix it with a quick flip of some switch or other. After its basement has been UNIT HQ and prior to its becoming the second most overfamiliar location in the series, this is a rare chance to see the Millennium Stadium in Cardiff as a stadium, albeit the wrong one.

Watch Out For...

• After a while, if you keep subverting a cliché the same way, that in turn becomes a cliché (see X4.6, "The Doctor's Daughter"). Thus, most British viewers would have realised that Edna Doré in *Doctor Who* wandering around warning everyone of something spooky is our biggest clue to what's happening. As we will see, Doré had been in practically every major drama, either playing old ladies with dementia (notably *EastEnders* and Mike Leigh's *High Hopes*) or old ladies who've seen something amazing, but aren't believed because they think she's got dementia (*Skellig*) or old ladies who get away with murder because everyone thinks she's got Alzheimer's (*Shameless*). The real shock in this episode, other than its inability to make any sense at the end, is that Doré's Maeve is actually a fairly small part.

• It's an unfortunate fact of science-fiction life that attempts to depict a near future are only really noticeable when they get it wrong. Children watching this story who can't remember the far-off days before BBC launched iPlayer may not spot that Chloe is watching the live coverage of the Olympics on her laptop. Similarly, the poster for *Shayne Ward's Greatest Hits* was intended as a joke at the expense of the *X Factor* winner who had just had his first No. 1 as this was being filmed. However, despite Simon Cowell dropping Ward from his label in 2011, there were seven UK top-20 singles (only one fewer than Billie Piper). The most impressive details are the one most viewers miss - T-registration cars (not on sale until August 2011) and the missing posters have dates of birth for the abducted children appropriate for eight-year-olds in 2012.

• There are some details they can't have foreseen, such as that the Olympic stadium is completely unlike the one actually built in Stratford, E15, and that a black guy with an East London accent repeatedly saying "bonkers" will be irresistibly funny to anyone who recalls Dizzee Rascal's 2009 No. 1 hit of the same name.

• With Steven Moffat apparently basing story-arcs on it, most fans are now familiar with the thought-experiment of Schrodinger's Cat. So here we see a cat go into a box and we aren't sure whether it's alive or dead. Even more appropriately for a story grounded in parental fear of children being abducted, the sound it makes as it vanishes is exactly like Charlie, the cat in the 70s Public Information Films, who reminded his chum always to tell mummy and daddy where you were going (a sample of which was the basis for the Prodigy's first hit). Writer Matthew Graham, also co-creator of *Life on Mars*, can't help making early 70s TV references; he, like Moffat, dreams of the day he can make a *Doctor Who* episode as scary as a 70s PIF.

• For the third time in as many stories, the ending has ominous forebodings of impending disaster concerning the Doctor and Rose. We can take a hint, thanks.

The Continuity

The Doctor He's able to detect ionic energy with his bare hands, and indeed his "manly hairy hand" reacts strongly to it by horripilating [see 3.10, "The War Machines" for something similar]. He's taken to using the rather 50s schoolboy phrase 'top banana'. He's quite good at squash, he claims [see X4.4, "The Sontaran Stratagem" for confirmation of this], as well as snakes and ladders. He's not fond of cats, based upon his experience with the cat-nuns [in X2.1, "New Earth", and in contrast to his sixth incarnation's affection for felines], but edible ball bearings make him exceedingly happy.

He is able, apparently with Chloe's consent, of

Was Series Two Supposed to be Like This?

Readers of Panini's *The Doctor Who Companion - Series Two* will have seen a version of the proposed second series that Russell T Davies presented to BBC Drama heads around the time that the first series was about to be broadcast. This is interesting, if incomplete (as this booklet went on sale before the second Christmas Special, the details of the first-draft of "The Runaway Bride" were left out, as were anything else they might have planned to bring to the screen). Attention to a few anomalous details in broadcast episodes, information we have now that wasn't public then, and - let's be honest - educated guesses complicate this, shall we say, slightly disingenuous account.

We'll begin with Davies' document, as published by Panini. This begins with the hour-long Christmas episode which is, right from the outset, a post-regeneration Doctor against the Sycorax (see **Did He Fall or Was He Pushed?** under X1.12, "Bad Wolf"). Harriet Jones is pencilled in as a returning character. As with many of the guest-cast being notionally brought back, availability and desire to return was assumed and a contingency plan considered. As we now know, Penelope Wilton, Elisabeth Sladen, Zoe Wanamaker, Shaun Dingwall and the semi-regular Noel Clarke and Camille Coduri all agreed to return. The first two episodes of the second series as shown were to have been what became "New Earth" and "The Girl in the Fireplace" (X2.1, X2.4), but not necessarily in that order. Whilst there was potential for Cassandra to have had an evil twin or a change of voice-box as part of her re-growth, Wanamaker's availability would have been a consideration. If she had agreed but had not been free until later on, the episode also could have come later, possibly as episode six. The story pencilled in for this slot was "The Runaway Bride" (eventually X3.0), but was here between the two two-part stories. Episode nine was Mark Gatiss' 50s-set story "Mr Sandman", about a song that steals people's faces. One story is exactly where it was in the broadcast run, notionally called "I Love the Doctor" and to be written last, on the understanding that whatever won the *Blue Peter* monster competition would be the antagonist and the Doctor and Rose would barely be in it. In at number eleven was something called "The 1920s", by Stephen Fry (see below). Finally, "Army of Ghosts" would be a two-part sequel to Tom MacRae's "Parallel World" story with the Cybermen (scheduled for eps four and five). There is no mention in this proposal of what is in the Void Ship or what happens to Rose...

The parallel universe and separation from the Doctor seems always to have been the planned exit for Rose at the end of a second series. The same plot, adapted from the Big Finish audio *Spare Parts*, was always to have brought back the Cybermen. The conversations that had crystallised into this document had been going on for about 18 months beforehand; other options for stories made in the first series can be added to the nebulous collection of not-quite ideas that were mooted and remained available as last-minute replacements. What became "Tooth and Claw" (X2.2) was a notion that had been kicked around since the first season but wasn't on the list presented to BBC drama-head Jane Tranter et al. The Series Three idea Matthew Graham had been asked to work on was hurriedly brought forward to fill the gap as Series Two's last episode before the two-part climax. The first idea for the eleventh story for Series One became "The Fires of Pompeii" (X4.2), although Captain Jack mentions "Volcano Day" in his debut episode (X1.9, "The Empty Child").

There are smaller differences from the broadcast versions that we can sketch in here. Davies confirms that Elton Pope (X2.10, "Love & Monsters") would have been female if either of the Doctor's celebrity historicals had fallen through and made the gender-balance different. The three historical-ish stories here were intended to root this new Doctor into the past; the consequences of his meeting with Queen Victoria would be playing out throughout the series, and he would be shown interacting with the start of television as a mass medium and the Coronation of the present Queen (in an episode shown shortly before her Golden Jubilee, a fact not lost on schools throughout the UK). Writer Toby Whithouse proposed an army base as the setting for what became "School Reunion" (X2.3). Early on, after seeing a pre-broadcast preview of "Aliens of London" (X1.4), writer Matt Jones asked to have the Slitheen in his two-parter, in the function that the Ood later fulfilled. These and others we have mentioned in each story's listing.

continued on Page 409...

X2.11 Fear Her

sending her into a trance in order to talk to her "guest". [This is done by a procedure like the mind-meld in X2.4, "The Girl in the Fireplace". See also 14.2, "The Hand of Fear", and 13.1, "Terror of the Zygons".]

• *Ethics.* Not many oddities to deal with here: he thinks he can help, so he does - albeit while being quick to assume that the disappearances stem from something non-human. He's a bit clueless about the rules of hospitality, helping himself to Trish's marmalade before Rose warns him not to. His interrogation of the Isolus [see **The Non-Humans**] is a bit harsh, but is done with Chloe's apparent co-operation.

• *Background.* This is the one where he nonchalantly tells Rose 'I was a dad, once'. [It's hardly news to anyone with even a nodding acquaintance with the programme's past (see Volume 1; 20.7, "The Five Doctors" or even 26.3, "The Curse of Fenric", although newcomers unaware of the basics almost melted the intertubes with ill-informed speculation - precisely how someone can be a grandfather without being a father is a matter for anyone with access to a time machine and a sympathetic partner to discover). Whatever the case, we have on-screen confirmation now - both here and in a conversation between the Doctor and Donna in "The Doctor's Daughter".

[Another thing we've wondered about: does the Doctor ever watch *Star Trek*? Apparently, he's at least got an idea that the Vulcan salute is known to kids in 2012. Maybe he only saw the 2009 film version[83], or perhaps the settlers who called an Earth colony 'Vulcan' (4.3, "The Power of the Daleks") taught it to him. Or maybe he, like Leonard Nimoy, picked it up at a synagogue. The complete absence of any previous reference to something so culturally significant in the Doctor's favourite time and planet has led to speculation that, as with the lack of any sign of people watching *Doctor Who*, it's proof that this series takes place in the *Star Trek* "universe". But then, is his silence on Michael Jackson or *The Two Ronnies* proof of anything? We have an essay on the *Trek* crossover theory for Volume 8, but it's worth noting that X6.11, "The God Complex" has Howie taunted for knowing Klingon.]

He went to the 1948 London Olympics. [The one where the home athletes had to pack their own sandwiches. Perhaps this Austerity-era comparison is why he's so enthusiastic about cakes with metallic balls on.] He enjoyed it so much he went again, and met the torchbearer then [whose name he can't recall - it was John Mark]. He has also been to Club Med, apparently. He makes reference to early seventies British TV, giving a spiel about the Scribble Creature reminiscent of Eric Idle as a door-to-door salesman in *Monty Python* ('breaks the ice at parties') and impersonating Shaw Taylor, host of *Police Five*, a short round up of appeals for eye-witnesses or information ('keep 'em peeled').

• *Inventory: Sonic Screwdriver.* It can turn a marauding scribble-monster the size of a space-hopper to an inert tennis-ball-sized lump. The psychic paper is brandished as ID [identifying Rose as 'Lewis', as in *Inspector Morse*] and works rapidly on an angry crowd. [This is noteworthy, as the emotional state of the viewer can have an effect on what is perceived (see X1.9, "The Empty Child"; X2.12, "Army of Ghosts") and because this is the largest number of people on whom it has been used.]

• *Inventory: Other.* The Doctor is carrying a pencil with a rubber on the end, just in case any graphite-based antagonists need erasing. He knocks up a gadget using odds and ends and Rose's chewing gum.

The TARDIS Apart from the problem with the Ship landing with the door facing an obstacle, the obvious point of comment is that the scanner system now has an analysis bay on the patch furthest from the door [cf X1.1, "Rose"], with the Scanner showing a completed analysis by having three of the indented circular sigils coinciding and seeming to lock together, with a chime, to indicate "analysis complete". Near this, apparently, is a store cupboard with spares with which he can construct a gadget to find the hidden Isolus Pod and a number of exotic tools Rose holds for him [in a scene resembling both the end of "The Hand of Fear" and the scene with Rodan building the D-Mat gun in 15.6, "The Invasion of Time"].

More intriguingly, the Isolus has the ability to "store" the TARDIS as a drawing. [Presumably, it can't know how much there is inside, so it must be the exterior "interface" with the universe (identified in 70s stories as the 'outer plasmic shell') that is being hidden (see 20.5, "Enlightenment"). This is in keeping with the impression we have from stories such as "Logopolis" (18.7), "Time-Flight" (19.7) and "The Masque of Mandragora" (14.1). However, the majority of the BBC Wales

Was Series Two Supposed to be Like This?

continued from Page 407...

Time for our first educated guess. Why does the Face of Boe haul the Doctor across space and time in "New Earth", and then not bother to make the big revelation he's got in store? It might be that the Series Three finale was originally part of Series Two. Well, some of it. The Toclafane are beings from a paradox - they arrive in their own past to wipe out their ancestors. If the Daleks hadn't been allowed to be in the new series, these new aliens are what would have been at war with the Time Lords (see X1.6, "Dalek"). Paradoxical ancient enemies and a parallel universe would seem like a natural fit. This also suggests that the Face of Boe might have known a thing or two about it. He comes from the Silver Devastation. Professor Yana was also from this neck of the woods, and if the first BBC Books *Doctor Who Annual* is to be believed, the phrase "You are not alone" was carved on a cliff-face at the (suspiciously Welsh-sounding) Crafe Tec Heydra, beneath hieroglyphs depicting the Time War. The precise connection between Boe and Yana is never explained, and the suggestion that Boe knows because he remembers this from when he was Captain Jack is troublesome (see X3.11, "Utopia", et seq). We can fairly conclusively rule out John Barrowman returning before Series Three - he was just too busy. Davies admits that the detail of Jack being called "The Face of Boe" was a last-minute improvisation when writing "Last of the Time Lords" (X3.13). Earlier plans would seem to have had a stronger link between these two strands.

The Cybermen were always going to have been the big returning enemy for Series Two, so it is unlikely that the Master would have been back as well. He would have been very unlikely to have sided with the antagonists in the Time War, whichever antagonists those turned out to have been. Even as broadcast as the climax of Series Three, the precise link between the Toclafane and the Master's plan to build a new Gallifrey on Earth is hazy. (It's a plan by the Master, do you really expect it to stand up to scrutiny?) Boe's revelation might have been something different, but his involvement in the "body-swap" episode was a given, which is interesting. Although we now know that the Face of Boe was popular with viewers and the two references back to him (billions of years before his actual appearance) made him seem potentially significant, there was no way that Davies could have known in advance that a non-speaking prop from "The End of the World" (X1.2) would catch on in this way. It might have made more sense to feature the Moxx of Balhoon, whom the Doctor had (apparently) already met and who was the focus of the pre-publicity for the forthcoming series. Boe's Last Message might well have formed to conclusion to the body-swap story, and his self-sacrifice could have provided a solution to the ethical problem of the "zombies". If he died helping the creation of a new version of humanity, it might have made a cleaner ending to the story than the Doctor's pseudo-laying on hands and then getting teased with the "textbook enigmatic" disappearance of Boe without any cryptic message being delivered as promised.

If we are right in assuming that, in the broadcast stories, the branching-off point of the parallel world was the assassination/infection of Queen Victoria, the fact that this story isn't there in the first proposal might also be significant. By the time the proposal document we have was written down, the Daleks had been brought back successfully. This was, as we've seen, touch-and-go for a while, and the contingency plan - or at least the need for flexibility - may have affected the plotting of the second series. There is no immediately comprehensible link between the Void Ship, the parallel universe and the Daleks, where there could easily have been one between these phenomena and the Toclafane. With them gone, there is a need for a new story to open up the storyline. Some version of the Queen Victoria story had been kicked around, possibly set in Buckingham Palace and according to some sources involving an insect getting in her eye and controlling her thoughts. (The optical theme might well have included the Koh-i-Nor and telescope as per the broadcast story - see **Are Writers Just Hired Guns These Days?** under X2.5, "Rise of the Cybermen".) Both the Toclafane and the Cybermen are humans augmented beyond any neurotic Victorian system of self-improvement - but clearly a development of the same Gradgrindish mentality. Following this line of reasoning leads us to "The Next Doctor" (X4.14), so we will hastily change the subject.

continued on Page 411...

X2.11 Fear Her

episodes assume that the Console Room is actually inside the blue box rather than the latter being a conduit to another dimension where the former resides.]

The Supporting Cast
• *Rose* is entirely nonplussed by the revelation that the Doctor, a 900-year-old man whose past is apparently full of former travelling companions he never mentions and one-night-stands with Cleopatra and Madame de Pompadour, might have been a father. [Blimey, she's thick!] She seems not to need telling when one of his gizmos will need chewing gum to stick it together, and enjoys playing up to the persona of a TV detective. The Doctor's homily about the main thing needed for space travel being a hand to hold strikes a chord with her: she worries when he doesn't return to the Close, and is smugly confident that they will always stick together.

On the basis of cousins she has never mentioned before, she has developed a low opinion of children. She deduces the location of the Isolus Pod, and seems to enjoy both swinging a pick-axe and irritating a council jobsworth.

• *UNIT/Torchwood*. Not a sausage. [Odd, given that the circumstances are exactly the sort of thing you would expect any alien-hunting agency to investigate as a matter of course. It's as if Torchwood doesn't exist by 2012, or has undergone a severe reduction in staff...]

The Non-Humans
• *The Isolus*. Despite the name, it's from a gregarious species. Millions are spawned by the matriarch and are bound together by an empathic link. They spend millennia riding solar tides, entertaining each other with the things they create with their gift for manipulating ionic energy. Once the Matriarch discards them, they feed on one another's love. About four billion of them flock together. Each travels in a pod the size of a bar of soap and approximate shape of a cardamom seed (the Doctor compares it to a gull's egg). The Matriarch, to judge from the drawing Chloe makes while explaining this, resembles a vast lily. The child that communes with Chloe looks like a cross between a crocus and a jellyfish, and floats away at the end.

History
• *Dating*. Another easy one: it's Friday, 27th July, 2012. The helicopter shots of the opening ceremony show Canary Wharf looking much as it did in 2006 [see next story for why this is impressive] and a London skyline lacking the Shard tower on the South Bank. There is now a collective 'East London Council' [rather than London Borough of Newham as Stratford has at the moment, or the neighbouring boroughs of Waltham Forest, Redbridge, Hackney or Tower Hamlets].

Nobody else in the Milky Way makes edible ball bearings, the Doctor claims.

Catchphrase Counter The Doctor is too busy using everyone else's.

Deus Ex Machina Everyone else is returned not only to wherever they were when they were softly and suddenly vanished away, but what they were doing then. The Doctor, by contrast, is magically made to reappear half a mile away right next to the Olympic Flame and beyond the grasp of the undoubtedly diligent security detail. [Be fair, they've had a trying day.]

The Analysis

The Big Picture We'll start with the bleedin' obvious: just after Eccleston's departure, the International Olympic Committee surprised everyone (especially Londoners) by picking London to host the 2012 Olympics instead of the widely-fancied favourite Paris. Once joy at beating the French at something kicked in, the idea that we were going to spend something like ten billion pounds on an event lasting less than a month was a bit of a shock. The following morning (7th July, 2005), four bombs went off in London, killing 53 people and making any questioning of the Olympics seem bad taste. In amongst the pledges of jobs and investment in an unfashionable bit of London (whether the locals wanted that kind of "improvement" or not) was the drip-fed message: children at school now would be the athletes representing us in seven years. As those same children were *Doctor Who*'s core demographic, it was an obvious and logical setting for a story. But why *this* kind of story?

In 2004, Sadler's Wells put on an opera based on the 1964 children's classic *Marianne Dreams* by Catherine Storr. This had already been adapted a

Was Series Two Supposed to be Like This?

continued from Page 409...

Episode six was a version of "The Runaway Bride" made before we knew what Torchwood was. It was scheduled to go in just before a story with a shaft to the core of a planet and something big, red and shouty lurking there from the Dawn of Time. That story is listed as "The Satan Pit", so this element of the story has to be assumed to be constant. Therefore, the whole Racnoss/Earth-formation element of what became the 2006 Christmas episode came later. The other odd feature of putting "The Runaway Bride" at number six is that it would be the fourth consecutive episode set in something like present-day London (even with the parallel world being more alien in the first drafts than as it appeared). Even the broadcast series having three markedly similar stories ("Fear Her", "Love & Monsters" and "The Idiot's Lantern") in rapid succession is less repetitive than that would have been. Once again, with nothing solid about the mysterious Torchwood any earlier than this, and nothing about its origins, we can play a hunch that we would have had the sort of background we get from Queen Victoria somewhere in that version of Donna's debut. Alternatively, it could have been at some point in the story set in the 1920s.

Many of the stories we got were planned logistically as well as aesthetically: the number of episodes set in something like present-day London was more to do with being able to afford armies of Cybermen than any Yeti-in-a-loo attempt at contemporary realism. Apart from one spaceship set in "The Girl in the Fireplace", there are two stories not set on Earth and one of these (the Jones two-parter) is self-consciously made to have a ventilator shaft, a quarry-like planet and recycled Slitheen costumes to keep costs down. Everything else was negotiable, so long as the ending with Rose and her curious nuclear family being stuck in the wrong universe was set-up and executed.

The great unknown is the precise detail of what Stephen Fry was going to have written. We know it was too expensive for that slot in the series. We know that he hinted it would involve an alien planet and the revelation that a well-known historical figure was of extraterrestrial origin. We know he had an idea of basing it on *Sir Gawain and the Green Knight*, an Arthurian tale that was partly a thinly veiled fertility rite and partly a meditation on mortality. We know he was unable to spare time to rewrite it for Martha. We know that he then sent an email saying "I can't do this", and then remained silent until he denounced the series as unworthy of any grown-up's time (unlike the terribly mature *QI*). Some have suggested that an alternative eleventh episode other than the notional Series Three story by Matthew Graham (the one that became "Fear Her") was touted, something about an alien force that absorbed colour. This sounds like Graham's first thought for a story. (Or one distorted by a Chinese Whispers process of rumourmongering. It could also have been Fry's story. It may even be a mis-remembered episode of *The Powerpuff Girls*.) It is also remotely possible that Fry's 1920s setting might have been a 1930s one, matching his recent directorial debut *Bright Young Things* (see X4.7, "The Unicorn and the Wasp"); Davies asked script-editor Helen Raynor to work up a 30s New York story, apparently at short notice. This became the two-part story "Daleks in Manhattan"/"Evolution of the Daleks" (X3.4-3.5). Assuming for a moment that a version of this without Daleks in was the Fry story, the positioning of this just before the two-part climax of Series Two might be significant. Then again, as with the broadcast run of episodes, it might merely be an effort at contrasting the present-day, big-budget epic season finale.

There's a lot of fun to be had speculating on which 1920s/30s celebrity would have been an alien in Fry's story (if this wasn't just mischief from a writer not overly fond of the press). The number of other possibilities make this an endless task unless you play the man, not the ball: Fry is a sufficiently knowable public figure for this to be worth a try. HG Wells might have been a good prospect - admittedly someone purporting to be him was in "Timelash" (22.5), but then, Shakespeare had been seen in "The Chase" (2.8) and mentioned several times since, and this didn't prevent "The Shakespeare Code" (X3.2). Virginia Woolf would have been a characteristic Fry choice, but tempting fate for reviewers to make the obvious "Bad Woolf" jibe (as everyone would have been gunning for him). It seems unlikely that Davies would have allowed Noel Coward to have been the clos-

continued on Page 413...

X2.11 Fear Her

few times, as a television play and the film *Paperhouse* (with a screenplay by Matthew Jacobs, who wrote the 1996 *Doctor Who* TV Movie). A girl who's confined to bed with Glandular Fever draws a house, then visits it (in her dreams, probably). She draws a boy in the window, and befriends him. But he appears to be real and thinks he drew her. Creepiness ensues. It's tempting to draw a straight line from this to "Fear Her", but Graham's first thought was about something leaching colour and beauty from the world. Davies rejected this idea, but what thought-process links that idea to the Olympics? A quick look at Graham's most famous work provides a possible answer: the appeal of *Life on Mars* and its continuation *Ashes to Ashes* is partly the we-had-one-of-those things we mentioned when discussing "The Idiot's Lantern" (X2.7), but also a constant dialogue between a colourful and straightforward era where police behaved in ways we couldn't countenance now and a bureaucratised, market-led present.

Dropping a dirty great stadium complex into the East End's last remaining un-gentrified area wasn't a universally popular move, especially with all the talk of the "legacy" for residents being about shopping and property-values. Graham, Ashley Pharoah and Tony Jordon, creators of these series, had 70s Euston Films programmes (notably *The Sweeney*) as their benchmark. These were set in London, and used the wastelands of the derelict docks (converted into the *faux* Manhattan of Canary Wharf and its ilk - X2.12, "Army of Ghosts") and railway sidings as their locale. The ur-text for *Ashes to Ashes* was the elegaic 1980 film *The Long Good Friday* about an old-school East End gangster (Bob Hoskins) failing to adjust to modern conditions and being killed by an IRA hoodlum (a promising youngster called Pierce Brosnan). Resistance to change is one of the key plot-motors of *Ashes to Ashes*, both with the unregenerate sexist DCI Gene Hunt getting all the best lines, but the various protest movements and rearguard actions that either cause the crimes or impede the investigations. It doesn't take Percy Bysshe Shelley to equate the loss of an unusual or defiantly out-of-synch lifestyle with the removal of colour from the world. The first series of *Life on Mars* had been trailed for the first time in the brief gap between the must-watch *EastEnders* Christmas episode and the must-watch *Doctor Who* Christmas special and emphasised the time-travel element. It had been made in Cardiff just after *Doctor Who* had ended its first production run, and, in case you were wondering, John Simm's present-day cop stuck in the Glam era - Sam Tyler - was named after Graham's son Sam and Rose Tyler. Davies famously asked Graham to write a story that would scare his little boy.

Objects moving by themselves are among the hoariest clichés of child-scaring, along with things changing when you aren't moving, noises in the cupboard and being made to un-exist. This last is fuelled by a constant stream of scare stories about strangers taking children. The press have whipped up a paranoia among parents, even though the overwhelming majority of child-harm and child murder cases are the result of people known to the family (and more often than not close relatives). Tabloids have always been able to sell papers and make their readers feel righteous by launching crusades; prior to the World Trade Centre attacks, the most popular bogeymen in the nation were paedophiles, who were alleged to hover on every street-corner. The Murdoch-owed *News of the World* generated the kind of mobs usually seen in the last reel of a *Frankenstein* movie, attacking anyone they thought was one of these (including a paediatrician - same first four letters, and it never occurred to anyone why someone would advertise an illegal perversion on a plaque outside their surgery). It is a staple of slow news days to rhetorically ask why today's children are so unhealthy, intimidated and cossetted, and to fear that parents are too risk-averse for the children to have "real" childhoods. Never mind that the supposedly cosy early 60s was the time in which the most prolific child-killers were active in the North of England (and the scary mug-shot of Moors Murderer Myra Hindley was routinely used to connote "evil"), parents seemed to believe that children were at more risk now than in their own childhoods. So parents were afraid, people who observed mob mentality and scapegoating were afraid. In the fingers-on-lips scene, Graham manages to exploit both sets of fears. The most high-profile recent child-murder case was in a small town called Soham, where someone with a prior conviction had been hired as a school caretaker. The inquest into this, as with the search for first bodies then the culprit, dominated headlines for months. Legislation to prevent a recurrence caused havoc in every organisation employing adults near children. That kept the wider con-

Was Series Two Supposed to be Like This?

continued from Page 411...

et BEM - BBC Books had published *Mad Dogs and Englishmen* by Paul Magrs, shortly thereafter put in charge of the prestigious Creative Writing programme at University of East Anglia, and this had featured Coward. Hitler being an alien is altogether too *Tomorrow People*, but Fry has written an alternate history novel, *Making History*, in which Hitler's father was infertile and a different Führer arose and was more successful. Some people have taken this to be a clue. The Gawain theme makes scholar/ writers such as TS Eliot, CS Lewis or JRR Tolkien possible, as they have all used this mythos in their work. Following the (admittedly shaky) line of reasoning in the previous paragraph, it may not have been based in Britain at all, but in Jazz-age New York. (Louis Armstrong? PG Wodehouse? F Scott Fitzgerald?) Fry still claimed, six months before his public dissing of "infantile" TV drama, to have a notion to finish the script, so he is still reticent on details. (This comfortably rules out Churchill.)

What we can say is that Davies never tried to move the story to an earlier production slot with more money; with the demands on Fry's time, this is probably a practical matter, but it could also be that the content of this story was meant to lead into the climactic two-parter more directly than "Fear Her" does. However, the prestige Fry brought, and might still bring, means that Davies might not have been able - even if he had wanted - to rewrite any of Fry's script to dovetail with any other story. It is thus more likely that this would have been effectively a self-contained script that could, had it been ready, have been recorded and broadcast at any point in the series - given the resources.

This last point is where a lot of other commentators have speculated about what would have been so costly (prosthetics, CGI space-battles and a big cast have all been mentioned), but none of these people has any more information that we have been using and the biggest expense is surely the period setting. At this stage in the production cycle, even a present-day London setting with a small cast and minimal effects was going to be touch-and-go. The eventual tenth episode ("Love & Monsters") had hardly any digital effects (and most of those were recycled from earlier episodes) and was given to a first-time *Who* director, Dan Zeff, who never returned to the series. The eleventh, also very light on special effects or vintage costumes, was given to the rising star of the series, Euros Lyn, to do back-to-back with "The Idiot's Lantern". Again, that story has scarcely any set-piece effects, but is diligently kept within a twentieth-century period that can, by virtue of being a period of austerity and a very ordinary street, be recreated relatively cheaply. The position in a series for a costume-drama with aliens is partially determined by the ratio of each: something relatively straightforward and off-the-peg, such as "The Unicorn and the Wasp" (X4.7), can be done later in the financial year than something with two periods colliding, for example "The Girl in the Fireplace" or "Victory of the Daleks" (X5.3). Putting any kind of period setting that wasn't essentially a street in Cardiff lightly retouched into this late slot in the series would make it prohibitively expensive to do anything else after. A period story with humans behaving oddly under alien influence would be as much as they could have afforded, and this simply isn't Fry's *metier*.

Until people start talking more openly about these matters, we are in danger of making bricks without straw if we carry on like this. It is obvious from the above that the relatively late insertion of "Tooth and Claw" was primarily a means to introduce both the parallel universe sub-plot and Torchwood, utilising a leftover idea about Queen Victoria being infected. Setting it in Scotland - possibly just an excuse for Tennant to drop the mockney accent for a bit - came as a result of the need to explain the name of the Institute. The entire story is an exercise in housekeeping to retain the shape of a series planned, it would seem, to fit together differently but in roughly the same sequence.

cerns a live political issue long after the eventual convictions.

A related matter was the regular occurrence, in the press and in drama, of the long-term damage caused by child abuse. If the nineteenth-century cult of Childhood as a semi-angelic state of grace had more-or-less evaporated, the idea that childhood could be damaged and that causing or allowing this was a worse crime than murder persisted in the media. However resilient real children often prove to be, the political rhetoric is grounded in Romanticism and the sanctity of an uncommercialised, unsexualised and easily tainted childhood. Anyone who knows any children realises it is more complex than that, and anyone who observes what governments and media actually do rather than say realises that children are a key market as much as they are an all-purpose justification for adults to be made to spend money. The idea that a child might not be saintly is still treated as if it's going to be shocking. Once again, the tabloid version is that any child who commits a crime must either be under a bad influence (in the 50s it was American comics, in the 60s and 70s television, in the 80s "video nasties", the 90s the Internet, now it's games consoles) or just afflicted by some unfocused force called "evil". (See 22.2, "Vengeance on Varos", **Did Sergeant Pepper Know the Doctor?** under 5.1, "Tomb of the Cybermen" and **Is the New Series More Xenophobic?** under X1.3, "The Unquiet Dead".) In 1993, a small boy called James Bulger was killed by two other underage boys, and the efforts to find a "cause" led to an attempt to blame the horror-comedy *Child's Play 3*. In "Fear Her", the entire story is concerned with finding reasons why Chloe Webber is doing such horrible things and it is all because the poor mite is lonely, which in turn is because her dad did something they can't discuss on a children's programme.

Which brings us back to *Paperhouse*. If you failed to see anything familiar in "The Brain of Morbius" (13.5), then it's possible you could watch *Paperhouse* and "Fear Her" back to back and not think "rip-off", just as you could have watched every episode of the BBC's story-telling show *Jackanory* from the 1970s and still theoretically have found *Harry Potter* original. *Marianne Dreams* is obviously a product of the late 50s, but in updating it to remove the governess and shillings, Matthew Jacobs introduced an entire Freddie Krueger-style subplot with a badly-drawn version of the girl's father who assaults the house and has to be destroyed by burning that bit of the drawing. This element is where the film ceases to be about the same topics as the book, but follows the usual Hollywood formula of a character "learning" and "growing" and getting "closure". Apparently, to be commercial, the film had to be about the child's maturation and relationship with her father (to the extent that - to nobody's surprise who remembers Jacobs' version of *Doctor Who* - eleven-year-olds start snogging just because it's reached that part of the story where the leads kiss). Graham reins in some of the film's slasher-movie urges, but still takes it as read that there has to be an unresolved "issue" with the child's father simply because that's how these stories are reckoned to work. (Indeed, looking at the film now, it's also noticeable how Anna, the film's version of Marianne, treats the boy Mark as if she has dreamt him, much as Alex behaves in the early episodes of *Ashes to Ashes* and the end of that storyline is about betrayal and an emotionally distant father.) The link between Chloe's father and the capturing of people onto paper is mainly that these elements were both in the film, but connected in ways that making it a *Doctor Who* story couldn't manage.

We'll just mention in passing that *Life on Mars* had someone purporting to be the girl from Test Card F (the classic BBC/ITV alignment-checker, shown for most of the afternoon in the 70s with light music and featuring Carol Hersee, aged eight in 1966, apparently losing a game of noughts and crosses to a stuffed toy) as the Grim Reaper.

English Lessons *Lewis* was the sidekick of the glum detective in *Inspector Morse*, the two-hour-long adaptations of the pompous detective books by Colin Dexter, another in the long line of people who fled Corby, Northants. In the fullness of time, Sgt Lewis got his own show (not based on novels), and his sidekick was played by Billie Piper's future husband, Lawrence Fox.

Oh, Isn't That...?

• *Huw Edwards*. BBC Television's senior newsreader, and thus one of the most prominent Welshmen in broadcasting. Life imitated art as Edwards was given Prince William's wedding (in place of the more usual David Dimbleby) and actually *did* the commentary for the 2012 Olympic opening ceremony. At the time of broadcast, however, this was one of the many instances of a real journalist being given slightly the wrong job in case any viewer mistook *Doctor Who* for a newsflash. (See **Why is Trinity Wells on Jackie's Telly?** under X1.4, "Aliens of London".)

• *Edna Doré* (Maeve). It's possible that there is some obscure by-law in the Equity handbook stating that if she is not given a role in something, the union can close the production down. She has recently been in *Gavin and Stacey* and *Shameless*, playing - well, there's a turn-up - old ladies who appear to be going senile (presumably the move into comedy-dramas is because Liz Smith retired, and all her old roles are up for grabs).

• *Nina Sosanya* (Chloe's mother, Trish). A lot of you will have tracked down Davies' *Casanova* and seen her as a woman posing as a castrato singer - inevitably landing up in bed with the eponymous lothario. She'd also been in spoof documentary series *People Like Us,* again opposite David Tennant, and worked with Piper in *Much Ado About Nothing*. There had also been a stint in Channel 4 comedy *Teachers*. Around the time this episode was shown, you may just have seen her as the only relatively likeable character in *Nathan Barley* and - odd coincidence alert! - she was most recently in the spoof documentary *2012*, about the Olympic build up (narrated by Tennant).

Things That Don't Make Sense We'll start with what's obvious for any British viewer: the Doctor finds it remarkably easy to snatch the Olympic Torch as it is being carried through East London. The security arrangements would mean that, even if everyone is a bit dazed after spending ten minutes as a drawing, the slightest interruption would result in an alert around Britain and, in all likelihood, the Doctor being picked off by a sniper. Let's not forget, the nearby blocks of flats had surface-to-air missiles on the rooves. Quite apart from the Queen, Ban Qui Moon and JK Rowling, there were several thousand people from across the world and a similar number of local performers. The global TV audience was close on a billion. We refer the reader to the absurd security overkill for the 2008 relay and the pro-Tibetan protesters with fire-extinguishers.

However, Huw Edwards, senior newsreader and experienced broadcaster, not only doesn't recognise the Doctor as one of the three 'Most Wanted' people implicated with the assassination of US President Winters a couple of years earlier (X3.12, "The Sound of Drums"), but is kept on air babbling when the stadium is emptied, rather than the newsroom cutting in with information from the rest of the massive coverage this event would be allocated. In the real event, there were cameras covering all the stages of the Torch approach, on the Thames, on streets nearby and in helicopters. As the whole torch thing was invented by Goebbels for the 1936 Berlin Games, you'd expect the Doctor to be a bit contemptuous of this event. More cogently, the story assumes that the Torch being carried is the sum total of an Olympic opening ceremony: even before Beijing, we knew that Sydney had put everything they had into the 2000 opening shindig and got huge tourist payback from it. London's was much bigger and planned well in advance.

Just at a basic level, anyone anywhere near the Stadium had their bags checked, not just for weapons but for anything potentially promoting companies other than the Olympic sponsors - people with cans of Pepsi were escorted from the premises by the Coke Police. That's the level of security attention past which the Doctor and Rose have idly slipped. And besides, the bit of the relay leading up to the Stadium was done on the river, not through the streets of Stratford. (There was a day of pre-Games torchbearing in Stratford the Saturday afternoon before the opening ceremony, towards the end of a two month peregrination during which Matt Smith bore it through Cardiff.) This isn't just hindsight: the announcement that London was to get the Games came the day before an Al Qaida assault on the city, during which we all got used to security-forces paranoia unseen since the IRA bombings were at their height.

This raises a bigger problem with the story's theme of keeping things hidden. With the Games being held in London, the aforementioned hoopla was magnified by a factor of 20. There would have been a news crew in Dame Kelly Holmes Place for weeks beforehand (just for the BBC coverage, let alone ITN and Sky, and the press), so the disappearances would have been covered in detail. One missing child can get a media feeding-frenzy going - look at the way Madeleine McCann's abduction became a freakshow for a whole summer. It might just have been plausible for half a dozen children to go missing with no reporters being even slightly interested if the Olympics had distracted the media, but as the Games are happening at the bottom of that street and are still getting about as much coverage as a school fete, even this is untenable.

The Government made provision for 2,500

X2.11 Fear Her

extra officers to take over a vast tract of common-land a few miles away and put a ten-foot fence around it: the Home Office tried to stop anything ruining London's big moment on the world stage (other than themselves), so any mass abductions of children would have a security black-out and the area would have been saturated with plain-clothes officers - the street would simply have been emptied for the 90 days of the Games and Paralympics. East London became like East Berlin as it was, so if something as potentially damaging as this happened, there would have been even more patrols by real police and G4S hired goons. The Doctor would spend the entire episode in a cell somewhere very far from London. More troops were deployed to augment the police than were in Iraq. Private security firms kept people off the building-sites, even former residents objecting to having their homes bulldozed, so it's hard to see how a new street would have been built that close to the Olympic Village anyway. (Yes, they said the Games would be the start of a major programme of urban regeneration, but none of the plans put forward at the time included streets that close to the Village, and even the bits that had social housing somewhere in the mix have been quietly dropped.)

On to more basic matters... the strong metallic smell accompanying every disappearance seems not to have been noticed by anyone else, although even a cat being vanished causes an overpowering aroma. Full marks to the crew, especially Graham and Davies, for devising a reason why late July looks so much like January (see **The Lore** for scripted comments about why breath is misting), but the heat-absorbing effect of the Isolus ship is a little wonky. Everyone who's come to cheer on the Torch is dressed for summer, so it must still be warm a couple of streets away (unless they're all Geordies - non-British readers will just have to accept that there are people who wear T-shirts in the snow to assert regional identity in the face of reason). But the cloud-cover and the footage of the Stadium indicate that the whole of London, possibly all of southern England, is in the depths of winter too. (It might seem churlish to mention this, but Edna Doré's breath mists after the spaceship has left, the Doctor's at the street-party too.) Let's hope everyone practicing for the (open air) Beach Volleyball starting next morning wrapped up warmly. If the rest of London is so much warmer than this one street, there would be a strong wind at all times (just as an aside, now we know what the Olympic Stadium and surrounding area is going to look like - and we've all seen the 'Pringle', as the Velodrome's become known - cut 'n' paste shots of the Millennium Stadium in Cardiff and the Manchester Commonwealth Games stadium simply won't cut it. We'll let them off for not knowing about the Shard - X7.7, "The Bells of Saint John".)

One of the odd features of the choice of venue for the Olympics is that the site is precisely where the fictitious Walford in *EastEnders* is supposed to be ('Walford' = Stratford+Walthamstow). Indeed, the Stadium is on a formerly derelict patch popularly supposed to be the real-life analogue of Albert Square (which is also where the circus was pitched during the filming of 8.1, "Terror of the Autons"). Maeve must have got utterly sick of people thinking she was Mo Butcher.

But our biggest concern is the lack of any real connection between two separate baffling phenomena that are presented to us as cause and effect. Chloe can make people go from the outside world to her land of drawings. With gritted teeth we'll accept that, especially as a similar scenario cropped up in *The Sarah Jane Adventures* with the Mona Lisa trapping policemen and Sarah in paintings (*SJA* 3.5, "Mona Lisa's Revenge"). Chloe's dad gave her a hard time and that caused her to imagine something bad in the cupboard. Again, a creepy idea better suited to *Sapphire and Steel*, but we'll go with it. Freeing all the people from being drawn somehow turns her conceptual bogey-man into a real entity. Regardless of whether it is dramatically justified, this doesn't follow from anything we've seen before. Maybe this could have happened via the Isolus, but that's now gone. The only way this works is if Chloe trapped her abusive father in a picture she drew in the cupboard and that somehow, during his confinement, he turned into a fire-breathing ogre. (One possible get-out is that the Isolus gave her the ability to realise anything she drew, such as the Scribble-Creature, but freeing the real children - and cat, and Time Lord - that had been imprisoned on paper also frees this entity in the wardrobe. If it is a manifestation of her anxiety about her father's abrupt disappearance then why is it even there, given that the Isolus homed in on Chloe simply because she was lonely too? A being that feeds on love would hardly make its 'host' more isolated.) Moreover, as all the children - and the cat -

returned to wherever they were when they were snatched, wouldn't the ogre upstairs have returned to inside Chloe's head? (Yes, the Doctor managed to translocate to where he was most needed, but any manifestation of anxiety worth its salt would have been more subtle about its intentions and waited until Mum wasn't around.)

Critique Oh dear!

Critique (Second Attempt After a Long Sit Down)
As with "The Impossible Planet" / "The Satan Pit" (X2.8-2.9), and the one before that, the episode seems to be a compendium of images from other places linked by a spurious rationale, but with the rhythm and causation all out of synch. The Matt Jones two-parter at least had pace on its side; it was full of sound and fury (we can take the rest of that line as read), so on a first viewing it was superficially more attractive. It was a pastiche of old *Doctor Who* as much as anything else. The Gatiss story had some affection working for it, with the pictures and the story moving in roughly the same direction. This has no such advantages.

Nothing Euros Lyn directs is a complete dead loss, but he's not really given much to work with, and so the result is flat. Maybe that was a deliberate policy to make this different from the next story he directed, "The Idiot's Lantern" (X2.7), but it's not a positive move. There's no real relish in any of the performances other than Abisola Agbaje as Chloe, and Tennant and Piper when in a scene with her. Such fatigue could have been surmounted, maybe turned into a moody atmosphere of menace, if the script had made any sense or any real feeling of, well, fear. Then when the climax comes, it gets unbearably cheesy. Anyone with any complaints about Peter Kay as a space-monster should have marched on BBC Wales with pitchforks and burning torches when Huw Edwards started bibbling about the Olympic Dream. And then Tennant lights the Olympic Flame. It's a miracle anyone watched the following episode.

This story is a victim of the mind-set that all children are interchangeable and they all have the same fears, fears which can be tapped ("exploited" might be a better word) in lieu of a new idea. Nobody who knows children thinks that they will all react like Pavlov's dogs at exactly the same stimulus (something under the bed, a shadow on the ceiling, a crack in the wall, a noise in the wardrobe, polishing a floor and putting a rug on

it...[84]). This is also a situation where the Law of Diminishing Returns applies, and so if every single episode is about things from an approved list of "Oooh... Scary" stuff, everyone gets bored (or forbidden to watch). "Scary" is a side effect of adequate-or-better storytelling, not an end in itself. If they do things simply to go "boo!", they lose their young audience. Anecdotally, this seems to have happened, and only the teaser of a Dalek-Cyberman shootout next week restored school playground cred to the series. Very young children were confused by the ending; slightly older ones just yawned.

Being in amongst a lot of near-identical Yeti-in-the-loo episodes doesn't do this any favours, but even seen in isolation, it's an unremarkable episode. Its only real talking points are mistakes. This makes any attempt to review it fairly difficult, because it just becomes a list of wrong things, and most of it is competent but bland. There's a vast problem with the grinding change of gears from *Sapphire and Steel* domestic fantasy (not really what *Doctor Who* is good at, but never mind) and the attempt at scale with the whole world being under threat, the red scary dad-monster and the Olympics being stolen. That's a different kind of story, and it used to be possible to go from one to another when there were cliffhangers and 25-minute episodes with a week between them, but all in one episode and that episode *still* seeming stretched is a sign of a big problem.

Just to get ahead of ourselves, it's a problem we've identified in the first paragraph and one writer Matthew Graham remedied. For all its faults, the two-parter he wrote for Series Six was one that began with a premise and developed the consequences and scary moments *from* it, rather than starting with other people's nifty pictures and stringing them together. Internal logic wasn't the problem there, it was strained father-child relations being used as a blunt instrument to make casual viewers "care more" about a situation that was already intense, but not in a soap-opera way. That's a problem here too. It shows a lack of faith in the viewers and their ability to get involved in a situation that isn't like every other drama on television.

That's where this story really falls flat. It lacks self-confidence, and so they over-egg it with that whole extraneous end sequence with the Olympics and the dad-monster. At the end of the second year of episodes, there's no real reason to be playing quite so safe. Over the whole year, we've had

X2.11 Fear Her

baby-steps: a nice safe alien planet just like Earth; a cosy parallel universe with tried-and-true monsters; a base-camp on a world made from old films; the all-purpose disembodied alien with the gimmick of retro television... only Davies himself, in a crisis, dares risk anything like combining Queen Victoria with a werewolf or doing a story about a Doctor-spotter's video-diary. No wonder everyone came away thinking of Steven Moffat as an innovator.

There's little here to engage with. Reviewing this story is like knitting with fog.

The Facts

Written by Matthew Graham. Directed by Euros Lyn. Viewing figures: (BBC1) 7.14 million, (BBC3 repeats) 0.5 and 0.2 million. AI was 83%.

Repeats and overseas promotion Londres 2012, Furchte Sie!

TARDISode A very energetic, very Welsh investigative reporter is covering the slew of disappearing children in Dame Kelly Holmes Place, with days to go before the Olympic opening ceremony. The series was supposedly called "CrimeCrackers", which had been the name of a real BBC series. There was a non-existent phone number to call. The clip ended with a glowing red light from a wardrobe. (NB, neither of the kids mentioned in this clip are in the list of children who have vanished in the episode.)

Production

One of the other series being made in Cardiff for wider distribution during the making of *Doctor Who*'s first Welsh year was *Life on Mars*, an ironic critique/affectionate pastiche of 70s British thick-ear cop-shows (see Volume 4 for *Target, The Sweeney* and all points west). With its non-realist moments and time-travel theme, *Life on Mars* seemed a good fit for *Doctor Who*, and lead writer Matthew Graham was asked if he had any ideas. Julie Gardner had been responsible for *Life on Mars* as well, and thought that Graham would have been a good candidate for Series One of *Doctor Who* had he been free. His previous SF-adjacent credits included an ITV series called *The Last Train* (although this had rapidly become a standing joke amongst Cult TV fans, and had indeed been ridiculed by cast-members on other shows even whilst it was being broadcast).

As with most of the writers Davies was now recruiting, Graham had done a bit of everything: soaps, cop-shows and what have you. He was sounded out for a possible Series Three slot, but most of his original notions were either too abstract or potentially costly, or both. His front-runner, an idea about a beauty-vampire sucking all the colour and joy from a world, was, apparently, too much like Science Fiction for Davies. (Although, oddly in this regard, Graham was later to say that the scenario Steven Moffat wanted from him in Series Six was more Science Fictional than he was used to writing, so perhaps that anecdote has been embroidered over the years.) Eventually, over dinner with Davies and Gardner, he was persuaded to focus on what his young son would find scary. Graham was told to get on with a script, make it low budget in case they had to bring it forward to the end of Series Two and, after the feedback from "The Empty Child" (X1.9), put a scarily powerful kid at the core.

Rather than write a story in a bunker or entirely aboard the TARDIS, Graham opted for *Doctor Who* in Brookside Close, a close analogue for the "ordinary" newly built street in the lurid Channel 4 soap. Thus a Yeti-in-the-loo present-day story about an ordinary street and a powerful entity stealing children was yoked to the newly-topical idea of a story with the forthcoming Olympics as a backdrop. Davies was most enthusiastic about the idea of the Doctor picking up the Olympic Torch, and relieved at how little CGI work would be needed. Worried that his story was halfway through and nothing scary had been seen, Graham took Moffat's comments in interviews at face value and added a noise from inside a cupboard, thus launching the whole subplot about Chloe's abusive father. So a script was ready within a few weeks of the meetings, and held in reserve from mid-September 2005 to be activated when needed.

• As is now well-documented, Stephen Fry's mysterious 1920s adventure had been scheduled to go in this slot. As he giddily included alien planets and Jazz-age settings, the sad truth that this would be too expensive for a slot at the end of the 14-episode series became obvious. Graham's script was complete enough (and cheap enough) to be used almost as it was, and was added to the production schedule in Block Four, the second

Euros Lyn stint, alongside a rapidly advanced Mark Gatiss script, now called "The Idiot's Lantern" (see this story's essay). This was middle to late November, with the script still only in its fifth draft (by their standards, that's almost improvised). The tone was set as being "*Edward Scissorhands* meets *Desperate Housewives*", and the Summer 2012 period was guessed to be brightly coloured for costumes and décor. However, aware that it was going to be made in January, they added lines about the Isolus Pod soaking up all heat from the close. A number of trims were made to the Doctor and Rose investigating the streets and a few additions were made to refer to earlier episodes (the cat-nuns, the Shadow Proclamation and so on). As negotiations continued to get the rights to the Olympic insignia and a possible cameo by Dame Kelly Holmes (busily rehearsing for ITV's *Dancing on Ice* - see 23.4, "The Ultimate Foe"[85]), it was decided that the script's description of Chloe as a pale, wraith-like figure was potentially too much like Reinette ("The Girl in the Fireplace") and that it was possibly more unexpected to make her black and outwardly energetic rather than yet another emo kid. This allowed them to cast Nina Sosanya as her mother, whilst Andy Prior came up trumps with an unsigned child actor from Southwark's Magic Eye Theatre, Abisola Agbaje.

- Work began on this shoot on Tuesday, 24th January in Page Drive, the main location for Dame Kelly Holmes Close. On the previous day (while Lyn was in London recording Maureen Lipman's inserts for "The Idiot's Lantern"), the area had been carefully rendered semi-futuristic, with the Missing Child posters giving dates of birth concordant with their assumed ages in 2012, cars with not-yet-used T-registration number-plates and that poster for *Shayne Ward's Greatest Hits*. Ward had just won a TV talent show when the script was being written, and he was one of the current artists they thought it would be funny to see as established veterans (another was then-fresh band Franz Ferdinand, whose second album had just come out and who had claimed to enjoy the first series of *Doctor Who* in interviews). Unusually, the interiors for Chloe's house were mainly shot inside the house used as the exterior, with bright lights used for the daylight from outside after it was too dark to do outside location scenes. The script had suggested that plasma screens would be standard by 2012, so the living-room had one (on which stock footage of the London Marathon was played), but Chloe had a laptop capable of showing television feed, something still not quite possible when this was made and added to the script late on. The third day on this location was the one where the second unit managed to get the first of two different torchbearing runners to run, seen from various angles, and then arranged for one of them to do a stunt fall.

Meanwhile, the main unit were finding out why it's proverbially difficult to herd cats. Predictably, this was the day Graham and his kids and the *Doctor Who Confidential* crew were around to watch. More second unit material, with another runner, was shot on the estate on the Friday, whilst the main crew went to the Millennium Stadium to get the Doctor to run up the red carpeted stairs to the fake flambeau, and take some shots of an empty stadium and commentary booth (the Media Suite that had been Van Statten's office in X1.6, "Dalek"). Tennant had spent the morning learning to drive his scooter for "The Idiot's Lantern". (Piper had been released to go to London, during which time she received an award: "Breakthrough Artist of the Year", voted for by readers of *The Times*.) On the Monday of the following week, the unit's electrician, Clive Johnson, provided a menacing male shadow (the voice is that of sound editor Paul McFadden, but that was later). February 1st was the start of work in the set for the Webber house at Q2. This is where most of the scenes of Chloe's bedroom and the inserts of her drawing were made. One of the set-dressers (Joelle Rumbelow) had an 11-year-old daughter, Indigo, whose artwork was used as a reference by the series storyboard artist, Richard Shaun Williams, for the pictures on the walls. The overall theme of the room was of space and flight, with balloons and star-maps. An art student from Bristol, Tinate Bilal, provided the arm and hand that did the sped-up drawings. That and interviews for the pop-mags took up most of Friday, and on Saturday the stars went to another award ceremony in London whilst the scenes of Chloe and her mum were completed.

On the 6th, the unit was all over the place. Apart from Page Drive, there was a non-residential road where the TARDIS landed (decorated with that Shayne Ward poster) and some open ground nearby, converted into a dais for the flambeau. Only the two leads and Sosanya were needed for these scenes. This was the day when the TARDIS landed in the wrong alignment, then was stolen by Chloe, then the Doctor finally reached the top of the stairs he'd been running up ten days earlier and lit the Olympic Flame. That last was at the local Rugby club, which had been the unit's base of operations throughout the location work in Tremorfa. February 10th was the unit's day at Blenheim Road, mainly for the scenes at Mr Magpie's shop in "The Idiot's Lantern", but for a few shots of back-streets in this story - notably the close-up of the torch flaring as the Isolus pod was flung in. The rest of the shoot required three days at Q2, concurrent with finishing off "The Idiot's Lantern". These were mainly the TARDIS interiors, although they finally got the cat to go into the box on Wednesday 22nd.

- As the design and precise location of the Olympic Stadium had not been announced - or, indeed, worked out properly - the team cobbled something together (although they would probably prefer a technical-sounding term like "composited") from stock footage of the Manchester Commonwealth Games arena and the material shot at the Millennium Stadium. By now, the title had been released as "Fear Her", which caused a lot of online kerfuffle and a resurgence of the perennial rumours that the Rani (22.3, "The Mark of the Rani", et al) was due to return, or even the Terrible Zodin (20.7, "The Five Doctors"; 22.1, "Attack of the Cybermen"; and the TV Movie[86]). An earlier title had been "Chloe Webber Destroys the Earth", so we got off lightly. It would appear that most of the cuts were less for timing (the episode is noticeably short) than to avoid defusing any tension that the potentially silly scenario might need. Almost all of the Doctor's anecdotes about unseen adventures are gone, including a zero-gravity picnic with Rose that was marred by a boy vomiting in free-fall and a space-game the Doctor was rather good at. Similarly, a lot of the taunting of Maeve was cut because it was too repetitive and delayed the action. Huw Edwards, who had narrated a Welsh Tourist Board promotion about *Doctor Who*, recorded his commentary just after Easter. Life has imitated, well, television: American viewers, who had a severely edited and dumbed-down version of Danny Boyle's £27 million opening ceremony via NBC, will have missed the sheer number of things in the ceremony that previous *About Time* books have mentioned and may also be unaware that Huw Edwards was indeed one of the three commentators. And although several people carried the Torch in its final approach, one of them was a skinny guy with big sideburns - British Tour de France winner and eventual Olympic gold medallist Bradley Wiggins.

Papua New Guinea didn't surprise anyone in the shot-putt. They didn't even enter.

X2.12: "Army of Ghosts"

(1st July, 2006)

Which One is This? The Doctor and Rose play at Scooby Doo (again) and go to Canary Wharf. And then, in the last few minutes we get the one thing the makers of *Doctor Who* assured us would never happen. Well, one of the two things...

Firsts and Lasts It's Jackie's first trip in the TARDIS, after which the Doctor tries to figure out if she counts as a companion or not.

For the first time, Russell T Davies nicks the name of an earlier, moderately-well received movie as an episode title - in this case, Jean-Pierre Melville's 1969 French Resistance film *L'Armée des Ombres*. This has been re-issued as *Army of Shadows*, but the other translation was used in earlier releases and was more appropriate - did the distributors retitle it to avoid US teenagers accidentally watching a good film in another language? (See also X3.0, "The Runaway Bride"; X4.0, "Voyage of the Damned"; and arguably X4.10, "Midnight", none of which exactly match the titles in practice.) There is, as we'll see in **The Big Picture**, another possible source for the title, more directly connected to the story.

We see an all-black Dalek, although without a New Zealand accent. And when the Doctor goes on the offensive against "ghosts", we get the first use of what will be the theme-tune for *Torchwood* (although in an arrangement that sounds like a spooky doorbell with a Linn Drum under it). We also get to finally see the elusive Torchwood they've been teasing us about all since X1.12, "Bad Wolf".

And look who's playing one of the Torchwood staff members, Adeola - it's Freema Agyeman. We'll see her again. Sadly, we will also hear the Doctor's new catch-phrase, "Allons-Y", rather a lot.

Watch Out For...

- Remember that copy of *Lovely Bones* that Rose was reading when the Doctor first visited her (X1.1, "Rose")? Well now we get a hook exactly

Army of Ghosts X2.12

What Are the Most Over-Familiar Locations?

There is a big problem when filming in Cardiff - namely, that there really aren't that many exotic locations. There are a few bits that can pass for London, or a generic Anytown, but these start to get to look a bit familiar after the second or third time.

This would be less of a problem if there hadn't been two spin-off series and an increasing number of other programmes being made in Cardiff with similar needs. *Doctor Who*, *Torchwood*, *The Sarah Jane Adventures*, *Ashes to Ashes* and its precursor *Life on Mars*, and now *Casualty* and *Holby City* have pretty much hoovered up every tasty-looking setting. Add to this *Sherlock*, *Being Human* and *Merlin*, and it's getting ridiculous. A casual viewer might not spot these, but most of these series have some fairly intensive non-casual viewers, and *Doctor Who*, *Sherlock* and the *Life on Mars* saga expected viewers to look very carefully indeed at tiny details.

There was a time, up to the location shooting for *Casanova*, when they could get away with using Cardiff for everything. Now, it's getting to the point when some of the less-well-made, more ill-conceived adventure series can make a point of not being made in Cardiff (in the case of Matthew Graham's spectacularly stupid *Bonekickers* - see X2.11, "Fear Her"; X6.3, "The Curse of the Black Spot"; and **What Are the Daftest Knock-Off Shows?** under X4.10, "Midnight").

One of the things this notional casual viewer will have spotted about *Doctor Who* lately is how weird the spaceships look (e.g. X5.2, "The Beast Below"; X6.12, "Closing Time"). Factories don't look quite right either, and the absurdity of this wasn't helped by the characters commenting upon the worst example (X6.5, "The Rebel Flesh" et seq) in ways that made the story's entire premise seem just that little bit more absurd. The fact is, it's easier to find a castle in South Wales than a good-looking industrial complex that isn't working flat-out, because all the others have shut and been demolished. There used to be one special factory, the Paper Mill on Sanitorium Road, Canton. Under Russell T Davies, it was the one-stop venue for all your spaceship / evil lair / industrial hell-hole needs, but they demolished it around the same time Steven Moffat took over (this wasn't cause-and-effect, by the way). Any alien planets the TARDIS might occasion upon are usually beaches with odd things matted into the sky. Despite eye-wateringly huge budgets even in the Moffat years, *Doctor Who* is made on the basis that as much as is possible should be done in the field, not in studio-sets or digitally grafted on. It's the art of the possible, the practical and above all the cost-effective. This means return engagements not just for costly aliens, but for convenient places that can be redressed to look excitingly different each time. Or not.

Full marks to the crews who managed to get so much variety out of Tredegar House. It is completely unrecognisable in each of its appearances as the same location. Cassandra's lair in "New Earth" (X2.1), the library in "Tooth and Claw" (X2.2) and two different buildings in "The Christmas Invasion" (X2.0) are the same place. In all, it shows up in nine stories. Similarly, Headlands School manages to be two totally different Victorian houses, the second time actually avoiding anachronisms (X1.3, "The Unquiet Dead" and "Tooth and Claw" again) and a theatre in New York (X3.4, "Daleks in Manhattan"). However, it isn't always easy to avoid viewers recognising places just the same way they spot returning performers. The Paper Mill is, in a sense, the true heir to John Scott Martin or Terry Walsh (see Volumes 3b and 4).

There are many frequently used locations that are never quite the same twice, such as the various bits of Cardiff Royal Infirmary, St Mary Street, Cardiff, Margam County Park, Port Talbot and the Llanederyn Maelfa Shopping Centre. They've managed to make Llandaff look fresh each time too. But when something you're told is Leadworth, in Gloucestershire, looks like somewhere in Sarah Jane Smith's neighbourhood in Ealing, and a hallucination inside the CAL computer, and a park in Colchester, Essex, where the Doctor learns to play football, it's time to worry.

Or is it? Maybe it's time to play a little game.

For anyone raised on 60s film series such as *The Avengers* and the various ITC shows (*The Prisoner*, *Department S*, *The Champions* and the original *Randall & Hopkirk (Deceased)* and loads more), the locale around Elstree Studios in Hertfordshire was almost as familiar as Cardiff is now. Looking out for Otterspool Lane, the International University or the Watford Housing Benefits Office was part of

continued on Page 423...

X2.12: Army of Ghosts

like that novel's gimmick. The novel's narrated by a murder-victim. Rose narrates another pre-credit sequence (X1.8, "Father's Day"), this time all about herself, in the past tense and in an affectless tone. We finally go from flashbacks to the present and a much older-seeming Rose, on a bleak beach with a washed-out colour-palette for the picture. And we hear her say "This is the story of how I died." Is Davies writing cheques he can't cash?

- Talking of cash and Davies, observe how The Mill has converted leftover effects of manta-rays and a shot of Tennant and Piper standing on a miserable beach into the kind of alien world we hoped they'd do more often, but knew deep down they could never afford. To his credit, Davies wrote one of the two cheap episodes of running around council estates that led up to this, rather than make other writers scrimp to make his own efforts look good (see Series Six). Nonetheless, it still looks like a sop to people who would prefer a series about someone with all of space and time as his backyard to occasionally leave present-day London (or Cardiff-in-disguise) for somewhere more interesting. (Sorry, no: a Portakabin in a quarry - see X2.8, "The Impossible Planet" - doesn't cut it.)

- Overt cost-cutting comes by picking a locale for the bulk of the story that has been used in many other series. What's noticeable, for BBC2 viewers, is the re-use of the helicopter shots of Canary Wharf that punctuate the UK version of *The Apprentice*. Whether the Cybermen are quite as horrifying as the smug yuppies who mouth corporate gibberish and make idiots of themselves or the grotesque Sir Alan Sugar, a real-life John Lumic who ritually humiliates these imbeciles in an apparent remake of Jonson's *Volpone*, is a matter of personal taste. (It's more than a passing resemblance, not just for Sugar's use of catch-phrases not too far off "Delete" or "Upgrade", but the whole power-dressing, acquisitiveness and casual xenophobia that pervades his organisation and Torchwood alike.) Torchwood and the Cybermen seem very at home in this soul-less district, and utterly alien when invading real people's houses or spying on an estate via CCTV.

- Cheesy as it might seem to some, the Powell Estate triangulation might be the quintessential David Tennant scene: Tennant crashing around the TARDIS set and running out to a playground on an estate wearing a deliberately-Bill Murray backpack with all the enthusiasm of a ten year old high on Jammy Dodgers, complete with high-speed technobabble and bouncy Murray Gold music intermixed with soap-opera emotional pathos.

- Jackie gets an unanswered point across to Rose, saying that if her daughter continues travelling with the Doctor, she'll not only cease to be recognisable as Rose, but will almost cease to be human. Rose doesn't seem to think of this as a problem. For most small girls watching, the idea of the former identification-character becoming not just cooler but more powerful as a result of experience and effort rather than off-world birth is deeply attractive. Slightly older girls force this into the whole relationships / Byronic-outsider-recognises-her-as-The-Special-One / soap-opera pattern, and want Rose to get off with the Doctor rather than become him. At the end of this story, Davies kicks the problem into the long grass, but it's worth noting how far he vacillates between these two views in Series Four. Did he make the right choice? See next episode's essay.

- Anybody who's somehow managed to get this far without knowing the cliffhanger will still be spoiled if they can remember what colour the villains were last series-ender. Logically, the sphere shouldn't be any colour, but they tried a blank white effect and it looked like a weather balloon - so observe that the entire Sphere Chamber is in the Dalek colour-scheme. None of this keeps the scene of the giant Malteser opening from being very cool, and besides, the end-twist was doubly spoiled by an extermination being included in the "Next Time" segment last week.

The Continuity

The Doctor He's seen *Ghostbusters*.

He's become positively comfortable in the domestic setting of Jackie's flat and even submits to a hug and her kisses, albeit with some mild protests. He's fine when confronted with a crowd of soldiers training guns on him - until it turns out they actually know something about him. Despite the leader of Torchwood, Yvonne Hartman, practically daring him to comment on the group's happy imperialistic atmosphere, he holds back criticism until future history seems to be on the line. Dealing with a planet-imperilling device he doesn't like first evokes shoutiness, then an explanation, then settling down to watch in a deliberately too-innocent mode [not the order the Doctor

What Are the Most Over-Familiar Locations?

continued from Page 421...

the ritual, like spotting Derren Nesbitt (1.4, "Marco Polo") or Ronald Radd or waiting to see how long someone in a white Mk II Jaguar could resist the urge to drive off a cliff. But Davies has pronounced these entertaining relics to be unworthy of anyone's time, openly sneering at anyone who could enjoy *Man in a Suitcase*. The simple and unavoidable fact is that since, until recently, the actors prepared to pop over to Cardiff were a small fraction of the available Equity roster, and these Welsh-made series all seem to use Andy Prior as casting director; Cardiff was the Borehamwood of the last decade. Pretending to be any better, or even in the same league, is hubris. Nearly half a century on, *The Avengers* is still watchable, whilst the Eccleston episodes are already looking a bit "vintage".

So instead let's embrace the ITC afficionado's habits as a new way to appreciate *Doctor Who*, and reward the ingenuity with which the same handful of locations have been applied to so many different times, places and uses. The casual viewer may only have seen these episodes once each and been dimly aware of vague similarities, but for anyone rewatching these episodes by choice, or because you're in a relationship with someone who can stand to revisit "Let's Kill Hitler" (X6.8), or simply to research a book about this series, it's a whole new dimension to the viewing experience. Surely, anything that helps you get through Series One of *Torchwood* without kicking in the screen is worth trying?

So here, to start you off, are the five that are most easily spotted and where to start looking for them. Good hunting!

The Millennium Stadium, Cardiff

X1.6, "Dalek"; X2.0, "The Christmas Invasion"; X2.11, "Fear Her"; X3.0, "The Runaway Bride"; X4.1, "Partners in Crime"; X5.12, "The Pandorica Opens"; X6.7, "A Good Man Goes to War"

This is the one you'd have to be blind to have missed. It was the main location for Van Statten's bunker, and then, a few months later, was UNIT's excitingly big HQ under the Tower of London. It must have been big, because a mile down the Thames it was Torchwood's secret underground lair, and Donna burst into giggles traversing it on a Segway in her wedding dress. For this, they tried to disguise it a bit by spraying the floor with water and bouncing coloured light off the wet surface. This would have worked better if they'd decided not to do that every time it's the Stormcage Correctional Facility and River Song decides to stop being a prisoner for a bit. When dry, it was the ancillary service tunnels for the Adipose offices.

And, just for a change, it appeared as the Olympic stadium, minus any commentators or spectators, rather than as a curved tunnel made of breeze-blocks.

RAF St Athan, Barry Island

X2.5, "Rise of the Cybermen"; X2.6, "The Age of Steel"; X2.12, "Army of Ghosts"; X2.13, "Doomsday"; X3.12, "The Sound of Drums"; X4.3, "Planet of the Ood"; X6.2, "Day of the Moon"; X6.7, "A Good Man Goes to War"

We're cheating a little bit here. There are two parts to this place, the airstrip and the hangar. The airstrip was used for the President of Great Britain meeting Pete Tyler, and the President of the United States meeting Harry Saxon, and a few zeppelin-related frolics. The hangar is the interior of Torchwood London, the place where the Doctor was chased by the Grab-Crane of Doom and, blatantly, a couple of hangars in the same year. But on different planets, so that's all right.

The Docks, Cardiff

We're going to be strict about this: most of the scenes in things that *look* like docks are actually shot in Newport (as in, for instance, X2.10, "Love & Monsters"), and there's one, Mermain Quay, that is not only the same each time but is used as *look, we're in Cardiff* scenes for refuelling the TARDIS or just hangin' with the Captain (X1.11, "Boom Town"; X3.11, "Utopia"; X3.13, "Last of the Time Lords"), but the one we're concerned with is only really noticeable in X4.4, "The Sontaran Stratagem". So why are we listing it? Because this is said in the dialogue, as the doomed Jo Nakashima tries to get her ATMOS-enabled car to take her to UNIT HQ, to be London. The car drives itself into "the Thames". But the place where this happens is familiar from practically every single episode of *Torchwood* as the bit of

continued on Page 425...

X2.12: Army of Ghosts

traditionally does this sort of thing].

When Yvonne demonstrates knowledge of him and the TARDIS, he starts using Jackie as an insult-punching bag as he usually would Mickey. He seems to knowingly pull Jackie out of the Ship to keep Rose safe, leaving her free to stage a rescue. He flatly orders Yvonne to stop using particle guns because it's only the twenty-first century.

He asks Rose how long she's going to stay with him, in exactly the way he's never challenged a companion before or since. When she replies 'forever', he smiles [instead of, say, wincing or running away very very fast].

- *Ethics*. He's horrified by the ghost-shifts, presumably because he knows whoever's behind it is deluding an entire planet; the way he phrases it to Jackie, however, makes it sounds like he's about to give one of those everything-has-its-time speeches. He seems positively enthusiastic about having prompted one of the ghosts to assault him.

He mercy-kills the three Cyber-converted office workers, saying they were already dead anyway, and gets grumpy over Jackie's protests.

- *Background*. His people referred to the interstices between realities as the Void; the Eternals (20.5, "Enlightenment") call it the Howling. [NB: He refers to the Eternals in the present tense. Maybe if you're Eternal, that's the only tense.] Others call it Hell [odd that he didn't mention this when confronting something pretending to be Satan a few weeks back]. Nobody, to his knowledge, ever came close to building a Void Ship.

- *Inventory: Sonic Screwdriver*. It's here used as a Cyberman-tracer, an over-ride for the TARDIS ghost-snare (on setting 15b for eight seconds), and a device that progressively cracks a handy glass sheet as a visual aid for to make a point.

- *Inventory: Other*. The psychic paper fails to work on Torchwood staff trained to resist psychic influence. But, it successfully works on automatic doors, as when Rose places it on a card-reader. [We don't know how she figured this out, but the Doctor does it on the Oyster-reader in X4.15, "Planet of the Dead", so she may have seen him do it on public transport.] The Doctor also has a set of cardboard 3D glasses, as used in 80s cinemas [we'll find out why next week].

The TARDIS The laundry is apparently broken. [Either that, or Rose is just making a nuisance of herself by bringing home all her clothes for Jackie to wash.] There's a Console panel opposite the door that has a socket for a cable to a force-field generator. To the left of it are three controls, one of which is a button for deep scan, and another (resembling a bean tin glued to the Console) will kill them if Rose operates it by mistake.

The Supporting Cast

- *Rose*. Once again ["Father's Day"], Rose is talking directly to us. She claims to have died [see the next episode].

Despite being a time traveller, Rose immediately thinks that Jackie's gone mental when she claims to have seen her long-dead father, Rose's grandad. She's sufficiently absorbed in her current life to dismiss the first 19 years of her life with the phrase 'nothing happened', but when her mother asks if she'll ever settle down, she throws the responsibility for that onto the Doctor - saying she can't, because he won't. Her mum's stereotypically boyfriend-related comment, 'You even look like him', is met with a sour look. Her instinctive response to Jackie's questioning of how much she's changed is to disparage having once been a shop girl. She again [X1.7, "The Long Game"] borrows information off the Doctor to make herself look clever in front of other people. More usefully, she does think of buying her mum a present [a weather-predicting Bezoolium barometer, exactly the sort of thing you'd think would be useful for a Londoner]. She has apparently stopped using her phone.

The idea of using the psychic paper to infiltrate and start a rescue bid occurs to her immediately, and she knows from the Doctor's glance that he's thought far enough ahead to trust his companion with this task whilst keeping the novice, Jackie, under his wing.

- *Jackie*. Post-"Love & Monsters" (X2.10), she seems to have extended her maternal affection to the Doctor as well as Rose; this dissipates fairly rapidly when she's accidentally brought along in the TARDIS. [It takes Rose to point out that Jackie is sitting in a tucked away corner, almost as though she didn't want to be seen until after take-off. This might just be to get in the longest conversation we've seen her have with her daughter since "The Christmas Invasion" (X2.0); she expresses concern about what her daughter's lifestyle will mean in the long run, but gets interrupted by the Doctor before getting any reasonable answers.]

Recalling the 'airs and graces' comment about

What Are the Most Over-Familiar Locations?

continued from Page 423...

quayside near the "normal" entrance. It's where Owen tries to drown himself (*TW*: "A Day in the Death"), after dying two episodes beforehand. It's where Ianto first stalked Jack with coffee (*TW*: "Fragments"). And it's where Jack was killed a lot more than usual by standing in the shadow of Abaddon at the end of Series One, leading into him running after the Doctor at the start of "Utopia". It's also visible from the air in the endless helicopter swoops over central Cardiff, especially the ones where Jack's standing on top of a tall office block at night, hoping to look a bit like David Boreanas.

National Museum of Wales, Cathays, Cardiff

X1.6, "Dalek"; X3.6, "The Lazarus Experiment"; X4.15, "Planet of the Dead"; X5.10, "Vincent and the Doctor"; X5.13, "The Big Bang" (plus *The Sarah Jane Adventures* about once a year)

An odd one, as it usually appears as a museum of some kind, just not always the same one. The big exception is when Professor Lazarus launched his sonic shower-cubical to reduce the seven signs of ageing there, and we got an exterior night scene so that we could identify it when it appears as the outside of a museum as well.

The Temple of Peace, Cathays Park, King Edward VII Avenue, Cardiff

X1.2, "The End of the World"; X3.3, "Gridlock"; X4.2, "The Fires of Pompeii"; X6.8, "Let's Kill Hitler" (plus assorted episodes of other shows, notably *Sherlock*)

It doesn't look much like the real Hotel Adlon in pre-war Berlin, nor does it really look like a Roman temple, but the Temple of Peace, at the Centre for International Affairs at University of Wales, Cardiff, is unmistakable. You'll have seen it most clearly as Platform One in "The End of the World". It's that hall with the high, honey-coloured marble columns. It's also where Novice Hame hid the Face of Boe. They tried turning the lights off so we wouldn't spot that one. Didn't work. They tried to cover it up with steam when it was the Sybil's Temple in Pompeii (although, let's be honest, you're all too preoccupied trying to spot Karen Gillan as one of the Sisterhood of Kar... er... Soothsayers). Nonetheless, it's really distinctive and any student having to sit exams there now must have to concentrate very hard to avoid thinking of the Moxx of Balhoon.

Henrik's [X1.1, "Rose"], it seems that any change in Rose is perceived by Jackie as rejection of Jackie's values.

She quite rightly snaps at the Doctor when he gets snarky about her in front of Yvonne, and convinces a staff of trained professionals that she really is a time traveller until Rose blows her cover; her comments and body language when the Doctor is being taken on Torchwood's grand tour are a combination of normal companion comments and her own cattiness. She can tell there's something funny about the Dalek sphere.

Jackie was close with her dad, and when offered the chance to imagine a deceased member of her family back to life [this is, more or less, what the Doctor claims to have been going on], she thinks of him rather than her husband. The 'ghost' seems to her to give off her dad's scent, mixed with tobacco. She rather likes having a bit more information than Rose or the Doctor do for once, and uses it to tease them a little.

- *Mickey.* He's infiltrated Torchwood under the name 'Samuel', and hidden a huge alien gun under a table without the ace alien-tech-hunters spotting it. He now works for the version of Torchwood in Pete's World [which, this being Bizarro-Britain, is competent and benign]. He relishes the opportunity to point out that the Doctor was mistaken about cross-universe travel. Rose merits a big grin just for saying it's good to see him, but he holds off from pursuing this further.

- *Torchwood.* Arguably ought to be filed under "The Supporting Cast (Evil)", as their express purpose is to scavenge alien tech from ships that they've shot down (with scavenged alien tech) and keep it for the downright perverse purpose of recreating the British Empire. Their Royal Charter, drawn up just after Queen Victoria and the Werewolf incident ["Tooth and Claw"], explicitly names the Doctor as Public Enemy No. 1. Nonetheless, Yvonne Hartman, the current head,

X2.12 Army of Ghosts

is delighted to see him as they have a problem with their beezer new energy-source (the thing that is letting ghosts in). They track the Doctor down by controlling every CCTV camera in Britain and detecting interference with their ghost-field.

They commandeer the TARDIS (under Yvonne's adage that 'If it's alien, it's ours') and add it to a large collection of found/salvaged objects. We see a sarcophagus [as per 13.3, "Pyramids of Mars"]; a Jathaa Sun Glider shot down over the Shetland Islands; and Gravity-Clamps captured from a ship that they brought down at the foot of Mount Snowden, North Wales. [See X4.17, "The End of Time Part One", *The Sarah Jane Adventures* story "Death of the Doctor", and "The Christmas Invasion" - the latter because the thing that shot down the Sycorax was in the same ship.]

On detecting an anomalous zone 600 feet over London, they stump up the money to have a huge office complex - 1, Canada Square, Canary Wharf [see "The Long Game"] - to investigate and capitalise on it. It's being renovated during this episode. In this is a mysterious and unsettling sphere, looking like a giant copper bubble, which Torchwood's instruments simply can't analyse. This and the ghost effect seem to be connected, but rather than wait for more information, they zap the anomaly with particles to activate it and generate energy (and regularly-timed appearances in homes and public spaces of vaguely anthropomorphic figures that seem to be relatives of the people looking at them).

Yvonne seems to want to be seen as modern, despite her organisation's refusal to use metric, and tries to know all her staff by name. She can certainly spot office romances that the parties in question think they're hiding. All the staff have basic psychic training, so their Sphere expert, Rajesh, is unaffected by Rose trying the psychic paper on him.

Like all alien-fighting top-secret organisations, they have a really distinctive logo plastered on everything. [See Gerry Anderson's *UFO* and *Captain Scarlet & the Mysterons* - wouldn't it be cool if Torchwood had an indestructible agent? Actually, no, it'd be silly.] It's a capital T made of hexagons, and seems to be leaning away from the observer so that the base is as wide as the top line - it looks like something from 1971.

The Non-Humans

• *Cybermen* have found a way of impacting on Earth from Pete's World [as it's named next episode] via the Torchwood scheme to heat Britain's homes with an inexplicable hole in space. They materialise around the world as 'ghosts', apparently using some sort of psychic feed to beguile the locals into thinking they are departed loved-ones. [Maybe they are, from the alternate history. Or it could be that the bereaved are kidding themselves.] Once enough of them have established a toehold on "our" Torchwood, they can over-ride the cut-outs and come through properly, in force, and take over Earth. They demand an immediate surrender from the overall World Control, believing that there is such a thing here. [Ironically, that's precisely what Torchwood is trying to establish.] The hands seem to have serrated edges, to cut polythene sheeting [that's probably not the original use] and they have equipment to insert permanent brain-control links through ear-pieces, rather than a temporary over-ride as on Lumic equipment. This equipment makes orange sparks and clearly hurts.

They now have built-in pulse-guns coming out of their right wrists [yes, just like the Ice Warriors - see 5.3, "The Ice Warriors" et seq] and the Cyber-Leader can control all infiltrated machinery by making a fist and pulling it over his chest [in the kind of not-quite-Nazi salute you used to get in *Flash Gordon* serials or *Star Trek*].

• *Daleks*. The Dalek Sphere seems to have a slightly mesmeric effect on people [although how this helps the occupants isn't made clear]. As they emerge, we see that one of them is black [see 2.2, "The Dalek Invasion of Earth" for the nearest we've come to that].

History

• *Dating*. It's about 'two months' since the ghosts started appearing, so it's been at least that long since Rose saw Jackie. [It's probably a Friday, because there's apparently just been a by-election (they're always on Thursday).] Leeds has just elected a ghost as MP, it seems. [Hmm... in our world, one of the MPs for Leeds was at that time International Development Secretary. Would he have been moved to his later real-life post of Environment Secretary under Harriet Jones? If there's one MP Torchwood would have wanted out of the way, it's Hilary Benn...]

The Ghosts have spawned a cult, with a sort of

Army of Ghosts

"Caspar" logo and T-shirts for excitable Japanese schoolgirls [is there another kind in popular culture?], plus 'Ecto-Shine', apparently a polish for the dead, advertised much the same way as "Mr Sheen" is in our world. The makers of the advert, and of *EastEnders*, have either learned to fake the appearance of ghosts, or have timed recording of these productions for when a co-operative phantom is scheduled to arrive.

The ghosts run to a timetable, and come in shifts that are advertised in much the same way that power-cuts were in the 1970s. In the two months since this all started happening, people have stopped being scared and have accepted the arrival of the dead on a carefully monitored rota. There are weather forecasts of spectral activity, and yet nobody has asked why this is so predictable. The living perceive these visitors as being the specific deceased they expect, and the more one believes the more they are visited, apparently; Jackie gets sensory hallucinations of tobacco-smoke when 'Grandad Prentice' arrives.

- *The Time War.* Everything that happens here is a consequence of that [but we won't find this out for another episode].

Catchphrase Counter We get an 'I'm sorry, I'm so sorry' when the Doctor terminates a zombified/already dead Adeola, but more importantly an ongoing string of 'Allons-Y' malarkey begins here, when the Doctor determines that it's a phrase he should use more often - especially if he were to meet someone named Alonso [see, inevitably, X4.0, "Voyage of the Damned"].

Deus Ex Machina More like the reverse of one; there's Daleks after they were removed from history with a wave of Rose's hand and a shower of orange sparkly pixie-dust [X1.13, "The Parting of the Ways"].

The Analysis

The Big Picture ("Army of Ghosts" and "Doomsday") The location of Torchwood headquarters at Canary Wharf is obvious. Not only is it exactly the kind of familiar London landmark they always use these days (cf the London Eye in "Rose", the Tower of London in "The Christmas Invasion", and the Gherkin in both that story and "The Wedding of River Song"), but this lump of fake America in the middle of Poplar is widely believed to be alien anyway. It's notoriously cold and impersonal, and all sorts of other kid's shows have suggested that it's secretly for something else. (The 90s relaunch of *The Tomorrow People* had Christopher Lee using the pyramid at the top as a base because he was a reincarnated pharaoh.) As we mentioned, this is also the trademark shot of the BBC's version of *The Apprentice*, and the rest of the country thinks that anyone who voluntarily goes to work in a place like that deserves all the name-calling this entails. (As it turns out, the rest of Lord Sugar's ritualised humiliation happens somewhere else entirely, and the helicopter shots of Docklands are a complete red herring.)

We have unfinished business with the previous Cyberman adventure. One of the source-materials Davies gave Toby Whithouse was the *DWM* strip "The Flood". Davies had a hand in this, to the extent of offering to make it dovetail properly into the run-up to "Rose" and give Paul McGann's Doctor, as redeemed by the strip, a proper regeneration. (The graphic novel version has some of the material for this attempt, although the editors ultimately decided to leave out the regeneration from McGann to Eccleston.) However, the two key things to mention here are that "The Flood" ends with the Doctor defeating the Telosian malfeasants by absorbing the space-time Vortex and temporarily gaining supernatural enemy-disintegrating powers (at the cost of his own current life, in this initial version) and that the Cybermen, who are mean-looking in ways hitherto impossible to do when actors are inside costumes, have invaded by slipping across dimensions invisibly and are revealed (by a secret alien-hunting agency that is itself compromised by Cyberman infiltration) to be at work in a London tourist haunt. (In this case, it's Camden Market.) The artwork for their manifestation is very suggestive of the "ghosts" in this story.

And with that in mind, let's return to the Big Finish audio *Spare Parts*. Quite aside from the name of the focal character in that story (Yvonne Hartley), the name of the Torchwood leader seen here - Yvonne Hartman - sounds suspiciously familiar, the way that someone retaining her humanity after the conversion is what saves the day might be worth considering. As we saw under X2.5, "Rise of the Cybermen", there is a thank-you to Marc Platt for *Spare Parts*, even though what remains of his story in Tom MacRae's script is simply the "Genesis of the Cybermen" notion everyone has done at some point, and much more like MacRae's script than Platt's.

X2.12 Army of Ghosts

There's a wider sense in which this story is raking over the coals of the tie-in series. A thread in many of the fan-fics that fed into Virgin's *New Adventures* and *Missing Adventures* books was the idea of sinister, *X-Files*-ish government agencies collecting alien tech from every incursion the Doctor had helped defeat. This was, after all, the mid-90s, where it was almost an article of faith that Aliens (especially the Whitney Streiber "Grays" from the novel *Communion* from 1987) had landed at Roswell and the authorities were hushing it all up. The default mental image of this was the end of *Raiders of the Lost Ark*, a stupid idea that was compounded and / or killed off by the filmmakers actually doing Area 51 in *Indiana Jones and the Kingdom of the Crystal Skull*. Inevitably, *Buffy the Vampire Slayer* did this storyline with the Initiative, a set of secret monster-hunters who adapted their powers for their own use. The most famous version of the sinister G-men taking alien stuff and making sure nobody knows or asks questions is the Men in Black - from the original 60s urban myth rather than the Will Smith films. (Those would have to wait until the pilot episode of *Torchwood* to be remade, with the protagonist being a cop who doesn't give up and gets recruited.) Eventually, these characters would make it into *Doctor Who* in both the animated "Dreamland" (see appendix in Volume 7) and *The Sarah Jane Adventures*. There's a more overt *X-Files* reference in the effect of the ghosts, which were explicitly requested to look like whatever it is in the titles for that series.

It was also mentioned a lot when this was broadcast how much the contrivance to get Rose out of the series resembled the end of Phillip Pullman's *His Dark Materials* trilogy. At the time of broadcast, this curious amalgam of Joan Aiken and the Albigensian Heresy was at the peak of its popularity, despite the gripes of self-publicist priests and US-based pressure-groups, prior to the misfiring film version of *The Golden Compass* killing it stone-dead. The last book, *The Amber Spyglass*, even has an army of ghosts (in a chapter of the same name) stepping through from a parallel universe, but they are on the side of the good guys (not quite the side of the Angels, as there's a war in heaven and the Angels are split fairly evenly). More to the point, the act of opening gateways between universes created malignant shadow-creatures that sap the souls of the adult victims, described like the Cyberman-created "ghosts", so this has to be remedied and all transit between universes ended once and for all, splitting up the couple at the heart of the story (who hail from different versions of Oxford - hers has Zeppelins, naturally). Underlying all of this is a complex speculation about the nature of creativity, the substance of imagination, Dark Matter, the origins of the Enlightenment and why children are different from adults - all of it bound up with a quasi-sentient substance called Dust that surrounds and communicates with people capable of asking the right questions in the right way. The eponymous Amber Spyglass allows a nun-turned-physicist to see it, much as the 3D glasses help the Doctor. The stage version, at the National Theatre in 2004, made more of this enforced parting than the book, and was cited as the main thing Rose's being dragged from the Doctor resembled. Pullman himself was full of praise for Davies and certainly had no objection to one of his other books, *Ruby in the Smoke*, being made as a vehicle for Piper.

Another book that used to be ubiquitous until the almost-whelming film removed it from book clubs' wish lists, *The Lovely Bones*, has already been mentioned. It begins: "My name was Salmon, like the fish: first name, Susie. I was fourteen when I was murdered." You get the idea. (Quite why the Doctor regards the narrator getting into Heaven and her relatives having children as a "sad ending" is another matter. But then, this is the same being who cried at the end of *Harry Potter and the Deadly Hallows* - see X3.2, "The Shakespeare Code".) Some might think that the film *Sunset Boulevard* is a precedent. However, we can't leave the topic without alluding to that year's tosh phenomenon, *Desperate Housewives*, which launched around the time Davies was writing this and had the gimmick in the pilot episode of the narrator's death. It was more talked-about than watched after the first week.

Similarly, the whole country was amused by a series of commercials that may have been deliberately cheesy or simply inept, for a product called Cillit Bang. There are lots of similar cleaning products around, with bad ads, but this was strikingly naff. Putting in a parody was a slam-dunk. If ghosts did manifest themselves regularly, though, a series a bit like *GhostWatch* would have happened, but not with that name. On Hallowe'en 1992, there was a spoof documentary called that which was too convincing for some viewers, despite meticulous efforts to disrupt the plausibility (one of the family in the supposedly haunted house was played by someone who'd just been in *Casualty* ten minutes earlier, for example, and it was clearly marked as a drama at the start). It being a Saturday night, not everyone was paying attention and allegedly some people were convinced and complained, so a few careers ended. Nonetheless, supposedly "real" ghost-hunting television is now accepted as a legitimate form of entertainment, as we will see in **Oh, Isn't That...?**

[For **Things That Don't Make Sense**, **Critique**, **The Facts** and **Production**, see the next episode.]

X2.13: "Doomsday"

(8th July, 2006)

Which One is This? We like the Daleks... and we like the Cybermen... but which is better? There's only one way to find out - FI-I-I-IGHT! (Oh, and Rose leaves.)

Firsts and Lasts It's Billie Piper's last stint as a regular cast member, although the number of non-regular / cameo / stock footage appearances of Rose removes a lot of the charge (and they're still at it; see X6.8, "Let's Kill Hitler"). It's definitely the last we see of Pete Tyler and Jake. As such, it's actually Mickey who gets the most interesting continuing story arc of any of them (his status in X4.18, "The End of Time Part Two" blindsided a lot of viewers, but is actually a more logical end than what happens to Rose next). However, this looks like Mickey's last stand, and he doesn't get a line after "Man, I told you he was good". He does, however, receive the series' first inter-racial same-sex kiss (unless one of the missing episodes - notably the remainder of 2.6, "The Crusade"; 4.1, "The Smugglers"; 4.5, "The Underwater Menace"; 5.4, "The Enemy of the World"; or 5.7, "The Wheel in Space" show up to prove us wrong.)

Something that's easy to overlook amidst all the soap-suds is that the entire planet has now become accustomed to the presence of aliens, and now to being invaded en masse, though this never really has the impact it ought to have had. Nevertheless, somewhere in the middle of this episode is the regular army fighting a pitched battle against Cybermen, the sort of thing that would have been the main sales-pitch for many Hollywood movies or almost any other TV show, and this is the first time since... ooh... 25.1, "Remembrance of the Daleks" that the "normal" sequence of bazookas having little effect on bullet-proof alien / robotic / giant-sized monstrosities is even attempted. (We might suggest 26.1, "Battlefield", but that's knight-on-knight action with UNIT as onlookers.) Prior to that, the last one to do it as a set-piece was 12.1, "Robot", in 1975.

This is the debut of the Cult of Skaro, a Dalek brains trust with silly names. They are going to be whittled away in subsequent appearances, so any effort in characterisation would have been redundant anyway. The black one, who seems to be first amongst equals, is Dalek Sec (see 3.4, "Daleks in Manhattan").

The full impact of Lauren the Schoolgirl, in a wedding-dress, shouting in the TARDIS Console Room will be lost on any foreign fan, but here is where Catherine Tate (credited as "the Bride") makes her first appearance as Donna Noble.

But we're missing the point - after 40 years, this episode has the first moment when a Dalek and a Cyberman are in the same shot, the first exchange of lines between them, the first exchange of gunfire between them and the very first time that the voice-artist for both has to do both sets of dialogue. And it isn't Roy Skelton doing it (which had the risk of it sounding like a lethal episode of *Rainbow*), it's Nicholas Briggs, and was broadcast on the day that Peter Hawkins - who created both voices and umpteen others from our collective childhood - died.

Watch Out For...

• Forty years. Forty sodding years we've been waiting to see what would happen if the Daleks and Cybermen ever met. And what happens? They stand around trading bitchy put-downs for five minutes. Small boys might think of WCW pre-fight taunting, but for anyone else, it's like a heavily armed *Queer as Folk*. The initial Cyberman-Dalek exchange bears all the hallmarks of a scene that the author conceived in all its catfight glory when playing with 70s Weetabix cards (see **Why Was There So Much Merchandising?** under 11.4, "The Monster of Peladon") and has been waiting to unleash ever since. With good reason, in this case. (Incidentally, Mickey's attempted quip about the voices indicate that this line was written before they'd decided what the Cybermen were going to sound like this time.)

X2.13 Doomsday

- The Cybermen have no emotions. The Daleks have hate and fear and nothing else. Yet both sides observe the niceties of a romantic reunion between two people who've never actually met, Parallel Pete and un-upgraded Jackie, to stop shooting for a long scene. We finally hear an "Ex-ter-min-ate!" and a gun going off, but that's an abrupt cut to a totally different place.

- After last year realised the long-held wish that a bazillion flying Daleks raining death on the world like in the 60s *TV 21* strip might look even better on screen, they try the obvious next step of doing it Yeti-in-the-loo style, with umpty-zillion Daleks flying out of a shaker-maker over Cardiff-pretending-to-be-London. Somehow, it looks less impressive than ten Cybermen stomping around back-streets, double-exposed to bring their numbers up to 20. In fact, CGI Cybermen falling to their death from a catwalk in a hangar during a pitched battle looks less impressive than that, despite costing an awful lot more.

- At risk of a spoiler, the Doctor's brilliant solution is to pull a lever. For anyone not a ten-year-old girl, the story ends eight minutes before the episode does. And yet, that eight minutes is the main thing everyone remembers about this episode. Murray Gold gives the whole sequence a Michael Nyman-like soundtrack and Rose is given a send-off longer than Susan's (2.2, "The Dalek Invasion of Earth"), more calculatedly a tearjerker than Jo's (10.5, "The Green Death"), and later undone as crassly as Peri's (23.2, "Mindwarp"; 23.4, "The Ultimate Foe"; and Series Four). In case you haven't heard, this was a national talking-point, even on the hottest day on record and when England's footballers had got through to the semi-finals of the World Cup.

The Continuity

The Doctor He takes two magna-clamps and then tells Rose that one will be needed to stop himself being sucked into the breach. He obviously expects her to participate, despite his attempt to get her to safety. When the 'old team' is back together, he'd rather be an elephant than a ghost [see **English Lessons**]. He prefers pain to numbness and is rather fond of hope.

He gets very excited about 3D glasses [far more than will ever make sense to future audiences of kids who have movies with these as a matter of course]. He's also started matchmaking. In the middle of a conversation about Cybermen invading Earth, he takes time out to suggest that Pete go look up his wife. And then proceeds to call Jake 'Jakey-boy', shortly before running off to find Rose and Mickey. [There seems to be a pattern forming.]

For once he says something nice to Mickey, right after he's opened the big CGI salad shaker of doom. [One wonders if their relationship would have gone better if Mickey had genuinely made more of a prat of himself in earlier stories.]

- *Ethics.* He thinks that he can dispatch Rose off with her mum and parallel dad without asking first, then tricks her into it against her passionate protests, silently approaching from behind and dropping a medallion on her just as Pete does the same to Jackie. [This ends about as well as you'd expect.]

Instead of moving on after being separated from Rose, he goes to quite a bit of time and trouble haunting her all the way to the parallel-reality Norway, where he tells her it's quite right for her to love him and nearly says Something Important before running out of time when the universes close. [Given that, as a Time Lord, that's just about the *last* problem he ought to be having, it's entirely possible he bluffed his way through that speech so he could leave her to imagine something. The production team all have their own theories on the matter, none of which are compatible. Rose is later told in X4.13, "Journey's End" something that *purports* to be what he was going to say, but the comment comes from the Oddbod Junior Doctor - and he's another person altogether, with a vested interest.]

He seems downright angry about the crossing-universes business. [Given what happens in X6.13, "The Wedding of River Song", this is possibly because mucking about with this sort of thing really *does* cause universal implosion.] Confining armies worth of Daleks and Cybermen to the Void forever seems like a really good plan to him. [It's left mercifully unclear whether this just means killing the lot stone dead, or if Hell actually is a good moniker and they're all left to suffer eternal nothing. In the light of X4.14, "The Next Doctor", though, at least some of them appear to land up *somewhere*.] In any event, he argues with Rose a bit about the chance of her suffering the same fate by sticking around.

- *Inventory: Sonic Screwdriver.* Promptly after announcing that he's above such things as using

Was 2006 the *Annus Mirabilis*?

The 27 episodes analysed in this book were made in a state of almost-permanent near-crisis, and yet for the people who saw them first time, on BBC1 on Saturdays at 7.00pm, they seemed flawless. Ask anyone who was around here at the time, and they all seem to think that everything after "The Runaway Bride" (X3.0) was a tailing-off. This perception is hard to shake, even though anyone who then goes to re-examine the broadcast episodes will be hard-put to find anything in them especially distinctive or different from what came later. The last scene officially made for the second run of episodes was of the Doctor and Rose telling Ida Scott that they were "the stuff of legend", and the production team and public seemed to agree (X2.9, "The Satan Pit"). That episode was the lowest-rated of the entire BBC Wales production to date, and when looked at now seems pretty flat. So where does this sense of Series Two being the Golden Age come from?

It can't be denied: for the British public, *Doctor Who* had lost whatever mojo it might once have possessed around the time the diamond logo and time-tunnel effect were ditched and student wit was replaced by technobabble. However much a nucleus of big-name fans claimed that the new approach was better, not even all the readers of the new *Doctor Who Monthly* were enthusiastic. For the next 25 years, the programme was a national joke. For many people who'd loved the series in the 60s and 70s, watching the new episodes in the 80s felt like visiting a sick friend in hospital. We pretended we thought that everything would be back to normal soon, but it became harder to lie to ourselves. The majority of the public thought it wasn't for them (see **What's All This Stuff About Anoraks?** under 24.1, "Time and the Rani"). Proportionately, fewer of the children who would normally have started watching aged five and stayed with the series were bothering. Those that did had fewer people to discuss it with at school. Once the plug was pulled in 1989, the legacy was split pretty evenly between being "kitsch" and "nostalgia" and being "cult". That second option was increasingly an obstacle to any widespread public acceptance that it had *ever* been worth watching or was worth reviving.

So the state of affairs at Christmas 2006 was bewildering to anyone who wore the scars of those wilderness years. There was the second hour-long Christmas Special, which already seemed like a regular fixture. The first series of *Torchwood* was just ending, and the first episode of *The Sarah Jane Adventures* was about to start. Billie Piper was doing publicity for her next project, an adaptation of a Philip Pullman novel that was another highlight promoted in the same package. Then after that, she was off to do ITV adaptations of Jane Austen and the blog of a scholarly prostitute. The traditional career-ending "curse" of being an ex-*Doctor Who* regular was dead and buried. On top of this, we'd had two subsidiary series about the making of *Doctor Who*, one on BBC3 detailing all the backstage effort they saw fit to broadcast (*Doctor Who Confidential*) and another for children on BBC1 (*Totally Doctor Who*) with activities for young proto-fans and background information, much of it accurate. (We've already gone into this in **Has All the Puff "Totally" Changed Things?** under X2.1, "New Earth".) These series were all moving to a big new purpose-built complex, rather than scrounging studio-space where and when they could. The prospects looked limitless.

The wedge between ordinary members of the public and the kind of person who'd be interested in watching *Doctor Who* had almost vanished. Everyone who had children was at some time in front of the telly on Saturday nights at 7.00pm in those three months, and the appeal of the series to teenage girls had been part of the pitch to BBC bosses. The casual viewer could usually pick up the thread of any episode, and any prolepsis or continuity reference would be amply explained in the dialogue. At this stage, the running threads of plot were generally cumulative details that came together, such as the throwaway references to "Torchwood" or "Mr Saxon". Any returning characters or adversarial races were either introduced as if for the first time or, more intriguingly, so changed as to leave the seasoned fan as much in the dark as a newcomer. Most people knew the basic set-up, and pretty much everyone in Britain knew who David Tennant and Billie Piper were (even if a few TV reviewers in newspapers seemed to think that her character was called "Billie").

The face of either star sold magazines. On top of this, 2006 was the year between John Barrowman

continued on Page 433...

X2.13 Doomsday

his sonic screwdriver as a weapon, the Doctor uses it to implode the doors so that bizarro-Torchwood can come in and shoot the Daleks. [Because there's a serious moral difference there, obviously.]

• *Inventory: Other.* His 3D glasses are a means to detect the residual energy [not even slightly like "Dust" from the works of Philip Pullman, then] on anyone who's been between universes. [Not only is this a remarkably handy thing to have just had in his coat-pocket one day - suggesting that he had his suspicions about the 'ghosts' early on - but it's a very odd thing for anyone to have around the place, if journeys between dimensions have been prevented by the end of the Time War.]

He has to use a sheet of A4 to make a white flag [so, he doesn't have a hankie].

The TARDIS It needs the power of a star going nova to send a cosmic Dear John to Rose. This uses a hologram projector. [What the Doctor literally sees while making this call is unclear. He asks Rose where they are, but *he* is evidently in the TARDIS, just next to the chair, with no screens or projected view of the bay.]

The Supporting Cast

• *Rose* has never been more teenage. She finally has everything she wanted when we first met her: a mum and dad (with money), Mickey in a cool job, herself defending Earth against aliens and a baby brother or sister on the way. And yet, she still acts as if she's come to the end of her life. Nor does being singled out for a telepathic summons to an inter-dimensional phone-call help her get on with her life, even now she's Defender of Earth. When forcibly removed to another world, she argues with Jackie and Pete, opting to return to the Doctor's side come what may. On Pete's World, she has a double-bed, but is seen sleeping alone in her new home. And she seems jokingly put out that the Doctor might believe she still works at a shop.

Before all that, though, she's quite able to take on the Daleks, talking them into stopping their killing-spree and staring them down. She's also quite keen on having been the Bad Wolf and killed loads of them, gloating about evaporating the Emperor and seeing them quake when they realise that it's the Doctor in the room upstairs. [So, apparently, her memory of X1.13, "The Parting of the Ways" has come back.] Her heart literally beats a bit faster when the Doctor appears on the screen. But, she now counts Mickey as the bravest human she's ever met.

That ominous, foreboding, smothering sense [particularly in X2.9, "The Satan Pit"] that Rose was going to die in battle? It turns out that after the smoke clears from the Dalek-Cybermen battle, the authorities recognise that she's gone missing and formally list her among the dead.

• *Jackie* knows that Rose is terrified of Daleks [although it's unclear exactly what Rose told her and when].

She manages to slip away from bemused Cybermen in the best companion fashion [and must be in far better shape than a woman her age and background ought to be, since she manages to run up 45 flights of stairs and still run to meet Pete at the end of it]. She's not sure what to make of alternative Pete at first and they proceed to quarrel about just about everything, but eventually they land up having a baby. She makes a big play of being unconcerned that he's loaded. Contrary to what some might have expected, her abrupt transition to wealth doesn't make her dress flashily.

Even after her daughter tells her point blank that she's staying with the Doctor for good, Jackie's insistent on retrieving Rose, whatever it takes.

• *Mickey* quite readily says that coming back for Rose is 'stupid', but even if he's fishing for a compliment, he's clearly moved on since we last saw him in X2.6, "The Age of Steel". [Maybe Jake's been helping him.] Nevertheless, he loves it when Rose talks technical. Mickey knows that all the Daleks are meant to be dead.

He trusts the Doctor enough that when Rose goes back for the Doctor, he doesn't help Jackie transport back again. When Jackie tells Pete there's not been anyone else since he "died", Mickey struggles to keep a straight face. He appears to have been the source for the ex-Preachers' knowledge of the Doctor's full range of abilities. He accompanies Rose to Norway, and appears to live in the Tyler household after returning to Pete's World. [Where he sleeps is anyone's guess.]

• *Pete* sticks to his belief that an alternative universe's Jackie can't be really his - until he actually sees her. Oddly, but conveniently, he is able in the heat of a full-on transdimensional armageddon-in-the-making to take time out and chat up "our" Jackie, after which he is better-disposed towards Rose. He comes back for his parallel

Was 2006 the *Annus Mirabilis*?

continued from Page 431...

becoming almost ubiquitous on panel-games, talent shows and occasionally freakish documentaries - and jokes being made about his ability to be on every channel at once - simultaneously. Unlike the end of the 2005 series, recorded before anyone had seen how the programme would look, this year celebrities were actively asking to be written in rather than agreeing to appear, sight-unseen. *Doctor Who* had so much goodwill directed towards it, even Michael Grade was watching. Everyone knew about it, generally approved of it and was happy to see something locally-made take on and beat the yanks at their own game. This extended to the whole BBC Wales / Russell T Davies operation, with Davies acknowledged in every end-of-year list as one of the top ten "players" in television (and one of only a handful who actually made programmes rather than running networks). As *Doctor Who* moved to a purpose-built studio complex, to be made alongside *Torchwood* and *The Sarah Jane Adventures* and a few others, it seemed that there was no limit to what might be achieved. The co-production deal with the Canadian Broadcasting Corporation was helpful in establishing a convincing global presence.

It was definitely a commercial giant in the UK. The reconfigured Panini version of what was now *Doctor Who Magazine* bore little resemblance to the *Monthly* of Marvel UK and had been joined on the news-stands by *Doctor Who Adventures*, which had gifts and strips very like the original Marvel *Doctor Who Weekly* in content if not style - *Doctor Who: Battles in Time*, which tied in with the collect-and-swap card-game (nothing like *Pokemon*, honest, guv) and the Panini sticker-book for the collect-and-swap stickers, assuming you hadn't got your free one in the *Radio Times* with the Cyber-Controller on the cover. It didn't stop there: even average-sized supermarkets now had sonic screwdrivers, Destroyed Cassandras and radio-controlled K9s. Two of these were things we'd not even had in the heydays of merchandising, broadly 1972-8 and 1984-6. (One was something even people who'd enjoyed X1.2, "The End of the World" didn't expect to ever see on sale in Tesco or Sainsbury's.) Chinese-made plastic toys, with chips in or not, were what small children wanted and could, just about, afford. There had been a fair amount of pre-launch sales in spring 2005, but that year's Christmas had been a bit embarrassing, with Eccleston-themed games, toys and books on sale just as everyone was gagging to see Tennant's debut. (We'll pick up this story in **What Are the Great 21st Century Merchandising Disasters?** under X5.3, "Victory of the Daleks".)

In bookshops, everyone had seen pound-signs and rushed out whatever they had lying around. Many of these were by experienced authors and hardened fans (and ideally by people who were both), but there were obvious hastily commissioned cash-ins such as *A Teaspoon and an Open Mind* (see **What Are the Silliest Examples of Bad Science?** under 10.4, "Planet of the Daleks"). Actor/writer Toby Hadoke began his stage-show *Moths Ate My Doctor Who Scarf*. Biographies of significant players, some containing verifiable facts, cropped up in the Media sections, whilst Billie Piper's autobiography - with "Eccleston" spelled wrong throughout - made the bestseller lists. BBC Books, back then a major player in the Christmas sales-figures, gave Gary Russell ample opportunity to exercise the skills he'd honed as editor of *DWM* in the 90s and co-founder of the Big Finish audios, with two hefty books by him coming out at once. Guides to old monsters, new monsters, and how to draw monsters and planets (with monsters on) came from the same source, giving the editor of their hitherto-ignored *Doctor Who* range, Justin Richards, even more to do. He also oversaw (and wrote for) the relaunched novels.

Which is where we have to draw breath for a moment. Nobody had a bad word to say about *Doctor Who* except a few, rather disappointed, old-time fans. But was it actually *popular*? Well, in terms of ratings, audience share, Audience Appreciation feedback and newspaper reviews, it was certainly holding its own. So were lots of BBC programmes of the time, and (despite some much-publicised flops) ITV1's Saturday night line-up was recovering lost ground too. The schedulers had decided to place *Doctor Who* at the heart of the Saturday night line-up and arrange all other programming around it. This would become less common as the years passed. By the time Steven Moffat and Matt Smith took over, it would be pre-

continued on Page 435...

X2.13 Doomsday

daughter [whether this is for her sake or Jackie's is never made clear]. He has taken over "his" London's Torchwood and recruited the surviving Preachers as commandos [expanding upon his previous role as 'Gemini'; see "The Age of Steel"]. He realises it's pointless trying to stop Mickey going back for Rose. His main concern is that the Breach is destroying his planet's environment; he's rid of the Cybermen and not too worried about the other Earth. In this connexion, he is keen to recruit the Doctor, abducting him at a crucial moment.

• *Torchwood*. Well... just about all of them are dead by the end. [Although somewhere in the building must be the partly converted Lisa Hallett - she'll show up in *Torchwood*'s "Cyberwoman" if you're a completist - and therefore Ianto Jones (see **Things That Don't Make Sense**). Jack, in X3.12, "The Sound of Drums", explains that the base was abandoned.]

There is a Torchwood in Pete's World, and Pete's in charge of it, using the Preachers as his elite strike-force. They have a means of traversing the Void with crystalline devices [appropriately for Pete as we saw him in 1987, it's a big medallion]. In his world, being more advanced in time [three years have elapsed since "The Age of Steel", while it's only been a few months for Jackie], the effect of the ghost-devices is to have accelerated global warming and caused Earth to come close to ecological collapse. The new President, Harriet Jones, has come to power apparently by silencing such fears and is credited with a 'new Golden Age' [again, ridiculously unlikely unless we posit goddess-Rose as an Infinite Improbability device selecting this one universe]. Parallel Torchwood is unlike the one in Jackie's world in being organised; it's also likeable and in favour of asking the Doctor for help. They have huge zap-guns that can actually work against polycarbide.

The Non-Humans

• *Daleks*. Reassuringly, they still have shells made of polycarbide ["Remembrance of the Daleks"] and count time in 'rels' [as in the Cushing films of the 60s and the *TV 21* comic strip]. In a curious development, the Genesis Ark is actually a Time Lord device, but is activated in exactly the same manner - same visual effect and all - as the Dalek trapped in Van Statten's vault [X1.6, "Dalek"]. They are unable to tell by sight which humans have the requisite Artron magic.

The four Daleks in the Void Ship are the Cult of Skaro, who are supposedly higher in rank than the Emperor. [They seem not to think so, and are concerned that Rose saw the Emperor destroyed, although less so when they hear that *she* did it. If the Emperor seen in "The Parting of the Ways" *did* originate as the Dalek seen in "Dalek", though, then it's possible the Cult and Rose are talking about different Emperors without realising it.] As an elite unit charged with thinking the unthinkable, they have names: Sec (the black-shelled one, who seems to be leader), Caan, Jast and Thay. The Doctor being alive, despite being the apparent reason for picking Earth at all, concerns them more than five million Cybermen. Indeed, they are openly derisive and catty about the idea of an alliance with the Cybermen, although Jast is tricked into identifying his species in a stand-off. [Only Sec is seen using an 'emergency temporal shift' to escape, but all four Cult members survive, and next appear in "Daleks in Manhattan".]

• *Cybermen*. They have a concept of design, and recognise another batch of cyborgs when they see them. They can tell that their technology is 'compatible' with that of Daleks [how this would even work is another question altogether]. They seem to have a plan to Cyber-convert the entire population of Earth all at once. [Although how they plan to do this without the factories they were dependent upon back in Pete's World is an open question. *TW*: "Cyberwoman" and the conversion of Adeola here suggest that they brought a few odds and ends along with them. These seem not to have been sucked into the Void.] They are vexed [as vexed as they get, anyway] that there is not a central global authority. When ordering a surrender, they offer freedom from anxiety and fear, an end to distinctions based on class, race, sex or creed, and no more pain or illness.

When their leader is destroyed, another is designated to download all the leadership software and takes over. One odd incident is that the original leader accepts that the Doctor is somehow special, and asks if he now accepts that emotions are a weakness. [It seems almost as if this one knows who the Doctor is and is familiar with his previous stated opinions, but none of the Cybermen say, "It is the one they call Doc-torr!", or any such acknowledgement of his difference, experience or previous form in Cyberman-vanquishing. The leader gets his head blown off by Jake before any further hint that this is the ex-

Was 2006 the *Annus Mirabilis*?

continued from Page 433...

empted and moved around from the 7.00pm start that had seemed set in stone in 2006. The point had been proved: family audiences watched things together on Saturdays again.

Muddying the waters for anyone looking to use ratings and AI figures to compare Davies and Moffat is the advent of BBC's online catch-up service, the iPlayer. As with almost all the Corporation's output, *Doctor Who* is available for up to a week after broadcast. The system was launched with "Voyage of the Damned" (X4.0). Whilst the overnight ratings are still collected in the old way, and are just as haphazard, the iPlayer figures are accurate. This cuts both ways: many people are now watching on iPlayer *rather* than on Saturday nights, now that the system has become more familiar. Other methods of streaming are available, and don't show up on the ratings. The collective memory of watching clockwork robots, Reapers and walking scarecrows as a family might make it seem to commentators that "nobody" is still watching *Doctor Who*, but 8.33 million nobodies saw "Asylum of the Daleks" (X7.1) and the following two weeks saw the series stay in the top ten most-watched programmes of that week - three weeks in a row never even happened in Hartnell's time, let alone Tennant or Pertwee. "Doomsday", which is posited as the high-water mark of the series' popularity, was actually only seen by 8.22 million on the first broadcast whilst "The Satan Pit" had the lowest recorded overnight ratings of any twenty-first century episode, at 6.08 million. (If more people had seen this episode, then Series Two would be less fondly remembered. Discuss.) Unless about four million people a week are tuning in religiously to a series they hate - and there aren't that many old fanzine editors in the UK - only people with negative opinions are bothering to share their views and the majority of viewers are either apathetic or quietly enthusiastic.

Ratings, as we've been saying since Volume 1, only tell a fraction of the story. In crude numerical terms, the first-night audience for most episodes in this phase were roughly the same as those of Hartnell or Pertwee, occasionally approaching the heights of Tom Baker's reign or, when the weather was good and ITV pulled out the stops, the average figures for Davison. This is hardly a fair comparison, though. The old duopoly system had shattered into five terrestrial analogue stations and dozens of others, either freely available via a set-top box or via subscription. This also complicated the ratings collation, as those of you following the stats in each story's listing will have noted. Technically, anything within the first week after a broadcast, whether recorded and watched back or watched on a digital catch-up system, counts to the ratings of the programme. BBC3 was repeating each episode of *Doctor Who* twice within the first week. Moreover, this and other digital channels with deals with the BBC, under the overall label "UK Gold" (later renamed with increasingly whimsical labels and promotional material) kept the new episodes in almost constant circulation for the next few years. The big question is whether it was the same people watching the reruns who'd seen it on first transmission or a new audience belatedly catching up. The kinds of viewing figures for these stations are so marginal that old-style fandom had been keeping them in business since the 90s. It's possible that only people who'd been watching repeats of 70s episodes they already owned on VHS or DVD were watching Rose and the Doctor being chased by Slitheen for the fifth time in a year.

People with the Freeview digital service (see **Why is Trinity Wells on Jackie's Telly?** under X1.4, "Aliens of London") could thus watch two different re-runs of Eccleston's run whilst Series Two was being shown, as well as BBC3's catch-up repeats on Friday of every Saturday's new episode. Add to this BBC3's very own *Torchwood*, being repeated on BBC2 for non-digital viewers. In fact, if we consider the calendar year 2006, beginning with the BBC1 repeat of X2.0, "The Christmas Invasion", we have 15 episodes of *Doctor Who*, plus another 13 for anyone who unaccountably missed the first year, plus all but two episodes of the first spin-off series and the pilot of the second *and* two different making-of shows, all repeated in some form, meaning that for the first time since 1968, there wasn't a single week when the BBC weren't transmitting some form of *Doctor Who*. One week - the one between the last two episodes of Series Two - saw something like nine and a half hours of *Doctor Who*-adjacent television shown on three

continued on Page 437...

X2.13 Doomsday

Jackie, or anyone else who might have taken an interest in the person who destroyed John Lumic's empire.]

Ultimately, the Cybermen's pulse-cannons have no effect whatsoever on the Daleks. The Cybermen themselves are bulletproof, but fall to the Daleks' weaponry and shoulder-mounted bazookas.

History (alternate) On Pete's side of the looking-glass, three years have elapsed since the Doctor left. Harriet Jones is President and the Earth's mean temperature has risen two degrees Celsius [that's the *mean* temperature, so the overall amount of energy being put into the atmosphere is colossal]. Torchwood has developed a trans-dimensional hop using a big yellow medallion. Things don't seem quite as futuristically clean any more; there is a shot of the city seen from Canary Wharf showing fires breaking out along the Thames [we hope it's helium in those airships]. Nonetheless, this is a 'golden age', according to President Jones.

• *The Time War*. The Cult of Skaro ran away with the Genesis Ark before the close of play, so didn't get to hear the final score. The Doctor talks about how he was fighting at 'the fall of Arcadia' to explain how he got out in one piece. [A planet by that name had popped up in one of the *New Adventures,* by the then-editor of the range. See X1.12, "Bad Wolf" for more on *Deceit*.]

Catchphrase Counter All the old favourites are here: 'Exterminate'; 'Delete'; 'WORRyuss', with a new one that will blight many later stories: 'E-mer-gen-cy Tem-por-al Shift'. And the episode ends with the Doctor doing a Colin Baker-style escalating-volume repetition of 'What?' (as will next year's finale).

Deus Ex Machina Isn't it lucky that the Void has a reverse? And how handy that the TARDIS is breached by an excitation of Huon particles *after* Rose has gone, rather than in the middle of pulling a spaceship out of a black hole or whatever [X2.9, "The Satan Pit"]. But the big one for now is Tracey-Anne Cyberman - the less-than-perfectly upgraded Yvonne, who manages to retain her own vocal cords, weep sump-oil from the "teardrops" at the sides of a Cyberman's eyes and gun down her new brethren right when the Doctor needs a distraction. [We have another that's so alarming and right out of left field, it gets its own annex built onto the side of **Things That Don't Make Sense**.]

The Analysis

English Lessons ("Army of Ghosts" and "Doomsday")

• *Snog* (n. v.): A proper, full-on kiss. (It's likely you'd gathered that from us using the term a lot in this volume, but in case you come to this episode cold and think they're doing a bit more than they are, it's best to have this in writing.)

• *Mount Snowdon* (n.): The highest mountain in Wales, and centrepiece of the Snowdonia National Park (location for 20.7, "The Five Doctors"). That ship that crashed there must have been a big one, because it has a Vinvocchi device for regenerating entire planets aboard, as well as a serious amount of weaponry. And this must have been before UNIT set up their new base under the mountain (*The Sarah Jane Adventures*: "Death of the Doctor").

• *Canary Wharf* (n.): As you will recall from "The Long Game", this is where all the newspapers relocated from Fleet Street in the 1980s. A tall building with a pyramid on top, 1, Canada Square, was constructed in the 80s in the derelict Docklands area (14.6, "The Talons of Weng Chiang"; 21.4, "Resurrection of the Daleks") as part of an initially risible attempt at bringing overseas companies to London. The original consortium that put it together was apparently composed of American financial firms (Morgan Stanley and First Boston). Hitherto, the Isle of Dogs was mainly known for sewage reclamation (X1.11, "Boom Town"; X4.14, "The Next Doctor"). Now, thousands of people work in this wannabe-Manhattan, even if hardly any of them seem to enjoy it and none of them live anywhere nearby. A lot of other similarly bland buildings have sprung up around it, and will often be seen in helicopter shots illustrating the financial news.

• *Queen Vic* (n.): The pub in *EastEnders* (see A3, "Dimensions in Time").

• *A4 Paper* (n): The standard size for office use, 29.5 cm X 21 cm, or half an A3 sheet (or indeed twice an A5 sheet - these things mattered in the 90s fanzine wars).

• *Shiver & Shake* (n): A comic. Or two comics. There was a fad for 70s kids papers (nothing like DC or Marvel, more like what Americans call "funny papers", but not really like them either) to have two titles conjoined and a fake rivalry

Was 2006 the *Annus Mirabilis*?

continued from Page 435...

channels. (There may have been more, with nocturnal reruns of Tom Baker episodes continuing sporadically until 2008, albeit sometimes without sound.)

And we haven't even looked at BBC Radio yet! Radio Two, the grown-up music station (as opposed to Radio Three, the music-for-grown-ups station and 6Music, the "adult" music station) ran documentaries on the return of the series and the recasting of the lead. Digital-only repeats station BBC7 (now Radio 4Extra, confusingly) started broadcasting the Big Finish audio dramas and the talking-book adaptations of Target novels, as well as, later on, Barry Letts' autobiography *Who and Me*. This whole movement took longer to reach its own saturation-level, and the peak time for Doctor Who related radio was immediately prior to X5.1, "The Eleventh Hour", but the notion of getting any of this, even at the programme's 40th anniversary in 2003, would have been laughable.

Meanwhile, the belated launch of the Eccleston series in other countries created a self-sustaining momentum for the programme. America, where the series had always been vaguely known-about, underwent a varispeed exposure. We'll develop this thread in an essay in Volume 8, but the situation is best described in Jonathan Lethem's last essay in his book *Manhood for Amateurs*. He runs into an English expat who, not following developments in the UK or on smaller cable channels, is incredulous that bright and seemingly well-adjusted ten-year-old Americans have Dalek T-shirts. This person is quietly ridiculed by Lethem for retaining the "anorak" notion of bygone years. Australia, with its own unique relationship with the 70s episodes and more particularly the 80s ones they (apparently unwittingly) partially paid for (see Volume 6) ran the episodes about a year after first BBC transmissions. More intriguingly, though, all around the world, people were watching illegal streams of each episode almost as quickly as they went out in Britain. Russia, with so much experience of secretly getting cool stuff from the West that the word "samizdat" is familiar here, proved to be enthusiastic about a BBC series after years of the Corporation trying to get the official channels to buy British shows. For obvious reasons, it's hard to get solid figures for this sort of enterprise.

Another thing for which we lack anything but empirical, anecdotal evidence is how far the stories are remembered *as* stories rather than as a hazy sense of *Doctor Who*-ishness. It's certainly true that people were more comfortable referring in passing to specifics in other contexts than before or, it appears, since. A noted rock music journalist cited John Lumic (X2.5, "Rise of the Cybermen"; X2.6, "The Age of Steel") when dismissing the latest manufactured boy-band; one of the contestants on that year's *Big Brother* was referred to by a critic as "The Face of Boe" ("The End of the World" et seq). It could be the case that the British public are responding warmly to the *idea* of *Doctor Who* rather than the content of any episode. The paradox is that in a lot of the stories in Series Two, the amount of what people think of as "typical *Doctor Who*" is actually rather small. Three alien planets are shown, one consisting entirely of corridors and a hole in the ground (X2.8, "The Impossible Planet"; "The Satan Pit"), one a beach in Wales with flying stingrays (X2.12, "Army of Ghosts") and one a beach in Wales with flying ambulances ("New Earth"). We have two straightforward trips to the past (Britain in both cases), one jump a whole seven years into the future (X2.11, "Fear Her") and that old cost-cutting measure, an Evil Parallel Universe. This leaves "The Girl in the Fireplace" (X2.4), "School Reunion" (X2.3) and "Love & Monsters" (X2.10). Two of those are meditations *about* the Doctor as much as adventures with him in it, and the other now looks like trial-runs for all Moffat's usual plot-gimmicks.

Davies is so careful not to make anything that looks like science fiction that he tends, even without budgetary wobbles caused by an unexpected Christmas episode, to try to ground everything in grotty estates in Wales pretending to be grotty estates in London. This isn't logistically much easier; those streets in Cardiff have residents and need to be redressed, barricaded and lit, before people start coming home from work if at all possible (night-shooting is worse), whereas studio sets and out-of-the-way locations are, in fact, easier to manage. There are usually rather more extras in a present-day story than in a future or past one. It's an aesthetic choice as much as a financial one. By

continued on Page 439...

X2.13 Doomsday

between them. The exemplar was *Whizzer & Chips*, but *Shiver & Shake* made more of a distinction between the two, with Shiver (a ghost) starring in a comic about spooky fun and Shake (an elephant in a school uniform) being more routine slapstick. No, you're wrong, it made absolute sense to Britain's eight year olds.

Oh, Isn't That...? ("Army of Ghosts" and "Doomsday")

• *Catherine Tate*. It was theoretically possible that some people watching this first time wouldn't have known who she was, but the entire scene is directed in such a way as to hint that we're all supposed to be thinking "Bloody hell! It's Catherine Tate! In a wedding-dress!" After a lot of stage work and a gig in the second series of *Big Train* (where she and Tracy-Ann Oberman were recruited to replace Tamsin Grieg - see how it all fits together?), Tate got her own sketch-show on BBC3 that transferred to terrestrial. As a result, there are several catch-phrases (one unprintable) associated with her various characters, and she was getting a bit sick of kids repeating them everywhere she went. We'll pick this up next episode, but by this time you could get birthday cards with her characters on.

• *Tracy-Ann Oberman* (Yvonne Hartman) was at this stage known for the second series of *Big Train* (see "The Long Game" and next episode) and a longer-term stint in *EastEnders*. Her character killed Den Watts the second time. (It's his ghost that turns up in the episode Jackie is watching - Den, as you probably knew, was Leslie Grantham from 21.4, "Resurrection of the Daleks".)

• *Derek Acorah* (himself). Off in the netherworld of the digital channels, he had been presenting *Most Haunted*. In this, he would go into a darkened room, with a night-vision camera and someone who believed the building had ghosts, and claim to be channelling the spirits. Later, he would participate in a grotesque televised séance to contact the recently deceased Michael Jackson, which cemented the downward spiral of his career about which Davies was already commenting in this episode.

• *Barbara Windsor*. From her early work with Joan Littlewood's theatre-group in East London (see 6.7, "The War Games"; 25.1, "Remembrance of the Daleks"), Windsor was typecast as busty blond cockney sparrers. She had other strings to her bow, but in the main she did this sort of part, notably in a long run of the *Carry On* films (we really ought to have had a piece on these in Volume 1) and as Saucy Nancy in *Worzel Gummage*. Then she got the main straight role of her career: as Peggy Mitchell (as she appears here), mother of the Sontaran-like Grant and Phil, in *EastEnders*.

• *David Warwick* (police commissioner). If you're struggling to place the police chief at the cliffhanger, he was Kimus in 16.2, "The Pirate Planet" - or, if you're old enough and lived in the UK, he was the dad in the launch advert for Kingsmill bread.

• *Freema Agyeman* (Adeola Jones). If you read the revised Volume 3, you'll know that there was a disastrous attempt (in fact, *two* disastrous attempts) to relaunch notorious Birmingham-based soap *Crossroads*. In the 2001 effort, there was a chalet-girl called Lola who tried to seduce her way to the top of the West Midlands regional non-chain hotel world. Agyeman, who played Lola, is one of the few people to crawl from the wreckage with a career.

• *Alistair Appleton* (himself) was one of the mainstays of daytime television at the time. He had begun on Channel 5's *House Doctor* (where his job was basically to go around apologising for the outspoken and clearly deranged American interior decorator), then he'd moved to *Garden Invaders* (sort of like a cheapskate *Ground Force* - see X1.12, "Bad Wolf") and *Cash in the Attic* (encouraging pensioners to flog their heirlooms and memories).

• *Trisha Goddard* (herself) had been doing daytime discussion shows for a while when the Jerry Springer fad came along and made her show look like an oasis of calm. (Perhaps because it was made by Anglia, dullest of dull regional ITV stations.) Davies had used her in *The Second Coming* in much the same way.

Things That Don't Make Sense ("Army of Ghosts" and "Doomsday") The Doctor and Rose work out in about 30 seconds that the ghosts aren't really ghosts, but merely somethings manifesting with a psychic link. In an unexplored aspect of the story's initial premise, it appears that humans *need to believe* that the spooky substances are their own dead loved-ones (maybe they are?) for the transition to work properly. Jackie's telly implies that the entire planet has all simultaneously jumped to the wrong conclusion about aliens they've never seen

Was 2006 the *Annus Mirabilis*?

continued from Page 437...

reminding viewers every so often of the kinds of story that *can* be told by this series, Davies has allowed himself the chance to restrict himself to more or less two kinds (the Celebrity Historical and the Yeti-in-the-loo) for most of each year's episodes. The 2006 season set the boundaries for the kinds of stories that the BBC Wales version of *Doctor Who* would tell, with the limits of each variety being staked out. Moreover, it left the pattern of the normal 14 episodes very firmly established, with no variation until 2009's four specials and the peculiar scheduling decisions of 2011 and 2012-13. Moffat's first year stuck scrupulously to the normal run of episodes. It also stayed firmly within the boundaries of what had been done in the first two years since the series came back.

Nonetheless, by the time Moffat took over the reins, it was becoming routine for him to win the Hugo Award for the best short-form SF production. Some years, three of the other four nominees were *Doctor Who* episodes. The competition wasn't always under-par. The first time this happened, it was so weird (for anyone who followed both the series and proper-written-down SF) as to be epochal, akin to the first time a former Soviet nation won the Eurovision Song Contest. Even though SF purists were pleased to see the show back, the existence of the series *per se* didn't make any given episode especially welcome. Under normal circumstances, this would be a matter of concern only to them, but 2006 was a year when the public were, broadly, beginning to see it their way. There may not have been much worthwhile SF allowed into the bookshops, but the TV approximations were getting steadily more popular.

2006 was a year when mainstream TV critics were confronted with the unpleasant fact that the kind of programmes at which they'd made cheap shots for years were now hipper, smarter and more popular than the rest of the television being made. Tiresome style-sections of papers proclaimed that it was now fashionable to be what they persisted in calling "geeky". Consider what imported US shows were getting all the attention - the relaunched *Battlestar Galactica*, the increasingly Skiffy-like *Lost*, the initially intriguing *Heroes*, then a seemingly endless stream of attempted reboots of old shows (see X4.15, "Planet of the Dead"). News broke of a relaunch / remake / regurgitation of ITC's 60s existential holiday-camp spy epic *The Prisoner* (see, amongst others, 4.7, "The Macra Terror") and 30s kitsch classic *Flash Gordon* without the 30s kitsch that made it watchable. In Britain, apart from the various me-too shows announced on the coat-tails of the BBC's success (see **What Are the Daftest Knock-Off Series?** under X4.10, "Midnight"), we had what has to be considered as much a companion-piece to Davies-era *Doctor Who* as *Blake's 7* was for the K9 years or *Casualty* was for Sylvester McCoy: *Life on Mars / Ashes to Ashes*. This took perhaps the simplest high-concept cop-show format ever and made it just intriguing enough to keep people watching whilst slowly ringing the changes to the formula and using it to make Big Statements about the role of the police then and now. The change of lead actor and period, with an unannounced shift in storytelling technique, cost *Ashes to Ashes* a slice of the casual audience, but proved that it wasn't just the Sam-Tyler-and-Gene-Hunt show.

This is relevant to *Doctor Who*, as the end of "Doomsday" was a calculated, known watershed. Although the change of lead actor at the end of "The Parting of the Ways" (X1.13) was alarming, it was still the Doctor and his relationship with Rose was changed but not severed. For a large proportion of the new audience the series had created, it was *about* Rose. Her departure, after the episode where Daleks had flown (*flown!*) around London and (at last) taken on the Cybermen, makes a convenient benchmark. People think back to that period and, whatever problems that they think the current version has, they lump it all up as "it was good when Billie was in it". In the backlash that followed, when the various mis-steps that blighted the characterisation of Martha dented the programme's sense of invulnerability, hindsight made the first two years seem more felicitous. The extent to which this is cause or symptom of a sense that 2006 was "better" as regards the actual broadcast episode rather than the general "aura" of the series is hard to gauge. It is definitely a running thread in online comments on each new episode, but that's a self-selecting poll.

Since 2008's economic woe, the budget for such risky programming has been almost non-

continued on Page 441...

X2.13 Doomsday

before, even though aliens have come at least twice in recent months and done spooky things. And yet, the kids play football around them, as if not really bothered that Uncle Chas has come back from the Great Beyond. One wonders what would have happened if the public had repudiated them instead. Presumably, Richard Dawkins has been appearing on talk shows pleading for scepticism but, really, has Harry Saxon been test-driving the Archangel network?

And then it turns out that these psychic emanations were Cybermen. So what was all that about Jackie smelling her dad's tobacco on one of them? Were they eliciting mnemonic/sensory hallucinations as part of anchoring themselves in this reality? Was there a real psychic phenomenon going on and if so, how are the Cybermen - the pureed remnants of people's brain-tissue - making telepathic links to people without touching them? And how is it that Torchwood decides that manifesting thousands of alien beings across the globe is a good idea? It's the worst possible way to keep knowledge of aliens quiet, and really only makes sense if they did want a public that was familiar with aliens. In which case, why?

We've looked in detail at the inadequacies of Torchwood over the previous century or so (see **All Right... Where Were Torchwood?** under 9.3, "The Sea Devils"), but if we can just focus on the internal logic of this episode vis-à-vis the episodes since "Rose", why is such a wealth of alien tech not being used to boost the British economy and cripple America and China financially? You want an empire, you start trading things people in other countries depend upon and reduce their dependency on things you haven't got, but your rivals have. So why not rid the nation of reliance on Russian gas, Middle Eastern oil and Polish coal? Well, they try that with the Breach, but that's causing global weirdness with psychic phenomena (the 'ghosts' seem to home in on the memories of the residents). There's a Jathaa Sun-Glider in the shed, with a power-source they could reverse-engineer instead of a mysterious blind spot with freakish and visible side effects. They've spent two months causing these apparitions without investigating them. The Void Ship has also arrived out of nowhere and they make some kind of link between the two phenomena, but still they press ahead with this as a potential power-source, despite it only generating 5000 KW (the weapon they used on the Sycorax in "The Christmas Invasion" would have been a couple of million times more powerful). Worse in that same story, Llewellyn's rocket group is struggling for funding and treat Guinevere One as an achievement. And while having a snog in a dangerous building-site - as Adeola and her co-worker Gareth attempt - might be thrillingly risky, doing so on the top floor of a notoriously high building is asking for trouble. The polythene sheets aren't rippling, so it's probably not exposed to the air, but if there's a bit of floor gone over one of the many cavernous service ducts...

There seems to be a correlation between where the ghosts arrive and where the Cybermen are in Pete's World. All other transfers seem to have this linkage. But if so, then Pete and his heavily armed posse have ignored a large number of Cybermen wandering around streets and having their photos taken at Westminster Bridge, the Eiffel Tower and the Taj Mahal. It would seem, from Mickey's synopsis of what we missed whilst following Rose instead of his apparently more exciting adventures, that the Cybermen were kept in holding-pens around the world. So their escape through the Void had an optional "tourist locations override" toggle.

This brings us to the big problem: what can imprisoned, decommissioned Cybermen do to access and control a supposedly sealed-off trap-door across dimensions and how, exactly, does their conquest of "real" Earth connect with the alarm-clock inside the Void Ship? Apparently, not a lot. It *just so happens* that they seep through the cracks caused by the Void Ship and their plan is timed to step up a gear at that point, and coincidentally, the Doctor shows up the same morning. And then the Sphere activates, but not when the Doctor goes up to it. We assume that something about the nature of the vessel's exterior detects changes in the nature of local spacetime - inside, there is 'no time', so the alarm would have to go off the instant the door shut, which could cover an interval, with respect to an outside observer, of three seconds, 20 trillion years or anything beyond or in between. Did the Daleks, with no idea of where their craft would arrive if it went through the Void and out the other side - nor indeed which of an infinity of "other sides" they'd encounter - plan the Cyberman assault on proper Earth (without being able to intervene, being in limbo for eternity) or was it a handy coincidence? If the latter, what *was* their original plan?

Was 2006 the *Annus Mirabilis*?

continued from Page 439...

existent and networks are playing a lot safer. *Doctor Who* in its present configuration is almost carrying on solo rather than competing with other almost-similar shows from around the world. Moffat, faced with savage cuts and increasing pressure to make more merchandisable "product", drew a line in the sand between casual viewers and the audience he hoped would pay closer attention. For many, the much-cut and borderline-incomprehensible storyline for X5.3, "Victory of the Daleks" was made worse by the story's apparent *raison d'etre* being to launch a new range of Dalek toys. This is not really what was happening, and indeed much of the Moffat era is coloured by the BBC's insistence on there being "sellable" monsters even when they cannot, for complex reasons bound up in their Charter agreements, give all the revenue from overseas sales and merchandising to the production team to make new episodes. Moffat has had to re-use old monsters from stock, and the ones developed for each new series haven't been the things kids want to play with. The emphasis, for sales purposes, has been on the adult collectors market, which has, for obvious reasons, contracted. In 2006, the first toys from the 2005 series were coming on-stream, along with a trickle of ones they knew in advance would sell (K9, the new Doctor, Cybermen) and the working, sound-producing sonic screwdriver was an obvious hit.

The BBC Books *Doctor Who* novels had been initiated in 1996 (and actually launched in 1997) when the prospect of a whole new, lucrative franchise on the back of the co-produced TV Movie seemed imminent. As the fall-out from this shambles cascaded down, and both Marvel's magazine and the hitherto challenging and complex Virgin *New Adventures* and the rights to original novels were co-opted by bigger players, the immediate impact had been a noticeable dumbing-down. Between this and the 2005 relaunch, the content of both had - once the money-men had stopped looking - regained lost ground. Moving to hardback tie-ins with the Eccleston/Piper year and using characters and situations from those 13 episodes where possible was part of yet-another reboot for the books. Similarly, after a blow-out of in-jokes and a climactic comic-strip for the McGann Doctor ("The Flood"; see "The Parting of the Ways" and "Army of Ghosts"), issue #351 of *DWM* was a fresh start, predicated on the idea that most of the new readers would be looking for hints on what was in the new episodes and what had happened in the old episodes that they needed to know about. A new agency, Orange20, took the reins. Evidently, with a new audience of children, there was money to be made from this publicly funded television programme. What's remarkable is how little this resembled the whole *Star Wars* industry, not how much it did at times.[88]

The significant feature of the novels after 2005 is that they are intended to function as stories without the reader necessarily having seen the television programme. Each works without any of the others. Moreover, whilst a stray one-line allusion to a planet visited in one of the books might worm its way into the TV dialogue, it would do so in amongst a slew of just-made-up-on-the-spur-of-the-moment references to entirely unseen adventures. Both *Star Trek* and *Star Wars* had alienated the general public by relying on the audience knowing decades of backstory (much of it unscreened and only known through tie-in books or a cartoon show only accessible on subscription channels), and both had ground to a halt just as the BBC Wales *Doctor Who* began. This iteration of Who began by assuming that any episode could be the jumping-on point for a new viewer.

That sense of inclusivity was gone by the time we reached "The Wedding of River Song" (X6.13). The Silence had finally been explained, with lots of heavy-handed hints about forthcoming adventures, two years after they were dropped into a clunky piece of dialogue (X5.1, "The Eleventh Hour"), but we still had no answer for basic questions such as whose was the crackly voice narrating the end of "The Pandorica Opens" (X5.12). Even the most attentive viewer was being told that the episode we were watching wouldn't actually make sense for a few years; casual viewers fled. Among reviewers and that portion of the public who felt moved to comment on newspaper sites, the consensus was that - as with the post-1980 episodes made in London - this was for anoraks only, and that 2006 was the last time they actively cared about anything happening in the series.

continued on Page 443...

X2.13 Doomsday

Well, apparently, the Daleks picked Earth as their hole-in-the-sky point simply because this planet, and specifically London after about 1900, is a good place to find a time-traveller who can open the Genesis Ark. (Which would mean that this is all the Doctor's fault.) But they picked a tempting gap in reality 600 feet over a river. Maybe less smart. And the Void Ship opens not because the Cybermen are anywhere around, but because Rose is in the room. Mickey, apparently, wasn't juicy enough. Except that he is, when the plot needs it. Likewise, having the Doctor peering at it at close quarters did nothing to affect the Sphere's readings. (Mickey must have been on a toilet break at exactly that moment.) Davies waited until the commentaries to mention this bit of plotting - and just as well, because it's silly. If the Void Ship needs someone with the altered DNA (or whatever having been in the TARDIS causes), and the Cult of Skaro hid behind the Breach before knowing that the Doctor was alive and that Gallifrey had fallen, why pick Earth rather than Karfel (22.5, "Timelash") or Tersurus (14.3, "The Deadly Assassin") or any other world the rest of the Time Lords used to use as holiday homes? They might not have quite such an annoying alternate version. And it seems rather silly for Time Lords to create a prison that can be opened by one of them crashing into it by accident.

Right, so this Void has no time, no space and no energy. Yet traversing it via cracks causes the global mean temperature on Pete's World to rise. Well, maybe Pete's World is copping the Thermodynamic aftershock of access to a different universe with a higher energy-state. Nope, he's only able to get to ours, and the local Torchwood franchise for this universe are using this "gap" as a source of energy too. So Rose's world and Pete's World are getting heated up by... each other? (Incidentally, mean global warming of two degrees is quite a lot in terms of ecological impact, but just about the lowest limits of what's been recorded lately.) If everything we hear is true, then Torchwood are firing particles into nothingness and getting power out. So maybe the nefarious Daleks are inside the Void sending out energy to tempt humans in either dimension to open the weak-spot. But if so, how? They're inside a Void Ship, with no idea who's there and no means of sending out energy. And they'd have to heat up the entire multidimensional Void to reach these weaknesses. The only way that could work is if they blew a hole in the walls of the universe(s) with their mighty ball-bearing, stepped out for a few moments to put some kind of cosmic brazier near each weak-spot, then got back into the Void Ship before Hell froze over and left them stranded and insane. (There is also the small problem that an interstitial dimension between all possible universes is going to be fairly big, so there's more chance that energy would follow the usual pattern of the Second Law of Thermodynamics and flow *from* somewhere that's got a lot of it *to* somewhere that has less per cubic centimetre - in other words, either version of Earth opening a gateway to an infinite space would *lose* energy real fast.)

The logic of the story suggests that this just happened to be the weak-point between realities caused by the Void ship's escape - it had some reason to be over London when it made the transit, some time before 1981 (several years, if Yvonne's story is accurate). So that's a weakness over London, another in Norway and a Time Rift in Cardiff. You'd think all these alien invaders would have Earth listed as a place to avoid at all costs. It'd be like trying to build an airstrip on an active volcano.

Why is Dalek Sec talking about square miles for the Genesis Ark when it's clearly designed to work in cubic areas? Having the Doctor say something is impossible before anyone else does must have seemed like a foolproof way of getting around the technobabble. Nevertheless, the question remains; how does light reflect off an object that isn't actually there so that people can see it?

A continuity problem arises when we cross-reference the backstory of Ianto Jones in *Torchwood* ("Cyberwoman" especially) with what's seen here. As a member of Torchwood London, he somehow escaped being upgraded, deleted or exterminated - but snuck into Canary Wharf and rescued his girlfriend, who managed *not* to be sucked into the Void despite being part-Cyberman. (There's a slim chance that this can be made to work: see **How Many Cyber-Races Are There?** under X2.6, "The Age of Steel".) He also got a few other goodies out of the base before shutdown and ferried them to Cardiff, so his security clearance must be better than you might expect (not that there was anyone around to check it).

The Doctor says that living life day after day is 'the one adventure I can never have'... so all that stuff with the Brigadier, Jo and Sergeant Benton was just a dream, was it? (See Volume 3b for years

Was 2006 the *Annus Mirabilis*?

continued from Page 441...

For this constituency, the two-part finale for David Tennant and Russell T Davies (X4.17, "The End of Time Part One" and X4.18, "The End of Time Part Two") was the last straw. The saturation publicity for this, with BBC1's Christmas idents themed around reindeer pulling the TARDIS in a loop-the-loop, and what Tennant called his "scorched-earth policy" of doing every single chat-show, game-show and interview prior to what he expected to be his Hollywood career, alienated a lot of people. Many switched on for the first time to see the last two episodes of this phase and were annoyed, baffled and contemptuous. This was more pronounced as, by 2010, *Doctor Who* was no longer one of a range of fantasy shows on British television: it was No. 1 in a field of one. People weren't judging it as being good or bad as an example of that sort of thing, but by absolute criteria: do I like it? Not everyone did. These days, anyone with an adverse opinion is able to get it known worldwide, and if there are enough, that in itself becomes a news story. Of course, there were still people who were judging individual episodes compared to other episodes of *Doctor Who* - and, after 2007, they were less reticent about saying if they were annoyed. The finale of Series Three, with what looked like three consecutive cop-outs in one episode, drew a lot of ire, and when the following year's closing episode compounded the felony (as they saw it) *and* undid the supposedly perfect ending of "Doomsday", newspapers and other outside commentators drew sharp comparisons with the near-universal praise heaped on Series Two.

Hindsight takes its cut in other ways. The financial constraints imposed on the BBC by the Blair government after the Hutton Inquiry were partly offset, in the case of *Doctor Who*, by the Canadian deal. Even though the 2006 episodes have some fairly blatant cost-cutting, they were still unexpectedly lavish. This continued as the Tennant episodes grew more ambitious, but ended abruptly when the Moffat / Smith episodes began. We will look at some of the catastrophic miscalculations (literal and figurative) in that first year of the new regime in Volume 9, but for now it's worth considering how the abrupt drop in production-values matched the fall in disposable income among the viewers. The ingenuity of Davies, Julie Gardner and above all Phil Collinson in making the episodes lends a retrospective glow to those episodes, whereas the painfully obvious cheats of Moffat, Piers Wenger and Beth Goddard recall some of the on-screen we-can't-afford-it moments of Season Six. (See, among others, the sound-only gunfight between an Ice Warrior and some alleged security guards in 6.5, "The Seeds of Death", and Tobias Vaughn's claim to have standardised even his luxuries, saving the bother of building a new set, in 6.3, "The Invasion".) In the 1973 essay, we argued that the Oil Crisis following the October 1973 Yom Kippur War, allied to the crippling inflation of the mid-seventies (see **Why Couldn't They Just Have Spent More Money?** under 12.2, "The Ark in Space"), left the stories in the run-up to "The Time Warrior" (11.1) seeming to come from a bygone age of excess. The BBC's purse-strings tightened even before the 2008 financial collapse.

Moreover, institutional changes were brought in as, in the wake of Hutton, the BBC Trust was formed as an oversight committee. This was led by Michael Grade. (Exactly.) His innovation was to set up reviews of value-for-money and how far any activity by the Corporation reflected the public service ethos of Lord Reith (founder and first Director-General). Grade didn't stick around long enough for a body formed to suit his own skills and beliefs to bed itself in, as a tempting offer from the ailing ITV1 came his way. The Trust's main findings were that many of the odd corners and nooks that the British public were paying for weren't really helping the British public en masse. Thus the BBC's websites were overhauled to suit the Licence-Fee payers (hence iPlayer) and the old Cult website, run by and for people who loved old telly (most of whom were long-term *Who* fans and former fanzine editors or Local Group leaders), bit the dust. This had been filled with nostalgic goodies and the *Doctor Who* section was better-informed than most commercially available sites (and lots sprung up around this time, few any cop). It also had tie-ins to each new episode, ostensibly by first Clive (X1.1, "Rose"), then Mickey, and with some bizarre details (see X2.10, "Love & Monsters" for some, and **What Were the Best Online Tie-Ins?** under X6.3, "The Curse of the Black Spot" for

continued on Page 445...

and years of him doing exactly that, punctuated by alien-invasion-of-the-month.) Quite why his holographic hair is blowing around aboard the TARDIS is probably connected with how he's seeing anything of Rose's version of Norway.

And, it appears to be daylight all over the world at the same time.

In the Universe Next Door to Sense ("Army of Ghosts" and "Doomsday") There is a question that, once asked, opens up a large number of others. That question is: "What did Pete *think* he was doing when he teleports back to 'our' Earth to snag Rose as she hurtles toward the Void, and how did he manage, at all, to do so?"

Look at the climax to the story from Pete's point of view. The Doctor has agreed to close off the Breach and suck the Cybermen and Daleks into the Void. To prevent anyone who's been between universes from suffering the same fate as the two invading armies, he has to put them safely on the other side of the cracks in reality opened up by the Ghost Shift. He also puts Jackie there, just to shut her up, or so it seems. So far, so good, and with Rose safe on Pete's World, he can take a few more risks.

But Rose decides to leave her mum and the not-quite dad and come back to help the Doctor, who handily has a spare magna-clamp. She reappears on "our" Earth a few seconds after she left. Now let's look at Pete's version of what happens next. Presumably, he has some way of monitoring the cracks and knowing if and when the Doctor succeeds in his brilliant plan to pull some levers. Presumably, this means Pete has to stay in the Parallel Lever Room and listen to Jackie wailing about her daughter. All right, this might be enough to prompt anyone to risk flying into Hell, but they don't have a CCTV link with their counterpart in "our" Torchwood - and yet, somehow, Pete arrives in the *exact* right place and time to catch Rose as she falls into Hell, but manages to avoid himself being sucked in. He can't have known this, can he?

There is a possibility that he saw that the Breach was closing and chose, at that split-second, to come and help - forgetting that if the problem rectified itself while he was in transit, he'd be lost. But this would require him to think, "Something's up, I'll jump unarmed into a room that's probably got a lot of annoyed Daleks and Cybermen in and see if I can figure out how to repair a scheme I needed to kidnap an alien genius from another universe to get up and running." So why not send Mickey? The only logic for the boss to go himself, other than some kind of lead-from-the-front mentality which is out-of-keeping with the Pete we've seen so far, is that Mickey and Jake have popped between universes too often to have any chance of standing upright if the Breach re-opens - but even that seems a stretch.

We can just about excuse the TARDIS itself not being pulled into the Void through if the Doctor's got the HADS working again (6.4, "The Krotons"), but not him deciding not to hide everyone vulnerable-but-precious inside his Ship while he enacts his plan to cleanse Earth of the Daleks and Cybermen. And isn't it lucky that *not one* of the thousands of monsters all being sucked into Hell thinks of shooting at the Doctor they're zooming past? It takes very little time for the five million Cybermen all around the world to be brought to London at what looks like 40 miles an hour. And they all come in through the one small window, so the pull of this irresistable force can't be as great as all that. (Wouldn't the Daleks all come through the particle-charged route they arrived? And the Cybermen ought to simply vanish the way they came, shouldn't they? They didn't arrive via the Breach, so whatever's pulling them towards it has just as big a chance of widening the cracks and blowing up Earth as it did when the Doctor broke the glass sheet to persuade Yvonne to stop.) Just at a basic level, why is the Sphere in a different room from the Breach? Did it materialise and then move down a floor? If Torchwood moved it, how did something with no mass, energy, Nectar Points or whatever give them anything to pull it with?

If you've ever stuck duct tape to wallpaper, you'll see the problem with the Doctor's Cunning Plan about the magna-clamps; there seems to be just as good a chance that he, the clamp and the wall it was stuck too would all go into the Void. Instead, the Doctor's apparent plan needs one man to operate two levers, 20 feet apart. Obviously, his ploy rather depended on Rose coming back to help him. But this would lard her up with *even more* Void-Dust - four times more than any Cyberman not in the initial undercover phase of the operation (assuming that the 'ghosts' got dosed). The Doctor must *really* want rid of her. Pete, on the other hand, can stand around right next to the Breach and not only not be affected, but hold a flying non-daughter as she hurtles

Was 2006 the *Annus Mirabilis*?

continued from Page 443...

more detail). It also had ebook versions of key tie-in novels, including Paul Cornell's *Human Nature* and Lance Parkin's *The Dying Days* (see "The Christmas Invasion" for what they meant there, and of course X3.8, "Human Nature" and its attached essay).

So we have a lot of before / after changes, some of which we can ascribe to the period between "Doomsday" and 3.1, "Smith and Jones", and some of which were later but emphasised what had altered. These are partly to do with the nature of *Doctor Who* itself, partly its place in the wider context of TV drama and partly global economics as the US Government and British banks found themselves flailing around. It's not nearly as clear-cut from such a short time afterwards as the change in the series before and after 1973 was.

Doctor Who is occasionally so closely aligned to the popular imagination as to be almost leading it. As we saw in the companion essay to this (**Was 1973 the *Annus Mirabilis*?** under 10.2, "Carnival of Monsters"), if the rest of the nation's entertainment and style seems like a slightly diluted version of the usual *Doctor Who* methodology, the whole package gets remembered together. We're less than a decade from this apparent high point, and already the conditions are so different that it can look further away. There used to be one sure way to test the water of any year and see whether *Doctor Who* was anything like the popular mood, but in August 2006 the unthinkable happened - the BBC cancelled *Top of the Pops*. Sales of physical singles were so low as to be easily skewed and the policy on counting downloads wasn't fixed. However, the year leading up to this was one in which the trend towards homogeneity that had been making the charts rather boring was arrested by a slew of local bands with unashamedly regional-British accents, energetic guitars or glitchy synths ("glitchy" in the sense that there was a sub-genre called "glitch", believe it or not) and lyrics using unlikely words. There was also, as befits a record-breaking heat-wave, a lot of camped-up trashy pop, at least two samples of which the Master has on his stereo in the episodes Davies was writing at the time, broadcast at the end of Series Three (one of the more endearing details in Davies' memoir *The Writer's Tale* is the 40-some-thing executive producer trying to keep up with the nation's youth). Even after *TotP* was taken from us, its traditional links to *Doctor Who* remained, up to casting one of the former presenters as Martha's brother. As we will see, the use of current pop stars who were willing to appear in *Doctor Who* peaked later[89]. (See X3.12, "The Sound of Drums"; "Voyage of the Damned"; and X5.4, "The Time of Angels"; but also 2.8, "The Chase" for the biggest near-miss of all time.) With an erstwhile pop-star in the TARDIS and a new Doctor who dressed like he was in one of those new guitar-bands getting all the coverage - and was played by someone keenly interested in music (to the extent of borrowing a stage-name from one of the more literate and quotable performers) - *Doctor Who*, for better or worse, looked aligned to the wider culture (see at least three essays in this very book).[90]

David Tennant's stage name, as you probably know, was derived from Neil Tennant of sardonic electropop act The Pet Shop Boys. He famously said that all new acts have "an Imperial phase" when they can do no wrong and every detail of their lives is headline news. Then it either goes wrong or someone new shows up and gets their go. *Doctor Who* had one around the time of "The Web Planet" (2.5). Because of the peculiarities of the series' ability to re-invent itself and get a new child audience for whom it's all fresh and "theirs", it also had one in 1971 and 1975-7. Producers and fans might think that there's something innate in the content of the episodes that makes it chime, but close examination of the recordings reveals that, if anything, the closest fit to any current obsessions comes when the ratings are sliding and the press reaction is adverse.

As far as the British public (who were paying for all of this) were concerned, in 2006 *Doctor Who* could do just about anything. That it didn't actually do that much, as far as the broadcast episodes went, is irrelevant. The "halo" around the series made it, for a brief time, bulletproof. This is something to bear in mind when watching those 14 episodes now or at any time in the future. Just as it's hard to see why everyone went so hog-wild over "The Chase" or "The Sea Devils" (9.3), so the context of 2006 is the missing ingredient for why - ratings notwithstanding - everyone seems to think that "The Idiot's Lantern" (X2.7) is some kind of high-water mark.

X2.13: Doomsday

towards him at a rate of knots. The weak link isn't the magna-clamps, it's the elbows of the participants. A Bronze in the Under 7's Gym Championships isn't going to cut it. And if Rose's arms aren't dislocated, then presumably there must be at least one Cyberman, somewhere, who grabbed on to a lamp-post or fixed object. And the Cybermen can over-ride the ghost-lever by making a fist in a B-movie salute - so why can't the sonic screwdriver, which can do bloody everything, not do anything to fix the lever when it slips out of position?

Hang on, though... Rose and the Doctor slipped between universes *inside the TARDIS* and got back that way too, so none of the Void-sparkliness ought to be on them. Thinking about it, if, prior to the Time War, all these parallel universes were accessible by TARDIS (and we know they were, because 7.4, "Inferno" and 26.1, "Battlefield" were partly set there and have the Doctor arriving and causing trouble), and you can't get to said parallel universes without going through the Void, then what's so special about a Void ship that makes it 'impossible'?

Critique ("Army of Ghosts" and "Doomsday") Of course Rose wasn't going to die. It was a huge, manipulative stunt. It worked well enough for Davies to do it again, ever more brazenly, until the public got wise and he actually had to kill the Doctor properly for anyone to be bothered (X4.18, "The End of Time Part Two"). Knowing this makes coming back to the Series Two finale harder, because the trick of Rose telling us she's dead is merely annoying. This isn't even the last time we'll see her. "Stunt" is also a verb, and that's what happens here.

The episode itself, bookended by this narrative ploy, has a lot of potentially rich ideas all squashed together and denied room to develop. Five years earlier, the idea that ghosts have come back and become accepted would have been an entire ITV series and Davies would have got a BAFTA for it. There may have been mileage in the idea of a secret scientific / military team collecting alien tech for their own ends (ideally, with Shaun Dingwall as their boss - watch his entry in episode thirteen and compare it to the Torchwood we got). Jackie's plea to Rose not to keep changing as a person is where they could profitably have put the whole weight of this series. Rose is recognisably stepping into the Doctor's shoes as this story develops, and the way she stands up to the Cult of Skaro is - to use a word they used a lot back then - "empowering". Having Jackie accept that could have been what they said they were aiming for: a genuinely involving drama using an unusual premise and where all sides have a good case. Here, they load the dice against Jackie, moving her back into comedy-soap-mum mode, and enforce an unnatural hiatus onto the story for her meeting with Pete. That in itself is an hour-long drama frittered away on a two-minute joke that squanders the momentum the rest of the story had built up by then. Davies is writing by the seat of his pants, getting this script in on time for Block Three, and director Graeme Harper is spinning so many plates by this stage that he hasn't time to argue. But one thing is clear: they've all decided that the main target audience of this series don't want long talky scenes, they want effects, explosions and monsters.

For anyone over 30 or under 12, the big event of this story was the Daleks and the Cybermen meeting at last. And it's embarrassing. School playground taunts don't sound any better though a ring modulator, and they don't even sound weird enough to be unsettling, the way "Would you like a cup of tea?" did (X5.3, "Victory of the Daleks"). All that build-up, and we're a step away from the Cyber-Controller getting a wedgie for saying to Dalek Jast, "You see that Bella Emberg? She's your girlfriend, she is."[87] On the plus side, it's fair to say that out of the (literally) millions of people who'd imagined such a confrontation over the previous 40 years, enacted it with Palitoy models, Weetabix pasteboard figures or in real school playgrounds, none had seen it coming out quite like that.

Right, with those caveats out of the way...

It's obvious that they planned this as an epic-to-end-all epics. That's going to cause them trouble when they try to top it each following year, but this is defiantly, unashamedly cinematic. Watched as a 90-minute blockbuster, the progression from domestic oddness to wide-screen chaos - from a kid's playground on a London estate to two separate Earths under threat from a concatenation of the two biggest threats the Doctor's ever faced, and an organisation specifically set up to apprehend him - is almost seamless. As two episodes with a week apart, the tension between the cliffhanger and the resolution is, for a whole new generation, a taste of why the supposedly naff twentieth-century series was a national obsession until 1980. Incidents that would have been the whole point of earlier stories or other series, such as the Cybermen menacing a family in their home or an army platoon taking on the invading forces, are almost nonchalantly tossed in alongside Derek Acorah and Japanese teenagers.

That sense of scale is present in the sets for Torchwood, most of which are, unusually, done in the studio. It's there in the music. Murray Gold's been idling a little lately, with only X2.10, "Love & Monsters" having a wholly new score that wasn't a bit perfunctory ("The Idiot's Lantern" is probably the low-point). Now, he makes a point of varying the styles, from brassy action-movie stuff to the *ersatz* Nyman of the end sequence. Unlike episodes eight and nine, there's nothing off-the-peg here, except in re-use of tags from the first half of this Block to denote Cybermen. People are paying attention to the details, the small effects in the corner of the screen getting as much care as the set pieces. There's no skimping.

But Daleks... Cybermen... in present-day London and elsewhere, in numbers beyond our comprehension. The *ne plus ultra* of Yeti-in-a-loo scenarios, and they concentrate on what's happening in an office in Canary Wharf. It's an enormous gamble and, on the day it was first shown, it paid off. Now, it's less successful. It subordinates the whole of the programme's history, and a lot of its immediate future, to the Cult of Rose Tyler. There's a piquant sense that the grown-up Rose we see on the beach isn't going to be around, that a more interesting version of this character we've already invested a lot in won't get to develop. A lot of this last year's episodes have relied on Piper to make her character more sympathetic than the script ought to allow. After "Love & Monsters", we also have a sense of Jackie as a more rounded character and here, where we see that money doesn't change her after all, there's a genuinely happy ending. Mickey's outgrown his pathetic hanger-on status. Everything tends towards this being equilibrium for everyone save for the Doctor and Rose, but the former is the one we'll be following. It means that the whole "I died" blether is left seeming like unfinished business rather than, as it ought to be, closure for everyone except the series' protagonist. This is going to poison the remainder of the Tennant / Davies years.

At the time of broadcast, this seemed like a satisfying answer to all the problems and riddles set up so far. Rather than, as many other stories from now on would, seeming to have a can of "emotion" as a pour-on sauce, the viewer's engagement with the story is at all levels - and any sympathy, empathy or irritation with the characters is a result of the situation, not an optional extra. It got Rose out of the series without killing her or seeming like a second-best. They made something that got everyone talking. It had a bit of everything, and in a combination only *Doctor Who* could provide. Now, it seems slightly less impressive. Seen in the bigger context of the whole series from 1963 to date, Rose's departure is less of a wrench than Ian and Barbara deciding to take their chances with a Dalek time machine to get home rather than stay with this odd "family" they've acquired. Jo Grant's departure ("The Green Death") is more effective for all the things not being said. Only a handful of the millions watching this on first transmission (ignore the official ratings, *everyone* saw this) knew that and, for them, this is the high-water mark of the programme.

The Facts

Written by Russell T Davies. Directed by Graeme Harper. Viewing figures: "Army of Ghosts": (BBC1) 8.19 million, (BBC3 repeats) 0.8 and 0.7 million. "Doomsday": (BBC1) 8.22 million, (BBC3 repeats) 0.6 and 0.4 million.

Repeats and overseas promotion Die Armee der Geister, L'armee des ombres, Der Weltuntergang, Adieu, Rose.

TARDISodes ("Army of Ghosts") A reporter goes to his editor with the "scoop of the century" about Torchwood, and is dragged off by Men in Black.

("Doomsday") A newsreader tries to give an emergency broadcast about the Cybermen (using footage of the bridge-battle and street assaults from the episode) as the Daleks enter the newsroom (unseen, using familiar dialogue from 2.2, "The Dalek Invasion of Earth").

Production

("Army of Ghosts" and "Doomsday"): With the rights to the Daleks finally negotiated and the Cybermen as this year's big re-introduced villain, it was time for a showdown between the two. This was the only thing considered momentous enough to write Rose out without killing her. Russell T

X2.13 Doomsday

Davies planned the entire parallel-universe storyline to reunite Pete and Jackie and give Rose and Mickey somewhere to be heroic off-screen. Noel Clarke was especially keen to get to use the gun we see in this story, although he probably had other reasons to want to be in the episodes. This meant that logistically, the best way to make this series was by having the season finale in the can before making the six episodes between the two two-part stories Graeme Harper was to direct. That in turn meant writing the end of the series at the same time as finishing the first few episodes. Although this allowed Davies to retroactively account for nobody in Torchwood knowing that Jackie wasn't Rose (by means of the "Bad Wolf" virus written into "Love & Monsters"), this was not a procedure they tried again while the Davies / Gardner / Collinson team was in charge. It was a matter of some debate who should rescue Rose at the end, with Collinson suggesting that this was the final way Mickey could be seen to have outgrown his "idiot" past. Gardner's suggestion that Pete had to accept Rose as his daughter (even though she clearly wasn't) was followed.

- Dalek Sec was the original Dalek from "Dalek" painted black. Edward Thomas' department had used the toys produced by Character Options and painted them in various permitations of black and another colour before opting to simply make it shiny black on matt black. Unfortunately, Sec and "his" operator, Nicholas Pegg (former leader of Nottingham Local Group of the Doctor Who Appreciation Society), had made an appearance at the BAFTA Awards ceremony and almost blown the big surprise (for some reason this time, it had a red eye instead of the usual blue). Pegg, David Hankinson and Barnaby Edwards were all returning from last year's finale, with occasional operator Dan Barratt. Stuart Crossman, as the Genesis Ark, was mainly ballast, as his planned stint moving the Ark across the hangar was reworked to allow the effects team to pump dry ice from the prop.

- We'll try to avoid too much repetition, despite this being made in the same block, and many of the same locations, as the earlier Cyberman two-parter. The first day's work exclusively on this episode was 2nd November, a return to the Brandon Estate for Rose's return to her mum's and the ghost-busting. The cones had TARDIS roundels as their bases. A fortnight later, there's a trip to Tredegar House for some street scenes and a studio session at Q2, for the briefing room material. Five days after that, on 21st, the location work at the Tyler Mansion included leaving for Norway, and the ad for Ekto-Shine was shot in the kitchen of that same house. The first solid block of work just for this episode was four days at Q2, starting on 29th November, for the sphere chamber and the corridors around it. The sliding door was recycled from X1.6, "Dalek" and kept sticking on the painted floor. On the first day of this, Piper was whisked off to London by helicopter for yet another awards ceremony.

We skip four days, and a second unit shot the Land Rover driving around Brackla, near Bridgend, which is where they were for the tunnels in "Rise of the Cybermen". Phil Collinson directed some of these, and Shaun Dingwall (Pete Tyler) had a bit of trouble driving the Land Rover. The next day, 7th December, was spent at Brackla Bunkers, the nuclear shelter used briefly in the earlier two-parter, as the corridor in which Jackie meets Pete (and a brief scene in episode twelve), and then on 8th, the action moved to the Lever Room. This was the same set as the Sphere Chamber, rebuilt and repainted. They began with the Parallel Lever Room, and shot Piper's distraught wall-thumping, before going on to do pick-ups for X2.1, "New Earth" (Collinson directed these too). The following day was the "real" Lever Room, which was the same set redressed, obviously. Some of this was a vertical green-screen, with Piper on wires "falling" towards the floor as she had done in X1.9, "The Empty Child". Other shots had her on a tea-trolley. There were huge wind-machines to make the Breach seem open, and Harper used a slow-motion camera for some shots. Freema Agyeman joined the cast on this day, and a few comments were sent from Harper to Davies. The regulars got a day off after this, and the crew went out into the streets around Bute Town (the shopping area of Cardiff Bay) for various reaction-shots, crowd-scenes and excitable Japanese teenagers with ghost T-shirts. Everyone took a day off at this stage, and on 12th, they began four more days of Lever-Room malarkey before Christmas. On 3rd January, they started again for three days, in the middle of which they recorded Alistair Appleton's "GhostWatch" sequences. 6th January was a day at the HTV studios for more corridors, the top floor of Torchwood and a "No Entry" sign.

The hangar scenes were mainly shot at RAF St

Doomsday X2.13

Athan's, which had already been used (and would again). The Egyptian sarcophagus seen at Torchwood was explicitly stated to be the one from "Pyramids of Mars", and the Jathaa Sunglider had originally been planned as the Doctor's exit strategy from the roof of Canary Wharf. The location allowed for a vast green screen to be erected for some shots, and everything above ground-floor level (even the Cybermen falling from gantries in episode thirteen) was done by The Mill. This location turned out to be useful for remounts of the Lumic zeppelin heist. The RAF staff lent some components of cockpits and fuselages to be used as alien tech props. The regulars weren't needed for the next day, as it was almost all scenes of "ghosts" arriving and Cybermen resisting the army on a bridge; this sequence was an enormous challenge to get into the one day they had. It was a Sunday, and the majority of the scene was at the Docks in Cardiff. (And meanwhile, Agyeman had been told that they wanted her for a part in another series, possibly the *Torchwood* spin-off they'd just announced, so on 15th January, they gave her auditions. Once this was over, they asked her to keep quiet about what it was they really wanted her for until the episode had aired, a wait of about six months.) Later that night, the basement of the Capital Arcade shopping centre was the site for the Dalek / Cybermen slanging-match. It was chosen for its flat floors and resemblance to other locations and sets used.

- The regulars went back to Bridgend, to Southerndown Beach, for the two coastal scenes, the alien world with the flying lizards and Bad Wolf Bay. A group of windsurfers wandered into shot at one stage, and Piper's long speech was done in two takes. The first was nearly perfect, but her nose was running; the second was dryer, but the wind sent her hair everywhere. It was unfair to ask her to do a third, so Harper composited these into the broadcast version. Nobody but the cast for this scene, the director, the producers and the costume designer knew the content of these, and the dialogue was on specific pages, for which Piper and Tennant had to sign on the location to prevent any leaks. (Dingwall seemed not to have been told to keep mum, and almost blurted out the ending.) The standby props manager, Phil Shellard, didn't know that the sonic screwdriver would be needed (but he had one handy anyway). This was Noel Clarke's last day as a regular cast-member.

Following that, there were scenes back at the TARDIS on 17th and at the Tyler flat set on 18th, both at Q2. On the latter day, at Gardner's request, they reshot Tennant's reaction to Rose being on the other side of a wall between dimensions, as he was insufficiently tortured-looking for her taste. They used the earlier take. There were also extra scenes in the Sphere Chamber and underground corridors. Most of the next day was the Cybermen menacing the public, including in a house in Canton, north of Cardiff, and a few scenes of Jackie running up and down stairs; later that night, Piper got on a London bus in the Haynes, Cardiff. Back at Q2 next morning, yet another scene in the Lever Room, followed by green-screen stuff of Daleks and Cybermen flying over London, some more ghosts and a bit more of Jackie's flat. Principal shooting ended at Thames Television's studios, Teddington Lock, London (look back to Volume 3b for why making *Doctor Who* there is piquantly ironic) and the *Trisha* sequence. Davies had used almost exactly the same trick of a morning discussion-show debating a freakish topical occurrence in *The Second Coming*, so Trisha knew the score. There were five more scenes to complete, one of which would be a major operation to keep secret. First, there was another Sphere Chamber scene six weeks after Trisha's guest cameo, on 9th March. A month after that there was another, and one more in the Tyler Mansion, and one in the hangar. That was April 11th, shortly before the new series began transmission. These had to be done at the Enfys studio as, by this stage, Q2 had been abandoned and the whole production was in the middle of moving to Upper Boat Studios (we'll tell you all about that in the next volume). But in between those was a short scene made on the day of the official end of production, and indeed during the wrap party for X2.9, "The Satan Pit" and Piper's official departure.

- The sixth episode of the second series would have been a story called "The Runaway Bride". Davies had decided to hold this back if there was a second Christmas special needed. This was the case, and secret negotiations had begun to get Catherine Tate to guest-star in it. The team decided that ending the second series on a downer was possibly counter-productive, so, the teaser into this Christmas episode was grafted onto the TARDIS scene at the end. On the last day at Q2, the introduction to this was shot. Harper had been given the script three days earlier, and a lot of effort was spent on getting a dress for Tate without tipping anyone off. Louise Page took the measurements and used Tate's birth-name, Catherine Ford, as a cover when shopping in London department stores.

• A few details needed tweaking. The box to operate the ghost-catcher was made using recycled ear-pod props, and this was only caught in the first edit; a new box was made and inserts of someone's hand (probably not Tennant's) operating it against grass were made. Gareth originally said that the TARDIS was "50 metres" from the CCTV camera; this needed to be redubbed to suit the retrogressive Torchwood policy of Imperial measurements. Similarly, nobody could agree which way Jackie's middle-name, Andrea, was pronounced last time, so they shot both but lost the correct take, needing a redub. Dalek Rabe (just about the most archetypal Davies-style alien name) was thought to sound too much like "Ray", so he became "Jast" (the second-most archetypal Davies alien name) in ADR. The alien world used an effect The Mill had left over of manta rays and coral, as a cheap way of making a suitably impressive vista (scripted as looking like a 70s Roger Dean album cover for Yes) beyond the initial budget and time allocated for the episode.

• Transmission of "Army of Ghosts" looked likely to be delayed, as one of the crucial matches of the World Cup threatened to over-run. As it turned out, they made the 7.00pm scheduled time. This was also the day that Andy Murray got plausibly close to making Wimbledon's Men's Final. (He didn't.) The *Radio Times* capitalised on the football link as "Doomsday" was due to come on just before the semi-final, in which England looked likely to be playing. They made two covers, one with Daleks and the FIFA-approved balls, another with Cybermen. The afternoon of 7th July was record-breakingly hot, but with two national obsessions back-to-back, the ratings held. Press and Internet speculation about what would happen to Rose grew. By this time Martha Jones, played by Freema Agyeman, had been announced to the public, with Tennant wearing a spectacularly wrong shirt for the photo-shoot. The episode itself was sandwiched between the Wimbledon Women's Final and the World Cup Semi-Final (England were still in it, at least for another 90 minutes) and the ratings withstood the heat and temptation to go out. The episode was bookended with trailers for that autumn's family-drama show, *Robin Hood* (see **What Are the Daftest Knock-Off Series?** under X4.10, "Midnight").

• In a momentary lapse, Davies agreed to write a 90-minute special about Rose's adventures as Defender of the (other) Earth, but with *Torchwood* coming to BBC3, a plan for a Sarah Jane Smith series for CBBC and a whole new series of *Doctor Who* to make - all in a new, purpose-built complex, Upper Boat, across Cardiff - this wasn't followed up. Clarke's first job after finishing work on this and promoting his film *Kidulthood* was to write an episode of *Torchwood*. Piper, meanwhile, was barely able to draw breath. Her next jobs were playing the lead in *Ruby in the Smoke* (the first of two adaptations of Phillip Pullman's Sally Lockhart Victorian adventures, with a sidekick played by a young unknown called Matt Smith) and Fanny in *Mansfield Park* (because someone at ITV had decided that it wasn't possible to have too many Jane Austen adaptations). Then came her next major role, as Belle in *Diary of a Call Girl*, adapted from the bestselling book version of a notorious blog by a prostitute. Smith was in that, too.

End Notes

1. Apparently, there's an American film star of the same name, but hardly anybody in Britain could pick that guy out of a police line-up, whereas the "real" (as far as we're concerned) Chris Evans is instantly recognisable. Assume throughout this book that we mean the *TFI Friday* bloke, and not the latest in a long line of Captain Americas. Besides, everyone knows that the "First Avenger" was John Steed....

2. A baffling "dark" sitcom of the kind BBC3 made a lot of back then, as we may have said. There's a *Doctor Who* reference every so often: in one episode, the inept part-time drug-dealer Moz is coming to on his bedroom floor and says "I may regenerate - it feels different this time" (21.6, "The Caves of Androzani"). There are a few actors who've done both series.

3. There's already a famous Russell Davies here, the one who's now presenting *Brain of Britain*.

4. Cheam is a district of South London, in the Commuter-Belt. It is, in television terms, best known as the locale for the (fictional) 23, Railway Cuttings, home of Tony Hancock and Sid James in *Hancock's Half Hour* (see Volume 1). Many British viewers heard the name and made the assumption that Jabe was from Surrey. American readers can try to imagine the Poughkeepsie rain forest or San Diego jungle for comparison.

5. We had spotted this and were very proud of making this connection, then the dialogue for X6.12, "Closing Time" makes it obvious. Grrr...

6. If your nerves can stand it, look up Crazy Frog and ponder that this was UK Number 1 for most of Eccleston's term as the Doctor.

7. Standard Trunk Dialling. This system replaced switchboards (see 2.1, "Planet of Giants") and is the source of endless schoolboy jokes about elephants in phone-boxes. The system doesn't need mains electricity, which is how Sarah managed to make phone calls in evacuated London in 11.2, "Invasion of the Dinosaurs". The Cabinet War Rooms had an earlier version of this. This is the only STD Churchill had, and anyone who says otherwise has an even shakier grasp of Wartime history than Mark Gatiss or Steven Moffat.

8. Needless to say, the Doctor's phone number, as seen on screen in this episode, is a fake. The fact that the BBC needs a non-existent prefix, like the Hollywood fake area-code 555, is a sign of how things have developed.

9. The Puffin Club: Puffin Books, the junior subsidiary of Penguin Books, was, when led by the redoubtable Kaye Webb, the one-stop source for imaginative and readable children's books. She is responsible for the careers of many of the most famous and respected authors from 1961 to 1980. The Puffin Club was a glorified order-form for such books, with jokes and puzzles as well as blurbs for the new books and slips to help you purchase them at reduced rates through your school. Other publishers in this field followed suit and tied to entice British kids into buying US imports. They undercut Puffin, which attracted less well-off schools to them, but failed to deliver what was ordered. When they did, the books were often less good than advertised. The unreliability of these is at least part of the reason the Puffin Club is so fondly remembered. The cartoons by Quentin Blake and Ronald Searle - later Webb's husband - are another.

10. In order to avoid a slapped wrist from Equity for breaking the rule about an actor playing two speaking roles in a series in under ten years, Gatiss selected the pseudonym "Rondo Haxton" when playing Gantok (X6.13, "The Wedding of River Song"). Anyone as trainspotterish as Gatiss - or us - about 30s horror movies would know that Rondo Hatton played the Hoxton Strangler.

11. The haberdashers in *David Copperfield* who have a sideline in funerals - Dickens' low opinion of that trade is so obvious that his acceptance of Mr Sneed's line of business is peculiar.

12. This proved so annoying to so many people that a successful radio parody was broadcast on BBC Radio 1. It was intended as a merchandising spin-off, and made with the collaboration of Twentieth Century Fox to cross-promote the film, but that's not how it was received. Even with the (German) director slotting in a few references to outside events, the jingoistic US-orientated script and the 4th of July iconography irritated anyone who wasn't American. The French response was

mainly outrage, Britain simply got sarcastic. Wunnerful Radio 1, the main Pop station, picks up on the Orson Welles vibe by having DJs playing themselves (and Patrick Moore as himself - X5.1, "The Eleventh Hour"; X1.4, "Aliens of London" - getting into fisticuffs with a BEM). *Independence Day UK* claimed to tell the "real" story of how the RAF did most of the work: the Group Captain - TV's Colin Baker - gets the last line, claiming "The Yanks'll take the credit for it, you wait and see."

13. The Whitechapel Foundry, where it was cast, is still in business. It also made the Liberty Bell, which was intact when it left London.

14. When it was launched in 1973, it was called *Why Don't You Just Switch Off Your Television Set and Go and Do Something Less Boring Instead*, and had been a show presented by children from a different region each series, during school holidays. It showed how to do things, make things and get to things. Davies took it over in 1993 and it became a strange comedy-drama, featuring child actors (the young Anthony McPartlan - half of the all-conquering Ant and Dec - was one) and a rival gang called "Liverpool Investigation 'N' Detective Agency". Mysteriously, the show was cancelled shortly after this...

15. A brief introduction to the institutional complexities, and how they manifested themselves in weird but memorable shows that anticipated the later discoveries by child psychiatrists, can be found in *The Cult TV Book*, edited by Stacey Abbott (IB Tauris, 2010). Not that we're biased, but Chapter 16 is a particular highlight, whilst Chapter 14 reinforces the distorting effect limited cable access had on the followings for some imported series.

16. *The Simpsons* began as a feature on *The Tracey Ullman Show*. That was, in part, a result of her work on BBC comedies, so when the cartoon segment got a spin-off show, it was offered to the Corporation for free. They were unsure about where it could be scheduled, so declined. Later, after Sky had misguidedly pitched it at kids, the BBC got terrestrial rights at favourable rates. Eventually, after they had shown all the episodes in rapid succession, twice, the series gained a huge following here as part of BBC2's "Cult" line-up and Channel 4 offered considerably more money to Fox. This move coincided with the return of *Doctor Who*, the end of the Cult ghettoisation - and the rather fine section of the BBC's website - and *The Simpsons* pretty much jumping the proverbial shark.

17. That Director General was John Birt, later given a peerage and a post with Tony Blair's government using his ability to spin management gobbledegook into a means to dragoon underpaid, overworked employees into doing even more paperwork into what passed for transport policy. See Volume 6 for more examples of this man's impact on the BBC's morale and ability to make watchable television.

18. And of course, back through Shakespeare and the Brothers Grimm. In fact, it's the staple of most of the traditional Christmas Pantomimes, which is a tradition Americans cannot comprehend until they've been to Britain and seen one, and even then it's a struggle. Just accept for the moment, if you've not come across this, that characters like Jackie Tyler are usually played by middle-aged men in drag and that the David Tennant Doctor would probably be a young woman in thigh-boots.

19. Well, the *very* start is a spoof trailer for what the Peter Cushing films might have looked like if they'd been made in the Pertwee era, with Bond as a model.

20. Akira Kurosawa, film director: famous for, amongst many other things, a string of American-influenced Samurai films - *The Seven Samurai* (recycled as *The Magnificent Seven*), *The Hidden Fortress* (recycled as *Star Wars*), *Yojimbo* (recycled as *For a Fistful of Dollars*), *Kagemusha* (recycled as, um, 24.3, "Delta and the Bannermen") and reworkings of Shakespeare. And, of course, he did *Rashomon*. In many of these, he used muddy battles in torrential rain to depict the unheroic nature of battles, and because he was using fast monochrome film-stock, he had to dye the rainwater black. Some see this as an allusion to the Hiroshima fall-out.

21. Sir Ridley Scott, famous for the 70s *Hovis* adverts, became a feature film director and pilfered Kurosawa's rain-sodden conflict trick for use in urban/industrial settings in films including *Alien*, *Blade Runner* and, um, *Black Rain*. We can

End Notes

file that under "full disclosure", or "overlong Michael Douglas movies".

22. Observe an embryonic art-form, and while away half an hour, by checking these out on YouTube or wherever. Appropriate early-80s snacks at the ready - the classic post-school crisps-and-salad-cream sarnie and Nesquik combo for any UK readers - and start with "Pop Muzik" by M or Queen and "Play the Game", which looked dead sophisticated in the era of Sid and Marty Kroft's *Electra-Woman and Dyna Girl*. Then see "Open Your Heart" by The Human League and "To Cut a Long Story Short" by Spandau Ballet to see what happens when you're not catering for Middle America any more, Kim Wilde's original "Kids in America" for that thin line between "aloof" and "bored", the aforementioned "Physical" for stretching a ten-second joke to three minutes, and then we enter the "we can afford film" stage with MTV opening up the opportunities for excess ("She Works Hard for the Money" and the magnificently silly "New Moon on Monday" - a video so OTT, even Duran Duran disown it) and the simple-but-effective "Shock the Monkey" by Peter Gabriel. After 1984, artists knew what they wanted and generally wanted what they'd just seen, so videos became increasingly homogeneous. Grant delivered what was asked of him on time and on budget but, like everyone else's, they're less memorable.

23. A nod in the direction of the groundbreaking book *The Uses of Literacy* by Richard Hoggart, which is - almost despite the title - as good an introduction into the pop-cultural world and basic assumptions about British identity into which *Doctor Who* was born as you'll find. Other than *About Time 1*, of course.

24. Ponder that: a working-class kid, fuelled by *Astounding Science Fiction* and *True Crime*, went to the college that employed FR Leavis. Look him up if you're unsure why this is, at very least, potentially amusing.

25. Adapted for television in the early 1960s in the *Out of This World* series, produced under the aegis of Sydney Newman - the tape is long-since wiped, but the version starred future household names Peter Wyngarde (21.5, "Planet of Fire") and Jane Asher, and was directed by Paul Bernard (see Volume 3). Three other episodes in the series had scripts by Terry Nation, making him a shoo-in a year later for a gig on *Doctor Who*. The original story is one of the most anthologised ever, and exemplified editor John W Campbell's approach to SF before he went bonkers - see 11.5, "Planet of the Spiders" for the Hieronymus Device - so obviously Robert Holmes knew full well what he was doing when plundering it for the *Blake's 7* episode "Orbit".

26. With good-quality colour film so useful for aeriel reconnaissance, anyone thinking to fritter it away on entertainment had to persuade the Powers That Be that it was somehow good for the War Effort. Brendon Bracken, wartime Minister of Information, filtered out the applications, but the decision was a military one and Churchill would often be the final arbiter. Thus a grand-scale enterprise like Olivier's *Henry V* had to be morale-boosting. It was two hours long, in sumptuous colour (costumes and all; tricky, with dyes at a premium) with literally thousands of extras - mainly active servicemen, something that needed a lot of logistical clout (Goebbels had sanctioned something similar for the 1943 *Baron Munchhausen*, and may have caused the Nazi defeat in Leningrad) especially to take them to Ireland to film Agincourt. It also pointedly cut out all the bits where Shakespeare makes King Harry morally ambiguous. So claims that Powell and Pressburger's 1942 *The Life and Death of Colonel Blimp* was made against Churchill's wishes may be Bracken spinning this literally and figuratively colourful satire on gentlemanly warfare. *A Matter of Life and Death* is emphatically romantic, in both senses, and set in a rural idyll where even the GIs are roped into the vicar's production of *A Midsummer Night's Dream*. So the few professionally made colour films from Wartime Britain are as far removed from the practical and mundane domestic settings where any evidence of colour in the home might be found as it is possible to get. The myth endures.

27. As *Doctor Who* fans tend to be the people most likely to have watched both series, let's just quickly point out that *Press Gang* had an American called "Spike", who was played by an English actor with a painfully unconvincing accent. In *Buffy the Vampire Slayer*, the roles were reversed.

End Notes

28. Everyone seems to assume that the "handsome Time Agent" mentioned in X5.12, "The Pandorica Opens", whose wrist is still in the bracelet, must be Jack. Yet we know of at least one other ex-Agent active in this time, and from him we learn that a lot of the other Agents have been killed. But the real question here, never addressed, is whether slicing Jack up creates lots of Jacks. We saw a number of baroque deaths in "Children of Earth", after which he was restored from nearly nothing, so it remains to be seen whether an army of indestructible fifty-first century charmers can be created with a chainsaw and a few petri dishes. But then, this opens up the whole problem of what happens when he shaves...

29. It is only when Jack first meets Ianto in a *Primeval*-style flashback that this is explained, but it makes everything about Jack more puzzling. Unless he has some kind of Zen training to avoid sweating when hot or anxious, this would mean that he is unable to do anything in a crisis because people are hurling themselves at him and ripping off his clothes. Let's just count all the *Torchwood* episodes that would have ended badly because they all dropped what they were doing to "dance". Then watch X3.11, "Utopia" and wonder why it wasn't a three-species orgy.

30. These days, with people attempting to cut down on sugar/ fat intake, or go vegan, or cater for people who are lactose-intolerant, a lot of World War II recipes are getting dusted off. A five-minute online search produced about 30 recipes for eggless cakes - including the standard carrot-cake now on sale in health-food shops across Britain at alarming prices - and Red Velvet cake, which uses beetroot instead of sugar. Carrots were also used as replacements for ice-lollies and - with the cover story for the officially non-existent radar being that they helped people see in the dark - were promoted as the quintessential "Victory" food. "Doctor Carrot" was "The children's best friend". This was, in part, because the "Dig for Victory" campaign had everyone rooting up their flower-beds to grow veg, this resulted in a serious glut of carrots. The Imperial War Museum, which has been heavily involved in the schools projects mentioned in **The Big Picture**, has posted a lot of the short films on this subject on YouTube.

31. And besides, so what if Tinky Winky *is* gay? There's only one other male Teletubby and that's Dipsy - and he's obviously up to something with Laa Laa when the cameras aren't rolling. It's those funky dance moves, and the hat. And *Teletubbies* is so last century - it's all about *In The Night Garden*... these days (see X3.11, "Utopia").

32. The 90s *New Adventures* novels dragged him in and sent him on a mission with Ace (see Volume 6), who by this stage had gone from spunky pyromaniac from Perivale to hard-bitten Starship Trooper. We'll look at the problematic relationship of these books to the BBC Wales episodes when we get to X3.8, "Human Nature".

33. Those not traumatised by seeing Jon Pertwee in the shower in 7.1, "Spearhead from Space" might not realise that the BBC let that go out 35 years earlier and repeated it the following summer. Of course, for all we know there may have been a full-frontal orgy sequence in 4.7, "The Macra Terror" that never made it to the telesnaps.

34. This was ITV's "answer" to *Big Brother*, a series where has-beens and nobodies get whisked off to Australia and are made to undergo ordeals involving buckets full of insects and eating unspeakable bits of marsupials (Colin Baker was in one and almost immediately kicked off). It looks exactly like a grotesque parody of bad "reality" television, but with one contestant in ten being someone you've heard of if you're from around here and over 30. As with all live ITV shows not featuring ice-skates, it's presented by Ant and Dec, op cit.

35. Apparently, he was asked to go on *Dancing on Ice* (see 24.4, "Dragonfire"), arguably the best of the "get people to learn a difficult skill and do it competitively" games because there is genuine difficulty and risk in ice-dance, as well as a complete lack of correlation between previous athletic skill or showbiz background and eventual performance. There is a long lead-in during which the contestants have to learn the basics, during which time John Barrowman became famous enough for people to have heard of him before this.

36. And his first line as Claude? "Fantastic." Some claim to have seen a police box in episode nine, but if you're the kind of person who uses the word "squee" in mixed company, the highlight is the scene Eccleston shares with George Takei and TV's Eric Roberts towards the end of that series.

455

End Notes

37. Watch the interrogation scene from 2.7, "The Space Museum" and his appreciation of the Beatles in 2.8, "The Chase" before dismissing the idea. It makes the latter story's line about "cinders floating around in Spain" take on a whole new meaning.

38. A weird piece of cultural history follows: the BBC is resolutely non-commercial, sort of. The charter prevents overt promotion of any company or product. However, Walt Disney had wangled a loophole, way back in the dawn of television. As so few people could either afford the first sets or receive a signal outside a small radius from Alexandra Palace, it didn't cost him anything to give five-minute Mickey Mouse and Goofy cartoons to the fledgling service, free of charge. In fact, a Mickey Mouse cartoon was the last thing shown before the closedown of transmissions when war broke out in September 1939 - the same cartoon being the first thing shown when they started again in 1946. As the medium caught on, these cartoons, like Muffin the Mule (see X2.7, "The Idiot's Lantern") were part of the way manufacturers used children to promote set-ownership. Disney, meanwhile, had told the new US television networks that he had experience of the medium from way back, and had thus got in on the ground floor and been ahead of the other studios in making material specifically for television, which the BBC got cheap as a thank-you. (During some cash-strapped years, the less-successful films became a lifeline, and the 1967 dud *The Gnome-Mobile* was the big Christmas Day movie of 1985.) So compilation shows of Disney films were made, presented by celebrities and shown on Bank Holidays. Other film companies found themselves unable to sell compilations and thus followed suit, providing free or cut-rate screen-time-fillers for BBC and ITV. The holiday *Disney Time* compilations started in the late 1960s and wore on until the 80s: as things progressed, it got increasingly sad as clips from much-loved old favourites were used to launch the rather substandard new releases in the late 70s. Jon Pertwee had done an edition as himself, because he was famous long before he starred in *Doctor Who*, but Tom Baker had to do it in character as the Doctor. And at the end, he was passed a slip of paper reminding him to meet the Brigadier at Loch Ness on Saturday...

39. Assuming they *are* playing that, and not an old Venusian Lullabye - 9.2, "The Curse of Peladon". And, in case you're wondering, the comma goes after "Merry".

40. One aspect of twenty-first century London life that would have been unimaginable even when Sylvester McCoy was the Doctor is that there are shops open on Christmas Day, run by Hindus or Muslims. It's handy if you get almost up to serving Christmas Dinner and realise you haven't got any asparagus or have run out of milk - as good a reason as any to skip the Queen's Speech - but they rarely stock specifically festive goods. Those that do run out really fast.

41. We thought about how to explain a middle-aged Glaswegian woman dressed as a schoolboy, but then we realised that we were in enough trouble trying to convey the weirdness of English pantos without dropping the Scottish ones into the mix. Just accept that The Krankies have been around long enough to not seem odd to us any more, and that John Barrowman usually lands up on stage with them at Christmas in Glasgow. They recently hit the headlines when it emerged that their off-screen life was more exotic than expected. They seem to have been a large part of the reason that Michael Grade cancelled *Crackerjack* - see Volume 1 for what you're obliged to say now - along with his general annoyance at there being a popular series he didn't green-light on "his" network.

42. The formal term for being sent to prison. We've been doing this for a long time.

43. Not what it sounds like, tempting though that may be. It's when there's near-enough a dead-heat in seats between two main parties, with a smaller party not really fancying either or being so small as to not make much odds. Harold Wilson held one together in early 1974, John Major effectively ran one - or let it run him - from about 1993 to 1997.

44. Just as Matt Smith's much-noted resemblance to comedian and deliberately-clumsy conjurer Tommy Cooper made it inevitable that they'd find an excuse to put him in a Fez: see X5.13, "The Big Bang" et seq.

End Notes

45. Harry Hill, doctor-turned-comedian-turned TV critic-of-sorts, observed that *Casualty* has two non-speaking nurses whose job is to cross the set - one moving toward and away from the camera, the other left-to-right and back again. Or, as he put it, one does widths, the other does lengths. Once this had become a standing joke, the directors of *Casualty* started playing up to it, since viewers were ignoring the dialogue to watch out for them.

46. The rule is a two-word phrase or name, the second half of which rhymes with the thing being encrypted, and then use the first. The ones that last have a fun aspect and take on a life of their own - what Americans call a "Bronx Cheer" is politely called "blowing a raspberry" by people unaware that it derives from "raspberry tart". People still make up new ones, so windscreen wipers are now called "Billies" in some quarters.

47. Perhaps unwisely, the pull-quote at the start of that edition was Moffat proudly proclaiming that this was the episode where "We've cranked everything up to 11". If you've not seen *This is Spinal Tap*, the combination of those words and a polystyrene model of Stonehenge is just over-selling a slightly embarrassing set...

48. Well, all right, Moffat is a special case, but he was still going to the Fitzroy Tavern right up until he was announced as Davies' replacement.

49. By lazy critics who've never read any of RS Thomas' stuff. The simple test of poetry, WH Auden observed, is whether that particular turn of phrase sticks in the memory for saying something that couldn't have been said another way. McGonagall is, by that criterion, better than Matthew Arnold or Kanye West.

50. We can't be bothered to keep up with leaving gaps for you to shout "Cra-Ker Ja-a-ack!" And besides, you might be reading this on public transport. And you may not have read Volume 1 or 2. The last series of *Crackerjack* with Stu Francis can be found online, but YouTube doesn't even have the clip of Peter Glaze singing "Bohemian Rhapsody", nor XTC's post-punk classic "Making Plans for Nigel" - although his rendition of "Golden Years" by David Bowie is sporadically available.

51. One of her characters was an old man who was evidently gay, but whenever anyone said out loud what they assumed his relationship with his friend was, he would take umbrage and say "How... very... *dare* you?". The make-up job on Tate to achieve this resembles both the aged Doctor in Series Three and the revised Davros in Series Four.

52. In the dark days of the early 90s, Cornes returned to stand-up and did a routine getting easy laughs from ridiculing *Doctor Who* - Daleks can't climb stairs, wobbly sets, you can guess the rest. He stopped this when hecklers reminded the audience that he'd been the Trickster in "Kinda", and has barely been heard from since.

53. Connoisseurs of bonkers mixed-up casts will recall that Cribbins is in the film with the most deranged cross-pollination of acting talent ever - the 1967 *Casino Royale*, a film where Ronnie Corbett and George Raft, Orson Welles and Derek Nimmo, Erik Chitty (14.3, "The Deadly Assassin") and Peter O'Toole coexist, and only Peter Sellers seems out-of-place; a film where Valentine Dyall (16.6, "The Armageddon Factor" et seq) does a voice-over for a character played by Woody Allen. So chaotic was the shoot that - allegedly - Cribbins was able to film A2, "Dalek Invasion Earth 2150AD" between his two main scenes.

54. *Goodbye, Mr Chips*, James Hilton's first novel, was a sentimental story of a disappointed schoolteacher realising that his pupils were getting the chances he thought he should have had. It was made into at least two films, notably one treacly 1930s version with Robert Donat (an Oscar-winner) and an execrable 1969 musical with Petula Clarke and Peter O'Toole.

55. These interviews from the 1990s keep cropping up online, but you have to be quick before they go again. He was trying, it seems, to impress his famous friends when starting out as a TV writer.

56. A sardonic description of how to tell a genuine aristocrat from someone raised properly. Nancy was probably the slyest of the six Mitford sisters, and the one whose only rival for turning a bid to escape the "curse" of this posh upbringing into a career was Jessica (see 22.6, "Revelation of the Daleks"). There is a recognisable Mitfordian

sensibility in the Graham Williams period of *Doctor Who* and thus in the tie-in novels of Gareth Roberts.

57. This ball being a fundraiser for the Seven Years' War, a campaign prolonged by putting rich aristos in charge of the army; another reason everyone blamed Pompadour for French humiliation after her recommendations didn't pan out.

58. The 1951 novel *Time and Again* by Clifford D Simak (a fix-up of an earlier serial) nonchalantly uses the term as a background detail.

59. The same name as a character who would have been the same age, from the E Nesbit Edwardian children's books *The Story of the Treasure Seekers* and *The Wouldbegoods*. Nesbit, a friend and colleague of HG Wells, was given to Utopian futures and time-travel in her more fantastical works - see Volumes 4 and 5 for sidelights on BBC adaptations of *The Phoenix and the Carpet* and *Five Children and It*. So Moorcock is using a collective memory of these books as a grounding for his sardonic fugues on other people's attempts at Utopia. A minor character called "Ulianov" shows up in *The War Lord of the Air*. We know him as Lenin. See also **Did Sergeant Pepper Know the Doctor?** under 5.1, "The Tomb of the Cybermen" for how 1960s pop culture reclaimed and detourned steam-driven moustachioed "progress" and the notes for 6.2, "The Mind Robber" for pre-school intertextuality.

60. Almost. Dido Twite ingests some peculiar tree-bark in *Night-Birds in Nantucket* and skips puberty, becoming an 11-year-old girl in an adult body for the remainder of the series.

61. Oh, all right - for what it's worth, our money's on Frank Cottrell Boyce. He was another *Springhill* survivor and had a CV like Davies', except that he went on to write films for Michael Winterbottom - usually with Eccleston in them - and had just done an ingenious low-budget science-fiction film called *Code 46*. Then he had his name taken off their next film, *A Cock and Bull Story*, and went off to write children's books at exactly the right time to be in on the relaunch of *Doctor Who*. The one thing is... he would never have passed up the chance to write a werewolf, surely?

62. An Evil Parallel London where the Branson figure is a familiar character using alien tech to facilitate an invasion by old monsters? That'll be *No Future* by Paul Cornell, published by, um, Virgin Books.

63. DA? Duck's Arse. Gent's hairdressing in postwar Britain is a complex story, but if he'd had that hairdo with that suit, he would have been beaten up or refused service in pubs. See 24.3, "Delta and the Bannermen" for the low reputation of Teddy Boys.

64. But not all of it. An anointed monarch is, as you will recall from *Macbeth*, semi-divine as far as the church is concerned. Even today, the Queen spends Maundy Thursday, the day before Good Friday, washing the feet of pensioners as a remnant of the ceremony when the King would cure scrofula by touching patients. Thus the moment when Elizabeth II received unction from the Archbishop of Canterbury was deemed too sacred to be shown to anyone not invited into the Abbey. For this reason, they switched off the cameras at this point.

65. Yes, we know we just said it went out live and most live dramas weren't recorded. In those days, a drama on television was put on twice, so they did a remount a few days later. If the initial feedback had been favourable, they did telerecordings (of the kind that preserved all those monochrome *Doctor Who* episodes) of the second run. This is how we have Kneale's *1984* from 1954. *The Quatermass Experiment* would have been one of these, but the picture quality for the first two episodes wasn't good enough, so they stopped. However, they had enough faith in this process to script its use to insert a reprise of the previous episode's cliffhanger at the start of each week's instalment, which needed a special arrangement with Equity and set the precedent for *Doctor Who*.

66. Although the puppet had been made for a TV show in 1934, it was as the star of a series presented by Annette Mills (who wrote the songs) that Muffin became a star from 1946 to Mills' death in 1955. Although Prudence Kitten got her own show after this, mercifully Wally the Gog, a minstrel-style character, didn't. Mills used to play the piano as Anne Hogarth, who pulled the

strings, stood on top of it out of sight. The character was revived in 2005 - the BBC had obviously run out of ideas for new programmes and were relaunching any old rubbish - but the DVDs of what survives of the originals shows why, innuendo aside, Sooty and Sweep and *Flower Pot Men* (1.2, "The Daleks"; X2.13, "Doomsday") are more fondly remembered.

67. In 1977, this ditty made the lower end of iconoclast DJ Kenny Everett's *Bottom Thirty*, now widely seen as the benchmark for terrible pop. However, it wasn't Adam Faith's version that did it, although his excruciating effort "Runk Bunk" was higher in the same chart. Faith, as you'll recall, was a protégé of Jon Pertwee and later an actor - see X1.2, "The End of the World" - and manager of Leo Sayer. The follow-up *Bottom Thirty* included another song from the film, "It's Legal". And here is where we make a shocking disclosure that will authenticate our assertion that none of the Cliff Richard musicals made in the early sixties contains the words "straight from the fridge, dad" - we sat through all of them as children, repeatedly, and endured again the five made before 1967 *and* the puppet performance by "Cliff Richard Junior" (*how?* Parthenogenesis?) in *Thunderbirds are Go!* last week just to make sure. Obviously, nothing could make us endure *Take Me High* again without medical supervision. Nobody, not Cliff, not Una Stubbs, not Melvyn Hayes, not even Jeremy Bulloch off've 2.7, "The Space Museum" and *Star Wars*, who was only in *Summer Holiday* and made half-arsed attempts at hepster jive, says any such thing. And Robert Morley certainly doesn't.

68. Pre-Decimal money is really simple if you just pay attention. We managed until 1971 (see 1.1, "An Unearthly Child" for how ludicrous the idea of changing was even in 1963). You start off with a pound ("quid" or "sov"), which was originally worth as much as one pound avoirdupois of silver. "Originally" means 700 years ago. Divide that by 20 and you have a shilling (or "bob"). Divide a shilling into 12 and you have a penny. For most of history, a penny is about the cost of a loaf of bread. Six of these would make a tanner, the sixpenny piece made of silver (or, later, something that looked like it) that was hidden in a Christmas pudding. A penny was denoted by the Latin "Denarius", so you'd have 6d (nobody pronounced it "dee", just "sixpence", or "thruppence"

for the 3d coin that came in later still, or however-manypence). The pound was denoted by the Latin "Librum" as in the Horoscope sign of the scales, and the pound-sign (£) is a fancy L. Hence L.S.D. being in common parlance even before Albert Hoffmann. A guinea was 21s, or a pound plus a shilling, and was for show-offy purchases. (The fancy hat modelled by the Mad Hatter in Tenniel's illustrations for *Alice* is half this, 10/6.) Most daily costs were in shillings and pence, so 7/6, seven shillings and sixpence, was three-eighths of a pound. That would be roughly what a 45rpm single would cost in the 1960s, so not an unreasonable amount a week for a telly. For comparison, a bag of chips, which would now be £1.30 on average, would have been 1/2 d fifty years ago. Ten bob was, until 1968, a note; other increments include the half-crown (a coin worth 2/6), the florin (the two-bob coin retained as the 10p piece until 1992), the ha'penny (half a penny, curiously a coin bigger than the penny) and the farthing (half a ha'penny, 1/4 of a d, and really hard to get out from cracks in the floorboards). The difference in size between a penny and a farthing wasn't *quite* as big as that between the wheels on a penny-farthing bike, but you get the idea. The half-crown was the SI unit for holes in trousers, just as Wales is for any geographical feature reported on the news. People would see 19/11 3/4 and think it was a bit of a bargain, even though it was a farthing less than a quid. So, from the Plantagenets to the time of 8.2, "The Mind of Evil", we worked with this system, then it all changed: a pound was worth 100 New Pence (for some reason, this was pronounced "pee") and thus all subdivisions were adjusted. 5p was worth a shilling, to begin with, the new 50p coin was worth ten bob and there were pennies, ha'pennies (a new one, tiny but worth almost 2 1/2 times more than its predecessor) and a new 2p coin. This meant that prices went up by much larger increments, and some claim that this is the kick-start for the 24% inflation five years later (see **Why Couldn't They Have Just Spent More Money?** under 12.2, "The Ark In Space"). Things that had been 1/- a dozen were 10p for ten, which is a *little* bit more. It is a lot easier to divide 12 up various ways than it is to split ten neatly, which is why eggs and cakes are still sold in multiples of six and why so many of the old idioms stay in the language.

69. The on-screen result looks to us like a

End Notes

1953 model Bush TV22, give or take a few amendations for artistic licence. The present author spent the summer of 1970 helping his dad dismantle these things for spares when Colour came in.

70. Victor Hugo's widow remarked that when he had been writing this book, he had worn a very long striped scarf to keep himself from going out. Make of that what you will.

71. American readers may not be aware that this is even ruder in colloquial English than in colloquial American English.

72. If the people of that planet have only got rivers, no other form of water, presumably they use it as a toilet. So the name could have come out as "Bog Standard" or "Elton John".

73. The Japanese Yakusa have a ritualised system of amputating fingers. There was a case, reported in the UK as a "funny" end-of-bulletin story, where a man was watching the homespun and once-wholesome animated series *Postman Pat* and, on noting that all the puppets had three fingers on each hand, believed it to be a warning and - if the reports are true - threw himself to his death from a hotel window.

74. Not just for building up suspense: the obvious way to denote all the possible languages on offer to the Doctor if this is true is to have subtitles everywhere. A less obvious one is to show the world through his eyes - and nose - occasionally and represent the entire world as language. Something close to this happened with the "Bad Wolf" message at the end of "Turn Left" (X4.11), but the nearest equivalent is in the pilot episode of Steven Moffat's *Sherlock,* when all the text messages the journalists were receiving appeared on screen at once. This presents a new and amusing challenge for foreign-language translations. The Argentinian film *L'Antena* shows a world transformed by such scriptomania, but the English-language broadcasts of this have been smothered in subtitles to the point of unwatchability.

75. Later on, the *Torchwood* novel *The Twilight Streets* by Gary Russell would further muddle the entire issue by claiming that Abaddon was actually a well-intentioned agent of good who happened to squash quite a lot of Cardiff flat en route. Your mileage may vary.

76. Sort of. Bisley's art appears exclusively on the monumental and much-admired three-volume series "The Horned God" (which changed the nature of its parent comic in many ways, not all for the better), in which Pat Mills finally lets his idiosyncratic paganism off the leash. Specifically, he tells us that the eponymous horned god isn't the devil. He's mainly represented by symbolism and genuine Celtic art, so isn't really a model for the Beast at all. There is one character who *might* be the inspiration; Slough Feg, who is basically an ancient and decrepit old man who typically wears an ox skull as part of his druidic costume. So if the Beast is based on anything from *2000AD*, it's the villain's hat.

77. Even though Lovecraft himself resisted any attempt at a Grand Unified Theory and August Derleth invented it after the author's death.

78. If we really want to get technical about it, Monarch's antics in 19.2, "Four to Doomsday" ought to have been enough to have halted the expansion of the Universe by making a Not-As-Fast-As-Light vessel get close to lightspeed without any means of removing the mass, thus letting itself get to near-infinite mass in a near-infinitely-small space and time. See **Four Whats to Doomsday?** But then we have to ask where his ship's getting near-infinite energy, and we'll start to cry.

79. *The Telegoons*: the deranged radio comedy *The Goon Show* ran throughout the 1950s and, as we saw in **Did Sergeant Pepper Know the Doctor?** (5.1, "The Tomb of the Cybermen") has as good a claim as Lewis Carroll to have been the key text for British psychedelia and Pop-Art. In 1962, a film company got the rights to remake old episodes with puppets - they were re-recordings with the original cast, but no studio audience or musical interludes, and many of the ruder jokes removed and replaced by sight gags. The characters, by and large, worked better as mental images unique to every listener but, perhaps surprisingly, when children had sent in drawings of what they thought Eccles, Bluebottle and Bloodnock looked like they were remarkably consistent. So, before

End notes

Basil Brush, Don't Scare the Hare, Roland Rat: The Series or *Lamb Chop*, the first puppet show to be on just before *Doctor Who* was something technically very sophisticated, but pretending to be crudely-made and laced with very *very* sly adult jokes in amongst child-friendly craziness. Ponder the fact that news updates about the fall-out from the Kennedy assassination were laced in between Count Jim "Knees" Moriarty trying to bump off Neddy Seagoon in that night's episode, "The River", and Ian and Barbara following Susan home and finding a police box in a junkyard. Ponder also that the visual version of Eccles (a voice that was basically Spike Milligan doing Goofy) was a raggy idiot with a big nose, sticky-outy ears and big boots, and apply this knowledge to the less-than-enthusiastic response the casting of the ninth Doctor got from older fans who - like anyone over 30 in the UK - know *The Goon Show* at least as well as its *real* TV equivalent, *Monty Python's Flying Circus*.

80. This was an attempt to archive and cross-reference fan-fic about *The X-Files*, and made several magazines more for the problems it was having with clogging up bandwidth on any host they used. As such, it was one of the first times anyone attempted to organise a community's creative output and has thus replaced Madonna as the Cultural Studies equivalent of *Drosophila*.

81. The thing is, the original purpose of slash was to "feminise" an assertively technological and pragmatic series, *Star Trek* (why technology is perceived as exclusively male is another problem for another day), and make it all about relationships. If you read the accounts of the start of this trend, in studies by Constance Penley, Henry Jenkins and others, it is predicated on an idea that these series were made for men and about conquest and control. The imbalance the slash writers perceived was something *Doctor Who* explicitly challenged in the broadcast episodes, so *Doctor Who* slash was as pointless as doing fan-fic about *The West Wing* that had more politics in it. However, a recent development has been that even the tendency of *Who*-slash to overtly eroticise the Doctor's adventures and rethink characters beyond what was broadcast has stopped. Steven Moffat has taken the basic material of fan-fic and is making it on screen, so fewer people are bothering online these days.

82. In a weird kind of way, both this and UK *Doctor Who* fandom in the 16-year interregnum were more like the first fandom, the Futurians, in New York in the 1930s. The very word "fandom" was theirs, as was "fanzine". Whilst their initial function was to act as a sort of textual Maxwell's Demon, sorting through all the crud being produced to exploit this new marketing wheeze "Scientifiction" to find the one story in 100 or one writer in 20 worth their attention, that ceased very soon to be the primary focus of their activities. With the pulp companies hiring their Western or Pirate-adventure hacks to change "horse" to "avitron" and give it feathers, but keep the rest of the story the same (because a flying horse and blue-skins *does not turn a Western into SF* - not even if you're James Cameron and can spend the gross domestic product of Venezuela on digital effects), they organised letter-writing campaigns to ensure that the gifted and imaginative writers got re-commissioned. Then they decided, not unreasonably, that any relatively bright teenager - like themselves - could do better than 90% of what was being paid for. They also got into politics, into complicated relationships and house-shares and, before too long, into World War II. You see the pattern: from consumption to production, from subject-matter to social-life. No Cons, no cosplay, no filking and, above all, nobody berating them for forgetting what originally connected them. The *Doctor Who* analogy continues when these kids came back from active duty. They got jobs to keep themselves and their young families housed and clothed whilst attempting to write the sort of thing they now wanted to read. (We had the same phenomenon with the *New Adventures* in the 1990s.) The standard of published SF just kept improving, especially when half the original Futurians were editing professional magazines (see Volumes 2, 3 and 4 for the impact of *Galaxy* on Robert Holmes and, thereby, Douglas Adams). The others went off and got influential jobs in government, media or university departments - again, rather the way *Doctor Who* fans of old are a sort of latter-day Freemasonry. Hollywood, meanwhile, latched on to the relatively infantile stuff these writers had all started off liking and pilfered the iconography, forgetting any logical connection between the pretty pictures. That's where the schism between proper-written-down-grown-up-SF and the 30s-derived collage that now dominates TV and cinema started, and when fans of one especially retro manifestation of that took

End notes

over their meetings in the late 60s, fandom turned ugly. Yes, the Trekkies had landed, with a thud, and things would become complicated and fractious. It wasn't their fault. NBC may have wanted them to be passive receptacles of television-as-product, but that product was, almost, Utopia. There were bits missing and compromises they had to lump because it was television, but by mixing with the old-guard SF fans, they had now got an idea of how to go about fixing that. And because there were so many of them (television being more of a mass-medium than books and magazines), they distorted everything around them. By the end of the 70s, the press had finally got hold of this phenomenon and took photos of the freaks in costumes, presenting this as the sum total of fannish activity.

83. The one where there's a Time War and Vulcan is destroyed, leaving Leonard Nimoy's version of Spock as the last of his kind, the only person who remembers the previous timeline. If the Doctor saw the sequel, he'd be even more confused at what Mickey's doing there.

84. The archetypal over-enthusiastic attempt by the Central Office of Information to make us scared of things in the home that might cause accidents. It's called "The Fatal Floor" - a seventies Public Information Film narrated by Patrick Troughton, which in 20 seconds tells you more about what the Pertwee era was like for those of us living here than anything in *Life on Mars*. Look it up on YouTube.

85. So desperate were they for minor celebs to teach ice-dance to, allegedly, that they approached Davies to be in it. This is according to Davies himself, so is to be treated with caution.

86. Eventually, they had to put in a line in *The Sarah Jane Adventures* story "The Mad Woman in the Attic" that the Zodin are a refugee race whose furry snouts are patterned with spirals, resembling *The Fimbles*, one of many close-but-no-cigar attempted *Teletubbies* knock-offs. With luck, this is the end of the matter.

87. Rob Newman and David Baddiel did a series of sketches, *History Today*, about two elderly and eminent Oxford Dons whose discussions on fourteenth-century agricultural reforms or whatever turn into name-calling usually beginning "See that (*names something unpleasant*)? That's you, that is!" This was part of a series called *The Mary Whitehouse Experience*, for which see also Volume 6.

88. We're not in the same situation as with Episodes II and III of *Star Wars*, where the plot only has a hope of making sense if you read a large number of books and watch a whole cartoon series on a TV channel you can only get if you've had a satellite dish installed. (See **Why is Trinity Wells on Jackie's Telly?** under X1.4, "Aliens of London", and remember that Rupert Murdoch owned 20th Century Fox and most of BSkyB.) Moreover, Episode III, *Revenge of the Sith*, begins with an otherwise hard-to-follow political gambit by Palpatine, Dooku and a third party. If you haven't bothered with this film, General Grievous is best described as a kitchen utensil with a bad Mexican accent. He looks like something a toy manufacturer designed and then said, "George, can you write this in?" Only one thing in BBC Wales' *Doctor Who* has the same taint of being made to be merchandised, and so far nobody's bothered making Gadget toys (X4.16, "The Waters of Mars"). Indeed, many of the action-figures on sale are downright weird as toys. Most kids could rummage in their own toyboxes and find Action Man dolls that were better Autons than the ones on sale. (Plastic effigies of plastic effigies? Well, if you save up and get a detailed 1970 moveable with hinged hand and gun, you're probably after it as a collector's item rather than to play with.) Across the board, the BBC's quality control and brand-management meant that the tie-in works were in keeping with the programme. There are worrying signs that the Moffat regime is thinking more like LucasFilms than 1960s BBC management, including a whole subplot of "Asylum of the Daleks" (7.1) that required one to have played a not-very-good computer-game to understand how Skaro was now magically exempt from the seal that kept the Time War out of everyone's reach. No mention of this was in the broadcast episode, leading to headscratching even among people who weren't exercised by the casting of Oswin.

89. The roster of artists who've appeared in *Doctor Who* and had a UK No. 1 has grown since "Delta and the Bannermen" (24.3) had two in one

End Notes

episode. Obviously, Billie Piper, Kylie Minogue, The Streets and McFly have to be added, but the real achievement was on 17th June 2010, when James Corden did both simultaneously. Contrary to popular opinion, Bernard Cribbins' three pre-Beatle singles with George Martin all narrowly missed the top-spot, as did the 1991 *Comic Relief* single "Stick It Out", wherein he guests on a song by a band named after his biggest hit, "Right, Said Fred".

90. This whole paragraph shows the legacy of writing for *DWM* when Alan Barnes was editor - the rule was that any article using the word "zeitgeist" was binned.

who made all this?

Since the far-off days of *About Time 6*, when "River Song" was just the track even hard-core Donovan fans skipped on the album *Hurdy Gurdy Man*, **Tat Wood** has been living within walking distance of the Olympic Stadium, watching it get built with more speed and less care than these books and marvelling at the missile emplacements on nearby tower-blocks. He has also, rather unexpectedly, got married. In between teaching and writing for other publishers, he's volunteering at a charity bookshop in Hampstead and helping a team of volunteers to re-open a local library. Confidentially, he thinks 1968 was the programme's Annus Mirabilis, and not just because he started watching then.

Favourite story in this book: "The Christmas Invasion". Least favourite: "The Impossible Planet"/"The Satan Pit".

Dorothy Ail enjoys, in no particular order, pub quizzes, Ace doubles, builder's tea, and anything made by Oliver Postgate. She also has a soft spot for the Cartmel era and Virgin NAs, but seems to spend a lot of time writing about Jon Pertwee instead. Her quest to read through the world's supply of nineteenth-century novels is continually being interrupted by the plan to finish enjoying all the womanist science fiction in existence, which is turn is often waylaid by whatever book happens to catch her eye on the way out of the library. Semicolons a speciality, and the use of the Oxford comma remains a point of dispute with the other writer of this book. Favourite story in this book: "Love & Monsters". Least favourite: "Fear Her".

Mad Norwegian Press

Publisher / AT Content Editor
Lars Pearson

Senior Editor / Design Manager
Christa Dickson

Associate Editor
Joshua Wilson

Designer (AT7)
Matt Dirkx

Beta Testers (AT7)
Barnaby Edwards, Steve Manfred, Cody Quijano-Schell, John Seavey

Cover
Jim Calafiore (art), Richard Martinez (colors)

The publisher wishes to thank... Tat, for being such an invaluable slushpile of knowledge; Dorothy Ail, for her superb writing assistance on this tome; Lawrence Miles; Christa Dickson; Matt Dirkx; Jim Calafiore; Richard Martinez; Shawne Kleckner; Brandon Griffis; Carrie Herndon; Jim Boyd; Allison Trebacz; Joey Wolfe and that nice lady who sends me newspaper articles.

mad norwegian press

1150 46th Street
Des Moines, Iowa 50311
madnorwegian@gmail.com
www.madnorwegian.com